TIME IN ITS FLIGHT

Susan Fromberg Schaeffer

PUBLISHED BY POCKET BOOKS NEW YORK

POCKET BOOKS, a Simon & Schuster division of
GULF & WESTERN CORPORATION
1230 Avenue of the Americas, New York, N.Y. 10020

ISBN: 0-671-82677-8

First Pocket Books printing June, 1979

10 9 8 7 6 5 4 3 2 1

Trademarks registered in the United States and other countries.

Printed in the U.S.A.

FOR THE REMARKABLE FATHERS:

Wayne Booth, Arthur Friedman, Gwin Kolb, Elder Olson, R. S. Crane, Ernest Sirluck, Edward Wasiolek, Ellen Bremner Williams, and Edna Heatherington Bergman.

Acknowledgment

I would like to thank the following people for assistance, tangible and intangible: David Hewitt, James Meritt, Evadne Lafayette, Gail Ann DeWitt, Harold C. Gale, Mary Eckroyd Hinkle, Daniel Mayers, Ken Perry, Charles Steiner, Christophe Castou, and Darlene Russ.

Truth crushed to earth will rise again,
but it is not so with eggs.

—Facetie, *Harper's Bazaar*, 1877

BOOK I

BOOK I

Ella: 1966

Odd to say it, but I can still *see* my sister's diary, only then we called it her "personal." I had a diary, too. None of our diaries were locked, and we often read one another's, but even Anna's diary was different. For one thing, it was not to be found. I unearthed it one day when I was looking for some velvet trim for my black delaine dress. That tells you something about us, I see now. Anna buried her diary where she least expected anyone to dig it up. But I found it almost the first time I went into her room. "This year I am going to be perfect." That was how she began. "This year I am going to be perfect. As Christ bade us in the Bible 'Be thou perfect,' so I am going to try to be. And by the blessings of my Heavenly Father I hope to carry my resolution out, and by this, my first Personal, show how much I have improved, how much I have done, and, at the end of the year as I finish the last page of my journal, I can say that I have been a better and happier person, that I am of some use in the world, and that I comprehend more the love of my Savior and give my heart to his keeping, and let these be my mottoes, to be Humble, Obedient, Gentle, Truthful, and Living for Others, and may Father in Heaven assist me in my efforts." Poor Anna! It all ended (although not that year) in an argument over whether her body could be laid to rest in the church burying ground, and I remember Father solemnly swearing to shoot the sexton if he said another word against it, and to make his point more strongly, picking up his rifle and shooting at the big bell in the church steeple. He made his point then. It rang; Anna was buried.

And I suppose even now, after years of chimes dissolving into the sullen sky, streaking it with gilt, Anna could have a more sympathetic interpreter. I picked up the diary and thought it was a pity we were only Baptists (if indeed we deserved to be called that) and how much better it would have been for my sister if we had been persecuted Catholics, and she could have hied herself off to a convent

3

and enjoyed true persecution and sacrifice. Who was going to persecute us properly in Williamsville? Or in New Bedford? Well, I suppose she did achieve perfection of a sort; at least she is perfectly quiet, perfectly calm, perfectly at peace. Gone Home. And I imagine she was those things, too, before she died. If what the old minister used to say was true, that only a minute sufficed for a change of heart, that only one minute was necessary to bring a sinner home to his heaven, then in the last minutes of her life Anna was made perfect; she was made perfect under the sight of the moon. How time achieves its ends!

And at that time there was a craze for telling character by reading the bumps of the head. You must forgive my wandering mind; it is a privilege I have earned, to start out for one house, and end up on another porch, rocking happily, and I earn it a little more every year. I am so old no one remembers how old I am. Even I don't remember. Nor is that lapse vanity. After one hundred years no one lies about their age unless they do their breathing in a lunatic asylum, and besides, I never was vain. Or, to be honest, I never was too vain. But it does seem unjust that I, who seemed, to myself, the most shallow and superficial of the brothers and sisters, the one least concerned with the veins under the skin of this world, should be left here alone to read the bumps and valleys of our old landscape: this was the Hill of Happiness, this was its peak (although we did not know it then). This was the river with the pull tide: it began so innocently in a pond, and its frogs were shiny and green. On warm days, we used to catch them and pet them and put them back; it was always so cool there, but a different story a few miles down, but who thought on to the course of the river while playing at its innocent head? And this was the pasture where the snow fell and fell. "How the mountains and the valleys are blanketed with snow!" I wrote during Composition Week. The others always wrote about "Life on a Farm," but really, we didn't live on a farm, although we had animals. We were rich. The neighbors pronounced: Everything we did was a hobby. "Their new hobby is keeping cows." "Their new hobby has a new bossie." "Their hobby is the crossest sow I ever heard tell of. Why, they were up half the night trying to keep her from eating her ten pigs. She was cross as fury, the hobby, all night. You'd think they could get something with a better character if they were going to have only one on the place. The hobby probably thinks she's in a palace, I never saw such a sty as that sty."

Well, the pigs lived. Perhaps that is the most one can ever say. They lived. He lived and she lived and they lived, and don't bother about the happily-ever-after. Wherever I went, during my life, I can't say I found too many people bothering about that, and they still don't. They have too much else to do. Yes, the snow blanketed the meadow. It covered her up. It covered her up right under her chin. I can see that, too, although I wasn't there, how she pulled at the snow as if it were a down blanket, how she closed those big green eyes with their delicate violet-veined lids, how she went silently to sleep. Yes, now that I think of it, Anna was perfect in the end. And it must have affected me. At least it changed the bumps on my head. I walked right into her room the next day and into the rafter at the edge of the L shape where she hid her desk, so while she lay cold in the parlor, I lay still on her bed. The bump on my forehead where the bones mended is still there; I always say it makes me look as if I have some brains.

Anna: 1865

Dear Darling Grandmother Edith,

I sit down this afternoon to write to you. I would have written before but I thought I would not until after New Year's and Christmas (O! what a solemn holiday is Christmas!) so I could tell you what kinds of times we had. Christmas we had a very good dinner and wished you had been here. New Year's I went to a Sunday School Festival at the Old Stone Church, we had a very good time, but not as good as we used to have them before Doctor Pierce went away. (Sometimes I think he didn't go away at all, least not in the way they tell us in the class, but you are going to say, "Now, Anna, you know you are morbid." But if he did just go away, why won't anyone tell us where he went or how we might direct to him even though the war is going on, a letter *might* get to him; why, I could even send it to Mr. William Moffat if his regiment got near Charlottesville, he could bring it there, if he really went away to be a Chaplain, and I don't believe he did. "Now, Anna," you are saying, so I won't go on about it. Unless you want to tell me. I should be happy if you would tell me.) We received your money and the letter all safe and were glad to hear you were well. I want to see you so bad I wish you could put yourself onto the cars and come down here. You said you wished I would send myself up, or send up some of our berries, but, Grandmother, you know our berries are gone long ago. Why, Grandmother, I am surprised at you. Nothing lasts, especially berries in the middle of the winter, and at Christmas time, too. But perhaps you were joking. O I forgot to wish you and Mr. Siddons a happy New Year, and you in particular. O say I can tell you some news. Edna Burrit that you saw at the Fair (Edna Burrit that was, she is Edna Brown now) is married to James Brown, and they are here yet.

I wonder what you got Christmas and New Year's, I will tell you all that I got. I got a coral necklace and a coral ring, and a jet necklace, even though Mother said I was much too little for jet, and besides, it was for mourning, but I got it, and you should see it, how it reflects everything back, just as if it were a whole string of mirrors, but everyone says they will not look at pictures in black mirrors, they are so mean, and some candy and some hazelnuts William sent down (but you need not start asking, we ate them right up first thing they came out of the box) and Hal had some books and some apples and a wooden train Mr. Cross made for him, and we all got some candy.

O say I can tell you some more news. I have got me a new bonnet (Momma is looking over my shoulder, and she says not to say I have got me, I have got) still, I have it, and it is the very type yours is, black felt trimmed and bound round the edge with blue velvet and a band round the crown of the same stuff and a very pretty bow in front and some feathers and in the middle of them a blue plum put on about the same as yours, I believe, and black ribbon strings behind, so long Father says I look like I have a couple of tails, and he says he never saw a bird with a tail like that before, unless it was a peacock, and he never saw a peacock in the first place anyhow, they are always teasing me, you know, and I don't care if the hat looks too old for me, everyone says I look pretty even if I put a Bible on my head, although I guess I oughtn't to agree I look pretty and specially not think much of them saying I look so with a Bible on my head, it is a sacred book, as you well know, but they will joke. I have described it the best I can, about how it is trimmed. It cost fourteen dollars without the strings. I took the strings off my summer hat and put them on my winter hat, and Aunt Ten is taking them right off again and putting them back on the old one, I tell you it is hard to be younger than most, but we all need these trials to strengthen us; if Aunt Ten touches my hat once more I shall be pretty strong about it, I can tell you. Now don't you take that as a threat against Aunt Ten, you know I wouldn't hurt her for anything, she is so much more than an Aunt, and where would Mother be without her?

I want you to write and tell me what you got Christmas and New Year's. Not sanctification, I guess. I know I shouldn't have said that. Don't write, "O Anna, you shouldn't have said that, joking with such sacred things." I would scratch it out now but I have no more paper, or at least none worth writing on; you'd think in a family like this they'd pay more attention to paper, but perhaps it is Christmas and they are thinking good thoughts all the time and paper is not one of them ("O Anna!" I can hear you again, I *will* stop it. If only Doctor Pierce was here. Do tell me if you know where he is, I think it is real mean not to tell us, and we are all missing him so much, and so many of the others gone from the village too, perhaps never to return, although we don't know one of them, not counting William Moffat of course). But you will return, won't you, dear Grandma, you tell Mr. Siddons that I wish him a happy New Year, and a Christmas. You tell him I am giving him the biggest kiss anyone ever got. Mother says Jim Halston's wife is dead and she thinks that Jennie Greene will have it all smooth ground now. We got a letter from Mrs. Powers some two weeks ago. She was well and she said she would have written before, but it had been typhoid and measles time there.

O say, Grandmother, you don't know what grand times

we do have sliding on the ice all around. Hal (Uncle, of course, not brother) has not yet got any sled, and Mother says put all the blame where it belongs, on Father, who is so busy with his knife taking the wrong things out of the right people, or perhaps Aunt Ten said that last part, Mother did say put all the blame on Father, but it doesn't matter. We can go on our feet. Martin and me and George went down to the woods to see about the foxes and the place we went through is all ice (now don't you tell about the foxes and the woods) and such fun as we had you don't know. We got on each side of Hal and away we went and we fell down more than thirty times I guess and on our backs too. I never laughed so much in my life. Hal fell down on the ice and tried to creep back, but he couldn't, so we got a long stick and pretended he was going under for the last time, but I cannot describe what fun we did have, we were heroes, don't you think, getting him out of the water like that, and not a drop on him either. Don't you think we have nice times? I am so partial to the ice and snow. Mother says to tell that by the time we get a sled we should have roses all over the house; well, I am coming to the end of the paper, and I suppose everyone will try to write on it and across it and over it and under it so you will not be able to see one word at all. That is always the way it is with poor Anna because she is not the oldest nor anywhere near it nor ever shall be.

Letitia is sitting here writing too; I am sure you are looking at her picture right now; she is so beautiful. I am sure you don't let her out of your sight. The Jones boy fell into a vat of scalding dye and got burned all over and died in the morning, and he was blue all over, so they kept his coffin closed. What do you think of that, and on Christmas Day too? Yet we must remember God takes what he needs and needs what he takes. O they are after me again. I shall be eleven years old the fifteenth of April, 1865. I shall be pretty old. I shall be a spinster, don't you think? (Aha! I have written up one margin myself! Aha!) I guess I have written you all the news (but I don't know, Mother is shaking her head, and Aunt is grinning at me as if I were a wet chick) so I will close with our love to all and remembering that the Savior loves us all too, even if he did have the Jones boy fall into the blue dye and get himself blue all over.

Aunt Ten says I must close on a more cheerful note, but there are some things I draw the line at, and I *will not*. Here comes Aunt Ten. Be prepared. She says she is going to cheer you to death. She is also muttering about how I must make haste slowly getting up out of this chair since last time I tipped it over with myself in it and hit my head on the wall, what do you think of that? She said it was a lucky thing the wall didn't crack, because the mortar man is as religious as I am and wouldn't have come on Christmas, and we should all have frozen to death, and then where would we be? Your granddaughter, Anna.

John: 1877

It certainly is smoky here, and dark, and I think I do the right thing not to let Edna in too often, or even to let her know how often I come here. I have no doubt the fumes from this hobby of mine, the daguerreotype, are dangerous, but somehow I don't care enough to see to the ventilation. Drummond writes from New York he has talked to Brady; they don't see why I do not use the wet-plate process by now and save myself time and trouble, but I don't want to do it. After being a country doctor for thirty years trouble and queer smells are familiar company. And it is the daguerreotype I like best in any event; it is not any kind of making faces that keeps my interest, but just this one sort, and I can see that its existence will be a short one. I intend to see, however, it lasts on this estate as long as I do. Still, I suppose it is true that for the sake of the family I should be more careful of the fumes. Yet I feel I have earned the right to be careless some of the time, even if that means I am selfish. My only fear is that my carelessness and selfishness will affect the pictures, and that must not happen. The quality of the work is paramount.

It is as hot as it can be today; that probably makes things sting more than they would in the dead of winter. I keep thinking about the winter today, and riding out in the open carriage to operate on that man with the tumor on his buttocks. They didn't tell me what I was coming for, so naturally, I had to choose that night to bring Anna with me. She was so interested in medicine and she had already found out about the women's medical college in Hartford. Ten years old and always at my medical books. I suppose that was inevitable. This family has always been involved with science in some way. Well, I took her with me in the open wagon because it was the lightest, and the horses would tire on a long trip easily enough without having to drag a buggy after them. How Ten raved! An older sister is always an older sister. She acted as if I was going to drown a kitten instead of taking my own daughter with me on a ride, and it was only when Anna burst into tears and told her how many times I had promised to take her the next time, and this was surely *the next time,* if not the next-to-last (we all started laughing at that. Anna was such a comical child).

Ten relented and went to get her clothes. I saw a bundle of high-fashion clothes climbing into the wagon, and there was Ten in the doorway, the light making a halo around her, as if she were a saint, her long blue shadow on the snow before her, as if she were trying to carpet nature's extremes for us, shivering in her blue woolen shawl, with one of her endless series of white nightdresses spilling onto the wooden floor. We waited until we were around the bend in the road before we put the lantern under the carriage robe to keep us warm, and then I told Anna how far we were going. Thirteen miles! Was she puffed up with herself! Her eyes were even more puffed when we got there eleven hours later. It was a perfect nightmare of washouts, drifted roads, riding through pastures, then back onto the road when we could ride on it, and there was Anna, a mass of clothes and curls, handing me the wire clippers so we could drive the team off the road and onto the flat as if she were already at the operation, assisting. What a dramatic streak the child had! In a better day, we should have put her on the stage and let her tear her clothes and rend her skin to some purpose, or at least have encouraged her at singing. But as Ten put it (my sister had such a way with words) Anna's voice was poor as a crow, and if she wanted to be known as the American Raven, instead of the Swedish Nightingale, that was entirely her business, but she washed her hands of it.

Still, we did arrive without setting fire to our lap robe or freezing our fingers or our noses off either, so that the operation would have been an anticlimax to me in any event. But not for Anna. This was the night she had been waiting for. And what was it we had been called for? A supposedly inoperable tumor of the buttocks; the thing must have weighed sixty pounds, and even I, with my lack of fatherly instincts, knew better than to let Anna witness this performance, especially since Mr. Weston could not sit down, but had to be operated on lying over the top of his grand piano (his wife was fussy; she took off the piano shawl. Anna did help there, but after that, Mrs. Weston put her behind a heavy curtain for propriety's sake; neither did she want the neighbors gaping at her husband's better part).

I took the tumor out piece by piece while Mr. Weston stood there under the influence of those spirits Anna had already decided were not heavenly ones, and after three hours of Mr. Weston's booming, "How much more time for this damn business?" and Anna's high, piping "O Mr. Weston, you must not talk like that, especially when so close to your Maker," that set me off into a laughing fit, I can tell you, and Mrs. Weston saying if it took any longer she should not be able to get the help's breakfast on the table on time, it was all accomplished and Mr. Weston's best end was as good as God ever made it.

But when Anna came out from behind the curtain, her face was long as the moral law. "*This* was not what I had in mind when I asked to assist at an operation." "Pompous little thing," Mrs. Weston muttered, and Anna burst into tears. And what could I rescue from that torrent? Something about how cruel was life, or fate, after waiting all this time to witness an operation, to spend it behind a curtain, and a dusty curtain too, and she wanted to sneeze all the time, but she pinched her nose so she wouldn't sneeze and frighten me and make my scalpel slip,

11

and she ached all over from standing up, and then I had to soothe Mrs. Weston about the state of her curtains and her housekeeping generally and force Anna to tell her she didn't mean to imply the tumor was caused by the dust, and Anna clamped her jaws together and I performed an operation on her that loosened them, and in the middle, I kept warning the whole Weston clan not to let the local doctor or the minister or Grandma loosen the bandages to see what was what, but I would return and do it myself, and Anna howling like a wolverine. No wonder Edna (my wife) kept saying parenthood came in with Adam and Eve and sin, and they had all kept rather good company ever since. It was a scene. I wish I had had my camera then. Still, I guess Anna had a right to be disappointed, although it wasn't every day I got to remove a sixty-pound tumor from such a scenic place. I think Mr. Weston sat still through the whole spring and harvest and let everyone else do the work, he was so happy to celebrate his new ability to sit down.

And we sat in the carriage going through the snow with the poor horses for eight hours; we were going back. By then some of the roads had been dug out and Anna was slightly pacified by our adventure with the farm dog who caught on to the harness ring. I threatened to shoot the mottled thing; I even had my rifle out. If the team had been one inch more frightened, we would have all been upside down in the snow, but Anna didn't really know that and her prayers for the vicious mongrel were too much for me; at the last minute, just as I was about to squeeze the trigger, the apologizing farmer appeared, seized the beast, and whipped him back to the house. Still, in the end (what a terrible habit, this punning) Anna had a right to her disappointment. Although I still suspect she managed to get a look through those curtains. But I don't think she could have seen much more than the back of some bare, hairy legs and her father in his Prince Albert coat leaning over the victim. How I would have liked a picture of Anna's face appearing from behind that curtain! Her face was a slate, and every tragic emotion was written on it. She had missed the salvation of a rear end. Still, she was only a child and she was heartbroken, and it was true, none of us were ever as heartbroken about anything as Anna was, and that only made her more despondent, because no one understood her. And I suppose no one did. At least not until afterwards when it was all over, and cold comfort it was then.

The Dickinsons

"My preference?" Edna echoed. "I prefer to leave this house immediately. I prefer no more nights spent under the roof of this house." She spoke to her mother as if to her landlady. Had she been speaking to her landlady, her tone, in all probability, would have been considerably warmer. "Are you speaking to me?" her mother asked, turning back into the room, away from the half-shuttered windows which faced out onto the street, the line of brick town houses facing their own. "I don't see anyone else in the room," Edna answered, "unless, of course, we count that monstrous potted plant lurking there in the corner." "That monstrous plant is very much admired; and"—her mother paused—"very expensive." "I want to part with house and plant this afternoon," Edna answered in her new monotone. "And why?" Edith, her mother, asked, "if I may be so bold?" "It might be better if you were less so." Her mother blushed.

Blushing, Edna had been told countless times, was very unbecoming; it certainly was unbecoming in her mother's case. With satisfaction, she watched the flush spreading slowly down her mother's neck to her dinner dress's low-cut bosom; the dress was a very expensive white affair, silk, its full sleeves covered with white lace trim, both sleeves and midband of the skirt trimmed with maroon velvet bows which hung down gracefully like so many tails. They looked, to Edna, like trophies, animals caught in a trap. "That *is* an interesting color," Edna commented; "where the red of your throat meets the ruche of your dress. I would call it perfectly startling, really quite paintable." Edith's flush deepened. She had not, as yet, shown any clear signs of annoyance, but now she moved her arm from the back of the side chair, moving more suddenly than usual to the small table next to her. Edna's face showed nothing. Inside, inside, Edith knew, her daughter was grinning; she was thinking a woman with auburn hair tending to common red did not look well in, as Edna had once put it, a purple fit of any sort of passion.

"You ought to remember I'm your mother," Edith finally said. "Indeed, Mother, I have a great deal of trouble forgetting it." "Then remember to watch that tongue of yours," Edith snapped. "You set such a marvelous example. I can be sure of not losing my temper." "I am not talking of your temper, I am talking about that tongue of yours," Edith retorted, beginning to drum on the carved wooden back of the gentleman's chair. "Don't beat the chair as if Father was in it," Edna said. "I want to know, *right now*, what this is all about," Edith insisted.

She could stare someone down, Edna thought; one had to give her credit for that. However, Edna was used to that stare. She opened her eyes wider, fixing them on her mother; she could manage without blinking longer than anyone she knew. The women stood there like two cats deciding whether to fight over one another's territory. Her mother decided against it. She broke the silence. "I should like to know what your father has to do with this." "What makes you think he has anything to do with anything? I can't remember"—and now Edna paused, as if to think —"hearing his name cross your lips within the month; no," she reconsidered, "not in the last two months." "How very precise," Edith mocked. "I'm not obliged to discuss your father with you. You know that." "Or talk to him yourself. Do you know," Edna said casually, "I think those ribbons are the wrong thing for your dress. They hang so . . . peculiarly; they remind one of skunk tails. It's a pity to spoil such a pretty dress by such a small thing. You're forever telling your dressmaker just that; it's the small details that count. You won't have them overlooked, you won't have them overlooked." She mimicked her mother's voice perfectly. "What an expensive hobby," her mother murmured, "raising a human parrot." She paused.

"I should like to know," her mother repeated slowly, "right now, immediately, what this conversation, if you want to call it that, has to do with your father." "And your husband," said Edna, as if reminding a feeble-minded old woman of something her impoverished brain caused her to overlook. "I would rather not ask again; I'm not a ship captain's parrot." "Of course not," her daughter agreed, soothing: "if you were, you certainly wouldn't be dressed in white." "You know," Edith answered, a touch of admiration stirring its feathers in her voice, "for a mere child of sixteen who knows nothing whatever of the world you do manage to be nastier than most women of society." "I'm flattered." "Perhaps," said her mother, studying her, "you're merely jealous. There you are in a stylish, but serviceable, walking suit, and here I am in a white dinner dress you never tire of criticizing, and the only other object of your remarks I can possibly discover seems to be your father, who, as I say, is my husband." "Yes. But you don't seem to remember that often; *that* is the point of the conversation, I think."

"Are you, are you," Edith asked, almost speechless, "accusing me of something?" "Oh, I'm sure that all your visits to that artist's studio downtown are perfectly innocent; after all, a statue of a woman of position can't be made in a day. Father certainly wants a marble model of you. The stone one we have now is getting rather decrepit." "And *you* are getting vulgar." "How reassuring," Edna said, "how very reassuring. I wondered if you recognized vulgarity." She stared at Edith as if she were a butterfly who had just accomplished the miracle of turning herself back into a caterpillar. "If you are implying," Edith said slowly, "that there is anything whatever between Mr. Siddons and myself, you are worse than wrong." She peered, miserable, at her daughter. "Nothing between you but air"; Edna hummed, staring off into space. "That is exactly right," Edith answered angrily. "And what is there between you and my father? Nothing between you but air?" "That's hardly your business, is it?" "I'm making it my business," said her daughter. "You aren't old enough to discuss such matters; I can't expect you to understand them." "From what I see," Edna retorted, "there is nothing to understand. Nothing. Nothing whatever. If there was something, this household wouldn't have the problems it has."

Edith turned back to the window, staring intently down into the street. Two hacks were approaching each other and would cross soon. The one on her side of the street would block the other from sight. At that instant, she hoped, the weather in the drawing room would change. The cars passed; the clouds remained. She stood motionless, staring out of the window. Two men were approaching each other on the sidewalk. When they met and passed each other, her daughter would no longer be in the room. Her daughter would leave her in peace. "If you continue to stand in the full sunlight," Edna's voice came from behind her, "that fresh ivy on your dress is going to wilt. Certainly," she continued, as if the ivy were the chief concern of her young life, "the lilies of the valley on the bodice are going to wilt. Even if the ivy should survive."

"Will you stop?" demanded her mother. "All right, we *will* talk about your father. *Against my better judgment.* What, precisely, in your mature view, is the serious problem shaking this entire household?" Now Edna was at a disadvantage. Her mother's green eyes were fixed firmly on her own. Edith had the satisfaction of knowing her own skin perfectly white while her daughter's cheekbones were red as a barn. It also made her feel more comfortable to be near the window, so close to the human traffic immediately beneath. The window had been opened several inches. She could hear the shattery music of two women's conversation, and then the unexpected burst of laughter, brought under control immediately, all in the prescribed manner. Further on, two men were talking, responses and counter-responses measurable as beats of a metronome. The sounds were soothing, little waves breaking constantly on the dark edge of the sand. In here, here, was the sound of the surf.

She remembered suddenly how afraid she was of swimming, and especially of the ocean, while her daughter plunged into any current as if she had been mothered by a water rat. No, that comparison was not flattering to either of them. I am not really so dreadful, she thought, not *that* dreadful. Am I? Am I so dreadful? Confused, she mechanically smoothed the flounces of her skirt. The instant her hand touched the fabric she knew she had made an error. Now Edna would explain her grievances, not to her mother, but to some imagined statue of domestic vanity. She *did* think; she was perfectly capable of normal human thought. It was unjust of Edna to take such a mean view of her, as if she had no mind, no feelings of her own, as if her only interest was her clothes, as if she lived for visits to the studio where a replica of her face emerged and emerged, chisel stroke by chisel stroke, out of stone.

But really, she had to admit it, she could not live without those visits to the studio, there, in the crowded business section of the city. There seemed to be more light; she seemed to breathe more easily. Yet she knew it was dusty and crowded; the streets were busy. There was the constant clatter of milk wagons, dogs barking. "The price of artistic life," she had laughed lightly the first time she visited; Mr. Siddons had not answered. He had merely stared at her, and kept staring as if *her* presence had turned him to stone. But he *was* carving a bust of her. It had been her husband's idea. She did enjoy going, even though she often had to wrap herself in a sheet before entering her own carriage, the streets were so filthy. She would never dare take a streetcar or hack back to her own home; the dust was that menacing, and Mr. Siddons insisted she pose only in white, in the same white dress. The dress she was wearing was white. She had a sudden impulse to change her costume. She continued staring at her daughter. Silence is white, she thought; silence is white.

I wonder if that woman ever thinks, Edna considered, watching Edith. I wonder if she ever thinks about anything but her dress, how low her neckline ought to be, how far from the floor her hem, how much of her splendid chest must be covered by that magnificent lace spencer. She always picks at it, Edna thought, when she's uncomfortable, as if she would rip it off, as if she wanted to stand in front of us virtually naked, as if she wants everyone to see her naked. Under the heat of Edna's stare, Edith began to feel hot, prickly. Without awareness, she began fidgeting with the lace ruffle of her spencer. Why is she smiling at me like that? her mother wondered. So bitterly? We have not even said anything; we haven't even charted a path which leads to the foot of the mountain. We have not found the first path to that last place from which there is no returning. Why is she smiling like that? So bitterly? As if she felt only contempt for me. As if she hated me.

"Something is wrong with Father," Edna finally said. "Look at his picture"; she pointed to the watercolor on the

17

marble-topped table. "It's not the same man Mr. Siddons sketched two years ago. For heaven's sake, Mother, look at the two pictures together." Edith looked, but saw nothing. She said so. She thought, I want to see what she sees, but I see a man two years younger in one, and in the next, the same man, two years older. "Edna," she said finally, "could we continue this inquiry sitting down? There are two chairs next to that table and that crush of pictures; we might as well make use of them." "Youth should defer to age after all," her daughter answered. Why had she spoken to her mother like that, and so sarcastically? She had not meant to say that, certainly not in such a way. Why was she always saying and doing these things she did not intend? Was it possible she moved through these rooms, through her life, like a clumsy visitor in a museum, unknowingly knocking precious object after precious object to the marble floor? Could it be true she was like that?

Unthinking, Edna sat down in the gentleman's chair. Seeing that, her mother sighed and sat down in the lady's chair. No, she had no idea where this had begun, nor how it would end. She asked Edna to tell her about the pictures. Edna was startled by her voice. There was something unfamiliar about it, something new. "In the drawing," Edna began slowly, "he looks happy. He is looking at the artist. His eyes are wide open and his fingers are lying along the stack of books as if he were interested in their feel, their texture." "The artist posed him that way." Edith sounded weary. "Not the *pose*," Edna said, impatient; "it's nothing as simple as that. His fingers are relaxed. But in the sketch, they're clenched. His tie is tighter. He's looking away, almost"—she hesitated—"as if there were something he was ashamed of, or something he didn't want to think of, or as if he didn't quite feel well, but was hiding it. His vest isn't buttoned properly. I just noticed it yesterday. That last button is open; he started buttoning it one button down." "The artist should have been more careful; it's his responsibility to see to those details." Edith had answered automatically.

Why did she say that? Why hadn't she thought before speaking? She decided against raising her head, against looking at her daughter, instead staring at the portrait.

From her position in the lady's chair, it gave back little

18

but her own face. It was as if her husband's features were swimming underwater, drowned, in a pond whose depths she had never thought to examine. "He does not look happy," she agreed; "no, he does not. Are you going to blame me for that? I know you can't believe it, but one person can't be held completely responsible for another person's happiness, even," she sighed, "if that person is her husband." She got up, restless, dress rustling, coming to rest in back of her daughter's chair. "Why, you can't see the picture from here at all!" Edith exclaimed; "bright light is falling on that portrait. It's blinding! It's only a silver square! You weren't looking at it at all!" "I've looked at it enough." "Yes. Yes, you must have. What, then, do you think is the trouble? Do you think the doctor should be called? Do you think we've been neglectful of his health? Do tell me." She knew her voice had the hushed, sad sound of a suppliant. "Not a doctor; we aren't paying enough attention to him. He's alone too much, even when he's in the same room with us. We're doing something wrong. Or worse, there's something we're not doing." Her voice was rushed, muffled. "Something *we* are not doing?" her mother wondered aloud; "*We?*" she repeated, astonished. "Yes," Edna said; "I suppose that's only fair."

"Your father," Edith began reluctantly—it did *not* seem proper, discussing her husband with his daughter—"has always been a very private man. He should never have gone into law. He takes all his cases too seriously." She saw her daughter's look. "Of course they *are* serious," she went on, "especially to the clients, but he cannot, I don't know how to put it, he cannot walk out of their lives, not even when the cases are settled to everyone's satisfaction. Even after the verdict, the people are there with him, and he doesn't forget them; he can't forget them. It's as if—sometimes I think—I don't mean to say anything against him, it's as if, once he meets them and talks to them, they stay with him"—she smiled weakly—"almost like country boarders, but they don't go home at the end of the season. No, I would say they never go home. His last case, you know, it was a divorce case. The man's wife was said to be overly friendly with a priest. Your father did his best to convince the man there was nothing at all to it, it was just the wagging tongues of the

19

neighbors; the Misses Corkscrew Curls, that's what he always calls them; and then he invariably says they should all be strung up, one right after another, hung from flagpoles in front of their own houses on their own best streets.

"But nothing turned out as he expected. The man was right. He followed his wife on an outing in the country, and there *was* a picnic all right, but there were only two revelers. The man found his wife and the priest"—Edith hesitated—"in a state of undress." "In a state of undress?" Edna repeated. She was smiling. I had no idea she was such a prude, she thought. "In a state of undress," her mother solemnly repeated. She saw her daughter smiling, attempted to do the same, but her mouth would not move. "I'm sorry," she told Edna; "I've gotten out of the habit of talking about things like this." "Things?" Edna queried. "Your father. You know I mean your father. I know how I seem to you," she went on quickly, "vain, silly, nervous, irritable, given to 'vapors' as they say in all those novels you're so fond of." "But do you love him? That's what I want you to tell me."

"Love him?" Edith asked. She was shocked. There was a silence. "Why, yes," she said, surprised; "I suppose I must." "But," Edna finished for her (I'm feeling sorry for her, she thought; I pity her), "you have your studio and your dressmaker and your fashion, and he has his courtroom and his divorces and murders and contested wills and illegitimate children and incendiaries." "Yes," Edith agreed excitedly; "yes, that's it exactly. Exactly."

She stared at her daughter, thinking, what a small child she was! But she wasn't a child. She gave the illusion of being a child. It is because she is so short, her mother thought; she is not even five feet tall, and she has such small bones. Whenever I see chicken bones, I think, yes, that is what Edna's skeleton must look like. And she is so pretty. She has such high cheekbones and such delicate skin. It always seems as if she's standing behind a pane of peach-colored glass. And then that black hair and those green eyes. She looks like a doll. She doesn't look real. But no, she is not a child. *I* am more of a child, she thought with a shock; my daughter is older than I am. And she had no idea where it came from, this odd precociousness about life, or most of life.

"What are we to do?" she asked finally. "I don't know," Edna said, twisting a long strand of dark hair around and around her finger, then watching it uncurl, an old childhood habit, so old neither she nor her mother noticed its reappearance. It was part of the fabric of their time together. "I don't know," she said again, "but . . ." "But what?" her mother prompted. "We will never continue to agree, to go on talking like this." "No," said Edith, "I suppose that would be too much to expect. But what are we to do *now?*"

"You can both stop worrying," Mr. Dickinson's voice said from the doorway. Both women jumped in their chairs. "Edmund," Edith protested, "it's not polite to sneak about like that; you've scared us half to death. Look at Edna. She's turned green." "Presume she will ripen soon," her father said, looking at her; "she certainly will if she goes to visit her cousins in Manhattan. Wasn't that what you were going to do?" he asked his daughter. "I don't want to go to Manhattan," Edna said. "I hate the city." "You never told us that before," Edith said. Would these surprises, these shaking, tiny revelations never end? "I would rather go to a farm," Edna announced. "A farm?" they both repeated. "I'm afraid your mother and I don't know many farmers." "There's always Ten," her mother suggested; "she never has enough people to take care of." "But Ten doesn't live on a farm; she lives out in Fredonia, and I thought you said she lived on its main street, if there is such a thing out in Kansas." "No, no," Edith said, impatient; "I must have forgotten to tell you. She's gone to live with her brother John. She's been living on his farm in Vermont. Ever since his wife died." "That was tragic," Edmund said, looking away. "Please," Edith protested, "don't sink into that again. We've talked about it often enough. I really can't stand it." Edna looked up with distinct dislike. Then, as if remembering something, an old song, a recent conversation, her expression slowly changed.

"It's real country there," Edmund explained; "there's no such thing as society. The nearest farm is ten miles away. It's all horses and dogs as I remember it." "Is the scenery pretty?" Edna asked. "Very pretty, the scenery is beautiful," her father answered, ironic. "It's even soothing, if you are interested in scenery and scenery only. But

John Steele, Ten's brother, has very little patience with women, at least so rumor says." "That won't distress me," Edna assured him. "You say that now," said her father. "I will talk to the trees; I'm very good at talking to trees." "Well, you will certainly have to be," Edith told her, "when you tire of talking to Ten. I understand John never says a word, at least not to anyone but his sister." "Will you write her?" Edna persisted. "If you insist," Edith answered. "If you are sure you want to go," her father put in. "I *am* sure!" Edna exploded; "but do you think she'll have me? She doesn't run a boardinghouse." "We went to school together; she's my oldest friend. I'm sure," Edith said, "that if I write and tell her you want to relax among the silent trees, she will be happy to take you in as long as you want to stay." Edmund noticed the bitterness in his wife's voice. He thought a moment, and decided, this one time, to ignore it.

"What were you talking about when I came in?" he asked; "you were staring at each other as if a rattlesnake on that love seat got you under his spell and you couldn't run away." "That's all nonsense," Edith protested. "That's how you looked, all the same." "We were worried about you; we thought perhaps you weren't well." Edna looked nervously at her mother; her mother nodded. "Not well!" exclaimed her father; "I've never been better. What gave you such an idea? I'm only"—he stopped—"tired. *You* would be tired with the court calendar filled up the way it is now." "I *am* sure that's it," her mother agreed, enthusiastic. "Are you?" Edna asked. She avoided looking at her father. "*I* am sure," her father said, "and I am the one who ought to know. Surely you can't believe I'm ignorant enough to make a mistake about something as important as my own state of mind? A good lawyer has to know the state of his own mind or his client is left looking up a tree in front of a crowd. No, no, there's nothing whatever wrong with me. I have only one unsatisfied ambition and that is to get one good night's sleep." They both looked up at him, troubled. "I mean one night's sleep that is long enough for *me*. I should have been born in Iceland where the nights go on for half the year." "You're *sure?*" Edna persisted. "Please not to cross-examine. I'm sure. Absolutely sure. There's nothing whatever the matter with me. I should have borrowed some of your mother's powder and stuck it under my eyes and you would have stopped worrying without even asking me." Edith was smiling up at him; he was smiling back at her.

Can I have been wrong? Edna wondered; right now, this minute, they seem so happy together. "Well, then," she said decidedly, "there is nothing for it. I will pack my trunks and Henry will drive me to the depot." "Do pack," Edith agreed, "but there will be no leaving for Vermont until we have Ten's answer in hand. It would never do if you went off and found yourself alone there with John." "No matter what his hatred of things in petticoats," her father agreed, "it would hardly be proper. And if they had both gone off somewhere? A fine time you would have learning to light a stove and then going out to discuss your dinner of cinders with the pigs. Do they still have pigs?" he asked, turning to Edith. "Who knows?" Edith answered, exasperated.

A week later, Dutch Henry drove Edna and her parents to the depot. She took the cars to Brattleboro and Ten's carriage met her at the station. Edna arrived in the middle of a state fair. She fell in love with Ten, with the patterned confusion of farm life. She did not meet John, who had gone to Harvard's medical school to take a course in battle surgery. "He expects there will be a war," Ten explained. "Do you?" "Eventually, sooner or later, don't you think so?" Ten grinned. "I suppose. John is a doctor?" "He is," Ten answered, frowning, "and of course, if there should be a war, he'll think he has to go. I should think he would have had enough of blood." She got up and closed the kitchen window. It was hot; the flies buzzed at it. "He's my one sane brother," Ten said, sitting down. "I see," Edna said, who did not. They did not mention John again.

In the country, on the farm, Edna discovered two things; silence and a cat. They seemed small enough. But the only silence she had known before, or remembered, was the silence which fell like a guillotine in the middle of raw, bleeding conversations. Her mother's friend Ten seemed to take it for granted that silence was part of her life, something as necessary as air, as deserved as the title she held to her land. "What are those voices?" Ten exclaimed, enraged. It was early morning; the house was still chilled from the evening's cool bandages. She jumped up from the table, peering out the kitchen window. "Tourists," she expostulated, enraged; "not another building for miles and they have to take their walks on our lawn. I'm sending Amos out after them; imagine going about disturbing people's peace like that!" "Peace?" "Well, train of thought then," Ten grumbled. "Bridget," she called to the cook, "will you go get Amos to get those people to scat off from here?" The woman nodded, leaving. In the silence, Edna could hear her own heart; it was a kind of autumn, she thought, as if here the mind shed all its unnecessary leaves desperately clinging to the branches from past seasons, weighing everything down whenever rain fell, or dew settled. Yes, Ten had been right; this was peace. She tried to imagine a whole life of it, but she could not; it was, she thought, like trying to imagine heaven.

Then she met Jimmie the cat. She had gone out to the stable for her horse when she caught sight of a huge orange cat, staring up at the world from a pile of hay, dissatisfaction with all existence written loudly on his broad face. Nothing so strange, so alien, had ever been permitted in the house on Beacon Street. It might go mad; it might scratch the furniture; it was, in short, inhuman. Edna immediately felt their kinship. She picked up the cat, marveling at how heavy he was, scratching him between the ears, up and down the length of his back. She would have to do something about the clumps in his fur. By the time her horse was saddled, the cat was purring. "Oh, miss," Amos gasped, his huge mouth falling open, "I wouldn't pick that critter up; he's wild as a mountain lion. It isn't safe." Edna looked down at the purring creature in her arms; it chose just that moment to extend a paw and touch her cheek. Amos leaped forward, prepared to defend her; he stopped, astounded. "Well, if that doesn't beat everything." He grinned. "It's too bad Mr. Steele isn't here to see it." "Doesn't he like the cat?" "Well, that's not it, miss. He'd be surprised as all get-out, I can tell you." It was clear he couldn't wait to report the cat's doings to the doctor, although why he should consider them unusual was beyond Edna's understanding.

In the time Edna stayed on the farm, she became fonder and fonder of the cat; the cat returned her affection. He began to follow her into the house and then into her room; he took to pushing her door shut behind him. His head, Edna thought, was large enough to butt a heavier door than hers. So the time went by, in silence and conversation, the two almost indistinguishable. They were compatible, she and Ten, she and Ten and the cat. She believed the cat had secret access to a secret world of savage vibrations, long lost to human perception. The beauty of the woods, the profusion of the unplanted flowers, their untended abundance, it was all so different from the carefully tended hints of life springing from small squares of earth which decorated Cedar Street; she fell hopelessly in love with the land. She never wanted to go back to Boston. She didn't know what excuse she could invent so that she could return to Ten, and the country, and the cat after she went back to the city. Finally, the anguish of the anticipated departure caused her to cut her visit short. She would rather leave than dread leaving. So she left early, in tears, as if she had lost everything she had ever had.

Edna arrived in Boston early; no one expected her. It was the fifteenth of April. She collected her traps and took a hansom to her house. When she rang the bell, no one answered; that was strange, but she let herself in. The house was absolutely quiet and still. Have they left? Edna wondered; have they gone on vacation without notifying me? Then she saw her mother's red head leaning over the side of the lady's chair. She walked around in front of it. Edith's head had fallen sideways; her hand both supported her cheek and covered her eyes. When she heard her daughter put down her case, she looked up. There was a huge ugly welt in the middle of her mother's forehead. "What happened? What's happening here?" Edna demanded. "Your father," her mother answered in a hoarse voice; her throat was so gravelly she could barely speak. "He hit you?" Edna asked, astonished. "No, I walked right into his feet." "His feet?" "He hung himself with his shoes on. The police said some people undressed before they hung themselves. I walked into his shoes in the bedchamber." "When?" "An hour ago."

Edna ran into her parents' suite. Her father was hanging in the doorway between the bedchamber and the inner room. His face was purple and black; his eyes were bulging. He was swaying back and forth, a pendulum about to run down. Edna ran out of the room. Later her mother told her the doctor had given her sedatives to stop her hysterics. The first thing she asked Edith was when they were to go to the funeral. "The funeral?" her mother said bitterly. "The funeral took place last Thursday. It was very well attended. It was a very interesting group. I doubt if so many criminals and so much of society ever gathered together without picking each other's pockets before." "What will we do now?" "Do?" her mother asked, smiling again. "Do? I called the doctor and the minister recited the burial service." "Who cut him down?" "The doctor." "Who read the funeral service?" "Dr. Sledd." "Would you describe it to me, please?" Edna asked, her voice thick with courtesy. "If you wish," her mother answered, and, meticulously, described every detail of the funeral and what had led up to it. The body had to be kept on ice during the heat spell preceding the funeral, and Dutch Henry sat up with the body to keep the flies off. Ten had come down; she had sat up with Edna. "Ten was here?" "Yes." "Where is she now?" "She went home." "Home," Edna echoed. "Yes," Edith said, "I know." "Home," Edna said again. It was getting dark.

Home, the family, Edith thought; now there was nothing left of hers but herself and her daughter. She thought about her friend Ten, their other school friend Nellie. Both of them, she remembered, envious, had come from such large families. Ten—how she used to go on about the advantages of a large family; *she* intended to have one, it was so much safer. Why, she had explained, a large family was like a brain, or a whole person. If one arm was hurt, there was another, but if you only began with one, well, then, suppose something should happen to *it?* It was always the small family which scattered, wasn't it? she had asked the nodding Nellie. They were like pearls on a string which had worn through, but a big family, well, that was a triple strand; it would take something to scatter all the pearls from a necklace like that. No, it was true, she would prefer a large family any day, even if she often complained at her family's neglect of her. There was still always someone in the crush who made a religion of

26

looking on the brighter side when things went wrong, someone who had a collection of proverbs beginning with "Sufficient unto the day the evil thereof," who solemnly quoted (and believed, yes, Edith, *believed*, it was true; they believed it) that one must forgive not only seven times, but seventy times seven.

How Edna parodied that command the evening they entertained Dr. Talbott. She went on and on about how severely men had been tried by such an injunction; she amused her father by interpreting it as a comment on biblical life, during which time, she said, families were so huge they were not really families at all, but tribes, yes, tribes, and therefore, Christ *must* have meant *people*, not sins. She beamed at her mother's religious "catch," cooling noticeably over his hot soup—and that was the first course, there were four more to sit through—so many sins could easily be committed in just one day. Society, she babbled pleasantly, gave so many opportunities for the sins of hypocrisy, self-pride, deceit, forgetfulness of duties to others, the too attractive life which could only lure others from Christ; yes, it was so obvious now, the more she considered it, the clearer it became, that even forgiving one person his weekly sins would free you to ignore that command for the rest of your life. For, in one week, would not it be possible to forgive *one* person seventy times seven, wasn't that possible, Father? And her father suddenly sat up straighter at the table, as if the actors had finally remembered to come upon the stage of an empty theater where a desperate audience waited for them hour after hour in an empty house. Yes, he said, logically, there was something to that, yes, she would have made an excellent lawyer for sinners standing at the bar of judgment.

Whereupon the gallant divine let his spoon fall with a clatter into his empty soup bowl. Dr. Talbott, in spite of his eminent reputation, had just endorsed Nervine Tonic; he had been convinced, he assured them, of the beneficial effects which would accrue to a suffering humanity, but now, he was featured in every prominent newspaper as recommending that nostrum, which, the ad assured its readers, would cure consumption, nervous prostration, the "blues," scarlet fever, and worst of all, "male weakness": Nervine, the tonic which makes family life

27

possible. So said the ad, also endorsed by a reputable doctor who claimed that, during his career, he had used it to save so many souls it was not difficult, Edna's father had remarked, to see why a divine was also chosen to endorse the product, since Nervine had evidently saved almost as many souls as Christ, this bringing on a sputtering fit in Edith, who knew there was something faulty in the comparison, but had no notion of how to attack it. "Oh, Mother," Edna said soothingly, "you know Dr. Talbott cares nothing for things of this world; we certainly don't mean to imply he had worldly motives for endorsing that remarkable cure. What is a Turkish room to him?" (Edith had just installed one in their mansion, a fantasy of gold-glittering tiled walls, draped blue silk threaded with gold peacocks—the thread itself real gold, and heavy—hassocks, footstools, couches, armless and low, to recline upon, and yet Edith always sat on them as if she were in any stiff parlor, receiving afternoon callers). "He is not concerned with fashion, with those things that make one sigh *sic transit gloria mundi;* oh no, he cares only for the immortal within us, and if he is concerned with prolonging the life of our mortal half, certainly his motive is pure, for the longer we live, the more opportunities we have to close with Christ, and," she continued, stabbing an oyster with her small special fork, "it would be quite unreasonable for us to suppose he accepted money for his services, or that he *enjoyed* sitting for the artist who made that excellent likeness of him for the engraving. Why, it is featured so prominently, I almost think Dr. Talbott himself has been folded into *The Reformer,* he pops up so unexpectedly, and in such a natural, inevitable way. No, I am sure he improved the time of his sittings composing those sermons for which he is so justly famous; I am sure he did. For the sake of the esteemed doctor, it is almost our religious duty to attempt Nervine, and I really can't understand why Molly's doctor threw a bottle of that excellent brown liquid through a third-story glass window just yesterday afternoon. Perhaps," she finished, pausing with oyster in the air, "he hadn't yet read the advertisement. It was so uplifting."

"Perhaps he had seen too many people uplifted," her father meditated aloud; "uplifted and carried feet first all the way to Greenwood." "I think," Edith interrupted, furious, looking from one to the other, "that will be enough. This is not proper dinner-table conversation. You needn't smile at each other that way," she went on severely; "both of you are insufferable and you know it. Is there nothing we can discuss at dinner without insulting my guests?" "We can discuss other things, certainly, my dear," Edmund soothed; he was sorry for her. This confused Edith, who coolly began eating her oysters as if her appetite had never been better; as if, in fact, it was impossible to spoil it. "The theater," she said, looking up, "has never had a more interesting season. Mrs. Hatch of the Star Course is speaking this evening on the new production of *Macbeth*. We were fortunate to have had such excellent seats." "I always say," replied her father, without thought, "that the best seats are nearest the fire exit. The Star Course," he repeated in an undertone: "so today is Thursday; I had lost track of time. One day is so much like another lately." Edith stirred, impatient. How her dress *rattles*, Edna thought, watching her mother in her new low-cut taffeta dinner dress; it *rattles*. It rattles, just as the snake rattled in the parade exhibition. Rattle, rattle, rattle, she repeated silently, the word giving her, each time, new satisfaction.

"And what did you think of the production?" Edith asked Dr. Talbott; she was at her most sociable. "Oh, *I* thought it quite remarkable," Edna cut in; "what particularly impressed me," she said (look how pleased Mother looks, Edna thought, look how pleased she looks now, this is just how she likes it, conversation well-done), "was how very unnaturally Lady Macbeth washed her hands. It seemed to me she washed them in the *most* unnatural manner possible. It didn't look like a 'wringing' of the hands, which might have had an excellent effect. She seemed to be suffering from a severe case of frostbite. She rubbed her hands so slowly, and created such awkward angles with her elbows, I couldn't help thinking she was following some doctor's instructions, and was warming her hands as slowly as possible, while at the same time revenging herself on the rest of the troupe. I believe she got Macbeth between the ribs." "Macbeth," Edith said, icy, "was not present during the scene." "Wasn't he watching somewhere?" her father asked innocently. "In any case, he was certainly not *jabbed*," Edith said, indignant. "Was he not?" her daughter asked; "then you can see how

29

vividly the scene impressed itself upon me, for I had the distinct impression she jabbed him between the ribs, and viciously, too. I can still see him, almost doubled over, a ridiculous position for a famous general." The renowned divine fidgeted.

"He was not *jabbed*," Edith repeated, now almost hissing, "nor was he a general. He was a king. He was the king of the country." "I wish you women would get your facts straight," Edmund remonstrated. "First, he was a general, then a king. He was both. If he hadn't been such a successful general, he wouldn't have been tempted to be king." Edith had gone pale with rage. "Then, Edmund, do tell us. Was he *jabbed*?" "Jabbed? I think not." Edith looked at her daughter, triumphant. "Although," Edmund continued, "he certainly looked as if something were sticking at him: *I* never saw such an expression maintained through an entire performance. Perhaps it was his liver. We ought to hope the man is well. The play has two more weeks to run." "Oh!" Edith exclaimed, setting down her fork so that her wineglass jumped. *"Do* be careful of the china, Mother," Edna warned; "I don't know how many times you've cautioned me against careless setting down of silverware. I've never forgotten that tale you told me."

"What tale, what tale?" her mother asked. "Oh, that old cautionary tale of Mary, who slammed down her fork, smashed her Sèvres plate, and ended with a sliver of glass in her eye and had to be led from room to room for the rest of her life." "Dear me," Dr. Talbott said, finally making use of his famous lungs, "is that what they tell children in the nurseries, Mrs. Dickinson? That hardly sounds like a moral tale; it reminds one of *Oedipus Rex.* I understand there will be performances of the tragedies next season." "The story is true," Edith answered the divine, and then, unable to stop herself, asked her husband and daughter, "Are you both finished with me? It is *impossible* to be sociable in such an atmosphere."

"You take everything too personally," Edna said sweetly; "you must learn to *forget* yourself more, at least so Dr. Talbott told the congregation in the South Church last Sunday, didn't you, Dr. Talbott?" "Dr. Talbott again," Edith said angrily as if forgetting he was there. "Edith, what *are* we to talk about?" Edmund asked; "we can't seem to hit on anything satisfactory. I believe you ought to begin our conversations." I have begun *twice,* and if I begin again, I will only end as Lady Macbeth. Washing my hands of the two of you." "Edith, your temper," Edmund reproved her gently; "there is no point in working yourself up over such trifles." "I *detest* that expression," Edith hissed, "working oneself up; it is a very vulgar expression." "So it is." Edna agreed, "and one should never do it."

The rest of the meal was finished in silence, white light slanting in heavily through the high, narrow windows, one shaft of light falling on each of them, so that they would have appeared, to an observer, as if they were at the bottom of an archaeological excavation, and all this was taking place somewhere deep beneath the earth's surface. "And I must say," Edith broke out, staring pointedly at her daughter, "that your recent reading of etiquette books has done nothing whatsoever to improve your manners. In point of fact, I suspect your motive for reading them." "You suspect my motives for everything," Edna answered. Edith did not reply. "Perhaps I shall improve at some later date," Edna said sweetly. "There is so often a lapse between the studying of a subject and the understanding of it," Dr. Talbott put in hastily. "And the *application* of it," said Edith.

"Well, well," Edmund said, as if trying to shake himself awake in time to grasp something important, he wasn't sure what. "Thursday. The Star Course. I suppose it is my night for cards tomorrow." "I wish you the best of luck," Edith replied, nasty. "And you with your lectures. There's nothing worse than being held captive by an enthusiastic lecturer as dull as his subject, is there, Dr. Talbott?" "Oh Lord," Edith sighed. "Father meant nothing by that," Edna said. "What have I done now?" Edmund asked, sincerely perplexed; "I only ventured to hope that your lecture would be an interesting one. You know they can be very tedious." "Of course, of course," Edith answered; "no one in their right mind would deny that." Edna beamed happily at the heavy linen tablecloth; the servant slid the last dish from her. She was unaware her face betrayed any sort of expression. "Well. Cook has done quite well. As always." Edith's tone clearly implied a grave dissatisfaction with the menu of guests, and her daughter understood perfectly how much happier her mother would

have been had Mrs. Brown put carbolic acid in their
wine, Paris green in their soup. Edmund rose and took his
wife's arm; Dr. Talbott gingerly took Edna's. Edna
stared at his arm sideways. It's like having a wet, creeping
vine tickling your elbow, Edna thought as the four of
them left the dining room. The room was already immaculate, as if no one had ever eaten there.

The removal of Edmund Dickinson from the domestic
scene did nothing to consolidate relations between mother
and daughter, although, as the etiquette books insisted, in
agreement with the tomes on practical religion Dr. Talbott
was forever bringing to the house, grief often brought
family members closer together. The books could only
suggest, Edith thought gloomily; they could not command.
Now there were only two of them; she always came back
to that. Mrs. Dickinson had no brothers and sisters. Mr.
Dickinson's two brothers had gone to California, evidently
with no intention of returning. Phineas ("Why did your
mother choose such dreadful names for her children?"
Edith had once asked her husband) was staying in California to improve his health. ("I never heard of such
rheumatism; if it was really so bad, it wouldn't change so
with the weather and the days of the week.") Edith wanted
Phineas to return and resume his practice with her husband, who, she felt, was overburdened handling it alone,
but then everyone around her was so unreasonable.

Martin Dickinson had followed Phineas out to California, writing Edmund that he doubted he should ever
return East; he was smitten with the landscape and the
climate, and until he and Phineas were both married, he
might as well remain where he was and look after poor
Phineas, who was now so lame it took him over an hour to
get out of bed, when he could get out of bed at all, and
then he was incapable of dressing himself, his fingers were
so swollen. *That* act could not decently be performed by
anyone else until Phineas married, but so far he showed
no signs of entering that holy state; instead, he was perpetually singing, when he had the strength to sing, "The
happiest life that ever was led is always to court and never
to wed." In Martin's letter, written almost a month before
Edmund's death, he had said he was "thinking of adopt-
ing two boys; I went down to the poorhouse to look for

help, and they looked so pitiful." *"They* looked pitiful!" Edith exclaimed, fixing her husband with a pitiless glare. Edmund got up and looked out the window. "Long, stringy clouds," he said; "do you remember any of the proverbs concerning clouds? I thought I saw an article about those proverbs last week. You can foretell the weather by the clouds." "A pretty useless occupation, I'd say," Edith fumed, glancing at the offending letter on the table, "for someone who doesn't know whether it's raining before he leaves the house." "Oh well," Edmund sighed, "I suppose I'll never find that article about clouds." "You should have told me you wanted it; I would have clipped it out," replied his irritated wife.

And perhaps she was right to be so irritated with everyone and everything, for with her husband's death, she was alone with an impossible daughter, and, unlike her friends, unoppressed by a large, meddlesome family forever delivering themselves of sentiments concerning duties of mothers, duties of daughters, how the two unfortunates were now cast upon the cruel sea of life with no raft to cling to but one another, how two people who had shared a life for sixteen years had done more than share a house, a mere shell, but must now cleave to one another as solemnly as if they were taking marriage vows. How she would have liked to hear such fulsome pronouncements! They would, in short, make it clear that only proper, helpful behavior would be tolerated; within the circle of family society, she and her daughter would be remorselessly persecuted if they did not live up to the expectations their relations had formed for them.

Nor is there any doubt that, under such unremitting, pitiless pressure, Edna and Edith might have been forced into a satisfactory, comforting sympathy. They would have begun emulating the form of behavior approved in the family theater, constructed without exits, so that, in the event of fire, the members would be obliged to stamp out the flames together, or perish without outside aid. And, burning under the focusing lens of the magnifying family eye, a bond of sympathy might have grown up between them: as prisoners in the same cell, no matter how unlike, and how likely to detest one another under ordinary circumstances, often become, before their trials, the closest friends they will ever have. Her sense of her situation, worse than that of other widowed women, made Mrs. Dickinson ever more resentful of her unfeeling daughter, and when, in her grief, which was genuine, she looked up and saw that doll-like creature with her cool, accusing green stare, she felt a desperation far worse than any she had ever before felt. If her daughter felt something similar, Edith did not know it, for *she* was the one now responsible for administering her husband's estate (although, now, there was some slight hope Phineas would reach Boston in time to see to business affairs and settle her husband's considerable estate, the practice, the trust funds, and the money coursing through its mysterious channels.

But as soon as he finished with his last responsibility to his dead brother, Phineas would leave. He had never grown close to Edith. Indeed, he had spent only two evenings with his brother after his marriage.) And this responsibility for a daughter who existed only to persecute her, certainly not to help or comfort, only made her more disconsolate. And finally, more dismal, so that even her friends from the Star Course avoided her. They did not disapprove of her; it was not a question of approval or disapproval—they simply avoided her. Edith understood why this was so, but nevertheless, understanding only made her state of mind worse. She spent afternoons crying, sitting on her upholstered bench looking out of her dressing-room window, telling herself that should a friend of *hers* ever fall into similar circumstances, *she* would certainly behave differently; *she* would know how to sympathize with them. The trouble was, she told herself, no one else she knew had been similarly afflicted. There was, unfortunately, not a single widow among her intimates. This only made her cry harder. Her eyes, as Edna often thought, going about the house, dry-eyed, eyes glazed, were usually redder than her hair.

It all ended, several months later, as most bereavements seemed to, in a removal of the widow from the scene of the tragedy. Friends persuaded Mrs. Dickinson that a trip was what was required, a tour, unfamiliar faces. It had been *months* since she had been in New York. She owed it to her husband's memory to dress properly in her widow's weeds, and where else could she better outfit herself than in Manhattan, that great city? Even Dr. Talbott finally professed himself helpless before her grief, sententiously announcing that, at crucial points in spiritual affliction, the patient must help herself, and, although it was no doubt comforting to be within carriage distance of her husband's grave, still, the sight of flowers, withering constantly upon the raw grave, would do nothing to heal the companion wound in her heart. And, when she returned from her tour, renewed in body and mind, freed from the excesses of despair, she would be prepared to mourn properly. Mr. Siddons, who had removed to New York City two weeks before her husband's death, leaving her marble bust (as everything else) uncompleted, also prevailed upon her by mail to come and take a suite in the Regency. There he could introduce her to new scenes and new faces, and would be in a position to help her through this season of trouble and sorrow.

Thus it was that mother and daughter found themselves seated upon a white wicker love seat in Mr. Siddons' studio, which was hardly described by that bohemian term. Mr. Siddons had bought two town houses, broken through the adjoining walls, painted everything snow white; the entire establishment was furnished, all four stories of it, with the most elaborate white wicker. "An artist's dream," Edna whispered to her mother as they entered. Edith ignored her. She was getting better at that. Edna sighed. They sat down on a love seat somehow reminiscent, with its arches and spires, of St. Paul's Cathedral; they arranged their voluminous black skirts. They both looked extremely well in black. Edna appeared taller in her new costume, and Mrs. Dickinson, auburn hair showing under her elaborately trimmed black bonnet, seemed positively regal.

She really looks too beautiful to live, Edna thought. Why can't I think charitable things? she reproached herself. Why can't I think *one* charitable thought? I should at least feel some sympathy for her as a woman unaccustomed to traveling alone. She might as well be alone, Edna thought, remorseful. And why can't I cry? I never cry. It must mean, she thought in an agony, that I did not love my father either. But *she*, she cries all the time. Who knows what she is crying about? If I knew she was crying for my father, perhaps I *would* feel some sympathy. But I keep thinking, now she is crying because she has to give

35

the butler orders. She is crying because she thinks she ought to be crying. She is crying because she has nothing else to do. She is crying because funerals, any funeral upsets her. She is crying because she doesn't know what kind of flowers to put on Father's grave, or who should be asked to see to that while she is on her tour. She is crying because she doesn't know how long she should continue in mourning. She is crying because she had to close the piano as a sign of her grief and she can't play without disgracing herself in the eyes of society. Who knows why she cries? I tell myself she is crying because she loved my father, and had to see him lying in her bed, stiff as a board (at least they say that's how he looked), his face turned into a gargoyle's thanks to that rope that ended his life. At this, Edna's mind inevitably shut down, a piano lid slamming on fingers.

"I suppose he will be down soon," Mrs. Dickinson said. "Yes," Edna said, looking at her gold pocket watch. (It had been her father's; it could be set to chime the hours. Her father had used it as a means of ordering his day. It had been given to him by his father, who had been a lawyer before him. It bore the statue of justice, holding its scales, eyes bandaged, the other side engraved with her father's name, the letters arranged in a crescent around the outer rim of the case, and in the center, an enormous book—Edna supposed, correctly, it represented a text of law, and in the center of the book, a remarkably good likeness of her father's face.) Her father's face. As he was once. As he had been. As he had been only a month before. "Yes," Edna agreed, finally looking up. "I give him," she said, "ten minutes. A longer delay would be rude; a shorter delay wouldn't permit him to make an entrance."

"I hope," Mrs. Dickinson said wearily, "you will change that tone before Mr. Siddons comes down." "He certainly has his sculptures prominently displayed," Edna remarked, "although all this white on white, I doubt if it's the most effective method of display. Since the statues seem to be the only form of decoration, it would be more advantageous to display his works in an entirely black house." "That would be morbidity itself," Mrs. Dickinson answered, her voice enervated. "Decidedly so," Edna answered, "but all for art, don't you agree?" "I do not," her mother said; she did not move. Recently, she seemed to have acquired the ability of speaking without moving her lips.

"Here he comes!" Edna exclaimed, touching her mother's skirt automatically, then withdrawing her hand as if she had put it down on a hot stove. O dear God, her mother thought, dear God! Why did I ever have children? She doesn't begin to resemble me; she's completely unlike her father. And they say chldren are tokens to remember loved ones by. I should just as soon travel with a swarm of bees. But, Edmund used to say it, I gave birth to her, I raised her. It can't be all her fault. She really is only a child; I should be able to feel *something* more for her. (Edith was unable to admit feeling nothing for Edna; nor did it occur to her that she felt far more than she knew.) And, if someone had suggested that she did indeed feel deep sorrow for her daughter, she would have been more disturbed had she been accused of detesting her.

She is my child after all, Edith reflected. She looked at her daughter's profile. Everyone *says* she is my child, she thought, puzzled; I remember giving birth to her, but this isn't the same thing; this is not the same person. Perhaps, she thought, slightly hopeful, I am losing my mind. She wondered, vaguely, what a prolonged rest cure at a watering place would be like. She would refuse to move from a wing chair. She would be wheeled into the surf in a bath chair. She would not move a muscle or utter a word. Her insanity would take the form of silence, fashionable, beautiful helplessness. It was something; it was something to look forward to. But I shall never lose my mind, she thought in despair. I do not have the right kind of mind to lose.

Mr. Siddons had now reached the midpoint in his curving, white staircase. He was dressed in a black suit, but instead of the ordinary frock coat, or swallow tail, he wore a black cape lined with red satin. Edna turned to her mother, satisfaction painted all over her. How long will it take him to descend? she wondered; there must be glue on the soles of his shoes.

"I am so sorry, madam," Mr. Siddons said, pressing her mother's hand: "and *Miss* Dickinson, to be left fatherless at such a tender age, what can I say?" "Nothing would be best," said Edna. Her mother sighed again. "I understand," Mr. Siddons sympathized gravely; "an artist must understand these things. The very transitoriness of life that drew me to the enduring perfection of stone." He waved his hand at the statues behind them, as if dismissing them, his life's work, as irrelevant and unimportant in the face of her grief. "Should you prefer," he stopped solicitously over Edna to peer into her eyes, "not to discuss it? The subject must be extremely painful to you."

Unfortunately, as he swooped down on Edna, the dome of his classical forehead jarred the rim of her bonnet. She adjusted it ostentatiously, peering up at him blankly. Is the girl mad? he wondered; she is not answering me. It was his bad luck to have been mistaken. "Absolutely I would not care to discuss it, especially with you." "Edna," Mrs. Dickinson warned. "Dear lady," said Mr. Siddons, confident in his ability to handle any situation, particularly those involving women, "I understand your daughter's feelings. Here, in the midst of what will one day be tributes to the dead, in this hall of statuary in which your daughter too shall one day take her place, the subject is too painful for a sensitive nature to touch upon." "That is the explanation, of course," Edna agreed acidly. "You see? I knew it," Mr. Siddons virtually crowed. "Madam," he said, bending over Mrs. Dickinson, "Miss Dickinson *shall* be better; she *shall* cope." "I *am* coping," Edna put in; "and so," she added, ironically, "is my mother."

"Shall we tour the studio?" Mr. Siddons asked. "Do you mean to say there is more of it?" Edna queried in mock astonishment. "Edna," her mother cautioned again. "Oh no," Mr. Siddons interjected; "Miss Dickinson must feel free to comment on my art. The artist cannot forever live on his own opinions. He cannot forever bask in the imagined light of his own creations. Other humans must bring their dissecting eyes to bear on his work." "Although it is hard to believe," Edna said, turning to her mother, as if she were an actress speaking in a stage whisper, "I believe we have found a secular Dr. Talbott." "Yes, that is very fortunate," Mrs. Dickinson snapped, glowering at her.

"Shall we go upstairs?" asked Mr. Siddons, taking Mrs. Dickinson's arm, and helping her up from the wicker love seat. Then he turned to the daughter. "I shall be happy to struggle up by myself, if you please." There was no mistaking her tone. A silence fell softly in the white light. The beautiful faces of the life-size statues and the romantic busts peered at them or gazed calmly aside. "Shall we go up?" Mr. Siddons repeated; "I have my most recent work on the upper floors, including," he said, "the bust of your beautiful mother herself." Edna did not answer. "Shall we go up?" he asked again. Mrs. Dickinson was about to answer, or burst into tears, she was not yet sure which. "How *long* will it take?" Edna asked. "What?" asked the startled sculptor. "How *long* will it take to climb a flight of stairs? You must have four flights. I believe it took you seven minutes to come down one flight. I timed your descent by this watch." She turned its case toward him. Mrs. Dickinson had turned scarlet. "Perhaps," Mr. Siddons said stiffly, "it would be best if we put off this tour until a happier time." "I believe the director of the funeral parlor used that very phrase. Happier time. He had quite a stock of such expressions. His caskets, too, were numerous, as are these statues. And expensive, very much so. How much," Edna asked deliberately, smiling slightly, "do these statues cost?"

For women of society, the rules of visiting a studio were as familiar as, if not more familiar than, the Ten Commandments. One *never* asked the price of the creations. Certainly, one did not ask as if one were inquiring about a joint of beef. "I am very sorry, Mr. Siddons," Mrs. Dickinson said, grasping her daughter's upper arm so violently that Edna found it impossible to shake loose, "but my daughter is not herself. There is no apologizing for her behavior. The best I can now do is remove her from the premises. Immediately." "I trust she will recover herself in the hotel," the sculptor said. Mrs. Dickinson didn't answer, nor did she release her grip on her daughter.

The artist saw them to the door. "What an unmentionable horrendous hideous devilish imp of a brat," he said to the closed door. He would have continued, but he had exhausted his share of adjectives, and worse, he was upset. Although he had a small fortune of his own, he was fond of Mrs. Dickinson, whose attractions had first come to his attention in the form of her willingness to pay his startling fees, and he had hopes of acquiring her himself. Once her period of mourning was over, of course. "Of course," he said aloud, as if someone had doubted his words: "I need not even say it. Of course," he said again. "But that daughter," he went on aloud, "that daughter." Mr. Siddons comforted himself; the question of Mrs. Dickinson was not, in any event, a matter of immediate concern. Still, the daughter was beautiful, anyone could see that, and intelligent, and it disturbed him to find how thoroughly she disliked him, and so violently. It was as if he had gone to the mirror and suddenly discovered a bald spot in the middle of his mane of golden hair. "Oh! Mr. Siddons!" said a Mrs. Case, just admitted by a servant. "There you are! Lost in artistic thoughts as usual." She laughed lightly, which, he thought, was quite an accomplishment considering her bulk. *Why* did such stout women insist upon wearing plaid? Why did such stout women insist upon going out of the house at all? Of course, his sculpture of her would show a fashionably slender woman. There was no question about it. Mr. Siddons was seriously vexed.

"Get into that cab," Mrs. Dickinson ordered her daughter as the driver brought his horse to a stop. "That's right, get in," she commanded, unceremoniously boosting Edna up the little pair of iron steps by a violent blow to her bottom. Even through the billows of her hoops and petticoats, Edna knew she had been smartly whacked. That made her happy. "Through the park, madam?" the driver asked. When he received no answer, he headed toward it. "The weather is lovely today," he remarked. And the ride through the park was longer. The two women stared straight in front of them; it was unlikely they saw more than the back of their driver's head.

"All right," Mrs. Dickinson began, coming into her daughter's room, "we have something to discuss." "Do we?" "Don't bother, don't bother to distress me," her mother retorted, her polish removed by the solvent of her anger. "I think it's completely clear that this tour will never be satisfactory." "I believe it would end in murder," Edna said agreeably. "Well, then, what do you suggest?" "I suggest you send me someplace." "Send you someplace? Like a parcel? Where am I to send you? You've already finished with school." "I could always attend a seminary. I understand the Cherry Vale Music Seminary is quite good." "You have no musical talent whatever. You cannot sing a note, and when you play, it sounds as if men are tinning a roof." "Then I can stay with a friend." "All of your friends have left the city for the season." "I can stay alone in a hotel in any city, so long as I stay there alone." "As your mother—much as I would like to—I can't permit you to do such a thing. I would like to very much, I can tell you." "No more than I would like it." "There is only one place I can think of to send you," her mother said, exasperated, "and that's back to Ten's farm. But I can tell you, if your behavior continues so horrendously there, she won't have you on her premises for a single day, not even one day!" Edith was practically shouting. "Don't raise your voice," Edna said. "You are going to Ten's *tomorrow;* I am sending someone out on the cars *this minute* to beg her permission, and if he comes back in the morning you are going, do you hear me, you are going!" "You're screaming," Edna drawled.

"You are going to Ten's for the season, and I refuse to hear another word on the subject," shrilled her mother. "Well, you know I am perfectly helpless, at least for another year," Edna answered, poisonous. "I am *warning* you," Mrs. Dickinson said, "for the last time, if Ten will not have you, I am sending you out of the country. I have reliable information. There are still convents in France that will accept horrors like you." "A regular fishwife," Edna said sweetly. Mrs. Dickinson rang the bell pull so violently that part of its sash parted company with the brocaded wall. "Send to Mr. Siddons," she ordered the bellboy; "please ask him to permit me the use of one of his servants. I will need him in the capacity of messenger. For an overnight trip." She seemed infuriated with the poor boy. "Take a hansom."

"A hansom, madam?" "A hansom," she ordered, thrusting a bill into his hand without looking at it. The boy looked down at it, and up, as if just granted a vision of heaven. "Bring whoever Mr. Siddons wishes to send straight back in the hansom with you." "Oh yes, ma'am." "I suppose you don't have much to pack?" Mrs. Dickinson asked her daughter. "I haven't *un*packed." "So much the better," Edith said, turning her back, sweeping out the door. The door slammed behind her, and, at that sound, a satisfied smile spread slowly over Edna's face, then was replaced by an uncertain look, the two expressions alternating like the crest and dip of a wave. She had gotten what she wanted. She was going back to Ten's

41

farm. Her mother's friend Ten, or Aunt Ten, as she called her, was the only person on earth for whom she now cared. If her mother had known how much she wanted to go to Ten's, she would never have given her the satisfaction of letting her go.

But what *would* she do at the end of the season? I have time, Edna thought; I'll think of something. It occurred to her that she could always follow the example of one of her poorer classmates and take a position teaching school somewhere very, very distant from her mother, and Dr. Talbott, and Nervine Tonic (she had meant to recommend a bottle of it to her mother, but it had proved unnecessary), and Mr. Siddons and his preposterous porcelain dolls, for some reason executed in marble. She replaced the few things she had taken from her suitcases and fastened them securely. She looked contented as a kitten on the warm fur of its mother. The room filled slowly with sun until the room was blazing with light. The light was cruel to the eyes.

The messenger had been dispatched to Williamsville; there was nothing the two women could do now but wait. By this time, they preferred not to wait with one another, and since it was still early, and there was yet some time before the hotel served dinner, both were relieved when Mr. Siddons sent his landau drawn by his prize black stallion. A bellboy brought up his card, on which Mr. Siddons had written, in his tiny, exquisite hand, that they were to consider the vehicle at their disposal, and, should the horse tire, to change horses at Mr. Wright's livery right off the park. Faced with the alternatives of either pretending to read or sleep for what might amount to two days, or touring the city in this handsome vehicle, the two women silently concluded to be civil, if not kind, to one another while still in Manhattan.

While they were still in Boston, Mr. Siddons had recommended they begin their tour, if time permitted, from Weehawken, New Jersey, where they would have a wonderful view of Manhattan if the day was clear, as indeed it was. It was the ideal place for picnickers. They need not even take a basket, for women peddlers were more than happy to supply their needs from their own baskets, although Mr. Siddons strongly urged they patronize only the peddlers in starched, spotlessly white aprons. Last month, he had told them, there had been quite a scandal involving what turned out to be week-old deviled eggs; ladies and gentlemen of fashion were doubling up on every sidewalk of Manhattan.

The view, he told them, was picturesque as could be, little wooded promontories jutting into the bay like islands, sailboats of every description on the blue waters, and the steeples of St. John's Chapel and Trinity Church clearly visible. "Well, Mother," Edna had said then, "Mr. Siddons described the scene so well it would appear redundant to see it." Her mother had made no comment, and Mr. Siddons had refrained from further descriptions of the wonderful city. Nevertheless, Mr. Siddons could not refrain, Edna mentally noted, from making further suggestions now, almost as if he were an invisible member of the party. He had drawn a small map charting "an interesting series of prospects," beginning in Brooklyn Heights. His accompanying note gave them the name, address, and directions to the house of an old friend who would be more than happy to allow them to view the city from his rooftop, equipped with an excellent telescope, and the landau's driver had several letters of introduction which they were free to make whatever use of they cared to.

"Shall we begin with Brooklyn Heights?" asked Mrs. Dickinson. "Certainly," replied Edna. To the driver, they acted and sounded like two acquaintances who, never having seen one another before, but now forced into one another's company, were at least determined to make the best of a bad business. The streets were not crowded; the carriage made excellent progress. They soon found themselves in front of Mr. Eddy's residence. It was a high, white rectangular house, brick, whitewashed, with a sharply sloping slate roof, a small rectangular addition whose roof formed the foundation for a pigeon coop, and a small, private promenade overlooking the bay. The street railings were constructed to resemble spines of a stairway, and, as had been promised, there on the roof was a small brass telescope fastened to a steel pole which could be swiveled for a better view of almost every residence from the East River to Canal and Wall streets. "So this is Columbus Street," Mrs. Dickinson said as the coachman helped her alight. "Yes," Edna answered.

Could that woman never think of anything original to say? A maid wearing a black uniform and starched white apron and cap admitted them; she and Mr. Siddons' coachman excused themselves. The letter was delivered and read, whereupon the maid returned, smilingly asking them to follow her. The two women began their stately ascent up the four flights of steps to the roof, Edna involuntarily pausing on the second-story landing, where, in front of an immense sunny window, deliberately left uncurtained, a huge marble statue, approximately twice life size, stood whitely in a flood of yellow light. "Mrs. Eddy," commented the maid, seeing Edna staring at it. "It's very unusual; is there some reason she's standing behind a huge marble tub?" "Oh, reely, miss, I don't know, I'm sure," the girl answered (one of the daughters of the Emerald Isle, Mrs. Dickinson noted to herself), "but I think she wanted something to"—she hesitated, trying to remember the proper, overheard word—"to commemorate," she burst out, triumphant, "her view of heaven."

Mrs. Dickinson evinced a sudden interest in the plastered stairway wall. Splash, splash, splash, Edna thought; God is in his heaven, all is right with the world. "Perhaps she pictures it as holding the bay she so loves," Edna said charitably. "Oh, that must be it!" the maid exclaimed, delight rouging her cheeks; "to tell the truth, madam, I always wondered at it myself. Now *my* mother," she confided, "thinks of baths as treacherous wicked things, you know, what with getting your feet too cold while the rest of you is warm or having certain parts of you too warm while the rest of you is cold, you know what I mean, miss, and those claw feet on that tub, well, until I came here, I never saw the like of them."

"What did you do for baths?" Edna chatted. "Oh, we all sat in a big wooden tub, an odd kind of thing it was, you know, coming apart into things like, like slats, and in the evenings it all holds itself together like those things fashionable ladies wear under their dresses, but before it came apart, you know, we sat in it and one of us poured pitchers of water on the other, we took our turns, you know." "In the same water?" asked Mrs. Dickinson, incredulous. "Oh yes, ma'am," the maid answered, while Edna's mother hurriedly resumed staring at the smooth plaster.

"Here you are, a good enough climb for you, I'd wager," the young maid babbled; she opened a small wooden door made of two broad slabs of wood, roughly joined. The two women were obliged to turn sideways to squeeze themselves and their billowing skirts through the aperture. "And there is the funny little pipe thing, the *glass,*" she corrected herself, prim. "Why," she burst out, "you can even see the little dogs running up and down the streets, you know, if you try hard enough. It's the little dogs I like to look at, you know." "You must spend a great deal of time up here," Edna said, sympathetic. Why doesn't she ever talk to me like that? Edith wondered. Why does she only take an interest in others? King or chimney sweep, anyone but her mother; she's sweeter than honey now; she's *kind*. Even if she is a little stiff. Yes, no matter whom she talks to, she is always a little stiff, a little unbending.

"Oh no, ma'am, no, I don't get up here near often enough; I'd been thinking it was the best place to hang the clothes, not in the garret, you know, but Mrs. Eddy won't hear a word about it, not one. She says no arms and legs flapping from the roof of *her* house like an emergency hospital, but if she wanted the fresh air for them, why then I could get up here so many more times, and I do like to see them freeze on the line, especially the underthings, you know, they look so comical when they're all stiff and silly, a regular society party, that's what I always say." Edna was positively grinning.

Edith suddenly remembered the artist posing Edna for a sketch; she was only a child then and was standing near a Sheraton table in their parlor, the magnificent woodland frieze painted on the milky glass behind her, flooding her little daughter in a green and golden light; she had been wearing a little plum-purple dress, with its neat row of matching covered buttons marching down its front like little orderly ladies, the bands of white velvet alternating with the tiny flounces, really more like pleats; the dress was so small, but it had been designed to resemble "Mama's," and there Edna finally stood in the oil painting, half turned into the room, the old beige lace, handed down from generation to generation, lapping just over her fragile wrist, her other arm encircling a precious structure of colored blocks, built while waiting for the artist to set up palette and easel.

At the time, Edith thought the little building of blocks looked more like a prison than a home. At least it was impossible to decide what the little architect was thinking of when she put the entrance to the building one third of the way up the façade of her building, so that no ladder could reach it. But perhaps Edna had intended the resident to stand on the back of her old elephant, which she had also insisted on placing upon the table.

It had been made from remnants of Edith's old purple velvet dress; Edna had taken it into her head to have the elephant's tail facing the painter, so that the rip in his back was clearly visible, as were all the pins and seams servant after servant had inflicted upon the poor animal's scarred back in their attempts to prolong his beloved life. Yes, Edith remembered, that contraption her daughter's arm rested on was a writing desk. It was her father's, a leather contraption, made especially for him, the edges banded with brass, the bands nailed on with brass pins, the leather embossed with an intricate crest, and Edna spent hour after hour playing in his study while he worked, trying to determine where one part of the design ended and the identical design again began. She never did discover that seam, the secret joining, but she kept at it year after year, as she kept after the servants and her velvet elephant. At one point, the poor tormented animal had sported two tails, so harassed was the maid by Edna's pathetic requests to refasten its appendage. That familiar wail. "The tail! The tail! My elephant's gone off without his tail!" And how she hugged him and cried and cried. Where was that elephant now? Surely we never threw it out, Edith thought; surely I would never have permitted the servants to throw it out. Could I have carried it out myself, she wondered, trying to trace some dim, but definite memory, during that epidemic of the typhoid? There was something we had to take from her after she visited that little girl who died two weeks later. There was *something* we took. I don't remember what it was. Why don't I remember these things?

She did remember, however, that although Edmund's desk was always covered with legal papers and unending correspondence, Edna would manage to play there without moving a sheet, and Edmund was very exacting. When he set down a neat sheaf of papers, he required it, for reasons Edith never understood, to remain exactly where it was. And since they lived on a busy street, on a trafficked street, there would inevitably be an almost invisible outline of dust which would reveal the smallest movement of any object on his desk. Yet he never objected to Edna taking his worktable as her place of play. He never minded if her elephant was found bleeding stuffing on his writing desk, if her blocks were placed squarely in the center of a stack of papers. Somehow, Edna played freely and happily without moving inkstand, writing desk, or letters, and Edmund never (no, not never—once he had swept the blocks to the floor, but the next week he had come down with scarlet fever, and all was forgiven by the queen of babydom) moved one of his daughter's possessions without consulting her as solemnly as he would a hanging judge.

And then there was that old painting she treasured so. It still hung in her own bedroom, but a heavy hanging concealed it; yes, she did look at it, but only after fastening the door behind her. In it, Edith was sitting at the shuttered window somewhere in Montpelier where they had gone as city boarders after the loss of her second child; the gold light flickered in through the heavy leaves. That was the color the past always seemed caught in. And she was sitting on a wooden chair holding open a children's book. (What was that book? Edna had been five; it must have been some tale of an animal. How she cried over tales of animals!) Edith hated to read them to her, but Edna insisted on hearing them. At the sight of her sobbing daughter, she would find her throat tightening and tightening, as if a hand had closed on it.

But in the picture, she was looking down at the book, her hair gathered up in thick curls pinned carelessly to the top of her head, and there Edna was, dressed in the purple outfit the elephant later grew from, a straight line of buttons down the front of *her* dress, a row of vertical tucks running down its length, and there was the book. Now it was coming clearer and clearer on the plaster wall: it was resting on her white apron, a hand-crocheted apron her own mother had made her when she had first announced her pregnancy, little round flowers stitched to suns, all attached with tiny fancywork stitches, open as air and lighter; how gracefully the apron fell. How delicate it looked next to the plain handwoven curtains of the room. And Edna, leaning in toward her, looking down at the book, her small body snuggled into her mother's boned bodice. The expressions on their faces! Oh, she could remember her own. She radiated; she was an ember glowing. She outglowed the sunlight itself, and even though the pose made her nose seem longer, and the lines in her cheeks deeper, she loved the light coming through the window, most of which fell on little Edna, dressed in her striped cotton dress, its little sleeves puffed at the shoulders, her starched little white collar with its red bow, cutting most of her chin from view; and it was odd, how old Edna looked.

She looked older than her mother, and more serious, with those deep-set eyes, and the painter had rendered the scene just as it was, all the tricks of the light, how it bleached the child's face, how it made her dark hair appear golden. It was the shine of the sunlight reflected on her mirrory dark hair. Edna seemed bleached out by the sun, pale and helpless, and her hair had not yet grown really thick, so that it was cut just below her ears and short over her forehead; that was very unbecoming to her, at least when she was a child. It was not so now.

Nothing was as it was then. Surely, Edith thought, agonized, it could not *all* have begun with that elephant. It could not all have begun because I tried to keep the typhoid from her. Children died that season, crops in a drought. She had lived in terror, real, immobilizing terror through which she managed to move through sheer exercise of will, and yet—and yet, perhaps her daughter had misunderstood the abduction of that beloved animal. Perhaps she had misunderstood her mother's emotional state. Perhaps she had not been deceived by the mannequin motions of affection she had gone through, all for the sake of preserving her daughter's tranquil state of mind.

But things were never the same again. Never. Surely it could not all have begun with that *elephant!* It was not fair. And she could no more ask Edna about the elephant than she could walk across the bay to the buildings she had been staring at so blindly. She thought of it; she thought of saying, Edna, do you remember? You had an

elephant made of my old purple dress. She thought of
explaining how it had happened and why, but she could
not endure the sight of that green gaze upon her. It would
rip her open, as the second child had ripped her open. She
could not bear to have that child, no, this child, born dead
again; no, not for the second time.

"The ships are very interesting," she heard Edna saying. "That long one steaming along, the one with that
long cloud of smoke, must be going south, and the
schooners, there's no telling where they're headed." "How
I envy the little yachts," Edith said with feeling; "they
could be going anywhere." "Or just drifting," Edna
agreed; "that would be nice, I think, just to drift on the
water, to bob up and down. I wonder," she asked, uncharacteristically mischievous, "if Mrs. Eddy ever fills up
that marble tub and climbs in with a little model just like
that one." She pointed with her gloved hand to a yacht
almost reaching the darker edge of the Manhattan shore-
line. "It is so lovely here," she thought aloud; "and the
air is so soft, almost like skin. And that smell, it's perfume." "Yes," Edith agreed, "the people here have rose
bushes potted in planters. They seem to be on every porch
and roof." "Roses and geraniums," Edna said, looking
about her. "What became of the maid?" "Mrs. Eddy
called her." "Did she? I didn't hear her. How odd." They
stood there, looking out over the bluish-gray water, over
at the white and gray buildings, punctuated by occasional
rose brick houses, the uneven little skyline. The city was
reduced to a miniature from this roof, an elaborate construction of fancily carved and fitted blocks, the steeples
rising from the roofs, the masts rising from the anchored
boats like pencil strokes, and in back of the island, another
stripe of water, this one slate gray, Staten Island, its buildings barely discernible, although to the right Edna could
see a road, rising up a hill, and what seemed to be a
climbing line of some kind of similar structures; slabs,
she thought, a burial ground. Odd how the best places
were always chosen for the dead. Not for the dead, of
course, but for the visitors. They must have *something* to
look at, something they believe the dead look at when
they awake and return, before they go back again to their
long homes. I suppose, she thought, I think it is true the
dead just leave the room, all the rooms, and roam about

perfectly free, out of everyone's sight, or at least out of the sight of their families. The living would not be used to them in their new state; I suppose that's why. A carriage, driven by a man in bright red livery, rumbled past. "Shall we push on to Castle Garden, then?" she asked her mother, polite. Edna felt a terrible sense of defeat, but at what? At what had she been defeated? "Yes," Edith sighed; "yes, we might as well." What is she thinking now? Edna wondered; I should like to know what she is thinking now. The two of them turned, soundlessly descended the stairs.

The landau was waiting for them, the driver sleeping peacefully, his chin resting on the gold buttons of his peacock-blue uniform. "Castle Garden," Edith said, and the horse set off, hoof clack after hoof clack, passing other open carriages, all of the ladies involuntarily swiveling their heads in automatic inventory-taking of spring fashions. "What a pretty place," Edna remarked, as she and her mother walked, side by side, over the little covered bridge to the island building with its round cupola for viewing the harbor, the sharp steeple rising from it, a needle picking the gray silk sky; it was going to storm. The whole sky had become one gray cloud. "Do you want to go up to the tower?" Edith asked. "Not really." "Nor do I." "I would be happy enough leaning over the railing looking into the water," Edna finally said. "Yes." They leaned over; they stared at their faces in the water. A trick of the light, or of the waves, superimposed one face upon another. Edith was reminded of her husband's likeness in its frame on the parlor table. There is nothing, nothing whatever, wrong with me. His voice had been so determined. Back on the cement walk across the little band of water separating them from the park, two little black dogs were fighting. A child was virtually pulling his father's arm loose in a fruitless attempt to free himself and get at the dogs, while his mother, dressed in rose, had attached herself to the father's other arm. Two ladies, one dressed in yellow, another in blue, sat on a long wooden bench while a little urchin tried to sell them something. Young men lounged against the rails. The railing was peculiar. It was constructed of stones which resembled arched tombstone after arched tombstone, fifteen feet apart, each connected by two parallel iron bars. "Peaceful," Edith said.

She was reminded of the temporary headstone for Edmund's grave and the plans for the family mausoleum Mr. Siddons was drawing up. What, really, was *her* view of heaven? Surely not a tub. Perhaps she should think carefully about its design: a family of three, arms clasped about each other's waists. That might be the very thing, the three of them with their backs to the little path. The faces, the expressions, no, they should not be visible immediately. Or visible only to those who were interested enough to walk around the statuary to look into the faces, the design of the clothes, the expressions. Those things, they were not important; it was the design, the three stone figures locked in their stone embrace. *That* was important. "Well," Edith said aloud, "we might as well be on our way. You've always wanted to see Wall Street; we can drive by that gallery you're interested in on our way to the park, unless you've seen enough of it." "No, I don't remember it at all," Edna answered; "we might as well be off." "It does feel strange," her mother said in a low voice, "to be on our own hook this way."

It was the calm before the storm. They both knew it. Insofar as they could enjoy anything, they both enjoyed it, for when they drove down Wall Street, right up to Trinity Church, which both of them had so looked forward to seeing, neither could help thinking of the Customs House and the treasury and the banks as huge, huge vaults. It was not difficult to imagine them filled with caskets. "Do you want to go in?" Edith asked, motioning in the direction of the church. "No, no," Edna said; "I've had enough of churches." The church has a clock, she noticed, startled; a church should not have a clock. A church should have nothing to do with clocks. "Can we go on to the park?" she asked aloud. "The little maid told me there was a gas balloon anchored above the Mall. I should like to see it." "To the park," Edith ordered, leaning forward. "I had forgotten the artificial lake and the refreshment tent," Edith said wearily; "we ought to see them."

The carriage began moving again. "The landscaping is much more formal than I expected," Edna remarked. "What odd banners," she continued, looking at the immensely tall Chinese flags mounted like archways over the steps going down to the park's man-made lake and the

pleasure boats waiting there. "I suppose we ought to return for our supper," Edith said; "Ten's answer ought to
be there by now." "Perhaps so," Edna answered, smiling,
her face, for the first time in weeks, almost sunny. Edith
noticed it and felt cold. "I should have taken my cloak,"
she said; "there's a chill in the air." "Perhaps you have a
fever," Edna said, looking closely at her; "we must call the
hotel doctor." "Nonsense," Edith retorted; "I have no
fever; I merely take cold very easily." Her voice had gone
cold. "My blood must be thin." "I might as well say it before she does, Edith thought. "I should like to sit under
that umbrella-like thing someday," Edna remarked in the
same frigid voice which had so chilled Edith when they
first left the hotel. The truce was over.

A letter from Ten was waiting for them. Edna could
come at whatever time was convenient for her. During the
night, she wrote, a hack could be gotten by one of the
station porters, and if Edna wanted to leave immediately,
she was not to worry about awakening the household, for
she slept so lightly, and fell asleep so easily, it would be
a pleasure to be awakened by a guest instead of the usual
demented bird flying at a glass hoping to get into another
world just like the one he already inhabited. Mrs. Dickinson, however, concluded (and her daughter) that a midnight arrival would certainly impose upon Ten, and her
brother, John Ashbel Steele, and it was agreed that Edna
would leave on the earliest morning train. "I think," Edna
said, avoiding her mother's eyes, "I would like to go for
a walk on Broadway and look into the shops." "Do as you
please," her mother answered; "I'm going up to my room
to rest. You had better stop for something to eat; you may
miss the supper hour here. Try Riboli's." "Yes, yes, I will,"
Edna agreed; she would have agreed to anything. "Please
take my daughter wherever she wants to go," Mrs. Dickinson instructed the driver, leaving the vehicle.

The landau set off briskly for Broadway where Third
and Fourth Avenue met. Edna wanted to see the famous
beer halls her father had spoken of so often. Both sides
of the streets were lined with canvas awnings which extended from the first stories of the buildings to the edge
of the sidewalks. Horse-drawn trolleys painted bright red
kept passing and passing; private carriages passed con-

tinually. There was the commotion of human voices, arguing and talking, wagons arriving with long planks of lumber, and, at the juncture of the street, wagons piled high with hay to supply the city's endless liveries. Edna abandoned her adventurous plan of asking Charlie, the driver, to escort her into one of the beer halls. There is too much life here, she thought; I shall be glad to leave. "The Regency, please," she called to Charlie, who reined in the horses and began the delicate maneuver of turning them around in the jostling street. "Will you want the carriage tomorrow, miss?" Charlie asked. "Yes, please. If you would stop at the station and check on the schedules; I should appreciate information—the earliest train to Brattleboro." "The hotel has a schedule," Charlie reminded her. "Yes, I know, but the railway may have added a car." "Not likely," Charlie answered. "Please check nonetheless." "My pleasure, miss; but it's useless, I can tell you." "Nevertheless," Edna repeated; "and whatever the time of departure, if you would arrive at the hotel one and a half hours earlier." "You'll have a long wait at the station," Charlie ventured. "I don't wish to miss the train." Charlie drove on in silence.

As Charlie had foreseen, Edna and her mother arrived at the depot far too early. Mrs. Dickinson could not prevent herself from commenting that the great iron horse must be lame today, and she hoped it would not limp all the way to Brattleboro, rattling Edna's brains beyond repair, but she was rewarded with a look which set her to carefully observing every lady present. Finally, she became so absorbed in that activity that she made careful mental notes of all new combinations of colors, all new styles of bonnets, as meticulously as any dressmaker or milliner. Primarily, she tried to avoid thinking her own thoughts. Perhaps because of the early hour the hotel parlormaid had awakened them—four o'clock in the morning—really, it was preposterous—but Edna had insisted on taking the six o'clock train—she was largely successful. The landau had rattled them along in what looked like moonlight, not early morning, although by the time the depot came into view, houses and horses alike cast great shadows, menacing carpets leading to their doors. The houses have the most interesting shadows, Edna thought; how the huge rectangles cross each other, as if someone had vandalized a cemetery and thrown down the headstones any which way. The shadows of the horses, lighter, more transient, flowed across those immovable rectangles like shadows of phantom beasts.

Edna occupied herself sitting primly on a bench, apparently indifferent to surrounding events, and, at predictable intervals, jumping up and walking briskly to the cement edge bordering the railway tracks, bending at a right angle from her waist (an activity, in her stays, which left her breathless) hoping for a hint of the desperately awaited locomotive. Nothing, as ever, she thought, returning to the brightly enameled green bench. *We* certainly are a blotch on the face of spring, Edna thought, looking from her own black lap to her mother's. How dead the two of us look; if her mother had taken up silence, Edna was now bent on torturing herself. This does not look, she thought, like a lap that would ever bear children, or a stomach that would ever expand to harbor them. I suppose it is all settled, really, she went on; I can feel it, that I am meant to be one of those childless old spinsters who find some little corner to make themselves useful in, or at least unobjectionable, except I shall have to build my own corner; there's certainly no one who would want to offer me one in a dwelling of theirs.

She had worked herself up into a state of mourning for her as yet unfulfilled destiny. Yes, she continued to herself, the future is like a train. I only have to sit here and wait for it. In each of the cars there is another version of me. I only have to sit here and wait for it. There I am, getting into the first car, in this mourning dress and bonnet, and in the second car, a little older (where am I going? the scenery stays hidden); the shades are pulled down; there is only the reflection of my face in the glass. And there I am in the third car. It's a long train, and there I am, wrinkled and alone, and I suppose, she thought, getting up, impatient, (why wouldn't *this* train of thought steam off over the horizon?) that if the train were long enough, there would come my coffin, and next the wagon, bringing it right to Cedar Street in Boston, and my dear mother. "Oh, Mrs. Dickinson," they would all be saying; "how tragic for a mother to see her child die before its time"; and my mother, no, it's not difficult to hear her. She would be crying into an elaborately embroidered black handkerchief (perhaps she has already saved some for the blessed event); "*Mrs.* Weatherly, to live beyond one's child! If there can be a greater sorrow, I do not want to know it. Ah, there goes Edna, so soon to join Edmund, and I, I am left to wander this earth alone, like a ghost, a disembodied spirit, a ghost God himself forgot about!"

And here Mrs. Weatherly would press her hand and ask, "*Dear* Mrs. Dickinson, what took your daughter?" She paused, thinking. "Oh, it was a silly thing," she heard her mother saying; "you know how my daughter adores riding, and we always thought it was so good for her. Well, she would take her favorite horse out to the apple orchard where there were so many snakes. . . ." "She was bitten by a snake?" interrupted the horrified Mrs. Weatherly. "Oh, not a snake," her mother continued, her tone tired, pitiful; "no, it was the horse that bit her. She picked up an apple, and I suppose the horse's eyes had become weak, but you know what my daughter is like, or was like; she would not be parted from anything. The horse thought her hand was the apple, and bit right into it; she died of the infection." "Yes," Mrs. Dickinson was finishing, fashionably dabbing at her eyes; "the doctor said the loss of blood had weakened her. The horse carried her right back to the stable, just as if she were the saddle." "She won't even let me die with dignity!" Edna thought bitterly, turning the justifiably withering look of an outraged ghost upon her mother.

"There's the train, madam," Charlie said to Edith. He immediately began to observe the locomotive with immense interest. Edna coolly announced that undoubtedly it was not their train at all: *she* would not scurry back and forth like a frightened lapdog only to find the train was departing for Kansas. "Kansas! Edna! How can you be so unreasonable?" her mother spluttered; "Charlie inquired of the depot master three times now and this train *is* bound for the Green Mountains." "Have Mr. Siddons' servant inquire again," Edna instructed hatefully. Mrs. Dickinson sighed, ignoring her. "What is that?" Edith asked Charlie, who was beginning to slump standing straight up. "What, ma'am?" "That red peaked thing on the front part of the locomotive." Is everything I say incomprehensible? she wondered, exasperated. Edna, she saw, was looking at her watch. Five-fifteen. Almost an hour before the train would be ready to board. "Beg pardon, ma'am, that's a cowcatcher," Charlie answered. "A cowcatcher? Why would the train want to catch cows?" It crossed her mind that perhaps the dining cars acquired their beef in that manner. Idiot! Edna commented silently. "Beg pardon, ma'am," Charlie said again, flushing, "they don't actually catch the cows, you see, but a cow will sometimes get onto the track and then that ironworks, the cowcatcher, it's supposed to pick the cow up." "And if there's a whole herd of cattle," Edith asked, noting with horror her own abnormal interest in the subject; "surely the train can't lift them all." She contemplated, puzzled, the picture she had conjured up; it was a locomotive covered with cattle, their brindled bodies mounting almost to the engineer's window.

"Why, then, ma'am," answered the increasingly befuddled Charlie, "the train stops, of course, until the men clear the tracks." "What men?" "The drovers who own the cattle, ma'am." "What?" Edna suddenly asked; "not Little Bopeep?" "Little Bopeep clears the tracks of sheep," Mrs. Dickinson hissed. The two women fell silent. Charlie stared at both of them. And women of such quality! he thought, pitying; it would be terrible to see them taken off to Northfield. Charlie's old Aunt Bertie, the one who had taken to singing, "Will my love ever come back to me?" in the garret under the dripping clothes had been taken off to Northfield by the minister. It would be just terrible to see these two ladies taken off to Northfield. He mentally wagged his head, although, there was no denying it, the idea gave him some satisfaction. It wasn't the nicest thing to drive two ladies around, both of them in a fit, even if (he remembered some of Mr. Siddons' other clients) he had seen worse days. Yes, he almost observed aloud, I have seen worse days. That's the truth; I have.

"I suppose," Mrs. Dickinson was asking, "that cowcatcher is also useful in clearing off the *pyramids* of snow they have falling up there all the time?" "Well, ma'am, again, like with the cows, you know, if there's not a huge amount of snow, just a drift or two, the cowcatcher will do just as fine as can be, but if it's a storm, then it's the snow plow they need." "I see," Mrs. Dickinson said absently.

The engine was beginning its chuff and cough. It isn't easy to believe all this began with Father's death, Edna thought. But then, what exactly *had* started? Perhaps, she thought, it was true the train of her old life had been interrupted, nothing more, temporarily sent along the wrong track, through the wrong, temporary scenery, not really wrong, but temporary, as when her father had once hung a tapestry of a hunting scene over a bathroom window when the house in Boston was undergoing renovation; he had refused to give up the convenience of using the room. But Edna could not persuade herself of this. Her father's death had done something that could not be considered temporary. It had shut the door to the way of life she had always known. The house on Cedar Street—that was someone else's house; the people whose lives had gone on inside concluded now, an impossibility. It was similar to her childhood belief that she *could*, if she only thought hard enough, live in the dollhouse her father had made for her. She will marry Mr. Siddons, Edna thought without resentment, as if her mind had become a winter scene, in which the gray of the sky and the gray of the snow, and the ice, and the pastures, all blended together into one tapestry subtly woven of different degrees of cold. If I stay away long enough, she will marry Mr. Siddons. There was little emotion attached to that realization, just as there was little curiosity, or even worry, devoted to her own ability to live independently of her mother. A pond had frozen over. Somewhere, in the old house on Cedar Street, there was an old pair of ice skates in a trunk in the attic.

Mrs. Dickinson, too, was oppressed by a feeling of finality. She is only going off to Ten's, Mrs. Dickinson comforted herself. She will tire of those blueberries; she has no patience. She will get tired of those blue fingers and stained clothes, and brambles catching on her skirt, and trotting around on that old dray horse Ten calls a riding animal; she will get tired of it. And then with Ten's brother John sitting across the table, radiating dislike of young ladies, why, if it were me, she thought, cheering, I would just as soon throw myself into the wood stove. She will get tired of it.

So they stood there, the daughter mentally bidding farewell to every stick and stone in the old town house on

Cedar Street, that tall pink rectangle, its high, square windows, evenly placed up and down its five stories, its high, steep flight of steps up to the massive front door, in shape and size exactly like one of the windows. And above the windows, their shutters thrown back, an upper set of shutters, in the shape of an open fan, the shutters closed unless the day was dark, then thrown open to catch every available particle of light, so that inside, the rooms seem filled with small cathedrals, cathedral-shaped squares of light arguing, usually victoriously, with the gloom inside. And the huge oriental rugs, and the gleam of the neatly placed furniture, the beautiful textures of the highly polished wood, the splendor of the European crystal chandeliers, lit every evening by the servant solemnly carrying in the long wick.

The army of servants saw to it that nothing ever moved. The square silver cigar box from Japan with its flying eagle always gleamed on the long table near the winged chairs, resting on the polished surface of the small chestnut table. The double candelabras shone perpetually on the oval dining-room table, wavering underwater in the grain of the table, and the magnificent carved chairs, one after another, down the length of the room, with their red and white striped velvet, the extra upholstered chairs in the corners, the filled vases of fresh flowers (they had always hurried the florist's bill from her sight), nothing would ever change in that room, in that house. I don't want a house like that, Edna decided, closing its front door gently, listening to it latch behind her: Now I am locking the door; now I am locking it forever. I do not understand that child, Mrs. Dickinson thought, looking over at her daughter. But I was a young mother. I suppose I shall have enough time to puzzle her out. I will, won't I?

It was a question, though. Mrs. Dickinson was a social being from the tip of her bonnet to the end of her polished, buttoned boot, and she swam as happily in society as fish swam in schools. But Edna was not basically a social being. She was given to her own thoughts, and generally to introspection. Nor was she particularly interested in herself, or in what moved others in the material world. Any subject in a book, though, that was different. It was likely to catch her up and hold her captive for month after month. She had inherited her father's scholarly disposition, although, as Edna herself had observed often enough, not his sense of purpose or direction. While her mother could induce sleep by pouring the flutter and chatter of a ball scene into her evening glass of milk like a powder, Edna, when wakeful, pictured a perfectly empty room, slowly filling with darkness, a single brighter beam striking the single wooden chair in the corner, then sliding back, up the wall, out the window. Then the darkness was perfect. She would wake many hours later. The pressures of life in society were not particularly inimical to her; nor were they congenial. But they exhausted her, as the constant effort to shut out irritating noises exhausted one desperately preparing to take his examinations. And, just as such a student would flee the noisy room for the patrolled silence of a library, Edna had lived with the unacknowledged but powerful impulse to flee to a quieter, less populated place. Or at least a place filled with other noises, so that no matter how many sounds there were, to her they would form a harmony, a kind of song, a bird on a bough, a music box; then she would be happy.

Had there been less tension in the house on Cedar Street, had she taken more after her mother, less after her father, so that her mother might have begun to understand her, or at least have called the proper physician whose prescription might have been nothing more drastic than periodical removals from the ordinary scene where silence itself would have been the most powerful curative: life for her small family might have run more smoothly. But no, she resembled her father, who did not understand himself any more than his wife understood him. She was forced, more and more, into a society of her mother's choosing, as was her father, her mother surrounding herself with chattery, apparently happy women.

Her father, if only because of the demands of his profession, was surrounded by an unlikely collection of petitioners, scandalmongers, either suing or being sued, men suing for divorce, wives suing their husbands, poisoners, stranglers, incompetent doctors, ministers under attack by vengeful congregations, teachers defending themselves against accusations of prudish, evil-minded parents, and most recently, a deputation from a church group, which wanted to prevent, legally, the other half of the congregation from changing the old pine pews in the historic church. The old pine pews were uncomfortable; that was their virtue. They kept everyone interested in what they were supposed to be interested in. No falling asleep and dreaming improper thoughts in *them*.

This society did nothing to cheer her father; neither could he abstract himself from it. Edna often thought of his clientele rising like a thick cloud from some huge bottle clearly marked with skull and crossbones, and in the background, stiff, bony women inveighing against the evils of such drink. Her father had become drunk on their society. Yet, slowly, they were poisoning him, and there was no temperance league to stop the imbibing of stories he heard: servants poisoning their mistresses (one right on Cedar Street, a "particular" friend of her mother's, with Paris green brought back from a visit to her sick mother in the country). Had her father wanted to get to the bottom of these distortions in life? Had he tried to become accustomed to the face of the gargoyle in the midst of the polished scenery? Had that face become his point of reference?

Edna saw the gargoyle; she was not attracted to it any more than she was interested in the society adored so by her mother. She had once attempted to draw her father into conversation about the law; she had had no luck. It was what had interested him first, he said, and nothing had come along to distract him since, and that was the end of it. And of her explorations as well.

As for her mother's way of life, the explanation given was simple enough: "*Everyone* lives as I do," her mother had answered, genuinely astonished. "*Everyone* does. The human is a gregarious animal. Everyone knows that." A sentence straight from an etiquette book, Edna thought; what was the use? She might as well talk to a woman from the moon. Or a tree. Or that chair. While Mrs. Dickinson, observing her daughter in various corners of the house, buried in various books describing Captain Cook's voyages, or the probable causes of summer complaint in young children, or suddenly coming upon her sitting on a bench in the park, under a heavily leafed elm, would think, what is that child doing there alone? Why does she always seem to seek out solitude? Something is wrong; it shows itself in her appetite for solitude.

Yet it never occurred to her that this was only a different nature, acting in ways completely natural to itself, and healthful in its exercise.

All around them, the depot was filling with activity, husbands and fathers heavily laden with packages, clearing the way for their harassed wives, each woman holding a child by each hand, many with one or more maids, each maid dangling an irrepressible child from each arm. There were straw baskets and leather baskets and huge tapestry bags with wooden handles; poorer women shouting directions to small troops of children, each woman holding a hamper filled with food. Smells, isolated people, domestic scenes, were rushing by the motionless train, a form of living scenery moving faster than the Lightning Express of Edna's imagination.

Trains had coasted into the depot, furnaces shut down before entering to prevent coal smoke from darkening the clothes of the ladies, the flying sparks from igniting the wooden structure housing the trains. Single gentlemen were fast coming to the aid of single ladies, offering to carry their parcels aboard the cars and settle the struggling traveler, knowing full well that no matter what their exertions, nor how interesting their traveling tête-à-tête, the acquaintance was meant to end, according to the rules of society, as the train reached its final destination. Charlie had tangled himself up in Edna's traps and hamper and carpet bag, and miscellaneous packages collected in haste by her mother, who hoped that the presents would do *something* to make life easier for poor Ten after her daughter's arrival turned the farm in Williamsville into an asylum. A young, handsomely whiskered man of about twenty-five promptly volunteered his services; he offered to assist the two women onto the third car, the first car, as he pointed out, like the second, out of the question entirely, thanks to the effusively embracing ladies who blocked the entrance of any other passengers, all of whom passed them, reproachfully staring, their disapproval doing nothing to separate them or hurry them on.

We shall not present such a spectacle, Mrs. Dickinson thought, gloomy. She would have liked, for once, to present such a reprehensible spectacle. "This is most kind of you, Mr. Helmsly," Edna heard her mother saying; "my daughter is traveling alone, and these packages will be far too heavy for her should she have to change cars or trains." "I am not anticipating any disasters," Edna said. Edith ignored her. Mr. Helmsly, whoever he was, looked curiously on. "Please do not put yourself out," Edna went on, irrepressible; "I can always find a porter." "You must excuse my daughter," said the weary Mrs. Dickinson; she was *tired* of finding excuses for her. "I shall be happy to assist her for *your* sake, madam," Mr. Helmsly said, "and then she will be free to enjoy her trip as she pleases." Edna blushed; she had managed to *blush*, Edith noted, astounded. Poor Ten, she thought; one gloomy brother and one impossible young woman. One brother who shuns the company of women and one woman who seems dedicated to making men miserable. It should be quite a rural scene. I am only glad, she assured herself, *I* will not be there to see it.

They had now reached the third car. "You will be happy to know, Mother dear," Edna said, "our cowcatcher is painted bright red." "How nice," Mrs. Dickinson answered, looking at the little flight of iron steps reaching up to the iron railings just outside the coach door. "And did you notice the shape of the smokestack?" her daughter continued; "a triangle with a gas balloon shape on top of it. What a hazardous arrangement." "There's no danger of your blowing up," her mother assured her, sarcastic. "And a whole car filled with coal, isn't that nice? We should be able to get partway there, at any rate." "I'm convinced you would walk if you had to," Edith answered; she wouldn't look at her. "Absolutely." "If you would not mind *too* much," Mrs. Dickinson said, "I cannot stand much more of this; it is altogether beyond human endurance. Why can't we just say goodbye?" "As long as we don't have to hug each other like those other females," Edna said, looking over her shoulder. "I hardly think there's any danger of *that*," Edith said, her skin firing. "Well, then," Edna said, awkward, "shall we shake hands?" Mr. Helmsly, looking on, blushed deeply. "We could even rub *noses*," Edith burst out, an unexpected attack of sharpness. Edna relented.

The train was shaking from side to side; smoke began puffing from the locomotive's funnel. Voices were shouting: All aboard! All aboard! A frantic woman was calling,

"Mr. Grimsby! Mr. Grimsby! What are you thinking of? You're going off with the children's satchel!" "Elvira! Elvira!" a nerve-shattering voice called. "Your black parasol! Your black parasol!" "Over here! Over here!" another voice answered, identical to the first in pitch and tone. The two invisible women sounded like two jays calling from different trees. "Well," Mrs. Dickinson said, barely audible. "Indeed," said her daughter. She hesitated a moment, threw her arms stiffly around her mother; Edith slumped against her daughter as if in a faint. Involuntarily, poor Charlie caught at Mrs. Dickinson's arm.

"What shall you do now?" Edna asked. "Oh, I shall probably persuade some friend to accompany me on a tour of the South." "In this weather?" Edna asked her mother's bonnet, its back crushed into her own hair. "It's warm everywhere," Edith answered. "I will write before I leave Aunt Ten's," Edna promised; she sounded apologetic. "Yes. Please do." Edith was at a loss. "I certainly shall," Edna said; she sounded like a creature of that society her mother so appreciated. "Well. I had better hurry along; the train seems to be moving." "Yes," Edith answered. "Yes," echoed the anonymous Mr. Helmsly. "A lavender train, how nice," Edith whispered; "you are to come home, of course," she went on, averting her eyes, "if you feel unwell, or if you are not happy there." "I will be happy there." "All the same," said her mother, "promise me. It's the last promise I will ask you to make." "I promise." Charlie and the helpful young gentleman sighed in relief. A long, shrill whistle split the air. "I have to leave," Edna said. Her mother slid from her grip. They separated like two identical pieces of black cloth that had lain, one on top of the other, and which, until the faint pressure, appeared seamless, indivisible.

Once inside, her packages neatly disposed around her, installed in a seat with a good "view," as the helpful gentleman assured her, disappearing, Edna automatically checked the depot seeking out her mother. There was the black bonnet and the unconquerable curls of auburn hair. Automatically, Edna lifted her black-gloved hand and waved. Her mother stood completely still, then raised her arm and waved back. Charlie, even from that distance, seemed distressed.

Well, thought Edna, that's that. We are finally finished

burying Father. Some of the cars are painted lavender; she was surprised. That's odd, she thought, settling back in her seat as the two huge wheels on each side of the locomotive began turning, and the whole train threw itself forward in its flight from the depot. Some coal smoke, some cinders, still burning, blew past Edna's windows, and then in, making her eyes burn and tear. I wonder how long it will take before we see some hills, she thought, settling herself with her brand-new copy of *Hearth's Bazaar*. She had meant to bring back issues for Aunt Ten, who adored them; she had complained that John's only interest was medical journals and *Farm and Fireside*. Edna gave the magazine a cursory look; nothing, she decided, could be duller. I shall get her a subscription, Edna thought cheerfully, to the *Bazaar* and *The Floral Cabinet*. She snuggled comfortably into her seat. The air now lifted and carried the smoke high above the speeding cars; her view of the passing scene was untroubled.

Although the cities seemed to promise an early spring, bulbs rising early from gardens, little shoots on the dead gray briars of climbing rose bushes beginning to redden and darken with new blood as soon as the snow was gone, the country was not so hospitable to the milder season. As the Lightning Express thundered out of the Manhattan depot, across the tracks, past all the buildings Edna had once been so anxious to see, the countryside imperceptibly became starker, more wintry. The great, jagged elms began to outline themselves against a cold gray sky as if etched, each tiny twig clearly visible against the sky's ice. The sun, as it rose, seemed to come only as far as the surface of an ice-covered pond, then shone coldly through the thick gray pane. Gradually, the train began to run its course along a cliff of ragged gray stone, and when Edna looked up from the story she was reading, which recounted how the minister's daughter had saved the wealthy family, who were her distant relations, from utter bankruptcy in whatever large city they supposedly inhabited, there were large patches of snow puffing and filling the crevices in the rocks. Every now and then the inevitable farmhouse would show itself at the edge of the horizon, each dwelling resembling the other, square two-floor dwellings facing the sun, triangular peaked third floors, their two rectangular windows, a smaller version of the same structure set at right angles to the larger ones, and, just to the rear of the main houses, the barns with their cupolas, either open or closed in, the necessary weather vane surmounting.

The train sped happily through its first four hours, and by ten o'clock the houses, when they began to make themselves visible, sported hills of snow on their roofs. The drifts sweeping up to the veranda were considerable and graceful, their wave-like nature announcing they had recently fallen, and had remained as they were in the icy, stiff weather. The trees, too, had the soft puffery of a recent snowfall. Edna was startled to see a gaily painted sleigh pulled by a team of horses, one brown and one white, dash up over the crest of a hill, disappearing magically. She swiveled in her seat, hoping to get another look at it, but instead saw another, this time running parallel to their train; it was enameled bright red, some kind of black and gilt decoration edging its swan-like body with scrollwork. "I suppose," said the young woman in the seat adjoining hers, startling Edna, who jumped nervously in her seat, "you must also find it depressing to see winter replace spring in this heartless way." The young woman had a soft, southern accent. Edna was surprised to see this young lady also dressed in mourning. So other people died, she thought; it had not occurred to her before. She looked at the young woman with more interest; she had blond, almost white curls and huge black eyes. Her cheekbones were high, flushed, almost hectic.

Edna, tired of her own nastiness, nevertheless could not bring herself to begin social conversation. She would say what she thought. And that would be bad enough. "No," she answered; "I find the change a relief. It has been one of those years," she heard herself continuing, surprised, "when time has just melted away somehow, like those snows in the city, and every time I saw the head of a bulb, I felt as if its sharp point was a threat to me, or reproaching me, because there was so much more I should have done before this spring came." She expected no answer; people rarely answered her when she said what she thought. "Yes, indeed," the blond woman said; "when I was walking through the park, I wanted nothing but a croquet hammer." "A croquet hammer?" "Yes"— the other young lady laughed softly—"the better to pound the flowers back into the ground. Every time I saw them, I thought of a board with nails in it, the nails just sticking up into the air, waiting like anything for some poor person's foot."

Edna began to take an interest in her. This woman didn't seem either older or younger than she was. She *did* have a bonnet more heavily trimmed with black net; her mourning dress was plainer, sturdier, as if she had been outfitted for a long trip before she finally was far enough away to cry herself out in privacy. "I am Miss Edna Dickinson." "Mrs. Byron Whitemore," the young woman said, extending her hand; there, under the fine hand-worked lace of her glove was the telltale peak on her left hand, the little rise denoting the peculiar status of a married woman. "Virginia," she added as an afterthought; "please call me Virginia." "Have you far to go?" "Not nearly far enough." There was a moment of silence. "The name of the village is Fetchburg." "Fitchburg," Edna corrected automatically. "Oh! You know where it is." "Yes. One town past Williamsville, or east of Williamsville, which is where I'm going." They stared at each other now in a friendly way.

"This is strange weather," Edna said, looking back out. The train was skimming the edge of a lake, heading back into the woods. Little puddles dotted the forest spaces among thickly growing trees; as the train went further into the woods, they appeared to be growing right out of the water, standing there, getting their feet cold and wet. "My grandfather used to tell a story about the War of the Revolution," Virginia said; she sounded as if she were talking to herself, speaking in her sleep. "They were looking for wounded in the woods, and there was a soldier standing right up. He looked mighty peculiar, and when they got up to him, they could see he was dead. So they drew lots to see who would pull him out, and my grandfather and his friend won, and when they pulled him out, his leg came right off. It just stood there where they found the body. They buried the body, but they couldn't bear to go after that leg. I suppose by now it's buried itself."

"You're a widow, aren't you?" Edna asked. The young woman nodded, looking at her, curious. "I saw the wedding ring," Edna explained lamely. "You're not wearing one." "No. My father was the one who died." "Perhaps that's worse." "Worse! What could be worse than losing a husband?" "Husbands," Virginia echoed; "if you've had one, you always know where to find more, but that's not so with fathers." Good Lord! Edna thought, shocked. "And besides," Virginia continued, "not every marriage is made in heaven. I believe," she said, glancing over at Edna's *Bazaar,* "that there's a joke apropos of that very subject on the last page of that issue. 'Some marriages, like matches,' " she quoted from memory, " 'are made in heaven, but others, like matches, are dipped in the other place.' " Edna felt a shock go through her; it was the first real sensation she had felt in some time. Virginia noticed the expression sliding over her face, and charitably added, "I was happily married, although it was hard to have everyone in town believing I poisoned my husband." Edna gaped at her. "Yes," Virginia drawled, "the coroner said I used strychnine. The maid said I used carbolic acid. It turned out so much simpler I think everyone was disappointed.

"My husband had taken most of my inheritance and invested in a coffin factory. You see, everyone thought there was going to be a terrible epidemic of diphtheria, and the last time that happened, oh, everyone remembered it so clearly, private parties broke into sidecars and stole all the coffins so they could bury their dead. Unfortunately for Byron, that was my husband, we had a very healthy summer. People came to Charleston to recover from miles around, and then Byron discovered his partner was bringing half of the caskets to store in our barn because he couldn't pay the storage bill. Well, I suppose he decided he might as well hurry himself up and fill at least one of them before I found out what happened, so he took some strychnine and drank some carbolic acid; I guess he wanted to be sure. He must have been terribly embarrassed. At any rate, he was dead in no time, surely before I got to him, and my daughter was at my mother's, so I had no witnesses, and a reputation for being a little witchy, and if it hadn't been for Ben, the darky's son, matters wouldn't have gone so well for me. This is my daughter," she said, handing the stunned Edna a small pen-and-ink sketch of a befuddled-looking child, her hair light brown, big black eyes, and two teeth protruding like a small tent from full little red lips. Virginia had followed her eyes. "Baby teeth. They're straight as a picket fence now."

Edna continued to stare at the drawing; was the woman mad? The child was standing next to an armchair. She seemed lost in her dress, a version of a grown-up sailor's costume. A little choker of black beads encircled her chubby neck, and a round collar mounted to just under the child's chin like a priest's collar. The skirt of white cotton she wore was stiffly starched, and the pleats stiffly ironed. The only reason for it Edna could find had to do with falling fits. Yes, she thought, looking at the dress again, they must have been afraid the child would fall down. I never saw such a costume, she thought. Nor was the dress the end of it. Black stockings, or leggings of some abnormally heavy material, protruded from its skirt; they tucked into the shiny tops of the little girl's leather shoes, which buttoned, like other shoes Edna remembered having seen, on the side. The chair, she observed with relief, looked entirely normal. It would be impossible now to invent an excuse for changing her seat. There was no one else she knew on the train, and she had imprudently revealed the identity of their destinations. Still, there *ought* to be a simple way to escape from a crazy woman. My mother arranged this, she thought suddenly; this is her revenge. No, she would never be clever enough for such a thing. Or so vindictive.

One black tree succeeded another, silhouetted against the milk-glass sky, the iced sun fluttering in and out like a blinded bird. "I *am* sorry," Virginia said, turning to her; "I'm not insane, you know. A bit unhinged by events, but not insane. I only begin to feel insane when I think of my daughter and how she's faring with my husband's parents back in the sunny South, and how on earth we're to manage without their help when I go back for her. I shouldn't have used you for target practice. A perfect stranger, it was not right. I'm sure you have your own sorrows." The trees continued their perpetual passing.

"How old are you?" Edna asked finally, blushing as she saw Virginia's faint smile. The height of impropriety, she thought; that question was the height of impropriety. "Nineteen." "Nineteen!" Edna exclaimed. "We ripen early in the heat, at least so your magazines say." "Nineteen!" Edna exclaimed again. "And already a mother, and al-

ready a widow; and already worrying about how to manage for the rest of my life—from day to day, I mean."
"Nineteen!" Edna said again. She promised herself that number would never form on her lips again. "Nineteen," the widow said for her, a mischievous grin lighting her face. She won't live long, Edna thought. She heard, as if he were there, her father's voice agreeing: she won't live long. "Would you care for some lunch?" Edna asked, motioning toward her hamper resting peacefully under her seat. "No, thank you. I'm sleepier than a maiden aunt in church." Virginia settled her bonneted head back against the chair. I want a peaceful life, Edna thought, staring intently out at the black and gray countryside. No matter what the price.

And in that moment it was decided. The young widow stirred in her light sleep, dreaming whatever dream had been chosen for her. Edna was certain she would have no other dream but peace. She stared out the window; there were three small children in red and blue winter coats on what was either a pond or a pasture. Under six feet of snow, it was impossible for Edna to tell whether they were standing on water or on solid ground. There should not be such uncertainties, not about such things as earth or water, she thought bitterly. She wondered if it really made any difference although it appeared to make so much of one to her. Yes, it did. If they were on land, they were absolutely safe; if they were on water, they were standing on ice, and the surface of what appeared to be the earth could give way, give way at any moment. As it had for the young widow sitting next to her. A row of stones, yes, a stone fence, bounded the expanse the children played on. A pasture, Edna thought, deeply relieved. No farmer would put up a fence like that to keep children out of the water. She remembered Ten's grumblings about her brother's negligence in attending to pasture fences; she had given up, she said, on a fence for her garden. Definitely, they were on land.

A peaceful life, she said again to herself, adding, for whatever the reason—she could not have explained it— at whatever the cost. The train sped on blindly toward Williamsville, unaware of them all, its rocking and clacking eventually lulling her, as it had her young companion, into sleep. When she woke, the train had stopped; there

69

was a confusion of voices, some of them angry, and snow, inexplicably flying up from the ground, arching up in front of her coach window, a white rainbow, falling back to the ground. Virginia stirred lazily in her seat; drawing on some half-lost reserve of energy, she told Edna the tracks were blocked by snow. The men were clearing them; all the able-bodied men were out shoveling. "And that's not all, misses," said an old woman, turning around and leaning over the back of her seat; "there's another train stuck right on the bridge in front of us." "Why can't this train push that one over when it comes free?" Virginia asked, groggy. The old woman looked grayly at Edna. "You see," Edna explained, "this is a trestle bridge. Once the train's on it, we're suspended almost one thousand feet over the river down there. I don't think this bridge —it's wood, you know—could support the weight of two trains." "Certainly not, ma'am," the elderly woman in front interjected, violently shaking her head; "that's how this very same bridge fell down the first time. You remember the first time. They were all spring finding bodies, and they haven't found them all yet. Terrible, terrible!" She sounded like a vulture, suddenly given the ability of speech. "Marvelous," Virginia whispered, nervously fingering her portrait case. "When they rebuilt it, they made it much stronger," Edna said, taking the girl's hand without any awareness of having done so. Inside her glove, Virginia's soft fingers began to relax. "We'll get there soon enough, if I guess correctly," the young woman said bravely. "Certainly we will," Edna assured her, fixing the old woman with a menacing glare; "we surely will." Yes, there were other people in the world with troubles. Would that old bat never stop hanging over their laps like a withered gourd? The old woman turned back and sank out of sight. "Hah!" she snorted defiantly from the cave of her seat. Virginia and Edna grinned at each other.

When the train finally crossed the trestle bridge, it did so without incident, although inside the cars there was anything but quiet. Women were scrambling over each other, and over men, too; they showed no compunctions whatever for their sharp elbows, their jabbing knees, all to get a better look at the river, running so far down under the trestle bridge. The watery depths they had just escaped! Oh, they were thrilled. "Well!" said the little widow, sinking back into her upholstered cushions; "I'm glad I didn't look before! Imagine falling down there!" The whole car filled with bird cries, delighted raw arias of "Look at how far down it is to those stones!" "I wonder how long it would take to fall down there?" "Not long, I guess." "But all the way to the bottom, I mean." "What a day for a train wreck! I wouldn't want to take the plunge today, no sir!" "Did you see that chunk of ice float by? Why, from up here it looked like a mere speck!" And so it went on, ladies and gentlemen in window seats unmercifully squashed, suffocated, used indiscriminately as bolsters, armrests, suitcases, and conveniently placed boulders, all for the sake of observing the horror so recently, but not quite yet, avoided.

"Well, they sound disappointed to me," Virginia said; "they positively do." "Some people don't know when to be thankful," said the old woman's voice from the seat in front of them, and rising with her voice, the iron-gray rim of her hair. "Why, I declare," the young widow said in a stage whisper, "I don't know why it is, it must be one of those things in nature, how some plants thrive in the sun and others climb so in the shade, but I cannot convince myself I like that old woman, no, I cannot convince myself of that," she finished in a heavier accent than Edna thought her capable of. The old woman's head suddenly sank from sight. "And do you know," she continued, making her voice more confidential, but without moving (she must have been an actress once, Edna decided), "I think she must be one of those *godly* women who spend all of their time, like the angels, looking out of windows, and peeping at people, and putting up picket fences and arbors all over so she can hide in them and make out her scrolls, and then, of course, trumpet her news all over town. You know those godly women. My father—*dear* Reverend, that's what those godly ladies all call him, and in such a tone, my dear, you wouldn't believe it—*he* says, even if he is a minister, he is going to spend his Sundays praying for their *immediate* perdition, that's what he's going to do, because damnation's waiting for them, but they'll have that warm place overcrowded, like one of their porch scandal dens in the summer. He does go on about them; oh, you should hear them. Why,

71

if he weren't my father, I wouldn't believe proper ministers could talk that way, no, I wouldn't."

The woven back of the seat facing them showed visible signs of agitation, which, as the vivacious young widow spoke (for now Edna had so dubbed her, and so she would remain to her), became violent buckings and rockings, as if a nervous horse had somehow gotten itself tied into a railway seat. *"Is* your father a minister?" Edna whispered directly through the black veils into Virginia's ear. " 'Course not," she whispered back; "he's the biggest tobacco grower in the state, and he swears like a steam locomotive. You can't see the sky for his curses." The two young women stared at each other, then Edna burst out in giggles; they were apparently very contagious, because the young widow followed her example, and soon the two of them were doubled up. The widow, first to reach her handkerchief, passed it over to Edna, whose face was streaming with tears. "It's a good thing," Edna said, trying to catch her breath, but bursting out in hysterical cackles again, "it's a good thing," and she began cackling like a hysterical chicken. "It's a good thing," the widow said; "it certainly is a good thing," and she doubled over in shrieks and gasps. "It's a good thing," Edna said, stopping to take a deep breath; "it's a good thing," and she dissolved in the warm bath of hysterical laughter. "Why, I'd wager you've forgotten what's a good thing," the young widow gasped out, amidst new peals. "Oh no," Edna cackled helplessly, again taking a deep breath and refusing to look at her companion; "it's a good thing we're both in mourning and both so serious, or what would an angel think of us?" Then, further intoxicated by this successful conclusion to her speech, she screamed helplessly with laughter, the young widow doing the same. People in the aisle seats in front of them began to turn around. "Tobacco!" Edna gasped, blowing her nose into her own handkerchief; it had finally materialized. The widow followed her example. They looked like two monkeys, Edna thought, one imitating the other. "Tobacco!" the widow whispered to her, testing. "Tobacco!" Edna whispered back. They were off again. "Disgraces, the two of them," came the old woman's voice, rising like smoke from an overheated stove, but she had made a mistake. She just started them up again. "Tobacco!" one of them whispered

72

and they were off. "And I thought," Edna gasped, "southern girls were so well behaved." "And I thought," Virginia puffed, "New England girls were so proper." "Tobacco!" she said suddenly, as if it were a curse, and out popped her small shiny pointed tongue. It was another three-quarters of an hour before the two of them had reached anything resembling a state of equilibrium, and then they could hardly congratulate themselves on their powers of control; they were simply exhausted.

At the train's first stop, and with the first exit of a passenger, the indignant old woman in front of them gathered up her packages and parasol and umbrella and, bearing a remarkable resemblance to a demented weather vane, set off in a gale of her own making down the aisle to the vacated seat far from Virginia and Edna, where, she told herself, out of hearing would be out of mind. Nevertheless, that horrible laughter pursued her. One of them must have said "tobacco" again, she thought, scandalized. And really, the poor old thing *was* scandalized. Why, they're both in weeds! she thought, indignant. At least I'll have a story to tell when I get home, she soothed herself; they do beat everything, the two of them. Why, they're probably not in mourning at all; they're probably hiding out from the law. She lost herself in such happy speculations as the train chugged inexorably on, snow flurries blowing up and down against the window like so many flakes of time, some of them sticking to the ground and the tracks and the window, others melting against the pane. Edna stared at a wet, high brown bank. The snow was sinking in as it hit, filling, she thought, the earth with time. Then she thought about tobacco.

"Virginia," she said, turning to her companion, "this friendship doesn't have to end with the trip, does it?" "Does it?" Virginia asked. "I don't know about your feelings. but you can be sure news of my trial got into all the local papers, and you know, it might not be so much fun what with plaid old ladies peering out from under every arbor and trellis." "I don't care about *that*," Edna said. "You say that now." "I don't care about that," Edna repeated with emphasis. "I bet you don't. I bet you don't," the young widow said, admiring; "and to think you don't even have red hair; I mean, to be so stubborn." "My mother has it; the red hair." "Oh well, then that explains

73

it. How far did you say Fitchburg was from Williamsville, from where you're going?" "About eleven miles. Can you ride?" "Like a saddle; the first thing I packed was my habit, although I daresay it will look mighty peculiar for a widow in 'society'."; she stared pointedly down the aisle at the old woman's cap, bobbing rhythmically with the train. She must have fallen asleep. "Oh, do you think it will look peculiar?" Edna asked, concerned; "I packed mine too." "At least mine is black," Virginia sighed. "Mine is maroon," Edna said, "but I decided, what, really, was the difference? Father's underground; Mother's somewhere in the South, and Father wouldn't care anyway." "The right ones never do." Virginia said sadly.

"Williamsville! Fitchburg! Dummerston! South Hadley! North Hadley! East Hadley! Brattleboro and all points east, west, north, and south! Next stop Bangor! All off for Brattleboro! Five minutes! Five minutes! All aboard for Bangor!" The two young women in black struggled into their cloaks. Giggling, they loaded each other up with packages. They had formed, for the length of the trip, a closed society; they wanted no further help from other people. They were all they needed in the world. But at the dark blue-black square that was the door, lit by the kerosene lantern, both of them paused uncertainly. The young widow stepped out first. She had a small, determined step. Edna followed right behind her. "Who's meeting you?" the young widow gasped, putting her hand over her mouth. She did not know how to recognize who was meeting her; that had just occurred to her. "Mrs. Byron Whitemore?" a gaunt young woman addressed Edna, peering through the white nets of snow, their noses almost colliding. "No, I'm sorry; this is Mrs. Byron Whitemore here." She pointed to the young widow. "Her name is Mrs. Permelia Churchill," the young woman told Edna; she averted her face as she spoke. Edna knew at once how comical the name seemed to her. "Would you mind, Mrs. Churchill," Virginia asked, "if we waited here with Miss Dickinson until her transportation comes for her?" "Of course not," the older woman answered rustily. *Her* cheeks could cast shadows, Edna thought; oh, I don't envy Virginia with her. A tall, thin gentlemanly snowman came up to Virginia. "Miss Edna Dickinson?" he asked. "No" —Virginia grinned—"*this* is your Miss Dickinson. . . . He certainly doesn't look like your Aunt Ten," she whispered daringly under the disapproving stare of her unknown escort. "Shall we try for Tuesday? We might meet then." "Oh yes," Edna said; "Tuesday, yes." "Well, I'll try riding anything, even a big dog," Virginia called back as the two of them moved apart on the railway landing, two cars, inexplicably joined, and now, inexplicably severed.

"I'm John Ashbel Steele, Ten's brother," John said. "Edna Dickinson. But I suppose you know that." Why did she feel so confused? I expected Aunt Ten, she thought; I expected Aunt Ten. "I'm sorry to drag you out like this," she apologized. "If you didn't, someone else would; the bigger the drifts, the more I'm called out in the middle of the night." "Oh yes," Edna said; "you're a doctor, aren't you?" "There's a certificate on my wall that says so." "It must be wonderful, helping people," Edna volunteered. She was surprised at her own eagerness; there was something in his face and voice. She was shocked; she wanted to please him. "I wish everyone didn't feel obliged to say that," he answered roughly. Edna blushed. "Why not?" she persevered, stubborn; "what else did you become a doctor for?" John finally turned to look at her. "To help people. Whatever else?" He was laughing at her. "Then why shouldn't people ask you how you enjoy it? Surely it must be something, knowing your life is benefiting humanity." "Well, you don't take no for an answer," John said, abrupt. "No gentleman *ever* talked to me like that," Edna blazed out; "*ever*." "Farm life has rubbed the gentleman off me, I guess," John said; he sounded a little bashful.

It occurred to Edna that she had just gotten all she was to get in the way of apology. She mentally reviewed all her mother's hateful comments about Ten's surly brother. For once, it appeared, her mother might have been right. "This way," he ordered Edna, as if talking to his dog; "no, not that buggy; my sister insisted I take the carriage because of your delicate health. She'll say anything to get her way." "What on earth does that mean?" Edna asked. "It means you look healthy as a dray horse," he said. "Which is more than I can say for that other lady in black you seemed so familiar with. *She* won't last long, that one. Don't pin your hopes on her." Edna was horrified. The exact words she had used! She won't last long, she thought again. "Why?" she asked, desperate; "Why won't she last long? Why did you say that?" "Because I know; my life is dedicated to benefiting humanity." His tone was bitter. "Why did you say that?" Edna asked again, her voice more shrill and insistent; "why did you say that?" "The flush on the cheek, the pallor of the rest of the face, the extreme loss of flesh all over the body. Consumption."

"You can't know that!" Edna protested, indignant; "you didn't even examine her!" "Does she cough yet?" Mr. Steele inquired in a bored voice. "Only when she laughs." "She will be coughing more soon." "This is ridiculous!" Edna exclaimed; "why am I listening to you? Your sister and my mother *both* told me you rarely if ever speak. I think I should like it if you fell silent at once!" Unexpectedly, Mr. Steele bestowed a friendly smile upon her. "Before I forsake the use of my voice, may I tell you which carriage to climb into?" His tone was far pleasanter than it had been. "It's that shiny blue one under the lantern, the one with the crescent-shaped roof; my sister has an artistic streak." "So do *I*," Edna said, nasty; "I suppose *you* exhaust your artistic impulses sewing up cuts." "On the contrary," Mr. Steele responded, looking more closely at his diminutive companion; "I merely try to sew as straight a line as the human skin will allow. I leave embroidery to the ladies." "How nice to give them credit for *something*." Ridiculous! she thought; he's an old man. I should at least show some respect for his age. He must be at least ten years older than I am. He *is* Ten's brother.

Still, she did not seem to think of him as an old man. She remembered Aunt Ten's telling her there was over twenty years, two decades, between herself and her brother John, and then, going on with the calculations, as people will, she finished by informing Edna there was a twelve-year difference between herself and her other brother, Hal. "Oh, he's quite old, your brother," Edna said in surprise. "Ancient," Ten agreed, grinning slyly. "Oh my!" Edna had burst out; "I didn't mean to insult *you!*" "You didn't, my dear; you didn't; I consider every year a victory. I'm almost fifty, forty-nine, almost half a century old. That *is* an accomplishment, no matter how you look at it." "My mother *never* tells her age," Edna gasped. "Oh *dear*," Ten said, covering her mouth; "it appears I let the kittens out of the bag." "Fifty," Edna said joyfully; "almost fifty." "You just keep quiet about that, you hear me?" Ten scolded; "otherwise I won't be able to open my mouth near you. Little pitchers!" "I'm not *that* young," Edna protested. "Young enough, and besides," Ten reflected, "it's all a state of mind. John, for example, is eighty-two this week. He's been eighty-two for two years now. It's dreadful. I should threaten to return to Kansas again; that always takes a few years off his life."

Edna looked up at her escort with more interest. What *had* happened two years ago? Her parents had hinted and hinted but never come out with it. She still hadn't forgiven him for his cold sentencing of the young widow. "You were married, Mr. Steele?" He stopped in his tracks, looking down into her face. The snow was now slanting down in thick chalk lines. They might as well have been two ghosts talking. 'Someone's been telling you tales," he said finally, resuming his step, tugging a little more violently at her elbow. Edna had all she could do to keep her balance. "I *was* married; I am not now and I never talk about it." "Never?" Edna asked; she knew she was cruel. "If you don't watch your step, you'll slip on that ice under the snow and break your neck." "Well, you can fix that," Edna answered, smug. "Necks are not my specialty, and it has been said I am better at breaking them." What an unpleasant person, Edna thought; he's not at all like his sister. That really is too bad.

"I heard that your father hung himself," Mr. Steele said, not even bothering to look toward her. "He must have looked dreadful. I wonder why he didn't try poison. I've always thought poison is easier on the family nerves." "How dare you!" Edna gasped; "how dare you!" "You don't talk about it?" he asked mildly. "Never!" said Edna. Oh, he's caught me, she thought; he has me just where he wants me. "Shall I help you into the carriage?" "No, thank you," Edna answered, beginning to clamber up herself, but her leather-soled boot slipped on the icy tread of the little iron flight of portable steps. The next thing she knew, she was lying flat on her back, a thwacking sensation fleeing the back of her head, looking up at the inky sky, the fast-moving clouds, and the crescent moon, which chose that moment to peer out and take a good look at her. "May I help you up?" asked Mr. Steele. The monster was definitely amused! Edna stuck up her hand. "Resurrect me, please." "What a demanding thing!" Mr. Steele said as if to himself. "You have your choice of a seat," he told her, having thrown her baggage unceremoniously into the back of the carriage (I hope *all* of Mother's presents to Aunt Ten were made of crystal, she thought viciously); "you can sit up here with me and see the view, what there is of it, or you can sit on the bench in back and stay out of the weather, which might be best for a city person." "I'll sit up front," she answered shortly.

They drove along through the thick snowstorm, huge heavy flakes sometimes falling so densely they blotted all scenery from sight, occasionally not falling at all where the carriage made its way. They seemed to be following an uneven wave of snow. Edna restrained herself from asking about it; just when she was about to give in, or to give up her attempts to make it out, some round stones glinted in the bright moonlight, the moon again having broken through the clouds, a successful digger of earth which had kept at the frozen ground just long enough.

"I don't see any cows." Edna commented without thinking. "Farmers around here don't get much into the habit of leaving their animals out in blizzards; that's what barns are for." "How do they keep their barns warm?" She wanted to restore polite relations before their arrival—for Ten's sake; definitely, for Ten's sake. "Often they set fire to them. The incendiary's good deed." "Oh, never mind," Edna pouted. "Coal stoves, wood stoves, anything safe that generates heat"; John reeled off the list. "Thank you *so much*." "I suppose," he said, "it is too much to expect you to know anything about the country." "*Or* the animals who inhabit it." The moon made another of its unexpected appearances. Mr. Steele was actually smiling. "There, at that farmhouse." Edna said, pointing excitedly; "they have a lantern hanging right on a stick. What does that mean? What is it doing there? Surely it will rust?" "That lantern means that as soon as I throw you and your traps in the front door, I throw myself and my bag into the buggy and go back to that house. It's a sign for the doctor." he finished wearily. "Poor people." Edna said, sarcastic. "I doubt if humanity will be benefited much tonight," Mr. Steele responded in an identical tone. "I can wait in the carriage while you fly to their aid." "That is just the point," Mr. Steele told her; "I can fly to their aid, but a lot of good it will do. I might as well deliver you to Ten first. At least you're already healthy. I'll get credit for one good deed done." "*And* for the bump on my head," Edna reminded him. "That was completely your own fault. I don't take responsibility for stupidity." Edna glared at him until the snow flying into her eyes began melting; then she looked more as if she were crying than glaring, and so they drove up along the curved carriage path to the front entrance of Ten and John Steele.

"Well, here she is," Mr. Steele announced to his sister. He sounds as if he's talking about a bag of potatoes, Edna thought, resentful. "Safe and sound and complaining all the way," he said, shaking his coat with his hands. "Who was complaining?" Ten asked. "She was," John answered. "He was," Edna corrected politely, glowering at him, then looking at Aunt Ten. Oh, did she feel foolish. What an arrival! Aunt Ten would believe every poisoned word her mother had written about her. Well, Ten thought; they've just met, and they're already fighting. What do you know about that? I think that's wonderful, she answered herself; I think it couldn't be better. "You had better get out of those wet clothes," she told Edna; "you too, John." "I can take care of myself." "So you always say, anyhow." "I've got to get back out right away," he said gruffly. "Well," Ten said, "there's the new carriage robe. Bertha trimmed the lantern wicks. You can go from here to California." "Good," John said, looking approvingly at the neat little heap on the chair in the entrance hall. "Don't rush yourself getting back," Ten said. It was, as Edna was soon to learn, her habitual way of saying goodbye to her brother. "Don't sit up wrinkling yourself," he answered, completing the prescribed exchange. "As for that one," he finished, "I presume you don't need me to tuck her up." Ten raised one eyebrow at him; Edna already envied her that trick. "Out!" Ten said; "out into the storm to do your merciful deeds!" John left grinning. A small grin flickered like a candle's flame around her lips. Hmmmm, Edna thought, worried; they look more alike than I thought.

It also occurred to her that, since they were, after all, brother and sister, they did, probably, like one another, however small was *any* reason for liking Mr. Steele; still, Ten's liking Mr. Steele was, she thought, inconceivable for the normal mind. So thinking, she followed Ten upstairs, into the large spacious room which was, Ten assured her, as much her own as her room in Boston. And so they began the process of chattering and unpacking, Ten periodically pausing to towel poor Edna off as if she were a bedraggled kitten found at the door. "Those windows look more like January than the beginning of May," Ten commented gloomily. "Poor John. He and the scarlatina have had a good run for their money this winter." She saw Edna's expression, and smiled happily. I may not have to threaten to leave after all, she thought, gleeful. In spite of herself, Edna looked out the window; Ten noted the worry.

The sky was the color of gray silk and the moon had disappeared. A milky-white light shone in the near distance. "The barn window," Ten said, following her gaze; "the hands are keeping a fire going tonight. As for me, it's a choice. If I don't keep a fire going all night, the plants will freeze. If I keep a fire all night, I'll freeze. I should probably choose the lesser of all evils." She paused. "And let myself freeze." "I'll stay up and watch the fire," Edna volunteered. "You'll do no such thing; into bed, fast, into bed," Ten ordered, turning down the corner of the bedclothes. As if it had just taken a step forward, Edna noticed the big wood stove in the corner of the bedroom. "Don't worry about that; Bertha will take care of it," Ten said carelessly. "You'll teach me how later? I don't want to be a burden," Edna said, worried. "Later, naturally," Ten agreed. They sat on the edge of the bed talking about this and that, until suddenly Ten jumped up like a jack-in-the-box, exclaiming, "It's me or the geraniums, me or the geraniums; I haven't come this far through the winter to let Mrs. Moffat get the better of me," and she flew out of the room.

Left alone, Edna found herself feeling isolated, as if Ten had walked out of her room forever. "Hello, stove," she whispered. It looked human with its silver claw feet, its elaborately worked potbelly, and something which looked like a little peaked hat resting jauntily on its top. It must have some purpose, that hat, Edna thought, studying it obsessively. Oh, I see, she said at last; that thing must direct the current of warm air. The room was comfortably warm, as warm as any room in the house in Cedar Street, and after all the warnings her mother had given her about freezing to death in the country, too.

It was also a well-furnished room, Edna thought, looking up at the immaculately starched canopy of her huge double bed. There was an abundance of pillows and the bed was already spread with two heavy down quilts. Edna looked around; the easy chair was filled up to its wings with more quilts. Those were patchwork quilts. She tried to imagine herself making such things; it was impossible. Probably Ten had made them, or her mother before her. Against one wall stood an enormous granite fireplace surrounded with brickwork, standing far out from the wall, beginning as a rectangular shape beneath the mantel, then growing into a triangle, and just before where the peak ought to have been, it developed into a chimney which continued right through the ceiling of her room, and, she presumed, all the way out of the roof of the house. But if they had a fireplace in her room, why had Ten brought a wood stove? She must have ordered it hauled in for her. She probably thinks I'm delicate; she probably doesn't trust me with fire. She looked at the empty fireplace. The inside was blackened with soot. In one corner of its slate floor, some gray ashes had escaped a broom and rested there.

The door of the room was the next object to come under study. It was made of wide, heavy slabs of wood and closed with a cast-iron drop latch; she went over and experimented with it. She lifted a little hook. The cast-iron bar fell into place and was caught by the little hook on the frame of the door. I should have known, she reproached herself, restless. Mr. Steele's house (already she had stopped thinking of it as Aunt Ten's house) *would* have locks on all the doors. In the unlikely event he should find himself in a room he usually did not visit, he could easily lock it and lock the rest of the world out. She got up and latched the door again and again. I had better stop that: I'll worry Aunt Ten, she thought, going back to her bed, and beginning the long process of removing her black basque with all its tiny cloth-covered buttons, then her long black skirt, with its tiny buttons, and then her slip, with its tiny buttons, and now my corset, she thought, bored, with its tiny buttons, and hooks, and laces, and when I get all through with that, she went on wearily, I can begin buttoning the endless white buttons on my nightdress. What a relief, she thought, to button something white. She went to the window.

The sky was in mourning, but the whole earth looked like a bridal gown. Snow, really, was a joyous thing; how it brought things together. The trees swept up like wind runes from the earth. The earth rolled on like a vast sea of calm tide. Nothing could be very far away in country like this. Everyone, when they looked out of their windows, saw the same thing. It was wonderful, Edna thought, how everyone must look out and see the same thing, think the same thing. It was as if they were all in the same room without needing one another's physical presence. Virginia seemed so near to her. She could see the young widow going through the same series of actions she had just completed, putting on her own long white dress, looking at her bed, climbing onto it. Now Virginia was snuggling under the covers. Now she was pulling the covers up under her chin. Now she was thinking about riding over to see her on Tuesday. Now she was falling asleep. If I had to die, Edna thought suddenly, I would want to die in the country, in the middle of a snowy winter, when everything was seamless, continuous, when the perfect wholeness of life made such a thing as separation impossible. How close the dead must be here! Edna thought happily; they just got under another blanket. They just sleep on another part of the big bed of the earth. They marked graves here, of course, but really, it must be unnecessary. She could feel it. This was a place for friendly ghosts. They would come to the doors and the windows. Their spirits could not have gone too far from their homes, for in such snow there were no landmarks to guide them. Like people lost in the woods, they would inevitably wander in a circle, and end, eventually, at the last door they had left.

No, there was no sign of Mr. Steele's buggy, Edna assured herself, peering intently out. What is this thing? she asked herself, picking up a jagged thick piece of white-painted wood shaped like lightning. It hung from the side of the window by a little iron link chain. I don't like it,

Edna fussed; what is it doing here? She tried to open the
window, but it was very heavy. She tried harder, and
pushed it up an inch. A blast of the purest, coldest air
she had ever felt struck her across the cheek. It would be
lovely, she thought, to walk in the snow dressed in white,
eating ice; it would be the purest thing, the purest thing.
How was she to keep the window open? She wanted it
open until she was too chilled to endure the cold, and then
she would *have* to jump into bed. *That* would put an end
to her unaccountable restlessness. Oh, the stick, she
thought; the stick. Ecstatic as a scientist who had just discovered the key to immortality, she propped the end of
the wooden stick on the windowsill, and lowered the window into its first notch. What a clever thing, she marveled. It had suddenly taken on a new dimension. It
seemed to embody all the special qualities of this house.
Now she would finally have a chance to explore all of it.
The quiet; it was infinite; its infinity made it beautiful,
magnificent. Even in the summer, it must be like this, she
thought, only the added noise of insects sputtering randomly, establishing no lines, no boundaries.

No, there was still no sign of Mr. Steele and his buggy.
Was he out delivering an elephant? I had better get away
from the window, she decided, picking up the candlestick;
I wouldn't want him to think I was waiting up for him.
Although, she hesitated, tempted, perhaps I ought to keep
Aunt Ten company down there with her geraniums. No,
she said I had to get into bed, Edna remembered. Involuntarily, she pulled down the corners of her mouth.
Well, there was nothing for it. She sat on the edge of the
bed, staring at the flickering candle. She blew it out. She
had not closed the white curtains.

A bluish light filled the room. Edna swung her legs up
onto the bed. She observed the qualities of moonlight as
if she were to be examined upon its nature in the morning. Yes, there were all ten of her toes. She wiggled them
at herself. They were cold: she had better put them under
the covers. She reluctantly slid her legs under the quilt.
Next she pulled the covers up to her waist. She was still
sitting up. Still completely soundless outside, she thought,
annoyed. What *am* I expecting? she asked herself in irritation: a herd of wild horses? She lay down on the bed,
rigid as a board. What is all that crackling? she wondered:

what's that cracking noise? *Another* cracking noise, she noted with rising interest. And another. Finally, there was a great crash outside her window. Edna jumped out of bed. Just in case there's anything wrong, I can tell Aunt Ten, she told herself, flying across the cold wooden floor. Outside the window, in the blue moonlight, she could see a huge jagged slab of ice sticking up from the snow. It must have fallen off the roof, Edna decided; look, there are real icicles sticking up from it. They look like glass nails. This time she had indeed run out of details to observe from her window. She got into bed, curled over on her side. I wonder where Ten's cat is, she thought; if I could only have that cat in my room at night. When I was here last time, she thought, sleepy, that big orange cat used to sleep on one side of my pillow. How he used to puff at me. That purr, she remembered, her body getting lighter and lighter and beginning to float away from her somewhere out into the snow; it hypnotized me. I have to remember, she told herself, making one last effort to grab at the receding world, to ask Aunt Ten for that cat tomorrow. Jimmie; the cat's name is Jimmie; there was something else she wanted to remember, but she couldn't. She was sound asleep.

Edna woke up floating somewhere in a sea of whiteness. Brilliant white light was pouring in through the two tall windows facing out on the pasture. The light was so bright the curtains seemed insubstantial, a texture overlaying the real fabric which was the solid white light. Edna picked up her arm, examining it curiously. What a white arm! she thought; it looks as if it were made of snow. Light splashed in patches on the geometric design of the woven rug. What an expensive rug, she thought. No, she could not think of one good reason for getting out of bed; but she began to smell the unmistakable odor of frying potato pancakes, the distinctive smell of frying bacon fat. Those smells will always mean this place to me, she thought, lazy, but she was getting hungry. I had better get dressed, she thought, looking at her black clothing, peering at her in an unfriendly way from the big oak wardrobe with its huge mirror in its tall door. Oh, I don't want to wear black, she thought, hopeless; I don't want to wear black at all. I feel bad enough without wearing black. She sat on the edge of the bed, the old, familiar feeling of gloom beginning to creep into her, apparently through her toes. There was a rap at the door. That must be Aunt Ten, she guessed; she sounds as if she's patting the wood.

"Edna," Ten began as soon as she entered (she never bothered with good-mornings), "I've been thinking. We're so isolated here. Nobody knows much about you, and your mother is nowhere around. You're not even seventeen. Well," she continued, coloring slightly, "I don't see why you have to wear mourning here. That is," she finished, awkward, "unless you want to. I never much liked mourning dress myself. I wore it exactly two weeks for my husband, and then I took the train for Williamsville, and as soon as we were a hundred miles out of Fredonia, I took out a little trap and changed my whole outfit in the dressing room. You should have heard the furious rattlings at the door," she remembered, smiling. "John says it's the likes of me that drive railway owners to take the locks off the doors to ladies' dressing rooms. Well, you see," Ten went on, "it all happened so fast, and I couldn't have felt worse, even if I had been dressed up like a country fair, so I didn't see any point in it. And then the outfitters, they never worry about how *warm* the mourning suits ought to be. They have to make things up in such a hurry, unless you're one of those dramatic ladies who like to look as if you've been mourning for something all of your life, and exist, like the clouds, only to weep; well, if you're one of those women, you already have all the proper clothes.

"Understand," she said hurriedly, "I don't want to talk you out of mourning, if that's what you want to put on." "I don't," Edna answered, vehement, surprising herself. "Well, that's a relief, that's settled then," Ten said; "we'll go into town and have Mrs. Grimsby make a whole new outfit for you, winter and spring; the weather's so changeable here." "Oh no," Edna gasped; "that would cost a fortune. I would have to write to Mother for the extra money, and she'd find out about it. I wouldn't want her to do that. She wouldn't understand." "Money?" Ten repeated, incredulous; "why on earth are you worrying about money? We have more money than we know what to do with. Why, unless John decided to build a replica of Manhattan right outside there"—she waved toward the pasture —"we couldn't even begin to make a dent in it. I thought your mother told you all about that. She always thought it was so funny, the story of how our grandmother had to get married in her shift to protect her new husband's estate; our grandmother was a widow then, you see." Edna stared, completely bewildered. "Oh well, we have time for that later; the important thing is to get you to Mrs. Grimsby. Or we get Mrs. Grimsby here. Yes, that might be the simplest thing: to carry her here. John could carry her here on his way back from town, whichever seems better in this weather. I never *saw* such weather!"

"But, Mr. Steele!" Edna protested; "surely he'll object to such an expenditure. I'm not even a member of the family." She burst into tears. Ten sat quietly on the huge goose-down chair. The sobs became quieter and finally stopped altogether. Still, she noted, Edna was not yet ready to look up. "As a matter of fact," Ten told her, rising, "John was the one who suggested it. I thought it was a very good idea, but then I thought, since you probably hadn't dressed yet, I ought to come in and ask you about it. At any rate, I can't imagine my brother getting to the point without confusing you so hopelessly you would never know he had come to ask about clothes." "How on earth does he manage with his patients?" Edna sniffed, raising her eyes; they felt heavy as the window. "Oh, if you were ill, that would be another matter, another thing altogether. Oh, he would be in here like George Washington, chopping down cherry trees right and left, all to good purpose, of course. Oh, he can convince anyone on a deathbed they'll be up in the morning, choring away in the doorway." Edna grinned at her. Ten grinned back. "That's better; put *something* on," Ten said, looking hopelessly at Edna's wardrobe, "and come down to breakfast. Don't fuss with yourself," she warned; "just come down and eat." "I suppose," Edna said, pretending to look through her clothes, "Mr. Steele has left on his rounds to minister to the invalids." "As it happens, he's sound asleep somewhere. I'm going to roust him now. I never know when he gets back at night," she complained; "I've asked him to leave notes on the mantel, but he won't hear of it. Either 'It's none of your business, Tenniel,' or 'You'll just worry yourself, Tenniel.' As stubborn as God ever made a mule. Well, I had better get down to the kitchen and see that Bridget doesn't burn everything to cinders." "Brid-

get?" Edna echoed; "I thought her name was Bertha."
"There's Bertha and Bridget and Maude and Nancy; oh,
it's a whole army. I told you there was no need to worry
about money. About the potato pancakes, definitely, but
about money, never about that." She went off down the
hall.

When Edna entered the kitchen, John and Ten were already seated before their big white plates, heavy oval porcelain plates which looked like platters. From the corner,
on the kitchen stove, came the snapping and spluttering of
bacon fat. There was a huge bowl of potato pancakes in
the center of the table; they bore no resemblance to any
pancakes Edna had ever seen before. From where she sat,
she watched Bridget. She dropped huge spoonful after
huge spoonful into the hot fat, lifting out the balls they
formed when they were brown and crusty. A dish of
tomato ketchup sat next to them. Next to that was a huge
loaf of white bread, and a large slab of butter resting on
rough chips of ice. Just then, Bridget went back over to
the fireplace, took out another giant loaf of bread with a
gigantic wooden paddle, and then, to Edna's astonishment,
thwacked it smartly against the wall of the fireplace. "That
takes off the ashes, miss." Bridget volunteered. There was
an enormous tureen of steaming cereal, a pitcher of cream,
and a platter of some kind of warm meat. Good Lord,
Edna thought, this must be the last meal of winter. John
had yet to look at her. Already repenting of his generosity,
she thought nervously; now he's probably wondering how
to get rid of me. He probably wants me out of mourning
so that some other gentleman will come along and take
me into *his* house.

"Where is Bertha?" Ten asked irritably; "I told her an
hour ago to get out there to the stable and see about getting that sleigh ready for Edna. I thought she could take
the matched team." John nodded and chewed, chewed
and nodded, still without looking up. "That girl is slower
than time in the primer!" Ten exclaimed, exasperated;
"she'll have the sleigh ready to drive through my tulip
garden." "I'll talk to Ben when I get out there," John said,
looking blankly at both of them. Why, he's half asleep!
Edna realized: I should have guessed as much. "If you
wait for Bertha," John went on groggily, "you might as
well sit there and wait for sanctification. You might as

well wait for the end of the world. You might as well wait for anything but Bertha." "Well, here I *am*," said the indignant object of their conversation; she was standing in the doorway behind them. "You must have ice-skated all the way," John said. "Oh, do go *on*," Bertha answered; "I can't be everywhere at once." How can they let servants talk to them that way? Edna wondered, but both John and Ten were smiling at each other. "Were you out at the stable? By any chance at all?" John asked. "Can't tell how far a cat will jump by looking at it," Bertha answered. smug. "Well, were you out there?" "I was." "And is the sleigh anywhere near ready?" "I forgot about the sleigh," Bertha admitted, face falling. "Well, as I said," he addressed Ten, "I'll fix it with Ben when I get out there." "Just what grapes did you find out in that barn to peck at, Miss Chicken?" Ten asked, more playful than annoyed. "Oh, missus, how you do go on," Bertha said, grinning in spite of herself. "You go on," Ten told her; "scat, scat." "Oh, about the cat," Edna said aloud. Both Ten's and John's head swiveled toward her; she found herself caught in the merciless cross fire of their gazes. Edna pretended to a sudden interest in the whereabouts of her last potato pancake.

"What cat?" John asked Ten. "Jimmie the cat." "You mean my cat?" John asked; "my cat wouldn't bother her. I can hardly find him long enough to get bothered by him." "He doesn't bother me," Edna mumbled, staring down at her plate. "What? Is he sick?" John asked. "I just wondered," Edna said, taking the plunge, "if anyone would mind if I kept Jimmie in my room at night, you know, the way I did last time." "In *your* room? At *night*?" John asked. "He didn't seem to mind it, Mr. Steele," Edna murmured, eyes fastened to her plate. "*My* cat didn't mind staying in the house all night?" the flabbergasted John asked his sister. "Why should he mind it, John dear? After all, he never got to sleep on a pillow before. The poor animal was in a fit after Edna left. He was under every ruffle and every bed. Every time I opened a drawer, he was in it, looking around, but I couldn't get him to chase a ball of yarn, or a stick, or a string. I guess he was just plain upset after Edna left." "My cat," John said slowly, as if he had just heard of a new pathway to the moon, "slept in the house all night, on that lady's pillow, and then he got up in the morning and ran around chasing toys?" "Well, he did make a few necessary trips outside," Ten considered straight-faced. "Ten, what were you thinking about?" John shouted; "the cat is *wild*. He might have gotten up in the middle of the night and wanted to go out and scratched her to pieces trying to get her up to open the door." "I guess," Ten answered, biting neatly into another pancake, "he forgot he was wild. I guess he forgot he was an animal. It was all 'velvet paws' from Edna, and all patting Edna on the cheek from Jimmie, and the only one who got swatted at was me one afternoon I went in there to wake her up from a nap. The wild cat seemed to have gotten it into his head I was going to strike her, or worse. You should have seen it; it would have done your heart good, how he slept on her hip all the time. That's because Edna sleeps on her side, and he stayed there as long as she stayed there, and I can't begin to describe the looks I got when I invaded the resting place. It's a good thing," she mused on, "he wasn't born a female; we would never have lived through any attempt on the kittens."

John stared from one to the other. No doubt about it, Ten thought; he's finally speechless. "You mean Jimmie?" John asked again; "my big orange mouser? The big cat I got from the Munyans to keep in the barn the summer there were so many rats?" "*I* know which cat is which cat," Ten answered, annoyed; "Jimmie, Jimmie the cat. How many Jimmie the cats do we have?" John turned his stare on Edna. Obviously, this was a dangerous woman. "Well?" Edna asked finally. "Well, what?" John asked. "Well, can I keep Jimmie? At night, only at night," she assured him; "I didn't know he was your cat." "Well, he was my *cat*," John said; "he wasn't my *pet;* there's a difference. You're sure he never scratched her?" "I'm sure," said Ten. John shook his head.

The tablecloth in the vicinity of Edna's chair began pushing itself in and out. Finally, John noticed a roundish bump pushing through the cloth. It approximated the size of a small pumpkin. He began to observe it more narrowly. The bump suddenly levitated. Edna started in her chair, sitting up straight as a stick, then relaxing. "Um, these are very good, Ten," Edna said sweetly. "What's so good?" Ten asked; "your plate's empty. Is there something in your lap?" she asked. "Lap?" Edna echoed. John stared

89

pointedly in the direction of that aforementioned object. Edna felt her body flushing hotly. "What *is* in your lap, Miss Edna?" John asked. "Yes, yes," said Ten, "don't be afraid to tell us what it is. Why, at least twice a week John tips his whole dinner into *his* lap." She was grinning like the crescent moon. "It's, um"—she hesitated—"it's who we were just talking about." Brother and sister inspected her in silence. "Who?" John demanded; "who could fit on your lap?" "Well, if you must know," Edna burst out, "it's the cat." "Let me see him," John ordered.

Edna slowly and gently drew back the white linen cloth, first disclosing the tips of two pointed ears, then the round, broad forehead, then the entire furry face of a huge, orange, ferocious tomcat. Jimmie squinted evilly at both Ten and John. "Good grief!" said John. "Poor, poor Jimmie," Edna crooned; "you have a little notch in your ear. That notch wasn't there before, was it? The rat got your ear, did he? Oh, I'll fix that ear," Edna chanted, while Jimmie, in a transport of affection, stood up on Edna's lap and put his paws around her neck. "There's a good cat; there's my handsome cat," Edna sang on. Jimmie stretched one paw past Edna's ear; his claws began to extend from their pads. John watched, as if hoping for deliverance from this amazingly revolting spectacle. In went the claws; out went the claws. "Why, he's flexing his claws," Ten said in a voice like maple sugar; "isn't that just adorable? Why, John, don't you think that's the most adorable thing you ever saw?"

John got up and looked out. "Where is my horse?" he asked, querulous. "Well, since he's not ready, why don't you sit back down and finish your breakfast? Don't worry so," she went on, looking John over. "I'm sure the horse spent the night in his own bed and is as normal as ever." Excited shrieks of children streaked somewhere behind the kitchen windows. "It's those Munyan children again," Ten sighed. "Don't ask me how I know who they are," she told Edna. "They're the only children in the county who specialize in invisibility. John, you know, while you were gone, the neighbors started to Frenchify them. All fall they were called the De Munyans; then some genius shortened it to the Demons." "Well, that's appropriate enough," he said; "what are they up to now?" "Aside from almost drowning the little Greene boy trying to cut a hole in the ice last month? Not much. Their last really good adventure had to do with our pear orchard. One of the Demons decided to pretend the branches of our pear trees were horns of cattle, and, after they lassoed them, they dragged them off home in a wagon." "I thought we lost those trees in a storm." "It was a kind of a storm, I guess," Ten said; "and I suppose there's no point in talking to their father?" "None. None whatever. He probably gave them the idea."

"Which reminds me, John," Ten said; "what are you going to do about putting a fence around this house?" "Why do we need a fence?" John asked absently, slicing up a piece of meat. "Because my bulbs and your horses and cattle and pigs and sheep don't get on too well together. The animals find my flowers underfoot all the time, and the flowers, well, they feel somehow trampled in the dust." "Flowers again," John grumbled. "It's that time of year. You can't blame spring on me; besides, it's unnerving to see those Canadian cattle with their huge horns peering in the kitchen windows. It's bad enough in the winter, I can tell you, but when they start sticking their great wet noses into the kitchen and licking me up and down, it's really beyond putting up with." "Next I suppose you'll want a new hen coop." "That goes without saying. The hens eat up everything. Then the cat gets after them and the eggs. Then the feathers start flying. Then one flies up on the back of a cow. Then the cow starts witching around the yard. You can't saddle up a horse without the creature getting nervous and coming down with a case of the blind staggers. You're not home all day, but I tell you, life isn't worth living in this house, and it won't be until I get a fence around it. I might as well move myself and my mending out into the barn." "That would be easier on me." "What kind of fence *is* it to be?" Ten asked; "if anyone thought to ask me, I'd say white picket with barbed wire on the barn side, and chicken wire nailed up high for the summer vines to run about on." "Well," said John, "since you've got it all planned, just give the orders." "When?" asked Ten; "when should they start?" "Today, naturally, since the ground's hard as a rock." "I'm serious." "I'll talk to Ben and Amos about it before I leave," he promised, getting up; "they can get the supplies in now. The store's not frozen up." Ten smiled blissfully at her plate. "And don't think I don't know you'll be out there in an hour checking to make sure they got the right instructions from me." "You do tend to mix things up," Ten observed; "mind, I don't want chicken wire on the bottom, and picket on the top." "No, when you said iron, I knew you meant iron."

"There's the sleigh," Ten announced, relieved. Edna got up to look at it. Why, if her face isn't a perfect model for an engraving of "Life's Disillusionments," John thought. Outside was a huge, heavy gray horse, less space showing between his legs and stomach than Edna had ever seen in a horse of such size; but he made up for it, she thought, in length. He had the thickest neck in the world, and ears the right size for a smallish mouse. His forelock was streaked with gray, and, standing there in the glare of the snow, he kept his eyes half closed like a septuagenarian who was tired of life. Look at those leg joints, Edna thought; another inch of snow and they wouldn't be visible. And the sleigh! Never had she seen such an apparition. No, she would never have guessed the vehicle in question was a sleigh, although the queer contraption did rest on runners. It must, she concluded, be some kind of converted buggy. Resting on the frame surmounting the wheels was what appeared to be a flat box, a small plain footboard rising out of one end, and what seemed to be an armchair and a half formed its back seat. Instead of armrests, the seat sported little rails, which looked very much like the fence Ten had just described, and above that little fence, rising from it, and fastening into the woodwork bracing the upholstered seat, was a little curved iron pipe. The most unsightly mongrel Edna ever hoped to see lay snuggled into one corner of the seat, eyes fixed patiently on the house, although the dog kept his back to it, preferring to gaze reproachfully over his thickset shoulder. What a thing to drive to Fitchburg!

"Don't worry," John broke in, as if reading her thoughts; "that's my sleigh and my dog Flag." "Oh," Edna said, not knowing whether to sympathize with him or compliment that weird assemblage of equipage and animalia. "Well," John said, buttoning up his coat, lifting his collar, "I'll see about your sleigh. It's too early for you to have formed any definite idea of a destination, I presume?" "I thought of going to Fitchburg," Edna answered nervously.

"Fitchburg! That's out of the question, out entirely. Well, Ten," he said, turning around in the rectangle of light, the light turning him from a three-dimensional figure to a black silhouette, as if he were already vanishing, as if his very existence had been an illusion, illusory, Edna thought, terrified; "don't wait up wrinkling yourself." Edna's eyes were stinging with salt. Why couldn't she go to Fitchburg if she wanted to? *He* was the *younger* brother; Ten was older. It wasn't his business to make decisions for her, as if *she* were his younger sister, or he was her father. Out of the question! she repeated to herself, trembling with fury.

"Well, dear, come into the parlor," Ten coaxed, taking Edna's arm. Lord, she thought; I forgot what it was like! They're going to be at each other like cats and dogs, and after that, it will be worse than trying to tell one snowflake from another. And the neighbors think I'm the one who keeps him away from the single women around here! Well, Ten comforted herself, it's still better than his ups and downs over nothing, and her ups and downs over empty spaces. Oh, Edith! she remembered; Edith won't like this. John will never go back to the city. Sitting down in the low chair, she cut short her grim reflections. Taking time by the forelock as usual, Ten, she scolded herself, as if she were her dead husband, Ed. You don't have a crystal ball. Trouble comes over the hill fast enough without your gasping yourself red and sweaty running up there to meet it. Ten smiled to herself. Ed. He was, had been—no, was—a remarkable man, but he did not have one thing: he did not have an elegant way with words. And now I guess I talk just like him, she thought, warmed by the idea.

She looked up to find Edna's face buried up to the eyes in the dusty, furry back of Jimmie the cat. "*Why* is Fitchburg out of the question?" she asked, voice quavering. "I guess because John doesn't want anyone else drowned in the river." "Drowned in the river? Drowned? Why, my friend told me it was a short easy ride from here." "She lives here through the year, I take it?" Ten asked; "she's not a city boarder?" "Actually she comes from the South." "The South. Then she doesn't know much about the Green River. It runs between us and Fitchburg. Well, there are two ways of getting across it. There's the floating bridge and there's the ferry and they're both impassable in weather like this." "But last night your brother said this wasn't even a blizzard." "It doesn't take a blizzard to put the floating bridge out of order. That's just what it is, my dear, a floating bridge. It's held on at both sides by chains, and if enough ice starts resting on it, well then, it floats off instead of floating where it's supposed to. It nearly got John last winter, but Gray wouldn't set foot on it. John went over it on his way to an amputation, and there wasn't any trouble about it. But coming back, he couldn't get Gray to get on it. He whipped the horse. He got out and dragged the horse, and Gray, he finally lay down in the snow and nothing would persuade him to get up. John tried to bully him by taking Flag off by the leash and pretending to walk on out to the bridge, leaving old Gray there in the snow, but then the dog set up a howl and pulled so he broke from the leash, and went and lay right down next to Gray; well, then, John decided he had better give in. The animals had the majority vote, and to make a long story short, he settled in with the other two; he wrapped himself up in every robe he had in the buggy, and lit up two kerosene lamps and set them down under the lap robes, saying a prayer for each one, and in the morning, when he woke up, the ice floe had broken and swept on down the river, and there was no trace at all of the bridge, and when John got back to Williamsville, they said it had been out since sundown. So he always says, I trust to the dog; I trust to the horse. Someday, if he's lucky, he'll live to have as much sense as they do."

"Well, then," Edna asked, "if the bridge is so dangerous, why can't I take the ferry?" "Just what are you imagining, a big pretty boat, with a long pier going down to it, big enough for a horse and buggy to ride out onto?" "Something like that." "It happens that a ferry in these parts is a great big raft and it gets pulled across the water by a man with a good strong arm who pulls at the ropes that go over the pulleys; they hook into two nice strong trees on either side of the river, but right now, I'd guess those holes are being used for sugaring. Well, Edna, think of it, trying to control a raft in weather like this. He'd be in whitecaps over his crown. The horse would never stay on, and everything would be at the bottom of the river that wasn't already floating down it before you even got your chance to drown yourself properly. No, brother or no brother, I couldn't let you set out for Fitchburg; of course, I *could* let you start out, but you'd only be disappointed, and what would be the point of that? No, no point at all," she concluded.

Well, Ten thought, taking a deep breath, that speech had given her a good opportunity to study the child. She didn't like the dark circles under her eyes, or the tendency she had either to sit still as a stone or to fidget like a pecking chicken, but there was something about her that was immovable, as something about John was immovable. And she was eerie at moments, the way she sometimes seemed old, older than all of them here. Some sort of emotional precociousness; probably it all came from studying her father. He had been old like that, too. But still, she was so much younger than John; she was twelve years younger. She wouldn't even know of what to be afraid. She hadn't had the time to become frightened of bats and shadows and shadows of shadows, the way John's wife had. Yes, Ten thought, satisfied; she'll end by being more than a companion to me.

There was a commotion in the yard. "That must be your sleigh. Now don't look right away," Ten teased; "I saw your face when you looked at John's. I want to see your face when you see this one." Edna shuddered theatrically. "Where shall I take it?" she asked cheerfully. She certainly could chase the clouds off fast enough, Ten observed. "Coe's Pond would be a good destination. Everyone will be out there somewhere. The Demons will be out there somewhere. You'll know where they are when everyone runs off in one direction to rescue their innocent victim. Try Coe's Pond. Yes, that's a good idea." "Why don't *you* come?" Edna asked suddenly; "you can lie on a sled as well as I can." Ten paused, one hand on her hip. She's remembering something, Edna thought. "Why not?" Ten asked; "why not?" "Bertha," she called out, "we're going sleighing." "Sleighing?" Bertha asked, sticking her bonneted head into the room. "With your rheumatism?" "It goes wherever I go," Ten answered philosophically; "get Ben after the sleighs and you go after my clothes." "Oh, Miss Ten," Bertha wailed, "what will Mr. Steele say?" "He'll be delighted if he knows nothing about it at all." "Oh, I see, ma'am," Bertha answered, grinning.

While they were waiting for the little wooden sleds and Ten's heavy clothing, Edna asked her if she thought John really would take care of that fence. "If he doesn't start in about the perfection of broken things," she said, resigned. "Come. Look at the sleigh." It was a brilliant red sleigh, graceful and light, sides sweeping back like wings, the wings decorated with flying birds. "And will that do, miss?" "As well as broken things?" Edna asked; "I'm not sure." They left, their laughter wafting back to the house.

How things happen, Ten meditated silently; one suicide by hanging, one bizarre death, one premature death, and we are brought together like this, and this is the beginning of a whole new family tree. Yes, she thought on, this will be an evergreen. I wonder how I will like it, really. They start out so small, like Mrs. Camp's big spruce. And now she complains she can't get any light in the house, it's gotten so big and spread out so, but when she first dragged it in on her wagon, she worried about it for two years, she was so sure it was going to die. And I asked her, why can't you get another one? The forest's full of them; what difference does it make? You could go one hundred feet and pick out a bigger one, and she looked at me as if there wasn't anything in the world I understood, and said, "Because I chose this one." As simple as that.

She chose that tree out of all the other trees and that was the important thing. I suppose that's the whole explanation of marriage. I suppose it's the whole explanation of parenthood, going out to avenge your injured dog, any kind of loyalty at all. Because I chose this one. Well, that does make all the difference, doesn't it? After that, the person's never the same. Once I chose Ed, she thought, absently sticking a cold cucumber from the big salad bowl, he wasn't the same man anymore. It was like having a new shadow. Well, I had to take responsibility for the shape it cast in front of me, or in back of me. And if there were any empty spaces in him, well, I filled them up. And if there were no empty spaces, and there were things I wanted to be rid of, but couldn't bear to part with, as when I'm cleaning out a clothes closet, there are always things I know I should throw out, but I'm so used to them, or they remind me of so many other things, well, and what happens to them? They go into a trunk, and the trunk goes into the attic. And then it all starts all over again when the attic needs cleaning out.

But, no, nothing ever gets thrown out in *my* lifetime; why, the very idea that someone might throw them out when I'm not here to stop them makes me go cold all over. So I suppose if Ed had no empty spaces to fill, I hung him all over with pockets on strings and he had to walk around with my worries and my hopes decorating him, whether he looked outlandish or not. And of course he did the same thing to me. So it was such a shock when he died like that. Everyone thought he just had a hard cold. He couldn't have been in bed more than two days. No, it was three, and then he got up and decided to go down to the local artist's and have his likeness done for my relatives back East, and they said he was just standing there, waiting for the horsecars, when his knees just folded up without any warning, and the next thing everyone knew, there he was lying on his side, and there were ladies murmuring about what a shame it was, how some people drank; they couldn't even stand up long enough to get on their cars and hide their shame at home. And then some gentleman thought to take a better look, and he must have known something about such things. He saw Ed's hands were blue, and he took his pulse.

Then, of course, everyone fell over everyone else trying to help out (they felt so sorry, so many of them had thought he was drunk), but there wasn't any helping, not him, not me. It went on for almost a week. The only thing I could seem to think was, it would have been so much better if he'd died *after* he'd had his likeness done. That would have been *so* much better; I could have had all the copies I wanted. Well, I wasn't going to have the artist draw a likeness of his headstone, a plain enough affair it was anyway, and out there in Kansas it must be scoured flat now by the dust and the wind. Or of his corpse. Well, that would have been pointless. But I thought at the time, well, I made this choice when I picked out Ed. I made this choice to be a widow. And when John's wife died, it seemed as if he had made the same choice, but I don't think he'll stay alone much longer. He's not suited to it;

so really, our choices weren't the same. I suppose they're not, for anyone.

And what shocked me most was the relief I felt once it all wore off. There was no one else but myself to think of, unless I chose to think of someone else. Well, wasn't that an odd thing, because I never thought I minded thinking about Ed. I thought I liked it. I never thought of it as a strain. But it must have been, once I was married and settled in, and chose him, everything felt all over with and settled, as if I had come to the end of a long book, as if I had begun reading the book during the late afternoon, and had read the rest of it in my sleep, and when I woke up in the morning, and settled down in the window seat to read it, there were hardly any pages left, and I was so disappointed.

I suppose there was something lacking in me. There must still be, to have so little imagination, to see the endings, not the beginnings. John sees the endings to things as fast as I do, but he never knows what will come in between. It's a curse, our mother used to say, that kind of acuteness, almost second sight of some kind, but as soon as he finishes looking at the end of one thing, he's looking at the beginning of something else. Well, she mused, I suppose that's why he's a scientist, and I'm an observer, a cataloguer, a good collector of data, but there's nothing much I want to do with it. Just preserve it, as if I were canning life, trying to put in just the right amount of sugar, trying to seal the jars so that no one doubles over poisoned, but I have no illusions about preserving life. No, that can't be done. I have no urge to prolong a life unless someone asks for some help in that line, as they would ask for help in getting the wash on the Monday line, no urge to experiment, no desire to take any risks, just to let things happen as they happen.

It must be a lack of imagination or nerve. Or perhaps it's just a character of some kind they'll find a name for someday. Ed had the same kind of character, although, if he had foreseen his own death, he would have risked a good deal to avoid it. But if someone told me today I would fall through the ice sleighing, and end up frozen, I would think, by the time I get home, I'll be a sight, icicles all over my head, looking like a witch out of *Macbeth*, dripping for hours in the kitchen until they dry me out and dare to put me in the parlor where I won't spoil anything. I would if I were wet. I'd think, what a way to die, so untidy, making such a mess, when the very last thing I did was to see the parlor was perfectly clean, what with Bridget sitting down on the carpet running a twisted rag through all the little holes of the carved furniture. But I wouldn't have tried to avoid it. It would have made me angry, though: very angry.

"What are you thinking about?" Edna asked; "you're so quiet. Did the skating wear you out so much? I probably kept you out there too long." "Nonsense, I stayed out just as long as I wanted to. I was thinking about it, though, what I must have looked like, at my age, getting pulled about, towed around like a wrecked train, at the end of that hooked stick. It was nice of those Munyans, really. They didn't even take me out far, did they? Mrs. Brown kept shouting, 'Now, Mrs. Richardson, you'll have no one to blame but yourself if you keep ahold of that tow stick and let those Demons take you out where the ice is so thin they drown you. You'll have no one to blame but yourself, you'll have no one to blame but yourself; she sounded like a regular parrot. And you. You cut out your name on that ice! I thought only country children could do that. That was something to see. When you went further out, you didn't look a bit bigger than one of the Demons. It was hard to keep track of you." Isn't it nice, Ten thought, what Ed always says; my face never shows there's a thought in my head. Sometimes I wonder if I think. Think properly, anyway.

"Oh, I liked the sliders," Edna babbled away; "I don't know how they get so very good at it. They went so fast, I kept looking for an engine hidden about their persons somewhere. There were the ones who went down the whole way on one leg, and then there was that very little one with the red pointed hat who looked like a devil and *he* spun around in line and he was looking right into the face of the boy in back of him. He went all the way down backwards!" "That, naturally," Ten told her, "was one of the Demon children." "They don't seem so bad to me," Edna reflected. "Well, neither do they to me, but we mustn't let that get around. It seems to be the one thing in town everyone agrees on, that there's nothing worse this side of hell than a Munvan, unless it's two Munyans."

"They do seem to get such satisfaction, complaining about them." "It's always better to complain about something outside of the house than inside it, but then the trouble is," Ten said, "the people in the house have to find the same thing outside of the house to complain about. Most people can't even manage that much." "I suppose not," Edna concurred.

Had that been the trouble at home, on Cedar Street; had it been so common, so simple? People just unable to agree. But that's not what she means. She means people always want to complain; there's something about living that makes people want to complain, as if they have some obscure disease, but no doctor can find it; no one can find it. They have no idea what it is themselves. If my mother and father had just had something to complain about. If they had neighbors who lassoed their pear trees; if they had worked themselves into a passion over that, then at least there would have been passion: there would have been a common cause. There would have been no hanging, no dwelling on poisonings, the impossibility of happiness on this earth, everything which finally led to the murders. They would have been so much calmer about the important things because they were so excited about the little ones. It would be terrible, she thought, desperately, if she's right; if it's just that simple. That stupidly simple. That *stupid*.

"Aunt Ten," Edna said, looking down at her plate, "we didn't have suppers like this when I was here before." They were eating grilled cheese sandwiches; Bertha brought in more warm ones as they finished the triangles on the platter. In the center of the table was a bowl of cucumbers floating in ice and vinegar, and next to it, a huge porcelain pitcher of milky, extremely sweet coffee. There was also a tureen of tomato soup, and Bertha came in with a tray of tomatoes on toast. "These are good," Edna said; "what makes them taste like this?" "It's the sugar they're grilled with. Summer food. I had to import the tomatoes. This is my own protest against winter. It's gone on longer than I approve of." "So you've decided against acknowledging it?" "Exactly." Ten answered; "and you can't imagine the pleasure, the vindictive pleasure, it gives me to eat these cold cucumbers with drifts almost to the top of the fences." Yes, there was a real understanding between these women. The thirty years separating them seemed irrelevant, except, of course, in practical matters and matters of common sense; then it was as if Ten had a different kind of stock in the same store, a store the two of them owned as partners. "I never wait for John before serving," Ten remarked, as if Edna was uninterested in such a subject; "a doctor's day is like the Arctic night. It goes on forever." The two women ate in contented silence, Edna unaware of thinking, although, she was to realize later, her mind had gone blank just because every fiber of her being was so concentrated on listening for sound, any sound that would mean a sleigh arriving. The door slammed.

From the hall came a storm of rustlings and clatterings and a noise distinctly like that of a boot being hurled across a wooden floor. This noise was soon followed by an identical one. "I wouldn't guess this was a good day," Ten whispered. Edna smiled at her plate. Why, the little thing isn't even intimidated! she noted. "Well, what is it now?" Ten asked, looking up at her looming brother in the doorway. "Those maniacal Westons," he exploded; "I'm going to have to settle their hash. They're beyond endurance, all of them." "You know you shouldn't talk about poor invalids that way," Ten egged him on. "Invalids!" John expostulated; "invalids! They're drunkards and hypochondriacs. There isn't a better combination to bury a doctor. And what was their urgent message this morning? I've got it here somewhere." John began slapping himself all over the front of his coat. "Well, I remember it without having to look at it: 'Father dying; come at once. Emma.' How many times has he died this year?" he asked his sister. "Oh, I'd say over twenty times; the miracle of it," she said, "is that you take it seriously each and every time." "He's going to die one of these days, isn't he?" John growled; "you can't expect me to guess which one. I can't just decide, oh well, today he's not dying, and turn over and go back to sleep and then go off like a respectable citizen to attend the funeral. I tell you, he has me caught. I've got to think of some way to even the score."

"And when you got there?" "When I got there! When I got there, the spiders had dropped off the walls; the bees had swarmed into the living room, and the only thing he had left to go on about was the infection of the brain that gave him such a terrible headache, and the big cancer of the stomach that made him vomit all the time, and as for his constant falling down, he knew that was a brain tumor as big as a squash, so I asked him what I, a mere mortal, could be expected to do with him. I wasn't a walking hospital, and the best I could suggest was that he leave right away for Germany and see if any of their research doctors had come up with something that would take care of the brain and the stomach and the tumor all at once. I told him I thought the brain was the hopeless thing, because, as far as I could tell, it was very nearly gone, and if he called me out again on such an errand, at least I'd have something to do setting some bones I fractured myself."

"But you've been gone since early morning!" Edna blurted out; "they must have locked you in a closet." "Closet, my foot," John snapped; "when you get into Weston country, you might as well start building a house. They go into such panics, those lunatics, they alert the whole county. By the time my sleigh even begins to move into view, every single house with an imaginary invalid in it has a real white flag swinging in the wind from its hitching post. So it's straight off to the maniacs, then hop one foot to one house and stitch up a cut that would heal by itself by morning; hop another foot to another house and dress a burn. Hop another foot to another house where the Bowens arranged I shouldn't just have my labor for my pains, and some good woman obliges by having a baby that instant, all to keep my life interesting. Hop another foot and it's some lunatic who thinks his father ought to be taken off to the Retreat because he threw his supper out the window. 'Oh, you'd think he'd be happy to have any supper at all, and a roof over his head, too,' says the sanctimonious son, and the walls of the kitchen are so covered with grease you could take them down and use them for skillets, and the food evil enough to poison a goat hog. The old man might as well have washed the slop down with carbolic acid. I told the better half that the old man ought to stay and look after the place and I'd be happy to take her husband off to the Retreat and throw away the key, so I guess they're put out, but the old man looked pretty smart."

"Who had the baby?" Ten asked mildly; "now that

102

you're finished with the county news." John glared, sat down, and began chewing. "Well? Who had the baby? The new arrival? The little newcomer? God's cherub? The tiny stranger?" More chewing. "John, you answer me; you know I can't bear curiosity." "The evening temper tantrum," John said to his plate. Edna had been grinning so long the muscles in her cheeks were beginning to hurt. No, she'd never been happier, and in the middle of talk like this. "Who had the little stranger?" John said finally; "Jane Munyan had the little stranger. Jane Munyan has a little stranger every nine months; I don't know why she needs help. The other ten children could be midwives by now and she's built like an I-don't-know-what; they pop out like cannonballs." "Another Munyan!" Ten said, shaking her head. "Just what everyone else I saw today said; you should have heard them at the post office. You'd think it was Lucifer himself who fell into that cradle." "Well, when I was there last time," Ten said, "during her confinement, I told her she ought to name that one Finis, but her niece said she better not, because she'd just have to name the next one Appendix and the one after Supplementary and the one after Index." "The girl was right," John said, tired.

"Appendix Munyan," Edna said, fork poised. Ten began laughing, then choked. "Don't do that," she gasped when she could breathe again. John shook his head at both of them. "Appendix, would you please get that book down from the shelf?" Edna asked the air. John choked on a cucumber slice. "Chew your food, dear," Ten gasped through her laughter. "Which one pulled you on the ice? Was it Appendix or Index?" Edna asked Ten. "Ice? What ice?" John asked, but the whole subject of ice sank under the unaccustomed tide of laughter lapping against the stone walls of the room, Bridget and Bertha materializing fast enough to see the incredible sight of Mr. Steele laughing so hard he had to wipe at his eyes with his pocket handkerchief. "Index, where's the cardamon?" they heard him ask in a ridiculous falsetto, and then everyone was laughing again. "I wouldn't have believed it," Bertha said; "I haven't seen him laugh like that since he was a little thing. Well, not *that* long. You'd think they were mad, all three of them. Unless you put something on the tomatoes." "Some people call them love's apples," Bridget said, starting to giggle herself. "Oh!" Bertha gasped; "love's apples! So that's what we've been serving up, is it?" "It is," Bridget said. The two of them went off down the hall, cackling softly, two old hens.

The snow, now that it had decided to go, was going fast; there was a terrible crash when John, Edna, and Ten were sitting in the parlor, each pretending to read. In all probability, only Ten was making progress through her precious *Isabella*. "*Isabella*," John had said, taking it up when he came in, turning to the title page: "By the author of *Rhoda, Minerva, Katerina, Maude*." John shook his head at his sister, giving the book back. "There must be some reason," he said, "the author refuses to put her name on the title page." "Not necessarily a literary one," Ten answered, grumpy; she did love those books. "She might be a minister's wife." This was a hit at John's friend who, after ordination, had gone to take over a parish in Dummerston. The last time he and his wife visited Williamsville, his wife had treated them to a description of the generous parishioners, and because she was back home in Williamsville, and thus sure nothing she said would fly from that particular birdcage and back to Dummerston, she had become more and more inspired in her runs at the various eminences of the town.

"Well, to begin with," she said, "you remember the 'handsome' salary they promised us? They neglected to tell us we were expected to pay rental for the parish house. You should have heard the sanctimonious old biddies explaining why, because none of their ministers had ever stayed on long enough, they hadn't thought it practical to buy us a house. 'We have been very unfortunate in ministers' wives,' one of them said, gazing pointedly at this object in question. I was disgusted, but what could *I* do? They always wait until Mr. Shepherd (he never should have been born with that name; it affected his destiny) is out of the house, and then the men send the biddies to do the dirty work. 'I do hope,' one of them said seriously, 'you will not refuse to pray aloud at our next Missionary Aid Meeting.'

"Missionary Aid Meeting! Go two miles back in the hills and there are little old ladies eating one boiled potato a day, deciding whether to freeze to death this week or next. Last week, an old lady froze to death up there on the hill; she was eighty-three. They found her frozen over the potato she was peeling (it was the last one; the house was completely empty), and in front of the fireplace there were the last two legs of the last parlor chair. The inside looked like a barn.

"But they're off to save the Chinese, and they want me to pray out loud. *I* should have preached the sermon before they made *that* decision. And after that, there was the terrible scandal about me. I thought it would never fade. It turned out one of our friends had put us in terrible jeopardy; he gave us a kitten, and I decided to play with him on the carpet, and the part of the carpet where the sun fell was under the window, and outside of the window walked one of the neighbors, and she double-quicked it into town, and it was all over town by dinner-time, my scandalous, undignified, unministerly-wife's behavior. I tell you!

"Then the Christmas donations for the minister! Crystal vases, rotted potatoes, oh, it was a disgrace. 'Well, you ought to live *now*,' one of them said meaningfully to me; and the others took up the refrain like a flock of geese. I can't even get sick. No one comes to visit me; they come to visit Matilda in the kitchen. 'Oh, I think she could have gotten up before now,' she agrees; she knows which side to fight on; they'll be there a lot longer than we will. 'Then she's a little sickly?' the visitor asks, and with such an excellent imitation of concern. 'Oh, very,' Matilda says; 'and she does tend to pamper herself. She does tend to that.'

"So we have no money and I'm trying my hand at writing books, religious ones, but not under my own name, of course. The commotion would be more than a saint could endure."

John looked over at Edna. She appeared to be absorbed in some story about "How the Orphans Ran the Household." She doesn't know what the ordinary things are like, things like that woman talked about; some people just can't stand it, the ordinary way. It's not in them to take it; they can't fight back. If they do fight back, then the rumor mill just has more to grind up. I wonder if she could take it? Now Ten and I, he thought, going over to the window, Ten and I just don't care. I sometimes suspect all the people here exist for my sister like characters in one of her novels. She likes watching them while they're out during the day; then, for all she cares, they might as well disappear into gopher holes at night. I doubt she even thinks most of them are human. I'm not much better. I never thought of most people as human. I used to look around the lecture hall at Harvard, and think there were, to be generous, three real people in the room. They might as well put all the rest in a stable.

John looked out the window; the soft gaslight stayed within the room, thrust back by the moon. That moon stands for no competition, John thought; I think about it when I'm out at night. In the country, the moon puts up with nothing but itself. It puts up with its attendants, the stars. It can afford to be so queenly because when it's gone, the dark is absolute. There's no point having eyes on a moonless night, not in the country. During the day everyone can see through everyone else's walls. At night, total blindness.

The country, it's more a state of mind than a place. All places are really states of mind, collective states. There are so many rules here; no one bothers writing them down. Everyone finds out what they are soon enough. It's the same thing in the city; there's only the appearance of freedom. "Oh, you can do what you want in the city; none of those gossiping porches to pass with those wire eyes." But, John went on, following his path, there are recluses in the country. I could be a recluse in the country if I weren't a doctor. "Oh," they'd say, "he's gotten peculiar," and they'd leave it at that; they'd leave me alone. Every now and then someone would leave a quarter of beef on my porch; loaves of bread, pails of milk, whether I wanted them or not. They have a formula for strange things up here: "He's gotten peculiar." "His wife's gotten a little peculiar."

And someone nearer the stove would say, "He sure is peculiar. He should have waited until the hunting season. Now, I wonder, where do you get that kind of license? As for myself, I wouldn't shoot at my own father, but I'd clean my gun and see if it would fire over my wife's mother's head, and I'm not even peculiar." "By now I guess she doesn't even duck," another one would joke back. And so it goes on, half hilarity, half seriousness.

They all go home, of course, and report. "You know Mr. Brown? He's having mother-in-law troubles. Shouldn't be surprised to find her staring at a green sludge in her teacup one of these days." Then the women press on for details. "How do you expect me to remember all those little things? I told you the main thing; he's having mother-in-law troubles. Now you have something to write up your diary about." "Well, it's too bad about your friend, Fred," the wife says sweetly, getting her own back; "and imagine giving *that* for an excuse."

Now she has him. His friend Fred? Giving that kind of excuse? "What are you babbling about now?" he asks his wife roughly. She stitches away on her quilt. If there's an aunt or a friend, they stitch on their quilts along with her. If there's an unmarried friend, she stitches. After a while he wears her out. "His mother-in-law found this green slime at the bottom of her cereal bowl; it made her kind of suspicious. So she took it down to the pharmacy. Arsenic compound. 'You have a lot of rats?' 'I sure do,' she said, and marched on with the bowl right down to the police station.

"The policeman was off waking up some man on the hill so he wouldn't miss his train to Boston. 'What do you want me to do?' the policeman asked her when she finally cornered him. 'Arrest him? Arrest Fred?' 'Is murder legal now?' the old lady asked. 'You want me to arrest Fred? In the middle of the haying season? No wonder he wanted you poisoned. I'd poison you myself if I had a farm and you wanted me arrested in the middle of the haying season.' The way men think!" his wife scoffs. "So off goes the officer to arrest Fred, takes him back to the jail looking so sheepish you'd never guess who had done wrong, and what does Fred say? 'I only wanted to frighten her.'

"Oh, it's in all the papers. Can you imagine? 'I only wanted to frighten her.'

"And that no good officer, you know what he said? He said Fred had better leave bear traps all around the old lady's room, and especially near the necessary. Why, anyone (the officer told him how to go about it), anyone could leave things like that lying around if he came home drunk and he'd have no particular intention anyone could speak to him about; it would be one of those lucky accidents. I don't know where it will all end." Well, I know where it will all end, John thought: with my taking Fred off to Northfield, or performing the autopsy on the old crone.

And what does the friend of the imaginary prisoner have to say but the truth: "You'd shoot that old goat yourself, and didn't think anyone would find you out. But now, you women have to stick together; you're so convinced everyone's putting arsenic in your soup. And who's doing the cooking? *Fred* should be worrying about what he eats, not that old crone." "Well, someone has to take care of the old people," the wife says in her Sunday voice, under the withering eye of her *own* mother. "Someone has to take care of the old people," mimics Fred's friend; "Fred, he'd have to take care of her if she was a rattlesnake, or go as far off as Turkey. He couldn't live in this county a day if he threw her out of the house. Well, he'd have an even chance if he put something in her soup, so I say good luck to him. And anyhow"—the friend pauses to think—"he probably *was* trying to frighten her. If he'd been better or worse, she wouldn't have found anything to take to the officer." "You'll have an excuse for poisoning me next," the friend's wife goes on, stitching away. "Well, and maybe I will," says her husband, stomping up to bed, *his* mother-in-law stirring the cauldron for tomorrow's troubles.

At least, John thought, turning with relief from contemplating the lives of people around him to considering the weather, when the snow goes, it goes fast. Like old people go. When they give up, they let go. I never yet had to pry one of their hands loose from life. They just let go, their hands colder and colder to the touch, and the next thing you know, they're gone. You have to hold their hands. They don't care about holding on to anyone—not after they've decided. They just lie there, waiting, getting cold as the snow, and the next thing someone's cutting a hole in it for them. They turn so white. First it's their hair; then it's all of them. The brides and bridegrooms of the snow-covered earth.

Yes, John decided, the best time to die is the winter. Then you don't have to hear all those relations standing around, pricking each other on: "Oh, to die like this, when everything is beginning to bloom. To be nipped in the bud in the middle of the spring. Not to last even so long as the crocus! The trees go on, the flowers come up, but our little Bertie . . ." and they sob themselves sick; and then there's always someone who doesn't think enough is enough, and goes on about the lilies and the roses and the lavender and the gooseberries and the elderberries and the trumpet vine: and some mother, or even some father, throws himself on the grave, while the one who ought to be under lock and key drones botanically on about the Dutch-pipe ivy, and day lilies, on how like a day lily, and all the rest of it, and then he starts on the animals, the raccoons, and the squirrels, and the bears, the goats and the lambs and the cows, and pretty soon the mother is almost distracted with grief, and she's lying on top of something all right, and if the droner keeps it up long enough, the father's lying there right next to her: the return of the blue jay, the first robin, who will train the bushes up the trellis now?—and then there's the whole spectacle to go through again, and the doctor; of course, the doctor gets the best seat. I shouldn't keep on like this, John thought, finally looking out the window, the imagined scenes fading from his eyes: I'll start to hate them all again.

"Well?" Ten asked, tearing her eyes from *Isabella;* "what *was* that crash? You've been looking out there for two chapters. Did the barn blow away?" "It's just the ice," John answered without moving; "the whole piece came off the west wing roof." "I saw a crocus today; you should have seen it," Ten said; "somehow it melted a hole for itself in the snow around the big fir. Now, I call that flower very intelligent." John couldn't help smiling. "The first crocus," he sang under his breath. "What?" Ten asked. "Oh, nothing. Some old song came back to me." Edna's eyes were drilling into him.

What old song? What was he thinking about? Was he thinking about his first wife? Some other woman? He must go to see every woman in the county. But he's a doctor; he doesn't see women in the same way. I've never believed *that;* she squirmed in her seat with dissatisfaction. "It's almost the middle of May," Ten said, looking up over the top of her glasses. Her spectacles, Edna thought, gave her such a comical look. "When do you think we're going to have some spring?" she asked, pushing her spectacles further back on her nose. "I don't know," he said, looking out the window, "but I guess we'll have some hot weather in two days." "Two days!" Edna said. "It's one extreme to the other here," Ten said; "hot, cold, hot, cold. John says you can bring the dead back to life that way; there's some reason behind it." "Yes, our elevation and our position in respect to the sun," John said. "Just what I said," Ten agreed, turning another page.

"Is that book really so interesting?" John asked, looking over at her. "Well, it certainly is," Ten answered, looking up, taking off her spectacles, putting them down on the little table next to her, rubbing the two red grooves running down the side of her nose. "This terrible man has chased Isabella out onto an ice floe where she fled to protect her virtue, but she didn't see the bear following both of them, so the bear is following them from one piece of ice to another. Then she climbs a tree." "Bears can climb trees," John reminded her. "Oh, I *know* that!" Ten said; "I'm just supposed to forget about it while I'm reading the book, that's all. The same way you get all interested when they start talking about immortality cures in the science columns." "Mortality cures." "Same thing," Ten sniffed; "those theories can't climb trees either," she added irrelevantly. Edna looked from one to the other. It was remarkable, she thought; there was a texture in the room, a kind of fancywork netting; it was invisible, but it was there. Every time they spoke, it covered more and more of the room, like a magic spider web from the old stories she used to read as a child, which protected the wearers, even made them invisible, gave them strange powers. While on Cedar Street, there had been nothing, nothing, either good or bad; just the empty spaces, and every day they made their sharp edges clearer, more ominous, until walking through a room there was like walking through a space hung with broken mirrors. In certain lights, the glass caught the brilliance and looked beautiful, and it was beautiful, if you were standing in the doorway looking in, if you had no reason to go in, or (if you were already in, through some failure of emotion or judgment or intelligence) had no reason to move.

"Well, we have to go to bed eventually," Ten said, closing her book. "I presume that means *Isabella* is off the ice?" John asked. "She's on the ice. The bear got distracted by a fish and drowned in the river." "There was a fish swimming near the surface in the dead of winter?"

John asked. "Oh, it's only a book," Ten remonstrated. "I hope so," said her brother; "does it have pictures?" "As a matter of fact, it does," Ten answered, reaching wearily for her spectacles, "but if you keep running at this book, there'll be nothing for it but to go to bed. John," she said, putting the spectacles down again, "Edna hasn't gotten to see anything but snow, snow, and more snow. If it turns spring, you ought to take her out in the buggy. There's the hill and the covered bridges; she hasn't seen many of them, and if they fix the ferry and the floating bridge, she really ought to see them." "I thought she wanted to go to Fitchburg." "Well, John, I never said she should try to go to two places at once, but she's going to be here a while, and she can go to Fitchburg whatever day you're not carrying her in the buggy." "How do you know she wants to go anywhere in the buggy?" "Well, I know an easy way to find out," Ten said. "Edna, do you want to get a look at the country hereabouts? In the buggy?" "Yes," Edna answered, flushing; "but I don't want to burden Mr. Steele; he's a very busy man." Ten groaned silently: oh, this was going to be impossible. "It's no burden," John said. Ten hurriedly picked up her spectacles and peered at him. "It's no burden," he repeated, looking away from his sister's eyes: "I've been wanting to get out on those back roads and see what's doing." "John! Don't take Edna on a tour of the sick list!" "I can take a book along," Edna said. She colored; she was sure she had been too eager. "John, don't you do it; it's not the way to introduce a lady to the attractions of the country." She sounds awfully solemn, Edna thought; I wonder why. "Don't worry about it," John said abruptly.

Three weeks later, and spring had really come to the mountains. The crab apples were flowering all over, randomly, like lace; forsythia was growing wildly along the lanes. The early daisies were beginning to show their yellow faces, but best of all was the grass. It was thick and green and Edna had to dig her fingers down into it to get at the scalp of the earth. She would take a picnic basket and her magazines and go out into the meadow, out of everyone's sight, lying on her back, watching those traveling clouds. Those poor clouds are going to Manhattan, she thought; those clouds are going south. When there were no clouds, she thought about the remarkable blueness of the sky. It was so brilliant, it was thin, tissue-like. It did not seem odd to see everything through the frame created by the two pointed ears of Jimmie the cat; he always sat on her stomach, petulant, as if sensing the meadow itself was a rival. Then Edna would turn on her side in the grass, and stroke it; she liked the feel of it against her face. She liked to feel the impress, the intricate pattern, of the blades on her cheek. She tended to choose the rounded meadow, which was itself shaped like a belly. It was, she thought, like lying on something human. The early warm sun was turning her bones to gold; she felt it throbbing through her. There were days when she came in from the meadow, Jimmie the cat preceding her, looking back, complaining every inch of the way until she got into the house, while she, feeling so changed, was startled to see that the color of her hair was the same. Her face, she thought, touching her cheek; her face was something that would never change. Then she would lie down on her bed. She had never dreamed that merely breathing in and out was such a joy.

And she was taking an unexpected interest in the flower garden. One day, helping Aunt Ten prune back the ancient pink rose bush, she decided to try sticking a branch into the soil near it. Ten watched with amusement; she played outside like a little child. The little branch rooted. Edna became intensely absorbed in the process of creating new rose bushes out of old ones. She tried rooting little cuttings all over the flower bed. They only rooted in one place. "It's the coffee grinds and the eggshells," she announced without introduction one night after dinner. "Oh, do you think so?" Ten asked; "then we should try other things there." I won't break in on *this*, John thought. "We're talking about planting rose cuttings," Ten thought to inform him fifteen minutes later.

"Well, if you're not too busy at your roses, and the weather holds, I can take Edna out tomorrow." Miss Dickinson and Mr. Steele, that was all over now. Ten looked out. "It doesn't look like the wind's going to get into the north corner; it should be fine." "The weather's one thing you can never tell about," John said. He always devoted a great deal of thought to the weather. "Well, look on the bright side anyhow," Ten suggested; "unless you want to spend the night imagining a storm, and then you'll feel better in the morning. That would be more like you, you know." And me, Edna thought, startled.

"Is that a letter from your mother?" Ten asked. Edna opened it. "She's staying longer at Magnolia Hall than she intended," Edna said, reading. She hasn't even read it, Ten thought, surprised. "Oh, this is fascinating," Edna said impatiently, turning the letter over to Ten; "she's busy describing every last statue and every last park and what the hop was like last night, which she couldn't attend, and how she got where she is, and what means of transportation is taking her off, and what kind of card games she's playing. She's getting tired of logomachy and improving at euchre. Really, Aunt Ten, when you write her you should tell her to put at least *one* bear in her letter." "She certainly does make you feel as if you were there with her," Ten said, reading on. "Yes," Edna agreed; "you feel as if you're taking each and every step she takes. It must be wonderful to have a mind for such details." "I believe," Ten said, "you could be more tolerant. Without harming yourself." "I *am* more tolerant," Edna said. John stood up. "Do *you* want to read the letter?" she asked him. "What? And be the last one to visit Magnolia Hall? I'm going to read that German article." There was a knock at the door. The two women listened. "Where?" they heard John asking. "Dummerston? What's he doing in Dummerston?" Another long answer followed. "What was he trying to shoot, a herd of elephants?" "Don't sit up," he started to say to Ten. "Don't you finish that sentence," she warned.

In defiance of the night sky, the hopes and optimism of three people, and most especially of Ten's prophetic rheumatism, it did rain the next day, and the next day, and the next. Edna found herself unaccountably depressed, a regular fit, although, as she told Ten, if there was anything she loved, it was a rainy day. John was there to hear this, eating his potato pancakes, but it didn't occur to him to ask Edna if she enjoyed riding in wet weather. "We'll just have to wait for a better day." Every morning he came into the kitchen, slumping slightly as he saw the thick drops splashing against the glass. He was also preoccupied with events of the Hill. (The Hill, Edna thought, resentful: the Point, the Flat, Slab Hollow. They might as well be talking about the Sahara Desert.)

"I don't know what's going on up on the Hill," John said, unaware he had already said this twice before; this time, however, he didn't look back down at his plate. "What's going on up there that doesn't usually go on up there?" Ten asked; "I thought, that last time after the scarlet fever, you burned their copy of that book *What to Do Until the Doctor Comes.*" "A lot of good it did," John said, mashing at his potato pancake. "Well, at least this time they're not treating someone for sick headache instead of scarlet fever," Ten said. "Oh, they're getting better at knocking at death's door"; he slammed his fork down. "This time it's a relative up from Boston for a little vacation and he just happened to bring his doctor bag with him." "It's that minister again, you just wait and see," Ten said; "those Methodists. They don't forget, you know." She looked significantly at her brother. "Well," she said, trying to fish the conversation out of the deep waters, "have they been immersing themselves recently? It's that time of year. Someone probably has the consumption and thinks it's heart trouble." "That's all superstition," John said; "I get immersed all winter, and what happens? I get wet." "Well," Ten said, "none of the other doctors agree with you." "The other doctors are sitting in their drugstores looking at one tongue after another in front of their coal stoves." "It's not such a bad idea," Ten said, briefly looking up. "And then giving patients little bottles, or tablets; they're really embalming them, not treating them. I've had that theory for a long time. I suppose they do it so the final liquid shouldn't be such a terrible shock to the patient's system—if any of it manages to get in their veins." "Hardly anyone tries that undertaker's nonsense!" Ten answered indignantly. "They're starting to, when there isn't enough ice in the summer." "There's *always* enough ice in the summer. Listen here, John," she went on, "it's because they're *Methodists.* And I know for a fact that doctor you're talking about is a Methodist. You're not religious enough for them, and besides, they remember the old times, and they're not going to take any chances on your getting even with *them.*"

"How do you know the quack's a Methodist?" John asked. "Bridget. She was off chasing that cow of Ben's, and she found herself up on the Hill, and Mary staring up there into space. Mary works in their kitchen. I don't know why working in a kitchen creates such a bond."

"What else did she find out?" "The eminent doctor thinks the child has cholera morbus, or perhaps an ascending infection of the toe." "What a set of alternatives!" John snorted; "the man's got less brains than a chicken." "Well, Mary thinks they're beginning to agree with you. There's another member of the family who's coming down with a fever, he doesn't have a cut anywhere on his body, certainly not on his toe, so you may get in that house alone yet.

"John doesn't have any doctor manners at all," she said, turning to Edna. "For God's sake, Ten!" John shouted, slamming down his glass; "if I went through that rigmarole every time I went into a house they'd all be dead of old age. First you press the hands of the mother and father, and give them a solemn look; oh, that's very important, the solemn look," he went on, enraged, addressing Edna directly for the first time; "then you press both of the grandmother's hands, the longer the more ribbons they have on their caps; you repeat that action if there are any honorary grandmothers about. Then you solemnly ask the mother and father who might be the patient, and what signs have made them think their dear one may be a little out of the ordinary way. Then you give them all a solemn, but very reassuring nod. If possible, and the patient's health permits, there should be more pressing of the hands. The important thing," he went on, "is to treat the family as if *it* were the patient. Then you excuse yourself, taking care to pat all the small heads in the room. Meanwhile, you try and find out what *they* think is the matter with the body weighing down the bed, since you probably have no idea whatever yourself, unless it's screaming with labor pains. Or was seen getting itself caught in a tractor. Or is all covered over with chicken pox." "That method has some advantages over striding in like the local police chief coming after a murderous scoundrel about to jump through a window," Ten said. John snorted.

"I suppose if I were sick," Edna said, "I'd just as soon have someone rush in, just in case there was any need for hurry, you know." "There! You see!" John answered, triumphant, staring at his sister. "She's *intelligent*," Ten

115

answered; "but with the rest of them, you act like the bishop with his eye on the Pope's seat." *"She's* right, anyhow,"* John growled.

"What *do* you think is the matter up on the Hill?" Edna finally asked, nerving herself up to enter the conversation directly. "Typhoid." "Typhoid!" Ten exclaimed; "John, if that's a joke, it's not a good one." "Well, I'm not joking. The two sick ones have sore throats, and they're dumpy and listless, and too tired to sit up or get out of a chair." "How did you find that out?" Edna asked. "I went down to the police station." "The police station?" "Everyone goes and sits there or in the store in bad weather; the store's doing some business right now, so it's the police station for a while." "The police station," Edna repeated. "John, look here," Ten said excitedly, "if it's typhoid, and they want that Boston doctor, you stay out of it." "That's enough, Ten," John warned; "I don't tolerate your telling me what to do about the doctoring business. We've been exposed often enough, anyhow." "But *she* hasn't," Ten pleaded. "I had it," Edna announced, "when I was eight. It was a very mild case." "Does that signify anything?" Ten asked anxiously. "Well," John thought aloud, "I've never seen anyone come down with it twice, but no one usually gets the chance to do it, either. I suppose, looking at it that way, having typhoid gives a kind of immunity." "That's not the way *I'm* looking at it," Ten assured him.

"It's typhoid they've got," Bridget said from the doorway; "beg pardon, everyone," she added as an afterthought. "How do *you* know?" John asked. "Well, Mary, up on the Hill Mary, she says the little boy who had the sore throat, there's something going over his tonsils, covering his throat on the inside part. They have to sit him up so he can breathe better. They say the doctor's got it too, but I don't think so. I got a look at him in the yard on his way to the necessary, and from the speed he was going, tearing at his pants and all, I think he's just not up to our water." "Well," John pronounced, "there you have it: the voice of experience. She's never wrong," he told Edna. "Well, Ten, any idiot can take care of it now, I guess; I just hope nobody rides down early to see about coffins and spreads the whole story all over the countryside." "Oh no, sir," Bridget said, poking her head back in; "Mary told Officer Pickett, the deputy, all about it, and he has them under quarantine." "Now if this rain would only stop," Ten said. Her relief was immense. "Why didn't they ask you?" Edna said, turning to John; "why did they want a Methodist doctor?" Ten and John looked at each other, then went on eating, as if they had never heard the question.

The next morning dawned blue and cloudless. By eight o'clock it was evident that the day would be perfect. It would be elegant. Edna slipped out the back door in her wrapper; the grass was still damp with dew. The far mountains outlined themselves in blue, but every tree on them was visible. There was not a trace of fog, or a cloud tinged even faintly with gray. The chill in the air was lifting with the sun, and it was apparent that by the time the sun made its debut, little patches of summer would be settling softly on the pastures and fields like dense clouds of pollen.

Edna slipped back in the door just in time to hear Ten scolding at Bertha; they were having a disagreement. Ten had called into question the thoroughness of her dusting; Bertha was indignant. From the hall, Edna watched, a happy, excited ghost. "You dusted *everything?*" Ten asked teasingly. *"Everything,"* Bertha answered, blushing. Ten began walking around the parlor humming, "Fee, fi, fo, fum, I smell the blood of an Englishman," and suddenly swooped down on a candlestick. "What's this nice little circle?" Ten asked; "it looks just the same size as the base of this candlestick"; she waved it menacingly at Bertha. "Fee, fi, fo, fum," she began again, circling the room like a mosquito deciding where to alight. "Oho!" she said; "I wonder if this berry dish has made an equal impression on the table"; she began to pick it up. "All right, all right," Bertha said; "I'll take more care with the dusting, although, what with all I have to do, I don't know how you can expect more of me."

Ten looked her over. "Is the work in the kitchen too much for you?" she asked; "we don't want to overwork you; you know that. Why, just down the road, at Mrs. Greene's, there's a young daughter who wants to hire out as a kitchen maid. We could have her in as your assistant." "I'm capable of doing by myself," Bertha said, indignant; "I don't need the help of the likes of her!"

Meditatively, Ten picked up a little glass dome, looking down at the polished surface which had been under it. "Oh, ma'am," Bertha exclaimed, starting to cry, "I said I'd take more care. I don't want anyone in my kitchen, messing it up, and not that Pamela Greene, either. She doesn't look strong enough to lift a fork, and her color! She looks like celery." "Well, we'll see," Ten answered evasively. "Please, ma'am, promise," Bertha pleaded. "Oh, all right," Ten answered, cross. Bertha retreated to the kitchen, her sobs lingering behind her. *I* could never handle servants, Edna thought; I'd be hacking through dust high as snowdrifts, and I wouldn't be able to say a word. Oh, what do I care? she thought; nice people don't pick up dishes to look for dust. She began buttoning herself into the basque of her riding habit, then suddenly paused. Nice people *are* the ones who pick up berry dishes to look for dust, she realized, fingers poised over a button. Oh, I don't care, she decided again, buttoning faster and faster. "Oh, wouldn't you know it!" she said out loud as a button came off in her hand; "*this* is what comes of hurrying." She sat down on the bed in a temper and began trying to thread the needle taken from her pincushion. Oh, is *everything* going to go wrong this morning? she asked herself, tears stinging under her lids.

"My, we're eating awfully fast this morning," Ten observed sweetly; "it must be the change in the weather. Everything seems so hungry. Ben turned the cows out in the back pasture, and how like witches they've been acting too. I suppose we could put them out on the flat someday if someone would only clear off the stones." No one answered her. "Oh, I do remember; today's the day you go out in the buggy," Ten said; "that must be why Bertha's spending so much time packing up a hamper. And I thought she was packing it to bring in here so she could do a proper job of dusting without disturbing herself unnecessarily." They weren't rising to the bait. "If you'll excuse me, I'll go look in that kitchen. I better put in a lot of fruit; someone always breaks the bottles in that hamper. It looks like a thirsty day."

"Why," John asked Edna the instant Ten had left the room, "do we have to ride around in the buggy? You told me you were a good rider." Edna looked up, surprised. "*I* didn't suggest taking the buggy," she reminded him. "Well, I don't see why we have to take it on a day like this when we have a stable of excellent riding horses." "Let's take the horses then." "You don't want to take the trotters," John cautioned; "they're fine for pulling the sleigh, but they're not good for a long ride." "I know, I know," Edna answered, exasperated. "You do? Then I'll get Ben to saddle the horses." "That's nice," Edna answered.

The intensity attending the dawn of this new kind of attachment had been heightened even more by the delay. John himself was noticeably different in manner. "We might as well walk the horses out to the meadow," John suggested; "that is, if you have no objection." "It would be nicer to climb on there without everyone watching from the windows," Edna said. "Is this all right?" John asked, solicitous, reining in his horse in the middle of a blazing carpet of dandelions. "Lovely." It occurred to John that the three little steps used to assist ladies in mounting were nowhere to be found in the meadow, but were residing heavily on stones in front of the stable. "I shall have to assist you to mount," John announced stiffly. Edna looked curiously at him. *Now* what was wrong?

Oh, John thought, beside himself, it's been so long since I've done this. No lady I knew could ride anything but a pony cart. "Are you ready?" he asked Edna, hoping she had developed a sudden fear of large animals and would suggest returning to the secure little stone steps, if not to the house itself. "Ready," she said cheerfully. John groaned inwardly. Edna automatically positioned herself at his shoulder, facing him. There's nothing for it, John thought, stooping down, holding his hand out so that she could put her little riding boot in it. Why does he look so sour? Edna worried; I was wrong to think he wanted to take me. A cloud passed the sun; just as quickly she was thrown into a state of acute vexation. "Well," Edna said, her foot still resting in his hand, "your arm will get tired; you won't be able to straighten up." "Don't be so smart; ready?" "I've *been* ready," Edna answered, touchy. Her feelings were hurt. All right then, John thought; there's no avoiding it.

"Get ready to spring," he told Edna, and suddenly lifted his hand as she sprang up, but with such impetus that, like vaulting ambition, she flew over the top of the saddle and landed on the other side of the horse. John stood in terror, transfixed by the motionless body in its maroon habit. "Oh no," he groaned aloud. "Are you dead?" he asked at last. "No, I'm not dead," she said, beginning to raise up on one elbow; "I just didn't expect to fall out of the nest before I was in it." John was dumb with embarrassment. "Are you going to help me up, or shall I lie here until noon?" John ran around to the other side of the horse; he looked younger, more vulnerable. "Please," he stammered, "accept my apologies; it's been some time since I helped a lady to mount. It wasn't my intention to throw you over like that." "Why didn't you say something?" Edna asked. She was still out of sorts, and was not quite over her suspicion that he had deliberately flung her, like a forkful of hay, into the air. Probably taking it out on me because Ten asked him about this ride, she thought, crabby. "Well, I thought I'd remember," John answered, irritation creeping back into his voice. "Well, you didn't." "You certainly are a charitable thing."

By now, Edna was sitting up. He does look humiliated, she thought, surprised. "You didn't mean to do it, truly?" "Of course I didn't intend to do it," John answered; "what sort of monster do you take me for? I don't need any new invalids to attend to." "Please forget it," Edna pleaded; "it was just a shock to find myself sailing through the air, that's all." John colored violently. I better not mention this again, Edna warned herself; I don't know why he doesn't have a bit of humor about it.

"Just hold your hand *here*," Edna pointed, "and I can scramble up without a boost." "You've done a great deal of riding," John observed, glum. "There aren't many other forms of exercise in the city." "You ride on my right," she reminded him. "I'm not completely ignorant." He was pouting, yes, pouting. "I didn't think it would hurt to remind you; you can't be expected to remember everything. After all, you have so many things on your mind." He looked her over warily; no, she was not being sarcastic. "Well, perhaps we should go over *some* of the details," he agreed, reluctant. "The lady sets the pace," Edna said, mischievous. "How fast can you go?" John asked. "Oh, I can go as fast as you can; I can jump, too." Good Lord, John thought. Jump, too! "Well, shall we start?" Edna asked. John handed her into the saddle, put her

120

foot in the stirrup, and smoothed the skirt of her habit; this caused both of them to flush. Edna beamed at him. John mounted his own horse. "We could head for the covered bridge near Dummerston," John suggested. "Is it a long ride?" Edna asked flirtatiously. "It is." "Is it a *very* long ride?" "A very long ride"; John grinned at her. "And you won't have to turn back for one of your invalids?" "Houston's taking over for me." "Then you have it all arranged." She had no idea John had such a capacity for blushing. "Not as thoroughly as I thought," he said in an undertone; "shall we?"

The sun, he thought; it was the sun. It was hatching whatever had been growing from the moment she arrived. The day was hurrying them along; no, it was seeing to it that they made up for lost time. "Shall we?" Edna spurred her horse on ahead; John went after her. It seemed as if everyone in the country was in front of his house. In the first fifteen minutes of their ride, they passed one stout woman sitting on a slatted wooden bench under an ivy arbor, her farmhouse at the top of the hill, the whole family apparently out on the porch, one contemplating the clothesline strung from one of the porch columns to the other, another woman looking down with considerable perplexity at the slate steps; a bewhiskered man sitting on the porch, a little girl on his lap, and a small boy throwing stones at a rock on the hill to the left side of the house. At the next farmhouse, things were more dismal. Something seemed to have eaten the grass from the front lawn. The stone well stuck up bonily; the farmer was guiding his flea-infested team along, breaking up furrows in front of the house. He can't have much land if he's doing that, Edna thought; still, he appeared to have a great deal of it; perhaps he's just greedy. Another farmhouse came into view, but the road suddenly turned, and the barn became the principal object, cedar-shingled, a huge heap of chopped wood leaning against one of its slatted walls, and an old farmer peering out at them from under his cap as if to say: Is that the doctor? Can that be the doctor? And who is that lady? Three of his cows, tethered together, gave them the same inquiring, curious look. Edna liked the look of those animals, the white triangles coming down over their foreheads between their eyes like tidies, their big, big eyes, the patient way they waited, the way nature had decorated them with patches of red and white. Like the hills when the snow melts, she thought. He's sawed off their horns! she noticed, horrified; what a cruel thing to do!

The next pasture revealed an elderly man, a cigarette drooping vertically from his lips, its end buried in his unruly beard, his head covered with a huge, drooping hat; he was standing with his horse in the middle of early Queen Anne's lace, ferociously glaring, but holding his horse under its chin as if it were a little child with whom he had to talk something over. The horse was tethered to a pole, the pole broken jaggedly at the top. That wood must have been part of something else; they don't let anything go to waste here.

The sun was climbing the steep steps of the sky. The air was warmer. Edna was warm in her habit. John signaled that he would ride on ahead; they veered across a road, on the side of which a young boy, not even eleven, was patiently slumped in a buggy seat, sleepily holding the reins to a team of matched golden bays. Wealth, Edna reflected, catching a glimpse of the huge mansion behind him, the barn not even visible, although the fields of corn beginning just behind the evenly spaced trees on the other side of the drive seemed to stretch on and on to the foot of the heavily wooded mountain. One tree was stark white, skeletal. It's dead, Edna thought; why should a dead tree stand out so from live ones?

There was the sound of running water; Edna could hear it over the rhythmic beat of the heavy hooves. John was motioning her to stop. He reined his horse up on her right. "Would you like to dismount? This is a good place," he went on hurriedly, not giving her a chance to answer; "up above the orchard there's a little path, and on the other side of it, there's a little meadow. No one else knows about it anymore. I found it years ago with an old friend, but he's dead now." He stopped as suddenly as he had begun. He was talking too much. "And there's a little brook running through the middle of it," he went on to his own surprise, "and back further there's a little pond filled with hornpout." "With what?" "Hornpout, fish; they're something like catfish." "I've always wanted to see a hornpout." "Then shall we stop?" John asked, embarrassed. "Is this the path?" Edna asked, pointing to a streak of beige and gray leaves; nothing had recently disturbed them. "That's it." Edna spurred her horse on down the path, waving gaily back. John went after her.

"The clouds are beautiful," Edna murmured, lying on her back in the grass. "They seem that way today." "Don't they always?" she asked. "Hardly ever; at least not to me." "That *is* too bad," Edna said lazily. "Do they always seem beautiful to you?" "Oh no," she said; "it depends on the weather in here." She tapped her head. "Now if the weather in there changed," she went on sleepily, "I'd lie here thinking lemony thoughts like 'What fashionable clouds; aren't those fashionable clouds, such veils, such trains. Clouds like that are meant for my mother,' and then the very next thing," she said, without thinking, "I'd be wondering about my father and why he hung himself, and remembering how he looked, and the cloud could get down into this field and walk right up to me, and I wouldn't even notice it." "Yes, that's how it is," he agreed; "I can't even say I knew there was a sky after my wife died." "Did you love her that much?" She was surprised, jealous.

It hadn't occurred to her that married people could love one another that much. Her father's death had hardly destroyed the sky for *her* mother. "I loved her in the beginning," she heard him saying; "well, I still love her. It's true, you know," he said, staring up at the sky; "you never stop loving once you start. Even when the person dies, you just keep on loving, just as if she were alive, but it's like"—he hesitated—"the buzz in this meadow; you don't notice it unless you listen for it. Or unless there's nothing else to look at. Well, and I married so young. Ten was dead against it, you know; I was only nineteen, and the way she died, it didn't help." It was as if he had been waiting for her, yes, waiting to finally say all this, to end these things, to start new ones.

Edna slowly turned her head; his profile was staring into the sun. How English he looks, Edna thought; that high forehead, that broad straight nose; those big deep eyes. It's hard to see into them. He looks like a portrait of one of those English kings. Ten has those looks too, imposing, regal. It makes them look like the last of a dying race. John turned slowly to face her. Edna was afraid to say anything. He had made it clear, so many times, that

123

his wife, anything about his wife, was not spoken of. Never. That was what he had said.

"If you *wanted* to tell me," Edna said carefully, feeling her way, "about how she died, if you would like to tell me, I would want to hear it." How many times had she listened to her father coaxing people into speech just like this? As if she had been in training all her life for this one day. "You're the worst possible one to hear it." "Why?" she asked gently; "why? I don't mind what it is." "It might frighten you; I don't want to frighten you." He fell silent. "I didn't mean to make you curious that way either; I didn't mean to tease you about it." "No, I know; I know that." She seems grown up so suddenly, John mused; she is so beautiful. "Why don't you tell me," Edna coaxed; "there was one good thing about my father's suicide, his own R.S.V.P., I guess that was what it was. Well, I became so much less, you know, *shockable*. And I never was, very." "If I tell you," John finally said, "it will be because it makes me feel sore inside. Still, after two years. It's selfish, but I *want* to tell you." "I can get over being frightened; really, I can."

"What do you think," John asked, "about pregnancy? Being in the family way? Gravid? That's the medical term." His voice had taken on the rough grating of metal against stone. "I hadn't thought about it for myself, not just yet," Edna said, blushing slightly; "although I suppose I will be with child, in the family way, big as a watermelon, all those things, sooner or later. It seems the inevitable thing." "Does the idea frighten you?" "No more than jumping a fence," she answered honestly; "I never seem to be afraid of the right things; I worry about people in fine weather, then I sleep soundly when they're out in the middle of a blizzard. It must have been my father. He inoculated me, yes, that's it, little bit by little bit, against fear. He started out by telling me all about fights over property lines, and chopping down boughs overhanging the next yard, and before we knew it, I was up to hearing about the stranglings, and the poisonings, and he even took me to see the display of the seven bodies of that mass murder in Newton. He was the counsel for the defense. What a job!" she remembered; "and how mad he was about their keeping the babies on display for everyone to look at. The smallest, it was a three-month-old baby; and they all lay there on the ice for most of the trial, and Father kept arguing with the judge about influencing public sentiment, how it was already inflamed enough, but the judge wouldn't grant the burial order."

"What happened?" "Oh, they hung Father's client; he was guilty as sin. I think my father was interested in the man, that's all. What kind of man could do such a thing? He kept on saying that. He thought it was so unnecessary, the murders; and then, after the conviction, the man confessed everything. For a stupid man, he was very clever, the way he lured those people into the barn one by one. And when they asked him why he had to kill the poor defenseless infant, he said he *had* to do it; he didn't know why everyone made such a fuss about that part at the trial. He *had* to kill the baby because it would have started in crying, and someone passing might have heard it, and come in to investigate, and he needed the time to get farther away. The baby was so small I couldn't tell whether it was a boy or a girl. But it did have its throat cut, just like the others, and an ax smash in its head." "That's ghastly," John said softly. "Even to you?" Edna asked, half smiling; "oh, we got used to it; or at least I got used to it. I'm not sure, now, that Father ever did. I'm not even sure it's sane to get used to those things. But you," she said, looking over at him, "you're a doctor. You must see worse things than that." "Not too many."

"Do you want to tell me about how your first wife died? Really, I wouldn't mind." "You're not terribly religious, are you?" he asked; he knew how irrelevant that would sound to her. "I'm a disgrace in that line." "Well, it began with religion; I met her at a sociable at the White Church; that's the way you're supposed to do things out here. Her name was Serepta. Ten kept saying there was bound to be something wrong with someone named Serepta, but she was so beautiful, so quiet, she had these deep-set blue eyes and her skin was really remarkable. The traveling artists were always asking her to pose for them. I don't know what it was. She radiated tranquillity. And she was like that; she was." He looked over at Edna, pleading. "I'm sure she was; she must have been." "She *was*," John insisted. This time Edna said nothing. "Well, then the next thing we knew she was expecting. I remember looking at a letter to her cousin somewhere or other saying, 'I expect to be sick in the fall.' Do they use that same expression in the city?" "Yes, yes they do." "Well, she was pregnant, and the next event was a religious revival. It started with the Methodists; they had church meetings every night. Serepta began going. She went to prayer meetings, inquiry meetings; she conferred with the minister. Ten didn't like what she heard of it, but what could she do about it? She was off in Kansas. She kept writing that I should take her away from the town, but Serepta didn't want to go anywhere, and I didn't give it much thought; I just assumed she'd get over it. But she didn't get over it. And then came the Drummelites; that's when everything went wrong."

"The Drummelites?" Edna echoed; "Drummelite? I heard he was dead." John paused. "He's probably just hiding. Well," he forced himself on, "he was a fanatic, and he had powers; there was no denying that. He convinced a whole group—my wife was in it—that he could crawl through a solid log. He used to crawl through a solid log every Sabbath. Well, it was preposterous, but the people, the people," he said, shaking his head, "swore up and down that he really did crawl through those logs. And he went on crawling through them until a loyal member of the audience decided to see what effect banging with a stick on the log would have. On Mr. Drummelite, where he was, there inside; the man said he wanted to discover if the Reverend Drummelite would be startled by the noises. So he got up and beat on the log, and practically beat Drummelite senseless. It took him a month to hobble around again. After that, there was no more crawling through logs, but Serepta didn't last long enough to see the end of it. It might not have made any difference anyway. Well, probably nothing would. The next thing I knew—I was away from the house a lot—and we lived on her father's old farm way up in the hills; it was awfully lonely, I guess. I should have thought more about it, but I was an apprentice to old Dr. Houston and didn't think about much but medicine—*she* was a Drummelite. They were a kind of offshoot of the Methodists"—he was trying to explain it carefully—"but they believed a soul was damned forever unless it was baptized on this earth.

"Well, I was gone most of the time, I said that, and Serepta must have miscalculated her time to be sick, and there she was, up on the farm, in the dead of winter—

you haven't seen one of our winters yet—with two hired girls, and impassable roads, and two Drummelite women. Well, one night when I got back late—it was the usual things, drifts all over the roads, the buggy at the bottom of the mountain while I led the horse up—the baby was almost delivered, and she was screaming like something caught in a trap, and blood was pouring out of her like water, it just poured over the bed, and the Drummelite women—" he stopped. "Go on; go on; finish." "The Drummelite women looked at the men, and the men held me by the arms. I could see from the doorway she was already mostly dead; she was gray as stone, and bluish. They said they were going to *tear* the baby out by main force so it could be baptized, since neither of them was going to live anyway, and they did; they tore the baby out. Serepta, she kept screaming. It wasn't a loud scream, she was too weak, but it sounded loud. One of the men kept telling me, 'That's how she wanted it; that's how she wanted it.'" He stopped again, and when he began talking, he was crying. Edna felt for his hand, trying to close it in with her fingers, as if he were the one bleeding. John looked down at his hand briefly, then looked away. "It was a girl, if it made any difference. It wasn't alive; blue, you know. It wouldn't have lived whatever they had done, and they grabbed the baby and plunged her into a pot and left Serepta there bleeding."

"Oh, by that time they'd let me go, but she didn't even know who I was. They were both dead in less than a quarter of an hour. The whole thing, the whole thing," John repeated, "was insane, completely, inexplicably insane." "Yes, it was," Edna said softly; "and then you blamed yourself?" "Of course!" he answered violently; "if I hadn't been a doctor, if I'd been a farmer, or a woodsman, she never would have gotten involved with those Drummelites. I wouldn't have let them . . ." His voice broke. "My friend Agnes married a logger," Edna said; "he's off in the woods for three, four weeks at a time. She had her first two children at her mother's house. Her husband wasn't there, and they couldn't have gotten to him if they'd wanted to." John was sobbing; Edna watched the spasms of his body; she could hear no sound.

She turned on her side. With her free hand, she began touching his cheek; then she began stroking it. Rhythmically, she began stroking his hair. This must be how she got Jimmie, John thought; it didn't help. He still couldn't stop crying. "I don't mind if you cry; I've seen lots of men cry." "All of them waiting for the hangman?" "Not exactly; no, of course not. Our doctor cried when his wife died of scarlet fever." She concocted that event spontaneously. "He did?" John asked through his tears. He had forgotten how salty they were. He was, Edna decided, a little more hopeful. "Oh yes; he cried so his mother thought he'd damaged his eyes, and his other friend, who was also a doctor, thought he would swallow so much, I don't know what he called it, mucus, I think, that he'd end with pneumonia. I used to cry every time I saw *him* crying; he had that effect. Mother wouldn't even go to visit at their house until he stopped because she had red hair and she hated it when her eyes were red. I remember when she had red-eye; she wouldn't leave the house for weeks." John had stopped sobbing and was inspecting her. "You're inventing that," he said. "I am *not,*" Edna contradicted. "It's very nice of you all the same." Edna couldn't help smiling.

John propped himself up on one elbow. Edna put her hand up to wipe at his cheeks. "You're a very beautiful little lady," he said; "how old are you?" "Sixteen." "Sixteen! I don't believe it!" "Well, I am rather old," she admitted, smiling. "I'm twenty-eight; don't you think I'm very old?" "You could be fourteen and an inebriate, and then where would we all be?" Yes, her father *had* trained her. What if I kissed her? he thought; she's so much younger than I am, no matter what she says. She might allow it only out of sympathy. "Are you going to kiss me?" Edna asked; "I hope so." She drew his head toward her with both little hands. What on earth am I doing? she asked herself. This is nice, she decided, refusing to let him go. They kissed again and again. "It must be the heat," John said finally. "The heat?" Edna said, grinning; "does that usually drive you to kissing young ladies?" "No, it does not," John smiled; "we feel the heat because of our clothes." "That is a terrible problem," Edna promptly agreed. He unbuttoned her first button. "But the solution," John said, hesitating, "is perfectly simple." "So it is." John unbuttoned a second. "That feels a *little* better," she said. She lay perfectly still. A third, fourth, sixth, seventh, came undone. Edna wore only a chemise under her habit; her form was so slender, so small, she barely ever bothered with stays. "Well," John said. Edna could feel him trembling. She reached over and loosened his collar button; then she began on the buttons of his shirt. "Cooler?" she asked, solicitous. "Not much." "It's cooler over here," she said, taking his hand and placing it on her breast. "Edna," he said; did she know what she was doing? "I know," she answered; "this is what comes of an irreligious life." John felt her nipple swelling under his hand. "But if *you* are still in mourning for your first wife?" she asked.

"Why do you always call her my first wife? Most people call her my late wife." "I must be assuming you're to have a second," she answered, moving his hand further down. "We hardly know each other," he said. He felt ridiculous; this was what a woman was supposed to say, but *he* was the one who seemed to want to jump up and run away. "You're not, I mean, you aren't interested in this just to find out?" he asked her nervously; "you know, to get over wondering about what it's like?" "Certainly not," she answered, indignant; "I'm very good at withstanding suspense." "I'm not," John warned her. "If I wiggled," she said, as if thinking out loud, "I could get closer to you. But if you turned on your side . . ." John stared at her. Was he insane? He knew what would happen now. There would be no going back. He turned on his side. He sat up, leaning over Edna. "You are a huggable man," Edna said; "I don't know why I never saw it before." "I'm a little too far off to hug," he said, stalling. "There's a simple solution to that," she answered.

John turned over, lying half upon Edna's body, fully clothed below the waist, stretching his body over hers. What is that lump? Edna wondered, feeling it through the fabric of her habit, pushing at her stomach. Now she was grateful for all the buttons keeping her clothes on. John stared at her to see how she was taking things. Edna stared up at him, and then deliberately moved her right hand to his belt, and began sliding it further down inside his clothing. "Edna, my God," John gasped. "I hope God is behind a cloud," she whispered, painfully sliding her arm further down under his belt. John stared again. He opened the top button of his trousers; he unbuckled his belt. Her hand slid down and in. "It's warm in here," she whispered;

"why," she murmured, surprised, "you're all bunched up!" "Are you going to straighten me out?" he asked, half gasping. Edna's hand grasped him, straightening him. She raised her head and looked at his "male organ." "Why," she said, "that's lovely! I had no idea it was so purple. Or so long. Or had such blue veins." "Edna," John pleaded. "Mmmmmm," she purred like a cat; "mmmm, it moves about just like a live thing. Aren't you afraid it will walk off somewhere?" "Edna," John begged; "I can't stand it." She continued stroking and looking, looking and stroking. "Feel this," she said, taking his left hand and putting it on her breast; "why, the nipple stands right up too; it's almost sore. Are you sore?" she asked, worried. "Not exactly," John gasped; he was gasping with excitement. Edna suddenly reached down and pulled his body down on top of her, his stomach against hers. "Oh, Edna," John panted; "you know what will happen. I'll ruin your dress. I can't contain myself much more." "I don't think I can either," she said, her voice deeper; she was taking deeper and deeper breaths. A warm sensation was moving up from her pelvis and filling her stomach. "Good Lord," she said; "I didn't think women felt things like this, not like this; it's like waves." John's body was helplessly moving up and down, up and down on her stomach. He was groaning. Edna involuntarily reached down. The groan became more uncontrollable, hopelessly intense. Edna began to feel something deep inside moving in and out, in and out, rhythmically.

"Oh God," John said a few minutes later, hiding from her eyes; "I've messed up your habit." Edna stared at him out of her green cat's eyes. "I suppose this means something," John said reluctantly. "What?" Edna asked. No, he thought; now she won't give an inch. "Are we engaged?" John asked. "Of course," she answered; "of course we are. Even if you haven't deflowered me. You can't get away now." "I could try," John said, playful. "Don't do it; I'll eat, and eat, and eat, and stuff pillows under my stomach, and no one will believe this was an innocent afternoon. Well"—she paused—"at least *relatively* innocent." "You would do all those things," John said, half joking, half amazed, "to have *me*? After what I've told you about my wife, my first wife? After you've seen what it's like for Ten sharing a house with a doctor? And I'm only her brother?" "Oh, I'll come with *you*, at least until the blessed events." "You *are* popping the question." John grinned dazedly. "I thought it had already popped."

Her smile was competing with the sun. "I'm much older than you are," John reminded her again; "you'll be a young widow." "I make friends with ease," Edna answered complacently. "What will your mother think?" John asked, desperate. "She wouldn't care if I married a gopher, provided our hole wasn't in her neighborhood." "Edna," John implored again, "this is serious. If we marry, I mean. Suppose I live another fifty years, and you live another fifty years; we might have to put up with each other for a good long time." "Only fifty? I hope that's not a professional prediction." "Edna," John pleaded again. "I suppose the question is, do we love each other?" John purpled. "I love you. I *adore* you," he broke out in surprise; "ever since you fell on your idiotic head at the station. And I know all your faults." "They are very obvious," Edna agreed. "You love me, then?" John asked. "Not exactly." John looked at her, pained. "No, I have to wait before the fog of worship clears off; then I can say 'love' is the proper word to describe my state." "Then we had better get married," John told her, serious. "Yes, I think that would be the best thing." "You don't want a big wedding, do you?" "I want *you*," Edna answered.

They drove back to Williamsville and home in the silence enforced by their separate mounts. John led the way, every now and then turning back, smiling. How had this ridiculous, but inevitable, state of affairs come to pass? But that was it; it did seem inevitable, not accidental, as his decision to marry Serepta had been. I wonder if she really will want children; she certainly seems to know what she wants. I've never seen anything like it. I wonder, Edna thought, if he's sorry. I guess he isn't, she reassured herself; he keeps turning around and smiling. They rode on; John's horse began to slow down.

"This is the prettiest burial ground in the county," he said, wheeling around, riding up close. Their hands clasped, as out of habit; "Serepta's not in there," he added, already protective. "Why is it the most beautiful?" "Because it's so unexpected here, in the middle of nowhere, and it's so well kept. And then there's only one piece of statuary." They both looked at it. Atop a pillar of three marble rectangles stood a woman dressed in what appeared to be a monk's belted robe. There was a garland resting on her marble curls; her right hand held a carved bouquet of lilies and daisies. She looks like Ten, Edna thought suddenly; she looks like Ten. "See how her feet are bare?" John asked softly; "how the toes just hang over the edge of the stone she's standing on, as if she could really step down, as if she were just about to? And her hand, about to drop the flower; she's tired of holding it. The flower looks so real, but better, as if the spirit had moved just far enough up to warm the whole stone; the whole body. And those eyelids, cast down, and something about the folds of the clothes, a shroud never looked the same to me again after I found her standing here." "No," Edna said, "no; she makes death look beautiful. But," she went on, unthinking, "that's because she isn't dead; or rather, the stone is dead, but the miracle is, it looks so alive." "Like all of us," John said; "the miracle is, we seem so alive." They stayed there, looking at each other; then they rode on into the reddening light. Yes, it was true; they understood one another.

"You know," John said after some time, "you seduced me." "I did not; you seduced me with all those growls and snarls and tempers. I believe you invented a whole new method of courtship." "We won't agree on this subject." He grinned. Really, Edna thought, she didn't understand what she had done. She had acted as a new mother cat would act, somehow knowing she could carry her kittens by the scruff of their necks. Except that John wasn't a kitten, and she wasn't a mother. She *was* bewildered. "Well," John said aloud, "that's one subject we're never going to agree on, never." "I guess we won't"—Edna beamed at him—"I guess we won't." The house was coming into view.

If they don't look like the cats that invented the canary, Ten thought, opening the door for them. "Did you have a good ride?" she asked. "Lovely," Edna burbled. "Cat got your tongue?" she asked John. He seemed to be eyeing everything in the household but her. "Actually, Ten, there's something I'd like to talk to you about." He sounded awkward. "In the parlor." Oh no, Ten thought, he's had enough of it; he's going to ask me to send her back to Boston. "Bertha's getting supper on the table, and she's in no good mood either," his sister said hurriedly; "we had that girl from the agency in, Ellen Wall, and she looked promising to me, so I decided to try her on Monday. Bertha doesn't like it; she'll be in a fit if we don't sit down to eat." "This is more important than Ellen Wall," John answered, obstinate. "Oh, all right; Edna, if you will excuse us." She glowered at her brother. "Um, actually, Edna wants to talk to you also." "Why didn't you say so then?" She was mystified. Of course, she teased herself, they might always want to send *me* back to Boston. That had never occurred to her.

"The best parlor or the everyday?" she asked, sarcastic. "What difference does it make?" John asked in despair. Why doesn't anyone ride up to the door now! he wondered, frantic. Silence, silence only, blew in from the front yard. "Shall *I* close the door?" Ten asked. He, no, they, she corrected herself, had her off balance. "Please close it," John answered roughly. Ten had already moved into the parlor; Edna was standing. Ten found it difficult to move; she sensed she had no desire to hear what was coming next. John walked over to the door and slammed it. Ornaments hopped on the whatnot. "Can't you be more careful?" Ten called; "those cups and saucers came all the way from England. Mother used to say they came on the *Mayflower*." "And I suppose you were right down there at the dock to meet it?" John asked, angry. "Well, if we're going to argue, we might as well get done with it," Ten fussed back; "every servant in the house is standing around wondering what the argument is about ever since you slammed that door." "It's not an argument, Aunt Ten," Edna assured her, but she looked at both of them like a woman facing two bailiffs arresting her for some unknown crime.

"Edna and I," John began. He broke off, looking pleadingly at Edna. "Edna and I," he began again. "You're going to visit Edna's friend, Mrs. Whitemore," Ten finished for him; she had never seen him take so long to finish a simple sentence. No, that's not it; they're not going on a visit. "No," John said, resolute; "Edna and I are going to get married." All life seemed to go out of him; he slumped against the parlor door. Well, John thought; well, what is she going to say?

Ten looked at him, deliberately turned and sat down on the horsehair couch, and began playing with one of the buttons on its tufted back. "I suppose," she said frigidly, "that I should be overjoyed your love of practical jokes has so suddenly returned, although I must say, I don't think this is one of your better ones." Why is Edna going along with it? she wondered. "It's not a joke," John said; his voice was tired. "No, it isn't a joke," Edna agreed. "You can't be serious," Ten finally said; "you hardly know each other." Why was she so surprised? Hadn't she expected this from the start? Still, she was more than surprised; she was stunned. "Besides," she addressed herself now to Edna, as if her brother were not present, "he's quite a bit older than you are. You haven't discussed this with your parents. I'm sorry, I mean your mother; why, I'm not sure you've discussed it with yourself." "I think that discussion is over," Edna answered; she smiled blurrily. "John," Ten said, a shade more hysterical. He said nothing, staring down at his toes. "Well," Ten said, "it can't be a case of marrying because the girl happens to be enceinte; she hasn't been here long enough, but I'm sure I don't know what it can be a case of." "Don't discuss this as if it were an illness," John protested. "Isn't it? How long has she been here? Three weeks? Four? You spend most of your time looking at each other, and none too pleasantly either, and the next thing you tell me is that you want to get married. It's a case of insanity, that's what it's a case of." "I love her," John cut in abruptly.

Now Ten was silenced; she stared at John as if she had just noticed a tarantula sitting on his nose. She searched her memory, frantic, like a woman on a streetcar looking for the fare as the car came closer and closer. Was this the right way? she thought; what possible destination could they be heading for? She should pull the warning bell; she should do something. But if she was wrong? She felt, illogically enough, that she was wrong. She had expected it. Perhaps she should relax and enjoy the ride. They had the reins. Yes, relax and enjoy the ride as if it were a holiday, and the company was providing free cars for the jaunt. Oh, she had found it, that coin she was looking for. No, she had never heard John use that word "love" before; she thought it had been removed, surgically, from his vocabulary. "But *why* are you marrying Serepta?" she could still hear herself asking; "she isn't the kind of woman who will do you any good; I can't believe you'll be happy with her." "I'm not sure of that," John answered. "Well, I am," she went on spiritedly. "That's only because you're my sister; you don't think any woman is the kind that would be good for me." "That's not true," Ten gasped; "that's just not true." But no matter how she went on, he had never once thought of mentioning love as a reason for marrying; no, not once.

"You say that now," Ten told him; "when the weather is sunny. Inside and out. But how is she going to take it, your moods when you come home late at night, these winters that go on forever; at least *she*" (Ten meant Serepta) "grew up here. She didn't have to get used to a whole new race. Who will she have for friends? Her friends won't come out from Boston to visit her in the winter, and she'll be lucky if they come calling in the summer." "I believe Edna reads a lot," John answered. And why *was* she going on so about it? Wasn't it because she wanted Edna to take John away from her, to take the responsibility for him away from her?

"Edna," Ten pleaded; "you haven't had time to think about it. There are weeks, *weeks*, when no one comes and I don't go out. Weeks when no horses or sleighs even *try* coming down the mountain. You'll be left here with me and the servants while John is out all over the country; you don't know what it's like, the isolation. Well, now, it's spring; even the trees seem to keep you company, and the birds and the animals; you might as well be on an ark. But in the winter! There was a woman who tried it in Dummerston, staying through the winter alone, but she left last year. She said she used to cry herself to sleep every night and do you know what she said she missed most? Not her family, not the museums, not the theater, the balls, the concerts, the lectures; she missed the *transportation*. 'Why,' she wailed to me, 'I used to go down to the corner of the street and wait for the horsecars; there wasn't anywhere I couldn't go, and now there's nowhere I can go.'

"And even if she could have gone somewhere, where would she have gone? On Mondays, the women here do their wash; on Tuesdays they sweep the parlor and the first floor; they have a schedule for every last day, and by Saturday night, they're waiting for the Sabbath so they won't have to do anything but listen to the minister and see what news is flying around. If the sermon turns out dull, or if there isn't enough gossip for them, the whole next week is already spoiled and they go home and take it out on everyone around them. They snap at the maids. God should take pity on their maiden sisters, but it doesn't seem he cares much.

"And then there's the other breed of women; you go see *them* on a Sunday and you might as well throw yourself into a bramble bush in the dead of winter. They're 'keeping the Sabbath,' 'doing appropriate things,' and they find it impossible"—she mimicked some women she knew—"'to concentrate on my reading with everybody chattering so; last Sunday no one came and it was quiet as a tomb and that's how I like it on Sundays.' And what is the household saint reading? *The History of the Reformation. The History of World Civilization.* And don't think she doesn't read every word either. I'd just as soon spend the Sabbath visiting a house of ill repute, but don't you think women can go in there," Ten warned, as if Edna had just expressed an interest in so doing.

"And that's another thing; religion. The Sabbath, the Sabbath, the Sabbath. They're all religious here. If they're going to kill their mothers, they wait until the Sabbath is officially over. The most popular time hereabouts for murdering is Saturday, because they're running out of time. And if they should see *you* in a rowboat, even if you're reading your pocket copy of the Sacred Book? Oh, the tongues start wagging so hard the gale blows the apples right off the trees. 'She spent the Sabbath lying in a pleasure boat, staring into the water, at her own pretty face probably; she doesn't care what kind of example she sets the young ones. I'm not having my children going up there near hers, I can tell you.' That's how they go on. You walk down a lane on a Sunday humming, and the next thing you know, the police station is full of tales about the doctor's wife shouting salacious tunes at the top of her lungs right outside the church gate.

"Then Bridget will tell someone you let Jimmie sit on

your lap once while you ate, and it will be the minister's wife all over again, your abnormal love of animals. 'Oh, people like that,' they wag on, 'people like that don't care a fig about other people. You'll see, the young thing won't have a child in the house; she'd probably strangle it and throw it down a well. No, the cat's all *she* can care about. *I* think it's too bad, the doctor works so hard, but she'd throw him right out if it came down to a choice between him and that cat.' And then they'll start in on John, and that's what he deserves for marrying a city girl, and not one of the fine ones brought up in the country; they might have been willing to have him if he'd only pressed his suit a little harder; why, they wouldn't even be surprised if Nellie Weston or some other horror wouldn't have him *now*, if he'd only have the sense to divorce her, but he probably won't have to. One day she'll get tired of the hard conditions; she's so small and delicate, and the next thing, he'll get a letter from somewhere in Virginia, asking him to please send all the family silver marked with her initials. Then one of them will sigh and say, 'I guess it will come out all right in the end, but I wouldn't want to be sleeping on his bed of coals for anything.' And then some hypocrite in the crowd will pipe up, 'We ought to think about *her;* she's sure to be taken off by the summer complaint or consumption, and if she has the misfortune to expect an addition to the family, that will kill her off for sure." John flushed. "Finished?" he asked. "*I'm* finished, but what I'm talking about hasn't even begun."

"You mean," Edna asked, "they really think about things like Jimmie sitting on my lap? They really care about little things like that?" "I'm sure they've been talking about nothing else since Bridget took note of it." "Good heavens"; Edna grinned; "what comical people. Why"— she beamed at John—"I should really give them something to talk about." "They'll beat their gums about something," John said; "for instance, if we don't marry, and by now someone in the halls knows what we intend" (behind him came the worried, rustling withdrawal of petticoats scurrying down the hall). "They'll start in on how Ten did it again, how she scared off a rival for her place in the house. 'She did it' "—John looked up at the ceiling as if reciting a passage in Sunday school—" 'just the way she always does; *she's* a smart one. *She's* not going to get cut out of all that money and spend her last years in an almshouse. That's one queen of the castle; no, I wouldn't be a princess if that was to be my castle, you can be certain of that.'" Ten reddened noticeably. "I have my own money," she told him, hoarse. "But they tend to forget that, don't they?" John asked; "still, you don't have any trouble standing for them, not that I've noticed." "I don't do all my complaining aloud," Ten answered. "Are *you* finished?" John asked again.

"Edna," Ten said, turning to her, imploring; "it's not that I don't want you here. I'm thinking of you. More than of him, and he's my own brother. He's got his medicine, but what will you have? The biddies aren't always wrong," she said, looking at John, defiant. "The snow *can* drive you crazy; it does terrible things sometimes, even to the animals. We have a horse in the barn John uses just to keep the little ones busy when he knows a bad labor's coming on. That's about the only time that horse goes any farther than the front yard; it's snow-blind, and it was a fine horse!" Ten burst into tears. "Ten," Edna said, sitting down on the couch; "Ten?"

The older woman refused to look at her. "Ten," Edna continued, "don't take on like that. Why, if marrying John doesn't work out, I can always divorce him." Ten looked up, shocked. The corners of Edna's mouth were curling uncontrollably upwards. John's face was also relaxing. "Or I could persuade him to be a society doctor." "He'd never do that," Ten sobbed; "he hates the city." "Well, so do I; that's why I'm here, after all." "You say that now," Ten cried again into her handkerchief; "just wait until the snow gives you cabin fever and you run out of the house with a knife trying to kill a tree that's been following you around at night. You'll come to miss the city. Everyone wants to return to the place of his birth." "Well, nothing would prevent that, once or twice a year, would it? You could even come with me and stay with my mother."

"But you have no idea," Ten said, looking quickly up, then down; "every day it's something else. Last week it was that crazy farmer who built a rat trap bigger than he was and then just walked in with his favorite dog, and he was three-quarters eaten before the hired help pulled him out." "John doesn't do things like that." "I know *John* doesn't," Ten sniffed with annoyance, "but you have to hear about it all the same. And then, the road that goes down the mountain and forks off into the hills, every time there's a funeral procession, it passes right by our windows." "That must save you reading the papers," Edna remarked.

"The papers!" Ten gasped, relieved as an unarmed person facing a bear suddenly finding a gun in her arms; "you haven't read a single paper since you've been here. Look at this," she cried, grabbing one from the wall rack, nearly tearing the contraption loose. John raised his eyebrows, looking quizzically at Edna while Ten excitedly turned the pages. "Never can find anything when I'm looking for it," she complained, leafing through it all over again. "Listen to this," she ordered Edna, who showed little desire to do anything else; "listen to this. Page three. General Notes. One whole page"—she paused for emphasis—"one whole page out of a six-page paper. General Notes," she began, poking in her pocket, thrusting her spectacles onto her nose. "Ten," John asked, impatient, "are you going to read that whole paper?" "You keep quiet," she ordered, furious.

"General Notes," she began again, staring John down. "'The funeral of Nora Davenport was largely attended at the church Tuesday afternoon, her second cousin, the Reverend H. P. Morgan, officiating.' Second cousin," she snorted; "very important. I suppose they put things like that in the Boston papers?" "Continue, please," John ordered. "'Mr. and Mrs. Osmer Cobleigh sang three hymns, one being a hymn which Miss Davenport sang just before she died. "When the Mists Have Cleared Away." Her death was very happy and peaceful. She not only sang but talked to those about her till the very last, thanking her mother for the kind and untiring care she had given her and telling them not to mourn for her, she was so happy and glad to go.'" "Maybe she was," John interjected. Ten ignored him. "'The floral offerings were beautiful, nearly covering the casket. Among them . . .' Just listen to this; who on this wide earth is interested?" Ten spluttered. "'. . . was a large bouquet from her father and mother, a pillow from her brothers and sisters

139

marked "Nora," a wreath of Easter lilies, small white flowers and fern from Harry Amidon, twenty-two roses formed in a crescent from Mr. and Mrs. Orestes Randall, cut flowers, carnations, roses, smilax from John Randall and family, twenty-two pinks from Mrs. Emma Taylor, a bouquet of lilies from Mary Johnson.' Well?" Ten asked Edna. "Well, what, Aunt Ten?" Edna asked; "not having been privileged to witness many dying scenes, that sounds rather interesting to me." "Including the twenty-two pinks, the three carnations, the eight lilies? What are they doing? Describing a funeral or taking inventory of a florist's shop? I tell you, the people up here have such *small* minds." "But you'd think them smaller if they didn't send anything at all," Edna suggested. "Probably," Ten agreed; "probably that is the explanation. Most people here probably don't send one thing, so when they do something generous, even sending one dandelion and two smilax, they go and put it in the paper." She resettled her spectacles on her nose.

"She's going to continue reading," John sighed to Edna; "it's astounding how those things stay on her nose with that little spring holding them. You always look," he addressed his sister, "as if you have a glass butterfly sitting right on the bridge of your nose." "At least my ears don't get pinched," she snapped; "and you, John, you just keep quiet until I get done." "I suppose there's no point in asking when that will be?" "Before Christmas anyway," Ten said, "not another word out of that mouth." She gave her glasses another pinch.

" 'Mrs. Elmira Smith is very sick with heart trouble. Mrs. Hollis Streeter is very feeble. Mrs. Ruel Nimmons is improving her tenement house on Kilgalley Street by putting in some new windows and painting the outside. Miss Annie Kiley and friends from Greenfield were the guests of Mr. and Mrs. Tilden over Sunday. Mrs. E. Lathan has packed her goods and will go to her new home in East Dummerston Wednesday. A huge adder was killed in front of Helen Eldridge's house in Williamsville; the adder was about three feet long. Miss Mary Bourke has entered the employment of the Retreat. Miss Mary Antin has been out of school part of the week, owing to trouble with her eyes. J. C. Tufts is now able to be out and is at Williamsville. Mr. Tupper's attempt to make applesauce from last winter's apples has failed miserably. Mrs. Louise Babbit has cleared her upper walk of the snow the plow deposited there throughout the winter.

" 'A huge nest of spotted snakes was uncovered in the west meadow of Mr. J. C. Emery's in Peru. The corn looks promising up on the high hills in Londonderry. At least Mr. Butler believes it to be the best crop in three years. Mrs. Louise Walker has left her millinery shop, and taken a post at the corset factory. Mr. Slater has returned to his duties at the meat market after his several weeks' illness. Mr. Albertson and his wife are on the sick list with hard colds. Mrs. Robertson has presented Mr. Robertson with a fat baby boy in Worcester. Mr. and Mrs. Lyndon's baby died on the third day of his life. Services to be held at twelve o'clock on the sixteenth of the month.' A lot of feeling they have, the way they stick these things together, and that's the exciting news for the week. From the whole county." "I don't care much for excitement, Aunt Ten. As for the rest of it, the dead baby, all that, it's foolish to expect much of people, isn't it? Probably someone just set the news as it came in." "News!" Ten snorted.

Time passed. "This silence is worse than your news," John said. "When Reason flies out the window, Love vandalizes the house," Ten quoted from some unknown source, staring from Edna to John and back again. "I have reasoned it out," Edna protested; "John is just what I want for a husband." "Her reasoning powers are stronger than mine," John added, trying to sweeten his sister's worry. She ignored him. "You *want* an irritable, moody, stern, arbitrary man? Also prone to insomnia?" She hoped the insomnia would be the last straw. "I certainly do." "John, she's a child!" Ten cried, her last appeal to the highest court. "Perhaps she is to you."

Oh, they are determined, Ten thought; this is worse than that purebred mare who ran off to mate with the iceman's horse. Oh dear, I'm not thinking right. I'm thinking, but I'm not thinking right. She stared down at her lap. What tiny little flowers go into making up the pattern, she thought, helpless. There must be, she went on inspecting the fabric, at least seventeen varieties here. And what's that? It's an oval shape, she concluded; not a flower at all. Perhaps it's meant to represent pollen. Or a bee. "Well?" she asked, looking up; "nothing will induce you to change your minds?" "Nothing," John said. "No," Edna agreed. "Then there's nothing to talk about"—Ten smiled weakly—"but the wedding."

"I'd prefer not to be married at home," Edna said; "I'd like to be married here. If you find such a plan agreeable. It would mean a great deal of work." "Why?" John asked; "why? We could just haul Dr. Pierce into the parlor here and Bridget and Bertha could stand as witnesses." "If you think I'm going to disgrace myself by a performance like that, you're mistaken altogether," his sister said; "I'd be making it look as if I didn't expect your marriage to last out the week." John was grinning at her. "Oh, have it your own way," she said, finally giving in and smiling back; "I can't say it's a *total* surprise." "You can't?" John asked. It was his turn to be caught off guard. "Well, you put two of the right sorts of cats with claws into a bag and there's either fighting or honeymooning." "What a novel way to look at it; in fact"—Edna smiled—"I think it's the only way to look at it." Inexplicable thing, Ten thought, looking at her; I hope she's not given to any queer fits Edith didn't tell me about. "I agree," John chimed in. Ten automatically slid her spectacles into her pocket. "Finished reading the will?" John teased. "So you'll be Mrs. Steele"; Ten smiled at Edna, taking her hand. "Go on as if I'm not in the room," John taunted. "And I certainly must congratulate *you*," his sister said, rounding on him; "if anyone ever needed a wife, you certainly do." "To sew on my buttons?" "To sew in your brains."

"Edna, can I come in?" Ten asked, closing the door behind her. Edna sat up in bed. "I've been thinking," Ten said. "So have I; I suppose that's what we're all doing right now." "Well, I can't help it," Ten apologized, "but I am worried. If only because your mother expected me to look after you." "Well, you have. No matter what, she's bound to be relieved. All I ever used to say was that my heart was free and I intended to keep it that way, that was just how I liked it, and the more I said things like that, the more young men she found for my partners at balls, until I thought to express my sentiments to the gentlemen themselves. She wouldn't have blamed you if I'd decided to marry the penniless undertaker.

"She used to express herself violently on the subject, you know. 'It's not difficult to marry wealth,' she used to say; 'in our set it's difficult *not* to do it. The mistake I see is in marrying for looks. What a terrible mistake to marry for looks! And then, if the marriage goes sour, to have nothing but the beautiful head to look at, shivering in the cold kitchen, resenting his burdens, the children howling in their thin clothes, the mother worrying about where the fuel should come from, then worrying over food, and after some time, the sad realization that one is living in a crumbling shack with a fine painting fit for a museum, but not for a husband or for anything else.' She could wax quite eloquent on that one subject. It must have been the topic of many of her magazine pieces. I suppose you've heard her at it often enough."

"Oh yes"—Ten thought back—"she never thought Ed was much to look at, and he didn't have much money either, so she never saw what there was to recommend him." "What did recommend him?" "You ask me now?" Ten said. "Well, I suppose a powerful recommendation was his interest in me. It's very hard not to return love. And the next thing was, he was a minister's son; he used to tell me about one sermon after another, and the behavior of one family after another, and he had this ridiculous theory that the dead didn't return because of their public humiliation the day of their funeral. I do think," she laughed, rustily remembering, "our courtship consisted of our screaming with laughter in every kind of conveyance, about every kind of funeral, and driving about in his open carriage, stopping at every single burying ground in and about Lowell. In Massachusetts, where our Academy was."

"What did he do?" "He sold shoes. That's how I ended up in Kansas. Ed could see the writing on the wall; he kept saying more and more people were going West, and all of them would need shoes. He was right, too. But he was a nasty one to do business with. Whenever someone came into his store with some shoes, he'd pick up the first pair, and look it over; then he'd pick up the second pair, look it over; then he'd start shouting, 'This is the worst, most sinful, ungodly reason for killing a cow I've ever heard tell of,' and throw them right out the door onto the street. There was one smart one, though; he used to put a bad pair on the top. They were all squashy, the left shoe bigger than the right one; one was dark brown, the other light. One of the laces would hardly go around your ring finger and the other was long enough to lasso a horse, and of course, Ed would automatically throw that pair right out onto the street. But the rest of the man's lot were perfect. Ed never even looked through all of them. I never knew if Ed was sure the man had caught on to his tricks. We were out there seven years, and he made a fortune in shoes. 'Step by step up the ladder of success.' That was his store motto and his best joke."

"Did your parents approve of the match?" "My parents? They believed in independent judgment. More common people call it making your own bed. They certainly weren't avoiding responsibility. Either of them would have come out to Kansas to paste things back, if that was what I needed. But Mother died the year after we went out, so it was Father who came out when Ed died, and talked me into coming back, and of course John had written so many letters saying the same thing I hardly bothered reading them, but I was so busy saying good-bye to every building and every tree, Father decided to crate everything in the house, and go on back alone and leave me to pick the train I could bear to climb on. Then, a year after I got back, he died. Ed died just six months after Serepta. Three in one year." Ten stopped suddenly, frightened.

"John told me about that." "He did? That's good. I won't have to, anyway; that's a relief." "It must have been a terrible, terrible thing." "You have no idea. One of the women there described it to me afterwards; there wasn't a fire this side of hell that warmed me for months. And then they insisted on burying the child cradled in its mother's arms and for some reason John took on about that, but he didn't say much, then or later, either. It seemed he didn't really think of Serepta as belonging to his family by that time; she belonged to those crazy people. And I know he kept thinking it might have made a difference if he had been there from the start. He really is a good doctor," she assured Edna; "well, it certainly didn't make me want to have children in a hurry, either.

It put a stop to my sitting in the parlor with the shutters closed crying my eyes out because Ed died before I had a little keepsake to take home with me. Oh, it was terrible, and no one in the county knew what to say to him. I guess they didn't know what to be sorry about—that she'd died, and the baby, of course, there was that too, or that she'd gone mad. That's what a lot of people thought and they weren't shy about saying so, either. Well, after that, his main concern was to get to the site of a call as soon as he could. He nearly drowned himself twice in two months, and he came near freezing three times that winter. Anyone could see what he was about. Edna," she went on, "he won't be an easy one for you. I don't mean because of the doctoring, either. He . . ." She stopped.

"You'll be all he cares about. If anything happened to you, he couldn't go on. Some people are like that, men especially. They fix on one person, and after that, there's no one else. Like the loon. Or the duck." Edna thought about what Virginia had said: "Once you've found a husband, you can always find another one, but you can't replace a father." She listened now with her nerves. "I don't mean to say he'd end up a suicide, not in any obvious way, but he uses himself up fast. Things use him up faster than they do other people. The way some logs do when you're building a fire. Two of them look just the same, but one of them burns itself up in no time. He's like that. He takes things hard. Well, I know a lot of people do, but they forget. Time passes and they forget. But if he got to be older than Moses, he'd remember every detail of every day. It has something to do with his sense of time"; she sounded as if she were talking to herself. "You know, he never uses a watch, and he always leaves on the second, as if someone fired off a gun at the start of a race. You can set your watch by John.

"Well, for me, time goes on, and the past gets vaguer and vaguer, the way curtains get bleached in the sun, but none of the scenes ever bleach out for him. I'm not sure he wants them to. The past is as alive as the present for him, not more alive, but as alive. It's a rare thing." "But not an easy one." Edna finished for her. "No, a terribly hard thing. Terrible. He can remember every death of every one of his invalids. They say a lot of doctors are like that, but he remember things that happened to him when he was five years old just as well. He was five when some older boys decided to play a trick on him because he was the smallest one in school. They took him out over on the little stone bridge, and made him stop in the middle and put out his tongue on the iron railing. It was sometime in March, and oh, it was freezing. The metal tore the skin right off; that was the whole point of the joke. The next day he was back playing with them. He'd heard about it before, how it was part of the ritual of starting school. So he didn't blame anyone. What I remember is waiting after school for little Phineas Weston and almost taking the eyes out of his head. He didn't complain about it either. I was a foot shorter than he was, and a girl on top of it. A young lady, really. I was twenty-five. I guess no one would have believed that Phineas creature anyhow. And John, he kept quiet.

"Well, don't you see, Edna? This is going to be the hardest part. He's never going to forget the way he feels now, about you, I mean. No matter how much time passes. With most couples, it's just not that way. Children come, and then they get sick; your parents get older, and they get sick. The potato bug gets the potatoes; everyone worries about that. If there's no rain a man can go half off his head if he's a farmer. They usually don't remember they have wives if it's the haying season, or there's a drought, or it's time for sugaring. The women start worrying about how to get the pantry cleaned and the clothes washed and how they're going to face their friends in church in last year's bonnet; letters keep coming that need answering. He won't build a chair that she wants, and she gets even by serving pork for six weeks in a row, and if they're lucky, they remember what it was like in the beginning, perhaps—once every two years. And you can't blame them. After marriage, nothing's the same again.

"Then, when they do come together, they worry about whether they're adding another addition to the family, and if they are, will that mean another addition to the house, and if the woman has had bad experiences in childbed, she thinks about that, and her husband does too, so if they get in bed at all after they have the right amount of chicks running around the house, there's that collection of shadows hanging over them. And then there's the woman who teased her husband with imaginary beaux during courtship, and he spends the next twenty years getting even with her in a hundred little ways, and she doesn't know what made him into such a monster after he started out so well. Then children die, and the wife can't stop mourning. The husband feels neglected. She doesn't think anyone understands her, and after a while, no one does. Or her mother dies and his wife goes into a positive decline, and the husband tries everything he can think of to get her more cheerful, and finally he just gives up and pays more attention to his grapes than to her. By that time, she starts waking up, and finds herself jealous of the grapes and thinks she's crazy for being jealous of the grapes and corn and cattle and wire fences.

"Well, all those things will happen to you if you're married long enough, but John won't look at you and see the daughter, or the chair, or the swollen joints, or notice that you're limping. He'll look at you and see you just the way you are now, almost seventeen years old, with that beautiful hair and those beautiful eyes, and he'll feel just the same way too. And if you change—you have to, somehow or other with time—he won't understand it. Or he will, but it will hurt him, that you've changed, that you don't love him the same way you did when you were married. He still thinks of me the way I was when I pulled him up and down in front of the house on a little sled. It keeps you young"—Ten smiled inwardly—"but sometimes it's hard to stay young, even for someone you love so much. Well, you know, he's like my own child. That's probably why I don't miss having children of my own. If you two have children, they'll be my grandchildren. It's hard, I tell you, Edna, to have someone love you that way, as if nothing could ever weather you or change you. It's hard for you to measure up yourself. It's so easy to start feeling guilty, or resentful. You'll start asking yourself, why can't he get behind the screen of everyday life; why can't the trivia of life protect him? But it won't.

"And you," she continued, looking at Edna, "you two aren't like the usual couple. You already have that—I don't know how to say it—that haze, of two people who shut out the rest of the world. As if you were the only two people on earth either of you cared about. I doubt," Ten went on, turning it over slowly, "if even children would break very far into that circle. A cat, or a dog, that might advance quite a way, but they don't last long at their best. This whole thing," she realized, surprised, "why, it must have begun when he found out about Jimmie the cat. For the last two years, it's been his sister and his cat. His sister could take care of herself, but he actually used to torture himself about leaving that animal alone. He used to have to *carry* Jimmie all over the house for the first hour after he was home. All that nonsense about getting him as a barn mouser! When that cat dies, *he's* going to need a doctor. I guess you both will.

"Well, that's the trouble; you're two of a kind. What kind of marriage will it be if the whole household, his medical practice, the needs of any children that might appear vanish in the double sorrow over that cat?"

"You don't have to worry," Edna said; "I'm stronger than I look." "Stronger than he is?" "I think so." "How much stronger?" "While he lives, very much stronger. You've explained it very clearly; he needs someone to take care of him. That's what I want to do. It's not even a question of my learning to be strong enough to care for him. I already want that. I think I know how. Do you think that's possible?" she asked anxiously; "I know how young I am. I know what a responsibility it is, but I want it. That's the main thing, isn't it? I never change my mind; at least I never have. Well, at any rate, I've never made it up before, but I don't think I'll change my mind once I've made it up. I want him; that's the main thing, isn't it?" "I suppose it is," Ten said slowly; "but even when the man is an easy one, even-tempered, practically bovine, it gets so hard, day in and day out." "It will be very hard to get bored by him," Edna joked; "he won't be home enough." "Is that going to be your salvation?" Ten asked, finally smiling. "Part of it"—she smiled back —"probably a large part of it." "And if he breaks his leg, or gets thrown from his horse, and ends up an invalid? He'll be in the house all the time then." "Anything can happen," Edna said; "*I* could die in childbirth; he has to take the same risks I do." "But if something like that were to happen to him?" "I think," Edna mused, "I could content myself with staring at his English profile." Ten stared at her, motionless.

"Edna," Ten said urgently; "you have to develop an interest. I don't care what it is, but do it quickly. Otherwise John is going to feel stricken every time he has to leave you alone in the house." "I *have* an interest: dollhouses. Not exactly dollhouses. I've never had the money to build real houses, so I build little ones. I'm a baby architect. I can work on one of those houses for fourteen hours at a time and it seems as if barely five minutes have passed." "Are you serious?" "Of course I'm serious. I'm surprised my mother never mentioned it. But she always thought it was abnormal. She wouldn't want to put herself in such a dreadful light: having raised such a peculiar child."

"John would let you build whatever you wanted; Edna, I'm serious. You have to tell him about it. We have over two thousand acres of land. If he knew you were looking forward to building a new house, his mind would be settled, not entirely, but it would mean a great deal. You have to tell him." "Oh no," Edna protested; "I'd just build a monstrosity. *Every* style of architecture appeals to me. If I built a house, one wing would be in the Revolutionary style; another would be oriental in influence; another would be the height of current fashion; another would be *my* idea of what things ought to look like. Strangers coming in would be afflicted with vertigo. No, anything I built would be known as the Lunatic Asylum before it was even half finished, and," she continued, "every time I had a new idea, or saw something else, I'd want to add a new room onto the whole thing. No, it wouldn't be the right kind of house for a doctor. Talk about wagging tongues! It would take a mass murder to get their attention away from the porticoes. And the arbors. And the statuary garden."

"Edna," Ten confessed, "I wasn't completely honest with you before. The usual standards just aren't applied to us here. We're too rich. They wouldn't even call such a house peculiar. 'When you're that rich, you have your own ways'; that's what they say. 'They've already got one foot in heaven or hell'; they go on like that about us. 'They can afford to be a little bit fly. They can afford to fly about.' You decide to live in a museum and Williamsville will make it a mark of their own distinction. Their standards don't apply to us. John says money reverses gravity on this earth. And all because our grandmother got married without her dress on. He's right; we could do anything short of murder—I'm not sure even murder is out of the question. Everyone would wag his head and say, 'That's how the wealthy do things. *I* wouldn't, myself; what with scraping out the leavings of the pan for tomorrow's dinner, I don't have time for murder.' And so on."

"But John is the country doctor," Edna protested; "they must judge *him*." "Only a little more, but that's because he tends to scold, interfere. He gives orders surrounded by the whole family. 'Your wife is overworked; you should have married a horse'; that's what he said last week. The wife's his friend for life, of course, and the husband will call him anyhow. if he has so much as a hangnail, and he does get some fun out of going down to the saloon and joking around. He used to. He grew up with everyone around here, and he played all those practical jokes. Practical jokes, they're a passion in the country," Ten explained; "I *hate* them myself. He's plotting something out right now." "He is?" "Ever since that Weston sent him a note saying he was dying and turned out drunk, he's been thinking up something; you just wait and see. When he thinks of what to do, *that* will be the talk of the county. He's probably waiting for the county fair. That's when he'd get the most attention."

The two women had relaxed; they were becoming gossipy. "What's this," Edna asked, "about your grandmother getting married in her shift?" "Oh, one hundred years ago, that was nothing; fifty years ago, it was just a little bit unusual. We come from a very old family; Father said if we came over as early as our family tree indicates, we must have been shipped out on the first schooner, and that means we come from criminal stock. Our grandmother, the one in the shift, Mary Tatum, lived in Pennsylvania and when her first husband died she came under the widow law." Edna was utterly baffled.

"It was all tied up with finances. If there were claims against a widow's estate, the creditors could take anything she owned. But if she got married in her shift, that was a public statement she was penniless. If she came dressed for a wedding, the creditors could have taken the dress right off her back. Then there would have been a question about *his* estate, and whether the creditors were entitled to any of it. So her second husband brought a wedding dress and a complete trousseau and dressed her in it as fast as he could *after* the wedding.

"At the time, the only odd thing about it all was Grandmother's decision to get married in the winter. She was so worried about her new husband's estate, she got married barefoot, and Father said all the guests swore she hopped from one foot to another right through the whole ceremony, and even put one foot on her husband's shoe near the end of the sermon. It was a very long one evidently. They spent their first hours of wedded bliss fighting a case of frostbitten toes." Now they were laughing. "Oh, I think you'll do all right," Ten said, exhaling relief, "but would you get married in your shift?" "I'd get married in nothing at all!" "Well!" Ten said; "religion has certainly gone out of the family now.

"Our grandmother, she was known for her religion. Her ship came over to this country in a storm. She was the only one who wasn't terrified because she knew her prayers would be answered. Sure enough, when they got into port, they found a swordfish wedged into a hole in the ship's bottom. *She* wasn't surprised. Nothing much surprised her. There's an old portrait of her in the parlor; she looked a little like you, only smaller." "Smaller!" "Smaller"—Ten nodded—"but I don't know if she would have had the courage to have taken John on. Not at seventeen." "She sounds capable of it." "Probably she was, but, Edna, please remember what I said. It's important. At least now." She got up from her perch on the side of the bed. "There's one more thing: are you going to call me Aunt Ten for the rest of your life?" "Oh, I think so; you seem like my aunt somehow." "As long as you don't start calling me Grandmother. But," she worried, "you must feel very young to want to call me Aunt." "Well," said Edna, "I'll probably stop sooner than you like. Or perhaps I call you Aunt because you

151

seem awfully old. Did you think of that?" "Imp." Ten grinned. "Sleep well, dear," she said, closing the door.

Edna slid under the covers; she tried to sleep. She had never been more wide awake. There was a sudden flurry in the hall, then the sound of doors opening and closing, feet running. Edna threw on a wrapper and ran into the kitchen. Amos was sitting at the kitchen table, his head in his hands. Bertha and Bridget were hugging each other, sobbing. Ten was pacing nervously up and down the room, glancing back and forth out the window in the direction of the barn. "What happened?" Edna demanded. John wasn't there; he wasn't there. "What happened? Did something happen to John?" "Oh, Edna," Ten said, reminded suddenly of her presence; "no, no, John is fine. He's out in the barn." She resumed pacing. "It's Ben that's the trouble; he must have been milking old Bessie and gotten kicked in the head. Amos found him out there. He's been dead for hours." "Kicked in the head? By a cow? An old cow?" "I told you it wasn't the same in the country," Ten answered, irritably. "John's out there now, looking him over."

The kitchen door opened, a gust of cool night wind following. "He's dead. I don't know how many times," John said in a monotone, "I told him to go around to the front of that damned cow. You can't walk in back of the cow." "It's not the cow's fault," Ten said; "it was Ben's fault. The cow's been like that since the day we got it." "We're getting rid of that cow tomorrow!" John thundered. "But why?" Ten protested; "it was Ben's fault. Always in a hurry, there was bound to be an accident sooner or later." "In the morning!" John roared. "Well, and who is to take it?" Ten asked. "The Westons. They're always having animals dying on them; they'll get something white to drink for a change. Maybe it will kick Tom in the head and the whole family a step up life's ladder." "You'll change your mind in the morning." "Don't you believe it!" John shouted. "Amos! You get that cow down to the Westons' before the sun's up." "Yessir," answered the hapless man. Ten shook her head at Edna. "And you might as well saddle up and get old Greenwood ready to bring one of his boxes tomorrow. Ben doesn't have any relatives, does he?" "You know he

doesn't; that's why we took him in the first place."
"Lucky for him, wasn't it?" John asked; "back to bed,
everyone. Go on, Ten, Edna." Edna stared at Ten, and
followed after her. "Well, you see now?" Ten asked,
pausing before Edna's door. Edna nodded and went in.
She was utterly exhausted; this time when she got into
bed, she fell immediately asleep.

A soft knock at the door woke Edna. "Who is it?" she
whispered; didn't anyone in the house ever go to sleep?
"Me," John whispered through a crack. Edna put on her
wrapper for the second time, and motioned John in. The
moonlight illuminated the room, painting it every possible shade of violet and blue. The colors of mourning.
"Come sit down," she said, patting the edge of the bed
next to her.

"I woke you up." "No, you didn't," Edna lied; "I
couldn't sleep." "There was something I wanted to talk
to you about." "What?" "Maybe the wedding." "Maybe?"
"Maybe not." "It was terrible about Ben," Edna said
softly; "you must have had him here for a long time."
"Since we were children." "Then you were friends?" "Not
really friends; I was used to him." "It's a useless way for
a man to die, isn't it?" Edna said; she was fishing. "What
difference does it make how a man dies? He's dead; that's
the end of it." "When you go out on your calls," Edna
asked, "is the invalid often dead before you get there?"
"Not often." "You must be cold," Edna said, feeling for
a quilt at the foot of her bed with her left hand, her eyes
fixed on his face. "I'm not." Edna carefully unfolded the
quilt with her free hand, her eyes fixed on his; she began
wrapping it around him. He looked at her, but didn't
resist. She tucked it firmly around his neck. "There," she
said; "you look like an Indian." He didn't answer. "I
should really," Edna said, "lay you down on this bed."
"It wouldn't look right," John answered in the same flat
voice that had jarred her so when he came in. "Well, I
don't suppose this does either," she said. Her right arm
circled his neck, her fingers pressing against his right
temple. Through the blanket, she could feel his body
relax slightly; he was trembling, as if half frozen. Cau-
tiously, she settled her left hand on the top of his head.
"Your head feels hot." No answer. She lowered her left

hand and began stroking his hair as if she were petting a favorite animal.

"I can't believe it," he said suddenly. "Why not?" "I must have assumed he'd be here as long as I was." "Well, then, you will miss him," Edna whispered. "I should have thought of that before and gotten rid of that damn cow." "You can't be expected to see into the future." "I could have been expected to know that damn cow," John said, tortured. "Ben must have wanted that cow on the farm." "Oh, he thought the world of that ugly beast; that was the whole trouble. If he hadn't gotten so attached to her when she was a calf, I would have had her gone long ago." "But Ben would have been unhappy if you'd done that." "He'd have sneaked off every day to look at her, the idiot." Edna said nothing, but kept stroking his hair. "How old was Ben?" "Twenty-nine; he was twenty-nine." "He wasn't a child, then?" "No more than I am." "Well, then, how could you take his cow away?" No answer. "Do you think he was out there alone long?" "He died instantly; his skull was smashed!" "That's something," Edna sighed.

"But it was so unnecessary!" John burst out; "if he'd only listened and gone around the front of the cow! But no, he never did listen to anyone but himself." "Stubborn," Edna commented. "I guess they'll put that on his tombstone." He had stopped shivering. "How," Edna asked, her own voice quivery, "are you going to sleep with that face in front of you?" He finally turned to look at her; his face seemed softened, younger. Edna suddenly thought of Ten's story of the boys who had forced John's tongue against the bridge. Does he always look this tortured? Edna thought; does he always look like this when someone dies? "I don't know." His whisper was hoarse. Edna drew his head closer. She was too short; she sat up on her knees and pulled his head against her. "We'll put out the lights; we'll go to sleep; we'll go to sleep; we'll go to sleep."

She sang it again and again. She could feel John crying without sound. She kept singing the same two lines, again and again, as monotonously as she could. She had no idea how long she had been singing; she was putting herself to sleep. "Edna," John mumbled. "Mmmm?" "What's that song?" "Oh, my governess used to sing it to me. I used to be afraid of the dark." "Sing it again." She did.

"It's a good song," John said groggily. "Isn't it?" asked Edna, beaming into the dark; "I've always loved it." "I should let you go to sleep"; John yawned. "And you too," Edna answered; "you should go to sleep," she repeated, hypnotic; "we should all be asleep." She kissed him on the cheek. "Yes," John said, getting up. "Oh," he said, surprised; "you'll want your quilt back." "You keep it," she suggested. "All right," John agreed, holding it closed with one hand, his other on the doorknob. "Tell me," he asked, "will Jimmie sleep on our pillow? After we're married?" "Oh, I'd think so, wouldn't you?"

Ten, peering out from behind her door, which she always kept ajar, heard the click of Edna's bedroom door, saw John going down the hall, a conical shape, a walking quilt topped by a large head. She watched him go into his room. For a few minutes, the light of his candle bled out from under the door. Then it went out. There was the creak of bedsprings, then silence. Ten stood there for half an hour. What *did* she like about Edna? She wasn't so interesting, really. And she was so young. But it was as if there were places in her waiting to be filled; they would be filled with anything. There wasn't anything she couldn't do. If she wanted to. Perhaps that was it, as if she sensed the deep currents in her the way the dousers claimed to sense water with their forked sticks. John's candle was not lit again. The bedsprings made no sound. Well, for heaven's sake. Of all things, Edith's child! Well, I'd do anything for her now, she thought, turning back to her own bed, pulling up her covers, staring at the wooden ceiling. Just as Edna was staring up at hers. If she could only *think* of what it was about Edna that caught her so. Eventually, the white hands of the moon closed both their eyes.

Ten woke feeling that something was wrong in the house. Well, there's no hurry, she told herself, tunneling back into the bedding. The gingerbread clock on her mantel began striking, and she went so far as to bury her ear in the goose-down pillow, pulling her satin quilt up over her other ear. Tired, she mumbled; the bed was so comfortable. Sun was beginning to break unpleasantly in. Ten shut her eyes and began breathing deeply, as if she were already asleep. Instead, she found her body growing more and more rigid. Oh, if I have to get up, she complained to herself. Well, what was it she had to do? She meant to show Edna her wedding sketches; was that it? That, she concluded fuzzily, was part of it. She sat up and turned her legs towards the bed's edge, but the floor might as well have been thirty feet below, so intense was her aversion to it. She looked around her room. It was comforting, finding everything in its place like this. All the same stones in the fireplace, she told herself, as if there was any likelihood they would have been changed in the night. In nightmares, the stones of the fireplace climbed down and began leaving the room, one by one. I have the most ridiculous dreams, she thought, irritated; it's no wonder I never tell anyone about them.

There was a legend that her grandfather, when he retired to Williamsville, spent most of his summer diving for rocks in the river, collecting the ones streaked with mica, so that at night, when the moonlight struck the stones, the fireplace would gleam as if it were still glowing. Well, and why not believe it? she thought, finally looking down at the floor. The entire family was given to obsessions; unless her grandfather had been a case of genuine madness and he had come to believe he was a fish. But fish didn't collect stones.

Stones. She wondered if the burial ground in Kansas really kept Ed's grave in order. She would have to stop postponing her duties in that direction, and get the order for exhuming the casket; it ought to be put in the family plot. It was about time for that, she thought, resigned. What was it, really, she wondered, this desire to be buried in one's native soil? She couldn't help feeling Ed didn't like it, lying out there in Kansas, that strange place. Why did it seem that he would be alive and closer to her if his dead body was in the family plot? He would be, though, Ten thought, sliding off the bed and into her slippers. She would be fifty this year. Why did her mind keep running to stones? Ben! Of course, Ben. They would have to bury him. She sat down weakly on the old wooden trunk at the foot of her bed. She pushed herself up onto the highest part of its curved lid as if she wanted to get as far from the earth as possible.

Yes, she repeated to herself, as if trying to learn a lesson she didn't believe (of course, China was said to be miles under her feet, but she didn't believe that either); and the time! How it had gone by since her first arrival. She thought back to that day, the day they all saw him first. "You brought *him* home from the poorhouse?" she could hear her incredulous mother asking. They were standing in the summer kitchen, her mother's back to the brick stove. "You brought *him* home to be the stable-boy?" "Julia," her father said to her impatiently, "*you* ought to know he'll get bigger." "And *you* ought to know how long it takes," her mother retorted, furious; "must we have a baby in the house every nine months?" "He's not really a baby." "He's not even an infant," Julia, her mother, flared out. The young man under discussion began squalling in his homespun blanket. "I don't imagine he gets his own dinner yet?" Julia asked; "I'm not taking him unless Ten agrees." She turned to her daughter. "It might be a good idea," Ten said; "John would have someone to grow up with; I'm so much older than he is. The way things are now, he'll be an only child." "An only child?" her mother turned on her. "There are four of you." "But John's twenty years younger than I am; we're hardly going to be crawling around on the floor together."

The infant bawled again. "Good lungs," her father muttered under his breath; "a fat one, too." "Kate, will you please get some nourishment into a bottle," her mother ordered, thumping the coffeepot violently on the table. "Here you are, little man," Kate crooned, putting something to the baby's mouth. "What's that?" asked her mother. "Cotton soaked in sugar and water"; Kate pouted. "I've told you and told you not to give children that unsanitary concoction; it gives them dyspepsia in later life." "Well, all the others had it, and they eat just fine." "Do you mean," Julia asked, "do you mean to say you went ahead and poisoned them with those rags after all the times you were told to stop it?" "Dr. Steele said it couldn't hurt them," Kate objected, looking at Ten's father half in fear, half in appeal. "Martin!" Julia exclaimed; "there are, there were, certain prerogatives in this house I insist upon!" "It's a dead horse, isn't it?" Julia didn't reply, glaring at him as if in hopes of turning him to stone. "Would you just hold him a minute while I look for the paper?" Martin asked her frostily; "I want to see what the trial period is." "What trial period?" Julia asked; "when did they begin trial periods?" "It's here somewhere," he answered, his back to her, methodically rummaging through the pockets of his coat. "Not here," he muttered; "I'll look in my bag."

Of course, by now, as her father had intended, her mother was peering curiously at the baby in the wrapper. "He must be hot in this kitchen," she observed. "Yes, ma'am," said Kate; "I brought out one of Harold's old summer gowns." "Does the gown fill up that whole box?" she asked, looking over at it. "He can't just go over to the privy, ma'am, you know that; even your own son can't do that, you know." "He has a dimple," Julia said, half to herself; "his eyes follow me. Good Lord, he smiles! Martin! How old is this child? Two days? That's remarkable." She moved her finger back and forth in front of his eyes; they followed. "Remarkable," she said again. Involuntarily, she smiled at the child. He smiled back. "Martin, he smiles!" "That's no smile," Martin answered, bored; "it's a reflex."

Julia smiled at the child again; he smiled back. "This one *smiles*," Julia informed him; "Martin, this will be like having twins." "Not exactly," Martin assured her; "Kate and Ten will take responsibility for this one." "Now I've heard everything!" Julia snorted; "I hope I don't live to see the day when those two take responsibility for anything this size while I'm in the house." "I'm sure you don't mean that," Martin said. "Oh, Ten," her mother said, looking up distressed, "I didn't mean you ought never to have children." Ten grinned like a pumpkin. "Well, are we to keep him?" Martin asked, seeing the baby had grasped Julia's index finger. "*If* Kate and Ten are raising him, and he'll be no bother to me." Martin sighed. "Wasn't there anyone else in the poorhouse?" Julia asked; "Martin, what I mean is, we could go back and get another one as well." "There was a very promising-looking girl and a sickly-looking boy about ten." "Sickly, how?" Julia asked, interested. "Thin, malnourished, sulky, not very promising." "Why not?" Julia asked; "there's plenty of food on a farm, and his sulkiness will have plenty of company here, I can tell you." "Should I go back for him?" "Not today"; she looked out the window. Thick flakes were coming down fast. "Tomorrow. Tomorrow. We can't let old Charlie go on alone in that barn. Did they tell you the other one's name?" "Amos." "Nice and biblical," Julia said happily.

"And how is the little baby?" Julia cooed at it, putting him down on the table, and beginning to unpeel him as if he were a banana, her palm automatically tucked under his head like a pillow. "Martin," she asked in alarm, "what are all these purple blotches on his feet, and his head?" She went on, inspecting the said creature more carefully. "A forceps baby," Martin confessed. "A forceps baby!" Julia exclaimed; "Martin, he'll be feeble-minded." "I guess so," Martin agreed, "if George was." "That was not fair," she said, not looking up. George, her firstborn, had died of scarlet fever during the dreaded second summer. She had always believed she would have ended up mad had she not already been carrying another baby.

Ten. That was Ten. ("Well," Julia used to say, "I didn't have to wait long for boys." Martin, Harold, and then John. And now Ben.) "Ben for better? Benefit?" Julia asked. "Why not?" Martin agreed. "Benevolent, bentwood, bent, benighted," Ten started in. "Enough of that," her mother interrupted. "Kate, give this child a bath: in the kitchen, where it's warm, give him his lunch, and put him in one of the old cradles. See that someone washes it down first and let me see it before he goes into it." "And where is the cradle to go, ma'am?" Kate asked. "In the nursery with John, where else?" Julia said. Why did she always have the bad luck to endure such weak-minded help? Well, Father's gotten exactly what he wanted, Ten thought, leaving the room. "Congratulations," she told him as he was trying to escape through the front door. "Watch out. We haven't cut the rose bushes back from the front door." "Congratulations for what?" he asked, guilty. "Do you want company on your way to Lima?" Ten asked; "now that it's all settled, I mean. You might not mind having a witness next time you go to the poorhouse." "A witness!" he snorted; "well, why don't you come along? I'm stopping to see my sanc-

tified friend; his son's home moping about something."
And that was how she had come to meet Ed.

Well, and John had gotten what he wanted, too, although he didn't know what he wanted at the time. How
he and Ben hated the neighbor at the bottom of the
mountain! The man used to rout out the constable if he
saw a boy on his way out of his orchard holding an apple.
The two boys also turned out to share a passion for practical jokes. Mother had always dreaded April Fools' Day;
she said it had been invented just for them.

They decided to get even with Mr. Probst one night in
the winter when the drifts weren't too high but the
weather was still menacing. The next day, the papers
claimed it had been the coldest November night for
twenty years. He had a favorite cow named Bossie, and
it wore a big brass bell around its neck so that it couldn't
stray far away enough to endanger itself. Mr. Probst certainly was proud of that cow! The two boys had gone
down on Halloween, smearing their faces with charcoal
like professional assassins, stolen into the barn, Ben leading the cow out, John muffling the bell in a cloth. Then
they took the cow up on top of the mountain, put it in
an old sugaring house, lit a fire to keep the precious animal warm, and went back down. How they ran around
ringing that bell! And good farmer Probst, he was up
and down all over the farm and the mountain, in and out
of the woods, after that bell, all the while roaring, "What
ails that cow? What can ail that cow?" The boys led him
quite a chase.

Then, when he finally went back into the farmhouse,
and they saw the light move up to the second floor, they
flew up to the sugarhouse, tied the bell around the cow's
neck, washed their faces in the snow, tied huge cloths
around their boots so that, in the morning, it would look
as if two monstrous animals had come down from the
mountain; and they went back up toward the house
through the woods, climbing in their bedroom window
on an old wooden ladder Ben had built, hinged in the
middle, apparently for the express purpose for which
they then used it: to fold it up and pull it into the room
after them. Most of their precautions, as it developed,
were unnecessary, since, after they fell asleep, the snow
covered all of the tracks but the very deep ones. Mr.

Probst never found out who had taken his favorite cow up to the sugarhouse, and used to puzzle out loud over whether it had made the journey up there on its own; but he suspected. As for our parents, they knew immediately, and so did the rest of the neighbors, but none of us ever told anyone. "Family secrets," Mother used to say, "ought to be kept," causing some disagreement at the table, since Father wasn't sure pranks ought to be included in that category. "What I mean is," Mother said, "if we're going to kill the boys for it, we ought to do it for our own reasons, not because the neighbors think we ought to." Father went along with her there.

It wasn't so nice, though, when they decided to revenge themselves again with Mr. Probst the next April by persecuting his summer boarder, a mild city gentleman born to be victimized. He used to trot across the little path to the little stone bridge over the creek and tap one of the maple trees, and the boys found out about it, sneaked down every night and dumped tin cups of water into the wooden bucket. "Well," John had said in his own defense, "I don't see what's wrong with it; he finds a full bucket every morning, and that's more than most can say." Mother had a fine time explaining the subtle difference between wreaking vengeance on the focus of one's hatred and getting even by tormenting someone else who was only associated with the victim through sheer accident— especially when she didn't believe in vengeance at all. "Well, Julia," Father said, "they'll grow out of it. We have to try to stop them, of course, but I think we'll just have to wait it out." "I don't think I can stand it," Mother said. "It's no worse than sending Ten off to a dance and getting a knock at the door from Mr. Brown's stableboy saying I better ride after him with our sleigh because Mr. Brown's oxteam was trying to pull Ten and her latest beau out of a ditch." "Oh, say," Ben said, looking up, "I'd like to hear more about that." "That must have been some driver, Ten," John croaked up. "Mother!" Ten appealed. "Martin," Julia appealed in exasperation, "there's a criminal element in the stones of this house. They're growing up to be monsters."

"I'd rather have that than see them grow up like the Probsts," her husband commented, unhelpful; "when I drove by there this morning, there she was, Mrs. Probst, with a face that would frighten a skunk. For amusement I think the two of them put their profiles to the grindstone. She had her hand on the butter churn as if she were hoping to drop someone from a scaffold, and that husband next to her coming out in that old straw hat. He got his hand on the wheel; she probably wasn't going fast enough for him, and every tool in the world scattered all over the yard. Everything there looks gray even in the middle of the summer. The devout," Martin went on, eating his cereal, "if that's the devout, I hope they do grow up criminals." "Martin!" her mother exploded, "what am I supposed to do with them when they start up the minute you're out of sight?" "Do they want to go to the county fair?" their father asked. "So they say." "Then when I get out of the yard, they'll experience a change of heart and ways, won't you, boys?" John and Ben looked glumly at each other; they nodded. "Well, the padlock's back on the cell," Martin reassured her. And they certainly did experience a change of heart. You would have thought they were almost Christians, at least until the fair was over and done.

In the kitchen, Edna was sitting alone at the table. Black, she thought, looking up at Ten; black again. I wonder if they would be any happier to have me out of the way for a while? This might be a good time to ride over and visit Virginia. If I don't get over to Fitchburg soon, I'll be lucky to find her alive. "Prepare yourself," Ten warned her, sitting down; "I'll be glad to see the sun go down on this day." John came in, stopping just inside the doorway, then he walked around in back of Edna's chair and put his big hand down on top of her head. She smiled up, but he was looking at his sister. I don't know how hands like that operate on anything but a barn door, Ten thought; then she noticed where his hand was. Good Lord, that's almost what you'd call affectionate. No, she didn't think he was aware his hand was there.

"We might as well get it over with," he said abruptly. "What?" Ten asked him. "Greenwood's here with the coffin; Pierce can perform the service today. There s no point leaving him in the parlor forever. He never liked it much in there when he was alive." "But people might want to see him," Ten protested. "What people?" "Didn't he make any friends when I was gone?" "Some old lady down the street from the church who makes dolls to send the Orientals; I'll go down and get her. She won't have anything else to do. Today?" she asked again. "Well, Ten, what do you want? Wait for his parents to show up? Wait for things to get pretty bad in the parlor? You want to go through the whole rigmarole of calling the iceman and laying him on the ice? What's the point?" "You're right, you're right," she agreed; "the place for the burial. That's all settled?" "He goes into the family plot." "Of course." "Well, Mother and Father named him Steele," John said angrily. "I'm not saying a word against it." "And nobody else better either."

"You said twelve o'clock?" Ten asked, pursuing a potato pancake around her plate. "High noon," John answered; "Edna, can you be ready by then?" "That's no trouble." "It won't remind you of your father's death?" Ten asked. "Remind me?" Edna smiled; "remind me? I never got to attend it. Perhaps this will be a substitute." "Should she wear mourning?" Ten asked. "That's hardly necessary." "Still, I think I will." "As long as everyone is on the gravel and into the carriage by twelve, that's all," John said, getting up abruptly; "don't forget Amos." The two women heard the sound of the parlor door, opening and closing. "Fine," Ten said aloud; "fine."

"Well, here we are," Ten said as the little group stood around the open scar in the earth. "Here we are and where is the Reverend Pierce?" John asked. "He'll be here," Ten said. "He's the only bad news I know that doesn't travel fast," John muttered. "Don't make things worse," Ten said. Edna slid her arm around his waist. If they aren't starting to look like an old married couple, Ten thought; if anything that young can look old.

Then there was the clatter of hooves, and the Reverend Pierce paced solemnly from his buggy, eyes on the ground. Edna felt John breathe in sharply. His arm crept around her waist. "I am so sorry," the Reverend said, pressing each hand in turn. Someday, John thought, weary, I expect to hear him ask which one is the corpse. "Shall we begin?" the Reverend asked the family. "What a lovely floral wreath," he said, grasping Ten's hand again; "this is your doing, isn't it?" he asked her; "you always had such a love for wild flowers." "We didn't have much

163

time for greenhouses," John growled. His sister reddened. Edna's arm tightened around his waist. Well, I wouldn't mind getting in on that daisy chain, Ten thought, miserable. "Shall we begin?" the Reverend asked. Neither of the Steeles answered. "Please," said Edna. The Reverend looked at her. Who was this new person? What was she doing with her arm around John Steele? Why was *she* telling him to begin?

"The text is one of praise," he intoned, "praise for God, for nature, and for a man of nature, who tended to its creatures like the faithful shepherd himself." He began reading from his small leather Bible. "Blessed is the man whom thou chooseth, and causest to approach unto thee, that he may dwell in thy courts: we shall be satisfied with the goodness of thy house, even of thy holy temple. By terrible things in righteousness wilt thou answer us, O God of our salvation; who art the confidence of all the ends of the earth, and of them that are afar off upon the sea." Here, the Reverend cast his eyes upon the five mourners, more out of curiosity about the young lady than concern for their loss. His face, however, was thoroughly disciplined in the ways of condolence.

"Which," he went on, "by his strength setteth fast the mountains, being girded with power: which stilleth the noise of the seas, the noise of the waves, and the tumult of the people. They also that dwell in the uttermost parts are afraid at thy tokens: thou makest the out-goings of the morning and evening to rejoice." Why should he care about Ben? John thought; he never did care. A regular psalm salad, Ten thought, looking covertly at John. "Thou visitest the earth, and waterest it: thou greatly enrichest it with the river of God, which is full of water: thou preparest them corn, when thou hast so provided for it. Thou waterest the ridges thereof abundantly; thou settlest the furrows thereof: thou makest it soft with showers: thou blessest the springing thereof. Thou crownest the year with thy goodness and thy paths drop fatness. They drop upon the pastures of the wilderness: and the little hills rejoice on every side. The pastures are clothed with flocks; the valleys also are covered with corn; they also sing. Blessed be God, which hath not turned away my prayer, nor his mercy from me. God be merciful unto us, and bless us; and cause his face to shine upon us.

Make haste unto me, O God; thou art my help and my deliverer; O Lord, make no tarrying." Why do they seem so angry? Edna wondered; are they angry because he died? Is that what happens when someone dies? Do people get angry first? Were they angry at the Reverend? He did sound smug, but then anyone would sound smug, at least they would to her, talking about goodness and mercy with a body lying between himself and his audience.

"And now," continued the Reverend, "we commend this soul, O God, into thy keeping, knowing thy mercy is infinite, and he shall rest in the valley of peace for ever and ever." That's all? John asked himself; usually he improves an occasion like this by taking off three more from apoplexy and sunstroke.

"Shall I accompany you home?" the Reverend asked, pressing Ten's hand. How limp and wet he always is, Ten thought, repulsed; like a leaf caught under other leaves all winter. That clamminess goes through any glove. "No, no," she answered politely; "our grief shall be private." "I do understand," Reverend Pierce whispered, looking at each one. "Now," his syrupy voice poured on, "there is one question I must ask. The place of burial. It *is* to be the family plot? Not many sites will remain." Edna felt John's body go stiff. She understood it now; the minister did not want the hired help buried with the family. That was what they had been angry about.

"Reverend Pierce," she asked sweetly; "I come from another neighborhood altogether and do not entirely understand the customs here." What is she talking about? the minister wondered; she makes this sound like Tanganyika. *Why* is she talking? "Do your parishioners here pay their pew rent promptly? I ask as a minister's daughter." Well, the nasty little thing! Ten thought. The minister flushed; the Steeles, if they did not attend the church, at least supported it. "Mr. Steele," he said, "I shall see to all details of maintenance myself." They stood silently while two workmen placed three stones together into the shape of a cross; they were excellent masons. They worked quickly. I shall be glad to get out of here, Ten thought, before the flowers wither. "Thank you, Mr. Pierce," John said, pressing a bill into his palm.

The five of them turned, retracing their steps to the

carriage. As soon as they were around the bend, as soon as the white church steeple was out of sight, John exploded. "That must have been one of his bargain sermons," he raved; "he would have gone on for hours if Ben had been one of the gentry." "Well, and what did you expect him to do, John? I thought he was mercifully short about it. He couldn't very well read the whole Book of Revelation." "He didn't have to pick a text that made it so obvious." "Made *what* so obvious?" "That he was burying a farm boy of no consequence." "For pity sake!" Ten flared; "he was quoting from the Psalms of David, and a generous number of them there were, too. I thought it was very appropriate." "You did not; you know you didn't. 'It is to be the family plot?' " John mimicked; " 'not pauper's field?' " "You're going to work yourself up, and over nothing, too, I must say." John slammed his fist down on the edge of the carriage. "A lot of good that will do," Ten said.

"And what's wrong with the Book of Revelation?" John asked, determined to quarrel; "there are some beautiful passages in it; God knows, he's droned them out before." "Well, then," Ten said, out of patience, "perhaps he was remembering the two of you as children; he *might* have chosen the psalms of repentance." "You were no angel yourself." "Is this going to stop?" his sister asked; "I feel dreadful enough without any more help from you. I'm sorry," she told Amos; "we shouldn't subject you to this." "That's all right, ma'am; I know it's because of your feelings." John slumped down.

"If it isn't sacrilegious," Ten told him, "I'd like to stop this carriage at the postal station. Who knows what might have come." "Go ahead. Get out and dance for all I care." Edna shook her head at Ten. "Well, I'll be glad enough to get out of *your* sight, if only for a few minutes. A fine tribute it is to the dead, going on like this." Ten sprang up and was out of the wagon and into the post office before they realized she was leaving. "The woman's part mosquito," John mumbled. Edna kept quiet.

"I don't like that minister much," she finally said; she could see Ten approaching with a letter. She wanted to forestall any argument over whether or not it ought to be read on the drive back from the burying ground. "It's from Hal," she told them, climbing back in and taking her seat. "Hal?" John asked, incredulous. "Hal. Your brother. He's coming back." "When?" "Tuesday. Five days from now. Hal," Ten explained to Edna, "is our brother. He's been working in the California orange orchards." "He's our *feebleminded* brother," John corrected. "He is *not* feebleminded; he is just slow." "Anyone that slow is called feebleminded." "At any rate, Edna," Ten spoke through him, "he will be here, if nothing prevents, on Tuesday." "Is that a good thing?" "He can take Ben's place; nothing could be smoother. Actually, that man there is very attached to his idiot brother." "I didn't say he was an idiot; he's feebleminded." "I'm not an expert on such distinctions." "Or on much of anything." Why don't they keep quiet? Edna wondered; why don't they just keep quiet? The carriage rolled on. The hills were brilliantly green under the flaming blue sky. Hidden streams sparkled just out of sight; another turn of the road brought the white church spire back into view. No, that would be worse, much worse if they kept quiet, Edna decided. Ten and John bickered on all the way home. Then they went to their own rooms. Edna saddled up the bay and left for the woods.

By the time she was back, John had calmed down considerably. "There doesn't seem to be much sickness about these days," he commented ironically; "we ought to go over to Fitchburg and see that Mrs. Whitemore of yours." "She'll be surprised." "I don't know about that; she looked as if she kept her eyes open day and night, and her ears, too." Edna kept seeing Ben's face behind the green flickering leaves of the woods; she decided to continue as if nothing unusual had happened. "It's a little late to start today," she said, looking up at the sky; "the weather should hold until tomorrow." "Then would you like to go down to the river and row? It's a nice river; the trees meet over it almost all of the way for two miles. They're trembling aspens, mostly. They'll be really something to look at in this light. There are a lot of frogs down there, too," he remembered; "it's a frog breeding ground. Once, when we went down the river on a raft, an enormous green frog was sitting in the mud and Ben decided to poke at it with a stick. We were terrified it would jump onto the raft and pitch us in; we weren't much as swimmers then."

"The water is nice; I'd like to go." "Horseback?" "I'd like that." "You're not tired of riding?" "That's never happened yet, although it might if I chanced to meet with an accident before starting out." They both grinned. "Hal, what is he like?" Edna asked as they walked over to the stable, hands clasped. "Saintly." "Saintly?"

"He's like a child, a good three-year-old child. But he can be hard; he does the strangest things. The trouble is, he doesn't know they're strange. One winter he took to going to every funeral in the county; he was too small to go alone, so he dragged Ten with him. I never saw her in a worse state. It was all our parents could do to get her mind out of the earth. Or he decides to sit in the cemetery and talk to the dead because they have no one else to talk to. That summer, some little boys tried to frighten him off by popping out from behind stones, but he ran after them because *he* wanted to talk to them. He wound up scaring them silly. Then one year he went to every church festival and baptism. Father began to get awfully itchy about the next life; he had a superstitious streak. I suppose he thought Hal's behavior signified something or other. Still, all things taken together, I guess I'll be happy to see him."

The surface of the river was so still it was disturbed only by water snakes and an occasional gnat. The rocks looked close enough to touch; they seemed just beneath the boat's surface, but the river was a deep one. Every now and then a small striped bass jumped out of the water and back again; sometimes Edna could see it start up from the bottom, fly into the air, and plunge back down. John had pulled in the oars, and they lay in the bottom of the boat watching the sunlight play with the leaves. "They have such beautiful veins," she said, reaching out to stop one moving past with the gentle current; "it's hard to believe they're not alive." "What, the leaves?" John asked lazily; "they are alive." "No, the way we are; the trees, too. They look prehistoric, with those trunks wrinkled like elephant skin, as if they were once some kind of relation to those giants." "As if they were elephant trunks that rooted," he teased; "maybe that's what happens when you bury an elephant." "Elephant seeds. Pack lots of trunks, we need a forest," Edna said.

They began laughing; the boat drifted on. A few old

beige leaves, swept into the river by the water's flow, drifted by them, aged by the fall and the winter. Edna swatted at one of them. "Don't tip us over," John warned. "It's so cool here, as if something with cold blood were breathing in and out. Something nice. Like the frogs." "Like the frogs," John repeated; "Edna, if the countryside doesn't decide to pop with babies tomorrow, do you really want to go to Fitchburg? There's nothing to prevent. Old Dr. Houston, he's only too happy to take over and drive up the mortality rate." "I'd like that, I would," she answered dreamily, swatting at another leaf, spiraling its way past the boat. "Edna, don't tip us over." "Oh, I'd never do that," she said.

I wonder why they named me Edna, she thought, staring into the long looking glass of her armoire. It always makes me think of eggs, Eds, plain people, fathers who wanted sons. She examined herself closely. I don't look like an Edna, she thought, relieved; but Virginia, she looks like Virginia. Six o'clock and no one had yet thundered up in the yard. We should be gone by six, Edna thought; we had better hurry. That would give them plenty of time to stop and walk the horses and water them, and talk, and no one around but the two of them and a few indifferent, beautiful birds. Dr. Houston was peacefully asleep in the extra room at the end of the second floor. I suppose they'll be opening up the third floor now, Edna thought, and the extra wing now that Hal's coming. And Lord knows who else, she thought, alarmed; she really knew very little about the Steele family. In the back of her mind, she sensed the approaching presence of a wedding, which would mean the arrival of her mother. Ten had already made it clear she intended *some* kind of wedding, although, she reassured John, she wasn't sending out two hundred calling cards like Mrs. Evans in Chatham.

Now, Edith, Edna thought, that name suits my mother; it sounds as if it were the original name for a corset. She thought about that again. A corset with stays and stocking fastenings hanging down over an attached skirt. The last time I saw one of those was on a headless dressmaker's form in the window of a Manhattan shop. She smiled, happy. It had been such a long time since Manhattan shops. Her mother's presence, though; that would spoil her wedding; well, not spoil it, but her presence certainly wouldn't improve it. She buttoned the top of her collar and looked at her pocket watch. Six-ten, she thought excitedly; in an hour, we'll be on the path going through the real forest. In two hours, we'll be near the river, riding along it. In five hours, we'll be in Fitchburg, and, she sighed, at this time tomorrow we'll be back; today will be over. Why, she asked herself, was she already annoyed with the innocent world because today, which had yet to begin, was already, in her own mind, coming to an end?

Ten watched them start off from the doorway. John started on ahead, and Edna appeared to follow, when suddenly she galloped madly around the corner of the house; John saw her from the corner of his eye, wheeled around, galloping after. The two of them emerged on the other side of the house, galloped in front of it, and started straight off down the path, waving back to Ten. Mischief, every inch of her, Ten thought; I hope it doesn't wear off with time. Well, and why should it? She was up here to get over her father's death, and before the month was up she was ready to be married and dragging that melancholy mule John around like an affectionate puppy. There's never any point in worrying over the future, she thought; I used to wish I could see into it, but it gets here fast enough for me now; too fast.

She went back into the dark of the house for her white parasol. Perhaps she should take a walk; it would be good for her. She started out purposefully, but as soon as she was out of sight of the windows, changed her mind and circled back to the house, going a little further into the woods and into the clearing, where the hammock was, and the rolled-up blinds of mosquito netting John had attached to the frame he built around it. There didn't seem to be any mosquitoes about today. She had something to think about. She swung in the hammock for what seemed hours, her fingers running over and over the deckled paper of the letter thrust deep into her pocket. Well, what *was* she going to do about Edith? She had to be invited to the wedding. Should she tell Edna about Edith's letter? Should she show it to her? Should she read it again? She would read it again; she ought to.

That way she wouldn't have to make up her mind, at least not right away. Or if she made it up, she'd make it up more sensibly. She continued swinging in the hammock. She was getting nice and sleepy; the hours were melting together like wax. When she woke up, the sun was almost overhead, but, she realized hopelessly, her fingers were still holding on to the edges of Edith's letter. Well, there was nothing for it. She took the letter out of her pocket. What had Edith been trying to do? she wondered, peering at it without her spectacles; make it long enough to take up a whole coach? She had never seen so many stamps on one letter. It should have been sent express, Ten thought, turning it over in the speckled light. She was running out of excuses; she was going to have to read it.

"Dearest Ten," the letter began, "you must excuse me for writing such a *long* letter, but it is a rainy day, and I am here alone in my room. You know I don't mean that the way it sounds, but I am going to have a chance to pretend you really are here, instead of somewhere I have never seen, in Williamsville. That is closer than Kansas; I suppose that is something. By now," the neat hand and brown ink continued, "you have probably gotten to know Edna rather well. I have no idea how much she has confided in you, but the truth of it is, Ten, I have no more idea what to do with her than I ever did with those geometry problems we had when we were in school. The truth is, I don't believe Edna likes me very much, and that is not an easy thing for me to say about my own child, or about myself as a mother. She preferred her father; he was deeper, and you know I was never very deep. Ten, the truth is, I am the same woman I always was, a goldfish in an ornamental pool, like the one in front of this hotel, and I like the gleam and the richness of the surface, swimming with the other fish of society. Edna, of course, hates such things and thinks my head is full of echoes. Her heroine used to be some lunatic in England, who returned from India and took to wearing Indian shawls and men's pants under her perfectly normal basques. I think her name was Cameron. At any rate, she turned her entire estate into a refuge for artists and they drew each other and wrote about each other, and suffered together. I believe they did a great deal of suffering. Edna used to go on about the beauty of their sufferings; of course, she had never suffered a single day in her life, but she kept telling me there was a magnificence about it. I don't even remember her running a high fever, not even with the typhoid. And then, when I met Mr. Siddons, who is such an excellent artist, she took one look at him and hated him. She is a very inconsistent child. Or perhaps the truth is, had I taken in every artist in Manhattan, it wouldn't have pleased her, because I was doing it, and I was such a goldfish.

"It will be the end of whatever family is left when I marry Mr. Siddons. Now, Ten dear, please do not be too shocked to find I am already planning to remarry, and my husband is only a month dead. Of course, I shall wait out the year and stay in mourning for Edna's sake, and to be honest, for my own. The judgment of society is very harsh. You were wise to escape to the country, dear friend, although at the time I thought you would only be cutting yourself off from everything and not getting anything in return, but we never really were alike.

"Do you remember Nellie Aldrich? I still keep her last letter with me; it was the letter in which she told me she expected to marry. It has been all notes from Nellie since then. I have no idea why I keep it, but perhaps you do, Ten; you were always wiser about such things. And do you remember at that time we thought her marrying was such a mistake? I guess we weren't entirely wise, were we? Oh, Ten, do you remember those times we had? They were pretty good ones, I'd say, and I don't think it's just remembering that gilded the lily, either. But it changed so with all our marrying, and yet we were so *restless* with each other, although I sometimes think I'll never love anyone as much as I loved you and Nellie; those were such young times and everything was so new for us. So today, it must be because of the rain, I feel selfish treasuring Nellie's letter, because you loved her, too. And it seems to me she might as well be dead; I never see her or hear from her anymore, unless it's to get a birth announcement, and of course, those have finally stopped coming. Well, and I suppose it could be worse, since she produced one of something every year, and if it's not children now, it's grandchildren, and regular as winter. I will copy out the letter, and of course, you don't have to bother reading it. I will write it out on a separate sheet, so you can keep it if you want it, or throw it out if you don't, but as I say, Ten, it has always been so important to me, and I don't know why."

"September 30, 1841. Dear friend Edith, Mrs. Thompson's windows are hung with the usual display of gay ribbons and flowers. Mr. Preston is at his old stand at the corner, as mild and clever as ever, but I can't say I've gotten used to Dudley yet; minister's families are such moving planets, you know, and now I'm out on my own, who knows how long I'll be here? I have not yet had the occasion to patronize anyone, as I wear my brown bonnet still, the same one I wore at school, only dressed up a bit, but I should be quite discouraged if I should try to get a new one among the many fashions and forms that are displayed daily on the street. I hardly dare to venture out in my old brown one, even with its new ribbons, so I look out the window at the others as if I saw them not, so little do they interest me. Oh, Edith, I see I am getting back to ego again. In my last, I said I would get off it, but I see I have not got off it yet. I tell you, the frost is already beginning to pinch my nose these cold mornings. I start for the shop about seven o'clock every morning and come home for dinner. I can stand the walk very well now, but I dare not look forward to the time when I shall be obliged to go through the snow. I believe I shall burrow down somehow. I have a horrible dread of the winter. Edith, do you not have sleigh rides? If you do, will you tell me about them? I should like to have them to think about while I am in the shop. I was in a sleigh once, but that was to attend the funeral of an old friend, Katherine Pike. She was such a dear, good girl. I miss her very much. She was the last of my shop mates left here that used to work for Mr. Coffin. We worked together almost a year, and we played together when we were children, although not for very long then, either. Mr. Coffin has dead three of the girls that worked for him. Truly 'we are passing away.'

"I have lived rather a monotonous life, haven't I, Edith? I go to the shop as soon as I can see to sew and work till nine day in and day out, or should I say night in and night out? I have not varied a day, have not been into society at all. I suppose that is never the case with you, dear Edith. You are always so popular and your family will see to it that you stay that way. It must be wonderful to have a family that stays in one place, and that can afford to take care of you besides. I tell you, if I had a choice, I would rather fall on pitchfork than marry a minister.

"When Mother was so unwell, I was obliged to be at home every moment I could be spared from the shop, and then Father came down with it, too. If I do not have some recreation soon, I believe my brains will just dry up. I shall not know anything, only how to make a hat and coat. Dear Edith, you asked about my playing. All it is good for now would be to frighten troublesome children out of the shop. Deplorable, is it not? 'No business to have any brains.' Or to play upon the pianoforte, either. I hope you will make all due allowances, for this is not a very interesting letter, I know, and your life is so interesting. I do wish I were in your place, but that is not a Christian thing to say, is it? You know I do not mean to take it from you, or wish you any harm, either. I hope you will make all due allowances when you consider this is from one whose life has been narrowed down to a tailor's shop.

"Dear Edith (as you can see from the date, I put this away and was about to begin to take it over to the post office, when everyone came in at once and wanted their coats and dresses all at the same time, and at night my eyes were too sore to write). Edith, I hope you will forgive me. It has been a beautiful day out of doors, but there have been many conflicting emotions in my own heart, which have, at times, rendered it almost cloudy. 1841! 'Tis gone! 1842 has come! 1842! The pen almost refuses to write it and thought lingers long over this new date, striving to read its unfolded pages. The old year is gone! Gone! And with it some, nay, many have gone too. Gone! Ah! Whither? The word strikes mournfully on the ear, and causes the heartstrings to vibrate almost painfully.

"Some of our friends here have left us. One dear aunt has been widowed and oh how we felt for her lonely situation and mourned for our own loss. Another, who has often been with us, one whom we loved, one in whom

174

we confided, you know who I mean, Edith, dear Minnie, full of youth and the dreams of life, is now sleeping 'neath the clods of the valley. Oh, how little thought I when I parted with her that I should never see her again alive. But she too is gone! She has finished her earthly work and whether life's great, most earnest, most important missions were performed, they are all undone. Her account is all sealed up, *forever sealed.* Oh, may we, dear friend, take warning, and when death meets us may we find our work for eternity *done* and *well done,* Life's missions all performed, and then we can lie peacefully down, having nought to do but 'to die.' Then shall we lie sweetly and rest quietly in peace.

"How many wishes for a happy new year have you had? Though rather late, I will add mine. May many years of happiness be your lot, and though clouds may cross our pathway, as cross it they must, in this world of changes, may they, like the light fleecy clouds of summer, which only enhance the beauty of the surrounding sky, rest lightly there. And, being quickly removed, cause the sun of happiness to appear more brilliant. Afflictions, which you have not yet known, are but blessings in disguise, you know, when we can trace in them our heavenly father's hand.

"Do you go over to the 'river' very often? If you do, do you drive your 'neighbor's' horse? Your *right-hand* neighbor's? What a time we had that evening!

"Edith, I know I promised I would have done with ego, and stop complaining, but I have begun, and well begun, my winter's work of 'climbing that hill.' I work now for Mr. Redfield at the upper part of the village. I have to walk so far and stay till nine o'clock at night. Oh, Edith! If I am *ever* to have a better half, I wish he would come soon and take me out of the shop. I shall die *outright* if I have to work as hard all winter. I have a good mind to say that if Mr. Wagner wants me I shall go to Lowell next spring. What think you? Would you not in my place? He is not a bad man. I think he is a good one, and he does seem to want me, and he is a farmer, you know, and if that wouldn't have me putting roots down, then I would like to know what would. I hope I don't sound sinfully coldhearted to you, but, Edith, I would make him a good wife; no one can say I can't sew, can they? And I have had my experiences with babies, what with Mother producing so many of them.

"One man is so much like another, as I see it, and I would as soon be mistress of my own house and life, as I have not been for some time. I don't know yet what I will do, but presume there is a spare corner somewhere for me to fill, and I might as well fill Mr. Wagner's corner, don't you think I should? I shall strive to occupy it as best I can. 'Tis but little I can do for myself, or for anyone else, either; that little must be well done, otherwise it had better be left undone.

"Now, Edith, don't go on to me about love, because my nose is so frozen it has already fallen in love with Mr. Wagner, and who knows but more of me will not follow its example? And don't think, Edith, I am after a fortune; I shall never have an opportunity for that, as you well know, but Mr. Wagner does well enough, and the farm produces so much of its own food, you could live on it and hardly take anything from the outside world. It would be a change, I tell you. And don't tell me I would freeze on my way to the barn milking the cows, because at least it would be *my* barn and *my* cows. And *my* nose, and *my* decision to freeze it off if I want to. A poor girl doesn't have a choice you know, and at least, I shall not have much to be disappointed about; that is something, don't you think?

"Oh, Edith! I have a horror of having my will read out, as they read out my Aunt Lucy's last week: Ellen (that is your dear friend, of course), set of teaspoons. Hattie, tea set. Frances, cream spoon, butter knife, and large spoon. Alice, two large spoons and salt spoon. Ellen (me again. Don't you think I am rich?), black silk dress (now I have two dresses worth speaking of, after I rip it up and make it over), Hattie, light silk dress, Frances, brown silk dress. Alice, chain. Ellen, the white shawl, ear ornaments to be divided between Ellen, Hattie, and Frances, yearling bay. Hattie, black silk dress to finish and to be used only on special occasions. Hattie to have the old bay, white silk stockings to Fanny, bosom pin to Ellen, unfinished silk to Hattie. Edith! Imagine it! To leave such scrapings after living out your life, I don't think I could stand it. It all seems so pitiful. So you see I have seen the writing on the wall, and even copied it out, and now copied it out again, and I think it is all on the side of Mr. Wagner; you must think so, too, at least for my sake, dear Edith. There are so few I have to even think about me.

"I know your life must make mine seem foreign to you, and you must find me very pathetic, as indeed I am, but if I had such an one as you to understand me, it would make such a difference, Edith, don't you see? You would be a spider web and perhaps I might get caught in one of the dew threads that are so brilliant in the light sometimes, almost like diamonds. That is all I want from you, dear Edith, that you will light up my corner with tales of your life and that you will not forget me, and write to me often, and make me know I am not to be entirely despised, no matter how low I may sink on life's ladder in the material way, though not in the spiritual one, I dearly hope; I give my duties in that line every attention, as I always did, even when we were in school together. Edith, the church bells are warning for the service and I must stop, but I will be down to the post office every day, waiting for your letters. Do you hear from Ten? She wrote me a rather curt epistle last week, but I suppose it is family trouble of some kind, and she never was given to expressing herself in writing. If she has some grudge against me, do let me know about it, because I could not stand it. Dear Edith, I must go. You must be happy this year, Edith, if only for my sake. Goodbye, dear friend. I sign myself as ever, your affectionate friend, Nellie."

"Ten, dear, how she did envy me! And I suppose I thought there was reason enough for it, for a thought never entered my head, unless it was something bad enough as a mosquito buzzing around my ear and annoying me while I was at the pianoforte. That was a sad event, wouldn't you say? And to tell the truth, I haven't had my share of tragedies, and somehow, I know I never will, either. For one thing, I don't take other people's troubles to heart, not even yours, Ten, and it's not because I don't want to, but I can't; I'm not made in that way. I like being with happy people (not that I mean you are not), even flighty, as long as they're always laughing and going somewhere, in and out of one carriage, in and out of one ball dress. That is my idea of heaven, and I seem to have found it on this earth.

"But then, when I think about it on a rainy day (as it is now) I sometimes feel the tables are rather turned, at least where Nellie and I are concerned. Well, we all know the rest of her followed right straight after her nose, and how she does love Mr. Wagner! And those children! People in Lowell talk about how many of them there are, but they love her. They do love her, and she loves them, and they talk to her about what happens to them, almost as if we were a friend. I often think it is because they are all so religious, but I know I am only fooling myself there, 'pulling the wool over my own eyes,' as Nellie used to say. Ten, if Nellie had had only *one* daughter, her daughter would not feel toward her the way mine feels toward me. I tell you, Edna could barely stand to say goodbye to me at the depot when she left for the mountains, and it wasn't because she expected to miss me, either. I feel so sad about her sometimes. I have failed her, you know, but the worst part of it, Ten, is that I could not have been any other way and never will change, either, so I cannot expect Edna to do more. I am just the same as I always was, and always will be.

"And after all I have done to Edna just by being myself, Ten, how is she going to take on about my marrying Mr. Siddons? He *is* a great artist. You would think so, too, if you could see his sculptures, but she treats him as if he would fail in an application for mason's work. The way she looked at me when I was in his presence made me feel quite as if I had fallen right into a puddle of mud. And if I did make an error in marrying Edmund? Well, he must have had a part in the mistake, too. And he was so morbid, Ten. We would be sitting at the table, before the sun was really up, and what did he want to talk about? A coroner's inquest. You remember from chemistry, I always had a weak stomach, and time did not improve it; well, not enough for coroner's inquests. And how was I to know he would go into criminal law and be so sensational in his ways? He was always in the papers, or his clients were, if you could call those creatures that; he had a positive passion for taking the most grotesque crime ever committed and then defending the villainous creature (believe me, the person would repulse any other living thing), as if his own life depended on it. But when we were married, I thought he would be just like Father, and content himself with quiet cases; well, quiet in their contents. You know what I mean. A corporation hardly ever turns up on the floor with its throat cut by an ax.

"Well, and I never had any religious faith to speak of, not like Nellie, but I did have such faith in people of our society, and those trials, they almost destroyed me. There were whole weeks when nothing felt solid under my feet, and at the same time, I would look down at the ground, to see if it had really turned to glass, and me in the middle of it. Oh, I was really frightened, I tell you. I didn't sleep for nights at a time. I saw everyone we had met at the theater or the opera going home and checking on his hoard of arsenic or Rat Away. They used to get hold of it during the summers and carry it home with them, and then when they came over to our house, I saw them pouring some of it into the ice pitcher. Well, you can't imagine what it was like, seeing a murderess under every party dress and a maniac killer in every swallowtail.

"There were even times when I would see Edmund looking into his closet and start to think to myself: Does he have something hidden in there? Is he planning to cut my throat and then tell the board of inquiry one of his clients killed his poor wife out of revenge? I think I was entirely insane for some time. And through it all, there was Nellie, writing me all those letters about how wonderful my life was.

"I suppose, Ten, don't you, that must be why I loved her letters so; they convinced me I was really living the kind of life she imagined for me. And what good would it have done to write her and tell her about Edmund and his hatchets and his axes and hanging ropes and pistols, and his arsenic in his closet, just waiting to go into my coffee. Or a morbid fear I had, one whole summer, when I was convinced he was going to pour lye in my washbowl and blind me altogether. I even went so far as to ask him to put his hand in and test the temperature for me, and it was spring water. I couldn't stop myself, even though I know I appeared ridiculous.

179

"So was it any wonder I began to take more and more satisfaction thinking about all the material comforts she used to go on about so? Her aunt's will made an impression on me, I can tell you. Almost as terrible, I think, as it did on Nellie herself. Well, you know how hard it is for me to keep my mind on any subject for very long, and I must have concluded (or so it seems to me now, copying it out for you, it makes it all seem so much clearer; as if writing it out in my own hand made it seem as if I had written it myself, I can squeeze into her place a bit more, even if it is late in the day for it, as you would say), the material things were important, a real legacy to leave behind. I must have thought I was building some kind of monument and the family that lived after me would have something safe and happy to remember me by, not just one white shawl and one black shawl and one pin and one unfinished dress.

"Then it came out Edna didn't care about those things. When we were up in the country, I used to think she'd manage to find an old cracker peddler to marry and shiver over a fire with for the rest of her days. She used to wait for his visits and buy practically every cracker he had, even if they were blue with mold, and then she never ate them. She just threw them out. Oh, I tell you, that made me furious! But I thought she would stop when she found out she had no more of her allowance left for those horse rides she liked so much, and those boating excursions on the lake steamers. I forgot about Edmund, though; he always gave her more money than she knew what to do with. That was one of the first things he always asked about when he left the house. He might forget to kiss *me* goodbye, but he always asked Edna if she had enough money to go about properly, and if she didn't jump up and down and complain she was so burdened down with money she could hardly move, out would come two bills, and into her hand they went, and into her pocket, and I never knew how much he gave her. But I suppose she would have needed to respect me before she bowed to my authority even in little things. From the time she was eight, I knew she was counting the days until her father's provisions for her would make her financially independent. He had such confidence in her judgment.

"I think he was clouded there, don't you? Even though he usually had such a fine mind and could read a person with one look. But no matter what I told him about how outrageously she behaved, how cruel she was, and how rude, it just blew from him; it didn't even *settle* on his skin the way bees settle on some people but don't bite them. I would have felt better if he had at least let the things I said settle on him for a few minutes. He could have waited until he was on the street to brush off my annoying dust, but he wouldn't even bother that much, not if I were criticizing Edna.

"Of course, if she was ill, or almost sick, or too tired, or unhappy at school, that was another tale altogether. His whole practice could fly straight out the window and everyone could hang for all he cared until he found out about the state of her headache. Headache! He came home from court during a recess one day to check on the progress of her headache when he knew perfectly well she'd gotten it crawling around under the table trying to find out what we were talking about, and I thought it served her right when she banged her head on one of the legs of the chairs. Well, you can see what I was up against. Instead of being punished, she was rewarded.

"Well, life is an odd thing and I have never been able to make much sense out of it, not for myself, anyway. There was Nellie in Lowell (finally rooted in one place), with her letters almost convincing me I had something to be happy about, and there I was on Cedar Street in that big town house wondering what would have become of me if I'd had a harder life and wouldn't I have been a better person for it. It's no use your writing to me to say I certainly would have been, for that's a conclusion I've come to myself, but life won't oblige you with tragedies any more than it will with happiness. If I died tonight, Edna wouldn't suffer over it, or mourn, as Nellie mourned, even for people she barely knew. She would be sorry, of course. She hates to see even a wild mouse die. She used to work herself up into hysterics if she found a dead chipmunk in the meadow.

"I'll never forget that. There we were at the Mountain View Resort, sitting on the benches and chairs under the trees, everyone sitting quietly, thinking their own thoughts, if they had any, and I presume they all had more than I did, in our flowered muslin dresses, the more adventurous ones sitting right on the moss; everyone was so quiet we looked natural as mushrooms, and there came Edna, tearing up to me, her face *covered, covered* with a sheet of tears, this dead chipmunk in her hands. It was stiff, and its eyes wide open and glazed, and I screamed at her, I was so disgusted, 'Throw that thing away,' and hit it out of her hand with my parasol. For all I know it might have died of rabies, and your father had told me that even a cut in the skin and a lick from a rabid animal, or a drop of saliva, and you had a case of rabies on your hands.

"And Edna! The way she looked at me! I'll never forget that look. As if I had gone out there and stabbed the chipmunk through the heart with the point of my parasol, and then she wouldn't talk to me for the rest of the time we stayed there. Later I got used to that, but I was much younger then, and I was embarrassed to death. 'Do you want a roll, Edna?' and no answer. And then she would dive across me and take it herself, or ask the gentleman on her side if *he* would please pass the rolls. That summer was a nightmare. Her father mercifully sent us out to the country while he carried out his trial for abortion, and my own daughter put me on trial. I know I always had a self-regarding streak, but I had reason to feel sinned against that summer, don't you think? I can't always have been wrong.

"And now, Mr. Siddons. Ten, I must have your advice. I cannot bear to begin a new life under Edna's stare, but I must have her at the wedding, and what is she to do but live with us? It will be harder than life with Edmund. At least we had some times worth speaking of, at least before she reached a certain age. And, Ten, you know I never intended to have only one child, and I remember, when the trouble started in with Edna, thinking, I'll have better luck with the next one. But she was all there was.

"Ten, I am not going to lie to her, any more than I am to you. I've had enough of lies, white or black, genteel or vulgar. It is hardly to be a marriage of passion, no, not at my age. I have accepted it; I shall never have a marriage of passion. How Nellie's cold calculations turned into passion has always been a great mystery to me, and very unfair to me it seemed, too. She wasn't even hoping for it. But I don't think I can hold up under Edna's criticism. She always makes me feel just the way I did the first time I went to a ball and was so sure I would trip right in the middle of a quadrille, in the middle of a fancy figure, in the center of the floor, and lie there like a puppet with cut strings, while everyone howled as if it were something out of *Punch and Judy,* and not the most important day in my life. I am as self-regarding as ever, Ten, and I have had time to think about it, and I know she would not hate me as much as she does if I had not hurt her in some dreadful way, but I have to protect myself, don't I? She is like arsenic to me, and she is my own daughter. I still love her as much as I did when she went toddling around crashing into everything, at least as much as I can love anyone. I don't have many illusions about that.

"Those magazine columns that go on about advice to husbands, and how they should not marry a doll of fashion who will be good for nothing after marriage except to display as one would an object on a shelf, and then what, after the passions cool (the man's, I mean)? Well, they might as well mention me by name—if the law didn't forbid it. But in spite of it, I *am* to marry Mr. Siddons and what am I to do? If I send Edna away, I shall not have a peaceful moment, and as if I didn't have myself to deal with, the whole street would get together to sing my condemnations.

"If she lives with us, the three of us will be miserable. I know Mr. Siddons wants no part of my daughter, and I can't blame him, either. If I live to be older than Methuselah, and believe me, Ten, that is now the worst fate I can imagine for myself, I'll never forget the scene she made in his studio. If a person could have perished from mortification, you'd have read of my demise in the papers before Edna reached you.

"Well, Ten, what more is there for me to say? I have wearied your poor eyes beyond all endurance already. I can see the ridges deepen in your nose as I write. You were the youngest one in the school to wear spectacles, and you were so cheerful about it, too. *I* would have taken on dreadfully, and have been run down by a horse trying to crush my spectacles in my reticule. That might have been better for everyone, don't you think so?

"I think of Nellie so much now, how she wrote she would finish her earthly work here and lie down for eternity, her work done and well done, life's missions all performed. I chant those words to myself sometimes, as if some of her goodness might rub off on me, but I am pretty free of virtue, I guess. 'Then shall we lie sweetly and rest quietly in peace.' Well, Ten, we shall all lie down, but I don't have much hope for peace if there's anything coming after. If there's any door in my tomb, I won't be in any hurry to open it.

"Well, I had better end with this sheet. It's not the bell ringing for church that's stopping me here, I assure you, but the dinner bell, and I apologize for this writing; it's slanting up the page more and more. As Nellie used to say, if writing uphill means you will be rich, what do you think I will be, a millionaire? I should have practiced writing the other way. How straight your lines are, but *you* should write uphill, that is, if Nellie was right in her saying. I expect you will write and tell me what you think pretty soon, won't you, and don't think I'm not dreading it, but tell me the truth of what you think; don't hold anything back. As you always used to say, you'd have to shoot me with a cannon to make a dent, and my skin hasn't gotten any thinner. I must stop and primp and fuss for dinner, even though I don't know or care about a soul in the place, but vanity will be obeyed. Goodbye, dear Ten. I know you can manage Edna, but I don't envy you the job. I cannot express my appreciation violently enough. Your loving friend, Edith."

Edith, Edna, Ten sighed; what a mess of chowder. She swung in the hammock, thinking. Yes, she decided, when Edna comes back with John, I'm going to show her this letter. Shallowness is no crime; no, it isn't. There are far worse things. I can't think of what they are at the moment, but I know there are. Oh yes! Edith is not evil. Her intentions are always good. She was *always* a lovable powder puff. You can't turn a woman like that into an Aristotle or a saint. Edna has to learn more tolerance, especially if she's going to marry my brother and live here among the Munyans and the Westons. They're all very amusing to her right now, but they're still a novelty, after all. And she only sees the outlines, but the fine lines—they'll show up soon enough. And if she becomes a mother? This should give her something to think about, she meditated, holding the letter up over her head, between herself and the light. It had better give her something to think about, she decided grimly. *I'll* see that it gives her something to think about.

"How far are we from Fitchburg?" Edna asked; she had ridden up abreast of John and their horses now stood still under the quivering trees. "How far are we from Fitchburg?" John repeated with amusement. "We've only been riding forty-five minutes, and you keep stopping me to talk about everything under the sun." "Well, if you're bored." "I'm not." "I'm tired," Edna announced. "You are?" "I am." "And I suppose that means you want to lie down on that green grass in that nice little meadow there?" he asked, pointing. "Oh, yes, that would be such a help." "It's certainly just what I would prescribe for a serious case of exhaustion." "If you don't want to stop," she said, "I can always force myself to sit up." "I wouldn't want you to risk a winding path like this sound asleep in your saddle." "I don't think I would like that either." "Then I guess we had better stop for your nap," John said, alighting, helping her down.

They tethered their horses on the far side of the meadow and lay down near the border of the forest where the trees cast their heaviest shadows on the grass. "Well, well," John smiled, "here we are again. I suppose you know I won't need much persuasion this time." His hand was already opening the top button of her habit. "No, it doesn't seem you will," she answered, smiling happily. "I do believe," John said, pausing, "you're almost contented when you're with me." "Almost? Almost? I don't know where you got that idea. Probably you've guessed how much of my time I spend plotting to raid your camp and carry you off alone." "Idiot, there's no sense in both of us plotting." "No; we should combine our efforts and have a unified battle plan." "Sensible," John said, continuing to loosen her bodice; "I will be so relieved when I can just come into the same room with you at night, and close the door, and get into the same bed, and get it all over with." "Perhaps we could tunnel

through the walls somehow; I mean, until the happy day."
John had already slid down in the grass, his body on
hers. I could kiss this face forever, he thought. "You
know," he told her, stopping, "I'm as addicted to you as
I used to be to brown maple sugar." "That sounds
delicious, but not very romantic." She drew him back
down toward her.

"This is getting to be a habit," he said a while later.
"I hope you're not thinking of breaking it." "I'd rather
give up my pipe; and this time, I didn't even bother your
dress." "It's your remarkable medical training"; Edna
beamed, stroking his hair." "It will be your first wedding
night; aren't you afraid?" "It will be my *only* wedding
night; oh yes, I'm afraid. I'm afraid you'll have a change
of mind." "Not very likely." He wanted to touch her
hair, her face, her body; even her wrists, he thought,
were lovable, but he was hypnotized by her touch.

This is love, he thought in some astonishment. And the
truly amazing thing is that I like her. I also like her. "I
like you," he said aloud. "I thought so; I wish I could
say the same." In spite of himself, he felt his brows furrowing. "You *are* fun to tease; I've never met anyone
who is so much fun to tease. You take everything so
seriously. I'm going to have to watch every word I say."
"Don't you dare do it; you're better than a novel." "But
am I better than a medical journal?" "Only time will tell
that," he answered; it wasn't easy to sound serious. Edna
turned over and began tickling him furiously. He managed
to lie still for a few seconds, then began rolling on the
grass trying to escape. "Say stop!" Edna demanded. No
answer. "Ha!" she giggled. "Stop!" John finally shouted.
"Ha ha ha," she laughed, tickling harder. Now John
pounced on her. "Stop, stop, stop!" she screamed before
he had a chance to ask. "Hmmmm; you're reckless; I
thought you didn't have a ticklish nerve in your body."
"Oh, I'm *very* ticklish," she gasped. "Don't do it again!"
she shrieked, jumping up in terror, and running toward
her horse. He went after her; they mounted and rode on
to Fitchburg.

"Well, there it is," John said at last, pointing down
from the crest of the high hill. The little town lay nestled
far down in the valley below. From this distance, it
looked enchanted, the white wood houses scattered amidst

the greenery, the flowering shrubbery and trees, colorful clouds settling against the hospitable earth. The church, at what must have been the end of the town's main street, bisecting it, rose gracefully, step by step, into the air, its beautiful white steeple immaculately entering the sky. "Things always look so beautiful from a distance," Edna murmured. "It's not only the eye that works that way," John said, thinking aloud; "memory is like that. The further away things move, the more beautiful they get. No matter how ugly they were at the time. Memory: there must be something, a kind of chemical or gas that's part of it, that envelops what happened, no matter what it was, so that just the passing of time, just because of that, what is over and done becomes beautiful. No matter what it was. It's nature's medicine; yes," he went on, more to himself than to her, "that's really what it is." "But some people are so tortured by their memories." "I don't think so; I think people like that enjoy their torture, so it comes to the same thing in the end. It's just that they find the pain beautiful. They get used to it; they wouldn't know where they were without it. The church knows that," he said, looking over at her.

Edna, who had been looking down at the town, had by now located two more churches, each considerably more modest than the one which had first seized their attention. "Yes," she said, "three churches in such a little town. Most people find life so painful, and they find comfort in a man nailed to the cross. It's curious. I should think more about it. Of course, he did it for them, but I don't see why that's as important as everyone says it is." How her mind snaps through things, he thought, almost as if it could accelerate time, as if it operated in some kind of space where there was no gravity to weigh it down. This too, he reflected, was something new to him, more than being able to say what he thought. He had done that before, but now when he said what he thought, someone understood. So easily and so quickly, that was the remarkable thing. No, I don't think I understand her that way, he thought, troubled; at least not yet. "Race you down," Edna said suddenly, digging her heels into the horse's side. John's horse flew after hers and passed ahead into a cloud of dust. It seemed as if they were standing still and the trees were moving. What

187

a strange thing perception was. A huge tree was lying straight across the path. "Jump! Jump!" John thundered back at her, his own mount rising easily into the air. With relief, he looked back and saw Edna sailing easily over. Serepta would not ride. She was ashamed; that was what it had turned out to be. She had learned to ride with her brothers and rode like a man. But before he found that out, he had everything but a doll's dogcart out in the yard for her use, stubbornly hoping *this* fear was one she would overcome; if she had done so, it would have been a beginning.

"Center Street," she said, "three Center Street." "Um, before we go," John stammered; "before we go, I want you to agree we can stay out of doors the whole time." "Out of doors? whatever for?" "It's a theory of mine." "A theory that all social visits should be conducted outside the house?" Silence; stubborn silence. "John, answer me!" "It has to do with a theory I have," he said uneasily; "I think your friend has a contagious illness." "You think consumption is contagious? I never heard of such a thing." "Nevertheless, it is one of my theories." He was embarrassed, pained. "All right," Edna agreed; "if it's one of your theories." "I suppose you're humoring me?" "No," she answered slowly; "I believe in you, that must be it, because when I *think* about it"—she stopped—*"then* it seems absolutely insane. But I believe you must be right, in some way." "No one else in the whole country agrees with you," he said bitterly. "Well, John, what do you expect? Even Christ began with one disciple. I think." "I think you should reread your Bible," he said, reining up in front of a large well-kept village house; "this looks like the right place."

Like the white picket fence which divided the house's yard from its neighbor and went around the corner of the street, the dwelling was painted an immaculate white. The shutters gleamed green. The front of the house was square, the door set between two bay windows which reached up to the roof, and on either side of the main structure, a small wing. On the house's left side, near the street's corner, was a large open porch. The side door retreated behind the pillar supporting a little roof, forming another small porch; a little wooden swing nestled against the wall. "Comfortable," Edna commented. "Yes, but there are no flowers in the yard." "No, there aren't," Edna realized, startled. "It's always a bad sign when there are no flowers in the yard," he said.

Good Lord, Edna thought, he does notice everything. I wonder what he can see in me. Well, something, anyhow. Maybe he's one of those people who like pain, and I cause him more than anyone else he knows. No, she concluded, as John handed her down, I'm only thinking this way because I'm worrying about Mother coming to the wedding. I don't know what I expect her to do, she thought as they tied the horses to the hitching post in front of the house; she's not a witch out of a fairy tale. She's not going to poison me with an apple. Or him. Or Ten. The trouble is, really, I'd like to poison her. But that's not true, either. It's Mr. Siddons I'd like to poison. Rat Away. That's what Father's clients always used. Why should I want to poison him? If I wait long enough, Father will become a happy memory. I hope I shall live to see that day.

A small woman in black flew out the side door of the house; she seemed moving faster than a tornado. "Edna! Edna!" Virginia was jumping up and down, kissing her all over her cheek; "why, I didn't think you were coming at all! I had absolutely given up! You were writing *letters*," she scolded excitedly, "and well," she went on jabbering, "I thought, if she's writing letters from Williamsville to Fitchburg, that little body has no intention in the world of appearing here. Oh, Edna, I'm *so* glad to see you. It's been worse than a jail!" She finally paused for breath. "You've left off mourning!" she exclaimed. "We decided I was too young." "Too young! They'd hang me from the flagpole here if I didn't dress every inch of myself in black. Oh, the long faces if one single blond curl escapes from my bonnet; oh, I tell you, they think I'm a positive disgrace, and all because I don't walk around the house with tears streaming down my face day and night. They'd be happy if I died of grief, just fell down in the hall and died of sorrow. Well, it's my own fault, coming to stay with two doting aunts of my dead husband, and then to have them find out I drove him to his death. Who are *you?*" she asked, turning to John; "I didn't see you standing there." "No, it didn't seem so."

"He's *marrying* me," Edna burst out. "Marrying!" Virginia almost shrieked; "why didn't you write me that!" "Will you stop that hopping; Virginia, stop *hopping.*" Virginia stood still, radiating at her. "Look," Edna said, "I want to do something very rude and ask John, that's his name, John Steele," she hurried on, "I want to ask him something, but I don't want you to hear me." "Rude! I should say so! Hurry up. Hurry up. I can hardly wait to get you and talk to you." "What are you doing?" John asked as Edna led him off down the walk. "I want to ask you something." "I know that; I guessed that." "Can she come stay with us? Just for a few days? Or a week?" "Or forever?" John suggested. "Oh, not forever," Edna protested; "no more than a week." "Stay at our house?" "Why ever not?" she asked. "Let me think."

Edna stood still, her green eyes boring into him. She looks better than she did at the train, John thought; that flush is gone. Her breathing is good. I can't remember anyone coming down with a case of consumption when the disease is in this stage. And, he thought it over carefully, I have to attend consumption patients; I can't protect her altogether. She might meet someone with it in the post office or the dry-goods store. It's hopeless. I can't start that, trying to keep everything from her, not so soon. And it's her friend. She probably needs a friend now. And the other one looks so miserable here. "Why ever not?" John said aloud.

He had to admit the possibility of Edna's death eventually; he might as well begin thinking sanely before the wedding. After it, he thought sadly, it would be utterly hopeless; it would be hopeless to try to reform then. "Well, go and ask her," he said, giving Edna a little push.

He occupied himself in studying the town. What drab-looking occupants. Edna said three churches? They ought to build another. Everyone was proceeding sedately down the street. It must be the heat, he thought. The silence was suddenly sundered by a little gang of children flying out of a yard, each with pears pressed against his shirt. Well, I guess it's no different than anywhere else, he decided, watching amused as an old woman exploded from her front door, waving a walking stick, shouting threats. "Constable Evans!" she was shouting at the top of her lungs; "Constable Evans!" The constable did not materialize. The children had vanished. She peered up and down the street time and time again. Finally, giving it up as hopeless, she closed her door. The slam shook the silence steeping the street, as if the town were painted on a loosely framed pane of glass.

"She wants to go!" Edna exclaimed as soon as John got within hearing distance. Virginia was alternately hugging her and looking fearfully at the windows of the first floor. The second-floor shutters were closed, but the ones at street level were open. John thought he saw light glint from the rim of a pair of spectacles. "Do you need permission to go?" Edna asked. "Permission!" Virginia sputtered; "I'm an independent woman. A *widow*. *Seasoned* by life's experiences. Oh, I shall be glad to come."

"I tried one of *your* tricks"; Edna poked at her. "You did? Which one?" "I said I was the minister's daughter at a funeral." "No!" Virginia giggled; "did it work?" "Of course." "It always does," Virginia said a little bitterly; "of course, it wouldn't if there wasn't always a wasps' nest of hypocrites to count on." John followed them up the steps. What a pair! he thought, shaking his head; what have I gotten myself into? Whatever it is, I like it; he smiled happily. Virginia was turning the bell knob as if she were trying to warn the inhabitants of a deadly fire.

"Prepare yourself," Edna whispered to John. They followed Virginia down the long dark hall. It reminds me, Edna thought, of "the narrow home." John shook his finger at her. He doesn't dare tell me to be quiet, she thought, amused. Really, the place was forbidding. Inside, the house had the air of having once been, and perhaps still being, the home of the three Fates. It is not hard, Edna thought, to imagine the three of them here, to imagine that this is their den, and in one of these rooms, behind one of these doors, the air looks as if it's filled with smoke, but it isn't smoke, it's white thread after white thread, each one tying a person to his life on this earth. How they must want to cut Virginia's! And how they will want to cut all of ours when they hear about our proposal. Why, she asked herself, should it be behind the façade of a house like this, so peaceful and respectable, inhabited by two elderly women, that such evil doings seemed most likely to occur? No, it would not surprise her to find a nest of murderers contentedly playing cards in the second-best parlor, the schedule of the house revolving around *their* schedule of setting churches afire, pillaging stores, vandalizing property for no reason whatever. "This is going to be a regular crow concert," John whispered into her ear as they reached the entrance to the best parlor, where there were, indeed, two extremely old women.

The two ancient creatures, dressed in rusty black, were sitting primly on an elaborately carved black horsehair sofa. Why was it so hard to see into the room? John wondered. His eyes were excellent. At home, he threaded Ten's needle when her eyes, as she always put it, fell out; in the dark, he was the one who could pick out the third tree or third fence post in the middle of a moonless night and swirling snowstorm.

Lovely, Edna thought; every shade of black, just the opposite of Mr. Siddons. The horsehair sofa was set at a right angle to the horsehair love seat; five matching occasional chairs were scattered around the room. One of them gleamed darkly from a corner. Edna had never seen walnut finished so blackly; in this parlor, it gleamed like ebony. An oriental rug with a maroon background, so dark in the flickering light it appeared black, relieved by an imperceptibly lighter pattern, covered the floor, which had been stained to match the wood of the chairs. Heavy velvet draperies covered the two windows. The shutters in this room, Edna saw, were closed. Nevertheless, some irrepressible beams of light managed to escape into the room, throwing a small set of bars onto the rug and striping the women's faces. Some trick of light divided the second woman's face into black and white, as if nature itself had bisected her.

Edna shuddered, remembering one of her visits to prison with her father. It must have been her first, the first time she saw the prisoners in those costumes. She had been shocked by the uniforms: the left side one color, the right another. Good Lord, the symbolism of it! Edna thought at the time; as if the wrong half of them had to be made visible. She had not liked looking at them. The uniforms made the nature of their deformity so obvious; they seemed more vulnerable than dangerous. She took note of the wallpaper; again she felt a sense of shock. It was the same pattern, the same color, her mother had chosen for the morning callers' room, that little parlor so far away on Cedar Street, but this background seemed darker, as if it had taken in the emotions of the inhabitants, had somehow drunk them in and blackened; she remembered a coroner testifying at the trial referred to as "the massacre," in the papers; venous blood was dark on its return to the heart for reoxygenation. It was impossible to think pleasant thoughts in this room. There seemed to be no air anywhere.

John, meanwhile, had busied himself studying the pictures on the walls. I'll have time enough to get a look at those two, he thought, surprised at the violence of his reaction. They were affecting him like the little pink worms he and Ten unearthed after storms. When he was still a child and too afraid to find them himself before he left for the river and its promising fish. I suppose, he decided, it must be because I don't want to think about death, at least not now, and I don't know what else anyone would think about in here. But what deathly pictures! The large picture in back of the sofa was round. As they advanced further into the room, John saw it was almost eight inches deep. It gleamed out from the dark, its white roses forming a garland around a painting of a young man's face. Of course, John thought; a mourning picture. Well, they would spare no expense for that. On the wall between the love seat and sofa was a huge, dark frame filled with dark, dead ferns and flowers which had blackened years ago. Over the love seat was a painting of a young woman dressed in white, and somewhat to its side, a wicker plant stand holding a huge pot of ivy, whose vines, in some better time when they had still permitted light to enter the room, had been trained up over the top and corner of the frame. Now the leaves had gone stiff and rigid. One vine hung straight down as if a weight were attached to its invisible end, the weight tucked somewhere out of sight.

And there it was, the inevitable marble-topped table, and the inevitable sewing basket, festooned as if it were trying to imitate a parade float in some dreadful kind of fair. That must be a gift; some of the ribbons were light enough to make themselves presences in the room, and the little paper roses decking it out, they were white. Or by now they had faded to white; who could say how long things had remained stationary in this crypt? As if to answer his question, as if to say defiantly that in this room everything could last forever, the oval picture of an old woman at the limits of mortality peered nastily at them from under her white lace cap. Not a strand of hair was visible beneath it; little white ribbons hung down from each side of that cap, as if to suggest the presence of the vanished hair. John imagined that the poor artist had done all he could to beautify her, but there were limits to the greatest abilities. The limits were a tribute all the same, he thought, to the unknown renderer's integrity. A third figure, unnoticed until now, was sitting in a motionless rocker in the room's far corner; the ornate black wicker gleamed like a casket. Next to the rocker was a black wicker wheelchair. No wonder Virginia had seemed so high-strung, so hysterical. One night in this room, John mused, and I'd be holding conversations with the dead, and without the aid of a medium, either.

Why, Edna was asking herself, did the black and white lambrequins, so elaborately and carefully draped across the windows, appear only black? She saw the round wooden pole running across the center of the ceiling, and then the thick black velvet curtains suspended from it, reaching the floor, pushed, as if violently, against each wall. "I am the resurrection and the life, saith the Lord," Edna found herself chanting unawares; it was as if the lines would protect her in here. That was it! That was what had been left out of Ben's burial service . . . those lines were never omitted from the burial service. No wonder, it finally occurred to her, no wonder John had been so furious.

Virginia, watching them, saw them both turn their attention to the old women on the sofa. Why, Edna realized, those two things, those mummies, are twins! The force of their disapproval, or hatred, yes, hatred, twice magnified! It was unimaginable. Yes, we will have to take Virginia out of here today. And then, she thought, John can diagnose some dreadful illness which requires warm weather and familiar scenes, and we can send her back

South. It won't even be her own decision. Her eyes were becoming used to the darkness; the two old ladies were coming into focus. John suddenly noticed the blackened ivy draped in hoops over the pole dividing the room's ceiling, its curtains, and the two white paper bells in the background. So that's what they were, he thought with relief. At first he had thought they were either spider webs or fantastic accumulations of dust. I'd bet, he thought, the dust hasn't been disturbed in here for over a quarter of a century. He was constantly fighting an impulse to sneeze.

What is wrong with those women's faces? Edna shivered. Their faces resembled the proverbial wrinkled apples used for grandmother dolls, but the bottom halves of their faces appeared to have collapsed inwards, as if already rotting. Oh, no teeth. She breathed in, relieved. No teeth, she told herself again, as if their lack of teeth made her safer, as if there had been any danger of being bitten. And one of them doesn't have a hair on her head, she thought, noticing the gleam beneath the black cotton bonnet; she studied that one with more care. Over her black dress she wore a little crocheted cape; that *was* fancywork, she thought, admiring. It was a miracle the old thing could still see, such intricate webs and overlays; the final product was three-dimensional, sculptured. Her voluminous black skirt fell weightily to the floor. A tiny flounce, or ruffle, finished off the garment, brushing the dark carpet.

The other woman turned toward her. She had a full head of white hair, pulled back over her broad white forehead; it was skewered into a rat at the top of her head. The wrinkled, loose flesh of her neck hung over her white collar. The collar's probably there to hold her head up, Edna thought uncharitably.

She could not imagine being so old, and, seeing them, she did not want to imagine it. This one, Edna saw, was dressed in what her mother never failed to call "the plain style," a black dress, small round collar, a yoke, the vertically gathered bodice reined in at the waist, a generous, round skirt which also reached to the floor and, like her sister's, ended in a plain ruffle. There seemed, somehow, to be less of her than the other one. She must be asking her sister who we are, Edna decided. Good

Lord, she thought, there are *other* horrid pictures; a second layer of heavy oak frames surmounted those she had already noticed, all of them holding faces rising out of black shoulders. It was virtually impossible to make out their features.

Virginia broke the silence. "These are my great-aunts," she said, her voice quavering slightly: "Aunt Lucinda," she said, bowing to the old woman in the bonnet; "Aunt Miranda." She bowed to the second. "And this is their companion," she said, turning toward the third woman in the dark corner: "Miss Jane Dalrymple." Evidently, the hierarchy did not require bowing to her. "Aunt Miranda," Aunt Lucinda," Virginia said, raising her voice, "these are my friends. Miss Edna Dickinson and her fiancé, Dr. John Steele."

"Dickinson, Dickinson," the one in the bonnet began repeating aloud; "Miranda, didn't we know a Dickinson?" "They lived here," Miranda answered. "Dickinson, Dickinson," the first continued; "Dickinson, Dickinson." "All right, Lucinda," her sister complained. "Dickinson," Lucinda repeated, as if deliberately annoying her; "it will come to me in a minute." Miranda snorted. "Dickinson," her sister said again. Lucinda glared at her. "I have it!" Lucinda cried in her cracked voice. "Well, blessed be to God," Miranda grumbled.

"Dickinson," Lucinda said again; "the wife was dragged out of the house by the constable. She shot her husband and her two little children; then she shot herself in the foot. Don't you remember *anything*, Miranda? Your mind is going, so it is, just as Mother's went." Miranda glared on. "*Can't* you trouble yourself to remember anything at all?" Lucinda asked irritably; "it was the event of the day. The constable told the paper it was not at all usual for a woman to use a gun. He said women usually made use of poisons. He said he couldn't imagine how she shot herself in the foot, because she couldn't possibly have mistaken her foot for her head. Don't you remember one single thing?" "I remember," her sister snapped; "I just never took the interest in murder you did." "You did, too," Lucinda said; "you were right there outside the jail with the rest of us ladies, all dressed up and carrying your parasol, fit to kill." "Are you going to run on about this forever?" Miranda asked; "I apologize," she addressed her guests, a trace of the old manner showing; "my sister tends to get herself stuck in a ditch. We should be thankful," she went on, glaring now at Virginia, "we have any memories at *all*." Virginia colored. Sharp old tacks, John thought.

"They weren't any relations of yours, Miss Dickinson?" Lucinda asked, unable to restrain herself. "Miss Jane can help you from the room," Miranda told her. Obviously, she had the upper hand here. "If you can't get yourself off that subject. Rude, Lucinda, you are being rude. Impolite." "Were they?" Lucinda persisted, ignoring her. "I'm afraid not," Edna said; "my father was rather on the other side of the tracks; he was a criminal lawyer. I'm afraid there have been very few murders in our family tree." "You see," Miranda hissed; "now will you quiet down about it?" "Dickinson," Lucinda repeated. At this her sister slumped like a melting wax doll.

"Wasn't a Dickinson the lawyer at that terrible slaughter case?" "That was my father," Edna said. "He defended them, didn't he?" the old lady asked greedily; "did he know anything the papers didn't get at?" "I'm sure he would have been relieved if he had." "What were they like?" Lucinda asked, leaning forward with something resembling animation; "the criminals, I mean. That one, especially, the man who killed all those people. Imagine, Miranda," she went on, "the man must have been exhausted after all that work." "Please excuse her," Miranda said, glancing over at Jane, who began folding up her needlework and pulling her work basket toward her. "*I'm* not leaving," Lucinda said; "Jane might as well stay right where she is. Don't you rattle her bones at me," she hissed at her sister. "What was he like?" she asked, turning back to Edna.

John watched her anxiously. "My father? Oh, he was a very quiet man." "Not your father!" the old woman puffed in exasperation; "the killer, the killer, the one they called the butcher, don't you remember him at *all*, Miranda?" "I am not *interested* in remembering him; can't you get that through your skin head?" "She's interested all right," Lucinda said in a loud whisper; "what was he like?" If she bends over any further, John thought, she's going to topple from that couch. I wouldn't like to touch that body. "Father said that Mr. Huebell was a very peaceful man; he never showed any signs of excitement, but he didn't admit to the murders or anything else until after the conviction." "I know that," Lucinda complained; "I read about that in the papers." "What *is* it you want to know, Lucinda? Are we never going to hear the end of this?" "Was he sorry? That's what I want to know; was he sorry about it?" "He told Father he wasn't; he was only sorry he'd gotten caught." "I knew it," Lucinda crowed; "I knew he wasn't sorry. He's always been my hero," she confided to Edna. Miranda raised her eyebrows threateningly. "Unbalanced since her childhood; because she came out second. Her head was squashed. Mother used to say that. Do you remember that, Lucinda?" "She also said she liked her second-born best, because she had to wait longer for it," Lucinda answered disagreeably. "She didn't mean it," Miranda pouted; "she said whatever came into her head." The memory of that dusty remark still rankled.

"Dr. Steele," Miranda said, turning her button eyes on him, "would you care for some tea? Miss Dickinson?" "No, no," they answered together. "Virginia?" Miranda asked, as if just reminded of her annoying presence. "No, thank you, Aunt." "Well, Dr. Steele," Miranda began sociably enough, "what brings you here? A medical emergency? Surely not our Virginia?" This one must have been the belle of the ball, Edna observed mentally. "It seems there is no one on the sick list today," John answered; "my fiancée was very anxious to see Mrs. Whitemore." "*Mrs.* Whitemore?" Miranda echoed; her tone was sticky with irony. "Miss Dickinson would like her help in preparing for the wedding," John went on. "Why? Why? Doesn't she have any family?" Lucinda cross-examined. "It is not our place to wonder about other people's doings," Miranda reproached her ambiguously. "I trust you are staying with relatives?" Miranda asked Edna. "Not exactly; I am staying with an old school friend of my mother's, for my health, you know." Miranda studied her. "Her name?" she asked coldly. "Mrs. Tenniel Richardson." "Now don't start repeating that over and over," Miranda cautioned her sister. "I *know* who she is; Mrs. Richardson of Williamsville. She was quite a light in amateur theatricals, only then she was called Miss Tenniel Steele," she said triumphantly.

"Is that true?" Miranda demanded of John. "I'm afraid it is," John said. "Afraid? Why should you be afraid?" Lucinda asked, missing the point; "she wasn't one of those painted actresses. Amateur theatricals are wholesome things," she went on didactically; "I particularly remember her in *The Old Maids' Convention*." "That's appropriate enough," Miranda said.

"Dare I ask," Edna began, "to borrow your great-niece for a week? Her help would be most welcome." "She's not our great-niece, only by marriage," Lucinda put in. Virginia colored again. "It will be quite a relief to you," John suddenly spoke up; "it must tire you, in your poor states of health, caring for such a young girl." "Poor state of health, Miranda, what is he talking about?" Lucinda asked in alarm. Miranda gave her a look. "Our state of health has never been better," Lucinda pouted. She did not like it, having such an observation made by a doctor. Next, Jane would be conferring with Virginia in the hall over the style of their coffins. It probably irritates him, she thought, furious, to see us looking so well, so *healthy*, and to know he has nothing to do with it. "When would you want her?" Miranda asked. She inquired politely, as if she wanted to know how long they would want the use of their house parlormaid. "Oh, immediately," Edna said cheerfully. "Well, it's up to her; everything always is." "It's up to her," Miranda echoed. They had finally found something to agree about. "I'll go and pack," Virginia said, jumping up; "excuse me, Aunts, Miss Jane," she said quickly, curtsying and leaving the room. Great strength of character that shows, John thought, not to run out.

"You really ought to see our ivy porch," Miranda suggested; "it's been a town attraction for so many years, I forget when people began stopping their carriages to walk around and look at it." "I'd love to see it," Edna said; "would you excuse us, please? Miss Jane, would you tell Virginia we will be outside admiring the vine?" "By all means go and look at it," Miranda advised. They can't wait, Edna thought, to get us out of the room to start in gossiping.

"It's a relief to breathe some air," John said, inhaling deeply. "That's right," Edna said, more gloomily than usual; "breathe deeply. You'll need all your strength to appreciate that vine." "Even the vine looks black," John sighed; "it's a monstrosity of plant life. It has intentions." "It's going straight from selectman to President," Edna commented, looking at it again; "I don't see how she survived this long in the house. You can think of some illness that requires her instant return to the South? After the week is up, I mean." "I've already given it some thought. But what we didn't give any thought," he said as they walked back to the front of the house and caught sight of their horses, "was how we were going to get Virginia back to Williamsville." "We could ride together." "Not side-saddle; it's not safe." "Oh, I don't know," Edna said, looking down at her skirt; "I think I could ride astride, but I don't think Virginia could do it." "Well, we'll need another horse," John said, thinking. "Do you have any acquaintances in Fitchburg?" John looked at her face; it was so hopeful. He began to concentrate on the question of the horse. "Mr. Cameron, the widower, he owes me a favor," he said finally; "I'll ride over there. If he'll give us the loan of his horse, Amos can bring it back tied to the buggy in the morning." "Well, go on," Edna told him, watching his retreating back, then staring fixedly at the side door. Was Virginia never going to come out?

The door opened a crack, and a bent figure showed itself, apparently pulling at something. "Wait, I'll help you," Edna called, going up the stairs after her. They took hold of the handles of Virginia's traps and set them on the walk. "It's like the arrival of Elijah's carriage," Virginia exulted; "I thought I'd have to wait until tomorrow until the train came. Where's Mr. Steele?" she asked, looking about. "He's gone off to beg another horse." "Do you think he'll have any luck?" "Well, I suppose so; the patient who has the horse lives alone all the way over here and if John doesn't come for him when he calls, he won't have anyone else. He thinks all the other doctors are criminals." "Oh, well then," Virginia sighed, relieved.

They waited, casting reluctant looks back at the house. "What a place!" Edna exclaimed. "And you only saw the beginning of what is a long, horrible tale," her friend said, shaking her head; "well, if the dead *do* want revenge, my dead husband ought to be satisfied; he ought to be sleeping in a cloud bed of happiness."

"Virginia," Edna said, awkward, "sometimes John wakes up at night and . . ." She paused. "Oh, I understand; I won't burst into your room." "No, no, it's nothing like that, but when he wakes up, I get up and talk to him." "And you want to talk to him alone? I don't have any inclination to prowl around at night; I always sleep like someone hit me with a stick." Edna still appeared uneasy. "Well, even if I should wake up," Virginia assured her, "I promise I'll climb out the window and walk around in the woods." "Your room's on the second floor." "Then I'll let myself down on a sheet." They grinned happily at each other. It was impossible that they had met only once before, and on a train.

"That was fast work," Virginia told Edna admiringly; "your Mr. Steele." "It just happened," Edna said, puzzled; "like a rainstorm. Or a flood." "An act of God, obviously." John appeared leading a black stallion. "I'll ride this one," he said; "you two take the other horses. We have to go back to Mr. Cameron's to feed and water ours; I'll tie those traps onto my horse." They set off. In the peaceful house, curtains twitched aside, then fell back into place. "Well, good riddance," Virginia said, mounting. "We don't have to go back at full gallop," John said; "we'll get there one way or the other." "If wishes were horses," Virginia said; "well, this one is," she said, patting the horse's mane; "the only trouble with this horse is that it can't keep up with a steam engine." "Some people are always complaining," Edna teased; "You've made your escape, and the posse's decomposing. Relax." "*That* will take some time," Virginia said.

In the Williamsville house, Ten was waiting for John and Edna; in minutes, she had Virginia installed in a room adjoining Edna's, and Bridget carrying in three of Edna's white lawn dresses to the new guest, which, she said, would be a healthy change for her, even if they only came down to her knees and burst at the seams. But she had already given orders to Bertha to begin altering three of *her* dresses to fit the young widow. "All this trouble for a week," Virginia had protested. "A week can be a long time," Ten reminded her. Virginia agreed, thankful.

The week went by very quickly. Virginia's arrival

seemed the signal for a long procession of foaming horses, wildly reined in before the Steeles' door, all of the riders pleading for the immediate company of the doctor. During supper, two men drove up at once. "You go on home," John told one of them; "I'll be over as soon as I finish with this one here." "Why can't you come with me? My wife's as important as anybody, I guess," the offended husband protested. "I always take children first; you know that, Tom. They don't keep as well as the older ones." So Virginia and Edna spent their first evening talking. Virginia did most of the speaking, raving on to both Ten and Edna's amusement about the wax mausoleum, and how the two sisters drank blood of adder every night so they would wake in the morning, venomous as ever. I do like her, Ten thought; I should wait a few days before I show this letter to Edna. It would be a pity to spoil the week for that other girl, poor thing; she looks as if someone just lifted the noose from her neck. Finally, they went to bed. It was clear to Ten, who thought of it as her consciousness began dimming for the night, that Virginia had not yet begun to realize her husband was really dead. Well, I hope she doesn't do it this week. We've had enough with Ben, she thought, and now Hal coming. And John, she thought groggily, he hasn't had any time to think about Ben. And he's seeing to it that he won't have any, either. It's a good thing, she decided, turning on her side, it's a good thing Edna is here.

Edna awoke as if she had been poked in the ribs. Yes, it was the sound of the horse in the yard. She settled back under the cotton quilts and began to doze off. But, after some time had passed, and she hadn't heard the familiar heavy footsteps going down the hall, she decided to get up. John was sitting in the library, writing by the light of a kerosene lamp. "Well," said Edna, "is any of humanity left alive? How is the baby?" "The baby's fine. He got my usual treatment. Convulsions are hard on the family, but they're not as bad as they look." He lectured automatically. "What are you doing up?" he asked, finally raising his head. "I couldn't sleep. Something about those old aunts, I guess." John went right back to his writing. Oh fine, Edna thought. "How *do* you treat convulsions?" "Something you've always wanted to know?" John asked, sarcastic. "Now that you've mentioned it."

"You should go to the next quilting bee; all the ladies there would be happy to tell you about my peculiar methods which have the even more peculiar effect of curing their children." "Well, what *do* you do?" Edna asked as if annoyed. "Give them castor oil, then an enema, sometimes another enema. If that doesn't do it, I throw the child into a warm bath. Then it's sol and bismuth. Tonight," he said, a little wearily, "I sponged one perfect little beast for six hours. He's going to end up shot fatally in the bottom trying to crawl through someone's fence before he turns fifteen." "The other doctors, what do they do?" "They sympathize with the parents for at least fifteen minutes, then dose the child with opiates or Dover's powders; the powders are full of opiates also. Then they send for the undertaker." "What does a convulsion look like?" Edna pursued, relentless.

"Are you going to keep at this subject all night?" he asked. "The little bodies contort into very strange shapes. You wouldn't believe the body could do such things until you see it happen. The children's eyes are half open; that gives them a fishy look. Their eyeballs roll up in their heads; their faces twitch and their skin is pale or bluish. Violent muscular contractions followed by relaxation, generally followed by more contractions. It can go on for hours, days. Then, if the parents are unlucky, there's the diarrhea, an emaciated skeleton alive in the bed, high fever, panting, the head unable to rise from the pillow. Coldness of the limbs, a slight quiver, the limbs relax, death; that's the *whole* clinical picture." "But the baby you went to see is healthy?" "I told you," John answered, exasperated; "he's fine. Physically fine. A criminal, but fine." He went back to his letter.

Edna stood, reading over his shoulder. "Impossible manners," John said, not looking up. But, Edna noted, he did not ask her to stop reading. "Dear Sir: I am writing you about your fence on Buck Hill. I *have* spoken to you about putting up a wire fence several times. You *don't seem* to pay any attention to it. I will give you one week to put up at least three strands of barbed wire. We had our cattle tested and don't want them with other cattle. The state veterinary said if our neighbors would not put up a good wire fence to report them to the head man in Montpelier. It is no more of a hardship for one man to have a good fence than another. Sincerely, Mr. John Ashbel Steele." "Finished?" John asked, looking up, defensive. "I didn't know you took care of those matters." "Well, I didn't, and I do now, and that's that. If you don't mind, I'd like to sit up and read." "If *you* don't mind, I'd like to curl up on the sofa with Jimmie here," she said; "I'd feel better." "You're not developing a case of country nerves?" John asked, unsympathetic. "I am *not*," she answered shortly, curling up on the couch and pulling the quilt over her. She *was* tired.

John pretended to read, every now and then glancing over at the curled body of his fiancée. If she doesn't look like an unpeeled shrimp, he thought, trying to read again. After an hour, he gave up. The clock began striking. One, two, three. At least *that's* still working, he thought, relieved. Some day or other he should tell Edna about the legends associated with that clock. Edna. She was still curled up. He got up, pushing his chair back wearily. What a beautiful thing that one is, he thought; she looks like a doll. Her hair. They always told us healthy hair meant a healthy body, but I go by the tongues. Well, her tongue was in her mouth where it belonged.

But that hair. It was brushed out and fanned out over her shoulders, reaching almost to the carpet. Such black hair, he thought, resisting an impulse to touch it; he didn't want to wake her up. He moved the kerosene lamp closer; Edna didn't stir. She sleeps deeply, he thought enviously. The light brought out the blue highlights in her jet hair. Remarkable; it's like the ocean before a storm. She's a phenomenon of nature. And that peach-colored tint to her skin, as if she were warmed by some internal fire. He had never come across that before in any of his patients. Such little bones, he thought, such little bones. She would be lost, he smiled, in the valley of bones. I don't think they would let her in it. They'd find somewhere else to put her. Such lovely bones. He wished he could touch her bones. I would like to swallow her, he thought; I would like to sew her to me. But she *is* strong, he meditated; she has a wide pelvic structure. Why, he asked himself, am I thinking so much about her bones? Well, it's her fault, after all, what with all those questions about children. They will probably have to tie me down, he thought sadly, when she goes into labor. Again.

But her hair drew his eyes back. It undulated, hypnotic, like a benevolent snake. She's part dragon; something oriental in her somewhere. I've never seen such hair. He was suddenly very tired. Nothing was ever going to happen to her, not if he could prevent it. He shook his head at the spectacle of Jimmie sleeping hugely on her tiny hip. He received a slit-eyed glare in return. Gingerly, he tapped the cat on his side; Jimmie refused to budge. He hissed at the cat. Jimmie kept his place. The cat's heart's in the right place, he thought; if they only lived longer. Cats. And dogs.

Well, that was the trouble with everyone, wasn't it; if they only lived longer. Then he thought of the old ladies. Yes, that Miranda would be lost without that bald egg she called her sister. It was a miracle, the ties of blood. And the clots that formed in the veins after a death. He wondered how many bedsides he'd attended, with no success, which had been emptied forever by the deaths of others. The hair undulated and fell.

Well, she can't sleep here all night, he told himself; she'll wake up in the morning bent like a camel. He sighed, stooped over, and picked her up as if she were made of glass. The cat jumped down in a huff, stretching his paws, defiantly scratching at the carpet, flexing his thick claws, and, raising his tail straight into the air, marched off down the hall. First. He was going first. That cat had his pride. John gently kicked Edna's door open with his boot; the moonlight fell on the bed where the covers had been turned neatly back. He lay her down on her side, covered her, and kissed her on the forehead. She knew he hadn't meant anything by his growls and snarls. There wouldn't be any explanations or apologies necessary in the morning. Thank God for that, he said under his breath in the hall, going into his own room, getting into bed without undressing, asleep before his head had even sunk into the pillow.

After breakfast, which Virginia, Edna, and Ten took together, John having left before dawn, called, as Ten casually told them, by the usual foaming steed (yes, reined in at full gallop), Edna and Virginia set off for the fields mounted on the two bay horses, a picnic basket securely tied around Edna's waist. Ten could never be casual about nourishment, especially nourishment to be taken in the hot sun. Under the red and white checked cover she had carefully tucked a wet linen cloth, and under that, a piece of old oilcloth. Was there any possibility John would return in their absence? Ten assured Edna that John, before he set off for South Hadley, had given her instructions for everyone. No one was to wait up for him, or even to worry if he did not return that night because his last visit to either North or South Hadley had taken place sometime in January. "'They pinch up their diseases like pennies,' that's what he said; 'I guess they'll make it even odds on the doctor and the undertaker.'" So it was with a clear conscience that Edna and Virginia set off together.

The day was so blue and so clear every tree on the far mountain outlined itself leaf by leaf; even the thick pines refused to blend together into one mass. The horses themselves seemed delighted to be out, having pranced all the way from the barn to the mounting steps. "What do you want to do?" Edna called out, half poised in the saddle. "Anything, so long as it keeps us out all day," Virginia answered gleefully; she had hopped into the saddle like a little jockey. "I tell you, Edna," she said, watching her companion settle down, adjusting her unusual waist ornament, the basket, "one more day in that house and I would have been seeing bars across the sun."

Ten watched as the two of them headed off down the path into the woods. They look like two mythical creatures; they seem to grow right out of their horses. There were things to be done in the house, but the day was powerful. It was using all its tricks to lure out all the company it could get. Well, Ten thought, it has comforted us often enough, the blue sky; I suppose I owe it something. She went back to her room for her white knit shawl; well, and there were three hard-boiled eggs that ought not go to waste, not to mention a jug of coffee, and the little bottle of cucumber salad, and there *was* that extra net bag hanging from the chair that had been too small for Virginia and Edna, but looked just the right size for her belongings, into which she slid four sheets of paper and a small, hard lead pencil.

Edith will just have to excuse the pencil, she decided; If I wait for a table, and a pot of ink, and a quill to run together all at the same time, Edith will be a grand-mother four times over before she hears the news. The mending, the checking on the pantry, the oven, looking into plans for the wedding, going downtown to Robbia's to discuss catering, conferring with the florist over decorations for the house, all that was certainly extremely urgent, and all that would just have to wait. The hammock shone in her mind like brazen gold. I owe it to the day to give it a little company, she told herself, a bit guilty; she wondered at her new tendency to think of everything in the world as alive. Well, it wasn't such a new tendency; it had begun, she knew, after her return from Kansas. Things had struggled so there, and the dust storm the day of Ed's funeral, blinding everyone on the road as if a blizzard had suddenly struck, three buggies running into one another, two overturning upon the third, and six runaways, one woman thrown right into a river, another through the front window of a store, and then to return here, the farmers endlessly complaining about the difficulties of raising crops in this hard climate, how it was impossible to keep roses alive through the winter, and Mrs. Camp, no, she wasn't even going to try anymore, and others who wanted to could wear themselves out with grape arbors, but she wasn't going to raise grapes for the Japanese beetles, and if they didn't get them, then the hens certainly would; it was no use raising anything but corn, and she wasn't half sure about potatoes.

But Ten, looking again at the high hills, rioting green with shade trees and evergreens, and the meadow next to the house seeding itself without effort, brimming with wild flowers, felt as if New England was nature's party. Even the winters were beautiful; there was nothing, no, nothing, that could match the sight of their big blue spruce weighed down with snow. Well, let those complain who will complain, Ten thought, mentally mocking Mrs. Camp (half of the town were either Camps or Thompsons), but there was something here in the country, vital, quickening, as if, at one time or another, lightning had struck everything in the countryside and electrified it with its force. The sky now, the brilliance of it, that was an example.

A small toad hopped off the path in front of her. She had a weakness for them, those little things that looked as if they had grown from a piece of bark which had taken root in the ground and then developed a life of its own. She looked back over her shoulder; yes, she was out of sight of the house. She stooped down and began looking for the toad. Nothing moved. Ten felt for a stick in the leaves and then poked gently in the pile closest to her. A small object jumped and disappeared. Ten followed after, her hands already domed, ready to catch and hold him. "Drat!" she exclaimed as her hands closed over him and he hopped out between her index finger and thumb, but on her second attempt, she was successful; she had him secure. What little bright eyes; what a small brain he must have. Had he thought it up himself, making himself look so like a tree? Or was there anything to her idea that he had somehow grown from bark?

She had never forgotten the first snowstorm the year she returned. It was impossible to tell where anything began and ended; there were no boundaries anywhere. Their absence was so absolute it was as if someone had intentionally erased them. The pastures resembled the ponds. It was impossible for the inexperienced eye to tell them apart. Even the earth and air were moving, as if evaporating, one into the other, for when the wind blew, the snow was blown up as a fine white fog, the blackboard of nature erasing itself into one chalky cloud. And the trees, too, disappearing, no matter what their size, even the houses discernible by the size of the mounds they made; they rose visibly, every now and then, from the general chaos, the drifting fog of snow pulling itself back, then dropping, shutting out the warm squares of yellow light. In the beginning, Ten thought; no, that was what it must have looked like before the beginning. Primeval matter, the original substance.

But it was so hard to remember winter in the spring or in the summer, just as, in the winter, the summer seemed a myth of memory, the hot days which pressed people flat as irons pressed cloth, erased out of mind, only the memory of the glowing bones sustaining throughout the days, the gray ones, the white. Yes, it was hard to remember the days, especially the ordinary ones. Ed, now. It was hard to remember him. When she tried to remember his face, it floated right out of the corner of her eye, but then when she dreamed, she would be talking to him just as if he were standing in the room. It was just as it had been when she was a child and dreamed she had gotten whatever it was she wished for: a colt, a special dress, a doll she had irretrievably broken, the certainty, on waking, that she had what she wished for. The terrible despair of searching the room, frantically ransacking it with her eyes, finally giving up hope. It had happened again; she had awakened. She had awakened out of a dream, and the important things, everything which meant something, locked in that lost world which opened its doors when it chose.

Yet that world seemed to come closer on those gray days, or rainy days in summer when the fog drained everything of its color and there was nothing but the wet, damp touch of the world against the skin. Well, was it any wonder she believed, yes, really believed the lost things lived in that mist, came closer in that mist so like sleep, lived with you again in that mist? It came as a shock to her, walking toward the hammock, to realize she had come to believe in the indivisibility of things, the impossibility of final separations; that she did, in fact, have her own kind of faith.

She sighed, lying down in the hammock, looking up at the sky. Faith. John would never stand for the Reverend Pierce, not after his performance at Ben's funeral. Perhaps Edith knew someone. Perhaps her old friend the minister from South Hadley would do. He was certainly in the business of creation, she thought idly, swinging back and forth in the gold light. John had delivered at least five of his children. Perhaps he would bring luck. She didn't know why; she hoped Edna would produce a tribe. Even though it would be best if she could produce them out of the air, without first becoming pregnant. John would prefer that. Well, probably she wanted a tribe about only because she needed more company these days, more than the day did, or perhaps both of them did, here on this hill, in these fields and pastures. *They* needed people; yes, she was sure of that.

And she had failed in her duties to produce a new crop. She supposed the country had forgiven her by now. She kept its animals going, and the flowers; she was good for something. She wished, for the thousandth time, that Ed had had his likeness executed before he died. All she had now was their wedding portrait, but when he had died, he hadn't looked at all as he did in that painting. She had no idea, she reminisced, swinging, a man could get so thin and live. Ed, though, he kept insisting the stringy ones were the strongest; the big ones were like cattle, good for slaughtering. He had been wrong about that. Ed, Edith, Edna, Edmund, she said aloud. All names beginning with the same two letters. Surely *that* had some significance. That was no coincidence. Ten shook herself. I'm getting to be a superstitious old woman, she lectured herself; next I'll be seeing ghosts. She sighed, realizing she had come to believe in them, too.

Time to write to Edith. *She* had become rather ghostly, before her last letter. But she had no trouble remembering Edith's face. It must be the time she met her; they were practically children. They couldn't have been more than twelve. New things, she thought with remorse, were never as vivid as old ones. Never. Well, and what would that mean about John's feelings for Edna? She would, after all, be a second wife. But she wasn't so sure of that.

"Dear Edith," she began, taking care to press the pencil heavily against the paper—if there was one thing she hated it was a faint hand that made the letter seem to come from someone already one hundred years old. Well, the letters *were* one hundred years old. That is, she paused, pencil poised—if one considered how many letters of this kind had been written since the beginning of things. It was a kind trick nature played, to make everything seem so novel, so new. *This* seemed novel to her, her childhood friend's daughter marrying her own brother, the same one who had announced his determination to keep Bachelor Hall for the rest of his days. So much for human intention. She suspected all these events had something to do with the land itself, that it had taken Edna in more efficiently than a trap took in a raccoon. Well, she had better get on with it.

Edna and Virginia had found their meadow, and spread out their cloth and their lunch. Virginia kept looking longingly at the sparkling, narrow river, barely visible through the thick trees bordering the grass, but determined to make itself heard. "Back home," she said, "we used to jump right in, with our clothes on, or without them. Not everyone," she assured Edna, seeing her surprise, "but some of us." "Well, you did, of course," Edna answered lightly, hoping desperately Virginia would not ask her to jump in that river without a stitch on her back. The aspens were trembling like sequins in a green and gold light. "What are those trees called?" Virginia asked. "Aspens; trembling aspens." "Oh," Virginia said, disappointed.

"How sad, she thought, to name something for its best quality. It stole away the possibility of surprise; it made it seem so common. No, she thought, the trees should have some other name. White barks, something like that. "Edna, if anyone asked us what our relation was, we would say we were friends, wouldn't we?" "I suppose so." "But that doesn't seem to cover it." "Names?" Edna mused; "they never do. Nothing ever means the same thing to everyone anyhow." "There's some kind of imbalance in nature," Virginia said; "nothing ever means the same thing to anyone else, but everyone reads the same markings on the trails, and they all mean different things, and everyone makes the same mistakes, just as if they had read the same signs. I suppose I'm starting to think about George," she went on, "except no one ever called him George; everyone else called him Snake. He killed so many snakes when he was a young man, they called it a holy war." "Snake," Edna echoed; "Snake? He must have hated that." "Oh no," Virginia said; "he hated being called George. Snake was a mark of their affection, acceptance, counting all the old days into the balance. I didn't find out how much he hated being called George until the day he was getting ready to swallow that tub of poisons. 'I've always hated the name George.' That's what he said. Which meant, I suppose, he hated something about living with me." A breeze played in the trees; there was the sound of a woman's silk dress in the leaves.

"Edna," Virginia said, "there's one thing I did learn from that ludicrous marriage. You shouldn't let them, husbands I mean, imagine *too* much about you. George, he imagined I was so proud of the house and the business and the old money. Well, my poppa could have driven over enough money to buy the town back from himself. George, though, he thought it was all the world to me. I

211

was used to dressing well; everyone always expected it from us, for as long as I can remember. Why, they used to go on about my christening robe and how important it was to have a good one, and just where they were keeping mine so I could use it for my children, and how I had to preserve it just the same way after it was finished with. I don't remember any time when anyone crept around the house looking like a wet mop. Even the insane were supposed to have their fits in a neat wrapper or morning dress. The morning dress was preferred; wrappers weren't so very proper for the street."

"You mean," Edna asked, "that John imagines things about me, dangerous things?" "Not that you like clothes or money, nothing as simple as that, but he can't see you for just what you are. No one can; but a husband or a wife, they're practically bat-blind. Flying into mountains that aren't there all the time." "But it can't be helped," Edna said. She was confused; she didn't really understand what Virginia meant. "I didn't say *that;* it's hard as putting spectacles on a cat, but I guess you could do it, if you tried hard enough." "Tried *what?*" Edna asked; "I wish you would just come out with it and tell me what you're worrying yourself about." Virginia turned, staring at her. She felt the wetness at the back of her dress; the day was a hot one. It made her homesick. She hadn't counted on being homesick. "I hardly know Mr. Steele"; she felt obliged to say that. She didn't want Edna to take what she said to heart. Edna did have a tendency to do that, to take things to heart, but she wasn't sure Edna knew what to do with things after she took them in. Like the lady back home with forty-three cats, half of them clawing the other half to death. "Then I won't expect much," Edna said. "Mind, I'm only guessing," Virginia cautioned. "Guess away," Edna encouraged.

"I'll just pretend I'm a fortune-teller," Virginia answered gaily; "they say whatever comes into their heads." "But they only say good things," Edna protested; "that's why people go to them." "Not the ones I know. Why, my crazy aunt, she went to a fortune-teller in darktown. And the old thing, oh, she had quite a den, black and sooty from a coal fire and a chimney that hadn't been cleaned since they cleared off the Indians, and she was so dark, she was like a voice, with this dirty white turban on her head, and she told my aunt her husband and son were going to die of the diphtheria, but her daughter wouldn't, and her daughter, she was Clara, Clara ought to get the coffins now, because there wouldn't be any later, and for a family of standing, burying their dead in a ditch, that wouldn't be proper. And my aunt, she went right over to the undertaker's with Clara and purchased two gorgeous coffins and brought them home and put them in the parlor. My uncle, he nearly died of fright, and then, oh, he was furious! He said everyone knew that dark old fraud worked hand in glove with the undertaker, and he wasn't keeping the coffins in the house; she could sleep in one outside if she wanted to, but of course there were more bugs and vapors out there, and miasmas, and all kinds of unhealthy things.

"And Aunt, she kept warning him how he'd be sorry, mocking the revealed word like that, and he asked her how he could be sorrier than he already was, looking at the casket his own wife was in such a flurry to buy for him, and how could he be sorrier than he was if he *did* believe her. Well, she said, he could prepare to meet his maker if he'd only listen to the writing on the wall. She always scrambled words up. And he said he'd been prepared to meet his maker since the day he married her. But he never did think, he said, she was going clear out of her mind: no, he hadn't been prepared for that. Her silliness, well, he'd known all about that, and kind of liked it, but why did she have to go clear crazy? She mumbled something about his never knowing anything she wanted to know, or at least his not telling her what she wanted to know. He asked her what things; he'd tell her right now, before she buried her own son alive, and she said things like the future, what would happen to them, would Clara live when she had the scarlet fever, things like that, and that was the first inkling he had that Aunt thought he *ought* to know things like that.

"So he told her only God knew the future, and he wasn't sure God knew what he was going to do in advance, because, if he did, what were prayers for, but by that time it was too late. She just got crazier and crazier, and when Uncle and her son didn't die in the epidemic, she went clear crazy from disappointment, yes, disappointment. There was nothing left for her to hold on to. It was certainties she was after. Well, and maybe Uncle could have stopped it, or at least roped it in, if he'd known anything at all about how she saw him, but he didn't.

"Well, Mr. Steele, now, he's a little bit like Uncle, or a little bit like Aunt thought Uncle was. He seems to think he *should* have certainties, or at least be able to give them to you. He must think you need them." She looked at Edna, who didn't answer. "Well, *do* you need them?" Virginia asked. "No," Edna answered slowly; "I don't think I do. I guess I don't think there are such things." "But my darky guess is that he *thinks* you need them," Virginia persisted; "it must come from wearing such a tight turban. The hazard of fortune-telling." "Well, I don't, I don't need them." "But if he thinks you do, then he'll try and try to keep it up, that look of being certain; and then, when he doesn't feel that way, when he feels lost, he wouldn't dare tell you. No, he'd wander around in the swamp, climbing over the alligators." In spite of herself, Virginia shuddered. "You wouldn't want that," she finished; "you better talk."

"Talk?" Edna asked; "the kind of talk they mean in etiquette books? Confide in your wife. Make her your confidante, that kind of talk?" "That kind of talk; that's the only kind that keeps you safe. You mean," Virginia asked her, "they *tell* you that in etiquette books?" "In every one, in each and every one. Ten just showed one to me. *The Marriage Ring*. That's the third rule it lays down: confide in your helpmate." "You read those books a lot?" Virginia asked. Edna flushed. "It's a hobby of mine." "A hobby like that," Virginia said, "could have saved my husband." "No," Edna protested; "no, none of it seems real. None of it means anything when it's just on the page like that. They always have ministers writing them, too; I suppose so the reader will think he's hearing a sermon, but it still doesn't seem real. It doesn't seem like the people they're talking about have any blood in them. Or it makes everything too clear. Well, nothing's ever that clear, is it? I don't know why," Edna mused, "I keep reading them; they always sound as if they're written for people on the dark side of the moon. And the people in them are so good. Or they would be so good if they listened. 'Gloomy and callous words can destroy a family surely as a knife,' " she quoted from memory; 'such looks and such glances must be resolutely banished from the heavenly domicile of family life.' They don't tell you how; they seem to think to read is to obey."

"Maybe," Virginia thought aloud, "those books aren't meant for you, or for me, not the young ones. Maybe they're meant for certain people, desperate people, sour mothers who don't want their daughters going sour. *They* buy them and read them, and it's all true to *them*, but it's true to them because they've already lived it out, but to give it to someone 'starting out on life's path'—the ministers always say that at weddings—why, I guess to the young ones it can't mean much. I guess it's about the same when I try to tell you things that happened to me?" Virginia asked, worried. "No, it's different; you're *real*." She poked Virginia in the side. "Sometimes I wonder; real enough to get hot, anyway," she said, sitting up suddenly. "I'm going swimming in that river." "But we don't have any bathing costumes." "Why, of course we do"—Virginia said—"we have our chemises and our petticoats. If anyone comes up, we'll say they're the latest style. No one ever argues with that. Do you think anyone will come up?" Edna looked about her. "Not here." "Then let's go," Virginia said, walking quickly to the woods.

"What you do," she explained, "is hang your dress on a branch in there, and then lie in the sun for half an hour on your front and back, and when you get home, no one knows one drop has gotten on you." They plunged in, their petticoats rising like clouds around them. "Lilies, lilies," Virginia sang out. "Let's race," Edna giggled. They struck out for the other side. Virginia, to Edna's surprise, was a powerful swimmer. Oh dear, Edna thought, swimming harder; I didn't count on this. She finished first, her hand touching the bank before Virginia's, her legs sinking into the mud when she stood up, the mud reaching almost up to her knees. Bubbles flew quickly alongside them, outlining their bodies. "What a smell!" Edna exclaimed. "Swamp gas," Virginia said. "Oh, snakes!" she exclaimed in alarm; "are there any snakes here?" "Ten says no, but John says there are still some rattlesnakes left." "Well, then, let's go," Virginia said, throwing herself forward, striking out for the opposite shore. Edna swam after, her white petticoats spreading out like a train behind her, and with every stroke, she thought, how do you do it; how do you just come out and say you don't need to live in a hothouse?

She remembered a passage from one of her books: "Humanity is so constituted that it does not thrive best in a hothouse." You start a fight, she thought, triumphant; that's it, a fight. People say anything during fights. Well, and what should she fight about? she wondered, climbing out of the river, clambering up the slippery, rocky bank, hair and clothes streaming. A bridal tour; that would just do it. Now it all seemed so simple. A fight about the bridal tour: raised voices, ugly looks, no swallowing poison for John. Yes, it was so simple; why hadn't she seen it before?

Ten had written and sent off her letter, and predictably, received an immediate, astonished, and almost pathetically grateful response, in which Edith said of course *she* would attend the wedding, but in light of her daughter's feelings, Mr. Siddons could not be expected to attend. Neither did she intend to do anything which might ruin her daughter's wedding day. She asked Ten's advice. Should she, or should she not, reveal her plans for marrying at the end of her year of mourning? Ten wrote back that she should, and that the house was large enough, and she could keep everyone busy enough—in fact, everyone would have to be so busy that Edith would barely have an opportunity to meet her daughter in the halls. Then she took a deep breath, and told Edna her mother would, of course, be staying with them for a few days preceding the wedding. Edna accepted this calmly. Ten was annoyed at herself for having worried so. After all, she ought to have known; the girl was living in such a cloud. She and John seemed to have special lenses which allowed them to see into it. No one else could. What she could not understand was why Edna refused, that was what it amounted to, to discuss the bridal tour, or even a short honeymoon. Whenever the subject arose, something far more pressing was certain to pop into Edna's head. She's up to something, Ten thought, but this time, she didn't have the slightest idea of what it could be.

Meanwhile, the week of Virginia's stay was drawing to a close. John had diagnosed a serious peptic ulcer, and a messenger had duly been dispatched to Fitchburg, saying poor Mrs. Whitemore had just come out of her coma and would have to return South as soon as she regained her strength. He hoped, he wrote, the family would not be too disappointed to lose her forever. A lot they care, he thought, signing and folding the letter.

Virginia was to leave Monday morning; Saturday night, Edna spent in her room, talking and helping her pack. "Do you think we'll see each other again?" Edna asked; "I mean, after this?" "Certainties, certainties," Virginia teased. They continued packing. There really was not much to be done, but they were both careful. "I don't know why," Virginia finally said, "but I think we will; I just think so." "And if we don't?" "Then it will mean we were not meant to," Virginia answered, solemn. "We could make a definite arrangement," Edna suggested. Virginia paused, a pair of white kid gloves in her hand. "There are no such things. That's what I've been trying to tell you." "We could make the arrangement anyway," Edna retorted defiantly, "and then if it didn't come to pass, we'd be disappointed, but at least our chances, they'd be improved." "That's different," her friend said, approving; "chances, we should try to improve our chances. We have nothing else to work with." "I think you're right," Edna said. "About what?" "About only having chances; I must want certainties." "You surely do," Virginia said.

Edna had barely seen John that week, but late that night she heard his horse plodding up in front of the house. She waited until sufficient time elapsed; when she was sure he was settled in the library she put on her wrapper and went to talk to him. Finally, she got around to her subject. "Do you still believe," she asked him reluctantly, "that Virginia has consumption?" "I could have been mistaken," he lied. "I want to know," Edna insisted. "Perhaps she does." Edna's hands suddenly went cold. This was it, she thought; this was what Virginia had meant. "I tell you what," she said cheerfully, "pretend I'm another doctor and give me your best guess." "Oh, you're my consultant now," he laughed; he looked so much lighter. She was right about us, Edna thought; how could she have known?

"Yes, I think she has it. I think she's in remission, but it could come back. It usually comes back again, like malaria," he explained, "except that consumption, when it returns, is always a killer. Sooner or later." He watched her carefully. She looked down at her hands. "I hope you're wrong." "So do I." "Well," she said energetically, "we're making indefinite definite plans to meet two years from now, so if you're right, we won't have to worry about the details of a trip, but if you're wrong, I'll plague you to death about going South."

"It won't be the first time a doctor will be happy to be plagued for having made that kind of mistake. How much longer?" he asked. "What?" Edna asked, shocked. Her mind was still running on Virginia's health. "I mean until Ten shakes out a wedding." "One week, two at the most." "We should talk about what to do afterwards." Edna smiled. It wouldn't be necessary to fight over the bridal trip, after all. "I'd like to do something exciting; we could go to South Hadley. Or Dummerston." "You're not serious"; John grinned. "Oh, I don't want to go far from here, not for any reason. Do you think there's an empty cottage to be found in South Hadley?" "I hope you don't forget me as soon as you forgot Dummerston." He was laughing at her. "Oh, don't you worry," she said.

John felt something; what was it? As if fate had intervened and lifted an imperceptible shadow. A cloud the size of a man's hand, he thought. It's gone. Gone for now, anyhow, he reassured himself, burying his nose in Edna's cheek. "Get to bed, rabbit," he scolded. "Rabbit? Rabbit?" Edna repeated; "do I look like the type that produces a litter?" "You look like a nice furry rabbit." "But my hair's the wrong color." "That's what you think," John said, pushing her out through the door, keeping his hand on the knob. Edna tugged at the door from the other side, just as he knew she would. "Good night, badger," she whispered, giving up. He went off down the hall. Virginia turned over in her sleep. She kicked off the covers, muttering slightly, but did not wake. Her body was dampening the sheets.

"Where did the time go?" Edna thought, standing stiff and straight while Mrs. Grimsby, Ten's second neighbor up the mountain road, as well as the local dressmaker, drew pin after pin out of a long white muslin strip she had Amos tack to the bedroom wall. Ten sat in the comfortable wing chair, snuggling into the cushions. "There's not much to be done," Mrs. Grimsby said, pulling a blue-headed pin from her bodice and pinning a seam along Edna's left side. "The dress doesn't even need taking up at the hem," she said, deftly slipping in another pin. "Are you sure," she asked Ten, "this was your mother's dress?" "Well, if it's not," Ten said, "they've been lying to us about it for over fifty years." What a temper, Mrs. Grimsby thought; bad as if she'd lived here every day of her life. Well, she did live here every day of her life, almost. It never seems that way, though. I suppose it's all that money, she meditated, slipping in pin after pin; the Steeles always seem as if they were dropped down from the moon.

Like my mother used to say about the dandelions. Watch, she'd say, when they go to seed, you'll see. You'll be able to tell they dropped down from the moon. Of course, Mrs. Grimsby thought, finishing with Edna's left side, and standing back to inspect her work with great satisfaction, Mother was always a little peculiar. Especially after she tried to walk there, to the moon, one night in the middle of the summer. Well, on some nights (Mrs. Grimsby mentally defended her), the moonlight *did* look like a path on the water. Still, what a sight she'd been, and so disappointed too. Crying like that because she couldn't walk to the moon. Never knew what she wanted to go to the moon about; she shook her head, beginning on Edna's right side. Wouldn't you know, she thought, pinning carefully, people swimming in money would go diving in the attic for some old thing of a bridal dress. Of course, they had spent all that money, or someone had spent all that money. Mr. Bowen *estimated* (Mrs. Grimsby stressed that word to herself; she was proud of it) almost two thousand dollars had been thrown out on her wedding outfit. Well, maybe not thrown out, she conceded to no one in particular; perhaps *this* marriage would last. She rather liked Edna, the way she stood so still. Most everyone she knew complained like the devil if the business took more than three pins. I wonder what she did to catch that doctor, she wondered, almost jabbing Edna with a pin; she must have done something. Don't believe in love at first sight, she thought, pausing. "Have to stock myself up," she addressed both women, pulling pins from the white muslin strip, and making a neat, double line down the front of her bodice.

"Can I sit down now?" Edna asked. "If you can," Mrs. Grimsby answered. "Well, then, I can *lie* down?" Edna asked, and proceeded to lay herself flat on the bed, without disturbing one precious pin. The dress was of white watered silk, the waist the old-fashioned wasp waist. This was Edna's first experience with such a dress and, she swore to herself, her last experience with the complete torture chamber of laces and stays. But she did like wearing the dress, as if she had stepped out of an old painting. Wearing it, she felt as if she had lived a long, long time. She particularly liked the wide belt with its ornate carved ivory buckle. She was perpetually carrying it off with her for further inspection, its endless roses and leaves and the tiny peacocks; it took a sharp eye to find them out. She was lying on the bed, looking for them again; there were four in all, but not in predictable places.

The huge leg-o'-mutton sleeves made Edna look even more like a doll than ever. She and Ten had inspected with amusement the wicker frames used to puff them out; from them, the shoulder lines sloped down to the bodice, which was very low, inches lower than bodices today, Ten had thought, watching Edna put the dress on the first time, understanding entirely why Edna flushed so when she looked down. The skirt was very full, gathered in sharply at the waist. A train of enormous length fastened on with a series of hooks and eyes, the purpose of it, Edna assumed, to make the wearer look tall enough to justify those leg-o'-mutton shoulders. She had decided to wear her hair like the woman in the portrait, Ten's mother, John's mother, she kept reminding herself. She had grown attached to the woman, as if life still clung to the oiled canvas, but it was difficult to think of the woman as their mother. It would be difficult, Edna decided, to conceive of any mere woman as John's mother. It didn't seem possible an earthly being would have produced him; or Ten, either, for that matter. Well, whoever she was, Edna thought, *she* would also part her hair in the middle and train a long curl to hang on each side of her cheek. She wouldn't need artificial curls for that, she thought sleepily; but the rest of her hair, that was a problem. She would have to pin it up against the back of her head in thick looped curls. Oh, but Ten did have those huge, heavy hairpins. She would have to remember to paint them black to match her hair. That was no problem, really. And the string of pearls, she thought; Ten had the same string the artist had painted in the portrait, but really, she thought, feeling sacrilegious, the other woman wasn't pretty.

Edna's mind was, two days before her wedding, like a hot palette. Warm shapes of paint suddenly formed into scenes and pictures, painting recent memories which, for some inexplicable reason, often seemed almost ancient, while events from the past had virtually ceased to exist. "If you don't stop delaying," Ten had warned, "Virginia will miss that train." "I guess that's what they're hoping for," John said from the doorway; he had finally gotten a good night's sleep. No one answered him. He wondered: Was there any chance they would be traveling South in two years? He remembered his old professor saying while there was life anything was possible. Well, they might be going, after all. With half the country throwing eggs after them and setting fire to the tracks because the peculiar doctor was leaving the neighborhood for more than two days. It had been the same thing for a week now, everyone asking pointedly after his bridal trip. "Three days," John invariably answered. "Three days!" was the incredulous answer, and then the expected response: a slow grin spreading over the anxious questioner's face, and then the pretense of disapproval. "Well, then you can't be going far," to which John always answered, "If horses had wings."

Then the man and woman would go inside and jaw on about how the doctor and his new wife would only have a bridal trip of three days, not anything like the bridal tour anyone had imagined for them; well, and that was what came of marrying someone who went into New

221

York with her friend and bought up half of the clothes the dressmaker had ever made, and all according to that *Godey's Lady's Book,* expensive creations as anyone could dream up. Why, the kitchen maid had told them it took Miss Dickinson's mother herself two hours to view the wedding display. Which was, in fact, rather considerable, Edna thought; she had gone through with the shopping tour, the fittings, the purchasing, all for John's sake. He so wanted her to have everything she would have had had she married and lived in the city, although there were times, as she stood there, watching the same speckled hand with its pin moving back and forth, regular as a metronome, when she suspected he wanted her to buy everything she would need for the rest of her life; then she would never have to leave again. That was agreeable to *her,* she thought, looking irritably at the fabrics lying on the dressmaker's fainting couch. And it had seemed to make Ten happy, too, as if this were something they had intended to do since the day they had been born, but life had prevented.

Odd, Edna thought, unsure whether she was asleep or awake, but it had been John's decision that she be accompanied by Virginia to Manhattan, so that her friend could supervise the acquisition of a proper trousseau. Edna knew he meant they were not to think of money, and he was right in his opinion of Virginia's shopping methods; she had been only too happy to disregard any such considerations when deciding on purchases. So the two ladies had packed to take the Brattleboro Express to New York. It was odd, considering how much he had objected to their being together in the same room. Well, it was all in getting the proper advice. Virginia had accomplished this change of heart with her talk about certainties. Of course, it would have been useless, Edna realized, if she hadn't believed her and decided to do something. It was so easy just to let things go on. So she and Virginia had set off for the station, Amos driving, Ten and John accompanying them, only to be met by the news that the trestle bridge had burned and was under repair and there would be no trains going to New York that day.

Like one of the Four Horsemen, sitting next to Amos, John drove the black bays back, the carriage swaying and rattling as it careened at full speed on its way up the mountain back to the Steele house. Well, if Edna was leaving, he thought, furious, he wished she would get *on* a train and get it over with, and then get on another one, and get back here. Where she belonged. Why, he asked himself, had she agreed to go in the first place? Mrs. Grimsby was a very competent dressmaker; hadn't Ten always said so? Of course, it *had* been his idea, but that didn't mean Edna had to jump at every suggestion he made. He might have been speaking without thought. He might have been entirely wrong. Why had she paid him any attention whatsoever? He reined the horses in tightly.

And then the next day, it was the same thing, and the next day the same thing. When Edna and Virginia were finally helped onto the train, John sat with Ten in the open carriage, saying nothing. "Well, it will be the last Edna sees of the city for some time," Ten volunteered cheerfully. Silence rewarded her. "It's amazing how time flies," she went on, as if talking to herself; "only three days and she'll be back. It won't even seem as if she's really been gone." A black, black look. "I guess *you'll* hardly notice," Ten said, sounding as pathetic as possible; "you'll be out all day healing the halt and the lame and the lepers, but it won't be so much fun for me, I can tell you." John stared straight ahead.

"Well," Ten continued, as if her brother were taking part in this conversation, "Hal will be arriving this afternoon. Now all the trains are coming through." How could he keep quiet like that? She had almost forgotten what he was like when he pulled one of his moods up over his head. "Of course," she remarked, casual, "they say the British invasion is not to take place for at least one more week, so Edna will be safe until then. An odd time for them to take the country back, if you ask me." He didn't even look at her. "Well," Ten persevered (he had to surface sooner or later), "don't you think it's a bit much to go into mourning over a three-day separation?" She was almost shouting, as if his inability to respond came from the onset of sudden deafness. He turned his head a fraction of an inch toward her, then resumed his staring. "You are just like those young women Mother used to threaten me with before I left for school," she scolded; "the ones who had no conversation. You remember. That was her precise phrase." I might as well please myself in this nonexistent conversation, she decided. " 'A young woman must have conversation'; Mother was at that even as she was packing me off to school and crying like a river. That was where I met Edna's mother," she said, as if he had missed learning that important detail. "And the examples of ladies 'without conversation'; she could concoct them at the drop of a pin; *she* ought to have been a writer.

" 'When I was young,' " she would begin, "don't you remember?" she egged on her brother; "it was the subject of *her* conversation for months, of course. 'I had a gentleman friend who had the bad luck to escort one of those speechless beauties to dinner. He asked her about painting and music. She found nothing in them. Well, and what of the habits of society? Oh, she said, that was no theme for her; her poppa approved only dinners, and dinner parties were all she attended. "Then I suppose you spend your time reading?" asked my friend. He was an inventive man, poor soul. "Oh! Indeed we do read!" "Light literature?" the benighted man asked, seeing some light. "Indeed! Light literature!" "Novels, perhaps?" "Indeed. We read novels." "Do you take to Fielding?" "We do not read Fielding." "Then you must like Richardson?" "Richardson? We never read Richardson." "Surely," he plowed bravely on, "you must be quite romantic in your tastes, and are a devotee of Aphra Behm." "Certainly not," replied the young thing, showing some signs of shock, which at least reassured my friend that his companion still lived. "Who, then," he asked irritably, "if I may be so bold, *is* your favorite novelist?" "Why, Defoe," she answered, going on with her eating as if she were an engine in need of constant stoking. "Aha," said my friend, taking heart; "Defoe is a very exciting novelist." "Indeed! We do like his books so much. Poppa read them out to us, but then he misses out all the exciting parts." '

"Then Mother would pause dramatically, fix me with that look, and say, 'Well, after that, was it any wonder my friend found his knife and fork better company than his neighbor? They were as well dressed with roses, and made a good deal more noise against the plate.' " Ten vainly waited for a response. "Well, of course, you take no interest because the subject of the lecture does not apply to *you*," she said nastily; "*you* were the one she saved her other story for, the one about the impossible father, the one who thundered at his servants, 'Confound you, will you take that dish to the other end!' He was the one with the poor wife, whose only refrain was 'My dear Charles, do be moderate,' which only brought on another tide of abuse. You must remember this story"; she didn't even bother looking at him; telling these stories was cheering her up, anyhow. It was as if Mother was back, watching. She would have liked to see this. "Then it was his daughter who came under fire, thanks to some innocent remark. I remember how well Mother used to impersonate him. ' "Really, you are quite a fool, Mary," he said, and turned on her like a wounded bear, and the poor thing burst into tears. Well, none of us knew where to look. Our appetites flew out the window, our indignation was hotter than the food before us, and we managed to sit through dinner by repeating Solomon's proverb about a dry morsel sufficing where love is, and swore off any further suppers of turtle and turbot at *that* man's house.' Yes," Ten finished, "that was the story Mother always saved up for you. 'Really, you're quite a fool, Mary.' I guess she could see how the branch was bending." Still no response. Ten sighed and settled back against the tufted leather cushioning. I shall consider this a temporary turn for the worse, she comforted herself. When John broke the silence she jumped in her seat.

"Whose decision was it that Edna return with her mother?" he asked bearishly. "Hers," Ten answered, monosyllabic. She had had enough; *she* wasn't volunteering one bit of information. He could extract it from her, if he wanted it, like meat from a lobster claw. Unfortunately, her desire for revenge was not to be satisfied; John asked no further questions.

The house was finally coming into view. Ten looked at it with gratitude. John could hug his silences somewhere in there far from her sight. John handed her out. Amos inquired about the carriage. "I'll be needing that for the three-fifteen train," Ten told him; "Hal arrives on that. Or so I assume," she addressed John's broad back; "since no other train is coming in from Manhattan." "I'll have the carriage ready, ma'am," Amos said. John stalked off into the house. Ten caught sight of Bridget, called to her, and asked for her gardening basket. "What do you want with that thing?" Bridget demanded. "Pruning roses," Ten answered irritably; "doesn't anyone ever keep quiet? Can't I take a step without giving someone an account of it?" What's gotten into her? Bridget wondered, watching her march off down the path as if she were after a murderer. I should have gotten after this wild bush long, long ago, Ten scolded herself furiously, beginning to clip wildly at all the brown branches; I'm going to get off every rose hip, she decided, piling up huge stone slabs to reach higher up. She spied some brown branches in back of the thicket.

"Neglected for years," she complained aloud; was there no one to take care of anything? These thorns look like they come from dinosaur backs, she thought, and then, disregarding them, dove into the bush, ignoring the thorns as well as the cuts they were inflicting on her palms as they pierced her leather gardening gloves. A saw, I need a saw, she concluded, starting for the barn. "Miss Ten," Bridget called from the window, "will you be careful in that bush?" Ten ignored her. Where was Amos? Well, she could find the saw without him. Bridget watched with alarm as Ten flew off down the path clutching her enormous prize. She made a mental note to go out and consult Ten on the menu for supper within the hour; why, a person could get killed on that bush. Ten, meanwhile, had disappeared as far as the waist into the brambles, and was enthusiastically sawing at dead branches, scratching her cheeks and pulling out dead, horned vines with the nerveless enthusiasm of a true fanatic. This will take hours! she thought, diving in for another branch. There certainly will be plenty of roses for poor Edna's wedding, she observed, wildly sawing at another branch.

John had gone straight inside, marched down the hall to his room, and not only slammed the door, but latched it. "What a pair!" Bridget exclaimed. John threw himself face down on the bed and burst into tears. How long, he asked himself, could it take to repair a bridge? How long could it take for a train to arrive? Was it unreasonable to expect them on the same day, or the day after they were expected? He beat on the pillow with his fists in a fit of tears. When he woke up, he was furious as ever but, as his slashed sister noted, somewhat more talkative. She decided not to mention Edna's departure again, and he decided not to ask any questions about the deep scratches covering her face, neck, and hands. If she doesn't look as if she got into a fight with an army of tomcats, he thought; she did look comical. Ten saw his glance, and could not restrain herself. "It was not *my* idea to send her to Manhattan for a trousseau." Her brother glared until she picked up her fork. Edna heard all about it after-wards, from Ten, from John, from Bridget. What impressed her the most was John's admitting to all that crying. I should have liked to see *that,* she thought.

And Manhattan, that seemed far away, on another planet, one she would not visit again. She was sure she would not return there in her lifetime, and the thought made her happy. She and Virginia certainly had a wonderful time, popping in and out of all the shops, buying whatever caught her eye; Virginia's eye, really. That was why she had enjoyed it so much, because Virginia thrived so on it. She had orders to buy whatever Virginia wanted, and present it to her, but her companion preferred to make use of her poppa's money. "He couldn't take it with him," she said, " 'cause if he did, there'd be no more room left in hell." So Edna bought pearls, and a diamond pendant, a new riding habit, which then became two riding habits, one black and one brown, three evening dresses, all with bared shoulders, an endless number of crinolines, a small hill of petticoats, three long shawls, two embroidered and two plain, two of silk, two of cashmere, ten lace spencers, and three scoop bonnets. Ten pairs of kid gloves. "They're impossible to keep clean," Virginia assured her; "you should purchase at least twenty," but the woman in the shop promised her they would keep records of her measurements; she could send for another ten whenever she felt she needed them: lace mittens to wear at dinner parties, wrappers of every description, several serpent bracelets, three lace mantillas, artificial floral wreaths to dress the hair, an assortment of knitted flowers, fourteen chemises, every description of hair ornament, two hoop skirts, three berthas, ten robes de nuit made of linen cambric and Valenciennes lace, one matinee of jaconet, one matinee of mull muslin trimmed with frills of needlework. To Edna, it resembled an elaborate basque for society dress, fastening at the waist with a ribbon rose and streamers, the sleeves trimmed in the same way, with its attached, beribboned hood, and finished at the bottom with a full flounce cut in small Vandykes and edged with braid, and, above that edge, a double row of braid. And marching down the front and the neck, a row of frilling, set with points inward, the sleeves also edged with frill, and gathered up inside the arm by bows of blue ribbons with long streamers.

"Oh, when you get up at night to talk, you should wear that," Virginia marveled, ordering two on the spot for herself. "Have you any embroidered screens? And fans? Very elaborate?" Edna was horrified; they might as well be ordering potatoes and onions for all the difference it made to her. "Well, Edna," Virginia lectured, "you must think of all the money you'll save by not having to purchase a wedding dress." Edna shuddered. "Fans in mother-of-pearl and lace, oriental in origin, I should think," Virginia ordered, looking up from her list; "and we need at least six robes of white cambric muslin for the hot weather; the same number of chemisettes to be worn underneath, and"—she paused to consider—"one dozen morning caps made of assorted lace designs. Something which does not cover too much of the hair, but throws the face into shadow." "Oh, I understand entirely," the agreeable designer said enthusiastically to Virginia, her pencil poised above the list she had been frantically scribbling, casting an appraising look at Edna.

"Have we forgotten anything in the way of vests?" the woman solicitously inquired. "Oh, vests!" Virginia cried; "we must have vests, blue preferably, satin, I think; she is small enough for it, and embroidered in peach, in green, I leave that all up to you. Gold buttons, of course." "Ours are set with turquoise," the designer said proudly. "That will just do"; Virginia smiled; "do you recommend the pelerine?" she asked anxiously. "It is wonderful for evening wear, especially if the lady does not want to expose her neck entirely, but there is also the basque for spring to consider. It makes a wonderful breakfast dress; we can make up some very pretty skirts for it. Why," Madame Jeannette exclaimed, "it can be sent to the common wash!

"But," she said gravely, "we have neglected the everyday bonnet. I think the straw-colored silks would suit her best, full-blown blush roses, mixed with tulle, inside the brim. Or a trim of field daisies in wreath, encircling the face, and the sides, they should merge just properly with a bouquet of May roses and foliage; the edges can be trimmed with pointed lace or covered with ribbon trim, the lace at the edge lying flat." "Several of each," Virginia decided. Edna felt her presence entirely unnecessary. She watched them through a fog; they were serious, as if they were drawing up the Declaration of Independence. "Yes," Madame Jeannette agreed, "a face like that must be on display." "And knitted lace undersleeves, the sort which fasten above the elbow by hook or button." "Puffed, I assume?" "Ten, of whatever is most flattering," Virginia ordered; "and white satin shoes, two pairs of day shoes, riding boots, embroidered house slippers, whatever is necessary for life in country and city."

"I understand," Madame Jeannette said; "I have just the shop to send you to. A Mr. Goodwin does all our work in that line." Virginia went on, indefatigable: cloaks, purses of fine mesh; "The marion, that is a cloak we must not forget, and the nightingale, one in violet, one in black; it is so pretty," Virginia babbled on easily; "taffeta and lace is surely one of the best combinations. Have we forgotten anything?" she asked at last. "If you have remembered the husband"—Madame Jeannette beamed— "I believe that will do. Oh, my dear!" she exclaimed; "we have forgotten the nonpareil garment." "What on earth is that?" Edna, finally, had taken an interest in *something*. "It combines chemise and drawers; its advantages are many," explained Madame Jeannette. "Well, at least one hundred then," Edna said. Madame Jeannette began writing, but Virginia stopped her hand. "Five will be fine, and shade bonnets, and I've forgotten straw bonnets, and if you could recommend one elaborate robe for the morning toilette, several hairnets, that's no difficulty, but I should appreciate your choosing an adjustable bustle."

"I recommend only Douglas and Sherwood," Madame Jeannette said solemnly, as if prescribing for a deadly illness; "their Patent Adjustable Bustle and Skirt is without rival, and nothing can express the advantages of their Tournure Corset. She will need that if she is marrying in a wasp-waist." "Then we are done," Virginia sighed in mock relief. "*If* you don't care for fans or feathers. We have some very pretty ones of pheasant feathers." "An assortment of fans and fire screens," Virginia ordered; "that ought to conclude our business. And one of all the items for myself, but mine must be in pale blues or dark crimsons." Madame Jeannette frowned; crimsons were definitely out of fashion. "I know how it will distress you to use such out-of-the-way colors," Virginia sympathized, "but I must think of my own coloring."

"Well," Virginia announced, triumphant, as soon as they were back on the street, their parasols bobbing above them, "now all you have to do is sit up straight and look at your Mr. Steele and you shall live blissfully ever after." "Or in bankruptcy," Edna scolded. "I solemnly foresee, in my invisible magic glove, that you will be used to all that money within the year. It grows on you, and not like poison ivy, either." "I hope you're right." "*Your* family wasn't exactly poor," Virginia reminded her. "But it wasn't like this; *this* makes me feel like a church mouse." "Some church mouse," Virginia laughed at her; "well, I can tell you, I like being a church mouse, although I suppose I could manage living as an ordinary wealthy being." She was mocking herself. They had almost reached the Astor. "Dinner?" Virginia inquired. "As long as they don't serve articles of clothing." "I shall ask them to remove the tablecloth." Laughter blew from them, but Edna was still alarmed. How *much* would that bill be? "John will think I'm after a fortune," she told Virginia over the cold shrimp salad. "Do you think so? He and Ten *insisted* you do your shopping with me; Ten said they were worried you would return with two ready-made dresses and no boots or winter cloak at all." "But didn't they set a limit?" "They certainly did, and *I* stayed within it. 'See that she gets whatever she wants,' that was what Ten said. 'Or might possibly need,' your fiancé added. 'Or whatever becomes her,' his sister put in. Well, if you want my opinion, I think they'd be terribly disappointed if anything less than a freight car arrived bearing the trousseau." "Lord," Edna gasped, dropping her fork. A waiter scurried over with a new one. "And," Virginia answered, "if you're doing any unnecessary worrying about what you're getting into, I'd say it's a wonderful assortment of fashionable items." "Fit for a princess," Edna said, ironic. "Well, isn't that what Mr. Steele thinks you are?" "Well, my dear mother does not," Edna said; "we take her on next."

While Edna was in New York, Ten made it her business to see about floral decorations for the house. She saw no point in consulting her brother, who remarked that he supposed a wedding at home would make extra cleaning for the maids, and then dismissed the entire matter from his mind. His sister, on the other hand, had very different ideas and thought that if the marriage party really was to be small, and was really to take place at their home, the very least they required was a floral arch set in front of the dining-room fireplace. Well, then, that meant a trip to Garibaldi's; she would take Hal with her. He had spent the previous two days sawing wood carefully into identically shaped planks, but when asked what he was doing, he looked bewildered, and went back to his sawing. When he had finished a pile of a certain size, of significance only to himself, he would crack each one in half, throw it in a corner, and begin on a new assortment of sticks, all of which in turn suffered the same fate. "John's getting married again"; Hal beamed happily as they drove off in their carriage. His sister glared at him; his face reddened as if it had been slapped smartly, and for no reason. Oh, he doesn't mean anything by it, she thought, remorseful.

She was beginning to remember how oddly her brother's memory functioned; he had an uncanny faculty for recalling details, dates, names she no longer knew the owners of, faces, where he had last seen them, but the meaning of all those things was lost to him. Either they were pleasant to remember, like the taste of maple sugar, or unpleasant, like the feel of slime on the water one hot summer. Now that she thought of it, Hal probably *still* would not swim; not after all these years. And it was over twenty-five years, too. That's right; he's thirty-seven now. And what a lecture we got from Mother, as if we could have been expected to know the green slime would have bothered him so. "Hal, dear," she said soothingly; "please don't say that again. Please don't say, 'John's getting married again' anymore. All right?" "He's always getting married"; Hal glowed. Hopeless, Ten thought; he makes it sound as if that's John's profession in life. "Hal," she said sweetly; it was a good thing she had time to get him in hand, before he began unnerving everyone, and the worst thing was, with the best of intentions; "Hal, please don't say anything about John getting married. Please." "Ten said please, Ten said please," he chanted with triumph. Well, she sighed, that was his idea of a promise. Yet after two or three weeks, she thought, watching the trees pass, he would become an indispensable presence, like the important family pet; if he left, he would be missed. Still, she would have preferred it if he had decided to reappear once the wedding was safely over.

The carriage stopped in front of Garibaldi's Floral Parlor. Ten chose an arch to be made up of pink and white carnations, and fourteen white standing wicker baskets to be filled with pink and white flowers of any description, but she did want gladiolas, and if they were past their season now, what was she to do? Was a special shipment from the South out of the question? It was. But, puffed Mr. Garibaldi, his colleagues in New York could ship enough gladiolas for the wedding ceremony if they shipped by express. Of course, the cost would be prohibitive; the bulbs would have to be forced, as would any lilies or tulips she wanted. Why, he lamented silently, did people who wanted spring and summer flowers always choose to marry just as summer was slipping over the horizon? Only two days left of July, and here she was, calmly talking of tulips and chrysanthemums. "Roses will be no problem, naturally," Ten was saying. Mr. Garibaldi sighed dramatically.

White roses would be blooming in the middle of August, but this wedding was to take place on the second of August. "Surely the nurseries have them as well?" Ten was asking. Mr. Garibaldi quickly estimated the cost. Ten appeared not to hear him. "And of course we need chrysanthemums, and pots of geraniums for the shelves and the brackets." "Chrysanthemums?" Mr. Garibaldi asked; "it's early for chrysanthemums." "Can it be done?" "Oh, well," he began, intending to explain the complexity of all of his efforts, but Ten cut in. "Yes, it can," he murmured. "Then we have that matter taken care of," she said complacently, looking down at her little list. "Why," she asked him, looking up at the tin baskets hanging by their handles from his walls, and the standing baskets, lined up like soldiers along the wall in back of him, "do wedding baskets and funeral baskets look so alike?" "I've often wondered about that myself," Mr. Garibaldi said; "but they aren't really alike. The funeral baskets," he demonstrated with an expert's precision, "are much stiffer, and generally made of tin. They try to soften the look of them by giving them that pleated appearance, but they look stiff all the same. And then to have them hang from handles, or rest on something; it's evident they're temporary. No one really intends them to remain in the house after the sad event. But the wedding baskets," he said, proudly appraising his stock, "they're fit to stand with any assemblage of fine wicker and they do cheer up a piazza. And of course, they stand by themselves, which makes them easier to distribute about a house." "Which the dead do not," Ten commented.

"Do not what?" asked Mr. Garibaldi. "Stand by themselves." "Of course not," he agreed. Why did his conversations with her always take such a peculiar turn? "But then it would be a strange wedding if the happy pair did not stand by themselves," he said. "They don't," Ten joked; "they stand together." The florist laughed; she was a witty woman, no matter what people said about her.

He watched her retreating back on its way to the post office. She certainly had a determined way. What a dusty day, he thought, watching the clouds of dust each step of hers stirred up. And there goes that Hal after her again, just like a puppy; well, that sight brings back memories. He watched, waiting for her to come out of the post office, but the door opened twice, and still, no Mrs. Richardson. Perhaps her brother had mailed her, he grinned to himself; then he laughed aloud. *He* was pretty witty himself. He should try his hand at cartoons for the local paper, but his pictures, he thought, looking down at a group of them, half covered by severed green stems, they looked like pumpkins after the rot set in. Well, she wasn't coming out of the post office. He had better get to work on his wreaths. That was one thing about his line of work; there was always someone who needed a wreath, usually for the wrong reason, he thought, measuring one strand against another, clipping it in the proper place. He wondered if what he had read in the papers was really true, that at a Boston funeral of a butcher, a floral lamb with a floral knife piercing its side had been the main object of display. Well, he could do well enough in that line, but a pretty picture it would make when weeping mothers came in demanding floral nooses for their hanged offspring, or floral rivers with floating bodies for suicides, or a floral patient sporting floral scalpel. His mind kept running along those lines. His mind was like most. He observed one kind of creation in the clouds and naturally tended to people the earth with the rest of the breed.

Meanwhile, Ten was lost in reading a long letter from Nellie which had finally come in. She *had* persuaded her husband to let her take two days' vacation from her ten children and thirty cows and God only knew how many pigs and hens and goats and grapes, and she would be coming on the two o'clock train on the day before the wedding. That would be a nice surprise for Edith, Ten thought, entirely contented with her doings. She hoped she hadn't tipped a balance of any sort by bringing them together again after all this time, but she imagined they would be happy as ever to be reunited. Nellie wrote she had grown "fleshy," and Edith—she would present the same smooth, cool, sophisticated façade Nellie always took such comfort in.

And then there was the way Edna had reacted to her mother's letter. Showing it to her, *that* had been a better strategy than she had anticipated. By the last page, big round tears had been rolling out of Edna's green cat eyes, and when she finished, she put the letter down in her lap, and sat there crying, looking at it. "Take it to your room and have a *very* good cry over it," Ten instructed sternly; "and a long time overdue it is, too." Well, after that night, she had no more trouble about Edith attending the wedding, or spending some time in the house before it, or Mr. Siddons, or anything else for that matter.

She was dragged back into everyday life by the buzzing of a crowd of men; they were talking about the county fair. Was it that time of year again? she wondered in disbelief, turning around to look about her, and finding herself buried in Hal's jacket. Had he been standing there all that time? And without complaint? John, beyond doubt, would have dragged her back to the carriage. He wouldn't have seen any reason standing in the post office reading a long letter when it could be read in their carriage on the way to wherever it was they were going. Well, she wasn't marrying either of her brothers, thank heavens. And now, with all the arrangements made at Tivoli's, refreshments, tent, band, she mentally ticked them off for the hundredth time, she had nothing to do but lie back in her hammock and inspect her chrysanthemums and her hanging fuchsia plant and her lily beds. Orange liles would be completely inappropriate for decorative purposes, and she was thankful she would not be called upon to sacrifice them.

In the lobby of the Regency, Edna and Virginia perched on straight-backed chairs waiting for Mrs. Dickinson, who should, just that minute, be receiving their calling cards. "I suppose I *could* have just gone up," she whispered worriedly to her friend; "it does seem preposterous to send one's own mother a calling card." "But you don't know her situation," Virginia whispered back. "You might interrupt something, a business conference, for example." "Business conference," Edna repeated. "Well, and what *do* you think about your mother's remarrying?" Virginia asked. Edna peered up the stairs and around the lobby; her mother was nowhere in sight. "I don't think much of Mr. Siddons, I can tell you, but from the time she went into his studio it was Pygmalion and Galatea all over again. If they make each other happy . . ." She trailed off. "And I don't think much of my mother, either, but whatever she is, she's a perfect specimen of it; I suspect I'll come to think of that as a real achievement—later in life. And she does the best she can." She was still haunted by the memory of that letter to Ten. If it was that important to her, having someone look up to her, the least she could do, she decided, was not to look down on her, or at least not to do so quite so ostentatiously. She didn't dare expect more of herself.

"Is *that* your mother?" Virginia asked, her twitching hand testifying to a barely controlled desire to point. Edna followed Virginia's gaze. Yes, that was her mother, coming down the curving stairs with her measured tread, her auburn hair haloing her magnificent face, her black robes flowing as if they were made of water. Really, Edna thought, the woman *was* a beauty. It must be difficult to be so beautiful; there was a perfection about her mother that was, in its own way, monstrous. No wonder her friend Nellie had become so important to her. Nellie, her daughter thought, is Mother's patron saint. She reassures her; she makes her feel as if her feet touch the earth, as if she had a body of flesh and blood and takes part in the real concerns of men and women. And hadn't *she* been seduced by her mother's exterior, assuming everything beneath such a perfect surface must exist in smug clouds of contentment? Well, in fact, what was her beauty but a magnificent dress she could never remove or alter, but was forced to wear, day in and day out, year in and year out, regardless of how she felt inside?

She was laced in forever by that beauty. She thought suddenly of the torture museum Virginia had insisted on visiting, and the iron lady, which at the time had reminded her of the famous Tournure Corset, except that its embrace was fatal. It was lined with iron spikes. Yes, beauty could be like that. People were always telling her how beautiful *she* was, but they always had some small reservation. She was so tiny; she had the look of a child. As if they were implying her particular breed of beauty derived from some perversion of nature, some arresting of growth. But, she thought, she did not feel *short* inside. It was her mother who felt short inside. And her father, who by most lights would have been considered homely (if imposing), she had considered him magnificent. Appearances mattered so little, she thought, and at the same time was intimidated all over again by her mother's approaching magnificence.

She rose and kissed her mother on the cheek. Edna was physically stunned by the grateful look she received in return, and then, when her mother had recovered herself, she presented her own cheek to be kissed and not in the usual way, either, as if she expected to be burned by a hot branding iron. Well, something has changed her, Mrs. Dickinson thought with relief; I only hope it isn't early suffering. She worried about that. She had never heard anything that would have led her to expect Edna to marry an "even" man; Mr. Siddons was "even," never given to moods. Mrs. Dickinson, now a few months short of her half century of life, considered that the paramount virtue one should seek in a spouse. She had written something of her worries to Ten, who had written back, assuring her Edna would die of boredom married to a genial man. "She needs something to occupy her mind," Ten had written, thinking it over carefully; she wanted to be accurate, and since John was her brother, that stood in the way.

"We used to chase the book peddlers from the door," Ten wrote; "they always have something new along the lines of *Immortality and the Joys of Eternal Life,* or *House and Home: Happiness Forever,* but Edna virtually runs down the path after them, buys the books, tries to get them to sell her their sample copies, and then is on the watch for their return with those remarkable objects, none of which are tolerable in my sight. And it's not the engravings she's after, either; she *finds* something in them, or she's looking for something in them. I think she has inherited her father's restless mind. If I guess correctly, Edith, it will be cat and rat with John and Edna. She'll be busy prowling around after him, as she has been since she set eyes on him, and I suppose that means they'll live happily ever after, or as close to it as she's likely to get, and probably closer than you or I ever will." Well, Mrs. Dickinson thought, it was certainly a novelty to see her daughter through another person's eyes.

She had assumed Ten would see Edna as she did, the two of them were such old friends, *ancient friends* as that dreadful Ten had put it; she shuddered at that phrase. Although lately, there were times she *felt* ancient, but her mirror never reflected it. I'm like the queen in that dreadful tale Edna translated, she thought, seating herself opposite the two girls; the one with the mirror that kept telling her she was the most beautiful of all. Well, and a lot of good it did her. Why couldn't she look ugly, or even sloppy? The midwife had assured her *she* looked beautiful as ever giving birth to Edna; nurse and the doctor had both expressed astonishment and admiration for a woman who could endure the "cataclysmic event" without disturbing a hair on her head. But it had made her feel as if she had no head at all. Yes, she thought, if she had her way about it, she would choose a talking mirror that was positively abusive. The closest she had ever come to owning such a thing was "owning" Edna, having her in the house, but now even Edna had reformed. The last critical voice hushed, she thought sadly. Well, where would she be now? Just where she had always been.

Everyone she knew worried about the changes that set in after death. Her fear, she realized recently at one of Mr. Siddons' countless dinner parties, or soirees, as he preferred to call them, was that there would be no change. She would wake up and find herself floating about with a harp, angels commenting, as they flew by, "What a magnificent-looking woman. She doesn't look real!" In nightmares, she saw herself coming before the bar of judgment, and God, before he passed sentence, turning to the angel Gabriel, saying, "What a magnificent-looking woman. She doesn't look real. I had a good idea when I created *that!*" And then, of course, he would cast her down into the flames, all for dear Edmund's sake, when really it had been his fault in the first place. Yes, she blamed God. She would have quite a bit to say to him if the condemned had an opportunity to speak up.

The three ladies decided to go out on their own hook and look for a pastry shop. There were, Mrs. Dickinson said, so many nice ones with tables set out on the sidewalks under brightly colored umbrellas, and it was a sin to waste such beautiful weather. She wondered how the weather liked it, every creature on earth constantly commenting on the beauty of the day (when it *was* beautiful; at least there were gray, unpleasant days, damp days, cold days, rainy days, sleety days, blizzardy days, cloudy days, overcast days. My mind is running on as badly as ever Edmund's ever did, she reproached herself. She had never expected this to be her reaction to Edna's miraculous reformation).

They chatted happily along, Virginia bubbling over Edna's trousseau, minutely describing every article. "Oh, Madame Jeannette's," Edith said, "you did stumble into the right robber's den." "Robber's den?" Edna asked. "Oh, I just meant she was so expensive, but, Edna, there is no one better in America." Her daughter seemed shocked. "Edna, you needn't worry about money, you know. Why, the Steele family must be one of the richest families in America, and there are no heirs in it, and John is the youngest. So you see, you must not feel any guilt." Edna blushed. I had better get off this topic, Edith decided. "Are you still doing translations?" she asked. Now Virginia looked bewildered; could she say nothing right? Virginia promptly rescued her. "What sort of translations did she do?" "Oh," Mrs. Dickinson went on, relieved, "she spoke French from childhood, but then it was German, and after that, Russian. She was about to begin on Swedish, but . . ." "But my father's death interrupted my preoccupation with strange stories," Edna finished for her; "and, probably, I wouldn't have continued in any event. I didn't like the German tales. They ended, after all that reading, in the end of the world. I wonder at the people; they seem to believe in their stories as we do in the Bible, and yet they have the world come to an end in the last of them." "Isn't a better one to begin?" Virginia asked. "I suppose so, but I was never quite clear on that; perhaps it was my clumsiness with the language."

"Do you read languages?" Virginia asked her mother. "French, what they teach all women of society. And," she said, somewhat playfully, "I know one line of Latin. Edna's father repeated it constantly. "Tiresomely," Edna put in. *"Sic transit gloria mundi."* "That *would* be tiresome," Virginia agreed. "You have no idea," Mrs. Dickinson said. Edna was looking at her with genuine sympathy. This so disconcerted her mother that, for the first time since childhood, she did not know where to look. She wasn't used to *this* kind of treatment. Not kindness. Certainly not sympathy. Not from her daughter.

They chattered on, about Virginia's widowhood, her feelings about returning South; the plans the two friends had made to meet again in two years' time, how John had agreed to it; what life was like in the country, how Virginia had reacted with fits, but Edna had taken to it like a fish to a river; how Mr. Siddons' gallery exhibition had been attended, and how excellent had been the reviews. They solemnly discussed what train would be best for Mrs. Dickinson and her daughter to take to Brattleboro the next day, Edna reassuring her mother that there were always hacks at the depot, willing to go anywhere, especially to the Steele house, Edna asking again and again if her mother wouldn't prefer to be accompanied by Mr. Siddons, her mother's answer always the same: "No, no, he is far too busy with his career. His next exhibition opens only six weeks from today." So everything was going smoothly, Virginia thought; at least she was doing some good. Not much, she had few illusions about that, but some. It would help her, when she returned to Charlottesville and everyone looked at her as if she had herself administered the strychnine and carbolic acid to her husband. Her dead husband. Her late husband, she corrected herself. And Edna's letters. They would help too. Life was such a series of accidents, she thought, resigned. "The world is a hospital," she mentally mocked the lugubrious Episcopalian minister who had presided, or better say reigned, over Byron's funeral. "The world is an infirmary and we are all invalids in it." She coughed involuntarily. Suggestible, she thought; they had always said that of her. Not that it made anyone more sympathetic. Was there anyone in the world, she wondered, who did not want more sympathy? Sometimes she thought all most people lived for was sympathy. Of course, there were exceptions. Edna, for instance. Curiosity, yes, that was it, that was what Edna lived for, that and for the passions with which she had been born.

Virginia, who was remaining in Manhattan for another week, "delaying the inevitable," as they thought, saw Edna and her mother off on the express. The two girls clung to each other, sobbing, while Mrs. Dickinson looked on speechless. How many times had she heard Edna inveigh against such vulgar spectacles? She didn't dare speak to her daughter for some time after the train left the station. She was grateful her only child had not been beheaded by a post as the train pulled from the station. Edna had been half hanging from the car attempting to catch the last possible glimpse of her friend; finally, her mother could no longer control herself and firmly took hold of Edna's belt. She wasn't going to have her fall out of the train, not if she had anything to say about it. Eventually, there was some polite discussion over who had the best title to the window seat. The conversation of mother and daughter never reached anything resembling intimacy, but neither would anyone have mistaken the two ladies for strangers. Her mother was, as Edna had told Virginia, the only mother she had ever known, and that meant something, didn't it? The two girls agreed that it did, indeed, although neither of them could decide what. Virginia's mother had died when she was too young to remember her, but she was sure, she said, had she lived and turned butcher, she would have meant *something*, whatever that might be. Mrs. Dickinson, for her part, kept reminding herself that she was traveling to attend her daughter's wedding. It was something she could not yet take in. No, she thought; no, she did not believe it at all. A wedding should make me *feel* older, she thought hopefully. But not *look* older, she concluded dismally.

It was *still* two days before the wedding; Ten had had enough of her hammock. There was something, something special. She should think of it, to mark this occasion which both bride and groom seemed determined to treat as commonly as parsnips. She had it! A wedding certificate! They must have a special wedding certificate! She set off for the barn. "The carriage again, ma'am?" Amos said. "*If* you please." "I will come, too," Hal volunteered cheerfully. "No, you stay here and help Amos," she told Hal, while Amos glared at her; she changed her mind. "No, no, you stay here and make more of those wooden things. Amos will drive."

At the printer's, Ten went through every sample of wedding certificate the harassed man could produce. He wanted nothing but to go home. Why did all his customers arrive at the end of the day, just as he was unbuttoning his vest? "Isn't there *anything* more elaborate?" Ten asked grumpily. She was dreadfully disappointed. *All* these seemed familiar. "Well, there is *this* new one," the overheated gentleman said; "but it's a sample, you see," he said, turning it over to show it to her. "It's stamped 'sample'; right there." But it was what she wanted. "I will take it," she announced. "My sample!" he exclaimed; "isn't there anything else in the entire shop?" "Nothing. What have you in the way of elaborate frames?" "Gold leaf?" he asked, exasperated. "Of course," she said, lost in admiration of the certificate as he trudged miserably off.

Well, this would just do, Ten thought; there in the center was a picture of the minister standing in the pulpit, the groom looking toward him, the bride looking down, a wedding party of seven adults looking on, and one small boy, with his back to the viewer, tugging at his father's shoulder. But on either side of this, which was rather the standard thing, were two more pictures, encapsulated in a dusty cloud of sepia, one showing a triumphant mother lying in bed, holding up a fat, jolly infant in its christening robes, and on the other side, the happy couple sailing off to a happy land in a boat pulled by twin swans. What a beautiful boat, Ten thought, admiring how gently the prow was pulled through the water lilies by the two lovely swans. What a beautiful curvature of their necks the artist had rendered, Ten thought; and how beautiful his rendering of their happy expressions. The whole thing was bordered with trellised roses and lilies.

The printer was returning with sample frames. Ten was immediately drawn to an elaborately carved one, rolling flowers, reminiscent of waves, and a design of chancels and bells scattered among the roses. In the center of the frame's top and bottom was the beaming face of the sun. "That one," she said without hesitation; "can you wrap it?" "Now?" "The wedding is tomorrow." "Oh, all right; you'll have to sit here in this oven and wait while I work on it." "That's fine." He began cutting angles in the frame's pieces.

Ten read the certificate happily. "This is to certify that blank of blank in the state of blank and blank of blank in the state of blank were by me joined together in Holy Matrimony" (that took up a separate line of three-dimensional letters, surrounded by a scroll design) "on the blank day of blank in the year of Our Lord, One Thousand Eight Hundred and blank. In presence of," and four lines drawn for as many as four witnesses. Exactly what mine said, Ten thought, delighted. "Well, can I have it?" the printer demanded; "I have to take it to put it in its frame." "Don't seal it thoroughly," Ten warned him; "we have to *use* the certificate tomorrow." The woman takes me for an idiot, he thought resentfully. "After sixty years in the business," he snapped, "everyone still tells me what to do." He carefully wrapped the certificate.

Well, he had to admit it, she was right to select this one. In all his time, he had never seen a nicer one. "Here you are," he said, handing it over; "but it's not the paper that makes the marriage." "After fifty years on this earth," Ten retorted, "no one has to teach me the primer of life." Lemon! he thought. What an old grouch, she thought, going out, getting into her carriage. But nothing could really bother her. There had been something missing, and she had found it.

Ten wondered idly if Virginia could really be counted on to keep a New England secret, and if she would really want to keep her promise once she was liberated in Manhattan. She would, Ten decided. She never had any basis for her opinions. They just existed, like the clouds. Well, they would all be arriving tonight, Nellie, Edna, and Edith. John was wandering about the house like a young beagle who had lost his duck in the swamp, but a call from South Dudley had taken him off her hands. Unconsciously, she checked the position of the sun in the sky. It must be at least four-fifteen, she thought, hurrying over to the stable. "Amos!" she called into its depths. "The carriage, ma'am?" he asked with the look of a man who had recently seen too much of the world and had recently become very tired of it. *"Two* more trips, Amos, just two more trips after this one; now you must admit," she said reasonably, "three trips to the depot is not many trips for an entire wedding." "It is if they're all made in one night," he grumbled; "is there a hurry?" "There is; we're getting the bride and her mother." "Then I'll get the black horses." "If you take them," she argued, "we have to stop the carriage *blocks* away from the depot, and then you will have to walk up to tell Miss and Mrs. Dickinson to wait for the carriage, and walk back to it. I'm not having John's horses racing any trains to the crossing tonight." "Well, we don't *have* to take them," Amos answered; "we can trot along with the oxen for all I care, but any of the other horses, and we'll have the two ladies standing around looking up and down the street for half an hour at least." Ten looked up at the sky. "And there's not a sign of lightning, ma'am."

He knew what she was thinking. One horse which raced

trains to crossings, another, storm-shy. She never understood what her brother was thinking of when it came to matters of horseflesh. Speed and strength, that's what he always said, and then he would buy some plodding, sway-backed horse old enough to have carried soldiers into Troy before the beast shrank down to its current size, and wheezed so noisily anyone could hear it on top of the mountain. And *then* it needed a good sleigh dog to give it a push up the hill. "Well, Ten," he had said when she had criticized his last acquisition ("Well, well, another grain-eating animal of some kind"; that was what she had said), "you should take this as a sign of how *you'll* be treated when you start wheezing up hills." There were times she believed half of what he said. Half! She believed most of what he said most of the time. Yes, he was a sentimentalist.

They set off for the Brattleboro station. It was getting dark as they rode, the color going so imperceptibly neither Ten nor Amos noticed when the greens of the trees suddenly gave up their identities, or when the deepening blues of the sky finally darkened to inky blacks streaked with haloes of silver and violet; the moon was up and giving some light. For such a clear night, Ten thought, there seemed to be very few stars. A deer shot in front of the carriage. Ten swiveled in her seat. Amos sighed. She insisted on riding up on the high seat with him, and now he'd be blamed if she went and fell off looking for deer. *He* couldn't see what was so unusual about them after all these years.

He wondered if she'd be out in the drift this winter feeding them again. It had taken her two years to tame them, but she had tamed over twenty, you had to give her that, and now she was after that foolish raccoon. It hadn't been enough for her to let in the animal, a mother raccoon and all her cubs; well, that was beyond imagination, but to let them in a second time after she had wrecked the summer kitchen with the doings of that animal. Poor Bridget! Life wasn't always harder in the stable; he wouldn't trade places and go into that house. Bridget had gone on about it for days, quivering all over until he had to give her some of his cough medicine. First, she had awakened, frightened to death by a horrible crash, and woke the whole house screaming,

"Tramps! Tramps!" For weeks, the servants and farm women had been drying their clothes in their garrets, regardless of the weather, all because of some tramps who were busy stealing clothes, and thieves, thieves, that was the theme of the day.

Amos came flying in from the barn in his nightsuit, hysterically greeted by Bridget in her nightdress. And there was Miss Ten, fully dressed, and an enraged mother raccoon on top of the kitchen hutch. By this time Bridget had realized there were no human thieves in the kitchen, and got out her broom, which only made the raccoon spring from the top of the hutch to the middle of the kitchen table, spitting and hissing and growling, while Amos and Bridget and Ten watched as the hutch, which seemed to be falling through glue, tipped over backwards against the stone wall, and then, striking it, began vomiting out porcelain canisters of flour, sugar, salt, and the simultaneous crashing of canned vegetables, currant jam, cranberry jam, relishes, peaches, as if the food in the house had suddenly declared war on the inhabitants, and all of them lost in a fog of flour. It took some time for the three of them to see through it, and meanwhile, all of them afraid to move, lest they introduce themselves to that wretched raccoon. By the time the flour had settled, covering the kitchen planks like snow, Ten had recovered herself, and ordered everyone out and back to bed. There was nothing for it, she had assured them, but to leave the kitchen to the raccoon and its family.

Amos had been only too glad to follow those instructions, but before breakfast, while he was combing down the horse she had been so busy ridiculing, Bridget was out telling him how Ten had stayed up, looking through a crack in the kitchen door, apparently greatly pleased by the good meal the animals were having. And there she had stayed until she realized the loyal mother had returned for her more distant relations, whereupon she decided to call it a night and beat a retreat. She surrendered the kitchen to the masked bandits. But had that stopped her? No, the next night, she was out in back of the house again with a long piece of pork lard, and that miserable animal, with her cubs hiding in the fringe of the woods, standing up to eat the lard, first grabbing its piece and running off, finally standing up and eating its piece right there. Well, he'd bet his year's wages she'd have the thing roaming the house by next summer.

He often saw her, swinging away in the hammock, crooning to something or other that didn't behave like anything alive he'd ever seen made a pet of before, and no, he wouldn't go over and look. *He* wasn't going to wind up keeping a fire to warm a raccoon while that animal with teeth like knives sniped at the horses. *That* was all he needed to shorten his life, and shortening his life was what both of the Steeles seemed bent on sometimes. "Six deer!" Ten crowed with delight; "six!" "Any of them have antlers?" Amos asked sarcastically. "Oh, you are an old towel," she pouted at him. He smiled into the rippling, whispering darkness. He liked these nights, the beginning of August, before they took on that cold tinge; that always reminded him of the first fringe of ice on the lake. Winter wasn't anything definite yet. It was so cool, so like the feel of one of the ladies' velvet cloaks when he helped them into the carriages. Everything seemed so peaceful, quiet, as if everything was resting, waiting. And who would believe that within four weeks, or even three weeks, he'd be hitching up oxen to the snow plow, clearing the drives to the house and the access to the big road at the bottom of the mountain? Or pulling the heavy roller, if clearing the snow off was out of the question.

What a place for changes! The people, too, were changeable. Maybe it was the weather. He wondered what they'd all be like if they went out to California and lived only in the gold and sunshine. Well, they all complained away by mail, even from out there, he thought, rounding a bend, the meadows stretching out on both sides of the road like black velvet. One lone cow, he could pick it out now, was wandering back to the pasture next to the house on the crest of the hill through the tunnel a farmer had dug under the road. The whole county, Amos included, considered him a genius of daring: everyone had predicted the tunnel would collapse under the first heavy snowfall, but he had lined the thing with brick. "Just like the little piggy," Ten had observed sweetly. And it held up all winter, although in the winter its main attraction was the shortcut it provided to the lake on the far side of the west meadow, and skating, and fishing through the ice, and sliding, and drowning.

Every year, drownings. There was one year, Amos remembered, when neither he nor anyone else, especially no one in the Steele family, wanted to swim anywhere in the West River for fear of bumping into a pale, bloated body. Well, children, he thought; they'd never learn. He was glad he'd never had any. He supposed there might be some coming around now, though. And how would he feel about that? They'd be a lot harder to argue away than a vicious raccoon he could always tell John he'd seen foaming at the mouth. *That* had worked for two weeks, before Mr. Steele decided the poor beast had probably eaten some soap in the kitchen or was drooling flour, since he'd seen no visible cases of hydrophobia. And I suppose he thought, if a child gets kicked in the head while I'm out in the barn they'll have mine for it. The imaginary urchins were already filling the stable like the children in the old woman's shoe. Well, he stopped himself, there wasn't any point in catching the family's habit of worrying about things centuries in the future. Centuries! It took only nine months. There could be a new arrival before next spring! But, he comforted himself, when they were new they couldn't do much. They weren't the same as horses; they didn't stand right up and start staggering around.

Ten's mind was off on an entirely different track. She was filled with visions of reactions to her floral decorations. John's and Edna's faces when they saw their wedding certificate, which had, to her, assumed the importance of the ceremony itself, and the other surprises, one for Edna, one for Edith. Oh, she had outdone herself this time. The carriage rounded another turn; the lights in the town blinked into view. Well, they looked enough like stars to satisfy a person. It always interested her, the way some of them clumped together, while others couldn't seem to get far away enough. Just like people on a train. She'd never understood it, why some people would enter a carriage and plop themselves right down next to the single soul inside, even if that soul was traveling all the way from Kansas to Vermont, and had a lunch hamper, a small pyramid of packages, a handbag, and a hatbox on the next seat. Two years later, and she was still angry about it.

"No train," Amos said laconically. "Well, do you think we can escape with our lives if you tie these beasts to the posts near the station? The *stone* posts. They can't race very far tied to rocks." Amos drove wordlessly up to the hitching posts. Women's minds. If the horses decided to take off, it would be the strength of the leather and the strength of the rope, not the stones. No wonder Mr. Steele always left such specific instructions. Not that anyone ever followed them.

A low thundering noise preceded a riot of gold and red sparks as the express thundered around the curve to the station, then screeched to a halt. Ten jumped out of the carriage and ran across the street. Amos went after her, sighing. In the excitement, she was likely to run under a buggy and he'd have a fine time explaining that. People were slowly trickling out of the train, moving darkly under the kerosene lamps lit for their arrival. Ten was prowling up and down like one of her interminable cats. Where was Edith? Where was Edna? A little body seized her from behind, squeezing her tightly around the waist. "Edna!" Ten exclaimed; "am I glad to see you!" "No one's sick?" Edna inquired anxiously. "Heavens, no," she answered, suddenly catching sight of Edith. "Edith!" she shrieked, flying over to her. The two women embraced and began hopping up and down, Amos thought, like two fleas on a dog. Probably some habit left over from school, Edna thought. She wondered if she and Virginia would jump up and down like that when they met two years later. If they met two years later. How many times, Amos was wondering, could they go on saying, "Let me look at you; stand back and let me look at you"? "Well," Ten was saying, eyes brimming, "you look the same as ever," and she squeezed Edith and held her as if she were in danger of ascending and it was her duty to hold her down. "You don't," Edith answered, admiring; "you look queenly, really queenly!" "Do I really?" Ten asked like a pleased child; "queenly?" "We always said you looked like a princess. Remember, Nellie, she used to look at you and say, 'The Princess is sad. What shall we do to cheer the Princess up?' " "Oh, she meant my money," Ten said, scoffing it off. "She did *not!*" Edith protested; "why, you always used to intimidate us, the way you always seemed to know what you were doing."

I wonder what happened, Amos thought. He was still remembering that miserable raccoon. Hadn't Mr. Steele told him it picked pockets? Something about it coming into the barn and picking his pocket of cigarettes? She *would* tame a wild pickpocket. Well, they would go on, and he had better get used to it. He leaned against a light post. "And is Mr. Steele home waiting?" Edith was asking. "No." "No?" Edith asked; "he can't be all that casual about it." "He can't choose birthdays for the babies, either, although since he's met Edna, I think he's even tried opening negotiations with the stork." "That could be taken a number of ways," Edith giggled. Amazing, Edna commented silently.

"Miss Ten," Amos spoke up; "you promised me I could leave off at eight o'clock. You know, for the raffle." "Oh yes, the raffle," Ten answered, recovering herself; "into the carriage, everyone." They drove back as quickly as Amos dared. If there was one thing he hated, it was Ten's decisions on what speeds were safe ones. Especially on rainy nights. *Then* she seemed to think he ought to get out and carry the horses. At least I have the driver's seat to myself, he thought happily, but was promptly rewarded with a poke from Ten's parasol. "Is something wrong with the horses?" she asked; "is this the fastest they can go?" "Inconsistent beast," he muttered to the impartial breezes, rounding the curve, sending them down the stretch at full gallop. Ten and Edith chattered away in the carriage; Edna, resting her head on the windowsill, looked up at the stars. She wished they had come in the open carriage so that she could tilt her head all the way back and look up at the stars. They were out now, thickly. The stars here were so beautiful; and they seemed so close on nights like this, as if they were really waiting there, like people, on the horizon, just as they seemed to be. The silences here, the silences. They flowed on one into the other in a kind of violet-blue music; they were all different. Such silence! That must have been what she was waiting for all that time in the city. Well, she couldn't *wait* to be married and left somewhere alone in these

249

silences, alone with John. She kept repeating that phrase to herself: alone with John.

He would be her husband. She would be alone with him. No one else could have him now. Well, it was wonderful. He could develop more moods, more tempers; what difference did it make if he was going to belong to her? She had come home. She heard, and did not hear, the chatter of the women in the background. Her mother would go away; the leaves would go away. There would be nothing but snow and a whitening, disappearing house in which she and John would be alone. Alone in their room. No matter what, no matter what happened, she thought, staring up at the stars, feeling the cool wind lifting and dropping her hair, they would always be alone together. Alone, what a beautiful word. They ought to find a place for it in the marriage ceremony.

Inside, there was the flurry of cloaks giving way in the warmth, the carrying off of parasols, showing Edith to her room, and then the three of them sitting in the parlor, Edith and Ten chattering as if to make up for over twenty years, Edna listening for the sound of a single horse. Ten suddenly interrupted herself to call Bertha and send her out to the stable for Amos. "Amos!" Bertha complained; "to track up the kitchen, and I suppose you won't mind, Miss Ten," she said, pulling her shawl tighter across her chest, "if there's no wedding cake at all." "I ordered one from Tivoli's." "It's not the same thing," Bertha retorted, stalking from the room. "This *is* an old house, isn't it?" her mother was asking, when Edna finally heard the sound of hooves. She jumped out of her lady's chair and flew off down the hall. John was standing there, bedraggled, muddy, exhausted, his sideburns unkempt, a thick growth of beard beginning to darken his cheeks. Edna jumped into the air, throwing her arms around him. He caught her, gasping. "Get down, Edna; get down," he pleaded; "I can hardly lift my arms." "Oh," Edna cried, "I am sorry. You look all tired out. You had better go right to bed." But she could not stop smiling. "Right to bed? With your mother sitting in the parlor with her microscope just waiting to get me under it? I think I had better get in my room and get to that washstand and put in an appearance." "Can I come?" Edna pleaded. "You go get Bridget and tell her to bring in some hot water. I waited all this time for you. You can sit there a half hour and wait for me." "I can't!" "In, get in there," John scolded, slapping her smartly on the bottom. "I'll get you back for that," she threatened, starting to follow him down the hall. "Back! Get back!" he ordered again, picking up his huge hand. "You're sure?" He nodded, smiling. "Absolutely sure, cross your heart and hope to die?" "Will you get in there? Before I fold up on the carpet and sleep right here in the hall." "Oh, you *are* tired!" "Just what I meant to tell you myself," he said, trudging off down the hall.

Edna's long face appeared in the doorway of the parlor. Both women looked up expectantly. "He's washing up," she announced. Edith looked questioningly at Ten. Perhaps he didn't want to be bothered meeting the mother of the bride. Her last memories of him weren't too pleasant, but then the circumstances hadn't been, either. "Oh, Mother," Edna exclaimed impatiently; "he is really a mess." "You shouldn't talk that way about your intended," said Ten; "in fact, from the minute that minister pronounces you man and wife you ought never to say a word against your husband again. Not in anyone's hearing, anyway." "That won't be hard," Edna burst out. "The voice of experience," Ten remarked to Edith. "Do say that again," Edith teased; "that does seem to describe her lately; the voice of experience."

Edna had never seen her mother so happy. It made a difference, almost as if the happiness were some kind of medicine which set her mind to functioning. Not in a way to marvel at, of course, but still, it was something of a miracle to see it working at all. "Amos has left, Miss Ten," Bertha announced from the hall; "if there's anything else you need, will you *please* call Bridget, and don't anyone come tramping into the kitchen so I wind up with a cake that looks like a pond when the ice falls down in the middle." She swept off. "What is John *doing?*" Ten wondered; "he must be hiring a stand-in. He never was much for public occasions," she apologized to Edith. "I just hope he doesn't fall asleep standing up."

"Spending your time slandering your own brother?" John's deep voice came from the back of Ten's chair; she jumped. Edith couldn't help smiling. Why, he didn't look so bad, after all. He certainly didn't look like the gloomy cloud she remembered. No, he didn't look that way at all. He was handsome; no, not handsome, distinguished. He ought to be the President of some country, not the country doctor. And he was so tall. This old house hadn't been built for him, she thought, watching him stoop down to come through the entrance. Well, now that *was* an attractive man.

Where, she wondered, would Edna come up to against him? She remembered standing Edna up against her white nursery wall, and the governess saying, "Stand still now, dear; stand still," and she took a pencil and put it flat on top of Edna's head and drew a line on the wall, then wrote down the date. Oh, she is going to be *short*, she had sighed time after time. That was over sixteen years ago. And she was still short, and still looked like the little girl who ran carelessly in and out of that expensively furnished town house with her little hoop, apparently not paying the slightest attention to where she was going, but never breaking a single thing. *I* was the one who broke things, Edith remembered; she made me so jittery running around like that. And now she was getting married. She looked up at John. Oh, you had to crane your neck to look up at him. "You know," she told him, "I still have the marks on the wall in Edna's nursery, the ones we used to measure her growth." "You should have tried stretching her," he answered. He had moved in back of Edna's chair and his hand was resting on the top of her hair; "did you ever get past three marks?" "I think we reached four before we realized we were raising a midget." "Mother!" Edna protested. "A midget," John repeated affectionately; "they're the next-best things to elves and brownies." He beamed down at the top of Edna's shining head.

Horses were abruptly clattering up in front of the house. "Oh no," John sighed. "Isn't Dr. Houston taking over yet?" Ten asked. "Not until tomorrow night." "Well, you might as well stand still a minute. If it's you they're after, Bridget will be right in." Everyone waited. No Bridget, but the excited babble of two female voices. "Well, what now?" John asked; this would be a marvelous time for Bridget's mother to come down with the measles. Or something worse. Then he'd have to think twice about going off with Edna and leaving Ten to fend for herself with Bertha. She was addlepated, that Bertha. A female figure finally appeared in the hallway, still in her traveling outfit. She was definitely shabbier than the others, but she belonged to the party; that was clear enough. "Nellie!" Edith suddenly shouted. John stared at her, then at his sister. "Nellie!" his sister shrieked, jumping from her seat. The three women flew together like blind bats, hopping up and down like children. "Nellie, Nellie, Nellie," Edith kept repeating; she was crying and talking, talking and crying. "Oh, Edith, don't do that," Nellie asked, but she was already beginning to sob herself, and Ten, too, John observed; it never took her long to strike up. Yes, there she went. He was off by three seconds. He had expected Ten to hold out three seconds longer. That's Nellie, Edna was thinking; she's much prettier than I thought she would be. But she wasn't really pretty. It was something about her. Edna supposed if she sat perfectly still, the way she'd seen women in the country sitting on their porches, apparently taking inventories of the miseries of life, she'd look homely. No, Edna decided, that face could never relax into that dreadful expression. Even if her white muslin dress was terribly out of date. No matter how skillful the darning, it was apparent it had been mended and remended and it was her best.

"So this is Edna," Nellie said, coming up to her, leaning forward on the tips of her toes; she was very shortsighted. "My goodness, you're even prettier than I thought you would be. One of my girls," she announced proudly, "has a chance of coming out half as well as you, and that should make her fortune, I guess." Which reminded her of her lack of one. "Oh," she said, miserable; "I know I'm going to disgrace all of you at the wedding, but, Ten, Edith, this *is* my best dress, and I don't have much occasion to wear such things, not even to church. We're snowed in so much of the time and if it comes down to a choice between a new dress, and I have to make it myself, you know, or twelve inoculations when there's smallpox on the mountain, well, you can guess what I choose. And one of the children is sure not to get a take until the fifth time, and then one comes down with something, and another breaks a leg, so I just keep putting it off. In heaven, if they dare dress me in white muslin wings, I'm going to pray for

stones and drop right down through a dressmaker's roof."
"Well, that sounds like the old Nellie," Edith said. "I
guess I was never much good at being the young Nellie.
Now don't you start in teasing me about my religion,"
she warned; "I'm as devout as ever. I just hide it more."
"Some things never change," Ten sighed, blissful. "I wish
I could say that about my wrinkles"; Nellie grimaced.
"Oh, you know you don't look like an unironed sheet,"
Ten said. "Well, I suppose that much is true," Nellie
agreed; "God should have struck me twice with the
point of the vanity star." "I think he got me three times
instead," Edith said ruefully. "Now don't get all solemn,"
Ten insisted; "imagine, the three of us here, and alive."
"Well, and I should hope so," Nellie laughed at her; "and
I don't intend to be laid out before the wedding, either."
This was better than the theater, Edna thought, looking
adoringly up at John. Edith saw the look; she relaxed
completely.

"Horses in the yard again," Ten announced; "well,
John, this time you better go." Her brother looked at her,
puzzled. "Well, what are you waiting for?" she asked.
Edna looked up, suspicious. "I'll be right back," he said.
That old cat had another trick up her sleeve; he knew it.
But lately, perhaps his mind was going, he couldn't keep
up with her. He opened the front door. A hired hansom
from the Brattleboro depot was waiting in the yard, the
driver handing down trap after trap. John went out.
They weren't expecting more guests. Not as far as he
knew. "Well, the bad penny is back," a head of blond
hair said, sticking itself out the window. "Virginia! Good
Lord!" "Are you that sorry to see me?" "It's like seeing
a ghost; I thought you'd be halfway to Charlottesville by
now." "Oh, Ten and I had an arrangement, but it was
hard, you know, going through the parting. It seemed so
real, and the day after tomorrow, I have to go through it
all over again. But it's worth it. I wouldn't want to miss
Edna's wedding." "It's mine, too," John said.

"Oh, are they letting you take part?" Virginia asked
impishly; "now, southern women wouldn't let you anywhere near the scene of the crime. They could go through
the whole business with just a dummy. They did that
once. They really did. The groom was on board ship,
and he signed the certificate and mailed it back, and the

bride was married by proxy." "How did it end?" "Oh, she divorced the sailor and married the proxy, but that's the South, you know. Everyone has malaria and acts strangely. All you Yankees know that." "I never can decide when you're telling the truth, or amusing us, or laughing at us, or doing all of those things at the same time." "Are you complaining?" "No, I like it; I'm just not used to it." "Well," Virginia said, "that was all true. Except for the malaria. You have to give a featherbrain like me a license to embroider the world a little." "Featherbrain, my foot," John said, pausing halfway down the hall; "why do you want people to think of you that way?" "Because I don't *want* to be taken seriously." "Would that be so bad?" "It would be damnation. Oh, every now and then it's all right, but I've had enough of that sort of thing to last me three lifetimes."

"All because of that one marriage?" John asked her. "When I was a child, my poppa took me to the circus. There was a horse there that jumped through a ring of fire. The first night the rider jumped him the wrong time and his side was burnt. The next night he was back, jumping through the same hoop. I could see the liniment. I must have been eight, but I remember thinking, I'd never jump through that hoop again, not after that first time. And I guess I never will." "You can't be sure about things like that." "Can't I?" Virginia asked; "can't I? I'm not like you, you know. Something pushes you forward. The same thing holds me back, as if there were strong arms around my waist, dragging me. No, I'm not a serious person. Or won't be. You understand, don't you?" "Yes," he said slowly; "yes, I suppose I do. You can swim so far and no farther." "Exactly; I'm a splasher. But you"—she looked at him, appraising—"you can swim for miles, can't you?" "Yes," he said uneasily, "if I have to." "I choose only to splash," she said. I'm disturbing him, she thought surprised. Ever since I talked about swimming. "Perhaps I'll find another splasher. Well," she whispered, looking toward the parlor, "let's throw me in." "The lions," he said, "are going to be delighted."

Ten heard them coming. "What is it now?" she called out; "a broken arm?" "I wouldn't say that," Virginia gasped, leaning into the room; "I think I'm pretty much as God made me, poor man." Edna looked wildly from

255

Ten to Virginia. "Say hello to your friend," Ten instructed; "if she's come all this way for some tea, the least we can do is give her a greeting and a room for the night." Edna jumped up; the two of them twined around each other, crying happily. "Everyone needs a bridesmaid," Ten observed. "Ten, you haven't changed a bit, not one bit," Nellie said proudly, as if Ten were one of her own children. "Look at them, Ten. They're like two snakes. It's hard to tell where one of them leaves off and the other begins. That reminds me, Edith. Do you remember the time they said we'd have to sleep in separate rooms because your grades weren't high enough, and Ten slept in your bed until they gave up and put us back together?" "Yes, up on the third floor; we nearly froze to death"; Edith nodded. "But we were down on the second, facing south, the next term; and we were lucky not to be thrown out," Ten put in.

They began reminiscing about their old rooms, old teachers, the play they had all been in, the new teacher who had decided to raise funds by putting on a tableaux display, and all of them had represented mythical figures. Ten was Achilles, and Edith, of course, Edith was Jove. "Well, Edith certainly made a terrible figure of a man," Ten giggled; "she developed so much faster than the rest of us." "You looked pretty funny yourself," Edith reminded her; "trying to stand there, holding on to that rope, with one foot up in the air and an arrow taped to it." "The rope was supposed to be invisible," Ten said; "don't you remember? Miss South had us paint it white because no one would see it against the white backdrop." "Well, *my* mother said you looked as if you were about to be dragged off like a bad dog," Edith said. "You never said that before," Ten gasped. "Well, and that's just what you did look like," Nellie agreed. "Like a bad *dog?*" Ten asked. "A *very* bad dog." "Oh dear," Ten sighed, "after all these years to smash my illusions about my one great performance. You two are *cruel.*"

"Is that another horse?" Edith asked; "what arrow have you pulled out of your heel now?" "My quiver's empty," Ten said, looking at John. "I'll go," he said. "What!" they heard him booming from the hall; "you did what? You just left him in the water?" A low voice droned pathetically on. "You only tried to kill him, and now you want to know if you succeeded? I haven't even seen him. Is he breathing?" The other voice droned away. "Well, let's go," John commanded; "whatever happens, the poor child won't have it easy with such idiots for parents." The ladies heard the door slam. "He's not known for his tact," Ten informed the silence. "Well, if you ask me, I wish we had a doctor like that," Nellie said; "I'd give a year of my life to have an excuse to stop in people's yards and scream like that when I see what they're up to." Ten just shook her head. Edith was watching Edna; she looked positively bereaved. There was a sudden tapping at the window. Ten opened it, swinging one pane into the room. "Well, what is it now?" "You have all tomorrow to sit around and gabble; I want everyone in bed when I get home. Everyone. Especially Edna and Virginia." "Attila the Hun," Ten snapped, slamming the window shut; "we old things can't be expected to take care of ourselves." John's face reappeared. "Edna and Virginia," he shouted through the pane, his face disappearing.

"Well, let's go unpack," Virginia suggested without waiting for an answer. Edna popped from her chair and the two of them scurried off down the hall. "Oh," Edna blurted out, running back in, "I forgot to say good night; please excuse us." "You're excused," Ten and Edith chorused together. The giggling faded down the hall. "I suppose we were once their age," Edith said. "Well, if we were," Nellie asked, "how did we get to be so much younger?" The three of them laughed so hard they ended up holding their sides. "Oh!" Edith gasped; "it hurts; don't say it again." "Younger," Nellie repeated. The three women screamed uncontrollably. Heads set to shaking in the kitchen. It wasn't so funny, that wasn't it. It was just all so familiar, so wonderfully familiar.

The next day, the day before the wedding, John was gone from early morning, first called out to check on the almost drowned baby, then on to another one with whooping cough, and then to reassure a hysterical mother her child did not have scarlet fever again, but probably did not want to go to Sabbath school. The month before, he noticed the little girl came down with scarlet fever every time the Sabbath-school class was due to meet, and further medical investigation revealed her public humiliation in class; that was just before her first dreadful recurrence of the disease. "Of course," John had explained to Edna, "she knew all the symptoms from first-hand experience, and she was pretty good at imitating them, too"; he had to admit that. Amos had mercifully taken Hal off to the stable, and then the west pasture. It was odd, Ten thought, how they never mentioned their dead brother, their other brother. Especially since John had told Edna all about Serepta; she would have thought he'd tell her about their other brother. She supposed, a little uneasily, he would. Eventually. Well, she wasn't going to mention it.

So he was gone, and the women were happily left to their own devices, peering over Mr. Garibaldi's shoulder, three faces pushing their way into the floral altar. "Please!" he finally protested; "I reach for a carnation and what do I find in my hand? A nose! Please! I am an artist! I cannot work with all these looks withering my flowers." Ten promptly began worrying over the arrival of the gladiolas. "Why," she moaned to Edith, "the wedding baskets would look lumpish, completely lumpish, without the gladiolas to give them height." "They are not due until the late-afternoon train," Mr. Garibaldi fumed; "you want me to put them in the baskets to brown at the edges? I'll put them in to brown at the edges. If I listen to you, everyone will be saying, 'Oh, Mr. Garibaldi. We can't have Mr. Garibaldi; he brings secondhand flowers to weddings. Right from the casket to the basket; no, we can't have him.' Ladies," he pleaded, "leave me in peace. I know my business. I shall keep them in my big icebox *in the shop*"—he glared—"until early morning, and I will bring them over then. And the lilies, and the roses. In the meantime," he suggested, "avert your eyes from the horrifying baskets and gaze upon this!" and he pointed triumphantly at his floral arch, but the three ladies had buzzed off somewhere near the end of his inspiring speech and were cooing over the wedding certificate Ten had just placed proudly on the table, Nellie standing sentry, keeping an eye on the door in the event Edna should suddenly appear.

"Oh, but, Ten," Nellie asked suddenly, "you don't think the picture of the woman with the baby will upset John?

I mean, after all that happened?" "Oh dear," gasped his sister, "I never gave that a thought." She sank down into the lady's chair. "No," she said at last; "I don't think it will. I've heard Edna on that subject and she seems to think she's going to hatch children from eggs. Her enthusiasms are contagious, I must say." "I can't say I've ever seen much of them," Edith said. Nellie looked at her. With one child, she thought, why couldn't things run smoothly? She had always thought her difficulties came from having so many. It was no easy thing to find time for each one when one had ten children; why, she had to count them at night. Yes, *count* them, especially when the devil was in them. And then go into their rooms in the middle of the night and count them again. Well, every family was different; that's what her husband always said. And, of course, there were so many of them it was hard for any one of them to get on anyone's nerves. Perhaps that was the difference; yes, she was sure it was.

Meanwhile, Tivoli's people had arrived and begun setting up a tent on the lawn. "But suppose it rains?" Ten asked Mr. Tivoli; "and the tent will be standing there all night and the dew will get it wet, if nothing else does." "It will be dry before nine," he answered, pointing at the spot for another peg. "But you haven't even *begun* on the band platform!" she exclaimed. "*Mrs.* Richardson," he said, "I have noticed it time and time again. The late-summer sun afflicts some people far more powerfully than others and it will all end in a dreadful headache for you. You don't want to be seeing spots at your own brother's wedding, do you? Why don't you, and your friends," he said, pointing to them as if she didn't know who they were, "just go inside and rest? And naturally, the feast will not be arriving until the happy day. We don't want the whole party coming down with cases of summer complaint, do we?" "There's no need to speak to me as if I were a child," Ten answered, huffy; "I have more than enough to do inside." Mr. Tivoli shook his head.

Well, someday, he should let those geese have it all their own way; let them set up their own tents. He'd love to see them creeping about inside the canvas, trying to get it up from the ground, and what a sight they'd be, setting up the band platform. They'd end up happy enough to have the band playing from the cupola on the barn roof. He couldn't even say no one had warned him. His own father had pleaded with him to choose another career. But, against all advice, he decided to take on the family business. "You work with women," his father had said, "and they'll be pecking at you all day like chickens and diving at you like hawks. Now, if you went into something like construction, you could forget to put in a flight of stairs, and if you were building for a bachelor, he'd never notice. Just give him a ladder. Tell him you bought it at your own expense and it cost three dollars and he'll be eternally grateful. But women, you get involved with women, and they spend days over whether it's to be a central staircase, or a side staircase, or a curving staircase, and what precise style of balustrade would be best, and then, in the middle of it all, they decide the wall at the head of the stairs should be broken through for an etched window, and they ask you to do it as if they were asking you to pick up a tack, and the next thing on their mind is the chandelier. It's not in the right place. It should have hung over the dining-room table, after all, or it was hanging over the dinner table, but she'd decided to move it, so please rip up the ceiling, but don't get any plaster dust in the air. I went through it all when I got married and did I learn my lesson? I did not.

"The business should stay in the family, but there are other brothers. Go into something sensible, like buffalo hunting. Yes," his father went on, dramatically clutching his head with both hands, "think of debating with women over a cake! They're all experts, even if they're celebrating the family's recovery from the poisoned tart they administered to them last week. 'Oh, I was sure the refrigeration was adequate,'" he mimicked in a high falsetto. "Who can stand that?" Well, he had decided he could stand it. Of course, he *did* get to attend a great many weddings, but at his age, he was tiring of them, and if the truth were known, he didn't see why couples didn't just walk around themselves three times, as they were said to do in some country or other. He had read about that in *The Reformer*'s column of "Curious Facts." But then, he also had a dim memory of having read that a three-day feast (or was it a seven-day feast—was such a horror possible?) followed the walking. Or was it the divorce that was accomplished by walking about? He would try to find the paper when he got home, if his better half hadn't used it to start the fire with which she would burn his dinner. What a profession! He couldn't even go to dinner, or sit down to one in his own house, without appraising every morsel on the plate. It had ruined his digestion. He no longer tasted his own food; he merely smelled it. There was only so much one could expect of the human body.

Ten gave up at last. They were obviously going to do exactly what they intended, and she doubted that even her body, impaled on a gladiola stem, would alter one movement of Mr. Garibaldi's. At least, she thought, Mr. Tivoli *had* the tent in the position she had chosen. Now they would not have to walk three miles from the house after the ceremony, or be so close to it that the whole wedding party would be overheated by the warmth of the two ovens inside. "Ten, dear," Edith said, steering her off, "let's all go sit on the piazza." Virginia and Edna materialized in front of them. "May we be excused for a ride?" Edna asked. "Oh, I think so," Ten said; "John won't be back until late." "We'll be back before then," Edna said. "Whenever 'then' is," Virginia quipped. "Well, by five then, on the piazza; we'll all meet there," Ten called out. The girls bobbed their capped heads in assent.

John did not arrive in time for supper; the others began without him. "Is this usual?" Edith worried. "Very," Ten answered. "Very," Edna chirped. "Very," Virginia repeated. "Oh, very," Nellie echoed; they dissolved in laughter. Everyone sat up in the parlor talking. It was getting darker. Bridget came in and began lighting the lamps. "The chandelier, Miss Ten?" she asked, and, at her nod, took up the lighting stick, setting the candles aflame. "Just leave the snuffer on the table," Ten told her; "we'll put them out ourselves."

Very likely, Bridget thought; now I'll have to get up and put out those candles before they burn the house down. She went off to bed; it was going to be a regular beehive tomorrow, and with four queen bees, too. Edna and Virginia sat up with heads drooping together like two tulips, whispering endlessly. "I'm so glad you came," Edna told her; "I didn't think I'd want anyone, but I guess I did, and not just anyone, just you. Aunt Ten is wonderful." "She certainly is; I'd adopt her and take her South, but she seems awfully attached to her garden." "That must be it," Edna agreed. "Tomorrow," she pronounced awesomely; "tomorrow I will be a married woman." "And not feeling one whit different," Virginia assured her. Edna looked dubious.

Sometime after the small party had retired to their chambers, Edna finally heard John's horse. Then she heard the sound of the library door opening and closing. She threw on one of her new robes de nuit and flew down the hall, tying ribbons as she went. That morning they had all inspected her trousseau, and quite a process it had been, too. It had taken them until almost noon, Virginia spreading out each garment with the expertise of a shopgirl. "Why," Edith said, "it seems a fitting out suited to a queen, and much of it more adapted to look at than to use." "Then someone will look at it," Ten said blissfully. "It is really a wonderful array," Nellie gasped in delight. "And this set of handkerchiefs," Edna said, picking up a long, elegant box of the fanciest kind, embroidered with delicate whitish-pink strawberries, "is you for." "For me?" Nellie whispered; "for me? The *box* is a masterpiece."

She sank onto a chair inspecting the box; it was enameled and hand-painted, a beautiful woman in a huge red hat, low-cut dress, and furs staring moodily out from its center, while roses, white sunflowers, and pink daffodils floated from her in all directions. Edith was smiling happily at her daughter. Ten was proud. "They can't be for *me*," Nellie protested; "you must have made a mistake." "No," Ten said quickly, "I asked her to select a present for a very particular guest." "Why, you must have thought she meant your mother," Nellie protested. "No, I did *not*," Edna said; "I selected something quite different for Mother. She brought out a slim black box. Edith looked at her quizzically, opening it. Inside was a double strand of blue pearls. "Good heavens, Edna! That must be five years of your trust fund!" "Three." "Three!" her mother gasped.

"And, Ten, this is for you," Edna said, pulling a huge, flat box from beneath the bed. "What is *that*?" Ten asked; "a platter?" She placed the box on the bed and opened it carefully. Inside was a giant oriental fan, the spines elaborately carved ivory, the frame inset with circles of beige handworked lace which bordered its rim, the most exquisitely embroidered flying pheasants, peacocks, dragons, and sea serpents set against a bluish-green background, and beneath the fan, a set of thirty long ostrich feathers which could be set into slots in back of the fan. How *did* they fit in there? Ten wondered. "You see," Edna showed her, "the ivory spines in the back are doubled; the spines of the feathers just slide into them; they're like pockets." "Oh, do put them in," Nellie implored, and then they all took turns fanning themselves with the wondrous object. "And how many years of your trust fund is this?" Ten finally asked, tears filling her eyes. I'm getting quite weepy lately, she reproached herself. "Seventy-three years," Edna said gravely. Well, Edith thought, perhaps I didn't do such a dreadful job with her after all. The three of them were still staring, hypnotized at their presents, and it was all Virginia could do to have them look at Edna's bridal dress.

"Well, and who can be lurking out there?" John called in a low voice. "Only me," Edna said, coming in. *"Only you?"* John repeated, staring at her; "what happened to you?" "What do you mean?" Had she stayed out too long in the sun? "You look so different." "It's only the robe"; Edna blushed. "I don't think so; it couldn't be *only* the robe." "John," Edna began, "I've been thinking; I'm going to be your second wife, but you're going to be my first husband. I hope I won't disappoint you; it worries me," she hurried on, "that you'll always have someone to compare me with." "But the woman I'll compare you with was *real*," John pointed out; "I have much more to fear. *You* can compare me with figments. Figments are more dangerous than real people. I can't say that figment *really* wasn't so handsome, was he? I can't say things like that." "I'm serious," Edna protested. "I am, too; there's no comparing you with Serepta. The idea is ridiculous; except for the events of that one day, you've made her a shadow. Not even a shadow." "Do you mean that? Are you sure?" She looked down and blushed. She had forgotten just how deeply these fashionable robes were cut. "As sure as I am that I'm breathing"; and he made a show of feeling for his pulse. "But you, are you *sure* you'll be contented with a three-day honeymoon? And in Dummerston?" "Dummerston?" "It's an ivy-covered cottage, and completely empty, not even a servant. Tivoli's is packing enough food for the whole time. But are you sure? Old Dr. Houston could take over for longer." "For a month?" Edna teased. "Well, yes, I imagine I could," John answered a little uneasily. "Three days will be just fine, just marvelous. After that, you'd begin pining for your invalids and I wouldn't be secure until we were installed here and I knew I was never going anywhere else." "Never?" "Never," she assured him; "not even into town." "I think I could stand for a trip like that; don't make promises you can't keep." "Try me." "Just what I intend to do." "Well, that's good," she said, content.

"John?" He looked up. "John, just suppose it does happen, suppose I did become, I mean, suppose I was soon in the family way. Would you be frantic? I mean, you *would* leave the house and not worry all the time?" "Not while I was working, but . . ." His expression had clouded. "I wouldn't like it if you worried; I can't wait to have children that look exactly like you." "Even the girls?" John smiled faintly. "Well, one or two could take after me." "They had better." "But, really, you wouldn't worry all the time?" "Well, perhaps the first." "And the second?" "Perhaps the second as well." "And the third?" "Perhaps that one, too." "And the fourth?" "Edna, what are you planning to do? Populate a city?" "If I can." "If you can," he echoed; "well, I'll be here to examine you." "And don't think I'm going to have you poking at me day and night like a worried hen," she scolded. "This is premature," John objected. "I don't think so; I just have this feeling." "You and Amos." "Oh? Amos thinks so, too," Edna squeaked, delighted. "I can't say he's looking forward to it. He seems to think they jump out of the womb into the stable and start climbing all over his animals." "Well, they won't." "I know they won't"; his eyes were bright, but he would not permit the tears in his eyes. Edna got up, went over to his chair, pressing his head into her bosom. "Don't you worry; I told you; I'd never upset our boat. I never will. Not for something so small as a child."

"You can't be sure," he answered. "But I am." "Well, if you are . . ." His voice trailed off. "Come, dear; come to bed," John got up; they clasped hands, wavering down the hall. "You do love me?" Edna asked as they paused before her door. He caught her up, lifting her. "Oh, do put me down," she finally ordered; "you're exhausted." She patted his cheek. "What a wonderful man! I don't believe it, such extraordinary luck." "You're demented," he said, stroking her hair; "I'm the lucky one. No," he considered, "I'm not lucky; I'm bewitched. Did anyone ever tell you what a magnificent bosom you have for such a little person?" She reached up to touch his cheek. "I do love you," she said again. "Love," he said softly; "I used to believe it was invented to fill out the pages of *Rhoda, Maude, Katerina, Isabella,* all those books Ten reads, but now . . . now I don't know how I escaped it for so long. Or didn't notice it in others. It's painful," he said, sad, "to love so much. It aches. As after an operation for appendicitis. Only in another place."

"Can you stand the suffering?" "Do I have any choice?" "I told you some time ago you didn't." "At the time I thought you were having a fit." "It was; it is," Edna said, "a very long fit. I intend to die right in the middle of it." "Then promise me something," John said, eyes filling now; "let me die first." "I won't let you die at all." "I'll have to, someday." "Then I'll have to follow Juliet's example," she said, pressing into him, her arms encircling him as best they could. "Would you?" John asked. She kept nuzzling. "Even if I didn't," she whispered, "I might as well have done; it would all come to the same thing." John bent down and kissed the top of her head. He kissed her head along the length of the part in her hair. "John?" Edna murmured. "Yes?" "Go to bed." "Yes, dear. I'll see you tomorrow. I hope." "You always have hope about the right things," she said, smiling up; "go on, go off to bed." Edna stood in the hall until she saw John go into his room. She waited until the door closed. Then she went into her own room and closed the door after her. In the moonlight, various articles of silk and satin gleamed like robes of the saints.

It was scurry and flurry all the next morning. The few invitations issued had set the time for four o'clock that afternoon, and the women in the house had decided it was best to be on the safe side and observe the old tradition which kept the bride from seeing the groom until the ceremony. However, neither the mother of the bride, nor the bride's adopted aunt (soon to be her sister-in-law), nor their old friend from school was prepared for the tricks of a seventeen-year-old girl who felt that, on the most important day of her life, she was unjustly being held captive. She *was* going to see John before the ceremony, although not necessarily in her wedding gown, and that was the end of it. Virginia, sitting on her bed, concluded that getting the two of them together, out of sight of the others, was her principal duty as maid of honor. She and Edna had waved away all mention of changing her title to matron of honor, and miraculously, no one had thought to bring up the subject of the possible impropriety, not to say bad luck, of a widow holding the post of assistant to the bride.

When a man further up the mountain rode up for the doctor, and was pointed toward Dr. Houston by John himself, Virginia promptly put their plan into action by walking casually outside to inspect the progress of the tent, her peculiar, sidelong look at John making it clear she wanted to speak to him. "Come around to the back of the house," she said, taking his arm, strolling casually down the walk. "Isn't it nice, how well they all get along together?" Nellie remarked placidly. "The back of the house?" "Edna wants to have a look at you," she said, pointing to the bandstand with her parasol. "You ought to do this professionally," John said; "were you once a spy during the French Revolution?" "During my last incarnation; during my next, I intend to come back as a toad under the wheels of the Emperor's chariot, or I'm sure someone intends that destiny for me." "Don't be so optimistic," he said, sympathetic. "Just realistic."

"But Edna, now, she's probably taking cold dangling out the window of her bedroom." "And how am I supposed to get up there? Climb up the trumpet vine?" "Oh, I think by the time you get there, you'll find her somewhere behind the curtains of the everyday parlor." "You children do have an instinct for the romantic." "Oh, I don't think that's it," she said; "young ladies tend to get a bit panicky; it's just the sight of you that's required."

"Edna? Panicky?" He sounded dubious. "The awful solemnity of the event," Virginia mocked, "has finally begun to descend upon her." "Good Lord," John sighed; "she isn't sorry?" "Sorry? Sorry?" Virginia repeated; "that has nothing to do with it. Just go see."

John went into the everyday parlor, leaving the door ajar. If he closed it, he knew someone would be there to investigate, but ajar, that could mean the wind, or a cat, or someone who had gone in and out for a book and not looked back. No Edna, but there was a lumpish russet velvet curtain shuddering in the far corner near the darkest window. "I really should straighten that curtain," John remarked softly to the walls; "really, I don't do my share of keeping a neat house." "John!" the curtain whispered urgently; "come in here!" "In where?" "Inside this curtain." John pulled the curtain aside and slipped behind it; he found himself staring down at the upturned bloodless face of his bride-to-be. She looked all of twelve years old. "What are we doing, Edna, playing tent?" "Oh," she wailed, "don't make fun of me," starting to cry, throwing her arm around his waist. "This curtain must make a pretty spectacle from the other side," he whispered into her hair; "anyone coming in would think it had come alive." "Oh," she moaned softly. "What on earth is the matter?" he asked; if she wanted to change her mind, he wanted her to tell him. Instantly. "We're going to have to stand there, in front of everyone, and then this man is going to preach at us, and warn us, and make terrible prophecies about the future, and I don't want to hear any of it," she sobbed. "Just don't listen," John advised seriously. "Listen to me, Edna; my sister got ahold of this old minister who married her, and the old thing is doddering off on his way to his maker, and this ceremony is just a detour. So we can be reasonably sure he can't manage droning through the first year of our marriage. But if you don't think you can stand up through it, or have some premonition you're going to faint away at the altar, we can meet Amos with the horses back in the woods and get married by the justice of the peace in Dummerston."

"Are you out of your head?" Edna demanded, tears forgotten. "But I thought it was the *ceremony* you were afraid of." "Not the ceremony," Edna said; "not the ceremony. But think of it, John, how many weddings must be taking place today. I tried to imagine it this morning, every wedding that was taking place on the globe, but I couldn't do it. So I pretended there was a wedding taking place in every house in Williamsville and on the hills. Well, don't you see? That makes us seem less special." "Edna, I hate to say this today, but you've gone off the rails. What is it you want? Do you want God to come down, and wipe everyone else out, and make us Adam and Eve?" "Yes," she cried. "Oh, Edna," he said, stroking her hair, "you are such a silly little kitten, such a silly little cat." "Kitten?" she asked, looking up. "All right, cat." "Eve the cat?" "That's right; Eve the cat. Every cat thinks she's Eve." "Then it's all right"; Edna exhaled, relieved; "and every tomcat thinks he's Adam." "I could put cotton soaked in warm oil in your ears for the ceremony." "You'll do no such thing," she protested; "I'm not a child." "How nice to hear it." "You must think less of me now," she said sadly. "Much less; if this continues," he went on thoughtfully, "I may see you as a real human being sometime in the next two years, not a mythical creature at all." "Well, it won't continue; it's just a fit."

"How long," John asked her, still stroking her hair, "are we going to hide behind this curtain? It's hot. I'll end up with the heatstroke." "No, we mustn't have that," Edna whispered, looking up; "I'll go out first, and then you sit down and pretend to read." "*I* don't know if I can sit still."

From far down the hall, he heard Edna's voice and Bridget's, the light, happy ripple of laughter, and the almost noiseless tread up the stairs, and then overhead. "Well, there's no need for me to sit in a chair," he decided, pulling back the curtain, looking out. Everything the same as ever, he thought with wonder, and everything utterly transformed. Well, and then there was Hal. He'd soon be following Edna about like a puppy. While they were gone, he'd better see to Ten's sitting him on her knees and giving him a good sharp lecture on the birds and the bees. *And* get Edna a large dog. Of course, it would begin as a very small dog. Ten would enjoy that, rescuing another panting, foaming creature in the interests of another tiny unprotected creature. He wondered what sixth sense permitted his sister to pick the puppy sure to end as the giant offspring of its midget mother, even if it began life looking like a premature mouse. One of those great big black dogs, that would be the thing.

He went off to give Ten her assignments. At the bandstand, he was told his sister had just left, went back into the house, and found her beaming at the floral arch and at Mr. Garibaldi, who was triumphantly arranging white gladiola after white gladiola in the wedding baskets and, with each one he placed, turning to look poisonously at Ten. Well, she had done a good job; who would have thought this house could be transformed into such a vision of heaven? It was a good thing, he thought, none of them went into seizures in the presence of flowers or they'd be carried out, stiff as boards, within three seconds after coming through the front door. John took Ten inside and gave her the instructions he wanted followed; she kept nodding her head, vexed but never removed her eyes from the florist, not for a second. "Can you hear me?" he inquired curiously. Perhaps women went into trances over these things. "I hear you; I hear you," she answered impatiently; "don't you have something important to do?" "For example?" "For example, staring up at your ceiling." "I'm going," he surrendered, wandering off.

Well, and that was not a bad idea, he thought, letting himself into his room. If he had one talent, it was his capacity for staring at ceilings. The sight of a ceiling, preferably plastered and free of cracks, made his mind as empty and blank as the roof above him. He lay down on his bed and let time wash over him, a quickly moving cool breeze.

"Are you feeling better now?" Virginia inquired anxiously. "Oh yes," Edna answered; she glowed at her. "Well, that's good; let's read." "Read?" "It passes the time," she answered placidly; "besides, if you go out there, you'll get yourself into a state all over again." "What shall we read?" "How about the criminal news?" Virginia asked, handing her the middle sheets of *The Reformer*. "You do think up the most peculiar solutions to problems," Edna said absently, but she was already absorbed in a bizarre account of a murder, in which the

269

smallest child of a family had attempted to dispatch all the servants by "diabolically," as the paper remarked, inviting them all to take part in her doll's tea party. The account went on for pages; then there was a description of the neighbors' comments. They inevitably recalled the child had been, in the past, given to "fits," especially when denied anything she had her heart set on, although everyone seemed puzzled. It was generally her mother or father, not the servants, who disciplined the "imp of the devil," causing her to throw herself to the floor, once even to throw herself half out a window. But she had been prevented from so doing by an old woman servant who had seized her heels, and since her nursemaid tied her shoes on very tightly, she was secured until help arrived. "Well, that's certainly turning things upside down," Edna said aloud; "usually it's the servants poisoning the family."

"That's what they're doing in this issue," Virginia observed, eyes glued. "Abortions, everyone's having abortions," Edna announced. "Are they living through them?" "Two yes, three no; one in jail, one released in custody of her parents. Next week she'll be in the suicide column." "Under local news, probably," Virginia murmured, "along with reports on the latest peach crop." "Well, it all goes together: peaches, women, crops, babies." "Oh, Edna, you're a cynic." "What's the difference between a cynic and a realist?" Edna asked, looking up. "Probably none. In a sane person. Except that a realist probably likes life better." "Like peaches," Edna agreed. "My mother didn't like peaches," Virginia remembered; "they told me it bothered her to feel them. They were so fuzzy; she thought they might grow beards. She used to call them 'male fruits.'" "Good Lord," Edna exclaimed; "some woman took the shoes off her horse and drove him all over Bald Mountain and the horse can't walk at all," Edna read out; "the veterinarian has the beast suspended from a sling in his hospital and is attempting to treat his hooves after having immobilized the legs. Veterinaries everywhere are eagerly awaiting reports regarding the success of this novel treatment, while everyone joins in deprecating this inhumane treatment of an animal; local authorities are investigating the case. It is believed the woman is demented." "Well, I'd say," Virginia said; "I'd horsewhip someone myself for that." "Me, too; what time is it?" Virginia took out her little watch. "Time to get dressed."

There was a gentle rap at the door. "The matron committee," Ten said as she and Edith and Nellie came in. "We won't pinch you to death," Ten said, "but we couldn't decide who was to help, so we decided the best thing would be for us to take turns buttoning each button." "And then leave her alone with Virginia," Nellie reminded her. Ten and Edith glowered at her. "How many guests are there?" Edna asked nervously. "Only fifteen," Ten assured her. "Then who are all those people looking in the windows downstairs?" Edith asked. "Local children," Ten said; "ignore them; they'll be peeping in the whole time. Precious little they have to do during the summer." Edith looked dubious. "Shouldn't we try to scare them off?" Nellie looked sympathetically at Ten. "It's almost a country custom," Nellie said, "and besides, Edith if we scare them off, the neighborhood would never forgive them. It's the children's privilege, and then the parents have to come for them to be sure they don't create a disturbance, so it ends up the parents' privilege, too. They keep quiet; it's nice, really, windows full of faces. It's probably the only time during the year they come near resembling cherubim." "Oh, well," Edith said. If nothing could be done about it, nothing could be done about it. There was no use in fussing. Windows full of faces indeed! On Cedar Street, the constables would take care of those faces without even being asked.

Outside, there was the sound of one carriage, then another "The minister," Ten said, looking out, "I had better go down; he looks nervous." "*He* looks nervous?" asked Edna. "Well, it's been a long time since anyone asked him to preach a wedding sermon." "And why is that?" Nellie demanded. "He tends to go on," Ten answered, vanishing swiftly. "Wonderful," Edith sighed, sinking into a chair. "Terrible," said Nellie. "I don't know," Edna said; "it's just what I expected."

Just as the last carriage drove up, the final touches were added to Edna's dress and hair. Virginia dangled from the window, reporting that the band was in place, ready to blare away. From downstairs the rumble of voices steamed up through the floorboards. Pleasant smells were beginning to waft up the stairs. "They're not serving the guests dinner?" Edna asked in terror. "No, no, just the house guests," her mother answered, impatient; "don't worry, this can't go on forever. Not with that decrepit creature presiding." "With the minister presiding," Nellie observed, "I fear it *can* go on forever." "Don't make Edna nervous again," Virginia said. "I'm not nervous," she answered; and it was true: she wasn't. The strains of the wedding march were beginning to make themselves audible, and Edna had just caught a glimpse of herself in the mirror.

In the old-fashioned dress, she looked as if she had stepped out of another century. The image she saw made her feel immortal, very old, very wise. She looked forward to wrinkling. She and John would wrinkle together, two pages of a book left out in the rain. Yes, she felt eternal in this dress. What a good idea Ten had had. "Ready?" Virginia asked. "Yes," she whispered. They started for the stairs, Edna's mother going down first to take her place at the altar. The wedding march took everything over. Edna followed Virginia down the stairs. Why, it's beautiful! Edna thought, seeing the pink and white floral arch, John standing on one side of it. It was as if they had been miraculously snowed in in the midst of deep summer. "Stop," Virginia whispered in back of her. A small choir of boys from the Old Stone Church began chanting a processional, and then, joined by members of the church choir, who had been invisible behind them, began the full choral service. When they fell silent, Edna proceeded the rest of the way to the altar, taking her place next to John. Why had she worried about the length of the ceremony? She wished now it would never end. She glanced shyly over at John. Yes, he was still standing there. She was suddenly seized by a fear he would take flight if the sermon went on too long, or bored him, or bothered him, but his eyes were fixed on her as if he had suffered a shock and was incapable of movement.

"We are gathered together, in the sight of God," the old minister began, hands shaking, "to join this couple together in Holy Matrimony. But before we seal the awful bonds which only God can set asunder, we must consider that this is the marriage of two mortals not yet sanctified and perfected by the Lord, our God. Rely not," the minister continued, "on the tides and sweeps of life to protect you. Everything is possible for he who strives to reach it, but strive we must. Pursue those sober and temperate diversions which God allows and recommends, for this is the surest way to preserve the love which now brings you to the altar. To a body in perfect health, the plainest food is nourishing, and to a soul rightly harmonized with its mate, everything affords delight. Rural retirement," he went on, "domestic tranquillity, friendly conversation, literary pursuits, philosophical inquiries, works of genius and imagination; nay, even the silent beauties of unadorned nature, a bright day, a still evening, a starry hemisphere, are sources of unadulterated pleasure to those whose lives have been joined, whose tastes have not been debased by criminal indulgences or by trifling ones. And when trials come, as come they must, you must be prepared to do your utmost, with the help of the Divine Grace, to correct your infirmities, to subdue your disruptive passions, to improve your understandings of one another, and thus of nature's grand plan, to exalt and purify your affections, to promote the welfare of all within your reach, for more *shall* come, and they may be many, to love and obey your Maker and your Redeemer; then is human happiness wound up to its utmost pitch, and this world has no higher gratifications to give. They are real happinesses, they are exquisite. They are what thousands have experienced, what thousands still experience, what you yourselves may experience if you choose.

"Your continued efforts will raise you above all low cares and little gratifications; it will give dignity and sublimity to your sentiments, inspire you with fortitude in danger, with patience in adversity, with moderation in prosperity, with alacrity in all your undertakings, with watchfulness over your own conduct, with benevolence toward each other, and to all mankind. Your continued watchfulness will be so far from throwing a damp on your other pleasures that it will give new life and spirit to them, and make all nature look gay around you. It will be a fresh fund of cheerfulness in store for you when the vivacity of youth begins to droop; and the only thing that can fill up the void in the soul left in it by every earthly enjoyment which is not consecrated to some higher purpose. It will not, like thoughtless worldly pleasures, desert you when you have most need of consolation in the hours of solitude, of old age, but once the holy flame of God's inspired life is thoroughly lighted up in your breasts, instead of becoming more faint and languid as you advance in years, it will grow stronger and brighter every day; will glow with particular warmth and luster when your dissolution draws near; will disperse the gloom and horrors of a deathbed, for there shall be no death to this love, will give you a foretaste of and render you worthy to partake of that *fullness of joy,* those pure celestial pleasures which are at 'God's right hand for evermore.' "

The minister paused, wheezing, to recover his breath. What a sermon for two atheists, Ten thought, but she was moved; even though she had never been able to resign herself to the good Reverend's habit of bringing death into the marriage service. Still, she supposed it belonged there. As she ought to know. Will he never stop? Edith was thinking. Poor Edna, she must be drooping there in that gown; and it is so hot. She restrained herself from the vulgarity of wiping her brow. Nellie doubted that the pair had heard a word of the sermon. The instant the minister fell silent, they stared at each other as if in obedience to some unheard command. But Nellie was wrong The sermon had deeply agitated both Edna and John; had anyone asked them, they would have been at a loss to explain why. It *was* true, as Ten suspected, that the mere mention of the Lord, our God, usually gave the two of them gooseflesh.

"My children," the minister began again, recovering strength. "before I recite the solemn marriage service, and you plight your troth, one to the other. let us listen to the words of David, who was punished by the remorse of his own conscience, by the deep affliction into which it plunged him, by the wretched consequences it drew after them, and by the heavy and positive punishment he inflicted upon himself. Hear how the repenting monarch bemoans himself in the anguish of his soul, and then ask yourself whether his situation was an enviable one; whether you would choose to imitate his misconduct as you enter into the holiest state, and whether you would choose the consequences which befell him, or instead meet with the rewards of the Lord, our God, already described." Oh no, Edith thought; here comes the other half of the Bible. But she had no desire to squirm. The rest of the audience, too, seemed fixed as if time had stopped.

Solemnly, the minister began chanting the Psalm of David. David, David, he seems to be everyone's theme lately, Ten thought. Was there some purpose in it? " 'Have mercy upon me, O God,' " the old man resolutely began, " 'after Thy great goodness, according to the multitude of Thy mercies do way mine offenses. Wash me thoroughly from my wickedness, and cleanse me from my sin; for I acknowledge my fault, and my sin is ever before me. Make me a clean heart, O God, and renew a right spirit within me. Cast me not away from Thy presence, and take not Thy Holy Spirit from me. Thy rebuke hath broken my heart, I am full of heaviness; I looked for some to have pity on me, but there was no man, neither found I any to comfort me. My God, my God, look upon me; why hast thou forsaken me, and art so far from my health and the words of my complaint? I cry in the daytime and thou hearest not; and in the night season also I take no rest. Turn Thee unto me, and have mercy upon me, for I am desolate and in misery. The sorrows of my heart are enlarged, O bring Thou me out of my troubles. Look upon my adversity and misery, and forgive me all my sin. Thine arrows stick fast in me, and Thy hand presseth me sore; for my wickednesses are gone over my head, and are like a sore burthen, too heavy for me to bear. I am brought into so great trouble and misery, that I go mourning all the day long. My heart panteth, my strength faileth, and the sight of mine eyes is gone from me.' "

The good minister paused again. Edna looked over at John, but he was staring down. Why, he described *me*, John thought; me, as I was. And I *have* sinned; I have wickedly remembered all the sorrows, wickedly, until just now. Until this miracle, this little person. He didn't dare look at Edna. He was shaken. Yes, he had to change. He had been blind. It occurred to him that he had experienced something of a miracle, a secular one, of course, not one the minister would consider worth discussing, but scales had been lifted from his eyes. He *had* experienced a change of heart. He felt a gratitude so overwhelming his head felt light. The room itself seemed suspended, like a cloud, somewhere in the strong, supporting sky. Edna was thinking, chilled, No, we must not. We shall not. She stood up even straighter. The minister resumed.

"Children," he began, "honor each other; live righteously with one another and an uninterrupted flow of health and spirit shall fill 'our mouths with laughter,' and our tongue with joy. We shall find ourselves happy. There shall be joy incorruptible, and through the trials of life, joy evermore. Remember always the words of our Savior: 'My yoke is heavy, but my burden is light.' From this day forward," he began winding up, "you two, joined in the sight of God, shall pull together as one, and, with the Help of our Savior, shall meet on the other shore, never again to endure partings or earthly trials. Today the immortal union begins and two hearts are joined which may never be separated."

The Reverend now began to intone the marriage service. During it, while giving all the proper responses, Edna was repeating silently, "I am the Resurrection, and the Life, saith the Lord. He that believeth in me though he were dead yet shall he live and whosoever liveth and believeth in me shall never die." Edna raised her left hand; John slipped on the ring. The glove's ring finger had been cut off, as was usual, to prevent unseemly struggling at the altar. This custom had always appeared comical to Edna, but she was unaware of external events. She was absorbed in reciting and reciting again, "I am the Resurrection and the Life . . . whosoever liveth and believeth in me shall never die." Why, I believe that! Edna realized, amazed. "Believest thou this?" she finished the passage mentally. Yes, she did believe it. Why did they recite this passage at funerals? *This*, she thought, should be the marriage service. This was when life began. Belief. What was it? she wondered. It had to begin somewhere. She believed in John. She believed in their life together. She believed in any life which would flow from them. Yes, she thought, we are Adam and Eve, and we begin again, and we go on until the end of time.

There may be judgment, yes, there will be judgment,

she decided, but there will be no end. World without end; she had just entered into it. The sudden hubbub of voices interrupted her. She found herself enclosed by John's arms, his face coming toward her as if descending from the sky itself; then her mother's body against hers, Ten's, Virginia's, Nellie's. Hal crept up, smiled down at her, saying, "You are so pretty. You are my mother now, you know!" "Oh, I do"; Edna smiled. John's eyes were on her. Something had happened; they had been transformed. He used to think changes occurred because of the public nature of the ceremony. Before, he and Edna had lived in their own world. The ceremony opened a door into it for the others. They could enter now and not be prosecuted. But the ceremony somehow changed their bodies, their souls, whatever they were; they were more permeable now, more visible. But that was not what had happened, that was not all of it. There was more. They had stepped into the river of time. Not time, he corrected himself; life. The common tide of life.

Time, he thought; that was the great riddle. The ceremony, the old Reverend's sermon, what had it done but cancel time? It denied it; there was no time, only eternity, time's opposite. He remembered an old theological argument. Everything had its opposite. If there was time, then there was immortality. But perhaps they were not comparable. Perhaps they were not opposites at all, as warmth was the opposite of cold. Perhaps time was something accidental, factitious. I don't believe in it, John realized; I don't believe in time. His thoughts were interrupted by an explosion of hugs, congratulations, whispered jokes. But now he knew what it was that had been at him; time, libelously called "the worm at the core." There was no such thing as time, he thought, feeling a consuming ecstasy; he reached for Edna, embracing her again. Somehow *she* was the source of the miracle; my God, he thought, how precious this little life was! "World without end," she whispered into his chest. He looked down at her garlanded head. They seemed to read one another's thoughts. No, it was coincidence. But it was not. He knew that.

Ten and the others were bustling everyone out onto the lawn like busy birds. The band had begun playing

gay music and the notes flew up into the air like gold
motes of dust. How lovely she looks, Edith thought; how
triumphant. Triumphant, that was it. She was sure *she*
had not looked triumphant at her wedding. She heard
John ordering Ten to stop kissing his bride; she would
wear her out. "Don't be so selfish," Ten was saying, and
now Nellie was kissing her, and John as well. It's hard to
believe he's standing still for this, Ten thought. Lord,
what a relief. She hadn't realized how thoroughly his
grief had invaded her. "Well," Ten was saying to John,
"you and Edna come back in and receive." "Receive?"
he asked; "there are hardly any guests." "Nevertheless,"
she answered, remorseless. She guided them into the
library; they stood under a floral bell of white roses with
Ten and Edith on one side, Virginia and Nellie on the
other. The mantel behind them was banked with pink
roses. Bridget and Bertha approached. They felt out of
place, that was clear, but it was equally certain Ten had
insisted upon their presence. She knew John and Edna
would want them there, and Amos, too, although he was
doing his best to make himself part of the far wall. The
minister was led up by Ten. "Thank you," Edna whispered, impulsively leaning forward to kiss him on the
cheek. It's wet, his cheek is wet, she realized. Well, that
was the source of his power, the riddle behind that sermon; he had been happily married. She should ask Ten,
but it was true; she already knew the answer. Bridget
and Bertha were duly kissed, then Amos and Hal, and the
women began all over again.

"Come," Ten commanded them; "Edna has to cut the
bridal loaf. Amos," she said, turning slightly, "go get the
rest of the servants. And the children, call the children."
Edna heard an excited giggle from behind the curtains.
She looked over quickly; it was true. The windows *were*
full of faces. "*And* any of their parents," Ten told Amos
impatiently. John stood by while Edna cut the bridal loaf,
taking the plates from her, handing them to the guests.
Now everything had become a blur. "All right, Edna,"
Virginia was saying, "come on in with me." "With you?"
Edna asked, dazed. "To prepare to leave." "Oh, yes,"
Edna answered vaguely. John's eyes followed her all the
way to the house. The same thought possessed the three
women simultaneously; they loved each other; they did.

"Well," John said awkwardly, "I had better go with Amos and see to the carriage." "Are you taking a pair of riding horses?" Ten asked. "They'll be enduring the indignity of following the other two." "Well, four horses," Nellie giggled; "you will look important." Mrs. Dickinson was also smiling at him. Everyone seemed so happy.

John turned and went off to the barn with Amos. Yes, all the luggage was in the carriage. Yes, the clothes were up on the rack. Yes, the boxes from Tivoli's were inside, wrapped in cool towels. Yes, he *had* wetted them down just now. Yes, he had watered the horses. No, there was nothing to worry about, and if John would only get out of the way, he would drive the carriage up to the front of the house and they could make their escape. John walked back to the tent. The next time he came home, he would be a married man. The house, he thought; it wasn't really suitable for a large family. And it had gotten so large, and so fast, or so it seemed, what with Hal back. He would have to tell Edna about his other brother, the one who had died. That was the only secret he had kept from her, what had happened to him. She had to know that. Hal would blurt it out one day, sooner or later, all the details, but even if Hal didn't do that, he had to tell her. Well, he supposed he would live through that, too. Edna was standing in the doorway in the most exquisite pale blue dress he had ever seen. He had no idea what it was called, though he thought he had heard someone call it a robe. He did not believe she would move, she looked so like a doll, with those heavily embroidered sleeves like a kimono's, and that beautiful skirt, it was in two layers, and all that lace. But what he liked best was that brilliant blue ribbon around her waist, and the little white roses someone had twined in that magnificent hair. What a beautiful creature, he thought for the hundredth time, when she startled him by moving, and moving toward him.

The women, meanwhile, were absorbed in all the details of the blue cambric muslin dress. "The corsage has no collar," Edith remarked happily; "an after-wedding dress *should* take a plunge." "It's the embroidery," Nellie gasped: "what do they call it?" "The arabesque design," Ten said. "Why," Nellie exclaimed, "the *whole* dress is open in front!" "Well, not exactly," Edith said; "there's an underskirt on the bottom half and a plain chemisette under the top. I think." She remembered she was talking about her daughter; Edna's lack of inhibitions often startled her. "Well, I am behind the times," lamented Nellie. "Oh, come, you're the only one who thinks so"; Ten hugged her. "Well," Edith said sadly, "let's send them off, say goodbye to the guests, and settle in for our supper." "In front of the fire, like three old dogs," Nellie agreed. "You know," Ten said, "I think it *will* be cool enough for a fire tonight. And the first day of August, too. How fast time goes!" "Shall we invite the minister?" Nellie asked. "Oh, I hope not," Edith cried without thinking; she covered her mouth with her hand. "Nellie, dear, you know what I mean. Just the three of us, that's what I want. That is, if the two of you do." "I do," said Ten. "So do I," Nellie said. "Well, then, a long speech of thanks to the minister; I really do feel grateful to him." "I know," Edith agreed, bewildered; "so do I." And then, John and Edna were driving off in the bright red carriage, a cloud of dust erasing them as they went. "Where *are* they going?" Edith asked in exasperation. "To some little town. They won't tell me, but I think it's Dummerston." "Dummerston!" Edith echoed; "as long as I live, I'll never understand that child." "Well, it's not necessary," Ten said; "at least that's what I've decided." "It's called resigning oneself to the inevitable," Nellie commented as they finally went in to say goodbye to the few remaining guests and sink in for the last two days they could be sure of together.

It was, or at least it seemed to the newly married pair, an unusual honeymoon. After a five-hour drive, both perched on the driving board, they found themselves stopping the carriage before a cottage which John had taken sight unseen. For the last few hours, he had worried nervously about what sight would greet their arriving eyes; he had been in enough houses where the fleas were the occupants most eager to offer hospitality to the new guests. He retained an especially vivid memory of one house in the South Hadley Hills. The sun had preceded him into the parlor, and not only were the fleas on a blond cat visible, but they could be seen jumping to and from the animals on the carpet. When he had returned home, he had to boil his clothes and scrub down out in the barn with brown soap, a performance he remembered (afterwards, his skin was more sensitive to the touch than had he badly burned it) was witnessed with great amusement by Amos and Ben, who suggested he bury his clothes and leave the boiling alone. But that was before Ten returned. After she came back—that was how he always thought of it—such crises had not seemed so looming, so overwhelming. Well, he certainly didn't want to introduce a bitten, scratching Edna to the marriage bed and bring her home, legs red, swollen, and scratched, all under the withering eyes of his sister. If there *was* a marriage bed. It suddenly occurred to him that there might not, or it might be what he called "a down bed," one with such dreadful springs it fell down the instant the exhausted occupant threw himself into it.

Well, he had worried unnecessarily. The cottage was spotlessly white, the shutters shining black, no sign of paint peeling anywhere on its wooden siding. And the owner had been modest, he thought, in calling it a cottage at all; the building was two stories high, and had an addition built onto the side, which opened onto a cedar-chipped path, and an arch, on the other side of which was the entrance to an immense barn. "Oh," he said, out loud, "you climb that hill," and he pointed the way out to Edna, "to get to the top story." "What's that door?" Edna asked, pointing to one that swung open into thin air. She seemed unusually subdued. "That one's for pitching hay; it goes up from the hay wagons. They fill the barn with it for the winters." "Oh," she said. "You'll like the haying season," he assured her; "the wagons get so piled up you can't even see the wheels underneath them, and then all those people perched on top; they look like people standing on top of the world." "I'm sure I will like it." Her hands, she noted, were clammy.

Was it possible, she wondered, the owner was still here? Everything was so perfectly in order. The trumpet vines grew over the windows in front of the house; the house was set off from the lawn by huge banks of purplish-pink and white phlox. Somehow, the owner had trained his vines to hang down on both sides of his windows in triangular shapes so that they resembled leafy draperies. A huge trumpet vine ran at right angles to the house, setting off a tiny apple orchard. The small red circles gleamed cheerily in the sun. In front of the house was a carefully tended lawn, and two smoke trees, both of them puffing pink clouds of flowers. When Edna had first seen them, she had thought they were on fire. And beyond those trees, more clumps of phlox, growing with no apparent plan, yet there was one, the grass deepening, becoming wilder, as the lawn spread out its colors to the meadow. Wild flowers, Queen Anne's lace, wild daisies, wild lilies, peeped from the high green grasses, and behind the row of trees and bushes and the stone fence was the pasture, the inevitable pasture, already the color of hay. No, it had not rained much this summer. The day was as bright as a day could be; it was very late for all this light.

She and John began exploring the grounds; they were hesitant to enter. "What peculiar-looking cabbages!" Edna exclaimed, stopping in front of the vegetable patch half hidden by the phlox. "That's rhubarb," John said, hugging her to him. He let go, bent down, broke off a stem and handed it to her. "Eat it. All the country children do." Edna bit into it, making a face. "Sour," she announced, chewing; "I like it." "Well, don't eat too much of it, not the first time, anyway." "Like green apples?" "Something like that." "Well, I wouldn't want to spend tonight clutching at *my* stomach," Edna said, poking his. "Look!" she cried, running off; "look at these vines. I have to tell Ten about them. What a beautiful way to ornament a fence! Don't you think," she went on excitedly, "it would be just the thing to cover her pickets?" He was laughing at her. "If she likes cucumbers." "Cucumbers; what do cucumbers have to do with these vines?" "Well, just look at them." She did. "John," she said slowly, "there are little pickles on these vines." She had also noticed the little strips of white cotton tying the vines to the sticks. "From little pickles little cucumbers grow," he chanted, mocking. "You mean these are *cucumber* vines?" "They are; here." He pulled off one of the larger ones, handing it to her. "We can eat it tonight. Take another. We'll have a cucumber supper." Edna picked two more from the vine, looking at them in disbelief. "Cucumbers!" she repeated in a whisper; "and they flower, too; the vines, I mean." She pointed to some yellow flowers. "They really *wouldn't* be a poor idea as decorative vines. I'm having trouble talking all squashed up like this," she complained. Squash, rhubarb! She felt ridiculous.

"It takes time to learn the country," John comforted her; "when we get back to Williamsville, I have to take you to see a Mr. Gale. He's been living in the town for over fifty years and he still thinks of himself as a stranger. And so does the rest of the town. 'Well, I love this place,' he always says, 'but I'm not really a native. Not born here, you know. It makes a big difference, a big difference, shouldn't you think so? I would think so, wouldn't you?' Over fifty years, and he still feels like a stranger. I suppose he is, too, when the La Marches had great-great-grandparents who were burned out by Indians. Is that sort of thing going to bother you?" "No, I was born here by proxy. I had that copied onto the margin of the marriage certificate." "Where did Ten get such a thing?" "I don't have the slightest idea, but I certainly treasure it." "You do, do you," he asked, picking her up; it was getting dark fast. They had better get into the house. "And how are you going to open the door?" Edna inquired from somewhere inside his arms. "Put you down, and pick you up again, throw you on a bed, take out the traps, light the lamps, put the horses in the stable, and hop into bed."

"In exactly that order?" "Not necessarily." "We should have taken Jimmie," Edna sighed, "but he might have gotten frightened and jumped out and we would never have found him." "Are you worried about being alone with me?" "Not exactly, but it would be nice to have something—familiar." "Familiar." "Familiar," she said. "I'm not familiar enough?" "That's the trouble; you will be. Jimmie is a perfect gentleman." "We could put it off." "Not on your life," she answered, snuggling up. "If we build a new house," she murmured, "it has to have a snuggery." "*You* are a snuggery," John answered, putting her down, bending to look for the key. "Third small rock under the large slab of slate," he recited out loud. He picked up the key; it worked. The tumblers turned in the door. He heard Edna's relieved sigh behind him. He picked her up, and walked directly into the parlor, depositing her in a chair. "Now, you sit there," he warned, "until I light some candles. I don't want you breaking a leg." "Well *something* had better get broken," Edna murmured from the depths of chintz flowers; she sounded like a little bee. He went on lighting candles. "Are you frightened?" he asked without pausing to look at her. "It's difficult, to tell the difference between that and excitement. Sometimes." She considered. "I'm a little frightened and a lot excited." "Well, then," John said; "it's safe for me to go out and see to the horses without worrying you'll go jumping out the window?" "I've got better sense than Jimmie; go on." He turned to look at her. Her huge green cat eyes were glowing at him in the dusk. She was something of a cat herself.

"Well, everything's done," Edna breathed after they finished their dinner of cucumber sandwiches and fancy cakes; "I've turned down the bed." She looked up at him. "And what did you find in it?" "Sheets. Sheets and pillows. It's very comfortable," she added, watching him sideways. "Is it?" "Very. And I unpacked all the trunks." "When did you do that?" "While you were in the stable." "Then we had better go to bed." "Yes, we had better." Her cat smile had suddenly reappeared. "Edna," John asked nervously from the bed, "what were all those nightdresses *for?* I mean, aren't you supposed to *wear* any of them?" Edna was standing at the foot of the bed, removing one article of clothing after another, placing each one neatly on the trunk at the foot of the bed, apparently with no use for anything as common as a nightdress. She stood at the foot of the bed, naked. "You're not going to put on a nightdress, are you?" "I have my skin on." "Well, is your skin going to lie itself down on this bed?" He had seen those breasts before, but never all of the body at once; she was so small except for those breasts. They were so firm and curved upwards; and the pink, sweet nipples. He noticed they were both erect. "Half of you," he said, "points in one direction, half in the other." Edna looked down. "So I do, but the roads all go in a circle and come back to the same place. It's just the signs that are confusing." She slid into bed, lying on her back next to him. "We must look," she told the ceiling, "like

the figures of a king and queen laid out on a sepulcher."
Now it was John's turn to be nervous.

"Edna?" he asked; "would it be all right if I told you
about something first? There's something I meant to tell
you." "Drowning," she said; "it has something to do with
drowning." "Someone told you?" he asked; he was outraged. "Told me what?" He fell silent again. She
turned on her side, pulling his arm across her chest.
Furry. He was furry. She began rubbing his chest right
over its central bone; it felt tight. "It was my brother
who drowned and I got the blame for it. We all went
swimming, and I was supposed to look out for him because I was a better swimmer, but then some of us decided to race to the other shore, and Hal was there, so I
thought there wasn't anything wrong with letting Hal
watch him. Hal could certainly do that. But then our
dog jumped in after us, and Hal forgot he was supposed
to stay with Martin and went in after the dog. Then Hal
started shouting for me, and I saw Martin coming after
us. He was too small to go so far.

"I don't remember the rest very well, just the swimming
back to him as fast as I could; and everyone else swimming after me. Hal kept calling to Martin, 'Come back,
come back,' and Martin, he would swim a few strokes
toward me and a few back. And there was a strong tide
that day. There usually isn't any to speak of in the river,
but the rain, when it floods the river, there's quite a current and it had been raining for almost a week before.
The banks were covered. Trees were in the water; flowers were just floating on the surface. By the time I got
near him, his head was starting to go under, so I stuck
my own head in, and forgot about breathing, but when
I looked up, he was gone." "Did you find him? Could you
dive?" "I got him out; I even tried all the things you're
supposed to do for a case of drowning." It was harder
and harder for him to go on.

"Well," Edna said, "it's a good thing the old festivities
of the bridal chamber have been dispensed with. Imagine," she teased gently, "Ten and my mother and Nellie
and Virginia coming in here with everyone else to throw
the stocking and listening to us talk. They'd never recover. And," she went on, rubbing his chest, "you never
really did 'pop the question.' And I was so curious to see

how you would do it. Well, especially after *all* the examples I'd studied in my etiquette books. There was one major rule: 'never lose an opportunity.' " "Well, *you* didn't," he answered shakily. "But you *cheated* me!" Edna complained; "why, I had one particular passage memorized. I was really hoping for something like it. 'Ah, Julia,' " she recited, " 'how happy existence would prove, if I always had such a companion!' " She paused for effect. "She sighs, and leans more fondly on the arm that tremblingly supports her. 'My dearest Julia, be mine forever.' This is a settler; that's what the book said.

"And then there was another, my second-best: 'Ellen, one word from you would make me the happiest man in the universe!' 'I should be cruel not to speak it then, unless it's a very hard one.' 'It's a word of three letters and answers the question: Will you have me?' The lady, of course, says yes, unless she happens to prefer a word of only two letters and answers no. And so," Edna solemnly intoned, "this interesting and terrible process in practice, simple as it is in theory, is varied in a hundred ways, according to circumstances and the various dispositions. My *least* favorite was: 'My dear Eliza, we must do what all the world evidently expects we shall.' 'All the world is very impertinent.' 'I know it, but it can't be helped. . . . When shall I tell the parson to be ready?' and after that: 'Have you any objection to changing your name?' and he follows this up with another, which clinches the significance of the question: 'How would mine suit you?' "

"You were much more direct." "*I* was?" Edna asked; "well, all right, there must be no deceptions between husband and wife. How nice you looked today in full dress; I never saw you in a dress vest, and black pantaloons, dress boots, black silk stockings, even white kid gloves and a white cravat. Well, you must admit, it was a remarkable transformation. But you should have had one or two grooms; that would have been only right. After all, I had a bridesmaid." "We didn't do anything by the book," he answered; "we were supposed to consider what we were about for a proper length of time." "We did," Edna protested; "but we can stretch time out now. You could dress up in that outfit once a day, and we could call in the minister weekly. We could make it *appear* we had spent considerable time considering." "Ridiculous, you are ridiculous"; he grinned. "What do you do for a case of drowning?" she asked.

John looked at her, startled. She must have been reading up on the shock cure they were currently advocating; throwing people into ice water for stroke. "The London Method. My father preferred it. Expose the face and the chest to the breeze. My God, he was so little!" "And then?" she prodded. "Well, then I turned him over, with his face down, this wrist"—he picked up his left hand— "under his forehead. He was so cold. Well, that was supposed to cause all fluids to escape by way of the mouth, and make the tongue come forward. So the windpipe would be free. It was supposed to do some good. But he didn't breathe; he didn't even begin, so we threw him on his side. Even though he was dead—it seemed so cruel to do it. I knew it was useless. But it still seemed so cruel. I was supposed to tickle his throat with a feather, – but I had to get a leaf, and use the stem, and then we dashed his face with cold water.

"None of it did any good. So we turned him back on his face. It seemed like we were turning him over in something invisible, like a mummy; it was ghastly, and Hal, that was the last straw, Hal kept asking, 'What's the matter with Martin? What's the matter with Martin?' So I screamed at him. I don't remember what I said, but he ran off into the woods crying, and someone else went after him. Someone ran for Martin's coat; it was supposed to support the chest. Then I had to rub his face; we kept turning him over and over, like something roasting, and each time we did it, leaned on his back, you know, right below the shoulder blades, they were so thin I thought we would break them, and then we stopped pressing just before we turned him over again. Well, that was when the respiration was supposed to begin. It didn't. I don't think Mother ever forgave me for it. Father, he took on about how just last year I had saved Martin from fire by wrapping him in a wet blanket and getting him to play a dog chasing a cat. I was the cat, and we crawled out under the smoke, down the steps, all the way outside. He didn't want to come at first, the fire frightened him. *I* was terrified.

"Father kept saying things like 'It was intended; last year he was almost destroyed by fire; this year by water. If it hadn't been for the water, the locusts would have gotten him next year.' But Mother wouldn't resign herself. 'Julia, you can't take over for God; it is my deep conviction'—he always phrased it that way—'God intended this.' Then he would remind her of the family up the hill who had lost all of their eight children in four days, and all the other families who met similar fates in the last diphtheria epidemic. It didn't make any impression." "Do you think *he* believed it?" "Believed what?" "That it was intended." "No. He didn't. He just kept saying it for Mother's sake. He blamed me, too, but he didn't think it was right to do it; he wasn't the same to me afterwards. When he came to see me at medical school, he said, I'll never forget him saying it, 'You chose the right profession. You can make up for things now.'" "Did you?"

"I don't believe you can make up for things." "Neither do I," Edna agreed. "Do *you* think it was my fault?" "Fault," she echoed: "blame. Suppose," she thought aloud, "nothing had happened. Suppose Hal had listened. Suppose *you* had drowned. Then it would have been the others who would have been busy blaming, and you were the youngest; they would have been worse about it. I mean, every year attaches a new thread. Sometimes the newest are the strongest. If it had been you, they never would have gotten over it. Not the youngest boy. No, I'm sure of that. And it *could* have happened that way, just as easily. Couldn't it? You make it sound as if you were reckless, very reckless. If I'd been your mother, I would have been frightened to death every time you left the house." "She was." He was thinking; she could tell that. "You do believe what you said?" he asked anxiously; "that it could have been me, just as easily?" "More easily." "I never thought of that," he said. "Blinded by guilt," she quoted from some forgotten tract. He was crying again. She hoped they wouldn't spend their entire married life with one or the other of them crying in bed. "Don't worry, Edna," John finally told her; "this won't go on forever." "I hope not," she answered, embracing him. "Still no nightdress," he observed; "still no nightdress." His hand reached her stomach.

"John," she asked, "can we pull back the covers?" "Why?" "I want to look at you." He sighed. A fine time for an anatomy lesson. "Do you approve of what you see?" he asked. But Edna was lost in inspecting him. "What an incredible thing!" she exclaimed while he lay there stiffly trying not to writhe; "it gets so much bigger and then smaller; it doesn't look at all the same standing up. Why, it looks like a little person; as if it could walk!" "It does have intentions along those lines," John said, turning over toward her. "Where does it want to go?" "I'll show you," John answered, and he did. "Edna?" John asked.

She was crying. No answer. "Why are you crying? You didn't get the sheets bloody. The blood didn't go through that towel with us; don't worry about that." She went on crying silently. "Will you *please* tell me why you're crying?" he demanded desperately. "Because," she sobbed, "it was so nice. It was so shocking. I'm possessed," she sobbed frantically. "You're just shocked at yourself, that's all," he said, impatient. "What are you talking about?" she demanded through her sobs. "You're not a proper young lady." "I *know* that." "Well, if you ask me," he said, his hand again on her breast, "I think you just found out." She turned over and peered at him. "Do you think that's it?" "I do." "It was like drowning," she said thoughtlessly. "And nothing *you* can do about it either," he said resolutely, lowering his hand, lowering it again. "There's a space between your thighs," he murmured; "are your demons back yet?" "Yes, yes," she gasped, "I think they are." "They may stay all night." "You think so?" she asked, beginning to move her lips over his chest. "I do, and," he added, "they may be back in the morning." "Do you think I'll get used to them? I thought we'd be spending the time here alone." "We are, more or less," John said, lowering himself onto her. "More, I think," she whispered; "more." "Do you want to get used to them?" John asked while he could still talk. "Don't ask such silly questions," she whispered back, beginning to undulate on the bed; "I think I'm getting used to them already."

Wednesday morning, as they were preparing to leave, Edna affectionately reached up to touch John's cheek, then his lips. "I don't think we left the bed for more than three hours; is that possible?" "No, but we did it all the same. Edna, can you, will you, love me?" he mocked. "I think I can," she responded, falling instantly in with his mood; "I shall try to be all you expect of me, and I must say yes. Only a heartless coquette finds the means of encouraging a man she does not intend to have." "And are you such an one?" "Let's hope not," Edna retorted; "did you know that, in one of my etiquette books, the chapter on 'The Etiquette of Courtship and Marriage' is followed by the 'The Raising and Breeding of Canaries'?" "How appropriate." He seemed nervous. Edna decided to avoid her new subject, but nevertheless she was sure. She was sure she was pregnant, and that John's little stranger had created another. Why, it couldn't be otherwise! she exclaimed to herself, as if answering some dubious inquirer. "What fee did you give the minister in that little piece of paper?" she asked irrelevantly. "Twenty dollars." It *had* been overdoing it, he thought. "He deserved forty; he deserves a room in our house," Edna teased.

They drove on through the misty day. "Edna, how *did* we get to this?" "Don't *you* know?" she asked, amused; "someone must. Maybe Gray, or Flag, or someone like that." "Someone like that?" "Oh, they seem alive to me." "Edna." he asked again, "really; how did it happen?" "I followed the instructions on 'How to Win a Sweetheart—True and Only Method,' page 402 of *Useful and Domestic Arts.*" "You did not." "I did." John shook his head. "Then I should have read the chapter on antidotes to the true and only method. What did your chapter say?" "*My* chapter told me that true love arises 'from a principle of *sympathy*, from a *oneness* of feeling, from a similarity in some points of character, although other points may be very dissimilar—from showing that you possess something which the other admires. Acting upon this, you may induce love in another for you, and *cement* the affections upon you.'" "That sounds sensible enough." he said comfortably. Three days, or three years, what was it?

"Oh, but *then*," Edna whispered dramatically, "they told you how to plot it out. They called in a phrenologist to make sure of that chapter. So I had an advantage.

'Find out the other's main passion,' she quoted: 'to one who has large intellectual organs do not talk fashionable nonsense, or words without ideas—chitchat or *small talk* —I mean the polite tête-à-tête of fashionable young people; but converse intellectually upon sensible subjects; evince good sense and sound judgment in all you do and say; present *ideas* and exhibit *intellect*.' They underline the important things," she interrupted herself. "Do go on"; John beamed; "so far I can't say I noticed you followed *any* of those instructions." "You're accusing me of sounding like a fashionable young person?" "I didn't say that; it's the conversing intellectually I'm not sure about; continue, my dear." "Well," she pouted, "if all this is to be lost on you. Still, you may come to your senses yet. 'This will gratify their intellects, and lay a deep intellectual basis for mutual love, as well as go far towards exciting it.' Perhaps," she considered, "it was your *lack* of intellect which kept you from noticing what I was about. After all, I did learn the *character* of the individual whose love is sought. 'That being known, success is to be obtained by bringing the batteries to bear properly upon the prominent traits of that character.' " "And *did* you find out my main passion?" "I did," Edna answered; "me." "And what did we have in common?" "*My* main passion was you." "Oh, I see"; he laughed. Well, that was a new sound, Edna thought. He hardly ever laughed. She had never heard him really laugh. She liked that laugh.

"He was very clever, I believe, that writer," she chattered on; " 'as one estimates himself and others not by a standard of wealth, beauty, dress, etc., but by a moral and intellectual standard, so your showing them that you really esteem those qualities which they prize so highly will cause them to perceive that your tastes harmonize with theirs, and thus turn their leading organs in your favor, and unite and endear them to you.' " "Their leading organs?" John laughed again; this time, he sounded less rusty. "That's what he wrote." "Do you memorize *everything?*" "I can't help it; if it's on a page, or said out loud, I remember it word for word." "That's because you're so young; just wait until you get older and things begin crowding themselves out. We'll see how your memory does then." "Well, you had better keep room for

me; after all, there was even more to that book. It ended
by reassuring the dedicated reader that 'by these and
other similar applications of this principle, the disengaged
affections of almost anyone can be secured, especially if
the organs of both be similar; for the command thus obtained over the feelings, will, and even judgment, is almost unlimited.'" "It must have been the similarity of
the organs," John said, turning toward her. "I see," Edna
said gravely, "that I should have spent more time on the
passage concerning men of vulgar passions." "True,"
John answered, rounding a bend; "you don't frighten me,
you know; you didn't have *time* to plan anything." "A
lot you know; it was you that didn't have time. You
didn't have time to escape." "A ridiculous little person.
The doctor has gone and married a ridiculous little person." "Say it again and I'll tickle you." He said it again.
Edna tickled. As if drunk, the carriage wandered from
side to side of the road.

"Aren't you supposed to stop on covered bridges?"
Edna asked; "to take advantage of the dark?" John
stopped the carriage. Yes, this was something, he thought;
this was like being hugged by the sun or the grass. This
was a burial and a resurrection. Edna's mind, on the
other hand, had been cleared of words. Her whole being
relaxed, bled into the man whose arms were around her.
Why had Ten worried? There's no one else in the world.
She was inside his arms; they were the clouds and the
trees. He was the horizon, the beginning and end. Oh
yes, she remembered, she thought I might die first. It
was likely they would have stayed there, under the roof
of the bridge, for hours, but the sound of hooves caused
John to start up their horses. "Oh, too bad," Edna sighed.
"We'll be there soon; are you sorry? You married such
an old man." "You're younger than I am. I checked into
it." "A ridiculous little person," he said again. "A ridiculous little *old* person." "Have it your way, Mrs. Steele."
"Mrs. Steele, Mrs. Steele," she repeated. "Ridiculous little
person," he muttered. "I heard that," she cautioned. "Mr.
Steele, Mr. Steele," she began again. "Worse than the
cuckoo bird." But they were turning the familiar bend
in the road. The old house was coming into view. "Ten
didn't tell you anything about my building a house?" she

asked, worried. He looked over, startled. "I didn't want you to think I was hunting a fortune." "I don't know what you're talking about; why don't you explain tonight? We can have another good cry over it." "Oh, stop." "Well, if you were hunting a fortune, you got the worst of the bargain," John concluded, "and that's that." "Don't say that." "What?" "That I got the worst of the bargain; it's not true."

Ten was standing in the doorway, waiting. One look at their faces was enough; she wasn't going to bother with silly questions. "He did talk to you in something other than monosyllables?" Ten asked Edna. "Oh, he never stops." She wanted desperately to tell Ten she knew she was pregnant, but she knew Ten would tell John, and they would both believe she had taken leave of her senses. She didn't want John to know until the last possible moment. She would eat less. Then he would worry less. Yes, that was what she would do. The three of them paused outside. "I can't *wait* until the winter," Edna exclaimed. Ten and John looked at each other, amused. It will be her first winter, Ten thought; her first winter. Now we wait and see. We wait to see if cabin fever develops. "And here," she said, handing John a long sheet of paper resembling a scroll, "is the list of invalids awaiting you. One of whom, I believe, is old Dr. Houston. He's prostrated on the second floor." "Will some sleep cure him?" John asked. "Him, yes," Ten said, looking over the list, "but I don't know about the others." "Well, it's back to the old yoke," John said; "you don't mind, Edna?" "It's what I expected." Her first winter alone, Ten thought again; her first winter alone.

She remembered *her* first winter after she had returned from Kansas, and she had lived here most of her life. She had been frightened by every squeak and crack and whimper. Well, she thought, if I so much as mention it to her, she'll shrug it off and reassure *me*, and tell me Jimmie will protect her. Edna was inspecting her curiously. Ten began chattering about suppers and dinners, and kitchen disasters, rose blights, and anything else which did her the favor of entering her mind, but she kept on at it: her first winter. It will be her first winter. Last year, a woman in the village had taken to walking in the snow barefoot, in her nightdress, up and down the common in the middle of the night. Someone took just such a walk each year. When the minister took the woman off, he asked her why she wanted to walk out like that. "The snow." That was all she answered. Yet everyone seemed to understand.

Ella: 1968

It is odd the tricks that memory plays. There is one picture I have always had so clearly in mind. I loved the picture so, and still love it. Once a year, the family turns the house inside out, looking in all the old trunks, through all the old drawers, through all the old papers, seeing if it can't be lurking somewhere, stuck between the pages of a book, behind some books, somehow slid beneath a carpet, fallen behind the refrigerator. Once a year, usually in April, everyone looks for it. It is because I want it so. No one finds it. There is the sound of hesitation outside my bedroom, subdued mutterings, while the decision is made: who is to come in and tell me now? I know what they all think, that this is all an aberration of somebody very old, but it isn't; there is something very important about that picture.

The picture is faded to tones of yellowish sepia. I doubt if anyone else would see anything very special about it. But to me it means everything. Whoever took it (did I? did Martin? did Letitia? There's no remembering that) must have had to walk a long way down the dusty drive leading up to our house, our new house, and the effect produced is strange enough. On the one side, blurred elms, completely out of focus, and fading into a mass of leafy cloud, and in back of that cloud the house, while on the other side, the right side, where so much less life took place, there is the barn, its one window a blank square, and in front of it, the second family car, and slightly to the right of it, the wooden swing suspended on its wooden contraption, Minnie's face covered by the shadow of a huge sun parasol, the bird fountain missing its top, and one folding canvas sun chair, with its awning still down. Someone must have gotten out of that chair, or been coaxed and pleaded with to come out of that chair and take the picture. Don't you think so? I mean, there is the chair, tilting slightly forward as if someone had just jumped out of it, and the chair was still recovering from the shock, or perhaps it was whichever of us had jumped out of the chair to drive off in the car which is standing impatiently as a horse right in back of it, the barn door still swung wide open to let it out. Well, if someone hadn't been in a hurry, the door would have been closed. Aunt Ten and Mother were always fussy about things like that.

At any rate, I should make some attempt to explain why, once a year, I am seized by a moon madness which sets me to pitilessly harassing the household, after them every minute to find that picture, find that picture. And I carried on that way every year before my sight was restored, too; only then it was worse, because one or another of the great-grandchildren would burst into tears and assure me that no one was burning my things or throwing them out just because I couldn't see. They never used the word "blind" when they spoke to me. But I heard one of the children telling a friend who had come to stay for the week, "We're so proud of Aunt Ella; at her age, to understand so much, and then to be so cheerful, and she's blind as a bat, too. Why," she whispered, "I can tell her anything. Things I wouldn't dare tell my parents." "Anything?" her friend had taunted. "Oh yes," she said, and there was some whispering, some giggling, and then a startled "No!" from her friend. How it brought old times back. Ella and Letitia waiting for Aunt Ten. She always knew the two of them waiting meant trouble. The only time, she used to say, we could keep from scratching out each other's eyes was when we were waiting for her with some trouble. Why, she used to wonder, did trouble for her mean peace for us? I still miss her. I thought Aunt Ten would live forever.

I still remember how she looked the last time I saw her, before she took sick, I mean. By that time, she had given up on frills. She said her mind hung enough bows and ribbons on the trees and the stones and she wore her hair pulled straight back from her face, skewered

into a knob in the back. It was our needling that finally
made her give in on the question of her hair; probably
the only thing she ever did give in on. I suppose it must
have been unimportant to her. She sat still as a good
child on the wooden kitchen chair while Letitia and I
performed the operation. Letitia (the lines she cut were
always straighter than mine) made a little part along the
front of Aunt Ten's forehead—she had such a high forehead—and drew some hair forward; then she parted that
long hair in the middle, while poor Aunt Ten pulled the
rest of her hair to safety back into her bun. She was
nervous as a chicken in a garret with a cat. "What are
you doing to me now?" she asked through the thin strands
of her hair we had covering her face like a demented veil.
"Cutting," Letitia answered absently. When it came down
to it, she was always the bystander. She handed me the
scissors; I think she would have made a very good nurse.
Or a dictator. "Straight across," she ordered me. "Straight
across?" Aunt Ten echoed; "you're going to make me
look like a little boy who's not old enough for pants."
I didn't answer her, I was so careful cutting. "That's it,"
Letitia said. (We all called her Lettie, except when we
were angry, or when she had a caller. She always had so
many beaux; that's what made what she finally did so inexplicable.) "No," she corrected herself, standing back,
"a little shorter; it shouldn't come down more than two
inches over the forehead." "I'm going to look like a
sheep dog," Aunt Ten wailed. "Sit still," Letitia said;
"you're moving the cloth. It won't be our fault if you
get hair down your back and hop around scratching."
"A sheep dog with fleas," Aunt Ten complained, sitting
perfectly still. I cut off another inch, and Lettie, seeing me nod, went to get the curling rod. It would have
been too much to expect her to sit still for hours with a
head full of curling papers. We curled the short hair into
a frizz over her forehead.

She wasn't displeased with the result. "I always had
such a high forehead," she sighed, looking into the hand
glass. I think she liked it. At least she never altered her
hair until we had to fuss with it again the day she died.
Aunt Ten had such beautiful eyes, but most of the time,
we worried about them; they seemed to see right through
us. But as she got older, they softened. We loved the little

wrinkles that formed in the corners of her eyes. Other women had crow's-feet; she had two deep lines that seemed drawn in with pencil. And how she used to complain! Other women had circles under their eyes; she had pouches of wrinkles. "And," she would invariably add, "ears like an elephant's." And that long, straight nose which seemed to grow directly from her forehead, the graceful arch of her eyebrows, even in the picture she sat for when she had to maintain her position in the torture chair; it was her characteristic expression. A softness about the broad, thin lips, as if she were both thinking and smiling, and her square, square chin. She did have a majestic face, but who ever thought of that?

Even when she adopted the style that was so fashionable and easy then, the starched white collar that looked like a priest's, the dark velvet dress, usually maroon, the big cameo set square in the middle of the collar. Well, that wasn't like everyone else's; it was blue and white Wedgwood, something her husband had once given her. We couldn't believe in him at all, he had taken place long ago, before we were even born. And the two velvet stripes running vertically down both sides of the brooch; if they didn't look like a priest's surplice, and of course, the neat row of buttons. Well, they showed how things were changing; they were uncovered. "The plain style," she used to say whenever we tried to coax her into something nicer; we always wanted to dress her like a doll. "Children," she said firmly one day, "I've spent seventy-five years dressing in the latest fashion, and now, if I want to wear a feed bag, no one's going to stop me." Well, that was the end of it. And when she finished speaking, her face would assume its usual expression, as if she were looking at a shining world we would never catch a glimpse of. Even now, thinking of it, it seems unbelievable, no, miraculous. She had seen so much. But if we had said something to her about it (none of us would have dared; perhaps Mother might have, but she was the only one), she would have said something self-exalting like "Some people are good at pickling and preserving and others have a talent for sewing." We were all reasonably old (for those days) before we no longer needed Mother to decode what we considered her gnomic utterances. Sixteen, seventeen. Oh, we were old.

Yes, the picture. You see, I remember Aunt Ten being in it, but she couldn't have been. She was long dead before the automobile began rumbling its way into ditches and creeks. Still, all these years, I've been sure she was there, in the rocker under the awning. Perhaps she was, in some sense or other. Perhaps we can't make any real distinction between proximity, what thing was actually next to the other thing, and what the mind perceived to be close together. If what I saw in the picture was a picture of my inner world, then of course she was there. And who is to say that those pictures aren't the real ones? But the reason I desperately want to find the picture is because my vision of it is so absolute. Mother and Father. Standing proudly in front of their touring car, each one resting a hand on it, as if it were their favorite horse, and one of Father's innumerable dogs standing at his feet. I remember the dog looked straight into the camera. Mother's long white arm was stretched out, and she was smiling, but not staring, like the dog, straight into the camera. Father, of course, was looking down at the dog. He never looked straight into a camera, although he was used to giving everyone else orders about that. And, I remember, Mother's arm was resting on the open door: the window must have been open. They must have been about to leave. As usual, something had gone wrong with the hood; Father had devised a contraption of leather strips to hold it down, and in back of Mother, the velocipede. All the children were afraid of it at first, but Mother wasn't.

Well, what I am getting at is this. Father couldn't have been in the picture. He died, like his sister, before the automobile came in. And I suppose it's unlikely Mother was standing there either, although she was still alive when we got our first car. In the picture, they are standing in a mist of life already lifting from the earth like a foggy morning, in front of the new house that Mother designed, the front of it facing out onto the road, conventional as any house in the village, but of course, it went on, wing after wing, into the woods. Oh, we used to get so bored with them, the way they would stand there, admiring the Dutchman's-pipe ivy which had finally pleased Mother by screening in the whole porch. That was what she had always wanted; privacy, but not a fence, not something that would give offense. Not that she wasn't capable of doing so if she so desired. Even the vine is fading at the top, just as the trees were.

Why is it that the things best preserved in the picture were the inanimate objects?—the two cars, the barn, the umbrella, the summer swing, the broken birdbath (there was a cement one, complete with top, one hundred yards off; Mother always had trouble throwing things out. "It's like Greek statuary," she informed Martin, who was going to do a good deed and carry the mammoth thing off to the dump; "you just leave it where it is"). It's useless to describe the extraordinary beauty of that photograph. But perhaps it was beautiful only to me; no one bothered framing it. They just kept it in the cardboard frame it arrived in from the photographer's. It was gray, I think, with a border of light gray and black stripes surrounding the picture. Every item in that picture means something to me. I suppose it is my Bayeux tapestry, which tells its own story in little symbols, like the open windows visible through the barn doors, luminous pictures of that lost, yellowing world.

Well, then, *why* was it so important to me? Of course, it brings, brought, back memories. No, it brings them back. There's only one way to describe that vanished object: the picture is important to me now, in 1968, while I am futilely trying to describe it. It has no past; it never permitted the past to become attached to it. Why do I dote so upon the border of phlox on both sides of the road leading up to the house, those beautiful purple and white flowers Mother grew, finally, up to the height of our corn? Because she grew them; that's simple enough. But then, why am I so certain Mother and Father are standing on either side of the car? Why do I want to see that picture so badly? It must have been Mother who used to say we must look for the truth in little things. It couldn't have been Father; anything that smacked of certainty was too much for him. Although I believe he ended wanting it; that was the terrible part. This picture, then, is my special thing. You see, in it Mother and Father are together, the proud parents of their car. It seems such a little thing, but that is it: they are together. As they were always together in life.

Always. Regardless of whether Father was sealed up

in his daguerrean salon in total blindness. Mother designed it and then dubbed it Hamlet Lodge. Well, I have a picture of *that*, fenced in by a gate strong enough to keep out a herd of stampeding buffaloes, a hitching post in front of the two gate doors, one swinging from the hitching post, another from the last fence post, and two more posts in the road. I wonder what Mother was thinking of when she built so many hitching posts. She must have been hoping Father would choose to escape from it.

And, for once, she followed orders in planning the Lodge, clearing out only enough of the wild bushes and trees to create a path and a small yard; the Lodge itself a replica of the larger Victorian house. And that was strange, too, because the more wooden carving and spindles that began to adorn its façade, the happier Father seemed about it. It was a beautiful place, the way the light fell straight on the Lodge, while the woods kept everything around it dark and cool, so that it seemed steeped in a pool of sunlight. Father wouldn't even permit the hired men to take down the poison ivy vines which had climbed to the very top of the great elm and were now hanging down. It looked so natural, he said; Mother didn't like it. I suppose she thought the whole tree would fall on the Lodge and he would scratch himself to death.

When she finished with the plans, Father asked sheepishly if the first floor couldn't have pointed windows, and when Mother looked at him puzzled, he explained he wanted little arches over them in the shape of tents. "Triangles," Mother corrected, making a note of it. None of us ever understood what was so important about the outside of the Lodge when he spent almost all of his time in it, and really preferred working in it at night. That was when he decided what he would photograph during the day—when he wasn't working on photographs he had already taken. I suppose it was knowing the Lodge was the one perfect thing, or perfect creation, at least in his eyes, and that he was working on it, so that something perfect would have to hatch from it. Perhaps it did. We will just have to wait and see, as Aunt Ten said: I suppose the provoking thing would be saying the same thing now, even though I've been waiting to see for almost a century.

But there was something special about *that* picture, too.

Mother took it, and Father couldn't bear the sight of it. Well, all that part is easy to remember. "Edna," he roared, "how many times do I have to tell you not to point the lens of a camera straight into the sun? You ruin the camera that way. You ruin the picture." And she would answer in that calm voice of hers, provokingly placid whenever she thought one of us had gone hysterical. "I'm sorry, dear, but I do like the picture; look, look," she pointed out proudly, "at the unusual effects of the light." "It's a *terrible* picture," Father growled, "terrible. I don't know what you can find so interesting about an amateur idiot's experiments." "Well, just look" (she would always try to explain and she was right to do it; no matter how loudly he bellowed, he never lost interest in the way her mind worked); "see how it's come out. It looks as if there are two clouds of sunlight coming from behind each side of the gates." "Edna," he said, beyond exasperation, "that is a mistake. A simple, technical mistake. Look, the Lodge is washed out. The trees look as if they've gotten caught in an insane dust storm, and *nothing* is in focus; only the fence. It's an excellent picture of the fence," he finished, throwing the picture down on the kitchen table. "Don't *do* that," Mother cried, beside herself; "*I* like it; I think it's very unusual." "It is," Father said, turning to leave, "but not for the reasons you seem to think." "You'll come to see its virtues later," Mother called after him. But he never did. Perhaps he was not intended to.

Now, to me, it was worth having my eyes operated upon just to be able to look at this picture again. To see all the pictures again. Daguerre, how I hated him, especially after Father's death. But now I think someone should build a marble statue of him in our yard; we could commemorate him, the same way the town commemorates its ridiculous war heroes. The photographers, Father. They knew what the real war was about. And it was odd that Mother, who took endless pictures of her thumb over the lens, and usually held the camera backwards, or was snapping happily away with the lens cover on, took the pictures that meant the most to us later. Or to me. As I see it now, the picture gives me something approaching the peace and resignation Aunt Ten seemed to have achieved in her life; I suppose I am getting more like her. Now when the children look at pictures of her, and then at me, and I am a sight, with my ghostly white face (but I have all my teeth), and my white bonnet (I don't have a hair on my head; it doesn't seem to bother anyone, and I'd rather have my teeth than my hair. I remember when Father first got dentures. He complained for weeks that it was like having a barn door in his mouth, and I can tell you, that made quite an impression on me). Every now and then one of them tries to modernize me, as if I were a house. They say I look like something that stepped out of the last century, and of course, I do, or did, if there is any point in making those distinctions.

But Mother's pictures, and this one in particular. It makes one think. Time *is* like dust. All our lives we were constantly battling against dust. We never won. And Mother, she always used to feel sorry for the dust. Well, I suppose the Munyan child down in the town had the right idea. His mother told him babies were made of dust; and he looked under the stove, and said, "Why, Mother! There's no reason I can't have a baby sister right now! You have enough dust to make three babies!" The poor child never did understand why she was so furious with him; she got enough criticism, one way or another, about her housekeeping from the neighbors.

But in this picture of Hamlet Lodge. The clouds of light look just like that, light and dust blowing quickly away. The longer I look at the picture, the more I think the answer is somewhere in it. In the picture, time seems like a substance, and the wind is blowing it away, and the more of it the wind blows away, the more the picture fades. The more the light is blown away, the lighter the picture gets, not darker. I look at that picture and think, time is like a mindless substance, swarmed by something else we never catch sight of, gathering the pollen it needs from the living and then flying on. And the more of that substance (I used to think of time as something intangible, but now I think of it as a living substance, migrating, like one of the Arabian Desert tribes) the wind blew, the less of life there was. If we had only known—perhaps Mother had guessed—that those winds of light were warnings, that there was something dangerous about the Lodge, that time blew from it faster, perhaps we might have stolen a little more honey from time's hive.

Well, now that I have gotten so old I want to know more about that ghostly world which seemed to invade so many of Mother's pictures, a world that seemed to live right next to the world we were so familiar with, that *I*, anyway, was always bumping into, that kept me black and blue; not Letitia of course. *She* was the graceful one, and she saw to it that she floated lovely as a cloud, even when she was carrying dishes from the pantry to the sink. "How that girl *wafts*," Aunt Ten used to say, exasperated; "she moves almost like one of the angels. It's too bad," she used to add, staring at Letitia (Lettie had always finished something Aunt disapproved of), "she doesn't resemble them spiritually just a little bit more." Sometimes I believe this whole world we are so concerned with is just a by-product of something else, the same way the ashes in the fireplace seemed insignificant to us after they produced a fire. They had their uses, of course, as I suppose our lives do, too; we could dump the ashes in the privies to keep down the smell; we could paint ourselves all over with them on April Fools' Day and Halloween; but they had no real purpose in themselves. The important thing was the fire. And it seems possible to me that we have got it all wrong, that we are of no more importance than those sticks which existed merely to warm others more intelligent, others of a higher order of life. It is even hinted at in the Bible, that we burn ourselves up like tapers; and Shakespeare also seemed to have an intuition of it, so perhaps I am not just a senile old woman. After all, Shakespeare had Macbeth stalking around declaiming, 'Out, out, brief candle; life's but a brief candle which lights our hour upon the stage, only to burn no more." I'm sure I have it all wrong, but that is the idea.

And then there is something about the nature of the past that always makes me think of ashes, and not because of that old saw "Ashes to ashes, dust to dust," either. No, it's Mother's pictures. If time was a kind of waste product, even a pollution of the air we breathed, and the people who used it were careless, it would keep circling the globe, and circling, settling here and there, perhaps even with bits of memories and lives attached to it. It looks positively sticky in the picture. So perhaps bits of life do stick to it. And I won't be argued out of this, either. I'm too old to be argued with. Mother always used to quote someone or other: We had come to the wrong place. We have come to the wrong planet. We have arrived at the wrong world. She never tired of repeating it, and there was one point when I gave serious consideration to strangling her, or putting something in her soup, if she said it one more time. She had reason enough for saying it, I suppose, but still, you would have thought she would have had more consideration. But by then Aunt Ten was no longer there to restrain her.

How Mother studied the subject! Time, it was always time. I imagine that was why she took her own pictures when Father was so much better at it. There was always something, a man sitting alone in front of his house looking over a ruined crop that she *knew* was very important, and was afraid Father would forget to record. Why, she was even busy with Newton; she had a scientific turn of mind. There was no doubt about it. How she used to puzzle over Newton's axiom "The universe is not twice given." I don't think, in the end, she believed it any more than I do now. She could sit for hours looking at her chain of pearls, while Father watched her over the top of his paper, attempting to discern what the necklace and the mind had in common. Then, one night, she became so exasperated she tugged at it and the pearls went scurrying like fleeing rats, all over the floor. Everyone went flying after them, even Father, but Mother just sat there like a beaming cat.

That was it, she told Father later, and we found it again in her notes; that was what the mind was like, memories strung like beads, and if the string broke, which it did every day, the beads rearranged themselves, and the present receded into the beginning of things, and the past shone out, as it were, brand-new. I believe that became one of her theories, and she relied on it more and more after Father died, especially since his death seemed to confirm her hypothesis; she must have been so desperate to find one before his death. She knew she would need something to lean on afterwards. She would have, I suspect, as soon poisoned herself if it hadn't been for the rest of us.

I expect she is delighted now, wherever she is, seeing my interest in her pictures, watching me work out their riddles, although by the time I finish, I will probably be too old to pass along any of the answers. But if she was right, or if I am, about time, it will not be necessary. But how the poor woman studied! She was ahead of her time, there is no doubting that. I suppose, in her own inward way, she was some kind of genius.

At night, outside the parlor door, I used to listen to her talking to Father about time, time, time; it was a subject that never tired her. And he never said a word—which meant he was interested. If he hadn't been, the teasing would have begun, that inexorable teasing, which just got sillier and sillier with their advancing years. I still think theirs was an enduring case of puppy love. "John," she said one day, after she had knocked a candy dish to the floor with her cup and saucer of tea (when she was concentrating, her clumsy genes took over, which is, I suppose, where I got mine), "did you see that?" "What, that you knocked down more crockery?" Even then he would put down his paper, take off his spectacles, and pick up anything she dropped. "No, no, the two things couldn't take up the same place." "If you expect me to be interested by that," he answered, "I have to tell you I learnt that rather early in college. Before college. Perhaps in grade school." "That's not what I mean," she went on, excited; "space, you see, things are different with space. Two things can't occupy the same space at the same time, but two things can occupy the same time at the same time." She looked confused. "If you see what I mean." "More or less." "I mean, you can think two thoughts at once, simultaneously, so time has to be different than space." "A whole new field of inquiry"; he nodded, picking up his paper again. "John!" Mother exclaimed, indignant; "don't you see? That newspaper can't be in two places at once." He was absorbed in something, and kept on reading. She jumped up and pulled away the paper. "What *are* you doing?" he asked, infuriated. "Well, go on; read the paper from there." "But *you* have it!" "I told you," Mother crowed; "the paper can't be in two places at once." "And I *told* you I knew that." "But," Mother went on, returning the paper absently, "when you finish reading it, I can finish reading it, or start it,

305

and the paper can be in two times at once." "Wonderful," Father said; he wanted his paper.

"But don't you see?" Mother persisted; "it means space is softer, I mean, more movable than time. For instance, we can say Dummerston is south of here, but we can't say that about the past." Now Father was paying attention. She would get to the point eventually. "Well, what I mean is," she explained impatiently, as if to a stupid student, "we could move your chair closer to my chair, but we couldn't move your birth closer to my birth." "Too bad, isn't it?" he asked; but she had caught him now. "Except in our minds," Edna qualified; "except in our minds." "That could lead to insanity," he said, looking up (he must have been reading the criminal cases), "if you started rearranging events of the past and present." "But, John," she protested, "memory does that, for everyone." She fell silent. He waited, looking at her over the paper (how his lion's mane has grayed; *I* remember thinking that). "Well, what I think," Edna said finally, "is that time doesn't move; it doesn't go anywhere. It just stays where it is and uses itself up. It evaporates, or something, like the water I use for my flowers. Because, remember, we found the bones of an old body in the orchard buried standing up and everyone said it was an Indian?

"But where are we going to find the dead body of someone who hasn't even been born yet? Well, they could pick up Dummerston, couldn't they, if they wanted to, and move it north, but they couldn't pick up the future and move it back. Or move the past forward. So I think," she concluded, "time is some kind of immovable thing. We walk through it, but it's like the water for the flowers. I'm sorry to keep going on so about the water, but it's like that, I think. Then the water gets to be too much for us, or it does something to our skin, like overwatering plants, like poison, and it kills us, or it can't get through to our roots because something of us freezes in us, the way the roots do in the ground, and that's why we die. So perhaps," she went on, "if something could be done with our skin, we *could* live forever. Someday. Not tonight," I guess, she finished, looking at Father, smiling; "I'm doing something to that skin of yours keeping you up so late."

"Edna," he asked, "why don't you ever write any of this down? There must be other people who think about these things." "Me?" Mother asked, incredulous, as if she were little better than the village idiot; "I couldn't do that. Who on earth would want to read it? I'm not a literary person." "What kind of person are you?" "A peculiar one." "Well, I'll show you what you're doing to my skin," he threatened (and I got ready to flee), going across the room and picking her up; "my overwatered skin is going to carry you to bed." And he did. They must have been quite old at the time. Father must have been almost sixty and Mother was almost fifty. Well, I used to wonder about it; all three of the girls used to wonder about it, I know that: which he loved best, her body or her mind. Lettie, I know, thought he loved her body best. Anna was sure it was her mind. I said it was both. "Oh, you," they laughed at me; "you're always the one for finding the middle of the road." But I wasn't. I still believe *I* was right. That Lettie never had any sense. And Anna, well, the spiritual was everything to her.

But Mother's pictures were that important to me. I believe now that she came to all the right conclusions, and the rest of her data: that was in her pictures. I think so. So it was worth having the eye operation, no matter what anyone said. Dr. Lucas guesses I was at least ninety-nine when the operation took place. Oh, the debates! They were the worst things I'd gone through since my arguments with Lettie over who could wear whose clothes. Cataracts, that's what they were after; they always made me think of Niagara Falls. "Was I sure I wanted to risk an operation at my age?" Yes, I was sure; Dr. Lucas had told me it was sure to work. I just didn't want to be knocked out. "Will I have to get drunk?" I believe that was the only question I thought to ask. I never could drink, and a fine mess I would make of the operation. He assured me they had much more sophisticated anesthetics now than when I was a girl. Well, I remembered Father going on and on about anesthetics. "Do you have to put me out all the way?" He assured me I could stay awake and watch the whole time, or not watch, considering what the operation was for. So the family argued on and on, but I was set on it, absolutely set on it. For one thing, I wanted to see the old house again since we were all liv-

ing in it, but they kept warning me it wasn't anything like
the same thing it used to be. I didn't believe them, more's
the pity. And then it turned out Dr. Lucas couldn't, or
wouldn't, take me to that fancy hospital called Massachusetts General because he had decided against such
a long trip; no, I had to be operated upon in the town
hospital which still had birdhouses hanging from the sills
of all the windows. The specialist was furious, but he
came around. After all, I told him on the phone, he was
only thirty-six, and I was very old, at least ninety-nine.

I could prove that by showing him my wedding certificate. And I had Mother and Father's, too. Aunt Ten,
before she died, said she wanted the girl who needed it
most to take it, and I decided it would be me, and Lettie
was only too happy to agree. Lettie was always very
polite: in her letters. And I got it. So the great specialist
came down and stuck some needles in me, and began on
my eyes; there was a lot of ice, and bandaging, I remember that, but we chatted along the whole time. It
seemed like the old days, when Father used to talk to his
invalids while he hacked away. But when it was over, Dr.
Lucas got worried. "Now, Mrs. Moffat," he kept warning
me; "now, Mrs. Moffat, don't you go expecting things to
be the way they were twenty-five years ago." "I know
time moves along," I answered. What a smart one I
was!

Well, I had no idea! Everything I had thought of for
twenty-five years took place in a house and a town that
looked just as it had over twenty-five years ago, and now,
the house was such a mess you had to climb over the
dirt; the great-great-grandchildren, or whatever they were,
were running around without shoes just like the Turners
used to when I was growing up (but everyone *pitied*
them), with skirts nothing more than ribbons around
their waists. And their hair! I used to find excuses to get
near their heads to check for lice, but, no, it wasn't that
they had a morbid fear of combs, they *liked* looking as if
they were growing storm clouds from their heads. And
the little children running around naked. Well, I could
tell they never had much on before, but I do suppose I
thought what they did wear was clean.

And those strange noises I used to hear in front of the
old house? They had built a highway a quarter of a mile

from us. A highway! I'd heard them all talking about it, but seeing it, that was something else. And the speed the cars went! "Shade trees, shade trees!" I kept ordering from the nursery; "just tear them out of the forest and seal off the house!" And they did, too. You can't see *us* from the highway anymore. But I was right about one thing; Hamlet Lodge is still the same, even if I have to practically beat on a tin pan with a tin spoon before going in, young people are so different in their ways now. I go there all the time, and if I can't make it there myself, one of the children takes me in the wicker wheelchair. I won't have a new one, even though it would make it easier on them. So the result is we have more ramps, but I'd rather have new ramps than a new chair.

And then there are Mother's pictures. I can look at Mother's pictures until the cataracts come back. Well, was she right there are no traces of the future? She was right about so many things, and wrong about so many, too. So here I sit, in Hamlet Lodge, hoping Father, wherever his dust has blown, isn't too annoyed. (Of course, I look at his, too; but it's different.) And I think the most important thing I've learned from them is hardly of any significance to anyone but myself. In the picture of the house with the two cars, Mother and Father aren't there at all. The two people are my brother Martin and his wife. But the important thing is, even when they are not in the pictures, they are always together; they are together in the picture even though they're invisible. And they were. They were always together. They were never separated. Why, it wouldn't surprise me to look right now and see Mother and Father standing in the doorway. Both of them, even though Mother rarely came here. Because they were always together, and that is how I will always remember them.

"Come into the parlor a minute," Ten said to the newly married couple. What *had* happened to them? Ten wondered. They looked as if they had swallowed lit candles. "John," she said, "I hope you won't be too angry with your aged sister, but I promised Dr. Houston he could treat your patients for tonight. Do you want me to go up and tell him you'll be going instead?" John thought; Edna watched him. "Not exactly." "Well, then," his sister breathed, relieved, "there's something I'd better tell you.

I'm staying the night with Mrs. Moffat. She's almost prostrated with grief over the fire in her barn, and Mr. Moffat is out with the others chasing down the incendiaries, so I thought I'd stay up with her; she's a high-strung person, you know." "That's the first I've heard of it," he answered; "I didn't know Sarah Moffat had a nerve in her body." Ten glowered at him. "From the sound of it," John said agreeably, "it sounds as if it would be best for you to go, even if you have to leave almost in the dead of night." "Better that than nothing at all." "As long as Amos will take you," John agreed; "and how long do you expect to be gone soothing poor Mrs. Moffat's nerves?" "Oh, just for tonight," Ten answered; "I expect they'll catch the incendiaries tonight." "*That* will be the event of the century," he commented sarcastically. "Well, we have an arrangement," Ten continued, without blinking an eye; "if the incendiaries aren't caught tonight, we women will take turns staying up with Mrs. Moffat." "I don't know," Edna put in, "but I think the incendiaries are likely to stay just where you found them."

Ten pretended not to hear her. Now John was grinning. "I'll be back in the morning." They noticed, suddenly, her case in the corner. "To make sure of breakfast, I suppose," John said; "you're not going to be like that jealous mother cat and refuse to teach Edna anything?" "You do worry about the most ridiculous things," his sister said. "Well, if you're going," he said, pulling out his watch; "although I don't see why you women have to sit up together. No one's sick that we know of." "We might catch a few winks," Ten admitted. "Do," John advised her; "going to court is going to wear you out." "Court?" "After they catch the incendiaries," John said; "you'll be needed as a witness." "That's true," Ten agreed, sighing dramatically. John shook his head. "Ready yet?" Bertha asked from the hall. "Well, good night, children," Ten murmured, kissing them each on the cheek; "it's good to have you back. I was rattling around in here like an old nut in an empty barn." "Which is why you're off to Mrs. Moffat's," John commented. "Don't be an idiot," she told him; he picked up her trap and followed her out the door. Edna sat smiling into space from what had become her chair, a low lady's chair Ten had once pronounced virtually useless, since it was too small for grown people, and children would never be permitted in *that* parlor. However, it just suited her.

"So," John said, coming back, his hand automatically resting on top of Edna's head, "we have the house to ourselves except for the forty cooks and the forty maids." "I think that's wonderful of her," said Edna. "I wonder what Mrs. Moffat makes of it, that's all." "Oh, she'll understand; she must have been a bride herself once." "That was one of the few things she did manage to accomplish; although how that Mrs. Moffat, whose house looks like the town dump, raised three such immaculate children is a miracle to us all." "Let that be a lesson to us"; Edna grinned, throwing some magazines to the floor. "Idiot!" he shouted, chasing her down the hall into his room. Their room, he thought, their room. "Oh, I like this room better than my room," Edna cried. "Just so you don't breed canaries in it." "Canaries, canaries?

"Do we need a fire?" Edna asked. John hesitated. "I don't think we need a fire," Edna decided; "your body heats up the bed so, and mine is always so cold." "You're talking about your skin, I presume?" "My skin gets very cold." "Well, get in bed and warm it up." "You're better than a bed warmer," she said a few minutes later. "Romantic little beast, aren't you?" "Aren't I?" "Well, compared to Mrs. Moffat." "Who is this Mrs. Moffat?" "An untidy sixty-year-old lady." "Poke," Edna whispered, tunneling in. "Any closer and you'll be inside." "Is that possible?" she asked, pressing even closer; "can I look out from inside those ribs?" "No." "Do you wish I could? John?" He made a little sound. "I remembered when I was getting undressed; I should warn you. That's when I always remember things. Your sister said something once about your going on about the perfection of broken things." "She did?" "She did. I believe it came up because of the fence. What did she mean?" No answer. Well, Edna decided, I won't pursue it.

She just lay there, enjoying the warmth of his body. "What a splendid body," she murmured. "Among the very many you've seen?" "And every one of them in Mr. Siddons' studio. And every one in marble. I wouldn't like to see Mr. Siddons in marble, though. Poor Mother," she sighed. "What she meant was," John said, "was—this view, I guess you'd call it, that life was built out of broken things. For instance, Ten's fence. Broken trees make whole fences. Broken boulders make stone fences. The wholeness comes out of the brokenness. I suppose the idea appealed to me more then than it does now; I needed to think that way." "But it's true," Edna objected; "everything new comes from something broken." "That doesn't mean it's the perfect way." "I suppose not." "And I felt pretty broken myself." "Well, *I'm* a good doctor," Edna said; "I was serious about wanting to come along with you." "We'll see." "No, I'm going." "You did say you'd go as long as you could." "Well, I'd prefer not to deliver in an open buggy." "Sometimes," he admitted, "I wish you wouldn't get in the family way at all." "I know that." It was her turn to turn silent. "Our wishes don't match there," she said finally. "At least it's not an immediate problem," John answered, reassuring himself; "it won't come up for a while." "Of course not."

She *was* feeling queasy, but it must be her imagination; no one showed symptoms this early. Although a friend of her mother's had claimed she could tell exactly on which night she had conceived, because by the next morning she was green and spent that afternoon dangling over her washstand. Why the afternoon? Edna wondered; she thought women always got sick in the morning. That's what they were expected to do. "John," she murmured into his chest, "let's talk a little more. About little things. Tell me what you like to eat and what kind of tobacco you smoke and what you would have been if you hadn't been a doctor." He didn't answer; then she heard the deep sound of his rhythmic breathing. Why, he's sound asleep! She smiled to herself, wondering when it would be safe to disengage her arm without waking him.

It looks like that's the end of his insomnia, she thought, contented; at least for a while. She was still afraid to move. Well, this was a new, tangly problem. When to move. Gingerly, she removed her arm. The breathing continued, deep and rhythmic. Then she moved her head back. Still asleep. She sighed with relief. She slid closer to the edge of the bed. Some slight stirrings. She waited, rigid, until the breathing became deeper. Slowly, she lowered her feet to the floor. She was sure she could hear some scratching; she had heard it just as he fell asleep. He was still sleeping. No, it wouldn't be safe to stand up.

She put her feet back, began rolling off the bed, feet first. He was still sleeping. She crept to the door. Just as she reached it she was overcome with a wave of nausea. Oh, for heaven's sake! she thought, opening the door. It squeaked. Sure enough, there was Jimmie. Well, she wasn't going to vomit into their basin and upset John. She stole down the hall, opened the back door, and slipped out under the sight of the full moon, Jimmie following, until she reached the woods. She went in, off the path; she was barefooted. This should be far enough, she thought, relieved, leaning forward, vomiting copiously. Instantly, the nausea was gone.

But the cat, the cat was in a panic, standing up against her nightdress, crying. She picked him up and started back to the house, at the same time washing off her face with some damp leaves. I know, she decided; I'll chew on an evergreen needle; that will take away the smell. She munched away. From her window, Bridget saw Edna leave and return. Good Lord! she thought, appalled; I hope this one isn't crazy, too. That's the saddle that broke the camel's back. Edna stole down the hall, carrying Jimmie. A board squeaked; she glared at it with hatred. She did not want to awaken John. She puffed at Jimmie; he didn't pull back his head. Well, the smell must be gone. She had finally reached their bedroom door; the hall seemed two miles long. She opened the door just wide enough to slide in, creeping silently across the floor. He sleeps as if he's in a coma, Edna noted. Gently she sat down on the edge of the bed. Safe so far. Then her feet. She waited three minutes, her hand out, warning Jimmie not to jump, not yet. After three minutes, she decided it was permissible to try lying down. That operation failed to disturb anyone. Drat! she thought, he's got his arm on my pillow. *Now* what was she going to do?

She had no idea going to sleep could be so complicated; why didn't people go on about this instead of the duties of the marriage bed? And he's gotten wrapped in the covers like a mummy! She gently began tugging them loose, trying to get her half. That operation took almost fifteen minutes. Finally, she had covers, but no pillow. At that instant, however, Jimmie lost all patience and jumped up on the bed next to her head and lay down right next to her cheek. He stood up once and looked irritably at

John. Squint, squint, squint. Finally, he resigned himself. After all, there was a place on the bed left for him. He turned on his side, settling next to Edna's head. A pillow! she thought in ecstasy, promptly burying her head in the cat's back, stretching her left arm across John's chest. It was an awkward position, but at least she was not disloyal to either. Jimmie began purring hypnotically on one side, John on the other. I'll never, she thought, get to sleep. She was thinking about her recent trip to the woods, but before she had time to repeat the sentence to herself, she was breathing as deeply as the two other creatures.

"Well, and how is Mrs. Moffat?" John asked the next morning, gobbling his breakfast. "Just fine." "And her barn?" He paused in his chewing. "Miraculously reconstructed, I presume?" "Oh, you know how fast things go when everyone helps at a barn raising." "In the middle of the night? My, the countryside is getting industrious." "So it is, so it is." Ten was watching Edna suspiciously; what was the matter with the child? She wasn't eating. She was giving her pancakes a grand tour of her plate. "You know," Edna said, "I think I'll eat later. I've spent the last four days stuffing myself until I feel like a turkey before Thanksgiving dinner. After a ride, I'll get hungry enough." John nodded, finished up, and left the table, kissed her goodbye, shouting out the window for his buggy. "Well, here we go," Ten said softly.

Edna decided to forestall any of her suspicions. "Aunt Ten," she said, her voice its most angelic; "I can't help noticing. You've been looking at me so peculiarly. You don't think John made a mistake?" "Good gracious, no," Ten expostulated, thrown off guard; "it's a miracle he found you." "I thought," Edna continued, "perhaps you went off to Mrs. Moffat's because you were unhappy we were married." "Why, you ridiculous little thing!" Ten exclaimed; "I just thought you should spend your first night alone. No one needs their older sister right down the hall the night of their homecoming." "We wouldn't have minded." "That's not the point, not the point at all." "Well, then, thank you. I feel much better." "I *knew* something was bothering you"; she was lifted up with relief. I'll have to tell her as soon as I'm sure, Edna thought, pretending to bite at a grilled tomato sandwich;

314

I'm going to need her help. I don't want John finding out until the last possible second. There must be a better way of putting that off than starving; perhaps, she thought, comforted, Ten will have some ideas. And anyway, he'd never let me go on rounds with him if he had the faintest suspicion. And he's *not* going to have it, as long as I, or we (that was a remarkable thought), can hide it from him.

Why was she so sure? She was already trying out names. Perhaps, she thought, if she had a boy, they should name it Martin, after John's drowned brother. That might make him feel as if he had somehow made amends. No, she didn't think he was superstitious, but he *was* the worrying kind. She would ask Ten what she thought. Eventually. It must have been hard on her, too, Edna realized; she had never mentioned Martin either. Well, Martin had been one of the youngest, and Ten the oldest; he must really have seemed like *her* baby, too. She wondered what Ten would think of naming the baby Martin. She imagined she would like it. But it was odd to be so sure. And so soon. "Do you want to ride out, Edna?" Ten was asking; "I have to ask Amos about the fence." "Yes, please," she answered, pretending to take another bite of her sandwich. Not hungry at all, she wondered; usually, she could eat an entire table, cloth and all.

It was the beginning of October. Something woke Ten early; perhaps it was the sound of rain beating against the glass. Oh well, in this weather everyone's sure to send for the doctor, she groaned. She peered outside; it was still dark. She had better wake Bridget and Bertha and let the others sleep. Was Edna getting enough sleep? she worried as she made her way down the hall. She was getting into the habit of staying up half the night waiting for John when she wasn't out with him herself. At least last night she had agreed not to go out with him today. She had clothes to mend, letters to write, something like that. Ten was relieved to hear it; she didn't like the look of her lately.

"Morning," Bertha said shortly, as she came into the kitchen. "Why don't you light some lamps?" Ten asked; "why do you want to work in the dark?" "We don't even *need* lights for our work anymore," Bertha snorted. "Well, you don't have to work in the gloom," Ten answered, lighting a wick; a yellow light warmed the kitchen, but it was a poor job. "What gloom?" Bridget asked.

Conversation in the morning always tended to the monosyllabic. Ten sighed, sank down at the kitchen table. There was a sheet of paper lying on it. She picked it up idly. "Perhaps," she read out to herself, "the right image for time is the image of the crucifixion." Wonderful, she thought, putting it down. "How long," Bertha was asking her, "do you estimate the good doctor's absence will be today, Miss Ten?" She was wondering about the evening basket; should it be one or two? "Shouldn't be surprised if he got home around noon tomorrow." Ten picked up the paper again. What on earth was it? "The roads are awful muddy, now," Bridget volunteered; "almost impassable up the mountain." "And how did we find that out?" Ten asked. She was forever curious about the servants' unending fund of information. "John Dale going down for the milk team; he stopped at the gate." "At this hour?" Bertha looked at Bridget with her distinctive "I told you so" expression. "And you just happened to be there? You must be part owl; does anyone in the room know at what hour Mr. and Mrs. Steele retired last night?" "They got home at four," Bridget answered; "Mrs. Steele was giggling like a baby. I guess your brother gave her some of his cough medicine to strengthen her up." "I'm sure I wish she would stop those trips," Ten said softly.

"Oh, she will, miss," Bridget assured her, "but right now, it's such a novelty to her; remember how excited she got the time they went out to set a fracture? I never heard anyone go on so about a broken bone unless it was the man who had it. It was Dr. Steele went into the barn, and Dr. Steele found just the right lumber, and Dr. Steele made a splint out of it with the aid of an old shirt, and the man felt better right away. Well, and I guess he did," Bridget added, "after the doctor finished tugging at his broken leg, poor thing." All that worrying about the winter, Ten thought; she wasn't sure Edna noticed it, except as an impediment to the carriages and buggies. She wasn't sure there was such a thing as snow unless it interfered with those infernal rounds.

"It's the other things I worry about," Ten said; "the

typhoid cases or childbed fever. I don't know how excited she's going to be about things like that." "If you ask me," Bertha called back, her head deep in the oven, "she's got a stronger stomach than the doctor." "And rounder," Bridget observed. "Well, at least she's not going today," Ten said, fiddling with the silverware. "Tonight might be a good night; I'm almost certain Mr. Steele is going to end in one of those hotels. She hasn't done that yet." "She'll get a chance soon enough," Ten answered, exasperated. "Yes," Bridget said, "but on a night like this one coming, two in a bed is better than one anytime." "He's likely to wind up two in a bed anyhow," Ten said, looking sadly out the window. Why, she couldn't even see the apple tree fifty feet from the house. "It looks like the middle of the night," Ten observed sadly. "Doesn't it just, miss"; Bertha nodded; "well, don't you worry; after breakfast, we'll go around lighting everything up. Don't look out the windows, is all. If it were me, I'd even pull the curtains. Then you can think anything." "Well, and what room do you intend to be in?" Bridget asked; "everything's so damp; even the kindling's damp. It's going to take more than three minutes, you know." "The best parlor," Ten said, tracing a pattern on the cloth with the spoon. "You have the right idea, if you ask me," Bertha said from the hutch; "most people's parlors are always so stiff. Well, and that makes sense, I guess. Either someone's sitting there courting, stiff as a board, or they're laid out on a table, even stiffer than that. I never saw the sense of it, and the dust this thick." She indicated a depth of five inches between her thumb and index finger. "Mmmmm," Ten murmured by way of answer; she was waking up slightly, looking again at that paper.

"What is that, ma'am?" Bertha asked; "some kind of theological tract the missus is writing?" "How many times have I told you," Ten responded automatically, settling her spectacles on her nose, "to keep out of other people's correspondence?" "Well, and I suppose *you* wrote that," Bridget said; "very likely, what with your interest in religious affairs." "I'm a new woman," Ten answered, without looking at her.

"The universe," she read to herself, "is a sphere, and everything in it arranged one way or another. The past creatures, the ones we call dead, go straight down, as in a vertical shaft; that could be likened to the vertical post of the cross. The present would be the post horizontal with the earth, what we call everyday life. This post, or shaft, is not steady in its composition, but is replaced constantly when old lives end, or when new lives begin, while the vertical shaft sinks deeper and deeper, and never changes. Perhaps this is why," the paper concluded, "people find the cross so comforting, when it is such a terrible image, because it is still the image of everyone's life. The moment of crucifixion for everyone comes when one's life travels along the horizontal shaft and superimposes itself on the vertical shaft and is nailed there by time passing. This is the moment of crucifixion, otherwise called death.

"I now believe that the fear of this instant is what drives men; Bacon called them engines. But from what I have now seen, most men do not fear death at the moment it comes. At the instant of death, all men are like Christ in that they feel no fear and no pain. I have seen John talking again and again to dying patients, as if nothing out of the ordinary run was occurring. What I do not completely understand," the paper went on, "is why, as the dying man talks, be he saint or sinner, as the preacher always says, all seem to die in the same way. As yet, the only man to die in terror was a deacon of the Church. John called him a sanctimonious old hypocrite. But the others, if they were strong enough, all seemed to chat away as if they were at a sociable.

"The other peculiarity I want to note is what they chat about. As death approaches, so does the past, as if it were getting larger and larger, or coming towards them like a comet. Perhaps this is what heaven is, being gathered into the folds of past time; not physically, but through some action of the mind. Although I should not overlook the possibility that the closer one comes to the earth and disintegration, the more the body and mind are suited to commune with those bodies which have already loosened themselves from their confining skins. Perhaps in the vertical shaft of the cross, all the cells of life move in and out, through one another, and have the freedom to take up with the ones which make them happiest. But I must admit, it puzzles me deeply, and I do not know what to read. When things end, do they go farther and farther away, or do they stay where they were, and do we move away from them? Or, in old age, do we travel back to them, as I came to Williamsville on a train? Perhaps the wandering minds of old men and women are really wandering through time? Perhaps they are *compos mentis* after all. This is a very knotty problem, and I must look into it further."

She felt a presence over her shoulder. Edna was standing there, looking down, paler than flour. "I'm always writing about something," she said, defensive. "This is new, isn't it?" Ten asked; "I thought you were still working on etiquette books, for whatever reason you're working on them." "We'll talk about it after breakfast." She looked, Ten thought, a little green about the gills. But that was because she was so tired out. She hadn't had a chance to work herself into doctor's hours. Well, what a thing to read in the morning, she thought, looking over at the paper again. Edna, following her eyes, snatched the paper up, folded it, and put it in the bosom of her robe. "You don't like people reading what you write, do you?" Ten asked curiously. "I do it for myself," Edna answered, trying to explain; "if I ever got to the end of something, perhaps then it would be different."

"*Do* you ever get to the end of things?" "Not usually." "Do you show these notes to John?" "Never!" Edna exclaimed. Why, Ten realized, she's terrified at the very thought! "Why don't you want John to see them? You two share everything." Edna walked over to the window, looking out. "I couldn't bear it if he thought I was silly." "He wouldn't." "Still, I couldn't do it; I couldn't stand it. Please don't tell him about it. You have to promise me." "All right, all right," Ten promised; "but I can't see the reason for it." "He doesn't need another dose of seriousness from me." "Or you from him?" "It's not that; not exactly, but it does take one down into deep waters." "And you want to drown there alone?" "*If* I'm going to drown; I don't think I will. You have to stay in the water long enough to drown. Well, you said it yourself. Yesterday: etiquette. Today: time." "Some people do think about two things at once." "Listen, Aunt Ten," Edna said, "just don't mention it. I'll have to start squirreling things away otherwise. I wouldn't like that." "Well, what about discussing etiquette on a rainy day?" Ten pursued. "Oh, *that's* fine; I've done a lot of thinking along those lines. I wouldn't feel such a fool." "After John leaves, then." A sudden rustling and fluttering made them look up in time to see Bridget flying out the kitchen's rear door, wrapped in a waterproof. "What now?" Ten asked.

"We're in for it," Bridget announced coming back in, her face a wet windowpane; "it's Mrs. Weston. She says her husband is so sick she doesn't guess he'll make it through the night." "John Dale saw him weaving all over the common last night," Bertha announced from the stove. "Oh, dear," Ten said; "we are in for it. John's been waiting for this opportunity all summer." "What do you mean?" Edna asked. "Well, Miss Edna," Bertha said, finally extracting herself from her cave of soot, "Mr. Steele, he conducts this war on people who drag him out for no reason when some perfectly innocent soul may be getting a call from his maker he wouldn't have gotten if the other one hadn't called him out for no reason at all." "War?" "He gets even, miss," Bertha went on; "he cures them of their tricks. He says that's the one thing he's certain he can cure them of." The women smiled at each other. "It's still raining," Ten observed; "how long can this go on?" "It just started," Edna reminded her. "It can go on until it starts snowing," Bridget predicted. "Well, it's raining down in Bennington," Bertha volunteered, "so it looks like we're in for it all right." "Anything that's not inside is going to rot," Ten warned them. "Anything that's in, miss, is going to mildew," Bridget said; "we're going to have that wash soaking in the tub for a week, and it was almost dry last night, too." "Well, we have enough dry clothes anyhow," Ten said. "That doesn't help the things floating around in the tub." "Well, if it's such a problem, get Amos and some of the men to put a stove in the garret, and set them drying up there." "Yes, miss," Bridget agreed; "I thought that was the best thing from the start." "Then why didn't you say so?" Ten demanded.

"Mrs. Weston's sent for you," Ten announced to John; "her husband is so sick she doesn't guess he'll make it through the night." "Again?" John asked, collapsing onto his chair. "And John Dale saw him weaving all over the common last night," she added. "With how many bottles tied around his neck?" John asked, beginning to eat. "If I ever retire," he said to Edna, "I'm going to attack those books of yours and find out how a gentleman eats at the table; I've forgotten altogether." "Now, John," his sister warned, "don't you do anything you're going to be sorry for." "Don't worry; I have a foolproof scheme." He reached for his bowl of cereal. "You're going to burn your throat," Edna cautioned. "It's made of the best leather." "Well," Ten said, "there's Mrs. Moffat; she has a stomach complaint, but she says it's nothing serious, and down at the Grimsbys', someone stepped on a rake and has a swollen foot, and then there's Mrs. Hornsby, who thinks her new arrival's arriving." "Who are you going for first?" Edna asked. All these details fascinated her. "Mrs. Hornsby last; a midwife could take care of her, or one of those crones in the house. I'm not sure about Mrs. Moffat; anyone who sends in saying it's nothing serious . . ." "She was fine last month," Ten reminded him. "I suppose that gave her a guarantee for the rest of the year." He stood still, thinking. "If anyone comes, I'm going to Mrs. Moffat's and then the Grimsby place. If the man there has what it sounds like he's got, an hour or two won't make any difference." "What does it sound like?" Edna asked. "Gas gangrene." Edna was impressed. "What do you do for that?" "Amputate, and don't you step on any rusty nails in a manure pile. Well, I'm going; don't stay up wrinkling yourselves"; he grinned, stroking Edna's hair one last time as he lifted his palm from the top of her head.

"Isn't his hand heavy?" Ten asked; "that piece of lumber would give me a headache." "On the contrary," responded his wife. "You must have strong bones in your neck." "And a head like a coconut." They finished eating in silence. "I'm going out for a walk in the woods," Edna said; "I don't know why; I'm so tired lately. I haven't been doing enough riding; on top of the horse, I mean; and sitting in that buggy, you get awfully knotted up." "Dress yourself warmly," Ten instructed automatically. "And let's have a good long talk after supper," Edna suggested; "I'll get out my latest book and bore you to death."

Ten shook her head, and looked out the window. Rain, and more rain. No, she didn't really like rain. It reminded her of her watercolor lessons, what the paintbrush water looked like after she had washed enough brushes in it. "No color anywhere at all," she said. "The parlor's lit up, miss," Bertha said. She must read my thoughts, Ten mused for the thousandth time. She settled into the comfortable chair with a copy of *Minerva*, the very latest novel by the author of *Rhoda*. Well, and it *was* a relief reading, without John keeping up his commentary like some nasty literary raven. He can be a pest, she thought, opening the book, purring with satisfaction. Jimmie stuck his head in the door. "Come, Jimmie, come," she coaxed. He didn't move. She patted her lap. "Jump, Jimmie, jump" He withdrew his head and went on down the hall. Why was it, she asked, that although she said the very same things to the beast Edna did, and was even reduced to mimicking her voice, that miserable cat would have nothing to do with her? He'll be scratching at the door in about thirty seconds, she decided, listening. "Oh, all right then," she heard Bridget saying; "go out and drown yourself." He's off with Edna, she thought, sinking in.

"Minerva was the eldest daughter of Lady Jane Hastings, a widow, whose purposed web of life had been broken to pieces by the unexpected accident of her husband dying before his father." Why was Edna interested in those etiquette books? She seems to think they have something to do with the Bible. Well, she was too absorbed with Lady Jane to bother herself with questions of literary taste. "By this untimely and, as Lady Jane had always called it, *unnatural* event, the title and fortunes which had determined her choice in a companion for life, had eluded her hopes, and had rested with a younger brother of her husband's. The several sons which had blessed the first period of the marriage had all died in their infancy; and several years having elapsed between the death of the last. and the quick succession with which she had presented Mr. Hastings with three daughters who survived him. Lady Jane found herself, on his death, in the wane of life, without having made one ascending step from the rank in which she was born, with a limited income. and three girls, who if they were to be countesses, or even splendidly established commoners, could only hope to be so by the favors bestowed on them by nature, or from the reputation imposed on them by education." How sad, how true, Ten sighed to herself. She heard the door open and close, the soft sound of Edna's voice in the kitchen, but she was so lost in sympathy for Lady Jane it never, for one second, occurred to her to surface. "Supper," Bridget called. "Oh, dear," she moaned again, reluctantly putting down the book. What was going to happen to that poor Minerva? Really, children were such a problem, and some parents were so heartless. She listened. Yes, it was still raining, pouring buckets was more like it, outside the warm draperies. Well, she did want to talk to Edna about her etiquette books, but she would be up all night finding out about Minerva's difficulties with her husband, who apparently had a secret corridor leading out of his room.

"You see," Edna was explaining, "they always used to sound so foolish to me, but Mother took them so seriously. It started when I decided to win at her game of cards. But *I* was the one who got caught. They have such a view of life, Ten, you can't imagine. I'm rereading another one now; well, it's not that I run out of them. There must be hundreds, but one of them seems to lay the bones barer than the others. I hate sermons," she went on, "and these books always seemed like sermons, except that the writer threw in knives and forks and instructions on ball gowns, and lists of what colors went with what flowers, and then the meanings of flowers. That used to annoy me terribly. But I missed the whole point." "You did?" Ten's head was spinning. "This isn't," she warned Edna, "a subject I'm very familiar with. I was finished off at school, you know, with Nellie and your mother, and the school believed in at least twenty coats of varnish; we never felt much need for much instruction." "Oh, it's not the part about the behavior—I mean, how to behave at the table—that's interesting," Edna said impatiently; "it's that a good etiquette book is like a Bible. A secular Bible. You know how John always takes on about those books called *What to Do Until the Doctor Comes?* The etiquette books, I think, are similar; what to do until the next life comes." "John thinks those medical tracts are very dangerous, you know," his sister said.

"But this is different," Edna said. "I used to get so *mad* when people would go around judging others according to their own ideas, people they didn't even know, but now I'm not so sure I was right. There have to be rules somewhere. And according to the Bible, only God can judge sinners. Isn't that right? But in daily life, everyone does it all the time. Just last week they tarred and feathered that man for—" She hesitated. "Licentious behavior; I read about it, too." "*They* weren't waiting for God," Edna said; "and whether they were right or wrong in tarring and feathering, and I don't think anyone should do that, I think they were right not to wait for Divine Judgment." "You don't believe in what's going on in the West?" Ten asked; "those spur-of-the-moment lynchings? I find them shocking." "I don't know," Edna answered thoughtfully, Ten staring at her. "You don't know, and you don't know if it's right or wrong to drag a man out of his house and hang him from a tree just because some self-appointed enthusiasts decide to play judge, jury, and grim reaper?" "No, I don't," Edna answered, standing firm. "Why?" Ten asked, outraged.

"I've been reading Lord Chesterfield again," Edna said slowly, "and primarily, he seems to think good etiquette exists to allow one to climb in society, things of that sort. But then he must believe in society, don't you think? Most of the books make one think the only reason for good behavior is to gratify personal vanity, but I think . . ." Edna wanted to be sure to get this right. "I think that the only way people behave themselves is out of fear of their neighbors. Punishment in the next world, that's too far away, and even if people *say* they believe in it, who knows if they do?" "They don't," Ten assured her. "Well, your Mrs. Moffat now," Edna considered. "Everyone deplores the condition of her house, don't they? But then everyone always adds what a good job she did with her children. So they leave her alone about her house. Society, if you want to call people here that, weigh her in the balance." "Well, they still find her wanting, they can't stop themselves from mentioning the condition of her house." "But they don't shut her out because of it," Edna argued; "there must be some people shut out by the society here."

Now it was Ten's turn to think. There was Mrs. Higham, the grocer's wife; everyone believed she had loose morals, and for no particular reason, either, but no one ever invited the Highams anywhere. She mentally reviewed all the tricks people had for taking *Mr.* Higham off alone. And, to tell the truth, if *she* had children, she wouldn't want them around Mrs. Higham, or her children, either, for that matter. "Yes," Ten said, "that's true; there are people shut out like that. Do you think that's wrong?"

"Only when it's a mistake; even whole juries make mistakes. But usually they don't. Father used to say society was pitiless, a pitiless censor, remorseless, things like that. There was some woman who ran off with another man, and even after she was divorced, and remarried, and even after everyone found out her husband used to beat her, and even burn her with hot irons straight from the fireplace, society just shut her out. It was forever, too; we all knew that. They finally left the country. Father advised them to do it; he said it was the only thing. He said judgments like that had no pardons; they weren't reversible. Well, I don't think they are, either. It makes me afraid, sometimes, to think something I consider very small could put me outside the charmed circle of husbands and children and maids, of people at the theater, of the butcher, the baker, the candlestick maker, of sisters-in-law." "You mean it makes you watch your step more; that's all it is?" *That* was hard to believe. "It does," Edna assured her, "but you never know when you may take the wrong one. It keeps you on the lookout."

"That's a grim view," Ten said. "Do you think so?" Edna asked; "at least it's better than thinking of people as irrepressible, mean-minded gossips who live only to destroy one another." The fire crackled; the rain fell. "I think of society as a great court," Edna went on, as if talking to herself. "It doesn't permit pardon; that makes it different from the Christian courts. *They* permit pardon, but usually, not on this earth. Well, and how would you punish someone who doesn't actually go out with an ax otherwise? If someone's a slanderer, or a drunkard, or a fortune hunter, you can't take them to court for *that;* there aren't any laws against it, are there? Or the seducer, and the cheat; what can you do with them? So *this* court has to go by rumor; it doesn't have any choice. How would you know, Ten, if Mrs. Moffat waited until night and beat her children senseless? But if someone found out about it and told you? You wouldn't feel the same. The trouble is," she went on, "the slanderer is the best and the worst reporter, and the sentence is sometimes pronounced on the wrong man, or the people are fooled and pass over some vices and go on about others. And it's so implacable, so ruthless, it drives most people to suicide. I think that's what's behind most suicides, knowing you're living in the midst of an inquisition, and it must be just as bad, whether you're right or wrong. At least, if you've done something wrong, you have the satisfaction of being punished for the right thing. I'd prefer that."

"And your father?" Ten asked; "his suicide? Did it have to do with things like this?" "Oh, I think so, or I think so now. Even in the real courts, the wrong ones walked out, and the right ones walked in, and Father, he never should have been prominent. You know; he was like me. He didn't like anyone's eyes on him much, but you can't hide yourself when your name is all over the front pages. Doesn't John have the same difficulty?" "Oh, he's on trial at every church picnic," Ten agreed, "every paning bee, every sociable, but he doesn't care. People could decide he was Satan incarnate and as long as they didn't try to burn him at the stake, he wouldn't care. That's one thing you have to admire about John," his sister said; "I wish I were more like him. I come pretty close, though. But it's hard to tell. We're so insulated by our money. Well, I told you before, it's always 'They can afford to be as peculiar as they like.' It would be a different thing if we started poisoning them with expensive imported substances, but that's about the only thing I can think of. Still," she meditated, "I don't think John would give a fig for their judgments anyhow."

"That's good," Edna sighed; "because if someone he takes care of dies, they must try to blame it on him." "Try? They blame him, and they're not shy about it, either. But then they won't call in any other doctor. I guess that's the final judgment, or sentence, whatever you want to call it." "But don't you see, Ten? People don't have any other choice, not even when it comes to judging John. Common report. That's all they have. No one opens their heavenly scrolls to us. People have so much to protect." She thought, involuntarily, of her outing this morning, and her usual daily vomiting. Now she could not remember when it was not a daily event.

"Children, most of all, and wives, sisters, the future of their sons; they won't have any of those things if they didn't have a reputation for being honorable." "But, Edna," Ten protested, "you know it yourself; it's slander, slander, and more slander always blowing about. Jealousy, greed, anything like that; it starts it right up."

"It's *very* dangerous. Gossip and scandal. I once had a beau who spent some time telling people about my terrible morals, and all because I wouldn't go to the Ceremonial Ball with him. Well, and it was lucky for me my friend's brother was there and practically threatened to shoot him. And there he was, on the bank of the Charles, with a line of people awaiting apologies. Now no one speaks to him. Something should be done about the likes of him. And those women who hear a name mentioned, and shake their heads as if they saw all the family skeletons rattling right in front of them. That's sinful, that behavior; at least, I think so." "But nothing can be done about it," Ten said, serious. "No, nothing," Edna agreed; "that's the trouble."

"Well," she said—she must have bored Ten enough by now—"the conclusion we draw from this is that I had better be a well-behaved proper young lady." "If I live to see that, I'll be a medical marvel." "I'm not so bad, am I?" "Oh, Edna, of course not; but if you start trying to behave like everyone else you'll end as a real disgrace. In fact," she thought, "we ought to give some thought to finding friends for you in the village. John and I won't be enough for you forever." "I have my letters from Virginia," Edna answered carelessly. "That won't be enough, either." "Well, you can't pick out my friends for me," Edna cautioned; "Mother used to try, but I never liked the right people. I was supposed to adore Mr. Siddons and that repulsive Dr. Talbott." She explained who Dr. Talbott was, and described him. "Oh no!" Ten screamed with laughter; "your mother never changes. Nervine Tonic, I should say. It's pure poison, poison. John says it's even better than Rat Away."

"Rat Away?" Edna echoed. "For killing rats." "Are there any around?" "Only in the barn. Jimmie, though, big as he is, prefers mice. A sensible animal in every respect." "He likes all small creatures," Edna said, successfully stifling a yawn. Why was she always so tired?

"Edna, if you don't mind," Ten said apologetically, "I really think I would like to take a nap. You won't judge me too harshly, will you? Rainy days always make me feel so sleepy." "Me, too; I feel chloroformed." "It's the weather," Ten said, getting up, picking up her copy of *Minerva*. "Well, anyway, we have one thing to look forward to, and that's find out what John did to poor Mr. Weston." "You really think he is up to something?" "I haven't had any doubt whatever since their last call," she said, leaving the room.

Edna woke up suddenly, hearing the clock striking five; someone was moving about in the parlor. She sat up in bed and waited. "Hello," John said; "you're developing nurses' sleep." "Nurses' sleep?" she echoed groggily. "Nothing wakes them up but the sound of the sick one, and then they're off like crackers. Before you ask," he said, sitting down on the bed, putting his arm around her, "the day was gruesome. Mrs. Moffat's stomachache looks like a big tumor, but she wants to wait until her daughter gets here from Chicago before I take any stabs at her. Mr. Grimsby's man was so bad off I had to amputate the leg, and I'm just glad I wasn't there when he woke up, but I have to go back tomorrow and make sure Grandma doesn't decide to check on the bandages, or the beloved minister doesn't suddenly notice some alarming signs and start prescribing himself." "Mrs. Hornsby's baby?" "Popped out like popcorn from a pot"; he grinned; "although I almost dropped him, I was so tired. They're very slippery when they're new. Usually, someone in the house reads a newspaper and I can use it to get a better grip until I have the creature on the table. This time I thought he was going to pop out of my hands and stick onto the ceiling." "But it turned out all right?" "It did," John said, beginning to undress, then getting into bed.

"John," she asked some time later, while they were trying to untangle the insanely twined ropes they had made of their bedclothes, "are you going to do anything to Mr. Weston?" "I did it." Edna could feel him smiling in the darkness. "What rain," he sighed; "well, Edna, on a day like this a man should have something to look forward to." "What did you do?" "Well, while I was on the way to Mr. Grimsby's, I had more time than I usually do to think about it, so I decided if he was really at death's door, he needed an undertaker, not a doctor, and since I couldn't get there until later, I decided to be economical about time, and stopped at Mr. Greenwood's casket factory, and told him that Mr. Weston was dying and arrangements ought to be made immediately. Edna, you wouldn't believe that man could move so fast when there's a prospect of a body; Greenwood must be half bottle fly. So he got out a casket and his sawhorses, and his white cloth, and off he went in his team, and it was on my way, so I thought, well, I better follow along, just in case there was something wrong.

"Well, no one came to the door when Greenwood knocked, and he never stands on ceremony; he went in, and there I was, peeping in one of the parlor windows like one of the Munyans, and Greenwood all busy setting up his sawhorses and board, and open casket with its white ruffled lining, satin, the very best quality for grief, that's always his philosophy, and when he had two funeral baskets hung on the wall where there were two pictures before, he went in and called for Mrs. Weston, but she didn't come down.

"So he went out in the yard to look for Mr. Weston's son, but he couldn't find him, either, and in the meantime, there came Mr. Weston himself, holding to the banister with one hand, and his head with the other, completely pickled. That's when he saw the open parlor door. It's a novelty in that house, I can tell you. But, Edna, you should have seen him when he looked in and saw that magnificent casket! He turned from green to white faster than you could close the lid, and ran right through the parlor, right to the window where I was crouching down like the dignified person I was, so I just had a chance to dive into the other bush near me before I had the gratifying sight of watching Weston come diving out through that window like he was shot from a cannon, right through the screen. It's a good thing the glass wasn't down, and I don't think he's stopped running yet. It warmed me up, I'll tell you." They both laughed. "Well, are you finished with him now?" "Nope. That was part one." "Part one! What is part two?" "Oh, you'll find out

329

later," he said, pulling her toward him. "You certainly are lighter than Mrs. Hornsby," he said.

"At least," he said, listening to the relentless pounding of the rain, "I didn't have to stay at one of those damned hotels. Oh, sorry," he corrected himself, embarrassed. Edna smiled into the darkness. "They're better than sleeping outside, but I guess that's the best you can say about them, especially if you're late getting to one. Those offices! If I never see one of them again, it will be too soon for me. The card table empty, the proprietor asleep, his lantern on the table. If you come in late, you take the lantern and go up and look for an open door. That's your room. I don't like it in the summer much, because those places get hot, and the ladies leave their doors open, and *that* can get to be like throwing a fox in with the hens. But if you're shy, like me, you look at the clothes on the chair instead of poking about at the bed."

"I don't think you better go anymore; I'm jealous." "But only in the summer," John reminded her. "Oh, all right, in the winter then; you can go then," she agreed, tunneling into him. "Edna?" he asked softly; he wasn't sure she was still awake. "Hmmmm?" "Would you like to go to the Brattleboro Fair sometime this week? It's the event of the year around here. Everyone makes more out of it than the circus." "Oh, yes," she mumbled, nestling again, "but I want to go with you tomorrow." "You know, I don't really like that so much," John murmured; "I never know what I'll find when I start out." "That doesn't bother me." "It should; you haven't seen enough to know whether you should be bothered." "Will I find you there?" "*That* goes without saying," he answered, reaching over to stroke her hair one last time. "Then I'm going," she assured him; she was barely awake. "I'd rather take you to the fair." "You can take me to both; in fact . . ." John waited for her to finish her sentence, but she was fast asleep. He circled his arm protectively around her waist; there was the thump of Jimmie the cat arriving at his customary station. John felt five nails needling the back of his hand. That cat, he thought, but Jimmie resigned himself without further protest, and within three seconds, the three of them were sound asleep.

In her room, Ten was falling asleep over *Minerva*. She could not bring herself to put it down. "It was then that

Mr. Willoughby saw the precipice upon which he had stood. Astonished, angry, mortified, yet pleased and grateful for his escape; all his better feelings returned with added force; and carried him impetuously to the feet of Minerva, there to expiate, by unremitted kindness and undeviating rectitude—so he had purposed!—the wrongs that he had offered to the claims that she had laid upon him." She fell asleep in the middle of the next sentence, the book falling over her face like a low little tent. A short while later, Bertha came in, saw Ten had fallen asleep as she knew she would, and put out the kerosene lamp. They'd burn down the house if it wasn't for me, she thought, pleased with herself. No, there was no light showing under Mr. and Mrs. Steele's door. Well, I can finally go to bed, she congratulated herself. In a few minutes, the house was mercifully quiet.

The first of October opened chilly and rainy. In spite of the stoves in their rooms, everyone awoke damp and clammy. And early. The Weston family had sent once more. This time, it was Mrs. Weston who was in danger of never rising again. Ten's soft knock on the door woke John, who immediately sat up in bed, listening to his sister trail back down the hall to her own room and further sleep. He turned to look at his wife. She was curled up in sleep, in her usual position, and, as usual, somewhere seven layers beneath the surface of the normal world. Her long black hair was falling over the pillow, over her arm, and under the quilts. He wondered how she managed it, rising without entangling her arm in her hair, or turning, wrapping her hair around her face in her sleep. It had become a nightly ritual now, when John was not too tired, or when Edna hadn't fallen asleep before him. He would pull the long black hairpins from her hair one at a time, while she held it up in back, and when the last pin was withdrawn, let it fall of its own weight. Or uncoil, slowly, until it had reached its full length. Long enough, he thought, to rescue a drowning man. Or if he had somehow missed a pin, they began the hunt, running through the masses of her hair in pursuit. John had heard of women whose hair was long enough to sit on, but he had never before seen one who, when so doing, had hair long enough to fall over the edge of the chair like a thick, fine fringe reaching to the middle of her calves.

He did not want to wake her up. Rainy mornings like this brought out the illnesses in people pressed down under the sunny days. These were abscess days, infection days, days of choring in the doorway when nothing of real work could be done, and the farmer's wife at last persuaded her husband to send for him. Although, he meditated, usually it was the other way around. He gently put his hand on the mound representing her shoulder. "Up, Doctor," he said. No response. He shook her slightly. "Up, Doctor. Toot, toot, toot toot toot toot." "Oh," the little mound yawned softly; "the bugler toots. What a lovely sound arises amidst the trees. Bird thou never wert," she assured him, sitting up, still beneath the covers. "Would you," she asked sleepily, "consider throwing that drape of clothes on the little chair at me? I just looked out the window." "Would you consider not going?" "Definitely not; you promised." "The Westons sent in." "Did they?" she asked, swallowing another yawn; "oh, good. I want to see them more than anyone." "Nothing will make you stay here and keep my poor widowed sister company?" "Oh, nothing." By now she was dressed as far as the waist; there was an elaborate Chinese screen shutting off one corner of the room. Edna never bothered with it.

She started buttoning her peach chemisette, which had been falling like magnolia petals over the top of her long black skirt. "Oh, look at that basque," she sighed; "that's not the kind of thing I'd want to put on in the morning." "What would you want to put on?" "Nothing. A blanket with a big pin." "You were meant to be an Indian." "True," Edna said, wiggling into the detestable basque; "then it would be more than proper for me to follow five paces behind you, carrying your case. It's the big case today, isn't it?" she noticed, looking over at the bed, while she stood still, as he buttoned row after row of her buttons. He has such skillful fingers, she thought, but she was so clumsy with hers. It was so early in the morning; they wouldn't work at all. She'd be buttoning up until sunrise. "Well, there you are"; he smiled; "I hope you never need as many stitches."

"In what, my love, are we traveling?" "We won't know

the answer to that," he told her, "until Bridget lets us know what John Dale found on his way to the cheese factory. You can sit on the bed and wake up, or eat, while I find out." "I'll lie on the bed," she answered, stretching straight out. "Draft oxen," he announced, coming back in. "Draft oxen," Edna yawned. "Mud, mud, mud," he said wearily; "someone started out for Brattleboro in a buggy, and was brought home with the buggy dismantled on an oxen cart." "We'll be gone a long time then," Edna realized. Nothing discourages her, he thought. An energetic little person. Still, *he* would be less nervous if he went alone. He had been less nervous when he went out the first times after his apprenticeship to old Dr. Houston.

John installed her in the covered cart. He came back out of the house, his face barely visible over three huge hampers he carried. "Three!" she gasped. "You said it yourself; a long day," he told her, climbing on, taking the reins. "Are we going to Westons' first?" she asked, excited as a child. "You bet your life we're going first. By now they've alerted the countryside; so we'll get to see some sick people." They started off in the gray drizzle. The day, apparently, had decided to sleep late. "When," Edna asked after a while, "is the fair?" "Next week." "No, I mean, what day?" "All week." "All week? What do they find to do?" "Coach parades, shows of needlework, blanket displays, knitted hoods and socks, contests of draft oxen, agricultural displays, trotting races, exhibits of creamery butter, things like that." He looked over at her. She was nodding, her eyes slowly closing, little pink shells. In minutes, she was sound asleep, leaning against him. He drove for three hours, Edna bumping gently, until he caught sight of the Weston barn and its little cupola. The entire household was out in the front yard, anxiously peering down the road, awaiting his appearance.

"Edna, wake up," he whispered. She sat up, wide awake, as if she had never been asleep. "Will you look at them," she whispered, suppressing a grin. "They certainly *look* alarmed." "They always look alarmed," he said; "if looking alarmed were an illness, this family has a continuous attack of it." "But maybe something *is* wrong," Edna whispered as they slowly plodded closer.

"They've had an early fall up here," she noted; "look, two big elms without leaves." "They've been dead for fifteen years; they're waiting for them to fall on the house, and then they'll move into another part of it," John explained wearily; "they're just like the Turners all over again." "Who *are* the Turners?" "On the way back, on the way back," he said, reining in the team, getting down. "Well, who's dying now?" she heard him asking angrily. "Oh, Doctor," the little girl sobbed, "it's Mother; she's doubled up like a hairpin." John turned around, deliberately plodding back to the wagon, his boots making a sucking sound. "You wait here; it's either overeating or drinking. I'll be right out." She sat back, resigned. She knew better than to argue with commands; he was captain of the road.

"Well, and I suppose you haven't touched a morsel," John demanded of the dying woman inside. "Oh, Doctor, not a thing," she wheezed, clutching at her abdomen. "All right," John said, taking a string from his pocket; "sit up." He wrapped the string around her waist like a belt. "The two ends don't meet," he said. Mrs. Weston flushed. "It's the bloat, Doctor, the bloat; I think the kidneys have given up on me." "Any vomiting?" "Oh yes, all the time, whenever I can get out of bed." "Only when you get out of bed?" he asked, pretending to take notes. "Well, I try not to mess up in it." "Naturally, naturally," he said soothingly; "I don't suppose it's possible another little stranger is on the way?" "At my age? After I've just begun getting rid of those rags?" So that's it, he thought; well, this was going to be quite a day. He had a premonition; and here was Mrs. Weston, brought into the kitchen to prevent her straining herself by additional movement. "This is serious," John said, pulling up a greasy wooden chair. "It is?" she asked, happiness rouging her cheeks. "Definite high blood pressure, with incipient complications; probably a dropped stomach. Have you any pain in the back?" he inquired anxiously. "Oh yes," she sighed, ecstatic. "I see"; he nodded, grave.

"Now, the question is, what is to be done with you? We do want to keep you alive?" he asked, his tone questioning. "Oh yes," Mrs. Weston answered, already a willing partner in his difficulties. "Sedation, naturally," he said; "but will you have the stomach for that?" "Oh yes, I think so; if it will keep me going for the sake of my married children. I hardly ever see them, but they have a dreadful habit of falling sick, and even the little boys, out with their father, they do get the worst cuts, and the only little one I have left, she's no trouble, but it's a worse tragedy to grow up motherless." "Tragic," John agreed, solemn; "we must overlook nothing." He pretended to think. "There are several things we can do," he said finally; "first, you must understand your unfortunate position of the stomach has nothing to do with your activities, and little to do with your complaints. You are," he explained to the great, statuesque woman, "frail, terribly frail. I do not see how you've gotten this far." He shook his head. Mrs. Weston looked positively bridal.

"Terrible family troubles for such a frail woman. I think these pills will help, but they are very potent; you must take them judiciously. One every two hours; keep an eye on the clock. Have everyone keep an eye on the clock. A dreadful case of overwork, a clear case of overwork," he lamented. Mrs. Weston pressed his hand. He noted hers were considerably softer than his. He doubted that she'd seen the sight of the laundry tub or a wet floor in years. "Now," he prescribed, "no more than one floor and one wall a day. Only one hour of washing per week." he said loudly, hearing the others enter. "We must build you up slowly, very slowly. You are not to overdo We do not want your health broken altogether. Do you think you can manage that?" he asked. "It's very important that you manage that much and no more; we must build up those wrecked muscles and soothe those ragged nerves. Step by step," he droned on, sententious; "the slowest runner wins the race. Tell me"—he bent forward. whispering in her ear—"do you often find yourself subject to fits of pity? Often accompanied by severe headaches?" "Oh, I do. All the time," she whispered back; "constantly. I think of my life and cannot refrain from weeping." "I do not wonder at it," the doctor said; "they must take better care of you. They must permit you to work about the house. There is such a thing as killing with kindness. Don't swallow that deadly arsenic, Mrs. Weston," he pleaded; "don't do it. For my sake; I beg you. And your soon-to-be-orphaned children."

"Which wall shall I begin with?" she whispered. "Any *one* will do, provided it is only one, and the floor that goes with it. It will get wet, you know, when you wash the wall, and you must not go on to a second wall." "I won't," she swore. "I think," Dr. Steele said, rising, "with proper care, Mrs. Weston should show definite signs of recovery by early spring. She must follow orders; that is of paramount importance," he instructed the little family group. He did pity them. What a collection: a chronic inebriate for a father and a stubborn mule hypochondriac for a mother, more selfish than a leech. "It's one pill every two hours; you can handle the responsibility?" he asked, worried; "if not, I know of an excellent nurse, but she is a great expense." "They can," Mrs. Weston pronounced; she was not about to have her household allowance cut down because of their laziness. "Then I must leave you to your own skill. Don't hesitate to send for me," he said, turning to Mrs. Weston, "if you sense the slightest indication of worsening." "I believe I feel better already," the poor woman breathed; but then, noticing the eyes of the family upon her, hastened to add it was the prospect of recovery which had so strengthened her. "And I assume," Dr. Steele said to no one in particular, "Mr. Weston will make his payments in the usual manner?" "Hay, definitely hay," Mrs. Weston hastened to assure him; "the wagons should be in Williamsville tomorrow." "That is more than satisfactory," the doctor said; "Mrs. Weston, do your best. That is all we can ask of you."

For some minutes now, he had been aware of the babble of an unfamiliar voice in the entryway. "Does someone else require the doctor?" Mrs. Weston inquired solicitously. "I shall go see," announced Dr. Steele; "Mrs. Weston, don't take on so over other people's troubles. It will be too much for you altogether." Pure curiosity, that vulture, he thought, leaving the room. A distraught, emaciated man was waiting in the entry, pacing frenetically. "Come outside," John said, steering him out by the elbow. "What's the trouble?" he asked. "Emma, my wife. She's very sick and the baby is, too; they look bad to me, but my mother said it was nothing, they would get over it, but they're not; they're so much worse, every minute." He was inchoate with worry. "How old is the baby?"

"Six days old." The man burst into tears. "Any swelling of the stomach?" The man nodded violently, unable to speak. "Mr. Weston!" John bellowed; "we need the use of two of your horses. Be quick about it, man." "After you dawdled here on those crawling oxen?" Weston growled. "The horses," John ordered; "one saddle for a woman. Hurry," he bellowed from the wagon's side, glaring in the direction of the barn.

A deep furrow had dug down the middle of his forehead. This was just what he hadn't wanted Edna to see. This was just what *he* didn't want to see. Sullen, Mr. Weston arrived with the two animals. Edna was already standing, ready to clamber down. "What's your name?" John asked the man. "Lucretius Sargent." "Do you know any wood paths, or mountain paths, Mr. Sargent? The main road is out of the question for these horses." "We can go back up in the woods and up onto the ridge," Mr. Sargent answered, voice quivering; "the ride down is hard. You have to ride well. It's very gravelly, very; the horses slip." He looked sidelong at Edna. "Let's go," she said softly. "We'll follow," John told him. The three of them set off, the Westons muttering about the high-toned doctor and how he always took care of anyone he took a fancy to, while they could die in a hogpen for all he cared, while inside, Mrs. Weston had decided if one pill would benefit, three would certainly cure. She happily swallowed the enormous sugar pills Bridget pressed late at night behind drawn curtains. She felt better already.

The three of them rode on through the woods. A milky, smoky light filtered in through the trees; here and there, an occasional boulder, carpeting itself slowly with green moss, made itself visible. Mr. Sargent carefully steered them through the maze of rocks and fallen boulders. There was the sound of a creek. Edna let her horse fall behind. She was getting very practiced at this, she thought, leaning over, vomiting expeditiously. She spurred on her horse, falling into line. The woods were smoking with fog and mist, as if there had been a terrible fire, recently put out. We look like three ghosts, Edna thought. Why did John look so worried? Sometimes, she couldn't help thinking it, she resented the patient. John ended up sicker inside than anyone on the bed. She knew he worried about her as well. He must know what it is already, she thought, automatically dodging a branch. She knew the woods were on fire with color, but they were riding through an interminable grayness. There was the sound of rain on leaves, but nothing touched them; the woods were too thick.

They had entered some mysterious zone, some uncharted place where nature manufactured itself, again and again. Nature's secret laboratory, she mused, guiding her horse around a fallen rock. Something jumped in front of her. Tree toads, she thought, on their way to becoming something else. "The ridge," Mr. Sargent called back. One by one they emerged from the woods onto a slanting sheet of gray rock. They rode on, the clack of their hooves mingling with the chatter of birds and squirrels. There was no drizzle here, only the endless haze. Edna could barely see John's mount ahead of her. They picked their way carefully along, the woods beneath them a denser cloud. "We're going down," John called to her. They began their descent.

Lord, Edna thought; that idiot should have given us mules. Her horse was sliding, panting, picking its way. A fine place for a horse to break its leg, Edna thought, giving the horse its head. It slowed, seeming to have less trouble. John had just done the same with his mount. They wove down, interminably. Boston, Edna thought. Boston was on another planet, another globe. They were spinning through the universe on a new course. This was limbo: this was the place where things went to be formed and re-formed. No wonder it protected its approaches so thoroughly. She thought, after some time, she could see a house taking shape before her. The ground was leveling; there was the smell of wet cedar. Cedar chips; the man must have emptied a wagonload of them on the trail. They rode into his yard.

"You picked the right day," John said; he shook his head at her, then helped her down. "You can't stay out here in the rain." Oh, he was worried all right. "I don't want to stay out in the rain; I could have done that at home." "This wasn't my idea," John said, angry, going in before her. "Where is your wife?" she heard him asking Mr. Sargent. They went down the hall. It was dark. Dark and quiet. "In there," Mr. Sargent said, pointing at a door. It was evident he would not open it himself. "Wait in the parlor," John told him gruffly. "Edna, come." They went in.

The first thing she saw was a woman lying absolutely motionless on a bed; the bed had been moved nearer the window, apparently so the woman could look out. But now she was lying, eyes wide open, fixed on the blank ceiling. Her eyes seemed to have fallen back into her skull, two burnt-out stars. Oh, Edna thought, it's her stomach that's the trouble; they've made some kind of tent out of hoops for her so the bedding won't press down. She moved closer, then went around to the other side of the bed near the window, facing John. It's not quiet here, she realized in astonishment; it's the tension. It makes things seem so still. No, it wasn't quiet at all; there was the sound of the woman's breathing. Edna had never heard anything like it. Little breaths, pants, in and out, each one a supreme effort. And her skin: it was blue, bluish and waxy. She looks waxy, as if she were made of tallow. John was carefully looking everywhere but at her.

"Emma?" she heard him saying; "Emma?" The woman's lips parted. Edna realized that she couldn't speak. John picked up the woman's hand, taking her pulse. His frown deepened. He tried again, higher on the wrist. "You try," he asked Edna; she was extraordinarily good at finding pulses. He had discovered that. "It's hardly there," Edna whispered, coming over to his side; "it—quivers; it's not steady. It seems awfully fast; I can't count it." John sighed. Without thinking, Edna put her hand on his shoulder, then lifted it. "All right now, Emma," he was saying, "we're going to pull back the blankets and have a look at you. This is my wife, Edna. She wants to help." The woman seemed to nod. John slowly drew the blankets back. "Puerperal fever," John murmured. What's that? Edna wondered; what's that? That's her stomach, Edna realized, stunned; that whole thing is her stomach. That whole globe is her stomach. My God, she thought, paling; my God. A chill seized her. She felt dizzy. Involuntarily, she took the woman's hand. It was clammy, cold, like a leaf buried under others for an entire winter. "It's all right, Emma, it's all right," she kept saying. She saw John going over to the cradle in the corner. Until now, she hadn't noticed it. "We're going to look after the baby, Emma, we're going to see to the baby," she said to the staring woman; "just lie still. Look out the window; the leaves are so bright." The sick woman blinked twice, as if to acknowledge the words; her head did not turn.

The two of them stood over the cradle. He took her hand. "You're cold, cold." He sounded heartbroken. She looked down into the cradle. There was a little waxy model of its mother, its belly distended in the same dreadful way, and, from the rapid rise and fall of its little chest, breathing even faster. But her color, that was different. This was not gray or blue; no, she was yellow, a funny color yellow. What would you call it? Ocher. "She's yellow," she whispered. "Cord infection," he whispered back. "What do we do?" "Nothing. Sedate them. Drops of opium and water. Whoever delivered her did this." "They just die?" "Unless you have a handbook of miracles." Edna stood still; her own skin felt frozen. Finally, she forced herself back to the woman's bed. "Emma," she called to her; "Emma? My husband's bringing you some medicine. It will help you. You'll feel better, much better." The woman's eyelids fluttered. "And the baby, too. She'll feel much better. She'll have medicine, too." The woman's eyes fixed on her momentarily. "Much better, much better," Edna repeated. The woman's eyes were fixed on the ceiling. Edna felt for her wrist. Her breathing was even faster, the pulse harder to find. I don't think she'll live long, Edna thought. She sat down on the chair next to the bed, holding onto the woman's hand.

John came back into the room with a little glass. "Can you get her to drink this?" "I think so. Emma, Emma," she called. "I know you can't pick up your head, so I'm going to put some drops of this on your lips, and you will lick them off, won't you?" She moistened the woman's lips. To her astonishment, her tongue came out slowly, and licked the liquid off. Edna repeated the process again and again until the liquid was gone. John watched her. Why hadn't he thought of that? He'd seen it work with animals. But it had never occurred to him. Edna sat down, holding the woman's hand. "Better now?" she asked after some time. The eyelids fluttered, more slowly this time. "More?" Edna asked John pleadingly. He thought. A few more drops would knock her out; a few too many would kill her outright. "Yes, all right." He disappeared, returning with a larger cup of water; this one had only two drops dissolved in it. Edna went through the laborious process of moistening the woman's lips. She sat down, taking her hand. "Better now?" she whispered. The lids fluttered once.

Frightened, Edna felt her wrist. No, she wasn't dead, just asleep. "Well, the baby," Edna sighed, exhausted; "I wonder if the same thing will work with her. If you held her mouth open," she thought out loud, "I could try the same thing with her tongue." Each time she moistened the child's tongue, John let its mouth close; the throat moved reflexively. "It's working," Edna told him, relieved. They continued. Finally, the liquid was gone. "They won't feel anything now?" "Nothing," John said; "nothing. We have to talk to Mr. Sargent." "I don't look forward to it." They went out; the two disfigured bodies slept peacefully.

"Mr. Sargent," Edna began, without thinking, "they're both out of pain. They feel no discomfort whatever." "Thank the Lord," he answered. "But I can hold out no hope," John said; "it's childbed fever in its last stage." "If you had come earlier?" "It wouldn't have made any difference." "None," Edna said. "Can he keep them comfortable?" Edna asked in an undertone. The man was staring into space, just as his wife had done. John nodded at her. "Mr. Sargent," John said; "Mr. Sargent." The man looked at him. "When they wake up, they will feel a great deal of pain. This is what you have to do. Four drops in a small glass for your wife; one for the child." He described Edna's method. "Can you do it?" The man nodded wordlessly; tears were splashing onto his coat. "They won't suffer," John assured him; "they won't suffer at all. They will be going to a better world." Edna looked at him, startled. He didn't believe in better worlds. "This may be a blessing in disguise," he went on; "who knows what God might have intended for them had they lived? Think what he may be sparing them. And Jesus said, 'Suffer the little children to come unto me.' Your child will be raised by our immortal Lord. Think what they will be like when you go to meet them." Edna listened, her body on fire. She went up to Mr. Sargent and kissed him on the cheek. "You mustn't forget the medicine," she told him softly; "God would not want them to suffer unnecessarily. You can help them," she assured him; "you can perform the greatest service of their lives. God would want that, wouldn't he?" The man nodded, helpless.

Edna put her arm around him. "Why does he have to have *mine?*" he broke out suddenly. John abruptly turned his back. He had heard that before; he would hear it again. "I don't understand why," Edna said; "I only know this is tragic, terribly tragic for you." "Why does he need *mine?*" the man screamed in agony. Edna stroked his hand. "My God!" the man sobbed, falling into a chair. "Have you other children?" Edna finally asked. "Five," he cried. "You must think of them," she said soothingly; "you mustn't forget them. Emma would want that." "No," he sobbed. "It's foolish to try and comfort you, isn't it?" she asked; "only time will do that. But there is duty. You have one, the medicine," she went on firmly, "and the children. They understand even less about this than you do. They won't keep; neither will the medicine, will it?" She's crying, John noticed, his back still to them; he could tell that from her voice. How can she cry in front of the husband? It will only make things worse. He was crying silently. Finally, the sobbing behind him seemed to die down. "Don't cry, missus," he heard the man saying; "you did all you could. I'll never forget either of you for coming. The other doctor wouldn't. I didn't even go for him. Don't cry, missus," he pleaded; "here, take a towel. Mop yourself off. Don't cry." He was still crying, but like the rain, he was beginning to stop. "Thank you," he heard Edna saying, muffled somewhere in the towel. What next? he wondered.

"If she dies," Edna was saying, "I would like to beg the privilege of attending the funeral; I know you'll want family. But I should like to come. If you will make an exception for me." "We'll send for you and bring you," the man promised, his voice rough. John heard the scraping of another chair on the wooden floor. He turned slightly and saw the two of them sitting close to one another, two conspirators. "Who delivered her?" Edna was asking. She's doing this for me, John realized; she knows what I'd be asking. If I could, he thought; if I could. "The new young doctor, Lindsay, from Jamaica." "Lindsay," Edna repeated; she had heard something about him from Bridget. Oh yes, he was raising chickens and hogs to enter in the county fair. "What kind of soap did he use? Green, I guess; to wash up with, I mean." "Oh, he didn't wash," the man answered nervelessly. "Not at all?" Edna asked. "No," the man thought back; "well, that's not really right, missus. After the baby, he washed his hands in the basin. I remember, he used his pants for a towel, and there was a towel right near him." "I see." "So do I," John spoke up, finally turning back into the room. "Will you be all right?" Edna was asking the husband. "Don't go worrying after me," the man cautioned her; "my mother, she's coming down the mountain, and there are the children to keep after." "You'll be very busy; you mustn't forget the medicine." "Oh, I won't, missus." They all heard the sound of a horse. John sighed audibly. "I won't forget to send after you; if anything happens, that is." "You did promise," Edna reminded him. The man nodded. What on earth will she do next? John wondered. She was better at these things than he was. "I better go see who's there," the husband said, getting up. John and Edna stood in the room, holding hands. A milky light was filling the dark room. The sun was somewhere, unable to free itself.

A young man came in. "It's my father; he can't breathe," he announced without ceremony; "a mile down the road." They said goodbye and left. An old man was propped on a bed in the parlor. "*That* one," the old man gasped when he saw John; "the one that scolds." He glared at his son. John was busy with some kind of apparatus. "That fluid has got to come out of your chest," John told him; "I have to cut an opening. Can you stand it?" The old man nodded as if at an idiot. Edna watched John make the incision with a knife. From where she stood, it looked as if John were stabbing the old man in the chest. John was wrapped in a blanket, which was promptly drenched by a stream of pus wide as a finger. It spurted out like a geyser. The old man's eyes stopped bulging. His grayish-blue skin returned to its normal color. His gasps stopped; his breathing had become normal. "You'll recover," John told him grumpily. "You had to get that one," the old man complained. Edna was astonished at the change, disgusted by the pus. But still, the old man was alive; when they had come in, she was certain every breath, every gasp, was his last. "Will you keep quiet, Pa?" his son demanded. The old man said nothing, glaring at John. "He's mad at me," John told her, "for stabbing him like that." "Well, how would you like it?" the old man asked; "and no chance to fight back!" "*I* wasn't dying," John retorted. "I don't see the difference," the curmudgeon grumbled. "And you wouldn't have seen anything more in a few more minutes," his wife said, coming into the room; "you just nail that mouth of yours shut." The general had come onto the field. There was silence from the troops.

"Say, Doc," she said; "down the hill, just over the bridge; there's a man broke his leg. You want to fix it?" "What a way to put it," Edna murmured. "Well, some of them don't seem to," the old woman said, turning on her. Edna didn't say anything. "Can you give directions?" John asked. "Take that fool of a son," the old man answered; "you won't need them directions." He looked over at his wife; she nodded. They started out again. "Watered and fed the horses," the young man told John. "Thanks," he answered. That, she realized, was to be his payment. Why, she thought, you had to be rich to be a doctor in the country. It seemed to her the horses were tired. They came up to another farm. By now, she was exhausted, utterly, as if her own bones were softening. John looked at her as he helped her down. "You go to sleep in the parlor; you've seen fractures before." "All right." She could see he was suspicious; she had given in too easily. "They are pretty boring," she added. "How soon the heart hardens," John joked wearily. "How much faster the body." "Into the parlor. Put my wife in the parlor," he told one of the daughters who had just appeared in the hall. "Well, and what's she doing here?" the girl asked. "Nurse," he replied; "see she gets covered up and gets to sleep."

Out in the barn, a young man was lying on some hay, while some chickens and rabbits pecked and hopped around him. "How'd you manage that?" John asked, cutting off the pant leg with his knife. A simple break, he saw, relieved. "Stepped on a rake and tried to jump off

344

it," the boy said; he was pale. "Get some blankets," John told whoever was behind him. He saw the beginnings of a trellis over against the far wall, went over, and loosened two boards. "Mother will be mad as fury," the boy said. "Too bad," John answered; "hold your breath. Just one pull." The boy took a deep breath and held it. John pulled the bone into alignment, and, with the help of the other son, bound on the splint with a torn sheet. "All right," John said, standing up; "carry him into the house on a blanket, with a piece of board under that leg; it's not to move." "Well, I guess we know what to do now," the other boy said. "I guess you do. If you see any swelling, red veins, anything peculiar, you come for me." "Don't worry, Doc," the patient said; "we even know when to take off the splint and start out on crutches." "I'll look at that leg first; unless you want it off. Any fever, anything like that, you come for me."

Well, what time was it? He felt centuries old. Inside, the mantel clock read three-thirty. He'd been out in the barn over an hour. "Want something to eat, Doc?" the younger one said. "I wouldn't mind." He wanted to give Edna some rest. "Is my wife asleep?" "Dead," the grandmother said, grinning. Something twisted inside. "Dead to the world," she said proudly; "everyone sleeps like the dead under my quilts." "Well, that is something to be proud of." "I'd say." He sat down at the table, wearily eating the boiled mutton. It would be some trip back. The horses were worn out. "We've got Weston's horses," he told them after he'd been eating for a while; "I don't think they'll get us back." "Wouldn't think so," the grandmother agreed, chomping away; "Elder, you get them two horses ready, one for the lady." "Yes, ma'am," the boy said, pushing back from the table. Edna wove into the room. "Sit down," the grandmother ordered her, piling some food on an extra plate. Edna noticed the woman looking her over. She held her breath. "You just get that strength up," the old lady ordered. Edna began eating. "Are you awake enough to ride?" John asked. "Why not?" "Why not?" he repeated, smiling at her. "Come on, Doc"; she smiled back; "*I'm* not sick." "Nothing that can't be cured," the grandmother agreed. No, John wasn't making anything out of that, she decided happily. They got back on their horses, following the younger son; he took them as far as the Sargents'. One of the Sargent children took them up the mountain, then back down to the Westons'. There was the oxteam. Edna felt as if they were returning from the moon. "Some way to pass the time, isn't it?" John asked. "Well," she considered, "I can't exactly think of a better one, but the minute I do, I'll let you know."

They set off in the oxcart, Mrs. Weston waving merrily from the doorway. "What a miraculous recovery," Edna trilled gaily. "Well," she summed up, "one life saved, one leg saved, two put out of misery, and one cheered up significantly. I'd say that's not bad." "I guess not," he said after a while; "but that woman and the baby." "I hope I never see anything like it again," Edna said. "At least this will be the end of your coming with me." "It won't."

"Not even after that woman and the baby?" "Especially not after *that;* they needed comfort as well as those drops. It is really interesting, too," she went on, "horrible as it is. There must be some way to cure it." "Not that I know of." "We could try to find something." "Aren't you too tired to have any more ideas?" "No, John; we could try; we could find out about it in the books and build a laboratory or something." She was odd, he thought; half theory, half emotion. It added up to more than one person. How could *that* be? A laboratory, of all things. "Well, and why couldn't we do it?" "Because I only have one life, and there are only so many hours in the day. You can't graft more of those on the way Ten grafts on roses. And that fever was rare; you don't see it much, unless there's a brilliant doctor like that Lindsay around to help out. The time in the laboratory wouldn't be worth it. So many others would be dying like flies." "Still."

"And don't think of taking it up yourself." "Why?" "Because it's useless. You'd do more good holding people's hands and crying over their invalids." "Don't mock me," she protested, angry. "I'm not. I can't get over it. I thought that was just about the worst thing you could do. To start crying yourself, I mean." "Well, but that doesn't make any sense," Edna retorted; "they're ready to kill themselves, and you stand there dry-eyed? Why should they believe you feel any sympathy?" "You're right; I just couldn't do it." "Because you couldn't stop crying, you mean." He drove straight ahead, silent. "You're right. I couldn't." "How much farther?" Edna asked. John looked down at the mud. "Two hours." Edna leaned against him, and went to sleep as if on signal. If I could sleep like that, John thought; but I would dream. I'll dream about that woman and that child. She won't, though. She won't forget it but it won't live in her. She washes it out, somehow: the poison in the experience. It can't just be the crying. He looked down at the neat part in her black hair, her head bobbing against his shoulder. It's more than loving her, he thought; I admire her. More than Ten. I admire her. He always came back to how little she was, such a little person.

Finally, they were home. He let Edna fall slowly onto the seat, got down, and lifted her out. From the doorway, Ten shook her head disapprovingly at him. He put a finger to his lips. She nodded, went down the hall, turned back the blankets, and covered Edna. They went out, closing the door gently. "Don't squeak," John pleaded. She glared at him. "Well, what happened?" Ten asked. "She takes to it like a fish to water; it's beyond me. She wants me to start a laboratory." "That's not such a bad idea. You used to be interested in all that research." "If it's product versus process, I'll take the product; you know I made that decision a long way back." "It's hard on you, though." "It's my way," he answered gently. "I know that; I know that; I just wish it weren't." They sat together, staring into the fire. Finally, John shook himself awake and went off to bed, creeping in slowly. Jimmie was already there. He was asleep the minute his head touched the pillow.

Some time later, Edna awoke. She saw a light under the door. Ten must be up. Yes, she had to ask for Ten's help. Especially after today. She crept gently from her side of the bed and skimmed out of the room. Jimmie picked up his head, put it down, having decided to wait for her return. Edna found Ten in the parlor, reading *Lucille: A Novel in Three Parts*. "I hate to interrupt that," Edna said; "should I go back to bed?" "Don't be ridiculous," Ten answered, putting the book down; "you had quite a day, didn't you?" "John's was worse. We saw a woman and her baby sick with childbed fever." "Oh." Ten took it in, shaking her head. "It makes me worry about him," Edna said. "I don't wonder." "Especially

now," Edna began. "Why now; why now particularly?"
"Well, I'm going to be, as they say here, sick, in confinement, carrying a new arrival: in short, pregnant." Ten
stared at her. "And I don't want John to know until the
last possible minute. There must be some kind of dress
Mrs. Grimsby can make, something in your fashion paper
I can take an interest in, something I can do to hide
things during the day. And you could comment on how
much I'm eating, that I'm getting fleshy, that you never
expected it of me." Ten was still staring. "How long have
you been pregnant?" "Two months." "Two months? How
can you be so sure?" "I'm sure; well, aside from the obvious things, I vomit once a day. Not much appetite and
I'm always sleepy." "Good Lord. It's not something we
can hide forever." "Maybe for three months more," Edna
pleaded; "maybe even four." "Three at the most, I'd
guess; you're too small not to show after that."

"Then you'll help me?" "We'll go to Mrs. Grimsby's
tomorrow." "You'll tell John you need my advice? Otherwise he'll want to know why I'm not insisting on coming
along." "I'll work myself into a state over what to have
made up for the winter; by breakfast, I'll be a barnacled
wreck. Don't you worry." "You think I'm doing the right
thing, don't you?" "The only thing; by the time he finds
out, most of it will be over, and if he sees there's been so
little trouble you didn't even seem to notice most of it,
well, he might not go off his mind altogether." "We'll see
to that." "We all will," Ten promised; "I'll even get
Bridget and Bertha in on it. It won't be easy without
them. They're farm girls. They'll notice; they might say
something out of turn." "Good," Edna said; "I'll go back
to bed." She bent down to kiss Ten. "Aunt Ten?" "What,
dear?" she asked, looking up from her perpetual book. At
times Edna suspected they were glued to her hands.
"Could I possibly borrow a nightgown of yours and
change in your room? I don't want to wake John." "You'd
better hurry," Ten said, looking at the doorway; "your
escort looks impatient." There was Jimmie, looking at
Edna, squinting. "If that cat doesn't look in a fit," Ten
said; "I don't have anything to suit *him*." "He'll be fine
in his fur suit," Edna answered, bending down to pick
him up; he stood up agreeably, meeting her halfway.

Well, this won't be a quiet house, Ten thought, resigning

herself to the new order: Edna, an enchanted cat, one enchanted husband. And, she remembered, the problem of what to do with John. We could give him sedatives for the next seven months, she mused idly. Well, and that wouldn't be a bad idea, would it? "It was some time before Lucille's father's knowledge of Lady Rachel confirmed this opinion of Mr. Heatherton's. Lady Rachel held the maxims by which Lucille had been taught to regulate her conduct in such sovereign contempt that Lucille was sometimes angry; and she treated as the merest trifles so much of what Lucille had been made to consider as the weighty matters of the law that Lucille began to doubt her wisdom. But she found such a charm in the spirit and originality of her conversation as nothing could countervail; and she solved all that appeared to her as strange, or imbecile, by teaching herself to believe that 'poor Lady Rachel' had lived so long out of the world that she did not know what was necessary to live in it."

Ten put the book down in her lap, looking into the fire. *Lucille* was a very good novel indeed; probably, she judged, even better than *Isabella* and *Minerva;* but somehow, it was drained of its vividness. A lot she cared right now about Lady Rachel, or Lucille either, for that matter. Well, and perhaps she had been living out of the world too long also. Like Lady Rachel. But Edna had hardly been in it, and *she* certainly seemed to know what was necessary. And at her age. She was suddenly tired; she heard the latch fall into place in the married pair's room.

They'd soon be asleep, the three of them: Edna, John, and that incredible cat. She'd never seen such devotion in an animal. Actually, she realized, confounded, it was four of them. Of course, she thought, standing up, unaware her book had fallen to the floor, she couldn't be so sure the fourth was asleep or not. Yes, it was true. There was a new book in the house called what? *Living in the World? Living in the World Again? New Life in the New World?* Well, she was too tired to read any more of it. She suddenly felt very ancient. And very decrepit.

It was with great relief she put her head down on her pillow, stroking its wrinkles with her fingers. The pillow was so cool, so nice. And wrinkled, as she was. Her version of Jimmie the cat. She was too exhausted to worry, although, really, she had no reason to be. She fell asleep immediately, and shortly thereafter, Bertha came in and put out the light.

The next morning found Mrs. Grimsby frantically searching through her fashion papers for something supposedly very new, and supposedly called "The National Costume," which was, according to Ten's description, very low-cut, sleeves set in below the shoulder, allowing great freedom for the arms, falling in loose billows directly from a band under the bosom. It could be made up, Ten lectured, in plain fabric, which made it excellent for housework, or in the most extravagant fabrics, and decorated equally extravagantly. She had just read about it, she insisted stubbornly; she couldn't quite remember where, but her brother had sat up later than she had and must have thrown the paper into the parlor fire. "Well, if it can't be done, it can't be done," Mrs. Grimsby said finally, pulling herself, panting, out of a cabinet. "Local dressmakers," Ten muttered under her breath, pulling a folded sheet of paper from her pocket. "It's a good thing I decided to sketch this out," she sniffed at Mrs. Grimsby, who took it from her with no good grace.

"Well, it's simple enough to make, *if* it's worth making," Mrs. Grimsby said. "Although," she went on, inspecting the sketch, "with the proper modifications you could pass through the street without anyone trying to dash it in the mud." Actually, she thought, it wasn't so bad, and it certainly did look comfortable. Moreover, once Ten Richardson began wearing it, she could make up a far plainer version for herself, and for once, be in the latest style herself. "Well," Ten said, watching her face, "can you make up a good number for Mrs. Steele? She is very taken with the garment, but she tends to the elaborate in fabrics. Still, Edna," she said, turning to the woman in question, "you might get two or three in flowered muslin. There's no point in dressing to travel with the doctor, or for learning the art of making bread. That's her new passion," Ten explained. "How long would it take you to make up several dresses for her?" "I have her measurements from the spring," Mrs. Grimsby mused; "I could have two or three done for her within the week, but if I am to work on yours first . . ." "Work on hers first. She's ruining her clothes day by day."

"Then I'll check her measurements to be on the safe side," the dressmaker said, retreating, coming back with a white card. Edna looked apprehensively at her sister-in-law, who looked away, as if this was all routine, nothing out of the ordinary. "They seem to have changed," Mrs. Grimsby said, from her kneeling position on the floor. Edna saw her steel-gray head lift, her face turning up to her, a fast-blooming flower; she was staring at her. "Well, don't they always?" Ten asked casually. "Not precisely in *these* places, Miss Ten." Ten remembered that Mrs. Grimsby had had eight children herself; she had been measuring waists, bellies, and hips most of her lifetime. "Mrs. Grimsby," Ten decided, "I want to take you partway into our confidence. No one at all is to know about any changes in anyone's measurements, not mine, not my sister-in-law's. Do you understand what I mean?"

Mrs. Grimsby peered at her through her thick spectacles. "I would not take to it, Mrs. Grimsby, if news of Mrs. Steele's measurements got about, even if they have only altered slightly. I should complain up and down the town about the lack of skill in seams; heaven knows what. You may remember"—she paused—"how my brother's first marriage came to an end." "No one is ever going to forget that," Mrs. Grimsby answered, drumming her fingers on the pin-covered table. "Yes," she said finally; "I catch your meaning. The style has more advantages than I realized at first glance. In some of them, Mrs. Richardson, am I to assume it would not be the worst of ideas to make very wide seams which would allow for enlarging? Or cutting down, either one, of course?" "It would be a very good idea." "Well, your measurements haven't changed at all," she assured Ten after another five minutes. "Then don't fuss with the seams on mine." "Are you sure you like this costume, Mrs. Richardson?" "Well, I had better, don't you think?" "I guess you had; I suppose you had better," Mrs. Grimsby answered, trying to rise from the floor. Ten thrust down her hand. My, but she is getting bent over, she thought; when I first came in to see her she was so slim and straight, and so pretty. Mother always used to say women came to resemble their husbands, and she went ahead and married that camel. Well, she remembered, he certainly looked solemn enough for a minister; the sight of him was enough to scare you into a change of heart. Poor Mrs. Grimsby. She was being hard on her.

Mrs. Grimsby was sitting at her worktable, making calculations. She was a small woman, really, even though she was so wide in the bones; still, she wasn't what you would call fleshy. And it was a deliberate choice, anyone could tell that, to make as little of herself as possible. She could as easily stitch up something flattering, not what she usually strung up. And that hair; she might as well be bald. Well, she'd never seen a part so straight, as if she marked it out with one stroke of an ax, and the rest of it so tight it pulled on the skin of her cheeks. She didn't wrinkle, though, Ten saw enviously; she just grayed, as if the sap had gone out of her body. As if the black of her mourning dress had been drawn in through the surface of her skin.

It was so much easier not to remember what others went through, to treat them as if they were the dressmaker forms filling this shop, headless and legless, immune to everything, even the vicious jabs of needles and pins. "Mrs. Grimsby," she said at last, "I wouldn't, you know, really care to gossip about the quality of your work." The older woman looked her over, then back down at the table. "I know that, Miss Ten. Why don't we say Mrs. Steele is getting so fleshy, and it's such a shame, when she was such a fine figure of a woman, things like that. I can start in on that subject in a few months, and everyone will be delighted. Overjoyed." "*We* will be," Edna said.

"Well, and why not let the gossips swallow their own wrong medicine once in a while, Miss Ten? Peck, peck, peck, that's all I hear all day. Of course, if anything gets around, it's me that's repeated it. Everyone's certain of that, but I hardly ever repeat anything. My ladies can take care of themselves. Last year, they were so busy over someone in a boardinghouse who was a little fly they didn't notice one of these dressmaking things had fallen on me, and I couldn't get out from under it for over an hour. Mr. Steele would remember; he had to come bind up my ribs." She touched her left side lightly. "I've been pretty mad about it since then; the gossiping, I mean. Why shouldn't it be put to good purpose, just for once?" Oh yes, the weather had changed in that room.

Mrs. Grimsby looked years younger, as if she had never heard of dresses and patterns and beading and lace, and hooks and eyes and covered buttons and staying in one room while outside the seasons changed and other women were free to come and go, while she, if she was lucky, got to stand in the doorway in between flurries and feel the different touches of the seasons against her skin. Of course, there were the walks in the morning and night, but every dress was an emergency, and she walked to her shop in the dusk before sunlight, and left hours after sunset. It kept her busy. That was what she always told herself. It kept her busy. No one would find her hanging from a beam in the barn.

"How is the doctor?" she suddenly asked; it was as if time had rolled up for her, like a carpet, and she was standing on the bright part of the pattern, protected from the sun by the piano and from the gradual wearing down of endless steps: steps to important events, steps taken waiting for events, and mostly, the determined step, step, step to the world of the trivial, the world which kept everything going. No matter what. She was thinking, as if of a double image, of a little boy not old enough for pants, and of the young man who had come into the kitchen where she had been waiting with her mother. Her mother had seemed so old then, but now she was older than her mother had been. The young man had told them that the typhoid had caused complications of the kidneys. That was why her husband wasn't passing water, and he could relieve the problem with a catheter; he had already tried, but mostly there was blood, and more blood. No, he had answered, without evasions, no there was no hope at all. Unless, of course, there was a miracle. There were always miracles. Well, she hadn't believed in miracles, not even then. Her family had always liked the Steeles; they might stab a sword into a bush, but they never beat around it.

"The doctor?" Ten answered; "he's in a heaven of his own. And we're trying to keep him there." "You can depend on me." "Yes, I know that," Ten said; her eyes were stinging. What was the past anyway? she asked herself, annoyed; it always affected her eyes like salt water. It filled her head as if she had stayed underwater too long.

And yet, it was always there, decorating the walls, warming them, when everything went blank. As it so often did. "Well, and I suppose we'll settle the bill in the usual way?" Mrs. Grimsby asked; "that means," she said, turning to Edna, "I buy whatever I think is best, ignoring the expense, make out a careful account and send it to your sister-in-law, who looks at the total and sends some-one down with the money. Someone's going to cheat her one of these days; someone should check up on her." "No one's cheated me yet," Ten said. "Not that you know of," Mrs. Grimsby observed. "I can't spend my whole life worrying about that. The sale of our farm, that would be a different affair altogether." "I suppose they make up for it cheating the doctor"—Mrs. Grimsby said—"the same way they did with my husband." "The country hasn't changed much," Ten agreed.

"Oh, hello," a sweet voice was saying to Edna; "you're Mrs. Steele, aren't you? The doctor's wife?" "Yes, I am," she answered, puzzled. "This isn't the proper way to in-troduce myself, I know," the woman went on quickly; "I'm Mr. Sargent's sister, Alice Moffat. We are all so grateful to you," she went on, to the bewilderment of the other two women; "I was coming out to see you this after-noon. The funeral will take place on Friday, and I will come for you. If your sister-in-law has no objections." Ten looked blankly over at her. "Oh, Mrs. Richardson," Alice Moffat said, "the whole town is talking about Mrs. Steele's kindnesses to my brother's family. I think Lucre-tius would have gone clear off his head if she hadn't been there. He keeps repeating little bits of things she said —well, in between his fits of crying—but particularly what she said about the little girl living on in heaven, and how they were in no pain, and how Mrs. Steele taught him to give the medicine, and she invented the way right on the spot, and how much calmer they seemed to him after she left, and how good she was to him. Well, and don't think I don't know where *my* obligations lie," Mrs. Moffat finished; "you see to it, Mrs. Steele. If you ever need anything on this earth, you send straight to me." "That's very generous of you," Edna murmured. How could that small time have meant so much? Of course, she had thought about it, but what she had thought most about was how surprised she was at her own reaction to the poor man. She didn't even know him. "Mrs. Grimsby, Mrs. Richardson, as God is my witness, I place myself under obligation to this lady." Everyone's eyes were shiny.

"I don't suppose my cousin's wedding dress has made much progress?" Alice Moffat asked; "she won't be happy in it now as she would have been." "Are they putting it off?" Ten asked. "Only a few weeks. Her prospective bridegroom has to leave for the West on business. It's always something. Isn't that always the way?" she asked them all; "some are dying and some are marrying and some are getting themselves born." "It's the way," Mrs. Grimsby agreed, "although I'd like more of the last than the first." "Wouldn't we all," Ten sighed. "Well, Mrs. Steele," the other young woman said, "I have to get about my business, but this was such a fortunate accident, and now if people smile at you on the street, at least you'll know you haven't forgotten to fasten your buttons. Oh, the dress," she asked Mrs. Grimsby hurriedly; "at what stage is it?" "Finished." "Isn't she the fastest thing you ever heard tell of?" Mrs. Moffat said; "well, good afternoon, ladies," she said, fastening her cloak; "there's that chill in the air again." She bowed slightly to Ten and Mrs. Grimsby, but stepped over and took Edna's hand. "Shall I send for you? Lucretius seems to depend upon it." "By all means." "And you may depend upon *me*. Well, good afternoon, again," she said, leaving.

"Does the whole town really know about that one thing?" Edna asked; "it was only yesterday." "Oh, poor thing," Mrs. Grimsby said; "you have a great deal to learn about the country. News travels faster than lightning here." "Even in the mud?" She was very curious; how did people learn of things so very fast? "Let's see," thought Mrs. Grimsby; "did you stop in anywhere on your way back from the Sargents'?" "Only at the Westons'." "*Only* at the Westons'," Mrs. Grimsby said, looking over at Ten. "Why, they fly around with news in their beaks like blue jays. One of the children probably swam the mud to another farm, and told another child, and that child told its mother, and so it goes on. I'd say in the Sargent neighborhood you were almost as remarkable as Lazarus." "But they *died*; the patients died," Edna lamented. "Edna," Ten cut in, "people who live on legends don't stop at details like that, do they, Mrs. Grimsby?" "They stop at nothing whatsoever." She remembered her early days as a minister's wife. "I'd say you're fortunate this is the first thing to get their little eyes fastened on again, wouldn't you, Miss Ten? Now, with me, it was the slaughtering of a hog. I couldn't stand the screams, so my husband had to have it done at the neighbor's, and everyone went on about that. I got myself compared to Abraham; he was willing to sacrifice a son, and I couldn't part with a hog. Such little things; they can really turn you against people. But my husband, he always had a way of throwing them into a better light, and I would wind up liking them again, even though, in the beginning of the fuss, if I'd had my way, I would have thrown them all into the fire." She paused. "Mrs. Steele seems to be getting fleshy." She was trying it on. "It will work," she assured Ten; "I'm sure it will." The two women thanked her and left for home. "Well, and now what are you going to do with yourself, fleshy miss?" Ten joked. "Sleep," Edna said.

Ten stole into her room at four. There was Edna, fully dressed, apparently motionless since she had lain down. She's been taking too much on herself, Ten thought; at least that's over now. "Edna," she whispered; "Edna, wake up." She shook her softly. "What?" Edna asked, sitting straight up. "John's home early; I thought he might get to wondering if he found you asleep." Edna hopped out of bed, and dashed some water on her face, briskly rubbing it off. "How do I look?" "Magnificent, not a bit different." "Let's go, then," Edna said. "No, you go; he has that 'I'm waiting for my wife' look written all over his face." Edna flew down the hall. Ten sank down on their bed. What a campaign this would be; but then, they had gotten off to a good start.

"Are you really going to that funeral on Friday?" John asked the instant she appeared. "Yes, and what are you looking so pleased about?" "Tonight I got the second installment of the Weston Revenge Campaign into action." "Are you going to tell me what it is, you silly cat?" "As soon as it's over." "What a tease you are; well, and what was it today?" "An enormous collection of broken bones, not more than one per person, and two very late cases of summer complaint, both with convulsions, both recovered. Well, it's lovely, as you ladies say, so little sponging; I'm home early. How about a ride?" "Where to?" Edna asked, getting up, draping herself over him. It was such a relief to see him rested. "To nowhere, absolutely nowhere." "That *is* lovely"; Edna beamed; "I know a wonderful meadow we can rest the horses in." "You do? Then we better hurry. I wouldn't want the sundown to interfere with the other sights." "Oh, the other sights are getting less sightly," Edna said; "Ten says I'm getting fleshy."

"Will you hurry?" John urged. He was standing, impatiently holding her cloak. They took Bridget's basket, and within minutes were on the little path into the woods. It was astonishing, Edna thought, galloping happily, how one day of sun brightened everything up and dried it off. And that was quite a scene Ten had made at breakfast; her nerves, she had sobbed, or the blues, she didn't know what it was, she was too old for the obvious thing, at least she thought so, but she couldn't decide on anything, not even a dress; really, she *needed* Edna, and she did such an excellent job of showering tears that the dinnerware actually rattled on the table, and John was thoroughly alarmed, absolutely relieved that his wife would be home with his sister. Yesterday's rounds had been quite enough for him. At least for a while. A talented woman, Edna thought, admiration renewed. Yes, her mother had said something about Ten's acting abilities, and so had one of those old crones in Fitchburg. One of them had said something about how dramatic she was. They were right. There was no question about that.

The funeral was over, and it was Monday, the day of the floats, the day of the parade. Edna was excited at the prospect, and John amused by her excitement. How days did pass, she sighed, patting her stomach in its "National Costume." Really, she thought, Ten ought to stop reading *Minerva* and *Lucille* and begin writing herself. She hoped, dimly, she would find Alice Moffat there. She did like her, although, lately, she didn't seem to like anyone. At least no one enough to talk to. Except, of course, John and Ten. The funeral, she remembered, buttoning the last neck buttons; really, she hardly remembered it. She had been so sleepy; a haze enveloped the event. But she remembered how lonely it had seemed, so few of them there, the men with their hats in their hands, and the abrupt break in the earth, much redder earth than she had expected, much more clay. Everyone had been so calm. Well, she supposed some people were like that when everything was settled and over, but she knew she would take on before, during, and after. Still, she would find the uncertainty the worst part; she knew that. But perhaps the calm was illusory. Perhaps later, when the shock dulled, they would wake up. Perhaps they had been in some kind of sleep and would wake some days afterwards. She knew what they would be doing now, though. Every routine task they could think up. Yes, that was the best way.

Finished, she sat down on the bed, waiting for John. He had thundered away from the house to inspect a suicide. She had asked Ten about it; she said sometimes the victims were not really dead or beyond help, but if they were, the family still needed to hear it from the doctor. It was a formality, really, and he would be back soon. She wished again that her husband's duties did not include so many duties of this kind. Probably it was the childbed fever that had set John off against the Westons. He couldn't help connecting their call with the scene at the Sargents'.

It had been comical, though, the way John had caught Weston in his own trap; she lay down, thinking about it. "Amos," she heard John saying again, "you gallop to the Westons', and tell Mr. Weston there's something very urgent I must discuss with him." "At this hour, midnight?" "Right now." So Amos galloped off. "Mr. Weston says he's not feeling too well, and he'll come in the morning," Amos reported. "All right," John said; "go straight back and tell him this is a matter of life and death, and if he values his, he'll get right on his horse and get over here. Tell him the matter will not brook the slightest delay." Wearily, Amos again mounted his horse. Within an hour, there came the sound of hooves. "Well, and what is it?" demanded a swollen-eyed Mr. Weston. "I thought it was of paramount importance," John said, "to ask you just when you intended to deliver that hay." An unrepeatable stream of oaths proceeded from Mr. Weston. "I really did not think it could wait until morning," John went on; "some things just cannot wait, even for an instant. They cannot brook the slightest delay. I used my judgment, of course." "It will come in the morning," Mr. Weston bellowed, slamming the door on his way out. "What are you grinning about?" John asked Amos, lit up like a lantern; "you had two hard trips back and forth." "And worth every minute, too," Amos chortled; "well, I'm off." He left for the barn. Shouts of laughter promptly began flying from the barn windows. Amos was obviously retailing the joke. "Well, Edna," John remarked, sheepish, "I suppose you think I'm a childish fool." He was actually blushing, she saw, amused.

"I don't; I think that's the best case of an eye for an eye I ever heard of." "But we're supposed to live by the New Testament." "I just wish you could pull off the same thing every few days." "Monster," he said. Shouts of laughter were still fleeing from the barn, losing themselves in the mountains. "They'll have the cows up all night," John said, shaking his head. "Satisfied?" "Not just yet; Ten's still up," he noted, blowing out their light.

"*Lucille: A Novel in Three Parts.* Good Lord," John said, lying down next to her, "whoever that anonymous writer is deserves a great reward in the next life." "Oh, do you think it's one? I've begun to think Miss Anonymous is really a factory of writers." "That would go a long way toward explaining the phenomenon. Edna, if you spent all that money on nightdresses, why don't you ever put them on? It gets cold. Even *I* get cold." "The down quilts are so comfortable, that's why." "I have nothing to do with it?" "Certainly not." She turned on her side and began kissing him, his hair, his ears, his face. "You always *taste* so good," she murmured. "That's because your bread tastes so dreadful," John said, in his turn moving toward her. Why, he wondered, did he always hold her so, immobilize her, until he could feel every inch of her, solid and real, before he could let her go for the rest of the night? Whatever it was bringing. He loosened his grip. "I do love you," he whispered; "fleshy as you are."

"Well, we're ready," John said, returning. "That was fast," Edna commented, waking up; "the man was beyond help?" "The woman; she drowned herself in Coe's

Pond. She had her mind on her business; she must have been preparing for some time. She tied on huge bags of slate; it must have taken her a good amount of time to carry the stones there." "Does anyone know why?" "No. It's the second time, too. The first time she tried to poison herself and her children so they could all go together, but I wasn't here then, so I don't know what she put in the food, but none of them would eat it. She got some down, though, and the story got out." "What did people make of it?" "What they always make of it: temporary insanity. Who knows what her life was really like. Or her husband. He wasn't home much, but she always seemed happiest when he was gone. Maybe he mistreated her." "Do you think so? I can't imagine that." "That's good," John said; "I have no idea what brought it on; I never do. It's a rare thing whenever anyone does." "You were going to tell me about the Turners," Edna reminded him. "I've changed my mind; I've decided to wait until you meet some of them." "You're so inconsistent." "*You* never seem to have any trouble making sense out of me." They stood, arms around each other, waiting. Ten, watching from the window, thought: How they go together, like trellis and vine. She was not going to the fair. She had put on such a convincing performance about how she looked like such a stick in all her clothes, working herself into hysterics even she could be proud of, John thought it best not to coax her. After that, of course, Edna hadn't dared, either; it would have been taking a chance, and really, she did not want company today. Not even Ten.

The road jostled along with every conceivable kind of conveyance. "It seems as if the whole world is going today," Edna said. "The parade is the most important thing," John said; "no one ever seems to get tired of watching it." They had taken the handsome closed carriage. With every day that passed, John felt more, not less, protective of Edna. It was getting cold; it would be snowing soon, and he'd have to get her a dog, and send Hal out with her all the time. He wouldn't put it past her to get lost in a drift somewhere, just walking. Perhaps, he thought, he should let her ride Gray. Gray could find his way back from the moon; he really ought to be breaking in another horse. It didn't occur to him that he was far more likely to find himself marooned in drifts than his wife was, and in the middle of the night, too. "Well, we can't get lost today," Edna chirped; "we just follow along after the line of carriages." "That's about the sum of it." "Well, and I get to look at you, and without that worried look of yours." "And I get to look at *you,* fleshy little thing." "*Am* I getting fleshy?" "A little; it suits you." Edna settled comfortably back, her hand on his knee.

"How long have we been married?" he asked. "Two months, and eight days." "It seems like forever, doesn't it?" "Somehow that doesn't sound happy." "Well, it was meant to sound happy. What I mean is, I am happy." "You better be," Edna said. "And what would you do if I wasn't?" "Come with you every day, and tickle you all the time." "I am *extremely* happy." "Then you're saved," his wife sighed; "too bad. I was looking for a good excuse to come along every day."

"We're a parade ourselves," John said impatiently almost two hours later. "Will we get there on time?" "At the hour we left? We'll be early. You can drag me to each one of the pumpkins." "Pumpkins? I wanted to see the knitted hoods." "Pumpkins," John insisted, and so they jolted along. Well, Edna thought, in three or four hours she had better think up an excuse to run off somewhere and vomit in privacy.

The parade was evidently meant to go through the main street of Brattleboro. "Why, I can see Brooks House already!" Edna exclaimed; "it looks different somehow." The carriage jogged along. "Oh, they're all decorated!" Edna squeaked. "It looks as if Uncle Sam got here early, that's all," John said; "they say they called in special artists from Springfield, Massachusetts." "Oh!" Edna burst out; "that must be why the color scheme is so uniform." "Red, white, and blue is hardly a flight of the imagination in this country," John said, but she was standing up in the carriage, holding on tightly to his jacket shoulder. "Just don't fall out." He had to raise his voice. The streets were so crowded, there were so many vehicles, it seemed like pandemonium itself. "I've never seen so many people," Edna said out loud. She wouldn't have been surprised to find her mother and Mr. Siddons strolling in the crowd, the crowd jostling its fringes into the street, but then she remembered that they wouldn't be found anywhere alive near a fair; it just showed, she realized, how far that train from Manhattan had taken her.

They came to the beginning of the decorations. "That's old Dr. Houston's house. He hardly ever stays in it." John pointed to a bay window and balcony draped in the national colors. The next house was covered with large red, white, and blue circles, half circles, and quarter circles, triangular festoons. The bay windows and the piazza were covered with them, and the next three houses, too. "Oh, look at the Town Hall! What's that on the left?" Edna cried. The Hall was festooned in the same manner as the other houses, but there was a huge portrait of the Goddess of Liberty hanging to the left of the building, framed in the same national colors. "A very patriotic state," John shouted above the noise. "Are we at war perhaps?" she shouted back. "Not that I've heard. There, look at that! That's different." He pointed at a huge house decorated entirely with autumn leaves and grasses. It immediately stood out from everything else. "I bet everyone's mad about that," John bellowed to his wife. "But they're supposed to be proud of their autumns." "But they all decide when to show it, at times like this, anyhow." "Oh," Edna said, bewildered. They drove on, Edna clinging to his shoulder, peering at each of the buildings. Finally they came to an enormous field where the carriages pulled off, and the spectators had a clear view of the empty road. How can they ever fill this field? Edna wondered, but before an hour was up, the carriages were gone from the road and a feeling of excitement was rising in those waiting.

From the road below, Edna and John could hear the excited screams: "Here they come! Here they come! They're coming!" "We'll be able to tell what's coming long before it gets here," John told her; they were accustomed to conversing at the top of their lungs. "The fairies! The fairies are coming!" came the next shout. Edna looked questioningly at John. He shrugged as if to say he had no idea of what that might mean. Finally along came a lone horse, bearing a sign, "Fairy Brigade," followed by a trail of little wooden platforms, each one sporting a little child dressed up in white, head to toe, little white wings attached to their backs, each child twirling slowly, like small figures on music boxes. "What balance!" Edna exclaimed; "they're too cute for anything!" She wondered how old *her* child would have to be before she could spin on a platform like that. "That's a detachment of special police," John shouted as the next group marched by, and then a marching band, playing as they went.

"Who are those ladies?" Edna asked; a group of mounted women, dressed, like the houses, in red, white, and blue, pranced by. "Mounted ladies," John answered, grinning. He was waiting for the carts and floats. "*Look* at these coaches," Edna said, pointing; "it must have taken them days and days and days to get them ready." "And days." Coach after coach went by, wheels covered in satin, carts so heavily laden with flowers their walls seemed like moving bridal altars; then a tandem, drawing a huge dogcart covered with wild double sunflowers and evergreen branches. A little girl, her hair covered with an ivy wreath, twined with orange and yellow flowers, sat in the middle, holding a wand. "Oh, that one is nice," Edna said.

Then came the floats. One bore a colonial house of yellow and white, trimmed with green. Another was the Swedish Float, the spokes draped in Sweden's colors, the tent made of red, white, and blue stripes. Then the fourth grade's Harvest Float, representing the Pilgrim Fathers' landing, a large black boat in its center, and the Pilgrim rock in the front, and everyone in the float poised to climb upon it, all garbed in antique style. Then came a float carrying a boat supposedly resting on green waves, decorated in yellow and white, its occupants entirely white. Finally came old Dr. Houston's float. The doctor had created an "Old Homestead," it's little house made entirely out of cornstalks, and a window and chimney in its rear. The doctor himself was guiding two oxen made of cardboard, and the family were in the yard standing amidst cardboard pigs and chickens, the five children in the yard picking vegetables, which they threw into harvest baskets. As the went by, John stood up, and also leaned forward.

The float of the Nine Muses drove up and began passing them. "Nine Muses?" Edna asked; "I thought there were seven." "Isn't it the Seven Graces?" "No, I think it's Muses." "They must have added two local ones, then." Just as the cart was about to pass them, the Muses in its center suddenly began sinking. "Oh no!" Edna gasped; she could see the bottom of the cart begin bulging. The coach stopped abruptly. Slowly, the next layer of Muses began its disappearance, and, instantly, the remaining three fell through the floor. "Oh, it's collapsing!" Edna was shouting, along with everyone else. People were running in all directions, diving under the cart, climbing over it, slowly pulling out angry young women draped in Grecian gowns of pure white.

"Oh, they do look so funny," Edna giggled; "we ought to feel sorry for them," she chided John, who was already laughing. "John, we *ought* to feel sorry," but she was laughing, too. "Oh, they do look ridiculous!" Edna shrieked with laughter. "It would have been better if the Old Homestead had gone under." "What!" Edna exclaimed; "and predict the end of the whole world?" The more she thought of the collapse as prophetic, the funnier the collapse of the Muses seemed. She couldn't stop herself from laughing, even when her side began hurting and she had to press her hand into it. She laughed until tears ran down her cheeks. John, watching her, felt the contagion, and was soon bellowing himself; whenever one came close to stopping, they looked at the other, and the laughter began all over again. John wiped his tearing eyes with his coat sleeves. "Oh, this is dreadfully unsympathetic," Edna moaned with laughter. John was breathless. The people on their left glared at them from their carriage. This only made matters worse. When the people on the right took it upon themselves to do the same, both lost control altogether. Finally, the wreckage was removed from sight, the women in white angry as wet cats, hissing at everyone who tried to help them. That was too much altogether.

When all traces of the Muses had disappeared, and the music float began its melodic approach, Edna nudged John. "I think we had better get a look at Floral Hall; I promised Ten." "Getting tired of it already?" "Well, a little. But I *do* want to see the pumpkins." They set off through the crowd, holding to each other like drowning men. "I'm going to make a list," Edna told him; "or I'll forget it all." "No doubt about that." There were doilies and crazy quilts and knitted hoods, veils, flowered ribbons, plush boxes for jewelry, pickle dishes, rag carpets, covers for sofa pillows, oil paintings, paintings on glass, rose lamp mats, coin collections, plus letter holders. To Edna, it seemed like a Noah's Ark of objects, except that she seldom saw two of anything, unless they were buttons. "There must be," Edna exclaimed, "one of everything under the sun here!" "There's one of me," a woman said at her elbow. It was Alice Moffat. "Oh, John," Edna said; "this is Alice Moffat." "He's met me before, but not at my best; I was usually in the process of adding another member to the town." John grinned at her. "You do look different standing up." "I suppose that's a compliment," Mrs. Moffat said shyly. "We met at Mrs. Grimsby's; the day I went there with Ten," Edna explained. "I hope my sister didn't have hysterics *there*," John said. "Oh, she was very good," Edna said; "John, would you mind clinging to the pillar a minute? There's something I wanted to ask Mrs. Moffat."

She had decided to take this woman, the only one she knew in town, into her confidence; she *had* said she wanted to be called upon if there were difficulties. "Go ahead," John said, puzzled. "Alice," she said, "I'm afraid I'm going to vomit. I don't want my husband to see me." Mrs. Moffat, without asking any questions, took her by the elbow and steered her quickly out of the room, out of the hall, then into the field behind it, over to a huge clump of elms. "I'll stand in front of you," she said; "go ahead." Edna promptly vomited. "You're expecting, aren't you?" Mrs. Moffat asked. Edna's pale face turned toward her. "I don't want John to find out about it." "Why? Doesn't he want children?" "Yes. But he wants a wife more." "Oh." "You won't tell anyone? Not even Mr. Moffat?" "Not even Mr. Moffat." "Oh, thank you," Edna gasped; "I was so worried about how to get away when this happened." "Well, we must be lucky for each other," Alice said; "come, I'll take you back." She was a little, plump woman, almost as round as she was wide, dressed in clean, faded muslin, carefully ironed. A farm woman, Edna thought; I never thought I'd have much to say to a farm woman. She wasn't sure she had much to say to one now, but she did feel better in Alice's company.

"Well, Doctor, here is your wife; she wanted to see the pumpkin and take you to it, but we couldn't find it in here." "It's in Agricultural Hall, you old biddies," John teased; "come on; I'll take *both* of you." "This way to the three-hundred-and-twenty-four-pound pumpkin," a barker was crying. Three hundred and twenty-four pounds! Edna thought; how big could anything grow? Unaware, she patted her stomach. Surely she wouldn't produce anything the size of that pumpkin. Alice was smiling at her; John's eyes were fixed on the pumpkin. "You could make a few pies from that, I guess," Alice said. "Where have you gotten to?" a male voice asked. "Oh," Alice said, "I'm sorry, Howard. I just seem to have wandered off. I guess you're champing after the draft oxen." He nodded. "Well," Alice said, "good afternoon, Dr. and Mrs. Steele." "Good afternoon," her husband echoed. "Enough?" John asked. "Missing your invalids already?" "As you see, they're all here. A nice woman, though, that Mrs. Moffat. Although how they get along is beyond me. Well, that's one family that won't produce criminals; sometimes I think it would be best to drown some of the others at birth." "Restless?" Edna asked again. "I suppose I am." "Well, I've had enough." They began the intricate process of finding their carriage. "Shouldn't we buy something first?" John asked, pausing. "I don't think I have the patience." "Well, that's good," John said; "we're almost there." They started home.

Shortly after the fair, the weather turned colder. Edna accompanied John less and less on his rounds; her husband assumed this new development had something to do with the inexplicable derangement of his sister's nerves. But just before Christmas, Edna decided she couldn't continue to keep her condition secret. She and Ten thought it would be better to have Edna tell John; if he guessed, they agreed, that would be worse. All one Wednesday, Edna prepared herself. "No Nervine in the house?" she asked Ten, pacing up and down the parlor. "You're making me dizzy," Ten complained; "you really will start my nerves up. Stop it. He'll live through the announcement." "If I could be sure!" "Well, *I'm* sure; he's not that bad at swallowing the inevitable. He won't choke; don't worry. Edna, sit *down*," she ordered, looking up. "Perhaps he'll come home very late." "Well, I certainly hope not; I'm not sure I could stand it." "What *will* I say?" Edna wailed for the hundredth time. "You'll think of something." But Ten was worried. "I could pretend I was frightened," Edna considered. "No, I don't think that would be a good idea." "Then I can't think of anything!" "But he's not even here yet; when he gets here, it will come to you." "Like the Seven Plagues." "Like the Nine Muses." "Oh, dear," Edna sighed, collapsing into her chair. "And stay there," Ten said. "Oh, *dear*." "Not more sighing!" Ten protested. She looked at the mantel clock. Eleven. Could she live through five more hours of this? She saw Edna's eyes fixed on the clock; apparently she was thinking the same thing.

At last, Edna retreated to her room. There was no reason, she decided, for both of them to suffer, especially since Ten had not yet finished *Minerva;* she couldn't understand that. After all, *Abigail* had just arrived from England. She lay down on her bed: just for an instant, but, as was usually the case now, fell immediately asleep. A familiar, almost inaudible squeak of the door woke her at once. "What time is it?" she asked hoarsely. "Five-thirty." "Five-thirty; is Ten up?" "She's not in the parlor, and the light isn't showing under her door." He sounded tired.

"What was it today?" Edna asked as usual. "Two suicides, both men, both dead by hanging, three cases of consumption, all under one roof, one woman with what's undoubtedly an ulcer, two cases of pneumonia, and the biggest abscessed boil I ever saw. And one old lady dying of old age while the rest of the family creeps around with rheumatism. Whatever the next world is, she'll be happy to see people standing up straight there." "Did I miss anything important?" "I did wish you were there for the abscess; I thought you could probably dream up a broom handle for the scalpel; then I could have operated from across the room." "It didn't get in your eyes, did it?" "No; by now I look the other way. It's automatic. I never make a mistake, either. Looking the other way is better than closing your eyes. I wonder why that is." "I don't know. Any babies; no babies?" "Not one. There must be no flowers for the bees to hide them in. That's everyone's favorite explanation for their mode of arrival this year."

"I'm pregnant," she announced suddenly. "What did you do?" John asked; "search through Ten's geraniums?

Are they hard to find this time of year? The one you got was very quiet, though." He pretended to listen, sitting down on the bed's edge. "John," she said, putting her hand on the hollow of his back, "I'm pregnant. I expect to produce something or other in April, the end of April. A spring baby. It will be coming out of a crocus, I guess." "You're not serious," he said flatly. "It's not a question of seriousness; I am pregnant." "No, you're not." "I am." He turned to look at her. "Why are you saying this to me?" "Because you're the father of the child; you're my husband," she answered, starting to cry. "How can you be pregnant? I would have noticed." "But you didn't want to notice!" "There would have been signs," he said faintly. "There were signs; there are signs." He suddenly fought a desire to jump out and run into the snow, just as he was, in his white wool underwear. "What signs?" he asked, barely audible. "Cessation of menstruation, vomiting once a day for almost three months, and that fleshiness we kept talking about, only it's all in one place." She tried to make the description as routine as possible; perhaps that would make it easier.

"I would have seen you vomiting," he said in the same flat voice. "You almost did, at the fair. Remember when I went off with Mrs. Moffat? That's why." "But your dresses; they're not any tighter. You're wearing the same ones you wore in September." "That 'National Costume'? Ten and I invented it to conceal the evidence. And her fits of the blues. We invented those, too. There's nothing the matter with her. We wanted an excuse for me to stay home more. I was so sleepy all the time." "And now?" "Now I'm very energetic; I never felt better. I should be out cleaning the barn. I have so much energy I don't know what to do with myself." "Five months pregnant," he said; "five months pregnant." "I guess so; that's right." From the heave of his back, she knew he was crying. "John," she asked, pretending indignation, "what are you trying to do? Scare me to death? I'm enjoying all of this. I like it, watching my stomach stretch out, and those funny little kickings; I like it. Why do you want to go and scare me like that?" "I'm sorry," he wept.

"I thought," she said piteously, "you'd like it, having a child." "But I want *you*." "It hardly comes down to a choice, does it? I've seen you go off on those calls almost every day, and you never make it sound as if you're going out to meet death and destruction. Why can't you give me a little credit? Why, the last woman you delivered was over forty, and it was her first child, and I'm not even eighteen; you said yourself: the younger, the better." "Eighteen," he echoed. "John," she remonstrated, *I'm* the one who's supposed to be frightened. And it's not as if there's anything we can do about it. And besides, I don't want to." "Mrs. Moffat knows," he said; "and who else?" "Mrs. Grimsby; we had to tell her. She saw the change in my measurements." "Oh, Lord."

"No one else knows," she burst out; "except Ten. I didn't know you thought I'd be such a dreadful mother; I didn't think you'd take this as a disgrace. I can always give the baby away to some sensible woman." "Give the baby away? Are you out of your head?" he shouted; "completely insane? Who said anything about giving the baby away?" "Jimmie will be awfully upset." "Jimmie! *He'll* love it. He used to mother all the litters out in the barn." Well. He seemed to be calming down. "You're sure?" he asked. "Feel," Edna said, placing his hand on her abdomen. The little creature obliged by a flurry of kicks. "He's angry with you," Edna righteously assured him; "he expected a warmer welcome." "Good God in heaven, she's right," John sighed. "Of course I am," she answered, annoyed; "we went to a great deal of trouble to keep you from finding out." "Are you sure you haven't had any trouble?" "Well, I can't sleep too well on my side anymore, and I'm forever off to the privy, but that's it. Now that the vomiting and the sleepiness are gone. I thought I was going to sleep for nine months." "I wish *I* could."

Well, thought Edna, enough was enough. "Do I resemble Serepta?" she asked abruptly. "Serepta? Not at all. What makes you ask that?" "It sounds to me as if you want her back instead of me. You can't seem to tell us apart, can you? I suppose you're sorry she died and I'm going to live. It's just as well I found out about it when I did." "You don't believe any of that nonsense?" he asked, turning to her. "Yes, I do, I do," she sobbed; "you're sorry she's dead and I'm alive. I guess I haven't been much of a substitute. You shouldn't have married me if you were still in love with her." She sobbed even more violently. She hadn't studied Ten these five months for nothing.

"Edna," he demanded, taking her roughly by the shoulders, "what on God's earth are you thinking of? If Serepta came back now, I'd put her in an extra room, lock the door, and throw away the key." "That's how you'd treat me," she cried. "And I don't believe you." "Edna," he said, his grip tightening, "will you stop? You'll make yourself sick. I love you. If I wanted a baby, I could have any of them tomorrow from the poorhouse." "You love *me?*" she wailed hysterically; "you dare say you love me, and in the same breath you don't want any baby of mine, but you'd rather go off and get one from the poorhouse? You don't care about me at all. I should have known, I should have known. I didn't know you at all when I married you. It's just like what happened last month." "What? What happened?" "That woman who killed herself somewhere in Michigan."

She's deranged, John thought, frantic. "What about her, what about her?" Her body was shaking so, the bed was beginning to quiver. "The Moffats were so happy she got married off, and then her husband left her in a hotel, taking some silver, saying he was just going out to have it marked, and he never came back, he just wrote her a note saying he never would live with her as man and wife, and he left almost everything valuable; he didn't want to rob her, he just didn't like her, and she killed herself. I should have known," she cried on; "it's the same thing here all over again. You're just taking longer to make your disappearance. It's your invalids that keep you here, that's all. You hate me, you hate me!" she shrieked.

Now he was positively alarmed. She could hurt herself and the baby if she kept this up. And could she possibly believe what she was saying? Could she possibly believe he hated her? "Please," he begged; "please. Stop it, stop it." "You're just saying that now because you're afraid I'll get sick and you'll have yourself to blame." "Saying what?" he asked, confused. "I don't know, saying anything, what difference does it make?" "Now you listen to me. I married you because I loved you. I still love you. I'm just frightened something might happen to you, that's all it is. I'll get over it. Will you stop that crying?" he demanded. She continued, even more loudly. In her own bed, Ten was sitting up, admiring the performance.

"Please," John begged, holding Edna tightly; "I can't stand this. You're deliberately torturing me." "No, I am not," she cried into his chest. "Then will you stop?" No answer. He sighed and marched over to the window with his wife in his arms, her nightdress trailing down like a waterfall. "Look at the snow, little person. See the big flakes." "All the better to throw me out in." "See the big snow flakes fly up and down," he crooned; "see how nice and clean it is. Baby likes the snow, doesn't Baby?" "Who are you talking to now?" she asked sarcastically, finally controlling her voice. "I'm not sure," her husband answered. "See the pretty mountains," he went on; "see the pretty barn." "That's enough of that," Edna pouted. She had stopped crying.

"Serepta never cried like this," he teased. "What *did* Serepta do?" she finally asked, poisonous. "She went crazy, just the same way you are. What a run of bad luck. Edna?" he asked, tentatively. "What?" "If I put you down, are you going to start up again? I'm very tired. I'm tired out." "You can put me down. I know how to walk. And I'm not off my head, either. A fine opinion you have of me." He put her down on the bed, sighing with relief, sinking down on it himself. "Five months?" he finally asked. "Five," she assured him. "And four to go?" "Four." "That's not so long." "You're not the kind who'll run away after the baby comes?" "Stop being ridiculous." He was thinking. Edna watched with satisfaction.

"Well, what is it?" he asked; "a boy or a girl?" "A boy." "You're sure?" "Absolutely." "What are we naming him?" "I thought we could name him Martin," she answered, blushing. "Martin. Martin. That would be a good name." "If you don't like it—the name, I mean—we can call the others names you like better." "The others?" "I want at least twelve." "I'm having my troubles with one; don't start up about twelve." "I have to start somewhere, don't I?" "Oh, you are a little idiot," he answered, getting up. "Where are you going?" she asked, pretending fright. "*All* the way to the vanity to get your comb. You look like a witch out of *Macbeth*." "Very nice," she said, dabbing at her eyes. "Well, that's just

371

what you do look like," he said, sitting down on the bed next to her, beginning to comb her hair. "Ouch!" she yelped; "you can't just pull my head off like that. You're supposed to brush it first." He sighed and went back for the brush.

"What did you do? Tie knots in it?" he asked, combing away. Jimmie was jumping at the ends of her hair. He kept on brushing. "Feeling any better?" "I suppose so." "Ready for the comb?" "I'll do that." She ran it through her hair expertly. "Do I look any better?" "The same as ever." "I told you so; I told you it didn't make any difference." "Then what's that kicking in your stomach? You swallowed a big frog?" "Very, very funny. And I suppose you won't want to touch me or anything. Well, Doctor, is it proper for us to carry on as usual? I want a medical opinion, that's all." "We can carry on a few more months"; still, the idea did make him nervous. Serepta hadn't wanted him within room's length once she knew she was expecting.

"It's snowing," Edna announced. "I told you that at the window." "I didn't hear you. It's so *quiet;* just like at the beach. This looks like a big storm." "You're not afraid of having the baby while I'm trapped in a drift?" "In April?" she asked; "a drift in April?" "Anything's possible up here with our weather. Perhaps you could write Virginia and ask her to stay with you." "I don't think so; in her last letter she said everyone was being as polite as could be and colder than Greenland. She was thinking of trying to get to California, something about starting all over again, and the weather being good for her. I don't want company, anyhow. I have Ten. And Jimmie." "A lot of help he'll be." "Oh, unusual events bring out the best in people." "He's not a person." "That's what you think." They sat on the edge of the bed, their arms around each other. "I think," Edna said, "we owe it to science to see how a pregnant lady behaves without her nightdress on." "Aren't you cold?" he asked. "I'm always cold; until you get in." "Then we had better make a dive for it." "It's a good thing this bed doesn't squeak," Edna said happily. "Sleigh beds hardly ever squeak," he answered, his voice thick with sleep; "can the three of us finally go to sleep?" "Which three?" "You, me, and the little kicker." "You forgot Jimmie." "The four of us. Can the four of us go to sleep? No one's going to stop getting sick just because you decided to produce a baby." "I decided?" She bit him sharply on the ear. "I hope you won't mistreat little Martin that way." "*He* won't be able to talk, at least not for a while." "Little Martin," John murmured, his eyes closing. Each time it was harder to open them again. Edna saw he had fallen asleep. It hadn't been as bad as she'd expected. This, she thought, this was more frightening than producing the baby. Life, she sighed. Still, she liked it. John was moaning slightly in his sleep; she put her arm over his chest. He slept peaceably on. Edna's own eyes were closing.

In the parlor, the poor geraniums were freezing to death. In her haste to remove herself from the scene, Ten had forgotten to light the fire for them. In the morning the first thing to greet her horrified gaze was pot after pot of crumpled green leaves, browning at the edges, the stems completely shriveled.

It was, Edna thought, looking out the window, a very snowy winter. In a few hours, sleighs would be flying all around. She would have to get Ten out of the house and into theirs. She had never seen such a delicate, graceful sleigh, bright red, with its sweeping, delicate arches. A snow swan; that's what she thought of every time she saw it, a red snow swan, if there was such a thing. Yes, it was time to go down to Coe's Pond to do some skating, although she might leave well enough alone, and not bother with the skating and the sliding. Perhaps Ten would want to slide, though; she smiled at the idea.

It was that strange time of morning when it was neither day nor night, but everything was visible once the eyes became accustomed to the light. The light reminded her of the feeling she had had in the forest, as if this, too, was a time when nature took note of itself only, mending and darning its elaborate fabric, thinking its own thoughts, letting those awake fend for themselves. If the world was a fabric, Edna thought, perhaps we see the wrong side of it. Perhaps if we could only turn it over, we would see the real tapestry, the real beauty. Although the wrong side, with its accidental threads forming trees and branches, mountains and valleys and roads, was beautiful enough. The snow was almost covering the tops of the high picket fence which ran around the house. The back door, she knew, would not open until someone shoveled it out; before that, members of the household would simply open the windows and leave through them. She loved the way the roofs were softened by the thick puffs of snow rounding their edges. All the houses looked like troll houses, and the fir trees were bent down under their own beautiful white weights. Confections. Magnificent confections. Yes, she thought, the snow was so deep one could just walk right off the porch, walk over the earth without touching it.

She wondered what the Munyans were doing, or what they had done. She hoped they had not been purified by the snow. Next year at this time, she thought, she would have a child eight months old. Some children were learning to walk and talk by that time. What would the child be like? She supposed she would prefer a Munyan child to most of the stick-in-the-muds she had met in this world. She was glad to be thinking this now, because, she thought, if there was a time nature was sensitive to human wishes, this must be one of them. She stood staring out the window so long she felt like one of the trees. The elms were completely bare except for the layer of snow lying along one side of each limb. They seemed so human in this winter; it was impossible to believe they would ever be green again. People, she thought, were more like evergreens; they chose their weather and lived in it. More or less. But their weather had less to do with climate and more to do with feelings. Hers, she decided, were summery, as if everything was already over. Over. She wished, fleetingly, she had more time to observe what was happening to her. But she supposed she would have other chances. She smiled inwardly; someone must have intended to stop the growth of the small round pine in front of the house. A ladder was still propped against it. It must have been there since August. Now it looked like an impromptu sculpture of the snow.

Everything, she thought, seemed a new creation of the snow. She should be out in it, without witnesses, just rolling over and over in it until she seemed part of the scenery. Jimmie wouldn't come out in *that*. Which was just as well. She wanted to go out in the snow alone. It was necessary to make peace with the seasons here. She had not yet done that with the winters. And their immaculate quilts. She was sure, she thought, it was a necessary ritual: lying down in the snow, on one of its quilts. Then she would become one of the snow's children. Protected, not endangered. It was a good thing no one could read her thoughts; she shivered, pulling her shawl tighter. She had always had a strange, mystical streak. Here it was, getting stronger and stronger. *Of course* she knew the baby would be a boy. She seemed to know other things, too, things which had gone before, things which had come after. They left their shadows when she closed her eyes; she hadn't yet learned to read them. And those faces she saw at night behind her eyelids before she fell back asleep. Who were they? Incipient souls? Souls which had come and gone? None of them were familiar. She had to ask John and Ten about the stories connected with the clock. Something was about to happen here, she thought, and it wasn't the fancy of a pregnant woman, either. She felt an arm creep around her waist.

"Don't you stay up wrinkling yourself," John whispered. "Can the baby stay up?" she whispered back. "He's wrinkled already." "Is he?" "Well, you would be, too, if you spent all your time floating around in the water." "What a way to think of it." "He'd be in pretty bad shape if he wasn't floating around," John said, tickling her side gently. Edna nodded, looking out the window. "Are you sure you're not lonely? You could invite anyone you wanted up here." "I have you and Ten and Jimmie and my books; I don't know where the time goes. Even if it does take me an hour to thread a needle."

She thought about the farm they lived on; it went on with its work, churning its butter, feeding the cows with grain and hay, the men watching for new little bossies in the barn, but it was impossible to get involved with it. It had a miniature, clockwork life of its own: cooking, and washing, drying clothes, ironing them. It had little to do with her. The farm was lovely, she thought, but almost a kind of scenery; they didn't really depend on it. Not like the farmers, the real farmers; the farm was their life. Her fascination with etiquette books was increasing, not diminishing. And there were always languages she hadn't learned; stories she hadn't finished, books she hadn't read. She supposed she was lazy, really lazy. Perhaps John was worried about that, the way he left her in bed with a book and found her there with another one when he got back. If he was, he never said anything; and it didn't happen every day.

She could understand his worrying over her preoccupation with etiquette; it seemed such an unlikely subject for a married woman, a married woman in isolation. "Don't worry about my reading," she had told John; "it's something necessary for me. Other people up here read the Bible; I have those books. I keep thinking there's something very important in them, some code everything is based on, some very important reason to have rules for every inch of human behavior. I want to try and find out what it is. But all I've learned so far is what everyone else has; that all of the codes are just elaborations of the golden rule. That, and they give some kind of protection to class structure. I'm not sure why that's so important." "Perhaps because the people who believe in those books feel more important in the elevated classes and want to make sure they stay there." "Do you think so?" Edna asked, looking up at him. He was tall as ever. "Everyone needs something to feel important about." "I suppose they do. What about the Munyans, then? What do they feel important about?" "How bad they are; they have quite a reputation. And it's not easy to stand out as they manage to." "Mrs. Grimsby, then." "She keeps going. Everyone marvels at how well she does it. Don't think she doesn't know it, either."

"But what kind of satisfaction is that?" "A sweet-and-sour one," John answered slowly; "it gives her a special position, but not special enough, so that even when she's congratulating herself on surviving so well she feels sour, empty, something like that: inside. And her dresses to be proud of. And funerals and weddings to attend. And that solemn feeling of importance you come across only at funerals because you're watching someone else lowered into the ground. 'What a nice person he was,' they say with their lips all pursed up. The corpse could have set fire to the state, and they go through it all: 'What a nice person he was'; such a pity to die so young, to die so old, to die leaving so many children, to die without leaving any, to die leaving a wife, to die without having married and tasted the joys of wedded bliss. They just fill in the blanks. Like the blanks on our wedding certificate. And it does make them happy in their sour way, belonging like that, everyone knowing just what to say, that feeling of belonging to something bigger than they are."

"We're not like that?" Edna asked. "Oh, yes we are; we're so special to each other, we can't imagine there's anyone else like us." "But there isn't." "Then we find our happiness in our differences." "But we're not sour," Edna objected. "I think we must be, somewhere; it seems to be the requirement of the human condition." "I don't think we are," Edna said, almost pleading. "Then why do we need people to disapprove of?" "We don't." "What about your Mr. Siddons?" "Oh, that ridiculous person," Edna burst out; "he's so pathetic in his silly illusions." "You see?" "But he is; he is pathetic." "Why are his illusions sillier than ours?" he asked, hugging her gently. Edna stared out at the snow, thinking. "I don't know." "At least," John said, "he has the courage to display his illusions and not hide them away like a miser. At least he doesn't feel superior because he thinks he has a treasure no one else knows about." "Am I like that?" she asked. "I don't know. Why," he asked, hesitant, "don't you ever talk to me about wanting to build a house? Ten told me all about it; you really haven't mentioned it."

"It would be so expensive." "You know that's nothing; and now, you have a splendid reason for building another house." "What will we do with this one?" "Let the servants live in it." "You're not practical," she sighed. "Neither are you; you're using economy as an excuse." "But suppose everyone in the county laughed at the house? How would you feel then?" "The same, I suppose." "Really? Is that true?" "It's true. I don't care much what they think. As long as you didn't design a giant igloo; the summers can be so hot here." "You really wouldn't mind," she asked, "if I started planning a new house, and sending to Boston for fabrics and furniture, and going off all the time with Ten to see to furnishing it?" "No. And it would be better than your living in whatever house somewhere in your imagination. People should try to realize their dreams, not live in them." "Why?" "Because you can't live on them."

"What's yours?" Edna asked. "Mine? To invent something that would keep faces, preserve them just as they were when they looked into the mirror. Some kind of mirror that didn't let the faces slide off, or change. A whole series of mirrors that kept the picture of each face as it was each time someone looked in it." "But that's impossible," Edna said; "there's no such thing. Except, perhaps, for painting." "Painting isn't accurate enough." "Well, and how will you realize that dream, then?" "I'll have to wait until someone invents the kind of looking glass I need, and meanwhile, I have the dream that someone will." "And meanwhile, are you happy?" she asked, tightening her grip on him. "Very; as happy as anyone can get on this earth." "Would you want the faces of the dead as well as the living? New ones as well as old ones?" Now the idea fascinated her. "All of them."

"It's like what Hal does," she mused; "going to all the funerals and weddings." "I suppose it is," John answered; "we're all half-witted, trying to get at the truth of things. My idea's probably more foolish than Ten's novels. But it's like your house," he realized; "you want one room of everything, a time machine to live in, a regular circus of the mind. The house would be a museum of your mind, wouldn't it? Except that people could walk through it. Or parts of it." "It sounds terribly egotistical," Edna said; "of course, the façade facing the road would be perfectly ordinary. It would be the façade facing into the pastures and the woods that would be strange. But it sounds so egotistical, no matter which way it faces." "It's more obviously so than winning the quilting prize at the fair, that's all."

"I *could* draw up the plans," Edna considered. "I wish you would; I keep waiting to see them, and I'm starting to feel as if we live in a rented house." "We can't have that, can we?" Edna smiled. He bent down and kissed the top of her head. "You had better hurry; you won't have much time with a new baby. And we had better see about a nursemaid." "Not to mention a tutor." A horse was wearily plodding up to the front of the house. "Well," John said. "Well," she echoed; "don't spend the day worrying." "I'll try; I may even succeed." "Well, I've got my robe on. I'll go out and get the message; you get dressed." He watched her tiny figure leave the room. "Something about fits," she reported, coming back, "and a little boy on another farm who stuck his arm in a vat of boiling water." "At least the sugaring season is over; water is easier than boiling sugar. I guess I'll eat in the carriage." "Take these lap robes, then," Edna said, pointing to the pile on the trunk at the foot of their bed. "Do you think the horse can pull all that?" "Put one on the horse; he'll trot along like a yearling." "I'd like to see that"; he laughed, kissing her goodbye. Edna stood immobile, watching him leave in the buggy, Flag sitting next to him, his furry back turned, as usual, to the rest of the world. She stifled a yawn, picked up a book, and slid back into bed.

A mirror that held onto faces. Would that be a good thing? Would it be right to interfere with the workings of memory? Well, she supposed only memories that *could* be interfered with *would* be interfered with. That was how things were. For most of the world, a mirror like that would change nothing. Something to sigh hypocritically over, something to moan over, the transitory nature of life, to moan how many that began the year with us, the old and the young, the rich and the poor, the learned and the unlearned, have fallen victim to the Destroyer—Death. As must we all. And then, of course, making themselves an exception to the rule. Yes, she knew what John meant about funerals. And such a mirror, well, it would alter very little, except for those whose minds already had such mirrors, uninvented, invisible, but there. The bed was so comfortable, and the room was so warm after John had put in that extra wood; no, there was no point in getting up just now. She could always start on those plans later. Later. She fell back asleep.

And so the winter wore on for them, Edna and Ten, sleighing and reading, reading and sleighing, poor Bertha doing her best to teach Edna embroidery, inevitably exhausting her supply of patience, seizing the fabric ruthlessly, stitching frantically away herself. Still, Edna would try again, and again, as if there were something important about the very nature of such activity. But she was that way about everything; even Bertha noticed it. And John and Edna, talking, warming each other, while every day Edna began to look, as she kept insisting, more and more like the three-hundred-and-twenty-four-pound pumpkin they had seen at the fair. There was no outside world. And then it was the beginning of April, crocuses bravely poking out of the cold earth, snow still clinging to its life under the evergreens, little green buds dotting the bare branches with point lace. And everyone in the Steele house waiting, as if everyone had taken a deep breath and had not yet dared to let it go. And, of course, it was Edna who seemed to feel the suspense the least. She had her duty to do, and she was doing it.

"Snow squalls!" Edna said, astonished, looking out the windows. Ten peered up from her book. "It looks like it's working itself into quite a storm; I'd wager it's going to be a later spring this year." "What is a late spring up here?" "The beginning of June." "I suppose they begin planting potatoes and things now," Edna said restlessly; "and hoeing out your flower garden." "Not until June, probably the beginning of June from the look of those windows." "Well, and what is the activity here all about, then?" "Sugaring. It takes them all over for the next month or so. They go up to the sap house and wait for the others to bring in the buckets; then they start boiling it down. It seems to me we make enough for the whole village, but John will have it done," his sister complained; "it's his supply of candy for the children and his source of eternal gratitude from the distracted parents. What they don't pour into little molds and stock up the pantry with, they keep for themselves." "We can go up there?" Edna asked nervously. "Why not?" Ten answered, beginning to observe her more narrowly; "when do you want to go?" "When they have more sap to boil." "Two weeks. That would be the best time." "Why don't we just go look today?" Edna asked, perverse. "All right," Ten agreed; my, but she seemed awfully edgy today. Fidgety. It wasn't like her.

They drove up to the sugarhouse. The drifts were still thick back up in the woods; the house itself was dark, smoky, and mysterious. "They've begun boiling sap," Ten observed. Edna was panting up the little hill after her. "My legs are so swollen," she complained irritably. "Then just sit down on the bench," Ten told her as they reached the house. One huge kettle was boiling on a tripod of some kind over a pile of blazing wood. "Is that it?" Edna asked, exasperated. "That's their lunch," Ten said. "Oh, miss," Bridget said, coming out; "I do hate sugaring time; it makes such slaves out of everyone. What's the matter with *her?*" she whispered to Ten, looking over at Edna, who was sitting on the bench, her expression distinctly cranky.

"It's too early for her to be sick, isn't it?" "I wish it weren't," Ten sighed; "I wish it were all over with." "It just might be, Miss Ten," Bridget said, looking over at her. "Not with my luck, it won't be. If you ask me, she's as nervous as a cat in a strange garret, but the minute my brother comes home, we have the Calm Madonna." "That's tiring her out, then," Bridget said. "If you ask me, the whole thing is getting like the sugaring season, she won't write her mother until she has something to show for it. That's what she said. I think she's getting downright superstitious. I wouldn't have thought it of her." "Maybe," Bridget thought aloud, "that's what happened to the pickle relish. The kind we chop up with tomato." Had they all gone crazy? Ten wondered. "Well, you know no one in the house likes it much, but we've kept on making it since Mrs. Steele, your mother, that Mrs. Steele—oh, there are so many Mrs. Steeles to remember now—since your mother died. She used to like it so much, your mother, I mean." "I know, I know," Ten answered. "Well now, Miss Ten, every time I go down cellar, there's another jar of it gone." "Rats," Ten said, dismissing it.

"Rats who come down with a spoon?" Bridget asked; "I found it there, yesterday, the spoon, and over in the corner, all those empty canning jars. There must have been thirty of them, and I don't think your mother's coming back for them, either." "Well, what is it you're driving at?" Ten asked; "do you want me to post Amos guard for the pickle-relish thief?" "Oh, Miss Ten; it's just that women get peculiar around this time. They get more peculiar the less time they have. That's all I meant about the pickle relish. We don't need anyone guarding it." She stomped off through the snow. Do everyone's servants talk to their mistresses like mine do? Ten wondered. Well, four weeks, or three, was not such a long time to live through. If the baby didn't arrive late; she'd heard John say hundreds of times that first babies came late. They'll be coming for me early, she thought, mocking the Reverend Pierce: in the Retreat. There will be rest for the weary. Personally, she doubted that last.

Meanwhile, Amos was pouring out ladlefuls of hot maple sugar onto the snow, drawing it into the most fantastic shapes, and Edna: she was gobbling it up, excited as a child. "Enough," Ten said finally; "you'll make yourself sick." "Just a little more," Edna pleaded. Amos looked at Ten. "*One* more ladle," she pronounced. Amos poured out two figure nines. "Very nice," Ten gloomed; "I thought you men were supposed to be oblivious to these things." "Some things are past ignoring, Miss Ten"; Amos grinned, going back to the sugarhouse. Odd, she thought; by now, she'd expected daily notices from Amos. Instead, he was taking the same interest in Edna he was taking in his pet spotted cow. Another Jimmie. "Edna," Ten scolded, "will you stop eating that? It will all end in a horrible stomachache." Edna was gobbling up the last of the sugar nines without bothering to brush off the snow. "It won't hurt her, Miss Ten," Amos murmured from behind her. "And is that your professional opinion?" Ten asked, sarcastic; "are you willing to explain a stomachache to Mr. Steele?" "I'll take my chances," he answered, pouring out more nines on the snow. Edna beamed at him. "And that is *it*," Ten ordered in a voice even Amos didn't dare disobey. Edna, chewing happily on the curve of another nine, looked nastily at her. She's still a child, Ten told herself. "Finished now?" she asked Edna; "we ought to be getting back for dinner." "Um," Edna murmured through another mouthful, holding the three other nines in her hand. "Well, come on, then," Ten ordered.

"Will you stop *poking* at me?" Edna complained as John felt about her abdomen. "Lie still. This is an examination, not a game." "Well, and how is the little stranger?" she asked, turning on her side in a pet. "He *seems* fine." "I wish you wouldn't act so surprised about it." "Oh, stop that now," John coaxed; "you just feel guilty because we can't carry on as usual." "It's not *all* my fault." He stroked her hair. Jimmie had learned to do the same, patiently pulling one strand after another through his mouth, a puzzled expression on his fuzzy face. He was used to fur coming to an end. But still, he kept on; he was washing *his* beloved pet. Between Jimmie and her husband, Edna finally cheered herself up. She was almost normal. And it was near the end of April. John, however, was again not sleeping well. He would wake in the middle of the night from dreams in which the funeral was going on all over again, except that it was Edna, not Serepta, in the casket. Or a little boy named Martin would walk up to him, dripping, and say, "Now you better take care of me." At such times, he would listen for the sound of Edna's breathing; if it was good and deep, he would wrap up in his overcoat and head out for the barn.

Amos was still keeping a fire for the animals. They would talk about rabies, runaway horses, anything that didn't have to do with birth and babies. "There's a woman over to Dummerston," Amos said, puffing at his pipe, carving away at something or other; "she showed all the signs of rabies, but she wasn't even bitten. She acted clear crazy and foamed, and the papers think she had a cut in her left hand and the dog licked at her and that must have done it." "Good Lord," John said. "Would that do it?" "Sure enough." "But she didn't seem terrified of water," Amos added; "at least that's what the paper said. So they're not sure." "I've never been sure that's a genuine symptom myself." "What do you know?" Amos asked the air, puffing. "I guess you'll be pretty busy tomorrow, boy," he predicted; "there's some kind of epidemic up on Lord's Hill." "What do you think it is?" John asked. "Well, if you're going after my advice, you must be turning gibbering idiot." He's like a second father, John thought; as Ben was a second brother.

Hal was sleeping peacefully on a hay mattress of his own construction, hay with a blanket thrown over it. "How's he doing?" John asked. "Him? Not so good; hardly any funerals about at all lately. He makes me read them out from the paper, the ones from all over the county." "Not many marriages this time of the year, either," John agreed. "It's too bad," he said, looking over at his brother. "Well, he has Edna to follow about." "You think she's safe with him?" "Couldn't be safer," Amos said placidly; "she's too small. He thinks she's a child. He's got more sense than to go near a child." "Well," John asked after a while, "what do you think it is up on the Hill?" "You will make a fool out of me, won't you?" Amos complained; "they had some kind of party got up for Grandma's anniversary, and now they're all having fits and seizures, everyone except Grandma, who knows more than to eat that food." "Summer complaint in the middle of the winter?" "I guess that's about the size of it," Amos nodded; "you go on back to bed. Everything's coming out just fine. Bad dreams, eh?" "I guess," John admitted, getting up. "Well, you're entitled. Go on now." And then John would go back to bed.

"Last day of sugaring," Bridget announced triumphantly after supper; "I'm going to bed early." Ten was exhausted. Should she go to bed and leave Edna alone in the parlor? "You look tired," she heard Edna saying; "go to bed. John's sure to get back soon." "Sure?" Ten asked. "I am, really." Lately, Edna had become considerably calmer. Ten decided to go to bed. Edna was left alone in the parlor, rereading Lord Chesterfield. She wasn't getting very far with her knitting. Still, she wanted to make *one* thing for the child herself. She decided to go out to the kitchen for a glass of milk. Just as she was going through the doorway, she turned around and saw a rat following her. It's awfully tame, she wondered, stopping to look at it, but it was very dim in the kitchen, the only light coming from the fireplace. She kept looking at the rat and the rat looked back at her. Edna walked all around it and tried to drive it back with a little broom she took from a hook on the wall, but the rat stood its ground. Edna was getting frightened. Probably the rat wanted something to eat itself.

She started to run, but the rat began running too; Edna put her hand over her mouth to stop herself from screaming. "Ten!" she cried, pounding on her door; "please come out! A rat's chasing me!" Ten, with a pair of tongs in her hand, appeared in the hall, ready for battle. "Where's your light?" Ten asked her. "Back in my room, on the other side of the rat," Edna sobbed. Ten went back into her room, and lit her own candle. "You hold this," she told Edna, wielding the tongs bravely. The two women hunted up and down the hall. "Here's the rat," Ten announced finally, picking it up.

It turned out to be Edna's knitting work. "He chased

me," Edna insisted; "I didn't know I had the ball in my pocket, the yarn, I mean." "You were just dragging the work after you," Ten said; "the faster you ran, the faster it ran." They went to look. "See; the ball fell out of your pocket when you came into my room and shut the door." "But I even saw his tail!" Edna wailed. "The needles are sticking out behind the ball." Ten pointed. "It's not a rat?" Edna asked, quavering. "It's a ball of yarn, that's all. Come on, dear, come to bed. I'll sit up with you. I want to finish *Lucille* or I'll never get on to *Abigail.*" "Is it a good book?" Edna asked piteously. "Very. So many mistaken marriages and fraudulent marriages; I would have thought the Pope would have been relieved to get rid of that country. Come on, into bed, and I'll sit here and read." She lit the wick of the kerosene lamp, and settled in her chair with a book. "Tuck up," she told her; then she decided to get up and do it herself. "There," she told Edna, stroking her head; it felt clammy. "There, you go to sleep. If you don't mind my sitting here." "I don't mind," Edna answered, her voice childish.

Every now and then she lifted her head to be sure Ten was still there. Ten pretended not to notice, but calmly kept turning page after page. She was too distracted to read a word. Finally, the sound of Edna's breathing assured her the child had fallen asleep. I'd better stay here all the same, she decided, beginning to read. "Lucille entered the sacred walls more at that instant impressed by the feeling that she was about to visit the last receptacle of the ancestors of her husband, than with any respect to the high destiny to which the building was dedicated. Nor was there any other thought in the mind of her companion, who led her straight to the recess from which descended the steps which led to the family vault. The sides of this recess were covered with various monumental notices of the Jameson family, but contained, in the imagination of Mrs. Evans, but the single marble which commemorated the virtues and the loss of her lamented superiors. With tears fast flowing and with a faltering voice, she began to comment and to explain; when Lucille's eye, glancing on an unadorned tablet of the purest white marble, read these words: 'Sacred to the memory of Jennie Rover! the only offspring of a widowed mother.' 'What is that?' said Lucille; 'had Lady Rachel Rover had a daughter?' 'Ah, madam, did you not know that she had?' returned Evans; 'I thought— I supposed— I thought you **must** have known all about Miss Rover.' 'Poor Lady Rachel!' said Lucille. 'Aye, poor indeed, madam!' replied Mrs. Evans; 'nobody knows what Lady Rachel has suffered! Nor how she has borne it!' Lucille became sick. She supported herself on an adjoining tomb. 'Let us go,' said she; 'I will come again some other time.' "

Why, Ten asked herself, was she sympathizing so with Lady Rachel and so little with Lucille? "Poor Lady Rachel," she repeated to herself; "nobody knows what Lady Rachel has suffered! Nor how she has borne it!" Just so, Ten thought; just so. The only child, too. The poor woman, to have all that responsibility. She was nodding over her book. Bridget peeped in, found both of them asleep, but decided to leave the light on. "Ten," Edna was shaking her; "Ten, wake up." "What now?" Ten asked wearily; "an army of mice drilling up and down the bedclothes?" She looks terrified, Ten saw, waking with a start. "It's this funny feeling," Edna hurried on; "right across here." She drew an imaginary line across her pelvis. "It hurts. I don't feel right." "It's not a stomachache?" She was already anxious. "No, I know what that's like. Isn't John back yet?" She saw from the look on Ten's face that he was not. "And it feels like something inside dropped down," Edna said; "but I'm supposed to have another week." "Women don't work like clocks; you get back into bed while I get Bridget. Can you stay here alone?" "I don't think I can walk," Edna half cried; "my back hurts, and something hurts when I try to sit up. It's like something's pressing down there. I have to urinate!" she wailed. "The chamber pot's right there; that's nothing to worry about." "But I don't think I can get onto it!" "Just wait one minute, one minute, and Bridget and I will help you." She flew down the hall, returning with Bridget, who had first shaken Bertha out of her bed. "This does sound like the end of it," Bridget whispered as they ran down the hall. "But she doesn't have any real pains!" "Now don't you get into a panic," Bridget warned; "that would be the worst thing for all of us. Some women don't have much in the way of pains. They just pop." But Ten was thinking of Serepta. "They're not all like Serepta," Bridget said, reading her thoughts.

They went in. Edna was writhing on the bed. "Oh!" she cried; "oh, it hurts, it hurts!" "Where does it hurt?" Bridget asked. "All over my belly; all over my body. My back. It hurts so. That's the worst thing." Bridget felt her forehead; it was damp and wet. "Where is Bertha?" she asked irritably. "You start in calming her down," she told Ten. "It's all right, it's all right, Edna," she chanted. "But I can feel something," Edna moaned, "twisting; oh, it hurts. Can't you give me anything for the pain? John must have something." "Edna, I'm not a doctor," Ten said; "just hold on. It will be over in a minute. It will all be over in a minute." "It's worse," Edna cried; "it's worse." "Describe how it feels." "Like a hot sheet pressing down on my stomach and something inside, hopping all around. I can't stand it; I don't think I can." "Here," Ten said, "hold on to my arm." Edna grasped it so violently Ten winced. "That won't do, Miss Ten," Bridget whispered; "not with your rheumatism. Here, Miss Edna, you hold on to this broom." Edna held on to the rat-fighting broom as if it were her only tie to the earth. "How are you doing now?" Bridget asked calmly. There was no answer, just the sound of Edna's gasping and panting. She placed her hand on Edna's stomach. It was moving about violently all right. "Oh!" Edna screamed suddenly; "oh! Something terrible's happening to me! Please help me," she pleaded; "something's tearing me!" Bertha had now arrived; Bridget automatically gave over to the expert. After all, Bertha had once been a midwife.

"Give me the lamp," Bertha ordered. "It's coming, it is. Look," she showed the other women, "there's the top of the head. It's not a breech anyways." They all stared. Edna was writhing and screaming automatically. "Go away," Bertha ordered Amos, barely turning around; "go get Dr. Steele if you want to make yourself useful." They heard him gallop off. "But the head's not catching," Bertha murmured; "I don't like that much." "Please," Edna was begging them again; "please give me something. Do something." She couldn't talk after that, just lay back moaning and holding on to the broom. Her hair, Ten saw, was soaking wet. So was her nightdress. Her body looked naked. "I think we should prop her up with pillows," Bridget ordered. "Don't touch me," Edna screamed; "I can't stand it; don't move me." "Now, Edna," Bertha insisted, "you be good; you be a good girl. You want this baby to get born, don't you?"

She let herself be lifted slightly; she was screaming like a wolverine, unaware she was making a sound. "It's worse, it's worse," she sobbed, and then the screaming began again. "Ergot!" she finally gasped; "I heard something," she panted, desperate, "about ergot." "That's dangerous," Bertha told her; "Dr. Steele always said that; it's to hasten labor." "Give it to me!" Edna screamed, flinging herself from side to side. "Edna, will you behave?" Bridget scolded; "we're not going to poison you. Not even if you scream your silly head off." "Please! Give me some. Anything, anything; I can't stand it." "The head's catching," Bertha said. "Now, Edna," she said gently, taking a towel from the shaking Bridget and slipping it under Edna's hips, "things are going to get worse before they get better."

"I'm going to die," Edna gasped; "I can't stand the pain." "It will get worse, Edna, and then it will get better," Bertha repeated. "Go get the sweet oil and some towels," she ordered Bridget quietly. Now Edna was screaming rhythmically; her voice had grown hoarse. "Why don't you try pushing down, Edna, since you can feel him?" Bertha said. "I can't, I can't," Edna screamed. The sound cut at Ten's nerves. She didn't know whether she ought to be grateful or terrified that John wasn't there. "Try," Bertha insisted. Edna took a deep breath; she tried pushing. Her head began swiveling back and forth on the wet pillow. "Dear God, dear God, dear God," she was screaming rhythmically. "Try again, dear," Bertha said; "you did such a good job last time." "I can't," Edna gasped; her moaning resumed, ascending, filling the room. "But little Martin is almost out," Bertha told her; "try once more for little Martin." Edna tried pushing again; now her shrieks were like gasps, magnified thousands of times.

Such agony! Ten marveled; such agony! Could she have gone through this? Could her mother have gone through this four times? Why did any woman have more than one child? "Again," Bertha instructed. Edna turned her head wildly on the pillow. "Little Martin is almost here," Bertha coaxed, while Ten stroked Edna's forehead. Bridget was returning with some oil and the flannel blankets. "Just put them down on the table near the bed," Bertha instructed without looking. "Oh, my God!" Edna was screaming; "oh, my God; I'm dying! You won't help me! I'm dying." "You are not dying," Bertha answered calmly; "push again." Little Martin shot from her body. Edna looked up, frightened. "What happened?" she asked; "it doesn't hurt anymore." "Little Martin has just made his appearance," Bertha said overjoyed. "Let me see him," Edna asked weakly. "One instant," she said, holding the baby by the heels, whacking him smartly on the bottom.

A new, thin wail filled the room. "He's all shiny and blue," Edna cried as they showed the little heir to her. "He's just not cleaned off yet, miss"; Bertha smiled, pressing her hand; "just wait until we wash him off. He has all forty of his fingers and toes." "Forty?" Edna gasped. "He's just fine, Miss Edna," she said, her back to the bed. She was expeditiously washing the baby down with sweet oil and wrapping him in a blanket. "Do we give him to her now?" Ten asked. "Not just yet," Bertha answered; "you hold him in the rocker. No, you're too shaky. Bridget, you hold him in the rocker. Keep him wrapped up. Now, Edna," she said, turning back to the bed, "there's one little matter we have to take care of, and that's little Martin's bathtub. See how big your stomach is? It hasn't come out yet." "Will it hurt?" Edna asked. "Yes, yes, it will. Almost as much as it did before." "All right," Edna said; she already sounded resigned to the process. "But it will be over very fast." Ten sat on one side of the bed, Bertha on the other, waiting. One stroked her hand, the other her forehead. "You did a good job," Ten said; "he's very pretty, little Martin." "Handsome," Edna corrected weakly. "Both," Bertha mediated. "Sleeping," Bridget put in. "Is he breathing?" Edna asked.

"Will you stop that?" Bertha asked; "they're so little you can see them breathe from across the room." Edna was about to ask that someone make absolutely sure, someone ought to get a mirror and put it in front of his mouth, but she was seized by a knife-like pain. "Oh no," she wailed; "it's starting again." "The bathtub, dear," Bertha reminded her. "It's another one," Edna screamed, writhing. Bertha shook her head. It had never been her luck to deliver anyone who didn't have much feeling for pain. Edna was desperately clutching at her abdomen, trying to sit up. "Lie back, lie back," Bertha ordered. The writhing began again. I can't stand any more of this, Ten thought. "Here it comes, here it comes," Bertha crooned; an enormous bloody mass began expelling itself. Edna was screaming as if they were boiling her in oil. "Just a few more minutes," Bertha said; "just a few minutes more. Just one more push." Edna shook her head no. "Miss Edna, you don't want to undo everything, do you? You want to be as healthy as Martin, don't you? Just one push." Edna pushed, screaming.

A wind rose in the trees as if the screams had stirred up the weather. "Snow squalls," Bridget murmured. "Snow?" Edna wailed; "isn't there any spring in this state?" She began twisting, helplessly clutching at her stomach. "Here it comes," Bertha said; "here it comes." Edna's breathing became less difficult, shallower. "I think we've got it all," Bertha sighed with relief; "the doctor can check on this when he gets back. Bridget," she said, "you take this out to the kitchen and put it somewhere safe; I want the doctor to have a look at it." "Is it over?" Edna asked sleepily. "All done now," Bertha congratulated her; "we'll just clean you up a bit." "Do you have to?" "You should see yourself," Bertha said. "All right," Edna agreed, peaceable. She had never, never been so tired. "John will be surprised," she said, almost inaudible. "I would guess so," Bertha agreed; "comfortable now?" "Very." She purred like a contented kitten. "Now weren't you foolish to make such a fuss?" Bertha scolded. "Oh yes," Edna sighed. Ten's heart, however, was pounding so hard she was shaking the bed. "And to think this all started with a rat," she said to Edna; "remember this? It's in one of your books: 'I smell a rat, I see him brewing in the air; but mark me, I shall yet nip him in the bud.'" "He didn't get nipped, did he?" Edna asked, giggling feebly. Was this it, then? Ten wondered; was it really all over? She stroked Edna's hair, combing it. Then she realized Edna was sound asleep. "Bridget," Bertha ordered, "you stay in here and keep an eye on the cradle. We'll take turns. I want to talk to Miss Ten." Ten shuddered at the idea; *she* didn't need any lecturing; she needed crutches. Or an iron rod tied up and down her back.

"And how is the proud grandmother?" Bertha asked. Ten could not answer; she sank back against the wall. "Well, Miss Ten, look at it this way," Bertha whispered; "we won't have any more of those terrible funeral sermons to listen to. She's a good one, and fast." "Fast?" Ten echoed; "it took all eternity." "Nonsense; sometimes it can take days." "I'm surprised there are any humans left." Bertha took hold of her elbow. "Now *you* push yourself into bed," she instructed; "you're almost in shock yourself. But we won't have any more of those silly sermons, will we? Remember that nonsense over Serepta? I hate to admit it, but I was terrified to burst out laughing. That Reverend Pierce. 'She was a woman of many accomplishments and virtues, graceful in her movements, winning in her address, a kind friend, a faithful and loving wife, and had she lived, would have been a most affectionate mother, and she played beautifully upon the pianoforte.' "

"She played terribly," Ten said as Bertha, not bothering to turn back the bedclothes, tucked some blankets around her. "And she wasn't graceful, either." "Well, he had to say *something*." "I suppose so; he was always better at weddings than funerals. At least," she said, closing her eyes, "we won't have to go through this again." "Don't close your eyes on *that* thought," Bertha said; "she's likely to have one a year." "After all that agony?" "Oh, you take it from me, she's already forgetting. By tomorrow, she won't even remember it hurt much. It's what happens when she realizes she has a baby I'm worrying myself over." Ten was sound asleep. Well, Bertha thought, this was a good night's work; she went into Edna's room, and took over rocking the baby. "Get a rag soaked in sugar water; and oil him," she told Bridget; "then you can sleep for a few hours." She rocked the baby. Its little hand crept around her finger. I've forgotten, she thought, surprised at herself. She *had* had two children and a husband, until that train went and crashed near Brattleboro. She never thought of them now, she realized. Well, and she wasn't going to begin, either. But still, she felt such a sense of relief. *Something new was alive.*

It was sometime during one of Bridget's shifts that the sound of hooves came faintly through the closed window. Bertha went to the doorway. John was grayer than a frozen river. "You have a boy," she told him, "and a perfectly healthy wife." He pushed past her, into the room. "Don't you wake her up, Master John," she scolded. He picked up Edna's wrist, feeling for the pulse. It was strong and steady. He looked at the baby in its neat wrappings; he saw, pulling the blankets back, that they had even tied off the cord properly. The baby himself, having tired of the sugar water, was sleeping happily against Bridget. There was no sound of wheezing as he breathed. John went back out into the hall, a sheet of tears covering his face. "Well, and what did we tell you?" Bertha fussed; "you come and eat." He followed her, dazed, into the kitchen. If anyone had asked him, the next day, what he had eaten, he could not have told them. Bertha decided to wait until morning, and until after John had inspected the afterbirth, before she said anything about the blues she expected from Edna. She put him to bed in the spare room as if he were the baby. That Martin, she thought wearily, taking over for Bridget, is the most grown-up person here.

"Well, how was it?" John asked, smiling down at Edna the next morning. "Just as nice as could be"; Edna smiled; "it wasn't any trouble at all." "That's good"; John beamed back. Well, in this, at any rate, she was like most of the others. "So you and Ten enjoyed yourselves?" "Ever so much." Ten was still asleep. John assumed she had gotten to bed very late. It occurred to him, fleetingly, that she must have been terrified something might go wrong, of having been blamed for it. "And the nurse-maid is feeding little Martin," he told her. "The second nursemaid should be here later today. I had them picked out weeks ago," he admitted shyly. "The women in the house were apparently afraid to give little Martin anything but sugar and water until I got here to approve every ounce." "I don't wonder." "How are you feeling?"

he asked again; why couldn't he get this silly grin from his face?

"John," Edna asked suddenly, "you said two nurse-maids? Why do we need two? Is there something wrong with the baby?" "The baby is as fine as a baby can be." "You better let me see him," Edna said, alarmed. "He'll be right in; he's eating his meal." "From a bottle or a wet nurse?" "A wet nurse; that always seems safer." "I don't really want to nurse." "I didn't think you would; you'll enjoy it more this way, believe me." "John," she said, hesitant, "I'm still very fleshy." She gestured at her abdomen. "That's all normal; it will take one week, or two, and then the swelling goes down completely. You won't even know you were pregnant." Her face darkened.

"I do want to see the baby," she reminded him. "You will, you will; you don't want to starve him to death. You don't want to start him out a society baby, making calls the minute after he's born." Edna smiled. "Ten even told jokes last night," she remembered. "She did?" "Yes, she did." There was a rap at the door. John got up and opened it. "The nursemaid with little Martin," he announced proudly. John took the baby and carried it over to Edna. She touched its face here and there with her index finger. "He's real," she marveled; "and breathing. Can he see me?" she asked John. "Not yet; he's seeing his own world, dreaming." "Probably of rats and maple sugar." "Rats?" Edna told him how her labor had started. "You don't follow anyone else's example, do you?" he laughed. "And it's a good thing no one follows mine. John," she said, her mood changing as suddenly as the direction of wind in the trees, "he's too little. He's yellow." Panic was seeping into her voice. "And he's purple all over, purple blotches. Look." "That's from coming through such a small door; don't worry about it. By the time he opens his eyes, the purple will be all gone. It's the same thing that happens when you get bruised." "Poor thing," Edna said.

"But, John, he's yellow. He looks like a lemon. He has cholera," she cried out hysterically. John sat down on the bed, taking her hand. "He has a little jaundice. You'll see; he'll be all pink in the morning." "Are you sure?" "If I'm not, who should be?" "Well, that's true; you are a doctor." John touched her cheek lightly, then the baby's.

"I never thought I'd have a child," he said. "You're sure this one is all right?" "I'm sure, I'm sure. You know me; I couldn't hide it if I were worried." "That's true enough."

"Well, and what about you?" John asked. "Oh, I'm so tired," Edna droned, "as if I'd swallowed a drug." "That's good," he said; "then we won't have to tie you to the bed." "No. I've never been so drowsy." "You've never worked so hard, either." "I think it was harder on everyone else." "I doubt that somehow." "But, John," she said. He looked at her; her eyes were filling. "Sometimes I feel so blue; I know I haven't been up very long yet, but sometimes I feel so blue. I don't know why I do. I feel a little—crazy." "It's a big change," he said, "having a baby in the house." "I don't know if that's it." "You don't know if what's it?" "If that's what's the matter." "Well, we'll just wait and see. Don't worry; you can get blue as indigo, but you're not going crazy." "Are you going on rounds today?" she asked. "Unless you need me here." "No, you go on; I'm so sleepy. I don't have much society to offer." "Well, then, you two sleep, and I'll try to get back early." "That's good," Edna said, surrendering the baby to the nursemaid, pressing her face into the pillow, falling sound asleep while he watched.

Sometime later, Edna woke up and found herself alone. Well, I can get up, she told herself, defiant. Oh, I'm sore, she thought, sliding carefully off the bed. She walked carefully to the window. She wasn't all that tired; they were making too much fuss. There was snow all over the ground, and almost the beginning of May. What a country! she sighed, suddenly feeling drained, exhausted. She held on to the windowsill; she was dizzy. "Edna!" she heard Ten's indignant voice behind her; "you get back onto that bed. What are you thinking of?" "I don't know," she said vaguely, letting Ten help her back; "I don't seem to think at all." "That's a change for the better." "I don't know. I don't know," Edna answered. She looked confused, lost.

Ten noticed the signs first. Edna showed less and less, not more and more, interest in the baby. Now they had to coax her out of bed into the chair next to the window. She hardly ever spoke, except to answer questions. "I told you, Miss Ten," Bertha whispered; "she wasn't pre-pared. In the head, I mean. She's worrying herself about something." Ten decided to talk to her. "Edna," she asked, looking casually up from *Abigail,* "do you want anything to read?" "No." "Are you hungry?" "No." "Lonesome?" "No." Ten tried again and again, always with the same results. She told John about it that night. "Would it make you feel better," he asked Edna, "if I gave up Bachelor Hall and came back into bed? Even if it is early. You're supposed to be resting and I snore and turn and twist around. Would it make you feel better?" "Yes." "Are you sure?" "Yes." "We should think about little Martin's school," he said, trying a new tack; "should we send him to the district school with the others, or should we have tutors?" "I don't know," Edna answered, bursting into tears. John sat down on the bed, picking her up and holding her. Her whole body was quivering. "It will be all right, it will be all right," he kept repeating, but really, he had no idea what was wrong.

The tenth day after Martin's birth brought no change in Edna's state of mind. Ten and John sat down to dis-cuss sending for a specialist from Boston. The only cheer-ful place in the house was the nursery, where Bridget, Bertha, and the two nursemaids, Ellen and Minnie, flitted in and out like angels on extremely important missions. But they had stopped bringing the baby in to his mother, and all of them felt some reluctance at bringing him to Mr. Steele, although he always took the baby, gently hug-ging it, rocking it, and, unaware, smiling everlastingly at the tiny infant, who had, by now, turned pink and could follow the track of a moving finger. It was in the midst of this discussion that they heard the sound of an approaching carriage. "It sounds so loud," Ten whis-pered. "That's because it's all stones again. The snow's gone out in front," John said; "I wonder who it is."

Bridget ushered Mrs. Moffat into the kitchen. "Oh, Mrs. Moffat," Ten said, polite, if cold; "how nice to see you." "I came to see Edna," she said, going straight to the point; "I've heard she's depressed. Is that true?" Ten said nothing. "Yes, it is," John said sadly; "we don't know what to do with her." Alice Moffat removed her own coat and was about to put it over the back of a chair, but Bridget swept it up. "Does she talk?" Mrs.

Moffat asked. "If you can call 'yes' and 'no' talking."
"Does she take an interest in the baby?" "No, no, she
doesn't." "Well, I had better talk to her," Mrs. Moffat
said briskly. "You'll only upset yourself," Ten said. "Oh,
I'll take that chance. There's something in her, you know.
It's a matter of finding the right bait, that's all." They
looked at her, despairing. "Well, it can't hurt to try, can
it?" John asked his sister. "Things can't get much worse,"
she agreed.

"Oh, come," Mrs. Moffat objected; "I would have come
in any event. If she won't talk to me, she won't talk to
me." "Well, come on, then," Ten said. "Let Bridget take
her," John interrupted. Alice opened Edna's door without knocking. "Don't move; it's only me, Alice Moffat,"
she said, pulling up a chair. "Don't say hello," she babbled
on as if nothing was wrong; "don't say anything. It's so
nice to have a captive audience who can't do anything
but listen to me. At least you can't get out of your bed
and run away the way everyone else does. Well," she
chattered, "you certainly have an ugly baby. But I suppose he'll improve. Probably by the time the potatoes are
dug up he'll look better than they do. I hope so, anyhow.
My last one started out looking so adorable, he was a
picture, and you should see him now. Put him next to a
pickle and it would take Solomon to tell them apart.
Edna," she asked appealingly, "I know I'm here to call
on *you*, but if you would only let me sit here and read
a paper without talking, I'd be so grateful I don't know
what I'll do. I haven't heard any quiet since the day I
was married. No, since the day I was born. There were
already four before me. Edna, I won't make a sound; I'd
give forty years of my life if I could just sit still and read
without one of the children coming in and getting after
me. Can I?"

When she got no answer, she opened her paper, and
began reading. "Good Lord!" she exclaimed to the air;
"three suicides in one hotel in one night, and all the
rooms adjoining. What a place it must be! I'm not taking up residence *there*. One, two, three, four divorces,"
she read out; "you'd think people would think twice before they tied that knot. Oh, well, I have the three back
issues and I can catch up with *Blackwater Mansion*." She
fell to reading. "Alice!" Edna wailed. "What?" Alice

asked, continuing to read. "There's something wrong with me." "Oh? Did the doctor say so? I always wondered what going off your head was like. I've thought about trying it, especially when it rains and the children are all inside, but I've never begun to manage it. What makes you think you're doing it? I'm envious." Edna stared at her. "I am; I am envious."

"I don't love the baby," Edna said, pulling her sheet up over her face. "Well, why should you?" Alice asked; "they're just little worms at this age. Eat, sleep, eat, sleep, dirty themselves." "But you're supposed to love them right away." Edna cried quietly. "Well, *I* didn't; and no one's ever told me I was a bad mother." "You didn't?" "No. I didn't. Sometimes I still don't like them much." "Do you love them now?" "Of course; most of the time, anyhow; you live with a rocker long enough, you come to love it." Edna kept on crying, but she was thinking. "Alice, suppose *he* doesn't like me?" "Give him away, the ungrateful beast." "I'm serious," Edna pleaded; "suppose he doesn't like me?" "He will," Alice answered, looking down at her paper.

"How do you know?" "Because," Mrs. Moffat answered without lifting her eyes, "they don't have much choice, do they? They only have one mother. You won't like him all the time and he won't like you all the time; it's only fair." "But he's all new," Edna sobbed; "I could ruin him." "You make him sound like a stew," Alice said, finally looking at her; "if you're worrying about ruining him, he'll come out fine. Most everyone comes out fine, and no one even thinks to worry about it. Why don't you come out of that tent? You look ridiculous." "Do you think so?" Edna asked, still under the sheet; "that he'll come out fine?"

"Well, dear, I can only speak from experience. I don't know any more than the next one, but I have five of my own, and that's something, I guess. And I don't sit up all the time worrying about them, either. They'd just worry because I was worrying. I do my best; what else can you do?" "Those suicides you read out," Edna said; "there was one somewhere in my family." "All families have accidents; I know mine has," Mrs. Moffat answered simply.

"Edna, how much do you blame your mother for this

fit of yours?" "My mother?" Edna asked, finally lowering the sheet; "what does my mother have to do with this? She doesn't even know I had a baby. She didn't even know I was pregnant." "Well, who did have to do with this?" "I don't know," Edna wondered; "I guess I worried too much. About John." "You should have spent more time worrying about yourself; he can take care of himself pretty well." "That wouldn't have helped." "Well, that's sure what I would have told you to do if I'd been your mother." "It wouldn't have helped," Edna repeated. "What would have?" "Nothing." "So there, you see?" Alice asked; "you can't think *you're* the only one who's going to spoil the child. You have to give the rest of the world its chance. And the child, too. It can do a good job on itself. You're not the only one who'll be around. There's the whole world to make a mess of him. And good things happen, too. Like when you went along with Dr. Steele and saw my brother. You probably saved his life. *I* couldn't have done a thing."

"Oh, but, Alice, he *is* so ugly; I must be a monster. That's all I think, how ugly he is, and after all we went through, and he's not even human. He just lies there." "City girls," Alice said. "What did you expect him to do? Get up and walk around the first day like a colt? They're all ugly when they start out. Just have a little patience. Everyone knows their baby is ugly, all squashed up and banged around; no one admits it, is all. And let me tell you, when I had my first, I didn't have any nursemaids, and the sight of that ugly, helpless thing, I used to think about strangling it, or dropping it. 'Accidents can happen,' I used to say to myself, and I got awfully near the stove and the washbasin, too; 'accidents can happen.' I thought *I* was crazy for a while, believe me. I probably was," she said, thinking back. "I used to scream at Howard for no reason at all. One day he didn't eat his supper and I started screaming if he didn't like my cooking, I wasn't doing any more of it, and I picked up his plate and threw it right out the window, and that was in the middle of the winter, too. The whole town was talking about it."

"What did they say?" "Oh, they all said what an impatient person, what kind of mother was that, but I tell you, the women in town were a lot friendlier after that plate flew out the window. We didn't come from such good stock, but that plate made up for a lot. Well, now, of course, if anyone tried to throw my son in a stove, I'd probably shoot him. I'm a good shot, too; it comes from shooting rats out the bedroom window." "Rats," Edna repeated. She suddenly began telling Alice about the ball of yarn and the knitting needles. "Oh, Edna," Alice said, laughing so hard she wiped at her eyes; "you *are* funny." "It was funny, wasn't it?" Alice was still giggling. "I sniff a rat, I see him in the air, say it again," she begged. Edna obliged. "Oh, Edna, you are a goose. I tell you what, if you don't like that ugly little worm after one year is up, I'll take him. We could even trade children; it would be a nice change. They're quieter when they're new, and that's something, I can tell you. Let's trade right now." "I better get a few more looks at him," Edna considered. "I guess," Alice answered, laughing; "I sniff a rat. That's just about how I talk. Oh, it sounds just about awful, doesn't it? Come on, Edna, come out of that bed," she said, getting up and turning back the covers; "come on out, you goose." She steered Edna over to the window. "There are buds on the trees!" Edna said. "If they improve, so can that horrible son." "I suppose," Edna said.

"And why haven't you told your mother?" Alice scolded; "she has a right to know. She's his *grandmother*." "Oh, that will just about kill her," Edna said; "being called Grandmother." "Your child isn't going to call anyone anything for some time; unless he's very special." "I suppose that's possible." "Definitely," said Alice; "or maybe he's the stupidest thing the county's ever seen, or even worse than the Munyans. Who knows? At least he's alive." "That's true." "I think you should tell your mother," Alice said again. "Why?" "It will all seem more —real; that's it, real. Not so much like a dream." "I guess it does seem like a dream." "Well, it's time to wake up and get out in the kitchen before your husband goes off his head." "Oh, John." Edna remembered suddenly. "Yes, the very one; come on. Put on this robe. Sit down. I'll help you on with it." "I'm not *that* weak." "Then don't *act* that way," Alice said; "come, Madam Pumpkin; there's a kitchen full of people waiting for you."

With surprise, Edna noticed that her stomach was no

longer bloated; her body felt normal. "See," Alice said, noticing what she was up to; "that's another reason it's so hard to believe you didn't dream it." "Does this happen every time?" Edna asked, hesitating at the door. "Just the first. At least I hope so. I'm not prepared for any more, but you can't control these things. Not short of shooting your husband." Edna laughed. "Well, that's better. Come on; you make Dr. Steele feel better." They went into the kitchen. John looked up as if he had just caught a glimpse of the sun after months of rain. "Well, I don't know what got into me," Edna said; "I have to apologize. I really do." "Don't worry about it," John said quickly. "Where's Martin?" "In the nursery." "Well, let's go and see him, and," Edna added, "if we really have two nurse-maids, I can go on rounds with you again." John shook his head at her. "Incorrigible, that's what you are." He hugged her, hard. He had his wife back.

"Well, what *did* you do?" Ten asked; "it's a miracle." "I wish I knew," Mrs. Moffat said; "I just said whatever came into my head. I wish I knew, in the event it ever comes up again." "You *are* a good friend." "It goes both ways, I guess; I wouldn't make much of it myself." "I suppose we'll be back to normal now," Ten sighed, relieved. "Until she's expecting again." "Oh, no," Ten gasped; "don't even say it." "Well, stranger things have happened." Ten was staring at her, aghast.

"Dear patient Edith," Ten was soon writing, propped up by pillows in the little conservatory attached to the house. "I thought I had better write and let you know about your daughter's newborn boy before you come on a visit of ceremony for his wedding. To tell you the truth, Edith, I can't think of any good excuse for not having notified you of Edna's pregnancy earlier, except that she was so set on my not doing it. I believe she expected to die, although, if she did, she never let on about it. We have had our hands full here, I can tell you; first trying to keep the news from John, and then trying to keep Edna quiet, and what does she decide to do: have the baby in the middle of the snowstorm in April with only the women of the house present. But really, I suppose we should be thankful; she may be small, but she is strong, and I don't believe the entire process took more than two hours, although it seemed more like two life-times to me. I don't ever want to have a baby again, I can tell you. And then, after it was all over, Edna sunk into such a fit of the blues we were thinking of calling in a specialist. But that's over with now. She's riding around with John, on his rounds, and when she's not out with him, she's feeding Martin. She has fits when she's away from the nursery, the nursery is all the world to her. And very busily trying to concoct a new kind of nipple for his bottles since she's convinced the ones available are long enough to strangle her child.

"I begin to see what you mean about her being a con-fusing one. There are days when she leaves the house as if there were nothing of interest in it, and others when she spends two hours feeding little Martin, and don't you doubt it, he can eat four or five times a day, too. She and John are the conspirators, as usual; she *will* have her way with the nursemaids, and he won't be the one to stop her. They go on and on about how Edna is spoiling the child by keeping him so long, and then she has John come in and announce the baby has digestive difficulties, and can take in food only very slowly, so that, on occasion, such feeding is warranted, not even warranted, but necessary.

"And of all the people in town I never expected her to take an interest in, why, she has taken up with Alice Moffat. I never saw anything in her but kindness, and more kindness, but what they find to talk about is beyond me. It seems that Mrs. Moffat is now expecting a new arrival, and they go on about that like two hens. I sup-pose Edna's vow of silence on that subject was too much for her, and the two women seem to feel extreme grati-tude toward one another, and loyalty, too. Whenever I see her staring over her book into space, I know just what she's thinking: how to smuggle something nicer into Mrs. Moffat's house without insulting her. She seems to be settling in here, though. Edith, I think your daughter must be part tree, and a taproot tree at that. If she never went more than ten miles from this house, I'm sure she would be satisfied.

"I must admit, too, Edith, I thought the arrival of a child would bring more of a change in her, but she's at her etiquette books every minute she's not drawing up plans for a new house, or up waiting for John, poring over her books on time. Last night, I was reading *Abigail*, when she suddenly looked up and said, 'Is it possible at the edge of the world to stretch one's hand out or not?' Well, you know how I always say whatever pops into my head, and I was almost nodding over poor Abigail's destitute state, so I said, 'We're always at the edge of the world.' And then was I examined! So I told her I meant we never knew what the future would bring, or if we could even be sure of tomorrow; that was all I meant. Well, she made something of it, scribbling on one of those endless papers of hers. Then she takes them off and pastes them in a notebook. I don't understand why she doesn't just write in a notebook in the first place. Well, I know she's been thinking about that silly comment all day, thinking if it's possible that we all live on a tiny strip of a flat world which our perceptions distort to roundness.

"I suppose I have dear Nellie in mind. Sometimes, Edith, dear, I think it must be true, that as one soul arrives, another leaves. We received the saddest letter you could want last night. Poor Nellie is dead. I think I must go down and help the family; they all seem distracted with grief. It was the younger daughter who wrote, begging me to write to you for her, so I am now doing that. Nellie was pregnant, and about to be confined, too, when their carriage had a runaway, and the horses dashed the carriage into a tree. Nellie was thrown clear, and broke her neck right away; the others were simply mashed. It is too dreadful even to consider. And to think if I had known she was pregnant, and at least fifty, I would have worried myself sick over that every day. I didn't think women could still perform those tricks at her age. She was not driving, either. It was her cousin, and the rest of the members of that sewing circle she loved so much. They were all returning from a demonstration of the use of the new sewing machine. Nellie's daughter, Helen, sent me a very good likeness of her, copied from one she had done just before her wedding day. I was very pleased, for I never expected to have it. Helen will be sending you one, but a poor substitute it is for the young girl we knew. I suppose she will always be that young girl to me.

"I will never forget the letter she wrote me the first time she discovered she was in the family way. She had expected to come here, you know, and it was such a blow to her. 'I might as well just tell you first that it has been one of my horrid streaks of good luck to get in the family way and that knocks the whole business on the head. I have very near cried my eyes out over it, I have felt so bad and disappointed; for I did want to go so much and it will be a long time now before I can go. I have come to the conclusion that a married woman need not make any calculations months ahead.' I wonder if she is at the edge of the world now, stretching out her hand. It does seem, lately, as if I could reach out and touch it.

"I know, Edith, that you will say I am just getting old and morbid. But, Edith, dear, I don't fear death, 'nor shake at death's alarm,' as poor Nellie used to say. Still, I should prefer enjoying all the rest of the sweets of life yet a little longer, for I am just at the age to enjoy myself. I have only myself to please, and that is saying something.

"I must tell you, Edith, I have had five teeth drawn since I saw you and I have three more that I want to keep as long as I can, for they will let my face sink in and I look old enough to scare Methuselah. I suppose I shall have to try to get false ones, although sometimes I think it would be easier to make up double quantities of little Martin's formula, and forget about that torturer, the dentist. If I fear death, Edith, it is because I suspect he is a dentist.

"And then, there is Edna's friend, Virginia. She sounds very badly to me, and I don't know whether to tell Edna or not; Virginia has left it all up to me. She has married again, although she was so sure she never would, but her new husband has been bleeding at the lungs two or three times. She says it makes her feel very badly sometimes when she gets to thinking of it, for she does think a great deal of him, and if he should be taken from her, what would she do? She writes that she has bled at the lungs once or twice herself, but thinks nothing of that, although John is more convinced than ever that the consumption goes from one to another by contagion, and is going off tomorrow without Edna to try persuading a family on Lord's Hill to send off their one son who does not yet have the disease in the hope of saving his life.

"I suppose Edna is getting him under her influence. He is all interested in puzzling out diseases again. He wrote a doctor in Boston about his theory, and the result was an invitation to testify at a criminal trial as an expert. Edna refused to let him even so much as think of it, and when he seemed to hesitate, she worked herself up so, he gave up the idea. The word 'court' or anything to do with it seems to set her off, I must say.

"It does make me feel so sad, Edith. Virginia is so lively, but John insists it is more lively than alive. I read her letter to Edna; she enclosed it for me since I was to decide whether to give it to her or not. 'Are you crazy, insane, or out of your head, or what is the difficulty that you write such an incomprehensible letter to me?' (She has such a style!) 'You say that you have your ideal baby, but you did not use the pronoun his, although I presume it is a boy. Why didn't you tell me his name, or residence, or describe his features, "his glorious features," so that I could have formed an opinion regarding your offspring? I presume he is better than all the world beside, in your estimation, is he not?'

"Oh, Edith, Helen has copied out Nellie's baptism certificate, and I send it on to you. I suppose there was little else to send on.

Miss Nellie M. White was Emersed at the Disciple Church in Bedford, September the 8, 1805, Age 13 years and 11 months.

> Proclaim says Christ my wondrous grace
> To all the sons of man
> He that believes and is immersed
> Salvation shall obtain
> Yet plenteous grace descend on those
> Who hoping in his word
> This day have publically declared
> That Jesus is their Lord.

Helen Abigail White, Bedford, Massachusetts

"Well, life would be a sad business, Edith, would it not, if things were not so various. Life on the farm here is like my garden, something always springing up out of the ground. And I suppose you are preparing to marry your Mr. Siddons? Be assured, dear Edith, I do not think less of you for it. I might have taken an interest in such matters, too, but things here have kept me occupied and still do. Well, *you* know your daughter and I know my brother. And don't think I feel superior, remaining faithful to dear Ed's memory.

"I don't suppose there's any glory in taking after the faithful shepherd's dog who moans over his master's grave, but that's how I was formed. I can't seem to attach myself to very many people. I suppose if my soul were held up, it would have very few threads weaving it, and should look like a torn lazy spider's web at the very best. Well, all this sitting around among the green things is making me feel young enough to hop, but I expect there's something in the house that needs looking after. You know you must come up here, though, and try to forgive Edna for not having told you as she ought to have. She is a person of forebodings, I think. I remain your faithful friend, dear Edith. Do let us know what train to come for."

Ten sighed, stood up, bent over, and rubbed her left knee. It's going to rain, she predicted, looking up at the blue sky.

"And how old are we now?" she asked little Martin, going into the nursery under the murderous glare of that Minnie. "We are eight weeks old, aren't we?" she cooed and, seeing he was awake, picked him up. She had to say something to John about this Minnie; she didn't like the way she acted. She seemed, somehow, peculiar. There was no point in taking any chances, not after all she'd gone through.

Seven weeks after Martin's birth, Edna found herself vomiting every morning. This time, she didn't think it necessary to mention the matter to Ten. She saddled a horse and drove down to Mrs. Moffat's. "Alice," she asked as soon as they were alone, "I couldn't be expecting again? Not so soon?" Alice was now in her fourth month of pregnancy. "You ought to know the answer to that one better than I do," Mrs. Moffat retorted. "Well, and would it be such a tragedy?" she asked, seeing Edna's face. "I had hoped," Edna said slowly, "to give John a chance to settle, to get calm, you know." "Well, are you going to keep it from him again? I don't think that's right, you know. And after you had such an easy time of it. Why, with my first, I was almost three days, and then, after the ergot, I bled so much I gave up on myself." Edna was developing a virulent interest in all these details, she wanted to know what happened. "Dr. Steele happened; he packed"—she hesitated, trying for the word—"the uterus with clean rags and a tallow candle; well, he didn't leave the candle there, he used it to push in the rags; and it stopped. And then, when my fourth came on in the wrong month, he did the same thing again, but the next day, a tiny little Moffat made his exit anyhow. You get used to it; it's something different for everyone, isn't it?" "Do you really? Get used to it, I mean." "If it happens enough. It gets to be like the potato crop. Sometimes they're fine and sometimes even a potato bug wouldn't want any part of them. Oh yes, I'd say you get used to it. It's like the fair for me, once a year." "Only more screaming." "*That* part doesn't last long. It all depends, I guess, getting used to it; your liking of children. And your husband's. But the whole county knows he's crazy over them." "Is he?" "Oh, Edna, are you going to tell him?" "In another month." "Go on and wait for the malaria season," Alice said.

But it was Edna who needed the month, who needed the time to feel all the changes. And she was angry at John now; *she* had been frightened that first time, but not enough, she decided, to try and avoid its happening again. Not that you could tell from the way she behaved. She still stayed up until John came home; she still woke up when she heard him coming. But this time, this time, she didn't want to worry alone, or worry harder than she had to. It made it all seem so terrible, having to keep it a secret.

June, the month she selected for the announcement, was hot and sultry. Everyone went about commenting on the terrible heat, how it was withering the crops, drying up the wells. There were epidemics of measles and mumps; there was the threat of typhoid up on Lord's Hill. And they were expecting Edith at the end of the month. Edna had harbored vague hopes that her mother's arrival had set her nerves on edge, giving her dyspepsia, but the vomiting stopped at the end of the third month, and when the sleepiness set in, she gave up such hopes. She hadn't, from the first, placed much faith in them.

"John," she began one night as he was turning on his side, settling into his pillow, "what would you say if I told you we were expecting another addition to the family?" He sat bolt upright. "What! What did you say!" "Sometime in March." "It's out of the question!" John shouted. "Why?" she asked frigidly; "we can afford it." "It doesn't have anything to do with money. Again!" he thundered; "it surpasses all imagination! Again!" "Well, you know what the Bible says; something about being fruitful and multiplying." "Not every nine months. It didn't say every nine months!" He jumped out of bed. "Well," she asked, appearing to consider, "do you want to abort it? No one would know."

"Abort? Are you off your head? Do you think I would take a chance like that?" "We might have a girl this time; that would be nice." "We don't even know what having a boy is like yet!" "They can play with each other." John stalked up and down the room, furious, every now and then turning to the bed to glare at her. "Well, I'll tell you now; no more going on rounds." "That's what you think!" Edna exclaimed, finally sitting up; "I'm going." "Don't shout, don't shout; you'll wake up Martin." "And little Ella." "And *who* is Ella?" Edna patted her stomach. "I thought I ought to name this one after *my* family." "We need separate rooms," John fumed. Edna sat on the bed, glaring at him. "Separate rooms, separate beds," he went on. "You'd just climb in mine." "Don't be so smart." "Well, you would." He paced up and down, silent. "Get back in this bed." John lay down on the edge of the bed. "What did you do? Sew yourself onto the edge of the sheet? You're defying the laws of gravity. Why don't you place your body on the mattress?" "I'm staying where I am." "You can't get me in the family way; I already am." "Fine," he muttered, clinging to his side of the bed. "John," Edna coaxed, beginning to stroke his back. "Don't *do* that! It tickles." "It tickles?" she asked, continuing. "It does." Well, Edna thought, she had nothing on but her skin. She got out of bed and walked around to John's side.

"Get back into bed," he warned her; "you'll freeze."

She knelt down on the rug, pressing his face into the space between her breasts. "I can't breathe," John complained; still, he sounded less enraged. "Can you now?" Edna asked, reaching for his hand. "You just stop that!" "I only wanted to know," she said, "if it was normal for them to swell up like this." She placed his hand on her breast. "You're starting again." "*Is* it normal?" "Yes, it's normal," he sighed, involuntarily beginning to caress her breast, its nipple rising to meet his fingers. She brushed her hair over his face. "All right," John said, giving up; "get in." "Will you get back on your side?" Edna asked. "I'll get back on yours.

"And how are the house plans coming?" John asked later. He sounded tired to death. "I'm adding another wing; and an architect is coming down from Boston for a conference." "You know it's that I don't want anything to happen to you," John said. "I don't want anything to happen to me, either; only good things." "And this is a good thing?" "It is." Flashes of the pain of Martin's birth returned; she shuddered. "I knew you'd get cold," John said, remorseful, holding her; "and how long are you going to keep this up?" "I'm definitely stopping at five." "You're always so positive about everything." "*And*," she told him, like a little general, "I am going on rounds; until I can't climb in and out of the carriage."

"Sometime in March?" "March." "That seems a long time off." "Well, it's only the last month that's so bothersome." "To *you*, inconsiderate mouse." "That is enough," Edna said; "what's done is done. And also, I'm sure someone or something wants things the way they turn out." "Well, that's a new thing, isn't it?" John asked, curious; "when did you become such a fatalist?" "Since I met you." "Then what are you crying about?" he asked, puzzled. "It's such a relief having told you, is all," she cried quietly. Good Lord, he hadn't realized. What those months of secrecy must have cost her! "I'm glad you told me," he whispered, holding her. "Why?" she asked, still crying; "so you can swallow your Paris green before the delivery?" "That is enough of *that*," he echoed, stroking her hair. "This time you can talk all you want. I mean that, Edna." She cried on. "Edna, I have to get out of this bed in three hours; do you think you could stop crying?" "Yes," she said, her voice small, nestling against him like a kitten. "A boy, a girl, we'll have our own school," he murmured, dumbfounded. "Well," he said, "we better hurry up and get to know Martin." They could have twenty children, he thought sleepily, and still, the children wouldn't open up to them the way they would to other parents. Or to Ten. No, he and Edna were the books with the pages already printed. The lives of the children would have to be written around the margins. Tomorrow, he decided, falling asleep, he would have to find out why Hal was swimming the river six times a day. What had he gotten through his head now? His eyes closed. Edna's closed. The moon's one eye stared on blankly.

BOOK II

BOOK II

1860

Could more have happened to the Steele family in the intervening nine years? Edna added four additional members to the family—the second: Ella; the third: Letitia; the fourth: Anna; and the fifth: John Ashbel Steele, Jr. By the time John Ashbel Steele, Jr., made his appearance, John had gotten used to Edna's rising and falling with the seasons, as the entire household grew used to the rising noise within the four walls. Living in a house constantly under construction also became a way of life with the Steeles, and a source of amusement to the rest of the county. John had interfered only to insist that the main structure be completed as expeditiously as possible, and Edna had inexplicably decided that the portion of the building facing onto the road should be as catholic in appearance as a country house could possibly be. For her model, she chose an "ideal model house" for a beautiful villa; it was a three-story gingerbread house of three turrets, one main porch, two bay windows, one enclosed porch on the second floor opening out from the side room, one open porch reached from the third-floor turret room.

According to *The Floral Cabinet*, which over the years, now nearing a decade, both Ten and Edna had come to adore, each for their own reasons, this "modest little villa" combined the Italian and Swiss styles, giving "the convenience of the former with the decorations of the latter."

"By reference to the plans on this page, the reader will see the rooms are of good size" (Edna's only change in the plans set down was to double all dimensions given) "and open easily into each other, or into the center hall. The kitchen has its numerous closets, pantry, and storeroom, with separate stairs, outdoor entrance, and passage to the dining room. The second floor is divided very economically into five excellent bedrooms all of good size, well lighted, an excellent closet room. In the third story,

413

there are three large rooms, with sides four feet in height, and closet room on each side. The height of the first story is ten feet; second, eight and a half. The roof of both house, the 'L,' and piazza is covered with slate of various colors, and the front part is decorated with gilded railings. Over the edge of the roof is erected a ventilator, which is not only a convenience to the rooms beneath, but also is quite an architectural ornament. The grounds around the house are to be laid out in lawn, flower beds, ornamental trees, shrubs, fountains, etc." Edna spent some time poring over the floor plan for two verandas, the parlor, dining room, sitting room, the kitchen with its pantry, back pantry, and closet, and at once called for the Boston architect her new father had recommended; that was how she always referred to Mr. Siddons now: "my new father."

During the week before the architect's arrival, Mrs. Steele, having time to study the issues in question further, decided to add what the magazine called "a pretty window garden," but, really, it was a miniature greenhouse. This structure, to be filled with stands of all sorts, ornamental metalworked arches, and high, arched windows, opened off the main parlor. *The Floral Cabinet* assured Ten, who took a special interest in this, that the addition would be adequately heated by the warmth from the parlor, which would enter the greenhouse through the open door dividing the two rooms. Still, Ten had insisted upon a brick floor for her greenhouse, and a coal stove, ordered after a trip to Boston. The stove, if possible, was even more elaborate than the façade of the house itself. Nor was there any reason, Edna decided, in her studies of the floor plans, not to add a second sitting room to the first floor, or to build two or more summer cottages, the designs for which were given on the next page.

Already in her second pregnancy, Edna had decided that John, as well as other members of the entourage, would often want refuge in the woods, and two rustic summer houses, which became three, and then four, were duly built. They were houses the size of gigantic rooms, their roofs peaked, each sporting two miniature steeples, elaborately decorated doors, and inside, a small couch, three or four chairs, and a good stove. Although the architect protested at the addition of a brick chimney to these structures, pointing out that their cost would almost equal the expense of the dwellings themselves, Edna could not see why members of the family would want privacy only during summer months, and fireplaces were quickly installed, along with a hidden layer of brick behind the oak walls. Edna had each cottage finished with trellises, which covered three of their walls. The people who chose them could make use of them or not, as they pleased.

The architect fretted over the ornamented gate and trellis for climbing vines which closed the road behind the house's bay window. It was elaborate as could be, and high enough at the height of its arch to require a weather vane to give it balance, and its metalwork repeated the arched design of the cathedral windows wherever possible. "It is too much, Mrs. Steele," the architect protested; "it looks like a doll's house; it doesn't look real. So many curlicues; it makes the head spin." "Just what I hoped for!" Edna clapped her hands, delighted; "there can never be enough curlicues for *me*." The architect prayed silently his name and this house would never publicly be connected; however, he was being paid extremely well, and if Mrs. Steele wanted a monstrosity, she had to live in it; he supposed that would be her punishment.

The eight huge bedrooms gave Mr. Steele some pause, since he had placed, he knew, preposterous faith in his wife's promise to stop at five; but Edna promptly counted things up for him: five bedrooms for the children, one for them, one for Ten, one for Hal, and one guest room. That made nine bedrooms essential, and others would have to be added sooner or later, although, Edna reflected, they could easily be added to the wings, which would then accommodate any further guests they happened to have. For most of the year, even after the snows had begun to fall, Edna and Ten's main diversion was to stand outside the new structure, admiring the progress of the men, keeping a better than adequate pace with the construction inside her swelling stomach.

By October, the entire outside façade, complete with decorations, had reached completion; Mrs. Steele stood there contemplating it cheerfully, her hand automatically supporting the small of her back. By the time she entered the eighth month of her pregnancy, the entire first and second floors were completed, although she and Mr.

Steele had decided not to move in until the following spring, since the workmen often had to sleep in the new house when the roads were impassable, and neither was up to attacks of billowing smoke from the new chimneys, filling the rooms, driving all of them out into the snow, leaks in the new roof, complaints from Bridget and Bertha over the difficulties of coping with a new kitchen. The cellar of the house, which ran its entire length, had also become something of a horror to the two maids, who claimed it was a regular catacomb, and they would not go down into it without a guide. All of this, Edna decided, her feet swelling, her stomach expanding as if to deny laws of probability, could wait until the spring and the establishment of the new baby.

This time Mr. Steele cooperated by remaining at home while Edna began her delivery, although, as he afterwards said, his presence was totally unnecessary, since his wife, seized with pains over breakfast, only had time to be helped to her bed before she was delivered of a second new arrival, a little girl they promptly named Ella. The same process was repeated with the third and fourth births, which resembled the second, and differed from the first primarily in the expeditiousness of the process, and the installing of Alice Moffat in the Steele household for one full week after the birth of each infant. Two nursemaids were hired and sent down to *her* house during her absence. "If that doesn't beat all," Mr. Moffat would say each time, seeing the arrival of two women in their neat uniforms, one of whom kept track of the children as far as was humanly possible, the rest of her time scrubbing the house of its accumulation of grease which lined the walls since the birth of the last Steele infant.

The town, needless to say, took quite an interest in these proceedings, but aside from commenting on the "peculiar" ways of the very rich, took far less interest than might have been expected, probably, as Mr. Steele correctly surmised, because they included the lives of a local family. Nor could they afford to judge the Steeles too harshly, because, unlike their ministers, who could be discharged for any conceivable reason, everyone knew how impossible it would be to secure another doctor of Mr. Steele's caliber. So it was concluded that he could live in a house of twigs for all it meant to them. It was a matter of indifference how the Steeles lived, although every new detail of their house building and decoration was promptly retailed along with the long licorice candies at the tobacco store and, during the winter, around the stove at the police station.

It was the birth of John Ashbel Steele, Jr., the fifth child, which put an end to additions to the family, if not the house. Edna, who was now almost twenty-six, awaited the event complacently as a cat, but when her pains began, she and everyone else in the house knew that this was not to be an easy delivery. Alice Moffat was immediately summoned; the doctor was recalled. Ten shipped all four children to one of the summer cottages with several of the maids. The house filled with screams, and more screams. By the end of the second day, Edna, too exhausted to scream, only moaned softly.

John had decided her labor was "nonfunctional," and was helping nature along with pushings of his own. His sister began to fear that even should their fifth arrive, it would arrive an orphan. She was not at all sure she wanted the responsibility of being mother and father to four unruly children, not to mention her own brother, Hal. Life, so it seemed to her, was beginning to resemble one of her own dreadful novels. By the beginning of the third day, Edna's pulse was, as she herself knew, weak and quivery. She was too exhausted to do more than moan and twist her head on the pillow. Alice Moffat had to be led from the room in tears which, on the third floor, turned into hysterics; Bridget was dispatched to care for *her*. And through it all, Edna tried to smile encouragingly at her husband, who was as gray as the skies over the villa. Finally, she was too tired even to do that.

Just as they had both separately given up hope, the baby's head suddenly emerged, and the fifth Steele child made his entrance. He was, all agreed, an enormous child, over ten pounds, and it was generally considered a miracle that even Edna, with her wide pelvic structure, had managed to separate herself from him at all. The birth was, however, immediately followed by a massive hemorrhage, which John, petrified, treated in his usual way: packing the uterus with rags and a candle, and then taking up his place at the bedside while Ten, opposite him, alternately watched or slept. The bleeding stopped, but several days afterwards, as Edna was recovering strength, she suffered prolapse of the uterus. The muscles of that organ, apparently ripped by the violence of the delivery, had to be tied and removed. So it developed that Mrs. Steele had been correct in her predictions: she was to stop at five. "Are you sorry?" her husband asked her. "No," she answered groggily; "no. Five is enough. For insurance," she went on in a weak voice; "even if we should lose one." The clarity, almost cruelty of her perceptions, still took her husband by surprise.

This time it was Mrs. Moffat who discovered the member of the family with the blues, when, going for an idle walk about the grounds, she heard sobbing in the farthest cottage, and Dr. Steele huddled as close to the stove as he could get without setting himself on fire. "But she's fine," Alice kept on repeating; "she's fine." He looked up as if he didn't recognize her; Alice finally decided he did not. Her husband, she decided, was better equipped to deal with this kind of crisis, and accordingly, she sent for him.

Howard promptly got the good doctor drunk, which was hardly difficult, since Mr. Steele rarely ever touched a drop of the "devil's fluid," and the next thing the amazed family heard was John and Howard singing bawdy songs at the top of their lungs. "Really, miss," Bridget complained to Ten, "we should put sweet oil in the children's ears; they shouldn't be listening to such things." "Nonsense," said Ten; "they'll be hearing it enough in their lifetimes. They might as well get accustomed to it young." "Daddy is all drunken up," Martin announced proudly to his mother. "That's good," she said, yawning; "are you all filled up?" "Oh yes," he answered, patting his stomach. "Then give me a kiss." Martin obliged. "That was a chocolate kiss." "Oh, Momma, Mrs. Moffat gave it to me." "It was delicious," Edna said, falling asleep. "Is Momma dead?" he asked Bridget, coming out. "Just sleeping, just sleeping," she repeated automatically. Ella and Letitia were constantly asking the same question, although no one was sure if they knew what it meant.

Edna woke in the middle of the night. "How is John?" she asked, finding Alice there. "Drunk. Howard and the rest of the police station mob have decided to keep him that way for another few days. The last time I went into the summer house, they were plotting how to overthrow the Temperance Union." "That's fine, then; what's everyone else up to?" "Oh, they're all sitting around in the kitchen trying to decide if what happened last month was an omen." "You mean that shot?" Edna asked, thoroughly confounded. "Well, Edna," Alice said, "that made some story."

Last month, as Edna and Ten were going to bed, each holding her candle before her, Ten, going first, suddenly stopped to listen to something, and, at that instant, came the sound of a shot, then the sound of plaster cracking right in front of her left ear. "Good Lord, Edna," she gasped; "someone's shooting at us." They peered around them and at the wall. It took several seconds to find the bullet hole on the left side of the stair wall, but there was no matching hole on the right side. Nor was there any in the other walls through which the bullet could have entered, nor any further holes through which it might have left. There was no trace of it in the walls. "You think it was someone shooting at the doctor, don't you?" Alice asked. Edna nodded. "Then why weren't there any other holes? There should have been more holes." "We just didn't find them, that's all." "But there should have been footprints in the snow; it didn't snow again after that shot." "The wind probably blew some from the drifts." "There was no wind." Edna fell silent. "Well," Alice concluded, "you wanted to know what the others were up to, and that's what they're up to. The bullet in the wall." "The bullet *hole*," Edna corrected.

"Alice?" Edna asked, waking up a few hours later. The other woman shook herself awake. "I want to ask a favor of you, but you must listen first; it's a very large one." "What is it, what is it?" Alice asked, impatient and sleepy. "John has been corresponding with a man in France about that thing, the daguerreotype, and I wrote to get a manual about how to make them, and a complete stock of necessary chemicals and equipment. They should be coming in from Brattleboro soon." "And you want me to hide them until you're up and about?" "Exactly. I have a note." Edna fished under her pillow. "The Express is to turn everything over to you. But I don't want John to find out."

"I thought you said it was a dangerous business." "The man swore it wasn't, not with adequate ventilation. And

John will have it regardless of what anyone says. My new father has even arranged an appointment with that Mr. Brady; he'll train him for a week if we can tear him away from here." "You're always up to something." "Will you hide the things away? I tried to get up this morning, but I feel like a leaden horse." "Don't worry; just go to sleep. I'll go down after the things tomorrow." "Oh, thank you, Alice," Edna sighed, falling asleep.

Ten had left everyone to his own devices and decided to sleep in the front turret room on the third floor. The older she got—she was almost sixty—at least so everyone said—the closer to the sky she liked to be. She would have to ask Amos and some of the other men to move her furniture up here permanently. It wouldn't take a nine-year-old child more than an extra three seconds to come up one more floor and roust her out. Well, she mused, drawing her thin legs into bed, she was shriveling, it seemed, from the toes up. Well, things had certainly changed. Or they had congealed, set, like a pudding. Which was it, she wondered, change, or hardening into their lives?

There were more children than ever, but Edna's attitude toward them all was really no different than it had ever been; it was only clearer. There was something in Edna, something which made her pull back from those she loved violently. Now Ten could see it in her growing addiction to her etiquette books and her preoccupation with time. None of these theoretical pursuits had ever interested her, but she frequently wondered why Edna did not *study* the children more; even *she* could see that time, at least the awareness of it, had not yet started for them.

Instead, Edna would busy herself with their strange grandfather clock; *she* had told her brother she would burn it if anyone mentioned it to her again. Ever since Edna's discovery of its dramatic acts—the way it flung itself onto the hall sofa the very minute their mother died, and when their father died, it dropped its pendulum to the bottom of the cabinet—she had been fascinated by that abominable machine. Last week, when the clock stopped, she had had her first attack of hypochondria, plagued all over by imaginary aches and pains as thoroughly as if she had come down with a new, invisible version of the measles.

And Edna, too. If she had looked like the little princess, now she looked like the little queen. Ten settled back against her pillow, staring out at the stars, thinking over her last conversation with her. Before this birth. Edna now believed more than ever that time was a substance of some sort which existence burned up like a fire, and, figuratively speaking, of course, the longer one lived, the taller one's pillar of ashes got. "Why, I must almost be normal height," Edna exclaimed; "if you think of us as accumulations of seconds, a kind of cone of time, like dust, settling on our heads, then I'm almost as tall as you were when I met you. You, of course, are taller. And John. I'll never catch up, not unless I outlive you. What a way to catch up," she said sadly.

Then Ten had found one of her scribbled papers. "At the moment of death, the person resembles a huge pile of seconds, not unlike an enormous pile of ashes swept into a heap in the corner of a fireplace. One of the qualities of time I am now sure of," the paper continued, "is its cannibalistic nature. As it passes, if it passes, it consumes. Perhaps it is the only immortal substance, one which feeds on us.

"Perhaps there is not one time, but a whole race of times, as if they were animals peopling the earth, invisible to us, but consuming us whenever they find it necessary, having their favorites, as people do, sparing those as long as they possibly can. I hope I shall not be more favored by these creatures than my husband, for the consumers of life are indifferent to us, and capricious; it may be" (here the paper veered off) "that all our affections are imitations of the cannibalisms of time; that our loving of each other uses each other up.

"But it does not seem that the isolated and the selfish live the longest. Still, I have read, recently, of people found dead of extreme old age in their homes, seen by no one but the occasional maid or woodman. Perhaps that is the answer, or at least part of it."

Ten sighed and looked at the cold stars. They never came nearer. Perhaps we exist to please *them*. Once you began thinking like Edna, anything seemed possible, although there seemed to be very definite boundaries to her own mind, its territory marked off by paths she would never think of wandering. Well, it did make it harder on Edna, to be different that way. For example, last week. John Probst, the farmer up above them on Lord's Hill, had driven by their house and seen Martin's black-and-white dog. Two days later, the dog had wandered up the hill, with Martin close behind, and for no reason ever discovered, Probst had suddenly taken a shotgun and shot Martin's pet. The child had burst into the kitchen, his face red, shining with tears, carrying the stiff, cold body. "Oh, dear God," Edna had gasped, looking up. "I'm going after him," Martin sobbed desperately, marching off into John's study and toward the gun rack. Edna had sat, frozen, at the table, staring down at her eternal etiquette book.

It had been Ten who grabbed Martin by the collar and dragged him back into the kitchen, murmuring about a proper burial for the dog, a new dog, how they would certainly have to do something about that devil Mr. Probst. Fortunately, John made his appearance at that moment; he took Martin and the dog's body off to Mr. Probst's. "I don't understand it; I can't understand it"; Edna kept repeating that. She had been completely ineffectual, of no help whatsoever. "John?" she finally asked, looking at Ten. "Oh, Edna," she had burst out, exasperated, "it's not John we have to worry about. Martin was the one who had the dog killed. And suppose Mr. Probst had shot Jimmie?" "Jimmie?" Edna repeated, stricken. "Well, don't worry about John," Ten scolded; "he always could take care of himself in a violent way; too well, if you ask me." "That's good," Edna answered, again absent, going back to her reading.

She could not stand too much of this world at once. Ten had supposed she would be up all night, trying to take it in. But by that time, Martin would have either recovered from this attack of reality, or he would not. Edna, she knew, would go into his room in the middle of the night and hold him. But she would not know what to say. She only knew what to say to John. But perhaps her presence, the holding, was enough. Perhaps there was something to be said for her emotional shocks, which kept her paralyzed at the moment of the event. Then, when everyone else was worn out dealing with the present, Edna was there, fending off the shadows of the future. Well, perhaps that was more important; she had no idea. She had fewer and fewer ideas with every year.

John, now. He didn't wait for the future. It was the present that concerned him, but that was natural, his sister thought, for a doctor. He had taken Martin up to Mr. Probst's and calmly asked the man if it were true he had shot his son's dog. Mr. Probst, rifle in hand, said it was. "Are you sure?" John asked. Probst assured him he was. "Well, that is too bad," John said, and the first thing Mr. Probst knew, he and his rifle were ascending through the air, propelled by John's heavy boot, in that part, as John said, where if nature had ever thought to favor him, his butt would have been situated. Mr. Probst ascended one way, his butt and teeth and hat in others. When he came down, and gathered up the fragments of himself, John asked politely if he was likely to shoot at any more of the family pets. Probst had unwisely muttered something about how it shouldn't be out of the way if he did, what with that army of unruly brats trampling through his flower garden. "I suppose your cows float through the air?" John asked, picking up the man's rifle, unloading it, then cracking it over his knee. "Here!" cried Mr. Probst; "that's my property you're destroying!" "You wouldn't fool with me, would you?" he asked Probst; "I thought someone lent it to you, just like the dog you shot. You must have thought someone just lent it to us, too, that he wasn't our dog you shot. You must have thought it was just lent to us, not our property, or you wouldn't have thought of such a thing." Little Martin was watching from behind a tree, his spirits soothing themselves.

"Turn around," John ordered Probst. "Why should I?" "Because otherwise I'll put your face through a coffee mill." That made Martin smile. His friend William Moffat, who was twenty, was already working in the chocolate mill, and his own parents had promised he could work there, too, after school: when he was twelve. "Are you turning around?" John inquired. "You wouldn't shoot me in the back? This isn't Colorado." "I know my geography; just let me see that backside of yours." To Martin's amazement, Mr. Probst turned his back, and John's boot lifted him into the air all over again. "You had better go after those teeth," his father observed, as if he had nothing to do with their travels. Mr. Probst muttered something about getting his own back for this. Martin was afraid. "You do that," John said; "it's an odd thing, but there's an oath we doctors take about treating the sick and the lame. You know that one? Treating the wealthy and the poor? I don't know how many tramps I've treated in the last year alone, and one of them was just up for trial as an incendiary. And they all owe me payment, too. I don't know how they're going to pay," he went on slowly, staring at Probst the whole time; "the only thing they have is their trade, and there's not anyone I want set fire to, not this instant, anyhow." Probst paled.

"You get off my property, and don't set one toe back on it," he yelled. "Then don't you call me," John told him; "I'll be busy fixing up the animals around here. The cattle seem a lot smarter than the humans hereabouts." Probst looked uneasy. John knew what he was thinking: his wife wouldn't like it. What if one of them got sick, and the doctor refused to come because he had been threatened with assault if he set foot on the property? "Good day, Mr. Probst," his father said, taking Martin's hand, raising his foot ominously, as if about to make good use of his boot again, and then just looking it over. "Awfully muddy up here," John commented. "I've seen many cases of insanity start out just like this," he went on amiably; "first a dog, then a wife, then hanging from a beam in the barn. You better watch out for yourself." "Get off my property!" Probst roared. John caught a glimpse of Probst's aproned wife running down the pine-needled path toward them. "Dr. Steele! Dr. Steele!" she panted, coming up; "whatever is wrong here?" "Nothing. But I'm afraid you need a new doctor. I can't come up here again." "What?" she exclaimed; "what! What did he do?" "You better ask him that," John said, turning, marching off with Martin in hand.

"You get out of here with that broom!" he heard the terrified Mr. Probst cry out. "I hope," he said, smiling down at his son, "she doesn't injure him too seriously, what with no doctor to stitch him up." "I hope she *kills* him!" Martin burst out. "Oh, she will: one way or another, something will." "But that won't bring back Spots," Martin said, starting to cry again. John stopped, sitting him down on a stump. "I think," his father told him, "Spots is very happy up there" (he pointed up at the sky), "watching Mr. Probst getting chased around with a broom. And perhaps, just maybe, when I kicked him so high, Spots bent down and bit him." "Do you think so?" "Yes, I do." "On his butt?" "I'm sure that's where he got him; Spots always was a smart dog." "You wouldn't really get someone to burn up his barn, would you?" Martin asked, hopeful. "Martin," John said, "do you think it would make Spots happy to smell horses burning, and kittens, and maybe even one of his own puppies?" Martin shook his head no. "Well, tonight, you tell Spots all about it; he might not have heard it all, way up there."

They walked the rest of the way home. Frightened, Edna looked up. "Momma!" Martin said, running over to her; "Mr. Probst flew up in the air and Spots bit him!" "What?" Edna asked, putting her book down, and Martin told her the whole story. "That's good," she murmured, stroking his hair; "I hope when Jimmie goes to heaven, he goes off with Spots." "Oh, Momma, I'm sure he will." Somehow, Ten thought, the children always ended comforting their mother.

John had now sobered up enough to take over for Alice. "Mmmmm," Edna murmured, waking up, seeing him. "Heaven," she said, reaching for his hand. "Don't mention any of those words," John ordered gloomily. "Oh, come," Edna said; her voice was almost as strong as it had been before her confinement; "you're having it all your way now. No more children." "That's something." "And someone invented your dream." "That's true." "You can't ask for more." "Not now." "I'm sorry," she whispered. "You didn't do it deliberately." "I guess not, but I'm sorry all the same. Well, anyway, it's over," she assured him. "Except when I wake up in an empty bed," he complained. "John, you selfish thing, I want you to promise me something. I have a new plan. If you dare die before me, I want a special tombstone." "You're off your head." "Actually, I'm serious; if you dare die before me, after all the worrying you've done about me, I'm going to get even; I'm going to have a picture of Jimmie carved on *my* tombstone." "Then Flag had better go on mine." "Oh, if you don't care whether it looks like an animal cemetery." "I'll be beyond caring." "I came through this," Edna teased him, "just to be sure you'll live forever." He couldn't see her face very well in the dim light. "I had better, then, hadn't I?" "And not take any chances if you start in with that making-faces business, those pictures?" "I'm not sure I like that description of it"; he smiled into the dark, taking her hand. It looked so white.

"Well, tell me what I've missed," she said. "Only the adventure of Lettie and the geese." "What geese? There aren't any geese up here." "Oh, she ran away from Martin, and went down that lane near the Moffats'. There are geese around there, and she was on one side of a hedge and persuaded herself there were geese on the other, and ran screaming down the path, so she thought they were chasing her, and by the time Martin caught up with Miss High Life, the vicious geese turned out to be the tips of the cows' horns showing over the top of the hedge. So that's how we found out she'd been prowling around the Littles' farm. And that cut on her leg? She was nipped at by a goose. We don't know where, or why she's all over the Littles' farm. Maybe it's their son, Dan." "Good heavens," Edna said; "don't they ever run out of trouble to get into?" "Not that I've noticed; they're very artistic in their bad behavior. They must get that from you." "And Anna?" Edna asked, refusing to be provoked. Anna was now five. "She's trying to read my medical books." "Can she *lift* them?" Edna asked. "Bridget gets them down for her." "Where will they all end?" "Probably as we have"—John squeezed her hand—"muddling through." "We do better than that," Edna insisted. "No, we don't; I'm just a country doctor, and you're a very short country doctor's wife. It would be funny, wouldn't it, if your new father outlasted us all? With his statues, I mean?" "Uproarious. Simply uproarious.

"You're not thinking of taking up any of those invitations to testify at trials?" she asked. She'd forgotten about all that for too long. "Only if they have to do with contagious diseases; I keep up that correspondence with Dr. Wittenstein, though. He's ahead of us here." "No American will believe a German," Edna thought aloud. "But I'm an American; I'll duplicate the experiments. Then I can testify." "I don't like it," she said; "one thing leads to another, and the next thing we know, you'll be involved

in those horrid murder cases we read about in the papers."
"Don't go invading the future." "You'll see." "Perhaps
I'll like it." "You won't; it would be the worst thing that
could happen to you." "I don't know why you're so
sure of that." "Because *I've* followed the course of this
disease before," she said. "I'm not your father." "That's
what you think." They fell silent, hands clasped. "I think
I should take you to the seashore," John whispered into
the candlelight. "The seashore? Whatever for?" "We
could go surfing." "Just what I've always wanted; to jump
into those huge waves and get myself pounded about."
Her free hand lightly touched her abdomen. "*I'd* like the
rest," he admitted. "Oh, well then," Edna said, "we'll go."
"To Cape Cod?" "Why Cape Cod?" Edna asked, already
suspicious; "not because it's near that court and that
attorney you're so busy with?" "It would be handy if
anything came up." "Don't say I didn't warn you"; she
yawned. He didn't answer; she was already asleep.

The white, milky light of an overcast dawn was filling
the room. Edna stirred, then turned to look at the chair
next to her bed. "Oh, Alice," she murmured; "is it good
morning or good night?" "Good morning." "John wants
to go to Cape Cod," Edna told her, stretching. "That
should be nice; you can turn brown as a berry in the
sun, and when you come home, you'll never know this
happened." "I don't want to leave home," Edna said,
sulky. Alice didn't answer. She was thinking how wonderful leaving home would be, leaving the children, her
problems with the farm, her problems with her sister-in-
law, the unending struggle to make ends meet. Just yesterday, Howard had ridden up to announce he had to
dig ten hills of potatoes for only one dinner, and they
wouldn't have any to store for the winter, *and* the apples
were all gone, too, or soon would be; he was afraid the
grapes he had hidden in the straw down in the cool part
of the cellar would soon be found out by one of the children, and their traditional Christmas treat would be eaten
before the leaves had a chance to fall. "You would,
wouldn't you?" Edna asked suddenly. "Would what?"
"Want to leave home." Yes, Alice decided, Edna was getting better, back to her old tricks of sniffing out differences, then needing the reasons for them.

"Oh, mostly because of my sister-in-law," Alice answered. "How long is she going to stay?" "She says she's staying long enough to convince her husband she's not coming back, but he doesn't seem to take the hint. I tell you, Edna, Lois Ann and those three children of hers are no joking matter. Last winter, she didn't get to church for almost three Sundays, and I tell you, that was tragedy enough for one household, I guess. I wish she'd run away somewhere nearer a church and have better folks to give her a roof over her head, poor mistreated soul." "I never did understand why she ran away in the first place." "The isolation on the farm was driving her crazy; that's what she said. So she left. She just put the three children in the wagon and drove them over to us, and she's been with us ever since."

"I don't understand it; why did she leave one isolated farm and go to another? It doesn't begin to make sense." "She says she wanted everyone to know she was leaving for good moral reasons, and if she'd gone straight to a town, who knew what people might think?" "But what were the reasons?" "Just what she told me: the isolation, always being left there alone with the little children. She decided to take on a job, and we were in Williamsville, and so is the textile factory, so she came to her brother's. Simple enough."

"And just when does she expect her motives to become clear enough?" "They better get clear enough pretty soon, or *I'm* running away to her farm in Massachusetts. It's beyond imagination what she's putting that poor husband through, but he won't divorce her. No, he keeps saying she's going to come to her senses and come back. He's just the type to try talking to a mad dog, except she won't talk to him. She waits near a window when she hears a horse, and if she sees it's him, latch on the back door, latch on the screen door, slam down the windows, and there he is, looking in, hands pressed on the glass, trying to talk to her, and all *you* can see are his lips moving. She stands there and looks at him a minute and then walks off into another room where he can't see her.

"And she doesn't let the children talk to him any more than she does. She wrote him a letter saying if God hadn't intended her to work in a textile factory, she wouldn't have been allowed to make the trip in safety, and it wasn't his business to meddle in the ways of Providence. Hypocritical old broom! With a face stiff enough to frighten off mosquitoes." "You have to get rid of her." "Well, it's not your trouble; I shouldn't even mention it. A fine thing, you lying there, and me going on like this." "No, I don't mind," Edna said; "it takes my mind off my own troubles."

Edna began thinking. They certainly had to get that Lois Ann out of Alice's house. "Well, and if they ate any more," Alice went on, indignantly; "I think religion must make them hungry. We're all going to be taking in seams and wearing crazy quilts. I guess there's no such thing as a new overcoat for any of us this year." "Oh, Alice, that reminds me," Edna said; "I wouldn't ask unless you were here, but there's all this fabric in the attic and Bertha just grabs it for polishing rags, and I tell you, I hate to see velvets and silks used to polish the furniture. If you can make use of it, please get Howard to carry it off before the squirrels get to it. I have nowhere at all to put the children's clothes. No one in the house ever throws anything out." She sighed ostentatiously.

"Up to your old tricks again?" Alice asked. "No, really," Edna insisted; "you ask Bertha how many scoldings she's gotten over those fabrics." Alice shook her head. "Well, but the main thing is how to get Lois Ann out of the house," Edna said; "I don't suppose she's afraid of ghosts? The children seem to be specializing in ghosts these days. They almost scared me to death last month. Martin hid Anna in the grandfather clock and had her start jumping it around, and you know all those stories they tell about that clock? I tell you, I was petrified." "She's not scared of anything, not ghosts either. She's too religious for ghosts. She expects to end up the first Baptist saint." "Did she say that?" "She doesn't have to, the way she floats above all of us like something that just ascended from a pickle barrel."

"Snakes?" Edna suggested; "Martin's rather dedicated to them, at least when he finds them one at a time." "She'd scare the snake. Oh say, Edna, Martin had his adventure with ringnecks yesterday. He went down to the swamp with my George. I've told George to leave him out of things, but Martin will follow after him. Well, you probably don't realize, but it's been terribly dry, and there are more snakes than potatoes, or anything else. George found some snake tracks going down to the swamp for water, so he came up here for Martin. He told him there were all sorts of birds' nests in the tree there, and off they went. Well, they just about fell over two heaps of snakes, about the size of a stack of hay, half a bushel, Dr. Steele said. Well, George said he never saw the like of it, all black snakes, full-grown, too, heads coming out of those piles every which way. I guess even my George got frightened, and they came tearing up here screaming, 'Ringnecks, ringnecks!' and poor Dr. Steele grabbed a stake and went back with those imps. Well, Edna, he hit at the pile, but all he did was get them back into their holes. Then, this is what George said, Mr. Steele grabbed one by the tail as it was going under, and the three of them grabbed and pulled, and they actually broke the thing in half. They weren't satisfied at that; no, they had to dig out the other half and pace it out and they all swear it was over five feet long, and a great adventure, too. I'm sorry for your Martin, with my George for an example." "He looks up to him," Edna said absently; "he's older."

"Well, I wish the older ones would look down on the little ones a bit better. William thinks an awful lot of himself because he's almost twenty. I tell you, he's getting mean. He takes our old buggy down to the grove, you know, where the birches line up in lanes, and just races up and down like the devil's chariot, and if one of the younger ones wants a ride, he says he'll run them down, and veers over at them, too. He's a good driver, though. You have to give him that." "I suppose," Edna said. She was still thinking about Lois Ann, how to get rid of her. "Alice, you know the old house? We need someone to stay in it to keep it up. Lois Ann could stay there and drive in to work." "She'll probably decide it's too far from church." "Well, it's closer than *your* house." "That's true." The two women fell silent, Alice wondering how to convince her brother to move Lois Ann, bodily if need be, into the old Steele house, and Edna, meditating, as usual, on the nature of her interest in everyone else's problems.

She was beginning to believe that everything, everything from "turn the other cheek" on, was invented to keep people's minds off their own troubles, their own lives.

Well, thinking about Lois Ann was a positive relief. She didn't have to think about what John had said about her moaning over her lost insides, that she was really like a chicken or a cat. She liked being pregnant, he said, and that was that. Afterwards, the children could pretty well take care of themselves for all she cared. If she really cared about the children, he said, she wouldn't want so many. They were not farmers, after all; they didn't need to raise a work force to manage the farm the way some families did who couldn't afford to hire help.

All that putting the others first: what was it but a preventive against being carried off to the Retreat or to Northfield? If you spent too long examining your own life, you were sure to go crazy, completely crazy. There was a great thing about taking an interest in the troubles of others. Their difficulties always seemed worse than your own. The whole Bible, she was sure, was invented because misery needed company. She, for instance, was wealthy, but that didn't mean her husband was getting younger; he was still twelve years older than she was, and always would be. So would Alice. All the money in the world wouldn't make John careful enough to avoid inhaling chlorine fumes. She'd already studied all the hazards. But it was useless, there was no keeping him from it. "Why don't we leave it up to John?" Edna suggested: 'he always could talk Howard into anything. He can think up something about your health." "Then *he'll* be the first Baptist saint," Alice said. "Are you still keeping a diary?" she asked. Edna flushed. Alice had picked hers up one day, accidentally, and tried to read it; it had made no sense at all to her.

"Edna, what is this all about?" she had asked, puzzled. "Oh, just things I think about." "Here's mine." Alice said, pulling a little trade diary out of her apron pocket; "look." Edna took it, hesitant. She hated anyone looking at hers. "Oh, don't worry, there's nothing in mine that the world can't look at," Alice said; "an ordinary life is an ordinary life. I'd guess the only interesting entries are about Lois Ann, and there are only three of those in twelve years." "Then why do you keep it?" "To remember. That's my life, isn't it? All those little things. I was looking at some diaries my mother left and I found the one for the year of her father's death, but the pages for the day he died and just after, they were blank. I wasn't sure I had the right diary. I was curious, you know, about how she took it. Mother's getting older; she's seventy-two. I guess that's what set me to thinking, her last birthday.

"But I couldn't tell when he died or if he did until I looked up the cash accounts in the back, and there it was: 'January 22nd: one funeral wreath, $1.50; one coffin, fourteen dollars; flowers for grave, 2 dollars, maintenance of grave, $2.00.' And then under that: 'One pound coffee, 30 cents, one pound tea, $1.50, one pound soda, twelve cents.' Coffee, tea, coffee, tea, death, coffee, tea, coffee, tea, and then eggs sold in 1851: 'Nov.: 12 cords wood drawed to Henry Belden.' Well, there was Grandpa, dead, coffee and tea creeping in over his wreath, and nothing stopped the drawing of that wood, I can tell you. Give it here," she told Edna.

"This is July," she said, beginning to read; "I guess the dates don't matter much, except my girl died in 1849, so that one had some different entries. Well: 'Cloudy this morning, but no rain. quite cool this afternoon. Too wet to hoe this forenoon so the boys worked up to the mill this afternoon. I hoed in the garden and in the cornfield. William got home just nine o'clock A.M. A beautiful day, though rather warm in the middle of the day. The boys hoeing corn, got most through. Two of Pat Sennet's cows got in our corn, eat off between 50 and 100 hills. He offers to pay all damage. I cut a white garibaldi for Mother today. Pleasant again today. Amos got through hoeing corn. Little Bertha Baldwin died this morning. I went down there this afternoon. Mr. Baldwin gone to Danby when she died. William taken to the village after tea. Got William a hat. Mrs. Lake to leave Robert. Went to Danby. Martha R. got me some red raspberries.' "

She stopped. "Ten years go by and I won't know who little Bertha was, or why I wanted to know what day I got William a hat, but I'll remember the red raspberries, and maybe the cows, and cutting out a cape. But why should I want to remember any of it? It wasn't interesting when it happened, was it? Maybe I guess it'll get more interesting with time, but it won't, I guess."

"Yes," Edna said, "it's like riding through a forest in a fog, reading those diaries, and every now and then you see one thing come clear. You must want—you must want to trace out all the other trees, the ones you can't see, so that later, you can get back somehow. You can get back by that blazed trail, there in those diaries." "I don't know what you mean, I don't understand a word," Alice said mournfully; "but I must have a reason, mustn't I?" "Yes, yes," Edna said; "that's what I meant." "Something about blazing a trail?" Alice puzzled; "it sounds as if I'm lost." "Probably we all are; probably we're all trying to figure out where, and if, we're on our way someplace, or if we missed the right place and can't find the way back." "The way back," Alice said; "the way back to the time before Florence died." "Something like that, I guess; back to the time before the worst thing happened." "It hasn't happened, not yet, to you, anyway, has it?" Alice asked. "No," Edna said slowly. "But you're afraid? All the same? Because you know it will?" "Because I know it will; yes, I do know that.

"I still keep it," Edna finally answered. "A careful little lady," Alice smiled; "clearing the road back to the place before you even lose it." Edna was taken aback. She was surprised Alice still remembered; she was surprised she had understood what she meant so well. But then someone had died, someone important to Alice. Perhaps even more important than Howard. Definitely more important than Howard. How could that be? Why, sometimes she was jealous of her own children, the way they ate up the spaces between herself and John; the way they swallowed up time with every mouthful they ate; the way John took Anna with him, without asking her, on sunny days. He didn't do it often, but each time it happened, she was pale with rage. And Anna was only five.

Alice, looking at her, thought, I was wrong all this time to think it would make any difference if she was poor as a mouse, if she was poorer than we were. She'd be out there digging twenty hills of potatoes, but she'd be thinking something about potatoes, or the eyes in the potatoes, about what they saw down there, about how they felt when the bugs came after them and they weren't able to move or get away. No, she wouldn't just go home and write, "Pleasant but chilly. I dug twenty hills of potatoes; got only enough for our dinner. Everyone else in bed; I had better get there, too." She'd be up thinking about sleep, what it was, why people had to sleep, what would happen if she didn't sleep until she fell apart. She'd even try it out. No, it's not the money; she's different. She's always thinking about something.

Alice's mind went back to the potatoes. Now, she thought, if I went on about potatoes, and their eyes open in the damp ground, and the worms, and the bugs (she shivered), I'd be crazy as a bedbug in ten minutes. It's different, thinking about Lois Ann: that makes me think about making over clothes and canning the blackberries up on Lord's Hill, whether we should stay on the first floor all winter and save wood money, all the things I put in those diaries. No wonder they call them Standard Diaries. And Dr. Steele, he's the same way, just like her. She wondered what would happen if one of them died before the other. They ought, she mused, to jump off a precipice somewhere together, like the couple she read about in Nevada; they did that when their parents objected to their marrying. Yes, Edna and John ought to do that before a Standard Diary caught one of them in its trap. Well, they certainly added something to *her* life; she never thought much about jumping off precipices before she met Edna, romantic things like that. She did like to think about it, stepping off into blue air, watching the solid rocks go by, holding someone's hand.

She guessed if she had to take someone's hand, she'd take Florence's. Florence had been company. Well, that was over, wasn't it, that working in the kitchen, watching her off to music lessons, boarding the teacher for her, hoping she would become something new and better, but would still want her mother all the same. No, she thought, it didn't do to think about these things, not when God in his mercy provided Lois Anns to think about. You couldn't mourn long with Lois Anns about. Or with cows eating the corn, and bugs eating the potatoes, and mosquitoes eating the noses of the horses, and salve to put on their noses to keep off the flies. When Florence died, Reverend Pierce had warned her not to paint the house of her soul all black, but who had the time to paint anything? If the roof was leaking, the porch was on fire, too. You didn't stop to paint. At least she didn't. Just here was where money might make the difference. The Steeles, now, they might have time to paint. She hoped they wouldn't have to, because if they did, it would be the end of them. The end of all of them. Except maybe some of the children; they didn't seem much different from hers. Or anyone else's. Was that good or bad? She didn't know. She supposed any family was like the ark; you needed all kinds. Well, and *would* they have any potatoes? And could Mr. Steele get Lois Ann out of the house?

"How many," Edna asked, "of our tribe of the devil have been down to your house when Lois Ann's husband was there?" "Martin, I think, and Ella. Not Lettie. She always goes off by herself somewhere, or she follows William all around. I don't think Lettie was; no, I don't think so." "Are the children frightened by him?" Edna asked. "Martin, he gets upset something terrible, but Ella, she doesn't mind anything; leastways I don't think so." "Not Anna?" "Anna? No. She's always off with Hal. Tags around right after him like a little dog." "I know," Edna said; "and then he has to carry her back, she gets so tired. Last time he carried her over three miles. I wonder why she goes all over with him. There *are* other children." "Probably because he takes her wherever he goes; she feels all grown up. They all like that." "I suppose that's it," Edna said. She was tired of lying in bed.

"I want to get up, or try getting up." "Oh no," Alice said, alarmed; "don't you move until I ask Dr. Steele." "You're frightened of him," Edna realized, amused. "Well, you would be, too, if you weren't married to him." She went off to look for John. They came back together and began walking Edna around the room. "Three times is enough," John pronounced, steering her over to the bed. "But I'm not a bit tired." "Well, *I* am." "Poor old thing," Edna whispered, stroking his hair. His whole body seemed to soften. Alice decided to leave while the going was good. "John," Edna murmured, touching his cheek, "you don't think Hal is taking Anna to funerals and weddings?" "Good God, I hope not." "We'll think about it later," she told him, snuggling up; "lie down next to me." They lay there, holding to each other. When Alice next looked in, they had fallen sound asleep. Alice watched them with envy; then she felt a sharp stab of pity. Oh, she

435

scolded herself, I'm just envious. Just envious. That's all that's the matter with me.

Six months passed and there were rumors of diphtheria up on Lord's Hill. The Steeles had not yet gotten to Cape Cod; John realized they were not going to, either. "Edna," he said, "I think we ought to send the girls down to your mother's; it's time to finish them up again. I think their shine is wearing off." "All right," she agreed; "Anna, too?" "Yes, why not start her out early? She must be tired of Hal even if she's too young to know it." Edna had finally made peace with her mother and her new father; she had sat down one day, and, as if making entries in the cash accounts of Alice's diary, had totaled things up. Her mother had not been much good with either her daughter or her husband, but she had done her best. Edna could not say that of herself. She was too selfish. It was she who wanted what was best. She kept hoping her children would grow up to be the same way, and would be strong, independent, capable of finding what they wanted—as she had. But she knew that was partly an excuse; it hid her obsessions with John, her lack of maternal instinct. And she had always believed she would be such a passionate mother.

She remembered Alice telling her that Jimmie would interest her ever so much less after her children were born, because the cat never changed, but the children were ever so much more interesting, when, in fact, it had turned out the other way around: Jimmie had become more and more of an idol to her with every passing year. He never changed. That was the special blessing of his nature. No matter what, Jimmie was always the same. He was no longer permitted to leave the house at all; he might catch and bite a mouse or a bat with rabies. Edna couldn't take that chance. She needed something secure, permanent. But she already had a mate for Jimmie, six years younger. That was her insurance. If anything happened to him. She kept his portrait hidden in a corner of the attic. She had had it done in secret; only John had found out about it. That was the one thing she hadn't wanted him to know, but he *would* come home as she was struggling up the stairs with the canvas newly stretched on its frame. It was true, too; she did want Jimmie's picture carved on her tombstone. The stonecutter could copy his picture from the portrait; sooner or later, she would have to let one of the children know about its existence. To be sure nothing went wrong with her plans. It would be terrible if someone carved the wrong cat.

And it was terrible she wasn't more of a mother, that she wasn't more excited by their changing and all the cute little things they did. Jimmie's companion, Ginnie the cat, still had two of her kittens. They were both two years old and she still dragged them about by the nape of their necks; as if they were still small as rolled-up socks. Edna studied the mother cat daily, but she couldn't bring herself to take after her. Ginnie hid the kittens whenever strangers came. If one escaped her vigilance, she stalked out, spanking the wayward offspring back to its hiding place. And they were twice her size, too. Edna didn't care that violently. Or if she did, she thought, uneasy, she could never begin to admit it. There was something wrong in her. Really, she envied Ginnie. She envied Alice. She had even come to envy her own mother. She *should* be more careful about Anna and where she went with Hal. Well, she thought, there was no point in worrying over it now. They were all, except for Martin, going off to Boston, and then on their annual trip to the dressmaker's in Manhattan.

Still, she kept coming back to it: Anna did seem different. She was almost six now, and going off to school; the board let her enter early because she was so precocious and because her parents contributed so generously to the district school. The Steeles even boarded the teacher in one of their wings. "Edna," Ten had said one day, turning from the stove, "this house is beginning to look and act like a creeping vine; it's wandering all over the hill." And that was true, too. The teacher was off on one of those tendrils somewhere or other. People just moved in and out of rooms as if the wind blew them, Edna thought, exasperated. It made it so much harder for Bridget and Bertha; they were getting on, too. Not that *they* didn't change rooms often enough. Still, they had better hire additional help to work under them. Ellen was still there, but Minnie had gone long ago, ever since she and John came home and found Ten pacing up and down in front of the nursery. "She's taking Ella home with *her*," Ten informed them; "she thinks there are too many drafts in this house." Edna insisted Minnie be on a train that very afternoon, before, as she told John, she did what all crazy servants did, and tried to poison the lot of them.

Before the children went off, she had better talk to Hal. That was one thing about Hal. He was like Jimmie. He never changed; he never lied. She found him out in the barn. "Hal," Edna said, perching on a wooden rail, "did you go to any funerals last week?" "Oh yes." She knew it. "Was it a good one?" "Oh yes." "Tell Edna what it was like." "Oh, it was nice, Miss Edna. The little boy died, and he was"—he stumbled—"contagious. And one of the likeness makers had his camera there but they wouldn't let him in." "That's too bad, after he came all that way." "No, Miss Edna. He took the picture all the same. Of the little dead boy, I mean. I thought he was sleeping, but they all said he was dead and that was why the man came to make his likeness." "How did he do it? If they wouldn't let him in?" "They made his bed go up higher. They put it up on stones. We saw him out the window. The man took his picture through the window."

"What a good idea," Edna said; "did Anna go, too? She must have liked it." "Oh yes, Anna said the little boy was her friend. She said he sat near her in school." "Did Anna cry?" "Oh yes; she was the best crier there. Everyone said she cried so much. Everyone gave her a handkerchief." "Did she take any?" "Oh no, she threw them down." "And then what did she do?" "She ran into the woods." "Oh," Edna said, "she must have gotten lost." "Hal got her out," he announced proudly. "Did you carry her home?" "Oh no, Miss Edna. There was another burying, so we went to that. I carried her there." "Who was getting buried that time?" "An old lady. She looked funny. She didn't have any skin." "No skin?" "She had lots of bones in her face." "I see." Edna's head was spinning. "Did Anna want to go to any more funerals?" "Oh no; she said they made her cry and she wouldn't go to any more with me, not to any of them." "*Did* she go to any more?" "Oh yes; she was just mad." "That's a good boy, Hal," Edna said, getting up. She had better tell John all about this.

She went into the cottage he had taken over and found him standing over towers of mosquito netting. "Are we expecting locusts?" she asked. She felt as if she had turned to stone; if she began to raise her voice she would be unable to stop screaming. She asked him what he was doing. "I'm trying an experiment; there's diphtheria, not typhoid, up on Lord's Hill. Dr. Gibson from Boston is taking over for me, and I'm finally trying out my theory. If we stay in one part of the house and don't let anyone in or out, and boil all the water, and keep the windows covered with stuff, and the doors, we may be safe. Completely safe. I'm going to try it out." "This isn't like you, John." "Yes, it is; you always said I should be in a lab finding cures for things. This is a prevention cure." "We're going to be living inside a spider web until this epidemic is over?" "That's about the size of it; we're putting a water tank up on the roof, and all the water that comes down gets boiled." "Everyone is going to think we've gone clean crazy at last." "I'd rather have them thinking evil thoughts over our live bodies than good ones over our dead ones." "But I'd like to see Alice." "Too late." "But Martin may be down at her house." "Ten has him under lock and key and Amos is already standing guard under his window." "You're really serious!" "You'd better get inside now," he answered absently. "No, there's something I want to talk to you about first."

She told John about Anna and the two funerals. "I don't like it," she finished. "Neither do I; neither do I," John grumbled, sitting down on a roll of netting; "but we don't know yet if the experience took. Some people get vaccinated twelve times before they get a take. Maybe this one didn't." "I have the definite feeling it did," Edna worried; "she's seemed different since then. That's what made me think of asking Hal about the funerals." "They photographed the boy in quarantine?" "Yes, I know," Edna said; "it seems terribly morbid to me, too." "I'm not so sure about that; that's the last they'll see of him. If they're like all the other parents I've ever met, they probably intended to have his likeness taken, and then he went and died and spoiled all their plans." "But to want to remember him like that?" "It must be better than not remembering him at all. Everyone's more afraid of losing their memory than their minds, don't you think so?" "I don't know. I'm worried about what Anna remembers." "I told you, Edna; we won't know until much later." "What do you mean?" she asked, beside herself; "we won't know what it meant to her until we find out if she reads the papers looking for death notices and spends her life going from funeral to funeral?" "I hardly think it will be that simple." Edna suddenly burst into tears. John picked her up, rocking her. It's because of that last delivery, he decided; yes, that had to be it.

"Why don't you stay here," he suggested, "until the men finish putting up the netting?" "Who's going to put up the netting over the door once we go in?" "One of the men." "John," she shrieked, "I am worried about Anna! Our daughter. The youngest one." "Edna," he said, taking her by the shoulders, shaking her, "what's the matter with you? The diphtheria is what we need to worry about and Anna's safe in Boston." "Good Lord, John," she burst out, "there are all kinds of diseases." "What do you want me to do? Ask Anna all kinds of questions about those funerals?" "Of course not; that would only impress them upon her more." "Then what *do* you want me to do? I can't tell her to forget it. Not without mentioning it again. Do you want me to talk to her about death?" "I don't want her *thinking* about death!" Edna exploded.

John looked at her, helpless. "Edna, look," he pleaded; "she's off in Boston with your mother and stepfather. They'll be taking her to the circus, shopping, for rides on ponies, on streetcars, and if she were here, she'd be seeing wagon after wagon passing the house on the way to the burying ground. So it just happens that she is, accidentally, in the best possible place *not* to think about death." "In the midst of all those marble corpses?" Edna wailed. "We can't do anything about it," John roared, finally losing all patience; "it's already happened. Can't you get that through your head?" Edna sank down on the floor; her hands covered her face. If Alice were only here, John thought. But he couldn't call her without breaking the quarantine. He wasn't going to do that. There had been enough close calls already. Edna finally stood up.

"John," she said, tentative; "this really is not like you. What are you up to?" "Nothing," he said, guilty," "nothing. I'm just trying to experiment." "I don't know," she thought out loud; "since John's birth, nothing's gone right. I don't even like calling him John. It makes it seem as if he's coming in one door and you're going out another." "Then we can call him Jack." "That's a good idea. Well," she asked, resigned, "how long do I have before I get sealed in the crypt?" He looked at his watch. "Exactly two minutes." "Are you sure we have enough food?" "It's all taken care of." "I think this is preposterous." "You thought it was preposterous when I thought consumption was contagious, but Virginia's husband managed to come down wtih it, and die of it, too." "That was just coincidence; that's all it was, coincidence." "It wasn't, and your time is up." "Oh yes, we'll have plenty of time to go crazy inside," she snapped, leaving.

What was wrong with her? There were times she never wanted to leave the house; why was she fretting so now? It must have to do with Anna. There was nothing he could do about Hal. *He* would be a problem, keeping him in the house when the caskets went by; he'd be jumping at the door like a dog. Well, there was nothing for it; he had better go in, too. He entered under the fierce stares of all the women. Martin was sitting in a corner of the kitchen, knees drawn up under his chin. The poor child looks terrified, John thought. They could do something about *that*. "Well, Warden," Ten asked, "are you thoroughly satisfied?" "You're just mad because you can't get into your turret." Ten went to the door, slamming it so hard after her the windows jumped in their frames. Edna looked at her husband and shook her head. "If everyone's going to treat me like a leper," he said, "I'm going into the parlor to read." "That daguerreotype book, no doubt," she said, sarcastic. "Exactly right," he answered, banging the door after him. Bridget looked down at Martin. "How about licking the gingerbread bowl?" she asked. "If you want me to," he answered. Well, this was a fine state of affairs, Bridget thought. She wondered if diphtheria could really be brought on by ailing nerves.

They had been confined to the house for well over a week now, and there was no one in the house who did not regard the doctor as tyrant and oppressor. Martin was continually moaning about George, who had no doubt discovered an even better nest of snakes, and, after working out all the puzzles for children in his *St. Nicholas*, had taken out his early *French's Arithmetic Books* and was methodically working his way through them; he was now almost finished with Book One. "What on earth do you want with *them?*" Ten asked; "I never could get you to look at them before your examinations." "I like them," he answered, without looking at her; "they make me remember how hard they were then and how easy they are now." He had turned back to the first page of the first volume and was involuntarily reading it all over again:

A. Easy Problems, Introducing the Numbers
in Order.

1. How many hands have you? how many mouths? how many noses?

* * *

8. How many horses are there in a pair of horses?
9. How many letters are there in the word CAT? If you take away the letter A, how many letters will remain? If you put back the A and the C, how many letters will remain? If you take away the C and the A, how many letters will remain?

Martin pointed to number 9. "I like that one, Aunt Ten; it's like a conundrum. If you take away the C and the A, what kind of drink do you have?" "Coffee?" "Oh, come on," Martin whined. "Tea?" "That's right"; Martin grinned; "tea." Ten began reading over his shoulder. He affectionately caressed the pages. "Problem 23. Joseph, Walter, and little Bob must carry into the cellar the wood which the dealer has dumped before their father's door. Joseph and Walter can carry two sticks at a time, but Bob can only carry one; how many sticks can they all carry at a trip?" "Remember that one, Aunt Ten? Remember how Daddy, I mean Poppa, always used to pick that one out to read to us when the wood came? 'How many sticks can they all carry at a trip?'" He grinned happily at the page.

Edna, rereading *The Guideboard,* was listening intently. Was it possible that Martin had already gotten old enough to remember things happening to him *as a child?* She thought back over her conversation with Alice. When did they lose that important place? How early did it happen? Had it happened to all of them without their knowing it? She was startled to see Martin smiling contentedly at her, and realized she had been sitting there, looking at him over the top of her book, beaming with pride like anyone else's mother. Perhaps John should lock us all up like this once a year, she thought: together.

Martin let the pages fly by to the last. "Aunt Ten?" he said playfully; "this one is for you. 'A man, being asked how many sheep he had, answered that if he had as many more, half as many more, and two and a half sheep, he should have a hundred. How many had he?" "Oh, Martin," Ten moaned, "you know, the truth is, I could never figure those out. They're like those other questions Ella was always busy with. 'If your sister's mother was your brother's uncle, and your grandmother's daughter is your first cousin, what is your relation to the pet cat?' " "Boy, I wish I'd thought up one like that," he murmured. "Why?" Ten asked, ruffling his hair; "so you could write it all over the board while the teacher was snoring?" "He didn't snore so very long," Martin mumbled, looking down at his book; "we fixed him. We knew he always put his feet up when we were doing lessons, so right after he fell asleep one day we put a board with a nail in it on the desk and when he put his feet down, he howled like a chicken in a cat cage." "How did I miss hearing about that?" Ten asked. "He didn't want anyone to know he was sleeping." "And the ball of yarn you used to kick around and then hide under that loose plank of wood in the floor?" Ten inquired. "How did *you* find out about that?" "A little mouse told me," she said, kissing the top of his head.

"Aunt Ten," he said abruptly, "if you never could figure out those problems, like the one about the sheep, how did you always get them worked out before me?" "I used to stay up all night," she admitted. "You should feel *sheepish*," Edna teased. "Well, *someone* had to do it," Ten said. "No wonder," Martin said, "you always seemed to have such long ways of getting through them." "Well, I got there, didn't I?" Edna shook her head, smiling. "You know, Ten," she said, "I always wondered why you didn't take on more after Martin got to the head of his class in arithmetic; even though it gave you more time for *Lucretia, Portia*, things like that. I thought you *liked* those problems." "Go on, make fun of an old woman," Ten snorted; "by that time, he had George to help him." "I never understood," Edna mused, "how that child could be so good at arithmetic and still could barely spell his name." "George is a hard name to spell," Martin piped up. "Oh, so that's it, is it?" Edna asked. "Well, one and one of you certainly made a good team," she remembered.

Eleven years. Time had certainly flown. She couldn't correct that habit of thinking that way, seeing time as a stream, winged water. A vulture, that would be a more appropriate picture for it. "Well, Mother," Martin said, getting up, "does this section on time help you out?" Edna took it. She realized she had never seen one of his books, at least not with her son attached to it.

" 'Change 5 minutes 20 seconds to seconds,' " she read out. Now, that sounded like an idiotic version of her theory, all those solid things turning into heaps of seconds, things which blew away, finally, like dust. She never liked it when her thoughts on the subject came close to anything religious in expression; for instance, ashes to ashes, dust to dust. And then back again. Why did they have to start over? Why couldn't they just keep on going? She looked up at Martin. Definitely, he resembled his father; he looked more like him every day. So the process was going on. Change this man, she thought, from a collection of forty-one years into a cloud of dust and blow him over the horizon's edge. She shuddered. Martin's small hand crept over hers; her knuckles, he noticed, were showing white. She was looking at the wheel, labeled, in its central circle, The Year. The next circle out was divided into summer, spring, autumn, winter. Well, what else did she expect? why did looking at this drawing make her feel like crying so?

There were Martin's little marks all over that circle; 58 in one slice, 88 in another, 69, 44. She supposed they were answers to problems. But it did look like a saw blade, that wheel, one spinning so fast the jagged jigsaw edges blurred into something smooth. And deadly. Autumn, winter, spring, summer, she chanted silently. Summer, autumn, winter, spring. She liked that best. "Don't cry, Momma," Martin was pleading; "you don't have to do these anymore." "She's just got the blues from being in the lockup," John commented from his darkness. "John," Edna remonstrated, "why can't you read in more light?" He didn't answer. "Can I look at the book?" she asked Martin shyly. He handed it over, pulling up the piano stool, sitting down. In his corner, John also felt like dissolving into a small, salty puddle. It was, he told himself, the isolation.

It was also, he finally admitted, seeing Edna with Martin like that. She certainly had lived through her pregnancies. She didn't look, he thought, appraising her with his photographer's eye, one day older than she did when he met her. Ella often looked older than her mother. You had to study her, he thought, to find the signs of age, and even those signs were so lovely; those little crinkles in the corners of her eyes. They reminded him of crinkles on the edges of pillows. *They* were so comforting when he went to sleep. And the red stretch marks on her belly. She didn't mind them, he knew, but other women did. To him, they had become the private maps and back roads of victories over dangers, arguments, all kinds of things. How she had fooled him when she was pregnant with Martin. Yes, she was a remarkable little person, he thought, gazing at her fixedly over the top of his book, as if he were already the camera he was reading about, trying, once and for all, to fix her image. How he loved her. Should he try to explain this quarantine to her? It would be useless, painful; she had had enough pain lately. If she had died. His mind emptied. That was not possible, not in this order of things. He pretended to continue reading, to breathe normally.

"What lovely pictures," he heard Edna murmuring; "how they do bring things back. I suppose they never meant much to you?" She looked at Martin. The first one displayed a country picnic, women walking under trees already half bare, carrying parasols, little children playing in the foreground; how the little children looked like shrunken adults! A little boy was playing with a hoop, a small, nondescript dog running up to him, tail erect. If you looked carefully, you could see the outline of the town, its steeple on the far horizon; it seemed to dissolve in the fog. "Oh no, Mother," Martin protested; "they meant a great deal." He always used such grown-up words, Edna thought; had John been that kind of child? "The little dog, now. He reminds me of Flag." "Flag?" Edna asked; "can you still remember Flag?" Martin nodded. "And this one," he said, taking a deep breath, "with

445

the little girls playing with a hoop, jumping rope, the boys over there playing marbles? It always reminds me of the Moffats, after George and I got to be friends. It seems so long ago," he sighed. "Eliza is eleven years old, and Hannah is two years older. How old is Hannah?" "As old as she will ever be, Edna thought; as old as Martin will ever be. As old as I am. She turned the pages gently, looking for the pictures.

Martin couldn't keep from smiling; if that wasn't what *he* had always done, whenever he got bored. He made up such stories about those pictures. For instance, the wagons leaving the mill. He used to imagine one was his father's, and then what dramatic things happened during the day. He could even hear the water turning the mill wheel, the clatter of hooves and wheels over the little wooden bridge. He had always put himself in the other wagon—going on some important mission. Usually rescuing something, or someone. He remembered now. He was often rescuing his mother. Or his father. They were invariably caught in a fire, and he got them out, wrapped in wet blankets. But Aunt Ten, he never imagined rescuing her. He guessed she didn't need rescuing.

" 'If three hogsheads of sugar make one load for a dray, how many loads will six hogsheads make?' John," she asked, "do you remember when I didn't know what any of those words meant?" "I remember," he answered without looking up. "It doesn't seem possible, does it?" she murmured. "Things never do, afterwards," Martin said. Was that *her* child talking? It certainly sounded like her child. Their spirit, she thought, their spirit was blowing into him like a wind, like strange honey filling an empty honeycomb. Poor child, she thought; poor us. "I like the picture of the barnyard," she said; "Martin, do you know when I first came here I thought everything with horns was a bull?" "You did?" It was hard for him to think of Mother as so ignorant. "Listen to this, Ten"; she read out: " 'how many feet have all the quadrupeds in this picture?' " "I know," Ten answered, "those books never did believe in keeping the children in suspense." "But what a strange mixture," Edna persisted; "quadrupeds in one line, and 'a ton of hay will keep six sheep nine months. How many months will it keep one sheep?' "

"You could probably figure that one out," John taunted his sister.

Edna went back to the pictures. There was a woman buying fruit at the store, a man measuring wood, children sitting on logs watching their fathers load wagons with boards, a butter churn being weighed, a round mound of hay going off to the barn, an apple cut in half, pies scored for cutting, a man with a globe. They were little books of life, all the seasons, all the scenes she knew, except, she thought, closing the book, looking uneasily at the cover, that picture of the devoted mother reading aloud with *her* five children. What an earnest expression the good woman had. She could never assume such an earnest expression, or lean forward with such concern over their lessons so anxiously. Well, she had never tried to convince herself she was the perfect mother. Never. "What *are* you reading?" Edna asked her husband. *"The American Handbook of the Daguerreotype."* She stifled a groan. "What part are you up to?"

"I'm reading backwards; they put an account of the early experiments with the daguerreotype in the back." That was like him, first things first. Orderly. "The early things are important," John said; "things get lost with progress. It's good practice to start with the beginning. A hundred years from now, even fifty, people won't know the names of the medicines we use. They won't know what they stand for; even if they work. For instance, potassium iodide for asthma, people are using it less and less, people will forget it and have to discover it all over again. Linseed meal, Venetian red, laudanum, soaking isinglass in water, gum ammoniac, decoction of logwood, saleratus, who can remember it all?"

"Do you think," Edna asked, "there was a time, a time when things were perfect?" "I thought you didn't believe in the Bible." He finally looked up. "I don't; it's just that it's not necessarily mistaken about *everything*. There *may* have been a perfect time, before the saleratus, or whatever, was forgotten. Or used up." "Ours has been good enough." "Don't speak of it as if it was over!" "It is, though, isn't it? More and more and more of the same, and fitting into shoes others lost the use for long ago, and then nothing at all." "You're all getting morbid," Ten cut in; "if you ask me, nature wouldn't dare fail to preserve traces of your life together; it's unique." "No, it's not," Edna said sadly. "Well, if you want to argue," Ten replied, picking up *Molly's Bible*. She had evidently graduated from one-word titles.

"Where did you get that?" Edna asked. "Anna." "Anna? She's not old enough to read that." "She was trying, anyhow; she seems to be getting very interested in religion. It makes me edgy." Edna and John looked at each other, Edna resolving, as soon as possible, to tell Ten about Anna's visits to all the funerals in the county. Perhaps she could think of something to do about it. Although it was like trying to prevent the formation of a certain footprint in the sand of a beach which had not yet even appeared; it would take such an effort, and no one even sure if the beach would appear in the first place.

"Martin," Edna asked, pulling a sketch out of the first book of arithmetic, "where did you get this?" It was a sketch of John on one straight chair, holding Anna, and Hal, wearing his perpetual pancake hat, right next to him. In the sketch, both men wore mustaches, and Anna: she was recognizable, but definitely a baby. It was not difficult to imagine John putting her down, to see her taking two steps, then falling. "I found it," he answered, awkward. "Is it one of your things?" she asked gently. "Yes, but I guess you could say I stole it." "You keep it," she told him, giving it back. She was sorry she had seen it. She felt she had read some part of a secret diary. Martin had retreated to a corner and, like his father, was peering at her from the shadows. "John, do you remember when he used to say, 'I like my skin on your comfy bed'? And then he used to say, 'My skin is all over me.'" John looked up smiling. "All this remembering is unhealthy," Ten announced; "if we're going to sit inside remembering, like corpses alive in a vault, I'm going to make my escape and take my chances outside." Everyone turned to look at her.

"That's a wagon," Ten said suddenly; they all jumped up and went to the window. Only John stayed in his chair. A long line of teams was slowly driving down the road in front of the house. "Six," Ten said; "there are six coffins in the bottom of that wagon." John got up and stood behind Edna. An unknown team followed, pulling an open carriage, three coffins propped up in back. "Two more," Ten reported as the next team passed on. The procession appeared peculiar, with its escort of men on horseback as if accompanying a military transport. "Who is in them?" Edna asked, frightened. She watched the drivers for the sight of Howard; he wasn't there. She relaxed slightly. Then it occurred to her he might be in one of the coffins. "It wipes out whole families," Ten murmured; "when John was eight, he had a little friend who had six sisters and brothers, and when it was all over, we went up to the boy's farm and the only one left was the mother and one baby; it couldn't have been more than five months old. She took that baby wherever she went. She never put him down, never." "It was a girl," John said suddenly; "my little friend was a girl. Helen. I was going to marry her. Don't you remember?" "No, not that part." "Well, are you sorry you're in here now?" John asked; "or would you all rather be in church moaning, 'The Lord giveth and the Lord taketh away'?" He got no answer.

"Do you think the Moffats are all right?" Edna asked. John put his arm around her. No one said a word. The procession kept passing. "How long do you think it will take them to get to the burying ground?" asked Martin. "An hour, at that rate," his father answered. "I wish we could get some mail," Edna flared up; "I have no idea of how the children are, what my mother's doing to them, what they're doing to her, what they're *doing*. I don't know what kind of *clothes* they're buying." "You can be sure they're safe with your mother. *And* Mr. Siddons. He treats them as if they were made of glass," Ten snapped. "Well, that's not good for them, is it?" Edna asked. Ten sighed, and went back to her seat. John and Edna stood, arms around each other, looking out the window, long after the last carriage had passed. "How many?" she whispered; "how many carriages?" "Twelve, I think." "Twelve; let's sit down. It's no use staring out there." They went back to their seats.

"One of those men was Amanda Hubbard's father," Martin said abruptly. "Who's Amanda Hubbard?" Ten asked. "She won the spelling bee last week." "Oh," said Ten, "that was Amanda Hubbard, was it?" "That doesn't mean," John said, "Amanda Hubbard was in one of those boxes. Her father might have been a friend of someone's family." "It was an awfully small box," Martin said. "All the same, it could be a cousin, a child of a friend, even a pet." Martin made no reply.

Ten picked up *The Guideboard* where Edna had dropped it. "Look," she said cheerfully, "it opened to a page on early marriages." They all stared at her. " 'Early marriages,' " she read, " 'by which we mean under twenty-three for the woman, and under twenty-eight for the man—are the misfortune and calamity of those who contract them. The constitution of the woman is prematurely broken down by early childbearing, and is broken down before she is thirty-five, the age in which she ought to be in all the glory of matronly beauty, of social and domestic influence and power and enjoyment. But instead of this,' " she read more enthusiastically, now peering significantly at Edna, " 'in what condition does "thirty-five" find the great majority of American women?—thin, pale, wasted, hollow cheeks, sunken and dark-circled eyes, no strength, no power of endurance, with a complication of peculiar ailments, which, while they baffle medical skill' " —she now stared significantly at John—" 'irritate the body, and leave the mind habitually fretful and complaining; or what is less endurable, throw it into a state of hopeless passivity, of wearisome and destructive indifference to family, children, household, everything. A woman who begins to have children at eighteen cannot have that vigor of body and mind which is essential to a well-regulated household; we say, therefore, to every young man— Do not marry under twenty-eight for yourself, nor under twenty-three for your wife.' It also says," she observed, "that the young wife 'drives the husband to wrack and ruin, diverts his time, drives the husband to do-nothing indulgence, or habitual drunkenness. The children increase in ignorance and idleness' "—she stared at Martin—" 'are more and more neglected; or, if learning at all, have the more leisure to learn but too well the habits and practices of ignorant, trifling, deceiving, blarneying, treacherous servants, for such the mass of them are, as we know by sorrowful experience.' I must take this to the kitchen for Bridget and Bertha," she observed cheerily.

"Ten, dear," Edna said gently, "don't trouble. It won't do any good." "She's right," John agreed. "Don't bother trying to keep my spirits up," Martin added gloomily; "if that's what you're doing." Ten got up and handed the book back to Edna. She had skipped, Edna saw, looking at it, the passage right above it: "In a few years their mothers and fathers will be gone. Brothers have formed new ties. One by one the associates of their former years are lost from their visiting list, by removal, or marriage, or death. Every year leaves them more and more neglected, more and more lonely; and soon thereafter the great world loses sight of them; their very names are only now and then mentioned, while all this time they are consuming themselves with sad memories, and anon pass unwept into a forgotten grave." Oh yes, Edna remembered, *that* passage had to do with the evils of spinsterhood. "I'm going off to see what Jimmie is up to," she said, getting up and hurrying upstairs.

Jimmie was, of course, just where she expected him to be: asleep on her pillow. She buried her face in his fur and cried quietly. "Jimmie," she whispered, "I can't stand more of this." The cat solemnly examined her, extended his claws, and patted her on the cheek. Automatically, she tapped at the pads of his paws. No, she thought, he never would understand why she objected to being petted while his claws were out; he doesn't know I haven't any fur, that's why. She fell asleep, her face buried in his side.

"What time is it?" Edna asked, coming down, rubbing the sleep from her eyes. "After three," Ten answered; she didn't bother looking at her watch. She nodded, and sat down in her usual chair. "What on earth do families do who live in three rooms?" she asked after a while. "Go quietly crazy, the way we are," Ten answered. "How long," she asked John, "can this epidemic last?" "Another three weeks; we'll see." "Three weeks before we find out if anything's happened to the children." "If anything's happened to them, we'll find out." "How?" she asked, desperate; "how?" "The constable said he would come up with an 'X' on a big piece of board." "I think that makes things worse," Ten considered. "There's no saying anything right today," Edna sighed. They sat there quietly; it was a beautiful day. Sun speckled the windows green and gold. The normally dark room was abnormally bright. The sky, Edna thought, how blue and innocent it looks! And John. What had gotten into him, catching them in this spider web? Perhaps it was true; perhaps he had gone crazy. She remembered the day in the meadow, John telling her about Serepta's death. No, he was just being careful. He thought this might be a way. Why, she wondered, was it so hard to remember other people's sorrows? Even John's. She never thought about Serepta; well, that was not quite true. She had thought about her whenever she was pregnant, but otherwise, she forgot her, as if she had never existed, had never made her impact on her husband. And they cared so much for each other. What must it be like for other couples?

Thinking back to that day in the meadow, she felt the same emotions she had felt almost twelve years ago. It wasn't fair, she thought passionately, that the daily things got in the way of remembering things like that; they covered up the meadow like dust, like a sheet pulled up over a face. He looked so tired, she thought; so worn out. Older. "I'm glad we're in here," she said softly. "Are you?" She knew this isolation was causing him more pain than the rest of them. "Yes, I am; really, I am." "I am, too," Martin announced. She looked gratefully at her son. John sighed and closed his book. "Edna, let's take a nap." "In a few minutes, dear." Martin was smiling. Everyone knew she didn't want to get up and disturb Jimmie, sleeping on her lap like a furry orange.

"There's this saying about cats," Edna said to the walls: "take in an orange cat and you will never have a fire." "That's true," Ten said; "we've missed that." "There's another one; take a stray cat and show itself its reflection in the mirror, and it will never run away." "There's something deep in that one," John observed. He sounded relaxed; "Edna, you had better give that one some thought." "I already am."

Their reading was interrupted by the whack of a small stone on the parlor window. "What now?" she asked. "Someone's throwing stones," Martin announced; he was peering out from behind the heavy velvet drape. "Who is? Who's throwing stones?" Edna asked, worried. "I can't see them yet. Oh, look," he called out, his voice muffled by the draperies; "it's Mrs. Moffat, and William. And George!" He was hopping up and down. The others flew to the window. Alice Moffat marched forward, carrying a huge sign nailed to a tall plank. "All alive and well." She waggled the sign. There was some commotion amidst the little group; the Steele family watched as they re-treated to the bushes. Alice marched back to the clearing's edge with another sign: "Expect to see us when you see us." "What does *that* mean?" Edna asked. "I think she means not to worry if she doesn't come every day."

But before there was time for further conjecture, the little group had withdrawn to the bushes; this time George came out. "Not to worry if we don't come." "They must have carried half the wood from the mill up here," Edna said, waving wildly. "Get me a piece of paper," she asked Martin. She kept gesturing to Alice, who hesitated, attempting to guess what she meant. Finally, Edna's fingers began forming the letters *wait* one at a time. Alice stood there puzzled but didn't leave. Just then Martin arrived with a huge sheet of wood. "Got it from the kitchen," he panted.

Edna hurriedly held it up to the window. Alice nodded her head to show she understood. "Here's some charcoal, Mother," Martin volunteered.

Edna began writing in huge letters: "Want to send a letter. Will you mail it? Will throw it out window. To-morrow." She held up the finished product. Alice peered shortsightedly at it, then motioned William over to her. "You're asking a lot of her, aren't you?" John said quietly; "we're sealed up in here, and they're out there, taking their chances." "They could have stayed with us." "We didn't ask them." "Mr. Moffat wouldn't have let them anyway," Martin said, defending his mother. "That's true enough," Ten agreed. William was now inspecting the sign with interest. He turned to his mother and began talking to her, apparently reading the sign to her, because, when he finished, Alice excitedly nodded her head. *Goodbye.* They could see the Moffats' mouths forming the words. As they disappeared into the woods, Edna anxiously asked her husband if they would be all right. "How can I know that? But it's harder to kill a Moffat than a rat." "Rats have always brought us good luck," Edna said.

"And how, Mrs. Baseball," John asked, "are you going to throw a letter far enough out for the Moffats to get it?" "*I'm* not," Edna retorted; "Martin is." "Martin?" John echoed; "no one can throw paper far enough." "They can," she insisted, "if you tie it around a porcelain figurine." "Aha!" Ten chortled from the depths of her chair; "I should have guessed she'd think of something. Why don't you," she considered, "use Mr. Siddons' little sculpture of that Venus there on the mantel, the one with wings? It's even heavier than porcelain." "She doesn't need encouraging," John said. "Oh, I don't know about that," she murmured. "What you need is a *nap*," John informed her, steering her up the stairs.

Jimmie followed after them, his tail straight as a pole bearing the banner of victory. "You know," John told her, "we won't be able to get any of their answers." "I know that," she answered, exasperated; "but now *they'll* know why they're not getting any mail from *us*." "Well, that's a good thing; in a few days, they'll be reading about this in the papers." "If the Moffats only come tomorrow." "They will; they will, hopefully, have the good sense not to ship the little Venus along with the letter." "Very funny," she said, slipping her fingers under his collar. "When do we outgrow this?" she asked later. John just looked at her and shook his head. Jimmie, seeing the peaceable nature of the bed, promptly jumped up on Edna's pillow and began cleaning her hair with his rough tongue. Finally, she felt his tongue scraping against her scalp. "Good cat," she said sleepily. "Look what you've done to my cat," John complained ritualistically. "He's surviving," Edna said. That answer was ritual, too. "You better get up and write your letter." "Later," she answered, snuggling in close to him.

The next day, shortly after dinner, the Moffats were back in the middle of a thunderstorm. "Go on, throw it," Edna instructed Martin. John gave him permission to pull the mosquito netting back just long enough for the letter to fly from the window. Martin threw it, standing on top of a table. Edna shrieked with delight as it fell at the feet of the Moffats. Alice picked it up. The Moffats, dripping, disappeared into the woods. George marched out with a new sign. The Steeles had just enough time to read it before the rain began smearing it: "Will return." Edna was jumping up and down like a child. "Well, well," Ten said; "how interesting life can get inside a spider web." "Do *we* get to throw out any notes?" Bridget asked behind them. Somehow, even inside the netting, which made the house look, from outside, abandoned for hundreds upon hundreds of years, the normal balance was re-establishing itself. It was Alice, Edna thought with feverish gratitude; she had given them the one normal moment. Now they were safe. "Mother?" Martin said tentatively. She turned to him. "I've been doing drawings of everyone. Would you like to see them?" When she said yes, Martin took her off to his room. Well, Ten decided, they could all catch diphtheria *now*. For all she cared. She, like everyone else, suddenly felt safe. "How long?" she asked her brother. "Who knows?" he said cheerfully; "get out your 'Advice to Mothers': the 'What to Do on a Rainy Day' columns."

Inside the Steele house, time passed, it seemed, slowly, but when the Moffats appeared in a blaze of autumn leaves, holding up a sign reading, "No sickness in county two weeks now," everyone was amazed at how quickly the time had sped. "Six weeks!" Edna said, again and again; "I can't believe we've been locked in here six weeks! It doesn't seem possible. I can hardly wait to get back to rounds." "You'd never guess who was the doctor around here," John said. He had just been thinking his first two days outside would be spent in setting up a studio for his first attempts at portraits; he would duplicate the experiments from the back section of the book, just as Ten had guessed; those goings back to the beginning of time. He knew she didn't like it. Edna wouldn't object much, he decided, not if she found out which chemicals were dangerous, and that there was a recommended antidote: a bottle of aqua ammonia. And there were other effective chemicals, prussic acid, for instance, vapor of chlorine, both recommended, and both to be kept "instantly at hand to counteract any bad effects."

Hal hopped out of the house like a rabbit; he wanted to get back to swimming the river from Crown's Point to Slab Hollow, and back again. Apparently, after Edna had told Ten of his trips to funerals with Anna, even to those of her schoolmates, Ten's scolding had done little to chasten him, or those lectures were no longer part of the texture of his private time. "Do you think he will stop now?" Edna asked nervously after Ten talked to him. "I don't know; it's so hard to tell anything about Hal. Of course, he believes every word we say is gospel truth, but it's impossible to say which passages he'll choose to remember when he wants something." "What did you tell him?" "That Anna was subject to terrible fits, just like his little dog, and if she saw a casket, she might get set off and he'd have to carry her home dead." "Did he believe you?" "Of course. But that's not the point; it's whether he'll choose to remember." She tried to keep herself from asking; she couldn't. "Do you think he will?" "I don't know." Well, and what other answer had she expected?

The day Dr. Steele pronounced them liberated, Martin was triumphantly posted off to Williamsville with a letter to Mr. and Mrs. Siddons which said that the return of the girls was now possible without any danger, and they trusted they had not worried too much, since, had there been trouble, they would surely have heard of it. Edna even added a postscript, asking if they would care to come down for a rest after almost two and a half months with her "terrible angels"; she assured both of them they would have nothing to do but look around and amuse themselves.

Mr. Siddons might even find inspiration among the trees, one of which, she wrote, she would be happy to show him, it so resembled a human being. Not to mention unusual rock formations up on Lord's Hill, where rocks seemed to be in the process of turning into human beings, or vice versa. She would be glad to give them the use of any carriage, any convenience, any number of servants, or to put up any of theirs. Until she wrote the invitation, she was unaware of how grateful to her mother and stepfather she was; they *had* taken her daughters out of danger. "Now, you meet us at the Moffats'," Edna called after Martin as he posted off. He waved his hand in acknowledgment. The Moffats', John thought; of course. He and Amos could spend the day setting up the studio without a pair of female eyes peering worriedly at every bottle he put up on the shelf. Which reminded him. He *had* no shelves.

A festive atmosphere reigned. Ten, Edna, Bridget, and Bertha rode dangerously fast in the carriage, down to the Moffats'. It seemed natural, somehow, to include Bridget and Bertha this time; they had been two of the inmates. "Well," Edna gasped, running to the door just as it

456

opened, throwing her arms around Alice; "we're out." She stood back. "How did it go with you?" "We're all here," Alice told her; "except Mother. She went up to visit her cousin Minnie and came right down with it. I'll never forgive them for not notifying us. It seems so sad to have her die away from home that way. And to take away my last chance of seeing her, too." "I don't understand," Edna said; "your mother died, and in the middle of it, you were still up at our house carrying those signs?" "Things had to go on," Alice said, looking over at Ten.

Edna knew that look. It was one of sympathy between two people dealing with a third who did not understand the common language. Edna, unable to think of anything to say, hugged Alice tightly again. "Oh, we *have* missed you!" she cried. This time when the two women looked at each other over the top of Edna's shiny head, their eyes met in pure delight. She still doesn't have any gray hairs, Ten noticed, but then, she reminded herself, Edna was only twenty-nine; she had no reason to have any, while hers was pure white. It was a strange sensation, she thought, looking in the mirror, brushing her white hair in the morning, as if she were already turning temporary and perishable. Like snow. Or smoke. Something which had burned up. She suddenly saw one silver strand in Edna's hair. Wouldn't you know it? she thought, amused; even if her hair turns, it will be pure silver. She had hoped for that.

"Well, and what's been going on?" Edna asked as they sat down, chattering, around the kitchen table; "I mean, aside from the funerals," she stammered, awkward. The others laughed at her, stirring the sugar in their tea. They heard Martin come galloping up. He came in without knocking, both hands full of mail. "Letters from Lettie, Ella, Anna, Grandmother, Grandfather, and some lawyer from Boston." "Let me see them," Edna said, trying to forget what she had just heard about the letter from Boston.

Alice watched Edna happily, as if she were one of her own children. She devoured the letters greedily, reading out little pieces. "Oh, they went to Madame Jeannette's," she trilled; "look, Ten, Ella's written in here, '*Barrels* of ornamented skirts; won't they be fine for climbing trees? Barrels of dresses for Anna; they look just like yours,

Mother, more flounces than snowdrifts in January.' They are growing up with the country in them, aren't they?" Edna asked happily. "You like that?" Alice asked; "I shouldn't have thought you would." "Oh yes. I do love it; they'll have two worlds to choose from, and they're never lonely. When people disappoint them, they have the animals and the mountains, and they get shipped off to civilization twice a year. Oh yes, I like it. After all, Alice, I wasn't happy until *I* got here." "Watch and see," Alice teased; "they'll all turn into society women. That's always the way." "And yours will be landed gentlemen."

"*That* would be harder," Alice said; "mine don't really have much choice." "Well, William does; John doesn't think he and Martin would survive a separation, not until they're old enough to be married, and he wants to send them both off somewhere to get educated together; if you approve of what they want to get educated about." Alice stared. "Oh," she stammered, "I couldn't allow that, Edna." "But William is already as interested in medicine as Martin." "Well, let's tell the truth, Edna; William was born into the wrong family." "He was born into *two* families, Alice; you know there isn't anything we wouldn't do for any of you." "That's just why I have to be so careful." "Oh, let's not be serious," Ten broke in; "you'll never change Edna's mind, anyhow, once it's made up. If she's made it up about William, she'll kidnap him; that's the long and short of it."

"Knitted lace undersleeves!" Edna exclaimed; "oh, listen to what they have to say about crinolines. This is Lettie"; she read: " 'They're charging ladies in hoops twelve cents more to get on the omnibuses in New York; Ella says she won't wear them anymore ever since her skirts forced some man right off the sidewalk into the street and he was nearly run down by a bus.' She says she celebrated the event by buying several dress caps for invalids since she's sure to be one by the time she gets back. Lettie's complaining Madame Jeannette won't cut them low-necked frocks. The doctors are all warning against it and she won't take chances with a doctor's daughters. Terrible, isn't it?"; Edna smiled; "Lettie says Madame Jeannette's done the best she can do to make country things fashionable and warm enough so the weather won't kill them."

"I guess," Alice said, "that means a lot of sewing for Mrs. Grimsby; that Madame Jeannette can't know what cold is, with that tissue of nerves they call trees standing here day after day like the miseries, and the snow coming down through the branches in the middle of May." "Something called a Saragossa cape; it's made of pineapple cloth. Pineapple cloth, mohair, fans. Good Lord, we'll need another wing just for their party costumes!"

She looked up at Alice, amused. The solemn expression she saw surprised her; then she saw it reflected in Ten. "Edna," Alice said, "two things. First, parties. I don't think you ought to worry about parties, not until everyone here gets over being so mad at all of you." "At us? What did we do?" "You didn't lose anyone in the epidemic, that's what." "But that's not our fault; we were lucky." "Well, they think you knew something. Because Dr. Steele knew medicine." "But he *told* everyone about it; he told them what he was going to do. He advised everyone to do the same thing; you know that, Alice. Everyone just laughed at us. *You* didn't listen to us." "You didn't believe him, either," Alice reminded her. "But the thing is," Ten said, picking up the thread, "now that it's worked, they're going to forget they laughed at the doctor, and they'll resent us all for being alive when their loved ones are filling the churchyard; that's it, isn't it, Alice?" She nodded. "But that's not fair! What did they expect us to do?" "Don't expect people dressed in black to be reasonable," Ten said.

"And another thing," Alice cautioned; "it looks like a real old-fashioned revival here, just like after that typhoid epidemic twenty years ago. You remember, Ten?" She did. "What does *that* mean?" Edna asked, looking from one to the other. "It means," Ten said slowly, "everyone's going to be out looking for God, trying to close with Christ, watching sick children to find out if God is in them, more Sabbath-school meetings, prayer meetings, inquiry meetings, Bible-reading meetings, poring over souls like primers, diaries to chart the soul's spiritual progress, examining each other for traces of justification; praying for unredeemed neighbors, people like us, sitting up at deathbeds and writing down pious words of dying men and women; even children. It's terrible." "I think so, too," Alice agreed, "but there's nothing we can do about it. It's already started." "Already started," Edna repeated; "what do you mean? Meetings, things like that?" "No, worse," Alice answered; "look at this." She took a little book from her pocket. *"Memoir of Florence Kidder, who died in Dorset, Vermont, April, 1855, aged 11 years."* "What *is* this?" she asked Alice. Eleven years. That was how old Martin was. "You had better have a look at it," Ten told her.

"It seems to be about a child," Edna said; "about her having attended Sabbath school most of the time since she was old enough to do so." She went on reading. "Oh, it's her teacher writing; she left her teacher a note: 'My dear Teacher, I am a lost sinner; can you tell me what I shall do to be saved? F. Kidder.' " "Read what the teacher did," Ten said. Edna looked up puzzled. They had so scrupulously avoided religion. Yes, their money, their position, had put them in a special, safe category. But this, this looked like something from the witch trials.

" 'In answer to my inquiries,' " she read, " 'what at that time made her so anxious for salvation?—she said, "When I was sick a few days ago, I thought perhaps I should die, and if I did, I knew I could not go to heaven unless my sins were forgiven, and I determined to try and be a Christian." ' So the teacher," Edna went on, "decided to take her Bible, and," she began reading again, " 'marked such passages as I thought would convince her still more deeply of her guilt, and others which invited sinners to Christ, with promises of acceptance to all those who were truly penitent.' That's *cruel,*" Edna whispered, looking at them. "She thought it was for the best, the teacher, I mean," Ten said.

"Oh, she writes her teacher another note," Edna told them, looking further into the book: " 'I believe, my dear Teacher, I have found Jesus, and given my heart to him. If it was God's will that I should die now, I think I should not be afraid, for I believe Christ would take me to himself in glory.' She dies, doesn't she?" Edna asked. The two women watched her. Bridget and Bertha had gone into the woods looking for mushrooms. " 'Never shall I forget that look—that lovely smile that played around those death-like features, as the deep struggle, which we expected would be her last, passed away; and as the little sufferer revived; and gazing upward in rapture, exclaimed in an audible voice, "All is light before me—" A few minutes before I entered the room, when, as they all supposed, she was in the last struggles of death, with an inexpressible look of holy triumph, she exclaimed, "O happiness! happiness! O death, where is thy sting? O grave, where is thy victory?"—"Who can weep for her," said her afflicted parents; "if we weep, can we weep but for joy? for her condition is far better than ours, or that of whom she leaves behind her." ' According to this," Edna said, "she gets happier and happier as death approaches." "Naturally," said Ten; "a fine thing it would be if it went the other way." "She says things like 'Angels now stand waiting to bear my spirit up to God.' Do things like this really happen?" she asked Alice.

"You ought to know better than we do," Alice said; "you've been at enough deathbeds with your husband." "All they ever say," Edna mused, "if they say anything is 'There will be rest for the weary.' No one goes into transports." "Well, they're going into them now," Ten said; "they're going to have transports with a vengeance." Edna seemed frightened. " 'Amid such joy as Florence experienced, she seemed almost to have forgotten that the clogs of mortality had not yet fallen from her.' I've never seen *that*, either," Edna said, almost to herself; "everybody I've ever seen complains about the pain until their hands start getting cold and they can't feel it anymore."

Under the eyes of the two women, Edna turned some pages. "It says her hands are cold," Edna read slowly, "but 'she still found means to utter the strong language of the spirit that struggled within her. As she saw her mother's tears, with a bright smile upon her countenance, but with no tear in her eye, she first looked up wishfully into her mother's face, and then, endeavoring to lift her little hand, she significantly pointed her finger upward.' " Edna skipped again. " 'To those friends who stood around her in this trying time, she exclaimed, "My sufferings are almost over." Then, looking upward, she said, "I am going. I am going; come, Lord Jesus, come quickly; O Lord, receive me," and, with this prayer upon her lips, she died.' " Disturbed, Edna turned to the last page: " 'There is something in the whole of this narrative which ought to awaken the deepest interest of all. *Especially* do I hope that all those who, like her, enjoy the privilege of Sabbath School instruction, may be led to think of this child's life and death, and to imitate her example. If she followed Christ, and thus obtained a peace which the world can neither give nor take away, so may you, by following Christ, obtain the same blessed portion. May you so live, that in the season of your last sickness and death, you may be able to repeat one of Florence's favorite hymns, and to die with heaven open, as it was to her: "All is light before me." ' " She closed the book, letting it fall in her lap, a leaf the winter would not take away.

"This is terrible," she said finally, "terrible. What are we in for? Are we going to be flooded with sermons, with this kind of thing? What kind of parent would want to preserve something like this? It's horrible, why do they do it?" She looked at the other two. "It's a travesty, pretending nothing happened! How can they let anyone print this thing up?" "Oh, probably they hope it will keep her from being forgotten," Ten said; "that, and to give the death some purpose." "Is that it?" Edna asked Alice. "I think so." "But nothing, *nothing*, can change the fact that she's dead," Edna cried; "Alice, you lost a daughter; would you do this?" "No," Mrs. Moffat answered thoughtfully; "death, I don't know, like love, it seemed—private. Not everyone's business. I couldn't do it," she thought out loud; "it would be like having poor Florence stuffed and sent around the country with a smile on her face. 'Let the dead bury the dead.' That's what I believe." "Do you believe in heaven?" Mrs. Steele asked; "the one they describe in here?"

"I suppose I do," Alice answered; "only I don't think you can do better than your best, and if you try living by the golden rule, that's all I ever found in the Bible, Christ will forgive everything else. Or so it seems to me. I don't think you have to act special; no, I don't." "When Florence died," Edna pursued, "did you go through anything like this?" "Oh, something like it," Mrs. Moffat answered, uncomfortable; "I even tried drawing pictures of heaven so I could see her there better." "Did it do any good?" "It kept me busy." "Busy," Ten said; "that's all I ever found." "Well, we won't know until we get there," Mrs. Moffat said. "*If* we get there," Edna murmured, looking down at the book. Without thinking, she picked it up and violently threw it across the room. She was white as any dying woman.

"I'm sorry for that," she apologized, getting up, giving it back to Alice; "it wasn't mine to throw." "Throwing stones at gravestones, I can certainly understand *that,*" Alice said. "Is that what I'm doing? I suppose I am." "It won't do you any more good than the rest of us." Edna sat, lost in thought. "I suppose," she said, "everyone's sprouting wings like cabbages?" "Probably more horns are sprouting than anything else," Ten predicted, remembering. Alice looked at her, shrugging her shoulders. "You explain it," she asked Ten wearily. "I'm sorry, Alice, but I've been locked away there in that web; I don't know what's been going on. You tell her what's been happening and I'll try to explain it. If there is any explaining it." They looked at each other, sympathizing.

"Well, first, it's practical jokes again," Alice began; "some boys went down to James's mill and asked if he would take a small bundle of grist if they came with it, and grind it; well, he knew just what they had in mind. Everyone's been going on so about Probst's dog and how it runs at them in the street and scares everyone half to death, and he said he would, so they asked him if he would grind it at any hour, and he said he would. So two days ago, they showed up at three o'clock at night with this little bundle. I guess they killed the poor thing first, at least I hope so, and the miller ground it up. I don't know how word got out about that, but it did.

"And then there's crazy James, the one who stays up all night, digging holes, and then tells everyone about them in the morning. Well, for I don't know how long, he's been going to the churchyard and crying, 'Arise, ye dead, arise!' and some of the boys waited for him behind the tombstones, and when he came, calling out the usual things, they shouted back, 'We're coming, we're coming!' and he ran off screaming for his life, so now his daughter has her hands full of cold compresses. I tell you, there's just no peace and quiet, robberies, it's either things like that, or endless praying. I don't know which comes first, the praying or the jokes."

"It's always like this," Ten said softly; "after so many deaths, I mean. They just get plain mad, if you ask me, at the way they're being knocked around and get so tired of worrying about the executioner, they decide to be executioner themselves. I can't think of any other reason for it, can you, Alice?" "No, I'd say about the same thing, if I could say anything clear. And more barn fires, beatings at night, all the rest of it. But I don't think it will last so long this time. They're getting a big famous preacher, a relation to Noah Webster, to preach at the Old Stone Church, and everyone's looking forward to it as if it were the county fair or better, so when it's over, I guess they'll be all worn out. I know that's all Lois Ann talks about, anyhow." "She probably thinks she's going to rise right out of her seat, through the roof, and straight on up, doesn't she?"; Ten grimaced. "That's about the size of it, all right; but I think everyone will calm down after that. Once the excitement dies out, they'll all get miserable as can be, and I know *I* get pretty quiet when I'm miserable." "Who isn't?" Ten asked. "The lunatics," said Alice. "True."

"But the children are coming back to this," Edna moaned. "Oh, stop it now," Ten scolded; "they're about as well inoculated against these things as anyone ever will be." "Except for Anna. Don't forget about Anna." "Well, we'll have to watch her," Ten said; "let her go to the sermon, that's interesting enough." George and Martin peered in long enough to say Mr. Steele was coming, and promptly evaporated again. "Well," John said, sitting down, Alice setting a dish of berries before him, "I'm about ready to make my portraits. I'm going to start with *you*," he told Edna; "I'm doing it the old way first. You have to sit in one position for six minutes."

"You've heard about the doings around here?" she asked. "It's what I expected; they'll be up to everything until the living bury the dead and stop throwing themselves into the caskets trying to get the others out. Guilt, that's what it is. Edna, I hate to break up this hen party, but there's an old lady dying up on Lord's Hill; do you want to come?" "Why should she want to?" Alice asked. "I don't know if she does, but she's a big help. She talks to them when everyone else jumps out the window. No one likes the final moment much. I don't think the invalids like anyone watching the others, either, at least anyone close to them. I don't know how they do it but they always contrive to die out of sight of their daughters and husbands. One old man held right on until his son left the room; he died the instant the latch fell into place on the door." "Well, right now," Ten told him, "they're busy publishing accounts of religious expirations." "They'll get over it," he said, "as soon as the religious fever dies down." "And if there's another epidemic soon?" Edna asked. "*Then* we have trouble," John said. "Mrs. Steele," he asked, "do you want to go?"

"I'll get my cloak. Unless you're going to mind staying behind," she said to Ten. "If Alice can put up with me, this is as good as heaven. As long as it's not our thready house. Besides, you wanted me to talk to her about what to do with Lois Ann." "Oh, that's right," Edna exclaimed; "I forget everything, I get so wrapped up in letters, strange books. The important thing, Ten, is to remember Lois Ann moves into the old house whether she wants to or not. Think of something to make it her Christian duty. 'Waste not, want not'; something like that." "That's not a religious saying," Ten objected; "oh, you go on. I'll think up something." Even with all this commotion, Ten thought, the pattern was forming The pond was icing over; it would soon be solid enough to hold their weight.

She was excited, too, at the prospect of the children returning. "Now, Alice," she began as the door closed on the Steeles, "you mustn't carry on if they come back with an outfit for you. They've come to think of you as another mother, you know, and Edna will be grateful in the next world for that letter you mailed." "I don't like charity," Alice said, staring at the floor. "You'll really insult them if you say anything like that; they always get things for everyone in the family, and that's just what you are to them. You better accept it." "It's beginning to sound as if I ought to have a legal change of name," moaned poor Alice. "Just so you understand," Ten said firmly; "now, about Lois Ann." "That is a knotty problem," Alice agreed. "Anyhow," Ten remarked, "you can't blame us for having all this money. We didn't ask for it." "And where am I going to wear all those things?" "Lord knows," Ten answered; "she'll think of something." "Just what I'm always afraid of," Alice said.

"What's she dying of?" Edna asked as they walked over to the stable. "Something very peculiar; it's called old age.

She likes to talk, though, and you're curious as a termite in a new piece of wood, so it should be a good time for everyone." "Are they part of this revival?" she asked, nervous. "That family? The Wards? No one bothers with them; public opinion decided they were damned two generations ago." He helped Edna onto her horse. "Is this the house?" she asked, dismounting. It bore a distinct resemblance to a chicken coop, except a coop, she thought, was cleaner. "Well, Mrs. Ward," he said, going over to the bed in the corner of the room which comprised the house, "how are you?" "Dancing in my pretty shoes. How do you think I am? I'm dying, that's what I'm doing." "Well, are you enjoying it?" "As much as anything else, I guess; more maybe." Edna sat down on a chair John pulled up for her. It was rickety; it needed gluing. "Who are you?" she demanded of Edna. "*His* wife."

"Oh, he's got another one," the old lady muttered; "well, I was my husband's fifth, and he was my third. People around here spend so much time dying I never thought I'd get so old. It's a pesty business, burying all those husbands." "You don't have to talk to me if you don't want to." "Well, it ain't likely I'll get many more chances, now will I, little lady? Everybody got religion again?" she asked. Edna nodded. "Damn loonies," the old woman sputtered. "You don't believe in heaven?" Edna asked. "Why, you a Baptist minister? No, and I hope there ain't no such thing. I've had enough life here; I don't want to go looking for any more anywhere else." "Why not?" "Why not, why not?" the old lady asked, crabby; "I'm ninety-nine years old. They all started mourning me when I was seventy-one and my leg broke on me. They're clear mourned out. I should have died and gotten myself buried thirty years ago," she complained; "no one's going to cry now except the rain. Foolish they'd be to do it, too; they'll probably catch their death, burying me in the rain, or drafts. Might as well just dig a hole in the backyard." "I thought it must be nice to be so old." "A lot you know," Mrs. Ward snorted.

"You've lived here almost one hundred years," Edna said, enviously; "you must have seen lots of changes." "That's right," she agreed; "worse and worse every year. Once people knew how to mind their own business or you just went out and shot them down. I sure as damnation liked that better." "Were you happy here?" "Happy, happy?" Mrs. Ward asked; "I lived here; who thought about it? Happy? I suppose I was as happy as anyone. I never thought about it." "What do you remember best?" She *was* incurably curious. "Fishing for hornpout; oh, they could get their stingers into you if you didn't watch out. Picking strawberries. We had a lot of strawberries. Putting eggs in our pockets. Seems like everything I remember had thorns on it." "Except the eggs," Edna said. "Well, we got the thorns right here"—she pointed to her hip—"if we broke one getting it home. Also Father went surfing a lot; that was a big thing, going to Rhode Island." She thought. "Well, and there were those Methodist meetings. My second husband, he took me, and ladies writhing all over the floor screaming away like they was having babies, and the minister got up and scolded at everyone; that was nice." Was it possible? Edna thought; was this all she remembered after almost a century? All that was important?

"I'd like to be as old as you are," she said. "No. You ain't got the right idea there at all. It's nothing good, just growing all over everyone like an old ivy till they want to cut you back to get some light in them windows. Don't do it," Mrs. Ward advised seriously. "I guess I won't have much choice." "It's luck, bad luck; no choice. Well, I'm sleepy," she announced; "don't have anything to say, either. Too bad, too. They let you say anything when you get as old as me." Edna smiled. "Nice little thing," Mrs. Ward said; "I guess you'll do for the doctor. About time he got a new wife. You'd think there was a shortage hereabouts." "I guess so." "Well, good night," Mrs. Ward said, closing her eyes; "never was much good at keeping company."

John got up from his seat in the corner, his hand resting on Edna's shoulder. "She's dead, I guess," he whispered. "Not yet, I ain't, but if that ain't the story of my life," she muttered feebly; "you tell me," she asked him, "why I never had the good luck to get the diphtheria?" "Beats me." "Nobody knows nothing; might as well close my eyes again." John gazed affectionately down at her. Suddenly, he bent over and picked up her wrist. "She's dead," he said. "Just like that?" "Just like that; I'd say she had a good life." "Why?" "There wasn't anything more she wanted." "Except company." "I'm not even sure about that; she had her rag carpets. They kept her going. Look." He picked up the carpet under her bed; there was a second beneath the first, a third beneath the second. They were on the walls, hung as curtains, used to divide rooms, for insulation. Her pillow was a little rag carpet, stuffed with more rags. The quilt was a rag carpet. "What an imposing woman," Edna whispered, getting up. "Yes, she was, in her own way. We better go out and tell the mourners." They smiled at each other.

"Well, that ain't no trouble," the younger Mrs. Ward said; "we have the coffin all ready, and the stone, too." Edna shook her head. "No sense in surprises," she said, looking at her. She was right, Edna thought; the old woman was right. Hornpout. Surfing. Strawberries. Methodist meetings. Writhing women. A scolding minister. Like splashes of sunlight on a wall, and then the sun moved on. Even after one hundred years of loyalty. No, she didn't like that. "Dr. Steele," Edna asked, pausing before the horses, "are you really going to start up those pictures?" "Tomorrow, if I can. Will you sit in the torture seat?" "The torture seat?" "I have to clamp your head to the back of the chair; you can't move at all for six minutes." "I look forward to it; it will do wonders for my posture." What *would* she remember—when it was all over with? Well, one thing she knew; she wouldn't be printing up little books about everyone's births and deaths and cute little tricks. She wondered if John's photographs were really like that horrid *Memoir;* she was too tired to think about it. She'd have plenty of time, she had a premonition, while she was sitting in that chair. And in two days the children would be home.

"So this is the famous studio, is it not?" Edna asked the next morning, which was mercifully free of emergency calls. "And that's the chair." John pointed at it. Oh no, Edna thought; it really *did* have a clamp for the head, right there at the top. A huge reflector had been set into the ceiling. "It tilts up and down," John said proudly; "just like the Walcotts' did. And there's the other one." He pointed. "There's something I forgot to tell you," he went on; "the light is too strong for your eyes, at least for five or six minutes, so we have to set screens between you and the camera." "That's nice. Are *these* the screens?" she asked a few minutes later, as John and Amos began setting thin muslin screens, one after another, in front of her. "These are the screens," he said, avoiding her gaze. The netting was secured to wire frames. "They're horrid," Edna announced; "it's like being put in a shroud." "Don't be foolish." "You're not in this chair." "I still have to look at you through them," he said. "Well, go ahead," she complained; "oh, they make me edgy." "You have to keep quiet and not move at all or we have to do it all over again." "Fine," she grumbled. "Ready?" "I am." "It will be a profile." He had already disappeared under the black camera cloth and begun exposing the silver plate. Edna didn't like the look of that cloth much, either. "Finished," he said, after a lifetime. "I'm staying to watch this miracle," Edna insisted; she knew he would want her right out because of the chemicals. "I can hold the chlorine," she said.

John began processing the plate. First, he mercurized it, removing the iodized surface. He explained each step, as if she were a student observing an anatomy demonstration: "You remove the coating with a solution of common salt," he continued automatically. "There I am!" Edna shrieked. "Don't touch it!" John roared at her; "I have to get it under glass. It's a silver-coated plate; it tarnishes if you even touch it!" He slid a piece of glass over it, and the whole into a frame. "It's *me*," Edna marveled again. John was ready to explode with pride. "Now I have two of you," he said, gleeful; he looked years younger, years, as if time had indeed been grafted onto him. "Look!" she squealed; "you have to hold it just the right way."

He watched her turn the image this way and that in its case. "Oops! I'm gone! I mean, there I am. It's a mirror. Oh, no! Here I come again. Oh, you can see my face, this one"—she tapped her cheek—"and this one, too, the profile you made, I mean. It's amazing! But," she asked, puzzled, "don't they already have a kind you don't have to print on glass?" "I like these better." Well, she understood that. Pictures of human beings *should* be on glass.

It was eerie, she thought, looking deeper and deeper into it. As time passed, the face she superimposed on this one in the frame would become more and more unlike it. They're like magic pools, the one that caught Narcissus;

that could be a danger, that you could tilt this, pretend it was a mirror, and always see yourself as you were. At the time. And the way its mirrory surface took things in, included them with you, just as life insisted on doing. Everything drowning in the same pool. "After I do more of these," John was saying, "I'm going on to the more complicated ones; there's a way of exposing part of the plate at a time, so there's one person on one half and one on the other. Or two versions of the same person." "I like *that*," she said; she wasn't ready to give the picture up. Really, they were better than Mr. Siddons' sculptures. They were so much more like life. "You said they fade?" "Not so much with the later processes, but this kind will; the clothing will be the last thing to go. But it will pit, and spot, even tarnish. As if it were covered with dust." Dust, Edna thought; always dust.

"Why," Edna asked, "does the clothing last longest?" "Because it has the highest contrast between black and white; the face is mostly shades of white." She thought of the old woman. Perhaps time was a bleach, whitening, eating spots in the fabric of life, as something did with these pictures. "You know," she said, "people will want you to take pictures of corpses, dead children, things like that." "That might be a good idea," John said; "to photograph everyone who dies. Future generations might be able to use them to find out about the causes of death. Although the other pictures, the kinds you were just talking about, might be better for that." "I wonder why no photographer ever set up here." "Too poor; he'd starve." "But you'll do all the portraits and won't present any bills?" "It's not a business to me, is it?" "No, I suppose not." "I'll take pictures of anyone who'll sit still, but I want to take pictures of things, the church, the stone walls, the house, clothes, everything." "A memory book." "I guess; you see enough of death in my profession." "Well, come on, dear," she said; "I hear a horse. It's supposed to be sunny tomorrow. So says Ten's hip and it's hardly ever wrong."

The horse was Alice's. "Did you do it yet?" she asked excitedly. "Here it is," Edna trilled, handing her the case. "Be careful," she warned, standing over her. "Ooooh," Alice sighed; "Dr. Steele, would you consider taking pictures of the children, mine, I mean? We could pay you in wood." "I was just telling Edna I'm not giving out bills for these pictures: images." He lingered over the word. "Oh," Alice said, "that would be wonderful! Wonderful! It looks just like her, as if you caught her in there. Just like a fly stuck on glue paper!" Well, how would he like that description? Edna wondered. "Six minutes of her, anyway"; John smiled. "Six *painful* minutes," she agreed, rubbing the back of her neck. "It's beyond believing," Alice gasped, awed. "I think so, too," Edna said. "And I thought you were so against it," he taunted her.

"As long as we do something adequate about the ventilation," she cautioned; "I'm going to design something better than open doors and windows and that cupola." "Don't meddle with *this*, miss." "You better let me do it," she threatened; "if you don't want me coming in and scratching your plates." "Never argue with a woman with long nails," he told Alice. They all went in, Alice and Edna to look over the children's rooms.

"Are you going on rounds?" Alice asked. "I certainly am." "I don't know how you stand it." "It's *interesting.*" Alice shuddered. "You get used to it," Edna said; "really." "*I* wouldn't." "Well, let's inspect the rooms," Edna said, giving up; "tomorrow they'll all be home." "Momma?" Jack said, toddling into the room. She snatched him up as he grabbed for her jet necklace. She felt too old for such a little boy, but she wasn't, not really. Well, I must care for them, she thought, to feel so warm inside. I just wish I could show it more. She repeated it again to herself: tomorrow the children were coming home. "I told Martin it was all right to go off to the swamp with George," Alice said; "was it?" "Certainly"; Edna buried her face in Jack's little breast. He always smelled so delicious. She hated it when they lost that smell. Even when they smelled sour, it was different from the sour smell of old age. "Yum," she murmured, pretending to bite his fat little arm. Jimmie squinted at her from the bed, tail twitching. Less than twenty-four hours and they'd all be back. Safe. So perhaps John had been right about the quarantine after all.

Two carriages went off the next morning to meet the children. Edna shuddered, standing on the wooden floor, putting on her robe. It was already getting cold. John was a quiet mound, sleeping. Let sleeping dogs lie, she thought affectionately, pointing silently at Jimmie, who had jumped up on the vanity and was swatting at some last wild daisies, which, if tipped over, would crash, waking the whole house. Her accusing finger, matched by her frowning stare, was too much; he squinted, licked his front paw, and jumped down on the rug. He stood up against her skirt, flexing his claws; one caught in the fabric of her flounce. I hope it isn't going to be one of those days, Edna sighed, bending over to loosen the yellowing, hooked nail. She went over to the window. Snow squalls were coming and going. She watched them, holding Jimmie. Little puffs momentarily blurring the image. Getting everything ready for what was coming. Warning everything. Another little squall swept by; the trees blurred, the gate blurred, the mountains behind hazed over. As John said his pictures would with passing time. Well, the country wouldn't; the house wouldn't. She thought that over. The mountains, no: they wouldn't change.

But she remembered, just before they had moved into the new house, she had been down at Alice's, helping her clip roses. Alice had said something about the house just below them. *It* had such magnificent roses. The whole countryside envied them. "The woman who lived there before them," Alice chattered away, "she used to work in her garden one hour every day, whether it was pouring down waterfalls or nice as could be, and you should have seen how beautiful that garden was. Just one hour a day." Edna, silently clipping, thought: Someday someone will say that about me. They'll say, she used to spend an hour there, clipping roses. That's why they're so beautiful. I think she was short. Edna felt chilled now, as she had then. Well, she had done a good job with her roses; they were blooming through the first snow. There was a woman, she repeated, turning suddenly away from the window. She stole out, followed by the cat. Let John have another hour's sleep; she settled in the parlor, reading further into her new translation of Aristotle's philosophy.

She loved the time she had in this room alone, before anyone else was up. She had it so rarely. Either John was up while it was dark, or Ten was *still* up from the night before; lately, she tended more and more to insomnia. It was odd, she thought, but she hadn't amounted to anything, not in the eyes of the world, anyway. Perhaps if she had written down her theories, as John once suggested. But she hadn't really followed any of her ideas into any particular ravine. Perhaps she was undermined by her own conviction that it was hopeless, that the things she wanted to know were beyond finding out. But that would be something: to be able to map out the road as far as it went, to say, we can go this far, and no farther. Well, she hadn't done it. Now what would survive her would be traces of her face in her children. She involuntarily smiled at that; her own face in those mirrory pictures. Which were the appropriate kind, she thought sadly; always one face blurring into another, the face visible only in a certain slant of light, and tarnishing, tarnishing in the light, every time you opened its case.

And the cases, too. She had seen them lined up, one after another, on John's second shelf. They were saved, she assumed, for pictures to come later. She was constantly struck by their resemblance to little tombstones, ready for their contents. Black and brown and shining. As were Mr. Greenwood's caskets. What was it Alice had said: had there really been looting of coffins? Had Mr. Greenwood really shot someone trying to break into his barn for one of them? She couldn't have imagined *that;* someone must have told her. And the pressed pictures on the covers; as if she were running her fingers over their embossed designs again, she felt them. The black one with the garland of wild flowers arranged so naturally and so stiffly within its ribbon frame. And the insides. Rose-colored velvet, lavender-colored velvet, padding out, little pillows for the faces to sleep on, waiting for someone to open the doors. Pillows with pressed designs of flowers, urns of flowers, flourishes, and on the other side, the portrait, framed in embossed gold, elaborated with burnished designs. She had read *The Handbook* now; soon an inevitable layer of tarnish would help frame the picture, bluish green, as the silver gave its sheen up to the air. Would people remember how to design them? Would they care? They were so fragile, so easily ruined. She was proud of her husband for seeing them, for understanding them, a reflection of life which made the way of his own life clearer. No, she wouldn't try to keep him out of the laboratory any longer.

Delusion: there was absolutely nothing truer than delusion. The value of the face in the picture, the delusion of that value. Even sorrow was a delusion, a belief in the importance of what was lost. Or what one didn't have, one's belief in its value. As, for example, God. Why, she wondered, was Lois Ann better than anyone else, lost in contemplating her own private picture of God in his heaven? What made that picture any more valuable than the ones John would be taking? You couldn't say Lois Ann's pictures were any better because they left more fields for the imagination to roam about in. No, even accurate likenesses did that. The mind saw what it wanted.

These pictures: they were a form of idolatry, after all. Perhaps, for a while, they would be used to preserve the past if there was any such thing, even while time was nibbling at its edges with its sharp rat teeth; then later, later they would be studied as if they were books, as perhaps one day their religion would be studied. Although some, as long as they lasted, would hypnotize the students. Some would retain an expression past ignoring. Then the student would forget his interest in their caps and their gowns; the mirrory surface of the pool would close over his head. He would talk for a while with the man or woman in the picture.

Some people, she mused, had that power; any trace of them retained that vibrancy, some halo of life which would not, could not, leave. She wanted to see the pictures of all of them. Perhaps it was already possible to tell who had that power, that ability to fasten themselves to the earth by strands of the sun, people who, for any given time of life, were best satisfied by what surrounded them. That was happiness, she supposed, not to imagine anything better, not to be able to. Different from what Mrs. Ward had described. It wasn't only that they didn't think about anything else, but when they did, they could not imagine a better world than this one. This life was the most golden, the most surprising, the most abundant, and everyone and everything in it, haloed by that light; it would shine out, it would, from some of the photographs. Yes, they were important, and valuable, and fragile. Even if someone opened them hundreds of years later and thought: Once there was a woman who looked this way, who wore dresses like this, who combed her hair in this way, who ate meals as we do, who may or may not have had children. Yes, something of them would remain. Because they had loved life so. Perhaps, she thought, smiling to herself, she ought to put Mr. Siddons to work on a person's hand. Before it had loved, after it had soothed children, after its body had felt childbirth, after it had felt the hands of others cool, after it felt itself cooling. Some hands, like some pictures, would bear their own records. Momentarily. It would take a genius to capture it.

"Well, Edna," Ten's voice said (how many times had she said that?), "it's time to come and eat. John's almost ready. We'll be leaving in a minute." "Martin?" "He's sitting in the carriage already." "We'll leave Jack here, then," she said; "its getting cold. He'll have plenty of time for trains." They went into the kitchen. Hal was already eating. "How many times have I told you," Ten scolded him, "not to start before everyone else?" "Anna comes home today"; he beamed. The two women looked at each other. "Don't you forget her fits at funerals. You don't want to kill her, do you?" Ten asked. "Oh no, sister Ten, I won't take her; I wouldn't kill my Anna." John came in and sat down. "Gobble like turkeys, everyone," he instructed.

By the time they got to the station, the snow squalls were thicker, more frequent. "Martin," Edna cautioned automatically, "get off those tracks." Five minutes later Ten, in a controlled scream Edna had never managed to imitate, called, "Martin, you get off those tracks or get back in the carriage and sit there where we can see you. With one hand on each knee." Sullenly, he came back and stood between his parents. Ten shook her finger at him. He pretended he hadn't noticed, staring down the tracks. "It's coming," he shouted, jumping forward. "Get back!" his father roared.

The train was majestically approaching, coughing great clouds of black smoke, orange cinders, taking everything over with its noise. "Where are they, where are they?" Martin squealed, running up and down the platform. "They're not on it," he wailed; "everyone's already off." Just then, a little parade began coming down the steps of the third car. "It's Ella!" Martin shrieked, darting off like a retriever. The three girls alighted, looked anxiously about them, saw Martin jumping up and down, looked around him, annoyed, for their parents and Ten. Then, to Edna's surprise, there was her mother, pausing at the top of the little iron stairway. Did the woman *never* change? Edna wondered.

She was moving toward her without awareness of it. The same statuesque beauty, the same beautiful auburn hair peeping out from under one of the bonnets Lettie's letters had described, the same sweep of her black dress. They hugged each other, while poor Mr. Siddons was left standing on the lowest step, unable either to alight or to move. "Well, how did you stand it?" Edna asked, leading her mother off. "Oh, they're very good, really," Edith answered; "we didn't have any trouble. Anna was homesick the first few days. She cried and cried. We couldn't tell what she was going on about, but Ella thought it all had something to do with some little friend she missed. And Lettie and Ella," her mother chattered; "Edna, they are *so* beautiful! You should have seen them in their new clothes. And I've done my best, really I have, to do something about their English. Ella is so good at the piano. We almost wore her out, playing all the time. I was surprised she had fingers for the milliners to measure. Oh, I tell you, it was fun. You know, I think it's more exciting than only having one; they do get into such things." "Squabbles, I presume."

"Squabble, squabble, squabble, about everything," Edith agreed; "and about the silliest things. All that fussing over who got what at Madame Jeannette's and two of them almost identical sizes. I finally solved it," she announced proudly; "I had Madame Jeannette make everything up with enormous hems; they can go up and down like balloons, everything with skirts, that is. Do you think they'll share things?" "They'll be too envious not to." "And we have all sorts of things for Martin; we had his measurements. Ten is so precise," Edith said; "she never changes. We thought we had better pack him a trunkful of games and books. Oh, he would have liked coming. Ten!" she squealed, catching sight of her; "you poor thing, locked in the house all that time!" Edith embraced her tightly, then held her back to inspect her. "You look just the same," Mrs. Siddons said, blissful.

"You've gone blind at last, Edith"; Ten smiled blurrily. "No, no, it's true." *"Do* you wear glasses?" Ten teased. "Only when I'm reading"; Edith blushed. *"You're* the one who's just the same," Ten insisted, holding to her hand. "Well, at least we're *here*," Edith said. "Poor Nellie," said Ten. "I can't believe it"; Edith shook her head. "We never will, dear," Ten answered. "No, I suppose not. But, Ten, other of our friends died, and I never took on so about it." "She was part of our childhoods; that made all the difference. We met all the others later." "I suppose so," Edith agreed softly; "I never have an explanation for anything." "A woman with your looks doesn't *need* explanations." "I do, for myself, I can say that much; well, you'll tell me all of yours, won't you?" "You'll have to ask me the questions first. If no one asks me the questions, I don't think of answers. What I mean is, I don't think of questions." "You were always so good at examinations," Edith remembered; "come say hello to Mr. Siddons."

Ten stopped her with a gesture. "You're really happy, Edith?" "Oh yes, I have such a *nice* time. And then Edna's children; Ten, who would have thought they would be so *nice*, so much fun to have around? We have such *times* with them, don't we? It does bring back the young days, doesn't it? Oh, don't grin at me like that," she scolded; "you have them all year." "I see you haven't replaced your dog," Ten noticed. "Well," Edith mumbled, uneasy, "is it a dreadful thing to say the children replaced him? And you mustn't tell Mr. Siddons. Promise me that, Ten. I never *did* like that dog, he looked so like a rat. I always liked the dog they had at school, that great red one. And here was this nervous little thing, eyes bulging, hopping up and down like a rabbit. Well, he was a nice enough creature, but I never could convince myself he was a *dog*. Is it true," she asked, "that Edna is giving us the old house? The whole thing? Mr. Siddons is so excited about it. She did get him on her hook with her description of trees and tombs and John's pictures and how he could use them as studies for his studio sculptures." "She's had it cleaned inside and out; *and* staffed. *And* a wing of our house made ready. You raised a woman of her word." "Will she mind," Edith whispered, "if we stay in the old house?" "Oh. I don't think so; she and John are pretty much as they ever were."

John and Mr. Siddons were already engaged in discussing his photographs, and John was agreeing, albeit uneasily, to photograph, not immediately, of course, but certainly before he left, landscapes, scenes, whatever Mr. Siddons thought might be an aid to his memory when he went back to Boston. Ten, Edna and her mother, Ella and Lettie, climbed into one carriage; Martin, John, Mr. Siddons, and Anna into the second. They set off, both carriages sounding like happy traveling birds' nests.

"Well, Lettie," Edna exclaimed; "you've gotten taller." "Don't call me Lettie any longer," the child responded in an affected manner; "I prefer to be called Letitia." Ella regarded her with distaste. "How about 'Let's Itch Her'?" Ella inquired. "Don't be vulgar," she sniffed. "She's a real stiff," Ella complained; "I can't wait until she tries on those airs at school. I just can't wait. Remember, Mother, last year, that little boy who came here for his lungs, the one who went on so, and how the others filled his lunch pail with horse dung? I suppose they'll have to do that with *her*"—she looked hatefully at her sister—"if they want to put a stop to this." "Don't make it sound as if good speech and proper behavior were diseases," Edith scolded; "a young lady *should* speak properly." Ella sullenly stared out the window. "Edith," Ten said, "if they're going to live here all year round, they have to fit in." "I suppose so, yes," Edith agreed, reluctant. "I shall always be called Letitia in the city," Lettie announced grandly. "Good for you," Ten said. Lettie squirmed under her aunt's gaze. "I bet Ella winds up marrying some poor farm boy, don't you, Mother?" Edna didn't answer her.

"Don't say such a thing," Edith scolded; "and to your own sister, too." "It's easier," Ten whispered, "to let them get it out of their systems. The more we say to them, the longer those children go on." "Young *ladies*," Lettie corrected in a huff. "Well, I'd never guess it from your behavior," Ten sniffed; "a lady is known by the way she acts, not by what she wears." Both girls kept quiet. Well, Edna thought, relieved, everyone was back in the nest. The palm of her hand still retained the feel of Anna's small, hot one; she was always so much warmer to the touch than the others, as if she were burning herself up faster, like a bird. She *had* seemed happy to see Hal; perhaps she had worried too much over Anna, after all. Meanwhile, Ten was telling Edith all the local news. "Oh, Mother," Edna broke in, "I won't be at home this afternoon; I'm going off on rounds with John." "You *still* do that? I was sure you'd lose interest." "Well, I haven't," Edna retorted, her voice tinged with the old defiance.

The arrival was a flurry of embraces, everyone hugging Bridget and Bertha and Ellen, everyone hugged back, Martin already running off to show Ella some of his latest creations, one of which was a puzzle of his own making; dogs hugged, cats picked up, Anna suddenly running inside to be sure Jimmie was still there, running out again like a winged creature. "Bridget will get you settled," Edna was telling her mother; "I imagine you can haul Ten off with you. And the children will be down at the Moffats' before you turn around, so just wait for us, wait for us, we'll be back as soon as we can." Edith shook her head; this was more confusing than life in the city. "And *do* get out of those hoops," Edna pleaded; "you won't fit on the little paths I wrote Mr. Siddons about." Edith sighed; she would feel naked without her hoops. But perhaps Mr. Siddons would like it; he did go on so about the apparent deformity of the body, and what would an audience at a studio think if he displayed a naked body which looked as it appeared to under a dress? It was different here; that was certainly true. "Where are you going?" she asked her daughter. "To see a crazy mayor. Oh, Mother, we should have a treat for you. There's a famous preacher coming; Noah Webster, or his son, someone like that." "Really?" Edith chirped; "I won't miss that." "*I* will," Edna assured her. "Can I go?" Anna asked urgently. "Certainly, dear," Mrs. Siddons answered; "you can always go anywhere appropriate with me." "And do you ever go anywhere inappropriate?" Ten asked, appearing at her elbow. "You do always make me blush so, Ten," she complained as the two of them went off.

The days, like the leaves, seemed to fly from the trees, as if this year was intent on its own destruction. It was the day before the sermon. "Well I don't think Anna should go," Edna protested; "she was morbid enough after those funerals." "Sermons aren't always morbid, dear," Edith said. "*This* one will be," John told her; "you mustn't forget, Mrs. Siddons, the town wants him because they've just come through this epidemic. They want an inoculation against anything worse." "You make it sound so complicated," Edith complained. "It is," John said; "they want to suffer for being alive, and they're proud to be alive, and now this Mr. Webster will tell them they're alive by the skin of their teeth because they lived righteous lives, and the worst sinner will believe him, and everyone will go home warm and happy with nice resolutions; you'll see. It's not like the city; it's not an entertainment." "But she is *set* on it," Mrs. Siddons pleaded; "and I did promise her." Ten sighed. "Edith, it *is* unwise to let a child do whatever she sets her heart on. Still, if we don't let her go, who knows what garbled message she'll get at that Sabbath school of hers?" "If she goes, I had better go," Edna decided. "That's nice, dear," Edith said; "isn't it, Mr. Siddons?" "Well, then," Ten gave in, worn out, "start out early; half the state will be here to hear him."

The next morning, the whole town was on its way to the Old Stone Church. "Mr. Noah Webster, Mr. Noah Webster." The name was on everyone's lips. "What is his text?" Mrs. Siddons inquired of her neighbor in the next pew. "I'm sure I don't know, but he has a title," the woman whispered, impressed: "A Plea for a Miserable World." After a wait of almost an hour, the Reverend Pierce introduced Mr. Webster to the awed congregation. "I shall no longer presume upon your attention," the Reverend Pierce was booming, "but shall immediately turn the pulpit over to one of the great pillars of our church, one who has warmed the chill streams which shall too soon swallow us, one who has brought life into the living dead after they placed flowers on the graves of their loved ones, one who has given hope to the hopeless, cheered the widows and the orphans, collected funds for the lepers in Africa, extended the magnificent, saving influence of Christ to the furthest ends of our globe." Edna squirmed in her seat; little Anna glowered at her. Edna sighed, sinking back. The Reverend Webster stalked slowly up the stairs, paused in back of the pulpit, then took his place behind it. He stared out at the congregation until even Edna began to feel a stirring of guilt.

"This is the condemnation, that light is come into the world, and men loved darkness rather than light," he suddenly boomed in his powerful voice, everyone startled, jumping in their seats, "because their deeds were evil. So said John," he continued, after a long pause. How did he manage it, Edna wondered; appearing to look into all their eyes? He must have trained as an actor. "The light is come into the world," he resumed; "men, all of you that are men, have preferred the darkness to this light. For this, ye shall be punished. For this, you have begun to feel the sting of punishment. And what is the reason for this perversion of mankind? The reason is," he roared, "your deeds are evil. They are evil in the sight of God. They are abominable in the sight of God. They are abominable in the sight of Christ. They crucify him again and again.

"Yes, I say, think on it; it is Christ you are killing, and only God in his mercy could have created a being so potent as to live through your plagues and tortures. Will you walk, will you always walk," he thundered, "by a borrowed light, a reflected light? Even when there is the greatest, the best light of the Gospel, whose province it is to 'govern the day and to lighten every man that cometh into the world'! Does the Gospel have too much light for your poor, blinded eyes? Have you become as bats who have lived so long in the caves of human custom that nothing will let you see? The true light not only reveals, it reproves. Will you reject Christ when he waits for you to close with him? Will you reject him and condemn your little ones, and their little ones after them, to fire everlasting?

"Christ," he whispered, "is like a prince. He can pardon you. He will pardon you, if you will only come to him. And when are you to come? You are to come immediately. Immediately." His voice winged to the top of the church. "Will you forever be like the foolish man with the plague who hears a miraculous cure has been found and says to those standing around his bedside"——he lowered his voice dramatically—"his dying bed, 'No, wait until I become worse, as I am becoming worse every hour. Wait until my pulse is no more. Wait until I am cold and stiff, and then, *then* send for the cure'?" The church was already filling with sobs. "Mothers," he roared, "you who have devoted your lives to your beloved children, you who have risked your lives giving them God's life, will you now die crushed by this tremendous thought? The tremendous, horrifying thought that you have become mothers only to people the realms of death? Mothers, will you people the earth with dead children, soulless creatures who shall stagger through life already dead? Shall you suckle these living corpses? Shall you give birth only to death? Fathers, shall you father dead children? Shall you people the earth with dead seed? For that is what you are doing, if your evil ways are to continue.

"What punishment shall be harsh enough for you? Must more die and be wrapped in the long shroud this earth shall never unroll before you see the evil of your ways? Can the lifeless corpse shake off its grave clothes and loose the hands of death? Christ, I say, Christ alone can do that. Christ alone *shall* do that. You have boasted of tomorrow, and seen it taken from you. But close with Christ, I say, and this very flesh which is mere dust and ashes shall be brighter than the stars. Then shall you murmur, 'Glory, glory'; then shall you shout, "Glory, glory'; then shall you forget those terrible words: What is your life? It is even a vapor, which appeareth for a little time, and then vanisheth away. Will you have nothing but the comfortless prospect of seeing your children become wild men, their hands set against every man, and every man's hand against them; nor is this the least; for, without the light of the Gospel, what is there for your little ones? Nothing but the blackness of darkness forever. Hang your harps, parents, upon the willows, and weep, for you shall not be comforted, not by any of the dead of this earth. Only Christ our Lord can do that." Now he had to raise his voice to make himself heard over the sobs of the congregation. Edna felt Anna's little hand close coldly over hers; she held on like a vise.

"Will you," he roared, "turn this good earth, this God-given earth, into a wild forest? And who are the inhabitants of this forest? They are our fathers and mothers, our brethren and sisters, our children, our friends and neighbors. They were born in the houses we occupy, they have gone from our families, or they shall be going, they shall be going from our bosom; they were the companions of our childhood and our youth. We took sweet counsel together, and went to the House of God in company. Hence the cry they utter sounds in our ears loud and eloquent as the shrieks of death. If we do not *hear* or *help* them, then we are all lost, then the mother shall forget her suckling child, and shall feel no compassion for the son of her womb. Then shall the sacred marriage bed be wet with tears, a rack of torture, a bar of justice; then shall there be no peace either in kitchen and fields. Do you, can you," he began, winding up, "say, 'They shall have a life of light; they shall come to Christ and life everlasting'? My heart responds, 'They shall.'

"And you," he whispered, scanning the congregation, "can you repeat after me, 'They shall'? Such words will be heard, people of sin," he thundered; "the sun sets in the west. Before darkness falls, shall you say it? 'They shall.'" An eerie silence, broken by loud sobs, throbbed in the church; its windows were darkening. "Can you repeat after me," he pleaded; "'They shall'?" He paused, tensely waiting. "They shall," an old woman's voice wavered. "They shall," the whole congregation echoed; Edna was astounded to hear herself repeating the words. "Now, now," Mr. Webster resumed, tremulous, "shall we be heirs of our Savior, to life everlasting, to the golden throne, to the lambs which surround it. Now shall we change our hearts, escape the first death, and the second death, and live forever with Christ risen and redeeming; we shall sing with the angels forever.

"Do not," he warned, "think it will be easy; the way is difficult, the road rocky. You must watch the citadel of your besieged soul every minute. Then shall you be as lights set on an eminence, shining. Then shall the rivers be free of suicides; then shall the hearts of parents mend, and shine out; then shall the children live forever; then shall death lose its power; then shall death itself die; then shall we all enter into the gates which shall never again open to expel us. Then shall we find peace." He paused.

"I beg you," he pleaded, "repeat once more after me, 'They shall.'" "They shall," answered the audience as one person. "Glory," he said, lowering his head into his cupped hands, "be to the Father, to the Son, and to the Holy Ghost. As it was in the beginning, is now, and ever shall be, world without end. World without end," he chanted. "Repeat after me," he commanded abruptly. "World without end." "World without end," the congregation repeated. "Amen," he thundered. "Amen," they called out. Then it was over.

A shaken congregation filed silently out of the church as from a tomb, the Reverend Webster solemnly clasping each hand as each person left the church door. Outside, Edna found herself shaking, her eyes burning. Her cheeks were wet; she didn't know why. "Here," her mother said, giving her a handkerchief. Edith's face, too, was wet; her eyes were rimmed, red. Edna noticed Anna, her body trembling, ague-like. "Anna," she murmured, shaking her. "Anna!" The child's eyes were fixed on some distant point, staring. "Anna!" she almost shouted; "Anna! Do you hear me?" Anna turned to her slowly. "Yes, yes, I can hear you," the child said, toneless; "but it is Christ I must hear now." The child is in shock, Edna realized. "Mother," she said urgently, "I think we better get her right home." "Heaven lies above us," Anna announced, pointing upwards. At that, they both hurried her into the carriage, wrapping her in a carriage robe as soon as she was inside. "I don't know, Edna," her mother fretted; she sounded worried. Edna shook her head. What was the point of recriminations? She had told her mother she didn't like it, Anna going, not after all those funerals.

At home, Ten took over, murmuring gently to Anna about ordinary things, singing her bits of old songs, reciting little pieces of *Mother Goose*, fussing ostentatiously over the whereabouts of her old toys. She finally got Anna to sleep and sat down by the bed. I should have known, she slashed at herself, crying silently; she'll never be the same after this, she thought, staring down at the white, sleeping child.

John came home to find Edna weeping in bed; he extracted the story from her. "It will be all right; don't worry. It will be all right; I'll take her with me more; we'll get her interested in other things." Finally, he had her calmed down. "Where is Anna?" he finally asked. "Ten's looking after her." "Then it's all right." Edna sobbed against his shoulder. He stroked her hair until she fell asleep. Why had she kept saying it was all her fault? She took too much on herself; she always expected to know consequences before the causes were even evident. Perhaps, he thought, it was because she so often could do just that. It was not a blessing; no, it was not a blessing. *She* should have been the doctor; it might have hardened her. But he didn't know; it might have destroyed her altogether. There was no knowing these things in advance. He stole into bed next to her, spreading the quilt over both of them. Edna stirred in her sleep, reaching for him. Mr. and Mrs. Siddons, he correctly supposed, had already talked the day's events over and come to their own conclusions. By tomorrow, they would not be worried. This would be past, and that would be the end of it. He sighed, putting his hand on Edna's shoulder. He began watching the thickening snow; it was hypnotic, just as she had always said. He fell asleep beside her.

Alice Moffat found herself alone in her own house. This, she thought, was her idea of heaven, and as rare as a vision of it. She went to her room, enjoying every leisurely unharassed step. Well, she had the Steeles to thank for getting rid of Lois Ann. The good soul was now at the old Steele house. And it had been accomplished so smoothly.

One afternoon, several weeks after the famous Webster sermon, the Steeles had unaccountably invited the Reverend Pierce to take tea with them in the afternoon. They had planned it so carefully, Mrs. Siddons arranged majestically on a love seat, under Edna's orders to remain absolutely mute, no matter what she chanced to think, and Mr. Siddons installed on the piano bench, his sketch pad spread out on the music stand, solemnly contemplating his country sketches. Altogether, it had not been an easy audience, Dr. Steele and Edna on one sofa, Ten staring straight at him from the lady's chair as if to say she had known him since he was a very, very small boy and he hadn't done much to improve himself since. The children had all been sent off with Ellen, picnicking in the snow, and Mr. Pierce's reception was as solemn as any the pillars of his church council could have given him.

"Well, Mr. Pierce," Edna began, "that was certainly a coup." She had begun innocently enough. At first, he pretended not to know what she meant. "Why, getting a remarkable man like Mr. Webster to come here in our time of need; how it must have depleted the church funds!" she said; "but, then, I suppose it will be worth every penny, spiritually speaking, of course, even though there probably will be no income left to pay the choir their yearly fee, or to decorate the chancel for Christmas holidays." "What! No decorations at Christmas!" Mrs. Siddons exclaimed involuntarily. Edna looked warningly over.

Mr. Pierce felt more and more uneasy. Were they, he wondered, taking a polite way of informing him they were withdrawing their support from a spendthrift church? That's what people always said about the rich; the richer, the harder they bit their pennies. "We shall need an extra pew," Ten said, on cue, "since Mr. and Mrs. Siddons shall be staying for most of the winter, and they are so used to spiritual comforts. I know," she went on, in compassion for his professional complexities, "how few pews there are, but if we could find just the right one for them, perhaps adjoining our family pew, or rearrange the pews altogether, we would be more than willing to compensate the church handsomely. After all, we mustn't neglect the rich man, must we? Even Christ took special pity on the rich man, and we wouldn't want Mrs. Steele's mother and father futilely trying to squash themselves through the eye of a needle, would we?" "Of course not," Mr. Pierce answered; why, he wondered, was he suffering from the definite impression they were up to something; that he was already caught in their web? Heaven, he decided, would have no congregation at all. And, therefore, no parishioners.

"This must have been a dreadful trial to you," Mr. Siddons said; "so many funerals, so many of the flock lost!" Edna had carefully coached *him*. Unlike her mother, he had a flair for the dramatic, and, she suspected, when money and having his way were at issue, he was probably unrivaled. "Yes," Mr. Pierce mumbled, miserable. He was thoroughly aware of the Siddons' social status. *The Reformer* had spent most of its first page announcing their arrival, fulsomely describing the eminent sculptor's accomplishments, accompanying its praise with sketches of the most famous, ending with a paragraph praising Williamsville, whose charms, obviously, had the power to attract such remarkable people.

"Well, Dr. Pierce," Ten began briskly, "do not think we are unaware of the hardships you have so recently undergone. It is our intense awareness of those difficulties which makes us so unwilling to implore you to once more throw yourself into the fires." She paused. Just what fires was she talking about? They had never gotten along as children. "You see," she said, narrowly observing him redden, "we must concern ourselves with the Moffats. Insignificant as they may seem in the eyes of society, they are important in the eyes of God, as are we all." "Of course," he agreed, peering at her; she always made him feel so ridiculous. She always had. "Naturally," she continued, "we did think of consulting the new minister from Exeter, but we felt this was rather a parish matter." Now he trembled in earnest.

So that was it. They planned to replace him. They were already beginning, collecting evidence of his incompetence. He himself could see the entire battle plan. Bruit it about that the Reverend Webster's extravagant visit had been an effort to distract everyone from his own ineffectiveness and indifference; hint that age was beginning to take its toll; his powers were certainly waning (although not, of course, his sincerity); comment sympathetically that tending to a sickly wife and so many children had distracted him in every way. Weakened by his duties, that's what he was. "We must do all in our power to help the Moffats," he assured them.

He wanted to jump up and beat them all over the head with his walking stick. "But I was unaware they were suffering." "Oh, but they are, terribly," Edna said fervently, interrupting; "and they have been such good friends to us, too. Heaven only knows," she said, lifting her eyes to the ceiling like the most seasoned Christian, "where I would be, where we all would be, if it hadn't been for Alice Moffat." "She means," Dr. Steele elucidated, now adding his powerful voice, "Mrs. Moffat saved her from despair after Martin's birth. What more terrible fate," he pondered, "then to fall prey to the sin of despair? And the good woman did save Edna's life; I had quite given up on her." Now the doctor was staring at him, as if noticing the first, fatal traces of a new disease.

"Tell me what must be done," the Reverend pleaded, wringing his hands; "I shall do everything possible." He saw Ten raise her eyebrows, as if to say *that*, whatever it was, would be worse than nothing. "The Moffats," Edna said, taking over, "are very poor. But they have taken on the additional burden of their sister-in-law, Mrs. Lois Ann Moffat; she is, as you must know, a very religious woman. I believe she rarely if ever misses a service." "She attends services twice on Sundays," he said. "But you see," Edna continued, "although you may be able to feed her *spiritu-*

ally, the Moffats are simply unable to support four more human souls." She looked down at her hands.

Was she expecting *him* to take them in? "What we had in mind, didn't we, Dr. Steele, was giving them, Lois Ann Moffat and her children, our old farmhouse. We feel she might be able to do her Christian duty there, for the farm hands live alone in one wing, without the heavenly influence of a woman's gentler nature, and then, too, my mother and father shall be living there, and we should feel quite uneasy without a guardian angel on the premises." She stopped, stricken. "Could you possibly," she begged, "could you possibly use your *profound* influence in persuading Lois Ann Moffat to take up residence in the old house? Where she will be most needed? Why, she has a mission there! *Some* would say it was her Christian duty, but I would not care to judge others spiritually. That is the duty of the pastor, of course. Nevertheless," she considered, "she would be, in her own way, a missionary." "Especially since," Ten added, "there are so few widows and lepers to attend to in the vicinity." The minister deflated noticeably.

"Does the church still have plans for adding a steeple?" the doctor asked absently; "my wife and I were just lamenting the absence of one, and Mr. Siddons had the same complaint. It would add much to the picturesque beauty of the old church. Mr. Siddons has expressed himself forcibly on the subject; *he* believes we ought to do *our* Christian duty and contribute to the construction of such a steeple." "Provided, of course," Mrs. Steele spoke up, "Mr. Siddons is genuinely convinced the church is effectively performing its mission among the people." "Of course, of course," the Reverend assented; he was attempting to get his bearings. And it was no easy job, not with Ten staring him down in that dreadful way.

"We thought," Mr. Siddons went on, "that if you would only help the Moffats, even though they have so little claim on your attention and feelings, the issue would be quite decided. I have known ministers," he continued sadly, "who seemed to feel their only mission was to preach to the already saved, or alas! to the wealthy. Of course," he hastened to assure Reverend Pierce, "I do not mean to imply you are such a disgrace to your profession." "No, of course not," Ten said. Her expression, however, had not altered. "Show me my duty and I shall do it," the Reverend Pierce said enthusiastically; "that has always been my motto. I hope to have it carved on my tombstone." "I myself shall see to that," Ten told him. "Well, Mr. Pierce," Edna intervened earnestly, gazing over at Ten, "if you could *only* persuade Mrs. Moffat's sister-in-law it was her *duty* to look after the sinners in the old house. I don't, needless to say, mean to include my mother and father in that description." "No, no; whoever would think of such a thing?" "Although there is no doubt we are very aware of our fallen state," Mr. Siddons gloomed; "we, too, should be glad of the influence of such a woman." "I shall go today," Mr. Pierce told them; "I shall not waste a minute in a matter of such paramount spiritual importance. I shall make her feel the urgency of immediately assuming her mission."

"We should be *so* grateful," Edna said; "we have been powerless to intervene; why, if *you* could accomplish such a miracle, your deed would be a *steeple* on the landscape of spiritual travail." "I shall leave this instant," he promised; he needed no further instructions. "Do you think I shall find her at home?" "Oh, she is *always* at home," Ten purred; "when she is not at church. And we would want her to understand that we would provide every possible means of transportation so that she may arrive at the church in the worst weather. My brother, you know, has to travel about, even on Sundays. I'm sure we could aid her in her efforts." "Well, I shall leave without delay. There is not a second to waste." Ten nodded, her metallic gray eyes as expressionless as a mousetrap. Edna got up and pressed his hand. "I cannot thank you enough; we all cannot thank you enough." "We shall find a tangible way," Ten said flatly. "And poor Mrs. Moffat," Edna went on, seeing him to the door, "she is fainting under her burdens. Just yesterday she said, 'It is eat, wash, eat, wash, all the time, just as it always is.' The poor woman," Edna said, "there is not a day that arrives for her without its note against her. If you could only relieve her of *some* of her burden, perhaps her spiritual nature could grow, not smothered so under the wet leaves of her washing and ironing and cleaning and cooking—as it is now." "Have no fears," he solemnly said, posting off at once to the

Moffats'. A steeple! It was the dream of his life. *And* an additional pew paid for! It was beyond all expectation.

At the Moffats' he found Lois Ann reading *The History of the Reformation* in the parlor and, after introducing the subject with proper seriousness, launched into such a passionate sermon on her duties that, within the hour, she was convinced she must at once retire to her room, there to begin packing. It was certainly true that the children would have more room in the old Steele house, and then, she thought, bitter, there was no overestimating the spiritual benefits they would receive once removed from such proximity with Alice's and Edna's children, who were, in her opinion, little better than godless savages. Then, too, she thought, pausing in folding a skirt, it would be some time before her husband came scratching at the screen door there; the men wouldn't put up with it. Not if she threatened to stop cooking. She would have her hands full, she concluded happily. And helping Mr. and Mrs. Siddons adjust to life in the country! Who would have imagined she would have been called on for such an important service?

Alice, lying flat on her back, luxuriating like any cat in the sun, loved telling herself that story again and again, just as Edna had told it to her. She wondered what heaven was, though. She tended to think of it as a kind of Retreat, except that the inmates were not insane. It would be filled, she decided, with grown-up children, all of whom had turned out well, but who only came to visit their parents during certain, set hours. There would be attendants soothing her forehead, carrying her meals, coaxing her to eat. "Do try to sit up, Mrs. Moffat," she could hear one of them saying; "do try to take just one step. Careful, be careful not to tax yourself." There would be no such things as runaway cows grazing at the edge of the road ten miles from the farm, eating themselves sick in the apple orchard, then dancing about like possessed things, or if there were, she wouldn't have to know about it. And everyone would have strict orders not to mention potato bugs, or Paris green, or dyes to her, or rag carpets, or children's illnesses, or husbands who needed persuading before they beat the carpets from the floors. There would be no leaking roofs, no shortage of wood for their stoves and fireplace. And certainly, there would be no Lois Ann.

Heaven would be a great restful bed. She turned on her side, caressing her pillow. Why have a bedroom, she wondered resentfully, when you got to spend so little time in it? She might as well sleep on the floor. Rest. Heaven would be rest.

She wondered what Edna's conception of heaven was like. That was easy; for her, heaven would be nothing more than a green meadow and Dr. Steele there holding her hand. With no one to interrupt them, of course. And Ten, now, she went on, becoming interested; what would be her conception of heaven? That puzzled her. Ten seemed to want nothing, to look forward to nothing. She lived every day as it came; she spent little time worrying about what was over, no time really, and little time worrying about the future. She must assume if she took care of the present, the future would take care of itself. She imagined Ten's heaven, if she wanted one (it occurred to her someone might not want such a thing), would be an endless sequence of days amidst people she had chosen. Perhaps Ed was still one of those people. She didn't believe Ten forgot much; probably he was almost as alive for her now as he had been when they were married. And how everyone had objected to that marriage! On every ground but the one which proved fatal to their union; no one thought he would die so young. Alice mused idly, staring out at the mountains.

She had had all the furniture moved, and it was heavy, too, so that she could see out when she lay on her bed. That was, for some reason, very important. And what would *dear* Lois Ann want? Well, she knew the answer to that one. She would want to float around like an angel in white robes, holding a golden trumpet, singing at the foot of God's throne. Well, she supposed, eyelids drooping, they would all get what they deserved, or what they wanted: it amounted to the same thing, no doubt. If they got anything at all. But if there was a next world, they would get what they expected; that would be the best reward, or the best punishment, she couldn't decide which. She was sound asleep. She woke up; a sound. Nothing but a bird hitting the window, poor thing: she supposed one of the children would rescue it eventually. At least their ministrations would keep them out of her kitchen.

They were odd, those Steeles; or it was Edna, perhaps.

She couldn't bear to see others in trouble, not when she could do something about it. And Dr. Steele, too. He was the same way. She didn't envy either of them their death-beds, but at least they had not yet lost anyone in their own family; that was something. Yes, that was really remarkable. Some force was definitely sparing them. Sometimes, she almost envied Edna, because of what had happened to her Florence, gone so long now, while Edna had all her children. But she hadn't gotten to the end of the story yet, and who could really envy Edna? Not when you knew her, anyway. And that business with her father; perhaps God, that miserable person, perpetually persecuting them with the weather, had decided she already had enough trouble. After that business of walking into her father's shoes. Alice shuddered.

And then these new murders of old people. *She* had better stay young. They had just found old man Aldridge and his wife dead in their own basement, and their spinster sister just barely alive. Everyone thought they were rich; she guessed that was what had done it. But three men, painting themselves black, jumping in on them like that and knocking them down, and beating them, and throwing the three of them down the steps that way. How could they be so cruel? Well, she would have done what the old man had done, picked up her sharpest knife, or what his wife had done; she had picked up a chair and made a run at them. But the robbers had such long knives they wounded them both, and then came a fourth and a fifth, also painted black, and that was the end of it. They stabbed the old man right where he lay on the floor, telling his wife he was an old miser and had lived long enough for two men. And then they tied the poor thing up, what with her rheumatism (they couldn't know about that), and just rolled her off down the cellar stairs.

As for Lima, the old spinster, they led her all over the house, threatening they would kill her at once if she didn't tell them where the money was. Everyone believed they had gotten more than two thousand dollars. Then they tied her up and put her down cellar with her dead brother, and her sister-in-law; she died of cold and shock within a few hours. What must *that* have been like, Alice imagined; lying there, waiting for help, her brother's body half on top of hers, and cold as a stone, her sister-in-law's turning cold next to her? No wonder she got herself loose. She told everyone about it; she couldn't stop telling them about it, how she had to climb over her brother's body, and then her sister-in-law's, and went to alarm the neighbors. Well, she alarmed all Williamsville, for all the good it did her.

And for a while she had seemed all right. The constables had done their best to cheer her up, but how could they? They said she must have been saved by her name. She just sprouted up like a lima bean, and even at the funeral, she seemed to be holding in one piece, whispering over and over "all that was mortal of them" had finally been laid to rest. But then she had been found wandering around the common in the snow. She had stopped at the sound of the sleigh bells and someone had climbed out. Alice couldn't remember who it was, and there she was, hair down, in her nightdress, no shoes, just wandering around in the snow. Well, they wrapped her up, and when they asked her what she was doing, she said she was walking, just walking, and her brother would be there for her soon. So Dr. Steele took her off to the Retreat.

And now there was another family gone clear crazy. The Camps, two sisters and one brother, promised their parents, on their deathbeds, they would never marry and always stay together. No one believed they meant it, and everyone so sure they were humoring their parents. But now Bertha had gone and turned down her second suitor, and there the three of them were, all summer, rocking on the porch, and in the winter, when you drove by in your sleigh, you could see them all at the table, playing euchre. Now what kind of life was that? Was it the times that were turning, she wondered, or did she just have more time to notice it? Now that she thought about it, there had been lots of women wandering around the common in her lifetime, all of them carried off; she just never gave it much attention. She felt sleepy again; this *was* heaven. She dozed off.

The crashing of kitchen pots and pans frightened her awake. Her heart, she thought, pressing on it, was about to jump out of her body. Oh, the children, she realized, hearing George's voice. She had better see what they were up to. She had a light, noiseless step. She heard them mumbling something about old Mrs. Luke (that was their teacher) and a closet, but as soon as they saw her, they fell silent. That was enough; she was convinced they were up to no good. And besides, she saw, they were soaking wet, dripping all over the floor. "George," she demanded, "what did you do to Martin?" "Nothing," George answered, glaring at Martin. "Nothing," Martin agreed, sullen. "Well, you look like you've gone out and baptized yourselves, and in the winter, too; you get out of those wet clothes and come right back in here." They scurried upstairs, dripping as they went.

"You better tell the truth now, George," she said, "you just come clean. I can always tell when you're lying, and it will be your father this time; he'll get the truth out of you if you don't give it over." "We decided to walk through a swamp." "It was a shortcut," Martin added, helpful. "A shortcut to where?" "Why, here, Mother," her son said. "What swamp?" she persisted. "Elder's Swamp." "Elder's Swamp!" his mother exclaimed; "you took Martin into Elder's Swamp? The water's 'most over his head!" She stared at her son.

He could see his next days were black ones. "Did you want to go, Martin?" she asked, putting her hand on his shoulder. Martin promptly burst into tears. "You made him, didn't you?" she asked her son. "I just told him if he didn't come with me, he could stay in the forest all night, that's all." "Oh, that's all, is it? You get up to your room. I'm taking Martin home. You could have drowned him, you imp of the devil. What do you think of that?" He didn't answer. "You get in your room," she shouted. "What are you going to do with me?" "Your father and I will decide." "You don't have to tell him," George suggested. "When you start your climb up the ladder to murder, it's as much his affair as it's mine," she said, picking up a wooden spoon and cracking him sharply across the knuckles. "You get on up there now, and if you try running off, I'd rather be boiled in oil, if I were in your shoes, which I'm not, I'm glad to say." She took the dried Martin, wrapped in a blanket, out to their carriage and drove him over to the Steeles'. "I was afraid of snakes," Martin announced. "I bet you were; *you* have some sense anyway." "One of the boys said there were snapping turtles in the mud there." "I don't know about that," Alice said, "but it's a good place to stay out of all the same."

"Here he is," she said, returning him to Edna; "not much worse for a dipping, but a little scared off swamps." Edna shook her head. "I think," she told Alice, "we had better have their likenesses taken right away; before they come up with anything else." Martin, holding her hand, smiled up at her. "Well, goodbye for now," Alice said, leaving. "Martin," Edna suggested uncharacteristically, "why don't you come take a nap with me?" "In *your* bed?" "Of course; come on."

She watched him out of narrowed eyes until he fell asleep. Why, she reproached herself, didn't she spend more time with them? She really didn't know what happened to them at school, what happened to them when they were with their friends. And lately, they were all behaving so strangely. Ella had begun a courting chain; she was all of ten years old, but every day she solemnly added a button. How she hounded John to get a different button at every house he visited!

And then her mother had told her she thought Ella was writing to a twelve-year-old boy she had met in Manhattan; she really ought to keep more of an eye on her. And Lettie. She was getting so selfish. She was so jealous of Ella; there was no accounting for it. She had even asked Ten about it. Ten said it was normal for sisters to be jealous. "But *so* jealous?" Edna asked; "she envies everything Ella does, everything she has; you'd think she didn't have anything herself." Ten thought it over. "It does seem a bit intense," she agreed at last; "you don't think it has anything to do with Ella's little suitor in New York? Lettie might be jealous of that." "At their age?" Edna asked, flabbergasted. "Well," Ten considered, "in six years she'll be as old as you were when you met John." "But six years is a long time!" "If anything, those six years will calm things down. Well, I hope that's not it, because once that kind of jealousy gets going, there's no telling where it will end." "What do you mean?" "Oh, that Lettie," Ten mused; "sometimes I think she'd cut someone's throat, even her own, to get what she wanted. She's got your will and John's all in one dose." "And if she couldn't get what she wanted?" "Then I wouldn't put it past her to try taking something from someone who did have what she wanted."

"Even if that person was her sister?" Edna asked, shocked. "Especially. But there's no point in trying to see through the snow six years ahead." Edna wasn't sure she agreed. Things set so early; people, she thought, their characters, were like the bones John set. Either they mended well or they didn't. It was a good thing everyone covered up their legs, so it didn't make any difference how they set. But character, that was a different matter altogether. She was beginning to think about it: her children were becoming people. It was an awakening. And Anna now; they had all decided to let her attend her precious Sabbath school and all its meetings. Anything seemed better than trying to upset her, and *she* was the only one who didn't believe in giving Anna her head; she didn't think that would help her expel her morbid obsession with death. They all seemed to believe such experiences were purgative. Yet she did not agree. She was sure they were poisonous, pure poison. Still, she had not fought them; perhaps she ought to have fought them harder.

But it would have been of no use; they were so used to making these decisions without her. And of course they had more experience with them than she did. But she didn't like it, little Anna sitting there embroidering a sampler for her room while the others were out playing. "Jesus is the silent listener to every conversation, the unseen guest at every table." She didn't like to look at the thing. And now Anna was up at Lois Ann's lamenting their terrible distance from church: "How I would like to hear the church bells." She had overheard Anna saying that; she sounded unnaturally old. "The first bell at nine o'clock," Anna whispered; "the second at ten o'clock; that means Sunday school, you know," she pompously informed the smiling, satisfied Lois Ann; "and the third bell, the blessed bell, calling us all to church." Now, whenever Edna saw Anna attentively listening to them, she suspected she was reciting that dreadful sampler's message to herself.

Of course, that was better than the child's insisting on keeping the Sabbath in her room with only her *Proverb* series for company, the latest *One Good Turn Deserves*

Another, and at supper, invariably announcing something like "Life is nothing but a preparation for death. Ideally, we must lead our lives as if they were in imitation of Christ, which means we must practice self-denial and good works." It was dreadful. During the first month of this, she had given them all the creeping shudders; that was Ten's name for it, and it was accurate enough. Now they were getting more accustomed to it. Just last night, Ten had gone after her. "Anna, perform a good work and finish your dinner. You're thin as a stick. You have to be alive to imitate Christ, don't you?" Anna nodded, gobbling her food as usual.

It was a good thing it was winter, Edna thought, or they would all be playing croquet on Sundays under that child's disapproving stare, boating under her reproving gaze, tending the sick against her advice. John had asked her, without thinking, if it was good Christianity to let someone die on the Sabbath simply because his work was that of a doctor, reminding her that Christ said the Sabbath was made for man, not man for the Sabbath, and unawares, threw her into a state of deep perplexity which necessitated several private councils with the Reverend Pierce in his closet. It had better end soon, Edna thought, before she and John moved in with her mother.

And then there was the problem of what to do with her mother. Mr. Siddons had decided that perhaps he might want to go into farming in a small way, nothing important, of course, but he felt the need of some nearer tie to the earth. As if he wouldn't have it soon enough, Edna had thought, unsympathetic. The problem was, he told her, to find a farmer who could manage things for him. They had duly ferreted out a family of good character: the De Witts, whose only sin had been changing their name to De Witt from Witt after a family quarrel; they were anxious to begin independent farming, but were unable to do so on their own. Still, difficulties had set in at once. Mr. Siddons wanted his fence, the one which kept his cattle in, to follow the contours of the country, and there was poor Mr. De Witt with almost fifty cows and three hundred chickens, and this lunatic, as he called Mr. Siddons, who wanted a fence that followed the contours of the country. Finally, he settled that matter by giving Mr. Siddons a good ladder, a hammer, and a pail of nails; after several falls from the aforesaid ladder, the contoured fence was abandoned. Regardless of how strongly he felt about it, he never said another word to the De Witts. That surprised Edna. How on earth, she wondered, had life suddenly become so complicated? She certainly hadn't planned on these complications. She remembered something from one of Nellie's old letters; Ten had shown it to her. "If I had known what it was like, Ten," she wrote shortly after the birth of her first child, "I would not do it over again for all the world. You never have a minute." No, *she* wouldn't say the same thing; although she might do some things differently. But what? That she could not say.

"Mrs. Steele! Mrs. Steele!" Bridget was hissing from the doorway. Edna slid off the bed as quietly as possible. "It's Jack," Bridget whispered. "Jack? What's wrong with *him?*" "Oh, come outside, miss!" Edna threw on her coat and ran outside after her. There was Jack, climbing the rose trellis, and almost up to the second floor. "I don't know how to get him down," Bridget wailed; "and Ten's too old for walking on walls." Edna shrugged and took off her boots. There was nothing for it; she had to go up and get him.

"You're not climbing that thing, Miss Edna?" Bridget asked; "it's no stronger than a straw." "If it will hold him, it will hold me," Edna said, not believing a word. She began climbing. This was one way of getting closer to heaven. A great deal closer than she wanted to, and she was going up higher. Climbing, she remembered a bit too late, always made her dizzy. Jack's little heels were beginning to come into view. "Jackie, Jackie," she cooed, coming up alongside him; "this is fun." He cooed back at her. "But your candy," she told him; "I think someone is eating it *all up.*" He began to wail. "If we go *right* down," she said, "we can get that candy." Jack smiled blissfully at her. "You come down with Mommy, then?" He nodded.

Edna went down one step, and reached for him. He took her hand and backed down, slipping. Edna clutched his wrist as he dangled in mid-air. She managed to install him on the trellis without slipping herself. "Mommy will carry you," she told him, picking him up with one arm, slowly beginning the descent. "Now you just put your arm around Mommy's neck and hold tight. Not *that* tight," she gasped. "A little tighter," she instructed, beginning again. "Just one more step, Miss Edna," Bridget called out. "Ground," Edna breathed with relief, handing Jack over to Bridget; "take him in and give him all the candy he wants." "All?" "Well, not enough to make him sick." "All right, Miss Edna." She led the child off. She turned around to see John staring at her in amusement; he was holding her boots. "Come on, Jacob," he said, picking her up; "everyone in the house doesn't have to freeze to death today." "How long were you standing there?" she asked. "Long enough. That was heroic, you know." "It was ridiculous."

"Did you know Alice is thinking of taking in summer boarders after this winter?" "How on earth will she manage?" Edna asked, her nerves inexplicably soothed by this lovely motion, this being carried by her husband. "You should do this with all your patients." "The woman wants me in an early grave." "Oh, don't say that," she wailed. Trouble, John thought; trouble with the children. He had better find out what it was, too. They went in, dried off Edna's feet, carried Martin gently back to his own bed, while Edna cried through her whole narration of domestic woes. "So that's it, miss?" he asked finally; "we can't do much about any of it at this hour. Why," he asked, "do you still wear those nursing gowns? You never did do much nursing. You never *did* nurse them." "Because they have the lowest-cut fronts." No, some things never changed, they both decided later, falling peacefully asleep.

In the morning, on the way to one of the Camp sisters, taken by a fit, they resolved to do the best they could in the way of disciplining the children. "I really don't see what else we can do," John told her, "even though that's a disappointing answer. For both of us." Edna, however, knew he was right. "We'll manage. Somehow," she said, squeezing his hand. "A fit of nerves," John told the other two Camps; "you ought to expect more of them, *all* of you." What did they expect after that vow of celibacy? "Alice wants you to take likenesses of her children," Edna told him, coming out of the house, deliberately distracting him. This was just the sort of thing he would brood over. Because it was all so unnecessary. In spite of him-

self, he was flattered. "I'm not sure I'm ready for that."
"Well, as soon as you reach 1850 in your book," she said.
They stood looking at each other, then climbed into the
carriage.

It was the summer of 1866. Everyone stopped everyone
else to comment on what a hot summer it was. Dr. Steele
still had his hands full filling out petitions of Union soldiers who wanted disability pensions from the government for injuries sustained during the war. He was, unaware of it, making himself extraordinarily popular by
granting almost everyone the benefit of the doubt and
then skillfully embroidering, for the government's benefit,
the disastrous consequence of even minor injuries. He had
been surprised to find that almost all had not been injured severely, but by a ball passing through the palm of
the hand; evidently, they had instinctively tried to ward
off injury. John pored over the newspapers, reading descriptions of yellow fever, even entered into correspondence with doctors in the South as to which treatment
seemed most effective. So far, all he could ascertain was
that quarantine was the safest measure; all recommended
the sick be taken as far from the healthy as possible.
Most treatment was primarily palliative; no real cure was
available, much less infallible.

The Steele children were now, according to their mother's etiquette books, young men and young ladies. Martin
was seventeen, Ella sixteen, Letitia fifteen, Anna eleven,
and Jack seven. On the day it occurred to Edna that she
had no more young children, she had gone down to find
Alice, only to see Ella and William returning from a
walk in the woods, looking suspiciously hazy. And if that
wasn't bad enough, Lettie, dressed as if for a society ball,
happened to drive by in an open carriage, and since she
was *already* there, thought she might as well ask William
to help her decorate the sewing booth for that Sunday's
fair. She was just not tall enough to reach *anything,* she
lamented. Letitia (she now insisted on calling herself that,
even though her wishes in that matter were scrupulously
disregarded by her family) had grown into a stunningly
beautiful young lady. She seemed to have skipped back
one generation and was almost a replica of Edna's moth-

er. She was, naturally, the grandchild Edith most doted upon.

The subject of her remarkable beauty had become a standard topic of conversation in Williamsville some years earlier. Now interest centered on whether she would choose the young lawyer she was said to have met on her last visit to Manhattan. It was well known that she regularly received tiny white envelopes addressed in his hand, posted from New York, the envelopes themselves seeming to be made of lace, pressed designs of winged sphinxes, or cameo faces, or winged headless statues adorning their upper right corners.

There was another rumor, too. She had no intention of having *him*, but instead had her eye on a senator in Boston, a close friend of the family. Ella, they always added, now that was too bad. *She* was certainly beautiful in her own dark way; she resembled her mother, but she had a more open air, sweeter, but only one year younger than that sister. Well, until Letitia married herself off, what hope could there be for her? No one had noticed Ella receiving such remarkable envelopes, although reputable sources, in fact the postmaster himself, said she had received several letters from William Moffat while the war was going on. And it was possible, agreed the nodding heads, she had received even more of them, enclosed in letters to his family. They had also noted the Steeles sending an endless series of packages to William, wherever he was: Antietam, Charlottesville, Vicksburg, but it was always Ella who took them down to the post office.

Edna herself believed Ella had fallen in love with William through the mail. When his letters first arrived, they were illegible, awkward things, their letters like chicken tracks scratched in the dirt with a stick. Then, as he wrote every day, they became more and more eloquent and moving until even Dr. Steele admitted preferring the letters to anything he could read in the papers; that was when he began to take an interest in William's future. The only trouble was, as Edna noted, the greater Ella's interest in William the greater was Lettie's, although all of them knew perfectly well she would rather be eaten alive by rats than marry "one of those Moffats," or anyone from a farmer's family.

Thus, while the rest of the countryside busied itself

commenting on Lettie's beauty, and what a wonderful thing it would be for a man of wealth to marry her, she was not only beautiful, but so wealthy herself, the constant refrain in the reigning beauty's home was Ten's: *Beauty is as beauty does.* Every time Lettie heard that, she would squidge her face up like a wrinkled lemon, Ten invariably telling her she had better stop or she would wrinkle herself beyond all hope of getting ironed out; she could just begin preparations for taking over as spinster of the house. *"That* will never happen to *me,"* Lettie promptly answered, and then, overcome with remorse, since Ten was one of the few humans on whom she seemed capable of focusing, tearfully assured her she hadn't meant to insult her or to injure her feelings in any way. Ten, sure *any* emotion other than vanity was salutary for Lettie, would let her suffer, and then assure her *she* was as fine as she would ever be. It was Ten's theory that too much suffering was unpleasant and only ended in hardening the heart.

Watching Lettie talk to the flattered William, while Ella stood by staring at the ground, her hands gripping each other over her skirt, Edna asked herself why they had ever permitted Lettie to buy that vanity. On a trip to Manhattan, she had seen "just the very one"; it was a cherry vanity, its top, three enormous mirrors, one inch smaller than the windows of St. Paul's, as Ten commented acidly, heavily carved with flying cupids, flowers, wreaths, and mythical scenes. Now she could study three times as much of herself as before, and she found every view equally fascinating. "How," Ten would ask, stentorian, outside Lettie's door, "can one human being take so long to dress itself? I fear she has early rheumatism of the fingers," she would tell an imaginary audience, "or that she finds buttoning too hard for her. We must contrive, Edna, to have her future dresses made up without buttons if at all possible. Perhaps they can tie with ribbons. Yes," she would go on to the empty hall, and the family's amusement, "we should have taken better care of the details of her education. Who would have thought buttons would be her undoing?"

After one of these performances, Edna appeared at her side, asking her to promise, to swear upon her Bible or whatever she held most dear, that she would not even consider dying until both Ella and Lettie were safely married off. "I think I can promise you that," Ten had answered; "*that* is a challenge that would keep anyone alive." Ten was now almost seventy; John forty-seven. Time, Edna thought, had not done much to them; it had only brought them closer to extinction. All of them: although the children found things just beginning, worlds opening like doors to sunken cities in the earth, while *she,* at Lettie's age, had already had her first child: Martin. Martin, she mused, smiling. He had John's loving nature, but none of his reticence. She was almost sure he was seriously interested in Alice Moffat's girl, Minnie. No, Edna thought, it would not disturb her if all her children married Alice's. Her mother's views on that matter, though; that was another story. Edith now insisted Martin attend them in Boston and Manhattan, parading a series of eligible young ladies before him, and then he would arrive at the Brattleboro station, and even while hugging her, look frantically over her head for Minnie. And what was Minnie like? A younger version of Alice, the same round red cheeks, straight blond hair, the same big, round innocent blue eyes, the same sturdy ability to survive. But she was unlike her physically; willowy, not round, in certain lights almost ethereal. No, Edna thought, there would be no interfering with Martin; he had his father's stubbornness. And hers, she added with remorse.

Thank goodness Anna was too young to marry; she was only eleven. She was going to be a beauty, perhaps even more remarkable than Lettie. She had jet-black hair, pure-white skin, red lips which always looked painted, and eyelashes thick enough to flutter older hearts whenever she lowered them. They cast shadows. Her green eyes shone out like skies, visions of another world, and she had what the others did not: a kind of presence or bearing. She seemed to float, to reassure, as if already part angel, ministering to needs of those still mortal. Everyone loved her. Yes, it was a good thing she was only eleven. Right now, she was madly in love with the Reverend Pierce, who, Edna thought, must be near seventy himself.

Anna attended church more regularly than Lois Ann, and, being younger, had the endurance to sit through three sessions of services, even if that meant, on some Sundays, hearing the same sermon three times. It was only there,

Edna noted (Edna felt obliged to accompany her, no matter what the hardship, as if she were chaperoning her daughter against God's advances), that she showed signs of fire. She disapproved of whispering over backs of pews before services, of young men and women exchanging fervent glances as services proceeded, even of the little refreshment carts set up outside on the common, soothing the more earthly thirsts and hungers of those who had come a long way. "Well, *it* is just terrible," Anna had told Ten, indignant; "there is the holy bell calling come to church, come to church, and then the way they *shop* in the cemetery, going from grassy mound to grassy mound, reading, out of *mere curiosity*, crumbling inscriptions on ancient headstones." "You're hardly charitable," Ten cut in; "how do you know whose stones they are visiting? Or why? Why, if I were there, visiting the tombstone of my dead husband, you would be busy disapproving of *me*." Anna flushed, and quieted, making a mental note to discuss her judgments of others with the Reverend Pierce when next she met with him.

"Well," Anna went on spiritedly, bright red spots appearing on each cheekbone (they made her look as if she were kept alive by fire), "you should *see* it again before coming to conclusions. Everyone comes in from the farms, from the villages, from the mills. They come on foot, in their farm wagons, some on horseback. They come through the dust on the highways, some walk through the meadows, some through the lanes" (Ten sighed), "and by the time they get there, the congregation is so immense, and it looks so promising!" Anna wailed. "But then, then they go into the churchyard through that little wicket, and go through the graves as if they didn't *care* the dead were there, and go in through the porch of the church. Well, the women go inside first, just so the men can gather all around the door to talk about horses, crops, wire worms, who knows what? Do you think that's proper conversation for a Sunday?" Ten stared without comment.

"And inside, what is it?" Anna continued, more and more heated; "the wives and daughters hanging over the backs of pews like the Monday wash, chattering about the most disgraceful things. And then the sexton rings the bell, the last one, I mean, and the men come in clattering like a herd of cattle into a barn, not like people into a house of worship at all." "Do they still come in through doors facing the congregation?" Ten asked mildly; she hoped to quiet her. "Yes, yes," Anna said, impatient. "And I suppose everyone just keeps on chattering?" Ten asked, remarkably solemn; "even after the elders and deacons sit down on both sides of the minister and look so seriously at the congregation?" "Oh, Aunt Ten," Anna sighed; "they are always quiet in the beginning; why, in the beginning, it's a true solemn hush. But those glances! Those whispers! Why, last Sunday," she said, pausing for effect, "the Reverend's grandson drew a naked man on a tablet and his mother had to scratch it out!" "Horrible," Ten said.

She was beginning to wonder if Anna would ever outgrow this fanatical streak. "Blessing, choir, psalm of praise, prayer and praise, sermon and doxology, who would think," Anna would go on, furious, "it would be necessary for a virtuous old lady to keep a small child quiet by *bribery?* By passing him little bunches of pennyroyal? She brings him herbs, she even"—she paused again—"brings him peppermint candies! It's dreadful, dreadful." "Little children," Ten could not refrain from saying, "don't understand every word they hear; after all, the Reverend Pierce is a monotone. He could put the quaking dead back to sleep, and the bees that fly in and out drone so, why, it's enough to put anyone to sleep. You don't mean to tell me, Anna," she asked, "that the sound of the wind in the leaves, the sight of the butterflies flitting here and there, horses swatting at flies—you can still see them through the open doors, I presume?—you don't mean to tell me that all those things, *and* the singing of the choir, never makes you drowsy?" "Well, and if it does," Anna answered, angry, "I don't need any old lady to give me candy. It's worse than a bribe!" "*You* used to need candy, I believe your mother gave you rhubarb stems to chew, and a lot of noise you made doing it, too." Tears of irritation filled Anna's eyes. "I don't believe that," she burst out. "Just ask anyone."

"Well," Anna said, happy to change the unexpected course this conversation had taken (rhubarb stems indeed!), "do you know what they're thinking of now? They're thinking of putting wood stoves in the Old Stone Church!" "I must be getting very, very old," Ten said gravely; "whatever is wrong with that?" "God's house is not a house of luxury!" "I don't think people get nearer to God, not spiritually anyway," Ten answered, "by freezing to death." Anna, in a pet, stared down at her lap. "Anna," Ten said, "you always look at things so simply. You ought to have been a Catholic martyr, you seem to adore suffering so. Now think of old Mrs. Weston. She's in her eighties and as religious a woman as I've ever met. Why should she end with congestion of the lungs because she goes to church in the winter?" "Well, if God wants it," Anna muttered. "And how do you know he doesn't want wood stoves? Even Alice Moffat goes to church most every Sunday she can get there, and she has such rheumatism of the neck. If she took a chill, how would she think about religious matters then? No, all she'd think about would be her neck and how much it hurt to move her head. Sometimes you're perfectly ridiculous.

"I suppose," Ten went on, "you're in agreement with the congregation about the Stained-Glass Window War? You think they should move the big one in back of the congregation out altogether?" "Yes," Anna admitted; "it's too beautiful. It distracts the minister." "If you ask me, the congregation is just jealous because the minister sees it throughout the service, while they, who paid for it, only get to see a plain little blue and red cross." "Oh, what a low view!" Anna exclaimed. "Have *you* noticed people turning around in their pews to stare at that window?" Ten asked. Anna admitted she had. Ten looked at her. "I am going up to my closet," Anna pompously announced. "And stay there," Ten called after her; "you need more humility and less pride."

Anna went up in a rage; Ten had so discomfited her she was unable to concentrate on private prayer. She decided she had better follow the Reverend's advice and, when she found her mind wandering as she tried to pray, to write out her prayers, then burn them. "Come to particulars, come to particulars." That was what he always said. "Come to particulars; then you will never lose interest." By the fifth page, she looked up, astonished. "More humility and less pride!" Why, that was just what the Reverend himself had said last week. She humbly knelt in the little space she had made behind her headboard and prayed for the subduing of her proud spirit.

Downstairs, Ten was thinking (as Edna now thought at least fifteen times a day), Anna was *already* fit to be nothing but a minister's wife.

Well, Edna thought, watching Lettie, William, and Ella, thank heavens Jack was only seven; he was taken with a little girl named Susie, but at least that was no more serious than his putting mice in her lunchbox or down the back of her dress. He was wild, though. Edna sighed, thinking about them all. Next to them, Alice's children seemed so sensible, even if they were wilder. Much more so than Martin or Jack, but sensible all the same. She hoped there would be no more epidemics; it would be the last straw for Anna. She didn't think she could live through another four weeks inside layers of net, nor did she believe she could endure another revival. Yet, if events were pointing to the future, like arrows, she suspected something of the sort indeed was on its way.

They were all fulfilling the prophecies of their smaller lives. Except, perhaps, Anna. It was still almost impossible to predict what would become of her. Enough bad things, she thought grimly, had happened to her already. She wondered if it was possible to drive a normal person crazy by having all the wrong things happen to him. Perhaps that was what it meant to be crazy; all the wrong things happened to you. Still, there *was* a man in town who had his left leg and right arm amputated during the war, and had come home, recuperated, married, and begun farming. But suppose his father had died while he was gone; perhaps he might never have gotten over that. Or if he managed to live through that, and then the corn crop had failed, perhaps that would have done it, while he might have weathered the death of his wife easily. Or even the death of a child. Some people, she went on obsessively, seemed immune to any number of deaths, while the slightest trivia, a delay in plastering, a leak in the ceiling, a well not even running dry but developing an evil smell, that would do it. That must be what it was to be born under an evil star; that must be what fate was, the events life brought on its tray of years. The right ones— then you had a good fate; the wrong ones and you might be unhappy, wrong enough, insane. Right now, it was Edna's guess that unless the intervening three years brought in events that were really antidotes to previous ones, Anna was destined to be unhappy. Unless, of course, she did marry a minister. But even then she would be endangered; even then.

And if another series of events, like those of the last ten years, should come to her; then who could predict what would happen? Or perhaps the events which could prove fatal would differ radically from those which had already so afflicted her. That was the difficulty, Edna thought, taking a deep breath; it was like the practice of medicine. The weak spots were hidden to everything but nature, as, in some cases, scarlet fever passed the patient like a soft breeze, but complications of the kidneys or lungs killed him. Well, and what could she do about it? Nothing. As usual. She thought, for a moment, of praying, of prayer, but then decided against it; *that* would be tempting the fates. Anna prayed enough for the entire family, not to mention Alice's prayers, and Howard's, and everyone else's. If she prayed and God listened, it would be unjust, as pushing past someone with a ticket into a crowded hall would be unjust. Unless, of course, the hall caught fire. Well, there was no point in going on like this, she thought, staring at Alice across the table. She had accomplished her purpose, she supposed, smiling at her friend. She *had* cheered herself up. She was not at all sure she regretted having no young children left. They all grew up into old children, otherwise known as people.

It was a very hot day, Edna thought, the kind of day Minnie always said turned her into a spot of grease. But now that it was night, it was unaccountably cool, almost chilly. She had decided to wait up for John, reading in their room. Lately, she realized both she and Ten were doing that more and more. Peace; it was probably that she needed peace, as Ten did, too. She kept trying to concentrate on Zeno's paradoxes, but her mind *would* wander. Her mind, she thought, was like the arrow which would never reach the target, in this case the end of the paragraph; it kept dividing the present, reverting to the past. Perhaps, she thought, that was how the mind solved St. Augustine's riddle, or at least it seemed a riddle to her, his belief that there was nothing but the present, the eternal present; she had supposed the past existed in the mind of God, that was what he meant. That was how the past avoided being lost forever, for humans, at any rate. The present existed, and then it was over, to be superseded by another instant of the present, which, if small enough, could be seen as one of John's pictures. But tonight her mind kept reverting to the past. That meant it must exist somewhere.

And how could the war, the Civil War, have gone past so quickly, and with so little effect upon them? Well, that was not quite true; it had its effect insofar as it intruded into the personal. At one point, John had decided it was his duty to join the Green Mountain Boys as a doctor, and no arguments regarding his age would change his mind. For days, she had walked around the house like Lady Macbeth, although, she imagined, if she had done any such wringing she had done so in a very natural way. Then there was a terrible commotion at their door; she and Ten had all they could do pushing it open against the snowdrifts. Two men carried John in on a stretcher. His new horse, Gray the Second, had run away and flown so close to a tree John's leg had been broken.

Well, that had been a fortunate thing; how quickly she had known that at the time. Amos and the others carried him in; after a stiff drink of whiskey, John sat up and examined his own leg, while the rest of them pleaded with him to call old Dr. Houston. No, he was intent on setting his own leg, even though, as Ten repeatedly told him, he was a deep shade of gray, something like the color of a tree trunk in summer, she elaborated graphically. After another drink, he sat straight up, took a deep breath, and pulled the leg, bones grating, into alignment. Then, half propped up, he instructed the others in the art of putting on a splint and, after that was accomplished, peacefully went to sleep in his own bed. Well, now he had a permanent limp; he didn't seem to mind it at all, and, of course, was more than ever a local legend. Martin, fifteen at the time, champing to enlist and follow William, had easily been persuaded that his duty was to stay and help his father; so that worry, too, had been quickly erased.

But of course she could not foresee or prevent everything. John *had* become involved in criminal cases; and it had all started because of their six weeks in the spider web. A Mr. Mueller, on trial for murder, had hired Mr.

Siddons' nephew as his lawyer. The victim died of what appeared to be a swollen throat, which had entirely closed, suffocating him. The prosecution claimed he had been poisoned, although the autopsy could not turn up any real traces of any such substance. It developed that the traces of arsenic they found were due to some patent medicine he had been taking for his "sore throat," allegedly brought on by some poison Mr. Mueller, deeply indebted to him, had administered. But then the victim's wife remembered her husband had had a high fever for some time before his death, and in his investigations, Mr. Siddons, the lawyer, unearthed the fact that the dead man had spent some time visiting his sister in the midst of a diphtheria outbreak. He argued that the man had died of diphtheria, or the consumption his sister so obviously had. He had called Dr. Steele as an expert witness on contagious diseases; he had powerfully expressed his belief that both diseases were contagious. The man had been acquitted.

But, in the course of the trial, John was revolted by the victim's past, his cheating of others, dealing viciously with them, as if they were not people at all. He was sleepless over it for months. Still, the bug had bitten; Edna knew every time the mail arrived John secretly hoped he was to be summoned to another trial. Another trial or two, Edna thought, would be as bad as another religious revival for Anna, but once John made up his mind, there was nothing anyone on this earth could do to prevent him. And that, of course, was one of the things she most loved about him. And where had *this* all begun? she wondered, walking to the window, staring into the blue-black night, little gold flies flickering on and off, as if to reassure the nervous that this darkness was not permanent. A soft wind blew past her cheek. That day in the meadow, she supposed. But no, really before that. Perhaps when she began blaming her mother for her father's inability to cope with what the spade of his curiosity unearthed. He had possessed, she now knew, the curiosity without the strength. It might have begun even earlier, when her father first began explaining the ins and outs of the law and court cases to her. Even then, she sensed that *she* had the curiosity and the strength.

But she must have realized, too, that her curiosity led her into different areas, ones more theoretical. Still, her father had always made her feel so protected, and then, when she met John, she sensed some of the same things in him, although John, she knew that at once, was a far stronger person. But not strong enough; that was why she worried about the mails so. She did not want him exposed to further trials. She could not rid herself of her belief that their effect upon him would be even more powerful than they had been upon her father. Her father had also been in the business of saving men's lives; whether they deserved to be saved, that was not his concern. He had explained that to her often enough. Not his concern or that of criminal justice, either. It had all been a game to him, whether they went free or swung from the gallows; it had been the process, the puzzle, which interested him. John had a streak of that, too, but he took the lives more seriously, more personally. The Camps, and their oath to remain single, that was going to take five years from his life. Even though the brother, Frank, had been sketched by a passing artist who thought him very picturesque, and his picture subsequently appeared in *The Ladies' Journal;* then he had been given a subscription to some magazine or other which cost seven dollars, and now that was all the town talked about: Frank Camp had a subscription to a magazine *which cost seven dollars.* The rest of his life they found too usual for comment.

And the war itself, she mused, reminded by the absolute peace of the house. They had seen it, absorbed what they had of it, through William. First, there had been letters filled with the usual complaints about delays in getting to battle. Orders and rumors would circulate; everyone would prepare, and then they were back to waiting again. Still in Pennsylvania, he wrote he had been in the river every day; "I suppose Hal is up to that, too." That was what he had written.

And then there was the terrible letter he had written his married sister, Julia, apologizing for pages on end because he teased her, saying she had all the comforts of life while he slept outside, rolled up in the large leaves the South abounded in, and he never would have done it if he had known her first baby had just died. He could never forgive himself for writing her such a letter; he could not have guessed that she had not written because her baby's cradle was empty. He had now reread her letter so many times he could understand perfectly her feelings of loneliness.

Perhaps he had an advantage in camp, he wrote, surrounded by so many, and everything now in such a hurry, there was no time to mourn the dead, or even to bury them. He thought of her often, he wrote, moving about the house, listening for the little cry she would not hear again, although he knew she must hear it, or think she heard it, from minute to minute. "I often ask myself," Mrs. Moffat read out to the two families, which now regularly assembled for this purpose, "again and again: What remarkable, inexplicable power of religion can so wonderfully support its believers in times like yours? How, Julia, can you, while the earth is still fresh on the coffin of your only child, and before the first blade is sprung on the grave of your closest friend, manage forgetting your own trials to feel such an interest in me, your brother, almost a stranger when compared with these. Oh, Julia," he went on, "I believe I need *your* sympathy more than you need mine. It is not possible for me to describe my feelings to you. I would be a Christian but I cannot become one. What I mean to say is that there is a vague longing for that unstoppable happiness I know must exist there, which you have surely tapped, and drink from as from a well, but there is an unwillingness on my part to have it for my own. I cannot," he went on, "even desire to be a Christian seriously enough to begin attempting the effort. You will wonder at me, but I wonder at myself more.

"You say, Julia, we all have idols. Well, dear sister, what is mine? If God should take my sisters or my brother or my parents, I could never bear it as you have borne your losses, but I do not think I have made idols of those I love. I hope I shall not wait to be driven into the flock by the snapping dogs, but I am afraid I shall in the end. If you can make nothing of this confusion of ideas, this character of stubbornness and longing, you are no more confused than I am. I do not understand my own heart. If I had your faith," he concluded, which set them all weeping, "I should be a better soldier." He then asked to be remembered to her husband, and in her prayers, although he was certain he already was. The letter, Edna remembered, had a remarkable effect on

Julia, who had the cradle carried into the attic, read-mitted her husband to her bed, and finally gave away the chair she used to sit in so long with her little daughter.

After that letter, Julia had her mission. To comfort her brother, who was so lonesome he considered himself a stranger to her, his own sister; how could she so have forgotten herself and her obligations to this world? In the middle of the war, Edna wondered at it, himself in danger of dying at any moment, he took all the time to worry about his sister. Now she suspected the letter had made an even greater impression upon Ella, because when he wrote of his narrow escape from death at Antietam, she was trembling from head to toe. He had decided one area was safe, and had gone to visit his friend the captain, sat there with him, smoking a pipeful of the tobacco they constantly sent him, and then, finally feeling restless, went off to inspect a different area of the battlefield. Fifteen minutes later, the captain had been carried back to the central camp, shot through the head, in exactly the same spot he considered so safe, and he had taken the body to the embalmer's and shipped it home. "So you see where curiosity can almost get you," he concluded.

Yes, William's letters had been the war to them. There were all the little things he mentioned, his observation that none of the dead ever fell in the same position. They remained, he said, as distinctive in death as they had in life. And the gray field the soldiers had wondered at from a distance, until they found it covered with Confederate uniforms, each with a body inside. He was glad, he wrote, there were no women there, for every time a shell exploded, they would think, especially Minnie, "There goes death and damnation for some poor man," but he and the others, he claimed, had grown calluses over their souls (and their soles) and no longer even noticed them. And how he had tried to keep up *their* spirits. He was too busy to worry and grow morbid, but they could only wait and wait again, a casket instead of a letter, one as likely to arrive as another. He assured them he knew he would not die in the war, although he might be wounded; and although he was down to almost ninety pounds, he seemed much stronger than those who had begun with far more flesh on their bones.

And they were happy, he assured them, unbelievable as

it must seem to them, and cruel, too, since his absence, and that of the others, made all those at home so miserable. There were some hours, he admitted, when the soldier removed his armor and allowed himself to think of home and all its pleasant memories, but, he went on, this was only done for relief. Generally, he went on, you will find us, and myself, careless of the past as of the future, irrepressible, each depending on himself only, and only aware of the present. Was there anything else? Edna wondered.

Every summer night was a variant of every other summer night, every emotion a variant of a previous emotion, every grief a repetition of a previous one. No wonder the first experience of anything, love, terror, melancholy, fidgets, was so important, so memorable. Every emotion of love she felt for John she had felt before. It was habit that was so odd, so strange, that things became so much dearer, so much more precious in the repetition. But she supposed that was not true for everyone, only for those who really loved things in this life. Not everyone did. William discovered that on the battlefield. "I don't know that I could honestly say that my bad temper is improved enough to cheer any of you up, but I have more control of it, in spite of the fact that yesterday I turned and cracked the man behind me across the face thanks to his valiant efforts to tangle his boots up with mine."

She could not forget his descriptions of picket fences disappearing like dew as his company pillaged the countryside for firewood. How they, unlike the Confederate soldiers, solved the problem of eating saltless meat by boiling their meat in salt water; the "secesh" threw their meat away, since they were too delicate to eat without salt, hence subsisting on moldy biscuits, and were, predictably, falling first. He had found a Confederate knapsack and a man slumped over a letter half written. It was all moan and complain; how could he, William asked, worry his family so, while he went into fits of guilt if he had to request extra sheets or shirts or stamps, knowing how much harder life on the farm must be without him there to help out? Edna spent weeks meditating over his descriptions of the battle of Antietam, in which, he wrote, all of importance took place in a cloud of white smoke from discharging rifles and cannons. Did he think about it, she had wondered, how perfectly he had then described life?

And, she had gone over it again and again, how sensible he had become. The worst letters, he insisted, were the "Do Come Home Missives"; they spoiled, he said, more soldiers than did any other thing. "The soldier answers he would if he could, and the very next thing, is preoccupied with home, and forgets to keep his head down under fire." But he had not changed, really. He was anxious to come home and drive those Copperheads back to their holes. "There is no middle ground; there never is. If a man comes in and talks peace, just drive him out with a broomstick as you said Mrs. Weston did. I wouldn't have thought the old thing had it in her." That had given them a good laugh. And with every letter, Ella more and more fascinated with their author, until she entered into a slowly growing correspondence with him, one on which William himself had come to rely, for, as the town had correctly surmised, she received countless letters enclosed within those addressed to his family. Ella alone knew he was in an army hospital, until he escaped from it, his arm only partially healed of its gunshot wound. He had deserted from his hospital bed and reported to his company commander. He guessed, he wrote Ella, no one would court-martial him for deserting the hospital.

And how he did joke with them. Yes, it was true. Life was repetition, nothing but repetition, and perhaps that was what made it so wonderful, the infinite variations possible on the same theme. Dangers narrowly escaped. The theme of all Ten's novels, the theme then of his letters, however diligently he tried hiding it. "My hat," he wrote, "has six bullet holes in it. But don't worry; they are all from one bullet. You remember the dent at the top of it? Well, the ball went in the rim first, and then through the top, which now has two dents. Of course, a quarter inch lower would have broken my skull, but it was too high." He wrote of anything that might amuse them, of finding a box of powder in a family graveyard. "Yes, the secesh had a grim sense of the appropriate." "Did Dr. Steele approve of soap pills for powder burns?"

Only occasionally did he yield to pity of self, and then, understandably, on his birthday. "Yesterday, I was twenty-three. It is time I became a man if I am ever to become one, but there is much of the boy in me yet. Still, I dread growing old, and the years fly by all too quickly. I begin to feel that women who would be wives are blowing by like leaves into some other men's gardens." (This set Ella blushing; then, for several days, into a depression. Either he meant, she decided, that she would marry *before* his return or it was nothing to him what she did. That was surely it; it meant nothing.) "The war may last another year and I shall be twenty-four and ready to start out in life for myself, with no capital at all, and only a small stock of brains. I have a horror," he wrote, "of being the head of a poverty-stricken family." (So *that* was it, Edna thought. He didn't want Ella to take his interest in her for interest in her money. And a futile campaign that would be; she remembered all too well how she had feared John would suspect her interest in him came from one in his fortune, especially when he heard of her expensive hobby: designing houses. No, little changed but the cast.) "Do you think," he had gone on, "I will be married before I am thirty and young enough to walk up to the altar unassisted? God willing, I mean to have a wife and home, but when is quite beyond my powers of divination." Tears and more tears from Ella.

And his description of the battle of Chancellorsville fought in woods called the Wilderness—was that right?—and of the final surrender of Lee's troops. What were they, she wondered, shivering, picking up her shawl from the chair, wrapping it tighter about her, but shrunken descriptions of life? It was all in knowing where to look for the evidence.

"The night before the battle was one of magnificent beauty such as I have never seen before. The men all lay asleep on their arms, readied for action at an instant's signal. There was a full moon, and it shone calmly on the scene, as if to say, this is life, this calm, and perhaps making some of us realize that never could there have been a greater contrast between men and nature than it revealed that night.

"There were times when the rattle of musketry would stop altogether, and then one by one, thinly and weakly at first, but each taking spirit from the other, the whippoorwills would begin their concert. The woods filled with their music and the night echoed with their mournful song, and then it would be as if we were in nature's own church. But the rattle of musketry *would* start up again, and come toward us down the line, and the birds would take fright, and the magnificent music would cease at once. So it went on all night, the beautiful chorus of the birds singing God's own song, and then the noise of the deadly guns. We shall always remember it" (and that was strange, too, because it was true; at the time something happened, trival or gigantic, it was somehow possible to know, absolutely, that this particular event would never change or fade) "as one of the saddest, most heartrending and strange nights in all our experience of war."

Well, and hadn't she always sensed that life was a kind of war? William had written home giving the melody and words to "Tattoo," later called "Taps," invented to keep noisy members of his troop quiet so that others could sleep. "Put out the lights, go to sleep, go to sleep, go to sleep. Put out the lights, go to sleep, go to sleep." What was that but another version of what she had sung to John the day he described his brother's drowning? Perhaps it was true you had to be a general, even a little general, to get through this life of contradictions. That description of the night, now. The world was like that: summer, winter, life, death, day, night. Martin's book. They lived at each end of the pendulum's swing, but somehow, in between there was an empty space, something preventing their motion from remaining continuous. Eventually, they ran down and stood still, the pendulum stopped in the heart.

She thought now about his description of the army's surrender. The little shelter tents on the slope opposite the Union troops taken down, carefully folded, melting as if ice, the things which men would need on their way home. Now they would carry their homes on their backs like the turtle, and that, too, was true of those who survived to the end of life. And the surrendering troops laying down their arms in a silence belonging to the dead. She supposed everything did. And in the morning, William had written, "the hills were busy as anthills, as if the earth itself had quickened, men, in groups, or alone, walking, or riding, each making their way home guided by the compass of instinct, each like an ant with its burden so much bigger than itself, each heading for its tunneled-out home. And how lonely they made us; they were so familiar they had become necessary; we didn't realize it until we saw them leaving. It was as if the sight of them had become necessary for each breath we drew; they had become the reason for our existence, and that reason was gone. We had no reason to live." "Isn't it odd," he asked Ella, "how we *will* find a reason to live, no matter how circumstances will conspire to pick our pockets of them?" Yes, Edna thought, that was it, that was the secret; to be able to find those reasons, or invent them.

And the letters had had such a salutary effect on John. He had become even more imaginative in his treatments of nervous patients. The Camps—they had become his despair—had finally yielded to his newly kindled hope that a solution to everything could eventually be found, so that when Jane Camp had taken to her bed for no reason whatsoever, giving up on the house, slowly piling with dust and bits of rotten food, and, on a hot day, could be smelled almost half a mile down the road, he did, in fact, come up with a cure. "My dear Mrs. Camp," he murmured, taking her hand, "there is only one known cure for this ailment, but I fear you will laugh at me." "Tell us, tell us," her brother Frank insisted. "Do so," she seconded, voice feeble. John looked dubiously at the three of them, while Edna, who knew what he was about, had already taken the precaution of keeping her back to them.

"Well, I have this magic little casket"; John removed a small wooden cube from his pocket. "Inside is a religious charm. I had to promise I would not reveal who gave it to me, and you must promise not to tell anyone you have it in your possession." They solemnly promised. How they enjoyed taking vows. That must have been how their parents had tricked them into that cruel vow of celibacy. "What you must do," John said in confidential tones, "Jane, if I may call you Jane" (she nodded), "is take this little casket and every morning go about the house touching every single object with it. Can you do it?" "We will help you," her brother and sister struck up. "No, no, she has to do this alone." Jane sighed feebly. "Can you manage such a task alone?" "I believe so," she whimpered. Definitely, he had aroused her curiosity. "You must start tomorrow morning," he said; "there is not a moment to waste, and I expect Mr. Camp daily reporting on your progress." They all nodded.

The next morning Jane Camp was in the attic; she had decided to start from the top of the house and work her way down to the porch, touching everything with her little wooden amulet. Gradually, she began to take an interest in the objects she touched; the more interested in them she became, the more interested in cleaning them. Perhaps she began cleaning them automatically. Whatever the reason, the results were immediately apparent. The house was the cleanest in the village. Jane Camp was once more visible on the porch, then at church, finally operating the fancywork booth at the fair (which was why Lettie had interested herself in that one), even doing the weekly marketing without the previously required attendance of brother and sister. All Williamsville pronounced it the most remarkable cure of an incurable depression they had ever heard of, and Dr. Steele's reputation rose higher than ever.

And what was *that* little victory, Edna wondered, but a winning of a small, almost invisible battle? Jane Camp, the spinster, saved by William Moffat's inspiration; she would certainly have held him in contempt had she permitted him anywhere near her. How would she feel, Edna pondered, if she knew how much he had to do with her magical cure? Life was such a strange interconnection of tissues and vessels, almost as if, she sometimes believed it, they were all part of one huge body. Yes, she imagined they had all developed from one amoeba, and only when they were reduced to skeletons (William had described a field of them in Charlottesville) was such a thing obvious. For some time after the letters, John had gone about his practice with more enthusiasm than she had seen in years, but now, she didn't know why, she was sure it was so, he was losing interest, almost as if he was losing interest in the flesh and blood he had spent most of his life preserving. For as long as possible.

The photographs lasted longer; the new work must be acting like a leech, drawing the dedication to medicine into his photographic studio. Still, his conscience would never permit him to change professions. Not unless something extraordinary happened. And by now, they had reached the age when very little extraordinary happened.

But perhaps she was wrong about that. Yes, she must be. The one thing William's letters had impressed upon *her* was the unpredictability, the infinity of surprises, with which life annoyed them all.

What surprises, she tried to imagine, could change the course of her husband's career as a doctor? If something happened to Anna, that was her constant fear, would that be a sufficient cause, altering the stream of his life? She thought not. No, she was sure that would change nothing. Tragedy was something he had grown accustomed to, as William had grown used to exploding shells. But then, what could it be? she wondered, ruefully reproaching herself for trying to peer into the future. As usual. Something he had never before come across; she could tell that much and no more. That was hardly much help. Well, she had better get into bed before she froze like Ten's geraniums, for which yearly, her sister-in-law grimly predicted chill death, but as far as she knew, they had perished only once, that first winter she was married, that first time she was pregnant. Imaginary disasters, Edna thought, pulling up the covers; *they* were certainly to be avoided. It was a terrible thing, wasn't it, Edna thought, picking up her book, determined to wait up for John, to think a whole war had been fought to protect the likes of her daughter Lettie. They should have shipped her off, tied up like a heifer, as a war nurse; yes, it would take a cannonball to penetrate that thick, beautiful skin of hers.

"Awake?" John stuck his head in. "As ever." "As ever, as ever," he whispered, sitting down on the edge of the bed, holding her. Something was up. "There are two mad dogs loose," he said at last, removing his head from her bosom, "and a good chance of yellow fever. There are three cases in Williamsville." "Does that mean we live in our web again?" "No, that's no use now; I've exposed the family to it." "Perhaps we'll be lucky." He just looked at her, blank. "We will; no one is going to die." She was, she realized, certain of that. "Come, dear," she said, "take off those clothes and blow out the light." When he didn't move, she began unbuttoning his shirt. When he still did not move, she got out of bed and removed his shoes and his stockings, and then, putting her palm flat against the center of his chest, pushed him back on the bed. "You just relax," she ordered; "there's nothing whatever to worry

about," she scolded as if he were a small child. "You
don't think so, do you?" he asked as she drew the covers
over him. "No, I don't," she said, blowing out the light
she kept on her side of the bed; "put out the lights, go to
sleep, go to sleep, go to sleep." He suddenly turned, holding to her violently. "*That* was a surprise," she said later.
"The doomed man's last dinner," he muttered; he sounded
sheepish. "Don't be ridiculous!" she scolded. "Where do
you get that impossible optimism?" "At Elder's store."

No one could convince her that more than a day, possibly a week, no more than that, had passed since that
day in the meadow when she had, in fact, turned his joke
into a serious proposal. She turned on her side, holding
his shoulders with one arm, cradling his head with the
other. One arm was beginning to fall asleep. It was, as
it always was, an extremely painful way to lie, but she
did not move until she heard the deep sound of his breathing. She forced herself to move her left arm. It felt paralyzed; soon it would be prickling as if stabbed by interminable needles. She kissed him gently on the cheek,
then turned on her side and fell asleep. She had often
wondered at it, why they always wound up sleeping back
to back; she always stopped at the same thought: at least
it made Jimmie happy to breathe into her face.

But he was dead now, and they had Archie instead; he
looked, she thought hourly, just like his father and took
after him, too. Edna still fell asleep with a cat breathing
happily at her nose. And how she had taken on over
Jimmie's death. It had nearly unhinged her. The slightest
thing, the most innocent conversation about a plant: she
would be crying uncontrollably.

Ten, still up, found herself thinking about that. At the
time, she had really wondered, not wondered, she corrected herself, but worried, if Edna would recover from
the blow. What a strange person, so violent in her affections. And so particular about whom she invested them
in. Well, Edna had told her, at least Jimmie had missed
the war. Ten knew she meant the cat had been spared
heartbreaking attacks of his mistress's blues and refrained
from comment. And by that time, Ten knew, Edna was
convinced that Jimmie was indeed human; such was the
violence of Edna's faith, whatever breed it was. She was

religious at heart, Ten thought, the way she loved all of creation. She did worship it.

If she were sure God had created it, Ten knew, Edna would worship him, too. Then she would make Lois Ann appear a godless sinner. But she would never be that sure of anything. Yes, Edna still interested her, while Edith, Edith, she imagined, must be something like Jimmie was to Edna. She hoped nothing would ever happen to Edith, or if it did, would happen after she was unable to see it. Everyone needed that idol asleep on their pillow, that strange little circle of glass which held their security. Edith was her last link with the past, her last living link. If she should die, she would be left alone with her memory. This way, they both kept it alive. It was much safer that way. She cried silently, for no reason. Yes, she thought, blowing out her own light, she *was* getting old. Old and sentimental. Emotionally incontinent, that was what John would say. Well, there were worse diseases, she meditated, staring defiantly at the moon's blank face. "Good night," she told it automatically. Somehow, it too had become human, almost a member of the family, a precious friend. "Good night," she told it again, trying to keep her eyes open, to keep looking at it, but her lids were heavier and heavier. She was sound asleep. The whole house was asleep, even the mirrors in Lettie's vanity.

There was now incontrovertible evidence of yellow fever in Williamsville, three victims already in the stages of "black vomiting." John, talking to Edna in the middle of the night, estimated that it would be ten days to two weeks before it was clear if he was coming down with the disease, or if any of the family would be. It was essential, he told her, voice flat, to quarantine the victims, to burn everything coming out of the quarantined room, and to make absolutely sure the victim was not allowed any exertion, even in bed. Then he paused, waiting for Edna's reaction. "I imagine," she said slowly, "we had better set up the little houses." "The *rustic* cottages," he mocked, trying to sound cheerful. "And there's no way of predicting? I mean, who will come down with it?" "None that I know of; except that people in good health are more likely to recover." "It's not necessarily fatal, then? Well," she said, "I suppose we had better stay away from the Moffats?" "No, none of that's necessary; Fred Elder came down with it this morning." "Oh no!" Edna gasped, lying back on the bed; "that means everyone's exposed who's gone into the store." She stared at the ceiling. "This is a real epidemic then, isn't it?" "It will be." "And any of us might get it." "That's about it."

"Are they closing the school?" she finally asked. Closing the school. When that happened, there was no further questioning the seriousness of events. "We just had a meeting today; it was the last day. Jack seems awfully happy about it; too happy about it, if you ask me; closing the school, I mean." "He's been awfully fidgety lately," Edna agreed; "he talks to Anna about everything, though. She was trying to get my attention about something this evening." "Why don't you talk to her? They say state of mind is important in this disease." "You mean," his wife asked, incredulous, "if he's unhappy at school, he's more likely to die?" She answered her own question, got up, and went out.

"Anna says," she reported, coming back, "that old Mrs. Whistle Breeches, that's what they're calling her now, has a new form of discipline, especially for the little ones. She locks them in the supply closet." "With or without a light?" "Without," she answered, collapsing on the bed. "Anna says," she went on, a disembodied voice, "that Jack's absolutely terrified of that closet; he thinks there's some kind of queer machine in it that's going to get him." "She's giving up on banging their heads against the desk?" "No, she still does that." "We better talk to Jack about the dark," his father considered; "you or me?" "You." "Why me?" he asked. "I have to talk to Ella." "Is Lettie still going on over William? I didn't think she could concentrate on anything so long." "She can manage it," Edna sighed, "as long as Ella stays interested. Do you ever have this horrid feeling we're breeding brainless rabbits instead of children?" He grinned at her. "Jack's heart is free." "No," Edna corrected; "he's in love with little Susie Webber; he puts mice down her dress. You lie down," she ordered him, "while I go and talk to her. They're all up." "If nobody comes," he agreed; "what are they all doing up, anyway?" "They're all celebrating the closing of the school. I don't understand that, either. Only Anna and Jack are still going." "The principle of sympathy," he mumbled, sleepy. "I wish there was more of *that* going around," she said, leaving.

She tapped gently at Ella's door. No answer. She opened it; the bed was empty, the room was empty. What now? she thought, desperate. She went downstairs and looked in the parlor. No one there. She went into the second parlor; she could hear the sound of voices in the dark. Gradually, they became familiar. Lettie and William. "Do keep quiet, Mother," Ella whispered urgently from the darkest corner, beckoning her over to the open window. They stood there listening. "Of course I care for you," Lettie was saying. "Then why don't I believe you when you tell me that?" William asked. Edna, feeling Ella's body trembling, put her arm around her daughter's waist. "Perhaps because you are unsure of your own feelings." "That's possible," he conceded, "but I thought I was." "You thought you were sure of your affections for me?" she coaxed. "I didn't mean to imply that," William objected. "Then," Lettie whispered, "you must mean you were sure of your feelings for Ella." "You know I can say nothing about that," William answered uneasily; "and you, what is the state of your feelings? The whole town believes you're good as engaged to a New York lawyer." "My heart is as free as it ever was," she said, the white shadow of her dress moving closer to his dark figure in the moonlight. "You're sure," he asked her, looking into her eyes—she had moved alarmingly close—"that you are not *playing* a game of hearts?" "No," Lettie murmured, tilting her heart-shaped face up at him. "I never had much talent for games of any sort," she whispered. "They also say," he persevered bravely in the sight of the moon, "that you've set your heart on a senator in Boston." "People here have the strangest fancies, William. William," she repeated softly; "that's such a lovely name."

Still, he hesitated, not moving toward her. "My mother," he said, "always warned me to watch out for beautiful women." "*Am* I beautiful?" "Now you *are* playing games," William answered angrily, stepping back. "Beauty is as beauty does," Lettie murmured; "I may not seem beautiful to you." He stood still. "There's a leaf on your jacket," she said suddenly; "in the middle of the summer, too. Isn't that supposed to bring good luck?" "I don't know, really." Lettie moved closer, pretending to brush something from his shoulder. She stared up into his face with the patience of stone. Edna, whose eyes had become accustomed to the dark, looked at Ella as if to ask if she should stop them; she could call to Lettie, but Ella shook her head no. "We've known each other for so long," William said, "and you've never been very interested in me before." He was straightforward, Edna thought; *that* was remarkable. Dealings with Lettie almost invariably produced maze-like approaches to the simplest issues. "I was not old enough to know any better; there are some things"—she hesitated, inclining toward him—"that improve so with age." "Yours or mine?" he asked, in a last effort to stop what was happening. "Why, both of ours, of course.

"At first," she went on, "it must have been my childish image of you as a war hero, a soldier of fortune, but all that is changed." "Lettie," he protested, "I work in a mill; I'm a farm boy. That's all I am. It doesn't seem logical that you should feel anything for me." "It's not logical," Lettie agreed, her voice deepening, "but it is the case. Is there a cure for it?" She stared at him, motionless. She should have been a hypnotist, Edna thought bitterly; *she* knew what her daughter was doing. So did Ella; that was the worst of it. "Some illnesses," William parried, "are like malaria. A serious attack, and then it passes off. If that's the nature of your illness, I recommend quinine." Edna, listening, had to admire his stubbornness; it pointed toward incorruptibility. But he would be no match for her. At least not right away. "I don't think quinine would do me much good," she answered; "I think I have something chronic." She paused. "Feel my cheek," she whispered; "feel how hot it is." William remained motionless. Lettie picked up his hand and placed it against her cheek. Oh no, Edna thought; it was happening all over again, but this time, she despaired, it was wrong, perverse. "You're cold as a stone." "Am I? Am I really cold as a stone? That's a dreadfully insulting thing to say to a lady." "Do you want the truth or don't you?" "I don't mind the truth, but I do want more."

Suddenly, William bent over, cupping Lettie's face between his hands, staring into her eyes. A shock went through Ella's body; Edna's arm tightened around her.

William was kissing Lettie, yes, kissing her. "Is that better than the truth?" "Almost," Lettie taunted; "almost, except I'm so cold." "And you wouldn't be if I put my arms around you?" "No, I think not." His arms folded her into his jacket; this time, when he kissed her, both Edna and her daughter felt as if an eternity were passing, as if they would surely smother before they surfaced.

"I think," William told her (he sounded almost angry), "you had better get inside. Some people here believe the night air is unhealthy." "I don't." "Well, I don't believe in taking chances," William answered, "not with yellow fever going about." "But we're so high up, and there isn't any water nearby. You're safer here. I don't think a miasma can climb up so high." "Nevertheless. I've seen yellow fever, and it's not pretty." "You didn't have it, did you?" Lettie asked, almost excitedly; "my father believes you can't have it twice." "Lettie," he said firmly, "it's time to get inside." "You're already giving me orders," she pouted. Edna noticed his body tense, as if with rage, but Ella, she knew, noticed nothing; she was quietly crying. "Just keep quiet," Edna whispered to her. They watched Lettie hold to William's hand until only the tips of their fingers touched. Then she turned, as if movement were agony, and went toward the door. Before she went in, she blew him a kiss. They listened to her go into the kitchen; she was apparently slicing something. No, Edna thought, nothing would spoil her appetite. It was business as usual. There were the methodical noises of flatware dropping into the washbasin, the icebox closing, the careless tread up the stairs.

"Well," Ella said after they heard Lettie's latch drop into place, "I suppose you're going to try and tell me she's not up to anything." Edna kept quiet. "Or that he's not up to anything with *her*." She spoke with such revulsion Edna felt cold. "No, I wouldn't say that, not after what we've seen. Come on," Edna coaxed; "let's go talk to Ten. Her light was still on when I came down." Ella followed her mechanically; she reminded Edna of those jointed paper dolls complete with elaborate kits for paper costumes. She was used to thinking of Lettie that way, she thought, but not Ella. Thank God, she thought, a light was still shining under Ten's door. "You sit down here," she told Ella, pushing her into Ten's armchair. "What's got everyone up with this old bone?" Ten asked, putting down her copy of *Great Expectations*. "I thought you read that during the war," Edna said. "We kept missing issues of *Harper's*, don't you remember?" "Oh yes, that's true." "Well, what's got you up?" Edna described what she had just seen. "That Lettie," Ten spluttered, pushing back the bedclothes, reaching for the crocheted shawl on the chair next to her bed; "she's no more interested in him than I am in bedbugs." Ella didn't say a word. "Ella, you listen to me," Ten said; "your beloved sister would no more marry him than she'd marry Gray."

This unflattering comparison finally set Ella crying. "She might," Ella said; "if she thought it would make me unhappy enough." Ten thought. "Then there's only one thing to do; you have to encourage someone else, or seem to, anyhow." "But that's not right," Ella protested. "Now, Ella," Ten went on, ignoring such scruples; "let's think. You've always been a wild girl, climbing trees with the boys. You don't have to pull the wool over anyone's eyes, not really. Isn't there someone who would go along with you? You could return the favor later." "You mean *act* as if I were in love with someone else?" Ella asked. "Exactly, exactly," Ten said impatiently. "What about that Tom James, the miller's son?" Ella made a face. "Don't be so sensitive; it's not as if he really *was* your brother. Everyone thinks he's a wonderful catch, and he's very handsome, too. What could seem more likely? It happens all the time, doesn't it?" Ten asked her; "something like what your dear devoted sister said. The scales were lifted from your eyes and you suddenly realized the swimming companion who went everywhere with you and your brothers was the shining light of your life. Do you think he would do it?" Ella looked desperately at her mother. Edna pretended not to see her.

"Well, do you?" Ten demanded. Perhaps Ten had benefited from reading all those novels, after all. "Yes," Ella answered. "You're sure?" "We always were partners in crime," Ella said, despondent; "but it won't do any good. I can tell you that now. I can't do anything against that one with her red hair and her green cat's eyes." "And the empty space where her heart's supposed to be," Ten added; "don't you think you're underestimating poor William? After all, his letters made it sound as if he had more than one grain of sense." "People in love don't have any sense," Ella said. "It's only hiding; you can coax it out from the walls with a few crumbs." "I wish I believed that." "Well, if you can't, you won't get anywhere, I can tell you that. When someone sets her cap for the man you want, you had just better tilt yours at a better angle." Ella sat in the armchair, lost in thought.

"*Are* you going to do it?" "What?" "Ask Tom James to help you. I hear he's interested in Susie Wakefield and can't get *her* attention; it might be just the thing for both of you. Well?" "I'll do it tomorrow."

"Good. That's all settled then," virtually licking her lips with satisfaction; "now that's taken care of, I can go to sleep." "It's *not* taken care of," Ella complained. "Not another word like that, or I'll give Lettie some ideas." "Don't do *that*." "Well, and do you think I would?" Ten asked, glowering at her; "even if you're willing to abandon William to that icebox? Go on to bed; you have your work cut out for you." "If I haven't been cut out already." "I warned you," Ten said; "one more word and I pay Lettie a visit with some helpful hints." "Oh, all right," Ella grumbled, waiting for her mother, who was bending over to kiss the top of Ten's head, its thinning gray hair.

When they left and went down the hall, Ella's step was already lighter. Well, now John was sound asleep, Edna sighed, beginning to undress. And all this about mad dogs; before anyone left tomorrow morning, John had better warn everyone about it. The girls would all be carrying pistols. There was the sudden sound of hooves in the yard. Edna went out. "It's me, Mr. Weston," he said, pounding on the door; "get the doctor up. Open up. My wife is freezing to death, trembling all over, just like the ague, but she's burning up. She feels like a stove," he babbled on hysterically. "What else is wrong with her?" John asked behind her. "She's nauseated and she's vomited twice, and she says she has a headache here"—he pointed to the front of his head—"and her back hurts her something terrible, and rubbing it doesn't help any." "Anything else?" John asked. This was the clinical picture of yellow fever, but some details were missing. She might only have a bad fever, an infection of some sort. "Well, her face is all red, and her eyes hurt, and if I bring in a candle, she shrieks and covers up her eyes." Well, there were the missing details. "When did her fever go up?" "A few hours after she got so cold." "You don't have much idea how high it is?" "Well, she feels about like my son did, the time you said he had a hundred and five." "I'll be back as soon as I can," he told Edna; "don't wait up wrinkling yourself." Ten was watching at the top of the stairs.

"More yellow fever?" Ten asked. "It looks like it." "Well, the Westons will be the first to go, mark my words," Ten said; "they can't any of them have much in the way of livers, what with all that drinking. If they still have livers." "Ten, dear," Edna asked, "would you remind me to warn all the children about the mad dogs in the morning?" "Rabies? Edna, I don't want to hear a word about it. I'll just remember to remind you." The two women went upstairs. Edna had not been in bed ten minutes before there was a little knock at her door. "Who is it?" "It's me, Jack." Edna fumbled for a match, struck it, and lit her kerosene lamp. "Come on in," she called. "Now," she said, settling him next to her, "what's all this about supply closets?"

He began a long recitation of how this time someone else had dropped a mouse down Susie's dress, but he had been blamed for it and put into the supply closet, and ended by confessing he was afraid of the dark. "Well, let's try and get you accustomed to it," his mother said, stroking his hair. "How?" "Well, you stay here with me until your father comes home, and I'll blow out the light." "You're not afraid of the dark, Mother?" "Not a bit," she said, blowing out the light. "Will I have to go back to my bed when Father gets home?" "Not tonight, dear." Why, she wondered, did she have so much trouble when they got older? In two years, she wouldn't have much idea of what to do with him, either. "Mother," Jack whispered, "what's that moving in the corner?" "A shadow." "Are you certain?" Edna sighed, lit another match, and held up the lamp. "It was a shadow, I guess," Jack murmured, relaxing. "What's that?" he asked a few moments later. "What's what?" Edna asked sleepily. "That noise." "That's what's called the wind," his mother said, stroking his cheek. "Oh, the wind," he repeated. "Do you think we can go to sleep now?" she asked.

She loved the way the wind blew the curtains in; she

loved the dark. It was dreadful, she thought, that a child of hers should grow up fearing it; it was such a magical thing. There was no answer from Jack; she heard the sound of his deep breathing. "Good," she thought, turning on her side, settling in for sleep.

The most unearthly pounding yet heard at the Steeles' woke the family. Had a patient finally gone mad right on their doorstep? Edna wondered, making the little jump to the floor, grabbing instinctively for her robe, which, like her clothing, was always laid out so that she could dress in seven minutes. The whole family, except Anna, who was up early, busy in prayer, had been flushed from their deep holes of sleep. Ten stood next to Edna, watching John hammer a huge sheet of paper onto the center of the front door. She was used to emergencies; it was not difficult to tell. She stood there wrapped in her light crazy quilt like an old Indian squaw. Edna looked at her; she just shook her head. Lettie, Ella, Martin, and Anna were standing on tiptoes, without success trying to read over their father's shoulder. Martin waited peaceably; Jack stared, quivering.

"Now," John said, turning to them with grim satisfaction, "I want everyone to memorize this list before breakfast. If anyone in the family comes down with symptoms like these, those on the list, someone is to find me wherever I am. Either Amos or that son of his, but someone, I don't care who."

John began reading out the list.

"He's not content with waking the dead," his sister muttered; "now he has to read his ninety-five theses out loud." "One," he read out: "Chill." He inspected them to make sure of their attention. In their nightclothes, everyone was watching him. They looked, he thought, like a small, underage army. "The chill may be absent. Rapid rise of temperature, following the chill, or coming on without it. That's two. Three. This is not a normal chill. It's accompanying symptoms are nausea, vomiting, frontal headache. severe pains in the back and limbs, a flushed face, shining and staring eyes, possibly accompanied by pain in the eyeballs, accompanied by a hatred of the light. Because it hurts the eyes," he elaborated, seeing Martin's questioning look. "I feel chilled already," Lettie exclaimed dramatically. None of them bothered looking at her. She was not suggestible; she did not, Ten thought, have enough nerves to be suggestible.

"This is not a joking matter," John roared at her; she paled. Edna nodded to herself. Lettie's father was the only person on the planet who could frighten that cube of ice. She wondered again at her lack of maternal sentiment. She remembered when Lettie was born; she had liked her then and until she was almost four. But by the time she was four, she found liking her impossible. Mothers, she scolded herself again, were *supposed* to like all of their children, but she did not like this one. She was not *likable*.

It was a disgrace *not* to like her with the threat of yellow fever in the neighborhood. But, even if she did like her, that would not protect her daughter against the fever. It would only, she decided, protect *her* later: from guilt, from self-hatred. If Lettie came down with it and she didn't. She was not superstitious enough to believe she would be punished with the fever because of her lack of love. If she liked her, she liked her; if she came down with the fever, she came down with it. Ella, though, *she* was suggestible. She was standing on the other side of her mother; Edna put her hand on her arm for an instant, a butterfly's touch; she was ice cold. "Get a hold of yourself," she whispered to her. "I know," her daughter whispered back; "I'm sorry." "Don't overdo it; there's nothing to be sorry about. Just don't start taking on in advance; you'll only upset your father." Ella nodded. Edna felt her body relax against hers. Well, no wonder she felt chilled after last night.

She looked over at Anna. *That* was what she expected; nothing medical fazed her, not in the slightest. At least nothing about this would disturb her, not unless someone she cared for was taken by the disease. Perhaps it was true that religion would protect her, spiritually at any rate, from the deaths, as her curiosity protected her from suggestibility, frightening premonition. She remembered asking Alice, one day after a letter from William arrived, the one in which he described his hospital days, whether she really believed in God, or whether she "practiced" religion, as she had once practiced the piano, out of habit or idle fondness. "Oh, dear," Alice answered, "just because I think Lois Ann goes to extremes doesn't mean

I'm not a religious woman myself. The older I get" (she stirred into patterns some salt which had fallen onto the tabletop), "the more religious I get; well, I guess it goes one way or another, doesn't it?" She looked at Edna. "It's the country, I think; it's seeing the way things work to hold on. And the lilies, for instance, I think that's what made it all so easy for me.

"That summer we almost fell down the far side of Lord's Hill going after those wild lilies I wanted? The ones that were taller than you were? You looked up the name," she prodded Edna; "I called them the winged lilies because of the way their petals swept back." "Oh, the turk's-cap lilies." "You always know the name for everything. Well, they were so beautiful, and they grew wild, in all the hard places, and before old Mrs. Ward died, I asked her about them, she had so many of them all over. She said you could start them out from seeds, remember? But it took almost nine years for them to grow full size. Well, it seemed to me if things grew like that in secret places, just waiting for us to find them, someone was up to something. Then, after we almost got killed getting them, I thought, whoever put them there didn't put them where they would be easy to get to. And we sure looked foolish, coming back without our shoes; I came back limping in one shoe, but you lost both." "Oh, I remember all that; I can still see them falling down the wall of that canyon; I mean, the far side of the hill." "Dr. Steele was right when he lit into you," Alice said; "we really were climbing around on a canyon." "Oh, I don't know," Edna objected. The memory of that scolding still irritated her, the way she had been treated as a senseless child.

"You don't know? When we had to lie flat against the hill and hold on to the grasses and there was almost an avalanche of pebbles going right past us, and then we had to creep up once we got them, and you kept complaining about how heavy they were. You kept saying they couldn't be that heavy; they were heavy as bodies!" "I remember." "And then you carried off some of their black seeds, and you said if anything looked like a death seed, then they did, and now you've got quite a collection." "I still don't see," Edna said, "why our almost getting killed hunting down wild lilies like two idiots would make any-one, not even you, Alice, more religious; no, I don't."

"Well, it seemed to me that the lilies were showing the way things always happened, living things, I mean. First they weren't there, and then they were. I don't know how I missed seeing them all those years. And the way things get born, or don't, but mostly the way they do. The weather, for instance," she went on, "it always seems so mysterious. Sometimes I think the weather is God, or part of him." She stirred the salt into figure eights with her index finger. "It decides if we live or die. Enough heat kills us; enough cold kills us. Fevers are like hot spells. If they go on long enough, they do in the crops, and if enough of them get done in, then we're all done for. I guess it's things like that. I can't help believing in God"; she stopped, helpless to explain further. "For in-stance, your appearance that day at my brother's. It seems as if God had something to do with that, but you know I can't explain it to you. You don't begin to think that way." "No, I don't; I can't believe there's much purpose behind anything. I can believe there's a force behind things, some kind of energy, even one that heats, the way fire does, but I can't believe it has anything in mind. It's a force, like the wind. It blows this way, then that way, creating things here and there, like the lilies, then wears them down. It doesn't *mean* anything. It heats things. It freezes them. It just plays, like a dim-witted child."

"I'll tell you one thing, Edna; you don't talk to anyone else around here like that. It's all right if you go to the Old Stone Church instead of the White Church, or if you don't go at all, but it's another if you say things against God out loud. Well, mostly the children would suffer. Now, you listen to me." Well, she certainly had done that.

Martin was calmly staring at the list; Jack was standing still, looking frightened. "Come on," Edna said, taking his hand; "I'll read it to you a few times. Don't worry," she said, guessing from his face; "you can't catch any-thing by reading about it." "All right." He had the most remarkable memory. When he was three, she had had a blue and white bathing outfit, and last week, while she was looking at a fashion paper, he looked over her shoul-der. "Mother," he said, "that's your old bathing outfit." "It does look like it," Edna said. He had inherited their memories with a vengeance. "Isn't it the same one?" he asked anxiously. How he hated change! "Your mother," Ten said, turning around in her chair, "has heard the old saw 'Keep a thing seven years and you'll have a use for it,' but I've never seen her living by it, not where her clothes are concerned, anyhow." She ruffled Jack's hair. "Well, she'll keep *you* for more than seven, don't you worry about that." "I'm not worrying about anything!" he exploded, leaving the room.

"He's too sensitive," Edna said mournfully. "He's the type who'll get it under control," Ten predicted; "but he won't outgrow it." "I wish he would." "It's good to have some of that kind around." "But," Edna objected—this was right after her conversation with Alice—"he might be withered by it, the heat of those emotions, I mean." "No," Ten disagreed; "there's a strength there that comes with it. He has both the sun and the moon. I wouldn't say that for Anna, though." "I wouldn't, either." Why, she now wondered, were they so sure of things in advance? And what was stranger, why did they usually turn out right? If they could only isolate the little signs and signals that made them know these things; now that, Edna thought, that would be something.

There could be preventive care of the spirit. Preventive care of the spirit; perhaps that was even more important, in the end, than care of the body. She sighed softly. It had certainly been a season of suicides, three on the Hill, one in the town, and it was only the beginning of August. The last had shocked everyone. The sexton of the White Church, one of the Camps' relations, said goodbye to his family as usual, dressed for work, said hello to everyone on the street, and then hanged himself from the bell rope. The peculiar pealing of the bells had alerted everyone. "Why the church, why the church?" everyone had asked. Edna asked the same thing. "It's probably nothing more complicated than picking the thing he was most used to," Ten answered without thinking. Suicide, as an action, dropped below the horizon of her imagination. "I don't think so," John said; "to hang himself from the bell rope he pulled for so many years, calling people to God, he must have had some sort of grievance against him." "Well, he's shaken up the godly, that's a certain thing," Ten said; "maybe he was trying to get God's attention in a hurry.

What do you think?" "Who knows?" John said; "he probably had something against the godly, I'd guess, anyway." "Yes, I think so," Edna said, "and at the same time, he wasn't taking any chances, was he? He made sure he got closer to God, and he certainly did get his attention with that racket." They heard a door slam. Anna had been eavesdropping. The door was her comment on the conversation.

One by one they filtered into breakfast. Martin picked up his spoon; he was ready to begin on his cold tomato soup. "Not so fast," John interrupted; "the catechism, please. Recite the list." Martin put down his spoon, mechanically reciting the document word for word. Anna and Ella repeated the performance. Then they got to Lettie. "Chill, fever, headache," she said carelessly. "Get out of that chair," John shouted at her, "and go back and study that list. I don't care if a bite doesn't go into that mouth for three days," he informed Ten and Edna; "I don't care if she starves until she learns that list word for word." Edna and Ten couldn't help grinning at each other. Her father was certainly immune to his daughter's beauty; probably, Edna reflected, she resembled *her* mother too closely. Anna, she was his favorite, and probably because she looked so like *her*. And she was such a good little medical student, going off on rounds, even studying medical books.

Edna and Ten had taken great care to avoid permitting the children to feel special—they were in danger of that because of their position and wealth—and they watched Anna more closely than the others. She was, really, precocious in every way. A lot of good it would do her, Edna thought, somewhat bitterly. A lot of good it had done her in her youth. In her youth, she laughed at herself; she still felt like Ella and Anna. But not like Lettie. Why couldn't she like that spoiled creature better? She knew the answer to that. What had they managed to produce but one of Mr. Siddons' statues, except that this one was capable of malevolence and moved about, and it was certainly just, Edna thought, that Lettie be the least intelligent. But she would only use that intelligence to persecute others. And, as people had often said of her mother, who, in contrast to her replica, seemed one of the living saints, a person of such beauty didn't need intelligence. No, Lettie probably didn't need a mind at all. It was too bad, though, that they couldn't stuff more heart into her.

Lettie came right back. "Out! Back!" John roared, "you haven't learned it yet." "But you haven't even let me try!" "Well, then, go on." "A chill," she said, "with a fever, or without a fever; then some vomiting and your legs hurt." "Out! Out!" he boomed, returning to his soup. Ella was beaming at her plate.

"Edna," John said, "I want to talk to you a minute." They went into the hall. "I'd rather you stayed home today." "You're not afraid I'll come down with anything? If you are, I don't want you going out, either." "No, that's not it at all; I'd like you to keep an eye on the troops, especially," he said, "that fleabrain we call Lettie." "Just today?" "Just today. I want you to rehearse them every three hours or so." "Why? What good will that do? If there's no cure?" "I'm not entirely sure of that; there's a drug called lachesis. The southern doctor I write to? He recommends it for every stage, and he has a theory about ice water and I have one about phosphorus for the liver; they may keep off jaundice and hemorrhaging. I think it may work, if we start early enough." "Where are you going to get that lachesis? Is that what's been in those fat letters you've been getting for months?" "I have enough poison to treat the county twice. I have that other snake poison, crotalus; its full name"—he grimaced—"is *Crotalus horridus*. They say it's worked in New Orleans."

"Those things are *snake* poisons? What's the antidote to *them?*" "You don't need any; it's the fever that needs the antidote." "I don't understand it," she said, shaking her head. "You and the rest of the medical profession."

"You do try," she said. "What else is there to do?" "I'll stay home today drilling them. Don't worry. What's this about hemorrhage? I didn't see that on the list." "Well"— he sounded embarrassed—"it's not exactly a warning; I didn't see the point of frightening them." "They're sure to hear about it." "Well, it won't hurt them to hear later." "What *kind* of hemorrhaging?" "Well, the black vomit, for instance; it's black blood from the stomach. Or from the eyes, nose, ears, and rectum. Or no hemorrhaging at all. It depends." "And they really turn yellow?" She wanted to hear the worst at once. "They sometimes turn the color of mahogany." "Mahogany! Don't tease." "I'm not teasing; that's the trouble." "Oh, Lord," she said; "well, I guess I'll get to see for myself." "That's what I was afraid of," he said, taking his leave in his usual way.

"Well, monsters," Edna announced, coming back into the kitchen, "your father wants you drilled every three hours; no one goes off longer than that between inquisitions. Is that clear enough for you, Lettie?" "Why is everyone always picking on me?" No one answered her. They finished eating in silence, interrupted only by Martin's jumping in his chair, glaring at Jack, who evidently had kicked him under the table, hoping for some response which would start something more to his liking. "Where are you going, Lettie?" Ten suddenly asked. "Into town; don't worry, I'll be back in three hours." "That one's up to something," she said; "and you, Ella, you better get yourself up to something pretty quick considering you've only got three hours." Ella flushed. Well, that wasn't a yellow color, Edna thought, relieved.

"I guess I'll go down to the Moffats'," said Martin. "You might as well wait for me," Edna told him; "I'm making my three-hour break for it, too." "I'd just as soon go alone, if you don't mind." "He's going to see Minnie," Jack chanted. Martin glowered at him. "Go on, then," Edna said; "Jack, do you want to come?" "Do you think George knows where the snakes are?" he asked hopefully. "I wouldn't be surprised if he does," Ten encouraged him; he might as well get out of the house while he could. "Ella," she said, "you might as well go on down, too." "I think I'll stay home and read," she answered, looking down at her plate; "it's hot for visiting."

Ten kept quiet until the others had left the room. "Now, you listen to me; you get on that white horse of yours and go down and talk to Tom James." Ella didn't move. "Miss, you take your bottom off that chair and sit it down on a saddle," Ten commanded. "It won't do any good." "Just get going; remember what I told you?" "What?" "That if you didn't shake yourself, I'd help out our dear Lettie." Ella reluctantly got up. "Where are *you* going?" Ten asked. "To the stable; that's where the horse usually is." Ten shook her head and went off to her room for her book. It was, really, very hot. She was surprised all of them had the energy to rush about like that.

Ten, hearing the noise of hooves outside the parlor, got up and looked out the window. Sure enough, there was Lettie with William; he was carrying a large package of hers. *Now* what was she up to? For someone who didn't have a scrap of brains in her head, she certainly was a cunning one. Perhaps they would all be easier if they just accepted the truth, which was that she was one cut below a raccoon, and then expected nothing of her. Of course, raccoons were, in general, less dangerous. Edna's latest padded up to her, and stood up, pulling on her skirt. He wanted her to sit down so that he could climb into her lap. "Little bandit," Ten whispered to him, "you'll have to wait until I find out what the master thief's up to." She went out into the hall, the raccoon following her.

"What's in that package?" she asked Lettie. "You see, William," Lettie commented in her saccharine way; "there's not a bit of privacy here, and with the house so large, too; there's more in yours, isn't there?" He blushed. He didn't want to get in the middle of anything. "Well, what's in it?" Ten asked again. "Wallpaper." "Wallpaper," Ten repeated; "wallpaper for what?" "Well, you know how Mother's always talking about papering the best parlor, and the paper's already steamed off, so I thought I would just surprise her, but then I thought, I'm not tall enough, and William is *so* tall, I thought he would help me." "If he's an inch taller than you are, there's something wrong with my eyes." Lettie glared at her. William blushed. "Come, William," Lettie said; "I'll show you where the ladder is and I've already mixed up the paste." Getting mixed up with that one, Ten decided, was worse than getting caught in amber. But there was a bright side to everything; at least now she knew what Lettie was up to. For two hours anyway.

This time, when she heard the sound of hooves, she went into the yard. It was Ella, back with Tom. "Well?" she asked. "She told me all about it," Tom said without further prompting; "you have the best ideas of anyone in town." "I'm glad someone thinks so," she said, looking at Ella. "Her sister," Ten said, "has got William trapped

into papering the best parlor; they're in there right now."
Ella looked as if her life had just come to an end. "Where's
the best parlor?" Tom asked. "Follow me, and drag that
lifeless rag along with you." They followed her around
the corner of the house, Ella walking as if asleep. "That's
the window"; Ten pointed. "A word to the wise"; Tom
grinned. "Well, I'm going in; I leave it in your hands. Just
jab her with a pin if she won't talk," she advised, turning
around.

"Ella," Tom began loudly, "remember when we were
little and I brought home the snakes?" She nodded. "My
father was going to beat me?" She nodded again. "And
you said you did it?" "Yes." "And the time I got you out
of trouble for spilling a bottle of ink on Lettie's head
when she was sitting in front of you in school? Well, it's
your turn to help me out." She nodded again. He wondered if she was really awake. "What I want you to do
is give the right answers to everything I say to you," he
whispered; "you just pretend I'm that William Moffat. I
know you can do it." "I can't." "Oh, come on, Ella. It's
time to pour more ink on Lettie's head, that's all." "But
it won't work this time!" "How much do you want to
wager on it? I know it will work; it has to work, because
if it doesn't, how am I going to get a hold of that Susie
Wakefield?" Ella stood there, thinking things over. "All
right," she agreed, this time enthusiastically. "Let's get it
over with." "You don't have to make it sound like you're
courting a snake!" "*You're* the one who's acting like a
leper's courting you." "All right," she said, making peace;
"there's no point in *our* fighting." They went around to
the parlor window. From inside, the sound of laughter
danced out of the window like the light skirt of a curtain.
Tom raised his eyebrows to the heavens. Ella was getting
into the spirit of things; this was like old-fashioned times.

"Ella," he said, raising his voice, "surely there is some
hope for me?" The sounds inside the parlor abruptly
ceased. "You see?" he whispered almost inaudibly. She
did. "I did not say that," she answered passionately. "But
you did not say there was no hope, either." "Oh, Tom,"
she exclaimed, falling in with his spirit. (This was the
way it had always been; he brought out the imp in her.
And she did like him, sturdy and tall, with that jet-black

hair and red cheeks. He was almost the spirit of the
country for her.) "How can we discuss the future at a
time like this? People are dying everywhere around us."
"I would have the ceremony performed even on a deathbed," he swore. She grinned.

Inside, the silence was absolute. "Tom, I must tell the
truth; I do not absolutely know the state of my own
heart." "But isn't it possible," he pleaded, "you are simply
confused by the state of things in general? You did speak
of the fever." "I may be, but I cannot tell." "But if you
are dragging your fears behind you like a train," Tom
protested, "then you cannot blame me for stepping on it.
It is only my eagerness to follow you." "I do not blame
you." "I hope not," he answered; "trains, even gloomy
ones, are such beautiful things." He was surprising himself; how much better at this he was than he thought he
would be! All those lies he told his father when he was
younger; they were standing him in good stead now. "It
is a rare woman," he said gravely, "who would not blame
the heel that trod upon her train." "I think I am an exception, then." It was fortunate, Tom thought, Ella kept her
back to the window. She could not keep herself from
grinning insanely with every exchange.

"Ella," he said, "you know there are some people who
prefer not to eat and talk at the same time. Perhaps something like that is the trouble here; you cannot worry and
love at the same time. Or you prefer not to." "A woman
must be a dull one if she cannot do both." "But, Ella, do
you want to do both? Where your feelings for me are
concerned?" She remained silent, signaling by opening
her eyes wide. They still knew the old code, as if only
seconds had passed since the third primer. "Ella, I fear,"
he continued, "that your imagination has been captured
by someone else. I hope I have not offended you?" "No,
you have not. You have every right to ask me such questions." Tom saw the curtains of the parlor moving twitch-
ily. "Well, then, I fear William has seized your imagination by distinguishing himself so in the war." "You were
in the war, too." "But I was not as heroic." "Heroism,"
Ella said sweetly, "is a matter of circumstance, of opportunity; my father believes the most heroic acts are performed without any thought whatever, and hence are not

fit subjects for idolatry." "And do you feel that way about William's heroism?" "I do," she lied.

They were referring to the time when part of William's brigade had suddenly found itself cut off from the rest of the army, which had returned to the nearest town; they were only protected from enemy fire by a small rise of ground and a small shed. Only when they lay on their stomachs were they really protected from enemy fire. The commanding general tried sending several men to the division commander for assistance, but one after another fell; he was unwilling to ask for further volunteers. William decided to go.

The only way to town, according to detailed newspaper reports of the incident, had been across an open field in full view of enemy sharpshooters. William scribbled a message on the back of an envelope, said goodbye, buttoned up, and started out. He scurried in back of the small shed, then out onto the field. The rifles started up. The newspapers boasted he ran faster than anyone had been known to run before. Then he was seen falling to the ground. "His comrades saw this," *The Reformer* reported, "with a thrill of sorrow." But just as the enemy finished cheering, he suddenly jumped up, flying across the field, and was out of range before they recovered from their surprise.

Thus, he was able to deliver his message, and now wanted to return with an answer; but this, he knew, would be harder. He would have to run back uphill; that would make it more difficult. First he had been running from the guns; now he would be running toward them. Worse, he would not have even so much as the protection of the shed. But this time Providence intervened in the form of an inexperienced, enthusiastic lieutenant who took it into his head to drill his men in the manual, and, as William peeped over the bank, the lieutenant commanded: "Fire by rank. Rear rank, at the brick house. Aim, fire! Front rank, at the stone wall. Aim, fire!" He was shouting as only a new soldier would. William heard him. So did the enemy; during the exercises, they decided to stay out of sight. Seeing this, William improved his luck, and was soon safe with the rest of his brigade behind the little rise. So he had become quite a local celebrity, and, because the people had little new to talk over after the war ended, this story was retailed over again and over again, embroidered skillfully at paning bees, until, according to some local authorities, eyewitnesses to William's race had seen misty wings sprouting from his back and heels, speeding him along on his godly mission.

"A man," Ella told him, "is not a hero until he is shot at and missed. I do not see how you could have been braver." "It was my unfortune," Tom answered, "to be the bugler; I was exempted from so much action. All I could write you about was the tents, and the muckets for our coffee, and dullish things, nothing that would fire the imagination. Why, by the end of the war, even I was tired of such mundane details." From the startled sound of the curtains jerking this way and that, moving without wind, even Ella could tell this description of their imaginary correspondence was startling someone. "Fire the imagination?" Ella echoed, indignant; "Tom, you must not run yourself down so. You know how little I am inclined to let my imagination soar off with me."

"But imagination," Tom answered, feeling like a player in some remarkable drama, "it is the safest companion you could have in your flight, and the one of whom you would least likely grow weary." "Tom," Ella asked, "don't you ever weary of your own thoughts—your own visions, your own companionship? I know I do. No, what I want is flesh and blood, not feathers plucked from innocent birds for wings of any kind. Imagination can be nothing but a sign of vanity, a belief," she went on, pressing his hand, "that the real world is not good enough, that one deserves better. No, I would not have the wings of birds plucked for my imagination. I would not sacrifice them to my vanity, or torture them in cages, either, waiting to be plucked."

"But, you are torturing me, for if you have not been caught by William's heroism, what prevents the acceptance of my suit?" "The heart, alas," Ella sighed, "will not run on a railway schedule." "But my train may perhaps yet arrive?" "Anything is possible." "Then I suppose I must be satisfied with that," Tom answered, taking her hand, leading her off to the path in the woods.

"Do you think that did any good?" Ella asked the instant they reached the woods' silence and safety. "If that didn't," Tom gasped, "nothing will; I tell you, I'm tired out. Even imaginary courtships are exhausting." "You *are* comical." She smiled happily at him. "If you want my opinion," Tom told her, "I think you just poured a casket of ink on that red head of your sister's." "Auburn, auburn!" Ella reminded him; "you know how she hates hearing it called red." "She didn't like 'carrot top' much better." They lay back on a small, leafy rise, laughing. A frog hopped onto Ella's skirt and off again. "That means good luck," Tom informed her. "When did you decide that?" "Just now." "That's what I thought."

Inside the parlor, the weather had taken a definite turn for the worse. Ten, standing outside the hall, heard William, impatient: "Lettie, will you hurry with that paper? The paste is drying up altogether. We'll make a mess of it." "And if we do? I can always buy more paper." "Well, *I* don't believe in throwing money out the window." "I can't help it," she whined, "if I'm not a papering expert." "Well, you better become a little more expert, or we might as well paste dollars on the walls." "*Must* you be so sulky?" "Just hurry up with the paper, and don't tangle it all up this time, either." "*I'm* not under your command." "Do you want help or don't you?"

Well, if that isn't just lovely, Ten thought, going back to the parlor and *Loves of a Demon Bride*. She had a feeling, she mused as she picked up the book, that her taste in literature was definitely degenerating. Actually, looking at the yellowback nickel novel, there was no question about it. "Do you want help or don't you?" she mimicked nasally. Well, it would be all rocky road for Lettie now. "I can always buy more paper," she repeated blissfully: that to a boy from such a poor family. Sooner or later, it would have come to light, that bamboozle's lack of sense, but it hardly could have done so sooner. And she wasn't going to permit the other two to let up, either; she was going to see that they mysteriously reappeared in William's presence, and certainly that they appeared whenever those two were together. Too bad for Lettie, she thought, completely unsympathetic. She looked at the clock; the three hours were almost up. Sure enough, there was the sound of hooves outside. Time for the quizzing, she thought unhappily, going to the door and reviewing the sheet. Her brother wouldn't even exempt *her;* she knew him well enough to be certain of that.

After the yellow-fever lessons were successfully completed, Edna was back on rounds with John. "This is a second-day case," he said before they went in. "Just remember, the mortality rate can be as low as seven per cent." "Or as high as eighty," she said. Well, he ought to have known she would have been reading, right along with Anna.

Inside, the victim looked as if he had been lightly painted all over with iodine. As usual, Edna took his pulse. "Fifty," she said calmly. How could a pulse slow down so, and the man still live? And how hot his skin was! "Give him this every three hours," John told the man's wife, giving her a bunch of packets, each bound with a string; "only one each time, hear? Otherwise it's poison. If you only give him one, one," he stressed, "you'll kill the fever, not your husband." The woman nodded, dumb. "And you must get him to drink all the ice water you can force on him; it controls the fever." "Ice water," she repeated. "I'll notify the iceman on my way into town," he said. "Some doctors," the woman said, hesitant, "have been giving things like camphor, belladonna, and exonite." "Aconite," he corrected; "and if I thought it would do your husband any good, I'd send over a drugstore in a wagon. But if you want my opinion, it won't help. I've studied this for almost a year. The death rate's higher when you take more of those medicines." "Death rate?" "The medicines do more killing than the fever," he said, blunt. "Oh," she said, reddening. "Every three hours." She looked down at the packets she held. "Just one," he reminded her, "and don't get them wet."

"What *was* that smell?" Edna asked, nose wrinkled the instant they were outside; "he smelled like a corpse." "The fever smell; it can be a lot worse than that." "Does it signify anything?" "Not really; it comes on the second day. Usually. Look, Edna, next's a ninth-day case, a hemorrhager. If it's bothering you, I'd rather you went back home when I stop off for the ice." "It's not bothering me." It was true, he thought; a phenomenon of life was no more and no less to her. "What do you think his chances are?" "I don't know; it's almost impossible to tell, but he was stronger than an ox when he came down with it, and he doesn't drink. Never has. All that helps." "That doesn't sound good for the Westons." "It isn't, and that's where we're going." How many times, he wondered, had he wished she would turn back? And how many times had he wondered what would happen if death invaded *their* family? Yes, he thought again, they had been truly fortunate. *He* had. Since their marriage. As if Edna herself were some kind of charm.

They arrived home, exhausted, a little after six. The family was waiting for them. "Well, in to supper," Ten announced. They all filed in. "Pretty yellow about, I guess," Ten commented, taking a good look at them. "My dear sister, an understatement." "Well," Ten said, cheery, "Jack has a good joke for us." "That's nice," said Edna; "we could certainly use one." Out of the corner of her eye, she saw Lettie glaring at Ella; she thought it would be the other way around. She preferred it this way, of course. "I read it in the paper," Jack shyly confessed. "Oh, get on with it," Lettie said. "Will you keep quiet?" her father demanded through compressed lips. She paled, toying with her knife. "Ignore your ignorant sister," Edna told Jack.

"Well," he began, encouraged, "I told Aunt this joke. An aunt asks a little boy to guess her age; she says if he gets it right, she'll give him this piece of candy. I forgot what kind it was." Lettie sighed dramatically. John glared at her. "Well, anyway, the little boy says, 'I can't; I can only count up to forty.' Isn't that funny?"; he laughed convulsively, tears running down his cheeks; "Aunt said she'd get me with a broom later for that one." "It's not *that* funny," said Lettie. "All right, Lettie. Leave the table," her father commanded. "What?" She was taken aback. It had been years since she had been ordered from the table. "You heard me," he thundered; "leave the table." She got up, face red as her hair, and ran up the stairs. "Don't be too hard on her," Edna murmured. "We are going to eat one meal in peace," John snapped; "even if that one starves to death." At this, Lettie, listening at the top of the stairs, ran into her room, slamming the door so hard the house shook. "Peace. At last." John began to eat. Ella, he thought; what was *she* looking so happy about. Well, they were all beyond him, and he was not going to think about a single one of them.

Several weeks later, near the middle of August, Edna woke in the middle of the night, shuddering. My, the weather has turned cold, she thought, getting up for her robe, getting back into bed wearing it, wrapping herself in the quilt, so that, from the door, she would have looked like something trapped in a cocoon. She shuddered so violently the bed shook; the ropes holding the mattress could be heard straining against the sideboards. Finally, she began warming up, took off the robe, and got back into bed.

Her head hurt and she was very warm. She kicked off the quilt. That didn't help; she unbuttoned the top of her nightdress. That was a little better. Finally, she got up and took it off altogether, standing to one side of her open window. She began to feel better and went back to bed. In the morning, she awoke with a slight headache, weak enough to give up rounds, but otherwise quite well. "It's funny," Lettie said after breakfast, "but the weather last night was so cold and then got so hot." "Do you have a headache?" her mother asked. "Why, yes, I do, but it's getting better every minute." "That's good," Edna said; hers was fast disappearing, too. "The same thing happened to me," said Ten. "Me, too," Martin said. "Me, too," Jack echoed. "I don't know what you're all talking about," Ella said; "the weather was perfectly normal. It was warm all night." "No, it wasn't, Ella," Anna said; "it was just as they said, very hot and then very cold. Father said something about that very thing this morning."

"Well, then," Ella mused, "I must have slept through it because I didn't notice anything of the kind." At the time, they thought the discussion of no consequence, and so ignored it. Especially since William chose that moment to drive up. They heard him ask Bridget if Ella might be at home. "I'll go out," Ella said, going down the hall. "I thought," William mumbled, awkward, "you might drive downstreet with me. I'm trying to select a birthday present for my mother and I need some advice. That is, if you're free." Ella hesitated. Lettie's voice cut in behind her. "Perhaps it would be better if *I* went," she suggested; "I seem to have much better judgment in these things." Ella said nothing. She didn't think it would put her in the best possible light if she turned around and scratched her sister from eyes to chin with all ten of her long, strong nails. "Ella is so much more like Mother," William said, diplomatic; "at least in this case I think she would really be the better judge." "Poor Mrs. Moffat," Lettie said, beating a graceful retreat. *"Will* you go?" William demanded, "I have to dig some potatoes, but I'll come back for you as soon as the stores open." "That would be fine," Ella answered.

"Well, we're off," Edna told them both; "the fever opens before the stores." "You wouldn't want to try tying up my wife?" John joked with William. "Not if I had to answer to *my* mother for it." "Well, don't forget to come down tomorrow and get your likeness taken, and keep quiet about it to your mother, too," John told him. "That's our present," Edna explained, "but you're missing from the series." "I'll be there." "The torture chamber," Ella said, "takes less time than it used to." "You wouldn't consider giving me a likeness of yourself?" William asked, shy; "that is, if you happen to have one?" "I would like to." Lettie, eavesdropping as usual, felt Ten's grip on her shoulder; she knew better than to say a word until they left the house. "I don't see what he wants with *her* likeness," Lettie complained; "he'd be better off with a good likeness of one of Father's headstones." "Why don't you just go back to your vanity mirror and drown yourself in it?" Ten suggested pleasantly. "I don't know why," Lettie whined, "you must speak to me that way." "When there's another language you understand, you just let me know."

John and Edna proceeded along to the Westons'. The area up above Williamsville and Tunbridge was reporting more and more cases of fever, although most of the cases they had seen there had been in their final stages for two weeks now. They both knew Mrs. Weston had little hope, worn down as she was by overwork, poor nutrition, and childbearing. There was constant argument concerning the actual number of children she had produced. Estimates varied from sixteen to twenty; no one could agree on how many had died in childbirth, of measles, of scarlet fever, of typhoid, of diphtheria, although, as the puzzled conversationalists generally concluded, if one child had died of each disease mentioned, Mrs. Weston would have had twenty-seven children, not twenty. "We could go to the burying ground and count the stones," one local wizard suggested; "and then add that number to the living ones," but for some reason no one had taken him up on his suggestion.

"What will they do without her?" Edna asked as they made their slow way. "Pretty much the same as they did with her. She was never much use as a mother. Either she was nursing one baby just born, or nursing one who was just sick, or bent crooked over the tub, or trying to keep the garden from growing half up the mountain. It would be worse if anything happened to Mr. Weston; at least he knows how to lay on the stripes with a beech wand." Edna sighed; that was not a bad summing up, nothing like what they would hear at the funeral, but accurate all the same. A gruesome enough epitaph. Fortunately, at the moment of death, or immediately after it, no one was honest.

"Well, and how is she?" John asked before they entered. "She's still vomiting, and it's black as coal, and whenever she's strong enough, she complains about her stomach." "What about bleeding?" "She's bleeding everywhere now," her husband said wearily, "and the ice you said to put in her mouth? We pushed it up against her gums and her tongue, but it doesn't stop it; she just keeps on bleeding. She doesn't sleep; she's wide awake all the time, staring at us. It gives us the shakes; well, then she stares at the ceiling. That's almost as bad." "I'd better have a look at her"; he had been reviewing the more drastic medicines he had in his bag.

Just as he walked in, one of the daughters ran up to the bed with a basin and her mother vomited copiously into it. As soon as her daughter cleaned her up, he got to work. "I'm going to turn your head from side to side," he told her; "you tell me if it hurts." No answer was required; the instant he began rotating her head, she shrieked weakly. The neck was stiff, there was no doubt about that. "Well," John said slowly, primarily addressing Mrs. Weston's daughter and husband, "this is arsenite of copper. It sometimes works after other medicines don't. It might stop the bleeding. Don't worry"—he looked up from his pad—"I'll write it all down." Gloinin for this, he thought; meningitis, that was what the neck indicated.

"This every six hours," he said, marking it down carefully on the chart. He got up and drew back the sheets. The lower part of the bed was covered with blood. "How long has this been going on?" "I'd say one day," the daughter answered. He added a packet of secale to the list, putting it in its proper time slot on the schedule, which, instant by instant, seemed to be growing longer. Well, she wasn't going to live unless nature pulled some remarkable trick from its pocket.

She might as well have the belladonna; he made another entry. "Now," he said, "unless you want to kill her straight off, don't give her more than one of these things at once. Just put an 'X' after each dose you give her; when six o'clock comes around, give her what it says in the line for six, and then make an 'X,' and then when it gets to be ten, make another 'X,' and at two, another 'X,' and so on until it's all used up. You have to be very careful." They nodded; that old Weston was unusually yellow. He'd be coming down with it next, but at least he wasn't drinking. He must care for his wife more than any of them would have guessed. There was no guessing at these things, really. "It's awful cold," Mr. Weston groaned. "As for you," Dr. Steele said, "this every three hours"; he wrote his name on a series of crotalus packets, "just for safety's sake." "That's good," Mr. Weston approved; "someone around here has to keep things going." "You should have thought of that before," John said. Mr. Weston started to say something, but outside there was the sound of a horse, then a pounding at the door. Edna turned white at the sight of Amos' face. If he hadn't sent one of his sons, something serious must have happened.

"It's Ella, Miss Edna; William brought her back shaking all over like she had the ague and Miss Ten said she was burning up. Come outside." "Why?" Edna asked; "did something else happen?" "Come on out," he pleaded. "Come on, Edna," John said, pushing her through the door. "I'll be back in the morning," he promised; "or the afternoon. Send in an emergency," he called back. "Well?" John demanded. "Hal and Anna," he blurted out. Edna slumped against John. "They have fever, too?" John asked.

"No; it's worse. You know that mad dog, Skip, the one Hal used to swim with? Well, he and Anna were down-

street, and Skip suddenly ran out from one of the buildings, and everyone was shouting, 'Mad dog! Mad dog!'
and running for their guns, but Hal, he saw Skip and
started running toward him. And Anna, she said they
seemed to be floating toward each other as if they were
moving through water, and when they got to the center
of the square, no one could shoot at Skip, they were so
close together, and Hal picked him up, and it all looked
so natural-like, and then Skip gave this funny growl and
bit him right on the neck and Hal dropped him, he was
so surprised, and he was calling, 'Bad dog,' and everyone
else was calling, 'Mad dog,' and then Martin came along,
he was down there for something, and he took them both
back to the house." "Where's Anna?" John asked. "In the
big house." "And Hal? Where did you put Hal?" "We
locked him in one of the cottages." "That's something,"
Edna said, almost inaudible. "Well," John said after a
minute, "you go on back first and we'll follow. Tell whoever's watching Hal not to let him out of there, just to
bring him meals, but not to go near him, have you got
that?" "Got it," Amos answered, mounting his horse.

Edna did not know what to worry about first. As usual,
she began with the one least frightening to her. "Rabies?"
she asked John; "what are we to look for?" "Whatever
we're looking for," he said, thinking how best to tell her,
"we'll be looking for it a long time. It can take three
days to three months, the incubation period, I mean."
"But you once said there were cases of bites where the
disease *didn't* develop." "That's if they were bitten on a
covered part of the body and washed off right away, but
it sounds like he got it on the neck and face; that's the
worst." "Amos said just the neck." "I doubt if Amos
stopped to examine him." "They die of paralysis, don't
they?" "After spasms stop." "What about Ella?" "That
sounds like the fever, don't you think so?" "They'll say
Hal got bitten because he wasn't, you know—" She broke
off. "Sexually fulfilled. I know," he said wearily; "there
are all kinds of superstitions; they never end." "What
about Ella?" she asked again. "Like the others. We wait
and see; we haven't seen her yet. We don't know if it's
really yellow fever, or how bad it is." "But if she should
end like Mrs. Weston," Edna wailed. "She won't." "You'll

stay home?" she asked. He looked at her. "Well, as much as you can then?" "As much as I can," he promised.

They drove on silently. She was thinking about Amos, how he had come all that way at full gallop, not even tired out. And he was almost as old as Ten. And last year when the new piano had come, Amos and his brother, he must have been two years older, were standing around watching the men from the piano company struggle with the instrument; finally, Amos got bored watching them fuss. "Try it this way," Amos suggested, hoisting the piano halfway into the air, looking at his brother, who had picked up the other end; they carried the piano into the house, tilting it this way and that, and then, still holding it, called for Ten, asking her where to put it down. As if it were a pillow. Up here, she thought, there were some who seemed inoculated against mortality. She had no idea of how it happened. Ten, now. She looked like the old queen who had voluntarily turned her authority over to the little princess, but still, she was the one who ruled; she was the one who had strength.

And now Ella; she had always seemed so healthy, and she was only eighteen. When the congregation finally decided to remove the great round rose window from the back of the church where it faced the minister, it was the sexton in his eighties and all his octogenarian cronies who went through snow up to their waists, carrying a round saw, and hauled the monstrous thing through the air with block and tackle, and then took it off to Mr. Siddons' barn. It might be out of the church, but they weren't going to see it killed. As if they had been picking up a child's toy. Ella; she was the only one who had no chills and fever that night. Perhaps that meant something. She asked John about it. "We might all have had a mild case," he said; "it's just a guess." "Then we're immune; the rest of us?" "I think so." "But Ella didn't have it," she said, not expecting any answer.

John had evidently spent some time deciding on the order of things to be done. "You go see Ella," he told his wife; "then Anna. I'll go look at Hal first. I hope your daughter had more sense than to let herself get kissed after that dog bit him." *"My* daughter." In times of crisis, he had a tendency to blame the flights of her stomach for everything. She wondered, briefly, why he was sending her

551

in to look at Ella; there was nothing *she* could do, either. She supposed that must be the reason. Well, Ten would need some help with Anna; John would be better at that.

Their hands locked automatically, then unclasped when they reached the path leading to the invalids' cottage. She went down slowly. Well, this *was* the garden path, she thought. All those hours of sponging down the children, of hearing them wake in the night, of hearing the knock on the door, invariably tentative, inevitably meaning the children's skin had the feel of one of Bridget's irons, all those frights over measles, and scarlet fever, and then that stay inside the spider web. And now this. There was no end to it. Why didn't they all tire of it, the inevitable repetitions of it, the variations on the same fear, loss, loss, or the threat of loss, which was worse? It was a miracle, she thought, turning the corner, coming into view of the little cottage, that all of humanity wasn't a tribe of compulsive gamblers; or perhaps it was odder that some of them were, when one considered the fact they were constantly casting dice, each loaded against them. Which only, she supposed, returned one to the riddle of perseverance. It must be the little thread of hope, the gambler again. The little thread could be anything: a miracle, heaven, a normal recovery, the passing of a wing without casting a shadow.

She went in. "William! What are you doing?" she exclaimed without thought. He was sitting on a chair next to Ella's bed, a sap bucket brimming with some kind of liquid, a distinctly alcoholic smell filling the room. "I'm sponging her down; she was awfully hot." "It smells like a saloon in here"; she sniffed. "Well, Mother says alcohol is the thing to cool people down and all she could find was some apple beer, so it's in that sap bucket." It was a good thing, thought the astonished Edna, the windows and doors were covered with mosquito netting, or poor Ella would be eaten alive. "She's cooled down a lot," William said. "She had the chills?" "They didn't last long. Maybe seven minutes, but she had something else first. She went stiff; I don't know how to describe it. But that was over before I knew it began. She told me about it; she can talk perfectly, can't you, Ella?" he asked, putting his finger across her lips; "but she's not allowed to. Except to open it to swallow ice." "Ice?" "Mother trotted up here with ice shavings; she says she doesn't like Minnie's looks much better than Ella's. She went stiff, too. Martin's down there." "Martin?" "Well, you know Minnie's not too hoppity."

"Sit down, Mrs. Steele," William said, turning to look at her; "you look worse than the patient." "Thank you," she murmured, dropping into a chair. Another perfect bedside manner. "Your daughter," he said a half hour later, "insists upon talking to you. I believe it has something to do with the state of her clothes." Edna got up; she *was* exhausted; yellow fever, mad dogs, what did she expect? Ella's abnormally bright eyes fastened on hers. "Your head hurts, does it?" Edna asked. "Yes," she whispered, "but that's not what I wanted to talk to you about." "Why are you whispering?" Edna asked, concerned; "can't you talk louder?" "I just don't want William to hear." Her voice was normal. "William, please go out." "No, I'm staying to listen," he said, sitting down. Ella sighed. "Then lower the blinds, please," she told him frigidly; "the light hurts my eyes." "Any vomiting?" Edna asked. "None." "Mother, *will* you listen to me?" Ella asked, irritable. "I'm sorry, dear," she said turning back to the bed; "what is it?"

"It's the indecency of this; he wants to drench me all over," she complained, flushing deeply; "he said I must have had over one hundred and six when he came in and he's sponging every inch of me. Why, look at this"—she gestured indignantly at her bosom—"I look like one of those marble statues. You can see everything." "I see you stopped him somewhere." Her skirt was drawn up to the edge of her bloomers; she had permitted them to be drenched so far, and no farther. "Well, and he says that's not far enough." Edna picked up her wrist. "Ninety," she told William. "Listen, Ella, I want you to tell me how you feel. You feel cool enough and your pulse is nice and strong. He must be doing something right; you just let him drown you in beer no matter how mortified he makes you."

"That's right, tell her, Mrs. Steele. Why, if it were her sister; you know Lettie would like nothing better than to have a real bath in beer so that she could show every line of her body, and I don't think it's a bit better than Ella's and not so round in some places, either." Ella threw herself about in bed. "He's right, you know; I think you should let him do whatever he wants." "That's dangerous advice to give a daughter," William teased. "Don't forget I know *your* mother," she said; "but you can't keep this sponging up forever. Even my husband draws the line at seven hours; I'll have to relieve you." "Only if I can sleep in here." "Where? On the floor?" "No, on that pile of straw; Amos brought it in for me." "Are you sure you're quite well?" "Those are my terms." "All right, all right, I surrender. Hit the straw." "In a half hour you get me up." "Is that straw comfortable?" Edna asked, curious; by now it appealed to her. "Absolutely." "All right, then," she agreed; "I'm going to look for Dr. Steele, but I'll be back within a half hour. Ella, behave. Let him have his will of you." "Mother!" "You heard me," she said.

"Well?" she asked John; he was already halfway down the path. "Oh, Anna. She's about to float away in tears." "And Hal?" "I'm afraid that's a lost cause; bites all over his face, lacerations really, and two deep bites in his neck. I guess that's the end of both their swimming; his and the dog's, I mean." "There's nothing we can do about him?" "Oh, we can have Amos keep him amused, with a revolver ready in his pocket." "Revolver?" "The next stage changes the personality; you know that. They go crazy as the dogs." "Yes, yes, I know. How is Ten?" "Oh, you know Ten; she's always saying things like 'What next?' and going right on about her business." "She always does what's next, doesn't she?" "I don't think you have to go in to Anna, not for a while anyway; the one thing Anna said that made sense had something to do with her aunt being her uncle's sister, so I guess that makes Ten the most qualified to stay with her." "For the time being." "No, I think that's the way it is with the two of them, Anna and Ten, I mean." "They're so unlike." "That probably explains all of it. Anna can talk to her; she doesn't have to worry about her, or shocking her; it makes her feel very—sheltered." "It's too bad we can't do the same thing," she said weakly, leaning her head against his shoulder. "*We* worry." "But Ten loves her as much as we do," Edna said.

"She's put together differently somehow," John said; "I never understood it. Even when Ed died, she didn't take on much. She cried a great deal and she couldn't make up her mind about things, that was unusual for her, but she didn't go on about it. It's almost as if she was born expecting to die, expecting that everyone else would. You know how she is with the garden. Sometimes I think she's part plant. She doesn't look forward; she doesn't look back. She takes what she needs right into this minute; she travels lightly somehow. The only time I ever heard her fuss was over that likeness of Ed's, the one he didn't get taken. I never heard anyone go on about anything for so long. But otherwise, she doesn't get stuck in the mud of what happened, why it didn't happen some other way, whatever it was that happened. She doesn't. I don't know how she does it. She should have been the doctor."

"You always think everyone else should have been the doctor." "Well, she wasn't interested; she just wanted a husband, a house or a tent, and children. The only time she argued with Ed was when he wanted to go to some frontier town where everyone lived in canvas houses, because she said if they had children, she wasn't having a lot of wild cowboys shooting up the air while her family lived in canvas tents." "It *should* have worked out that way for her." "She has more children now than she ever hoped for." "But it's not the same; she once said so herself." "I think she prefers it that way," John said; "who knows what goes on in that mind of hers? Perhaps in her mind she's already had children and raised them and parted with them. She's quite capable of thinking, without thinking, if you know what I mean, that if it didn't happen, she might as well imagine it did, since by now it would be all over with, the children gone off and married, the responsibilities over, and this way she has the best of both: your children and her children." "But *her* children are imaginary!" "There's nothing so real as the imagination," he quoted from one of her old papers.

"Those papers," she sighed; "they sound so silly later. It's so hard to make sense of things." "*You* keep making sense out of them, on paper anyway, and then *I* understand them." "But you understand them differently," she said; "I only understand them in theory." "Well, everything has its purpose, everything exists for a reason"; he grinned. "Egotist!" "We better go on and see Ella."

They opened the door, dropping the netting in place

behind them. William, they saw, had fallen asleep, his head on the edge of Ella's bed. John looked at his wife and raised his eyebrows. She nodded. He went over to the bed, gently placing the back of his hand against his daughter's cheek; it was cool, slightly damp, as if she had been walking through dew. He smiled happily at Edna. "It doesn't look bad," he said, cautious. "But only time will tell," she mocked. "Well," she said, "I'm taking turns with William; I'll go to sleep on that straw there." "Amos will bring down a real bed." "No one's bringing anything in until they wake up." "I'll tell him that," she said, turning around. She settled down on the straw.

"Mother," she heard a voice calling in the middle of the night. "Yes, dear," she said, getting up. Odd, she had a pain in her shoulder. She *was* getting older; just last week Alice had teased her about her stiff fingers, saying it was rheumatism and she ought to know because there wasn't a joint in her body that didn't give a good home to it. "Mother, would you make him go to sleep?" William was swaying on the edge of his chair. "Onto the straw," Edna ordered him; "didn't your mother tell you we antique creatures needed less sleep as we got even older?" "Women will say anything," he said as he crawled wearily off. She admired him, she thought, taking his place on the chair; the way he could joke under circumstances like this.

"Come on, Ella, ice," she coaxed; "otherwise I'll wake him up again." She noticed John hadn't prescribed anything. He had left some lachesis with William to be used if her temperature went up before the fourth day; after that, he told him, it always rose, but that was called the second phase, and then, higher fever was normal. There was even a name for it: reactionary fever. "Maybe I had better read up in your books," William suggested shyly. Amos had been duly instructed to carry them over with the bed. Edna helped him with it, while William slept as if in hibernation for the summer. The raccoon came in to pay its visit, jumped into her lap, went through her pockets, and followed Amos back to the house. Well, Edna thought, it was nice to know the rest of the world had stayed where it was. She promptly fell asleep.

"Mother!" "What?" "I smell terrible!" "Couldn't you complain about it later? Well, you do smell like a fish," she said, sitting up; "but it's normal, dear. Except I've never smelled that combination before, fish, apples, and alcohol; that's some fragrance." "I don't want William smelling it!" "Too late," he called from the straw; "I've been sniffing for the last hour." "You have not!" "Oh, yes, I have; it's better than ether." "Anyhow," Edna interrupted, "you better save your strength, I hear the family is visiting today." "Not Lettie," she moaned. "We haven't excommunicated her yet." "I'm going back to sleep," she whined, closing her eyes. Edna and William smiled at each other.

Edna beckoned him outside. "I think we should keep mirrors away from her," she whispered. Ella had turned almost saffron, a day earlier than usual, too. "It's not necessarily serious," William said; "it's just a complication. And she hasn't done any vomiting; that's the most important thing." "You've been doing your reading, haven't you?" she asked, rubbing sleep out of her eyes. How like a child she looked, he thought. She was only twelve years younger than his mother, but she didn't look much older than Ella. Except when you looked very closely at her skin. Then it seemed to have puckered slightly; but even that didn't seem permanent, almost as if there was something wrong with eyes noticing it. "She's been urinating very copiously, too." "*That's* a very good sign," Edna agreed. "Well, if you keep up the ice and the bedpan"; he smiled again. "It's so hard to get her to drink." "I don't even bother with water; I stick to the ice."

"You really should be a doctor," Edna said, not thinking. "Oh, I would if I could, but it's not the kind of thing for the oldest son of a poor family." "No," Edna agreed, but she was already plotting.

"Let me see those gums," William demanded, unceremoniously pulling down Ella's lower lip. "You don't have to treat me like a horse you're thinking of buying; you're taking advantage, just because I smell like this." "I don't see what one thing has to do with the other; if you smell like a fish, and I treat you like a horse, that doesn't make much sense. Her mind is affected," he told Edna. "I can't wait to get out of this bed and get after him." *That* notion, Edna thought, was probably the best medicine she could take.

Around noon, all three were roused by the babble of voices outside the door. It was the rest of the children, all except Martin. That did not augur well for Minnie. Well, at least the children of both families had sympathies; she and John had accomplished that much. She supposed that was more than most managed. "One at a time," she instructed through the netting; "and Lettie last." Hearing this, Lettie retreated gracelessly to a bench, sitting there watching them as if she had never laid eyes on them before.

"You'll be better soon," Anna promised Ella; "I've been praying for you. Do you want to hear one of my prayers for you?" "No, she doesn't," Edna answered, pushing her out the door. "I have a book for you," Jack announced; "they said you couldn't read, but Mother could read it to you. It's a very good book. *Fred Martin's Voyages to the Amazon Jungle.*" Ella fervently thanked him. "You don't look bad at all, even if you smell funny." Ella grinned. "I'd give you a kiss," she told him, "but I don't know just how this yellow fever travels around; look at my foot," she told him, raising it from under the sheet and letting the sheet slide back to her knee: "I look like an old banana." "Only your skin," Jack said. "You come back soon," Ella said; "maybe I can kiss you later." "I don't want any *kisses.*" "You'll change your mind," William said from the straw, where he was propped on his elbow. "I don't think so." "He saves his kisses for toads," Edna told them. "Toads are different." "Go on and play," his mother told him, giving him a gentle push. Well, she thought, she had run out of children.

They would have to let Lettie in now. "Hmmm," Lettie said, wrinkling her nose in the doorway, "you smell like a dead fish. I don't know how William can stand it." "There are times, Miss Lettie," he answered sharply, "when some odors are invisible to some noses just because they've become so used to them." She decided it was safer to deal with her sister. "You certainly look horrible, but they say you'll live. Is that color permanent?" she asked, flicking open her pocket mirror; "look, you're the color of the piano, on top anyway." Ella squinted; the light still hurt her eyes. Tears began filling them, spilling onto her cheeks. "Are you satisfied now?" Edna de-

manded; "out. I'll speak to your father about you later."
William was looking contemplatively at Lettie. Perhaps,
he thought, Jack could deal with *her.* He'd have to see
about it.

During the next ten days, while the fever took its
mildest course, William rarely left Ella's bedside. On the
fourth day, a low fever returned, coming and going, but
the yellow color gradually began fading. There were no
hemorrhages, and from Ella's increasing restlessness, she
was clearly growing stronger. She had taken no medication, showed no signs of stomach disorder, slept well,
showed no signs of incipient coma or nervousness. Her
pulse, which William by now took as skillfully as Edna,
was regular and strong. She was often drowsy, but whenever she awoke, she seemed better than before. Still, no
one was willing to believe her recovery was certain.
Anna, of course, insisted she had been sure from the
very beginning, and had no idea why anyone worried in
the first place, or why they continued to do so.

It was Jack who broke the gloom, although, as they remembered occasionally, there was still plenty to worry
about. Hal was now showing signs of restlessness and
irritability. Amos reported that the slightest thing irritated
him; there was no pleasing him at all. Either it was too
hot or, if he opened the window, he whined about the
breeze slapping at his skin. "And he doesn't even want to
drink beer," Amos complained. Jack, however, appeared
at Ella's cottage with a small red cow, not much bigger
than a rat; he was oblivious of Hal's predicament. "What
is that?" Edna asked, coming out; "it looks like a cross
between a dog and a cat and a chicken." "It's a brindled
cow," her son announced proudly, seemingly unaware it
was red, its brindle a small white spot just beneath its tail.
But it did have graceful horns and beautiful eyes. Mr.
Siddons, she thought, would appreciate those features. "I
want to take it in to Ella." Edna sighed. She knew he
would never forgive her if she forbade it. "All right; just
let me spread out the red carpet for him." She went in
and conferred with William. They took a roll of canvas
and spread it from the doorway to the bed. "Ella," her
mother alerted her, "Jack bought a new cow." Ella sat
up, interested. William promptly slid two pillows behind
her back. Yes, Edna decided, it was about time she took

this business seriously, unless, of course, this was his vicarious way of playing at doctoring, but somehow, she doubted it.

"What a beautiful cow," Ella cooed, evidently meaning it. *Anything* new, Edna realized, even a tarantula, would look beautiful to her. "Where did you get it?" "I bought him. At an auction." Oh, he was proud of that cow! "Where did you get the money?" "Oh, that was hard," Jack rattled on; "I don't get enough for a cow in my allowance, you know, so I had to figure it out myself, and I thought the bank, you see, well everyone knows the doctor, so I went in and identified myself," he said, as proud of the word as of the action, "and I told them I needed a loan to buy the cow, and my father would come and pay them the money as soon as he got home, and they just gave it to me, and the man at the auction was so nice and trusting, he saved the cow for me." "I bet he was trusting," Edna said. "Well, don't you think I did a good job?" Jack asked Ella. "Oh yes, I do, and you got one just the right size for you, too." "Yes, that's just what I thought, except that Lettie keeps saying such mean things; she says his eyes are crossed, and they aren't, not even a little." "No," said his mother, "I'd say that's the one thing not the matter with him." "Anyway," William said (there was a strange look about *him*), "it's not a she, it's a he." "Then we won't get any milk!" Jack gasped. " 'Fraid not," said William; "would you mind coming outside, Mr. Steele? There's a complicated operation in mind; I have the need of a very resourceful person such as one who buys cows at auctions." Jack trotted out after him, the little calf blundering along behind.

"This won't be easy," William whispered to Jack; he wasn't going to give the game away too fast; "I'm not sure you can do it." "Do what, do what?" Jack asked, excited and flattered. "Well, first, how many friends can you get to help you?" "Well," Jack considered, "there's Tommy and George, and Bobby and . . ." "In numbers, how many?" "Oh, twelve at least." "Well, that should be enough." "Come on, tell me," Jack pleaded. William bent over and began whispering in his ear. Jack's face brightened; he was transformed. "I think I could just manage that! I think I would just like to manage that! I think that would be the most fun I ever had. But will you tell

Father you suggested it?" "I will; but afterwards. I don't want to give away any secrets." Jack ran off, the little calf hard on his heels. Edna, observing from the door, wondered what plot was in the making. It was, she supposed, harmless enough. Still, she felt sorry for Amos; he was going to have his hands full with that red animal. She'd never seen anything looking so starved before. She'd only read about such starved things in *The Foreign News Column.*

"Mother! Mother! Come out here, come right out here now!" Lettie's hysterical voice woke Edna from her nap. Was someone else sick? Something was definitely wrong with her eyes, she thought, rubbing them; from the doorway of the cottage, Lettie seemed to have turned bright red, so red she clashed with her own hair. "What's the matter?" Was she going blind? she wondered. "What's the matter!" Lettie screamed maniacally; "my own brother and a gang of little boys with masks on tie me down and paint me red, screaming that I'm a squaw and they're Indians, and you want to know what's the matter!" "Oh," Edna said sleepily, "you *are* red." "Of *course* I'm red," Lettie howled; "and it won't come off! I'm going to kill him! I'm going to kill that calf of his!" "You touch either one of those creatures," Edna said, "and I'll have you painted black with yellow stripes, and I mean that. I'll have your father shave your head to protect you from lice. I mean it, Lettie; I'm warning you. If you touch either of them." "Everyone hates me!" she wailed, running off into the woods. "I wonder how that happened?" Edna said. "She certainly looks peculiar," Ella said, delighted. "You get back into bed," she ordered, but William had already gathered her up like a pile of clothes and was settling her in.

"You wouldn't have had anything to do with that, would you?" Edna asked him. "Well," he said, smiling down at Ella, "I wouldn't blame someone else for it, if that's what you mean. I had one idea last week, and that was the one about the red cow." Edna collapsed on a chair. "How *will* we get that paint off her? Well and who cares?" she said finally; "Amos will think of something, I suppose. I hope it burns," she added. "Good for Jack," she said sometime later. As the day wore on, she suddenly burst into laughter and couldn't stop. *"That,"* she gasped, "was an *inspired* idea." Even that sentence was too much for her; within seconds she was helpless with laughter again. It proved contagious, for when John walked up to the cottage to break the sad news of Lettie's change and the caustic scrubbing she was now enduring, he was almost driven back to the house by the tide of laughter pouring from the door like an unexpected flood after a drought. "We better let him in on the whole thing," Edna told them; "come on, William. Come clean." "That's more than some people can do," he roared. Ella was breathless with giggles and hiccoughs. When Ten came down on her routine visit, she got caught up in the tide herself, and so it went on. The cottage had become the gayest part of the farm. "Well, I like the cow, anyhow," Ten shrieked, and then everyone was off again.

Ella was finally moved back to the house; William retreated to his own family. Martin was still absent. "It's touch and go with Minnie, but I think she'll get there," John said; "it will be a recovery and a half, though, I can tell you. There's hardly anything left of her." "I'll go down there in the morning," Edna promised; "Martin's probably in as bad shape as anyone." "Worse. He wants to marry her, even if she's dying, that's what he said." "That's a rather futile gesture, isn't it?" Edna asked. "But touching." "More than that. Perhaps I had better go down there tonight." "Tonight you sleep on your own bed."

"John?" she said that night; "John? Are you awake?" He mumbled something. "Remember during the war days how interested you were in William's letters? Well, one of those days in the cottage, he let it slip out that he wanted to go to medical school, but it was nothing to think of, he said, not for the oldest boy of a poor family." "Well?" "I think we should send him. Martin wants to go, too; they're practically inseparable." "Martin may not want to go if anything happens to Minnie." "Oh, I think he will." "But how would we manage it without offending every one of the Moffats?" John asked; "and sometimes I think that means half the town." "We'll think of something," Edna said, turning on her side, putting her arm around his shoulders, another around his head. "Your arm there? You know what it always reminds me of?" "No, what?" "A halo," he said groggily. Edna smiled into the friendly dark. It had become friendly after she decided the dark only drew a line which seemed to mark them off from the world they thought they knew. He would never have said that about the halo if he'd known he was really awake.

How were they going to manage getting William off to medical school? Well, that wasn't hard; Martin would simply have to suffer a nervous collapse and require a companion who saw to it he didn't overstrain himself. Martin would just have to wait, she decided, until Minnie's fate was clear. Ella wouldn't like it, though, if they sent William off to Boston, and with Martin, too. The two of them were so close. Well, *she* could perpetually visit her beloved grandmother. That would take care of her. And, for that matter, she had better think about shipping Little Red Lettie Hood off there as soon as possible. She was beginning to worry about what would become of Lettie's nerves if anyone called her that again. And of course, no one was likely to stop, not with Jack so proud of himself. Ten would take care of that overweening pride, she thought comfortably, falling asleep.

Anna was lying on her bed. She stared at the wallpaper. Yes, she thought, it was very prettily papered and the floral design was so delicate and lovely, and the green ivy border around the wall just under the ceiling; that was lovely, too. She could still see, when the light fell correctly, the brushstrokes where she had lacquered the ivy trim which seemed to wrap up the gay little room like a box. Well, she was beyond all that now. Even the pretty frieze of nymphs which covered the fourth wall; how many hours had she spent imagining she had entered into it, playing in the sun with the unicorn, walking to the edge of the wood, lying down with the lion and the lamb while the tiger and the elephant, a small adorable monkey on his back, stood happily by. Aunt Ten had pointed out that, really, the symbolism of the frieze was religious, the unicorn after all did stand for the Virgin Mary, but that was not part of *her* religion, although the lion and the lamb lying down together, that certainly was. Still, she thought, she would prefer some other kind of scene, such as Christ rising from his winding shroud, or an exact replica of her favorite engraving of the moment, a bereaved mother in black collapsed over the recent mound of her buried child, the distraught father half turned from the pathetic scene. And the stone, with its granite angels, and hovering just above them, barely visible, almost a formation of mist or cloud, the *real* angels God had sent down to comfort the mourners, as yet unaware of them.

No, whenever she suggested painting out the scene she now had, no one in the house would hear of it, even after she threatened to do it herself. *That,* her father told her abruptly, would certainly put an end to her going on rounds. It was a sign, he said, of a disturbed imagination, and, he had gone on, troubled, it was all his fault, too, because he took her with him when she was so young and impressionable. What he was blaming himself for was beyond Anna, since, if he had been the instrument of any change in her, surely it was (as the Reverend Pierce said it was) for the better. But she did not want to upset her father, and so the discussion over changing the frieze ended abruptly. She sighed. They didn't understand her.

And it was so sad, too. Why, just last week, at prayer meeting, one man had stood up and confessed how he had come to change his heart. It was (there was no doubting his sincerity; how he had perspired and wrung his hands, and his voice quavered so) the conversion of his own daughter which had done it. She had come home one day and told him she was now a Christian, but she cried because they would never again meet after this life was over, and he had found that so unendurable that he had prostrated himself, yes, prostrated himself, at his daughter's feet, and at that moment, the awful conviction of sin washed over him, catching at his throat until he felt he was drowning, and he saw, as if in a vision, the ship of Christ sailing toward him, and he knew—he went on with tears in his eyes—this was his last hope. Christ risen and beckoning. How his heart had jumped in his bosom! And how grateful to his little daughter he had been. He hoped, he said, eyes downcast, he would have the power, with the help of their prayers, and his and his beloved daughter's, to bring his wife and two other children of sensible age to the same understanding he had been fortunate enough to reach before it was too late. Especially now, he quavered, when death was stalking the land and there was no safety anywhere. Would they pray with him? They would.

And what had happened when she had come home and attempted the same thing? *Her* father, instead of dwelling upon the awful aspects of their separation for all eternity, had simply said he would save whom he could in this life, and if God was just, he would not separate those who loved one another. "*You* cannot preach to God!" she had cried; "or attempt to teach him his duty! It is your duty to listen to *him!* We might be separated for all eternity, all eternity!" she pleaded feverishly; "why, who is to say that it was not my prayers for Ella which made the difference? The ways of God are so mysterious." Her father had paused to agree with that, but methodically continued replacing medications and other supplies in his black bag.

"Father!" she pleaded, falling to her knees; "just think! You might never see Mother again, never, never, never. How awfully that word falls upon the ears, how it tolls, nevermore, nevermore. Is there a more awful word than that?" "Anna," he said, "get up. You'll get splinters in your knees and I'll be trapped here taking them out while others scurry needlessly into eternity." He tucked a huge book under his elbow. "Anna," he said, softening for a minute, "not everyone is ready for your kind of belief." "But that is just the point," she exclaimed; "that is the very point they make in all our prayer meetings. 'When,' the Reverend Pierce always asks (he always begins that way), 'are you to believe in Christ? You are to believe immediately, that is when you are to believe.' Father," she went on, prepared to continue into the early hours of morning, "let me come with you on rounds. Let me attempt to bring you to the true way. You *must*, you must," she said, bursting into tears, "become a Christian or I shall never see you again."

"You shall see the palm of my hand all too soon if you don't get off that floor. I have sick people to attend to. Christ," he said impatiently, "was compared to the great healer. I'm only following in his footsteps, in my humble way." Why did she always let him confuse her, she thought resentfully, especially when so much was at stake? There were times she resented his thorough knowledge of the Bible, when he could pervert it so and use it against her, but surely, she thought, puzzled, *that* was wrong. The Bible was, according to dear Reverend Pierce, the only true oath to the one God. It was like a vast, ancient carpet which could descend and descend, while the Holy Ghost paced slowly and majestically down into the evil and struggling heart, freeing it from sin, giving it Grace. Perhaps she was not really a Christian yet, not if she wanted to deprive her own father of the sacred, radiant book.

She would reread, she decided, the prayers of David. Why, she wondered, did Aunt Ten always say those psalms depressed her? She said she found Ecclesiastes, with its grim predictions of doom, more uplifting than David. Aunt Ten even said his despair seemed so very genuine it was impossible to believe him when he claimed God relieved such immense spiritual distress. What misfortune, she sighed, being born into such a godless family. But that, that, she agonized, was wrong, too. It was not her place to judge them; only God could do that. Yes, she was still riddled with sin. Her heart was a corrupt house; her tongue was truly the most unruly member of her body.

Still, she could wish (there was nothing wrong with wishing, not if one acknowledged, while wishing, that God's ways, his Providence, were most just; *then* she could wish and perhaps God would hear her—but should she wish, or should she pray?) that she had been born into Lois Ann Moffat's family. How much easier it would be, or have been, to bear the travails of a broken marriage, the round white face of her husband at the door at night (he looked so like a deformed moth), than to see the fires of hell already lapping at the hems of the family she loved so.

Perhaps she did not place enough confidence in them. Perhaps her own manner was *too* unsympathetic, and so, unknowingly, she was turning them from the correct path. She stared into the frieze. No, this was not a maze she could find her way out of alone. She would have to consult with the Reverend Pierce. But not today, she realized with a shock; today was Sunday! How could she have forgotten that, after attending three services with Lois

Ann? And then she must not neglect her earthly duties. She read her sampler to herself: "Christ is the unseen guest at every table, the unseen listener at every conversation." *He* would want her to look after Hal; he would not want her intruding her selfish demands upon the Reverend's Holy Sabbath. No, indeed. He would not want that. She turned on her side, impatiently kicking at her quilt.

At his house, the Reverend Pierce was sitting down to dinner with his wife; the children, thank God, he thought, gone out to do something or other. If the truth were known, he didn't care what they were doing. "Well, Mother," he began unctuously, "and how go things with you this week?" "A lot you care," she snapped, concentrating on her plate. "What is that supposed to mean?" he asked; "and why," he continued when he received no answer, "must you start an argument over dinner when that's the only peaceful time we have?" "And is that my fault, too?" she asked; "the children are little better than criminals, and all you care about is prayer meetings and special meetings with every pretty little thing in the parish. You wouldn't notice if I fell on my knife and bled to death in the kitchen. You would go on, though, if the blood somehow stained that precious collar of yours. As if I didn't have to wash and iron them," she said, petulant. "A very good job you make of it, too," he snarled; "I can't hold up my head in these wrinkled clothes you call ironed; it's a good thing I have my religion for starch and iron." "I wish I had an iron right here," his wife said, raising her voice; "I know what I'd do with it." She stared at his forehead. "Don't you threaten me," he warned her.

"And don't you threaten me; I'm only an instrument of Providence"; she imitated his sanctimonious voice with provoking accuracy. "And if I choose to throw irons, and they choose to hit their mark, that's all God's will. We must not chafe at the bit," she went calmly on, inspecting her soup as if she expected to find Jonah and the whale swimming about in it; "after all, *my* burden is heavy but my yoke is light. I do have that right, don't I?" she inquired, now mimicking one of his younger charges. "If anyone is going to throw anything," he said,

"I'll do the throwing." "A man in your position, dear, throwing things, and all the mothers haven't even been in asking *you* to help, as part of your God-given duty, with nursing the sick. That, the blessed ones have concluded, is my duty, *too*." "I have good aim," he said; "I'm telling you for the last time." "We must always," she mocked, "consider how our actions appear to others on the Sabbath." Yes, she decided, gleeful, he was reddening. How like a diseased tomato he looked. And what satisfaction the thought gave her.

"Throwing soup," she went on in an innocent falsetto, "may indeed be a Christian action, a type of feeding the hungry, or a type of the legend of loaves and fishes, but who, looking into this *innocent* kitchen, would know that you were throwing a bowl of soup at your wife for her spiritual good? Or to make more vivid the impressions of such paramount importance which the Bible grants us?" Beside himself, the Reverend picked up his bowl of potato soup and threw it at her head. She ducked so skillfully it was clear this performance had taken place more than once. Tinkling glass fell behind her. "Ah," she said, "you have broken through the spiritual ice with my soup. I do hope you remember, dear, that it was *my* soup which gave you such spiritual warmth." "You call that slop soup?" he roared; "it's salt water with a few moldy potatoes drowning in it." "Well, then," she asked in her normal voice, "why don't you just preach a good, thundering sermon about pew rent and the congregation raising the minister's salary so that his poor, starving family can live without being given over to a life of crime?" He glared furiously at her. "I suppose," she mused sadistically, "that God's paths are easier for some men to tread than they are for others. Poor dear."

"Why didn't you marry one of those men, then?" "It's a question I often ask myself, but then God's ways are beyond my comprehension." He stared at her; now he had gone white. Murder, he thought, murder was expressly forbidden by the first commandment, but surely there must be exceptions. No, he decided, sitting silent and glaring, God must want him to suffer; she was his cross and his crucifixion. And besides, God had never forgiven Cain. Why should he forgive *him*? A poor country minister. Although killing a wife, he thought, surely that was less serious than killing a blood relation. Although it was true there were numerous injunctions against treating a wife cruelly. Yes, theirs was a harsh God.

A neighbor who had passed by minutes before had seen the plate sailing out through the window. Poor Minister Pierce, she thought, tears filling her eyes; I don't know how he manages with those children. And now, no doubt, one of the parents will have to miss their dinner. It was really a disgrace, she meditated, pacing sedately on in her best black summer dress, how those children went on, but then she supposed one ought not to complain of them; it was for their sake he was not more often at home with them. Still, it was too bad neither of them had a parent who could stay home and administer the grandmotherly birch. They should, she thought, take old Mrs. Higgenbottom, the teacher, in to board.

Except now she had a family. She could remember back to the days she was considered a hopeless spinster. *She* would have taken care of those children for them, although even she had trouble with the Pierce children; it was their heads, Mrs. Higgenbottom's granddaughter reported, which most frequently hit the desks, and just last week, she had locked the schoolhouse door and refused to teach while they were in her presence. And the school board had backed her up, too. But finally the children promised to reform; they had actually made good on that promise! Unbelievable. Yes, it was.

Perhaps it was because Mrs. Pierce had been taken with a fainting fit and could not get up for two days after the door was locked against her children. Well, she supposed those monsters had *some* human sympathies, although it was too bad, she said, nodding automatically to a passing couple, one of whom was reading aloud from what she unthinkingly assumed to be the Bible, they had to kill their mother before they improved on their opportunity to receive education. No, she did not blame him for calling in other ministers, exchanging, even straining the funds for one more distinguished than himself. *That* showed true forbearance, true humility. Times were certainly changing, she thought, spearing a brown leaf

with the point of her parasol and throwing it back into
the woods, when humility was mistaken for arrogance.

Anna's thoughts had reverted to her Uncle Hal; there
was no point in saving him spiritually, she had decided
that long ago. It was evidently God's will that he remain
untouched by this world, although he spoiled in the sun
like any other of the world's apples. She often thought
this unjust, and often struggled with her tendency to
judge God, which she knew to be dreadful blasphemy.
She could not help seeing it; she saw it whenever she
closed her eyes. One instant she had been standing on the
sidewalk holding Uncle Hal's hand (it was never clear
who was holding on to whom; Ten had said that more
than once) and the next thing she knew he was floating,
yes, floating across the street to that dog. Probably it was
all those cries of "Mad dog" that had made him run so
toward the beast. He never could tolerate anything being
hurt. Perhaps that was why he seemed to like the dead
so. They were beyond all that; that was nice, the way he
sensed the greater truths, when the rest of the family, supposedly in full possession of their faculties, did not, but
then how was she to reconcile herself to his tendency to
confuse weddings and funerals?

His understanding. It might be deeper than theirs, since
he felt with his heart and mind; they could not get in the
way to confuse him, as hers so often did. He must see it
all at once, the wedding, the beginning of the grand procession, producing in the inevitable grandeur of things
more and more souls to be taken off to God, and death
only the chariot in which they safely arrived at their
destination. Yes, he must surely know better than the rest
of them that it was necessary to die if one was to be
born again. As it was necessary for the seed to die to become the crop, although he never would be able to put
such things into words.

And he did believe in God, even Father agreed about
that, although, as Father said, he seemed to think God
was some large toy carved to protect him. Well, and was
that so bad? Was that so far from the truth? She had
better go and look at him, she decided, wearily sitting
up. They wouldn't let her in to see him now, even though
Amos had a pistol ready, and they wouldn't let her in

even if she promised to take her own pistol with her, because they knew she wouldn't use it. But that day, the dog and Hal floating toward each other right in the middle of the town square, with the three-tiered birdbath right in back of them. They met right in front of it, the amazed crowds frozen on the walks, just as she had been, while Uncle Hal, in his innocence, tried to comfort the bad dog. It had all seemed like a ballet, she thought, going down the path toward the cottage, just like one of the ballets Grandmother took them to in Boston. They had moved toward each other so slowly, and yet, there were other times when she remembered it as if it were over with, settled, beyond repair, in an instant, when Uncle Hal appeared to have leaped into the air and the little dog appeared to have leaped into the air, and they caught each other high, high above the ground, as if for years they had been trained in that intricate dance. And then they shot the dog, right in front of Hal, and dragged him off and locked him up.

He was now, her father warned her, knowing she would have read his books, in "the final stage of excitement." He didn't seem to want to drink, although he didn't show a real aversion to it, a symptom which the books described as classic and decisive. He said he didn't like drinking it because it made his throat hurt. She had given up hoping he would recover, even after all her prayers. He did have every other symptom; there was no point in quarreling with the inevitable, which would only mean quarreling with God. She kicked a stone up above her head; she kicked another one harder.

She went up to the window and looked in. Aunt Ten was sitting inside with Amos. Ten looked up and saw her. She had a pistol, too, and she would use it; Anna knew that. She probably hates me for it, Ten thought, but what could she do? She loved Hal as much as anyone in the world, but he was, she hated to say it, no longer human. And Anna's face perpetually at that window, that white face. Edna was right; it was Lois Ann Moffat's husband all over again, peering helplessly through the screen, only worse, because this time it was not Lois Ann's husband, it was a member of their family, and there would soon be a death to deal with. Lois Ann's husband, too. He had died out of sheer grief; that was her diagnosis, and for once, her brother hadn't contradicted her. Why, she wondered, was Anna always drawn so to scenes like this? She would give ten years of her life to be spared these days in the cottage with Hal, but Anna hung to the window of the cottage like a leech. There was something terrible about it; at least, it chilled *her* blood.

Hal, Ten saw, was terribly restless, terribly. He did not stay still for an instant. At times he seemed to recognize neither of them. They had tried to give him some water (she had read somewhere of a woman who had lived forty days on water before she died), but this had only produced the most dreadful spasms of his throat, and afterwards, he could barely breathe. And it was hardly a pleasant procedure—since it had to be performed at arm's length, and required two people, one to restrain him, another to administer the water. At times, he seemed altogether in another world; then he would talk happily about their mother and father. He would promise their father he would become a doctor just like John and help him, and why wouldn't Mother take him sleighing? Just because she was coughing, that was no reason. She could dress up real warm, just the way he was. At other times, he would play quietly in a corner with a concoction made of straw; it resembled some kind of idol, but he called it Flag or Spots; then he threw another bunch of straw he had tied for the first bunch to chase, throwing the toy idol after it, evidently convinced that was the dog chasing the bone.

"Oh, they shouldn't have called you bad doggie," he lamented again and again until both she and Amos were ready to leap right out of their skins. At other times, he would turn on them, accusing them of having hidden "Hal's doggie"; then he would start crying, threatening to tell Mother. She was real mean, he said, and so was Amos. If he upset himself sufficiently, he would try jumping at them and shaking them, hitting them, anything to make them give him the dog. During these periods, Amos would usher Ten out behind his back and slip out himself, locking the door until Hal calmed down, usually from the exhausting effort to breathe; lately that had become harder and harder for him. And now, he was foaming at the mouth, just as the dog he had tried to protect had done.

Anna had murmured something dreadful, she couldn't forget it, about the dog's spirit having passed into Uncle Hal, but John had been home; at least she had been set straight on that. The saliva, he patiently explained, was increased by the disease, and because Hal had difficulty swallowing, he tried not to, but instead let the saliva drool from his mouth. Still, she remained convinced some exchange of spirit had taken place. She denied it now, but Ten knew she believed it. Well, he had fallen asleep now. She might as well go back to the house. This was certainly a long death watch, she thought, bones aching. As she got up, a sharp pain caught her in the hip and she gasped; Hal's eyes swiveled toward her, but it was obvious enough he did not see her.

"He's sleeping," she lied to Anna, taking her hand, the two of them returning together to the house. Anna certainly had bad luck, she thought; first becoming so attached to Hal, who tried to entertain her as best he could by taking her to those funerals and weddings. Well, she thought, discouraged, how was that different from his attempts to rescue the poor bad dog? He always meant well, that was the trouble. Her mother had foreseen it. She had warned all of them on *her* deathbed: "Don't let him get away with things, just because," she rasped, her hand cooling; "it won't end well."

Well, they were younger and they had not listened, and it had turned out just as Mother had said. John had given him two forms of medication, and one, she thought, was as inefficient as the other; but they did seem to relieve him. And all this after Ella, and Minnie still not out of the woods. This was life, after all. As Alice had written in one of her journals inadvertently left at their house: "Some are dancing and some are dying." Still, it was hard to get used to that way of thought. When it actually happened. "Where are you going?" she asked Anna. "Up to pray." She should have known better than to ask. She had no idea of what to do with her. She knew what *she* was going to do; she was going to bury her troubles under the deep waters of *Abigail: The Story of a Young Woman Deceived and Destroyed*. There would be no foaming at the mouth in *that* book.

Two days later, as poor Abigail, who thought she was merely getting fleshy, was thrown out into a dreadful

573

storm when her unsympathetic employers discovered the true nature of her condition, there was a sharp rap on her door. She knew it was Amos, and before she even got up to open the door, she knew it was the end of her brother. "Miss Ten, he's been drinking all the time, but he looks awful stiff to me; he's drinking up *pails*." "You had better get Anna," she said; "who else is home?" "You and Anna is all." Wouldn't that be just the way? Not only was Hal dying, but Anna would have to be home to see it, and she would have to be home watching both of them. Life was not fair, she thought, her eyes filling with tears. By the time the three of them reached the cottage, Hal was completely paralyzed. It had crept up on him, she thought, aghast, like a sheet. Now it covered everything but his face. Anna had already fallen down next to the bed and was crying hysterically. "Anna," Ten scolded, "have *some* sympathy for the feelings of the dying. He feels bad enough. There's nothing he can do to comfort you now; it ought to be the other way around." She got up, her hand creeping into Ten's.

"Flag?" Hal whispered. "Flag is fine," Ten assured him; his lips were starting to form another question. "He and Spots went on rounds with John; you know they always do that." "What a pretty little girl," he said, looking at Anna; "who is she?" "A friend of Flag's," Ten answered. Anna was sobbing again. Oh, well, what did it matter? He didn't know who she was, after all; her state wouldn't matter so acutely to him. "Mother, when is she coming?" "Mother is busy right now; you remember, she scalded herself with some tea last night. She's dressing the burn on her leg." "Oh yes," Hal said; "Mother was not careful." "No, she was not." "Where's Father?" "On rounds, just as usual." "Father will come see Hal?" he asked more weakly now. "You know he will." "That's good," he said, closing his eyes. How quiet he was, Ten thought; the spasms were gone now. She felt his hand; no, he wasn't gone yet. He was still warm. "Ten won't go and leave Hal?" he asked, opening his eyes. "Certainly not; you close your eyes and go to sleep." "Hal has the measles," he announced proudly. Now she was crying silently. "Don't cry, sister," he reassured her; "Father said the measles were not bad for me." "I know," Ten said; "but

I broke my doll and I am *so* upset." "Hal get you new one," he promised, closing his eyes.

She kept hold of his hand; yes, it was cooling. She saw his eyelids flutter, as if he were trying to open them again for one last look at something he thought was important, but they did not open. His hand was almost cold. His mouth, too, seemed to be forming words. She bent over closer. "Not too far, Miss Ten," Amos warned her. "Nice Flag." His lips formed the words. "Nice Flag." But he had no voice.

"He's dead, Miss Ten," Amos told her. He had been holding Ten's other hand. "No!" Ten screamed, turning on him; "I don't believe you!" Amos and Anna turned to her in astonishment. "I don't believe you, I don't," she kept crying convulsively as they led her back to the house. They kept her in her room, trying to get her to talk, but all she said was "He was like my child, my child," and then the sad, hopeless sobbing would resume, constant as a river murmuring over its bed of stones.

"Now we'll have Ten to worry about," John told Edna that night; he had already made the necessary arrangements. "What do you mean?" "You watch," he said; "she'll come down with something, catarrh of the lungs, as they call it here. Coughing, choking, high fever. I tell you, Edna, I'm dreading it." "But why do you think that?" "It seems to be her way of mourning," he said lying back, unhappy. "But she promised me to stay alive until Lettie and Ella were married off!" Oh, now John would be angry with *her*. What a selfish, thoughtless thing to say. "Did she?" he asked, smiling; "well, then, perhaps we don't have to worry, after all. She always keeps her promises. She may go to the edge of the grave," he said slowly, "but if she made you that promise, she'll keep it. I wish I knew what made that woman tick." "But you've lived with her most of your life." "It doesn't make much difference, does it? If it were possible for a doctor to dissect one living person and not hurt them, I'd choose her." Edna pressed down some hurt feelings. Was there no end to egotism? Sometimes she thought a bit of Anna's training wouldn't hurt her in the least. "Well," John asked, "are you going to let me lie here freezing to death or are you going to hold on to me?" She turned on her side, holding him, as she always did, until he was asleep. She could not sleep, not for some time, especially after she heard the unmistakable sound of Ten's coughing.

"Well," Edna said the day Ten's fever broke, and she was finally able to take something more than warm chicken water, "you did give us all a scare." "I did?" Ten asked; "I'm sure it was good for you. How is everyone?" "Everyone is fine; even Minnie is on the mend, but it will take her a while to get back where she was." "How long has it been?" Ten asked, looking around slowly; there was a fire in her stove. "Almost three weeks, that's all. You do things with panache, but John said if you promised not to die before Lettie and Ella were married, you'd keep your word." "He was right," Ten answered, exhausted, drawing the blanket up a little further. Edna finished doing it for her; she was still very weak. "Hal's funeral?" "Well, that's over with, too," Edna said sadly. "Is Anna still crying?" Ten asked, crotchety. "Not as far as we know."

Ten fell silent, her breathing now audible from the effort to talk, not from the illness. "Something about," she said softly, "I am the resurrection, and the life; he that believeth in me, though he shall die, shall live forever." "That's how he began"; Edna smiled. "And something about how Christ said, 'Suffer ye little children to come unto me,' and that Hal was really a kind of child, and he would be one of the first taken into the folds of the heavenly father." "That, too." "Well, I didn't miss anything at all," Ten said. She was positively cranky; "after you go to enough of them, they become predictable. Like death, and then the promise of the afterlife, as if everything were to be canceled out as it happened, just as life does things." "Ten, dear," Edna remonstrated gently, "we'll talk more later; you must rest." "And the worst of it is," Ten whispered, "that I still don't know what happened to Abigail." "Would you like me to read to you?" At the suggestion, Ten seemed positively rejuvenated.

Edna got up and found the book. "Where did you leave off?" "Where I put the bookmark," Ten answered. Edna began reading. "Abigail, finding herself in a terrible storm, as if God's hands were stirring the elements to fury, knew not what to do. She had found so little compassion in the walled houses that she decided without thinking to search out the wilder places; accordingly, she found herself making her way toward the deep wet forest. She gave no thought to the dangers which might await her there, to the inevitable presence of the prowling beasts. Somehow, she knew, there would be safety in the forest, and the wild creatures, would they take worse care of her than the Huntingtons had? A child! They had insisted she was to have a child! But where, wondered the innocent girl no more than a child herself, could it have come from? She had not been bitten by a bee, not stepped on a snake." Edna looked up at Ten; she looked like an ancient, radiant bride, reunited with her long-lost book. She continued reading the adventures of the poor, innocent child. The next time she looked up, Ten was already asleep. "Well, how is she?" John asked that night. "She wants to read *Abigail*." "We can stop worrying about *her*."

Several months later when Ten was again up and about, Edna asked her if there was likely to be another religious revival. The thought of it, she said, turned her blood to ice. "You mean because of the yellow fever?" Ten asked; "no, I doubt it very much. That was too much of a shock to everyone. Nothing will happen right away," she thought out loud; "I would guess they'll be more in the way of prayer meetings, more people getting themselves dunked, more going to church, but nothing serious in the way of a revival," she considered. "Until something milder comes along, when everyone's too far from the fever not to remember it too well. Something like a measles scare, or the mumps; in three years, or four; that should do it. But not right now, no; not right now. Everyone has had too much. I suppose there will be more marrying instead."

"You're right about that; you should have heard about some of the marriages that took place when you were sick." "I can hear about them now, can't I?" She was more irritable lately, Edna saw; that seemed to be the only consequence of the congestive fever, or whatever it was called. "Your Uncle Calvin, or Cousin Calvin, you know I can't keep these things straight," Edna said, "married someone named Mary Wade." "Well, if that isn't about time; they've only been making up their minds fifty years. I didn't think they'd make it to the altar this side of seventy." "Well, they did, and we got a list of all their presents. I'll dig it out for you." "Don't bother; get on with the rest of the news." "Well, Nellie Wakefield married someone from Ohio; she met him while she was visiting her married sister, and Jane Weston, the Westons' oldest daughter, married Fred Higgins, and of course everyone in town believes she did it because she had too much to handle on the farm with her mother gone." Ten nodded as if in time to a metronome. "But the best of all was our post-ma'am, who thought it best to forgo a twelve-hundred-dollar salary with a pension, all for a poor man with three little boys. How is that for getting married?" "Not bad," Ten agreed; "what else did I miss? I have to ask about everything before anyone thinks to tell me about it."

"You missed the Apple Adventure down at the Moffats', but you've probably heard that one before. Alice's been drying apples for years. She had the roof of the back portico spread full of apples two weeks ago, and then in the middle of the night it began raining, and she and the rest of them had to get up and take down all the apples; George fell off, of course, in the middle, and that livened things up, and then she had to dry them all in front of the stove, and all she did was complain about how now she had no time to sew, so we sent Mrs. Grimsby down. Then she was busy drying a bushel of elderberries and swearing up and down she would never again dry anything that didn't fit in the house, and in the meantime Minnie kept on complaining about how sore her joints were, and all grown out, and John told them it was just a complication of the fever and she should soak all she could in hot water, and probably all but one finger would be back to normal again. They also painted the parlor and the bedroom white, the ceilings light pink, and they papered it light blue. The sitting room is now light-straw-colored, although I'd think they'd have enough of that shade, and the chambers are now painted pink with striped paper. They think they're very fancy, that's what Alice said, except she's fussing over carpets. They're not down yet, and they're all hunting up rags; they're cutting up so much I'm afraid to go close to any one of them with a scissors.

"And things between Ella and William are really going

on. We had a talk with them last night." She paused. "They want to get married, of course," Ten put in. "Yes, they do," Edna said, "but it's complicated." "What's complicating *that?*" "They want to wait until Minnie is better because Martin is so set on marrying her, and they think it would be the cruelest thing for them to get married while she's still tied to her bed." Ten nodded. "So they'll wait and have a double wedding," she said finally. "Yes, that's it." It was such a relief to have her back and thinking. "And," Edna continued, "Martin and William are going to start medical school in Boston, probably for the second term; they'll never make the first one now. That will be something; when Mother hears that two of our children are marrying Moffats."

"Has Lettie decided what to do to get attention over to herself yet?" "No, but she's leaving for Boston within the week." Probably to poison Edith against William. "I tell you, Ten, I'm worried about my mother; she can make the Moffats awfully miserable with her society snobbery, and the worst of it is, they won't know how to protect themselves."

"I'll handle Edith," Ten said peaceably; "if she doesn't change with age, neither do I. Don't worry about Edith." Edna sighed with real relief. "So you think they're definite on it, the two of them, or the four of them, however you want to count up." "I think so." "It's about time William got settled; and Martin, too; I think they'll be happy," she calculated on some mental abacus of her own; "what are they all like together?"

"Well, there's not much to tell about Martin and Minnie, except that he's there forever looking after her, and William and Ella," she said, beaming, "they're confirming all my theories about love." "Theories," Ten said, contented; "I don't know how I survived three weeks without them, even if I was unconscious." "Well, it's not a new theory; it's all in the story of Ruth. 'Whither thou goest,' that sort of thing. Ella goes out to the fields with William; she helps him husk corn; she helps him with Minnie; she even helped him slaughter a hog. I would have thought *that* would kill her, but she managed to find it all very romantic." "That's love," Ten said, "when you find slaughtering a screaming animal romantic." "But it's the going everywhere, together—you know, John and I did that too—it's some kind of pledge, some kind of public avowal, that nothing the other one does is too small, too insignificant. It's like," she went on, "one of John's pictures. You see the signs developing, the faces moving into position, coming closer, taking up one pose, finally becoming so fond of it they hold it for life. No matter what other noises and disasters happen around the margins of the studio."

"Mr. Pierce, I always think of him in this connection, because he's so in love with himself, I mean. When he came for his sitting, you were sick then, the skylight came crashing down and almost killed him, but he wasn't a bit frightened; no, all he worried about was how long it would take John to sweep the glass up and get things back in order because he wanted his pictures of himself that very day. He looked, he said, so very much better than usual." "The heavens could fall, and that man wouldn't notice unless he saw it in a mirror," Ten agreed; "not even if the angel Gabriel tried getting his attention with his golden horn. He's another Lettie. It's true, though, what you've been saying. When I met Ed I didn't care if I ever wore a shoe. They used to threaten me with taking me off to the smithy, I lost so many shoes. I liked the way the grass felt, things like that. Everyone said I'd be taken off for lockjaw, but after I met Ed, what a passion I developed for shoes and all kinds of leather, and inside linings, and stretchings, and dyes, and finishings, and laces; why," she mused, surprised, "even today I could write out a manual concerning their manufacture and sale. No detail was too small for me."

"We were all," Edna said with apparent irrelevance, "terribly worried about your illness—after Hal's death; I suppose it was an illness in honor of his death, wasn't it? None of us expected you to take it like that." "Who can understand another person's heart?" Ten laughed. "Well, it wasn't something I was accustomed to talking about, how I felt about him. He was young enough to be my child, after all, eighteen years younger than I am, two years older than John. I depended on him more than he did on me; oh," she said, eyes darting away, "I knew from the minute he decided to come back. I knew it the instant I heard about the dog biting him. It's so important, to have someone need you the way he needed me.

And it was lovely, wasn't it, the way no one seemed to know about it? It was almost something religious, it was so private; Hal couldn't give it away, could he? It was something like faith." "You cared for him more than John?" "No, no, you miss the point entirely; it was different, different.

"There will never be anything like that again. And I feel so much older, now that he's gone. He never seemed to age; I suppose he was my private fountain of youth," she continued painfully. "Well," she said, brushing some imaginary crumbs from her skirt, "that's all over now, all dead and buried, as they say." Her eyes were glazed. "Don't be sorry you asked," Ten told her. It had happened again, Edna thought, that eerie way she had of entering her mind. "I had to talk about it sooner or later." The two of them sat there in silence, watching the darkness stir and thicken its inks. Too many pages, too many pages being written, at least to my liking, Ten thought uneasily. Yes, it was true; she was getting old. She would be seventy in March.

"Well," she said after some time—by now they were comfortable as two old cats together—"there's no point in making wedding plans until they make the announcement." "No, they might think we were pushing them along." "Wouldn't they, though; I suppose it has been all lazy days for William and Ella?" "Oh yes; whenever they can find them. They've had their share of lying in the bottom of a rowboat and floating down the part of the creek just after the bend where the trees meet overhead, and it's not been unusual to see them head off somewhere, Ella's head under the parasol, the two of them struggling to keep both their heads under it; Ella's five inches shorter; that doesn't make it easy." "Poor William must have a crick in his neck." "Yes, and Ella's got the stiff arm," Edna laughed.

"I wonder," Ten said, "how Minnie and Ella will take to being students' wives, especially Minnie. She's hardly used to the big city." "A great deal will depend on my beautiful mother," Edna said, forehead puckering. "I promised you I'd take care of that, but, Edna, it's only fair, if you're going to hold me to my promise of keeping alive until they're all safely married, you have to promise me to keep alive until John goes." "That's odd, Ten; he

once asked me to promise the same thing." "Did you?"
"Of course. Although I don't want to outlive him, you
know. Although I suppose I could if I had to. But I'd
rather drink down those noxious chemicals of his." "It
would be terrible for you, wouldn't it? Yes, worse than
it would ever be for the rest of us." "Let's get back to
something more cheerful." "As, for example, *Julia: Lost
and Abandoned.*" "Is that what you're up to now? I don't
understand why those things cheer you up." "Because
they have nothing to do with life, that's why," Ten replied, picking up the book and falling into it, Edna
thought, the way stones fell into deep water.

Well, she had better get back to her own notes. Her
mind, she was sure, had stiffened to burnt wood from
disuse, all these sicknesses in the family. Of course, she
resented them. Still, she would resent herself more if
anyone had died. Why was it always a choice between
two fires? She sighed. Ten looked up briefly, and went
back to her book. Edna thinking. A familiar enough
sight. Perhaps, Edna thought, that sort of choice was all
that kept anyone on the path. And when, she wondered,
would they decide to get married? She would have to
remind Ten tomorrow, about writing her mother. There
wasn't much time to lose, even if no one had officially
declared his intentions. Lettie was leaving within the
week, and, although she might appear perfectly normal,
she was still, Edna knew, bright red inside. Well, she
thought, annoyed, when everyone went off to Boston she
would have plenty of time to think. Undoubtedly too
much. She would know something was wrong when she
began pilfering copies of *Lucille* from Ten's room; yes,
that would be a sure sign her mind had gone altogether.

Toward the middle of November, John decided to go to
Boston "after all" for a conference with the lawyer, a Mr.
Tulliver, who, sight unseen, Edna loathed. She was sure,
she repeated, until John forbade any further discussion
of him, that he would cause trouble for them in the end.
Ten decided it was time to write Edith a letter when
Edna, beside herself with fury at her husband's departure,
refused to see him to the station, but announced she was
going to see Alice. If he didn't care about the course the
family was taking, Edna said, and wasn't satisfied with

two careers, doctoring and photography, but now had to become an expert testifying in repulsive court cases, *she* was going to attempt staying on the rails of her usual life. She had hopes she would wake up one morning, she said, glaring at him, and find herself somewhere in the middle of Wyoming, with cactuses like hitching posts, without the slightest idea of what she was doing there. Life here was impossible. So it was with relief that Ten turned to her letter.

"Dear Edith, as you know from Lettie by now, we are likely to be having a double wedding in the family here. William and Ella, Martin and Minnie. Both boys are set on going to medical school, although we did have a time persuading William; I'm not sure if you can call him 'persuaded,' dear Edith. We pulled half the wool of a textile factory over his eyes. Martin—we thought he had absolutely no talent for theatricals—put on an admirable performance as a distraught lover on the edge of nervous prostration. And finally William actually pleaded with his mother to forgive him for leaving her with the farm and so many additional chores, but he would never feel right if he left Ella's brother alive and had to return and find him in one of those oblong boxes. Now, I don't have to tell you, do I, Edith, that this letter is for your eyes only, and not for any of the grandchildren who may be visiting you *at any time*.

"Now, I must tell you the truth of the matter, and, Edith, I think we are both old enough to know better than to suspect the other of lying. The years have bound us together more surely than they tied us to our husbands. Life is queer, isn't it? Lettie set her cap for William when she saw Ella wanted him. We all knew that as soon as she had him, and had Ella prostrated somewhere in the house with eyes permanently swollen, she would have abandoned him as carelessly as she would a torn dress. But she didn't have a chance for all that because William found Ella more to his liking. Now I know that when you look at Lettie, you see yourself, and of course, dear, it goes without saying that you cannot imagine yourself doing such a thing, but you must remember that, however great the resemblance, Lettie is *not* a younger version of you. Would that she were! That would certainly be a comfort to me in my rheumatic old age, and more a comfort to you in your beautiful advanced one. And, Edith, no matter how much we love and respect Mr. Siddons' inspired sculptures of magnificent women, more triumphant in marble than we shall ever be in life, we must not forget that a living woman with a heart as cold as one of his statuary's (and I don't imagine he bothers carving hearts in them) is not to be given free rein.

"Why, you should see how cruelly she treats little Jack, who is so much a replica of your own child. Before she left, Jack was playing with a little girl he likes so much and he permitted her to mix together several of Lettie's little perfume bottles. I know you will say it is not right to meddle with other people's property, and, of course, I quite agree with you, but very young people really cannot conceive of such little beakers and their contents as so very rare, especially when they are only five years old.

"Lettie did make a terrible fuss over it. I believe I shall not forget it until the day I die. It is the sort of thing you see once and never need to see again. 'Look what she has done now,' Lettie kept crying, until, I tell you, Edith, we all felt we had a mad parrot trapped in the house. Then, right in front of the little child, she shouted (oh yes, she is quite capable of shouting, if not shrieking in a high-pitched voice good enough to call all the wolves in from the mountains, although I am sure she never raises her voice above a whisper in *your* town house; we always think it is such a pity she gets all her good behavior out of her system while she is with you, while we suffer on with her better side the rest of the year), 'I believe the child is a natural fool; believe me, if all of you are going to pamper her into criminalhood, *I* shall find an opportunity to get her alone later, don't you worry,' and she didn't stop threatening until the poor little thing had her hair, yes, her hair, wet with tears. Little Jack, having such a sensitive nature, was soon hysterical as his little companion, and then what a scene we did have, and how long it went on, until we finally convinced him it wasn't his fault; he was not old enough to act as host when the bad fairy came to the party uninvited. (You remember that fairy, Edith. We used to call Martha Scott, with her elastic face as long as she was, the Bad Fairy of the Fourth Form, the way she always used to appear in our doorways before examinations and stare at us like a prophetic angel, determined to spoil the day for everyone.)

"Moreover, I do not believe Lettie will ever resign herself to what she believes to be the greatest insult of her life, and perhaps that is just what it is, since it was an insult to her vanity, and I believe vanity is her animating principle. I *do* remember how you used to cry when people accused you of vaingloriousness, and how Nellie and I used to stick to you, and you know, we never would have, Edith, not with Nellie's being a minister's daughter, if we hadn't believed the others were wrong. But if Nellie was here, I tell you she would not say one word, not one word, in your granddaughter's defense.

"Now, you are their true grandmother, Edith, and you have responsibilities to the others, not just to Lettie, who was the first to arrive with her bill of complaints. You always used to say you did the very best you could, and I guess you will have a chance to do that now. Hovering on the brink of the grave as we are, we cannot afford to have extra bad marks set on our slates, can we, Edith? The truth of it is that William and Ella have become as close as John and Edna used to be, and separating them, even thinking of such a thing, would be, in my mind, the same as contemplating murder. Ella knows little of Boston, Edith, but with you as her teacher, she will learn quickly. She is a very independent and very strong girl. William is even stronger and more intelligent, but he knows cows, cows, and more cows. It would not be hard to make him miserable for the length of his stay there, and he would endure it all for Ella's sake (you know how she loves you, although she never *professes* quite so much as her auburn-haired sister), but when they returned here, and they do plan to, William would never forgive any of you, and Ella would naturally cling to him. It would be a terrible rift in the family, and one which, at our age, I would not care to see.

"The case is more delicate with Martin and Minnie, Edith, and I only hope that, at your advanced age, you will be able to cope with it. She is a farm girl through and through, although she is quite amazingly beautiful, and delicate as can be. She could certainly pose as the doomed heroine of any number of plays, but I doubt she would do it, she is so shy. She needs bringing out, and not in the ordinary way; at a party, for example, I believe she would be found dead of strained nerves by the end of the evening. Edith, you must be her fairy godmother. I do not see how she can possibly endure the three years in Boston without your assistance. If you could make things livable for her (mind, I am not asking you to attempt the impossible, and make a fish waltz in air), Edna would never forget you for it. You know how you have kept on sorrowing over the years because of your relations with your only daughter, but even you must admit she has done everything in her power to make both you and Mr. Siddons (and you know she never had much love for him) as happy as she possibly could. I suppose you remember, because you have always been a grateful person; that was always one of your most endearing qualities, if not one of your silliest; we used to joke about how grateful for trifles you were. And do remember how Mr. Siddons won his most important prizes both here and in England for work he did in the old house on our farm, and that was all Edna; I had nothing to do with his installation here. Not that I was against it, of course; I simply never thought of it.

"Oh, Edith, I do not want to sound like a pale imitation of our beloved Nellie, but you know how impossible it is to stop the planets in their course, and these two courtships are moving on with the irresistible grandeur of two small planets, each with its own intentions. Changing their course, well, you see, my dear, it would be impossible if not sinful. When nature chooses, and experience places its seal, there is nothing left for us but to obey. I know how many hours Edna has spent crying into her pillow when John has been on rounds, and why? Out of remorse for the way she treated your Mr. Siddons. She was too young to know any better, she cried, tears streaming down her face. Edith, *will* you be outdone by your daughter, and worse, will you make the same mistake for which you resented her so bitterly?

"Well, my dear, I suppose, if all else fails, I can take you up on your invitation to visit Boston, and manage to remain most of the three years, with time off for good behavior on holidays"—how Edith would dread *that,* she thought—"but surely I can rely on you to manage your own grandchildren. I can go to *my* grave saying I have done the best with them I could all these years, and now, Edith, dear, I am afraid it is your turn. And you will have the best of it, too. Don't think I am not jealous of you, dear friend. Having watched them grow from yellow balls into the lovely creatures they are now, taking their place in the world, like new marble statues in the drafty museum we call this world, and you will be the one to see it. Only think of it, Edith! Martin a doctor like his father! And such a gentle, loving creature. Nor will he have to suffer as my brother John has, for he will have a companion in William; they intend to open a practice together, and should anything happen to John, what satisfaction it will be to Martin to know he is carrying on his father's great work.

"And to Edna, too; it will give her something to go on for. I cannot shake the feeling of terror I have for her should anything happen to my brother. So you see, Edith, what a grand scheme you were the sower of. Your one seed has led to all these children and all these destinies; your one cracked little egg has brought forth such a flock of chickens. And is it right, again, as Nellie would say, for the hen to push all of the eggs out of the nest and warm only one? For that is what they all are, eggs, still, and we do not know how they will turn out, and really, it will be years before we do. And think how terrible you will feel if you take Lettie under your wing and give the others cold comfort and the shadow, only to find her turning her back on you, as she seems quite capable of doing, if it suits her, for she does care about what suits her—deeply.

"In memory of dear Nellie, Edith, I beg you to hide whatever prejudices you may have against the Moffats (for, after all, was her family of any better standing than theirs, really? And did we owe them anything, except for the fact they created dear Nellie? I tell you, we owe the Moffats everything, Alice in particular. She has seen Edna through some black times. She chased away that black streak she inherited from her father. I tell you, she is as good at that as any cat after a honey-covered rat) and try to make the two our children have chosen as happy as possible. They are warmhearted, Minnie and William, and they shall never forget your efforts, nor will Martin or Ella; they are all so loyal, really, I do not know where it comes from. You would think each of their spouses was a country, they are so patriotic about them. You stand in the way of that, Edith, and you might as well fight Civil Wars on two fronts. I do not mean to say, either, that you should permit Lettie to drown while the rest of you float merrily off on a raft, but I beg you not to forget them. I know you will regret their lack of social status, but they will make it up to you, and, as I said before, if they do not have such standing when they arrive, I am certain, with your training, they will have it when they return.

"I am sure John has written you of my dreadful illness; I did not expect to see another winter, really, so all these things are very much on my mind, and I know I should gain so in strength if I knew once again I had you as my ally." Ten paused and looked up. The afternoon was moving along. This, she thought, looking at the letter, was not so bad; Edith was very vulnerable, really. It was all a matter of knowing which old ivory keys to play. It was possible, she knew, to produce harmony out of Edith's actions, although Edna would never believe such a thing. So she continued writing.

Edna drove up through the drifts of snow to Alice's, her horse picking his experienced way through the shallow places, stopping and refusing to proceed before places of danger. "Well, Alice," she said, shaking herself loose from some late-flurrying snow, "how are you?" "Is your horse tethered?" Alice asked blackly. "Naturally; I wouldn't want to try walking home in this. How are you?" "Better not ask; you should have come earlier, before the day got its claws into me." "What on earth is the matter?" Edna asked, sinking down on a chair. "Oh, you wouldn't understand"; Alice glared down at the table. "I'm sorry, Edna; I didn't mean that the way it sounded." "Well, at least tell me what happened; I'll nod in all the right places." "Even if you don't know what I'm talking about?" "Especially then."

"Well, you can't see it from here, but we have a new guest," Alice began; "it's called an apple tree. It blew right into George's room last night; he woke up twittering like a vulture on a branch, and more scared than the bird that was stupid enough to fly in the window. And we just finished papering that wing; it's been a dirty mess for two months here, dust and mortar," she went on tearfully, "and now we have an apple tree for an ornament, and the wind whistling through the whole wing. No one else wants to be there. Well, Edna, it's more than a human can be expected to bear."

"What else?" "What else! What else! Well you may ask," she went on, furious. "That tree was only the beginning. The minute I saw it was an apple tree. All bad things start with apples. I should have known it was only the beginning." Edna looked down at her lap, hiding a smile. "Well, our old cat, Jumps, she's taken to eating eggs. Howard is threatening to shoot her, and I told him he might as well save his bullets and I'd stand in back of her and he could shoot both of us with one ball, and now he won't come out of the outhouse and says the farm can look after itself for all he cares. So the boys, and your Martin, too, are down in the barn and all over the place, and every five minutes in here, and then William says the well smells something awful, and he's sure something fell in it and died, and I tell you, I wouldn't be disappointed to hear what fell in was Mr. Moffat himself.

"Then someone comes by and just has to tell me the little Taylor child died deaf and paralyzed, and how lucky I was with Minnie, and the best of families have the worst problems; the Probsts' oldest son and daughter have parted. Oh, she announced that with enthusiasm, that some old friend was the curse.

"Then Howard came out of the privy just long enough to threaten me with selling Trick, our farm dog, the one who counts the cows when they come in? And if he doesn't get them all, he goes out into the fields and chases them down? And now some lunatic from New York has taken a fancy to Trick and wants to buy him for two hundred dollars, and Howard is actually thinking about it. No, he's threatening to do it, too, and he's as lame as a half-dead horse; he'll freeze to death hunting down one of those creatures. Then someone came by and stopped at the gate and wouldn't be satisfied until I came out and half froze so I could hear Fred Field's child had probably died; she wasn't sure, but she thought so. She thought I would just want to know. And then the boys took off to dig trenches, trenches in this snow, because of incendiaries; did you know"—she glared at Edna as if she were the party responsible—"that five buildings and two barns in Williamsville have burned to the ground in the last two nights? Well, they're trying to build up a snow reservoir, whatever that is, to protect against incendiaries." "That's terrible." "There's nothing terrible about reservoirs; what's terrible is the fires." "Oh," Edna said; "I thought that was what I meant."

"And," Alice went on, "we were lucky enough to be treated to a long visit by Lois Ann, who couldn't get to the factory, so she decided to come here and twist some threads. She wanted"—she paused—"to share some of her 'deeper thoughts' with us. They all turned out to have to do with death, especially Hal's. You don't want to hear about that, though." "Actually, I do." "I should have known." "Well, what did she say?"

"Well, what didn't she say? Actually, she didn't say anything. She had most of it written down in that horrid journal of hers, and she read it out to us as if it were the sacred text, and then I got on my ear, and lit into her for picking on wounds, and Howard got into a cat fight with me, and back into the privy. Well, anyway, the only good part of all of it is that she gets sick headaches all the time now on Sundays, and if you want to know what I think, I think God is squeezing her head like an orange for being so religious and driving everyone else out of the fold.

"Well, the dear lady's journal. She didn't start right out with it, though; I tell you, Edna, you've found me in a very depressed state. She went on and on about the oldest Taylor girl; the bell tolled this morning, she didn't know for whom, but then she found out, alas; imagine being buried on a day like today, with the ground frozen so hard, she thought it was a terrible thing, but she supposed it was better than being packed on ice the way Hal was, someone watching over him all the last few days to keep the flies off him, even before he was dead, and this was all introduction.

"It's tedious enough out of doors, isn't it?" she asked Edna, as if suddenly seeing her there. "Oh, I don't know; the snow's flying rather merrily about, I thought." "I'm glad someone has something to be merry about," Alice said, gloomily looking out the window; "the world is still there, is it?" "Afraid so." "I miss the teams of city boarders; they always stop and say something nice about my flowers, but now, it's all funeral processions, and who knows who's in the caskets? Howard's mother's been carrying on because she has no salt pork to grease pans, and nothing else will do; there were five tramps here last night, and I didn't like the look of them, either. I refused to let them stay, and Howard said I was getting pretty peculiar; there are times, really, there are, when I wonder why I ever married that man. I should have known better after I met his sister." She tapped the table so vigorously her fingers produced a small call to arms. "I expect I'll do my Christmas celebrating washing," she announced, looking out the window again; "old Boreas has been roaring so long I'm sick of his music. 'The bourne from which none returns,'" she exploded. Edna looked at her, quizzical.

"Well," Alice explained, "Lois Ann would make Hal's death the theme for the death of my first child." "Florence?" "No, not Florence; it was well over twenty years ago, but still, I don't care to be reminded of it, especially by Old Lemon Face. If she said, 'For it is as if the rose had climbed our garden wall, and bloomed on the other side, once more I would have gone out for an ax. She's just getting even with me because her middle son isn't over the fever complications yet, but I tell you, I can't endure it." "I never could bear her; she's not one of 'my particular friends.' " "Well, when she picks up a phrase, it has a friend for life," Alice snorted; "and the clothes froze on the line, and what with Lois Ann in the house, you'd think you were already in the land of the haunted. Well, Howard, he's a big help, isn't he? He says if I'm not used to her yet, I'm never going to be, and that's the long and short of it." "What about the journal?" "Oh, please. I don't want another case on my hands." "You know you don't have to worry." "You are asking to hear this? Don't say you didn't order your own meal.

"Look." She held up the offensive object. "She even left it here for self-study, such a wonderful opportunity for me, that's what she told me. 'Oh! The day! The crushing blow! The terrific realization that Hal was dead! The innocent! How hard to believe it. He did not rally at all from the bite. After all things were in readiness for his last moments on the surface of this earth, he was taken down for a last look at his face, innocent in life, and lovely in death, for he looked very natural, and was indeed beautiful, even though a man, he was beautiful, for he was one of Christ's chosen. What a weight of sadness hangs over everything. Oh! What a changed state of things! What a weight for all to carry! Ten had one of her poor turns in the morn, but is better again this evening, as she has been every day since her dear brother died. She is taking no solid food, but keeps in bed. And everyone sick at the Moffats' and the Steeles'.' " ("Everyone?" Edna said, looking up; "isn't that an exaggeration?") " 'I am the only one at present that is able to come and go regularly. Such a number of invalids in the families and with such a collection of strange complaints.

" 'And the hopes of the young blighted; ashes filling the path to the altar that should be covered with tender blooms of roses.' (In November, Edna?) 'It seems too bad after all they have endured to have this new blow come. And Freddie' (that was my first child, Edna) 'has been dead twenty-four years today. It seems so hard to realize that he would have been twenty-four had he lived.' And you know, Edna," she broke off her narrative, "Howard will not let us say a word while she runs on at the mouth." She began reading again. " 'I must find some flowers to put upon poor Freddie's grave, when it seems the others have forgotten him.' How do you like that?" Alice exclaimed. " 'Ah, what a cruel world it is! Just two months since Mrs. Ward was buried, and all the mortal frame of that dear sweet girl was deposited in the burial ground.' Can you imagine anyone, anyone, describing Mrs. Ward that way? And I had to sit still and listen to it, even though the bottom of my ash barrel just fell out and I had all that cleaning up to do, but I didn't dare mention it, before the ashes became the theme for another sermon. Well, let me get this over with.

" 'But I must return to my theme; how difficult it is,' " Alice read out, " 'for the mind to concentrate upon the awful solemnities of life. I stopped, of course, to see the face of dear Hal, and how much more natural he looked than he did in life, so disfigured by the ravages of his disease.' She interrupted herself here to tell us that Mr. Ross's wife gave birth to a dead child and it weighed ten pounds and was two days old when it died, and five when it was buried.

"'I was deeply impressed,'" Alice resumed reading, "'with the floral remembrances daily sent to poor dear Hal and many of them really beautiful, not just bunches thrown together. Ah! How soon we may all be covered with such remembrances!' She'll live to be two hundred if she lives another day," Alice sighed. "'Just yesterday, Mr. Knowlton's mother was killed by a runaway horse.' And just today," Alice said, looking up, "our colt ran away with our wagon and went flat against a tree, smashing everything up, including itself and Martin, who's black and blue on one whole side, and the colt's ruined for the selling now, but we must not mind," she said bitterly, "such little tragedies. 'Ah! When I think of Freddie, so long dead, I cannot help but remember the dream I always have in connection with him. Why is it,' and here she always pauses," Alice told her. "'Why is it whenever I think of him, I dream someone close to me has died, my dear son Phineas was parted from me just last night? I woke up bathed in tears. Oh! It is a peculiar dream, but I hope not a prophetic one.'

"Now Sennet's cows have gotten into our fields again, and are trampling the rose bushes," Alice said, interrupting her narrative. "Howard came out of the outhouse long enough to take the wagon down the hill and lose a wheel, so you can just imagine. And we have to clean the pantry, and you know, Edna, that is the worst part of housekeeping, and on top of it, Mrs. Chapman up on the Hill is sick, and I'll have to take my turn watching with the rest of them, and George went out to look into the sap house to see to it, and see if it needed cleaning out for the spring, and found Mr. Skunk there. Do you think," she asked, "I will *ever* get to the end of washing old pants? Oh, well, I don't really expect an answer to that. And the sewing machine has gotten bewitched again; there's nothing I can look at," she cried, "that doesn't bring me to the edge of distraction!

"Bradshaw's old horse fell down in the road right outside our house, you know, and Howard helped to get him up. Poor old horse. Then some rowdies took our gate from the front fence and put it somewhere down the road; a lot of good it did them, I hope. A lot of chance

I have of regulating this house. The straw I needed to fill the beds? Well, it's moldy, or will be soon, thanks to that apple tree, and we had to cook the old rooster, so I guess his scratching days are over. Oh, I tell you, Edna, I feel more like quitting home than working." The poor woman burst into tears. "Isn't there *anything good* that's happened?" Edna asked. "Well, none of us got struck by lightning, or the horses and cows, either." "Alice, what *is* the matter?"

"Oh, to tell the truth, I suppose it is Lois Ann and all that business about Freddie; I don't know why her passage about last year affected me so," she sniffed. "Read it." Alice picked up the little black book as if it were a live coal. "Some people ask for whippings," she warned, beginning. " 'The year that has just departed has had much more in store of pleasure for me and I feel profoundly grateful that our family circle has not yet been invaded by that great enemy of all mortals, and that I, personally, have enjoyed that boon of health. Sometimes I think I have more than is deserved, that is, in earthly comforts, and then again, it comes to my mind that circumstances may easily be altered (so it seems to me), that my existence might be far pleasanter and better than it is now. But believing that whatever is, is right, I become somewhat contented with my lot and trust that in some happier sphere somewhere, sometime, the fruition of our highest and best desires may be fulfilled, and then we may discern that the past has been all for the best.' "

"What," Edna asked, "was so dreadful about *that*? It hardly sounds as if it compares to the day's events." "Don't you see?" Alice wailed; "it's as if she put *my* thoughts into words." "Oh, nonsense," Edna exclaimed; "you don't think that way at all. You're much more cheerful and happy on this earth than your sister-in-law. What is getting you into such a depressed state?" Alice looked at her, a child, caught fooling with the best china. "Everyone getting married," she blurted out. "Everyone getting married? Is there something wrong?" Edna asked, anxious; "have any of them had second thoughts?" "That's just the trouble; they haven't." "I don't see what's so dreadful about that, either. You'll still have George and the two little girls. Amanda and Permelia?" "I remember their names," Alice sniffed. "Well, then?" "Well, then, it makes me feel so old! You're twelve years younger. You don't have to feel old; besides, how could you, looking the way you do?" "Alice," Edna said, "they *will* be coming back here after medical college, and they don't just say that now. If you have no objections to the matches, I don't see what you can do but resign yourself to it." Alice glared. Well, and what should she expect, with that Lois Ann on her errands of horror?

"Alice," she said abruptly, "if you're upset because Freddie won't be here to see the weddings, you're a religious woman. You ought to know he'll be here in spirit." "Do you think so?" "Certainly." "Then I might as well tell you William said he intended to talk to his father and then to Dr. Steele; I assume he meant about marrying your daughter." "I suppose so. I just hope he can find him long enough to ask him. I never thought John's rushing around so would prevent him from marrying off one of his daughters." "And Martin is going to talk to Howard; *if* he comes out of the outhouse." "Well, everything will be better when it's all settled." "Won't that just bring Lois Ann out of the woodwork?" Alice worried; "if there's one thing she can't bear, it's seeing other people happy." "Then I don't think you should let her win this card game by letting her make *you* unhappy. After all, she'd rather see *you* depressed than one of the children. She is like that." "I suppose so; oh, the wind's gotten into the north corner again." "White, the color of weddings," Edna said, cheerful. "Well, it isn't something to go into mourning about, is it?" Alice asked. "Hardly." "We have to plan; I don't know anything about these things. I'm going to disgrace you."

"Well, I know some important things; Jack hovers around doors so. He told me they want to be married at one of our houses and keep the ceremonies very private." "Will your mother agree to that?" Alice asked. "I don't see that she has any choice." "No. Well, it's a relief to know I won't have to learn being a society lady." "You're fine as you are. They consider me a disgrace, anyhow. I'm not sure my mother would want to take her chances with *me*. It will all be over with before you know it." "That's what Dr. Steele always said about the babies," Alice murmured. "Come on, Alice," Edna coaxed. "Well, you be cheerful," she grumbled, "but before you know it, you'll be marrying Anna off." "Anna? She's waiting for the beloved Reverend Pierce."

"That man!" Alice exclaimed; "she should have some private meetings with his wife." "Fortunately," Edna said, "he's likely to expire before she's the right age. It's amazing how people forget how he disgraced himself in the war. William told us how he tried to hide himself under a leaf when a gun went off, and remember how happy they were to get a new military chaplain?" "It didn't get in the papers; no one believes it," Alice said, weary; "but tomorrow you'll read all about my ash barrel and the runaway colt; there's no justice in the world." "Providence, my dear, Providence," Edna teased. "If I never hear that word again, I shall die happy." "Well," Edna asked, "my house or yours?" "Considering that ours was just invaded by part of the orchard, I think it's a sign our house is not intended. And that's just fine, because I would only make a dreadful mess of it anyway." "Don't be an idiot." "Well, between Lois Ann, a skunk, a runaway, and the ash barrel, you mustn't expect much of me." "I must say, when you lump all those things together, it sounds as if Lois Ann and the skunk are just about the same." "Oh, dear, does it really?" Alice asked, finally smiling; "it's good it's settled about the children." "Isn't it? You sit still and I'll make the tea." "Now we'll all die of poisoning." "Well, I can do some things," Edna protested. "Just let me add the tea to the pot."

"It sounds like the boys are nerving themselves up right now," Edna told Ten that night; "I do wish you would write that letter," she said, jumping up, beginning pacing. "I bought something today." Ten barely looked over. "Well, it was rather large." "All right," said Ten, putting down her book, "what was it?" "A man from Rutland is selling out his daguerreotype shop, wagon and all." "And you're buying it." "The whole thing, including the wagon. It should get here tomorrow. Anyway, it's bought."

"I really think, Edna, you're going to *such* lengths to keep John out of the courts. Suicide isn't catching, is it? If John testifies in the same court your father practiced in, it doesn't mean he'll end the same way." "Do we have to wait for a man to commit suicide before we become alarmed? Isn't there some passage in the Bible about the watchman who falls asleep at the gates being responsible for the city's destruction? I'll ask Anna," she said, nervous. "It's nice to live with a walking Bible. I *still* think I'm right." "All right, all right," Ten muttered from her chair; "just stop that pacing. I'm not looking up, but the trouble is, you still cast a shadow." "At least you know I'm not a vampire." "What an enormous relief," her sister-in-law sniffed.

"Do *you* have any idea of when your brother is returning?" "My brother? Well, he asked the substitute to stay for three weeks, if that's any indication." "Why doesn't he just fall out a store window, the way Mr. Camp did last week, just get it over with?" Over her book, Ten shook her whole head. "You know, you're acting the same way my brother did when you were about to have Martin." "And I have just as good reason now as he did then." "Look, Edna"—she must be winding down; it was taking her longer and longer to cross the room— "you know if John is set on testifying at some of these cases, you won't be able to change his mind no matter how you dislike it, and then, if anything does happen, of the sort you're afraid of, whatever that is, I can't tell what, there will be a schism between you, and you won't be able to help him." Edna crossed the room again. "You know," Ten remarked, "you make quite a picture, pacing up and down with Archie there. He keeps his tail up the whole time. Have pity, for heaven's sake, on poor Archie's tail." Edna stopped, looked at the cat, walked two steps, and sank into a chair. "I haven't noticed," Ten said, "John tearing etiquette books out of your hands, although one might get the idea they might make a person morbid.

"I marked some passages in your favorite, *The Guideboard*. Listen," she ordered, beginning to read: " 'One thing is clear, that men are not so sure they are absolutely right in all their opinions and customs as they were when they knew less and were narrower in their range of observation. Increased knowledge not only makes them more tolerant but less sure that they are altogether right.' Then there is this extremely interesting passage on reciprocity. 'The great human law of life is mutual helpfulness.' And I found it quite interesting on the home: 'The inspiration of all labor comes from the home. There are our personal wants, the wants of our dear ones, and the tastes and pleasures of the whole. There is the companion we love and are glad to toil for; there is the baby we would die for, and the little boy who is our pride, and the little girl who is our joy, and the blessed old mother'—that must be me—'whom we venerate, and the grand old father whom we honor, all inmates and a part of our home'—sorry we couldn't oblige with a grandfather —'we toil for them and would think meanly of ourselves if we did not. It is called sacrifice to do this, to spend our life and strength for the dear ones at home, but we do not count it so. It is our life and joy. We feel the more manly and honored'—you make that 'womanly'—'the more we do our best to make a good home, and its inmates good and happy. This thing of toiling for home, how it sharpens one's wits, toughens one's muscles, magnifies one's brain, augments the forces of one's character, and quickens and enlarges all that is best. *It so happens,'* " she read with emphasis, " *'that man is not a plant that grows and fruits well in a hot bed. Frosts and storms, heat and cold, wet and drought, somehow, put qualities into him which he gets only in hard experiences; this home-making and home-keeping necessity, which seems to be upon us all, keeping us hard at work—in our push, enterprise, and power—is the key to all our good fortune.'

"I never thought the day would come," she said, looking at Edna over her spectacles, "when I would find comfort and sense in one of your books. But this," she said, refastening her spectacles, "I thought deserved particular attention. 'Everyone is most himself in his home, because there he is freest from restraint, least repressed and most spontaneous and natural.' Well, Edna, haven't you found that so?" Edna flushed. " 'He knows his home friends and they know him. They are used to each other and can bear with and help each other better than strangers. This sense of freedom and mutual understanding gives the essence of home feeling. The charm of feeling at home with home friends and home things is the delight of human life.' I suppose," she asked the air, "that John was always transported by your accompanying him on rounds, and it took no sacrifice at all for him to get used to you on the sickbed, or near the deathbed, either. Five children, my dear! Five children!

"It seems to me," Ten went on, "that *your husband* would never absent himself from his duties so long unless there was some powerful need in him to testify at those courts. People do what they have to, don't they? Where has your perspective gone? Well, it's not surprising if it's gone off after that epidemic, and now with two of the girls going off, but really, Edna, John never kept you on so tight a rein. It isn't the fair thing to do to him." "But why," Edna cried, "why can't he just stay here and do his photography? He's gotten so good at it, especially the double pictures; people have come all the way here from Boston to see them." "I understand your losing your balance," Ten said, "but I'd certainly blame you if you don't try to get it back." "I *am* trying; why can't you see that?" "Because you're trying to avoid the inevitable; well, really, Edna," she asked, "isn't that what you're doing? There's something he's looking for in that courtroom and he'll find it if it kills him. Well, when your stomach became the inevitable, John didn't try aborting the babies." "The two cases are hardly comparable." "Aren't they? I think they are precise parallels." Edna fell silent.

"Well, I've gone along with his photographs, no matter how morbid they seemed to be growing. His last ones are chilling; he's learned to expose one part of a plate at a time without leaving a mark or a seam—that's what I call it—to divide the two portions, and he has a man gazing at himself, as if he were looking into the mirror, each face with a different expression, and his latest is horrifying, absolutely it is; there's a man, I think he used Fred Camp, lying flat on his back with his hands folded over his chest as if dead, and then, on the other half of the plate, is the same man staring down at what looks like his dead body, and somehow, he made the picture look like the dead man was much older than the living one. Then there's another one which I can't get out of my mind. It's just a field in early spring, one of those immense fields that slopes and is divided by a rock fence, and a man sitting on the far end, where the fence disappears over the horizon. He's smoking, or something like that. He's too far away to tell, but it's the loneliest picture I ever saw. Well, I suppose I *could* call those things morbid, too, but I don't mind them somehow. Not even the picture he took of the six-week-old twins who died of

the fever. Their mother wanted them photographed on a
bear rug their father shot, the bear, not the rug. John
thought there was something very revealing about that."

"Well, think about it," Ten said; "you don't mind the
pictures because you like them; they fit in with what you
think. And it's obvious enough, isn't it, John's trying to
express some view of life he has through them. After all,
he's spent most of his life saving other people, and the
only record of his effort is a funeral procession, or a
moving body, and that's finally commemorated by a blank
stone with a name and some dates. He must want to preserve more. He remembers so much about them, and when
he goes, those memories go, and then there's just family
to remember, and we've all heard him say often enough
that strangers remember longer than people in the house.
And you said something about what he does when he
mounts the daguerreotypes, I wasn't paying much attention, but it was something about leaving messages in them,
or messages in bottles, or their being like Jonah and the
whale; I didn't have the faintest idea of what you were
talking about. I was trying, too, but I was so feverish at
the time, it was beyond me."

"He sticks little notes in back of the pictures; he writes
down the people's names and their birth dates, and death
dates, if they have any, and if anyone in the family wants
to write anything, they write it down, and sometimes he has
a struggle fitting all the epitaphs, or sentiments—that's
what he calls them when he's with the others—into the
back of the cases. I didn't know why he did it at first; I
thought surely Mrs. Gibbons would remember who her
husband was without a note stuck to the back of his
picture as if it were a book she was sure to lose in select
school, but then John said something about how, with
luck, they could last five hundred years, and he rather
liked the idea of imitating the Egyptians and burying the
dead with all their loved ones around them, in spirit, anyway.

"Well, it reminded me of Jonah," Edna said, "and you
know how the story ends with God telling Jonah he
won't destroy Nineveh, because the people were so ignorant they couldn't tell their left hands from the right,
'and also much cattle'? Then the cattle would have to go,
too? I always thought that was the best part of the Bible,

because if it showed anything about the world, it showed that whoever dreamed up its creator understood that only someone who loved all the little things in it would have made it this way. Even if he had two left hands and was half blind. Well, and now John is taking pictures of cats and dogs, and farmers holding their best horses. You'd be surprised how many men would rather be photographed with their horses than their wives, and dead children in their caskets. Last week, after he developed a huge one of those, he spent hours burnishing the plate of the Castou baby in its coffin; it was propped up, you know, for viewing against the side of the house—they were keeping it there because it was so cold outside—he said daguerreotype was the right name for them; they were, the pictures, I mean, recording the real war. He was sure there was some purpose in the inventor bearing that name. But I can't understand," she finished sadly, "what the court can do to explain *that* war."

"Why don't you just wait and see?" Ten suggested; "hasn't it occurred to you," she said slowly, "that largely he's seemed more and more torn between the pictures and the people? Well, Edna, as you say, the pictures have a chance of lasting five hundred years, but the people spoil a great deal faster. And he just lines the pictures up on his shelf; you know, when I went in there, I've been in exactly twice, they looked very like trophies to me, as if no matter what happened to the people, he still had shelves and shelves full of little sparks of life in his cottage, and I thought, it was a silly thought, perhaps he was hoping if he could collect enough of those sparks he would ignite a good sun, a warm sun, one which wouldn't let those dreadful erasures happen, first from memories, then from life altogether.

"Well, death always makes me think of my mother folding raisins inside her dough. They seemed to disappear so easily, and then when they swelled up and jumped out, if they did, we always ate them up first. I used to think the raisins were like people and the dough was like the earth, and after Ed died, I thought if I went crazy I would start seeing little mouths in the earth everywhere, like traps, you know, just snapping at everyone's heels, trying to get them into their stomachs, as if they were food. And you know how blood blackens after death? After Ed was gone,

I was sure that was why the earth stayed dark instead of growing paler every year.

"If there had been anything I could have done then to fight it, death, I would have done it. But I realized it couldn't be done and I gave it up. I'm not sure," she considered, "you can go on being a good doctor, a really good doctor, and come to the same conclusions about death I came to." "But the pictures seem to be drawing him to that same conclusion," Edna worried. "I know," Ten said; "perhaps the court is the element which will resolve the conflict." "Good Lord, I never thought of that!" "Well, you can't be expected to think of everything, can you, dear?"

A loud crash interrupted their reading; the pendulum of the grandfather clock, previously under discussion, had dropped straight to the bottom of the wooden case. "What next?" Edna asked, picking it up and fastening it back on. "Something," Ten said. "Well," Edna sighed, supporting her back with the palms of her hands unawares, "how are William and Martin going to tell John their intentions if he's going to be holed up in Boston for three weeks? *We* have to make plans, at any rate." "The trains are still running." "What?" "The trains are still running. Put William and Martin on the cars. They can talk to your husband in Boston just as well as they can here, and they can come back with presents. I think they should do that in any case, and it will be an easy dose of Edith they'll get, too; she's never happier than when she's guiding some ignorant goat through that maze of stores and then letting them collapse and gather what wits they have left at the Parker House." "Heaven forbid anything should stop Mother in her appointed course to the Parker House," Edna agreed. "*Lunch* at the Parker House," Ten mimicked mischievously; "in time to finish and take the three forty-five back to Brattleboro." "You *are* bringing back horrible memories." "Well, if you can just remember all John's been through, and how he put himself through so much more for you, everything will be just fine." "You make me feel ashamed." "Good." "I'd like their wedding to be a little fancier than ours was," Edna said, changing the subject. "Yours was pretty fancy; as I remember, you complained about it."

"Never mind dredging the river altogether; *our* wedding was a summer wedding; this one, or these two, will take place in the dead of winter." "Oh, we can think of something. Your mother can ship cartloads of flowers from Boston and Mr. Garibaldi can start the minute we tell him, and then we could entertain everyone by taking them on a tour of this whole house, right from the medieval torture chamber to the world of the future where people fly around like bumblebees." "Don't make fun of the house," Edna said; "we'll have to cordon off most of it to avoid embarrassing the Moffats." "Well, Edna, how special *can* you make the wedding? Any wedding? We can have a choir and the last word in wedding gowns and the important part comes after that's all over; you remember that part, I guess." "I guess I do." "Then stop worrying; we just won't have the band from the firehouse and everything will be just fine. Leave it to Tivoli; that's what he always said, and believe me, I've come to trust him. We can get him to make something special. How about cakes shaped like historical figures?" "You do have the best ideas." "Well, the Moffats would be impressed by that even if I wouldn't." "I suppose it's better than little cakes made up to look like corpses." "Bite your tongue," Ten chided. "We *could* have a few made up to look like Jimmie," Edna said. "You see how contagious the idea is once you catch it?" Ten said happily. "A regular epidemic, Ten, dear."

1869

Three years later, Martin and William returned, doctors and married men. Both the elder Steeles and Moffats argued that it was not right for newly married couples to take up residence with their in-laws; for at least several more years, the two couples each ought to have their privacy. Nevertheless, William and Martin were excited at the prospect of three doctors residing under one roof, teaching and learning from one another, so another wing was duly added to the house. Edna, John, and Ten, meanwhile, found themselves with four new additions to the family—although, as Edna remarked, it was a miracle they had *only* four to contend with. That state of affairs wouldn't last, Ten predicted. The three intervening years had brought many insignificant changes in the family and some significant ones. Mrs. Siddons had been far more cooperative in dealing with her new in-laws, the Moffats, than anyone had expected.

When John heard of Ten's letter, he said it all reminded him of St. Paul and his threats to visit the Thessalonians, or whichever city was misbehaving at the time, the mere threat, as he remembered it, bringing everyone to their Christian senses. Mrs. Siddons, it developed, had her hands full with Minnie, although not precisely in ways she anticipated. Oddly, Minnie, more easily than William, fit into Boston society as if she had always been there, primarily because she became Mr. Siddons' extremely famous model. His statues of her in various mythical poses had become all the rage, and six months before her final return to Williamsville, he had personally supervised the crating of Minnie, turning into a tree, all two thousand pounds of which was to be shipped to an eccentric collector in Reno, Nevada. Her pictures, or at least marble likenesses of her, were in every magazine the Steeles opened. Why, as Ten exclaimed, there she was right in the middle of a garden in her precious *Floral Cabinet*.

Minnie, her languid, almost liquid figure, her delicate cameo face, which would someday round into the apple shape of Alice's, was actually becoming a style which other artists found worth copying, so that Mr. Siddons, who had always lamented his lack of original ideas, and the sporadic nature of the attacks of inspiration he longed for, now suddenly found himself regarded as an original, and an original worth copying. At the sight of the copies, he would regularly go into rages. Then Mrs. Siddons would soothe him, saying, "Come, come, dear; the struggling must be allowed to pay their homage, no matter how perverted, and there is no point, really, in playing into their hands by dying of sheer aggravation." Then she would promptly lead him back to their town house, where he would instantly prostrate himself on his green velvet fainting couch, which, he insisted to William and Martin, was indispensable to professional men of all schools, since it gave such remarkable support to the neck.

But Minnie, for all her cooperativeness, and for all the pleasure of being petted by high society, whose motives she of course supposed disinterested, if not pure, and only what she would expect of people of higher spiritual and intellectual pursuits, was still seriously weakened by the fever. Mrs. Siddons, after witnessing a fainting fit at a formal ball, decided something would have to be done and that the child must rest in other surroundings; yes, indeed, she told Mr. Siddons, poor Minnie worried more than dear Martin ever would. It simply never *occurred* to Martin that he might fail, while Minnie, having seen little but failure all her life, could barely swallow from the moment an examination was announced, and there was nothing William, or Ella, or Martin could do to calm her nerves. So it was up to them. After all, Minnie *had* put herself out sitting all those hours in the studio.

Surely, she quizzed Mr. Siddons, he had *some* propertied relations in the country. Well, Mr. Siddons said, thinking, he did in fact have an uncle and aunt who had extensive property in Westminster. That would be, he told Edith, his Uncle Fayette and Aunt Lavinia Bates. But, he said, brow furrowing, it had been almost thirty years since he had been to see them. On the other hand, he turned it over, they had never really considered him normal, and he had gone along with the family's belief that artists were always aberrant. Didn't she, Edith, think that was a rather peculiar way of thinking of things?

Edith expressed herself rather violently on the subject of the property in Westminster; the phrasing with which they discussed him could be taken up later. Well, he admitted, they did write him every three months; it was that kind of family, he said, as if they were some kind of disgrace. Once you belonged to them, you might as well try to change your skin color as abdicate. Edith sighed. For him, the Civil War might as well have been a cloud formation. Still, she did not believe in criticizing one's husband, especially over political views. If one began on that, she thought, it might even end in the divorce courts. The courts; she shuddered.

"Well, and can you write to them?" she asked. Mr. Siddons, whose vision was clear enough to see his wife's intentions—she would simply ship Minnie back home unless her health improved, and then what would become of his statues?—wrote immediately to Aunt Lavinia and Uncle Fayette. They responded with such enthusiasm her husband was positively intimidated, but when Edith suggested *she* go down alone with Minnie, he hurriedly ordered the servants to pack all their things. If there was one thing he did not need, he told himself, it was domestic discord, discord of any kind for that matter, anything which might cause his chisel to slip in its crucial work.

Did Martin have any objections to their taking Minnie off in this way? No, he certainly did not; he was worried enough about her health. There, Mr. Siddons thought, went his last hope. They duly set off for the Bateses', were met at the station by their covered wagon, a Miss Whidden in attendance and several other relations under her charge, all of whom were relaxing from one strain or another. They spent a great deal of time blackberrying and raspberrying with the others until he found the pastime wearisome, and there was no ignoring the fact the bushes scratched his hands intolerably, and no, he would not consider Uncle Fayette's suggestion he borrow a pair of Aunt Lavinia's garden gloves, even if his hands were just the same size.

He thereupon retreated to a hammock in the shadow of the woods, sketching the old house, drawing curlicues around the margins of every sheet of his drawing pad. No, it was not so unpleasant, and Minnie did seem to be strengthening; undoubtedly he was wrong thus to torment himself over time passing him by. His wife was right, after all; it would never do to have his model die and all society turn against him as the murderer of that beautiful innocent, killed by his selfish, uncontrollable ambition. And the irony of it was, he thought, Minnie was completely unaware of what importance she had assumed, and would continue to assume, in the public mind. She was like a spring leaf; all the publicity evaporated from her marble skin like morning dew. Well, he thought happily, Westminster was bringing out his literary talents. Who would have thought he had any in that line? He purred away in the sun like a contented cat.

Minnie and Edith, meanwhile, drifted down the winding country paths in their white muslin dresses and huge white straw hats like two visions loosed from a book, each carrying a little straw basket fitted out with little silver shovels and a pair of fancy scissors, the handles elaborately carved with bunches of grapes, snipping at anything, wild flowers or berries, which caught their fancy, and then making perfect sauces of themselves in the ancient kitchen, attempting, to the endless amusement of Aunt Lavinia, to can currant jelly, blackberry jelly, peaches, pears, whatever they could get their hands on. Mr. Siddons found their second attempt perfectly sickening since they had persuaded themselves to try using honey instead of sugar, and honey, honey, honey was what everything tasted like.

It was stunning, he thought, how nothing had changed here in the last thirty years, as if time itself had stopped, and when Edith and Minnie floated back, their baskets full of red and yellow flowers, his eyes filled with real tears; why, he had not seen anything like that since his mother died. He became quite fond of the rhythm of the weeks, or lack of it, he could not decide which, one of which was no different than the other, except, perhaps, for differences in the weather. On Sundays, they all drove off to the Methodist church. When it rained, they stayed inside and read newspapers aloud to one another. On some days, they attempted driving up to the mountain house, getting down from the wagon before they reached the top, walking up the rest of the way. It was usually too hazy for an extended view; then they would sit about for a while, drinking ginger ale, then start back along the carriage road, while the "gents," as Uncle Fayette called them, visited the stores, or not, as they pleased. It was, as he wrote William, a quiet, restful place, and a free and easy one, "as each can go his own way without interference from anyone."

Edith, at her age, had fallen in love with tennis, and the untended courts just suited her. He loved watching her. She avoided cracks as if there were eyes in the soles of her shoes, and she was graceful. It struck him all over again how graceful she was; she made it seem as if she floated through the thickening air to meet the ball. At night, the ladies sewed; he had never seen women so intent on embroidery, or so quiet so long. He was astonished at Edith's lack of boredom, although Minnie's happy acceptance of it was quite predictable. They drove to Princeton in an open carriage, going on one road, coming back on another. They went to Uncle Fayette's grandfather's house up on a high hill, a beautiful view of the brilliant and dim valleys, the house unoccupied, partly in ruins; then it was reading again in the old kitchen, tennis and blueberries, tennis and blueberries. A man could lose all ambition here, he thought comfortably.

They went to Athol to see another aunt his wife never knew he had; he was surprised at how fleshy she had become, and how old. She was so round-shouldered and her health so poor; she coughed continually. *He* would not consider life worth living, bent over like that, a birch that could not pick itself up. Still, it had been good to see her, although something of a strain, and he lay on the lounge the rest of that afternoon with a sick headache, while everyone else went about his business, picking berries, chasing after butterflies they called tennis balls. They sat on the old porch in the morning; they had suppers of crackers and berries and milk on the big flat near the wood house, sitting out until dark trying to keep comfortable. It was terribly sultry at times, and at such times, someone would invariably remark how much worse it must have been in the city. When it got chilly in the evenings, they put on warmer dresses and suits and lit a fire in the sitting room, looking into the flames for hours. Mr. Siddons found himself reading a great deal; he had read most of *Nicholas Nickleby* and showed every sign of having the capacity to finish it. This in itself, he thought, was remarkable, and a true measure of the profound effect Westminster was having upon him.

It had never occurred to him to wonder why he had never finished a worthy book before; he merely assumed he submerged himself so in his own branch of art he had time for none of the others, although, as a child, before his talent had made itself known, he had never once been detected reading anything which would not bring on a whipping if not studied on schedule. The last day there, they looked about the whole house, went out, played tennis again for the last time, everyone said that, and later played on the old piano in the old kitchen. A little before eight, soon after supper, they all left for Boston on the cars, Edith proudly carrying home the eight quarts of blueberries she and Minnie had picked. And Minnie was so much stronger; why, when they arrived, she could barely lift a tennis racket, much less chase after the ball, and poor Edith had been forced to stop every ten feet while she leaned against a tree as they sought after berries.

But by the time they went back—four whole weeks! how they had gone!—she could run around the courts like a mouse and walk up to the mountain house and back down without even losing the rhythm of her calm, regular breathing. Yes, the visit had been a success. Who would have thought, Mr. Siddons wondered, that the sight of the sun, after three damp, cloudy days, could be such an event? Yes, he decided, he had been spiritually renewed. Although, as the rural train rattled along through the picturesque scenery, he wondered what Edith really did have in mind; she and Aunt Lavinia had been thick as four Irishmen in a bed for the last two weeks. He had his suspicions about Edith's doings, but they were not under way more than four hours before she revealed the contents of those suspect conferences.

Aunt Lavinia did so want to meet the rest of the family, Edna and all the other children, the Moffat children as well. Now that Edna's children were growing up so fast, Westminster would be the perfect place for them, too, didn't he think so? Mr. Siddons, unaccustomed to changes in his routine, felt absolutely unstuck, wrenched from his familiar niche, as if he were a statue suddenly required to respond to swiftly moving events. Yes, he agreed dazedly, yes, that was a splendid idea. Perhaps it would never come up again, he comforted himself, settling in. But he knew that was synthetic comfort, since Edith was, he knew, nothing if not steady once she fixed on a course; that, he concluded, was undoubtedly what made her such a splendid navigator in the yacht races on the Charles. At any rate, he assured himself, lulled to sleep by the rhythm of the cars, it would not be coming up for a while. What would be coming up, he thought, surfacing partially, would be a visit to Williamsville. He did like Williamsville, he thought, closing his eyes, nodding off. Edith and Minnie smiled at him indulgently.

So the three years had passed peaceably, Edith thought, no more than that. They had been warm years, not at all what she had anticipated after that letter from Ten. Well, Ten; she did believe in preparing one for the worst. It was just as well, Edith decided, that she didn't try the opposite. That, she thought, would only lead to anti-climax, disappointment, possibly heartbreak.

Well, Ten had been right about Lettie. Lettie was a married woman of society for almost three years now, and so far had one child, which she promptly handed over to the nursemaids and then forgot. She produced it for Edna's amusement, but showed less interest in it than she would in a doll. She had done, Edith realized, swinging in a hammock at Westminster, exactly what Ten had said she would. She married as quickly as possible, and even to Edith, it seemed her principal object was to marry before her sister Ella. Fortunately for her, Edith thought, the senator had gotten to her first. He was, of the two suitors (the other was the New York lawyer), the more likely to put up with a beautiful porcelain doll adorning his house. No, she would never have believed she would come to see Lettie as so cold, so heartless. Why, one day, she even found herself mesmerized by her, a slightly younger image of herself, loosed from the looking glass. "There but for the grace of God go I." That was what she had heard herself whispering.

Edith knew Lettie had fastened onto the senator the first night she met him at a ball. She chattered on, Edith remembered, like a society macaw. "This is our dance, I think," her poor husband-to-be, Mr. Knowles, had said to her. "How did you guess that?" she asked; "surely you cannot read my card upside down?" And of course she was one of the principal sights of the evening, her magnificent white dress trimmed with pale yellow flowers, pale white butterflies pinned to quiver in her thick auburn hair.

She and Mr. Siddons, waltzing near them, overheard almost all their conversation. "How I envy that butterfly close to your ear," Mr. Knowles had whispered; "what a chance to whisper secrets, lucky butterfly!" To which her beloved granddaughter had answered, "Oh no, the butterfly is not so happy as you think; I shut it up in a velvet case when I go home lest I should lose it. You see how possessive and cruel I am? Now, *you* could not be shut up, for you would not like it, even if you could. Or perhaps"—she smiled—"unlike you, the butterfly may have no feeling, so it does not appreciate its happiness, a trait, I believe, characteristic of butterflies. You"—she batted her eyelashes ostentatiously—"*you* ought to know something about that." "Oh," Mr. Knowles answered, "you are kind enough to anticipate my future. I haven't found my wings yet. I believe I am still in a chrysalis state." "Then," said Letitia, for she was definitely Letitia now, "*you* are safer to hold, if not so pretty as my butterfly to keep in a velvet box, and I do not think"—she beamed up at him—"you could do better than remain a chrysalis for the present."

Of course, Edith thought, Lettie had the last word, and she had been lucky to have it, too, especially since the first thing she did upon arriving at Cedar Street was to head like a red setter for their dictionary, frantically looking up "chrysalis." Things had moved quickly to the wedding after that, so quickly she herself, even though forewarned, was positively startled. And she saw to it that hers was the most elaborate wedding possible. Why, Lettie insisted upon what was really a cathedral, not a church; only the Queen of England would call All Saints' Church by such a humble name. And All Saints' Church was nothing if not overwhelming, and it did not bother Lettie to convert to Catholicism, not in the slightest. She would as easily have converted to Mohammedanism if that suited her convenience.

Two hundred invitations, she remembered with a shudder, had been sent out for New Year's Day calls alone, and that was only the beginning. It was a work of time to get to the church and then inside it, thanks to the crush of people. The chancel, approximately the size of the city courthouse, had been elaborately decorated in white and green and was said never to have looked lovelier. It certainly never looked more elaborate. The bridal procession was headed by the entire choir of All Saints' Church, all in their black robes, all carrying bouquets, and everything sung to the *St. Matthew Passion*.

Well, no one could say the ceremony was not impressive, not with the Archbishop himself preaching the sermon and performing the service, although he did seem to be on an hourly salary, or celestial time, one or the other. The reception, which took place in Mr. Siddons' studios, was striking and unusual in every way, the statues, to her husband's horror, festooned with flowers, those which were capable of holding floral arrangements, most of them sporting the most elaborate wreaths for necklaces, crowned with the most expensive floral displays.

Lettie, Edith thought, looked more like a conquering queen than a happy bride standing under the floral arch of white and pink roses, receiving guests as if she were indeed a visiting monarch from a fabulous country. They left within forty minutes, Letitia apparently having concluded there was no point in spoiling a perfect impression with warmth or friendship of any kind.

And now she was living in Boston; the season in Washington, she decided, was too inconvenient for permanent residence, although she did spend most of the season there, enjoying the impression she made on her husband's political acquaintances and thriving on the homage the men so automatically paid her. Then, when the Senate closed down, she would return sourly to Boston and her poor child, little Mina. For some reason Lettie was unable to fathom, no one in her family, or her husband's, either, expressed any great desire to have the child named after her, so she had done the politic thing and named it after her husband's mother, the one most likely to cause her trouble.

"Mina? Mina?" Ten had asked on a visit; "isn't that the name of one of the characters in *The Monk?*" Whereupon she had to retail the entire plot of the novel to Edith. Lettie told Ten she had seen the Museum, the Smithsonian, the Fish Commission, the Horticultural Department, the Library of Congress, the Pension Office, the Patent Office, the Treasury, and a score, a score, of other places, and what *knowledge* she had assimilated, too! Ten, holding Mina—they now all referred to the child out of Lettie's hearing as poor little Mina—said she trusted that was the longest list Lettie had ever committed to memory, and she supposed the visit to the Fish Commission, whatever that might be, must have been the most edifying part of her tour, although the smell could not have been enviable. And then it was so hot, too. She also hoped, she said, that Lettie would be somewhat original in her design of a home, wherever she built it, since she supposed the White House lawn was already spoken for, and would refrain from asking poor Senator Knowles to build her an exact replica of the Vice-President's house, since *that* would make the poor official nervous and unwanted, and perhaps even give other Washingtonians the idea the two of them were interested in the most blatant social climbing.

Now, three years after their wedding, William and Ella, Martin and Minnie, had traveled far enough from the event so that it had settled peaceably, free from dust, under the glass domes Edna had bought each pair for their wedding-cake ornaments, far enough so that even Lettie's unmerciful teasing about their wedding, which had previously reduced both Ella and Minnie to tears, William and Martin to sulks and fits of temper, no longer bothered them. Instead, much to Lettie's annoyance, they now remembered the event with amusement, and certainly affection. A double wedding, Edna agreed after Tivoli's men began clearing the ruins, certainly had its hazards. At the last minute, the two couples forgot which was to descend the stairs first, and William and Ella had nearly pitched down to the first floor head over heels. Then there had been the confusing chorus of "I do's," not to mention the twisting of arms at the reception line, or the near fatal accident when both brides attempted slicing the bridal loaf at the same time. Now, in 1869, none of the Moffats or Steeles could discuss the blessed event without ending in hysterics. And poor Reverend Pierce; well, as Ten had said, he deserved it.

It was about time he had to preside over a circus. Afterwards, the two couples went their separate ways on their separate bridal tours, Martin and Minnie departing for Providence, sending back a series of pictures, each showing Martin in his bathing costume, and Minnie, dressed in white, usually perched on the edge of a rowboat, inspecting an oar, her beautiful dark bonnet trimmed with light flowers, looking for all the world as if she hoped someone would tip her into the water and let her enjoy herself. The second photograph, as Ten had said, told the whole story. It was the same scene and the same day and the same photographer, but Martin had moved over to the rowboat and Minnie, and was gazing down at her with the unmistakable look of adoration, while Minnie had partially raised her head and was either looking out to sea or about to gaze up into his face. Yes, they all concluded, it would take Minnie as long to accept the fact of Martin's absolute love as it would for her to get into the water. Of course, they had been wrong about that.

And Lettie. They all, children and parents, regarded her as some sort of permanent appendage to the family who must be visited and included and invited, but she had become as unfamiliar to them as the lobster or the aardvark. And then, of course, there were the apparently endless photographs of William and Ella, so many that John decided either William or his new wife was sending him specimens of the new process in hopes he would change his medium.

They had traveled up to Maine, and were brilliantly visible in the midst of the crowd gathered on the wharf about to board the small steamer-ferry *Edmund Burpee* for an outing to one of the smaller, wilder islands. Another photograph, which did indeed give John ideas, showed William and Ella calmly sitting in a rowboat, each facing the other with a pair of oars, while a smoking pipe from another rowboat clouded the left hand of the scene as if a finger or hand were already erasing the picture, blowing it off, like dust. John had become interested in the effects smoke might have; it might permit making a statement in a daguerreotype, and he was soon busily rigging up what he called a smoke machine, after which Amos refused to help in the cottage unless the monster, as he called it, was out of fuel for the day. If not, he threatened, he would not even send in his son. John would just have to hire someone else to smother to death. Edna again busied herself with designs for improved ventilation devices.

During the years the children had been in Boston, John and Edna missed them far less than they expected. As John remarked one morning as they left on rounds, this *was* more like old times, wasn't it? And Edna beamed her agreement. Anna was perpetually busy with her school, and her Sabbath school, and teaching younger children, and Jack was up to every imaginable sort of mischief. He and a new friend, Edgar, had invited another, Roy, to camp out in one of the cottages and cut partly through the rope supports of his bed. Roy and the other two hobbled into breakfast the next morning, everyone doubled up laughing, saying, "That was a real *down bed*, a real down bed." Apparently, they had never heard anything so funny in their lives, and John expressed himself forcibly, saying it was his joke in the first place, and his professional opinion that any further laughter on their part would end in a collapsed lung. "A real down lung," Roy shouted, and the adults promptly beat a retreat. Then they would become inexplicably industrious, deciding to pick and peddle berries. The inseparable trio had managed to pick twenty quarts of blackberries, setting out promptly to sell them, marching all the way into Williamsville, until finally the Camps took pity on their flushed faces and dragging feet and bought all the berries and they returned happy as discoverers of gold in the forest.

They worked in the mill, slept on the newly roasted chocolate in its bags as soon as it began cooling, tamed several wild rats, and drove the miller half mad with their jokes. The poor miller used to boast that no one could enter his mill once he had shut it up, so the three friends made it their business to sneak in, and it did seem to the town as if they could materialize on the other side of solid wood. And then, after making a horrendous noise to wake the miller, they would flee from him with their hats pulled down over their faces, screaming, "Slim Jim! Slim Jim!" while he frantically chased them in all directions, but they were, he said, impossible to catch as bats. The next morning he was the butt of the county, but nothing could persuade the boys to stop. Still, John and Edna agreed, two children, one almost grown, although who knew how, and one wild as a north wind, but old enough to be left to his own devices, two children were far less to cope with than five. Infinitely less, Edna sighed one night as the moon shone in; she no longer felt they ought to roll logs in front of their door, or that someone was drilling holes in the walls to watch them in their beds. Yes, she thought, rubbing her palm in circles over John's powerful chest, two were almost nothing. Compared to five. So the three years had proved idyllic for them. And now, it was fun, Edna supposed, although not the same, not so intimate. Measles up on Lord's Hill, and Ella having gotten herself pregnant the instant she stepped in

615

the front door. Edna was again persuaded the pregnancy had something to do with the land on which the house was built. At least Ella had measles as a child, they remembered, relieved.

Unfortunately, just as Ten predicted, the measles epidemic released the forces locked in coffins since the yellow fever epidemic. It had all begun when a man stood up in the middle of church one Sunday and announced there was a shadow on Lord's Hill. He had done this, everyone repeatedly said, right in the middle of the sermon, not only interrupting the poor Reverend, but demanding to know what he was going to do about removing the shadow. When he received no answer, he turned to the rest of the congregation, demanding to know what *they* were going to do about it. John was promptly sent for, and sedated him, providing the Reverend with enough opiates to cart the unfortunate off to the Retreat.

But that *had* set it off. The shadow, so long delayed, had fallen. Edna noted the familiar ominous signs with dread, fledgling ministers arriving to help the old minister in his time of crisis: increased Bible classes, inquiry meetings, prayer meetings, public prayer meetings, additional services, and endless, endless sermons on the necessity for true baptism, and the more that were baptized, the more insistently the sermons went on.

Ella's predicament interrupted Edna's concentration on the new religious fervor. Her confinement was dreadful, uncontrollable vomiting, perpetual nausea, wrenching headaches, continuous bleeding, and she was so enormous everyone was surprised each time she managed to enter through a door. The unanimous advice of all three doctors confined her to her bed. It was obvious to Edna she was continually in pain, and amazing to her how well Ella hid it. She had been a dreadfully healthy child, except for her bout with yellow fever, and had no opportunity to become familiar with pain. Fortunately, everyone was still home the day Ella's labor began, and it began innocently enough, but within three hours she was screaming in agony, the three doctors conferring in corners about opiates: was it advisable or was it not to give them to her when they tried to turn the baby?

After the second full day of labor, they decided Ella was too worn out to need opiates, although Edna, remembering Jack's birth, doubted it. Just as they were ready to begin turning the baby into its proper position, the baby suddenly turned itself and began emerging, Ella's voice regaining its power, the screams flying madly through the tall trees. Ten and Edna stayed with her, sponging her, petting her, until she fell asleep. John came in a few minutes afterwards. Except for the exhaustion she was fine as she had ever been; she would have no trouble with later children.

"*Later* children?" Edna demanded, getting up and dragging John over to a corner; "later children?" she asked again. "This one died." "Died! Died! That's impossible!" Edna protested. John pulled her out of the room. "There was a membrane over the baby's face; it never started breathing." Edna collapsed on her bed. "How is William?" "Depressed enough, but he'll be over it in the morning." "Tell me the truth," Edna insisted; "can she really have more children? I mean, John, it wasn't like that time with Jack?" "No, no, it wasn't." Sometimes she did carry on like a cat mother. "It was a perfectly normal labor and delivery, except that the baby died." "She *can* have others?" "As long as William's capable of producing them." Edna thought suddenly of her wedding ring; she stared down at it. How many times, she wondered, had her arm, wrapping itself around John's body, rested briefly on the back of his neck on its way elsewhere? Yes, she supposed, Ella would have more children. If John was telling her the truth. "I *am* telling you the truth," he almost shouted, seeing the look in her eyes.

The next morning, William was sitting in Ella's room next to her bed when she woke. Edna, watching from across the hall, had an awful sense of *déjà vu*. "You're just fine," William told her; "you'll feel just fine in a few days." "I know," Ella said; her voice was surprisingly strong; "I also know the baby died. I heard Mother and Father talking last night." "You're just following in the Moffat tradition, Mrs. Moffat," he said lightly; "all the first of Moffat babies die. Then you produce fifty." "I hope so." She did not sound convinced. Later, when the Three Stethoscopes, as Ten had dubbed them, finally departed for measles unknown, Edna went in. "Well, Ella," she said, "this is some way to begin, isn't it?" "It's the Moffat tradition," her daughter answered, trying to joke. "Ella," she said, "don't you pretend with me.

"After Jack, when I knew I couldn't have any more children, I was nearly off my head. I kept thinking about black water, cold snow, falling out of office windows, Paris green; Alice Moffat knows all about it. Ella," she said firmly, "the baby *died*. It was a little girl. What were you going to name her? If the baby was a girl?" "Tenniel." She looked at her mother and began to cry; once having begun, she could not stop. "Oh, Ella," her mother moaned, "it will be all right, but don't pretend, please don't pretend. You don't have to, you don't have to"; now *she* was crying steadily. She leaned over her daughter, holding her in her arms. She finally felt Ella stop crying, the rhythmic breathing of her usual, familiar sleep. She kept on crying until she fell asleep with her head on her daughter's chest. Later, Ten came in, took one look, went for Amos, had Edna carried off to her own bed, and took her place at Ella's bedside. Within a week, Ella was up and about as if nothing had happened. No, she told Edna, she had no real desire to go on rounds with William, but she wouldn't mind teaching school if they would have her, at least until she had her next child. Ella's eyes filled; yes, thought Ten, inside it was rain, rain, rain. And there wouldn't be any sun there until she was pregnant again. She supposed that wouldn't take long. And so the family focus swung back like the beam of a lighthouse to Anna and the religious revival gripping the neighborhood.

"We should send her to Boston tonight," Ten announced peremptorily; she was in no mood for taking chances. "Edith will be delighted." "But she'll never go without a reason," John told his sister; "that will never work. She'll know what we're up to. She's sixteen, after all. She's too old to be ordered around as if she were still only two." "I wish she had *stayed* two," Edna burst out. "No," Ten decided, "we have to trick her. I don't like it, Edna; she's getting too thick with those young ministers, and she's old enough to get married herself now, you know." "Anna? Anna married?" "Well, you never looked at marriage as a disaster before," William said. "But the child doesn't have a grain of sense, not a grain," Edna wailed; "this is different." "You try and tell Anna that; you might as well talk to Lettie," Ella put in. This was their first full family council, and all of them possessed by the premonition there would be many, many more.

"She has to be sent away," Edna agreed, "but how are we to do it? We can't just chloroform her and put her in a box for the baggage cars." "Mother," Martin said, "I have an idea. You can go to church with her this Sunday and come home filled, and I mean filled, with religious feeling. Then you get a letter from your mother about some dreadful illness which has her prostrated. We'll think of the correct one, and you add the pitiful sentiments about how Lettie has abandoned her in her time of need, and we can't send Ella, of course, because she's still so weak, and Minnie can't go because of Martin and she's still helping her mother on the farm when she's not going off on rounds. So it would be Anna's Christian duty not to let her grandmother die unattended, or attended by strangers." "But will she *believe* it?" Edna asked.

"She'll believe it," Ten said; "I'll send Amos' son down to Boston with a copy of the letter, and Edith can write it over in her own hand, and Amos can explain the whole thing to her. Your mother won't want the child in shock again. It would be the worst possible thing for her, especially after Hal's death." "She's bound to have shocks later in life," Ten added after a moment; "she might be able to get through them. I mean, she will be able to get through them," she hastily corrected herself at the sight of Edna's expression, "if we can keep them from coming too closely together just now." "You made it sound like babies," Ella said. They all stared at her. "Don't worry about me," she said, brusque. "I have a right to be preoccupied with babies, at least for a little while." Well, Edna concluded, if Ella could talk about it, then there *was* nothing to worry about. But the more Anna talked, the more there was to worry about. Although she was being quieter about her enthusiasms than usual. *That* was even more alarming. And what, she asked herself, wasn't alarming about Anna?

"This is ridiculous," she said, jumping up. They were all hiding out in the house's pre-Revolutionary wing, taking turns watching at windows and doors. "This is like waiting for Paul Revere." "Well, Edna, if we want to fool her, we can't have her listening to us. Isn't that worth sitting here in the dark for? With lookouts?" Edna sighed and leaned back against the wall. "Do you think it will work?" she asked John. "I think so. Look, everyone go back to bed. Act as if nothing happened, except to Ella, of course. Ella, if it wouldn't be too much for you, you could start acting up. No," he reconsidered; "Anna might decide she ought to stay here with you. Strike up when the letter from Edith comes. Take on about how good she was to you, and how sure, absolutely sure you are that your losing the baby brought this on, and if anything happens to Grandmother, you'll never forgive yourself. Can you do that, or is that asking too much of you?" "I can do it." "The whole family should be writing novels," Edna grumbled. "Do *you* think she can do it?" she asked William.

William peered at his wife in the dim light. "I can, William, really; and besides," she announced casually, "this is as good a time as any to let everyone know I'm pregnant again." "Oh no," Edna gasped. "Mother!" Ella exclaimed. "Oh, I am sorry, dear," Edna answered, preoccupied. "And how do you know so soon, miss?" Ten asked. "I have all the symptoms; sometimes I think I can tell the morning after." "A medical marvel," William said, eyes fixed on her. "She's the second; her mother was the first," John said, going over to Edna and putting his arm around her as if *she* had just made the announcement. "Peculiar, all of you," Ten commented; "well, Edna, now I suppose you want me to promise to live until Anna is safely married." "You may be sure of that." She sounded exhausted.

"All right, everyone to bed, everyone," John ordered, going over and tapping his sister on the shoulder. "Are you sure, Ella?" he asked her before he went out. "Oh yes; I'm like Mother. You know that." John shook his head sadly, took Edna to their bedroom, pushed her down on the mattress, and went out to get Amos. "No, you have to go tomorrow morning," he said; "you're the only one who can explain properly." "It won't do any good, mark my words; letters go all ways, you know. If she's already interested in someone, I mean." "Don't even think it," John said sternly. "You're getting soft in the head, Doc," Amos mumbled. "I'm not arguing; just get one of the boys ready to go; see that he leaves early and let him bring back your horse. You don't need it on the train." "Yes, sir," Amos said wearily; "I'm surprised you don't want me leaving tonight." "No trains are leaving tonight." "I should have known it; such a terrible, unholy delay." "Well, now you know what it is, I hope you're happy," John said, closing the door.

"Well, Edna, it looks like you're in for another visit to the Old Stone Church." He dropped one boot noisily, then another, finding grim satisfaction in watching them drop. "It could be worse." "Let's hope so; but *you* better plan out some story to tell yourself during the sermon or you'll go crazy from boredom. From what I hear it's baptism, baptism, and more baptism." "A little water never hurt anyone," she mumbled, half asleep. "That's what you think; how many times can you listen to the differences between baptism by the Holy Ghost and baptism by immersion?"

It made him remember his dead brother. Almost every family he knew had a dead child in it. He turned to tell Edna something, but she was sound asleep. I don't know why she needs to sleep now, he thought, irritable, when she has all of Sunday services to sleep through. Well, wasn't he getting old and cranky? he thought, lying down flat on his back next to her. He should lie on his stomach; he had just read lying on the stomach prevented the back from curving. Fifty-five years old, fifty-five years old; when he was Martin's age, he assumed anyone who had reached such an age was well into a second lifetime. And Edna, he thought, looking over at her, she was forty-two; she would be forty-three in March. Had that small person actually lived almost a half century? And twenty-five years; they had been married almost twenty-five years. It was definitely time, he decided, for a secret raid on her etiquette books.

What had he been thinking of, to neglect all those anniversaries: paper, wood, silver, ash, arsenic, whatever they were? Well, they would have to do something special when this August came around. And was she really as sound asleep as she looked? He bent over her and began slowly pulling the long hairpins from her dark hair; she didn't stir. He became interested in the activity itself, pulling them, one at a time, from the masses of her hair. Yes, he could do this just as well with his eyes shut.

Finally, fate, in the form of the moon suddenly emerging from behind a cloud, as if to illumine one of her most beautiful creations, rewarded him. Just then, her long hair began its slow, then fast, cascade over the edge of the bed. Like black water, beautiful, fast black water, and too safe to drown in. Yes, he loved her, he thought, angry at himself because of the tears stinging his eyes.

No wonder they had not celebrated anniversaries. There had been none, just events, marking off the seamless fabric of their life together, like the soap marks Ten used to make when she fooled with the children's clothes. They just washed off; they left without a trace. And then they were left. They were left. *They,* he repeated; it was one of the most beautiful, most underrated words in the language. He had better, he thought, looking at her delicate profile against her carpet of hair, begin a new series of portraits of her, although except for the pose, he could see no difference in any of them, certainly not as far as age was concerned. No, it would take a better camera than his to record signs of aging in her. If he didn't know better, and if he didn't have such a clear conception of the limitations of Mr. Siddons' talents, he would not find it hard persuading himself she had been carved by him, out of ivory.

He watched the snow, dancing outside the window. Well, after all those years of battling its drifts, shoveling "the beautiful" from his path, nearly freezing to death with Gray in its ditches, he still loved it—especially the first time the drifts swept up to the tops of the little picket fences, and they seemed, all of them in the house, adrift on a strange, pure sea in an ark of their own. Yes, he would have to get up before the others, before anyone went out and spoiled the purity with footprints. Tracks, though, they were different. The animals had made their peace with the snow. They had not. It was so evident in the marks left by people's boots, the holes they made, no, tunnels really, as if little stovepipes were sprouting from the ground trying to warm the earth, to bring it back to some condition more suitable for men. There were some things worth fighting, but the weather was not one of them. It had a life of its own and was entitled to it. Even on the worst days and for the best reasons, he had never felt it proper to invade its white veils and gowns. He should tell Edna about it; she would understand.

Why, he thought, exasperated, was she asleep? He knew she would not mind if he awakened her. She might even be relieved, but there was something about her sleep tonight which resembled the snow: it was not to be invaded. She had gone, he knew, into her cave; by Sunday, she would be ready for anything. Eleven o'clock on Sunday. They were all looking forward to Sunday at eleven as if it was the hour set for an execution. How much simpler it would have been had they only been able to believe in religion, if they had been able to take it in through their roots, the way the Moffat family seemed to. Nothing, nothing disturbed their faith, not even the aberrations of their own religious sect. Well, that was faith, wasn't it? No, their problem was they found too much in each other. Except for Lettie. She was a true pagan; she worshipped little idols dressed in ceremonial costumes. That was a woman of fashion. Well, he wasn't tired at all. He got up in four stages, creeping from the room, leaving the door ajar; he didn't want the latch waking Edna.

Ten was up in the parlor. "Well, here we go again, old goat," he said, sinking into a chair. "Do you want to talk to me or just look at me?" Just what she had always asked him when he was a child, and frightened. "Just look at you," he admitted, sheepish. She went back to her reading. When she looked up some time later, he was still there. "John," she volunteered, "we've always managed; we still will." He shook his head. "Don't *do* that." Ella drifted in wrapped in her robe. "Don't you worry," Ten instructed, without looking up; "there are more of us than ever. We'll manage; we'll manage." Ella looked questioningly at her father. "What choice do we have?" he asked his daughter.

"Choices do seem to be made for us," she said. "My, my, you are growing up." "Well, I'm not too old to sit on your lap," she threatened, instantly making her threat good. She nestled into his shoulder. "You always made us feel so safe." "I did?" John asked, incredulous; "*I* did?" "Mmm," Ella sighed; "you're just like a nice warm wall. It's been very nice of you, Father, to let us little vines climb over you all these years." "Ten," he appealed, "do you know what she's talking about?" "I do; your children don't have peepholes into what came before. They see you as you are now." "I'm not as Ella says." He stroked his daughter's hair. "Yes, you are; and you'll be a wonderful grandfather. I hope you'll live forever." Ten's eyes glistened. "Another one," she said. "Another what?" Ella asked sleepily. Over the top of Ella's head, John shook his head at his sister.

"Well, John," she said, looking up at last, "you always used to say you ought to adopt children, because, if they were even half of you, they were sure to be monsters. Now what do you think?" "I think they must be all Edna." "You are a cake," Ten teased; "Grandfather Steele." "Just don't expect me to start chiming." "Well, Daddy," Ella said, stirring, "I better get back to my bed. And you to yours." "Looking after your doddering father already?" "Just both of you go on to bed," Ten said. It had been years, John thought, pulling up the covers, since any of the children had called him Daddy. He had not realized how he missed it.

How many things did he miss, things he was not even aware he had lost? No, he couldn't think of any more. And that, he decided, closing his eyes, was Edna's real achievement. The sound of his name when she said it; the air was golden and warm and the bees buzzed, and the drownings, the deaths, burned up in the flames. He couldn't, he thought, fighting off sleep, see anything clearly with Edna there; her presence was a kind of heat. Everything rippled in the heat she radiated; everything was seen through the waves of her special sea. Whatever there was in the air; nothing could ever change that. If he ever prayed for anything, he thought, eyes closing against him, he would pray that nothing would ever change that heat, that rippling, that blur. The magic lady, he thought, looking over at her. He wanted to keep awake, watching her, but the harder he tried, the deeper into the warm waters of sleep he sank. And it had been this way, his eyes closing for the last time before sleep tucked him under its wing, for over twenty-five years.

The next morning, Anna woke up earlier than usual, and in time to see her father ordering Amos and his son off somewhere. From the way Amos glared at everything visible, particularly the snow, she knew something was wrong. She hated to see her father upset, and she knew he was; otherwise he and Amos would never be arguing. It made her heart beat faster to see her father upset, or her mother, or Ten, or anyone she cared about. She would, she was sure, feel better if they would only tell her what was wrong, but she knew better than to ask. She knew they thought her "too sensitive." Whenever they said that, she went into a rage.

She wasn't that sensitive; she had, she told herself, already lived through a great deal. There had been Ella's illness, and the loss of her baby, and Uncle Hal's death, and she was still here. What more did they want in the way of proof? Would a house have to fall on her, and would she have to walk out from beneath the rubble, before she could convince them she wasn't about to be blown off by the slightest breeze? They had, she thought bitterly, convinced everyone. Even Jack would not take her with him when he went to hunt ringnecks. "I'm not getting into trouble over *you*," he announced, turning his back and stomping off with George. She had followed them down to the swamp anyway, but they had been so mean. They pretended she wasn't even there, and then when they caught their wood snakes, they wouldn't let her see them. "Oh, no," Jack had shrilled, "don't you try to get me into trouble again. The last time you came down after me, you went on so about the slimy wet leaves and how they felt like dead things, and mushrooms growing like dead bodies, they wouldn't let me out with George for a week. You just get away from this basket." No, they were not fair to her.

It was true she took on about things, but then, didn't they drive her to it? They saw her that way, so naturally she tried to act as they expected her to. She stood looking out at her father, thinking that, really, she did try to please them. Now they made such a fuss about how religious she had become. To listen to them, you would think churchgoing was the real sin. Well, it made her feel better, her faith in Christ, trying to become a Christian. Why, she asked, defensive, wasn't that as good a goal as any other? Lettie was happy dressing herself up like a doll; no one really liked her much for it, but no one went on and on about it to her, either. And Ella, all she wanted to do was stay home and have children. Why, just last night she had said something about there being only two proper sizes for families: one should either have an only child, or have twelve. How was *she* so different? She wanted to have children; she wanted a home. It wasn't as if she thought her religion made her special.

She knew she had been insufferable when she was younger, but, really, she was calmer about everything now, and still, if they heard of her attending an extra meeting, or a member of the family passed her door and thought they heard the dread sound of prayer, all of them went on as if she were conducting some kind of black mass replete with a burning wood fire right in the middle of her oak floor. As if she had no sense at all, no strength whatever. Why couldn't they see how insulting they were to her? And why couldn't she bring herself to tell them how she felt? Well, if she couldn't, perhaps they were right. She *was* too sensitive; she didn't want to cause them any additional trouble. She knew she had caused too much already, and there was always enough without her creating more of it. And wouldn't she be doing just that if she shattered one of the mirrors they were so used to looking into? Then every time they passed that mirror they would have to stop in their tracks, and think, oh yes, that's Anna; and they would be puzzled, comparing the picture in the new mirror with the old picture so firmly drawn in their imaginations.

She stood, watching the relentlessly falling snow. It was determined, she could see that, to blot out all boundaries, to make everything look insignificant, to whiten the revival, to take out its dark tones, so that finally only the ghost of its original spirit would remain. Well, that did bother her, especially since this was the first Sunday the carillon was to be rung in the new steeple for which her parents had paid; almost everyone in the town was preparing to go to hear it, regardless of the weather. She could see them already, all dressed in their variegated clothes, and some of the women, she knew, half dressed, half frozen, out of vanity. After a lifetime here, she did wonder at it, there were still women who refused to make concessions to the weather. Well, that was all vanity, wasn't it, and it did seem unjust to her that it was those very women who never took cold, or a chill, or ended with congestion of the lungs. No, it seemed one had to be a pillar of the church before one came down with lung fever. Well, it was thinking like that, that was what made the family worry over her so. But still, the things she thought were still true, and none of them ever tried glossing over any of the truths *they* perceived. It was not fair that they muzzle *her* on the subject of religion.

Her thoughts took a happier turn. She did like the young Reverend Matthew Hewitt; no, she more than liked him. He was such a kind person, such a gentle one. He had the air of having only one foot in this world, his other in a better one. There was, she thought, settling deep into her chair, a radiance about him. It was impossible not to be drawn to him. It was foolish of her, she knew, to hope he was sincere in seeming to return her interest, although how could she reconcile what he said to her, when he wrote her, as insincere and false when she held him in such esteem? Still, every young woman of the town had fallen hopelessly in love with him. It seemed so foolish, now, to remember how enamored she had been of the Reverend Pierce.

He seemed old enough to be her grandfather. He seemed more like a grandmother. And lately, the little things: the way he snapped at his wife, cooed at the old soprano in the choir, the way he purred at her parents, the very type he should, according to his own principles, be denouncing from the pulpit. He was like a snowman, and that was sad, really. She had believed in him for so very long, and now he was choosing to melt down in front of her, and, as if to make the awakening as painful as possible, he was choosing a blizzard to melt himself down in.

Well, if the truth were known, she didn't really like him. It wasn't that she suspected him of worldly ambition, although he seemed tangled in its ribbons like a maypole, but that she suspected him of having a bad heart. That was the worst thing she could think of: inability to sympathize with others. And then to pretend to! Surely that was the worst form of hypocrisy. Even someone not religious, her own mother, would agree with her, she was sure of that. When her mother didn't understand something, she never claimed to. She would sit there with that helpless, stricken look; that look broke her heart. Her father, though; he was another sort of creature altogether. He understood everything, and, as

he took it in, she could see the faint twinge as the knowledge slipped into him somewhere, as if understanding
were a sharp knife. He was brave, she had to say that
for him. She supposed her mother was also, in her own
way. Stricken or not, she did what was necessary; that
was bravery, too.

And now, she had somehow been stopped from going
on rounds with her father. They must have decided *that*
was bad for her as well. No one had asked her if she
wanted to go to medical school, and they had certainly
seen her reading and reading about the women's medical
college in Connecticut. They couldn't have missed it, not
after she had read the same article from the same magazine day in and day out, and finally had taken to leaving
the magazine open to the proper page, the article marked
heavily in red. If they *had* asked her, and if they had sent
her, perhaps she wouldn't have had an opportunity to become so confirmed in her religion, although still, no matter how she looked at it, she could see no harm in it.
What, she wondered, was wrong with believing a human
needed additional strength, strength beyond his own, to
help him through life? After all, her own grandfather had
been a lawyer; he had spent a career trying to extricate
people who had not survived through their own efforts,
and at least set them back on the path, even if they were,
by the time he arrived, like horses with cases of the blind
staggers. What did trouble her, and of course there was
no one in the family she could talk to about *that*—although she could to Matthew—was how frequently she
wondered whether she really believed in God, or if she
just needed to believe in God, the way children needed
to pretend dolls turned live in the dark, or their stuffed
puppies began growling at intruders, turning protectors
with the fall of night.

But Matthew. He didn't seem to think less of her for
her doubts. When there was so little difference between
illusion and reality, he said, there was no difference at all.
But perhaps he said that out of partiality to her—although surely she was foolish to believe that. Still, *she*
was the one he chose to see home, regardless of the
weather, and he was undiscouraged by her insistence he
turn his horse back on the road before they came into
sight of the house. He asked no questions at all; he

trusted her. That was what made him so unique, the way he trusted her. And that was not all. There were his spiritual qualities which struck everyone.

Although when she had shown the family a picture of him, what did they say? Aunt Ten had asked her if there was something wrong with his heart. She assumed there must be, or why else would he have his hand thrust into his jacket between the third and fourth button that peculiar way? And the way his eyes narrowed; yes, Ten said, looking at it sagely, she was sure he must have been in pain, at least when the picture was taken. And then Ella said that anyone who wanted to look so serious couldn't possibly be sincere, while dear Minnie, who said whatever came into her head, no motive at all, said she altogether disagreed with Ella. Actually, he seemed to be holding back a smile. And she supposed it must be extremely difficult to hold the same pose, not to mention the same expression, especially when a person wasn't used to it.

Her mother said he resembled Heathcliff, and her father, that he looked like everyone else, except for the collar, and he couldn't understand all the fussing; after all, her father said, when William sent back tintypes from the war, there were plenty of soldiers who posed with hands thrust into their jackets, and no one thought they were trying to hold their hearts or livers inside their bodies. She snatched the picture from Martin's hand before he had a chance to comment on it, taking it off to the safety of her room, bursting into furious sobs behind her locked door. Of course, it was just such events which confirmed their ideas of her delicacy. But what did they expect when they ridiculed her so? She turned from the window as the Three Stethoscopes began leading their horses toward the main path.

It was a lovely picture, though, she thought, looking more closely. Matthew was such an impressive-looking man, a rugged peasant from the moors, much as Mother had said, his heavy eyebrows, his deep-set eyes, his long, straight nose, and that mouth, in the photograph, so like a straight line, but anyone who knew him could tell he had pressed his lips together. That was obvious from the little fold of flesh in one corner of his mouth, and the deepened cleft in his chin. She had fallen into that ravine,

TIME IN ITS FLIGHT

she had to admit, as every other young woman in the parish had. And he was so tall, so big. He reminded her of Johnny Appleseed, not some poor heart patient who ought to be sent to Poland Springs, a true type of the old apostle, a strong man, a good man, and all they could do was ridicule him. Still, she could make up her own mind, no matter how weak they considered it.

The trouble was, she kept coming back to it, she could not believe his intentions were truly serious. In the family, she could consult with no one, except, perhaps, Minnie, but she was such an innocent, she would probably blurt it all out to Martin, and then the chickens would be pecking all over the yard. Perhaps she could talk to Alice Moffat. That was the most promising idea she had yet had. Of course, she was her mother's closest friend, but she was a religious woman; she did like Mr. Hewitt and certainly she respected a confidence. A rare virtue nowadays, thought poor Anna, her cheeks firing. She took out his recent letter, and read it for the hundredth time.

It was ridiculous to be writing letters when they saw each other every day, but under the circumstances, it was the only way. Neither of them wanted their religious convictions viewed as a cloak for a courtship. They had managed to say that much to each other conferring over the arrangements for baptism services. It was obvious, they both agreed, people could not be immersed in the dead of winter without first warming the water, the problem being *how* the heating was to be done. Here, Matthew said, was a description of his latest plan; then he handed her the letter she was now clutching. It was watermarked, she thought, looking at it affectionately, by the infinite pressings of her fingers on its pages. She opened it slowly, looking up to be sure her door was thoroughly secured.

"There is nothing so appalling to a modest and sensitive young man, which I flatter myself to be," Matthew wrote, "than asking the girl he loves to marry him, and there are few who do not find their moral courage tasked to the utmost. Many a man who would lead a forlorn hope, mount a breach, and 'seek the bubble of reputation e'en in the cannon's mouth,' trembles at the idea of asking a woman the question which is to decide his fate. It is worse, far worse, dear Anna, when that man is a minister, and can offer his wife nothing but a good home, steady love, and the trials and tribulations, not only of his own family, but the families of all in his parish.

"I take some dim hope in remembering you are the daughter of a doctor and have become used to some of the hardships a minister's wife would inevitably encounter. There are parallels in the two occupations, are there not, dear Anna? One ministers to the body, the other to the spirit. And the spiritual keeper of the flame must be present at the deathbed and the sickbed, at the wedding and at the funeral, as must the doctor so often be. But a man must still tremble at asking a woman, a beautiful, sensitive woman, even to put the merest toe of her shoe into such cold, muddy waters. Better, Anna, I sometimes think, to let you float from me on the blue waters like a happy leaf, or seed, headed where some milder destiny will take you. Yet I cannot refrain from obeying this selfish compulsion to ask if you will consider sharing my life. It is a hard, desolate thing for a man to contemplate his future as a desert, the oasis he so loves forever beyond his reach.

"Dear Anna, if I may so call you, a man conforms to the disposition of the woman he admires. But I believe in such secular, though sacred matters, there is one maxim of universal application, and I should never forgive myself should I neglect it—never lose an opportunity. What can a woman think of a lover (now, Anna, dear, I know you are blushing, and perhaps even outraged, your delicate higher sentiments leading you to seize a candle and fire this offensive page) who neglects one? Women cannot make direct advances, and, Anna, even if they could, I know *you* would not. In every case, it is fair to presume that when a woman gives a man an opportunity (and I blush, for I seem everywhere to be hinting at aspects of your nature which do not exist), she expects him to improve it, and though he may tremble, as I am trembling now, and feel his pulses throbbing (believe me, I never knew the body harbored so many) and tingling through every limb, though his heart is filling up his throat, and his tongue cleaves to the roof of his mouth, yet the awful question must be asked, the fearful task accomplished.

"But, dear Anna, imagine now my perplexity. The

heart's work is thorough and takes little time, and though I know mine is set on yours forever, I cannot guess whether you are serious only, or serious and lively, or serious, lively, and sentimental, as well as practical. I simply have not had the time, dear Anna, to plan the correct campaign. So I must throw myself on your mercy, fearing, as I do, I shall not prove equal to your satisfaction. You must, you *must*, reflect that I am but human, for the collar does not do much but stiffen the neck, and that is not always desirable, especially in delicate matters such as these, and am subject to imperfections and temptation and not altogether free of that selfishness which abounds in the feelings of all the human family. How else could I even ask you to consider sharing your life with me?

"So do not, I beg you, let your love of me induce you to consent to live with me if you feel that it is impossible to be happy and content with the little I have to offer you, although I feel that I should be unhappy, nay, miserable, without the enjoyment of your sweet company. But perhaps I should not say that, since I do not want to prey upon your all too ready sympathies, which, if enlisted in the wrong cause, would only end in making you miserable for life, and I should perish watching such a fate unfolding. You may well scorn me, Anna, justly reproaching me for loving too soon, but then you must do me the favor of informing me of the proper time to commence loving since I am very ignorant on that subject and have always been ignorant enough to suppose that love is a spontaneous production of the heart which is impossible to regulate by any special law in regard to time and place, that it is like any other emotion such as pleasure, pain, fear, and hope (all of which I now experience at their most intense) and regulated only by circumstances beyond human powers to control. Neither can I bring myself to consider anything wrong or reckless in admitting to loving so soon, to a love formed on such short acquaintance, for if the miracle is to happen, and you reciprocate my affections, we shall certainly, by the grace of God, have sufficient and more than sufficient time to learn the alphabet of each other's character and expectations. Our only duty, as I see it, is to unite our destinies in the hope of the promotion of our happiness.

"I beg you, dear green-eyed Anna, to give this matter your most serious consideration; do not enlist the affections only in these serious deliberations, but also discretion, prudence, and common sense. Discuss, if you can, this matter with those who are nearest and dearest to you and who know your heart far longer than I have known it. Once you set your foot upon the path, either toward me or away, there is no going back, and so, too, is the case with me. I have taken all the steps toward you I can; now it is all up to you. If you are willing to consider my suit after a seasonable amount of time has passed, please signal me in some way. Wear, perhaps, your hair in that delightful manner you once wore it, parted in the center, framing your face with two beautiful black falls. Then you need nod to me, Anna, dear, and I shall fly to your side to hear, with fear and trembling, your decision, for yours it must be. Be assured, I shall accept it, whatever it may be, quietly and with resignation, regardless of the subsequent state of my feelings.

"As I look over this letter, I cannot help but think it is cold, cold, a minister's letter of love. But do not think, because of that, my affections are not powerfully attached to you; nay, I shall tell the truth, my deepest passions as well. So I must close, my little helpmate, trembling next to the stove, praying to Him we hold most dear, awaiting your answer."

What, exactly, Anna asked herself, was there to think about? Surely his intentions were not in question; those were plain enough. No, it was her fear of her family's reaction. If they heard she was considering engaging herself to a minister, they would be sure it was the end of her. She had better confer with Mrs. Moffat. She got her cloak and began dressing. "I'm going for a ride," she told Ten, who seemed lurking about in the hall; "I do so love the snow." Ten looked suspiciously after her. She led her horse out to the path through the crunching drift.

Well, she thought, entering Alice's kitchen, it was certainly quiet enough. "Where are the children?" she asked Mrs. Moffat. "Trying to slay one another with snowballs in slingshots." "Mrs. Moffat," Anna burst out soon after they were seated at the table, "I desperately need your advice. You know my family's fear for me; you know how unsteady they think me. But I am not, really I am not. And now," she said shyly, not daring to look at her, "Mr. Hewitt has declared his love for me, and, Mrs. Moffat, I do love him! But I dare not encourage him if it will mean disturbing the minds of everyone in the family; that would not be right. Oh, I do not know what to do! If I were an orphan, I would not hesitate. I would throw myself at his feet as quickly as society would permit. My mind is made up, and believe me, I have one," she went on. "I want no other husband. I am sure I shall never marry if I cannot have the man I adore. Why, he is a vision to me, Mrs. Moffat. I could not have imagined a man more perfect, a man I could love more deeply. He is more than the fulfillment of my wildest dreams. But I suppose you will tell me I must give him up." She sat still, staring at the checked oilcloth.

"Anna," Mrs. Moffat asked, "are you quite sure of your feelings?" "I am; I would stand in front of the congregation and declare them publicly if necessary. I would fast for months. I would do anything! But I shall have none of those opportunities." "Nonsense, nonsense," Alice scolded briskly, "a minister is no more a burden than a doctor." "That is *just* what Mr. Hewitt said in his letter." "I only worry," Alice said, "that this is an infatuation, not unlike your infatuation with poor Reverend Pierce." "No, it is *not* the same," Anna said despondently; everyone would think the same thing. "Well, you see, Anna, my children grew up with those they married; I have had so little experience with things like this." "But you didn't know your husband forever!" "It might have been better if I had." "But you can never be absolutely sure before the event!" "That's true; that is very true."

"You do know him some," Anna insisted. "Yes, I do. But not well enough to judge his suitability for you." "But surely, you have formed *some* opinion of him? Do tell me what it is, never mind how dreadful." "Whoever said it was dreadful? Why, if I were your age, I should be prostrated at the sight of him. But, being in my fifties, the clouds clear off a bit of the time. I would say he is a very good man, and a sincere one, too. It's obvious enough he could encourage all the women in the parish if he had a mind to, but he does nothing of the sort. He doesn't even give them an opportunity to throw themselves at him. Really," Alice wondered, shaking her head, "I don't know how he manages it."

"You don't mean to say I threw myself at him?" "Don't be silly. And it wouldn't have done you a bit of good even if you had, not if he hadn't set his heart on you in the first place." "Do you think so?" "There's no question about it. Anna, I think I will talk to your mother. If you give me your permission. She does worry about you; she's afraid you tend to fanaticism, but Mr. Hewitt does not, and what could be better than to have you under *his* religious influence? Why," she finished, "a tree would more likely be swept away in a religious revival than he would. No, it all makes perfect sense to me; it does, indeed. May I talk to her?" Anna traced the borders of the oilcloth squares.

She was, Alice saw, in terror of her parents' reaction. "Of course you may; but I would be so grateful if you would wait a few days. So that I have a chance to prepare myself for the storm, you know." "I do know." "What do you think their attitude will be?" "Oh, there's no predicting that, but they are good at taking what comes after them, and this doesn't seem bad, not at all. It's all in presenting it to them properly. Believe me, Anna, my dear, I've seen enough of my own children's peculiar approaches to subjects; they've made me something of an expert in circling in on a target." "What a dreadful way to describe it."

"Well," Alice asked, "would you prefer if I just blurted it out as if I had read it in the papers or heard it at Elder's store?" "Oh, in heaven's name, don't do that!" "So I will circle in, and you get ready for the storm. Bank up your house. Are you going to tell Mr. Hewitt anything before I speak to them?" "Only what I've told you; that all depends on my family's reaction, and I cannot encourage him further until I know conclusively how they will react." "You are a good girl, Anna, and in this case, a lot better than I would be in your place, I can tell you. But I shouldn't say that, since your mother and I are such old friends. Still, I think you are too good.

"Let me take care of it," she said, pressing Anna's hand; "I am so used to Edna, and if I bring her around, she'll bring your father around, and Ten will adjust within seconds, and as for your brother and sister, I'll talk to their husband and wife, who happen to belong to me, and I don't expect they'll be much trouble about it." "Oh, I do hope you are right." "The important thing is not to agitate yourself; if things do work themselves out, and they have a way of doing that, then you want the strength to walk down an aisle to an altar." Anna nodded her streaming face at her. "Smile," Mrs. Moffat ordered. Anna obeyed. "Well, that's a pretty poor specimen," Alice sniffed, "but I daresay within a week you'll be much better at it." Anna smiled brilliantly. "*That's* better," Alice congratulated her; "are you ready to go home and face the walls? They know more than anyone else." "I'm ready." "Now ride carefully." "I will," her happy voice called back.

All was confusion when she arrived at her house. Edna, in tears, was standing in the middle of the kitchen, while John was staring bleakly at a piece of stationery in his hand. Amos' son leaned miserably against the wall. "What's that?" Anna asked, looking at the paper in her father's hand. "It's a letter about your grandmother," John said. "She's not dead, is she?" "Oh no, just sick," he said, giving her the letter to read: "Mrs. Siddons made"—no, that was meant to be erased; someone had drawn a line through it—"taken sick at Westminster." Both the words "taken" and "Westminster" were underlined three times. "My father went out to Westminster," Amos' son said. "Oh, fine," Edna sighed. Ella and Ten looked equally distraught. "You're all acting so strangely," Anna said, bewildered; "if Grandmother is sick, why does everyone look so disappointed? I'd think you'd be miserable." "We are disappointed," Ten said quickly; "we wanted to leave immediately to see her, but the roads to Westminster seem blocked. We won't be able to get a real report for two days now. Amos is still in Boston, and even if he goes on to Westminster, I don't know what good that will do, if—" She broke off, her voice shaking.

"Well, who is with her?" Anna asked. "That's just the trouble," Edna moaned; "we don't know. We presume Mr. Siddons is there, but he isn't much good in the way of nursing an invalid." "I wouldn't imagine so," Anna agreed; "when do you think we'll hear further?" "Well, we sent Amos out this morning," John said, "and he should get to Westminster today; he'll have to go by horse. Ten has everything confused. But a minimum of two days to hear from him, as we said. Today is Friday; if Amos writes instead of returning—he might stay if they need his help—we won't hear anything until Tuesday." "Except the bells in the carillon," Anna reminded them. They all stared at her. "I don't know," she explained lamely; "it just seems that ought to bring her luck, whatever is ailing her. You made the carillon possible, you know." "That's true," Edna said, pretending to cheer slightly. "Well," Ten cut in briskly, "there's no point in everyone worrying themselves into fits before we find out if she's done more than sprain her ankle running after a tennis ball in the house." Minnie could not suppress a smile.

"Well, I tell you what," Anna said as brightly as possible—this was the last thing she wanted to do, but who else could?—"if it does turn out to be anything serious, I'll go and look after her." "Oh, but that will be such a strain," Ten protested. "I'm *perfectly* capable of looking after her," Anna said. There they went again, she thought. "There's no point in opening that book before we finish this one," Ella said. She was always so calm it was infuriating. "Mother," she said, turning her back on the rest of them. "I hope you haven't forgotten your promise to accompany me to church this Sunday." "Under the circumstances, I will certainly keep that promise." How worried she looked, Anna thought, how miserable. "At eleven; and in this snow, we'll have to leave hours and hours before." "Will we have to leave the day before and stay in town overnight?" "Don't tease," Anna said, and swept out of the room.

"Good work," Ella murmured. The rest of them nodded their heads. "I wish there wasn't this delay, though," Edna said; "I'd like her to leave immediately. Why did Mother decide to visit Westminster at this time of year?" "Probably Mr. Siddons wants to sketch hills and trees in the snow, and besides, we can't have everything," John replied, putting his arm around her. A shadow went by the window. "It looks like we're off somewhere again," he told his wife; "if you want to come." "I certainly do; I feel guilty as Judas in here." "It's the right thing to do, sending her," Ten assured Edna. "Well, let's go," Edna said; "what are we looking forward to now?" "Frostbite and a broken leg for starters." Martin grinned down at his mother. Edna shook her head, puzzled. There were so *many* of them.

Now what were they up to? Anna wondered; she had never seen the family take such an intense, peculiar interest in the snow. And they thought *she* was the one to watch. Perhaps it was only that two of the Three Stethoscopes were so anxious to get to their invalids. It had occurred to more than one member of the family that when sleighs summoning them to bedsides failed to materialize outside their door, both William and Martin were almost sick themselves.

Sunday, Edna sighed at four in the morning, and still no signs of Amos. He had decided, he wrote to John, to report from Westminster, and a letter was less likely to give the game away than his guilty face. Looking out at the yard, the fences sunken from sight, Edna wondered how long it could possibly take his letter to arrive; could it take so long she would be forced to keep her promise and attend the prayer meeting with her daughter on Wednesday? She was dreading the sermon enough. It *was* terribly cold. As John said, it was frostbite and burns, frostbite and burns. He had never seen so many cases of frostbite; he had never seen so many cases of burns. Still, that was always the way it was.

He repeated this rather unimpressive bit of information to the other two fledglings; fledglings, that was how he thought of them, not doctors. Was it possible, he wondered, to raise a child and still see it as anything but an incompetent butcher? He doubted it. All one's doubts flew into the child like bees hiving; that was why he had more confidence in William than Martin. Whenever he looked at Martin, he thought of all the wrong things. He remembered the entire household turned topsy-turvy by the women (when Ten and Edna took on about the children, especially when they were free of symptoms, he thought of the two of them that way) when they decided Martin was never to be housebroken. In despondent tones, they bemoaned his destiny; he would be the first child in Vermont ever to enter medical college with pins forged by the smithy. "Just wait," John said, "until he sees William perform the mysterious actions. He's so impressed with William; you'll see. He'll catch on at the end of the day." Well, William had valiantly demonstrated his skills, and John, at the importunate pleas of the women, had set Martin on his knees on the bottom step, and said, "Well, Martin, do you know what to do now in the privy?" "Oh yes"; Martin had beamed at him. "And what is that?" cooed Ten. "I paint." Yes, that was what he had said. "I paint." They had forgotten how recently he had seen William painting the Moffat privy. Now, he thought, shaking his head, this Michelangelo was in charge of human lives. So life went on. And now poor Edna trying to do something similar with Anna, trying to wean her daughter from what she thought the poisoned milk of religion. Well, good luck to her, he thought, turning from the window.

"Mother," Anna announced petulantly, "it's almost seven o'clock; are we never to start out?" "Why must I freeze for hours in church? Every house is a house of God, and *ours* is better heated. Thank goodness you lost your battle over the coal stoves. I should freeze to death altogether. I guess that's something, the stoves." She shivered. "Oh, Mother," Anna complained, "do hurry up. It's almost seven." "We'll go, we'll go," Edna said, buttoning her second boot; "I'll just remind your father where I'll be for the two or three extra hours, so he can take me off on rounds before the late services." "Mother!" "Don't worry; I'm not intending to escape." "Well, you will have to sit still there while I help decorate the church; that's one of my duties. I help Mr. Hewitt this week. It's right on the duty schedule." Edna looked up wearily.

"Well," she said finally, "you hair is certainly becoming, parted in the middle like that; you haven't been doing it up that way for some time. Actually, Anna, that's an interesting hairdo for you, that part in the middle. It makes you look more spiritual, or older, I'm not sure which. It's called the waterfall," she told her daughter. "I don't see what's so interesting about it; the two curls always reminded me of horse's tails folded under." "Really? That observation's worthy of *Godey's Lady's Book*. If they don't take it, you can send it on to *The Ladies' Journal*." "I'll do no such thing," Anna answered, fretting up and down in the shadow carpeting the area just inside the front door. "All right, let's *go*," her mother finally said; "I hear the sleigh bells."

Inside the church, Anna immediately busied herself with one of the ministers. They had so many baskets of geraniums, Edna thought; they must have cornered the world market. Well, religious people, she thought, resentful and already bored, what did they care if no one else in the world had a flower in the house? Anna had wanted her to read until the sermon began; very well, she *would* read. She took out one of Jack's yellow pamphlets: *The Life, Confessions, and Atrocious Crimes of Antione Wolff, the Cruel Murderer of the Wellman Family. A Graphic Account of Many of the Most Horrible and Mysterious Murders Committed in This and Other Countries.* She began reading it. She preferred reading Jack's scurrilous pamphlets to Ten's endless novels. It said something, undoubtedly, about her own mind, probably nothing too flattering, either. She lost herself in the stabbings with pitchforks, axes, knives, and every other conceivable instrument of doom, while above, the risen Christ observed her in the brilliant, immovable, fluctuating colors of his stained glass.

"Anna," Matthew was saying, "does your change of hairdo signify a change of heart?" "It does," she answered, bending over for another pot of geraniums; "it signifies it has changed and shall change no more." Matthew Hewitt turned the same rose color as the church window above them. "Do you mean that?" he asked; it seemed his heart had stopped beating, but if it had, there was no explaining his continuing existence. "I do." "Then when shall we set the happy day?" he asked, deciding to get it over with at once. "We cannot, not yet; I have to go to my grandmother in Boston, or in Westminster, wherever they are to keep her. She is very very ill, and she has been so good to us." Matthew looked over to see the brightening tears; they brimmed; they did not spill. "Anna," he whispered passionately, "I will wait for you. Even if it takes two years; even if it takes five years, ten years!" "Stop; add any more years and we will be too old to consider such matters." "I do mean it, Anna; I will have no one else." "And I will have no one but you."

"Remember," he said, "you say this to me in the sight of God."

"Now that's a curious scolding, since I'm the one leaving and you're staying surrounded by the town's most attractive young women *and* their mothers." "Mothers?" "Most mothers want to marry their daughters off." Oh, she was ashamed of herself. "My parents don't worry, because—" She stopped herself. "Because you're so pretty and so wealthy," he finished for her. "You had better get another pot; we're working too slowly." "*Your* mother seems absorbed in something." Anna turned, saw the yellow cover of the pamphlet, and shook her head. It was hopeless, she knew, to try reforming her mother. "Converting." She knew that was the word she ought to use, but "reforming" seemed so much more apropos. "I'm not worried about Mother; she'd never suspect me while I was under her very nose." "And a very pretty nose she has, too," Matthew said; "I'm prejudiced in its favor; it's just like yours." "I think the credit goes the other way around." "Anna," Matthew said miserably, "you can't mean what you were implying. You know I will wait for you, no matter how long it takes. I do hope," he said, fixing her, "it will not take half a century for your grandmother to recover." Anna promptly handed him another pot of geraniums.

"Will you write?" he pleaded. "If I could only believe you were sincere . . ." Her voice trailed off suggestively. "Anna, what will convince you?" He slammed down the pot of geraniums. "Clay vessels, clay vessels," she warned. "What *will* convince you? I'll stand up today," he threatened, "and announce our betrothal before the whole congregation." "Don't do that," Anna pleaded hysterically; and hadn't she told Mrs. Moffat she would do the same thing? "Why not?" he asked, calmly taking another pot. "Because my family is worried about ministers; I need time," she continued, blushing furiously, "to convince them you are in your right mind." "I won't be if you don't answer me; would you mind pushing that white pot over to the edge? Are you going to write me?" "Yes, yes, I will," she answered hurriedly, fleeing. "Where are you going?" one of the other girls asked. "Into the vestry; I think there are additional flowers there."

She leaned against the cool hall outside the vestry door.

From inside, she could hear the voices of Mr. and Mrs. Pierce. They seemed to be arguing about something. Yes, they were arguing about eggs, something about the price she paid for eggs, and not even fresh ones; he didn't like the speckled ones, either. She could hear perfectly, now that the blood had stopped thudding in her ears: ". . . no matter what the farmers said about their being no different than the uniformly colored ones." No, she had no delusions about ministers any longer. It was Matthew that she loved. She would have loved him if he had made shoes like Aunt Ten's dead husband. *She* had changed, she knew. And she had better get back. Matthew saw her enter out of the corner of his eye, but did not look at her. She fussed about the flower brackets fastened to the aisle seats, eventually appearing at his side. "Matthew," she whispered, "if you will wait for me, I pledge myself to do the same." "Thank God. There's one thing I wanted to ask, though. It's very small of me," he admitted, abashed. Anna waited. "Your Aunt Ten was ordering a wedding certificate last Wednesday." He looked sidelong at her. "Oh, that. That was for Lettie. She's my married sister in Boston, but Aunt thinks it's never too late to remind her of what marriage signifies, so she got her the most old-fashioned one she could find. She believes in keeping after the sheep. Lettie won't like it at all, but her husband will insist on having it framed and she'll try to get a house painter to slip up and paint it over." "She sounds terrible." "No, only empty."

"I'll write. Don't give it any more thought, especially if it causes you to go on as you have just done." Others were coming in. "Well, you can hardly blame me for *some* anxiety," he pleaded, knowing this was his last chance for some days, "when you may be going off any minute." Anna nodded, hearing other voices close behind her. "I do," she said daringly; "I do understand that." "Then," Matthew said, stooping down for his last pot, "I am the happiest man on earth." "I hope you will live to believe that. Well," she said, "I had better get to Mother. The services are about to begin and she looks at the pew as a prison." "Go; I think you ought."

She left, settling next to Edna like a bird. "Well, you *do* look happy; I never could understand," her mother puzzled, "why anyone would feel happy *before* a sermon."

Anna looked at her. Edna decided she had better be quiet and sit peaceably through the service. "The congregation shall be seated." She had always hated the way men sat on one side, women on the other. It seemed so unnatural. She stood for the Prayer of Invocation, the reading of Scripture (passages from Galatians and John; *they* brought back faint echoes), the singing of "My Country 'Tis of Thee." So far, she thought, all appeared routine, not a revivalist enterprise at all. But she would wait for the sermon.

The minister was finally standing at the communion table. Edna's consciousness began winking on and off; why, it didn't seem like a sermon; no, it was more like a Bible lesson for Sabbath school. But perhaps, she thought, looking at the others around her, eyes glued to Reverend Pierce, that was the important thing; they felt like children. They needed to be guided as children, to feel secure as children. He was going on and on and on, defining the differences between Holy Ghost baptism and water baptism. Apparently, he had decided to baptize, or rebaptize, the whole congregation next week. But what was astounding was everyone's response; they shouted their answers to his questions as if he were Daniel Webster himself.

"Christ," the Reverend went on, "preached the necessity of baptism and the indispensability of baptism. So, too, his Apostles preached that the lack of baptism stood between, as a stone wall stands between a cow and his pasture, man and the City of God. Christ said he would save all through Holy Ghost baptism, although he also told us he alone could do so; his Apostles could not. Under the new dispensation, ordered and issued by Christ our Lord, there is a definite, yes, a definite and distinct difference between water baptism and Holy Ghost baptism. Water baptism requires and demands a *burial*, a burial, an entrance into the earth, a conversation with the beige worms, an annihilation by the small worms. That is the meaning, the only true meaning of total immersion." From the way people leaned in toward one another, children climbing their mothers' sides, Edna saw the worms had indeed come alive for those inside the church; they were *there*. As in drunkenness, Edna thought; as in advanced drunkenness.

"There are several soul-saving distinctions which I must

raise with you, as I hope you will raise your souls. There is a crucial, lifesaving distinction between Holy Ghost baptism and water baptism. Holy Ghost baptism was a promise, but only a promise; Christ *commanded* water baptism for all. A promise is to be believed in; a command is to be obeyed. I tell you, water baptism is a *command*. Who in this congregation dares disobey Christ's command? Shall you disobey him?" "No," the congregation thundered. "Shall you obey him?" "Yea," came the answering shout. To Edna, they were gladiators watching bodies enter the mouths of lions.

Finally, he ordered them to open their Bibles; yes, just as if they were children again. "Open the great books before you, and let us study these great truths together, so that you may no longer fall into the many pits and hollows awaiting you, the snows which may smother and freeze you; the heats which may scald you." Well, Edna thought, opening her Bible—she was almost ashamed of how new and shiny it obviously was. This *was* hypnotism, swinging the words back and forth, like a gold watch, Holy Ghost baptism, water baptism, Holy Ghost baptism, water baptism. She did not like it, but, like the others, she was powerless to resist. The congregation roared again and again. It reminded Edna again of childbirth. Once the pains began, there was no stopping it. That was it; he caught them up in the inevitable rhythms of life, the one unstoppable rhythm. He gave that rhythm meaning. She shuddered slightly. Anna put her hand over hers.

"Ye shall be clean!" he continued in a lowered voice; "shall you come to the water?" "We shall," everyone answered. "Next Sunday comes the water," he whispered; "shall you come in?" Edna wondered how many would actually come out in weather like this, and for a baptism. Anna would, she knew. She looked carefully at what faces she could see. Yes, most of them would. Why did that frighten her? *She* would come: to witness. No one would mind; they would all hope she, in her turn, would enter the water. And her reactions? They were paradoxical. Perhaps even perverse. Why be so horrified at everyone's belief? No one here could doubt they were not comforted by their belief. Still, she was convinced, she felt her nerves knew, somehow, that in the end such belief had to be harmful.

But he told them there was no end. Perhaps that was the secret. There was no end. World without end, she thought; world without end, amen. She would give anything to believe that. But she did not. She believed she ended when her heart gave its last squeeze and contract. At least, she thought she believed that. Perhaps she didn't really believe in what she assumed she did. Perhaps she, too, needed delusions to live. She squirmed uneasily, listening to the choir singing "Blest Be the Tie That Binds"; there *was* always the possibility, however small, it was not delusion. Wasn't it, she wondered, a form of arrogance not to believe, not to believe with such smugness? Surely, they had done their daughter an injustice. When there were only theories, theories which could neither be proven nor disproven, a person had a right to choose. Yes, they had been unjust to their own daughter.

She suddenly became aware, during the Benediction, of various smells which filled the church. When they were finally outside, she felt unable to move; she asked Anna about them. "I thought I smelled fennel," she said, dazed. "Oh yes"—Anna smiled at her—"everyone uses fennel to keep awake. It is so hot sometimes," she went on as if apologizing for these subterfuges, "and some of the people are so old." "There were other smells," her mother said tonelessly; she *was* dazed, she knew it. "Well, no one minds the nibbling," Anna explained a bit uneasily; it was, she thought, like trying to explain this religion, her mother's own religion, to a Hottentot. "People," she began, "use dill for hiccoughs; they seem to disturb the mood"; she smiled faintly. "And then people *will* get hiccoughs in church, so those prone to them carry along bark or prickly ash; it does help." "I must remember to tell your father."

Anna inspected her, confused. She seemed so weak. "Are you well, Mother?" "Oh yes, dear. I think it's the effect of the sermon. Strong meat, as he said." "More likely the stuffiness; the church does get stuffy with all those coal stoves and the windows and doors closed; we should look into the pipes leading from them." "Yes," Edna agreed; it was easier to agree; "that must be it. What else do they use?" "The only other thing I can think of is sassafras, sassafras root, you know; oh, you probably don't; well, it's used to make saliva flow more freely; it keeps you from getting too thirsty. I hate it, though; it always reminds me of Uncle Hal and that dog." "Yes, I imagine it must."

Anna looked up; Matthew was standing almost in front of her. Suddenly he bent over, pretending to fasten his boot. When he stood up, Anna called to him. "Mr. Hewitt," she said, "I would like you to meet my mother. She is the one who gives me her precious red sleigh so I may attend church." "I can believe that is quite a sacrifice," Matthew said, smiling down at Edna. "Not so dreadful; I'm a good rider. I prefer horses to the sleigh if they can manage the snow." "You are a hearty woman, then." "Not really; I just do my best." "That," he said, looking more carefully at her, "is what I call heartiness. Whatever strength is, I think that must be it." "You have found no other kind?" "No." How simply he answered; there was no pretense about him. "And *you* do your best; one can tell that by looking at you." "For that I must thank you." "I would like to shake your hand," Edna heard herself saying; "I've never quite gotten over my Boston upbringing; if we do not shake hands, I won't feel we are properly introduced." He immediately extended his. Edna could not begin to understand the sympathy she had for him, the feeling of protectiveness, the feeling he gave her of being protected. "I wish you luck in life," she said softly. Both their eyes were bright.

Anna watched them; she would not have been more surprised if the heavens had chosen that moment to part and reveal a glimpse of the heavenly city. Perhaps the road would not be so rocky for Mrs. Moffat, after all. "Mrs. Steele," Matthew said, "you're shivering. I must insist you climb into your sleigh. Has she adequate rugs?" he asked Anna. "Oh yes, we have many," Edna assured him; "I do hope we meet again. I like so few people." "Especially ministers?" "I'm afraid that's true. I hope you will permit me to make an exception, and you will make one for my daughter." "You must be careful," he laughed, helping Edna into the sleigh; "once you make an exception, there's no telling where they will end." "As I said" —Edna hesitated—"I do the best I can. If religion will break down the door, I shall not complain." "That would indeed be foolish," he answered, handing Anna in. Edna leaned across. "Do come visit; really, my invitation is sincere, isn't it, Anna?" "It is, especially since this is the very first time Mother has found a good reason for anyone outside the family to set foot inside the door in twenty years. More than twenty," she couldn't help teasing; "unless, of course, they've come for the doctor. Mother lets anyone in who comes for the doctor."

"Shall I fall ill, then?" "That won't be necessary," Edna said, slapping at her daughter's gloved hand. "Then I shall come." "If Mother will not open the door, we usually have the entrance facing the flat unlatched." "Anna!" her mother exclaimed; "please don't give such a disgraceful report of me!" Anna was grinning at her; Matthew was smiling, too. He did look transformed when he smiled. But Anna. Truly, she was amazed at her. Such mischievousness! Teasing! Really, it was unbelievable; she would never have thought her capable of it. Yes, she thought, holding the reins in one hand as the horses started up, waving back to Mr. Hewitt with the other, she had been unfair to her daughter. How dreadful could the Church be if it drew men like that to it? It was true, she had so far seen the worst of that profession, beginning with Dr. Talbott, and then all the others, interfering with John's work, hoping to make themselves indispensable to those who provided their living.

"Are you sure this bandage is fresh enough?" one of those monsters of God asked a week after John finished treating a wound, and solicitously proceeded to remove it; it took over a week to save the patient from death by infection. And then all the others who came to comfort the dying, to reassure them of heaven's existence, when, as even she had known perfectly well, what was needed was a conviction they would live, would recover. John was particularly good at inducing that belief. He would go on so about the piteous plight of widows, citing Judith, imaginary cases invented on the spot, or instantaneously embroidered from memory, but he excelled in his pathetic descriptions of orphans. Fatherless children: how often she had heard him begin with that, until, ending his sermon (yes, that was what it was; indeed, it was), *she* was in terror of *their* own lives and what would happen to their own poor children.

Other people, she thought, smiling inwardly, talked about how they were frightened to death. John frightened

647

people alive. He was something of a resurrectionist himself; she ought to remember what was in his bag of tricks should he ever fall ill. Well, that would never happen, she thought, reining in the horses as another sleigh approached. Those people were in for a spill, she thought, going that fast, if they didn't hit a tree or another sleigh first. And who would be the first to hear of it? The Three Stethoscopes. But she did so like Mr. Hewitt. She would have to tell John about him. It was so peculiar, her liking him. Perhaps there was something wrong with her: sentimental senescence. But she didn't think so, observing their shadows, even their shadows blue with cold; she ought to be fair.

It must be something was right with him. How she loved this bluish-white snow, its peculiar lights. Anna was right, too. He was the first "outsider" she had taken in since Alice. It was odd, certainly, she thought, watching the shadows. She looked over at Anna. Well, *she* was in a world of her own somewhere, but from the look of her, it must be a happy one. She would talk to the others about her. She no longer wanted to send her off to Boston; she would convince the others it was right to keep her home. In the pre-Revolutionary wing, complete with lookouts, she thought.

Of course, as things worked out, she had no time to alter anything; the machinery had been set in motion. Now there was no stopping it. Who should come from the barn to assist them but Amos, looking as if this world and the next had ended. "Oh, Mrs. Steele!" he said; "Mrs. Siddons is hovering." "She is doing what?" "Hovering, just hovering, between this world and the next." "I will go; where is she?" Anna asked. "In Westminster." "What, for heaven's sake," Edna asked, "is wrong with her?" "That's just the trouble, Miss Edna," he said. Oh, Edna thought, he had been well coached. There would be no undoing this mess. Now they would have to go through with the whole charade. They had made their own beds this time, and in a nest of thistles, too. "That's just the trouble," Amos moaned again; "no one can tell. And they've called in the best doctors. She has no fever, no ague, but she can barely breathe or move, and every bone in her body hurts her. It's pitiful. She has to be assisted, almost carried, really, from her bed to her chair. Mr. Siddons is distracted almost to death."

Edna could imagine how dramatically his grief would express itself. No, poor Anna would go off on this idiotic, unnecessary trip; she would never see through any of them. "Well, if you're going," she told Anna slowly, "perhaps you better pack. But if she has a good nurse," she said, desperately fishing about, "perhaps it's unnecessary for you to go." "They can find no one at all; Mr. Siddons says everyone they find is worse than no one. Imagine," Amos said.

Why, he wondered, was Mrs. Steele glaring at *him* like that? He was only following their peculiar instructions; he supposed they had their reasons. They usually did, or thought they did. Maybe, he soothed himself, Edna didn't realize she was glaring. But when she turned around at the front door and glared again he knew she was angry. She was getting peculiar.

Well, she was getting old, too, he thought, as he went into the barn. There was no doubt about it. His feelings were badly injured. To go so far and go through all this acting, then to be glared at, glared at! It was not nice; no, it was not even proper for a lady like Mrs. Steele, he thought resentfully, lying down on his bed. She must be, he thought, getting peculiar. He repeated that comforting sentiment to himself until he soothed himself asleep.

Anna floated off to her room to pray in private. That, she soon decided, was impossible, although she hoped it was less a sin to let one's mind and heart wander to a minister than to an ordinary man, since the minister was at least primarily occupied with love of God. She was embarrassed, making such excuses for herself, but the truth was, she did love Mr. Hewitt, and when she closed her eyes, her hands clasped in prayer, she felt she was clasping his hand; she blushed at the thought of *that*. These were not proper thoughts, she reproached herself, for the Sabbath. But, she reasoned, surely an exaltation of love, such as she now experienced, was an emotion acceptable to God. So it was decided, she thought. If he was sincere. She shuddered; that, that was the only hazard of short acquaintance (*if* six months was a short time, and she did not think it was, although everyone, including

Matthew, insisted it was). But they had been through so much together, and things had taken such a surprising turn when he was there.

When Abigail Grafton was dying, one of her well-meaning neighbors decided to record her final words. Matthew had seen to it that the fanatical soul had not harassed the woman into the next world, but, Reverend Pierce had decided, since Matthew would be entering a regular hen's nest at the Graftons', he had better take someone with him for protection; Anna, he thought, was the best choice. Both Matthew and Anna had set out in the Pierces' wagon. The snow had not been so thick then, but a lot of good, she thought, with unusual bitterness, the remarkable mildness of the winter weather had done Abby Grafton. Her husband had met them outside the door; his most pressing problem, it seemed, was Mrs. Helen Knott, who believed his wife would make best spiritual progress if her husband and children were excluded from the sickroom.

Anna and Matthew explained that Reverend Pierce had sent them to assist her. "Poor Reverend Pierce," Mrs. Knott murmured automatically. Anna doubted she had heard a word about him; no, she thought, she was enveloped in such a cloud of perfection, manufactured by the fogs of her own mind, there was nothing anyone could say about him that would easily penetrate. Unless, of course, she smiled inwardly, Matthew should casually mention the Reverend had just murdered his wife and two parishioners with an ax. On second thought, *that* might take over a week to make its impression; the good woman would simply conclude Matthew had taken leave of *his* senses.

Well, Anna thought, certainly Matthew had been right to compare the professions of minister and doctor, although, she remembered, when he had first drawn the parallel, she had believed some unnecessary storm of humility was causing him to underrate himself. She had underestimated both Matthew and her father. It took strength, she saw now, to maintain one's beliefs, to hold fast to them, and yet allow them to be handled by others who were, she thought, resentful, not worthy to touch them. Yet they never felt their beliefs soiled; they did not feel discouraged. She had always taken such strength for granted. They did their best; that was what Mother always said. That was what Father said when they went on rounds, instead of happy faces, finding blank ice faces, staring at the white sheet drawn up over the body.

And now, she remembered, picking up the missive of Mrs. Knott's, the very, very long letter—long enough to be a book—transcribing Abby's last days, this record was still having a profound effect on men and women of the parish. Still, she was sure Mrs. Knott, for all her devotion and sacrifice, was little but a hypocrite; yet now she was a true instrument of God. His ways, they were mysterious. And she had even begun to suspect Mrs. Grafton. If she were really sure of her faith, why did she have to go to extremes, seeking out evidence for it. Faith, well, everyone had explained to her since she could remember, did not need evidence. Her own father believed in the curative powers of faith; he had told her so. Although he had also said he seemed unable to procure such medication for himself. The world, he had once said, was evidence enough for him. He saw nothing beyond it. She saw the same world, but she saw beyond it. And *she* was not forever picking up rocks, looking for sprouting miracles. That kind of search, it had the odor of death about it, as if one were looking for the seeds of death, not eternity. The seeds of death were so much more in evidence. It was almost certain what a diligent search of the material, palpable world would turn up: death, death, and more death. It was the invisible that held faith, that kept life uncorrupted. Anna was surprised, still, that she had found faith. Perhaps it had something to do with the Moffats, their influence. But, she now admitted to herself, she was more afraid of losing it. When one didn't know how one found something one could never be sure how to keep it. Well, she would do her best. After all, what else could she do?

"Two weeks before her death she sent for me to come and spend afternoon and night with her. I accordingly did." How *good* she sounded! "She appeared glad to see me and immediately began to converse with me about the state of her soul and the near prospect of death. She appeared much exhausted with what she said." I had better, Anna realized, raising her eyes from the page, hide this from the family. They're sure to decide, she thought with less rancor than usual, this poor pamphlet will end driving me off to the Retreat. And why, she asked herself, did she still expect them to understand? That was the child in her; she would have to fight against it.

The reading of the Scriptures. That had been odd; it had seemed immoral. Mrs. Knott had read passages, and then insisted Abby pray God intercede in behalf of her family and friends. At the time, both she and Matthew had strongly objected, insisting she was unnecessarily burdening a dying woman already concerned for those she would leave behind. But she had stubbornly insisted that such agony was the better part, the valuable part, of dying. Matthew's reaction, or lack of it, told Anna he believed the woman right. Still, neither of them had liked her any better for it.

She resumed reading. How articulate poor Abby was in this description! How clearly she expressed her desire for Scripture, for the comfort it gave her! It had been another state of affairs altogether on the deathbed; and it was remarkable, really, how often people did die in peace, comforted and convinced they were only going to sleep, although they did not usually leave this world speaking like texts of sermons or passages from encyclopedias. And how desperately she wished for Mrs. Knott's presence while she prayed! "About twelve, she asked me to pray with her, saying, 'My cough shall soon wear me out,' or 'I hope I shall have patience to bear all God sees fit to lay upon me without complaint.'" Anna's memory was excellent; those requests had not been nearly as spontaneous as they were here described.

"I asked her what I should pray for in particular. 'Pray,' she said, 'that my hope is a good one.'" Yes, faith was the hard thing. She and Matthew had appeared when Mrs. Knott began praying in Abby's stead. The poor woman, she had probably been expiring of loneliness. "'Oh,' said she, 'I do love Christians. I love their conversation and their prayers.' I asked if she could pray. She inquired the day of the month. When I told her, she said, 'How short the time is; if I live until the third of March, I shall be twenty-six years old.'" Anna thought about that; a little less than ten years older than she was now. But ten years was a very long time, she comforted herself; an eternity. It was too long to even imagine the end of, as when she had insisted on going to school the day she had come down with the measles (that was before the spots made the diagnosis official) and the road to school lengthened and lengthened, an infinitely long snake, uncoiling, its tongue with its poison waiting for her at the end. Yes, the missive was upsetting her. It had all been dreadful enough at the time, but this varnished version: it was worse somehow. It must not be that way for everyone. Of course, everyone had not been there to witness the actual event, but vanish was necessary to make things acceptable in most people's sight. She hoped it would never be for hers.

"Dear friends," Mrs. Knott went on, "I feel much for her. I love her much but I shall not see her again in time. I hope God will make this stroke of Providence result in her salvation, and that we may hereafter never be separated. Said she, I cannot bear to think my Husband will leave the world in an impenitent state; or my father. I hope to see him once more before I die,' and she spoke of all her dear friends who were shut out of the ark of safety. I desired her to get a little rest, as I found it would make her much worse to talk." Had Mrs. Knott's mental arm been twisted black and blue when she wrote that sentence? " 'Dear girl,' she said with a smile, "what if it does tire my poor body and wear it out a little sooner?' " (Yes, eventually she *had* come to look upon this life, this body, as a dress she would hang in the closet, as if it were something she hoped others would put on and wear, give glimpses of to the world: after it no longer fit her.) " 'I must talk. I must have many strong and tender ties to tie me to this earth but I feel and trust I am willing to go and leave all in the hands of God. If I am not deceived, I have given up my dear Husband and babes and all my dearest interests and feeling, willing God should dispose of all as he sees fit.' " Who, really, talked like that? And before she and Matthew arrived, no one would have guessed the poor woman had a husband, much less children.

Still, Abby had gone on about her husband and her children and her father, even about her long-dead mother. At the time, Anna would not have been surprised if she had begun worrying over her cat, the fate of her quilts, the plight of the spider in the dark spiritual corner of her room. It had made her uneasy. Such concern for others, she told Matthew later, she couldn't help thinking Abby was hiding behind it, hiding from the real tragedy, the real horror, the real truth: that she was dying, and knew even less what would befall her than her family. Was faith, she wondered, only a distraction? Matthew said he didn't know. If it was, it was so universal, then it must be part of God's grand plan; perhaps faith ought to distract, hide one from the present, which was, in any event, an illusion. The main thing, he considered, was to have faith in God. It was useless, he thought, to understand the ins and outs. What he believed, he had explained to her uneasily, was that it was the business of those who had such faith to make those on earth happy and comfortable as possible. God, he thought, was joy, and only through an extreme experience of joy could one find him. It was impossible, or almost impossible, at least this was what he believed, although he knew others took the opposite road, to have faith in God while one lived in fear and terror. Although that did seem to drive *some* into God's house, where they huddled before the fire like tramps warming themselves in a barn. But somehow he could not believe such faith was real, or as real as the faith of those who were not necessarily happy, but able, yes, that was it, to make their peace with the world.

She believed they needed each other's presence. But her grandmother's illness, that was Providence. She knew she had to believe in that. Belief in Providence, she had long ago decided (she had to tell Matthew that, too), was the better part of faith.

She went back to her chair, determined to finish reading.

Abby was bitterly lamenting her absence from prayer meetings. But could she really have believed that was sin, staying home to care for her children, for her husband? Would she really have been happier leaving them bitter, perhaps feeling neglected, while she prayed herself into a state of self-assurance? What *ought* one to do? She was happy Matthew would be there to help her. They both wanted to do the right thing, or the best possible thing; yes, she would have to learn to think of it that way. They were not miniature Gods.

She sat, motionless, the missive in her lap, the white

sun glare of the snow falling on her. It was very quiet in the house. The quiet made room for memory. Her father had said the same things; well, almost the same things. You treated a patient, he told her (that was when he still hoped she would attend the medical college, and she resented it, the way he had needlessly abandoned that hope, that faith in her), whether you liked them or not, and sometimes you even did a better job with those you disliked just because you disliked them. It put you on your guard; you were more careful not to make mistakes, such as administering the wrong medicine out of nothing but dislike. A great deal of incompetence, he said, was really uncontrolled aversion, and that, he believed, was unpardonable arrogance. If that was true, why did people, some people: well, to be honest, her own family, see religion as so alien to life? The codes of the good and the generous were so like the codes of religion, its dictates. It was faith, then, the ability to trust, to lean back and trust the waters to hold you and float you, that made it so impossible. But then if there *was* nothing to trust? It was impossible, she felt guilty to think it, to know that in this life. So perhaps it was wrong not to have faith; or if it wasn't wrong, it was presumptuous and arrogant. To say that you knew more about the world than anyone else, more about it than any human being could know.

"She prayed for all her friends, present and absent, then for those without God in the world. But what difference did it make? None. None. She was dead. She had expressed faith. She concluded by reading with great emphasis the Lord's Prayer. She appeared perfectly collected and expressed much fervor and sincerity."

At the time, Anna had thought how very convenient it was for Mrs. Knott that Abby regained the use of her voice just before her death, but Matthew had assured her that Mrs. Knott was only human in her delusions. She could understand Abby's need for delusions; but Mrs. Knott—God did not want you to overlook the world and live in a rival one you constructed in your own seven days and seven nights. It had been impossible for them to believe in Mrs. Knott's sincerity, and since they could not, it was their duty to acknowledge the evidence before their eyes. Otherwise, he asked her, how were they to know what to do, to whom to minister? Anna had gone on and on standing in the snow: it was so pitiful, her fright for her children. And even to envy them for going on, and she believed Abby did indeed envy them, and the friend of whom she spoke so often. Was it right to expect someone to die without fear? That would mean blindness to events; anything could happen after death, anything. Abby knew that, coughing and burning with fever. How could she not know it? Why should she wish for such a frightening existence as hers for her children? Surely the prospect of their living through experiences such as hers ought to terrify her, and why did they all assume that such fear meant lack of faith? They did, after all, have to get through this world before they got to the next one. She got up and went out to look for the others. The house was utterly silent. Anna went back to her room and lay on the bed. Where were they? Probably sliding down a hill, she thought, if no one had decided to die that very moment. If the children were on sleds, then her mother and father would be, too. Well, they did enjoy life; perhaps that was the beginning of religion, or even the end of it, but they refused to read the middle of the story. She could not judge them any longer, or even pretend to understand them. Her mind went in circles as hopelessly as Abby's had in those last days. She might as well go to sleep.

Not more than five minutes after Edna and her daughter returned from church, Alice came riding up. Edna had intended to talk to John; perhaps it was still possible to change the plans for the Boston visit, but the short conversation they had convinced her any change would be worse than the original deception. She might begin to suspect the truth of the original reports of her grandmother's illness; she would certainly resent their attempts to control her, to treat her as if she was insane. What, he had asked her, would Anna think if she discovered they had gone to such lengths to keep her from the house of God? It would undermine her confidence altogether. He kept insisting on that; that would be the worst thing, and she had to agree. "But when you come back from rounds," she said, "we have to talk further. I think we've been very wrong. Now we have to make it up to her; if she has been suffering for our mistakes." *"If,"* John said, pausing in the doorway; "I hope we've made them," he said, peering out at the snow. "Even if it means we've treated her badly?" "No matter what it means. If she's stronger than we thought, we won't feel *very* badly, will we?" "No, I suppose not." And just as he went out, Alice came in. She glanced at Edna and saw she was in a very depressed state. Perhaps she should wait for a better time to discuss Anna.

"Edna," she said, "you look quite off the hooks today." "I might as well have no top on my head," Edna said; "everyone can read my face. Soon everyone will read my thoughts, poor things. It's Anna," she said; "come on into the other wing." *"Which* wing?" "The pre-Revolutionary wing; it seems to be the place for secret councils." "That's because it's the farthest away." "I suppose, but it's also the coldest." "Well, at least *one* of us knows how to build a fire. Shall we carry out wood?" "It can't do any harm, but I think there's plenty there." "Well, if you're thinking badly, we'll freeze," Alice said, and they went out to the woodpile and each carried as much as they could manage.

"Well, what about Anna?" Mrs. Moffat asked, relieved not to have to bring up the subject. "I think we've been wrong about her," Edna said; "please forgive me, Alice. I'm thinking out loud. It shows how little thinking I've done. Well, I went with her to church today, and I couldn't help thinking, she seemed so sensible, really, and so happy, not at all staring into space the way some of them do. She looked just fine, and she seemed to be having a fine time, too. And I've been thinking, Alice—oh, I feel very uneasy about everything to do with Anna right now—John and I don't believe. We'll never be Christians —that's what Anna is always going on about, you know— but we can't know certainly that she's wrong, or that you are, and we've been unjust in trying to force her thoughts, to make her think as we do." Alice sat as if entranced.

"And the other thing, we may have mistaken her altogether. Perhaps we mistook a part for the whole. I mean, when she went into shock after that sermon, well, we blamed it on religion. But then the way she took on after Hal's death. I think we mistook impressionability for fanaticism. Well, anything might have produced the same effect. Any part of the whole world. It was probably Hal's taking her to the funerals, and then the sermon; we would have been better off protecting her from Hal than from religion." She looked at Alice quizzically. "Edna," she said, "I'm not an educated person, but I have no trouble understanding you. Stop putting everything," she instructed, "every which way. It's just like what you said you did to Anna. So you think religion has very little to do with your worrying over her? It's her nature worrying you?" "Yes, that's it, that's it; and if it's her nature, then we can't protect her against anything at all. And if that's true," she said, miserable, "then we were wrong to separate her from religion, because that does seem to comfort her and it gives her more strength than we can."

"The dear Reverend Pierce," Alice said, ironic, "always finds one thousand occasions to recite his favorite text: 'Man must have leaders. As a child is led by his father's hand, as the pupil is led by his teacher, as the soldier is led by his commanding officer, so are all men led by their leaders. Men without a teacher are always looking for one. This need of leadership is so absolute and so universal that it is accepted in man's life as a necessity. And,'" she continued quoting, eyes fixed on some anonymous point, "'all this is so methodical and universal and perpetual that it points to the Great Head who is Leader of All, to one universal law in force in all, and one end—far off, but beneficent and grand—to which human affairs are tending. There seems to be no chance, but purpose in this; no chaos, but law; no fate, but Providence.'" "How did you ever learn all that?" "Don't look so amazed," Alice chided; "a stupid parrot would learn all that if it heard it often enough, and I heard it enough.

"Well, I believe Reverend Pierce is right. Most people need a leader to get them out of some wilderness they create for themselves; that's his phrase, too. I apologize for quoting him at you so much; I know you don't like him and I can't honestly say I do, either, but he's usually right. So," she thought aloud, "if it's true Anna has this sensitive streak, then she better have more strength than most of us, and if she doesn't have it inside"—Alice tapped her chest—"then you're right. To be safe, she's got to get it somewhere. In fact," she said casually, "she came on over to talk to me about that very thing." "She did?" She looked so relieved to hear it; well, Alice hadn't expected that. Maybe it would not be necessary to creep up to the subject, Anna and Mr. Hewitt, like a frightened inchworm along a big tree.

She told Edna everything they had said. "Oh no!" Edna wailed. "Now what's wrong?" Edna jumped from her chair and began flying around the room. "I met Mr. Hewitt today, and I liked him very much! It surprised me so. Why, Alice, I even asked him to call on us!" "Then why be upset? You like him; your daughter loves him. You've decided God won't kill her. Everything is coming out just fine." "Oh no, it isn't," Edna gasped, sitting down. She told Alice everything about the arrangements they made to send her away. Alice sat back, thinking. "Well," she said at last, "make arrangements to get her back sooner than you intended. And it won't hurt them to be separated if you can't. Well, Edna, if she's impressionable as you say, it won't hurt her to wait a little. Perhaps this is Providence. Now they'll write one another, and if they survive a correspondence, I doubt you'll be worrying about much of anything." "But I feel so dreadful!"

"Stop that gasping and face up to things," Alice said impatiently; "if you convinced your mother to fall ill, you just persuade her to arise healthy. The thing is, you better explain it all to your mother before Anna gets wind of it. She's not stupid." "That's the trouble!" "Nothing is the trouble; you've just gone and complicated things. But it's not so bad now, is it? Now that you've come to your senses, I mean?" "You don't beat around the bush, do you?" "Well, you've known that for over twenty years," Alice answered.

"You better call a war council in here tonight," Alice said. She thought a minute. "Wait a day or two to send her off; otherwise she might just guess." "Do you think the others will listen to me?" "That's a silly question, isn't it? But if you're hinting you want me to come, I'll come." "Even at five in the morning, tomorrow? I'll have to talk to John when they get home, but five in the morning is when I'm sure to trap them all." "Even Ten?" "Oh, she's been keeping doctor's hours so long she doesn't know there are any others; sometimes I think she doesn't sleep at all." "She catnaps." "How do you know?" "Well, I've known her since I was born; oh, I did envy her in church. She was older, but still, I did envy the way she could just close her eyes, fall sound asleep, sitting up perfectly straight, tilting her head so no one who wasn't next to her even knew she was sleeping, and then, when you had to stand up? She would get up right on time, like a person who walks in his sleep." "A somnambulist." "That's right; what a fancy word for it," Mrs. Moffat said. "Well, you'll have nice times unraveling this sweater, my dear friend."

"While we're here," Alice said over her shoulder, having gotten up to tend the fire, "how are my children doing with your children?" "Magic, absolutely." "Ella, though," Alice asked, "is she all right?" "Better than all right. She's a strong one, spiritually, I mean," Edna said. "I don't know what would have become of me if I'd had a child die." "You'd probably have surprised yourself and been just like Ella. I surprised myself, but then, no one really gets over it, you know. It just takes its place on the shelf with everything else, and after enough time goes by, it stops sticking out and calling attention to itself, and makes itself at home just as if it was always there. Well, after it gets to that, I guess you'd begin to miss it, even the death, if it was taken away, it's so much a piece of you." "That's because you're strong." "Well, so are you; but Anna—she's another kettle of fish. And it's not because she's not as strong as we are," Alice said; "she just needs more because she's different. She's like an animal, a skinned animal, but still alive and going about. Everything that touches hurts or makes her happy. She doesn't get any peace from the day as it goes along. I think that's the way it is." Edna nodded. She always, she thought, *always* underestimated Alice. She was glad she would be at the family council tomorrow. And what would they do with Anna? Lock her in? John would think of something, or one of them could stay out and distract her.

It would not be such nice times, she thought, speaking to John tonight. He took things to heart almost as Anna did. Alice was watching her face. "Don't torture yourself," she told her; "all you did was embroider the wrong fabric. Well, a scouring rag looks silly all embroidered, so all you have to do now is take out the stitches. It's a nuisance, but it isn't anything to worry over much. Unless you want to." She stirred her cup of tea. "I don't." "Then stop." Edna leaned on her little hand, staring at her friend.

She was collecting her forces, trying to take it all in. She had, she decided, taken in a great deal. But, she knew, there was a great deal more she would have to think about herself. *That,* she knew, would be worse than thinking about Anna. So many mistakes to have made! Yes, if Alice was right, she wouldn't be punished for them. Perhaps there was a kindly force in life after all; not God, of course, but a force. She wanted to believe that, she thought, only because she was on the verge of hysteria.

No, at this minute she did not like herself very much. The two women fell to chatting about the usual matters; finally, it was too dark to see one another. Mrs. Moffat put down her spoon. She had to hie away home like the ladybug, she said, even if her house wasn't on fire, but the stove wasn't, either, and if she didn't get to cooking something, Howard would set fire to her, but she'd be back in the morning. At least, she thought, riding back, it was a relief to be on Edna's side. And she hadn't had to do anything. Wasn't life full of surprises? But her husband's face at the sight of a dinnerless table, no, there would be nothing surprising about it. She rode on faster through the narrow lane between the huge blue walls of snow. What a job, digging them out! Oh, it *was* cold.

Was everything going to go wrong at once? Edna asked John after telling him about her conversation with Alice and her own experiences with Anna at the Old Stone Church. "Well," he said, tired, "if a bad beginning means a good ending, we shouldn't complain." "Whenever you resort to old saws," she said, "I *know* there's something to worry about. There's also the old saying that all bad things come in threes, and we've only had two, Ella's illness and Hal's death." "It depends on how you count; some people," John said, "would count Lettie's wedding a third bad thing, or Ella's losing the baby a fourth." "*I* don't count those." "Have it your own way," John said, turning to look at her; even in the moonlight he could see that furrow. "I don't know why you're worrying; if what you think is right—I'm won over, anyhow—and what Alice told you is true, it's just a matter of time until she and Matthew get back together. Then," he said, "we'll have something to worry about." "Why?" He grinned into the dark. She had been lying flat on her back, and she looked like a corpse risen to meet an emergency. Well, there wasn't anything he didn't expect from *her*. He didn't answer immediately. "It isn't," she asked, suspicious, "you're afraid she won't be able to tolerate the fears of a pregnancy?" "No, no; she's just like you there. She'd worry about something happening to everyone else but herself; I don't think she'd give a thought to whether or not she'd survive; it would be all worry about leaving Matthew alone. Or if anything happened to him: that's what I don't like thinking about.

"No, she's one of those creatures like that sister Abby everyone's talking about; she'd die peacefully enough if she had just herself to worry about, but if someone else died, the door would be off the barn altogether." "It's ridiculous," Edna said, "to worry that far into the future when we haven't even decided how to get her back here. She hasn't even left yet. She's going Tuesday, and I had to promise to go to the baptism services and write her all about it, and I have news for you, Old Stethoscope, you're going, too. I can't write anymore, I've gotten so out of the habit of writing, but I see you at it all the time, so *you* can just plan on describing the whole scene for her."

"You *are* in a fit about something." Edna kicked at her covers like a bad child. "*That* made me feel better," she said, "you told Amos all about revising the length of Mother's illness, and getting Anna back here within two weeks?" "I did." "You explained all the whys and wherefores?" "I did." "Are you sure he understood?" "He always understands *what* we're doing; it's why we're doing things that always gives him the sick headache; lately, though, he's tending to dyspepsia." "Oh, stop," Edna complained; "not one more word about a disease." "Well, what *is* worrying you?"

"Aside from your correspondence with Attorney Tulliver? Just that he will, Matthew Hewitt, I mean, get taken off by one of the other young ladies of the church. They have their own way of interpreting the commandments. 'Thou shalt not covet thy neighbor's wife' doesn't really apply to sweethearts, anyhow." "No one even knows she's his sweetheart"; she was certainly irrational tonight.

He supposed it was the blame she was so busy heaping

upon herself. "So they're likely to take their time, the young ladies, don't you think? I mean, they won't hurry around doing obvious things like setting out beaver traps for him in front of the Reverend's house, because they think there's no hurry, and the less we talk about it, the more everything will stay that way. Those religious girls," he observed, "they never want to make fools of themselves. I don't know how many suicides we've had here from just that, girls who threw themselves at men, or who caught the men when they jumped, and then the men went off, and the next thing everyone knew, the girl was taking her last bath in the river. Jilting; sometimes I think that's the most common cause of suicide." "Among the women?" "Both." "Are you trying to tell me Anna's likely to drown herself if Mr. Hewitt's intentions aren't serious?" John sighed.

There *was* no talking to her tonight. "Edna, we're sending her away for at least two weeks. At their age, two weeks will be like twenty years. And you didn't get that impression of him, did you?" he asked a little anxiously; "that he was the kind of scoundrel who went around collecting women's hearts for the fun of it?" "That wasn't my impression, but then I'm usually wrong about things." "Look here," John almost shouted, "if you want to wear a hair shirt and pour ashes on your head and stick your hands in boiling oil, go ahead. I'll even tie you with iron chains. But there's no *reason* for it; you keep it up and I'll be more worried about you than Anna." "How *could* I have made such a mistake?" his wife wailed. "I don't know why you go on about Tulliver when you're trying to kill me with lack of sleep." "Oh, all right," Edna said, "go to sleep; I don't have anything more to say." He was, he was actually going to sleep, Edna saw, outraged, watching him turn over, facing the wall. She supposed she was worrying over nothing, but there was no point in getting up and talking to Ten; she would just repeat what John had already said, and then both of them would be out. How her mind did run on a track once it was given a push!

A week after Anna left for Boston, Mrs. Moffat came riding up just at evening. "Anyone home?" she asked, peering around. "You're in luck," Edna said; "the Three

Stethoscopes went out after a drowning, and they must have found plenty more to do in the area." "Where are they, anyway?" "Cavendish, Castleton, something like that; it seems they get called farther and farther away every week. I can't tell you what a relief it is having Martin and William backing up the old war horse." "We've never been able to thank you about William," Alice murmured, looking down at her wedding ring. "Oh, Alice, it's the other way around. John doesn't know when to stop. But now if he wants to stay home and make his faces, that's what I call his pictures, he lets them go in his place —unless he thinks it's something too new for them, but lately, he doesn't seem to think that. He's more impressed with William than Martin, you know, and he used to worry so about who would be taking his place when he was gone; it isn't easy to get a good doctor up in the country. If he said that once, he's said it a thousand times. So that weight's off him, too. Ten's scooting around somewhere," Edna remembered; "do you want to go off and hide?" "I certainly do; I'm at the end of the one wit I have."

"More wood?" Edna asked. They tramped through the snow to the old wing carrying their bundles. "Don't they wonder," Alice asked, "Ten and the rest of them, who-ever's home, when you go off like this?" "Oh, they're used to me, and besides, if I can go hide out, so can they. When Anna was about three, she used to go up in the attic and sit on the chest behind the dressmaking form, and we never found her when she hid there. She didn't even tell us where she went until last year." "It must be nice to go into the walls like a mouse." "Usually all you find are a few crumbs. I used to think a lot more of solitude than I do now. Ten used to say I was formed for it. I still like it. I can't take too much of living things; some trellis I make for a whole family"; she grimaced; "I still take so much"—she opened her fingers to show a gap two inches wide—"and then I have to fly for the open spaces. Sometimes I just get into bed the way children do and pull the covers over my head and tell myself over and over, 'There is no world, there is no world, there is no such thing.' It works." "It does? I should try it." "You look like you need to," Edna said, sympathetic; "What's going on in your bear den?"

"George. He is going on. He's been off the reins since Anna left." "Anna; does Anna have something to do with him?" "Well, you know, Edna, right now you're the last person I want to bring more troubles, but I have my suspicions about George. You know how he was when Ella married William? That's when he threatened to go off to California, but Howard was flat on his back from dragging those sacks into the house, and he wasn't so set on it then, but now California, California, that's all he talks about. He seems all set on it. He's been writing some old friend of William's from his old regiment, and collecting all sorts of information about some place called Centerville, and he knows the train fare, and he's making out lists of what to take for starting up a farm, and he says he has enough to buy a farm himself from all that work in the sausage factory and the chocolate mill; well, it sounds like he means business."

"It does, but what does it have to do with Anna?" "I think he fixed on Anna after Ella went off and married herself to his own brother." "But Anna never knew anything about it," Edna exclaimed; "none of us did. *Ella* didn't know anything about it. I can't believe it." "Well, he did come home one day, and told William someone—he wouldn't say who—had given him the mitten (you know what that means) and he wouldn't be fool enough to try again, not unless she came after him, and we looked all over the country to find out where he'd been, and he'd been down to your place, and Ten and Anna were the only ones to be found. Well, Howard said he doubted Ten had given him the mitten, or anything more than a cookie, for that matter." "But if Anna rejected him," Edna said, "she didn't even know she was doing it." "No doubt, but that doesn't change anything about the way he is. I'd push him in the lockup myself. You'd think he'd been born to punish the whole world, the way he's going on now. You know we have the same boarders we had last time? They decided the country was relaxing. Well, he's taking it out on all their children, especially their little girl, Lucy. The poor thing's in one fit after another. Well you may look puzzled," she said, looking at her friend.

"Just what *is* he doing? Surely he wouldn't hurt her. She's only seven." "Well, he hasn't taken a broom to her,

665

if that's what you mean, but he's thought of just about everything else. He's the first one down after the newspapers, and Lucy, he calls her Silly, loves stories, so you should just hear what he tells her. Why, it makes my blood run cold. First off, she has a cat. He found this story called 'An Uncanny Bedfellow,' and read it to her in the barn when it was getting dark. Here, I have it," she said, pulling something from her pocket.

" 'If I had been told,' " Edna read, " 'that tame, loving old pussycat would sometime attempt my life, I could not have believed it.' " "It goes on," Alice interrupted her, "with the author's description of how she always fed the cat everything good on her plate. The whole story doesn't make sense, not to me, anyway. The woman should have starved, not lived to write the tale. But I suppose anything makes sense to a seven-year-old." " 'In the dim light,' " Edna continued, reading the charcoal-marked passage, " 'I could see my old cat crouched on my breast, her ears laid back, her eyes flashing with yellow fire, and her tail fiercely lashing as though on the spring for prey. Her nose and mouth were pressed close to my nostrils, while she sucked my breath with fierce, greedy eagerness. She sucked faster than my breaths came—great, strong sucking gulps that even after all these long years I remember with vividness and horror.' Why, the writer's demented!" Edna exclaimed. "Go and explain that to Silly," Alice groaned. "The way Lucy screamed when I came in, I thought her heart was stopped altogether. Well, Howard reddened his rear end, but it didn't stop him. No, he had to read her about a cat who froze her paws, and then her brother had to drown it. Well, and if he hadn't enough of cats; it's all because she has a cat called Gingercat, and she loves that cat beyond life, he had to go and *cut out* something about a cat farm and guide her finger all along the lines to make her sure it was all true. Something to do with somebody named Mrs. Jameson in Pomfret who started a cat farm because a medical school near her needed specimens; the students were stealing the farmers' cats to get specimens for other students, so this lady decided to raise her own cats, the way some people raise daisies, and then sell them to the medical school for cutting. There was something about how next year there promised to be a good demand for the commodity." "I suppose she cried herself sick over that," Edna said, shuddering; "kidnapping cats!" "Worse, worse," Alice said, furious; "she got into such hysterics I came near sending for Dr. Steele."

"Well, you tell her," Edna said energetically, "that there's no such thing as a cat farm. You read the papers the next week, and they printed something about how some mean person had made it all up. And you tell her that if there was more than one cat alive in the snow watching for a dead body, you're amazed to know such a thing is possible, and if anything jumps on *her* face, just to roll over, and tell her the woman who wrote all about that is in jail right now for publishing lies and fooling the paper." "*You* always have such good ideas." "Only where others are concerned. He's stopped at cats, or has he gone on to the more complicated beasts?"

"Stopped? Stopped? I don't think he's going to give the child any peace until he goes and leaves for California. He told her one about an old woman who had a premonition she'd die of a spider bite. 'She lay down on a sofa, and something bit her, and when she brushed it off, she saw it was a spider; then she had sharp pains which got at her nerves'—oh, I tell you, Edna, he's getting at mine —'and her whole face swelled. Two days later she staggered on the steps'; that's what the thing he found says. 'I am so weak,' she moaned, and then, 'My heart acts queerly.' Heart failure, induced from the spider's bite, had killed her.'"

"Good heavens! Why is he doing it?" "I told you, he's mad at the whole world because of Anna giving him the mitten, and he doesn't even know a thing about Mr. Hewitt. I think he's even getting up a file for you, but a lot of good *that* will do him," his mother said blackly; "I stole it right out of his room this morning." "Alice, I'm not sure that's proper." "I'd worry more about what's proper if he didn't have that little girl practicing faints on the stairs and holding her heart, grabbing at her face; who knows what he's doing to her imagination? And the worst of it is, I can't tell her parents; they wouldn't listen. They've just given her over to us, and they think she ought to learn, while she's still young and strong; the long and short of it is, they think suffering will be the making of her." Edna shook her head. "Now don't *you* go feeling guilty about it, that's not why I told you. I thought if things ever got settled with Anna, then she might be able to talk to him." "It won't work." "We don't know that; he does admire her so much." "But then Anna will feel at fault." "Well, *I* don't know what to do," Alice fussed; "I'm half distracted by him, and Howard's ready to get at him with the pick. A nice state of affairs."

"What's in *our* file?" "Oh, there's a clipping about a reverend shot dead at a spring because his sermons bothered someone in the congregation. They tried to send the man off to the lunatic asylum, the killer, I mean, but he was found sane as anyone else, so he's behind bars. Then there's something about the minister's still having strength to roll into his wagon and start up his horses, and how they hauled him home dead." "Perhaps," Edna suggested without much hope, "he's thinking of writing a book." "A book with articles on long courtships, turning down the wrong suitor, a clipping about how most causes of insanity in Taunton's Lunatic Asylum are given over to spiritualism and religious excitement, the failings of modern ministers, girls who marry too young; you think he's writing a book?"

"No, I guess he has it in for us," Edna agreed. "You haven't thought of anything yet?" "No. But my guess is he knows something about Mr. Hewitt; he has so many clippings there about ministers." "But you will think about what to do?" "I'll try; four heads are better than one. I'll get John and Ten in on it, too. I don't want to find that little girl dangling from a ribbon in one of your rooms." "Do you think that could happen?" "Well, no; it sounds as if she's too interested in George to do any dangling from ribbons." "Do you really think so?" "I can't imagine how else he got such a hold over her." "You may be right there; the more I think of it, the more I'm sure you have a point." "Well, if he can't get even with Anna, he'll pick on something smaller; isn't that the way they usually are?" Edna asked. "But *he's* old enough to know better." "Tell that to him," Edna said. "You might as well talk to the well; at least it has an echo." "We'll think of something," Edna said. "You don't think we can count on his outgrowing it?" "Oh, I don't think people ever outgrow anything." "That's just the difference between us; you always take the blackest view of things." "*I'm* too old to change; what's going on lately? Life seems too peaceful. Not counting your George." "That's because you don't read the papers. Well, what's your news? We have a duty to keep it flying about."

"Oh, except for Anna, just the clock. It's taken to telling the weather. We always wind it on Thursdays, just before bedtime, and now the wheels squeal sometimes. It sounds just like a rat in trouble, and after the squeal, there's sure to be a storm in forty-eight hours. We owe this remarkable information to Jack; he keeps a chart on his calendar. He says he wouldn't sell it for his life." "Do you think there's anything to all those stories about that clock? I half believe them myself." "I'm beginning to believe anything," Edna said; she sounded tired. How could it happen that Anna, who had hardly lived in this world, could have caused such trouble at the Moffats'? Really, she thought, it was true; there was no protecting anyone. She had, she knew, always found that hard. Anna must, too, otherwise how did one explain her comfort in religion's promises? It was certainly safer than to put all one's faith and assurance in the temple of one man, as she had done. But still, she hoped she would go on as long as she was needed, even if anything happened to him. That would be the crucial test of her own strength. She hoped she would never be tested that way.

"Alice," Edna asked, "are you going to the baptism services this Sunday?" "I wasn't going to; were you?" "Yes, I promised Anna." "Well, I might as well creep there with you." "John will be the happiest man on earth when he hears that, unless he decides to go and photograph the whole business." "Oh, if he's going to do that, he better get the Reverend's permission, and not only his, the pillars'; you know, the ones Ten calls the pillars of the church, the ones losing their paint? You better get their approval, too." "How do you do that?" "You convince the Reverend Pierce, then that angel on earth convinces the others." "I better leave that up to John." "No, Ten; he's terrified of her. She still remembers how he cheated on arithmetic exams." "He did?" "He copied from *her* slate," Alice said, grinning. They went back to the main wing; they were both more cheerful. "I'll think about George," she promised. "It's too bad about Anna; I mean, her missing the baptism services," Alice said. "I can think of worse," Edna said, waving to Alice as she rode off up the hill.

Anna was bewildered to find herself in Boston, even though, as she could see, and had been thoroughly persuaded, she had her work cut out taking care of her grandmother. Edith had been thoroughly coached in moans, groans, and silent, pained looks by her husband, who, as he told his wife, had spent a great deal of his life coaching models in just such activities. Therefore, she *was* to adjust her pose, or lower her pitch when he instructed; he was an expert when it came to demonstrating how to arise from her bed, apparently in great agony, and an expert was there to be obeyed. When Edith remarked that she was having a great deal more fun than she expected, and she couldn't understand why she hadn't been more interested in theatricals while in school, he informed her to thank her lucky stars she hadn't been destined for such an occupation. There wasn't a model, except for dear Minnie, of course, who didn't complain of everything under the sun: the light was in their eyes, their necks were getting stiff, they were bored. If the scenery was not cheerful they became depressed; no, he told Edith, he agreed with them; it was not easy work. However, he was not one to miss an opportunity, and as Edith went obediently through her paces, he was not above sketching her for a statue he would execute later. By the time Anna arrived in the family barouche, Edith could do everything but faint dead away on the floor. It injured her pride, she admitted, to need the assistance of furniture, but then, at her age, he couldn't expect a circus acrobat, could he?

Anna was immediately set to work. Although she thought of the city as a giant store to be raided for needs in Williamsville, then fled with all possible speed, she soon came to see it as a house on Cedar Street where everything conceivable was going wrong. The day she came, the house furnace completely broke down, and she found her grandmother in bed wearing old-fashioned mittens she immediately recognized, since Ten constantly knit them while she read. Her grandmother had greeted her weakly, saying she had intended writing Edna, but it was so hard to write with such pain in every joint, and then the cold;

she shuddered pathetically: she simply was drained of strength.

She could not begin to apologize to Anna for this dreadful inconvenience, especially since she knew how she would miss her sleighing and skating, not to mention her church work. *They* went weekly to church, she assured Anna, but, of course, she might not be altogether happy with the church they attended; it was so much gentler in its approach. "Oh yes," Mr. Siddons said, "it has become something other than a church, but what could one expect when the whole congregation consisted of men and women of society?" The minister, he went on, could not preach properly, for if he made them feel too guilty, or too sinful, he was shipped straight to some local parish, where, the cynical ladies commented, he could treat the entire parish as if they were children whose hands he had caught in the cookie jar. No, it was unreasonable, although tragic, to expect men and women of society to give serious thought to the state of their souls, except, of course, when they fell ill, and then, as Anna knew only too well, it was often too late. How glad they were, he said, she was there, for poor Edith was inconsolable; yes, she was absolutely morbid. He was sure, he told Anna, taking her aside, much of her depressed state was due to the constant pain she experienced, but the sight of a young woman, her own granddaughter, that would bring youth back to the house. That was just what the doctor *should* have prescribed; why, he told her, he wouldn't be a bit surprised if she made a miraculous recovery under Anna's watchful care.

"I'll have a cot put in her room," Anna said. "Oh, no," Mr. Siddons protested; "I don't want two invalids to care for. Mrs. Siddons has a lovely silver bell, but you mustn't be fooled by its size. When she first began ringing the tiny thing, people rushed to their windows to see the firemen with their pumps. No, no, it doesn't take much strength to ring a little bell. She keeps it on the edge of her bed, right next to her hand." "But if it should fall?" Her father had considered the possibility of undiagnosed rheumatic fever, asking his daughter to suggest that possibility to the attending physician. She might say, for example, she had just read an article on that very subject in one of the daily papers, but on no account, he warned her, must she name the paper, lest he check, and then the cat would be out of the bag. "We could," Mr. Siddons considered, "tie it to her arm." "I'll go and do that right now," Anna told him, hurrying off.

At the sound of her step, Edith let her left arm drop limply over the bed's edge and began breathing more deeply, as if each breath were an effort. Did Edna know what she was asking of her? she wondered. She was used to running about, a gadfly; her daughter had once called her that, and she was: confined to bed for almost two weeks! How on earth would she live through it? It would be altogether different if she were ill, but there was nothing wrong with her.

"I'll just sit here, unless you want something," Anna said. "All I want is to talk," Edith said, feeble; "who knows how many opportunities I shall have?" Anna's eyes filled so suddenly Edith instantly decided to modify the script set down for her by Mr. Siddons. "What I most like to think about are the old days; what fun we used to have, Ten and Nellie and I. Our school was in the country." Now this, Edith thought, was not so bad at all; it *was* warming to think back to the beginning of things. "And times they were," she went on, enthusiastic, but careful to keep her voice quavering; "all those dark covered bridges, and blackberrying and worrying over examinations, and amateur theatricals. We had a friend," she meandered, "named Susan. She married straight out of school and she went off crying. We thought she did the wrong thing in marrying him. Oh, for some time it was a sadder sight to see the living than the dead, she was so miserable." "Why did she marry him?" "She was so tired of being a floating leaf, that's what she called herself. She came from a soldier's family. She used to say how she envied us, having stable homes, while she felt as if she lived on a raft. She was such a nice girl; I think Ten has kept up with her, or kept up with her while she was alive. I'm not sure she still is.

"And then, after she was married—she was a year ahead of us, you see—what do you think happened? Her husband decided to sell the farm they lived on and go further west, and we got the most piteous letter about how she could see no way for her to do for the present but let her things remain in her cousin's attic; she wanted her mother's blankets because her mother made them, and then everyone was after her because she said she wanted a chair, and she said she never even asked for one. She always had such odd complaints. Well, they seemed odd to us at the time, but we were still in school, and she was out there struggling with everything at once, a child, a new husband, and not a very nice one, either; we heard from someone with whom they boarded. The whole town called them the battling boarders, and not with words, either, but objects. And then things calmed down, and she wrote letters about how needles got stuck in her.

"Poor Susan! It all seemed so wonderful at the time, though; getting her letters, I mean, not her getting the needle stuck in her thigh. She used to phrase things so comically, too; why, I remember whole parts of her letters and my memory is so bad, too. She used to write things like this: 'Can you write letters any time and in any place? I think I shall learn to concentrate my thoughts while here, for surely if I do not, I shall suffer mentally, as there is constantly some kind of confusion or something to be done or some subject to be discussed which attracts the attention as easily as the magnet. We have a good room. The only objection, and a small, cold one it is, too, is that we have no fire. The mercury has stood some below zero, but now we are having an Indian summer.' Then she would go on about her neighbors; she had the kindest heart, but she had a tongue like a knife.

"She wrote us a long, long letter—it was so long we had to pay extra postage, probably that's why we remember it so well—about a Mrs. Johnson was having her house papered and painted, and she couldn't understand it, she said, because the woman was so sick and she had to stay upstairs all the time, and then she couldn't understand why she would want to have the room her mother had slept in for so many years. She thought it would bring back terrible memories, or that she hadn't liked her mother in the first place, and the man who was doing the work had to carry her up the day before in a sacking chair, and got all her things into her mother's old bedroom. Well, Susan wrote: 'Her room is all painted and papered now. And the floor is painted, and she is not going to have the floor carpet down this summer; she thinks it will be better for her.' And she would go on about the smallest things. She wrote they had a new organ for the Congregational church. They had put it up that week and it would be played that very day for the first time. They had just gotten up new chandeliers, too, and all in the church was very pretty indeed. Then she went and visited it, and the organ was very large. She told us it had eight power stops and twelve pedals (a lot that meant to us, you know) and Mr. Alexander was going to play on it for nothing, at least for a while, and the Musical Convention was going to meet in the church. Why," she asked Anna seriously, "do you think things seem so much better just because they happened so long ago?"

Anna hesitated. "Grandmother, promise me not to tell Mother about this. When I was younger, I used to sit in the hall outside the parlor and listen to Mother and Father talk, and the minute I heard them get up, I scurried down to my room like the worst little rat in the world. They were talking about all that one night and I nearly got myself caught. Mother said she didn't think it had anything to do with the things themselves. It had something to do with what happened to you as you stayed alive, soaking in time. She said time was like an embalming fluid, but that it didn't get into things that were over, so they had a special radiance of their own, and that made them so remarkable; even disasters were remarkable.

"She said something about her father's suicide; how she even remembered *that* with a sort of affection, and something about a fight she had at a hotel with you; how all the bitterness, or most of it, seeped away, and now she felt remorse, regret, all the emotions she hadn't felt at the time. Oh, they went on about it much longer, but I didn't understand most of what they were talking about.

"I remember thinking that was probably why I never liked my new dolls as much as my old one, and why I didn't like Archie as much as the other cat; his name was Jimmie, I think. I once described him to Mother, you know, and she said he didn't look like that at all. He was really a barn cat, and not very handsome; some people even called him ugly, but she thought he had character. You would have thought we were talking about two different cats, but we knew it was the same one. Oh, I got very upset about it, too, and I didn't have the slightest idea why, but I think I must have known what she meant, really: nothing could be replaced. You had to leave them behind and find new things, and comparing new ones and old ones, that was forbidden. Well, I don't think *I* could live that way; Mother is so much stronger than I am." Edith, lying palely in her bed (Mr. Siddons had carefully powdered her with marble dust), did not understand much of what Anna was saying, but whatever it was about, it was soothing, as if Edna was there, talking to her, and so openly, in a way Edna would not talk to her, not even now. Well, she thought, her daughter had certainly tangled the yarn of this one's romance. It was comforting to know Edna had failings; she so rarely saw any evidence of them.

"Grandmother," Anna asked suddenly, "what do you remember first?" "First?" "I mean, first in your life." "Heavens; I never thought of that before. Well," she considered, "the first thing I remember was tearing up paper to make into rags, paper rags, you know, for a paper carpet." She thought intently. "I can't remember anything before that; I must have been four when I did that; four or five." "I can remember almost everything," Anna mused; "I don't know which is better. I remember sitting in my white wicker carriage, the one you shipped me from Boston, the one with the big wheels, and looking down at my elephant on the floor. Mother was so determined I have a stuffed elephant. I don't know why." "She had one." "I didn't know that." "We manage not to know the little things," Edith said, "and in the end those are the ones everyone else remembers; it's strange." "Creepy, that's what the children would say in Williamsville." "Are you homesick?" "Not yet." Well, she was honest, too, just like her mother.

"Anna," she asked, "would you mind if I spent some time alone with Mr. Siddons? Just until I fall asleep? I have so little time to spend with him now that I'm sick and can't go sit in the studio." "Oh, I am sorry; I should have asked you to tell me when you were tired of me." "I'm not tired of you, dear; I'm just tired of missing my husband." "Well, I'll go get him," she said, jumping up; she had a letter to write. This would be the perfect time for it. Her room, she thought, discouraged, was hardly fitted up for correspondence. The vanity wasn't wide

675

enough for sheets of paper and ink. Finally, she took the vanity chair, piled it with her books, climbed on top of the tower from the vanity's surface, and began writing on top of the bureau. Before she left, Matthew had managed to tell her that their marriage might mean a removal from the scenes of her childhood. His father was not well and refused to leave New Bedford; he wanted her to think it over carefully—if she could really bring herself to leave all the dear familiar scenes and faces. He was not sure, he said, he would be willing to make such a sacrifice himself.

While she wrote, Mrs. Siddons, her door bolted, was literally running around the room with her Lhasa apso. "What *are* you doing?" demanded her husband. "I *have* to move. I feel like a mummy," she whispered, trotting up and down, the little dog trotting after in ecstasy. "You're making me dizzy." "Don't look; you can't imagine how wonderful it is to feel blood moving through your veins. Two weeks of this! I don't think I can stand it!" "I'll take her out as much as I can"; his wife was still flying around like a bird mistakenly having flown into a cage. "How long are you going to keep that up?" he asked; "you look hilarious."

"For the first time in my life," Edith retorted, rounding a corner, the little dog leaping into the air, growling, "I really don't care what I look like." "That's because you know you'd look magnificent standing on your head." "That's a nice thing to say," Edith answered, flying by in her nightdress. "Oh, dear," Mr. Siddons said, "I am going back to my studio. Everyone stands still there." "Well, if you put those precious statues into this bed," Edith retorted, "you'd see them running around the room, too." She flashed by again. "Edith," he remonstrated, "you'll make yourself sick." "I suppose I've had enough," she agreed, climbing back onto the bed, gasping slightly; "how do I look?" "Much too rosy," he answered, getting out a little cloisonné pot from her third drawer; "prepare for powdering." Edith grimaced. "The least you could do is to wash my face off first. I still have to think of my skin." "The vanity of the mortally ill," he said, going to the washstand, moistening a cloth. "After two more weeks of this, no, after two more days, you are going to come in here and find my hair snow white." "Somehow"—he smiled—"I can't bring myself to believe that; you'd use a crayon on your hair first."

"Dear Matthew," Anna began, "I think you would laugh were you to see me writing by a high bureau on a chair upon a pile of books. But, as you anticipated, I have reflected much upon my duties as a wife. I fear I shall not come up to your expectations, not even with the help of books elevating me to such unaccustomed heights. But I shall endeavor to educate myself in all the domestic arts about which I must confess I know nothing, and will try to fill my station with honor. Dear Matthew, it is not wealth or distinction I idolize. I have had enough of both. And I must ask you to reflect on how you, a minister, will feel when my family makes its customary marriage settlement upon one of its daughters. It is quite as hard, I often fear, to resign oneself to unaccustomed wealth as it is to unaccustomed poverty. If there is anything I idolize it is your warm loving heart. I do love you enough to join my destiny to yours for better or for worse, for I know if trouble comes, I shall have a strong, manly arm to support me in all trouble. As you do not urge a speedy union and wish me to make up my mind without haste, and as I have so little choice now that Grandmother is so ill, but still is so lovely to stay with, I think it would be best to postpone discussions of our wedding for the present.

"I should like to be more prepared, Matthew, in every way. You did say something about your father's interest in his new housekeeper. I hope he will get married and then you can be released, and we can make our decisions with freer minds. I do not mean to say I will not come to your home, but, if I must be honest, I would prefer to remain in Williamsville. It is all I have ever known, and I am attached to it by threads too numerous to count. Yet if you must return to New Bedford and want me there with you, I will come. Still my wish is that something may intervene before spring and such a move will not be necessary. But if nothing does, I will come. You must know that. I tell myself, when I feel lonesome, and it does seem ridiculous to feel so lonesome after only one day has passed, I must keep up a good heart and time will soon pass. I wish very much I could see you and tell you so much more than I could write. But I hope my honesty will not cause you disappointment, because, Matthew, I cannot believe that when one half of the pair is your own self, all will not be best in the end."

No, Anna thought, looking at the letter, it would all sound meaningless; she hoped he knew the letter contained more than mere words. She sealed it, stamped it, and slid it into her pocket. She looked in at her grandmother: sleeping. "Kate," she asked the maid, "could you sit outside Mrs. Siddons' door, just until I get back? I'll only be gone a few minutes." "Of course, Miss Anna; I'll just get a chair and sit in the hall." Anna threw on a coat and flew out onto the street. Oh, she was lucky the post office was just a short way down. She flew back in the front door within ten minutes hot and flushed. Letters to her family, she knew, could be dispatched by family servants.

"Oh, Anna," Mr. Siddons said, passing the entry just as she came in, "I have a letter for you. Odd, though, it has no directions for returning it to the sender. Well, here it is, anyway." Anna closed her door and read the letter standing against it. "Dear Anna," Matthew wrote, "even though you have not yet gone, I have begun to fear that you shall be prostrated with illness, unable to write, or that some accident will happen to you. I hope my fears, which I know are foolish, will prove equally groundless. There have been many letters from my father which have caused me many disagreeable feelings and made me fearful of your affections; yes, as you will guess, I am lonesome and despondent. Oh, Anna, how much do I now need your advice and sympathy, and how ridiculous I do feel requiring them, since before I met you, I felt so strong and independent. Love undoes us all. But it is impossible to lay the subject of my family responsibilities before you in the line of an ordinary epistle so that you would be able to comprehend fully.

"Consequently, you would be unable to advise me properly, although I do sometimes think the voice of your heart needs no information. I am sending you the ambrotype of myself taken by your father last week. Yes, I have taken up your mother's invitation, and on the very morning you left, too. You will perceive I am a lot thinner (or perhaps I just think I am). I shall return to my former self if you will only promise me that you will not weary of expressing your feelings at leaving your river and home. I, too, love that old river and that old church where we first met, that meadow landscape, those grand mountains, grand and yet so comforting beyond, and they will seem doubly dear if you must leave, for you will think you shall never see the old homestead again. But I should never be so cruel as to remove you with no hope of return. We shall contrive, somehow, to spend part of the year in Williamsville; that is, if you will have me. I know it is arrogant of me to assume it, even though you did promise, but you seem so far away, and certainly we shall have your family visiting us in New Bedford. An ocean is something of a substitute for a river. An inadequate one, I know, but my despondency over asking you to make such a sacrifice makes me think there will indeed be no substitute.

"You will be pleased, I hope, to know that your parents and I seem quite happy together. It was not what I expected at all. I had heard they were likely to go into fits at the sight of a minister, but we had very nice times, especially since one of my hobbies has always been photography: thus the ambrotype. I taught your father how to make them; he still prefers his daguerreotype. I only hope you will be able to put up with my father. That is the best I can expect, I know, but still, it must cheer us to know that your family, which I confess I expected to oppose us, seems so willing to like me. I hope they will continue to do so when they find I seek a more intimate footing in their household. Until I hear from you, dear Anna, I remain ever faithfully yours, Matthew."

Their letters had crossed in the mail! She would have to write him another. Just then she heard the chime of a handbell; she had better wait until later that night. But for several more days she was not to have time to write. Mrs. Siddons was taking her duties very seriously, even enthusiastically; Mr. Siddons thought a good deal of her enthusiasm was due to the novelty of such responsibility. Perhaps, he thought uneasily, she really had been born into the wrong sphere. Well, he had his work to do, and in any event, it was too late to think of that now.

After two days passed, and Anna still had not heard from Matthew, she began to convince herself she had taken too much for granted. Perhaps, she tortured herself, she had imagined much of what had transpired. Of course, when she was with her grandmother, she put the absence of letters out of her mind, but finally she could no longer endure it and, perched on top of her books, wrote an anguished letter, scolding herself with every word she put on the page, revealing her anxieties; she was going to sound, she thought, unable to stop writing, like a jealous witch. That Saturday, a letter finally arrived. She read it as if it were food for a starving man.

"Dear Anna, your affectionate letter came to hand last evening. And the perusal of it gave me the greatest pleasure imaginable. I read over and over again the closest testimony of your affection for me and then after kissing the precious missive, as I would have kissed the fair writer had she been in its stead, retired to bed, there to dream of future bliss and domestic happiness. It seems that you have been deeply distressing yourself in regard to my constancy, struggling between hope and fear and doubt and love until at last (blessed be the moment when it comes) love will prevail and you will blossom, permit to blossom, your long-suppressed feelings of love, which I assure you will meet with the warmest responding return from the innermost resources of my heart. But, oh, Anna, it did grieve me to think that you could doubt the sincerity of my declarations of love, since I cannot believe I could ever give you cause for so doing. Had I, after succeeding in winning your promises of love and marriage, endeavored to entice you from the path of virtue to joy (and, Anna, if you will only look in your glass, you will see how great is the temptation, even for a man of the cloth) for a few moments of sensual passion, then you might with justice have doubted my sincerity, and believe me, Anna, there was no one else, there will be no one else, who has ever so tempted me. Had there been, then there might be justice in your doubts of my sincerity.

"I believe, dear Anna, we have had little opportunity to know one another, and these vapors of your imagination come from this lack of knowledge. And you, too, must own that I have not had any advantage of you in that respect. I think it is our duty to inform each other, without any reserve, of our habits, tastes, and feelings so that we may know whether we are calculated agreeably, for we had better remain apart, as we are now, than be tied together in mutual disagreement. Still, I cannot believe we will find anything that will make such a prospect, one which would break our hearts to contemplate, necessary. There is much I wish to say to you, but I will defer it until next time. One of the young women baptized has come down with consumption, and her family, I am sorry to say, blames it all on the winter immersion. The Three Stethoscopes (the whole town calls them that now) insist that the girl was already in the disease's last stages, but it is not difficult to read the embittered hearts of the parents, so I have not only had Jane Walker to watch with, but now her parents to manage. I am not at all sure we will manage them. I do wish you were here, Anna, for I am sure you would find some way. And I do wish you had been at the baptism; it was a very moving event. But nothing shall be so moving as the day on which you return."

Anna wrote back immediately. "Dear Matthew, I do not know where to begin apologizing for my doubts. My only excuse is the depth of my feelings and the distance which separates us. I know, Matthew, I should show my feelings, but I should not express my worst. I have tried as mightily as I can to express my best, but I am afraid I cannot. I know it must seem to you, as you read my letters, that I should show my feelings more, make them more real to you, and I will try very hard after this, not to express the worst side of my nature, but my best." She had a chance to test her resolve sooner than she expected. There was another long interval between letters. But, she though, it was worth waiting, scrunched up on the window seat, reading his last. *He* must have stayed up all night writing it. His mood was lighter; she could see that immediately. And Grandmother was so much stronger; her own spirits began brightening. Yes, she had been tarnishing here, here in this house in Boston. For the first time, she understood why wedding rings had to be made of gold. Some things, though, she thought, reading on in the letter, did stay the same. As things went on, there had to be something reminding you of that.

Now she had his letter explaining the unpardonable delay of his letter. "Fred Weston gave me your letter today. The postman had given it to him, and after reading it, I told him it arrived at least two days ago. 'Well,' he said, 'it must have been put into another box.' I told him it was his fault if it was. 'Why,' said he, 'is anybody killed?' I told him I guessed not, but I couldn't promise there would be no one killed if it happened again. How things have changed."

"I remember when my room seemed a perfect heaven, but now the dreary solitude of this room has nothing whatever pleasing to look on except your picture, which stands before me now (I must admit to 'borrowing' it from your father's cottage). My only enjoyment now while here is hoping for your return, of seeing you, of coming closer to you. I wish you could help me subdue these foolish feelings of mine (and you reproach yourself!) but I cannot. I am lonesome without you. Will you call this a love letter or what, dear Anna? You will, I suppose, call it an 'or what.' But, Anna, how much I miss you; how much I long to see some sweet smile from your beaming face. Yes, Anna, I do truly love you, else, as I write these impossible words, the tears, by one single impulse, would never reach my eyes. Pray tell me, what is the use of the world's enjoyments if those enjoyments cannot be reached? And aren't these dreadful sentiments for a minister to express?

"But, Anna, don't you think I have a naughty picture of you? I do. I wish it could have been taken in such a way so that it was capable of smiling every so often. But still, it is a great consolation as it is, and it is more to me than any ornament. I look upon it as bringing more happiness than anything short of heaven. I tell you, Anna, it is a good thing I have a room of my own. I am forever jumping from my bed since I must receive some consolation from some quarter, and then it must be either your picture or your letters. Anyone observing me would be sure I was plagued by bedbugs and fleas.

"I thought it best to stop the hopping and take a walk last night, so I rode over to Lord's Hill and then went up on the high mountain in back of the village. When I was partway to the top I could see the steeple of our old church, and oh, it was such a pleasant sight to me! I was far away enough to imagine you inside, handing an undeserving young man pot after pot of geraniums. I believe they will be my favorite blossoms forever; I think of them,

Anna, as the buds of promise. I knew, somehow, I was near you. Then I thought that by going higher I might get a glimpse of Boston (you see how idiotic love makes me), but I did not. Still, I stood some time with eyes fastened on the old brick tavern in Dummerston, trying to convince myself it was the house you are now in, but it was a cold night, and soon I turned my eyes away from the sight my imagination had made so dear, and began to pace slowly homeward, when suddenly a distant sound fell upon my ear, and I listened, and lo! 'twas the ringing of the uptown bell.

"What can it mean? I asked myself. Still it rang and rang. I looked for a fire but none could I see. I wondered if it were you, ringing for me to come.

"You know, you told me how loudly your grandmother's little silver bell rang, and the distraught heart will seize on anything; I have had time, and more than time enough, to find that out. Finally, I went back to the village and made inquiries, and found, to my great relief, that a meeting had been called to discuss the problem of the baptism controversy. It was the first walk I've taken here since you've gone, and the first outside the village altogether, and a rather sensational one it was, for the first, don't you think?

"Well, my dear Anna, I do run out of things to say to you; it is *you* I want. The Scripture may generally be true when it says, 'The desire of the slothful killeth him, for his hands refuse to labor,' but I am afraid I shall kill *you* if this letter continues for one more page. I must ask you to excuse me, for it is the nature of my passion which drives me to this improper, ungenteel show of feelings. You will discipline me, or save me, and I suspect they will prove the same in the end, when you return. Your brother Martin stopped by and led me to hope you might be back within a few days, but I refused to listen to any rumors, for even if they were correct, I could not meet the train until we have settled things entirely. This is not a good time to cause more gossip in the church. What a thing to worry you with in a letter!"

Anna went on to the letter from her mother; she was so relieved, she wrote, to hear *her* mother was returning to health under her care; she had known that would be the case, and as for the picture of Mrs. Siddons, she could barely believe it. Surely Anna must have had a strange influence on her grandmother. It was impossible, Edna wrote, to imagine her mother, Edith, could reach such a state of—she did not know what to call it—but there was a lack of dignity about the picture of her Anna had sent them—a happiness she had never seen in her mother before, sitting there in her fancy wicker love seat, holding her two Lhasa apsos in her arms, one of them nestling its head into Edith's bosom, the other hanging its sulky head over her arm. "You have bewitched her," Edna claimed, and then went on to explain how Mr. Hewitt appeared to have bewitched the entire family. "It is too bad, dear Anna," Edna wrote, grinning like a cat, "you cannot find someone like him to take to your heart. It seems almost preposterous to think of him as a minister."

Well, Anna sighed, Grandmother was walking around. Today they had even been to the shops, and tomorrow, she was going home. She was afraid to think of it; anything might happen to the train, to the trestle bridge; she might be crushed to death in an avalanche. She might miss the train. Why hadn't she thought of that more mundane possibility? She would certainly have to arrive at the station well before departure time. Why, anything might happen to Matthew. Life was so fragile; it was the most fragile thing. That was what her father always said. And how was she to know he was alive at this very minute? She went to the window seat and stared up at the stars. They were indifferent and far off. Still, she thought, shivering in the cold draft, they were there. She would simply have to calm down. Nevertheless, she was up almost all night, worrying herself into a fever over, she knew, nothing whatever.

How quiet everything in the house was, Ten thought; she was dressing for the evening's dinner with the family and Matthew Hewitt and his father, Simon Hewitt. It was hard to believe, fastening the little black satin buttons as always, that tomorrow all the children except Jack would be safely married. It did seem strange to be dressing specially for dinner. She couldn't remember when she had last done so; probably, she wryly concluded, the night before the last wedding in the house. But this time the wedding would be in the Old Stone Church; everyone had seemed so nervous about it. She had quietly seen to it that Tivoli's would take care of everything. Why, she wondered, did everyone in this family decide to get married as if they were simply stooping to pick a daisy which had attracted their attention? The wedding, she thought dismally, had a funereal air about it. She supposed that was because the actual ceremony was going to take place in a church, while usually the house was such a beehive of activity.

Well, at least Edith and Mr. Siddons were somewhere in the house, and by the time she was dressed, everyone would be in a state of suspense awaiting Matthew's arrival with his father. That would seem more like the natural state of affairs. She had to admit, though, she didn't like this wedding because, although it was uniting two perfectly suited people, Anna was the first of the children actually leaving the nest after the ceremony. At least, she corrected herself, leaving permanently. And for New Bedford.

Her father used to go down to Rhode Island for surfing; he swore he saw a sea serpent as well as a shark. After that, Ten had preferred their river, with its occasional hornpout, their spiky spines, whiskers, and all, to the more dangerous waters of the wide blue ocean. And then there were all those shipwrecks she was always reading about. She thought, looking for her cameo, that it must be a very depressed town, since so many of the women were married to sailors and every day a ship was lost or sinking. Well, not every day. She knew she tended to press some events closer together at her age, or perhaps it was that the texts separating the individual events erased themselves, and the pressed leaves moved together into a bouquet, some fragrant, some smelling of dust and decay. New Bedford; *that* was dust and decay.

She sat down on her chair, automatically setting a copy of *Arabella* on her lap even though she had no intention of reading it; the dust and decay probably belonged to her bouquet, she thought sadly. No, it wouldn't be so unendurable to think of Anna going to housekeeping in New Bedford if it weren't for her sense of her own antiquity. She was almost seventy. Well, they could talk all they wanted about how easy it would be for the family to pile into a wagon and take the cars to New Bedford, but she knew it would not be that way, at least not for her. Why, most mornings, and she did hide it very well, she had to congratulate herself on that, she could barely get out of bed. Sometimes it took her twenty minutes, that was how long it took her some mornings. And that was a performance, wasn't it? she thought, looking ruefully at the bed. She would have to turn over, from her stomach to her left side, then curl herself up until she looked like a cooked shrimp. After ten or fifteen minutes of that, she got up the courage to grab hold of the headboard with her right arm and swing herself up into an upright position. Then she leaned her head against the board, gasping, until the pain began settling down. Then it was one foot after another onto the carpet, but that didn't mean she was up; no, all it meant was she could reach the bureau and, holding on with both hands, drag herself erect.

Eventually, all her joints would grind out some sort of treaty with the rest of her body; but, she had to admit it, there were some mornings they would not make peace on any terms, and then she had to creep around the room for the longest time, going from the chiffonier to the washstand, from the washstand to the armchair, from the armchair to the bed, and once around again. It was hardly worth going to sleep when mornings meant waking up like that.

She could just imagine what would happen the first time she tried taking the cars to New Bedford. She would delay the train for an hour while everyone tried to pry her out of her seat, twisted up like a coil of barbed wire. Well, it would be all letters and one visit a year from Anna; she might as well accept it. And if Anna followed in the tradition of the other girls in the family, she would have something to tend in a cradle before ten months were up and a lot of traveling she would do then.

Yes, as the inevitable approached, she was less and less skillful at accepting it, age also approaching, advancing on her like a determined assassin. She didn't like him at all; to this day she still thought of death as William Platt, who had set fire to his house when he was alone and killed himself in the fire. Except William Platt hadn't taken anyone with him, but that was what death did. He waited until you were alone in the building, the guards fallen asleep, and then he lit his torch. *He* had come from New

Bedford, she recalled suddenly, even though he had come to live in Williamsville after marrying Arabella Wheeler. She supposed the others knew how she felt, although she doubted they were willing to think about her reasons; just last week, Edna read her a long clipping on protracted courtships. They did tend to treat her more and more like a child. But then that was her fault, too, wasn't it?

She didn't want to bother anyone with the details of her aging. That was her personal business, but, of course, her silence left them to puzzle out her strange ways. Her ways *were* strange, too, especially since her worsening rheumatism was such a well-guarded secret. She had been coming to breakfast more and more irregularly. Bridget sat in a rocker with knotted hands, ordering the younger maids to keep her breakfast warm; *she* knew what the trouble was, but only because she had the same trouble herself. Ten saw her staring down at one of her swollen knuckles one day, and after that, there had been no further questions from her, just meals kept warm in the oven. And her own brother, who was a doctor, after all, he didn't guess what made her arrivals as unpredictable as those of the trains. Why should he want to think of it? It would be another matter entirely if she weren't his sister.

There was no conceivable reason, she kept telling herself, for looking forward to this wedding as if it was to be her own hanging, but still, she had premonitions about it. She was sure she dreamt about the wedding and what came after, but when she woke up, she would be short of breath, aching all over, and the first thing which swam into her sight was Anna's face, staring out of the huge daguerreotype on her vanity. And why had she given it such a prominent position? It was as if she were already treasuring the picture as an artifact which would permit her to remember her niece. She was getting to be a superstitious old woman. Unlike Edith. Even rheumatism barely dared approach her. Yes, she told Ten last night, she had one attack, but then she had tried a bottle of Trask's Magic Ointment and the ailment had fled forever. Mr. Siddons, too, had one severe attack, but his had almost immediately yielded to Tomlin's Galvanic Batteries, although he had to go for a series of treatments. John refused to let her touch any of those things. She supposed he was right, too. He usually was.

Perhaps she ought to meditate on the little clipping on long courtships Edna had read her; and then the imp had left the clipping on her vanity tray. She picked it up, fastened on her spectacles, and drew the paper closer and closer until it virtually pressed her eyeglasses. She would not, in this lifetime, change her spectacles again. She was making no further concessions to old age. The joys of old age, she sighed, squinting at the clipping. How Edna's etiquette books went on about *that!* And how they omitted all the true blessings, feeling a twinge in her shoulder, such as the spiritual strengthener, rheumatism. It did give her something in common with every other old woman in the parish. Never, she thought bitterly, had she so much in common with everyone else her age. They also read with books pressed like scales against their eyes.

"Long Courtships," she read painfully. "Beyond a certain point there is no progress in courtship. When the parties to the affair have arrived at the conviction that they were 'made for each other,' and cannot be happy apart, the sooner they become 'one and inseparable,' the better." How true, and how many times had she thought the very same thing? That was another blessing of old age; how little new there was under the sun. "Antenuptial affection is as mobile as quicksilver, and when it has reached its highest point, the safest policy is to merge it in matrimonial bliss. Otherwise, it may retrograde." As if it were a train sliding backwards on the track. "Very long courtships often end in a blackout on one side or the other—the retiring party being in most cases 'inconstant man.' And we would hint to that unreliable being that he has no right to dangle after an estimable woman for years without any fixed intention of marrying her. The best thing a lady can do under such circumstances is to bring matters to a focus." (That, Ten thought, was a new way of putting it; that was something.)

She supposed the author meant the young lady should procure a pearl-handled pistol, thus settling the issue immediately. Bring matters to a focus, indeed! These articles were always long on theories and short on advice. Bring him into focus in a rifle's sight; that would be the best thing. Oh, she had forgotten. They did instruct you on how to bring matters to a focus. What was wrong with her, she wondered, that she could not stop repeating that phrase? They were to ask "the *no point* gentleman *what* he means, and *when?* She can either do that or dismiss him altogether. Perhaps the latter plan would in most instances be better; for a man who is slow in matrimony is generally slow in all concerns of life."

Where, Ten wondered, did they find the authors of these articles? On the dark side of the moon. The article painted quite a picture really. There was Minnie, or Anna, demanding what and when the gentleman intended; why, their nerves would shatter like glass at the mere idea. And if they could not nerve themselves up to do that, they must at once throw the hesitating suitor out the window, giving no thought whatever to his feelings, his uncertainties, his state of mind. It was no wonder the men cast such hideous looks at magazines taken by the ladies of the house, nor was it any wonder magazine covers were becoming more and more elaborate. Lately, they were almost impossible to tell from paintings hanging on the wall, except for the fact that they tilted forward at a suspicious angle, and, if one inspected more closely, there, inside, was the offensive corpse, variously called *Home Circle, Family World, Hearth and Home.* Well, they inveigh a lot, and cause a great deal of trouble; they were just like in-laws, except people went to such lengths to have them arrive once or twice a month. She was becoming too violent on the subject. Nowadays, she did have that tendency.

Well, and Anna? Why *was* she in such a state over her wedding? She liked Mr. Hewitt; she liked him as much as if he had always belonged to the family. It was too bad she couldn't say the same for his father; he was an old curmudgeon if ever there was one. Above complaining, but not above making pained faces: the worst kind. From the first, it had been clear to her he would never move his ancient bones from that old homestead in New Bedford, not after that piteous speech he had delivered himself of last month; how he had built the farm up from nothing and had hoped his sons would inherit it, or at least one of his children would want to go forward with it, but then, after two of them were killed in the Civil War, and the disappointment of his youngest going into the ministry, that had nearly killed him—that gruff voice of his—he had to abandon all hope of having the farm stay in the family past his lifetime.

But he would not see it pass from their hands now, not while he lived. He would die there alone, if that was the way God wanted it, he lamented, staring accusingly at his son, but he was going to die on his own land, and be buried there, too. Well, and who would have thought the young could be so cruel? His two remaining children, he whined on, had started all this fire and smoke over his housekeeper, Hannah Wade; if rumors were dollars, he had gone on, he would have his fortune made for this world and the next one. What were they thinking of, he grouched along, to think he was even interested in such matters at his age? They were just clutching at straws; he knew it. They would do anything to keep from returning to the farm; and where would they be without it?

You'd think, to watch them, they didn't say much, they were subtle ones, he went on, he'd sent them off to the poorhouse instead of doing the right thing by them even after their mother died, and it wasn't every child who could say so much of his father. How much sharper than a serpent's tooth, he had trailed off, glaring at Matthew. Well, obviously there was no fighting him, and he would probably live to put flowers on all their graves. She wondered, though, what he had been like when he was younger; it was hard to tell things like that through the thick, bubbled glass of age. What was he, what was she, but some mockery, some child's drawing of them, distorted beyond recognition, yet with something comically recognizable about them?

Still, for all her rage at him for removing Anna, he did remind her of almost all the young men she had grown up with; it was, she supposed, the way he walked. He was a huge, hulking man, hair snow white, but when he was younger, she knew, he walked just as he did now; oh, perhaps a little faster, but head down, as if inspecting every inch of ground he covered, his arms swinging in that flappy way, palms facing backwards. She had wondered about that all her life, how they acquired that habit of keeping their palms facing whatever was behind them; she had supposed it came from being surrounded by animals, always having to push them back so they could make their way, but John had said that wasn't it. Of course, he didn't know what did it, but he didn't think it was perpetually pushing away cows. She preferred her own explanation. After all, hers *was* an explanation. But now, when old Mr. Hewitt got up, it seemed as if his palms were pushing away life, or at least the present; yes, he was pushing away the present.

She should get up and go downstairs; it was different now. She would get over Anna's departure in a few days at most. It seemed as if events taking place in the present sped off like express trains, while events from her past sped toward her like the lovely carriages she remembered from childhood, faster, even faster. It was lovely, that was the lovely thing about getting old, how some things traveled to meet you. Why, last night, her wedding day had come up in that precious carriage and carried her off; she supposed senility was next, but she did love it, the way the past came back now, missing none of its details, dresses, tones, odors: how it came back complete, inviolable.

John and Edna were sitting in their room, perched silently on the edge of their big bed. There was only Jack left now; each of them had said that. The bed seemed emptier now, Edna thought, now that all that had flowed from it was rushing away from its source, faster and faster, like some unstoppable flood. "Well, old thing, I guess we did a better job than we thought. Or than I thought. I was so horrified, for so many years, at what a bad mother I was, and now, look how well they've turned out." She certainly didn't look as cheerful as her words. "At least they've turned out well for now," he said; "we couldn't have expected more. From now on, what happens isn't our responsibility." "Isn't it?" she asked uneasily. "I don't think so." Each of them fell back into the dark pools of their own thoughts.

Her mind wandered to the baptism services. That was, she thought, the least they could do, to go, after sending Anna off for no reason at all, and they had promised her. Of course, John *would* cause all the trouble he possibly could if he had to go to church, setting up his daguerreotype camera near the pulpit, off to the side, diving in and out of his black cloth as if he were baptizing himself somewhere inside it. Would she ever get over feeling so foolish when attention was drawn to her? She supposed life would give her far more things to feel foolish about.

Eventually, their shipping Anna to Boston would seem trifling, like dropping a pin on the carpet, picking it up. Nevertheless, that didn't mean she didn't feel a perfect fool this very minute, and would continue to feel a perfect fool throughout the ceremony tomorrow. Still, if she had to pay a price for her daughter's happiness, she had gotten off cheaply, more cheaply than she deserved.

As she would have guessed at any other time, John was lost in contemplating pictures he had taken at the services, comparing them with what he had actually seen. How the daguerreotypes changed the face of reality; even while he was taking the plates from their cases, which would eventually surface as images of the event, he knew there would only be an apparent similarity between what he photographed and what he saw. Why had the services seemed so strange to him? He had never seen total immersion before; he remembered his mother saying that three people were dipped last week, that was how she had put it, but she hoped she would never be fool enough to have the same said of her. So he had never seen the services. Probably they ought to have left Jack at home. He had seemed terrified; creepy, that's what he called the baptisms. Well, he supposed they were. Most of the people baptized were twelve or thirteen, although there had been some very old people who had crept into the waters. The church, that was what created the effect. It was snow white inside; the only color in the church came from what flowers the Ladies' Aid Society provided, and that Sunday they had chosen white geraniums.

It was as if everything had taken place in a snowstorm, or somewhere inside a snowbank. At the proper time, the Reverend Pierce had stepped back; the pulpit had been moved by two of the young ministers. Then Matthew had taken up the rug, and underneath it, a vast vat. It was there all year, John had realized, half in horror, half surprise; a pond waiting to be stocked. It seemed bottomless; it seemed bottomless even after the Reverend Pierce had gone up the little flight of steps to its edge, then down the steps into it.

He had been dressed in robes, black robes; against the cold whiteness of the church, it had seemed like a wintry religion, a frozen event. The water must have been cold; he remembered the good Reverend shivering as he went

down. There seemed no end to his descent; John thought
he would descend and descend until the waters were over
his head, but he had stopped, the waters just above his
waist. He was a tall man; age and white hair had made
him appear a human version of the church that Sunday,
white and black, an edifice. Then he turned to the congregation, said his prayer: Yes, they would be born again.
They would have to die to be born again, but after this,
there would be no death, there would only be life everlasting, and everything looking so bleak, so black and
white, like the country in the dead of winter, when the
sap sank to the center of the earth and everything waited
out the frost, waiting it out, the trees silently watching
those who succumbed, unable to help.

And then his voice ringing out, asking, "Do you testify
before this whole congregation your faith in Lord Jesus
Christ? Do you swear forever?" and then the person to be
baptized answering, "I do," just as one would in a wedding ceremony, only this wedding could never be undone.
It was a wedding with the dark water and the weeds,
underneath and tangling, the newly born dressed in white
robes only, no clothes beneath them, one by one entering
those black waters, as old Dr. Pierce, one hand about their
buttocks, one hand circling their waist, tilted them over,
all the way back into the water, their faces going under.
John had wanted to run when he saw that; he supposed
they were taught to take a deep breath, but the Reverend
must not have trusted all of them. He held the noses of
some of them, his large hand also covering their mouths,
so they could not swallow the water, as if it were poison;
and the people sitting in the church—they could not see
the Reverend slowly tilting the white bodies back into
blackness, the burial, the water burial, and how easily
the waters opened to take them in.

Instead, they saw them when he stood them up, and
they were streaming, streaming. Their hair, the women's
hair, was streaming, the clothes pressed against their
bodies, outlining their breasts and their pelvis, as if all
the tears in the world were running from their bodies,
back to the sad waters. It was that he couldn't forget, the
streaming; how the waters poured down over their faces.
They seemed mad, that was it; he never saw women with

their hair down that way, all wet. Only his own wife, but that was different, that had a context.

This was taking place in the colorless, floating space of the church; and then they walked back up the steps, very, very slowly, as if the water had entered their veins, and was heavy, and weighted them down, even as it streamed from them, their hands in the position for prayer, to be greeted at the head of the steps by Jane Camp, the same woman he had given the magic casket, and she quickly wrapped them in a great blanket. The wool blankets were white; nothing, nothing was permitted to threaten the frost, the whiteness: hurrying them into the vestry. That straight, streaming hair: it was an amazing sight, how it transformed familiar features. It reminded him of childbirth, that was it, how some women's hair dampened and dampened until it became straight and wet, how they became unrecognizable versions of their usual selves.

And the pictures: they had been a shock. As if they had gone into the flesh, or through it, deep into the bones underneath; it must have something to do with the light, the way it had drifted in through the high church windows, and the shadows it cast, but the people did not look alive. They looked as if they had seen the other world, and the other world was horrifying. In the pictures, they seemed skeletons, huge of eye, big-boned, the flesh only temporarily assumed for the occasion, then only for the benefit of the spectators, and some of them seemed only faces floating on bodies barely corporeal; that, he supposed, was because their robes were white and the wall they stood against when he took their pictures was white, but the folds of shadows in the robes, they had created the illusion of bones showing through soaking-wet gowns.

And the bones in the face, how they seemed to have jumped forward, past the eyes, which sank back into their sockets. It was all a trick of the light, the aberrations of the camera, but it was horrifying, and the absolute silence while the procedure went on, as if all life on the planet had been suspended for this miraculous event, and the miracle, a rebirth into the same pain and suffering from which they had just died. He would not forget it, not the event, not the pictures, and he did wish all of it was not so connected with Anna's wedding. It was, in his mind, the whiteness of the baptism robes, the whiteness of the wedding dress, the whiteness of the ceremony in the church amidst the dark waters, the whiteness of the wedding in the church on a dark winter day. No, he was getting foolish as his sister; if his mind chose to liken those two events, the linkage said nothing about his daughter, only about him.

"What are you thinking about?" Edna asked. He was still surprised by it, how she always asked at the right time, just as he started to feel like someone who had set foot on a steep bank, sure of his footing, only to find the mud slippery as glass; in his worst nightmares, that was what happened. He stepped onto the bank, and no matter who called to him, or reached to him, or threw ropes or sticks, there was the black water, waiting. Nothing would discourage it. "Just the pictures of the baptism services." "I can't look at them," Edna said; "they turn me cold inside; they make me feel like this sheet feels on a cold night, and the same color, too. I wish," she said, "you would put them out of sight. They look like bodies coming back from the dead." She shuddered. "Are you getting used to them?" she asked; 'is that why you're keeping them out like that?" "Yes." "You will never get used to them." "You're probably right; if a camera could photograph nightmares, those would be the photographs." "I couldn't agree more. For my sake, close them; I've gotten so I dread walking into that cottage. It's like an embalming parlor," she said after a minute, "only worse, because the bodies are dead and alive at the same time." "I'll close them; I know just how you feel." "They're like" —she paused—"they're like pictures of memory itself; things dead and alive, both at once, but it's all right, I mean, it isn't so frightening, when the memories are where they belong"—she tapped the side of her head— "but to see them so touchable; it's a horror, as if you invaded some misted world. Oh, I wish you hadn't taken them. I keep thinking they're evil somehow." "Don't be silly," he said, out of patience.

And he was impatient because that was just how the pictures had seemed to him. He had not phrased it so well, and was annoyed at Edna for doing so. It only made matters worse; the clearer their view of the pictures became, the more they were terrified of them. But that had never been their way. As soon as they understood, they were reassured, they were confident. But these pictures reversed everything; it was as if they presented a negative image of the world: before it was developed into a positive one, something clear. He wished there *was* a negative of those pictures to look at; he suspected they would be images of the world as he knew it. He shivered slightly.

"Do you really think," Edna asked, feeling the tremor in his body, "Anna will manage to come here once a year? That father of Matthew's seems determined to hate everything about Williamsville. Last week, I had the definite impression he was trying to convince all of us that Williamsville was more dangerous than Durango, the way he went on over a shooting at the Junction."

"You know," Edna said, "I think we're all taking on so strangely because Anna is almost the last one left. I never thought she'd get married. I never thought she'd get *old* enough to get married. Did you?" "I guess not." "And soon Jack will be going through the same paces," his mother lamented. "Don't even say it." "Well, not for five years at least; men tend to marry older than women. There's more hope with Jack. I suppose it's selfish of us to want to keep them home, like the Camps; I wouldn't want them to be like the Camps." "No, but don't forget, we have two of them living in the house with us and not trying to shoot us down in the halls; we've turned out luckier than most." "I just hope it lasts." She touched his hair lightly. "I'm glad you kept your mane; I never did like bald husbands." "You probably paste the hairs back on at night. It's too bad *you* can't wear your hair down." "At my age? Wouldn't I be the sight? Everyone would say I was competing with my own daughters." "Well, you could, you know." "You're prejudiced, my dear face maker," Edna said, leaning over to kiss him; "do you think Anna will have our luck?" "If she's lucky," he laughed. "Do you think she will be?" "She can put up with that old codger, and she couldn't be better matched. I suppose life will make up its mind about her luck. As usual." "You make it sound so nice and predictable; as if there was nothing to worry about." "I didn't say that; I said there was nothing we could do about *anything* from now on."

"These weddings are making me feel old," she fretted. "You are." "Well, thank you," she said, turning to glare at him. "Compared to a newborn infant." "Impossible, you always were." "But, on the other hand, you're very young compared to the one-hundred-year-old frog." "Now what are you talking about? What a time machine of silly information you are." "The old frog up at the Ritchie place. There's a pool of cold water in its springhouse, and that's where the old frog lives." "What frog? What frog?" He *could* tease when he put his mind to it. "The hundred-year-old frog. They know it's the hundred-year-old frog because old man Ritchie says it's the same frog that lived there when his grandmother was a child and his grandmother always said that the old frog's voice was a rain sign; it sounded like thunder. You can hear the frog for almost a mile," he told her; "and moreover, it is a very active frog and shows little if any evidence of the century or more of its life. So you see, you don't have to worry; compared to the frog, you're just a baby." "Well, I *feel* like a baby, a baby about to have a temper tantrum." "That's only because we have to go to a church wedding." "Will you stop?" "I'm not looking forward to it, either; it takes all the solemnity out of the occasion when it takes place in a church." "All right," Edna gave in, "you win. I'd rather go downstairs and face the music than sit up here and listen to this." "Come on, then," he said, getting up first, handing her down from the bed as from a carriage.

The evening passed peaceably enough, Ten thought with relief; she hadn't been at all sure she could endure any further diatribes on the number of criminals and lunatics in Williamsville, not with the way her elbow and jaw hurt, especially, since to look polite, she had to go on with her chewing no matter how much it hurt. She supposed old man Hewitt was happy enough; he was having his way, after all. The newly married pair would be going back to New Bedford after their honeymoon trip to the mountains; that was all he cared about. But by the third course, she felt more mellow; it must have been the effect of the hot soup.

"You know," Edna was saying, "the entire parish thinks your son is just short of a saint." "It's no wonder," the old man said; "everyone here is shooting or poisoning everyone else." A bleak silence fell over the table as members of the Steele family looked at each other under half-lowered lids. "It was very nice of you, Matthew," Edna tried again, "to bring me your mother's button collection; I've gotten very interested in them, especially the Della Robbia buttons. They look Grecian. No, no," she hurried on, seeing his face, "I do mean it. I hope to start collecting them." "Then I'll give you some to begin with," he promised. "Go ahead, give away everything," the old man muttered. Matthew glowered at him. Ten smiled into her soup. "How does it feel," she asked the old man, "to have such a distinguished son?" "He's not so saintly; I could tell you lots of things about him that would tear his wings right off." "What, for example?" Ten asked, ignoring Anna, who would, had she been close enough, be kicking her under the table.

"Well, for instance, the time he painted up the little girl he used to play with." "Painted up?" Ten asked, putting down her fork. "Oh, the two devilish imps were playing out in back, and I left out a couple of buckets of paint; I was painting the house. I always worked hard on that place," he said, glowering at Matthew. "One pot was red and one was green, and the two idiots took the brushes and painted the barn stall red but that didn't wear them out, so they painted one wheel of my wagon green, and finally Matthew decided they should paint each other. So he painted one of her feet green, and the other foot red, and then she painted up his legs, and then she got jealous because his looked nicer than hers, so they rolled up her stockings and painted up to her knees, and then they decided they'd look better striped, so they wound up striped green and red like a barber pole. Martha, that's my poor dead wife, I thought that was her last day," he went on with something like good humor; "she had to try and get the paint off this one here, and then the girl went home to show her mother the scenery, and she was over howling like a wolf at her house.

"The little girl jumped over a fence right ahead of the handle of her mother's mop. Well, we got them and warmed them, I can tell you, and they *would* have had to pick paint with some new kind of drier that made it hard and shiny and we got out the benzine and he was screaming, 'Murder! Murder!' until people on the highway came running over to see him. It burned something dreadful;

anyway, he wasn't much for painting after that." "All I did," Matthew said mildly, "was transform nature into high art." "I hope you'll leave off all that now," his father grumbled. "I'll leave the artistic things up to Anna."

And so the evening went off rather well, the old man telling his favorite jokes, which ran to stories about a man who was so round-shouldered he had to use sticking plaster to keep his shirt on. At least he kept himself amused, Ten thought, listening to him roar with laughter. She would end with a sick headache if he told one more joke. And something in Anna's eyes told her she could expect her later that night. She was giving Anna her little book *The Wedding Ring,* the same one her mother had given her when she had been about to marry. It wasn't much bigger than John's daguerreotypes, the little ones; probably it was smaller. She couldn't imagine anything in it would upset Anna, but then, it was Anna after all, and one never knew.

Ten waited up in her room, telling the time by her bones; it had to be after midnight or her hip and knee would never ache this way. Probably she was so superstitious about Anna because she felt so achy. There was nothing to have premonitions *about;* everything had gone so well for her. *That* was just what bothered her. When one considered Anna's nature, a smooth course was the last thing to be expected. It must be, she thought, resettling herself carefully, avoiding a twinge, her own memories coming back and settling on Anna, one hornet from her own nest. The whole fuss over George had been settled now for some time, and Anna *still* didn't even know about it. When Edna and John had no ideas for Alice, they had called in the rest of the family. Really, it was comical to see how she, her brother, and one cat had multiplied into the contents necessary for several arks.

William, who had made it his business to know Matthew, said the solution was simple as could be. He would just tell Matthew all about George and they could slam it out in back of someone's barn. "Well, don't look at me as if I've gone off my head," William protested; "George is my brother, and he's just plain mad. He'll have it all settled if Matthew knocks him down, or the other way around." Deliberately setting them to fight. Ten could see that didn't sit well with Edna. "Edna doesn't like it," she said. "What do you think?" they asked Minnie; *she* was George's sister. "Oh, Bill's right," she answered without hesitation, "Ma always said you had to put an idea on the end of a nail and drive it into his head for him to pay any attention to it." That from gentle Minnie! Well, she had certainly settled it. "I'll talk to Matthew tomorrow when we go to church," Martin said. Whenever he could he went to church with Minnie; she attended as habitually as the others ate breakfast.

Several days after their conference, Matthew had come in, holding one of his hands in the other, looking pretty ashamed of himself. "Well, what happened?" Ten asked; and to think, she reproved herself, how she ridiculed people who took such an interest in pugilists. "The other one looks worse," Matthew said, sitting down at the table, while Bridget and Ten carried over an enameled basin of cold water with a big chip of ice floating in it.

"*How* much worse?" What a vulture she still was! "Let's see," Matthew said; "I appear to have been following the wrong testament; 'if thy eye offend thee, pluck it out.' " "Hand, hand," Ten corrected automatically; "you hurt your hand." Oh, he was running at her, she realized, blushing. "George's right eye is all swollen shut; he won't be able to see out of that for two weeks, and I can't take the credit for his arm." "His arm?" Bridget asked. "Well, he fell on that when he fell down. The good earth will have to take all the credit for that." "What, is it broken?" "Just a sprain, but his mother and father won't like him much if he can't carry the old milk pail. He can still turn the well handle and get the oaken bucket up with his left hand." He grinned down at the tablecloth. "We all thought *you* were going to be murdered," Bridget said.

"Me?" Matthew asked, surprised. "I grew up on a farm, too, and besides, I used to earn money to help out the family by fighting in amateur pugilistics. But I was fair," he insisted to Ten; "I didn't use any professional tricks except when it came to ducking." "I guess George is, too, by now," Bridget said; she looked over at Ten. They all looked happy as pigeons with a piece of bread. "What about that hand?" Ten asked. She could just see him assisting at services, with a blue and green hand complete with cut-up knuckles. Everyone in the parish would know what that meant. Matthew picked up his hand from the basin and looked at it. "It will be just as it ever was by tomorrow morning," he assured them. They looked dubious. "That was the voice of experience," he said. "So you think," Ten asked him, "George won't bother Anna now?" "He won't bother anyone," Matthew assured her; "we had this little heart-to-heart talk while he was lying on the ground. Well, not heart to heart, exactly; I was sitting on him." "Good Lord!" Bridget exclaimed. "This is one thing the Lord had little to do with," he said, picking up a piece of buttered bread they had set in front of him. "Have you any sugar?" "Sugar? For what?" Ten asked. She saw Bridget's sympathetic look. "Poor man's cake," he said. "Oh," Ten said, getting up creakily, taking the sugar canister down from the hutch shelf. Yes, she could see Anna had a strong shoulder to lean on. Well, and what could be better for her, after all, than a minister who wasn't above knocking someone down to make his point? Yet, she worried.

Anna gave her little code knock, one long, three shorts, and came in. How had these peculiar habits ever developed? Ten was sure when death came for her, he would have some special tap of his own, probably three scratchings and one mew of Jimmie's. "Come in," she whispered in a low voice. "You're awake?" "No, I'm sitting here talking in my sleep." Cranky, she was cranky. So much for her forebodings. "I can always go back to bed." It was selfish of her to keep Aunt Ten up so late. "You just move that little body of yours nearer the door," Ten threatened, "and I'll show you how good the aim of a sleepwalker is." Anna sat down on the chair near Ten's little table. "Well, Aunt, it's your fault, you know. You did too good a job with us." "Don't try to blame your bliss on me; your mother was around every once in a while." "It wasn't the same; Mother always had part of her mind on something else, and then when she turned it on us, it was too hot. As if she burned the skin. It's awfully hard to explain; I don't mean to blame Mother for anything, but she just wasn't as suited to things as you were. Where would I be without you?" "Just where you are now."

Anna shook her head hopelessly. "You'll never convince me." "Nervous little ladies are given to strange imaginings the night before their weddings." "I'm not nervous." "Did your mother ask you about that?" "Did she ask you about your wedding night?" "There you go again," Anna sighed; "that's what I meant. No, she did not ask me about anything of the sort. She expects matters will just take care of themselves. I suppose they usually do." "*Are* you nervous?" "Terrified." "Well," Ten said, "no one in the history of our family has ever bled to death on their wedding night." "No?" "Definitely not; if you have ideas of backing out along those lines, you'd better forget it." "Backing out? No, if I'm afraid of anything like that, it's that Matthew will think things over and decide to disappear." "In his profession, he'd have to disappear all the way to Africa, and he can't do that because of his father. No, we're stuck with him, Anna; I can't think of too many ministers who would dare leave their intended standing near the altar of the church. Just last week I read an article about a congregation tarring and feathering their minister for wife beating. You're not worried about Matthew beating you?" Anna just sighed and tapped on the table. "Well, then it must be something worse." No sign from Anna. "Then something harder to talk about." Anna nodded dismally. "Are you going to make me guess away all night?" "Probably," her niece said, blushing. "Aha, blushing. Fee, fie, fo, fum. That can only mean one thing: the act of physical union. Is that right?" Anna nodded, staring down at her fingernails.

"Enlighten me," Ten requested; "you've been around animals all your life. You know exactly what the process entails. I've washed you in enough tubs so I know you have no deformities to worry about. You're not going to frighten anyone off in your skin suit. So what is it?" Anna hesitated. "I can't." "Oh yes, you can. Try harder." Anna took a deep breath. "Well, I'm not clear on some things. Horses and men aren't *exactly* the same." "Well, what is the difference?" "I don't see how we're supposed to fit together," Anna blurted out. "Fit together? As in a jigsaw puzzle?" Anna nodded miserably. "I think you'd better explain that further." "Well, a horse, you know— Anna stumbled along—"its private parts point straight ahead, and it climbs up on its mate, but if that's the way it is with humans . . ." Ten regarded her with amusement. The child did look ready to perish of embarrassment. "You never were very good at geometry, were you?" Ten asked. 'Oh, please, stop grinning; it's not at all amusing." "I suppose it depends on your point of view.

"Well," Ten began, settling down to business, "when a man is not interested in bodily union" (in spite of herself she could not help stressing those words), "his organs just dangle." Anna turned fire red. "But when his interests change, then he sticks straight out, or on a slant. Why, I could hang a towel on my husband's unmentionable." "Aunt Ten!" "So that when the male of the species places himself on the female of the species, it's about the same thing as placing a spoon into cake batter, more or less straight, or slanted, depending on the body of the woman, the man's unmentionable being rather flexible. That's it; you can come out of your coma now," she coaxed Anna, who had almost slid from her chair.

Poor Anna! She did take everything so to heart. How had the other girls found out these little secrets? Lettie: well, nothing would surprise her about that one. Ella probably found out all about those things from Martin. They had been inseparable. Oh yes, she did remember the beating Ella had gotten when she had followed Martin and some of the other boys down to Slab Hollow after school and watched them all experimenting with their unmentionables, and then she had gone and had the senselessness to tease him about it in front of all of them at the table. Well, she had been only nine at the time, but that had undoubtedly cleared matters up for her.

"Why," she asked her niece (for some reason she could not really put her finger on, she liked thinking of her that way tonight), "do they call that little valley between Williamsville and Dummerston Slab Hollow?" "I don't know. I never thought about it." She was never surprised at any turn her aunt's mind took. "Maybe there was once a burying ground there," Ten said; "or an Indian war." "Or they dug up stones for slabs." "Maybe," Ten agreed; "imagine living here so long and not knowing why it has that name." "That's just why we don't know." "True." "Well," she started up in her brisk way, "I wanted to give you the same little book my mother gave me when I married Ed." She took it from her pocket.

It was a tiny beige book, embossed all along the edges, the gilt worn off everything but the central design, a wedding ring surrounded by a garland of roses. *"My* mother had it," Ten said, watching her open it; "that's why it says Julia Steele above my name." "It's like a family Bible," Anna said softly; "but it's so small." "Big things come in small packages." So this was what Edna's rabbit-like habits had led her to, a perpetual spout of truisms.

"You've underlined a lot." "Well, I read in it a great deal." "Some of the underlinings," Anna said, looking through the little book more carefully, "are in violet ink; they're faded." "Just like their scribbler." "But some of the underlinings are in pencil; they look much newer." "Pencil always stays looking fresh," Ten said, guilty; "that's why so many people keep diaries in pencil." "Some of these pencil underlinings still smudge," Anna went on remorselessly, running her finger over one page. "Will you leave that poor book alone?" Ten snapped; "it's old, like its owner. You're not supposed to treat it as if it were a new shovel."

"Aunt," Anna said decisively, "I do believe you've underlined some of these passages in the last few days." "Why on earth would I do that? I wouldn't dream of marrying again at my age. Can you just imagine the spectacle? The minister joining two hands from one casket to another while we try to whisper, 'I do'?" "I don't intend to be distracted," Anna said. "You could at least thank me," Ten said grumpily. "For the underlining?" "For the book. I don't know why anyone in this family worries about you; your mind has teeth like a bulldog." *"Did* you underline it for me?" "And if I did?" Even she could hear the guilt in her voice. Anna looked sadly at her, then began inspecting the book. "No one in this family ever changes," she said without looking up. "Well, and what do you expect. You don't change either." Anna shook her head.

"All right, then," Anna retorted; "I'm going to look for those passages right now." "Go right ahead and kill me with lack of sleep," Ten said; "if I'm not at the ceremony tomorrow, you'll have only yourself to blame." "That old trick doesn't fool me anymore," Anna answered, turning pages. " 'Many, I believe, act toward the deity as they do toward their friends; they make up their own minds and then ask to be directed.' I don't see how that applies to me." "So, Miss Smartypants, my mother underlined that for *me*." Anna tested the passage with her finger, and went back to turning pages. "Now *this* smudges," Anna announced, triumphant. "I don't like this," her aunt protested. "Then you shouldn't have done it." How fast they grew up, Ten thought. Sometimes they seemed older than she was. She supposed in a way they were. They were so involved in the webbing of life, while she observed it from a distance. She looked at life now as she looked at things through her spectacles when she came in from the cold and her spectacles misted over, and she saw everything through a fog, picking her way more by memory than by awareness. Only now and then, she thought, did her eyes really open.

"'A family,'" Anna read. "'How delightful the associations we form with such a word!' What's wrong with that?" Read on, read on." Why, if it weren't for her lace cap, designed by dear old Mrs. Grimsby so cleverly to resemble the fall and drape of hair, she would look positively like a man. She was getting to be a skeleton, she thought, looking down at her wrist. There are no differences in the grave: hadn't that been the recent theme of one of Reverend Pierce's interminable sermons? What on heaven or earth kept that old bag of bones going? "'But, alas,'" Anna continued, "'of those who, in the ardor of youth, start for the possession of this dear prize, how many fail! And why? Because the imagination alone is engaged upon the subject. It is a merely lovely creation of a romantic mind, and oftentimes, with such persons, fades away, "and, like the baseless fabric of a vision / Leaves but a wreck behind."'" "Now, Aunt, that is not fair. I *have* seriously considered the suitability of our characters and I don't see how I could have made a better choice." The poor child looked furious.

"It wasn't your choice of husband I was worried about." "What, then?" "Just about everything else that can go wrong," she said bluntly: "leaky roofs, Japanese beetles, deaths in the family." "Deaths in the family? Aunt, just because your husband was taken from you doesn't mean the same thing will happen to me." "It doesn't mean it won't, either; or to a child or a pet." "I'm sure that won't happen." "If it's not a good idea to look for trouble, it's still worse to imagine it doesn't exist. Considering what this life is." She was making Anna uncomfortable, she could see that. "What's this?" Anna asked, pausing at another page. " 'Precious, indeed, are the joys of a happy family; but, oh, how fleet! How *soon* must the circle be broken up, how suddenly it may be! What scenes of delight, resembling gay visions of fairy bliss, have all been unexpectedly wrapped in shadow and gloom, by misfortune, by sickness, by death! The last enemy has entered the paradise, and, by expelling one of its tenants, has embittered the rest to the scene. The ravages of death have been in some cases followed by the desolations of poverty; and they, who once dwelt together in the happy enclosure, have been separated and scattered to meet no more. But religion, true religion, if it be possessed, will gather them together again after this destruction of their earthly ties and conduct them to another paradise, from which no joy shall ever depart and into which no calamity shall ever enter.' "

Anna let the book slip into her lap, its two covers spread back like the wings of a fallen bird.

All this had happened to Aunt. Did Aunt Ten have some premonition about her, about her future? Or was she worried about her own coming death? Probably both. But the implication of those passages seemed clear enough. Aunt did not think she was ready to face anyone's death; anything else, apparently, she thought, reviewing the subjects she had already flipped through. She looked at her aunt. She *was* awfully old and, lately, she looked even older. She must think, Anna guessed at it, one step of ours toward the future is one step of hers toward the edge of the grave. Anna shivered slightly. She could not imagine life without her aunt. But people in her family lived so long! Most of them lived to be one hundred; there had been one aunt who had died at one hundred and five. She remembered that because of an old uncle who had come staggering in to look at the face of the dead woman, although he hadn't seen her alive in twenty years. He thought it was remarkable how well she looked. That was what he said, as if the sight of her face, somehow concealing the ravages of age and pain, convinced him he had nothing to fear.

It was just as well, they had all thought at the time, he hadn't gotten too close, or he might have been able to see too well; he might have noticed the youthful look was due to hair supplied by the undertaker, and the lips and cheeks were fuller than they had been in years, thanks to another trick compensating for the loss of her own teeth. Yes, Aunt must be worried about herself. Perhaps she had forgotten the difference in their ages; that must be it. She resumed her thumbing through the book; nothing less would satisfy Aunt. "Are you through?" her aunt asked. "Not until I read the page with the corner turned down. Now that was obvious, wasn't it?" Ten glared at her. " 'Let her guard as much as possible against a gloomy and moody disposition, which causes her to move about with the silence and cloudiness of a specter, for who likes to dwell in a haunted house?' Is *that* your view of me? Someone who moves about with the cloudiness of a specter? Who makes a house into a haunted house?" "Well, you do manage to produce something of that effect sometimes; just remember how you went on after Hal's death." "Well, there was something to go on about!" "There was also something to stop about!"

She had raised her voice; it surprised her. She was *still* angry about it, how much worse Anna had made it, adding worry over her to their grief over Hal, making the rest of them feel as if there was something wrong with the rest of them carrying on with their lives. And suppose she were to act that way if something went wrong in *her* new family? If she were to lose a first child, as Ella had? Perhaps, she meditated, that was not so dangerous. The affections did not really become entangled with the newborn child, only the threads of the imagination. They were easier to pull loose without pulling apart the wound they held together. But an older child? Or her husband? Why couldn't she imagine Anna going through those woods, coming out onto the flat? She could not; and none of them would be there with her as they always had been. But there *was* no reason to worry, she told herself again, as she had already told herself one hundred times that evening. If any of the children were to worry so far in advance, she would give it to them with a broom. Age was melting her brain. Even her emotions were addled.

"Aunt?" Anna said, trying to get her wandering attention; "you mustn't take on about this wedding so. It won't be the last time we'll see each other." "It may be." "Don't say that!" "Oh," Ten said, "I didn't mean to imply your wedding and my health were connected in any way, but my health isn't what it used to be, and time presses on me more than it used to. You must promise me," Ten went on anxiously, "that if anything happens to me you will go on as if I were still there. I will be, you know. Somewhere inside you." "You are not going to die." "I have to die sometime or other." "No, you don't." "Anna, when you say things like that, you make me worry. I do. I do have to die sometime. It isn't easy, when you know your own death will be the next-best thing to the murder of someone else." Her niece didn't answer her.

"Sometimes, Anna," she went on, exasperated, "I think the best place for your honeymoon tour would be Palermo." "Palermo? Why Palermo?" "Oh, because it's so cheerful. It's the burying place of the Capuchins. It has vast subterranean apartments in its convent; it's so very interesting," she said, avoiding Anna's eyes. "They divided the apartments into large galleries and hollowed the walls out on both sides, and put niches in them—don't they sound industrious? It's marvelous how industrious they are, isn't it? Well, in the niches they put dead bodies instead of statues. The bodies stand straight up on their legs. They fasten to the back of the niche somehow. There are about two thousand of them, I think, maybe more by now. They're all dressed up in the clothes they wore every day. It is a strange place, like the Egyptian tombs. They have some kind of preparation and it makes the skin and muscles hard and dry as leather. Some of them have been standing up there for over two hundred and fifty years. It must be hard on the knees," she said, caressing her own, "even for a skeleton. Some of them look better than others; probably they looked better when they died.

"Well, Anna, the people who live in Palermo pay daily visits to their dead friends, just as if they were calling on them for afternoon tea, and it makes them happy to remember all the good and bad things from the past. It must be their way of getting used to what comes next. You know, after the little clock in here"—she tapped her chest—"stops ticking. Well, and I don't believe it starts up again in another world, you know that. But the point is, they get used to death. They even think they're choosing the company they want for themselves in the next world. They choose their own coffins and monuments and even climb in to see if their bodies fit. That way"—she smiled weakly—"no one has to alter any of their arrangements after their deaths. They're very practical, don't you think? Some of them even *stand* in the niches for hours trying to get used to it. Well, the families have keys to the niches. They say they like to go, too, that they learn all about humility there, and they say the visits don't frighten them at all. It seems to have something to do with the likeness of the dead body to the living person, so they look—how shall I explain it?"—she thought—"as if they were just a part of a great gallery of original portraits drawn by an unflattering artist, an uncompromising painter.

"Well, of course the colors fade, and the pencils the artists use are the world's most pleasing, but still, they say the pencil of truth draws those lines. And some of the visitors say they couldn't get through life without the visits, because they make them see all aspects of life at once, and they believe, whenever someone becomes too confident, or starts in strutting, or gets above himself, or decides someone is never going to die, he ought to be sent for a talk with his friends standing there in the gallery. And if their conversations couldn't bring him to his senses, then they would just give that person up as insane or incorrigible. Some of the Capuchins," she said, looking up at Anna, "sleep there every single night, and they say it's the best hotel in the world, or something very like that. They also have visions, they say, and revelations, but of course no one believes that. At any rate, I think it all started with a lady who was very vain in her youth. She was supposedly everyone's admiration, but then something or other happened to her, and she decided to atone for her vanity. She bequeathed herself as a monument. They say she hoped to curb vanity in other people.

"Then, on her deathbed, she started worrying about the adulation people had paid her, and she hadn't deserved it and felt like a thief for having taken it all those years, and gave orders that her body should be dissected after what she called 'the fatal change'; and she wanted her bones hung up for inspection so all young women could look on them and think about where their inclination to vanity is leading them. Lettie should go there,

709

definitely; yes, I think so. Well, I myself think it's too bad she wasn't put in the gallery. It would have been better to have preserved her features than her skeleton, don't you think? One skeleton looks so much like another, but if her *features* had been preserved, their powers all gone, well, charm, that would be out of the question. That would have made a much greater impression on people. Sometimes I think we need something like that here." Anna was staring, dumbfounded.

"You don't like the idea, do you?" "No." "Don't you think going might do you some good?" "It might; but I think it's horrible all the same." "Religious people oughtn't to see death as horrible. It's only the beginning, not the end, stepping from a patch of shade into the sun. That's what the Reverend Pierce always says, at any rate. Well, *you* are not dying, anyhow." Ten looked her over and sighed. "You study that little book."

"Can I come in?" a little voice asked from the hall. "That *has* to be Minnie," Ten said. Anna got up to open the door. "Oh, I will miss you," Minnie said, sinking down on the bed. "But you're going to be the first one visiting me." Ten watched them both happily. Minnie— if she had been Edna's daughter, she would have been her favorite. "Why should you want me first?" Anna laughed. "Just because you say things like that." "I don't understand why all of you take on about me so," Minnie said, looking at Ten, puzzled; "I'm not really very intelligent, or remarkably good-looking. There must be one of me on every farm." "I doubt it," said Ten. "It's that you fit in so well," Anna said; "wherever you go, you just fit in. Everyone feels happier when you're there. You're like a candle." "I don't understand any of that." "You don't have to; it's enough that other people understand it."

"Fit in," Minnie repeated; "that's because I'm so unremarkable; I have no edges." "No, that is not it," Anna contradicted; "it's as if you're something natural, like a river or a tree." "With as much brains as a stone," Minnie sighed. "Will you stop running yourself down?" Ten scolded; "really, Minnie, that's your only bad habit." "No one at home saw anything so very remarkable about me." "A prophet," Ten said, "is rarely honored in his own country." "I don't understand that, either." "Well, Minnie," Ten told her, "Alice said after you left she was sure it was one of the cloudiest years we'd had in ages, but then she checked her diaries, and it wasn't the weather, after all, so all it could be, she decided, was that you weren't there." "I was hardly *ever* there; I was usually out in the woods or with Martin. That was later, though." "But they always knew you would be back soon," Anna said. Minnie shook her head vigorously. "Just another mouth to feed," she said, mournful.

"Minnie," Anna asked suddenly, "what things are you afraid of?" Minnie thought for some time. "Why, nothing, I think." "Perhaps that's it, then," Anna said, looking at her aunt; "aren't you afraid you'll die?" "No. No," Minnie repeated, "but I am curious about when. A lot of good it does me to be curious." "But aren't you afraid Martin will die?" "I hope he doesn't," Minnie said solemnly. "But if he did," Anna persisted. "Then I'd see to it that his grave was nicely kept and I would visit it all the time, and it *would* be nicer if he died after we had children, so there would be something of him left." Ten's eyes flicked from one of their faces to the other.

"Would you marry again?" "Not right away," Minnie said after some time; "it would take quite a while to resign myself. But then I would have to do it." "Why?" "Because I wouldn't have any choice." Now she looked at Anna as if she were the simpleminded one. "You don't believe there's one perfect person for you?" "Oh, heavens no," Minnie answered; "why should anyone bother so much with me? *I* think Martin is perfect, but then, I love him; he's my husband." She made it all sound so simple, Anna thought, and the truly astounding part was that for her it *was* just that simple. "Like a river or a mountain," Ten quoted. Anna flushed. "A river or a *tree*," she corrected. She did sound miffed. "You will visit me first?" Anna asked Minnie. "I suppose I shall have to; I seem rather backward in getting in the family way." "That's only because you're comparing yourself to our family," Ten said; "and all the people in our family breed like rabbits." "I hope I shall have children," Minnie said quietly. "And if you don't?" Anna asked. How could she cross-examine her so? Ten wondered. "There are always children in the workhouse," Minnie answered. "You would do that?" "Of course." Anna shook her head. She was bewildered. "You study Minnie along with that

711

book," Ten scolded her. "You will visit me?" she asked Minnie again. "Of course I will." Why, Ten wondered, was Anna so insistent on an answer? There were things about that child she would never understand, and she had certainly been trying, right from the day she was born.

A tremendous crash, accompanied by agonized shrieks and strange chimings, came from the first floor. The three women rushed out onto the landing. "Go down," Ten told Minnie and Anna; "I'll crawl after." "Oh, heavens!" she heard Minnie exclaim; "it's Jack. He's gotten himself caught in the clock!" "What?" Well, life was not going to leave her alone, not until she finally got free of it by donning the good old wooden suit. "He's been playing with the grandfather clock," Anna called up. From the sound of her voice, Ten could tell she was absorbed in something. "He's caught his lips in it." "I'll get your father."

John, Martin, and William materialized instantly. "What on earth were you doing with that clock, and at three in the morning?" Ten demanded. "He can't answer you," Anna reminded her. "Wonderful," Ten sighed; "I'll never have such an opportunity again. Jack, you are a born idiot," she inveighed; "that poor clock is too old to put up with your onslaughts." He twitched slightly to show his annoyance. John was bending over him. "This," she said, "should look interesting at the ceremony, bringing Jack in with a grandfather clock soldered onto his face."

"We're going to have to take apart the whole damned clock," John swore; "he's gotten his lips stuck in the wheels. We have to take the whole machinery apart. Well, boys," he said, turning to look up at Martin and William, "go get the tool kit. The medical kits can wait."

Edna came down in her white robe. "Oh no," she gasped, looking down at the sorry spectacle. She couldn't decide for which she was most sorry, the clock or the child. "Does this mean," she asked Ten, "that the clock is trying to make a prediction?" "It means," Ten said grimly, swatting at Jack's leg with her walking stick, "that Jack is making an excellent prediction about giving up all sleighing and sliding for the next month." Edna was relieved. Yes, she had begun to believe in the predictive powers of that peculiar clock. The three men busied themselves with screwdrivers and wrenches, carefully putting each piece they removed into a box. It was a regular assembly line, Ten thought, watching them dismantle the old clock, dipping each piece in warm water and alcohol to remove any blood so that the clockmaker could reassemble the old thing at some more convenient time. If he *could*, she thought; she would not like to see anything happen to that clock.

"I think," John said finally, "we have *liperated* the mouse from the instrument of torture. Will you look at that lip!" he exclaimed. In addition to its deep cut, Jack's lip bore the imprint of the saw edge given him by one of the round cogs. "Just how did it happen?" Edna asked. "Well, in some way," Jack said, "I got too close to the clock and it caught me." "In some way," Ten snorted. "Well," John asked, "who wants to sponge him off and pack him up with ice? I'm going to bed. My last daughter is getting married tomorrow." "I'll do it," Minnie volunteered. *"We'll* do it," Martin said. "Up to bed, everyone; you'll catch up with the hours pretty soon," his father threatened Jack, starting up; "I'm going to show you just how fast time flies, especially when it takes the form of a stout strap." "A lot of sympathy I ever get for anything," Jack complained stiffly, trying not to move his lip. "And a lot of sympathy you deserve," Ten sniffed, going up.

"You can visit Anna, you know; after she's married, I mean," Minnie told Jack as she was sponging off his mangled lip. She was trying not to smile. He did look like a foolish raccoon, caught in a snare. Jack said nothing. "She told me she hoped you would," Minnie went on. "She did?" Jack asked finally, grimacing with pain. "She certainly did." Minnie continued sponging, while Martin was busily threading his needle. "Would you tell them I'm sorry about the clock?" he asked her, seeing the dreaded needle's approach; "I only wanted to get a good look at it." "You got a good look at it," Martin said. Minnie looked reproachfully up at him. "I'll tell them you're sorry," she said. "Maybe they'll believe you." "I doubt it," Martin said. "Martin, don't," Minnie protested. He took one look at his wife and decided to keep quiet. She picked things up; later he'd ask her what she had caught in her claws. "Well, probably they will believe

713

Minnie," Martin muttered, as if changing his mind. Minnie smiled at him.

"Children!" Edna said to John, getting into bed. "We're due for another round, at least one more in about six months." "You know," Edna said, "the best thing I ever did was surround them with better mothers than they already had. Ten, and Alice. They were better mothers than I was." "Not everyone could have done that, that's not what I'd call a small accomplishment. Most women would have driven the others off. You've managed to keep them; not to mention having made their lives better." "It does seem all the other way around." "Ten and Alice wouldn't say that; they know what you've meant to them." "Don't put anything in the past tense!" "Everyone is certainly queer around here tonight," John complained, coughing. "What's that cough?" "A cough," he answered, turning over, readying himself for sleep. "You spend too much time in that cottage," she said, peevish; "I'm coming back in, and then I'll see for myself, about the ventilation, I mean." "I'd rather you didn't." "Well, I am. At least for a while." "For a *short* while." "We'll just see," Edna said, turning on her side. They took up their accustomed postures, falling asleep. Ten, settling into sleep (this was her normal bedtime now: four o'clock at night), wondered about the clock. Of course, she had said what she had to comfort Edna, but there was no doubt, anything involving that clock still gave her the creeping shudders. For once, she was too tired to think about it.

Edna awakened with a start; yes, John was there. Her heart was beating very fast, very hard. She must have been dreaming, that was it, but about what? Probably about what a bad mother she had been; wasn't that always what she dreamed about? And now she was going over it all again, even in her sleep. How she had never been a proper mother. She had spent four, perhaps five, days with one or more of the children, all alone with them, when they were young, usually because she had decided she *ought* to spend more time with them. But even when she was alone with one child, with Jack when he was only two and a half, she couldn't tolerate it for long. Two hours, perhaps three, that was all she could stand and no more. After three hours, the small child began to seem like a moon person, existing only to ignore her. Were other mothers like that? She asked herself that question times past counting. She never *had* to stay alone, caring for children. She still didn't understand how other women did it: Alice, for instance. Why didn't they all go mad? It was such a strain. But then perhaps it wasn't such a strain for them. Perhaps they had gotten used to it because they had no choice. She did not think she could have gotten used to it. She would have disappeared one day, as Lois Ann had one day vanished from her house. Perhaps, she thought for the thousandth time, she was being too hard on herself; there was really no telling how she would have existed were circumstances different.

Still, she had known only one kind of life; yet, she was sure she had not been a proper mother. A proper mother would have done more than reproach herself over inadequacies. She would have spent more time alone with her children. But she loved them; she was sure she loved them. She could not have been any other way. What was wrong with her? she asked herself in an agony. Just thinking about this, it set her nerves on fire; it squeezed her heart. Absolution: she wanted absolution from her own nature. She knew she was never to have it. That, she thought, was why she was so irrational, so convinced the children married to punish her. And Anna in particular. While she was a child, she was frequently very dear. But more frequently an oppressive entity, something to escape from. Now she could not imagine a household without her. Should she wake John? She hated to wake him; he was always so tired.

Edna woke John in the middle of the night. He automatically reached for his trousers, neatly folded on a little stool on his side of the bed. "No one's here but me," Edna said sadly. John sat up and looked at her. In all the years of their marriage, she had never awakened him unless she thought someone might be dying in another house. "We'll be saying that a great deal soon," Edna said; "there's no one here but me." "Us." "Us is still a great deal smaller than we." "I don't think it's very motherly of you to say that," John scolded; "we have two of our own older children, and two of Alice's, and another one on the way." "Do you remember," Edna finally said, "the time you came home and Martin had torn up your anatomy book and taken the colored plate of the digestive

715

system; he said it looked like a flower?" "I remember."
"And you said you were going to teach him a lesson he
would never forget, and he came downstairs trailing the
plate and said, 'I love you, Daddy,' and threw his arms
around your knees and you forgot all about punishing
him?" "I remember," John said, smiling into the dark.
"And now he's a doctor," Edna said, confused; "and
that time we were all home and someone came and we
had to leave Anna in the kitchen and we told her not to
touch the eggs, and when we came back, she was dropping
one after another on the floor, saying, 'Anna mustn't do
that.' Do you remember that?" "Who could forget that?
We ran across the floor so fast to get at her we nearly
broke our necks when we hit the egg pond." "That's
right," Edna said; "I nearly forgot that part." "It was too
bad they didn't have photographs right from the beginning, wasn't it?" John asked. "It was; it certainly was."
She was beginning to sound sleepy. John waited for her
to say something else, but her breathing slowly deepened,
and when she didn't turn toward him, he realized she was
asleep. He supposed they would have to paint the whole
house black when Jack married; he ought to start ordering the yards of crepe now. He fell asleep on his back.

It was all confusion in the Steele household the next
morning, Ten constantly reiterating it was only the grace
of God that had led Mr. Hewitt and his son to stay at the
Reverend Pierce's. Anna got into a fit when she couldn't
find a copy of the Bible; then she misplaced *The Wedding
Ring;* then she couldn't find the flower basket they were
supposed to bring to church. When Minnie accidentally
began fastening the first button in the front into the third
buttonhole, Anna became frantic. She knew it, she said;
she had become fleshy. The dress wouldn't fit. There was
no point in leaving the house; she just couldn't get married in a print dress, and she wasn't getting married in a
fancy black one, either, whereupon Ten came in, gently
pushed Minnie aside, looked at the front of her dress, declared the buttoning was all wrong, and if Anna could
only calm down, she would teach her how to button a
dress. She thought she knew *that* much, she said.

"I suppose everyone is angry at me because I'm getting
married in church," Anna said, looking at her aunt. "Not

that I know of; at least no one is angry *yet;* oh, dear," she gasped, pulling her pocket watch out and flipping it open; "Mr. Hewitt is going to be terrified!" "Terrified of what?" Anna asked, curious. Oh, she did rise to the bait, Ten thought; as ever. "He's surely going to think you've changed your mind; really, Anna, it is very unkind of you to leave him standing out there in the cold with the whole county thinking his bride didn't make enough of him even to send a note to tell him she changed her mind." "Oh, dear!" Anna cried, hopping on one foot like a stork, trying to stuff her other foot into the lace wedding shoe.

"Will you sit down before you break your neck; *I'll* put the shoe on for you." "Oh, no, no, no," Minnie interrupted; "all your bones will crackle and snap, you know that; you're even worse off than Ma. I'll put her shoe on." "I can put my *own* shoes on, for Lord's sake!" "Well, then, let's see you do it, Miss Wise Apple; isn't it a good thing," she asked Minnie, "she never had to play the part of Cinderella?" Anna glared up from her intense concentration on her ankle. "I am ready," she announced; "now will everyone stop running at me?" "You're not setting foot out the door with your hair looking like that; you look like a headful of snakes is nesting up there." "*Give* me the comb!" Anna said, seizing it, tugging it through her thick hair. "Ouch! It's all tangled." "Minnie," Ten said, "would you brush out that sad cat's hair, and I'll pin it up. If she can't stand the pain, I'll get the box of artificial curls." Anna glared at her. "Anna," Ten said, taking up the comb, "what about the waterfall? Matthew's always seemed so fond of that hairdo, and most of it won't be seen under the headdress; you might as well start pleasing your husband now." "That's a good idea." Storm to shine, storm to shine, Ten thought, mentally shaking her head, concentrating on Anna's hair; how it shone! It was remarkable as her mother's. "Well, there," Ten said, standing back, "go look in your glass." "It looks wonderful," Anna said gratefully. "Now we're ready to go," Ten pronounced.

"Let's go in the open carriage," Anna pleaded; "I want to look at everything one last time." "No open carriage, but you can sit next to the window in the closed one," Ten told her; "you're not supposed to let the groom see you before the ceremony." Anna was glaring again.

"And you'd be quite a sight by the time we got there," Ten went on; "you know how your hair curls up in the wind, and if there's a drop of dampness, we might as well shave your head as let anyone see you." "It's only to church," Minnie reminded her; "you can come back in the open carriage." "I'll be coming back as a married woman," Anna said, toneless. Minnie sighed. "If the idea upsets you so much, we won't go at all," Ten snapped. "Oh, let's go, then," Anna grumbled. "I don't believe Minnie acted this way on her wedding day," Ten commented. "Don't start with that," Anna protested. "Minnie," Ten replied, "Minnie was very, very good. *She* didn't carry on about her hair, or scream about her buttons, or lie down on the floor and drum her heels into the carpet because she wasn't going in a closed carriage, or whatever kind of carriage she couldn't go in. Tut, tut, tut." Minnie was grinning at both of them. Anna went out of her room. "Mother!" she called; "isn't everyone ready?" "Everyone is ready but you and Ten and Minnie." "We're coming," Anna called down; "Aunt has been fussing so." "You just watch out for my hairpins, miss," Ten threatened her.

Why, Edna wondered, was the crowd in front of the church so large? Alice's family was already there; there was Alice's brother, Lucretius, his new wife, and his five children. His new wife, Edna thought, a bit ruefully, had been his wife now for fifteen years. It was odd how, although two of her children had married two of Alice's, the rest of their families had not really been drawn together. Why, she hadn't seen Lucretius since the last wedding in the family. As for Howard, he was as much a mystery as ever. He seemed to consider her friendship with Alice something which the two of them owned, and, aside from his meetings with John when one or another of the family fell ill, he seemed to have little desire to deepen the acquaintance. She supposed it was just as well; she couldn't imagine beginning to sympathize with Howard and his ways. He was always flinging out of the house, banging the screen door or the wooden door after him. If a cow was loose, he looked blacker than a rain cloud, and no one lived in peace until the animal was under lock and key. He would cross-examine everyone to discover who had been the culprit; usually, it turned out to be Howard himself. But, Edna thought, leaning forward, there were more people here than both of their families could account for.

She turned around to look at her mother and Mr. Siddons; they looked beautiful enough to be mistaken for the happy couple, she thought merrily. Well, her mother's second marriage had ended far better than she would have predicted; it was miraculous, really, that the never-aging Edith had managed to unite herself to the never-aging Mr. Siddons. She hoped if her father was anywhere to mind, he did not. He would not be surprised, she knew that. He had known human nature too well; that had always been the entire trouble. He hadn't been suited for such knowledge. It had been worse for him than the original apple in the garden. But he did do well, or had done well, she corrected herself, while he lived; yes, while he lived, there had been none better. Could anything have been done? No matter whom her father had married? She doubted it. Her father had been established in his profession before he even met her mother. She supposed he had been set in his ways. Weddings, she thought resignedly.

She remembered some client of her father's who referred to weddings as the much-dreaded events. Well, they were, the way they dredged the river, or the mud, of the past. She never thought of her father, really; she tried not to think about him. Although there were times she would wake up in the middle of the night and see the mark on her mother's forehead, the one left after her mother had walked into his swinging soles. She had not been kind to her mother, not after all that. The way she had complained of her mother's lack of sensitivity! Now, she thought, she considered insensitivity one of the greatest blessings in life, although she had no illusions about the likelihood of having it conferred upon her. She didn't deserve it, either, not after the way she had carried on.

By the time the Steeles' carriage had drawn up to the church, the crowd had gone inside. They got up and went into the Reverend Pierce's house first; when everyone was inside, the family would go in and be seated. Then the ceremony would begin. Anna kissed them all and let Mrs. Pierce lead her off. From the shiny pews, they could see the chancel, elaborately and elegantly decorated in white and green and pink. The murmuring, Alice noted; everyone must be wondering where the carnations and roses had come from. She was sure everyone in her family was talking about that. The bridal procession was beginning; she heard the muffled strains of the organ, and the high, pure voices of the boys' choir chanting their processional, and then the full choir filling the church with their winged voices. Weddings, Alice sighed. She wasn't sure she liked them. Of course, they did have the advantage of making things final; then everyone could go ahead and get resigned, just as they did at funerals.

She found herself, as she always did, thinking of her own wedding. Well, that had been no fancy business, just the minister and her parents and two cousins in the old kitchen. How her father had gone on about the importance of a gentle nature; she'd never heard him use such words before. He must have been reading up in a book. But then he started to tell her how he'd made her mother suffer with *his* nature: how he never took things as they came, but was always fighting them, and then he would get himself into a depressed state, and nothing she could say would ever cheer him up. And then, when her mother decided to visit her grandmother when she'd fallen ill, he'd threatened to divorce her, and he had really meant it, he told his daughter. Yes, he had. So her poor mother went off to look after her mother, all worried that she was going to get there after the body had turned cold, and in back of her, what was waiting? A husband who threatened the family with divorce. And this was only the beginning of his sins and her mother's sorrows, he went on; Alice was dumbfounded. She had never heard him talk that way before, and apparently her mother never had, either. Alice had never seen a human look more astonished at anything.

Most of the time, he told her, he was about as grown up as a new baby. If things didn't go his way, he had a tantrum and took it out on everyone. Why, he told her, as if she didn't know it too well already, the slightest thing and he could sit for days in his chair, glaring at everyone, without saying a word. No matter what they said to him, he wouldn't answer. And could he take care of himself if Mother was sick? No, he couldn't so much as find a sock. When Mother had been sick after Alice was born, he had stopped eating altogether, except for vegetables, and complained so much at the jail the neighbors began leaving hot meals on the steps and in front of the porch door. And didn't she think Mother was embarrassed to death? Why, that was just the way they treated charity cases, old people, and the mortally ill; that was what Mother had said, and she was right. But he ate everything up all the same. And when Dr. Steele, John's father, said to carry everything in to her and not let her move in her bed, then the trays were so greasy they practically slid out of her hand, and Mrs. Steele (that was John's mother) had to come down and clean the whole house with two of her maids. Otherwise, Dr. Steele said, he knew Mother would be up killing herself trying to make the house look respectable. "Regulating things, that's what kills them all," Dr. Steele had told *his* mother, as she set off for their house. Then, when Dr. Steele found out *what* her father was bringing in for her to eat, he threatened to take him out in the yard and knock him down, or drag him down to the jail on a rope and have him written up for murder.

Well, he'd gone on and on: he'd spent his whole life on a farm, working a farm, and his father before him, and *his* father before him, and if one thing went wrong—if the potato crop failed, if the pumpkins weren't big enough, if the corn wasn't heavy enough, if there were too many raccoons in the corn or moles in the garden—he would just sit down at dinner and start in as if he were Job himself. "Now, Alice," he told her, "you don't want to go and marry another one like me." That, she supposed, was the first time she had ever been sure her father really cared about her as much as he did about tomatoes or hay. Well, and she had gone and married someone impossible enough, not the same as her father, but close. Howard was never home at night: at least if her own father had been glowering and not talking, he was there; but Howard wasn't happy unless he was off every night after supper collecting and retailing news at some poor soul's house while *she* stayed up keeping the fire going in the parlor so the plants wouldn't freeze; she and Ten still carried on over who had the best geraniums, she thought, watching the couple approach the altar, then staring down at her wedding ring; it was so silly, but there it was. They took it seriously, too; the year *her* geraniums had frozen because she had fallen asleep, she had taken on as if there had been a death in the family, and what was the result? She had come down with congestion of the lungs.

And if everything had gone wrong with the children at once, it was still her business, unless Howard saw a good prospect of Mr. Greenwood sniffing about. Then he would come in and talk to Dr. Steele, but unless the doctor told him to start readying the family plot, he'd go off as if there were nothing to do but wait. She had all the sponging, washing, feeding, cooking to do herself, and if she worried, and who wouldn't worry, the way they burned and shivered, their smooth skins hot as irons, she stayed there, worrying alone. But he had been a good man, she thought, feeling discouraged; he had provided for them. That hadn't been easy. He hadn't gone after any other woman, or ever made her worry about that. He didn't drink; he didn't gamble. That was the trouble: if anyone asked her what she liked about her husband, she wouldn't be able to tell them one thing. Not anything. She could tell them what wasn't wrong with him, but she couldn't tell them what was right with him.

She guessed, half an ear on the ceremony—she never listened to them; a lot of difference they made—she didn't like him. Well, that was a hard thing to admit. She didn't like Howard. If he were loose around town, and she were a widow, she'd never pick on him for a friend. But she supposed she did love him. How was that possible? Not to like him, yet to love him? She supposed it was that they had gone through so much together. Especially Florence's death. Well, when Reverend Pierce said death was often a blessing in disguise and all the rest of the length of the ribbon that fell from his mouth, she had almost picked up a pot of her bleeding heart plant and thrown it at his head; but he had been right, at least about their marriage. Things had run smoother after that. At least they were always awake in bed together after she got over crying herself to sleep. Howard must have decided she'd get over Florence faster the more children she had; he'd been right, too. She supposed he was a good man in his way.

It was too bad there were other men in the world to compare him with. If there weren't, she could actually convince herself he was a fine person. She was happy, though, her children were doing so much better than they had. Although she didn't like the look of things for George; there he was, squirming away. He was just like his father, only more willful. If that was possible. He was determined to leave for California in the morning; that was what he said, and that was what he meant. Prices of land had gone up in California, so now he planned to take up logging until he saved up enough, and then he would buy that farm in Centerville. She pitied the woman he decided to marry. *If* he ever decided to get married. Someone would have to hogtie him. Well, there were always plenty of women ready to do that; she hoped he got one with good teeth. There had been a divorce up on Lord's Hill last month, and everyone said it was because the wife had taken on so over her teeth she had made her own life a misery, and finally her husband couldn't stand it, either; he'd threatened to knock the rest of her teeth right out and get it over with. That was too much for the poor woman: she'd run out of the house in her night-dress, and as luck would have it, the Camp wagon was going by. They took her back to their house, and she said she never would go back, not after what he'd said about her teeth, after all she'd been through with them. Well, Howard had never threatened her or beaten her. So there was something good about everything, if you only had a big enough lantern to find it in the dark.

How beautiful the ceremony is, Edith thought, how impressive. She would never have expected such effects in a country church. And Anna. She was the very picture of her mother. It was like seeing her own daughter marrying again. She looked over at Edna. Her hand was clasped tightly in John's; no, Edna wouldn't mind doing it again. She would do it *all* over again, even if she had to jump through rings of fire first. And how, as a child, she had insisted she would never, never have children. Why, Edith remembered, she used to worry about all that, Edna's diatribes about how her heart was her own, and it always would be; and she had seemed to mean it, the way she rejected one suitor after another. It had looked like the same thing with Anna, too. Every time someone in Boston declared himself, Anna would appear in tears, asking what she could have done to encourage this one or that one, and really, even Edith couldn't think of what she had done but stand there. There was something about her, though; it was a good thing there were no harems in this country. But that wasn't right, was it? It was the men who had all the wives, not the other way around. Anna had gone on and on about dedicating her life to God; going to Africa as a missionary (to catch leprosy, Edith supposed); at least she hadn't had to put up with such foolish ideas from Edna. Although Edna had a sharper tongue.

Anna and Matthew did make a lovely couple, though. He was so tall. If there was one thing important in a husband, it was that he be tall. She could never understand women who respected husbands whose heads barely came up to the little purses they fastened to their belts. They must have to stoop down, she thought, to see their faces. Although she imagined they could see them well enough in bed. But still, *how* could those women tolerate it? Why, she had seen some of them turn right around, looking for their husbands, and there they were, right under their elbows. It was a preposterous arrangement, really. Now Anna would not have to look under the carpet for *her* husband; for what more could one ask? And she did look lovely in her mother's dress; it was a good thing she had thought of having its hem taken up so deeply.

No matter what Edna had said at the time about giving birth to trolls or midgets, she had expected the children would be utterly normal, and one of them might possibly live to wear the gown. Well, this was the second time it was being worn, she thought, delighted with herself. Lettie had to have the latest things, so they hadn't had to fuss with hems for her; and it was a good thing, too. She would have taken the dress off and thrown it in a corner, and after that, it would have been good for nothing. Anna stood up so straight in that cream satin and old pane lace; the wasp waist was as lovely now as it had been when Edna wore it. Edith was proud of her. She imagined the minister's eye could not help straying to that diamond pin she had given her; it was a wonder. Anna wasn't clumsy, either. She held the bouquet of bride's roses and maidenhair fern as carefully as if she were holding a baby.

And Ella and Minnie did look so magnificent, dressed in their white gowns. Well, they were a bit preposterous, especially with Ella's stomach the size it was; she hoped she wouldn't bump anyone and throw him off the platform. Still, it *was* a beautiful wedding, especially when she thought back to Minnie's and Ella's. That wedding had so many comical touches it had been impossible to take seriously, although the contracting parties certainly hadn't seen anything amusing about it. She turned, unobtrusively as possible; yes, Lettie was there, two rows back, late as usual, without her husband, again as usual. He was in Washington on some official business or other. Edna was right about her, really. Her husband ought to put her up on a marble pedestal with the rest of his statues where she could do no harm, and leave her there. Lettie did pout about Westminster, and just because she hadn't been asked to visit. Mr. Siddons put a stop to that. He asked her last month if she would like to go, that was all, and she looked as if he had suggested she throw herself under a passing carriage. But she did collect insults along with her calling cards. Nothing, Edith sighed, could convince Lettie to give up that habit: it was horribly vulgar. Well, Edith thought, shaking herself, it was actually over. A minister's wife! It was past understanding. But how happy she looked; Edith admired her as she and Matthew began wending their way out of the church. Everyone followed them out, and the kissing and congratulations began, and the babble; yes, she still liked weddings. They were so much nicer than funerals, and you saw all your old friends. It might have been years before she saw Ten again if it hadn't been for this wedding.

Now they would be going back for the wedding supper at the Steele house. What a beautiful sleigh; she had never seen so many ribbons. That sleigh must be covered with every color under the sun. Was it a new one, or had they painted the red one white? No, it must be a new one. Ten wouldn't start in painting sleighs, not at her age. Anna and Matthew stood under a lovely arch of green and white, from which two lovely hydrangea bells swung gently. Edna told her Alice had provided them. Edith wondered how she preserved them so long past their season. Why, she wouldn't be surprised to see a bee flying merrily about right in the dead of winter. She wondered why Edna had refused to have a complete dinner, but had insisted on sandwiches and coffee, and of course the white and gold wedding cake with its gold design of a wedding ring in the center, but she ceased wondering when Ten blinked at her three times, and then three times again, the old signal, meaning "Help, help!" She was cornered, or had cornered (that seemed more likely) old Mr. Hewitt; she was keeping him busy, that was obvious to Edith the minute she came up to them, and she needed help with it. Seeing her step up, Ten sighed with relief. Edith could flirt anyone into the grave.

So the social hour, mingling with the music, went off smoothly. And, of course, when Matthew and Anna were ready to leave, they would sing, "God Be with You Till We Meet Again." "What do you expect?" Ten whispered into Edith's ear; "there are so many wings in here you'd think we were in a hive." Well, Ten thought, it might as well be snowing. Ella and Minnie and the rest of them had thrown out enough rice and old shoes to feed and shoe half the world. Now there were flowers all over the sleigh; oh, that was too bad. They'd be brown before they were out of Williamsville. "Aha!" Ten said aloud, noticing the new, large card on the back of the sleigh. "We are just married," it proclaimed in large, irregular capital letters. *That* had to be Jack's work; she was sure he wrote with his feet. With his feet and with his shoes on.

"Come on back in," Edna was saying; "it's freezing out here." The guests who had come out of respect for Matthew promptly made their excuses. The rest of the family settled into the parlor, eating this and that, nibbling at odds and ends Bridget brought in, talking about everything but the couple themselves. "Did you know," Alice was asking Mr. Hewitt, "that some drunken railroad man shot and killed a coal man and shot the selectman who tried arresting him?" "I don't know what the world is coming to," said Mr. Hewitt. "I'm sure I don't either," Alice answered. She had evidently caught on to the state of things, Edna thought, looking over at her; she was taking her turn. None of them would have put it past him to try jumping on a horse and pursuing his son on his wedding trip. Some trip, Edna thought sadly. They didn't dare leave the codger alone for even a week. "They say all the murdering came out of an argument over who was to stay up and watch; there have been so many incendiaries around here lately." "You don't say so?" Mr. Hewitt asked; "I've often thought it. Everyone in Williamsville is a lunatic or a criminal." "Well, your son spent a great deal of time here," Alice replied, "and he doesn't seem to be the worse for it." "Got out in the nick of time," the old man grumbled. "Surely," Edna asked, leaning over, "you can't believe Matthew would have turned criminal if he'd stayed here longer?" "Course not; no such thing. He's one of the lucky ones, that's all." "I see," Edna said. "How anyone sees anything clear here is beyond me," Mr. Hewitt mumbled. "You'll be home soon enough," Ten said in her icy voice. He calmed down. After all, he wanted to go back to New Bedford, but he didn't want to be thrown out in the snow. That Ten, he thought; she was a miserable one. He wouldn't want to come home and find her in the dark.

Edna saw Mr. Siddons and John get up, put on their coats, and head toward the door. She and her mother looked at each other, nodding. They went off to hold a consultation over his pictures. Neither of them, Edna thought, would care if they froze to death doing it, and all for the sake of some image of life. As if life wasn't enough. Edna slid over into the chair next to her mother. "Well, Mother," she said. "Well, dear," Edith smiled. They still could think of nothing to say to one another, but at least they were happy together.

"Oh, I do not like Anna leaving," Ten complained; "I'm getting to be a selfish old woman." "Well," Alice said, "it's all in the way of seeing. You've got one of my daughters and one of my sons in the hive; and one of Edna's daughters, and there's still Jack. You don't need the whole Fourth Regiment. I should be the one who's envious." "Are you, Mother?" Minnie asked. "Oh no," Alice assured her, "not about your being here." Minnie smiled, happy. Edna, of course, wondered what, exactly, she meant. "Bill," Minnie said, "wasn't it nice of Mrs. Lawson not to have her baby just now?" "It was; it was nice of Ella, too." "Oh, I don't expect anything of the sort for two months," Ella protested.

So the talk went back and forth, from births to murder, to the arrest of Mr. King for smashing up a livery team he'd taken without permission; he'd whacked it all around the hills, someone was saying, and torn up the harness and worn the whip half down on the poor animal. Students were returning who were homesick; Louise Williams was back from Northampton, pure homesickness. Abby Prouty was back from Baltimore; she couldn't keep away from that old beau of hers. They should have known better than to waste money on her in the first place. Someone was enthusiastically recommending Dr. Shenk's Seaweed Tonic; it was good for everything. A barn had been fired in Brookline; what next? They had routed a regular den of vice in Putney, though; they must have gotten three thieves and two rum runners at once; that was something. Someone had come back from a visit in Brooklyn. Poor Mrs. Martin had to go all the way to Maryland to tend to her daughter, she was such a wreck of a woman after that first child finally came. And so the talk flew, as essential and inevitable as the snow, and as transitory, melting as it touched the ground. Yes, Edna thought, the snow was blowing merrily. She controlled an urge to rub her eyes; the room did seem swirling with snow, and everyone disappearing behind it. Was death like that? The snow, the illusion of snow, it made everyone in the room look like Mr. Siddons' statues. Was something wrong with her eyes, or had time suddenly made itself visible to her? It was piling up in drifts near the north window, climbing up the curtain, and the velvet was darkening with it as it drew it up through its veins. What was wrong with her? Edna wondered; was she losing her senses at last? And what a time to have it happen.

"Will someone *please* close that window," Ten called out; "before we're all buried under an avalanche. Martin left it like that after he stuck his head out to talk to the man up the Hill," she told Ella; "I guess Mrs. Lawson decided not to continue waiting, after all." "Well, I'm not following her example," Ella answered complacently; she was eating sandwich after sandwich. "Eat some more of those," Ten told her, "and you can plan on building a pen for an elephant." "That would be nice," Ella said peaceably, picking two more sandwiches from the tray. She was always hungry, she thought; always hungry. "Why don't you stay all week?" Edna was pleading with her mother. "Oh, dear, I don't know," Edith answered; "Mr. Siddons is right in the middle of something. He's calling it 'The Dark Side of the Moon,' except," she said, puzzled, "it has people in it." "I think," Ten suggested, "we could persuade him to stay if we could get John to let the other two stethoscopes take over. Then the two of them could work with pictures in the cottage." "He *is* partial to winter scenes." "Then it's settled," Ten said comfortably. Edna beamed. "Well, almost," Edith agreed.

Really, Edna thought, she wanted as many people in the house as possible. This endless procession of weddings; it was beginning to make her nervous. Still, hearing the clattering of a wagon and the sound of the horses outside, she knew without looking—it was a funeral procession. What a miserable day to be buried, and with the ground so hard. Still, there were worse kinds of processions. She sighed, reaching for a sandwich. If she so much as saw Jack mooning after some ten-year-old imp, she thought bleakly, she would take to her bed for a month.

John and Mr. Siddons came back in puffed up with themselves. "That is revolutionary work," Mr. Siddons boomed with enthusiasm. "Why do you let him keep it hidden away?" he asked Edna. "He makes his own decisions; you might as well argue with the sofa there." "They belong to the world," Mr. Siddons announced dramatically. "Well, you better get him to put that in his will, because he's not giving them to the world now," Edna laughed. "*That* is a good idea," Mr. Siddons said. "Creations from the world beyond," he went on, irrepressible; "I don't see how he does it." Every eye in the room was on him; that, Edna knew, was just how he liked it. "The same way he does everything else," Edna put in; "he forces himself." John smiled at her painfully. It still hurt him, he thought, wondering, when he had to admit how well she knew him; there was no protecting her from *him*. But then, she didn't want to be protected from him; from everything else perhaps, but not from him.

The next few months passed smoothly enough. Everyone was waiting for Ella's new arrival. Anna proved a remarkably faithful correspondent. Her letters were full of details of life in New Bedford; she sketched characters for them as if she were a born novelist. She was proud, she wrote, of Matthew's abilities. He penned the most remarkable sermons, and then, to everyone's horror, she would transcribe them entire, and that, they all knew, meant she expected comments upon them, and not vague ones, either, but ones which showed they had read them with all proper attention. Mr. Hewitt was not such a bother, after all, she told them; he had, in fact, taken up with Mrs. Wade, although whether he would bring himself to the question she could not yet say. But she did believe it was all Aunt Ten and Grandmother's fault. After meeting them, he must have decided he wasn't so old, after all.

Letters arrived almost as regularly from Matthew; he must have sensed how worried they all were over Anna's departure from the family circle. He gave them minute accounts of Anna's duties; she accompanied him, he said, to parishioners who had been taken ill, and she was very good at comforting people. She kept watch with him at deathbeds and wasn't a bit frightened; he was gratefully surprised to find her so strong, both spiritually and bodily, but he supposed he owed most of his happiness to her parents. They had accustomed her to rounds, and scenes that would freeze the blood of someone less experienced. He had received an emergency call; one of the women had run the full three miles down to their house to call him for help, but she was too hysterical to say what was wrong, and they had taken her back in their carriage, and there was her husband hanging from a beam in the barn, and Anna hardly batted an eye. Well, no one liked the sound of those visits and the sights of Matthew's rounds, but it was inevitable, and from the feeling of both sets of letters, it seemed Anna was having trouble getting on with things.

Then, sometime in June, came the "happy tidings," as Matthew called them; Anna was expecting a baby sometime in December. "What could be better than a Christmas baby?" Anna's letter babbled happily on, just as if she were there. "We've decided to name the baby Minnie if it's a girl, which is *almost* like naming it after Matthew, or Matthew if it's a boy. We hope to go through all our families in this way," she wrote cheerfully, "and I am not even a bit sick. I expect to have as little trouble as Ella did with her second. Why," the letter complained, "don't I have any pictures of him yet? It's unreasonable with a face maker right there on the premises. I hope Ella and the baby will be able to visit me soon." Ella sighed when she heard that. The idea of a journey anywhere with a six-month-old baby, especially without her

husband, held no appeal whatever. But it had been decided, before Anna married, that there were to be visits
every four months. So Minnie said she would go, and
then, to everyone's astonishment, promptly burst into tears.
Ten led her off.

"She's afraid she'll never have children," she reported,
coming back in; "John, you better talk to her. I put her
to bed." "Don't you think Martin should do it?" John
asked. "No, no," Ten said; "she'll only think he's reassuring her because he's her husband." John went up and
assured Minnie that, after her serious bout with the fever,
it was to be expected that her body would wait before it
undertook the strain of childbearing, and she should think
herself lucky, he lectured her, because her body *was* having time to recover and strengthen itself, and if she were
pregnant right now, the child might not have the best possible chances. She wouldn't want that, would she? No,
Minnie agreed, finally turning her head on the pillow to
look at him, she wouldn't want that; that would be selfish
of her, she knew that. "Well, then," John said, "you
must have patience. You're not even twenty. You have
twenty years to grow an army."

"Mr. Steele," she said (she still could not bring herself
to call him anything more familiar), "you are telling me
the truth?" "As far as I know it." "Then I must be satisfied with that." "I doubt that's all you'll have to satisfy
you"; he squeezed her hand; "you don't have to be the
one to visit Anna, you know. By the time you get there,
she'll be as green as someone who ate green apples; I
doubt she'll be much fun." "Oh, I want to go; I promised
Anna I'd visit her first." "You did? I didn't know that."
"Oh yes. She made me promise the night before she got
married." "Then you're just the one to go; besides, there
have been times I've thought pregnancy was contagious.
My wife took one look at your mother's stomach, and the
next thing we knew we had Martin." "Oh, I do hope that's
true." "Just wait and see."

Still, he did wish someone else were going down to look
Anna over. Minnie was so sweet and good; she did sense
things. He agreed with them when they said that, but she
wouldn't know what to look for. On the other hand, if
they sent someone else, William, Martin, Edna, or himself, Anna would be sure they were worrying about her,

and that was the last impression he wanted to give. "I better go down," he told Minnie; "listen to that cough. I don't like the sound of it. I wonder who's come down sick now?"

"Edna feels queer," Ten said, hearing his step. "She can't seem to stop coughing." John felt her head. "Into bed," he said, picking her up. Well, this would be a bout. It was like her to come down with something like this in the spring; everyone else coughed to pieces all winter. He was worried, though; apparently, everyone noticed it. They were in their room every ten minutes to check on Edna's progress. By the third day, she was delirious, and everyone was walking around the house silent, looking sideways at one another, then averting their eyes. She would argue with an imaginary enemy about how she would not go here, but she would go there. They eventually realized, horrified, that she thought she was arguing with her mother, their grandmother. Martin and Ella stayed up late that night, not entirely for unselfish reasons; they were stunned to see this side of their mother, or rather, to realize there was so much about their mother they had never known and might never know. Somehow, they had taken it for granted that everything had always run smoothly in her life. There were times, Martin admitted, when he had resented it (Ella confessed she had, too), but really, it had given them a tremendous sense of protection; they both agreed on that. They also agreed only William need know about the two disasters in their father's life: the death of his first wife and the drowning of his brother. Edna had revealed those family secrets before Martin began practicing; she had been afraid that otherwise they might say and do things which would strain their father unnecessarily, but they were to keep this knowledge to themselves. Over Edna's delirious body, they decided to share the secrets with William, who, by nature and upbringing, was more likely than they were to rush in where angels shivered in terror on thresholds.

When Ten and John took up watch, they could make no sense of Edna's mutterings. She had now been sick five days. Finally, Ten realized she was trying to sing "Old One Hundred." "She must have heard that hymn when she went to church with Anna," she whispered. "Don't whisper," John said; "we're having trouble waking her up." "Once in a lifetime," Edna muttered; "once in a lifetime." They looked at each other. "Washed away, washed away," she said, turning to them with bright eyes as if she saw them; "reborn," she said more clearly; "reborn, once in a lifetime, sins washed away, real water, nearer to thee." The muttering again became inaudible as Edna fell asleep.

But she woke them reciting, "Do you accept Jesus Christ as your personal savior? I do. You do? I don't. I can't. You do." "She's conducting services from her bed," John told Ten, trying to smile. "I don't understand it; she's never taken an interest in such things." "She was never exposed to them much, either." "But she said she didn't accept Jesus Christ as her savior." "She also said she couldn't." "What difference does that make?" "It sounds as if she wants to." "Do you think," Ten asked, "both of you will meet in the next world?" "Oh, you know Edna; she says she doesn't, but she's not taking any chances, either; she's decided we're both being buried in the same grave, and not only in the same grave, the same coffin." Ten thought. She was about to say something, then stopped. "I don't know," she said aloud. "Don't know what?" "Perhaps she really does believe it, but can't let herself." John looked at his sister. "Are you going to meet Ed?" "I don't know," she said simply.

Edna had started talking again. "I baptize thee," she said hoarsely, "in the name of the Father, Son, and Holy Ghost." "I hope," Ten whispered, "she's not going to go through the whole ceremony. Was Anna ever delirious?" "A little. That time after the Webster affair." "What did she talk about?" "Cats. She was sure someone had taken Archie, or was going to shoot Archie, or eat Archie; it was Archie, Archie, Archie. And my wife," he said, puzzled, "goes through the baptism service." "With an invisible hymnal." They were trying so hard to keep up their own spirits, Ten thought, they would end sicker than Edna. Edna chose that minute to turn and look at them. "What are you both doing up at this hour of the night?" she asked clearly; "it must be three in the morning." Ten, stunned, looked at John's large pocket watch, hanging outside his vest from its gold chain. It was five minutes past three.

"Well, welcome back, Sleeping Beauty," John said

weakly. "Sleeping Beauty?" Edna asked, automatically pushing her hair back. "Good Lord, it's all stiff. Have I been sick?" "Have you been sick?" John echoed; "no, it was only acute lung congestion, accompanied by coma, high fever and verging on convulsions. It was really nothing," he teased as much as his exhaustion would permit; "William and Martin and I didn't mind taking turns holding you up so you could breathe, or sucking that muck out of your throat. Just a touch of something." "I don't believe it," she answered in her usual voice. "Try and get up then." Edna managed to push herself up with two hands. "Oh, I can't keep it up," she cried, sinking back; "things are going around. I feel funny; you've given me something." "I have not."

She lay there, considering matters. "I was delirious?" "Yes." "What did I say?" Curious already, that was a good sign. "You performed the whole baptism service," Ten said. "*I* did?" They both nodded. "Did I do it right?" "The minister couldn't have done a better job." Edna was staring at John with her great green cat's eyes; she had lost weight. She looked so young and so helpless; she might have died; he admitted it for the first time.

"Ten," he asked, "would you please go tell the others their mother is busy asking questions and feels cool as rain?" Ten began to get up, then sank back. "Oh, John," she said gloomily, "I can't." "Can't what?" "Can't get up; my hip won't seem to hold me." "What next?" he sighed, going to the door. Ella and Minnie heard him knocking at their husbands' doors. The boys came in and, shaking their heads at Ten, carried her bodily off to bed. Minnie was dispatched for food and drink on a tray, a lamp with a new supply of wicks, and several books, all of which bore women's names as titles. Then Minnie stayed behind while the rest of them went in, one at a time, to look at Edna. "I wish you would come in in larger groups," Edna complained querulously; "you make me feel as if you're taking leave of the corpse." "I'll tell the others to pile in," William snorted at her, "and then you'll only have two minutes of visitors." "I like it better this way." "What you like won't matter much for a while." "How is Ten?" "Except for a bad attack of rheumatism, she's fine." "Magnetic Ointment," Edna murmured, feeling very tired.

"That's right," Martin said, noting the drop in her energies.

He summoned everyone in at once. They were to go in and out, that was all; she needed more sleep. "What next?" asked Ella. "Whenever anyone says that in this house," John said, "there's sure to be trouble." "You're not getting superstitious?" William asked. "I just have a good memory." Minnie sneezed suddenly. John got up and felt her head. "See?" he told William; "carry this one up to bed. Well," he announced, "whatever Edna has is contagious, so everyone who isn't sneezing or coughing, off to the cottages." "What about rounds?" William asked, coming back down. Martin was already installed at his wife's bedside. "Martin won't come down anyway," William said, hearing of the new order. "Well," John said, "that's only fair." He thought. "Ella, William, and the baby, the three of you are definitely going to the cottages; it won't be a laughing matter if the baby comes down with this." They didn't take much persuading after that.

It wasn't thirty minutes before Amos was back, carrying Jack over his shoulder. "Broke his leg jumping a fence," Amos said, plopping Jack on the sofa, glaring at him; "you'd think by now he'd jump in the center instead of snuggling up to a tree." Well, John saw, Amos had already fastened Jack's leg to a board; it was immovable. No wonder he threw the rest of him around with such impunity. "If you ask me," Ella said, turning back in the doorway, "it looks as if Anna left just in time." "Out," Jack ordered her. "You heard it straight from the little pitcher," Amos growled; "I tell you, John, I have my hands full now with Tufts strung up in a hammock in the barn; *she* has two legs in splints and I've never seen such cuts. She looks like old Mrs. Whistle Britches gave her a whipping." "Will the horse be all right?" John asked. "I would guess so, wouldn't you? She's lived this long." "Well," Dr. Steele said, "as soon as this one here is better, you do what you want with him. He knows how we feel about cruelty to animals." "You better check on that leg, Doc," Amos said, smiling a little; they all knew he was better at such business than any doctor in the state.

"And when you're through, you better get on down to the Moffats'; they're in a pretty poor way." "How do *you* know?" John asked, busy with his son's leg. Jack shrieked the instant he touched it. "What's wrong with you?" he demanded of his son; "that's not even where the break is! Bite the bullet, cowboy." "Lois Ann was down here; she said there's something wrong with all of them. They can't even get up, and the place smells a mile off." "Well, is she there?" "No, the blessed woman said she couldn't afford to waste time today when she had to prepare for the Sabbath school." John sighed. "Amos," he asked, "would you stay here with this crackhead?" "Go on," Amos said; "my son's out with the horse." "How's the new Gray?" John asked, getting his bag. He wouldn't be surprised to hear he'd been eaten by a skunk. "Take him."

"Well, how's *my* family?" William asked later. "Your family had a horrible case of rhubarb-pie poisoning; the only one who doesn't have it is your baby sister. She said the pie was too sour. And guess who baked it." "Lois Ann." "You hit the nail on the head." "That's one nail I'd really like to hit on the head; she's descended from a nail in Christ's cross." "Well, William," Amos said, looking up, "if it hadn't been for people like Lois Ann, we wouldn't have gotten Christ down here to take a look." William grinned.

"What did you do for them, anyway?" he asked; "I mean, besides warning them off any more of Lois Ann's cooking." "The same thing I do for babies with summer complaint: castor oil, enemas, salol and bismuth. They weren't hot enough for sponging." "Ma must have loved that; who's helping out down there?" "No one; I sent down three of the maids." "It sounds like old times," he said to himself; "Pa's sick, too?" "Sick as can be." "Good; then he's too sick to bother anyone." "That's right." "I don't envy anyone trying to recover in a house with him." "I can't say I do, either," Amos pronounced, going back to the barn; "why, just this morning, he was down here insisting one of our cows (mind, we have only one) was eating up his grass on the flat." "Was she?" John asked. "And if she was?"

John shook his head. No wonder they had so little trouble with the farming end of things. "They couldn't convict that one there," he said, pointing at Amos, "of murder if they found him over a body still stabbing at it." "Don't put ideas in his head," William cautioned. "You better get on to the cottage; as for rounds, I don't see why you can't go. It's got to be safer anywhere else than it is here." "Ella's going to miss Minnie," William predicted. "Ella can make signs to hold up to her window; remember all that?" "Spider-web days?" Bill grinned; "they're beyond forgetting."

Someone was clattering up to the front door. "Typhoid at Slab Hollow," Bill reported, coming back in; "what are we going to do now? We can't seal up again." "Not for typhoid," John agreed; "everyone here's been around it so much. But you're not going. I'll set Ten on Minnie and Martin can go. I'm not taking chances with a six-month-old baby. You go to the cottage and stay there. Martin and I can take care of it." "Minnie will perish of loneliness," her brother answered uneasily. "No one perishes of loneliness with Ten around; of exasperation, but not of loneliness."

"Maybe it would be better," Bill thought, "if we turned things over to Dr. Chumley; they say he's a very good doctor when he's not drunk." "But when isn't he drunk?" "I guess you and Martin better go," Bill said; "but it's too bad about Minnie. She'll never get in the family way at this rate." "It won't hurt the two of them to have some time alone. Sometimes I think Edna and I are making plans to live forever so we won't have to sleep with something in a cradle at the foot of the bed. Any news from Anna?" "The usual thing; she's sleeping all the time. Matthew said she doesn't wake up except to eat. He thinks he's married a sleepwalker. Oh, there *is* something new. I forgot all about it after Edna got sick. George never got to California."

"What? Did something happen to George, too?" "He got as far as New Bedford and no farther. He told Anna he was more interested in whaling than he ever thought he would be, so he's taken a room in some family's house —about three blocks from Anna. Ma doesn't like it much." "I can't say I like it, either." "Well, I knew all about that other business before Anna got married. Ma says if George wants to stay there and torture himself, he better do it and get it out of his system. But she doesn't think he'll bother anyone; he just wants to be near her." "I didn't think that ruffian had a romantic bone in his body," John said; this *was* an amazing development.

"Well, I don't much like the idea of his flying around there like a vulture."

"That," John said, "is the worst view of it. He won't be flying around there much if he takes off on a whaling vessel; at least this way we'll get some more news." "If we got any more news, we'd have to build another wing to hold it." "You think we're making too much of Anna?" John asked. "I can't say," Bill answered; "she always reminded me of a little doll Minnie had. I sure got warmed for breaking it. But she seemed different; I mean, after she met Matthew. No. She seemed different a long time before that. She's stubborn, too; I remember when she used to follow us around. She didn't do it too often, but when she did, there was no getting rid of her." "Well, it's pointless to worry about her now," John said; "we have our hands full here." "I never saw so many invalids with so many strange complaints under one roof; Lois Ann said that once. What's that cough of yours? You're not coming down with Edna's sickness?" "No, it's something from those chemicals."

The eight years following Anna's wedding had been busy ones both for the Steeles and the Moffats, who were, as Ten was given to noting, becoming more and more indistinguishable. It was strange, one of them said, as they sat around in the huge parlor, how the younger ones in the family had more trouble accepting their ages than the older ones. It wasn't likely anyone would forget the night before Minnie's twentieth birthday; she had cried herself to sleep after a full two hours of moaning about life passing her by and how she would never have children, and as soon as the people in the poorhouse heard she'd had the fever, they wouldn't let her have any of the ones there, either. Now, with three children of her own to look after, Minnie insisted it had all been due to the sound of the words sixteen, seventeen, eighteen, nineteen. Then twenty; well, it sounded so different, as if you were counting years on another kind of string altogether. That, she explained, was how her children came to arrive. Martin, she said, had taken his twenty-eighth birthday very well; that was almost thirty. But she still had eight more years to face that.

Edna thought the reason she and John didn't take on

over birthdays was that they'd stopped thinking about them, or they wouldn't think about them; besides, it had always been her theory that if one staggered on to thirty, you were almost sure of safety until one hundred. Still, it was hard to believe she was forty-six, which meant John was fifty-eight, and Ten was eighty. For some reason Ten seemed younger than the rest of them. Except when it rained, Ten put in, whereupon both John and Edna commented on their dawning ability to predict the weather also. "Yes," said Edna, "I can tell when the weather's changing right here"; she pointed to the angle of her jaw. "I can tell here," John volunteered, pointing first to one elbow, then another. Why did the boys think he'd turned so much surgery over to them? Why, there were times when his thumb stiffened up so he couldn't pull it back to the rest of his fingers; unless things went the other way around.

They asked Ella how she was going to take turning thirty; she had only three more years to go. Ella, who had four children, said she doubted she'd have time to notice. They all wondered how Lettie was doing; she was twenty-six now. From what they heard from Edith, Ten said, it sounded as if she was just fine; her main accomplishment, as far as they were concerned, was her disinclination to visit Williamsville, that and her having stopped at one child, although she might still have more. One was enough to ruin, Ten pronounced. And wasn't it hard, Minnie asked, to believe Anna was twenty-two? They all agreed it was. Edna, they all said, still looked only sixteen; she looked younger than Jack, and he was eighteen. They thought he must intend to marry in his dotage; he was off at the medical college, but had decided to go out West. "I hope he'll get further than New Bedford," Bill remarked. "George's been a help, really," Edna said, "but he's wasting his time. He must be thirty-one." "That's right," Minnie agreed; "thirty-one; he's three years older than I am." "Every family should have a bachelor and a spinster," Ten pronounced. "And a photographer," Edna chimed in; "we like it here because of the isolation, and Mr. Siddons sends streams of people to look at John's daguerreotypes." "And they spend half their time deciding why I'm working in such an outdated medium. I wish they'd all stop at home." "He just can't imagine your not wanting publicity," Edna said. "Well, I don't."

"Then you shouldn't spend so much time writing that Tulliver." "She's starting again," John warned; "why don't you complain about the boys publishing articles under my name?" They had done just that, and now, in 1877, there was more and more evidence supporting John's original theories of contagion. Typhoid, diphtheria, and smallpox were suspect, and a host of others as well. John was corresponding with doctors all over the country.

What concerned Edna particularly, they all knew, was John's increasing involvement in the Florence Gilman murder case. For weeks, the papers had been covering every development in the investigation on their front pages. It *was* a very mysterious case, John insisted, and anyone would be curious about it, especially, he said, a medical man; no one could decide if murder was the issue, or natural causes. Well, that was an interesting question, wasn't it? Edna didn't answer. Tulliver was defending the dead girl's boy friend and he needed all the help he could get, John told them. "But you don't know whether or not he's innocent!" Edna protested. "I'm not supposed to; not before the trial, am I?"

Stubborn as a stone, that's what he was, Edna thought. A thick silence muffled the room. John began going over the details of the case. One of her brothers had noticed Florence Gilman's disappearance; a search party had duly been formed, and they eventually discovered her lying in a pasture not far from her farmhouse. When her brother had picked up her legs to lift her onto the stretcher, he noticed blood on his hands. Another man had found a cigar near the right side of the body, and the papers claimed it was the same brand her boy friend, or fiancé, no one was sure what to call him, had bought the day before. She wore brown slippers, but no hose. Near the body, tracks pressed into the grass as if a horse and carriage had gone by, and the girl's apron lay on the ground, folded into a pillow, her head resting on it. Jack Shannon, the man who found her first, put the apron over her face. Later, he noticed a black stain on the girl's dress.

The girl's fiancé, Millie Griffin, was the main suspect. Witnesses testified he had gotten some medicine and said he was going to use it. When asked if the medicine was for Florence, he said he would not give it to her. He had only asked her to meet him in the pasture. *She* had asked for the medicine. But the dead girl's sister, Mrs. Nora Aetna, insisted he had gotten medicine from a doctor in another town and had given it to Florence himself. Her dead sister, she said, had brought the medicine in to show it to her; it was in a cologne bottle, a reddish bottle; it was reddish brown in color. They had arrested a doctor from the neighboring town, as well as Nora Aetna's husband, who, it had developed, went with Millie Griffin to get the medicine. Mrs. Gilman had not been home the day her daughter died, but she was by the time the body was carried in; she had not looked at it because the officers had told her not to do so.

On the day of the murder, someone had seen Millie Griffin running through the old cemetery and had called to him, asking if he had become a gravedigger; he said he hadn't and continued running. The man didn't know Griffin and Miss Gilman so much as knew one another. Then it developed Millie Griffin had gone off to a second doctor, asking him for a speculum and catheter; it was now suspected he had attempted to perform an abortion upon her, thus causing her death. Griffin contended he had done nothing of the sort; he and Florence had paused to talk on the meadow's bank; he gave her the speculum and catheter because she told him she needed them, and he had not walked more than ten feet when he heard her cry out and fall to the ground. He had, he claimed, rushed to her side. He thought she had fainted, and fanned her with his hat. Then, when he saw she was dying, he fled in terror from the girl passing into the next world.

An autopsy disclosed a fetus of about three months' growth; an examination of the body, previous to the autopsy, disclosed masses of matted leaves stuck to her left hip, evidently held in place by some sticky substance. The original doctor called in to testify could find no evidence of the cause of death. He could not find evidence of an abortion. Her genital organs, he said, were normal; there was no sign of injury by instrument. The bloodstain on the right ear, a slight wound on the head, came, he believed, from her head striking a stick on the ground, but there was no indication that any blow had been struck. The spinal cord, brain, esophagus, lungs, stomach, liver, kidneys, spleen, uterus, ovaries, and tongue were removed. The autopsy could disclose no poisonous substance in the stomach. The doctor believed the girl's early history, which indicated considerable trouble with fainting spells, indicated some previous disorder of the heart; the report showed that the organ had indeed suffered a spasm. But another doctor disagreed; the contents of the stomach had not been properly examined at the time, or analyzed adequately at the postmortem. Everyone, the papers now revealed, was awaiting the results of that examination with feverish interest since it might throw some light on the matter. The girl was fifteen years old; Millie Griffin, her fiancé, was eighteen. The papers concluded there was reason to suspect others of complicity in the case since the young man seemed to have had remarkable access to medical assistance in his attempts at an abortion. Suspicion seemed to be falling on everyone; the latest report read that the girl's sister, Nora Aetna, as well as her husband, Robert Aetna, boarded in a house with a doctor; they lived in Dudley, fifteen miles from the Gilman farm. Altogether, John thought, it was a puzzling and fascinating case. Edna read several of the articles concerning the matter, pronounced it repulsive, proclaiming she had no further interest in the case, but, as John noticed, she seemed as familiar with its progress as everyone else.

"Why don't you," Ten asked, looking up at her brother from her paper, "go in for something nice and common and local? For instance, that suicide attempt of the young mother in Dummerston." "What young mother?" Edna asked. "A Mrs. Elm; she had a four-month-old baby, and she waded into the river at St. Petersbury after taking a huge dose of laudanum and tried to drown herself, but was rescued by parties who saw her going into the water. It sounds as if *she* meant business." "What," Edna asked, "do they say is the cause?" "Despondency is the supposed cause of this attempted suicide," Ten read out, pressing the paper up to the edge of her nose. "That's what they always say," Martin observed. "There *is* so much of that," Edna scolded; "wouldn't it be more useful to investigate the causes of this so-called despondency? You would certainly save many more lives, and more worthwhile ones, too." "I don't think anyone is going to do much good for a woman who rides off on a horse, takes poison, *and* tries to drown herself." "Well, she's still alive," Edna protested. "Next time she'll take poison and hang herself after she's sure no parties are around, that's all; if she's going to kill herself, no one is going to stop her." "But this girl is already dead!" Edna protested, raising her voice. "I am not interested," John said tonelessly and menacingly to the air, "in medical research. This case simply happens to present an interesting medical problem, and it happens to intrigue me. Neither will it go on forever."

"Well, who goes to see Anna next?" Minnie asked, trying to change the subject. She was rewarded with gloomy silence. If *they* were going to sit and brood over that horrid trial, she wasn't; she thought back to one of her earliest visits to Anna. That must have been over seven years ago; no, six. Anna's first child had been almost a year and a half old. Well, that had been a shock. She had expected to find Anna polishing the ceiling, but the house was upside down. She had nearly skidded into the parlor on one of little Minnie's toys. The icebox was filled with things turning green and blue; empty bottles thickening their contents, fortunately out of reach of the baby. Dead plants rested dustily on the shelves. Anna couldn't be bothered watering them. The only thing in the house which appeared uninfected by that strange disease called dirt was Anna herself; it would be impossible for her, Minnie thought, to look a dirty mess. How, she asked Anna, did Matthew put up with this? Why, the whole parish must be talking of nothing else.

Oh, Anna answered, it *was* a great inconvenience living in town after the seclusion of her old home. There wasn't anything, she went on placidly, that escaped notice. If your lawn wasn't mowed on the proper day, someone was sure to say something about it right outside your window, or knock on the door to be sure you were still alive. And you had no freedom of your own; why, when old Mr. Hewitt decided to marry Mrs. Wade, Mrs. Wade that was, and they wanted to build a small house for them on their own property, and adjacent to their yard, too, the whole town council had to meet, and there had been one discussion after another with the selectmen. It was ridiculous, she told Minnie, obviously unruffled. Now that Anna had a seven-year-old and a one-and-half-year-old, Minnie thought, you probably had to shovel your way from room to room.

She still remembered Edna's face after her first visit. "We must send her hired help," she kept insisting to John, who was only too willing, but Anna absolutely refused to have any further invasions of her privacy. She already, she wrote, had to lead prayer meetings, inquiry meetings, Sabbath-school classes, fill in for the choir minister, accompany Matthew on calls, and she had her own two children, although they did seem more an army than a pair. She was perfectly capable of hiring someone by the week when things got out of hand. Edna and John had gone down soon afterwards. John took his daughter aside, and told her the only more unhealthy place he knew of was a cemetery which didn't bury its victims deeply enough; the emanations here, he scolded, were worse than a swamp. If she wanted to live in a swamp, or better yet, the city dump, why didn't she move there?

So Anna had finally decided to take in help, but the problem was, as she complained in letter after letter, no one would stay. Finally, a granddaughter of Bridget's had been sent down, and hired two girls to work under her. It was a good thing, she wrote *her* grandmother, they got to stay at a boardinghouse at night, because living with Anna was something, she could say that. Anna didn't care whether there was food in the house unless she happened to notice someone was losing too much weight. If there was a spider web on the ceiling, that didn't bother her, even when it got long enough so she had to walk through it each time she went through the door. Well, if some poisonous ones were in the web and decided to bite the children, she would take notice of *that,* but otherwise it was all up to them, and it was a wonderful thing to get back to that boardinghouse, where the landlady, who everyone said was mean as a shark in a washbowl, at least saw to it that the roof over their heads didn't leak and took note if the front porch started to slide into the street. She'd never seen such housekeeping; well, it was silly even calling it that, but they were happy together, the family; she had to give them that.

And everyone in the parish loved the both of them, so they decided to overlook the decaying heaps in the house;

there weren't any more *now*. The house was neat as could be. You could eat off the floor. But she didn't think Mrs. Hewitt liked it that way; every time she walked into a room they'd just finished cleaning (and they were just cleaning a room every time Anna or one of the children walked out of it), she looked around as if someone had just stolen her best friend; why, she looked as if she *missed* the mess. It was a good thing for her, the granddaughter said, she came from such a wealthy family, or she would have been killed long ago by the dirt falling on her or choking her, or flies eating her all up. And now with the little boy beginning to run wild, it was harder work than ever. If it went on, she complained, they would have to have another girl. It took three, she said, just to keep the backyard clean. And Anna let the children pull up everything in the garden; she didn't care what they did so long as they enjoyed themselves.

That had been a pretty fair description of the situation. They had all been called down by endless pleas to witness the first and second babies' testaments in the church; unfortunately, what they all remembered was the unearthly state of Anna's house (at least when little Minnie and Matthew were walking around. So did Bridget's granddaughter, Kate, and the rest of the troops). They had a dim memory of Anna and Matthew bringing little Minnie to the front of the church (at least you could see the floor *there*, Ten thought), and the minister from Fall River asking, "Do you dedicate this child to Christ, his teachings, will you try to raise her so that she will lead a Christian life?" "We will," they said. And the baby so plainly dressed. "Oh, that was necessary," Anna explained; the people in town thought even a stitch of embroidery on the little thing's robe smacked of popery. It was too bad, though, that the baby had to wait until the age of belief to be baptized; she had come to like the other way, baptism right after birth. It seemed so much safer. Nothing could have astonished them more. Anna disagreeing with doctrine! Of course, she warned them, they must not breathe a word of what she said to anyone. It was heresy, she knew that; but she only felt that way because she had a child.

If anyone had told them, Ten remarked, after they returned home, that they ought to have worried over Anna's housekeeping, not her morbid tendencies, what *would* they have thought? Ten's mind was also running to Anna; they did seem so happy, she and Matthew. Lately, she waited for Anna's letters the way she used to wait for new novels by the author of *Isabella*, although recently they *had* changed in character; in fact, she realized, most of the letters now came from Matthew. In his last one, he had said Anna was not going with him visiting parishioners as much as she once did; she had the two children now, of course, and that was enough to explain it, but lately her father's profession seemed to be getting more and more ahold of her.

Why, she had even set up a little laboratory in the cellar and was doing some kind of work with cell life. She was constantly writing a Dr. Johnston Gale, whose latest book, *The Immortal Life: How to Achieve It,* had received a great deal of attention. Since he was somewhere off in Indiana, Dr. Gale and Anna were conducting their educational exchange through the mail. Now when Anna went out with the children, she returned with all kinds of specimens, usually of simple life forms. She was busy scraping algae and moss from the rocks and she was expert at preparing slides; she had a very good microscope, too. She had gotten it when Dr. Bennet's widow was preparing to auction off their estate; Anna stayed with her husband while he was ill, and later, with the widow, to comfort her.

The only thing about the whole business he didn't like was Anna's hours; now they were even worse than his. She was not willing to take time from the children, or from her work, so she was up with the children all day, dropped off for a nap after supper, and then was up into the small hours of the night. She must have remarkable eyes, he wrote them; she worked by candlelight and lantern light, and the new doctor, who came in and looked over her drawings from slides, said she was talented enough to get a job as a medical illustrator. It surprised him, though, that Anna, whose faith was so strong, was interested in this type of research. But when he asked her about it, she only said not everyone's faith was strong as hers, and if she could contribute something to the path toward belief, then she would believe she had repaid some of the blessings God had seen fit to shower upon her.

Matthew was sure Anna was steady in her beliefs; she went on and on about how, if he were to die first, she would never forgive him, just as if he would be somewhere in a corner and remain unreconciled to argue with. Why, what would she feel like, she asked him, coming to heaven old and gray, while he would have entered just as he was when he died? He might not even recognize her. How would he like finding himself married to an old woman in heaven? she asked, indignant; the Bible said there was no aging in heaven. He would arrive young and handsome, as he was when he died, while she would be white as winter.

Matthew thought it the most ridiculous argument they ever had, but the worst was how seriously Anna took it. He had gone on and on about how the Bible promised they would be transformed, and would not have the same bodies, but would somehow recognize one another. Still, Anna refused to be pacified, insisting she would come marching in rheumatic and gray, and there he would be, handsome as ever, with that distinguished beard and presence, and it would be more than she could bear. He attributed it all to the fits of late pregnancy, but she was still on the subject after little Matthew was born, looking in the mirror for signs of age, and it was soon after that her correspondence with Dr. Johnston Gale had begun.

Did Dr. Steele know anything about him? Was he reputable? He seemed so, from all the information he had collected, but then it was difficult for someone outside the profession to make a true estimate. Dr. Gale said he had heard of Dr. Steele; he had read his articles on contagious diseases and was impressed. Dr. Gale had told Anna that he had every intention of writing the estimable Dr. Steele; he had, it seemed, a theory ancillary to his. He believed some organisms were more susceptible to disease because of their greater tendency to admit dirt particles into the cells of life, which, taken together, constituted the organism as a whole. He hoped Dr. Steele would be anxious to prepare slides of some of the deceased members of his practice in hopes of discovering evidence which would support or violate his new theory. Well, all of it was beyond him, his business was with the soul, and he had a great deal of trouble imagining it covered with dirt particles, much less smothered by them. It *was* something incorporeal, after all, and the idea of dusting it off, or preventing it from getting dusty (all he could think of was putting the soul in a china cabinet, which was not at all what the doctor meant), was too silly for him.

But then Anna had read him quite a lecture about how the soul, while it was on earth, was indissolubly tied to the gross organism (that was the body), so that the more the cells of the body were purified, the more the soul would be purified *before* it left this earth. And, she defied him, picking up their Bible, to find any passage indicating the whereabouts of heaven; it didn't even hold that heaven need be located anywhere but on this planet. How did they know, she asked, this very planet was not meant to be the earthly paradise? After the second death, she meant. After all, it *had* been the earthly paradise once, and perhaps it still was, and when the veil was lifted from their eyes by death, they would see they had been living in it and had been unable to perceive that truth all their lives.

So now, Ten thought, Anna was annoying her husband with some crank and his addled theories, and John would have to be bothered with it, too; she knew him. He would not rest until he had checked out the methods and the motives of this Dr. Johnston Gale. Still, what worse could come of it than exhaustion? If Anna wanted to stay up at night peering at slime, that was her business. What could they expect, really? John had them all isolated in mosquito netting; getting Edna's attention usually meant prying her away from some book on time or etiquette. Anna probably felt as if something were missing from her life unless she was frying her brains over some hot stove.

She wondered what the poor children made of Anna's collections of slime and mold? Nothing much, she supposed. Children got used to their parents so quickly; it was some time before they had anyone else to compare them with, although little Minnie was about to reach just that age, and then Anna might find herself on the hot seat. More likely, Ten thought regretfully, it would be little Minnie who would get nowhere; Anna was as stubborn as her mother. She would explain it all, make it

748

sound perfectly adorable to collect mold and fungi, and the child would go out and play with her hoop and that would be the end of that.

Ella had picked up her writing tablet and begun a letter to Anna. If everyone was going to sit there in silence, or go on about the Gilman trial, well, she had just had enough of that. Besides, she had just taken her four children down to the photographer's and wanted to send Anna their likenesses. Naturally, her own father would not be bothered with anything as mundane as healthy, living children. She ought to tell Anna about this Gilman trial anyhow. From the look on Edna's face, she wouldn't be surprised if Anna received a surprise visit from Mrs. Steele. Edna would have a tantrum if Dr. Steele went off to Boston for any length of time, and she might just decide to pack up and go to New Bedford. She could get to Boston easily enough from there. She would never go far away enough from Father so that he was really out of reach. No matter what trials he might choose to testify in, she would go no farther than a train ride of one or two hours. Still, she might as well warn her sister. She might want to chase the cows out of the living room or something. Although, Ella thought, Anna did seem to be improving in that department. She slipped the little picture of Matthew out of her pocket; he *was* an adorable child. You would never guess he was a boy from looking at his picture.

There he was, propped up on pillows, his little gown spread out around him, resting on a raccoon rug. He looked just like a tiny version of Anna, except his hair was much straighter, and his ears stuck out further. But he had such big round black eyes; and he would have her coloring: that was clear enough, even in the photograph. His little lips looked red with kisses, and his eyebrows were beyond understanding, each one straight, slanting up toward the center of his forehead, stopping wide of each side of his nose, giving him an air of perpetual astonishment. What fat cheeks he had! Well, she thought, taking up her pen, she should be writing all this to Anna. And so she went on, about how little Matthew's chin was so plump and round it overlapped the little gown he was in, but the cutest thing, didn't Anna think so, was the little folds where his wrists ought to be. Why, from the picture, it appeared as if he had on two little bracelets, and those dimples in his fingers, and that round little stomach, he would not be safe around Aunt Ten; she was absolutely turning into a cannibal, although so far she stopped short of biting them; she buried her nose in their fat little cheeks and nuzzled into their stomachs. The children adored her right back. It certainly seemed to keep Aunt Ten young, having all these little creatures around, and as for their mother, she supposed she might as well grab the opportunity of telling Anna some news before everyone else did.

Mother had taken the new horse out yesterday; Amos got into such a state over it he flung himself down on a pile of hay, refusing to talk about it when Father went out to ask him what on earth he was thinking of, letting Edna take that wild Arabian beast. Well, Prince (that was the beast, and Mother was still the beauty) had decided to make a run for Arabia somewhere between their home and Williamsville, and Mother had flattened herself out on him like part of his skin. Everyone told Father, when he set out in pursuit, his wife had managed to get her legs swung over the saddle. They didn't know how she did it; the horse *was* running in a panic, they were sure of that, and he was jumping everything he saw, and Edna just went sailing with him, and he was headed (the horse) toward the covered bridge, and that really gave Father a scare because the sound of his hooves on that bridge was sure to panic the animal, and he might decide to try slamming Edna off, but when he finally caught up with her somewhere near Montpelier, there was Mother, sitting on the ground, glaring at the exhausted horse, who was tied to a stump.

"She *caught it* from Father," Ella wrote, "although, when they came back, they hadn't seen fit to do more than tell them about the barest details of the journey." Mother thought Father had the worst of it, though; didn't Anna think so, too? The next day, when she took the children into town for their likenesses, one of the women told her that Father looked as if *his* heart had stopped. When he brought Mother back, Ella wrote, he said he was going off to his cottage, and they all thought he was going off to work, but when Bill went out to the cottage to ask him something, he was lying there on his cot, completely prostrated, staring at the ceiling. Mother was a little old for runaways, didn't she think? But still, she was sure none of *them* would have stayed on that horse, even when they were in their teens.

Martin, watching his sister writing, began thinking of all the letters which had passed back and forth between Williamsville and New Bedford over the years. The postage alone would probably be enough, if they could collect it all now, to build a bridge from one town to the other. That was sad. Anna was constantly writing about clambakes, and how they barely had enough of them in Williamsville; and they barely had enough in New Bedford, for that matter, she had written, the trouble being, the more of them you ate, the more you wanted to eat. She didn't understand why she wasn't the size of a barn, but she was lucky. And she guessed he knew it wasn't from working too hard cleaning house.

In her last letter to him, Anna said she hoped Amos had taken a reef in his jaw, for if his lower one dropped any further, it would take such an immense quantity of tobacco to fill it up, that cavern in the lower part of his face, he would ruin any firm attempting to supply his wants for that weed. Martin grinned. He had worried Anna would become intolerably prudish as a minister's wife, but on the contrary, she seemed to have lost her stays altogether. She cautioned them about being careful with Amos; they must not let mortification set in by sending him out in bad weather, "especially when there is so much exposure of the vital organ through the mouth cavity as there is with Amos."

George, she wrote, was in from his recent whaling trip and had been playing with the children. He didn't have much sense himself; he let them stand on him and jump on him just as if he was made of wood. They couldn't wait, either, for him to come and see them (whether he brought them presents or not; wasn't that remarkable?) and right now George was interviewing hash houses, as he put it, at one of the many hash factories. Whaling was rather dull, so she expected he would go up into the logging camps for one of the long pulls; that would almost kill little Minnie. She was in love with George altogether. Well, she wrote Martin, she wouldn't tell anyone else about this, but they had been trying to get little

Matthew out of diapers, and were quite at their wits' end about what to do with him. She supposed she ought to warn the family right now he was likely to leave for medical school making use of a sheet for a diaper; big Matthew had decided to let George take the child into the privy, for a demonstration; that's what they called it. Then they sat Mat down on her husband's knee, and Matthew solemnly asked his son if he knew what to do in the privy now, and he said, "Yes, I do," clear as could be. "What?" his father had asked, smiling, filled with hope. "I demonstrate," little Mat answered, although he said "demonstrate" none too clearly. George roared for an hour, but they didn't think it was so funny.

Still, she guessed they would think it was funny if they could see George changing diapers; who would have expected such a sacrifice from him? She worried, though, sometimes; they might have a bad effect on him. He often left them in a depressed state, as if, Anna thought, he just realized it was not his family, after all, and if they were not there, perhaps he might just shake the water from his fur a little faster, and begin a family of his own. Still, it was good having him there, and she decided it was not so selfish of her to let him in as an honorary uncle, even though she long ago guessed what he was about, because she thought he was just one of those bamboozles who wouldn't settle down until someone caught him in a good strong bear trap. Oh, there was one more bit of news: little Minnie. Really, didn't Martin think they ought to stop naming their children after one another? Half of the time she felt prematurely feebleminded, she got everyone's names so confused, and now her Minnie had gone and made matters worse, and named her new cat, or kitten—it was definitely a kitten, wasn't it, when you could hold it in the palm of your hand?—Ella. She had gone and named it Ella.

No wonder George had settled in there. He did wish he would settle into a house of his own, though. And they had all been so sure it was puppy love, or something even milder. Well, there was no telling about anything, that was what Aunt Ten always said.

He did miss his sister, but he never said anything about it. He imagined everyone did, at least as much as he did, and there was no point in making matters worse going on and on about it. They were still, he knew, mad at Mother for going on one night about how death and distance were really indistinguishable. When someone got far away enough, there was no way of getting in touch with them, and then, what difference did it make, she asked, whether they were dead or alive? She was thinking about Anna, he knew, but still, George's ship had just been reported missing in a storm, and it hadn't done Minnie or William much good to hear that little speech.

Then they saw her up at night, writing away at her notes. He knew she was trying to decide if there *was* any difference between death and distance, or if distance wasn't an element of death; if time wasn't some kind of barrier, which, when it grew tall enough, formed a wall no one could surmount, and it became impossible to see the person on the other side, something like a mountain, so that what was commonly assumed to be death was only a separation. She had the severest doubts, she wrote, about this new theory, but she had noticed it again and again, how the two, distance and death, seemed the same to the mind; it made her think of Virginia. That was nearly thirty years ago, but she seemed dead before she had actually died: well before. Just because she had been so far away. She concluded proximity was essential to life; perhaps it was possible to kill someone simply by ceasing to believe he existed.

She wondered what would happen if everyone decided to believe some living person was really dead; would he actually die if they cut themselves off from him? She supposed they would never find out since no one was likely to try such a cruel experiment. It was interesting, though, that Virginia died just when she ceased believing in her existence; her last letters might have been penned by a ghost or an impostor for all the belief they generated in her actual physical existence. Well, thought Martin, it was wrong of him to have read Mother's notes, especially when she hid them in the book she was reading, but he had been furious with her. Still, at her age, it was preposterous to expect change.

He hoped everyone was doing what he and Minnie were, carefully preserving all the letters from Anna. Why, taken all together, they were almost a history of the families. It was odd how *he* liked the little details Anna or the children wrote of; the others always fastened on the larger issues. Little Min had written that on Christmas night she went to singing school, and the next night to a Baptist Anniversary, and New Year's night she went to a Disciple Anniversary. That little one didn't seemed reined in by being the minister's daughter. And George had gotten her a subscription to *The Children's Hour*. "I have got a nice sacque hood and veil," Min had written in her last letter to him; "My sacque is a nice warm one for winter; my hood, I bought the stuff and crocheted it. It is made square and then a border put on. I wear it for nice things, so I have no hat, and Ma says I am vain as can be." Well, it had been a long time since that child wrote him. He would have to get after his sister about it. *She* had complained noisily enough whenever she didn't get her daily letter during their medical-school days. She was probably too busy with her piano and her molds; but he did like her letters.

"I have had the organ moved into the sitting room so I can practice when I want to without building a fire. I suppose you still have a fire in every room. I can't imagine Father sitting in his cottage evenings with his foot on the stove, smoking his pipe, and thinking and talking about ague medicine, although perhaps that is what he's doing, for all the writing he does me. The children," she wrote, "went on a sleigh ride with nine little boys and girls and it really seemed as if the sleigh was made of India rubber, it held so many. I enjoyed it so much more than I do a party of grown people. They all came to our house and played games until tea was ready, and after tea, Grandfather Hewitt had a frolic with them, and then it was oranges, you know what a rare treat that is, and they all sang for us before going home." They *all* got at his letters, Martin thought, annoyed; he was the only one who got letters like that from Anna.

They had always been so close, that must be it; she knew he missed all the little minutes together, but he didn't want everyone else taking them off, too, as if they were cookies on a plate to be passed around. She wrote him about apple blossoms, how it seemed they were living in a world of flowers. She wrote *him* about robberies: there had been one at Marie Dawson's. He had met her, she reminded him, on his last visit two hundred years ago. Marie said there was someone in her yard at half past eleven last night, and that her husband had twelve men out looking for them. Marie said they got nearly a thousand dollars' worth of silks in the back of the house; that was nearly every piece they had, too. They were in such a hurry, they dropped some of the things and Mrs. Dawson found some umbrellas, shoes, and other things. It looked, Anna wrote, as if some people undressed themselves in the grass, and were in quite a bustle about it, too.

And it was thanks to Martin's letters from Anna they felt they knew Matthew so well; he resented it. He would get letters about the amusing incidents of their married life, probably, he thought, because Anna trusted him not to laugh at her for thinking them so remarkable. Martin knew, she wrote, what a passion for fresh peas she always had, and Matthew had surprised her one morning coming in with a big mixing bowl full to the brim with them. She was so excited she was jumping up and down as if there were snakes flicking at her heels, and she sat right down at the table, and what did he do? He took one pea and put it in the center of the plate. Thanksgiving, though: that was his favorite time for jokes: everyone's plate, and then, when they got to his aunt, Jane Hewitt, he would solemnly put a tiny sliver of turkey in the middle of it and pass it down to her.

It happened every year, and every year it seemed funnier, although she didn't suppose it would to them. She had been worried about little Minnie when the tree fell into her room, not because a tree had fallen in, that happened often enough, but because it was covered all over with tent caterpillars, and Minnie ran out into the hall screaming, "Shrouds! Shrouds! Shrouds!" and it had taken them some time persuading her they really were insect webs, and they had their hands full, too, taking them up after they got rid of the tree and burning all those miserable insects in gasoline. "Shrouds! Shrouds!" Minnie awoke for nights screaming that. No wonder Mother had worried about *her* so much after the Webster sermon. "Shrouds! Shrouds!" she wrote Martin; sometimes she found herself walking around the house repeating that to herself.

Well, thanks to George and his constant shepherding of

the children off to farms, they said when she and Matthew kissed, they sounded just like a cow pulling its foot out of the mud. So they were getting pretty rural, after all, even if they had to live in the town. And she was so greedy for details of his life! It was a good thing, he thought, Minnie hadn't known how many nights, supposedly up studying, he actually was writing his sister. Anna was sure he was having incomparable adventures in Boston, so if anything came up, he immediately wrote it down and sent it off to her.

And it had been worth it. She had never forgotten anything he wrote her of, and often now she referred to those days in Boston; he lived them over and over again because of her letters. She never would forget, she said, his account of the professor and the chickens. "One of the German professors here at the medical school," he wrote her just as a term was beginning, "had his jaw broken while chasing a chicken thief just before his class started. He was raising some very choice chickens in his yard for the poultry show. The thief tried to steal them; the professor heard him and ran after him and fell into a hole where they were digging a sewer, broke his jaw, blacked his eye, and got his cheek cut open. The thief got away and also the chickens, for neither the professor nor the thief got them. I am afraid it will spoil this professor for life, for he always used such jawbreaking words it is liable to break again. We suggested he be the exhibit for a course in setting bones, but he didn't take to the idea too well." Every time she looked at that letter, Anna said it made her laugh.

Well, he might as well write Anna a letter. Ten, seeing more and more sheets of paper appearing, decided to pick up her book. The silence between John and Edna was thick as lamb's wool. She wouldn't miss anything if she read *Isabella*; this must be the third time she'd read it, but it had been so long since the last time, she'd forgotten what it was about in the first place. Just what they'd say about her and her own life in a little while.

Martin, meanwhile, settled down to his task. "There have been a lot of suicides here," he wrote, rushing through the mundane details; "Caroline Rivers and her four children killed themselves (or rather, she killed them) by putting some salt of arsenite in their food. The little one didn't eat enough, but she must have been determined they go together because she had them all in bed with her, and literally strangled the little one. No one can think of any reason for it, either. Everyone says her home was happy. Then someone from New Haven came all the way here to jump off a bridge, and must have changed his mind, because he started calling for help. He came up to the surface once or twice, but he didn't try to swim and they couldn't get him; the tide was too strong.

"Then there was a Mr. Flagg you didn't know who got married Thursday morning and killed himself jumping out of the honeymoon suite at the Brooks House the very next day. They say an acute attack of mania made him do it, because the neighbors in the next room didn't hear them quarreling, but his bride said her husband had become greatly excited over something and rushed to the window to jump out, and she tried to grab his foot and hold on to him, but he pushed her aside. Some people think he had financial troubles, but his new wife must have recovered fast, because she was a hospital nurse the day before she married and she was a hospital nurse three days later.

"I guess Reverend Temple—he's taking over for Dr. Pierce for a while—is afraid this is becoming a resort or watering place for suicides. At least he's taken to giving sermons on suicide, which he calls a sin and a cowardice. 'It is the life of faith that cures this evil,' he preaches; 'God is a good, a faithful keeper, a friend in need. He who feels this will wish to live.' But I am afraid *his* mind is disordered, since he didn't end there, and he should have, don't you think? Instead, he ground on about how education is no cure for suicide, because, as compulsory education becomes more common, so does suicide. Mrs. Tewksberry was so furious afterward she swore she was not returning to church until she could again look on the sensible visage of old Reverend Pierce, and then he meandered on some more about how May, June, and July, the months of greenness, flowers, and sunshine, give the greatest numbers of self-murders, and here we are, right in the middle of July, and the whole parish worried to death the beauty of the countryside will be the end of someone in their family.

"Well, it certainly has been queer times around here.

Mary Brown started barking like a dog last week and frothing at the mouth. They called us in, but she hadn't been bitten by anything bigger than a mosquito, and Father thought it was some kind of hysterics, but then she kept drinking large quantities of water, so we didn't think it could be rabies. The vet came out and looked over her three dogs, and when one of them died, he did an autopsy, but *he* couldn't find any sign of rabies, either. Mary Brown died two days after the dog, but the autopsy showed that although she was not bitten by a dog, as far as anyone can tell, she did die of rabies. Well, everyone's talking about it; you can imagine, I guess. *Spirits* this and *spirits* that.

"Then they just arrested two people for stealing bodies right out of the town churchyard; they were selling them privately to some doctor for one hundred and ten dollars, and nobody knows what the doctor was about, or can seem to find out. Wherever we go, we hear of people found dead in rooms, and not by suicide, either. Mrs. Elvira Camp was found dead just sitting in her bedroom with all her noon work done. Then Mr. and Mrs. Blenton went out to look at some roses and came back to find their nine-month-old baby dead in the crib, and we can't tell what ailed it. It didn't die of strangulation because it didn't have a pillow or any blankets, so the cause of death is a mystery to us, I can tell you. The poor mother is half prostrated with guilt, and the father, too, I guess.

"Did you see the article in the papers about the lady in France who has the artificial skins? She has a third skin made of silk, and it's said to be so exquisitely fine and close-fitting almost no one has ever detected its presence. They say it covers her whole body, from ankles to chin, and all the sets are woven especially for her. Aunt Ten says she hopes Lettie never sees that article or she'll be having webs woven for *her*. They are supposed to be flesh-colored, and they hide all wrinkles and ravages of time, so I guess Mother has one and we just haven't discovered it; it even hides natural discolorations of age. They also say she wears a collar of jewels where the skin leaves off and never takes off her gloves even while eating dinner; that must be a nuisance, I think.

"Then Alfred Culpepper—you remember him, I guess (he used to try peeping at you when you were getting dressed)—just died horribly. He was down at the mill last week and didn't think there was any danger and stepped into a bin that had five tons of corn, but he started to sink, and his friend tried to pull him out, but he was up to his waist in corn in no time. His friend ran down to turn off the machinery, but when he got back, Alfred had disappeared under the corn. They cut away one side of the bin and shoveled out some of the corn, but it was too late; he was suffocated, and nothing could be done to revive him. His mother was hysterical when she heard he held his hat in front of his face to keep the corn away from his mouth and nose, but no air could get to him when the corn went over his head. I tell you, Anna, it *is* queer times here. Everyone keeps going on about what a strange and horrible death it was, but I think one kind is bad as another. What do you say?

"But I do have some good news for you. Remember the man who was killed by a swarm of bees when we were children, and they had to pick the bees off the dead body, and the bees swarmed right into the hive? Well, they say now that if you hold your breath, wasps, bees, and hornets can be handled with impunity. The skin is supposed to become stingproof, and you are supposed to be able to hold the insect by the feet and give it full liberty of action, and if it drives its weapon against the impenetrable surface (that's your skin) nothing whatever will happen, but if you let even a tiny quantity of air escape from your lungs, the sting will penetrate at once. The man who made this discovery (I don't believe him, do you?) claims his theory is based on his learning that the pores of the skin close when the breath is kept in. He also says his experiments in that direction have not been exact enough to have much scientific value, and Father agrees with him there.

"It's a good thing that Father agrees with someone, because he and Mother have been fighting like cats and dogs over that court business again, and Father seems set on getting involved in the Gilman case, and Mother is at her wit's end to know how to stop him. I've never seen them fuss at each other like this, and I tell you, Anna, it worries me, just because Mother is usually right about Father. Ten says we should stay out of it, because once they get started there's no stopping them, and they'll just have to fight it out like two cats, but I don't like it, and if you have any ideas, I hope you'll put them in the mail."

Martin sighed, looking over his letter. It was a good thing there were no family censors to look over the mail or his letters would never leave the house; they wouldn't approve of his writing Anna about such morbid matters, but he knew what would interest her, and besides, they'd always told each other whatever entered their heads. He looked up just in time to see his father look at his mother in their own way, and they suddenly got up, announcing they were going to bed. Everyone breathed a sigh of relief as they left. "I wish they'd settle down," Ten said without looking up; "it's like living in a haunted house." "They'll settle down when the trial's over," Ella said, "and not before." "I don't like to hear things like that; I'm stuffing my old ears with oil and cotton for the next few months. You just hold up a headline announcing the verdict. I'm too old for this nonsense. You'd think," she said, looking toward the door, "*they* would be, too."

In the relative safety of their room, Edna decided to try reining in her temper and make the attempt: she would try to talk to her husband. "That was quite a picture we just got from Anna," she began innocently; "Matthew and George sitting there like two mummies on straight-backed chairs up against the side wall of the house; was Matthew holding Minnie, or was George? I can't remember who had which." John didn't answer. "All right," she said, "what *is* it about this trial that concerns you so much?" "I don't think you're interested in hearing about it." "Well, I am." "I don't believe you." "I don't care; I would like to know what's so interesting about it, if it isn't too much trouble. If it isn't too much of an inconvenience to talk." "If you promise not to interrupt." "I promise, I promise," Edna said in a temper; "really, John you're just like a child." "And you could follow Sir Isaac Newton's example; you're always so interested in him. Remember Diamond?" he half taunted; "his dog who overturned the almost finished labors of so many years? You used to tell the children about it all the time. And the loss was *irretrievable;* how you used to emphasize that word—because he was so advanced in age. And all Sir Isaac said was 'Oh, Diamond! Diamond! You little know what mischief you have done.' Would that Sir Isaac were here tonight." "Are you going to get on with it?" Edna asked icily. "All *right,*" he shouted.

"When I was in medical school," he said, turning on his side and staring at the wall, "there was an old Austrian professor who developed a theory about the powers of imagination. He thought people could be frightened to death, but he was short on evidence. He did have a huge list of people who died of joy. We got on well. He used to talk to me about the powerful influence of passions and affections on the human frame. He thought too violent an emotion, bad or good, could paralyze the heart; it was like an excessive stimulus. He had a list of examples.

"It went all the way back to the Greeks. Someone in Lacedaemon died on hearing his son had won a prize in the Olympics. Sophocles died when a contest of honor was decided in his favor. Diagoras had three sons who were all crowned victors the same day, and the sons carried their father on their shoulders through the crowds, and everyone threw flowers at him, but he died in the midst of his sons' embraces and all the congratulations. There was something or other he found in Livy about an aged matron who was suffering because she thought her son was dead, but then, when he came home, she died of joy in his arms."

Edna began taking an interest. She should not, she scolded herself; she should not let him interest her. "Leo the Tenth is supposed to have died of a fever brought on by happy news; he heard Milan had been captured; he had been hoping it would be. Then there was someone unexpectedly pardoned during Henry the Eighth's reign; he died of shock, or the same thing, a transport of joy. The professor said they were the same thing.

"He also studied the effects of grief. He thought excessive sorrow might cause sudden death, melancholy, amnesia, imbecility, nervous fever, hypochondria, pretty much everything. When Plautus saw his dead wife's body, he threw himself on it, and died right then. Some woman heard of her closest friend's death, cried out, and fell down dead. Then there was a Duchess of Burgundy who knew she was dying and told her husband she knew he couldn't live without a wife, so she wanted to know whom he was going to marry next. He told her he hoped God would never punish him so, but if he did, he would not take a second wife, since he would die within a week of her. He did; he died the seventh day after her death. Are you interested?" "Yes, yes," she answered tonelessly. "Do you see what I'm getting at?" "Yes, yes, *yes;* go on."

"Well. He collected as many extraordinary cases of powers of the imagination as he could. That's what he called them. He had a patient in Austria burning with fever, and was ready to give him up. Then the man pointed to the door and said if he could only swim in that lake, he would cool off. So the professor humored him, and the man walked all around the room saying he could feel the water going up to his neck, and finally said he felt cool and well and it turned out he was right.

"He'd come across people who thought their arms and legs were made of wax or strange shapes, or even thought they were dead. He found an account of someone who believed he was a rabbit and wouldn't let any bell ring in the house; he was afraid the noise would drive him off into the woods. Then, other times, the same one thought he was a plant and stood up in the garden to be watered. Everyone was so afraid he would die of the chill, so they dressed up two people and they convinced him they were shades of his dead relatives so he followed them to a cellar. He ate a meal with them. Well then, after that, whenever he was in a state, or stood about in the garden, he ate in the cellar with some noble ghost.

"And there was a man who thought he was so gigantic he couldn't go through a door, and the attending doctor thought, if they forced him through one of them, he would get over it, so they struggled away with him, and when the man saw he was inside the doorway, he started in screaming just as if his bones really had been broken; well, he died almost immediately. There were files and files of cases like that. At the time of the Camp business —you know, when I gave her the magic casket? That brought all of it back."

He looked over at her. She nodded. "So, you see, that's how I've gotten more and more interested in emotions and what they do to the body, and I've wondered"—he looked at her warily—"perhaps this Gilman case just might have the answer. The girl *could* have died of fright.

She was only fifteen; she does sound very suggestible. It's not just a matter of my wanting to see her evil fiancé swinging in the air. I'd like to find out if you can be frightened to death." Edna nodded again. "Well, are you going to keep on opposing me?" "No, I don't think so; you're going to pay a high enough price for your answer to that question without help from me." He looked at her quizzically. "Before you get near the answer to that question," she said, her voice far away, "you'll wade through a lot of sewers. That sister of hers; you'll see." "It will be worth it," he told her, positive. "For all our sakes," Edna said, "I hope so." "Then can we make up in the usual way?" "Will I cause a fatal excess?" "Get in bed," he ordered, smiling for the first time in days.

"I believe we heard the sound of horses' hooves," Edna said, just as they were falling asleep. She held one finger up in the dark. "Shssss!" John hissed. "Grandma says it's the scarlet fever," a voice was saying; "the whole house is full of it, and it looks like all Slab Hollow's got it. You better come quick," the man's voice insisted. "We'll be right there," Martin's voice answered. "Let the boys handle it," John whispered to his wife; "I never worry much about scarlet fever." "Probably because you hardly ever lose a patient to it." "That's a good reason not to worry."

"Did you see," she asked him, "the new batch of pictures Anna sent home this week?" "I'm not sure. I've been an outcast lately." "All right," Edna answered curtly; "I thought we agreed to stop talking about that." She told him a long story about Minnie and a chipmunk. "What are you getting at?" he asked. "Getting at? I was just bringing you up to date after the long silence." "I don't believe that, somehow." "Well, if you must know," she retorted, defensive, "I was thinking about what you said before. Which reminds me, I think you ought to suspend your principles for once and take likenesses of the whole family tomorrow." "The photographer from town would have an easier time of it, and you'd have less trouble sending his pictures through the mail. Besides, if you call him, you can have all the copies you want." "That's what you always say." "It's the truth." "All right, all right, we'll send Amos out to get him here; it's not worth disputing." "What *were* you thinking about?

Before you decided we needed pictures of the whole family."

"The Austrian professor. I don't like him. Especially if he was right. We're all on the ends of pretty shaky branches anyway. Everything's dangerous. Emotions are dangerous; everything, fear, love. It sounds as if we never should feel them. Feel nothing but mild things, no high points and low points. That's a terrible thought. It oughtn't be that way. It makes us sound destined for monotony; you know, forever sitting in Sabbath school, listening to endless stories about sweet, darling baby Jesus, singing hymns, anything to keep our minds off things like real life. Well, real life won't stay monotonous. That Austrian professor—he put life on trial. Emotions, life; they're antagonistic.

"Criminals, murderers, suicides, they just have too much of life, not enough monotony; then there's no blaming them. Then the papers are right when they keep on saying all these crimes are performed in states of acute dementia; there isn't any cause or no cause smaller than all of life taken together." "You see where his theories lead once you begin thinking about them." "Wherever they lead, they're frightening." "But they explain a great many more things than crime. Crime, well, perhaps it is a disorder of the body. Or the mind. It prevents it from taking experience in properly, as with children or adults who can't digest some kinds of food. You came with us the day we went to see that woman who accidentally ate the strawberry, and by the time we got there, her throat had swollen shut; don't you remember? We had to make out the report. She died of asphyxiation.

"Life must affect some people that way, except they run to fits, firing barns, pouring poison in porridge, but it's a question whether life's the cause of it or the person's constitution. What people *do* to keep off the dangerous things, the peaks and the valleys, that's what you called them? That's what interests me. How much human activity is an attempt to get rid of them? To restore monotony? The Pyramids, for instance. Well, those were peaks, literally, but what were they *for?* Just so the people who died and moved into them could live there with their cats and dogs and jewelry and maids in complete museum monotony, day after day? All that embalming, that was its point; so the mummies could live in absolute certainty of sameness, no surprises, no shocks, no further births or deaths, additions perhaps, but they could never leave or move. But no losses, no further disintegrations, no disappointments, no further changes.

"That's what interests me, really. Possibly all our lives take one of two courses. One attempts to arrest the inevitable. My daguerreotypes would be in that category. They try to hold the present moment, but the moment passes, and if the picture does hold it, I'm not sure it does so in a much more useful way than the Pyramids hold the mummies. Except, of course, it's possible to look at the pictures. But there's no future for the people in my little casket cases, any more than there's a future for the mummies. Still, I forget the futility while I'm working. I don't think about whether or not it's a symbolic activity, or a useful one historically or artistically. What is history to me, really? I won't be here to take part in it, even tions, paradoxical reactions, that's the medical term. But history's a dead study, like the mummies. If it could be artistic, I suppose it would be better because at least art gives people pleasure; that's an unusual thing to have in this life: pleasure. I suppose that's why everyone is so grateful to the artist."

"Or hates him so much," Edna murmured. "The really good ones bring that on," John said, "the double reactions, paradoxical reacations, that's the medical term. But the ones who just make people feel more comfortable about the way they're living, the people who carve statuary for tombstones, or give glowing eulogies over the bodies of mass murderers; they're always taken to everyone's bosom. Mr. Siddons manages to make this earth seem like a paradise; no one tries attacking him. Why should they? It would be stupid as attacking someone trying to save your life. But the others; they're different. They take away the picture of paradise; and there goes the ground under your feet. Well, that takes skill, but no one has to like them for it."

"And the other course?" "The other must be *your* way; to try and find an explanation for things. An explanation is close to a cause. Once you discover what went wrong, or is wrong, there's some chance of doing something. Time, your theories about time," he went on, "how the dust sinks into the skin, weighs down the bones, keeps the pure fluid out, well, if that were true, there might be some way to prevent it from happening. It's not really a matter of pure science. It's not altogether altruistic, that interest of yours. No, now that I think of it, you've probably been more concerned than we have, the doctors among us, I mean: about rescuing us. I wrap the house in mosquito netting, but that's for the moment, something for the moment. But what you're up to is stopping moments, or at least stopping them from bruising the skin. And the soul, I suppose. You must know how things bruise the soul or you wouldn't be so set against religion. It's harmless enough.

"And now that you're collecting those Della Robbia buttons and courting chains, it seems our interests are coming closer. You must be giving up in your attempts," he said gently, "if you've started in on taxidermy the way I did." She didn't say anything. "If you ask me," he went on, "that's what Anna's up to also. After Webster's sermon, I thought she'd end up as one of the professor's cases. She couldn't take in extreme things; they're only like heat and cold, nothing more unusual, except that the mind feels them, not the skin, and the mind is so sensitive. But now that she's passed that point, she's trying to find some way to stop time in its passage.

"Do you remember when you were reading St. Augustine, and he was trying to decide what time was? He said he was only measuring time in its passage: once the present moment passed from one place to another, it was no longer there to be measured. 'Therefore,' he said, 'it is time in its passage I am measuring.' There was also something about the future proceeding from some secret place, and then receding into some secret place. She seemed fascinated with that; where those places were. Well, these new experiments of hers, if what Matthew writes is true, and I imagine it is—then it sounds as if she's trying to stop the passage of time. If she could, she could keep experiencing the same thing over and over again. I think that's what she wants. I think that's what she's always wanted." "I'd think," Edna said, "*that* would be monotony." "Whether it is or isn't," John said sadly, "I've come to believe that's all she cares about. It's the length she'll go to—that we'll all go to, to achieve it—

that's what interests me now. Hence this Gilman trial you go on so about."

"And if the lengths are longer than your measuring stick?" "I don't know how I'd take that," John considered; "it might turn me against life. That's what you're afraid of, isn't it?" Edna said nothing. "I had no idea *at all*," she said at last, "you knew what worried me." "Well, it had to be something serious, it had to be something connected with your father; otherwise, there was no explaining that insane aversion of yours to any kind of court; otherwise"—he smiled into the moonlight—"you'd be more like Lettie, delighted out of your skin by all the publicity I was getting. So I put two and two together; it wasn't so hard. It was just another diagnosis," he said, squeezing her hand; "you were frantic over my appearing in court. You never got over what happened to your father. You know I would never kill myself." "Not like him, anyway," she interrupted. "So it had to be you thought something similar would happen to me. You never would have worried so if you only thought I'd be unhappy; you didn't think I'd hang myself. I don't think you think I'm the type to end in a lunatic asylum, so I assumed you thought it would suck the lifeblood from me, you know; like some kind of leech."

"Well," Edna said—she sounded exhausted—"it may begin to seem more that way to you after a while, especially after you listen to them trying to explain their horrors away; oh, they even resort to claiming the person they murdered wasn't dead when he or she was buried. They make the court give an exhumation order so they can see if there was any activity in the casket, and you're right, the judge sits there in his black robes, and he looks just like that. A giant leech. They kill themselves with alarming frequency, you know that, don't you? My father used to complain about it; how every time a judge killed himself, he had to learn a whole new personality, a whole new set of rules and calculations. It was like learning a new language when he had to cope with a new judge. So you see what good it does the leeches, sucking all that poisoned blood."

"But I have to know more about it; I know it's obsessive. It became an obsession after Jane Camp. After all these years as a doctor, almost thirty years, I have to know how much of what I've done is medicine and how much superstition. I tend to think most of it's been superstition, suggestion. I keep coming back to Jane Camp and the magic casket. I can't stop myself."

"Why do you think her parents asked her to make that vow? I mean, the three of them. Why did their parents want them to stay unmarried and together that way?" "I don't know, but once when Fred Camp had a high fever and was raving, he said something about blood being the only decent thing. Maybe their parents thought nothing tied people closer than the same bloodline, and if they stayed together, nothing could hurt them."

"But if they married, why couldn't the ones who weren't blood relations just live there?" "No one knows much about Mr. and Mrs. Camp, but there used to be a story about Mrs. Camp's running out of her back door and across the common into Mrs. Pierce's house. They said she told Mrs. Pierce her husband tried to kill her with a pitchfork, and the thing was supposed to have been caused by something small, something like an argument about one of the in-laws, whether he should come to live there with them or not. Well, after that, no one ever saw any sign of trouble between them again, but someone or other remembers seeing her start a bonfire one night, and they swore she threw a pitchfork on it. They used to fight over the children, too. Ten would remember that more. I think she once said something about how their parents disgraced themselves one winter by deciding to go to different churches, and they started up every Sunday, and waited to see which one of them the children would choose to go with; they always went together before. It was a big thing, I guess. Everyone waited for Sunday to see which one of them the children would pick. Ten said, I think she said, the children solved it all by taking turns. One Sunday, they went with their father. The next Sunday, they went with their mother. I guess they took the fun out of it because then the parents stopped. It's funny how it comes back; I haven't thought about it in years." "The Camps," Edna said; "*they* started you on all this." "Not really. It was the old professor; but the Camps put the seal on things. It just happened that way." Edna sighed. "Trials," she said, "are very boring; they drag on and on, just like dragging a river, and they drag up all the wrong corpses, and if a trial goes on long enough, I can tell you, if they dragged up Queen Elizabeth, you wouldn't even care." "That's just why I want to see it," John said, excited. "The whole process sounds like life in miniature." "It feels like two lifetimes, especially if you're sitting on a hard seat."

They fell silent for a while. "Are you going to flee to New Bedford the way the children think you will? If I go to Boston? For the whole trial?" "How do you know they think that?" Edna asked, flabbergasted. "You don't think they're the only ones who listen at doors, do you?" She could tell he was smiling. "No, no. I'll come down on weekends. We can stay with Mother some of the time and the Parker House the rest of the time." "I don't want to stay with our dear daughter, either," he answered in response to something left unsaid; "she'd be there every night with some new personage to introduce. I don't think I could stand it; you'd be sitting through *my* trial next." "She *is* a bit of a ghoul." "So are all the social climbers; we got away from an awful lot of that by staying up in the country this way. You don't have any regrets? When you think of all the openings of ball seasons you've missed?" "The more I think of them, the more I remember the ones I didn't miss, and the happier I am to be here; really, it's true. I was a misfit in that house on Cedar Street if ever there was one."

"You and your father; he'd have been happier in the country." "Oh yes, I think so; I've thought about that. But I think your Austrian professor would have pronounced him incurable. His power of imagination would have been fatal anywhere." "I suppose." "You're tired." "Well, that's nothing new." "I know," his wife retorted, "but I'd like to see it get to be something old." Silence again fell like snow. "Turn over on your side; how can I hug you otherwise?"

The next morning, Edna, resigned to John's attendance at the entire Gilman trial (which she fully expected to last until next spring, if not next summer), sent for the local photographer. She had no idea why she wanted pictures of the family at that very instant; she knew only that she wanted them and intended to have them before John left. If she had to tie him to his bed. She was, luckily, very satisfied with the results. One picture particularly appealed to her. It was a group picture, taken on the slate slabs forming the steps to the old kitchen of the pre-Revolutionary wing. Martin sat next to John; Ten was right in the middle. Then came Edna, and next to her, Ella. A tree was reflected in the windowpane behind Martin; it seemed underwater. Martin was sitting in his usual way, straight, but managing to look as if he were slumping. John sat up straight, knees apart, his pose identical to Martin's. He was wearing a cap; it was very hot. For once, Edna saw, his doctor's coat was off. His deep-set eyes stared out at her as if he were inside the picture itself. Time had not changed the original impression he gave; he still seemed more a force of nature, a dynamic, than a human. When she looked at his pictured face, she still thought of trees, mountains, streams. He was natural and inevitable as a storm.

She was not sure she liked seeing pictures of Ten. In the pictures, she looked her age, although she never seemed to in daily life. She stared straight into the camera, making no concessions to sunlight, although she had made some to vanity. She was not wearing her spectacles. She drew the line there, though; she sat there, holding her walking stick, and, while the rest of them were obviously warm enough in the sun, she wore a dark crocheted shawl which Anna had sent her. Anna sent a note with it, telling her a parishioner made it up; Aunt Ten, she knew, would understand she couldn't keep more than one stitch together at a time. "Sensible woman," Ten pronounced, examining the garment; she hadn't been far from it since.

Well, she *did* look funny, Edna thought, looking at the picture of herself. Even with Ten stooped over as she was now, *she* was still shorter and she was sitting one step above Ten, too. She wished, looking at the picture, her hair would turn gray; it would give her a more dignified look. She did do her best to look dignified; she parted her hair in the middle and swept it back in wings. It only made her, Ella said, look like a retired stage actress. Ella looked so astonishingly stern. Really she wasn't like that at all. She had, more than any of them, nerved herself to face the days as they came. She supposed that kind of strength took its own kind of toll.

She particularly liked one picture of Ten; they had sat her on a chair in the middle of the pasture, half shaded by the apple tree. She was there, neat in her elaborate print cotton dress, the fingers of one hand stretched out; they must have felt more comfortable that way. Her other hand was curled in her lap. She looked into the lens with that half-humorous, half-comical look she always had. Her hair had thinned; now it looked like a light fall of snow on her head. She hadn't realized, not before, how perpetually Ten's eyebrows were raised, as if she were constantly surprised at the world.

She asked John about that before they fell asleep: "You remember what we were talking about last night? The different kinds of people? What about Ten? How does she fit in?" "I'm not sure; sometimes I think she's part animal. Oh, I don't mean that in any negative way; but she suspends judgment about everything. That gives her more balance, or ballast, than the rest of us; I've never been sure what to call it. I remember, we were all children and there was a terrible hailstorm and apples began raining down with the hailstones; Mother took on about it. She probably expected the whole house to blow away. No one in the country reacted very sensibly. Mrs. Moffat, Alice's mother, insisted on moving them all into the barn, and that was a lot more likely to blow down than the house.

"Ten was very calm about it. Especially since she'd never seen anything like it before. She would have been out trying to catch apples and hailstones in her apron if Mother hadn't been afraid a tree would fall on her. Well, after everyone was through moaning and groaning about the apples, the poor apples, she asked us what we were all complaining about because now we wouldn't have to bother climbing up to pick them." "Well, she was right." "It was the easiest apple crop we ever took in, but she was the only one who thought of it. It's not called looking on the bright side, either, that kind of thinking. She's an instinctual thing." "She's getting old," Edna said. "I imagine her instincts are telling her that." "I wish they'd think of something else to say." "It won't be the same around here without her." "No, it won't." "But you said some women in your family live to be over one hundred." "Some."

As she was falling asleep, Edna found herself thinking about how much Ten's picture did, in fact, resemble one of the apple dolls the women in Hill houses were perpetually making. They made the faces of apples, so that, when they wrinkled, they would look like old women. On one of her rare visits, Anna tried to comment on the resemblance, but Edna cut her off. It was as if Ten, as she now was, stressed some kind of underlying unity: between male and female, between animal and vegetable. She wondered if Anna noticed that; if Ten's appearance had anything to do with Anna's study of vegetable life, her beginning attempts at investigating human immortality.

Her mind wandered off to another picture: of Martin. She kept slipping it in, mentally, with ones they had just gotten made up. It was a picture taken the winter before he married Minnie; he stood there in his dark wool outfit with his farmer's cap, a dark outline against all that snow. He was the only thing in the picture not covered, at least partially, by snow. It had always interested her, the way the snow chose to leave some things untouched, as if those things were immune to its fall.

Those beautiful trees: how the winter reduced them, black nettings against the sky futilely trying to hold something back. The rose bushes were nothing but vague sticks. Half of the barn seemed to have disintegrated; it was covered with snow and didn't show itself. It was the same color as the sky and melded with it. The far hills, the ones she had spent so many hours watching spring and summer, were shortened, shorn of their majesty, not even like shorn lambs, continuing to exist, but looking altogether like some new kind of animal; they were shrunken by the snow covering them, and except for the evergreens, they too sunk under the white sea of the gray-white sky. A blighted pearl; a huge, blighted pearl. Martin stood in the middle of that vastness as if he were inhuman, a protest against the general eradication. He appeared surrounded by more footprints than had been necessary to transport him to his frozen, defiant position; as if, she thought, he had trampled the snow to see how he liked doing it, after it had trampled so on the earth. Well, she hoped John *did* learn something at this trial. That was the best she could hope for. As for her uneasiness, she decided, hearing John's deep breathing, and withdrawing her arms, turning on her own side, sleeping as usual, back to back, she would just have to live with it.

The Gilman case dragged on and on, just as Edna had predicted. It introduced its cast of characters rather briskly: there was Florence Gilman, the rather nice, rather simpleminded fifteen-year-old girl; Millie Griffin, who was being tried for her murder. Inexplicably, by the time the trial began, there were over two hundred witnesses subpoenaed to testify. The prosecution was to be conducted by the state attorney, George Taggart, assisted by M. A. Powell, the defense represented by George P. Tulliver. The trial began on Tuesday, and by the end of the week the court had evidence given by the father, mother, and brother of the dead girl as well as that of a few other witnesses, who told the courtroom about her life the day she had gone to the "fatal pasture." No one claimed to have found injuries which caused the girl's death, nor that she had died from poison, only that her collapse was the result of poisoning or an operation for abortion, or both.

Mrs. Ella B. Gilman, Florence's mother, testified to finding two bottles containing liquids in a bureau drawer on the night before her disappearance; they were later sent to Professor Heinz of Harvard. On cross-examination, her mother testified that Florence corresponded with several young men from time to time. Dr. Adolphus P. Gilman, father of the dead girl, corroborated the evidence of previous witnesses. The defense, as Tulliver said it would, dedicated its energies to breaking down the father's testimony and trying to discredit his character since *he* had instruments similar to those which caused his daughter's death, or were said to have caused her death, and which she might easily have gotten into her possession and used. Her father testified that no one who did not have a key to his office could get the articles, and he always carried the key with him.

James Triteman, a farmhand on the Gilman place, was also testifying; he was arrested as an accessory, and turned state's evidence. He was said to have been the go-between for Griffin and Miss Gilman, and testified that he made various appointments for them to meet and had arranged the last meeting of the two in the pasture the afternoon of Florence Gilman's death. He then testified that he went over the mountain to Benson at Griffin's request, and got from Horace Chesterfield, the paramour of Florence Gilman's sister, a small cologne bottle partially filled with reddish-brown liquid. (When John heard that, he couldn't help thinking of Edna's original reaction; it would all come down to the sister, she said, just as if she had been talking of an ordinary novel and decided the butler had done it.) Chesterfield asked Triteman to tell Griffin to mix the two tablespoons of liquid with half a pint of alcohol and then give Florence the mixture to drink. Triteman delivered these instructions to Griffin, and was then asked if Florence Gilman had taken any of the preparation. Triteman said, as far as he knew, she had not, because Triteman mixed the fluid with brandy, and she had said it was too strong for her. Triteman said he knew the mixture was strong since he had done the mixing himself, and all he had at the time was brandy. He also testified that he frequently saw a small box in Griffin's possession, and he guarded it as carefully as he would precious jewels, and one day told him he had an instrument in his pocket, but would not tell him what kind of instrument it was.

Griffin's employer, as well as Triteman, testified to his drunken habits and his immoralities with women. There were several other important witnesses, John noted; it seemed to him the jury's main task was to keep them straight, but by the end of the week, that seemed the least of the difficulties. Griffin's brother-in-law said that Griffin boarded with him the month before the tragedy. Griffin, he said, was not at home the night before Florence's death, but came to dinner as usual the next day.

Charles Griffin, a brother of Millie Griffin, was put on the stand, and everyone agreed that, so far, he gave the most damaging evidence against the prisoner. He related how Griffin had appeared at their father's house in Northfield at about nine o'clock at night three or four days after Florence's death and said he walked from Cambridge Junction, a distance of about twenty miles. Griffin was all broken up and wanted to see his folks and then get back to Morgan, the town where Florence's farm was located. Griffin had talked about Florence's death, although his brother Charles had tried to stop him. Charles Griffin testified that Millie described the circumstances under which Florence had died in the pasture. He said he was of the impression death was almost instantaneous. He also told him he had offered to marry Florence, but she had refused him. Charles Griffin said his brother Millie was arrested the same night shortly after midnight.

By the end of the second week, there were five persons under arrest for complicity in the crime which caused Florence Gilman's death at Morgan: Millie Griffin, her alleged betrayer; James Triteman, his chum, whom he had sent for the fatal dose; a Dr. M. P. Joyce, a Shrewsbury dentist; Harold Grimsby, a Rutland painter who posed as a traveling doctor, both of whom were accused of having advised about, or furnished, medicine or instruments for the abortion; and Horace Chesterfield, by now called the lover of Nora Aetna, Florence's sister. Horace Chesterfield was accused of having been accessory before the fact and was virtually under arrest, a warrant having been issued for him, and Nora Aetna, Florence's sister, was now kept under strict surveillance.

The circumstances of the arrest itself, as the papers said, gave much food for thought. Chesterfield was arrested at Green River at Alder's Livery Stable on Friday. When searched, he was found in possession of a loaded revolver and a part of a box of cartridges was found in his pocket. Investigation revealed that Chesterfield had been working as a farmhand in Benson in Lincoln County, just across the mountain from Morgan. He had been intimate with Mrs. Nora Aetna, Florence's sister (they kept stressing that), and it was on Chesterfield's account that Mr. Aetna, Nora's husband, had left her. According to the story told by James Triteman, Millie Griffin's chum. Triteman had driven Mrs. Aetna to Benson and met Chesterfield, who there gave him some red liquid in a bottle to be given to Griffin. Chesterfield said the liquid would bring about the result which Griffin desired, and Mrs. Nora Aetna seemed relieved to hear it. Chesterfield had given him the directions for taking the medicine, and told him to relate them to Griffin, which he had done, as he had already said.

Mrs. Aetna had lately been working in a hotel at Morgan Junction, and Chesterfield had left the farm in Benson where he had been hired out for the season and worked for a time at the Morgan Junction Inn, and then at the livery stable, but boarded at the hotel, where he used the name of Smith. On Saturday, Mrs. Nora Aetna went to her home in Benson, where officers were now watching her. The prisoners, at the command of the judge, the Honorable Mr. Fitzhugh, were to be kept in separate jails to prevent communication with one another. Griffin, Triteman, Dr. Joyce, and Grimsby were in four jails in four towns.

When Edna arrived for the weekend, she found poor John pacing up and down the length of the studio. John told her he could hardly be more confused; it sounded as if half the town had been involved in the girl's death. At the last minute, before the court closed for the week, Chesterfield, who was about twenty-eight and very distinguished in appearance, decided to produce a signed statement from the jail where he was currently lodged in Newport. *His* main concern seemed to be Mrs. Aetna. John read his statement to her: "In my judgment, she is as nice a woman as I ever met. If I were to die this moment. I could not say one word against her character. I admit I have been with Nora quite a little, which has perhaps led people to talk, but our intimacies were always a matter of friendship." "He seems to protest too much," Edna said; "at this point in the case." "That's what *I* thought," John said, relieved, "but by now I don't trust myself to think at all. Whenever I try to think I get a headache."

"Wouldn't the defense be happy to hear that?" Edna said; "that's Tulliver's whole idea, you know. Confusion and more confusion." "It's working," John said, desperate; "and you don't have to look so happy about it. And, *please*," he begged, "*don't* say, 'I warned you.' " "Oh, if you insist; who is the judge?" "Someone named Fitzhugh." "Fitzhugh! Is that old vulture still flying around the bodies? Well, you'll get a lesson in justice," she said, thoughtful. "Father always used to say even if someone saw the murderer dispatching his victim, he had to present his evidence in a legally acceptable way, admissible evidence, that's what they call it, or he wouldn't admit it for consideration. Father used to go into tantrums if the inadmissible went against him."

"Well, anyway," John said, "Chesterfield now claims

776

Griffin and Triteman are trying to put the blame off on him. And I don't know *what* to make of the sister; she's about thirty, and she's been around Morgan since August. She claims she didn't know a thing about her sister's condition until she was getting ready to go home to Benson. But," he went on, puzzled, "there seem to be letters no one's brought into court yet, and *they* are supposed to prove conclusively she knew all about it long before she says she did. She also told a reporter she never saw any intimacy between her sister and Chesterfield, which was the first anyone knew *that* was even an issue, much less suggested, and she never knew her sister took chloroform to induce sleep—no one knows what that has to do with anything, either. But these letters seem to contradict her altogether."

"The letters no one knows anything about," Edna summarized, "contradict her claim she didn't know her sister was in that condition, that her sister was not intimate with Chesterfield, her own lover, and that her sister took chloroform to get to sleep?" "That's right," John said wearily. "And *none* of these things were ever mentioned in court; the chloroform, the possibility of a relationship between Miss Gilman and Chesterfield, or the knowledge of her condition?" "No." "Well, Father would have said all that was suspicious; he always started sniffing about after things people denied before they'd even been accused of them. This sister sounds like an interesting character."

"How can you be so clinical?" John groaned; there was something comical in the way the tables were now turned, although the humor of it failed to affect him. "She sounds like a monster. If everyone's suspicions are true." "What else," Edna asked, "does that dear lady have to say for herself? You can't find out anything useful reading the papers." "She says she hasn't lived with her husband for six months, and that *she* caused *him* to leave because of his cruelties to her, and she has borne him two children, too. She also says Triteman's story about getting the medicine from Chesterfield isn't believable because she was there at the time of the interview Triteman described, and no bottle of any kind was exchanged." "Well, no one else seems to agree with her." "And then there's all this business about the doctors; three of them, no less, and the only real one in the bunch is the girl's father, but no one suspects him. I don't understand that. Joyce says he never did get any instruments for Griffin, but no one believes him, and now it turns out he did go to Northfield after them—that's where Griffin's family comes from—and he got a speculum from a Northfield druggist.

"He told the druggist he wanted to use it on a member of his own family and that's why he got hold of one. Well, they've dragged in half the state," John went on, exasperated; "we know from the jailer Griffin complains he'd like to be able to look out of doors, and he thinks Nora knew of her sister's 'deplorable' condition for a long time and he even talked to her about whether or not she would give her sister that medicine. Griffin says he got the instrument on the Thursday before the girl's death, and that it was a tube-like instrument with a wire attached to it. He told the papers he was very sorry the affair had ever happened."

"They all say that," Edna interrupted. "I suppose they would. He also says his fault was going with such a young girl, and *that* wasn't his fault, either, but he won't tell anyone what he means, and he says even if he did go with such a young girl, no one could say he was any worse than a lot of other young men. He also says he can't stand the disgrace of being in jail. Then they dredged up an old sweetheart of Griffin's; she's a dressmaker. Her name is Tanner, I think, and *she* testified that he stayed at her house in Cambridge the night of Florence Gilman's death, but didn't tell her what caused the death; he only said he was going back to Morgan to give himself up because otherwise people would certainly suspect him."

"And you don't know what to make of it?" "No," John said miserably. "Don't worry; by the time the lawyers finish, they'll have these pieces fit into two or three stories, and you can choose between them like pieces from *Mother Goose*. Plenty more will turn up, I can tell you." "More! And they haven't even found out what killed her yet! They don't even know if she was murdered, and they're trying everyone in sight for murder. They don't have any medical evidence to sneeze at yet." "Well, don't lose your temper at me; I didn't set this trial up. It's always like this, anyway." "That's hard to believe." "Nevertheless, it's true. You'll see." "Don't say it." "Well, Old Bones," she murmured, ruffling his hair, "I have to get back and see how well the household is going without me." "I'll go sit in Mr. Siddons' studio," John said, mournful, feeling somewhat abandoned; "it's wonderful the way no one in there ever opens his mouth."

The next week of the trial brought further embroideries on the same theme. That, John thought, was not a bad way of describing the progress of this trial—or any trial, if this one was at all typical. He remembered his mother laboring over a tapestry which now hung in the main parlor; how, she lamented for over two years, had that miracle, the Bayeux, ever reached completion? What he recalled was coming up to her chair, standing near her elbow, taking care not to jog it, watching the outlines slowly fill in. That was not only like a trial; it was like life. It was also like photography, watching the image surface slowly on the negative, gradually becoming more and more distinct, finally, fixed forever. He wondered if trials, by the time the verdict came in, ever gave that illusion of fixity to the portraits it drew of its main characters. He doubted it, he thought wearily.

This week, Horace Chesterfield and Nora Aetna were arraigned before Fitzhugh on a charge of adultery. The testimony of witnesses established that Mrs. Aetna was very attentive to Mr. Chesterfield, as he was to her; and that he frequently took her riding. To John's amazement, the prosecution proceeded to read thirty-eight letters which had passed between the two for the benefit of the jury. Before permitting this, Fitzhugh cleared the court of spectators and newsmen; they were steamy letters, he thought. Yes, it was obvious the two of them had been lying so far. They had sounded so convincing, too. The defense, which had decided to represent only Millie Griffin, now claimed the letters were not properly obtained, but the prosecution claimed otherwise.

Justice Fitzhugh admitted the letters; they could hardly have been more incriminating. Perhaps that was why he admitted them. On the other hand, John had been able to make no sense at all of the objections to their admissibility and he was beginning to suspect Justice Fitzhugh could not, either. The lawyers became quite hot on the issue; Fitzhugh warned them both that should any such information, comments, or rumors surface in the papers, they would be before the bench right after their clients. Edna told him this judge had been young when her father was practicing; he wondered what growing old in *this* profession would be like. He had felt far too sorry for himself for having chosen medicine as a profession.

The question of admissibility held up the progress of the trial for almost two weeks. It was now becoming clear that Justice Fitzhugh, for all his granite impenetrability, found something about this trial particularly distasteful; or perhaps, John reconsidered, it was obvious only to a few. He had seen enough faces holding back expressions of disgust, especially when it was those they loved best who disgusted them. That made him wonder; was Fitzhugh drawn to these matters out of some sort of perverse love? It made him question the nature of his own interest in medicine.

Neighbor after neighbor testified that Griffin told him about Florence's condition; that was all Griffin had done, John thought, gone about the countryside complaining of the girl's state. Apparently the case would be complicated beyond all human understanding, thanks to Griffin's compulsion to discuss the events of his rather sordid and pitiful life.

John was shocked to find himself judging the man in that way; he had been trained by profession and inclined by nature to suspend moral judgments, to do what was necessary to keep the patient alive. The moral nature of the man rarely came into focus. It never came into it for him, at least not until now. The episode with Weston: that hadn't involved judging the man; he was just getting even. If he had been asked to pronounce on moral issues at the time, he would have said one man was as good as another. That belief had, he mused, something to do with an intuitive feeling, which he never examined, that the most scurrilous people were often responsible for the greatest advances of humanity. No one would have accused his old professor of excessive morality: he was to be seen with a new young girl draped on his arm weekly, while his sickly wife, who had borne him fourteen children, lay like a corpse on their couch in the parlor, dying slowly of boredom.

Apparently, Griffin had told a reporter he had gotten some pills for Florence after he found out she was in trouble. It was interesting how each bit of testimony added another sliver of glass to the shattered mirror; how many, he wondered, would one need before anyone could construct an accurate picture of even the most ordinary events? Griffin had said he was nearly crazy when he saw her lying on the ground, and threw the speculum into the brook nearby. Yes, he answered in response to a question, he said he had thrown a speculum, not an instrument, although what significance that had was entirely beyond John, since by now even the feebleminded would have been able to chant the name of the deplorable instrument in their sleep.

Griffin told him that if it came to hanging or a life sentence, he would just as soon hang. That sounded pretty pathetic; he noted Griffin's appearance. Usually, he seemed the coolest in the room. His composure was only rivaled by the dead girl's sister; John had taken quite a dislike to Mrs. Aetna, although that must all be part of it, the emotional judgments. They were impossible to chase off, and, perhaps like wounded animals, human judgments became more and more accurate the tighter the corner they were pressed in. Griffin's testimony exhausted the day's and the week's supply of witnesses, and at four forty-five a recess was taken until nine o'clock the following Monday morning.

At least Edna would be waiting for him at the Siddonses' house, John thought, getting up creakily; he only hoped his daughter Lettie would not be waiting to ambush him as she often tried to do, but then he remembered a ball of great social moment was taking place that evening. That would dispose of his beautiful offspring. To his surprise, he discovered that, as the trial wore on, he had begun to dislike his own daughter more and more. He strongly suspected that if something were to go wrong in her life, the spectacle of seeing Lettie suffer would afford him great satisfaction. Perhaps, he comforted himself, walking to Cedar Street as he always did, hoping the dust from the trial would rise from his suit like a fog, this was similar to his early reaction to medical school: when he had come down with every disease he studied. One night, he had made a positive diagnosis of leprosy and tuberculosis of the lungs. This, he hoped, might wear off, too. While walking he tried to remember what the boys had come down with while they were away at the medical college. There had been a piteous letter from Martin, asking if it was likely someone could catch malaria in the middle of the winter; then he went on to complain that William was becoming a hypochondriac. Last night, he found William counting the hairs in his brush; he was sure he had alopecia. Premature baldness, and still, it was impossible for anyone to drag a comb through Bill's hair.

When he reached Cedar Street, and Mr. Siddons' studio, he found Edna perched happily on the newest creation, a white marble unicorn streaked with pink; she was sitting astride it, smiling broadly. "Perhaps you *ought* to have put a woman on it," Mrs. Siddons fretted, looking at the total effect. John noted the furry nature of Edna's clothes; it must be getting much colder than he had realized. Of course. It *was* much colder in Williamsville. He stood there admiring his wife; she looked, in her fur-trimmed outfit, like some wintry nymph about to ride off from civilization forever. He never really believed she was flesh and blood. "Oh," she cried out, "I have so much to talk to you about; let's go for a walk." She clambered down like a child. "It's awfully cold out," Mr. Siddons fussed. He had taken his cue from Mrs. Siddons and, unaware, the two of them tended to treat Edna and John as if *they* were the children; well, Edna thought merrily, everyone was enjoying it. They were taking years off each other's lives. And to tell the truth, she admitted, *she* enjoyed it. She couldn't remember when she had been treated as a child before, or if she had. And, watching her mother now, she wondered if she had ever given Edith a chance to act as her mother. It was too bad her mother hadn't been able to produce someone to take her place in the nest. She was, after all, Edna realized, a hatcher. Poor hatcher, with her for an egg!

"We're used to the cold, Mother; it feels like spring here to me." "Oh, well, if you insist on living in Greenland"; her mother smiled. "Greenland?" said Mr. Siddons; "I'd call it the Arctic Circle. Still, I like it," he pronounced. "Well, right now," Edna told him, "you'd be complaining away about how long it was taking the hands to shovel paths from your wing to ours. The drifts," she said, turning to John, "are about an inch above the windowsills;

I've never seen such wind and snow together. And so much ice. We're putting nails through our shoes or we'll be blown down the mountain." Mrs. Siddons shivered.

"Did you have any trouble with the trains?" John asked. "I never have trouble with the trains"—Edna almost giggled—"I have a very satisfactory new arrangement with the cheese wagon. It stops for me on its way to the factory." "Enterprising thing." "*And* an arrangement with the stationmaster, who lets me put my feet on his stove, but I had to swear not to tell any man in the village about it. These," she said, lifting one booted foot, "are the first woman's feet to rest on that stove since he had it brought in." "Well, if you *must* go for a walk," Edna's mother said, "go now. I don't want to listen to more of Cook's complaints. She's getting old," she said, as if unconscious that she, like Ten, was almost eighty. "Come on, John, you deserve a good meal," Edna glowed, slipping her arm around his waist. "But, Edna," Mrs. Siddons protested, "the poor man just got in." "That's all right; that court makes you feel awfully cramped." "No need to tell *me* about that," Mrs. Siddons sympathized.

"I tell you, Edna," John burst out the minute they set foot on the sidewalk, "the jurors and the others feel like the real prisoners in there." It was getting dimmer and dimmer; the town houses were losing themselves in a bluish-gray light. The dim glow of streetlights was beginning to shine palely in the streets. Some rose-colored streaks were dying slowly against the horizon; they looked like ribbons, tying up the day. "Prisoners?" "That's just what I feel like, and I haven't even done anything." "There's probably a reason for that," Edna sighed; "the judicial system seems to have a reason for everything." "If you can think of one for this," John retorted, tapping his bottom, "I'd like to hear of it." "Perhaps," she suggested playfully, "the idea is this: you are *supposed* to have an inkling of what it's like to be a prisoner; then you're more sympathetic with the accused, and so more careful." "Very ingenious." He smiled down at her. "If that's the reason, it works. Although, I can't help thinking jail is an improvement over the court. They seem to talk to half the world in there." "I know; they used to smuggle in mothers, easy women, reporters, Easter bunnies, Santa Claus. It used to make everyone furious, but they haven't managed to stop it yet." "Probably because the guards sympathize with them; you should have seen Griffin's brother this week. The first time he testified he couldn't remember much of anything. This week he could practically recite the court records, certainly every minute of the evening his brother came to see him; it was as if he'd been hypnotized." "You *can* bring back a lot if you try." "I suppose." He wasn't really concentrating on anything; he was enjoying the sensation of Edna against him, the physical reality of her presence, the gentle blendings of colors softening the sharp edges of the buildings. He missed the country, he thought, finally giving a name to the sadness.

"What's been going on at home?" "At home? Thank heavens, everything is just about the same. I can't think of anything new." "That's good." He looked down at the top of his wife's fur hat. He was trying to imagine her acting like Nora Aetna; it was impossible. She would climb on a marble unicorn, but she would never be up to the tricks of a Mrs. Aetna. He wondered about that woman. Probably she was a result of no imagination at all; that must be it. She must not feel the ordinary sensations of life. She needed the extraordinary, the violent ones. She must have felt very alive while she was carrying on with her sister's boy friend—that did seem to be what had happened, (although he wasn't absolutely sure) —and at the same time frolicking about with that Chesterfield fellow, and all the time knowing how she was torturing her husband. Probably every inch of her was resurrected now, he thought cynically: with the eyes of the world fastened on her, as Tulliver had dramatically thundered yesterday.

"Oh! There *is* something new!" Edna said, "it's a letter from George in New Bedford. Bill gave it to me. I'm supposed to give it to you, but I'm not supposed to read it first. You'd think they'd know better than to expect one of us to listen to instructions like that." "You would," John agreed, leading her over to a bench at the end of a little circular park of grass. The horses could turn around there. That was why they had built it; it was nice of them, too, she decided, sinking gratefully down on the bench. "*Have* you read it?" Edna raised her eyebrows. "All right, then"—he smiled—"*you* read it to *me*." "Actually," she

said, blushing slightly, "I'd rather you read it to me."
John took it. " 'Dear brother William. I guess you think
I'm dead and buried by now, but I am not dead of old
age or of the cholera or of the measles, either. I guess
your brother is as full of the old cat as ever.' " John
paused to look at his wife. "Don't worry, don't worry,"
she said; "it has nothing whatever to do with Anna." "I
should hope not," John snorted, resuming his reading.
"Well, I better let the cat out of the bag before it claws
its way out all the way to Williamsville. The long and
short of it is, I have gone and got married. Now don't
remind me how many times I swore I would never do anything as foolish as that, because I remember all that well
enough.

" 'I suppose you're wondering where I found my ministering angel. Well, stop wondering. *She* found me. Mind,
William, if you breathe a word to our parents, I'll come
down there and shoot you along with a bear; I won't
waste more than that one bullet. Well, the long and short
of it is, I went up to the logging camp in the mountains,
and it gets pretty lonely up there in the snow, what with
all the men sitting around complaining about how they
miss their families, and they never knew what loneliness
was until they signed on for this trip, and then the gloom
after the mail comes when someone doesn't get a letter
he was waiting for and sits down in the snow and gets
himself ready to freeze to death, or better yet, starts in
imagining catastrophes that would fill thirty years of the
Farmer's Almanac or the curious-facts section of *The
Farmer's Home and Hearth*. Well, and what should happen to me, your chaste, blameless, innocent brother?

" 'There I am, getting ready to fall asleep, not expecting
any letters, just waiting for the logs to pile up the right
amount, when in walks this very fancy lady. I mean, this
very fancy lady walked right into my tent. Oh, you should
have seen her! I never saw such a coat, or such a bonnet,
either. It looked like it had half of spring in Vermont on
it, and a feather boa hanging down on all sides of her.
She looked like an angel. She had enough feathers to fly
all the way up without any help from Our Lord, I can
tell you. So there I was in my red suit, looking like the
devil without his tail, and she says her name is Ellen
Mellors. So what? says I. So I need someone to stay with

for the night, she says. Why me? I asked. You can see I haven't gotten more polite with advancing age, can't you, William, but you know all those tales they used to tell us about fancy women and how everything we owned would fall off and we'd go clear off our heads; so I was, I have to admit, a little worried, even if she was a woman, and they don't worry me much, not unless they're chasing me around the room with a knife.

" 'Anyway, she started unbuttoning her coat, and I was so amazed I didn't say stop, or anything that would lead her to believe she ought to seal herself up tight and trot back down the mountain, and the next thing I knew, here was this person crawling into my bag with me, without a stitch on her that God didn't put there, or a doctor, either. Well, I'd been up there five weeks, so I guess I forgot about all the warnings and a pretty warm night we had of it, too. Then in the morning, I thought: What am I going to do with her? And she must have guessed what I was thinking, because she told me not to worry; there were plenty of men who would take her in, and pay for it, too, but when she got up to the camp last night it was too dark for her to find them, but she sure could now. So then what would happen but I decided to talk to her to find out what made a fancy thing like that tick. She seemed like anyone else to me . . .' He certainly can tell a story," John said; "is this true?" "It is." "Well, if it's true," John said, "I guess I'd better get on with it." "I'd say so."

" 'She seemed like anyone else to me, only a lot more discerning, she paid so many compliments to my more intelligent parts, if you know what I mean, and I thought: Why stay up here alone watching them all wait for letters when I could watch her? So we went a little way down the mountain and routed a justice of the peace and now we are hitched. I guess we'll have to move back to Williamsville since my better half, and you can believe she is, is pretty well known in these parts, and I gather she's not too popular with churchgoing folk in New Bedford. She was up at the camp in the first place because the selectmen told her she'd have to get out of her boarding-house; too many complaints from the Godly. We all know how that is.

"Don't read me any lectures on the subject of our

marital bliss, either, because I *know* we'll be perfectly happy. My beloved wife Ellen is clear on what fate awaits her if she steps from the straight and narrow. I thought up fates and tortures you wouldn't believe and even ran around my tent in a mad, jealous fit, but I don't think I needed to do it, she seems so happy to be quitting her line of work.

"'Well, and it all comes back to Anna; wouldn't you know it? The local papers reported the death of a George P. Moffat, and Anna naturally thought that was me, even though the middle initial was wrong, but she thought it was a misprint, and Matthew, in the course of his appointed rounds, happened in at Ellen's boardinghouse, where she was prostrated with despair and swallowing all manner of things, and persuaded her to go up to the camp and look for me so his wife would have some peace. So up she came and that's why she is sporting a gold ring.' Anna did this?" John asked. "Anna Steele Hewitt, your daughter," Edna said. "Yours." "You saw her first. Read."

"'So your younger brother is an old married man and you should meet the happy couple sometime next week when I get down off the mountain and am back on praying ground once more. I'm happy about it, now you don't get me wrong, and don't you let others start sniffing around the rat I just caught for you. So we'll be down next week, or two weeks at most; it depends on how long it takes to get some normal-looking clothes for fancy Ellen. She can cook, too. She says she wasn't born wearing feathers and jumping into tents. She's real funny, I can tell you, although you may take some time getting used to her sense of humor, but don't you worry about anything, because I'm not as stupid as I look, and I had a doctor look her over even though I had to tie her down and she practically scratched my eyes out afterwards and cried her silly head off and there's nothing the matter with her to worry about, so if anyone in Williamsville goes off his head, it won't be for the reasons Ma used to worry about. You better be nice to her, is all. Anyway, I'm saved from a lonely old age you're always predicting for me, and that ought to shut you up and resign you to the fateful course of events. I guess you could say I surrendered and lay down my arms and picked them up again. Well, you should see Miss Mellors here in the snow, picking her way from drift to drift. Can't you imagine it? I remain your affectionate brother, Married George.'"

"Well?" Edna asked. "Well, God works his wonders in mysterious ways, his wonders to perform." "I think there's something wrong with that wording." "I hope there's nothing wrong with *George*." "I think it's the best thing that could have happened to him." "I am shocked at you, my virtuous wife." He leaned over and kissed her. "Shocked, and acting like this in public, too?" "We better take advantage of this freedom. When we get back, we'll have your parents listening for the porch swing." They clung to each other until Edna's breathing became suspiciously deep; John shook her before she fell asleep in the cold.

"You really do have to go back?" John asked her, seeing her off at the station three hours before court opened that Monday. Edna grimaced slightly. "The trial can't last forever." "Don't worry," she said, her foot already perched on the first little iron step; "it won't." "I wish I were so sure," he called after her; "write!" He watched the bright red and blue train fade into the dim bluing grayness, and his wife, leaning out the window of her coach, waving until she was out of sight. More and more of that Florence Gilman business, he thought, and they hadn't even begun on the medical aspects of the case. He trudged back to the Siddonses'; everyone was sound asleep. He lay down on his bed, knowing he would wake, automatically, in time to walk to the courthouse.

The week proved to be an eventful one in court, even though, as John later realized, little was new in the way of evidence. "Griffin, Griffin," the prosecution insisted, "appears to have visited the scene of the terrible tragedy *twice* that fateful afternoon." Would they ever, John wondered, stop calling that day the "fateful afternoon"? Once more, and *he* would be seized with fits.

"Now," said Taggart, "nearly all those who examined the vicinity with a view towards discovering evidence are unanimous in the opinion that Griffin moved the body. He doubtless," Taggart went on, "moved the body. He had left Miss Gilman in an unconscious condition, was uncertain as to the outcome, then returned and found her dead. Dazed with fear, as well he might be," Taggart continued, glaring at the accused, "he moved the body first to a more secluded spot; then he picked up her hat, her apron, and a little pail of berries and put them beside her. In stooping to lay the body on the ground, he lost a cigar which fell out of his vest pocket." Taggart demonstrated the act bodily; the jury, John saw, seemed very impressed. "He set down the pail of berries upright so people would think she sat down to rest and died of heart disease."

The next day turned out to be a shocker. Tulliver moved quite a way toward establishing his theory that the death of Florence Gilman was the result of a conspiracy between Nora Aetna and Horace Chesterfield. Those two, Tulliver maintained, were really responsible for everything. Chesterfield, he claimed, pointing accusingly at the aforementioned party, was responsible for the poor girl's condition, and when he and the girl's sister discovered she was in trouble, they went to work to seduce his client, a hitherto innocent and inexperienced young man, exemplary in every way, and they seduced him, yes, seduced him, into undue intimacy with this young girl, only fifteen years old, and then made him believe he was responsible for the young girl's condition and also the tragedy that followed.

Was it possible, Tulliver demanded rhetorically, that two such evil people could exist? Was it possible that, granted the fact of their existence, they would find one another? Yet they had. Griffin and Florence Gilman were, by the untiring efforts of those two, brought together in ways which resulted in the improper relations between the two young people, and they were always together at Mrs. Nora Aetna's house in Benson, and not infrequently did Chesterfield spend the entire night with Nora; so, too, did Griffin, who was then easily tempted into habits of excessive drink previously mentioned. Those habits were mentioned to cast doubts upon his character, but really showed the characters of the infamous Chesterfield and Mrs. Aetna for what they were.

Griffin constantly avowed his intention to marry Florence. That, Tulliver claimed, was beyond question, so many witnesses having testified to that effect. "He even," Tulliver continued, "advised her to consult with her parents, but she kept on insisting there was no trouble. Apparently, her sister had managed to convince her such was the case. He had, as we shall see, procured the medicine and the instruments so much discussed, at Florence's request, but with the understanding that they were to be used only for purposes of examination at a local doctor's. When he gave them to her in the fatal pasture, he gave them with the advice that she must not attempt to make use of them, but must only satisfy herself of her condition. And, having taken all these precautions," Tulliver said solemnly, "imagine his surprise, his shock, his heartbreak, when he heard a noise that attracted his attention and found it was not a groundhog, not a squirrel, not a badger, but his beloved Florence herself, lying back in a dead faint, and then going to find her dead, dead! Is it any wonder," Tulliver asked the jury, "that he fled in fright? Who in this courtroom would not do the same?"

After lunch, Griffin himself took the stand and testified in a manner supporting Tulliver's theories. He had told Mrs. Aetna he wanted to marry her sister; he asked Florence to find out if she was pregnant. He said he had bought Florence the pills she asked for since she told him she had taken them before and he had no reason to doubt her. "If the doctor had found her pregnant," he swore, "we agreed I would marry her immediately. After some trouble, I finally convinced Dr. Grimsby to get the instruments himself. Then Chesterfield got some medicine, and I sent Triteman over for it, but I hadn't asked for it, and I didn't give it to her; I didn't know what it was.

"When I came to the pasture," he continued, paling, "I saw Florence right away, and she looked almost ready to drop down. She went to a shady place and sat down and we talked quite a little while. She seemed to go on and on about her sister, and I didn't understand why she was concerned with her sister at such a time. She asked me if I had the speculum and the catheter in my pocket, but I wouldn't let her have them until she promised me not to use them herself. I finally got up, after we agreed again that if she was pregnant we would marry at once. I got up just to light a cigar, not to go away, and was only about ten feet away when I heard a groan.

"I ran over to her and found her unconscious. When I fanned her with my hat, and she didn't get up, I thought she was dead. I threw the speculum and the catheter—

they were lying by her side—into the brook. I didn't," he said piteously, "know what I was doing. I think I was out of my head. Then I thought things over and I couldn't believe Florence was really dead, so I went back to the pasture, and she was really dead. That was when I got frightened and went into town for some money. I was sure everyone would think I had done it since everyone knew about our intimacy. But I never gave her any medicine or got any instruments for her to use for the wrong purpose." He sounded sincere, John thought. "And I don't think Florence would have used the instruments for the wrong purpose, either," he said defensively. He also appeared loyal. Taggart then busied himself trying to break down Griffin's testimony in cross-examination; he was attempting to undermine the defense's claim that Horace Chesterfield had been intimate with Florence Gilman.

By the end of the day, everyone was so exhausted by absorbing new information the judge dismissed the court early, instructing them to reconvene at nine in the morning, when, he announced, nodding slightly in Dr. Steele's direction, expert testimony of a medical nature would finally be introduced. John left, excited as a schoolboy. Tulliver stopped him at the door; he wanted to warn him that other doctors would naturally be called on to testify. The prosecution would have its own doctors, ones which would support their claims. Things would get tangled. "So get a good night's sleep," Tulliver told him. John promised; nevertheless, he was wakeful most of the night.

The next day, the research doctor from Harvard testified that the stomach and intestines, which had been sent to him, contained no foreign or suspicious substance. They then called Dr. Steele, who said that if the first doctor's testimony had been correct, and he had found signs of some irritant in the stomach, but had not been willing to state such mild irritation resulted in death, or that it was even worth considering as a cause of death; if that was the case, then there was only one way of accounting for the death: death from some kind of shock. There had not been enough uterine bleeding, he went on, to justify claiming the girl had bled to death; nor had there been any blood in the peritoneum or the reproductive tract.

He had no idea, he said frankly, whether or not the girl did or did not have heart disease prior to this incident, but he *had* witnessed cases where severe emotional shocks had almost certainly caused death. Just before coming to this court, he said, he attended an elderly couple. The woman was perfectly healthy, but the husband was in the last throes of tuberculosis, and he had been in the room when the woman's son informed her of her husband's death, and she had fallen over the bed, just as Florence Gilman was said to have fallen over in the pasture. When he took the old woman's pulse, she was dead. They had made all strenuous efforts to revive her, but it was of no use whatever. The two had been buried together. A murmur went through the court; John was aware of it, and not. From Tulliver's expression, he gathered he had made an impact on the jury. He returned to his seat like a somnambulist.

Nora Aetna was called, to murmurings and growlings of the court populace. She testified there had been frequent visits between her sister and Griffin. There were audible murmurs from the jurors complaining that this was hardly anything new. She insisted, as she did before, it was only three weeks before her sister died that she learned of Florence's condition. The judge then warned the jury that, since the evidence was now in, they would soon be secluded and soon be called upon to make a decision as to Griffin's guilt, as well as the necessity of trying Mrs. Nora Aetna and Horace Chesterfield at a later date. Everyone filed out in a subdued mood. Even the reporters seemed chastened. He wondered if that would have any effect on the sensational nature of their reports in tomorrow's paper; he thought not.

Edna did not come down that weekend; everyone in the house, she wrote, had come down with hard colds. It had gotten so you could hear the house all the way from the Moffats'; it sounded as if a crowd of people had been dropped into a pepper factory. George Moffat and his new wife were expected back daily. Everyone was highly excited, and from what she observed, William would not be the one to give the secret away, and she wouldn't either. There had been no letters from Anna for over a week now, but she noticed his were taking longer and longer to arrive in Williamsville; she supposed it must be the snow. Trains were coming in later and later; if they managed a few more delays, she wrote in her precise little hand, they would soon turn day into night. She was following accounts of the trial in the papers. She was making less and less sense of it, she hated to admit it; but she certainly had made sense of the last report saying it was over, or almost over (the papers were coming through late, too), and he could not imagine how glad she was to know this would be his last week away from home. John sighed when he read that. On Monday of the trial's last week, as he continued walking toward the court he took it out, read and reread parts of it, and put it back in his pocket. He would wear it out, he thought, tucking it away for the day.

The last testimony was give on Wednesday, Attorney Taggart opening for the prosecution and Tulliver for the defense. Taggart asked Griffin: Had he not said he used the instruments before named? But he denied any such action. Then Taggart questioned him in detail: Had he not said he did not move the body? Was a towel used? Did he not actually have intercourse with the girl? Did he not cover her face? Griffin denied the last. He admitted he knew doctors lived near the "fatal pasture" but he did not try to call on any of them for help in reviving the dead girl.

Tulliver recalled the arresting sheriff. He did not think Griffin had been in his right mind when he was brought into jail. His friend Triteman testified he had visited Griffin in jail and thought him mentally unbalanced. The sheriff in charge of the jail also testified he saw Griffin in jail and he was badly excited when put in it. The prosecution was offering one J. P. Badger as a witness since he had been in jail with Griffin. Tulliver duly objected that this witness should have been brought forth before, but the state claimed a new fact had developed since it rested its case, and the new evidence should be admitted. To John's horror, this raised some legal point which the court decided to take into consideration during the recess that followed for dinner. When the court reassembled, Justice Fitzhugh overruled the objection; J. P. Badger, alias F. O. Hogg, a jailmate of Griffin's, took the stand.

He swore that Griffin had told him he had used the speculum on the body of Florence Gilman, and had only told him this since the beginning of the trial. Tulliver contended, with some force, that if Badger had indeed been told this, he would have come forth with the evidence earlier. Therefore, he argued, he was probably making his own bid for attention, trying to gain the public's sympathy before his own trial. John saw a number of nodding heads.

That Saturday, the charge in the case of Millie Griffin, accused of accomplishing the death of Florence Gilman, was delivered in County Court in Boston, and the jury retired. They came back in a few minutes, or so it seemed to John. He looked at his watch; it was exactly three twenty-five. They rendered a verdict that Griffin was guilty only under the fourth count in the indictment for the lesser offense, which turned out to mean, simply, that he had been found guilty of furnishing the instruments. The sentence was not to be suspended under exceptions. Mrs. Nora Aetna and Horace Chesterfield were then bound over to court officials, to be tried on a number of counts, chief of which was conspiracy to seduce and murder, and remanded into custody until the beginning of their trial, which would take place after the court's recess ended in March. Triteman was given a suspended sentence as accessory to Griffin in procuring the instruments; both doctors were to be kept in prison pending the trial of Nora Aetna and Horace Chesterfield. So, John thought, getting up, they had settled on one thing they thought to be true. If that piece of truth were land, he thought, it would be just large enough for a fly to land on.

Tulliver thanked him profusely; he insisted his testimony had evidently been decisive as far as the jury had been concerned. They were obviously leaning toward Griffin, but they needed a reason to find him innocent, and John had provided one for them. He hoped he would want to testify again in the same capacity. "No," John said slowly; "you'll never see me inside a courtroom again." "Never?" Tulliver asked, his eyebrows raised. "Not unless *I* commit a crime," John answered, attempting to smile. Tulliver, puzzled, watched him as he left the building; well, he had other things to think about. He had come off rather well, very well, much better than he had expected.

John was surprised to find Edna standing outside the court's door; she was wrapped in her winter coat, her hair covered with a thick, furry brown hat, her little hands buried in a fur muff. "I thought you couldn't come down," he said wearily; he had never been so relieved to see anyone, but he didn't have the energy to tell her so. "We borrowed back some servants from the Moffats; I thought it would be best." He nodded. He didn't want an explanation. "When do you want to go back?" Edna asked, tucking her arm through his arm. "When does the next train leave?" "In exactly two hours." "Then we're going back in exactly two hours." "I thought so; I've had all your things packed and sent ahead to the station." "Uncanny." "I'm no such thing; I'm just in a hurry to get you back." "I ought to warn you," John said, trying to rally himself, "I'm much better at catching lying than I used to be." "As long as you learned something," she answered, feeling for his fingers through his glove.

There was something sad about this farewell, Edna thought, lingering in her mother's embrace; she had come to look forward to these weekends with her more than she had realized. And, she thought, holding her mother at arm's length, the better to fix her image, this would have to remain fixed for some time. She had a premonition of that, and no matter how hard she tried, she could not make it vanish. Yes, her mother was an old woman; you had to have good eyes to see it, though. Or perhaps it was that she made no concessions to her age. She was not the type, Edna thought, to begin mourning for her life before it ended. Certainly no one would ever pronounce her mother a genius, but she did expect a great deal from each new day. Martin, she remembered, had once suggested Edith and Mr. Siddons come to live with them; her mother reacted as if she had just received an engraved invitation to spend the rest of her life in a mausoleum. No, no, she exclaimed; it was the closest thing to panic Edna had ever seen in her. She had her own ways, she told Martin, and she didn't mean to interrupt them before she had to. Although, she added, after she calmed down, she was grateful to him for wanting her there, but she would bore herself and everyone else to death; didn't he think so, too? Martin, not sure what trigger he had pulled, hastened to agree with her.

"Well, goodbye, Mother," Edna finally said, disengaging herself from those slender white arms; they felt so dry and thin now. Even her mother's arms were mottled with the brown spots of age. "I have a houseful of invalids, all sneezing up clouds of dust," Edna said regretfully; "please settle for a peck on the cheek. I'd never forgive myself if you had to stay in bed two weeks on our account. You've been awfully good to us, you know, Mother. You did put yourself out," she said. "Nonsense," said Edith; "we loved it. I'm sorry it's over."

"We enjoyed every minute of it," Mr. Siddons said; he sounded unusually subdued. "At least," he asked, "you will accept the service of our carriage?" "Of course," Edna answered, clasping his hand. Who would have thought she would get so fond of this silly peacock? She no longer thought of him that way. He, too, had aged; his skin had grayed; his hair had silvered; his elegance had the air of another time about it. She would see them again, she told herself; she was being foolish. It was only that she was worried about John. Something had happened; she had no idea what. That, she decided, was what disturbed her most of all.

She and John went toward the carriage, turning around every other step to wave to Mr. and Mrs. Siddons, outlined like icons in a golden painting filling their front door. "I'll miss them," John admitted. "So will I." "I'll miss the time we spent here. It was like turning back the clock. It was wonderful. The rest, well, that's something else." Edna said nothing. He handed her into the carriage, and climbed in after her. He moved more slowly now, more carefully, as if keeping his bones safe from sharp edges, sudden jars. She did the same thing, she saw, observing herself as from a far distance, carefully settling herself and her cloak in the carriage seat. Why, ten years ago she would have plopped in any old way; it would not have occurred to her that she might sit down on the back of her coat in an uncomfortable manner, giving her neck a painful jerk that might keep her up all night. And she would not have worried so over her muff and her gloves and her scarf; the cold would not have brought on that stiffness in the bones. Did they get more porous with age, as Martin seemed to think, or did they get heavier? She thought the latter; they seemed so much heavier, so much harder to manage.

She took off her hat; it seemed to weigh down her head. There were times when her hair felt too heavy for her neck; more and more often, she let it down. It grew just as quickly and thickly as it had ever done. It was almost mid-calf when it fell. The children liked it; they never failed to remark on how much younger she looked. How would they know that the weight of one's hair could become oppressive? She looked over at her husband; he was staring at her. Yes, something was wrong, "You know," she said, "we're in for a long trip, at least four hours. The snow is just dreadful. It's stop, stop, stop every three miles while the crew digs out the tracks." "Is it snowing in Williamsville?" "What a question!" Edna laughed; "is it ever not snowing in Williamsville?" "I'll be glad to see some snow." "You've seen snow in Boston." "Not the same. It doesn't seem to win out against the buildings; it doesn't get anyone's attention. Unless, of course, it's a blizzard. No one pays any attention to it.

"There was a blizzard when I was in medical college," John said; "everything but the snow seemed unimportant, defenseless, too. I still see the view from my window, you know, when I think of it. The main street was impassable; no traffic and it was so quiet and the only thing I could see was a woman with a black umbrella; she was almost bent double against that wind, trying to get to the other side of the street. There was so much snow falling she looked sketched in with slanted lines, or as if she were beneath some kind of slanted netting. It was so beautiful, so unearthly." How pale his voice sounded, Edna worried; it wasn't like him to reminisce like this, not unless they had already been talking for some time. She saw the station approaching with relief; sparks were already flying from the train when they entered the terminal and found the proper track. It had taken longer to say good-bye than they had thought; really, they had almost missed the train. She was glad they had not. She wanted John back in Williamsville; she wanted the four hours alone with him.

"No news of Anna?" John asked as they settled into

their seats, Edna setting the hamper Mr. Siddons' servant packed for them on the empty seat across the aisle. They were the only ones in the carriage. "Not yet; no sign of George, either; it must be the snow." "I suppose that's it." "Of course it is." "What else could it be?" he asked, as if talking to himself. "Nothing, nothing," she said. He looked so worn out, so tired; it was not the sort of tiredness she knew; it was another kind of tired. "Try to sleep," she said softly, squeezing his hand. "I'm wide awake." Edna decided to pretend she was asleep. After all the raving she'd done about these trials, she didn't want him thinking she was sitting beside him glorying in whatever suffering he endured simply because she foresaw it. She better give him some time, some time to realize he was going back to Williamsville; the faster and farther the train went, the easier it would be to talk to him. She kept herself as still as possible, her face as expressionless as possible. "Are we out of the city yet?" she asked, pretending to rouse herself a half hour or so later. "I can't tell; we must be. You can't see anything through this snow; there were some lights for a while, close together, but they've been gone for miles now. We must be out in the country." She closed her eyes, again pretending to sleep. Finally, she felt John's body moving restlessly, as if he had just regained consciousness.

"John?" He looked over. "The boys will be glad you're back. They're very good doctors now. Everyone says so, but they feel much better when the Raven is there to sit on their shoulders." "Is that what they call me?" "Didn't you know?" "No. They keep their secrets very well. Howard Moffat still doesn't know everyone in Williamsville calls him Old Mushmouth." "How did *that* happen?" "Well, you know how Alice is always complaining about how he roams about like a tomcat; he's usually chewing some poor soul's ear off." "What does he talk *about?*" Howard doing anything but slamming screen doors and front doors and windows—it was hard to imagine. "Anything. He'll talk about little green men on the moon if silence gets a toe in the room. He goes down to the police station, and if the constable's too tired to talk, he goes off and talks to the prisoners. Even ones too drunk to talk. If someone collected all his conversations with criminals, they'd have the beginning of a whole science of criminology based on firsthand report." "Why doesn't he talk to Alice?" "Who knows? At least this way, he has friends all over. He thinks he does. He's not the type to rely on one person. It would be like planting one potato and expecting a crop. He doesn't take chances." "You're giving him too much credit." "I don't think so."

Edna sat silently, thinking things over. "Well," she said, at her wit's end (she had no idea where to begin), "the boys really *will* be glad to see you." She was relieved he was returning for other reasons. Ten's cold was not improving. When she left for Boston this morning, Ten had been feverish and restive. She had not even wanted to get out of bed. It was the first time since Hal's death she hadn't wanted to get out of bed. That news could wait. John would hear her coughing the minute he got in the door; such a dry, hard cough. There was nowhere in the house you could go without hearing it. The children, too, had begun observing the grandfather clock with more than their usual attention—although, as Jack said, some of its magical powers must have been removed when it was repaired after it caught his lip. Those powers, he insisted, claiming he had studied it, came from all the years it had ticked along without being tampered with.

"I'm not so sure the boys will be glad to see me," John finally said. "Whyever not?" "Because I'm giving up medicine. Permanently," he went on, looking at her. She sat, staring and frozen. "Well, say something." "I don't believe you." "You can believe me; I won't change my mind." She looked down at her lap. Was this the same world she knew? Was her husband ill? Had he been keeping that from her while the trial went on? She didn't think he would do that. "Why?" "I don't know; I'm not sure. I know that's how it is. I thought," he went on miserably, "if we talked about it, it might come clearer." "You're not ill?" "Nothing that simple; I can always say I've retired. That will make sense to everyone. Everyone knows how interested I've gotten in the daguerreotype, and Martin and William are there, so no one will think I've gone queer in the head, neglecting things." "I don't give a fig what other people think!" "*I* care, insofar as it affects Bill and Martin." "Will you forget Bill and Martin?" Edna exploded; "I want to know about you." She clasped his hand, sliding her fingers through the spaces between his. He looked down at the interlacing.

"You were right, after all." She waited. "I began thinking about what was happening, during the trial. It began when I first realized Tulliver wasn't interested in the moral issues of the case; the moral implications, well, those were beyond bothering him altogether. He took on the case because it seemed so cut and dried. Everyone expected Millie Griffin to hang; there were people selling tickets to the execution almost a month before the trial was over. It was all an intellectual game to him, a chess game: how to move this one here, how to get this one there. How to paint this one black, how to lighten the shadows on that one's face. It was all a game. It was irrelevant that he ended by finding out the truth, or an important part of it. It was irrelevant that his client was really innocent, even though he'd been swearing to that for months. He didn't bat an eyelash when he found out the dead girl's sister was guiltier than Nora's lover. He didn't blink when he found out Chesterfield had relations with the dead girl first. It was all useful, that was all it was; it gave him an advantage. He didn't even have to go for stalemate; he could win. That was what he was fastened on all along. It was a game, a complicated game. The people weren't even people, they were pieces; nothing more important than checkers Jack plays with." *"Everyone's* not like Tulliver; my father wasn't like that."

"I know, I know. But Tulliver, he was only the beginning. It started me thinking about the difference between a doctor and a lawyer and an ordinary person; someone like Ed, who made shoes. Well, I began thinking about how doctors couldn't make moral judgments. His whole career, his whole integrity, depends on suspending them while he's working. I began to think I was amoral, not much better than the people on trial. All I cared about was saving lives, using any trick I could to do it. If Nora Aetna fell over in that courtroom, I would have done all I could to keep that human bomb ticking; then I started in wondering why I would want to do it, or *why* I would do it. *She* ought to be dead!" he said violently. "Can you imagine what it feels like for someone like me to start thinking like that, feeling that way? The more I looked at her, the more I wished I *could* kill her, not cure her. Chesterfield, he was something else again; I wouldn't have minded giving him a lift closer to heaven; but the woman! She was the girl's sister, her *sister*. The more I watched her, the more she resembled a perversion of nature, a cancer. I suppose I would have tried killing her myself, if I'd been certain I wouldn't be caught.

"And then I started thinking about the others and what their lives were like and none of them seemed worth much. Just like empty bags, all of them, people perpetually waiting for Santa Claus to fill them up, and then having to live in an empty stocking for the rest of their lives, with that crisscross netting, like a double set of bars. And Tulliver, I thought about him all the time. I don't remember much about his house, but I think of it as a hunting lodge except he has human heads mounted on plaques covering all the walls.

"Well, the upshot was, *he* began to seem as bad as all the others. And I didn't seem so worthwhile, either, thinking things like that, after going through a whole lifetime like a stone, giving as much thought as a tree to the moral side of my profession. Oh, I don't mean," he explained, seeing his wife's look, "I would ever have decided to let someone die because I judged them unworthy. That's God's work, if there is a God. It's not human work. But I should have thought about it. I should have *thought* about it. But no. All I've ever thought about for thirty years is how unhappy people are at funerals—most of the time, anyhow—and how nice it is to avoid children growing up without parents, and parents without children, and husbands without wives, but I never got beyond that."

"That *is* moral thinking," Edna objected; "that's the basis of morality. Isn't it? Being able to see other people's interests as well as your own? Or better? All those years wearing yourself out saving people's lives; you had to pay a price! All the times you nearly froze to death in snowdrifts, all the times your team overturned on the roads, when the horses ran away with you, when you nearly drowned in the river because the floating bridge went out, all the chances you took on coming down with diseases yourself; that's sacrifice, and sacrifice is at the bottom of morality, any morality. Especially religion. That's why everyone believes in Christ and thinks he's so important. Because he's supposed to have given up his life for us, and we're less worthy, and he did it of his own free will." She was desperate; she couldn't endure the way he saw himself now.

"I'm not sure you can call what I've done sacrifice," John persevered wearily; "you have to think about what you're giving up before you make a sacrifice. I never thought about it. It was what I did. And after I married you, well, then, I never had to think about sacrifice much; you never complained. Everything always went so smoothly. No one ever seemed harmed." "You thought about it after Serepta died." "No, I felt guilt. That was different. I was still sure I was doing the right thing. As for Christ"—he smiled bitterly—"the comparison goes through to the bone. The Great Physician, that's what they call him. He considered, and reconsidered, didn't he? He even cried out asking if his sacrifice was necessary. I never did anything like that. I was good at what I did, better than almost anyone else. Someone had to do it; it made me happy when people were less unhappy. What makes my life any more worthy than a clown in a circus?" "That's ridiculous!" Edna expostulated. "Well, then. *Why* am I better than a clown?"

"I don't know *how* to answer that; a clown, well, he cheers you up for an hour, perhaps two, but he doesn't stop anyone from bleeding to death. He doesn't add years to his life. He doesn't keep half his audience from ending up widowers or orphans. On the scale of accomplishment, there's no comparison." "That's not a moral scale; on the scale of accomplishment, I'm a black sinner compared to the Pharaohs who built the Pyramids." Edna didn't know what to say; his arguments were logical. Worse, they made sense. In more ways than one. "The netting," she said; "when you made us stay inside the netting. You were protecting us. You were going on instinct. Your instincts were to preserve life. Your morality, it must be the same order of things; instinctual." "*You* should have been the lawyer," he said, as he had so many times before.

"I don't judge, either," she expostulated; "I'm always uncomfortable with the Bible. It's so confident when it lays down its rules. That's why I prefer etiquette books. They're really bibles for daily living. I only understood one thing in the Bible—why it harped on getting along with one's neighbor, loving thy neighbor, turning the other cheek; and that was because I saw all the consequences of breaking those rules." She thought, picking at the fringed end of her hood tie. "I always believed," she said at last, "the first and only commandment ought to be 'Tolerate thy neighbor.' I didn't think, I don't think, anything more can be expected, not of human beings." "Then how can you justify hangings, trials, executions, the whole business I just sat through?" "By arithmetic. One murderer erases more people than he's permitted. He's not permitted to erase anyone. Murder, well, you found that out, that's a kind of judgment. No one should be permitted that kind of judgment. If anyone takes it and insists on using it, you have to dispose of them." "Dispose of them?" "The same way you would a mad dog. I've never heard you going on about the shooting of mad dogs." "They're not even dogs; they're only walking diseases. They're mad."

"And the people you saw on the stand? Did you think they were sane? Did you think Nora Aetna was sane?" "She wasn't insane," he said, puzzled; "she knew what she was doing; she didn't care. Her emotions got cut off somewhere, like a broken string of beads. The beads rolled off, God know where." "But if that's true," his wife asked, "just how *does* she differ from a mad dog? If she were a dog and went around biting her sister, wouldn't you shoot her? I would." "I suppose," John agreed. He sounded despairing. "John," she said, shaking him physically with her free hand, "listen to me. I went to worse trials than that one. Some of the men suffer. I went with my father to that famous trial of the mass murderer. The judge was in agony, agony, before he pronounced the death sentence. And everyone wanted him to pronounce it. There were people outside the jail chanting and holding candles; no one thought the man would live to reach the gallows. The crowd was so thick they had police in from all over the state. They were terrified of riots. It fired everyone's imagination. It was almost as if the people thought they could get free of any feelings like this by killing *him*. It seemed to us in the courtroom as if a sea of murderers was beating against the court; well, the walls of the prison, too. I never forgot the closing speech.

"The judge went over all the atrocities the man committed, how he committed them of his own free will, how all procedures had been scrupulously followed in his case, how he had been protected from popular violence; how the law itself had become his friend. 'All this was secured to you!' That was how he started; I never heard such a toneless voice; there was no inflection at all. It sounded as if it floated out of him, as if he were a mannequin, and a ventriloquist was speaking through him. 'By none other than legal evidence, not in the least degree by your confession, but by evidence from which there was no escape, most conclusive in its character, you have been found guilty of one of the most appalling crimes of which the records of civilized jurisprudence make any mention.' Well, he went on and on, almost as if he was still trying to justify the sentence to himself, and not only the sentence: to make some sense of the crime.

"He went over things much longer than he needed to, much longer than anyone had patience for, really. 'Almost without motive you went at your work, self-imposed, and eight innocent victims you slew. Not suddenly; not in a tempest of relentless passion; but in the coolness of a premeditated design—one by one at intervals with solemn pause, with calm deliberation, and with a quenchless thirst for blood, you ceased not until all that you set out to do was fully accomplished, and you found yourself alone with the dead. Your triumph was then complete.' Well, I told you I never forgot it; but even Father said his language was more biblical than usual, and he began to bend forward, as if he were worried about the judge. The thing I remember best," she said, mesmerized by some invisible sight, "was something he said near the end of his remarks. Or in the middle. He went on and on for so long it's hard to remember. He kept wondering if it was possible for the murderer to realize the enormity of his deeds, and if he could realize it, could he bring himself to ask for pardon? It bothered him, that the man couldn't *realize* what he had done. And then he said, 'No one may limit his power to forgive, but you can find mercy only in redeeming love. Man cannot, dare not, will not, pass by unavenged a crime so fearful as to be almost nameless. Society demands protection, and violated law its vindication. But the Omnipotent God hath said, "Whosoever will, let him come." ' I can tell you, he didn't sound as if he approved of the Omnipotent God at that moment.

"Then he said, 'To his mercy I commend you.' I think he was relieved to have someone else take the responsibility. It was clear to all of us, and I was very young, I couldn't have been more than fourteen, that it was all more than he could understand. And he was trying. Trying to understand was part of his work. He tried much harder than most; that's why everyone still says he was such a great judge, but in the end, he couldn't. In the end, he had to fall back on the effect the crime had on ordinary people. 'All that which must be done shall not be long delayed; you had your success in the execution of your fell purpose; but it demands its triumph now in the detection, exposure, conviction, and promptest and severest punishment of the criminal, who has defied alike the laws of God and man, and outraged all the nobler sympathies of his nature.' He meant man, not Christ; that was clear enough. Christ was ready to pardon the most hardened sinner provided he repented. But man was not; it went against his nature. Men had to protect themselves, and when it came down to important things, what did they go on? Instinct, emotion. Well, and what have you been going on for thirty years? Instinct, emotion. So if you didn't ask why you were doing what you were doing, you were driven to it all the same. And you drove yourself by what that judge would have called the nobler sympathies of nature. It seems to me," she said, her forehead still wrinkled, "you asked and answered the questions without knowing it."

"But it's not the same; it's not good enough," John insisted; "now that I've gone and asked them, nothing's enough. I don't care anymore. I don't care enough anymore. That one woman poisoned my feeling, whatever you want to call it. My intuitions won't get through that ice anymore. That's why I'm giving up medicine. I can't trust myself anymore. I don't want to, either. That's what it comes down to." He looked over at her, expecting a storm of scolding, persuasion, reproach. "Well," she said thoughtfully, "your instincts have always been right. If you want to give up medicine, that's what you ought to do. Don't worry about me," she assured him; "you won't have me for a dissenter in the house." "You think I'm right, then?" "I think it's right for you." John took a deep breath; he felt as if the courtroom itself had been sud-

805

denly lifted from his chest. "I suppose," Edna said, grimacing, "this means you'll be living in that cottage." "I'll come back to the house to sleep." "You'll have plenty of company there before bedtime rolls around and, it had better roll around sooner than it did when you were practicing medicine." "It probably won't." "That's what I was afraid of"—Edna smiled—"some things about you never change." "Nothing about you *ever* seems to change." "Well, don't forget that I haven't been through many of the other kinds of trials." "I'll forget it." "I don't think you ought to." *She* had something on her mind; it would be useless to ask her about it. She wouldn't tell him if a log had failed to ignite until she was sure he was over the trial. She could have been a priest as well as a lawyer, he thought, grinning to himself; she certainly could keep confidences, especially her own.

"How is everyone at home?" he asked again. "I told you," she answered a little uneasily; "everyone has colds." "Ten, too?" "Everyone means everyone." Something was wrong, he was sure of that. He supposed he would find out soon enough; it couldn't be too bad or she would never have left home. But he wasn't sure that was true. The train chugged and puffed its way inexorably on. "You can't see anything but yourself from these windows," John complained. The snow was falling so thickly it seemed solid. "That's life," she said casually.

The Brattleboro station looked the same as ever, John thought, relieved; at least what you could see of it. "Do you think Amos got here?" he asked Edna. "I suppose he did, even if he had to pull the sleigh himself and teach the oxen how to shovel." They stood, linked together, while a large, gaunt figure began materializing from the solid atmosphere. "Finished dispensing justice?" Amos asked grumpily. "You can bet your boots I am." "You could have picked a better time to finish," Amos grumbled; "I've got the draft oxen out, the ones that pulled that supply wagon out of the mud last summer, and they're going to need a doctor when they get back to the barn. If we don't wind up carrying them back on our shoulders." "It can't be that bad." "It will be by morning." "We hope to get home before that," Edna said. "Hope away," Amos said; "a lot of effect it will have on the weather." "Did you pass any other sleighs?" she asked. "I didn't hear any sleigh bells, if that's what you mean; you can't see a thing." "Well," Edna said, "we might as well get in, unless you want to go off gossiping with the stationmaster." "Gossiping with the stationmaster? Mrs. Steele, what do you take me for? I want to get these animals back where they belong, that's all I want." John smiled down at his wife. She usually picked up the thread when he dropped it. He was, he thought, overly domesticated by all those women in the house. He supposed, handing Edna into the carriage, he would have to tell her all about his horrible thoughts concerning Lettie. He wasn't up to that yet.

"Any news from Anna?" Edna shouted, leaning forward. "Not unless you call this blizzard a letter," Amos called back. "What about George? Hasn't he appeared?" "Don't you think I'd tell you *good* news?" Edna's free hand clenched. John thought Amos was getting more original in his comments, but made no more of it. The rest of the journey was occupied with climbing in and out of the wagon, clipping fences with wire cutters, driving the team across the pastures when the roads became impassable; that, John thought sadly, was a luxury he would soon be giving up, that and the tacit permission everyone had given him to shoot dogs annoying his teams when on call.

Finally, in the middle of their eighth pasture, the team stopped and refused to move. "Now what?" Edna gasped. "I'll just go and see," Amos said, getting out, taking a long stick with him. "Water," he announced, coming back; "it's covered over by the snow. We'll have to go back and try another pasture." The oxen were only too pleased to retrace their tracks. The instincts of animals, Edna thought. They were like doctors in their way; she would have to tell John that. But now she was anxious to get home. "Are we going to get home tonight?" she asked in exasperation after another hour passed. "If I have to move heaven and earth, miss." What on earth had gotten into him? John wondered. He didn't think he was the type to fall for revivalism, but then one never knew.

"Good Lord, is everyone in the house still up?" John asked as the oxen finally rounded the bend, lowering their heads still further for the final long pull. There was a golden glow in almost every window of the main wing. "They wouldn't want to miss your return," Edna said; "what are you going to tell them?" "About giving up medicine?" "What else?" "I'm going to tell them I'm retiring, not more, not less." "Not one word about the rest of it?" "One word, perhaps; that should be more than enough." "You're not looking forward to it, I suppose?" "Would you be?" She shook her head.

"Well," Amos shouted back to them, "I told you I'd get you home, and a lot you deserve it," he bellowed at John; "I was beginning to think you'd gotten caught up in all those fancy ways." "You ought to know me better than that," John said, climbing out, helping his wife down. "Nobody ever knows nobody until they're dead," Amos growled. "I guess you missed me." "I never said that; I just got sort of used to getting orders all the time and then what with only animals snorting and blaating, I kind of missed the noise of the biggest goat of all." John laughed. This *was* beginning to feel like home; no one in Boston ever thought to compare him with a sheep or a bull or an ass. "Well, have a good night," Amos said, stomping off; the snow was over the top of his boots. Edna and John watched him make his slow progress to the barn, going after one of his sons, heavily picking up one foot, then sinking it into the snow again, then the next foot, each step leaving deep holes like vertical tunnels, visible in the bright moonlight when the snow swirled the right way, giving the landscape an eerie resemblance to the moon's surface on a clear night. John was puzzled; he sensed that Amos had been attempting to give him hints and signals, but he had no idea about what. He looked down at Edna, but she was lost in the scene, in having her husband back, his arm around her waist. "Let's go in," she finally said, looking up.

"Who's coughing like that?" John asked the instant they climbed over the drift and were in the door. The dry, hacking cough filled the house. "Ten." "Ten?" John asked; he seemed, at once, inches shorter. "Where is she?" "She's on the lounge in the second parlor." "She let you put her in there?" he asked, incredulous. "We didn't have much choice; she doesn't seem very strong." "I'll be right back," he said, automatically picking up his bag, resting just where he had left it: on the seat of the coat stand. Some retirement, Edna thought.

"Well, well," John said, looking down at his sister, his hand on her forehead; it was cool and dry; "I can't leave the house for five minutes without your starting up; you never change." He pulled up a chair, his sister smiling weakly at him. He didn't like the look of her; she was positively emaciated. He knew, without bothering to think about it, the others wouldn't have noticed how dramatic the change was; they had seen her day by day. She had already, he thought sadly, taken on that look familiar to all people her age who were dying: her cheeks had fallen, sunken, the bone in her nose was more prominent. There was less and less color in her face to define where her flesh left off and the pillow on which her head rested began. Both of her hands were so thin, so knotted with rheumatism, they appeared claw-like. "A returning brother's privilege," he said, putting his ear to her chest. Crackles. It was as he thought. "I'm turning you over," he told her; "don't complain." She made a face at him.

He wanted to be sure. He tapped her back, listening to her lungs. Crackles in both of them. Both lungs thoroughly congested. If this didn't kill her, he thought, it would be a miracle. "How long," he asked her, "has this been going on?" "Two weeks," she whispered hoarsely. "That's all? Fraud. Nuisance. Family burden. When are you going to stop acting and get out of bed?" "As soon as I can talk properly." "Well, that makes sense; you wouldn't see much point in being up and about unless you could order everyone around." "I can't," she told him slowly, "even talk this well all the time." "Can you talk better at all?" he asked casually. "Sometimes," she said; her sentences, he saw, were becoming very elliptical. "Well, what are you doing up? Waiting for me?" "You?" she whispered; "I'd given you up." "Just about what Amos said." "Two old frogs," she croaked.

"*This* old frog looks like it jumped into the wrong pond," John said, looking at her. "Can't always be right," she whispered back. "If you weren't waiting up for me, what are you doing up?" "Sleep, wake, sleep, who knows the time?" The effort to talk was wearing her out. He would give her up this minute, but her fever was not high; she was a tough old turkey, he thought admiringly. "You get some sleep, little sister," he ordered menacingly; "I'm back, and I'll be after you, flipping you around like a pancake. I guess the boys didn't dare, did they?" She shook her head from side to side on the pillow. "Well, your vacation's over now," he warned. She smiled, this time more cheerfully. "You're going to be working pretty hard," he finished, "drinking the hot concoctions I'm making up for you." "Poison," she rasped. "You just keep quiet. If you keep quiet," he joked, "they'll never think of suspecting me, not the devoted brother. Our secret," he said, turning to leave. "Do you want someone to sit up with you?" he asked, pausing in the doorway. "Not a corpse yet," she gasped. "And I suppose you want your light out, too?" She looked relieved; the others must have unsettled her with all their attention. "Dark," she gasped; "not reading." "I'll blow it out; you do have peculiar ways."

"Well?" Edna asked; she was waiting on the other side of the door. "It doesn't look good," he said in a low voice; he was sure Ten still had ears like a bat. He half pushed Edna into the other parlor and shut the sliding doors. "Congestion of both lungs, swollen glands in the throat, severe difficulty talking, severe weight loss. It's the lungs; they're bad. She's likely to die of suffocation." "Should I have called you earlier?" Edna asked anxiously; "the boys kept saying she'd get over it. They thought it was severe congestion of the lungs, but they said she'd come out of it." "She might yet," John pondered; "if it were anyone else, I'd give them until morning." "I would *never* have forgiven myself if you'd come home and anything had happened to her." "There's no use in looking out the window for Greenwood yet; she's strong. She'll rally, I think. I'll set Ellen to making her hot concoctions she's never had before and she'll take to it. You'll see." "But for how long?" "One week, two weeks. If there isn't a drastic change, that's all we can hope for; more, really." "I thought you were giving up medicine." "I am. This is different; she's my sister. You don't think I'd let you cough yourself to death?" "Why don't you trust the boys?" "They haven't been around as long as I have, and," he repeated, "she's my sister. She won't dare die in my presence." "What are you going to give her?" Edna asked at last.

She could hear voices outside the parlor; they knew better than to come in when she and John closeted up together. "Things she won't like much"; he grinned; he was looking more and more familiar, as if her eyes were getting used to him all over again. "A decoction of pine needles sweetened with white sugar; that's one. The vinegar drink, though, that should do her the most good. She'll hate it. She hates vinegar. The recipe goes like this: a large teaspoon of flaxseed with half an ounce of licorice extract and a quarter of a pound of raisins, dried, in two quarts of soft water, simmering over a slow fire until it's only one quart; then you add a quarter of a pound of brown sugar candy and two tablespoonfuls of white wine vinegar. You could use lemon juice, but she likes lemon juice. But if you add the vinegar at the last minute, it tastes poisonous. *And* you have to drink half a pint whenever the cough bothers you." "It sounds perfectly repulsive." "That's the general idea." "What about alternating it with something she likes? That always worked with the children."

"That's not a bad idea; I'm trying to remember if there's something she'll like. There is," he said; "you roast a lemon. Then, when it's all hot, it gets cut up and squeezed into a cup on top of three ounces of sugar candy after powdering it. That should keep Bridget busy, anyway. Then there's another one the grandmothers like: two ounces of syrup of poppies; we ought to have some of that in the storeroom. The same amount of rose jelly, one spoonful for as long as the cough lasts: before going to bed. They're all ridiculous, but the point is, she'll think we're doing something." "Maybe the vinegar's not ridiculous. That time I was coughing after Anna was born, and I was out in the kitchen and we were making some kind of spiced beef? The vinegar felt like acid, and I thought the cough was getting worse, and the next thing I knew, there was some stuff in my handkerchief and the cough was gone." "Maybe we'll give it to her hot." He was always agreeable to suggestions.

"You don't really believe—" Edna hesitated. "That she might die?" he finished for her. "Yes, I do. It's the most likely thing. She's eighty-one, or almost eighty-one. How did it start?" "Oh, you know Ten; she decided there was something down-cellar she wanted, some kind of yarn or other, and we couldn't get her out of there. It was freezing cold. Martin threatened her with everything he could think of. He told her he wouldn't take care of her if she got sick, so she told him she'd just take care of herself." "They should have threatened her with a letter to me." "I told you; they really didn't think it was that serious. They never thought it would go on this long. What are you going to tell them?" "About what?" "About Ten." "The truth. At her age, she's particularly susceptible to this kind of disease. It's not their fault. If they're going to worry, they might as well worry about something useful; I'll concentrate on my retiring."

Edna sighed. "Edna," he said sharply, "don't start resigning yourself to the inevitable before it comes. She'll sense it and try obliging you." "You're right. Of course." She sounded tired. "I suppose," she said, "we might as well let the others in." "If we don't, they'll just keep Ten up all night." He got up to open the door. There they all were, Minnie and Martin, Ella and William. There was the usual flurry of kisses, hugs, holding each other at arm's length; Ella, John saw, was in tears. "So you didn't think I'd come back, either?" he asked gently. "I was beginning to worry," she answered between sniffs. John sat down and pulled Ella onto his lap. "You're heavier than you were when you were four years old," he complained. "You didn't think I'd be lighter, did you? I feel foolish," she sniffed a few minutes later. "Well, I'll have more time to make you feel foolish from now on," he said softly. "What does that mean?" his daughter demanded. "Your father has a surprise for all of you," Edna announced brightly. She had sounded just like that, Martin remembered, when she came out of Lettie's room and said Lettie had the measles, and now they would all have it, too, but wasn't that wonderful, because they would be able to stay home from school.

"Well, I don't know how surprising this is," John said; "I've decided to retire and treat my photographs." There was a stunned silence. "Well, I'm over sixty." They were still staring at him. "Is there something wrong with you?" Minnie asked shyly, voicing all their thoughts. "There's nothing wrong with me; I just want to get on with my pictures. Don't worry; I'll be coming on rounds often enough with the black hood over the camera and you'll have your hands full convincing your invalids I'm not there taking their death portraits." "You're really serious?" Bill asked. "Determined." "I don't believe it," Martin finally said. "You'll believe it after the first week you two go off on your own." "That makes me feel shaky," Martin admitted. "You'll get over it. You were on your own while I was gone. I can always come as a consultant in emergencies. I just want to get on with the pictures before I'm dead, that's all." "Are you planning on dying?" Ella asked, still suspicious. "Not that I know of," he answered, refusing to let her up. "Well, that's it, then," William said; "I don't think it's fair," he announced to the air, "to put pressure on someone who's spent thirty years trotting around the country to keep it up until he expires in a snowdrift at ninety." "No," Martin said slowly. "No," Minnie agreed. Ella, however, kept inspecting his face. "No," she finally agreed. They sounded, John thought, like a jury coming to a verdict.

"Well," Martin asked as the rest of them settled on love seats and chairs, "how was the trial?" "I'd rather spend my time in a leper colony." "What makes it so bad?" Martin asked, surprised. "The kinds of diseases you see there aren't curable, not in this world, anyway." "Did it," Ella asked from her seat next to William, "have anything to do with the trial? This retirement?" "No; but that reminds me of something I wanted to tell the boys. You two know how to treat your patient without asking questions about his character. Now," he said, hesitating, "I think they ought to be asked. After the work is done." "Why?" asked William. "Because sooner or later it will become clear that some diseases have to do with a person's worth, or their intelligence, or personality, and at least now, I can't help but think, the more you know of the person on the bed, the better job you'll do. You won't feel so much like machines later, either." Martin and William regarded him carefully. "You have a point," Martin conceded. "I'm not sure," William said. "Well, dear," Minnie suggested, "why don't you think about it later? Your father must be tired after the long trip."

"What about Aunt Ten?" It was Ella who asked; John wondered which of them would bring her up first. "Her condition isn't good; if I was a gambling man, I'd say she had one chance in ten." "Is that a pun?" Martin asked.

"No, an estimate." "What's to be done?" William asked. He was the practical one. "I'll write out a list of concoctions for Ellen and Bridget; keep her comfortable as possible, and drinking as much of the stuff as possible, and, since she has to stay still, we're got to keep her cheerful as possible."

"Maybe," William said, blackly, "we should call back *my* father." John raised his eyebrows. "His father seems to cheer her up," Ella explained; "he came up three nights ago when she was talking better. He told her she looked terrible; I thought Mrs. Moffat was going to strangle him right there in the sickroom and he'd fall on Aunt's body and do her in, and then he said something about if you wanted nice clean oats, you had to expect to pay a reasonable price for them, but if you wanted oats that had already been through the horse, they came a lot cheaper. Mrs. Moffat was spluttering and telling him to keep quiet, but Aunt Ten was finally smiling.

"What *did* he mean?" Ella asked; "I still don't understand it." "He meant," William explained, "that she'd had a good life and now she had to pay a price." "What a way to put it," Ella said; "I thought his mind had just wandered off to farming. She did ask him to come back again." "He would make her feel cheerful," John said; "your aunt would think anyone so honest and careless wouldn't think she was in any great danger. The rest of you have to stop sitting up with her. It's scaring her witless. She thinks you're getting ready to sit up with the body; and more than one of you in there with a candle, her heart will probably stop. She doesn't want a light on in her room, either; not at night. She says she doesn't see any point in it since she can't read." "Oh, my," Minnie said; "we've been doing everything wrong." "I wouldn't say that; Ten's not an easy one to track. You were doing the right thing for everyone else in the world. She'll be happy if she hears loud noises in the kitchen, loud noises in the parlors, loud noises outside her door, outside the window; anything that makes it sound like an ordinary day, that will be good for her."

"We *have* been creeping around," Edna admitted. "Well, then, enough of that; start slamming doors, and if you have anything you want to fight about, fight outside her door. She'll have something to think about. Just to be safe, keep the children out of the room, but don't try keeping them quiet. Keep things usual, that's the main point. You could read to her, if she's not too tired." "We didn't want to wear her out," Minnie moaned. "Stop worrying about it. It's up to nature now; if she's tired and you're reading, she'll fall asleep. I wouldn't put it past her to live to hear the end of the story, so look out for big books."

"We *have* been doing everything wrong," Edna echoed. "If she lives, she lives," John said; "if she's not going to live, there's nothing any of us can do to prevent it. Except those things I already mentioned." He began writing on a pad as he spoke. "These prescriptions will keep the kitchen cheerful, and that will cheer Ten up, and there's always some chance they'll do some good; they can't do any harm." "No opiates for that cough?" Ella asked; the cough had been scraping steadily at their skins. They felt raw. "Not unless you want to kill her outright." He would have thought she knew better; opium for such a weakened condition! "It's painful to hear her coughing," Edna said. "She's not coughing now," Ella said; "I better go look." "I told you; none of that. Just sit down. You go rush in on her every time she's quiet, and it will be the end of her." "How long *do* we have to wait?" Edna asked. "No more than three hours, and no less than three, either, unless you hear something unusual, or unless she calls you. Is that understood?" he asked, glaring at Ella. "Oh, all right." "I know her better," he insisted. "He's pulling rank again," William said. They all seemed brighter. "Well, you go up to bed," Ella said; "don't worry. The big children will follow your orders." "Good. Do you think," he asked William, "we can get your father back for another visit?" "*That* will be only too easy."

In the morning, Ten's body was cool and dewy; she could speak plainly, although her voice was far from what it was, and she was still racked by coughing. "You are a case," John told her; "I knew it was all bamboozling; you're just trying to scare us to death so you can bury us all." "Get on, you old scoundrel." "Well, I guess you're not ready to scrub floors yet." "I *never* knew how to scrub floors." She did seem more herself. "Whatever this is," she went on hoarsely, "it's good for my rheumatism; nothing hurts." "Probably it's the first time you've kept still in over a century." "I suppose," she said, "the others are waiting outside to view the dear departed." "What do you think?" "Let them in and let's get it over with." John went out and told the assembled group not to stay more than five minutes. It was, he said, a surprising remission, but it didn't necessarily mean anything.

He stopped William on his way in. "You're sure your father cheered her up?" "He sure did; I don't know why, either. I look at him and think of carbolic acid or Paris green." "Where is he?" "Outside." "Outside, outside where?" "Outside this house. He said something about liking your sister since she got him off for chicken stealing." "Chicking stealing!" "Well, when we were young, I guess when they were, too, we used to pretend we were out hunting a wild animal; then we'd hunt up a chicken and roast the wild beast off in the woods. My father caught a chicken, but Probst caught him, and Ten went down to the jail and said it was her chicken they stole, and the constable got so confused about whose chicken it was, and from whom it was stolen, or if Ten should be considered the thief, he decided to let the boys go, especially after Ten paid Probst for the chicken. Then she told Probst not to bother selling her family more eggs. And that's when your family started raising chickens." "I never heard anything about that." "I guess your sister doesn't tell all her secrets. I'll get Father; he's still out under the big pine unless he turned blue and went in with Amos."

"Here he is," William announced, dragging his father in. Howard hadn't bothered changing from his work clothes; that was a good thing. "I'm here to visit Ten," he announced. "Well, the rest of us don't mind seeing you," John said, slapping him on the back. It didn't work; he was as stiff as ever, as set on his purpose as ever. "Is she any better?" "Today." "Well, it's one day at a time, one foot at a time up the apple tree." *His* voice sounded rusty, as if he were unused to talking. "Can I see Ten?" he finally asked. "I brought her over some of my favorite clippings." "Dad," William warned. "You keep out of it," his father growled; "she's as much a ghoul as I ever was." Would this process of learning about his sister never end?

"Poor Ten," Bill said. "That sprout never knows what

he's talking about, anyhow," Howard growled; "is anyone letting me in, or should I yell through the door?" "Go on in," John said; "the others were in to say hello; you'll have her to yourself." "Just the way I want it; I could be a jailbird today if it weren't for her." He went in. John and William stood in the hall, grinning. "What do you make of it?" William asked. "If he went in there and read her the obituary list and it cheered her up that would be just fine with me." "Maybe we ought to press our little ears to the door and make sure he *doesn't* do that." "My, my," John scolded; "big pitchers have big ears." "You're going to trust that man in there?" "Your mother's survived this long with him." "Yes, but we practically locked him out of the house; don't you remember? You once told us to do it." "No two cases are the same; what do I make of it? I think it's incredible, but I'm not asking questions. I'd like to be a fly on that wall, though, I can tell you."

Inside, Howard inspected Ten from the doorway. "Don't stand there gaping at the remains," she said; "come sit down. I won't bite." "I guess you won't; not today, anyhow." "What do you mean?" "You bit a little boy who bit you when you were eighteen." "So I did; there's a hole in my mouth," she announced horrified; "did those monsters pull out a tooth while I was dead to this world?" "Is it there?" "No." "Then they took it away; unless you swallowed it." "Swallowed it!" "I wouldn't guess you swallowed it; I'd guess one of the wolf pack out there decided to try dentistry on something and you were closer than the barn." "Hmmm," Ten considered, testing the hole in her gum with her tongue. "I brought you my clippings," Howard volunteered bashfully; "like I said I would."

"Oh, good," Ten said with something resembling animation; "did you get the best ones?" "*My* best; William says I'm a ghoul." "I like the ghoulish ones best." They sounded like conspirators. "Read, read," she hurried him on. "I'll start with a short one," Howard said; "I read awful slow; this reading-aloud business is a new thing with me." "That's *fine*." "This one's called 'A Baby Killed by Rats.'" "Read, read," Ten ordered dictatorially, seeing him look over at her. " 'Three big rats attacked the two-month-old baby of Mr. and Mrs. Isaac Raskin of Baltimore, Maryland, Saturday night, and gnawed its face, head, and neck to such an extent that the baby died in a short time. Mr. Raskin lives over his store. He was looking after his business and Mrs. Raskin had gone to market when the rats started to make a meal of the helpless infant which was snugly tucked in its crib in the second story of the dwelling. They tore the flesh from the babe's tender face, head, and neck. He died immediately.' " "That's a good one," Ten said.

"I don't have any more about rats; I guess you remember what happened in Dummerston when the farmer built the big rat cage and caught, say, two hundred and fifty big rats in the corncrib, and he and his dog got eaten up when they went in?" "Yes, that's old news; it reminds me of a joke: A little child says, 'I'm tired of my rag doll; I want a meat baby.' " Howard roared with laughter; Ten started to laugh, but her cough made her stop. "It's a good thing they're not in here," Howard said. "True, too true," Ten agreed.

"There are two good ones on this one piece," Howard went on; "what do you want first? An infidel, or a dead man driving?" "The dead man driving," Ten answered happily. " 'Benjamin P. Lewis, seventy years of age, fell dead in a sleigh on Harvard Bridge, near the Boston side. Heart disease is given as the cause. When his heart stopped, Mr. Lewis fell from his sleigh and the horse ran away, continuing up Massachusetts Avenue. At the junction of Beacon Street, it knocked down nine-year-old Fabian Ashald, and bruised him badly. As the horse ran along the avenue, he overturned the sleigh, and at St. Botolph Street, disentangled himself from the wreck and, after running through various South End streets, finally brought himself up at the door of the stable of A. T. Robinson, where Mr. Lewis had hired the outfit.' " "The horse knew where home was," Ten observed. "I used to think a lot about what would happen if I died driving the team," Howard confided. "Well, now you know."

"Now," she instructed happily, "for the infidel." "Oh, that's a good one. It's called 'Infidel and Proud of it.' 'John Snap, a famous character, died at Middlebury, Vermont, aged fifty-seven. He was a bitter enemy of the Christian religion.' " "That's nice," Ten said. " 'In the city cemetery, where love and faith in the future were inscribed on tombstones, he erected no less than ten tombstones bearing inscriptions the most shocking and blasphemous the mind could devise. On the tombstone erected for himself, he caused to be inscribed: "I have died as I have lived for forty years, a thorough infidel and unbeliever in all ancient and modern theological humbugs and religious myths." For twenty years he had been erecting these tombstones and awaiting his death. His wife, stepchildren, and one nephew are in the gallery. Whenever the old man felt unusually vindictive toward Christianity, he took a day off and cut an inscription on his tombstone.'" "Oh, that's a wonderful one," Ten chortled; "could I ask a great favor and keep that one to copy out for Anna?" "Well, I don't know; it's one of my best ones." "I'll have Edna do it and send it right back." "All right, if you have to have it." He gave in with no good grace; "mind, this is the only one." Ten nodded.

"It sounds like nice times, doesn't it?" she asked; "carving those things whenever you get mad." "It does to me, anyhow," Howard answered, managing the closest thing to a smile anyone would ever see. "No suicides?" She was disappointed. "Oh yes," Howard assured her; "there's a good one about a man who killed himself so he wouldn't have to go to his fortieth anniversary party. They found him hanging from the church tower's bell rope." "What do they say caused it?" "'Aberration of the mind, due to poor health and some recent financial humiliations, is supposed to have been the cause, as he is a very sensitive man,'" Howard read out. "'He had been acting strangely for some time and his friends had noticed this and spoken of it among themselves.'" "And didn't bestir themselves either, I guess." "Guess not," Howard agreed; "they held the funeral just two days ago."

He looked over his little collection; she seemed somewhat tired. "You like romances?" She nodded violently. "'Reunited at the Verge of the Grave.'" He stopped. "Alice is always at me to read more, but I guess you understand what I say." Ten nodded again. "'A most romantic courtship has been ended by the marriage at Dummerston, Vermont, of F. L. James and Mrs. John Sherwin of Watertown, New York. The bride's age is ninety and the groom is but one year younger. In their school days, they were lovers, but a quarrel parted them, and they did not meet again until a short time ago. The courtship was renewed and a quiet wedding soon took place.' There's hope for you yet." "Oh, I never want to get married again." "Can't say I blame you," he agreed sourly; "one is enough for anyone, I'd say." Ten grinned in spite of herself. Poor Alice. "That was a little disappointing, though," Ten said; "at the edge of the grave. I thought they'd be getting married on their deathbeds." "Well, headlines."

"Well, I have one for you; it's called 'We Never Shall Be Missed.' " "Read it." " 'There are almost a billion and a half people living on the planet which we inhabit. And yet there is now and then a man who wonders what the rest of us will do when he dies. There are people in "society" who honestly think the world closes its eyes when they lie down to sleep. There are men who fear to act according to their own convictions, because perhaps ten persons in a crowd of a billion and a half will laugh at them. Why, if a man could only realize what a bustling, busy, fussy important little atom he is in the great anthill of important, fussy little atoms, every day he would regard himself less, and think still less of the people around him.' " "Why, I could have written that myself!" Ten exclaimed. "It had the sound of you." "I can't understand why they take on so about my dying or not dying. It won't make any difference. And a lot of good I'd have done them if I'd thought any other way the rest of my life." "That's the truth, but my family, they don't like it much, my thinking like that. They don't think I take them serious enough. I take them as serious as I take any living thing, but they can't figure it. It makes a man bitter."

"I know." "You do?" *"I* just keep quiet about it, and I take them seriously enough from day to day, but I don't tell them it's day to day. Maybe," she considered, "that's where you made your mistake. Letting them know how you think." "It's too late now." "Try." "For how long?" "For however long it takes." "I guess; it's hard my way, I can tell you." "Try." Even on her deathbed, she thought, she'd be stuck telling people what to do. "Howard," she said warmly, "thank you. They've been killing me with quiet. This was just like old, old times; it was like having Mother here to read to me. Not that you look like her," she added quickly, seeing his expression. "So you're dropping off, are you?" "I'm afraid so; but you'll come back?"

"You can bet your britches on it." "Good, I'll get some britches." "You always were a silly one." "I'm too old to change now." "Well, don't; I always liked the chicken woman." "What?" Ten asked, rousing herself momentarily. "That's what we used to call you." "Imagine!" Ten said, her lids closing heavily; "come back," she said, mustering strength for those few words. "I gave my word."

Outside, there was great excitement. A letter from Anna had finally arrived. Howard looked out the window. "Snow," he pronounced positively. "You didn't kill her?" Bill asked. "She's no worse than she was, and maybe better; I have to get back to choring. *You* do the miracle work." He left, insulted. "Don't you want to stay and hear Anna's letter?" Bill called after him. Howard glowered over his shoulder, stomping toward the barn and his horse, through the heavy, suffocating snow.

There was such relief at the arrival of Anna's letter, Martin thought, no one could have known the difference between its importance and news of the beginning of the new world. "I've been writing and writing," Anna said, "but no word from any of you. What are you thinking of? I am almost sick with worry, and little Minnie asks every day about letters, letters, letters, until the word makes my ears burn. She is getting smarter and cuter every day and looks just like me. Little Mat looks just like his father, and he is after Minnie all the time, and would you believe it, he can walk by himself and even say some words, though I doubt if he'll be up to testifying in court for a year or two. Father is the only one I'm sure is alive and well and that's only because he's been in the papers so long. Why don't the rest of you get yourselves in the papers if you've forgotten how to write?" "Oh, dear," Minnie said, looking up; "she hasn't been getting our letters." "The drifts," William said, "are just terrible." She went back to her reading.

"The whole congregation here is in an uproar and Matthew is disgusted with them, and they say they don't know what to make of him any longer. Last Sunday, he had just enough of church behavior, and had to speak of it at last. I don't know whether it's the custom in all congregations to bob the head around as soon as the door opens, or a footstep is heard in the aisle, but from what used to go on in Williamsville at the Old Stone Church, I suppose it is. But in New Bedford, I tell you, it is worse, and don't think I'm exaggerating. Half of the time you can't tell if you're at a circus or inside a house of worship. Here, every head turns at everything and stays that way until the look is long enough to satisfy. All a dog has to do is bark, or a baby to pipe up, or a cow to bawl out in the street, and you'd think they'd never heard such things before, remarkable things like a horse snorting, and that sets all the young people to giggling. If anyone should have the good luck to fall, or blunder, well, then, the amusement is just about infinite. If such-and-such should happen to sit in the pew occupied by a young widow, then the younger ones will wink and blink at one another, and send notes or write comments in their hymn books. It's all very unbecoming, especially considering the day, the place, and the occasion. So Matthew decided to devote a few moments to the subject. I thought it was a good idea, too, since no one would be tired out listening at the rate they've been going.

"Oh, I tell you, I am tired of New Bedford ways. Matthew plainly told them that nothing annoyed the minister more than people turning their heads at every sound as if their heads were set on pivots; he said he often drew inspiration from a pair of attentive eyes, but that well had certainly dried up, and if they only knew how much their attention contributed to his assistance, they would give it most devoutly. Then he related something he'd overheard one of the beautiful young 'ladies' say one evening going home from church. It was very dark, and she was walking in front of him, so she didn't see him. Her arm was linked in another girl's. 'I always like to sit in front so that my eye can take in the whole congregation,' she said. 'I like to see people when they come in, and if there are any strangers, well, then it's so nice to see how they're dressed. It's such a convenient way to see new fashions, and I get more ideas for new contrivances that way than any other, don't you think so?" The other girl did, too. 'It's a big help when I have to work over my old clothes into new ones; I do such a good job even my own folks don't think they've ever seen them on me before.'

"And then what does little Minnie have to say when it's all over? 'I do wish, Momma, I could make myself mind Poppa while we're sitting in that old church. I want to think about what he's saying, and what the hymns mean, I'd like to know all that, but I try so hard, and then I'm thinking of my stories, or how little Mat is with his cold, or I wonder how much that lady paid for her hat, it's so big, or that I had a blue feather, not a black one, but I'll try some more.' I don't know how far she'll get; at any rate, everyone's been behaving for two weeks, but that's probably the end of it.

"Now there's a real hornet's nest. Matthew preached a sermon about the value and uses of prayer and wondered why mothers kept at having their two-and-a-half-year-olds learn prayers when the children couldn't understand a word they themselves were saying. He went on about how children could become too familiar with sacred things. 'Be not thou overly familiar with sacred things.' That was his text. He asked them if some of the children weren't being fed meat too strong for babes, and told the story of a little girl he'd scolded who said, 'Oh, well, it's not *my* fault. Eve was the one who gobbled up the apple; you should blame her, you know.' He went on about how the child firmly believed Eve was responsible for all her pranks, and this gave her a marvelous freedom from responsibility. How, he asked, could she ever become a Christian thinking that way? He said a child of five was too young for such things, and then you should have heard the rumblings and grumblings. 'Before they learn the importance and solemnity of things, they have learned to look upon them in such a light as to make the whole course of so-called religious instruction almost a farce.' Mumblings and rumblings now almost approached roars.

"He went on with anecdotes he'd collected about the parish. One mother told him she was in the next room when she heard her son saying his prayers. 'Our father,' the boy said ('Let me alone, Tom Pewling!'), 'which art in heaven.' ('Stop that!'), and so on. It was dreadful. Her children, she told him, were both old enough to know better, but it didn't strike Matthew that they did, or their mother, either. 'Then,' she said, 'one night I had the little one on my lap, putting her into bed. She knelt on my knee and, clasping her hands, solemnly said, "A, B, C, D." "Well," I said, shocked, "Carrie, that is your alphabet, not your prayers!" "Oh," asked my little girl, "won't that just do? I'm so tired," and she put her head down and went to sleep. I didn't even try to talk to her until the next morning, and you can guess what it's like reasoning with a three-year-old mind. Now she was obstinate. 'I should think,' Carrie said, "my Father in Heaven would like to hear me say my ABC's once in a while, so as to know that I know them. Poppa does,' she told me smugly. "I should think He'd get tired of hearing me say 'Now I lay me' every night." '

"Her mother said the climax of it all was the saying of Grace. She had always taught her children to say, 'We thank thee, O Lord, for all thy bountiful provisions this day.' 'They used to say that,' she told Matthew, 'just as soon as they could talk, and long before they knew enough to quarrel with their food if it did not suit them.' But one day, one of the children had some kind of argument with his mother, and he came to the table looking like a cyclone.

"He kept quiet while the others said their Grace, so his mother scolded him. He jerked Grace out with a vicious, ungrateful smile. 'Phineas, will you have some potatoes?' his mother asked him. 'No!' said the dear child; 'I hate mashed potatoes. I hate everything that's on the table; you needn't give me any dinner.' 'So much,' she said, 'for Grace in the mouths of children.' Matthew told the congregation he would rather see children heathenish from ignorance than irreverent from overfamiliarity. 'The latter,' he said, 'is far harder to eradicate than the former.' He mentioned a woman who had not taught her children Grace or their prayers until they reached an age when they could understand them, and she never has to tell her children to get back out of bed because they forgot their prayers; they always say them. Matthew said he believed that if one leaves such teaching till a child is old enough to understand what he or she is about, it will not be forgotten. Well, you can imagine what *that* started up.

"Everyone wants to stand up and have their say on the subject in church; our Sundays are now like some revival gone demented. I suppose we should be grateful there are no more swiveling heads, at least while this continues. Some mothers stand up and heartrendingly describe how their children died, and how dreadfully they would have felt had they gone on to the next world with no knowledge whatever of prayer. 'When we asked Annabelle' (that was one of the daughters), 'seven years old' (which is a lot older than three, if you ask me, and not really to the point), 'a few hours before her death, "Annabelle, aren't you Jesus' child, and don't you love him?" what a thrill of joy and peace was in my heart when her face lighted up and she answered. "Yes, Poppa; yes, Poppa!" Did we then regret teaching her of him she was so soon to see? Ask our little boy,' she went on, 'what he expects to find and do first on reaching heaven. "I'm going to find Jesus first and kiss him, and then my little sisters, and we will run all round heaven's pretty streets." ' "

She went on, chatting about sermons, reporting some tidbits of her research on cells, asking if she'd remembered to tell them she had baked her first sweet potato during the summer and, to show how good she now was at managing the oven, she forgot to poke holes in the potato, and the potato exploded and it looked as if orange paint was all over. The cooks did have a laugh and she guessed there was plenty to laugh at. She wrote that she'd almost done the same thing with chestnuts, but they'd stopped her before she'd blown them up.

The whaling vessels were not going out yet, she said; the ice was too thick, but new ones were coming in, and the ice was thick enough so that teams could go out on it and get the men and supplies. George hadn't come down from the mountain yet, but he couldn't be up there much longer; none of them could. It was too cold to hold on to anything for more than a minute. Then she again fell to scolding them about their lack of letter-writing ability; she hoped the house hadn't burned down with all of them in it, although she imagined she'd have read about that, but she would have to stop writing now because *this* Sunday everyone would expect to hear her views on teaching children prayers and Grace at an early age, and she didn't know what to think, really. She didn't actually agree with Matthew; some of the children, she thought, were just plain wicked, and it wouldn't make any difference when they learned anything, if they ever did learn. She would send her regards to all the children separately, she concluded, "but it would be worse than copying out the Book of Genesis." "That's a relief," Edna sighed. "True enough," Ella agreed, slowly exhaling. Everyone looked as if they had heard news of a war ending.

"Well," William said, "I'd better be getting back to work. There's Mrs. Lawson to check on and some supplies to pick up in the village." The others nodded at him.

There was the sound of Ten's handbell. "I'll go," Minnie volunteered. "Do you think," Ten asked, her voice uncommonly strong, "I could have some soup? You could soak some crushed bread in it." "I'll go ask," Minnie said, going back to the parlor. "She wants soup with bread in it; can she have it?" "I should hope she could," John answered; "well, that sounds better, doesn't it?" he asked, looking around; "it looks like we should be in for a good day."

The next day, however, Ten was not as strong. She was hot and restless, her cough as bad as ever. "Peaks and valleys, peaks and valleys," Edna sighed as they were getting ready for bed one night; "she's beginning to remind me of the scenery." "You always said she fit in like a tree." "I wish she'd fit into the meadow a little bit more. Oh, good Lord," she exclaimed, clasping her hand over her mouth; "that sounds dreadful. I didn't mean she ought to get under it." "I know that." "If she does die, or when she does die, two years from now, or whenever, are you going to take a portrait of her?" "Yes." "Why?" "There's something about pictures of people who have just passed from one state to the other; they still look alive. If they didn't, death probably wouldn't be so hard to accept. Mine are different than the usual ones; I won't have them in natural poses, or photograph corpses taken out of their beds and propped up on chairs, or children sitting in their rockers holding their favorite dolls. That's taxidermy, not photography."

"What," Edna asked, stepping out of the rest of her clothes, "would be wrong with stuffing the dead body of a loved one? I mean, it might be a good thing." "Have you lost your senses entirely? Don't you think you'd get tired of walking past the statue of your husband or your child and never getting any response? Unless, of course, you developed acute dementia and then you could talk to the human statue all the time; it would save exhuming bodies, I suppose." "But you might get accustomed to them being dead," Edna argued; "and until you did, at least they would seem to be there." "And you could keep the wound open almost indefinitely," John retorted, getting into bed; "do you think that's a good idea?"

"I don't know if it's a *bad* one; if you died, I think I'd want you stuffed." "Good Lord; Edna, can you imagine explaining why I'm standing there stuffed in the hall, to the grandchildren, I mean? They'd think I was a doll and try to play with me, and how would you like to come home and find them all over my stuffed body pretending I was a soldier who'd just been shot, or draped in white material because I was supposed to be a bride about to tie the knot?" "That's a dreadful idea; I suppose I could keep you in my room." "If I didn't know better," John said seriously, "I'd think you couldn't put up with anyone so much as coming down with a cold. I never heard of anything so outlandish."

"What's outlandish about it? They stuff trophies, animals—they were once alive; they cover the walls of hunting lodges with them." "That's to show the life was taken *away*, not to remind them of their happy memories of a deer they never saw before in their lives." "Oh, well," Edna said. "Unless, of course, you regard me as a trophy," John said, managing to sound serious. "Don't be ridiculous." "Well, and what would happen to the stuffed shirts after a while?" John asked; "more and more generations; more and more people, less and less room. They'd end carrying all the stuffed up to the attic or throwing them in the ash barrel. I think I'd rather be buried." "It won't be up to you; after you're dead." "I sincerely hope I will not die before this ludicrous moth of an idea stops eating holes in your brain."

"Wouldn't *you* want me stuffed?" Edna asked. "I like you just the way you are; and you wouldn't be the same stuffed, would you?" he asked, putting his hand on her breast. "I'd be *almost* the same," she contended, pushing his hand away. "I've never been interested in necrophilia," John growled; he was annoyed. "Necrophilia? Who's talking about necrophilia? If you can take pictures of dead people, I don't see why you can't just keep the whole body and not bother with the pictures." "For one thing," John said, throwing himself down on his back, "after a while you hardly look at pictures, but I'd guess a full-length stuffed version of a husband or child would hold the attention a lot longer, and, for the last time, Edna, I don't think it would be good for you. Or for anyone in their right mind."

"Some people stuff their pets." She wasn't going to drop it. "All right, Edna, if you want to stuff your pet, go ahead. As you said, I won't be there to stop you. And I hope you enjoy kissing me every night before you go to bed. I should feel something like old newspaper." No answer. "I suppose you're right," she said finally; "but there should be a way out." "There isn't, not in this lifetime, anyway." "I suppose." She was sobbing in his arms.

His absence, Ten's illness, they had taken more of a toll than he thought; he should have expected it. He began stroking her hair. She finally lay quiet and still. "John?" "Yes?" "I'm glad I don't have to worry about having you stuffed." "That's good," he answered, rubbing the small of her back; "I thought you'd made a diagnosis and were afraid to tell me." "You're mocking me again." He didn't reply. "I suppose I deserve it." She took his hand, putting it back on her breast and its erect nipple. "I suppose," she said, squirming closer to him, "I wouldn't do that if I were stuffed." "No, I don't think so." "Is the door shut?" she asked out of habit. "Locked, bolted, and barred; a runaway team couldn't make a dent in it." "Good; do we ever get too old for this?" "Not until we're stuffed." "You're *always* stuffed." They lay back, happy in each other's presence. Having him back, she thought; that was the most exciting thing. "Do you hear sleigh bells?" John asked suddenly. "No," Edna said, blissful. "You still don't hear them?" "No; I think you're just missing your old harness." They lay quiet in the darkness. "There are people downstairs," Edna said, sitting up straight; "I heard the front door open." John was listening beside her.

They heard someone running up the steps, then the slam of a door, and two indistinguishable voices, then the steps returning to the first floor. "What's going on?" Edna asked. Someone else ran up the steps and knocked at another door down the hall, the same muttered conversation, the same running down to the first floor. "I'm going to get up and see what this is all about," Edna decided. "No, you're not; you're staying right here." He put his arm across her, pinning her down. "I didn't give up medicine to have my wife start hopping in and out of bed like a rabbit." "All right; if it's anything important, they'll call us."

Edna settled comfortably in, but no sooner had her head touched John's shoulder than there was an anxious tapping at their door. "Who is it?" John called out. "It's me, Minnie; would you come out here a minute, Dr. Steele?" "I'm coming, too," Edna said. They both dressed instantly. "What's happened?" Edna demanded; "did something happen to Ten?" "No, no, come *down*." They went down after her. "Anna's outside in a sleigh," she said at the foot of the stairs. "Anna, our Anna?" Edna asked. "Anna and George." "Anna and George?" John repeated; "what on earth are they doing here?" "Matthew's dead," William said, seeing his sister hesitate. "What!" Edna exclaimed. "And little Minnie," William went on; "there's diphtheria all over New Bedford. She hasn't been talking since Matthew and Minnie died within two weeks of each other. The other women there decided the best thing to do would be to send her home."

"What about little Mat?" Edna asked, scrambling into her cloak with John's help; "where is he?" "The Perkinses took him in; George didn't think he looked too promising when they left." "Who? Who didn't look too promising?" Edna asked, frantic. "Little Matthew," Minnie said softly. "Don't get hysterical," John ordered his wife. "You mean to say," Edna asked, "George and Anna are sitting out there in the sleigh? In the middle of this snowstorm?" "He can't convince her to come in," Minnie said, "and he doesn't think he should drag her in bodily; she's holding on to the side of something or other and she won't let go." "My God!" Edna gasped; "and we just got a letter from her today!" "They've been coming through awfully late," Bill said. "Edna," John said, tugging her arm, "we better get out there." She looked at him, dazed.

They opened the door. Snow was slanting diagonally and thickly across the entrance to the house as if a curtain were separating those inside from those out. John and Edna walked outside. To those indoors, it seemed as if they had stepped into a void, the Milky Way, some uncharted territory. The sleigh itself, not twenty feet from the door, was barely visible, the figures in it blurred and concealed by the snow. "I don't see her," Edna gasped anxiously; the snow was flying in their faces, closing their eyes, melting on their cheeks, running down their faces. "What a storm," John said, shaking his head. "I think I can see her now," Edna told him; they were almost at the side of the sleigh.

"Anna," Edna called as she reached the sleigh; her daughter's clothes were so thoroughly covered with snow she seemed made of it; her hat was snow-white. She looked, Edna thought, while waiting for an answer, like a bride of winter, a frozen bride of winter. She had apparently been sitting in the snow in one position for so long the snow was beginning to cover her face, sticking to her cheeks in patches; to Edna's horror, one patch suddenly slid from under her eye, falling onto the front of her cloak. "Anna," Edna repeated; "it's very cold out here. Won't you come inside?" Her daughter didn't move. John tried. "Anna," he began firmly, "your mother hasn't been well. It's not right to keep her out in this weather." They thought they noticed a movement, but still she said nothing. "I don't know what to do," George told them desperately. "Try," John asked. "I think," George whispered, bending close to them, "I told her Matthew wanted her to go with me." John nodded.

"Anna," he said calmly, "we had a long letter from Matthew; he said he wanted you to stay in your old room when you came home." Her head turned stiffly toward him. "But you have to come inside to get into your old room," he said reasonably; "don't you?" She nodded woodenly; she seemed made of something other than flesh. "Are you going to let go of the sleigh?" She nodded as before. "All right, then," John said, opening the door; "give me your hand." She remained motionless. John took her hand and looked at George; the two of them lifted her down. "Can you stand?" John asked. She nodded, but her knees gave way beneath her. George held her under one arm, John under the other. "Thank you," Edna whispered to George, walking next to him; "you must have had a frightful time." "I don't know what was worse," he told her candidly, "what came before or this." "Didn't she talk at all?" "Not one word the whole way; it was like driving back with a dead body." Edna shuddered.

"Here we are," Edna told Anna as they entered the hall, unfastening her cloak and handing it to Ellen, who took it off to dry out. "Sit down here," Edna instructed, helping Anna onto the hall stand. She stooped, removing Anna's boots; they were soaked through. So were her stockings. Her flesh felt frozen. Edna removed her gloves. Anna lowered her eyes suddenly; Edna realized she was staring at her wedding ring. "Ten?" Anna said through stiff lips. "Aunt Ten is sleeping," her mother answered gently; "she has a cold." Anna didn't answer. "What's that you have in your hand?" Mrs. Steele asked. Anna was toying obsessively with a little packet wrapped in brown paper and tied with string; she had evidently taken it from her pocket. "Can I look at it?" Edna asked patiently. Her hand met no resistance as she extracted the package from between Anna's fingers; she unwrapped it efficiently.

It was Ten's copy of *The Wedding Ring*. "Ten will be glad to see it again," Edna said. Anna's eyes flicked to her mother's face, then back into space. To all watching, it seemed as if she were beginning the painful process of defrosting. John saw William had taken his brother George aside, and the two of them were talking quickly and seriously. "We had better get you up to bed," John said in his doctor's voice; "would you mind if your mother got in with you? She's half frozen herself." "I don't want to," Anna answered stiffly. "Don't want to what, dear?" Minnie asked. "My old room," Anna said tonelessly. "Would you mind getting into bed with your mother in our room?" John asked. "No." At least, he thought, relieved, she was talking. She had always crept into bed with Edna when she was upset, after he went off on rounds, sometimes even after they had both fallen asleep; he would find her there, like a ribbon on the edge of the bed, as he was getting dressed. It was because of Anna, he remembered, they still had that large screen in their room. "Well, you can keep your mother warm, then. George, you get William and the others to look after you. Martin, you make sure he has a big fire in his room; someone has to go out to the woodpile," he reminded them as he and William supported, or half carried, Anna up the steps; "we have to heat two more rooms. *Really* heat them."

In their room, John watched Edna begin undressing Anna. "My gowns will be too short for you," Edna wailed, looking over at John. "Anna won't mind, once she gets under the quilts, will you, Anna?" She shook her head no.

"John," Edna called, "I meant to ask about rounds to-morrow." "What?" He moved closer. Edna pretended to go to the chiffonier for something else. "I don't trust her; if she should wake up and I don't—" She broke off. "I'll have the children stand guard outside." "Don't let Ten get wind of this," she pleaded. "She'll know in an hour; don't ask me how, but she'll know. It's those bat ears of hers." "I wish she were better," Edna said. "It would help, but she's not, and that's that, and there's no point in exposing her to diphtheria in her condition." "I hope *she* goes along with that decision." John massaged the sides of his temples with both hands. "You're right. Christ, if she wants to see Anna there'll be no stopping it." "We'll worry about that tomorrow," Edna decided. "We might as well get a good night's rest. We can start worrying in the morning. We'll have time to make a profession of it, from the looks of it."

Edna settled into bed next to Anna. She tucked the comforter around her as tightly as she could. "Mother?" Anna suddenly said. "What, dear?" "I want my book." "What book?" *The Wedding Ring.* "All right," Edna said, getting up, sighing to herself; next she'd be asking for another drink of water. She opened the door and found herself staring into Ella's eyes. "Your sister," she told her, "wants her copy of *The Wedding Ring.*" "I'll get it," Ella said, going downstairs for it. "Thank you," Edna said, going back in. "Here's *The Wedding Ring,*" Edna said, giving it to her. Anna took it without a word, turned on her side facing Edna, and curled herself around the book as if it were a stuffed toy. "Are you ready to go to sleep now?" Edna asked from her side of the bed. "Yes, Mother." She sounded as if she had just learned to talk. This was more than shock, Edna was sure of that. She was wide awake for at least an hour after the sound of Anna's breathing told her she was really, finally asleep. Some household, Edna thought. If Ten wasn't expiring already, she would be when she got a sniff of this. Although, she thought, trying to keep her eyes open, Anna might present something of a challenge. But she was worse now than she had been before John came home. She fell asleep, dreading the morning. She missed John; she was amazed at how resentfully she noted the pressure of Anna's elbow. She was too old, she decided, to begin hoping for an unselfish nature.

Early the next morning, Edna awakened; outside, it was still dark. She could hear the muffled sounds of voices in the parlor downstairs; they were, she knew, talking about what must have happened in New Bedford. Her daughter was still sound asleep; she slid out of bed, reaching for her robe, opening her door a crack. Minnie was sitting on the chair. "Do you mind sitting here while I go down?" Edna whispered. Minnie shook her head no. Edna began stealing down the steps. John, William, Martin, and George were there; Ella was there, too. She noticed her suddenly in the dark corner. "Oh, good, you're here," John said; "we were just asking George about how things happened."

"Whole families were wiped out," he said; "I don't know why Anna didn't get it." John asked him who got sick first. "Minnie. She was feverish; she didn't want to do anything. Anna couldn't get her to play with her hoop outside; she didn't want her doll inside. She started complaining that reading gave her a headache and threw her book at Anna. Anna didn't know whether to spank her or call the doctor, so she didn't do either one. She didn't have a sore throat; she ate everything, even though she didn't eat much, so Anna really didn't think it was diphtheria. But then she started having trouble breathing, and Anna knew it was more than a cold. Then that membrane showed up and she could hardly get any air at all. But about six days after she was really sick, she seemed to be getting better, and Anna and Matthew thought there was no more danger for her. Anna, though, kept trying to remember something you told her about recovery being only an apparent recovery if she was still having trouble breathing, but they were both so happy, they didn't think too much about it.

"Then a few days went by, and she got weaker and weaker and could hardly breathe at all; near the end, it looked as if she gave up trying, and then Anna came in to bring her some chicken water to drink, and she didn't move, and when Anna felt her hand and it was cold and just fell back on the bed she started screaming, and Matthew ran in and got her. Well, it looked all right for Anna for a while; he kept on at her about how Minnie had gone on to blessings so rich they cannot be prepared for us in a day. He said she had special duties as a minister's wife; that they were the mirrors and in them men saw the beauties of God, and there were too many broken mirrors already. Blessed are they that mourn, for they shall be comforted; I don't know how he kept it up, because no matter what he said, at least at first, she kept saying, 'Why Minnie? Why Minnie?' It was enough to make a grown man cry. Well, I guess I did," he admitted, seeing all their eyes on him.

"But Matthew did go on, and he was feeling it just as much as she was, and I don't think he was really well just then, either. He said shared grief wedded hearts; he told her they would never really get over their deep griefs; that they would never be the same again now that this had happened. He said it was sinful to stop in the midst of life and sit down by the coffin and stay there while the rest of the world tried to lead its life, and it needed just as much help as it ever had. He told her if she kept up this way, she'd neglect him and little Matthew and then how would she feel? Going on that way was a perversion of life; and gradually, she started coming around. He reminded her of their family motto: 'Do Ye the Next Thynge.' He kept insisting there was never more than one next thing at a time; for instance, what did she want Matthew to eat, or didn't she care?

"So she went into the kitchen and told the cook what to make up for the day, crying the whole time. 'Iron sharpens iron,' he said; 'life sharpens life.' He quoted Scripture; he scolded; he petted her. 'Which of you, by being anxious, can add one cubit unto his stature?' He told her it was the character of the human mind not to be able to stay in suspense on any question for long; it had to decide at once. He told her she was trying to accept Minnie's death. That was why she kept asking, 'Why Minnie?' He told her about a man he had visited on his deathbed who reminded him of her and who died saying, 'In all my sorrows, I had not a right sorrow.'

"Then he took another tack and told her the human mind was made in such a way that when anything took hold of it, anything strong in its emotional impact, such as the loss they had just suffered, it operated immediately on the body and could sometimes produce strange phys-

ical sensations, even illnesses. He said he'd seen cases
where emotions disrupted the senses, and everything was
illusion and more illusion, and then what kind of mother
could she be to her living child? He said he could understand why she wouldn't care about him, but he couldn't
understand why she didn't care about her own son. He
said it was universally true that when she felt her entire
existence depended on God, she would begin to improve.
She had to believe this was God's will; she had to be able
to say, 'It is the Lord's work and it is marvelous in our
eyes."

"Well, she looked at him as if he were the devil himself, and then she started sobbing into his vest, and after
that, she walked around white as a winding sheet, but
every day she was getting more and more normal; they
spent hours talking. I used to drop by all the time and
they'd be talking, talking, talking. Well, I went over with
Ellen, that's my wife, you know, and after about a week
she seemed on the way back. She wasn't exactly smiling
and laughing, but she was a lot better than we thought
she'd be. Matthew, he kept the funeral service simple and
quick as he could, without making it look as if they were
trying to throw the coffin in. There were wild flowers all
over the coffin; they kept the casket open. I guess they
had to: everyone was muttering about what a sin it would
be to close it and deprive them of a chance to say goodbye to the dear child. There was an organ playing, no
hymns, nothing like that. Then there was a procession to
the cemetery. We went with them, and Matthew's father
and Mrs. Wade. Everyone else had to stay behind; I
don't know how he made that clear, but he did. Matthew
said something like 'Our Heavenly Father, we commend
this sinner to thy care, secure in our hopes she will reach
that golden shore and will live forever in thy abounding
grace.'

"He skipped a eulogy. I guess you don't really have to
have them. Then he took Anna home with his father,
and Ellen and I, we stayed after to see them lower the
casket; they hadn't dug out the hole yet, just a little dent
in the ground. It was a small box; it gave me the shudders, it was so small. I don't know why we stayed there,
watching them dig out the grave. I can't think I'll ever
hear anything worse than the sound of earth hitting that

coffin, and then they were clumsy; you know those things are hard to handle? I never thought about any of it before. They bumped poor Minnie back and forth; God only knows what she looked like in there when they finally got the thing down to the bottom.

"Well, back at their house, it wasn't so bad. The people turned out better than I thought. The house was filled up with them and their stews and casseroles and breads. I never saw so much food in my life. It was a regular bounty; Thanksgiving couldn't come up to it. And there was one lady who told her she didn't think she'd live after her husband died, but now she slept in an attic room in the turret on the north side, and there was a new star there she'd never seen before, and it made her feel so much better, she said; she felt as if it were taking care of her, you know, watching over her somehow. That gave Matthew a rest, because they kept telling her things like that, and she started eating, and pretty soon it was shorter times before she closeted herself up in her room, so that was just when Matthew came down with it."

He looked at their horrified faces from out of a nightmare of his own. "This is one story I'd like to change around," he pleaded, almost as if they were going to blame him. "George," Bill said, "you did all you could with her. With all of them. Everyone knows it. I mean, we won't chop your head off like they used to chop off heads of messengers who brought bad news." "They really did that?" George asked. "A long time ago," Ella said. "Well, I guess I feel better," George admitted, rubbing the back of his neck.

"I guess I better get on with what happened to Matthew?" he asked, almost imploring them to release him from his task. "I think so," Edna said gently. "Well, right after he preached a sermon about how Christians were tried in the crucible of suffering, it was all about Job, he came home and said something about how he was tired out from shouting over the voices of the congregation, and the next thing Anna knew, he was burning up with fever. She knew how to take a pulse, I guess, and she sent for the doctor, and she kept wailing about how she wished her father were there; if you were there," he said to John, "she was sure everything would be all right. Then she sent one of the servants over to get Ellen and me and we went right over. I don't know why we were so sure we'd never get it, but I thought Ma told me I had it, a mild case of it, or something like that, and Ellen said she'd been exposed a lot." "You had it," John said.

"When we got there, things were in a pretty bad way. There was no getting Anna from his bed, and I can't say I blame her, either. I never saw anything like it. The doctor there said something about a major membrane and that it was going across the windpipe. I never saw," he said painfully, "anyone fight so hard to breathe. Just to breathe. He would seem to give it up, and then he'd see Anna and start in fighting, just to get some air. It was like watching someone drown, and there wasn't even any water." John nodded; he had paled. "Then he got delirious; he tried saying things like 'We'll meet again'; I think he was trying to sing 'Amazing Grace' and 'Nearer My God to Thee.' There was something about a good fight." George flushed. "I think he had something else in mind," John said.

"Well, then he stopped talking altogether, and he just got bluer and bluer as if someone was painting him over. His eyes started bulging right out of his head; Minnie"— George looked at his sister piteously—"he looked just like those frogs we used to go after in Coe's Pond." His sister shivered. "Well, by that time, Ellen wouldn't think of leaving the house, even if she didn't get along with some of the biddies there, and then it seemed like he couldn't see us at all. Well, it must have been toward two, we heard the clock striking. It was late at night, anyhow, and his head and shoulders just pulled back on the bed, and his hands kept on twitching like he couldn't stop them. I guess Ellen thought he was trying to get up, but all of a sudden he was lying there relaxed as could be and his face wasn't as livid and it took all of us a time to know he was dead. Well, that was when the trouble really started with Anna.

"Well, we could talk to her the way he did, and Ellen said something about how time made everything better, and that just sent her off into hysterics, and then old Mr. Hewitt, he said something about how only Catholics had hysterics and she picked up a basin from the bed next to Matthew's—she'd been sleeping there—and threw it on the floor. I think she wanted to throw it at him, but she didn't have the strength. Anyway, all she got by it was a good cut on her leg when a piece of the glass jumped up at her, and then she got into fits over whether she had cut Matthew's skin, and she had to look all over to make sure she hadn't and we didn't see what difference it made. By the time the undertakers had the sawhorses set up in the parlor, and the casket on them, she was trying to climb in first, saying she'd always gotten into bed first, and insisting he really wasn't dead, and no matter how many times we took her in to see him and got her to take his pulse, she kept on about it, how he wasn't really dead. He just seemed dead. She was going to get her book about people who had been buried alive; she wouldn't permit him to be buried for five days.

"She made us all swear that no matter what happened to her they wouldn't bury him for five days. She wanted to read to us from some terrible book about the people who were buried alive; she went on about how she had clippings about people buried like that, and they were all new; the clippings, I mean. I don't know how it happened, because half of the pillars of the church were there holding up the building, but she actually managed to climb into the casket on top of him and we found her curled up on her side, and when we pulled her out, dragged her, is more like it, she let out this shriek. I never heard the like of it even from an animal in a trap. I guess that was what she was. But even when we first got her to go to the sleigh, we got her in because she didn't think he was dead and she believed us when we told her Matthew wanted her to go home. Before, just as we were leaving the house, she said, 'The Lord giveth and the Lord taketh away,' and all of a sudden she grabbed on to the rose bush. I think she was trying to pull it up but she cut up her hand pretty bad; anyway, I bandaged it. I'm pretty good at it, but someone should look at it. Her left hand," he added, conscientiously.

"So that's what it was," Edna said; "I thought she'd tried something." "Just with the rose bush," George said, managing a smile. "Do you think," John asked, "she still thinks he's alive?" George thought; it was the longest time, William decided, he'd ever seen his brother keep quiet. "I think so," he finally said; "we couldn't get Matthew's eyes closed and she kept trying to talk to him and she didn't even believe he was dead once he was in the casket, and then we had to get her out of there so fast she didn't even see the funeral. I think she believes it: that he's still alive." Edna and John looked at each other. "What about little Mat?" Edna asked after a pause; "did she mention him?" She didn't even seem to know he was alive." "Well, she'll remember soon enough," John predicted; "what are we going to do with her?" No one spoke. "Fine," Edna said; "just fine." Ten's handbell suddenly rang. "I'll go," Edna told them, getting up.

"What's all this about Anna?" Ten asked. Since last night, she seemed nearly recovered. "Anna?" "Anna, your daughter; I know she's here. I heard her, or someone talking about her. Who died?" "Her husband and Minnie." "Oh, Lord," Ten sighed; "that's not right. They just began, and I'm still here bothering everyone to death. Minnie, too?" "Minnie first." "Get Anna down here." "Oh, Ten, you're hardly in the bloom of health and she's a wreck; you can't take her on, not now." "Down here, now," Ten answered firmly. "She's sleeping." "Wake her up," the old woman said implacably. "She *needs* the sleep." "We'll all have plenty of time for sleep soon enough. Now don't you start," she warned, noticing the brightness in Edna's eyes; "just get up there and wake her up. Wait," she ordered; "what about the little boy?" "They had to leave him behind with the neighbors; George Moffat brought her home. He said the little boy didn't look any too well, either." "He's gone, that's for sure." "Don't say that!" "The truth is the truth," Ten answered flatly; "go on, get her down here."

"Did she bring anything with her," she heard John ask as she went through the room. "We didn't have time for packing. She took a book and a picture of Minnie and another of herself and Matthew; that's all there is. The people there promised to send pictures of all the family in their caskets, and all the other pictures, too. That cheered her up some, for about one second, I'd guess." Edna went upstairs. She had no idea why she listened to Ten, especially now. Almost eighty-one, probably dying herself; why did she believe Ten's mind was what it had been? Still, she trusted her more than anyone else in the world, and if Anna were a colt, Ten would be the only one to break her in. Edna awakened Anna and led her down; it was like leading one of the dear beloved stuffed ones, that was how much human response she gave. "Aunt Ten wants to see you," she kept repeating as they descended. "Aunt Ten?" Anna finally said; "Aunt Ten?" "That's right, dear. How many aunts do you have?" Anna appeared to nod. "Well, here we are," Edna told Ten, glaring at her in her bed, settling her daughter on the chair near the bed. "You can go out now," Ten told Edna. "Ten, for heaven's sake!" "You have so much to do; I'm surprised I have to remind you." "John is in the next room; don't worry, dear. I'm leaving."

"I know all about it," Ten said at once, looking straight at Anna. "No, you don't," Anna said slowly, as if just regaining her voice; "you don't know that Matthew's not dead." "Of course he's not; he's waiting for you on the other shore." "He's waiting for me *here*." "You know more about those things than I do," Ten answered from her pillow; "the golden shore may be right here somewhere." Anna's eyes suddenly seemed to focus. "Just what did you do out there to make them drag you home in a storm?" "Nothing." "Nothing?" Ten asked, raising her eyebrows. "They made a fuss over some things." "What things?" "My climbing into the casket with Matthew. He wasn't dead." "Whether he was or not, people don't climb into other people's caskets; it simply isn't done. What awful manners." "I'm sorry"; Anna blushed. "You ought to be. The people in that crazy town probably think Matthew put vulgar ideas like that into your head." "They wouldn't." "Well, were you married to a minister or not? You know they will. And *where* is little Mat?" she asked severely. "Someone took him." "Took him. Who? The Gypsies?" "The neighbors." "Aren't you even interested?" "Of course," Anna mumbled. "Can't you talk any faster?" Ten asked, irritated; "I'm not going to live long enough to hear you finish these sentences." "What's wrong with you?" Anna asked, her attention seeming to return suddenly, a falcon settling on its master's glove. "Acute congestion of the lungs, and of course, my age is against me; I'm so young.

"Why isn't little Mat here?" "They wouldn't let him go; in case he had the disease; they weren't too happy about my leaving, either, but George made them." "How?"

"He shot out some people's hats; I suppose it looked odd. I didn't seem to notice it at the time, the way their hats flew off their heads, and the way they started walking backwards. It looked so funny, as if everything were going backwards, as if someone was winding up my life, back to the beginning, you know. It did look funny." "Are you planning on going completely mad?" Ten asked, as if that were an ordinary question. Anna didn't answer. "You know," Ten continued, "in the book I gave you, it says, 'A wife may be supplied, but a mother cannot.' You still have one child to account for. Of course, if you don't care . . ." "I do care," Anna burst out passionately. "Then I suppose your behavior better show it. Not to mention the rest of your family; they have me to worry about, and now you, and your father has gone through tortures with that terrible trial and your mother suffers right along with him *and* I know all about you, miss. Every time you see one of your nieces, you're going to start in on yourself about why theirs are alive and yours isn't, and you'll have yourself to answer to if anything goes wrong here, I can tell you. You're not going to be selfish enough to kill me off before it's absolutely necessary to speed me on, are you?" "Of course not," Anna said slowly.

"Well, then, get out there and tell them how long you think it will take you to get over it, and how you'll seem pretty strange from time to time, but that you're going to try and stay here instead of in the Retreat. Can you do that?" "I don't know." "What!" Ten exclaimed in astonishment. "Yes, yes, I can," Anna said more quickly. "Well, before you go," Ten said, "I want to remind you about part of *The Wedding Ring*. Did you like that book?" "We lived by it." "Then this should mean something to you," Ten said sternly; "unless I've been taken in by some pretty fancy hypocrisy of yours. 'The worm at the core of the Christian,' " she quoted. " 'Those married pairs that live as remembering they must part again, and give an account of how they treat themselves and each other, shall, at the day of their death, be admitted to the glorious espousals, and then, when they shall live again, be married to the Lord and partake of his glories.' Did you and Matthew live that way? Was Matthew aware that he might have to part from you?" "He always said so.

Especially when we went to tend sick people and when there were epidemics." "And you?" Anna didn't answer. "*You*," Ten said accusingly, "just forgot that part; I know all about it. Well, you better start thinking it over now. As for me," she said, almost smug, "I intend to meet Ed any minute."

"You're supposed to be prepared to meet your maker." "Same thing," Ten answered, suddenly tired; "get out there and make your speech or I'll take care of you later." To the astonishment of the collected family, Anna promptly went out and did what she was told. They were, of course, worried about what she meant by how her behavior would, from time to time, seem strange, and what she meant when she said she would try to stay out of the Retreat, but then, they decided after she went back up to Edna's room, she seemed realistic about her state, and was talking and acting something like herself; that was more than they expected. "Well, that's Ten's work," Edna sighed.

"What does she mean about getting on with her work?" Ella asked; she had changed places with Minnie, but now it seemed they might be able to suspend guard duty outside Anna's door. "She's been doing some kind of research on immortality and cell life; and she thinks she's gotten to the stage where she can begin theorizing on the basis of her evidence." "They should be some theories," Ella said sarcastically. "As long as they keep her busy, I can't say I care," Edna said, getting up; she was going in to see Ten.

"Well, you did it," she said, sitting down next to her bed, taking her thin hand. "For a while; there's no point in fooling ourselves. She's as much on the edge as I am, maybe more." Edna was chilled. "But the longer she keeps going, the better chance she has," Ten said; *"she's young."* Edna sat quietly, thinking things over. Why, she wondered, did she worry herself about Ten's mind? It was strong enough, she sometimes thought, to survive death itself. "You know, Edna," Ten said after a while, grinning affectionately, "you made me make the wrong promises. You should have gotten me to promise to live as long as Anna." "Promise now," Edna asked, half teasing, half serious. "I'll try," Ten said wearily; "although I'd just as soon get it over with. It's not such nice times hearing about life like Polonius through a tapestry." "It's better than not hearing at all." "Sometimes," Ten reflected, "I'm afraid I'll have the bad luck to hear what goes on even if I'm buried twelve feet deep." "Don't be so pessimistic." "Well, I'm getting sleepy. Just promise *me* you'll make the most of Anna's good behavior while it lasts." "Don't you think it will?" "I don't have a Ouija board; promise." "I promise," Edna said; "I also promise to let you get some sleep." "Good," Ten answered, closing her eyes.

In the next two weeks, Anna seemed better than any dared hope. The first week, she either kept to her room or sat next to Ten's bed. This caused no little concern amidst the rest of the family. Edna finally took her aside and warned her they had given up sitting with Ten because her aunt was afraid they were really beginning a death watch early. But she must have been standing too near Ten's door when she spoke, because immediately there was the sound of the handbell, and when Edna went in, Ten told her to let Anna come in and sit whenever she wanted to; Anna might not know it, she told Edna, but *she* was watching *her*. Anna's visits were more or less perpetual, although no one had the slightest idea of what passed between them. Eventually, they began to notice Anna's visits did not vary in frequency with the state of Ten's health; she took up her post regularly as a trained nurse whether Ten was feverish and incapable of speaking or apparently healthy except for her inability to leave her bed.

The visits, too, seemed beneficial for both of them; John and the others saw no medical reason to limit them, much less stop them. As John had guessed, Ten spent a great deal of strength giving Anna good tongue lashings, and consequently, Anna felt free to reveal her feelings to Ten. In spite of her sense that her state of mind was a special one, somehow more elevated than that of others, Anna still knew, somehow, that self-criticism was no longer possible to her, and without any awareness of it, turned her conscience over to Ten, who lectured her as part of herself.

Gradually, largely thanks to Ten's indefatigable taunting, she began to accept the retinue of children under the care of their various nursemaids, and even to take an in-

terest in one of Minnie's children. She particularly liked
Annie, who was six, and Ella's oldest girl, Wilma, who
was nine. Annie resembled Minnie, her mother, and had
the same sweet, unthinking disposition. There was little
difference, Anna thought, between Annie and her pet
puppy, both of whom climbed into her lap and dispensed
affection as if from the heavenly source itself, while
Wilma, at nine, already reminded her of her sister Ella.
She was quick, intelligent, but she had the Moffat streak;
she was mercurial. Anna could not remember what she
said to her after she had been home a week, but whatever
it was, it sent Wilma off to her room in tears, and it took
poor Anna more than two hours to coax her out, and
then, when she did, she found Wilma, in a fit of temper,
had broken the head of her favorite doll, and was inconsolable over that loss, even though, she told her aunt,
she knew she ought not to be because she did it, and it
was only what she deserved. Slowly, Anna's maternal feelings began asserting themselves like unruly weeds in an
untended garden in strange soil, as Annie persisted in
climbing all over her as if she were some kind of tree. She
was spending, as the family noted, less and less time in
her room.

Edna unwittingly caused things to take a sharp turn
for the better. "You know," she said one evening, looking
up from *The Ladies' Home Journal;* "we've never tried
any of these games they say are so good for families."
"Which ones?" John asked; "which ones would you suggest?" "Oh, I don't know," Edna answered, without lifting her eyes from the page, "but there's one they're describing again; it sounds like the one Mother and Ten
used to talk about playing when they were in school."
She went on with her reading, unaware anyone was paying her the slightest attention. "Well, what game *is* it,
Edna?" John finally asked. "Game?" Edna said, looking
up, confused; "have all of you been waiting for an answer all this time?"

"What game did Ten and your mother play at school?"
Minnie asked; "that's what we want to know." "Oh, I'm
sorry; I've gotten into the habit of saying things without
expecting any answer at all." John smiled at the others;
that comment, coming from anyone else, would sound like
criticism or, at the very least, self-pity. "It's just *tableaux*

vivants," Edna told them; "everyone dressing up like statues, or impersonating objects, or scenes, famous paintings, scenes from plays, things like that. Mother and Ten said they wrapped themselves in brown paper and had pin-on knots so they could pretend to be trees, but they thought they made a very bad choice because their arms ached for weeks afterwards." "That might not be a bad game for the children," Ella said. "It sounds like a great deal of work," Edna answered, going back to her reading. "Still," Ella persisted, "it would be fun for them; they could dress up and pretend to be whoever they wanted to be. They like costumes, and they're all so dramatic." "Yes, but who's going to do all the work?" Edna asked. "I will," Anna volunteered. "You?" Edna asked, incredulous. "I don't have much else to do." "Well," Ella said, "don't suggest it unless you intend to go through with it; they won't give you an instant's peace once you mention it. I've never seen such memories." "I'll go through with it," Anna promised.

From the complaints which came pouring in from Amos by the next day, it was apparent Anna did, indeed, mean business. "What does she need with all those bathtubs?" Amos demanded; "she has all my boys dragging out used tubs and troughs, and now she wants us off to the dump to find more. What's she doing, holding baptism services in the snow?" "She's having some kind of theatrical for the children," Bridget's quavery voice explained. "Very exciting it should be," Amos snorted, "what with everyone sitting around in tubs looking at each other. Doesn't even sound decent." "Well, do as she says," John said. "Even about the whitewash?" "The whitewash? What whitewash?" Edna asked. "She wants about eight wagons of whitewash and I don't know how many yards of white cloth and how many pounds of flour." "Fifteen," Bridget volunteered. "Perhaps she intends to make a soup of them," Edna suggested; "the bathtubs for the pots, and the whitewash and flour for the white sauce. The children for the dumplings." "That sounds dull enough," Amos grunted. "I was only joking; I wonder what the gauze is for, though." "Perhaps," John suggested, "she's going to make mummies out of them." "Mummies in bathtubs?" Edna asked, puzzled.

During the week, more and more objects began disappearing from the house. One night, Edna mentioned at dinner that she was missing two pairs of hose, although she never kept good track of them, but still, she was sure she had set these aside because they were particularly warm. This brought on a storm of complaints about other missing objects. Ella said one of the children's white summer caps had disappeared from the top of the chiffonier where she left it for mending; John said he was missing two sets of long underwear, which he was sorry to have to mention at the table, whereupon William and Martin felt free to report the same loss.

When the subject was mentioned to the children, they could extract no information, although they did produce convulsions of giggles. Finally, they all concluded the mysterious case of the disappearing objects had something to do with the coming theatricals they were all in such a fever about. "I hope this lasts," John sighed as they were getting into bed one night, "although I can tell you," he said, looking ruefully at the next day's clothes laid out on the chair, "I for one will be a happy man when they present the results of their efforts and I can go about dressed decently again. It's a good thing we don't wear white suits or all the men on the place would be in robes all day." "Which reminds me," Edna said, removing her dress, "there are some sheets missing as well." "What next? I suppose," he considered as Edna slid in beside him, "losing one's underwear is a small price to pay for someone's sanity." "That depends on where you lose it, and whose sanity you're speaking of." If she could joke like that, John thought, things were certainly on the mend.

But two days later, George came riding up to the house just at dark. Where was Anna? That was the first thing he asked. She was out in the old barn, rehearsing with the children, they told him; they were putting on a play. "I have more bad news," he said hopelessly. He didn't seem, John observed, able to rid himself of the idea he was responsible for bad news. "What now?" Edna asked; she had gone pale as the snow they stood in. "Little Matthew died five days ago: of diphtheria. They said it was a terrible case and the Perkinses, the people who kept him, are beside themselves; they keep saying Anna will blame them all for it and they did the best they could, but the child was worse than the father. That was what they said." "When did you find out?" John asked. "When Ellen got here; about twenty minutes ago. She brought this packet. Mrs. Perkins gave it to her."

It was the size of a small box, about six by four inches, but, Edna realized, it wasn't a box; the contents seemed to slide against one another. "Family pictures," George said, noticing her preoccupation. "They took death portraits of Matthew and little Mat. I don't know what you want to do with them." "It's her right to have them," John insisted, sensing the opposition in the air; "she doesn't have anything else left of them." "They're not all photographs of the family, at least that's what Ellen said. The Perkinses took some pictures of their old house and some of the rooms; they didn't imagine she'd want to come back." "I suppose the funeral is already over?" Edna said. "It's been five days," George said simply. Edna and John nodded. "I'm sorry you had to go through all this, especially," John told George, "under the circumstances."

In the bright light of the snow, reflecting back on their faces in the dark as if they stood on the light, not under it, they could see his dark flush. "My duties in that line are over now; she'll never remarry. It's probably just as well," he added after a while. "At least the way things have turned out," Edna said. She meant to remind him, he knew, he was now a married man, although she doubted if that would stop him if he thought he still had hope. But then, she didn't know; her sureties about people were disappearing faster than objects in the house. "Should we look at the pictures first?" Edna asked, trying to change the subject. "That," George agreed, "might be a good idea."

That night, after Anna had gone to sleep, they had the first conference in a long time in the pre-Revolutionary wing, although this one, everyone thought, was more hectic than the others. There were forever two people coming and going, one to sit outside Ten's room in the parlor across the hall, another to sit at the foot of the main stairs should Anna wake and begin looking for them. They all agreed they might as well let Anna sleep; she would be better off hearing this news after a good night's rest. Then they took out the pictures and began passing them around. The first one was a shock to everyone. The Perkinses had called in the Donner Brothers, photographers famous enough so that John knew of them. It was a photograph of little Matthew; he had been photographed in his burial robes.

John saw it first. The child seemed to be floating; the hem of its garment seemed, where it folded, to rise out of the picture. The length of the child's body, almost at a forty-five-degree angle to the rectangular lines of the picture, as if defying gravity, lay back against black space. He supposed the photographers wanted to suggest the rising movement of the spirit was already taking place. But what struck him most forcibly was the length of the robes; they were so long for the body. They made the child appear almost the size of an adult, and that was almost the saddest part: the little hands, resting at the sides, making the child appear as if he had died a midget who had not had time to grow into his appointed destiny. The child's eyes were closed, but his mouth, indeed his whole expression, seemed to express annoyance, if not fury, at what had happened. And the face seemed so much deader than the hands; his little nose was so sharp. His bottom lip had sunk so far beneath his upper one. That was probably what gave him such a disapproving expression.

The more he looked at it, the more it seemed as if someone had pushed the little head back at an unnatural angle to capture the features clearly; or perhaps, John thought, that was a result of the stiffening sometimes taking place at death. Still, he wondered, examining the photograph more closely, the body usually relaxed at the moment of death. This would disturb Anna; and why not? It was disturbing him. Somehow, the photographer had contrived to make it look as if the infant was looking for someone through closed eyes, and had shut them in annoyance at the sight of the perpetually empty, perpetually disappointing room. Probably the child had seen heaven and this was his expression. His little shoulder looked so stiff and small, even with its padding, as he floated there on the dark waters. Well, he thought, finally passing the picture on, parting with it as sadly as he would have the body of one of his own children. It was, in a way, part of the body of one of his own children.

He began looking at the other pictures; the Perkinses had evidently arranged them so the most recent ones were on the top; going through them was like going back in time, to some impossible place which had been forever changed. It was still marked on the maps, but it was no longer there. There was a picture of Matthew's funeral cross; the people had evidently carved it from a tree. It was heavily decorated. The longer he peered at it, the more he saw. It was odd that the same process of examining the living should apply so closely to observing things of the dead. It had taken him some time to notice the little white paper silhouette of Matthew's body at its apex, its arms raised imploringly toward God. Beneath the crown on which that stood was a round plaque bearing the inscription "God is light"; the horizontal bars of the cross were covered with wild flowers of every kind. He supposed they were dried, kept by the undertaker for such occasions, these deaths in winter. There were other objects whose meaning he could not find, and he supposed he never would, since none of them would ask Anna, although she might volunteer the information, but he doubted it. One of them, he concluded, must represent the fount of life; the rest, as far as he could see, appeared to be tributary baskets. Some peeped out from behind the cross as if to say there were so many of them they could barely be contained.

Next came Matthew's death portrait, his face reposing in its coffin, looking exactly as it had in life. He wished it had changed. The photograph, he thought, shaking his head, made it appear as if they had indeed placed a living man in the casket.

His eyes were open under their heavily hooded brows; in death, his face had relaxed into its habitual expression. The eyes, the mouth, seemed smiling at something; the high forehead amused at the doings of the world. Yes, the mouth was definitely puckered in an incipient smile. If he had seen heaven, John thought, he had definitely been more pleased with it than his little son had been. His beard was full and neat; they must have combed it. John wondered when he had decided to shave all but his chin. He remembered him more heavily bearded. In the next picture, he was standing, much as John remembered him, his arm on a chair, the same semi-serious expression.

Then came a series of small pictures of Anna. In the first, she was holding up little Minnie. The child, John thought, looked fat enough for slaughtering. Anna was beaming into the camera, but there was a stiffness about her all the same; from the position of *her* hands, it was evident she feared dropping the child. He could not make out what scene they had been photographed against; he wondered about it, if it gave any clue to what was coming. Well, he was getting on, too; he was beginning to think like his sister. Next came a tintype of Anna, sitting on a chair, but leaning toward little Minnie, who stood with her hands touching her mother's skirt, seriously pushing her little head forward like a chicken. She did look exactly like her mother at her age. He had forgotten Anna's fat little cheeks.

Then came a picture of Anna holding to a chair, hair parted in the middle, her face unusually full; she was obviously about to give birth to Matthew. He had no idea she had been so large. Then little Minnie standing alone in a fancy white hat, matching collar, and crocheted muff, which looped across her neck; the arm of the chair came most of the way up to her shoulders; Minnie leaning seductively against a chair, dressed in white, her black curls pulled back with a bow; one could already tell what she would look like as a young woman, one foot poised, tiptoe, in back of the other, her head resting on her extended arm, her arm resting on the chair's arm; Minnie in a gingham dress with flounces, her hair parted in the middle and put up, her skirt flounced; Matthew sitting in his mother's embrace; little Matthew sitting gingerly on a stool carefully placed against the wall; he was still in skirts, much too young for pants, his hair still long; finally a picture of the two children together, Minnie on the edge of a love seat, leaning sulkily toward her younger brother, collapsed plumply against the softer, unholstered arm of his sister's chair; a sepulchral picture of Anna, evidently slipped in at the wrong place, wrapped in a black shawl, her eyes so prominent and deep-set they seemed to have taken possession of her face, almost separate, alien beings; someone must have taken that picture while she was sitting at Matthew's bedside. Someone who knew the outcome and was not surprised. He wondered who it had been. There was a small picture of Ten, wearing her lace cap with its lace streamers, glaring, he supposed, at Anna, who was forever persuading her to sit for her portrait. Ten *must* have been angry, John thought, to have been photographed with her spectacles on, although, he saw, she had put on her best earrings.

Well, he supposed he had mustered the courage to go on to the larger pictures. There was one of Minnie sitting in a porcelain bowl; she must have been taking a bath when they decided to move her to the top of the piano and its shawl and photograph her. She wore a little chain of black beads, almost entirely hidden by the folds of her fat neck, and a nipple in her mouth, a long cord of some kind attached to one end, the other end fastening to her toe. Then a photograph of the two children in little Matthew's wicker pram, Minnie staring out in amusement, biting her lower lip, Matthew looking uncomfortable, and no wonder, John thought, catching sight of the pillow holding him upright, his little hand clutching the braided edge of the carriage. They were posed before a gate and some steps, something, he supposed, meant to represent a trumpet vine, but bearing a far greater resemblance to a huge snake, twining up its height. He supposed there was no clue in that backdrop, no clue to anything.

A picture of Anna in her own living room, amazingly elegant in the plainer style she must have adopted once she fully realized she was indeed a minister's wife. The velvet of her basque looked soft enough to touch. He realized he had been examining the picture of his daughter as if she was already dead. Then Matthew in his fireman's uniform; that must have been before he realized *he* was a minister. A picture of old man Hewitt, who had grown so old the flesh of his face resembled parchment soaked and permitted to dry, and the familiar androgynous look of one his age; a funeral portrait of Matthew's mother set behind a frame of crossed iron bars forming a rectangle, live flowers pressed behind it. One tulip in the left-hand corner looked especially beautiful. Matthew, he thought, had been fortunate in avoiding inheriting her prominent chin.

Anna posed with a tiny basket next to the expected granite fence with its dead ivy; she looked so young and so happy. So young, and she must have been married two years, and with no idea that tiny basket would be the proper size to hold her life. Anna in a white dress holding her baptism certificate; that was before she married. He recognized the room; that must have been taken at Mr. Siddons'. And the elegance of the dress; that meant Edith somewhere about. Anna would never have permitted them to seal her up in gloves and bows at home that way. A picture of Ella, Anna, and Lettie and three of their school friends; that had been taken in their own parlor, Anna sitting on the floor with Ella; Lettie, naturally, sitting on a chair smack in the middle of the picture; a picture of some friends of Anna's, the Perkinses, and Mrs. Perkins' mother, the two women sitting on mock stones, Mrs. Perkins holding their pride and joy, the famous Perkins parrot. The older Mrs. Perkins bore a startling resemblance to Ten. He wondered if that drew her to them so quickly when she usually kept her distance even after years passed.

More pictures of the children, Matthew resembling a driveling idiot, one finger in his mouth, slumped on something resembling a tombstone; it must be a fence post; Minnie sulkily sitting beside him. Then a picture of the two children: they had evidently grown old enough to understand and resemble one another; then a series of family pictures. They began, he realized, after Ella and Minnie had begun their visits. Six children in one picture, and all staying still; that *must* have been *someone's* moral triumph. Of course. Those were Ella's children. That probably accounted for it. One of Anna and Matthew with their two children, and the first two of Minnie's; it had never struck him before how much Minnie's daughter resembled her; how beautiful both of them were. He would have to say something to Minnie; it was so easy to take these things for granted. The child lay back against Anna like the happiest, most relaxed little thing in the world, as if her bones had softened out of pure affection, she looked so fluid; yes, she was her mother all over again.

Then a tintype of Anna and Lettie; it must have been taken on one of Lettie's rare visits home. She and Anna had covered themselves with every kind of flower imaginable. The brims of their hats were weighed down with them. They wore garlands around their necks. There were garlands hung at an angle from shoulder to waist. Lettie was facing the camera. Unfortunately, she had placed the white flowers so they resembled horns. She had one hand on her hip. Anna was holding one flower as if to smell it, her other hand full of flowers; *she* had been picking them to take home to her room. She could look at them for hours. As for Lettie, they could blacken and die the instant they finished adorning her. He supposed it had been Lettie's idea, a Queen of the May picture, with Anna, of course, the attendant. Then a picture of George, timidly holding his hat, posed in a studio as if about to enter a gate in a stone wall and go into a garden, but stopping just short; well, *that* had turned out to be prophetic. He sighed; he would have to look at the rest later.

He looked wakefully around the family circle and the expressions flickering over their faces, as if they sat before a fire of every human emotion. "I had no idea she had such a collection," Ella murmured. She had stopped at one of them; he wished he knew what had caught her, but he couldn't see. "She was always so sentimental," Ella said, with shining eyes. She was doing it, too, he thought, disturbed: talking about Anna as if she were already gone. Still, it was nothing but the influence of the pictures. He became aware of Edna's hand pressing on his. "All right, old thing," she whispered. "The crones are going up to bed," he said, getting up; "the rest of you go, too." "We'll stay here and talk a while," Martin answered, his voice smothered. The rest nodded agreement. They ought to leave them to their own horrors, John thought; it was all different to them, so much newer. Probably to Edna it was, too. "Well, Edna?" John said questioningly as they got back into bed. "You'd think disaster would get tired of us," she said, promptly bursting into tears. Now she would cry herself to sleep. In anticipation, he settled himself as comfortably as he could. The first rays of morning were already creeping in through the curtains.

In the morning, they broke the news to Anna. "I thought as much." That was all she said. They all looked at each other; everyone would have preferred hysterics. "If you will excuse me," she said, disappearing. They knew, from the fall of the latch on the door, she had gone in to see Ten. "It's one of her good days," John said aloud. "We've been lucky that way, at least," Edna said. "We can't count on it; it's like counting on good weather in the wrong season." Edna nodded miserably.

"Well," Ten was asking Anna, "what is it that's so bad about this one?" "This one?" "Yes, this one; you're not even crying. That means it's worse." "I should have been there." "Why? So you could have come down with the disease and gotten buried with him?" "Yes," Anna answered, her voice flat. "Do you think of no one but yourself?" Ten asked; "don't you ever think of your family?" No response. "Well?" "Frankly, I don't really care much about anything." "Right now," her aunt scolded, "you're a juicy morsel for the devil. You keep thinking like that and you'll never meet them on the other shore." "They're there and I'm here," Anna said. "Would you like to have them in the family plot?" "Yes," Anna said, brightening. Why, Ten thought, hadn't that occurred to her before? "Do you think the old bat will object? Your father-in-law?" "Not if you pay the expenses," Anna said bitterly. "Go out and get your mother," Ten ordered her; "we'll make the necessary arrangements. Would you like to design the monuments?" "Oh yes," Anna breathed with relief. "I think that would be an excellent idea," Ten said. Edna came back with her; John was sent for. One of Amos' sons was dispatched to New Bedford to make traveling arrangements and procure the exhumation orders. Perhaps he had been wrong all along, John thought; perhaps Ten ought to have been the doctor.

The week ended peacefully; Friday night was to be the night of the theatricals and the children persuaded Anna, as the reigning genius, to take a part. At six o'clock they all gathered in the double parlors, emptied for the purpose; Amos had constructed an unnecessarily sturdy stage which ran the length of the room; the stage and the walls on the three sides of it were covered in white. "There are the sheets," Edna whispered, leaning over to John. A white curtain suddenly fell like a stone, covering the stage. "Someone must have lost their grip on a cord," Ella whispered to her mother; "that came down like a guillotine." Edna grinned back at her. They *had* missed something all these years, overlooking the more common amusements; they were all beside themselves waiting to see what the children came up with. Finally, the curtain jerked and flew up as if it were a bale of hay flying erratically into the loft.

Little Annie's head peeped out, then the rest of her flew onto the middle of the stage. One of the older children had given her a push; that was clear enough. She raised the enormous sign she carried. "Famous Historical Scenes." She peered at them to see if they had read it and ran back behind the curtain. It fell again with the same hysterical fervor. "Every time it does that," Minnie whispered to John, "it reminds me of a bird that's been shot." "They're not at their best with that curtain," John agreed.

An enormous commotion was now taking place behind it. "Get that thing off my foot!" one of the boys cried out passionately. "That," Ella said, "sounds like one of mine." "I can't stand on something so high," came another voice. "Will you get out of the way?" "Don't push me!" "They sound as if they're going to enact a war," Edna said. The complaints, accompanied by the sounds of dragging and pushing, and the familiar gruff voice of Amos, blended into the general chaos. "Will you stop?" they heard Amos roaring. "Will you move?" he thundered; "I'm not trying to run anyone down with this foolish tub." "This is better than the spectacle," William laughed, turning from his row. "I'm afraid it's going to go on as long, too," Martin said, turning to face them. "All right, all right," Amos roared; "Miss Anna, will you please stand aside? You're worse than the children. Stand still on that crazy thing." And so it went on for ten minutes. "You kicked me!" "I didn't!" "I didn't! She did!" "She doesn't have any shoes." "I hope they begin before they kill each other," Edna whispered into John's ear. "All right, get your own coats," Amos said; they heard his heavy boots stomping off the stage. "Wait!" they heard Wilma call out desperately; "you have to pull up the curtain." Inaudible mutterings from Amos. This time the curtain went up smoothly.

When it reached the top of the stage, the audience sat there transfixed. Anna had managed to make each of them look as if they were made of marble. Stockings were stretched over their faces and then powdered with flour.

All the children wore white wigs; any exposed parts of their body were painted over with a whitewash of flour and water. Everything on the stage was white and frozen as if they had all been caught in a storm of time, each scene blown in from a different time, preserved like the Egyptians, unable to get out. In one corner, two of Minnie's little ones were the two little princes in the tower, murdered in the tower by Ella's oldest boy. Another child stood over Annie, stabbing her in the bath. That, they knew, was supposed to represent the death of Marat.

Another of the children, draped in a Grecian toga, sat solemnly with a little cup, obviously hemlock, raised to his lips. For some reason, they were all in bathtubs, even little Socrates, although he must have been sitting on something placed inside it; probably, John thought, a keg. In the forefront of the stage, Wilma was poised, knife in hand; she, too, wore a toga and was stabbing a large doll representing Agamemnon. Anna stood on a pedestal, evidently meant to be rubbing her hands, since there was a little sign at the pedestal's bottom labeling her Lady Macbeth.

"John!" Edna gasped; "it's horrible! It's the most morbid thing I ever saw. All they need up there is a real body. How could she do this to the children?" "The children probably don't have any idea what this looks like." "They will later!" "Stop that whispering," he whispered back; "if we start clapping, they'll lower the curtain and get out of those shrouds." He and Edna began clapping noisily; the others, startled, jumped, then followed suit. The children jumped from their tubs, bowing and grinning. Little Annie turned away, took something from one of the tubs, and began throwing flowers at the audience. Everyone laughed nervously, trying to catch them. So this was what Anna had been up to all this time. Things were not going as well as they thought; that was obvious. She was going to persuade John to get at Anna's journals; *that* would take some doing. Perhaps they had made a mistake in allowing her to go about so, unobserved. Something had to be done.

The children were hopping all about, chattering about how they had painted each other, how they had stolen all the things. Hadn't they done a good job? Didn't they think they had learned a lot of history? Weren't they too amazing to believe? They couldn't have done it, they babbled on, without Anna, she was so clever. Little Jack, Ella's boy, suddenly turned on Wilma. "You were supposed to get her down," he said accusingly. They all turned back to the stage. Anna was standing still as if petrified. "Go on, Wilma," her brother said, giving her a push. "Come on, Aunt Anna," Wilma said, holding up a hand. Anna took it and stepped down. "I'm so sorry I forgot you," Wilma whimpered. "That's all right, dear," Anna reassured her. She sounded, Edna thought in a panic, perfectly normal. Yet Minnie told her that morning Anna left her door ajar, which she never did; Anna had a notebook in her lap and a gold pencil had fallen to the floor. She was turning over the pictures which George had brought as if they were cards in a deck, but she wasn't looking at them; she was just staring straight ahead, and when she got to the end of the series, she started over again.

Everyone finally got the children to bed, and then, as if by instinct, gathered in the parlor. There was no doubt of it; they all agreed something had to be done. "Minnie, please look out the door," Martin asked. "All clear," she reported. "I think John and I ought to get at her journals," Edna said. John looked pained; he did not disagree. "Well," Martin said finally, "I've never liked that sort of thing, but I don't see we have any choice." "It's the lesser of the evils," Ella agreed. No one had the slightest desire to ask what the greater evil might be. "When?" John asked. "Tomorrow," Edna answered. They all went to bed like mourners leaving a funeral.

John was still asleep when Edna woke up. She had no desire to get out of bed, as if doing so would mean remembering something better forgotten, an invading dream, which, by staying in bed, she could keep within the confines of a small space. She began, looking at John sleeping, to feel panic, an obsessive impulse to check, to see if he was still alive. Fortunately, he turned slightly in his sleep, moving his arm across his eyes.

She ought to be enjoying this sight, Edna scolded herself, her husband asleep after the sun was up, but as soon as she was up, there it was: the whole white snow-cold spectacle of the children, either dead or dying, killed or killing, frozen through time before their eyes, almost as if they had been used by the hand of the snow itself, purposely writing out some message about evil forces managing the world, as if, in some way, Anna sensed that each one of them was each other's destroyer, or, Edna thought, getting up, buttoning her black silk dress, that everyone obeyed forces beyond any control, which, in last night's indoor blizzard, happened to be Anna herself. Guilt, Edna decided, getting to the end of her basque buttons, beginning to hook it into her skirt, which, like a magic circle on the floor, she had been standing inside of. Anna must feel tremendous guilt. If that was all it was, Edna concluded, hoping against all convictions to the contrary, they might be able to do something with her. John was inventive; William very much so. They might be able to think of a thousand and one punishments which, disguised as good deeds to be done in the world, might keep Anna alive, sucking at her guilt like so many leeches.

The pendulum on her clock was swinging comfortably. It was almost nine. The performance, she thought, looking back at John, must have exhausted them all. She might as well start immediately, and with Anna's room. If they were going to make a felonious attempt on her journals, they had better have Anna used to their tripping in and out; they had allowed her too much privacy. "Oh, Mother," Anna said excitedly, without bothering to lean over the wing chair's arm to look at her, but recognizing her step, "the papers have something very exciting this morning." Probably another war, Edna thought. She sat down on the vanity bench near Anna's chair. "Sit on the bed; it's more comfortable," Anna instructed, without raising her eyes. Edna sighed and did so.

"Matthew wrote you about some of my experiments," she went right on, eyes glued to the paper, "and there's a minister in here who's come to some conclusions similar to mine." "What's it about?" Edna asked, trying not to sound as furious as she was. "The incarnation. He says that all Christianity must believe in the doctrine of incarnation, for it is a scientific fact supported by the authority of the Bible. I better read it to you. I don't want to get it wrong. 'In the thought of the older theology the process of incarnation was a purely mechanical one; it meant the arbitrary, miraculous coming of God in the flesh in the person of Jesus, that through this humiliation and sacrifice eternal life might be secured for humanity. In these days a larger meaning is placed upon the incarnation. It is now regarded as a more universal, a more eternal, a more natural process. We think of it'—this is the minister talking—'as the coming of God into the life of man from the very earliest days of conscious life as the inflowing of the Holy Spirit into the various channels of human activity; as the life of God welling up in human consciousness. Wherever there has been or is anything of truth, honesty, purity, and faithfulness, we see the process of incarnation at work.

" 'The great fact of religion is to be seen not alone in the personality of Christ; with greater or less conspicuousness it appears in every individual. It is not a miracle but a purely natural process, which was operating centuries before the advent of Jesus: God was in the world long before the Master came; the divine wisdom, intelligence, and love gradually developing in humanity through many prophets and nations.

" 'The incarnation is a growth, and therefore it is intimately associated with salvation. These are simply different words for the same fact, the realization of the life of God in the life of man. This view does not rob the man of Nazareth of any of his greatness or glory, he being the primary example of the ideal incarnation, the God-man of the ages. His splendid life must be referred to the fact that in him the incarnation had reached its highest development; he concreted onto finite human existence the eternal laws of the spiritual universe.'

"Isn't that wonderful?" Anna breathed. "I don't understand," Edna said firmly; she felt dizzy. She ought to have eaten breakfast before talking to Anna; morning sickness, that was what it felt like. "I don't understand what this has to do with any of your theories. I thought you were working on something called the cell of life which was supposed to hurry along human immortality." "Well, that's just the point!" Anna exclaimed; her cheeks were flushed with excitement. "If Christ developed as a purely natural process, the way some cells change into better cells, or some people's children into better people than their parents were, then it's possible we will all be like Christ. Not this generation, of course, but eventually. If we make the proper discoveries. Christ *did* say, 'Ye shall be as Gods.' " She lifted her own green eyes to her mother's.

"But some children are worse than their parents," Edna said; she knew her mind refused to follow Anna one step further into this desert she was exploring. "Who?" Anna asked curiously; "not the Munyans?" "The Munyans?" Edna echoed, astonished. She hadn't thought about the Munyans in years, probably almost twenty years. They had become so wrapped up in themselves, in the Moffats, in the trips to Boston and New York, the rest of the countryside had ceased to exist except as a series of illnesses to be treated. Occasionally some stood out as people: Old Mrs. Ward, Alice's brother Lucretius; he wasn't a patient, rather the husband of a patient; but the rest of the people she had been so sure she wanted to get to know, somehow they had been swept aside in the onrushing thunder of their everyday carriage.

"You were always going on about the Munyans when I was small." *"They* turned out better than their parents, at least from what we hear. Oscar Munyan is a selectman in Dummerston; Fred Munyan went out to California and patented some kind of spraying device which made him a fortune; Edmund Munyan went after him and became the sheriff of some county or other, Alameda County, I think. He's always in the papers for hanging someone or other, but they say he keeps a peaceful town.

"The girls," Edna said, searching her memory, "are all married; they didn't marry here. They married out West. They all live near Fred; people here say that's so their brother can make sure their husbands behave or give them a foot up the ladder to heaven. The parents still sit on the porch a lot; they're too old to bother anyone." "Then people *do* get better," Anna crowed. "That's only one family," Edna said sharply; she didn't think her own daughter was any proof of her own theory, although she knew better than to say so.

"Then every day," Edna said as cheerfully as possible, "we come a step closer to purification?" "If we continue to improve. Through methods like selective breeding, improvement of food, spiritual strengthening, things like that." "I'd like to hear much more about it," Edna lied; "have you eaten yet?" "No." "Do your theories recommend starvation?" "Of course not." "Then let's go down to the kitchen and eat." "Not yet," Anna said lazily; "it feels so peaceful up here." Edna stifled a groan. If her daughter was going to sit in her room meditating on the incarnation as a form of evolution, then she was going to choose her own subject.

"How was the trip back from New Bedford?" Anna seemed not to hear her. She repeated the question. "I didn't like it," Anna said, speaking slowly; "the trees. George kept commenting on the trees, how beautiful they looked. I thought how I hated them, they all looked alike. The monotonous, monotonous trees. They stood there like people who had forgotten where to go, like Indians who had been buried standing up, but the ground wore down around them, and now they were only bodies, or bodies with spirits, exposed to everyone's gaze. There was something wrong with them; I could see that; standing there so long and not learning how to move. But then they might not have been able to decide where to go. They might have been everywhere already.

"Then I felt very sorry for them, if they were so old and so wise and still didn't know where to go and just stood still in the middle of what must have been a desert for them, and for everyone else those were the beautiful places, and George kept pointing out that it all looked gray, but really there was lots of color, but he was wrong, there wasn't any color anywhere in the countryside. It was all the color of ice, and the water underneath was the color of ice, and the sky was the same color, and the longer we drove, the more our horses and sleigh became the same color, and when I looked at George I could see he was becoming the same color, which meant I was, too, and we were both the same color of little Minnie's skin when they put her in the casket, and that was when it occurred to me, because I started crying, and I knew the tears were the same color as the water, and my face the same color as the ice."

Edna listened, horrified; Anna didn't even know she was there. She had gone into some kind of trance. "What occurred to you?" she finally asked. "That the dead didn't stay buried; there was a place for them when they turned that color, and it had to be a place where there was a great deal of water and a great deal of snow, and they went into it and continued their lives while we continued ours; the only difference was that theirs had no color, but if we knew where to look for them we could find them. So I didn't want to come home, because I knew where the place was and George was only taking me farther away." "Where was it?" Anna didn't answer her. "Where?" Edna asked again. "What? What did you say?" "I asked you where they live." "Where who live; the Munyans? You know that better than I do." She did not have the slightest idea of what she had said. "I'm sorry; my mind must have been wandering." "Don't worry; it happens to all of us," Anna said cheerfully.

"You know," her mother said, "while you were gone old Mr. Munyan became pretty eccentric. He used to go to hotels and tie one end of a rope to a doorknob of the room, or something else equally immobile, and the other end to his ankle." "Why?" "So that in case of fire he could jump out. We thought he was a bit foolish, not because he was taking measures against getting caught in a fire, but because he seemed to think he could keep his own fate from catching up with him. Well, he's dead now, anyway," she finished, looking furtively at Anna from under lowered eyelids. "How did he die?" "He fell out of a hotel window trying to see if his rope was long enough." Anna stared at her. "Are you trying to tell me something?" "Just what happened to one of the Munyans; you seemed so curious about them." "But it *may* be possible to avoid one's destiny; or one's destiny may only apparently be inevitable."

"I'm not up to intellectual conversations before breakfast." "Well, Mother," Anna answered sensibly, "there's a simple solution to that problem; we go down and eat. You know," she chatted as they went down, "Minnie made up a conundrum before she died; one week before. 'Life is a circle.' No, it was 'Why is life like a circle?' We tried guessing, but she had the strangest answer. 'Because it viciouses and viciouses.' " "Had the epidemic started when she thought that up?" Again she got no answer. Now Edna knew better than to try. She wondered if little Minnie had been trying to warn Anna, to prepare her. Children, she had long ago learned, were preternaturally sensitive.

"Oh, excuse me," Ella's voice cut in, her hand arresting

Edna's progress; "there's something I must ask Mother about. I'm a bit embarrassed, too," she said, looking over at her sister. "A word to the wise," Anna smiled, going into the kitchen. "I talked to Ten," Ella whispered nervously; "and she's going to pretend she wants someone to stay with her for two nights, but she says it's up to us to make sure Anna doesn't get out of the room when she sleeps, because she's not going to stay up all night watching her, not in her condition." "I take it"—Edna said, smiling—"this is one of her good days." "She's never been crankier." "John will be able to think of something to keep Anna holding a chair down all night; I'll get him later. Is Ten going to tell Anna herself?" "Naturally. She's spent the morning working out the whole thing. Making up stories must be the bright side of Anna's state, at least for Ten," Ella said, amused. "She was *always* very dramatic; I suppose you never saw her up to her tricks. She had such hysterics over staying alone when I was first pregnant. John didn't even notice I looked like a whale until Martin was almost here." "Over staying alone? She loves it. She has nerves like a wolf."

"Well, she convinced him hers were gone forever and she needed constant company; I've never seen anything like it. She had me worried, and I knew what she was planning all along." Her mind went back to visiting Virginia at her maiden aunts'. That was what one of them remembered Ten for, how dramatic she had been. "She used to act," Edna said absently, her imagination lingering over the scene with Virginia as if she were still there. Oh, she could use her now, with her foolish pranks, her acting, pretending she was the minister's daughter, retailing her scandals, fleeing with them from that deathly house; perhaps she might have been able to tell them what to do about Anna. She seemed, she had seemed, to know what to do about everything. Except, of course, death. That was one she could not cope with. She and Ella went in to join Anna; only William was there with her. Martin had already left for Centerville and would send back if he needed help; John came in as they were beginning to eat. Edna picked up her fork, put it down, and repeated the gesture. John raised his eyebrows to show he understood. They could have invented the Morse code, she thought, after the birth of their children. Now they would go out to the cottage alone and she would have to tell him about the morning's conversation with Anna.

"She didn't remember *anything* afterwards?" "Nothing. At least she didn't remember she had talked to me. It happened twice; the second time was smaller, so small, if she hadn't spent so much time talking about the ride home I might have thought her mentioning Minnie was a good sign, that she was beginning to cope with things, with the idea they were gone. But she doesn't think they're dead." "No, it doesn't sound like it, not from what she said to you." "So I think it's urgent we get at her journals. Ten is thinking up some scheme to keep Anna watching at the bedside for two nights; that should be time enough, shouldn't it?" "Yes, Edna. I don't think we're going to like what we find." "That goes without saying." "It does, doesn't it?" He thought for a while. "Would you mind," he asked, "if I spent the day doing fascinating things like burnishing plates?" "No; I'll go see Alice." She always, he thought, went to see Alice when life in the family got unmanageable.

He imagined she would be gone most of the day, but she returned in two hours. "John," she told him, "George told Alice he didn't think Anna was in her right mind, and that was before the theatricals and everything else. He thought it was beginning long before Matthew died and that was why he was so worried about her experiments. He thought it began, or Matthew told him *he* thought it started, after they went to see a little boy who died of scarlet fever, but Matthew couldn't understand why that should have set anything off because they couldn't see the child, or the family, either; they were all in isolation." "It's our fault, then," John said. "What do you mean?" Was he losing his mind, too? "I never should have let her go anywhere with Hal. I knew all about his passion for funerals and weddings." "You couldn't have known how she would react." "It doesn't make any difference," John said savagely. He was looking at her as if he hated her. "I knew, you knew, anyone in their senses would have known that a steady diet of funerals was not right for a young child." "We didn't *know* it was a steady diet." "We shouldn't have taken any chances," John said angrily, cutting her off; "I wouldn't have taken any chances like that with patients." "But she wasn't *sick,*" Edna protested desperately.

"She didn't have to be exposed every day, either; now you tell me," he demanded of his wife, "how I am one bit better than that Nora Aetna. I used my own daughter to keep my own brother busy and I destroyed her. I'm as much a monster as that woman was." "You *are* being ridiculous; you're just in shock." "No, I'm not. You just don't want to hear the truth." "What? What truth? That you're as much of a monster as Nora Aetna? What she did was deliberate. It was criminal. It had to do with sexual appetites. She planned everything. She had a motive. I'm sorry. I don't see any parallels." "Not in the legal sense perhaps; *your* exposure to the law deadened your moral sense." "That is insulting," Edna exploded. "It is still true." "There is nothing wrong with my moral sense!" "Shouting won't change anything." "Will you stop being so preposterous? Accusing me won't do any good; what happened, happened. It's no one's fault. If Hal had taken Ella, it wouldn't have had any effect on *her.*" "But he didn't take Ella." His voice was unpleasant, nasty; he sounded as if he were talking to an idiot.

"All right! He didn't take Ella. But we had no way of knowing how it would affect Anna. At the time," her own voice sounding in her ears like the gong of hatred, "we thought she was interested in anything that had to do with doctoring, and that included sickness, death, corpses, funerals, everything." "An eight-year-old isn't *ready* for it, and she started a lot earlier. It was just too easy for me to ignore what Hal was up to; I had peace of mind and Anna was losing hers. Until we agree on that, we don't have anything to talk about." "Agree on what?" Edna shouted, slamming the table; "that you're as much a monster as Nora Aetna, that it's all your fault?" "Yes." Edna sat still in a fury. "Shouldn't we change that to 'our' fault?" she asked coldly. "I imagine so," he said, glaring; "you were her mother, after all." "I *am* her mother." If anyone referred to Anna in the past tense once more, they might as well take *her* to the Retreat. She said as much. "That might not be a bad idea," John answered. "Perhaps Anna and I might share a room," she said, remote. He didn't answer. "Are we going to spend all our time blaming and blaming," Edna screamed suddenly, "or are we going to do something about it?" Her voice was shrill, out of control, squawking, like a demented violin.

John sat looking at her. "You sound foolish." "I don't care what I sound like," Edna shrieked; "I want to know if you're going on with this blaming and blaming and this guilt and more guilt or if you're going to do something about Anna. Or at least help the rest of us. We all know," she went on cruelly, "**how** guilty you still feel over your other brother's drowning, and how that made you more indulgent with the one left, more than you should have been, but that's hardly an excuse for neglecting your present duty." She never should have said that, she thought, looking down at her ring, beginning to twist it round and round; now he would never forgive her. He would be no help at all. How could she have said such things? And in such a tone? But she couldn't apologize; she believed every word of what she said. "You're right." John sounded defeated, worn down. She looked up at him. He seemed suddenly to have aged. He was holding with both hands to the table he sat on. "Come into the house and rest," she pleaded. "No," he said stonily; "you go in. I want to stay out here alone for a while." "All *right!*" "Edna?" he called softly. "What?" "I'll get over it." "I hope so." "I hope you can accept your portion of the truth. It was our fault." "That may be, but that doesn't make us Nora Aetna; still," she said, unbending slightly, "I'll think about it." She had better, she knew, trudging back through the snow, if she wanted to understand her husband from now on.

Inside, the household was predictably topsy-turvy. Ten had evidently smashed her bowl and basin, complaining they didn't care if she lived or died and if Anna wouldn't stay up at night with her, no one was coming into her room and she wouldn't eat anything even if they tried to push it down her throat, and that was the end of it, she wasn't discussing it further with anyone; why, she went on querulously, they had even stolen her lamp and left her alone in the dark and someone pulled the curtains so there wasn't any moonlight, either, and if they thought she was dead why didn't they just get it over with and bury her right there and then; she would never have thought it of them; she would never have believed it; the least they could have done was get her some impossible nurse who at least would let them know if she'd stopped breathing, but what else did a woman her age have to look forward to but listening for the owl, not that you could hear *him* much in the dead of winter. Anna, predictably, was hysterical.

Nothing (she was crying frantically) could be done to calm Aunt Ten down; Ten would aggravate herself right into the grave, and it was all her fault. Ten had spent so much time with her, this was why she was so worn out and so unreasonable, and Ella had pleaded with Aunt Ten, telling her it was her own idea that no one wait up with her at night; *she* asked them to take out the lamp, and then Ten accused Ella of lying to her. She hadn't lost her senses yet, she told Ella menacingly. She still knew what was what. She wanted to change her will; they had to call the lawyer and so on. No one, Anna sobbed, knew what to do.

Ten had never mentioned wills or lawyers before in her life. What, Anna asked, did Ten want? Edna had better go ask her. She came back saying all Ten seemed to want was Anna; she wanted Anna to stay up with her for a few nights, at least until she felt better. Would Anna do it? Of course she would, she cried hopelessly. "Why don't you go in there now, and tell her so, dear?" Edna asked; "it would make her feel so much more secure." Anna ran in. Ella was now left staring at her mother. "You were right," she admitted, shaking her head, as if to clear it of mist; "I had no idea Ten could act that way." "Thank goodness she didn't think of trying it more often." "She wouldn't," Ella said, eyes bright; "she's an awfully good woman. I only hope I end half as well." "You will, you will," Edna said. She did believe *that*.

"Where should we meet?" she asked Ella. Ella had agreed to collect the diaries and bring them to the family council, but they already decided meeting in the pre-Revolutionary wing was not a good idea, because, should anything really happen to Ten, and Anna needed to find them, they would never be able to go there again. "What about my room?" Ella suggested; "you know we have the largest one." "And the largest child in the room next door." "She's sleeping with Annie tonight; no little pitchers

at all." "But it's just down the hall from Anna's room,"
Edna protested. "She'll be down in the parlor with Ten."
"That's right; this is all so unsettling." "Don't worry,
Mother; do you want me to go tell Father?" "No, why
should you be the one to walk into the lion's den?" She
put her boots back on, then her coat. She looked so
defeated, Ella thought, watching her mother walk out to
the cottage across the empty field of snow.

A silence hung over Ella's room; no one seemed anxious
to make the first cut into it. "Well," Edna said, "I'll read.
Can anyone tell which is first?" "They're dated," Ella
said, handing her mother the first one; "I only looked at
the dates, just the first pages," she quickly assured them,
as if already accused of violating a sacred tomb. Edna
opened the first notebook. " 'Theological questions,' " she
read out; " 'Why is evil permitted? Jesus was the exact
counterpart of the perfect man Adam who stood in Eden
unscathed by sin. His sacrifice was the redemptive price
for all men; otherwise each would have had to be re-
deemed separately.' " She looked up. Everyone was waiting. " 'When will evil end? After God has had time to
develop a new creation. This might be considered analo-
gous to selective breeding. Then, during the one-thousand-
year reign of Christ on earth, Adam's stock will have a
fair and impartial trial for life under favorable conditions.
It will then be decided that death is the great enemy but
while the people have been dead, if they have been dead,
none of the dead would have been suffering.' " "That
doesn't sound crazy to me," Martin commented; "pedantic,
but not crazy." "Well, shall I stop?" Edna asked, sharp.
"Go on, go on," John said.

" 'There is no such entity as the devil.' " Now everyone looked up. " 'Satan was perfect in the beginning, but
he was a free, intelligent, moral being. If he hadn't been
able to choose between good and evil, he would have
been a machine. He could have become evil, even though
he was perfect in the beginning, by making evil choices.
God did not create Satan. He created Lucifer; Lucifer
created Satan.' What a legalistic mind!" Edna said. " 'God
created man, as he created Lucifer, in his own image; for
God to have understood evil, he must once have per-

formed wicked, evil deeds and rejected them.' That's heresy, isn't it?" Edna asked. "Yes," Minnie answered.

" 'There is no such thing as an immortal soul.' " Edna stopped, stunned. They all stared at one another. "I'd like to hear how she proves that," Bill finally said. "Well," John answered—sardonic, hard—"I'm sure your mother is about to tell you." "If a creature is immortal, not even God could put him to death. There is a definite distinction between living forever and being an immortal entity. There is no scriptural passage in the Bible declaring man inherently immortal. There is, however, contrary proof. "The soul that sinneth, it shall die."

" 'Soul and being are synonymous. Every creature that breathes is a soul. No creature possesses a soul.' 'Possesses' is underlined three times," Edna interjected. " 'Every animal is itself a soul. The Scriptures describe animals as souls because they are all breathing creatures. Man is a soul, but he does not possess one. This does not mean man is a cow, although it may be possible that the soul of a man might enter that of a cow, and vice versa. When a soul creature dies, it goes to one place, the same where all go.' " Edna paused, remembering what Anna said about Matthew, how he was alive somewhere near New Bedford. " 'The difference between men and animals is that for animals there is no hereafter. But God has permitted redemption and resurrection for man.

" 'Satan originated the sinful doctrine that man's soul is immortal. This was the first lie Satan ever told. All other false doctrines sprang from this. Satan wanted men to believe that their souls were immortal, and so they could not die. But only God is immortal. Immortality is the great reward of the faithful. The Scriptures claim, "In Adam all die." God was always immortal. Jesus Christ and the Church were granted immortality. No other creatures will ever be immortal.

" 'The Scriptures give ample evidence of this. "God so loved the world that he gave his only begotten son, that whosoever believeth in him should not perish but have everlasting life." Anyone immortal could not perish. The coming of Jesus would have been unnecessary otherwise. This brings up the question of resurrection.' I can't believe," Edna said slowly, "she showed *this* to Matthew." Was anyone going to answer her, or was *she* talking to the dead? That was how she felt, in this silence, as if they had reached the place where souls went after their deaths. "Matthew only mentioned her research on cells," Martin said. "Do you think she showed *this* to him?" Edna asked, insistent. "No, I don't think so." The others nodded their heads in assent.

" 'The body is never resurrected. This was Satan's second deceptive doctrine. An immortal cannot die. An immortal cannot be resurrected. "For as in Adam we all die, even so in Christ shall all be made alive." What, then, is resurrected? Not the body which dies. Just as one cell replaces another, and the body is still perceived to be the same, so the body which God resurrects is not the one which died, for it is not fit to be immortal. Nor is there eternal torture of the dead; it is also unlikely man can communicate with any of his dead brethren. These doctrines deny the meaning of the great ransom sacrifice, which is the only salvation of the human race.

" 'Protestant clergy,' " Edna read out in astonishment, " 'teach that the soul is immortal and that the dead are somewhere, conscious. They say the good dead are in heaven, and the bad and wicked in eternal torture. But if man does not possess an immortal soul, then he cannot be conscious after death. God sent men down to death, not to immortal torture. Death is only the absence of life. The Bible plainly states, "The dead praise not the Lord, neither any that go down into silence." "The living know that they shall die, but the dead know not anything." "Their love and their hatred, and their envy, is now perished." '

"There's more of this," Edna said, looking up. "Skip it," William instructed. Edna, relieved, did so. " 'The hell of the Bible, properly translated, means *tomb*, the condition of death, oblivion only, the grave. Hell is translated to mean grave as often as it is translated to mean hell. Hades and Gehenna are translated as hell. Hades is the condition of death from which there is no resurrection. Gehenna is that condition of death from which there is no resurrection. Therefore, the retribution God inflicts on the wicked is total annihilation. The worthy shall live forever on the earth. This is established in the Book of Revelation. There is no heaven. This earth will be heaven after the second death. All human agencies tending to bring this about must necessarily be a failure.' Well?" Edna asked.

"Well," William said, "it sounds as if she was getting into some pretty deep waters, especially with her husband being a minister." "I wish some of you would get into some deep waters," Edna flared up; "we're trying to decide what's wrong with her. If anything is wrong with her. How much is wrong with her. What to do about her." She glowered around the room.

"I don't see," Ella said, "what's demented about what you've read. It's very logical; it's heretical, but it's logical." "It is not *logical* for Anna to become heretical," Edna snapped. "I suppose not," Martin agreed. "Well, we better look in the second book," Ella sighed. "Give it to me, give it to me," Edna said. "This is dated almost a year later, a year ago. 'How to Achieve Immortality in This Lifetime.' I think," she informed them icily, "we are about to leave logic, or at least to pervert it. 'All matter has feelings. It is not lifeless. A tree is not lifeless, nor is a stone. All matter possesses elements of conscious feeling; it has either lost much of what it had, or it has not yet reached the level of conciousness man possesses. Dr. Gale's experiments on these points are conclusive.' She doesn't describe them," Edna said sadly.

" 'In higher forms of life, we are seeing the miracle of insentient matter transforming itself into consciousness and intelligence, matter simply raising itself to a conscious state, a primary consciousness, one barely discernible, but one which will eventually reach full expression. All matter which appears lifeless, *and this is true of the dead,* only seems so because conscious properties of matter cannot break free and display themselves in a form we recognize as living. This is the meaning of evolution.

" 'The great truth which we must recognize is that life is a potentially observable property of all matter which strives toward consciousness and finally rises to higher and higher levels of intelligence. Thus, telepathy, clairvoyance, intuition are possible. All this comes from the consciousness of the cells-of-life, all of which have consciousness in common with all other cells-of-life which constitute the entire universe. This is what the hope of immortality must rest on—the eternal constant, which is the intimate, conscious life of matter.' "

"That's quite a shift in belief," John observed; he was thinking. Edna could tell that from his bored look; vacant, she corrected herself, it was a vacant look, as if he had emptied his mind of everything else to concentrate on this. "It goes on quite a while," she half apologized. "I think we better hear it now," Ella said; "I don't think we want any more surprises."

" 'The prolongation of life,' " Edna read wearily on, " 'is a purely physical problem. Man has to learn to set aside all natural laws. He can set aside the natural law of death. The best scientific evidence we now have shows that the brain developed as a result of a series of accidents. The brain was once composed of simple cells which began to do something peculiar. People do not want to believe this is possible because death has so long been made the cornerstone of religion. Jesus himself believed in a shared life of the human race. We have to work together to achieve immortality. Immortal life had already been initiated. We live longer now. There is no inherent limit in matter which determines a finite life span. There are tissues which live a century. If all cells did so, humans would live to be more than eighteen thousand years old, but the failure of other tissues, which are made up of cells, to cooperate and share with one another, causes the breakdown of the body and death.

" 'In higher forms of life, cells surrender their individual lives. First one cell combines with another to perform a more important, complicated function. Then these cells combine with the others, and are then called multi-cells; they surrender their own primal personalities for the sake of perplexity!' Oh, I'm sorry," Edna said, "she crossed that out and wrote 'complexity.' 'The most perfect example of cell sacrifice is the brain, in which thousands of cells surrender, or sacrifice themselves, to create the personality of man and his soul. This seems to occur as a result of some electric contact. But the moment the separate cells resume their separate lives, the human mind ceases to exist; unconsciousness now appears. This is what happens in sleep.

" 'In sleep, each cell breaks its contact with every other cell. It unclasps its hands, as it were. The cell now lives again as it once did, simple, restoring its powers. Upon waking, the cells join together in their common cause. The body is a type of Jesus' heaven. Without sacrifice, there would be no human personality. Many millions of cells must sacrifice themselves to create one human life; to save its existence, as Christ had to sacrifice himself to permit human life to become, ultimately, immortal.

" 'In strokes, personality continues, yet the person who has had the stroke usually feels a stranger to himself. This is because the contact between the sacrificing cells is now imperfect.' " "Interesting," John murmured. " 'Old age, too, comes from a similar loss of contact but, in this case, cell death is the real cause. As the cells wear out, the personality becomes vaguer and finally seems to vanish.' " Edna paused, exhausted. "Do you want me to read?" Bill asked. "No. 'Cells are psychic. That is because they all originated from the same source. But the more complicated the organism, the less likely it is to notice psychic messages from the cells. The brain dims and becomes older and acquires habits which cause it to perceive things in one way only. Children often show an ability to see through the ether, as do animals. In telepathy and clairvoyance and similar phenomena, the cells perceive the whole cooperative effort of the life on earth; the cells see the future and the past. They are a type of what will be immortal life.

" 'At death, the personality does not disappear, nor does the soul. But because the soul is a bunching together of lesser lives, at the moment of death they separate, as when a thousand people disperse even after Jesus himself has preached a sermon.

" 'But we must assume that personality is not separable, but detaches from the body at the moment of death, and that personality survives the death of the body.' " There were murmurs around the room; there was no logical reason given for that statement. " 'The primary question we must ask is whether or not the more complicated, highly developed tissues, those which have striven hardest to reach Christ, will someday be able to redeem the less developed tissues. We should now be able to assemble evidence they can.

" 'Dirt is matter in the wrong place. It interferes with cell life. Food is imperfect. A more perfect food would mean longer cell life, and hence longer life. Sex excesses drain away the life of cells; so does improper reading.

Pure sleep becomes less and less possible. The cell decomposes, poisoning other cells. Under favorable conditions, not to say perfect ones, the cell is capable of achieving immortality. Gravity, too, may cause an unnecessary strain on the cells; perhaps it may be suspended.

" 'We are,' " Edna read, unconsciously counting the number of pages left, " 'all mediums. We are like some large crypt, such as the tombs of Palermo. In each of us, all our ancestors are stored away. We are each a Book of Genesis. All those who went before us, or those whom we loved, are only sleeping in us quietly. Sometimes a shock, a death, will cause one of those old people to wake up, to take over, and to rise above the rest of the human personality, taking command, re-entering, in its resurrection, the oceans of light. For everyone is down there, buried in us, asleep with their fathers, waiting for us to call them up. Somewhere in us are the forgotten tongues of the Aryans, the astronomy of the Chaldeans.

" 'Life as we now live it is immoral. So few die of old age that there is some probability there is no such cause of death. As it is now, we have to be devoured by our young, who say, move over so we may live. This is not moral. Reincarnation is now only possible for us through our children. "Give me children or I must die." When we have children, the life of the race continues, but we do not. Thus sex is evil. It cannot resurrect the life of the person. It breaks the person into individual cells and reassembles its contents into a new being. This is the equivalent of death of the parent; the only individual is now the child.' Edna, looking at the next entry, gasped.

" 'We live only on the surface of the earth, as on an egg. The egg is ancient. Inside is only black mold. After time passes, it becomes clear that, if you wanted to, it is easy to put your foot down and put it right through the shell, like ice that hardens over soft snow, and it is so deep, you are stuck because your ankles are caught, black dust rising to your knees, and there is no getting out. We are possessed by spirits we do not understand. Sometimes plants take us over; other times the dead use us.

" 'I have seen dead trees covered with grape ivy; one was in the shape of a cross. One killed the other by depending on it. We should never depend on anyone.' " Absolute silence now possessed the audience. " 'There is a place near Coe's pond which is a frog hatching ground. There is a place near New Bedford which is a hatching ground for human life. I think I have found it. The dead seem to be buried, but they go there. It is possible to go and see them, although not right away, because the brightness of our colors disturbs them. They are all gray, especially if they died in winter. They went underground only to hatch again. Shadows go across the ceiling like rats, and they are rats. It would be terrible to die in a borrowed bed. I have thrown out many pictures of family life so that they cannot repeat themselves. This has also liberated bits of the people caught in them. Voices come out of empty houses, but no one listens to them. I have been guilty of this. There are no boundaries to anything. No matter how far the human mind imagines the universe stretching, he can always imagine it stretching further; he cannot imagine an end to it. This is terrible, since it accounts for the separations we call death. We can move objects around in a room, but we cannot move the past in front of the future. This is not right.

" 'But perhaps there is some purpose in this. Everyone sees the same things differently. No one ever sees the same thing, which means the thing is never truly itself to us. Perhaps this is because the nature of the thing, or person, is unimportant to whoever created us and the universe. Things cannot happen all at once; first there must be the present and then the future, whether we like it or not. This must mean what we like does not matter. Perhaps the whole world is an unimportant thing, as vapor rising from a pot is unimportant; what is important is what is being cooked. The cook does not care about the vapor even though the vapor may care about itself.

" 'If our minds were not put together the way they are, we might not even know there was time at all. There are no two identical instants in life; this is not right, either. We would have to lose our memory to go back to another moment which is over. This would mean our memories would have to die and so too our minds. The only eternity there is, is an eternity of death. There is a real world behind this one but it does not care about us. The faster we go, the smaller we get. Yet if we stop the heart, we also continue to grow smaller. There is no solution. We are ghosts standing next to the real world which we cannot see.' " Edna suddenly paused and stared blankly at them. "What is it?" Minnie asked. "My eye just skipped down; first there's this part about how Plato must have thought he could have done something about the future, but he put his foot through the surface of the egg as we are now doing." She stopped again for a moment.

" 'I am a great sinner. I should have contrived to eat some of Matthew and Minnie. Then we would have stayed together more easily. Then George could never have gotten me into the sleigh.' She must just have written this," Edna said, almost inaudible, the book in her lap. William came over and picked it up, continuing the reading. " 'If I had eaten part of them, I would have become part of their time; their memories would have become part of mine. They will have come out of the holes in the earth by now. If I had eaten part of them they would look for me. Now I must look for them. I should have cut some of my flesh to be buried with them. We would have been buried like seeds in the same bed. I should have had more buried with them because they will need it. The work of time can be unraveled by this eating. At the moment of death, man sees his whole life. I should have been alone with them and eaten them at that precise moment.

" 'Before I left they had come back as far as the forest, but they would not come out. I have to go back to them where they are hidden in the trees. None of us are animals. Our bodies are not real.

" 'The dead bodies should be preserved until the spirit is taken from them. Corpses are helpless; they should not be buried. There is a cemetery in Germany where the dead are buried just as they were when they died and a bell is tied to their toes so that should they wake they will not be frightened and will be found. The bell has only rung twice. People are buried every day and they are alive. Exhumed bodies have been found which have changed positions; women have been found who clawed their faces and clothes when they understood what happened to them.

" 'I have made an extensive study of this. Who is to say if Mat was not alive when he was buried? I was not there. Our world as it is is not acceptable to the human mind and spirit. Our religion has conspired against us; it has not taught us what to do to keep death away. It is necessary to find the dead ourselves. The Greeks seemed to have made discoveries concerning that difficulty. I must study their legends.' That," William said, "is the end of it."

"She's completely mad," John said softly. The sentence floated through the silence like a feather; it refused to settle. "We can't leave her alone," said Minnie. "No." That was Ella. "What are we going to do?" Martin asked; "I could try talking to her." "Talking to her?" John said, his voice rising; "what would you be talking to? Someone who believes you should be eating pieces of dead bodies?" "But we have to do something. Otherwise she's going to find some way to get back there and start looking for the dead; she thinks they're alive." "Probably in Fall River," Edna said; "she keeps mentioning Fall River." "I think you should talk to her," Martin told his father. "What good will that do?" "Anything's better than nothing," Edna said. "Maybe," Minnie suggested, "if you tell her we read her journals?"

"Tell her we read them!" Edna exclaimed; "then why are we hiding up here in this room?" "Well," Minnie bravely persisted, "it might catch her by surprise, and while she's surprised, she might do some listening. Ma used to do that to us a lot." "That's not a bad idea," Ella considered. "It seems to be the only one we have," John said, staring at his hands on his knees. "Then will you do it?" Martin asked.

"It might do more harm than good." "I think we have to take that chance," Edna said, hesitant. "And if it doesn't work?" John asked, looking at his wife; "if something happens to her?" "What worse can happen to her?" Edna cried. The others were silent. "I presume," John said, "all this quiet means you want me to talk to her. Is there anyone who doesn't want me to talk to her?" No one said a word. "That's what I was afraid of; all right, I'll talk to her tomorrow. She'll have to stay up with Ten tomorrow night, though; Ten put on such an act." "You know," Martin said, "this feels like it happened once before. When we decided to send her to Boston and then couldn't let her stay home because we'd convinced her Grandmother was sick." "Does that mean you don't want me to talk to her?" John asked. "No," Martin answered. John took a deep breath. "All right, then; let's all go to bed." When they were back in their own bed, Edna asked if he wanted to talk about anything. "No," he answered, turning over on his side.

"Anna," John said as he was stoking the wood stove, "last night we read your journals." "You did what! How could you? Those were personal!" "And I want to talk to you about them," he continued implacably; "what is this about your eating people?" "You wouldn't understand," she whispered; "you're a doctor." "Try." "It was just an idea." "Anna, other people have lost families before." "That's different." "How?" "They weren't chosen specially for each other." "And you and Matthew were?" "Yes." "Doesn't that seem egotistical?" "Nevertheless, it's true." "The creator of this universe deliberately took time out and brought the two of you together?" "You can laugh at that if you want to," Anna answered, "but that is just what happened." "Anna, that is sinful; it's the sin of pride. All are equal before God. It says so in the Bible." "It says a lot of things in the Bible." "In your notebooks," John persisted, "you wrote that when a man died he ceased to exist until God chose to resurrect him and you also said that when a man died he went to stay somewhere else." "That's right." "Don't you see any contradictions? Any contradictions at all?" "No." This was hopeless, John thought. He decided to try another tack.

"When your aunt's husband died, she was half dead of grief, but she went forward with the living." "That was her destiny." "It seems to be the destiny of all human beings," John said sarcastically; "why shouldn't it be yours?" "I don't know; that's an unanswerable question." "Don't you think your aunt loved her husband?" "She must have; she loves everybody." "She loved him more than everyone else," her father said quietly; it was getting harder and harder to control his temper. "Then there was no reason for her to go on living." "*She* thought there was. Because she didn't think she was so special the laws of nature didn't apply to her." "Maybe they didn't and she didn't realize it." "Matthew wouldn't have liked to hear you talk that way; I know that. Everything you're saying, everything you wrote down, would be torture to him." "That would have been true when he died, but now I can explain it to him; he'll agree with me."

"How are you going to explain it to him? He's *dead!*"

John roared, suddenly losing control. "How can you be so sure? You haven't looked everywhere. He's alive with everyone else who died. They're in a village near New Bedford." "How do you know that?" John made a great effort to sit still, not to grab her and bang her against the wall. "I saw them. Sometimes they stay in the graveyard at night." "What graveyard?" "I can't tell you that." "Why not?" "I'm not supposed to." "Anna," he roared, "do you have any idea what you sound like? You sound as if you've lost your mind altogether." "I suppose so; but that's because you don't know the truth about things yet." She was so calm. "Such as biting dead people?" John shouted. "Things like that," she said, fidgeting with a button on her skirt, refusing to look at him.

"You're rebelling against all nature; that's Satanic, demonic; what's the difference between you and Lucifer, or Satan, whatever you want to call him, and *your* rebellion against the order of things?" She looked confused. "Demonic, demonic," he repeated in a fury; "keep it up and you'll never be reunited with them. It will take millenniums of their prayers to do *you* any good." "I am not committing any sins," Anna said softly. "You're the worst sinner *I've* ever met; special afterlives for you, special worlds for you, possibilities of escaping death no one else has; you want to be God." "No, I don't; I don't like God." "That's why you're rebelling against him," John shouted, banging the table; "you think *you* can do a better job." "I never said that." "But that's what you mean." "You can say anything you like." "And don't you talk to your earthly father that way; you're not too old for the birch stick."

"You could have been there," she said accusingly. "And what good would I have done? I'm not God. Most people who come down with diphtheria here die of it. I would have stood by and watched the inevitable happen." "It wasn't inevitable; you could have done something about it." "No human being, *no* human being, could have done anything about it." "I don't believe it." "Would you like," he asked, "to read my record books? I've listed every disease, every patient, the outcome of every illness. One out of twenty who came down with diphtheria lived and what I did had nothing to do with the outcome; I treated everyone the same way." His daughter did not respond.

"If you're angry at me," he went on, scanning her face, "that's no reason to start a war against the world and God." "I'm not angry with you." "Yes, you are." "And if I am? I have every reason to be." "Not enough to destroy yourself." "I haven't done anything to destroy myself." "Well, your mind, then." She stared blankly, as if she were listening to some other voice.

"Anna," John tried again, "you met Matthew when the church was preparing for its baptism; you remember that?" "Of course." "Well, what did it mean to you? Did it mean anything? What did it mean when the Reverend Pierce asked if you were willing to give up everything for Christ?" She didn't answer. "I want to know what it meant to you!" he shouted, hitting his fist on the table. "*You* know what it means." "What? *You* tell me what." "It means," she said monotonously, "you must be willing to submit to God's will, to submit to whatever providence He ordains for you, to value Christ above all material things, to value and love Christ more than anything of this world, including human ties. It means there must be nothing more important than Christ in your life."

"When you were baptized," John asked, "did you have any exceptions, any special privileges you thought you were entitled to? Did you have secret reservations? Did you believe you would have to give up everything but your horse?" "Of course not!" She blushed, furious. "Well, then, did you secretly believe you wouldn't be expected to give up too much? Your husband, for example? Or your child?" Silence. "*Did* you think about it?" "No, I didn't," she finally answered; "it never occurred to me that things could happen, not things like that." "You'd seen them happen to other people. You *must* have had reservations," he went on, remorseless; "you just weren't aware of them. That means," he said, fixing her, "you were *never* a Christian. Never. You were *almost* a Christian; you *never* were one." "No," Anna wailed. "It's the simple truth." "But I can pray," Anna said feverishly; "I can pray to become a Christian!" "Then you had better concentrate on praying, don't you think? Not on those theories of immortality. A woman who claims she's a Christian!"

"You're wrong," Anna said suddenly, her voice strange; "I'm a Christian; I do have faith. My terms are not the same as everyone else's; it is the *faith* that counts in the eyes of God." Her invulnerability had closed over her again. "I am *not* wrong," John shouted; "there are no two ways of looking at God, not for a Christian. There are no two ways of looking at faith. You can't believe in God's omnipotence and in your own as well." "I don't understand you," she answered; her voice was remote, as if it were coming to him from another cold, far star. "Well?" he asked. Was this what Edna had meant? This sudden darkness in a room full of light, whatever flame that Anna was, suddenly blown out by some wind, igniting again in a new, terrible forest? He was frightened. "Well, what?" "Are you trying to be infuriating? Don't you think your sister was angry when her first baby died?" "It was the child, not the husband." "Would you have been happier if all of their husbands and wives and children had died?"

"Yes," she said suddenly; "yes, I would! Why should it have happened to me? Why should I care what happens to them? Especially in this life. Do you think they really care about me?" she went on in a rage; "they can't care because they don't know what it's like; they think they know, but they don't." "I suppose," John said after a while—he was stunned by the force of her fury—yet he had known it was there, or thought he had known—"I suppose you just expressed Christian charity." "Don't bother me with that," she answered abruptly. "I could have you talk to people who have gone through the same things you have," he suggested. "I don't want to talk to anyone else. Why should someone else have the same feelings I have?" "Why should yours be so remarkable?" "I didn't say they were remarkable; I said they were mine." "It comes to the same thing." "I'll get over it in time." Her tone, her expression, he saw, had changed; she looked calculating, almost criminal. "You can't imagine—I want an honest answer, now—anyone else having such terrible things happen to them?" "No." "Then time is the only thing that can cure you," he concluded sadly.

She nodded; there was an old, satisfied look about her, as if she had trapped him, as if she had made *him* say what she wanted him to say. "Are you going to watch with your aunt tonight?" "If she wants me to." "She does." "Then I will." "You might as well get back to the house," he told her wearily; "the snowstorm's getting worse every minute. Tell your mother I'd like to talk to her." "I don't want to talk about this anymore," Anna warned him. "Don't worry," he answered brusquely. John told his wife the sum of his conversation; they decided to send for the others. Edna went, having concluded her comings and goings would look most usual. "It sounds hopeless," Martin said; after hearing of the conversation, he was surprised again at his father's memory. "I'm not sure," Bill thought aloud; "there *is* a possibility that time will cure her." The rest, however, did not look cheered.

After Anna had watched with her two nights, Ten suddenly decided it was impossible to sleep with an observer in the room. Anna therefore retreated to her own, although she frequently peeped in at Ten, and once even resorted to looking in through the window wrapped in a blanket like an Indian squaw. But on the fifth day, Ten took a serious turn for the worse. She was barely able to breathe. Everyone walked about silent, restless. All that was missing, Edna thought, getting up, beginning to pace again, was wringing of hands. She supposed that would begin soon enough. Still, Ten would not permit anyone to stay with her at night. Sometime during the day, Anna, alone in her room, decided she heard Matthew asking her to come see him in Fall River. "I'll leave in the middle of the night," she promised him; "when they can't stop me." Outside, the snow drove at the earth as if trying to hammer important messages in. By 3 A.M., she was dressed and ready to leave; she had her boots in one hand.

She didn't want to wake anyone up. That, she thought, would be inconsiderate. She would not be inconsiderate, no matter what her father thought. In her other hand, she had Ten's old copy of *The Wedding Ring*. She decided to give it back before she left, while she was saying goodbye. She opened her door; the house was completely silent. She had no trouble getting into Ten's room; the only light was the reflected light of the snow, but she had no difficulty finding the chair next to her bed. "Aunt Ten?" she whispered. There was no answer, but there was no sound of labored breathing, either. She must be better, Anna thought. "Aunt Ten," she said, "I have to go and find my family. Matthew called me. The others don't understand." She took her aunt's hand; it was ice cold.

"Oh," she murmured, rubbing the hand between her own, "I'll warm your hand up. They don't understand I have to go back and find the others before it's too late and they become angry and go further away. You must have known that when you sent for your husband's remains, didn't you?" "Yes, dear, I did," Ten answered. "You think I'm doing the right thing?" "A wife should cleave to her husband," Ten said. "That's just what I thought," Anna whispered happily; "are you going to let them bury you?" "Certainly not; they will think they've buried me, but I'll come right out and find you in Fall River." "Oh, that will be nice; that will be such excellent timing." "I think so," Ten answered. "You don't think there's anything wrong with my walking to Brattleboro in this weather? It really isn't so far, and if I ask for a horse, they'll try and stop me." "No, go," Ten instructed her; "as long as you have your boots." "I have them," Anna said proudly; "and your book. I wanted to give it back to you."

"That's a good girl; I'll need it after I get out." "I thought you would"; Anna smiled. "I can't take it now; just put it next to my hand." "As soon as I'm ready to go; your hand is still so cold." "I shall always be cold," Ten said; "you have to go to Fall River. Don't worry about me." "All right," Anna answered; "I had better say good-bye, then." She bent down to kiss her aunt; her cheek was as cold as her hand. "Thank you for the book," Ten said again; "you better hurry, though. It's a long walk." "I'm going right now." "Have a safe trip," Ten called after her. Anna crept to the front door and slid out into the storm.

Once outside, it did not occur to her to put on her boots. She looked up at the sky; there was no moon. Probably Aunt Ten had been looking at it when she stared up through the ceiling that way. By the time Anna crossed the north pasture, she was exhausted; she was cold. She could no longer feel her feet. The snow was so white; it looked so comfortable. She had never seen sheets so white; she decided to rest in the snow for a minute. It was so sweet lying there in that incredible purity; it was so wonderful to stop struggling against the snow and feel its little lips all over her face. With a great effort, she extended one arm and swept enough snow under her head to make a pillow. It was soft, she thought, ecstatic. She felt an overwhelming sense of comfort, trust, security, protection; she knew they would forgive her for taking a short nap. She would be on her way soon enough. It was not a dark sleep, she thought, her lids getting heavier; it was a bright white sleep, as if the sun had blazed out, temporarily blinding her. Yes, she would see them later, she thought, turning on her side, settling in, sleeping.

The constant chiming of the grandfather clock woke Edna and John early; it was still absolutely dark. "Oh, for heaven's sake," Edna muttered, turning over on her back; "we really should get rid of that thing." "Or stop it," John grumbled, his voice thick with sleep. Just as he was about to ask what time it was, their own gingerbread clock struck six. "Six!" Edna exclaimed; "oh, I would like to get ahold of that clock!" "Mother! Mother! Get up!" It was Martin's voice calling through the door. "He *still* can't be afraid of that clock!" Edna muttered, hurrying into her robe. "Well, what is it?" she demanded, jerking the door open; she knew the instant she got out of bed her mood had not been improved by a night's sleep.

"Aunt Ten. She's dead. She must have died last night." "Dear Lord," Edna gasped; "John, get up, hurry up." "I'm standing right in back of you; just go out into the hall and I can get out of the room."

The family stood in a little group at the foot of the stairs. "Wilma," Ella ordered, "take the rest of the children out to the barn and tell Amos to take them off sleighing and not to bring them back until this afternoon. Stop at Mrs. Moffat's for lunch and tell Amos to talk to her. Can you do all that?" Wilma nodded self-importantly. "Let's wait for them to get dressed and out," Minnie pleaded. They all nodded. Bill slapped Tenney's bottom as she went out. "That's the last one," he sighed with relief. "Worse than the district school," Bridget mumbled. Edna had forgotten about her; she would be extremely upset. What *had* happened, she wondered, to Bridget's granddaughter? Was she still in Anna's house? In the general confusion, they had forgotten all about her.

"Kate," Edna asked; "where is she?" "Where is Anna?" she asked suddenly. No one heard her. "I'll go for George later," Bill said; they all conversed, in emergencies, in shorthand.

"Where is Anna?" Bridget suddenly asked in her flickery old voice. "Anna, where is Anna?" The question went around the circle. "Who saw her last?" No one knew. Then it appeared everyone last saw her when they went to bed. "I'll look in her room," Edna volunteered. "Everything's there," she told them, puzzled. "Her coat is gone from the rack," Bridget said, "and I didn't see her boots under the hooks where she usually keeps them." "I'll look in her room again," Edna said. "They're not there," she told them, coming down. "She's probably out there communing with the snow," John said sardonically; "first things first." It was just like Anna to cause a disturbance in an emergency. They followed him into Ten's room. From the instant he entered, he knew his sister was dead. He must have hoped, hoped, Martin had made a mistake. There was no sound of labored breathing, but it was the familiar gray color of the face, the way the bones had suddenly ascended, taken sudden dominion over the plains of her flesh. The nose was sharp; the cheeks were hollow. The lips were white, eyes wide and staring. So this was his sister now.

He picked up her hand. Goodbye, Ten, he whispered to himself; then, to give himself something to do, he automatically felt for her pulse. There was none. The waters had stopped running; the fountain had dried at its source. This land was desert now. He supposed she had enough of hot and cold. "She's dead," he said aloud. Edna had slipped up beside him. She was crying soundlessly, shaking her head back and forth as if to say no, no, but there was the body, saying accept it, say the right word; don't keep shaking your head that way. John led her away from the bedside and sat her down on the vanity bench. She kept crying; she kept shaking her head. She tried to say something; she wanted to tell him how much she would miss her, what she meant to her, but she could not talk. "You'll have plenty of time to talk later," John said, stroking her hair, just as he had said it thousands of times in the past, to strangers, about people who were strangers.

Her hair, he saw with a shock, was down. The others had surrounded the bed like a living curtain. "Don't worry, don't worry," he kept murmuring over and over; "you know what she did. She stayed alive until we were all in bed, and then she decided she could go ahead and die in peace and give everyone a good night's sleep." It was heartbreaking; it was like losing his mother again. Edna squeezed his hand, crying, shaking her head in dissent, no, no, this had not happened; this could be undone. "We should send for your mother," he said. "No," she said, taking a deep breath; "no, it's too cold." Her throat tightened. She made a little choking noise; she began weeping again.

There was a sudden flurry in the five people standing around the bed. They looked, Edna thought through her tears, like five pigeons just thrown crumbs in a Boston park. Why did such incongruous images always pop into her head? Ella and William moved around to the other side of the bed; the five of them stood in a tight knot, murmuring, looking down at something. "Father," Ella called softly, "would you come here a minute?" "Excuse me, dear," he said, letting go of his wife. Edna nodded miserably. "What is it?" he whispered as Martin moved over to make a place for him. "This." Martin handed him the little book, *The Wedding Ring*. "That's Anna's book," John said, confused; "where did you get it?"

"It was lying right next to Ten's hand," Martin whispered. "It wasn't there last night," Minnie whispered. "How do you know?" "I was the last one in and I smoothed down the sheets and I asked her if she wanted a lamp or anything to read and she said she'd read enough and guessed she was as smart as she would ever be. There were some books on the table, but they were big ones. No, I would remember," Minnie went on carefully; "I had to pick up each of her hands to smooth the sheets down, and then I kind of tucked her in. After I turned her over on her side to smooth the sheets, that's when I tucked her in, so she couldn't have been lying on it, either, and she would have felt it, she was so thin, you know." "Anna must have left it here," Martin said, "after the rest of us went to bed. "Then she must have been the last one to see Ten alive," Martin said. "Or dead." That was Ella. "Or both," John put in; "she could have been here when Ten died." "I can't believe," Ella said, "Aunt Ten would have died while anyone was in the room." "Neither can I," her father agreed. "Then," Ella sighed, "she must have come in and found her dead; that was just what she needed." "But if she was dead when she came in," Minnie puzzled, brow wrinkling, "why did she leave Ten the book?" They stared at her. "I think," they suddenly heard Edna saying, "we had better start looking for her." "For whom?" Bill asked.

"For Anna. She's not in her room; her coat and her boots are gone and she left her book with Ten. She left almost everything else in New Bedford, but she brought that book. Someone go out to the barn and see if she took a horse." "She didn't," Bill told them, coming back in, stamping his feet up and down; "no one saw her near the stable all night. All the horses are there except the ones Amos took with the children." "No one could have come for her?" "There's only one set of tracks and they leave straight from the barn." "But there might have been more," Edna protested; "it's been snowing all night. There are still flurries. If there were tracks, they'd have been covered up."

"I don't think anything would have gotten past the stable without the dogs starting up," Minnie said practically; "they bark their heads off whenever George comes around, and they know *him;* they were even barking at Anna for the first week she was home." "We might not have heard them," Edna argued; "we were so tired. Someone said something about that before they went up to bed." "Mother," Martin said firmly, "Amos and his help have large, pointed ears. A squirrel couldn't have gotten past them, and not a butterfly, either, not if the dogs were barking." "Then where *is* she?" Edna cried, agonized. "Mother," Ella took over; "she might have gone off to another room in the house. She used to hide up in the old attic; don't you remember, that was how the extra wood fell on her and broke two of her ribs? You said it was like Mrs. Grimsby and the dress form, and Aunt Ten started in calling her 'Mrs. Grimsby, dear,' and she would get so mad about it." "The rest of the house is unheated!" Edna cried. "Mother! She knows how to light a fire!" "Or she might have gone out to one of the cottages," William suggested. "Why don't we stick together

887

through the house?" John asked Edna; "you know it better than anyone else, and the rest of you check the cottages and then come back; otherwise we're going to be crashing into each other in the halls." In the silence, they all turned back to the body on the bed. "She almost kept her promise," Edna said softly. "What promise?" Ella asked. "To stay alive as long as Anna did." "Perhaps she did," John whispered. Edna nodded, saying nothing. Ten. Yes, she had probably died the instant Anna closed the door.

She and John searched the house. They looked under dust ruffles; they poked the canopies; they looked in the wardrobes; they looked under love seats. It was more, Edna thought, like looking for a lost kitten than a lost child. A grown lost child. Finally, they had to conclude she was not there. They went back and sat automatically in Ten's room; they had stopped calling it the parlor. Any room Ten was in automatically became Ten's room. "When do you think they'll be back?" Edna asked. "Not long now," he answered; 'they'll check out the cottages; and they'll remember some place they should have looked, then Bill will decide to look in the loft, and if he leaves the woodpile alone, we should see them in ten minutes." "If they don't find her?" "Then we'll look until we find her; she could have gone anywhere. She could have gone down to the church; she could have gone down to the Pierces'." "That's true." Voices flew in from the hall. "They're back," John said. "They didn't find her," Edna answered dully; "I can tell. You can barely hear them." "Well, then, we'll do just what I told you; we'll look everywhere else." "She's not at the Moffats', either," Ella told them, coming in; "oh, it *is* cold." Their cheeks were bright red; they looked so dear, Edna thought, like children grown too large for their clothes. Why did they ever have to grow out of their lives?

"Your father," Edna said, "thinks we ought to look in at the church and the Pierces'." "I don't think so," Bill said; "if she went out there, she had to get there. I think we ought to take out sleighs and look over the grounds. If she didn't take a horse, she must have been walking. She might have fallen or something." "All right, get the sleighs. You four go together. Bridget," he asked, "do you want to come with us?" "No," she answered after some thought; "Anna always took the shortcuts. She liked the flat, the one right after the north meadow." "She liked everything," John said. "All right," Bill said, cutting off discussion; "we'll go over the north pasture and the flat and the south pasture; you take east and west and the first mile up and down the road. It's passable, for some inexplicable reason." "The milk wagon," Minnie said. "Probably," Martin agreed; "since we don't believe in miracles." So they started out.

The four left first; none of them had anything to say, or would not. Everyone's eyes were stuck to the ground. Minnie would look up suddenly and scan the horizon; the others kept looking at the snow. "We've been all over the south pasture," Bill finally said; "we're crossing our own tracks." Martin wordlessly turned the horses in the direction of the flat. "We're cutting our own tracks again," Minnie told him. They didn't like it, Martin thought; that was why they were so quiet. "It's the north pasture, then," Martin announced. He didn't know why he was sure that was where he did not want to go, why he felt a sense of dread the closer to them it came. "Let's try something different," Ella suggested, trying to lift the heavy air that seemed pressing them down as they sat; "let's go around in circles, starting with the trees and going into the center; it should look pretty when we're finished anyhow."

Martin started the outer rim of the circle. "A person could get lost in those woods," William observed, carefully casual. "Not Anna," Ella said impatiently; "she knows every inch of this land." "We'll end by searching the woods," Martin predicted, beginning the second circle. "How many circles do you think it will be before we get to the center?" Minnie asked; "let's guess." "Let's not," Martin called back. "About six," Bill volunteered. "Oh, well," Minnie sighed, settling back. "Nothing," Martin announced; "circle three." "What's that?" Minnie asked, bending forward sharply. "What's what?" Martin asked wearily. "That mound. There," she said, pointing to her left. "I don't see anything," Ella said, bending forward. "There it is," Bill cried out excitedly; "it's a mound of some kind." "We're looking for Anna," Martin reminded him. "I want to look at it," Bill answered, stubborn. Martin shook his head and reined in the horses. "Climb down and get yourself wet," he growled restlessly. They watched

Bill bend over the mound. For a moment, he was motionless.

Then he suddenly lurched forward and began pawing snow into the air as if he were a dog looking for a bone. "Get down here, Martin," he called back. He went on pushing snow aside frantically. "It's Anna!" Martin gasped. Bill had unearthed her face and her shoulders; "she's frozen to death." Bill looked at him. "Is that what we're going to call it?" Martin asked. "What do you want me to say?" Bill retorted angrily. "That she froze to death; let's dig her out." "It's Anna," Martin called back to the two women; "she slipped and fell. She's frozen." Ella and Minnie looked at each other; their two husbands kept digging. Finally, Anna's body was completely exposed; she was lying on her side, curled, like a crescent moon, her head on her arm. They hadn't heard Minnie and Ella come up behind them; the snow muffled all sounds. "She slipped?" Minnie asked. "And fell?" asked Ella. "Yes," Martin told them, not turning. "She was as surefooted as a goat," Ella said angrily, "and she's not wearing any boots. That doesn't look like a simple fall. It doesn't look like any kind of fall."

"We don't have to tell Mother that," Martin hissed, furious. "I don't think we should try and hide things from them, not anymore," Ella said. "I'm putting her boots on, anyhow," Martin insisted, struggling with them. "Bill," he demanded, "will you help? I can't get them on." "We'll break a bone getting them on," Bill told him, standing up; "she's solid as a rock." They stood still around Anna's body. "She looks so lonely in the snow," Minnie whimpered; Martin took hold of her. "She looks so little," Minnie cried; "she wouldn't have been twenty-five for a long time." "Three months," Martin said. "What does she have in her hand?" Minnie asked. "I don't know," Martin said; "we can't open it." "It looks like a ribbon," Minnie said. "She had that kind of ribbon around her pictures when she came home," Bill said. "That night we read her journals," he asked; "didn't she say something about destroying them? The pictures? Maybe she was sorry. That was all she had left."

"There's no telling now," Ella said; "we have to decide how to bring her back. I don't know about the rest of you," she hurried on, "but I don't think I want to stand the body up in the sleigh with the rest of us." "No," Martin agreed slowly. "Well, how will we get her back?" William asked in exasperation. "We better go back and get a big board and some rope," Ella said, taking over; "and some strong rope to tie the board to the back of the sleigh. We can bring her back that way. Is that all right?" They took the silence as a sign of agreement and began to get back in the sleigh. "I don't want to leave her here," Minnie said abruptly, stopping short; "not alone." "Someone's coming." Ella pointed. It was a man. That was all they could tell; the figure plodded steadily toward them. "Oh, it's Father," Minnie sighed in relief. "What's *he* doing here?" Bill asked, annoyed. "You just keep quiet," Minnie snapped at him; "*I'm* glad he's here."

"So she's gone, too, is she?" Howard said, coming up to them. They nodded. "Minnie, what are you doing out in the snow?" "I'm waiting with her until they come back to get her." Howard nodded at his daughter. "I'll wait with her," he announced, looking down at his boots; "get on, get on." Reluctant, Martin started up the sleigh. "Well, Minnie," Howard finally said; "crying won't do no good," he scolded, putting his arm defensively around her. "I guess not." "I sure will miss Ten," he admitted gruffly. "But you hardly ever saw her!" "That didn't hardly make any difference; you don't need to see some people. They get in your blood like the malaria." "She gave you the chills," Minnie gasped, trying to joke. "Nah; she could stand a joke, though." "How do you know, anyhow?" Minnie asked, swallowing a sob. "Ella and some of the others stopped by our house looking for Anna; I guess they don't expect anything too sunny, from the look of them." Minnie shook her head. "I always liked Anna so much; I don't know why. She said I was soothing."

"Soothing?" Howard repeated; he wondered what that could mean. "She was only twenty-four," Minnie whispered. "You keep on with those things and you'll be lying down next to her," Howard warned. She leaned against her father's rough wool coat, sobbing. Howard patted her roughly, exactly as he would have gentled a nervous horse. "Gonna have any more children?" he asked when she stopped crying. Minnie was astounded; that was the first time she ever heard him mention any such things. He saw his daughter's eyes on him. "I just used to think what a pity it was Ten never had any," he mumbled. "Well, I'm only twenty-eight; I don't imagine I'll get much choice." "Not the way all of you carry on." "Maybe if she had stayed at home," Minnie began tentatively. "Don't *you* start up that nonsense. Maybe this. Maybe that. The Steeles are pretty good at sticking pins in their own skins. Look, Minnie, next year, we might get the cholera and all go, and everyone in New Bedford, they'll say, if we had only stayed home. Or if only we'd decided to go traveling. A lot of difference it makes if life has it in for you."

That was, Minnie thought, probably the longest speech she'd ever heard him make. "I guess," she sighed, drawing a deep breath; the cold air stung her lungs. Going to sleep in this! "Cold?" he asked. "At least I can warm up." "That's a good girl," he said, approving; "one peck doesn't lose the cockfight." She let that pass; she had given up on her father's sayings. "There's the sleigh," she said. It came steadily, unstoppably forward; if only it would stop, Minnie thought; if only it would turn around. She looked down at Anna. She looked so peaceful; it was hard to believe she wouldn't wake up and climb in. When she looked up, the sleigh had already reached them. If she had watched it, would it have stopped? She sighed. Foolishness and more foolishness. "I'm going to help them," Howard told her; "you get in the sleigh with Ella there."

The men tied Anna's body onto the flat board, then tied the board onto the end of the sleigh, tilting it so that her head was higher than her body; she looked as if she were floating, more and more as the snow settled, whitening the board, whitening her clothes all over again. "Squash in," Bill told his father; "we might as well go back together." "I want to pay my respects," Howard told him. "They're pretty upset," Bill cautioned his father. Howard looked at him. "Well, and what did you think? It ain't the Fourth of July." They fell silent, Ella and Minnie unable to keep from turning to watch Anna's body following after them, but all they could see were her toes, her toes and the outline of a body from the waist down. It was as if the snow were burying her all over again. No, Ella thought, life had never taken enough hold of her. She was going under again; and then there would be one more time, and they would have their pictures, their memories, their bitterness, which was so easy to feed on. She worried about her parents. They would never get over this. She would have thought, by the time they reached their age, they would be safe from miscellaneous blows of life, but not, she supposed, while they had children. Or each other. Yet she still believed they had paid a small price. The final bill, she could hear William saying, had not yet come in. Inside her cloak, under her fur carriage blanket, she shuddered. "Cold?" Minnie asked. "Aren't you?" Minnie nodded. The house was coming into view. They looked at each other. Both felt colder. The two women clasped each other's hand.

"Maybe Mother and Father aren't back yet," Martin said hopefully; "we could get her into her room and make her look better if they're not." "Don't get your hopes up," Howard grumbled; "there comes their team; bad timing, bad timing." Martin reined in the horses before the house, John pulling his sleigh up alongside. "Where was she?" he asked. "In the north pasture," Howard answered for them. "What happened?" Edna asked. "She went for a walk without her boots on," Martin told them, not daring to look at the others in the sleigh. "Without her boots?" Edna echoed; "she had them with her?" "They're on the sleigh with her." "Is that what you call it?" Edna asked, smiling strangely; "it looks like a portable slab. So she killed herself," she said slowly. "I don't think she knew what she was doing," William said; "she had her boots but she forgot to put them on. She was headed toward the road; we were all afraid she would try to go back. I think that's what she did. We knew she wasn't in her right mind; you can't call that suicide. She was dressed for the weather. Except for the boots," he finished lamely, "and she *had* them. Clutched in one hand." "He's right, Edna," John decided. "What difference, what earthly difference can it make?" "Please," John begged her. "I know," she said; "I know. Don't worry about me." "I believe Anna said something like that," he said savagely. "We only looked the same," Edna reassured him. "Howard," she said, rousing herself, "I suppose you want to see Ten." He nodded. "Come on in, then. The rest of you will bring your sister in? Put her on the bed and don't worry about getting things wet."

Edna went in with Howard; he strode right up to the bed and then stared down at it as if he were stuck deep in a shaft of glue. Suddenly he reached out and touched Ten's cheek. "I always liked her," he said hoarsely. "Very much, I would guess," Edna said softly. "Oh, that's an old story, goes back before the beginning of the world." He sounded so sad. "But she was twelve years older than you were." "Wouldn't have made no difference to me," Howard answered, looking at her, defenseless; "but she went off with that shoemaker. Ladies don't have time for you to grow yourself up." Edna patted his arm. "I'll leave you here."

"Are you going to change her room?" he asked abruptly; "I guess some people don't like to keep the rooms after the people. After our Florence went, Alice had to go and drag everything out of the room. She whitewashed it; well, it didn't do her much good." "I guess it just made the room seem emptier." "That's about the size of it, miss." "No, we won't change Ten's room," Edna considered; "there was something about her. You know what I mean. Whenever I was unhappy about something, and she wasn't there, I used to go sit in her room. It was just like sitting with her. I guess we'll keep it the same way." "With the canopy bed, and the trunk at the bottom, and all those chairs? I never saw a woman with such a desire for chairs." "You were in there?" "Oh, I came on up one day; Alice was going on and on. I asked Ten; she told me." "Told you what?" "What to do. She always did." Edna couldn't help smiling. Ten was always up to something. Wherever she was now, she was up to something.

"And Anna's room?" Howard was asking. "If the others don't object," Edna answered slowly, "I'd like to change that. I don't think I could stand it. And I couldn't seal it up; that would be—ghostly, like having a tomb in the house." "A child is always different," Howard said, finally looking at her. "Yes, yes it is." "Very much, you'll see," Howard said; "Ten, she said Alice and me did most of our arguing over Florence." "Do you think that was true?" "Sure do." "Well," Edna began tiredly. "Mrs. Steele,"

Howard interrupted, putting his hand on her arm to hold
her in place; "the burial services; the church is peculiar.
They don't like it, insane people, suicides. We'll have to
fight them." "We?" "I came this far; I'll back old Doc
up." "Thank you." He had touched something far away,
years away, the reason she had first come here. " 'Thank
you' isn't enough," she said, lifting her eyes; they were
brimming. "Don't you cry over it, now, Mrs. Steele; I'll
go and change my mind." Edna rubbed her eyes and
pulled a smile over her face. There wasn't any need to
cut into that hide of his; she hadn't realized how much he
needed it on, on and firmly in place.

Two days later, Mr. Greenwood's caskets, one carrying
Ten, the other Anna, made their solemn procession, escorted by the family, along with the Moffats, on horseback to the church. A cousin of Matthew's had come
down to preach the sermon. Reverend Pierce was over
eighty-five, his wife informed them nastily, and he wasn't
going to start fighting with deacons and sextons at his age.
They moved steadily forward until in sight of the church.
Edna had never before realized how lonely it looked. It
was similar to the other houses, only much larger, and
distinguished by its tall, thin steeple; that, at least, seemed
able to pierce the impenetrable sky. The high gray and
white mountains rose behind it. They looked, in this
weather, behind the church, behind the town burying
ground, like giant tombstones eroded by the weather. On
one side of the church, the burying ground; on the other,
the pasture. Edna wondered why the Steeles had never
built a family tomb on their own grounds; they certainly
had enough land.

She supposed it was their way of saying they belonged with everyone else, no matter how they acted.
Well, everyone seemed to understand that, judging by
Howard. The pasture was so empty, so white. And in the
summer it was covered by cows and lambs grazing and
bleating and mooing and children dancing up and down
behind them, taking chances on getting themselves trampled; booths set up for fairs to benefit the church, the
Ladies' Aid Society, the Sewing Society, the Missionary
Society; it was a place of such color and noise. Now it
had been bled white. Yet she did love the snow. Even

though it had taken her daughter. But the snow was kind. If it was a killer, it was kind. It had only covered Anna in the robes she had chosen. It had not harmed her; it had preserved her as long as it could. If only it didn't stiffen things so; it reminded her of time. If time became visible, it would be like snow. She had thought that before, the day of Anna's wedding. That event was as difficult to accept as this. All important events were unacceptable, as if the mind went blank, canceled any great changes, sensing the horror inside the pod. But the perfume, when it broke open, that finally overcame everything. As it did when they covered the casket with flowers in warmer weather. They had covered Anna's with pine boughs. Only the Moffats and the Wards had come to see the bodies. Howard had been right: the question of suicide, insanity; it kept people off. And that was too bad. For once she would have liked to see more people.

The little cortege drew up to the gates of the cemetery. The white frame houses with their dark green shutters watched silently; Edna could see faces in the windows overlooking the cemetery. The houses were stark and bleak as the mountains, like the tombs. In the summer, they would be rioting with color, as if there was too much life, too much color. Trellises would be hammered hastily together; vines would climb them. Wild rose bushes. Ivy would hang in upside-down cones from pot after pot along the porch railings, pots of red and pink and red-pink geraniums between them. The scarlet poppies would flame; the air would be thick with the smell of wisteria, honeysuckle, the dusty, irresistible odor of bridal wreath. The trumpet vines would play their unheard hymns; the porches would come alive with furniture and people.

The people would call to whoever was walking up the steep hill to the post office; the postmistress would put out her wicker table and benches and chairs for the older ones to collapse upon after they had climbed the steep hill and received their mail. The gossip would fly through the air like a rising of birds; life would be warm with the buzzing of bees. Mosquitoes would bite. Everyone would meet together in the heat; the blood would slow and simmer. More and more life would bubble out of the cauldron. No, she did not want to think it was winter, with nothing to take the edges from this scene; everything sharp, clear, definable, not subject to change, not even in memory. She did not like this day, the sky so blue, the snow so white, the steeple clock so easy to read: two o'clock. The faces peering out at them, as if the houses were tombs, the people buried alive. It was not right that Anna should be in that box: exactly half her own age.

A sudden picture of Ten's room, as she had just seen it before leaving that morning: it was still before daybreak. Snowy light seeped into the room, through the thin white curtains with their frilled edges, their frilled tiebacks, the green and pink striped pattern of the wallpaper, which made the walls appear covered with one ribbon after another, the border just under the ceiling of bright green ivy, which Ten had herself recently varnished, although everyone expected she would break her neck in the process, but she had no trouble, except, of course, when she had to let go of the ladder after she reached the last step. The wing chair, its recesses so dark it was difficult not to imagine someone sitting in it, but the footstool clearer and definitely empty; a small square of light falling just next to the chair like a little rug. That was where the cats always went when she was not home; oh, dear God, she would miss her. That sarcastic, ironic, impossible person. She would miss her. Well, she would just pretend she was alive, she decided, defiant; the carriages were coming to a halt.

"Which of the coffins belongs to your daughter?" the sexton demanded. "What business is it of yours?" John asked; "of any of yours," he snarled, looking around at the others. She had no idea he could sound like that. "We don't want no insane people buried in here; this is a respectable burying ground." "The dead are all respectable," John growled, lifting his lap robe. The sexton speaking watched him warily; he had known John for years, but he didn't trust him. He knew what he'd been like as a child. He was wild, and they didn't change much.

"I hate useless arguments," John told him flatly. He lifted a rifle out from under his robe and put it across his knees. The sexton paled, but stuck. "You want to add murder to everything else?" "If this went off just as it rests here," John told him in a low voice—no one else could hear him—"the shot wouldn't kill you. It would only cripple you. I'd have the devil's own time taking out the bullet, and if I didn't, well, I guess you'd just bleed your-self out." "You've gone clean crazy, too," the sexton answered. "The dead are not crazy," John said. "That doesn't make no difference," the man answered stub-bornly; he turned around, beckoning to three of the deacons lurking in the background.

Howard spurred his horse forward. "I suppose," he asked laconically, "you don't mind answering to me?" "What do you have to do with anything?" the sexton de-manded. "These people are my friends, and my wife's friends, and my wife's brother's friends, and my daugh-ter's husband's in there, and my son's wife. We're family. I guess I have something to do with it. You watch it, you hymn-singing lunatic. All you Probsts are the same thing, dog killers, cat murderers, anything smaller than a beetle. They get buried in here, or you do. Go get the sheriff," he taunted. Everyone knew the sheriff refused to put bullets in his gun because he didn't know how to use it; he lived in terror it would go off. "Just thought I'd test mine out," Howard announced, raising his rifle, taking aim. The sexton's hat flew from his head; he grabbed for it auto-matically. "Shouldn't think you'd want your bones in the way of a bullet," Howard drawled. "Poor skinhead"; he grinned; "likely to freeze your brains out." "Get over here," Probst roared to the other deacons. The three of them crept forward.

Howard looked at John, who picked up his rifle. "A lovely steeple," John considered loudly; "such a perfect symbol of Christian charity. Such a reminder of Mary Magdalene. 'Let those who are without sin cast the first stone,'" he roared; "I think I'll fire a stone," he thun-dered. "That's not casting a stone, is it, wise ones?" he asked the deacons in the same booming voice.

He picked up the rifle and took aim. The bell rang out eerily. "Nice sound," John said approvingly, sliding in another bullet. The bell rang again and again and again. "Howard?" John asked; "you want to go for the chorus?" "Sure thing, Doc"; Howard grinned; the bell rang again and again. "I wonder," John addressed the air, "if we could go in now. 'Do not judge lest ye be judged,'" he roared; then, on cue, he and Howard burst into an ear-splitting, off-key chorus of "Amazing Grace." "They've all gone crazy," one of the deacons muttered to Probst;

"let them in; let them in. God will be the judge in the end. I don't think he wants a blood sacrifice over this. We don't even know, do we," he went on intently, "whether she fell, or went crazy, or committed suicide? I mean, no one but them was there." The others nodded. "We'll stand aside"; Probst glowered, moving back with the others. "Wise, wise," John murmured. He and Howard grinned at each other.

What a scene for a funeral, a double funeral, Edna thought; still, there was something comical about it. The opposition, in some odd way, had made it appear as if there was opposition to the deaths, something attempting to prevent ending the two lives. But now they were driving on into the graveyard, past the plain stones, high rectangles, some square, some shaped like the church steeple, others shaped like crosses, the arms oddly rounded, some flat against the ground, gray against the greenish black of the pines, and, in their turn against the gray and black of the mountains, and the sky, mocking them with its vitality. Someone had placed a basket of ferns in front of one tombstone, but the wind had blown it over. Some frozen little flags were wedged into crevices of others; she had never understood their significance. "John!" she exclaimed suddenly; "there are two holes already dug out!" "Amos and his sons during the night," he answered shortly. His nature—why hadn't she realized it?—was basically violent, and Howard's too; she wondered what strength it took to keep it under control. "I suppose we don't go into the church?" she asked. "There's no point in looking for trouble, and I wouldn't set foot in it, anyhow," John said.

Amos and his sons took down the caskets; the other men joined in carrying Ten first, then Anna, setting each casket down to the left of the excavations prepared for them. The minister was already standing at the burial site. He had thought it best, he told John, to enter by the back door of God; he had too many parishioners to leave in the lurch. "I'm sorry," Edna said, "but I really don't know your name." "James Hewitt; Matthew's cousin. I followed him into this black suit." "Oh," Edna said. No one had ever mentioned him before. Which meant Anna had not mentioned him before, but then, what had she ever been concerned with but her own family, the ones who lived within her own four walls?

"Our heavenly Father," Reverend Hewitt began, "we commend thy sisters to thy heavenly care in the certainty that we will meet upon the golden shore and they shall live forever in thy abounding grace. Everyone whose lives were touched by the lives of these two women were as cold shores warmed by warm waters. The world was fortunate in Tenniel Steele Richardson, in having her with us for eighty years, sustaining those around her after losing the man she loved best in this world; and in Anna Steele Hewitt, who, during her short lifetime, blessed the lives of all those who came in contact with her, who left her own home to help a devoted minister in the work of God, who fulfilled her duties with wisdom beyond her years. What price she paid for that sacrifice, none of us will ever know. We can only know how great was her comfort, how sustaining her generous heart. We commend these two women to the earth, which not only holds, but treasures, and which will abide with them, protecting them in its frosts and its fevers, until the great day of resurrection.

"We commend them to the earth secure in our faith in them. 'I am the resurrection and the life, sayeth the Lord; he who believeth in me, yea, though he may die, yet he shall live.' Amen." "Amen," everyone echoed. "And now we leave the cemetery, looking once more at the beloved caskets" (at a signal, the plates over the faces were opened, and those in command of their limbs went to view the dead first, the rest following after), "leaving the sad work of the interment to be done after our footsteps have ceased to press on this sacred soil, so that we may better remember them as they were in life, and, as they miraculously seem alive in their last, narrow homes, so shall they be on the day of resurrection." He lowered his head in silent prayer. The others bowed their heads, prayed, spoke with themselves, or felt the smash of their blood against their bodies, surfs gone wild. Edna felt John's hand gripping hers almost cruelly. She must have been swaying. She was dizzy.

She would be glad to leave. She had to keep her balance, she told herself as they turned to go, to remember trying to view John's pictures upside down; perhaps if

900

she looked at them that way, as he saw the images when he looked through the lens of the camera, under his dark cloth, she might find something; she hardly knew what. Some kind of clue; yes, that was it. Some kind of clue. What would she be like, she wondered as John handed her into the carriage, when the enormity of these events finally reached her, as a long delayed letter announcing the death of the intended might arrive immediately before the ceremony? She supposed it would be like that, like an event straight out of Ten's novels; but then Ten had always said her novels were totally unlike life. And yet, they had everything in common with it.

She had not, Edna remembered sadly, admitted to the second part of her theory until last year. Well, everyone had their timidities. She settled back for the long ride home. She still could not believe they had done more than simply "carry," as the people here said, Ten and her daughter to town, that they would not be returning for them, bringing them back. She looked over at John. From the grim, entirely unfamiliar expression on his face, she imagined he had already come to believe in the finality of those boxes, those caskets. She could not, except with pain, bring herself to use that word. And then that strange, strange tolling of the death bell, tolling from the rifle shots. She looked at Howard, who was sitting next to her. "The cold makes my eyes drip," he muttered hoarsely, looking the other way. "Here," Edna said; taking her handkerchief out, she wiped his eyes.

From the back seat, Alice looked on. She would have to think about Howard; was it possible after all these years she had permitted herself to overlook him somehow? Well, she decided passionately, time would not sustain them forever; she would try to change, old dog that she was. For the first time, she knew he deserved more; she also knew she had known this from the start. Did it take a tragedy to make her aware of other people's pain? What kind of monster was she? She leaned forward and squeezed her husband's shoulder. He looked back in surprise, which then faded into gratitude, a warm blurriness. Alice looked down at her own hands. She was incredulous to find herself wishing she had been born a Catholic; she would like to confess everything now, to be absolved of all her sins. All at once it seemed to her she had many to account for; the deacons, she thought cynically, would call this a change of heart. A lot those vultures knew about hearts. At least her children were taken care of; she could turn her attention to her husband with a good conscience. It was good of God, she thought, dabbing at her eyes, permitting her to live long enough to reach this place, this place from whence one began.

"What's this?" Edna asked wearily; she was the first one in the door. The hall was dark. She had never noticed it before, how dark the hall was, even on bright days. She was holding a little square envelope; it had her name written on it. "No doubt," Edna said, "something's happened to my mother." Edna stared at it. John took it away from her; she was obviously afraid to open it. He opened it while the others waited uneasily. "It's from Mrs. Grimsby; just Mrs. Grimsby. She says," he went on, taking in his wife's frozen figure, "she wanted to come up here to see Ten before she died. She wanted to come after she and Anna died, but she's too sick to go out, and no one would take her even after she asked, so she hopes it won't be too great an imposition to ask in such a cruel time if we would send one of the family down to see her. She says she's been in a very depressed state since Ten died, and she knows we all must be, but if we could spare one of the family to see her, she knows she would feel better because she thinks otherwise it would look as if she didn't care, but she wants to see one of us because it would be almost like seeing Ten and Ten cared so much about us."

John stopped suddenly and thrust the note aside. Bill took it. "I'll go," Minnie volunteered. She always, Edna thought, volunteered to do everything. "No, you're not, not this time," Bill contradicted; "I'm going. I'm going to get those people and this is the best way to do it." What was he talking about? Edna was surprised how like Howard's his voice sounded now. "Then you better go with Ella; she went to school with her granddaughter." What on earth were they talking about? Edna wondered impatiently. She didn't have the energy to ask. "That's right, I can talk to Sarah," Ella agreed; "it will look perfectly natural." "Those deacons are going to have cold breakfasts now," Bill growled. "Leave well enough alone," John told him, tired. "We're finished with them." "I'm sorry;

I can't. I grew up going to that church and sitting next to those people, and believing they stood for all the right things, and then they go and act like this, and after all the sacrifices this family has made for them, no, I can't let it go. You heard what that deacon said when you said something to him. " 'I can carry my head as I please; after all, it is my head.' Well, I just want to see him get it on straighter." "It's useless," John said; "what are you going to do? You can't fight the whole church." "I wouldn't think of fighting the church; it's the people I'm tilting after." "You won't get anywhere." "I'll bet you one day's rounds. Give me two weeks," William said. His spirit seemed to be returning. "You've got it; and what do you do when you lose?" "Clean out that cistern you call a cottage." "Well, get on then, before Mrs. Grimsby goes to bed." Those two would be glad enough to leave the house, Edna thought, watching William and Ella turn back to the sleigh.

Mrs. Grimsby was propped up in her bed; a big, toothless smile spread over her wrinkled face as they came in. "If you'll excuse me," she mumbled, disappearing under her blanket, reappearing with her false teeth in place. "I never could get them to fit," she complained. "You're too old to have to worry about other people," Bill teased. "Tell me what else to do," she flew back at him; "I can't take up fancywork with these hands. Sit down," she said, gesturing to a bench near her bed; "Just because you're younger doesn't mean you have to wear yourselves out early. It was something for you two to pay a call, on the day of the funeral and all. I heard you had trouble at the burying ground." "How did you hear that?" Ella asked; "we just got back." "Sarah was in town after some foolish berry spoon; she heard it at the post office. Well, tell me about it; there aren't many of us old trees left in the woods. I can't say it's so decent, this peeping curiosity of mine, but I did care about her, about all of you," she finished quietly.

They told her all about Ten, then Anna, omitting everything about the notebooks and the experiments. "Poor Anna," Mrs. Grimsby sighed; "she really did believe she could get there." Bill and Ella looked at each other, dumbfounded. Did she understand? "Well, Moffats," she sighed, "Anna wasn't made for heavy loads. A purebred

903

thing, not draft oxen like the rest of us. I always thought she was special. What *did* they do at the burying ground?" "Really?" she said, after they told her; "they really shot at the bell?" "And they got it each time"; Bill grinned; "not one miss. I tell you, I was surprised." "*I'm* not," Mrs. Grimsby said; "we always used to say your father and Howard, they'd turn out to be the best or the worst. They used to shoot blackberries off the bushes just to spite the birds. They never shot the birds, though." She thought. "They won't get off that easy, not with just a few bullets pinging at their bells; not that easy." She shook her head. Ella was afraid to look again at Bill; could the woman read their minds?

"Why don't you talk to Sarah?" she suggested to Ella. Ella left. Sarah had gotten so old, she thought when she saw her. She saw the same thought reflected on her old schoolmate's face. She repeated the story of the burying ground, as Mrs. Grimsby had intended her to do. Sarah shook her head, lips narrowing and whitening, just as her grandmother's always did whenever she was angry. She had taken over her grandmother's dressmaking business; there was no woman in town to whom she didn't talk. "You know," she told Ella confidentially, "Lucretius Sargent told the man with the milk wagon he wasn't going over to the church anymore; he was joining up with the Methodists and the new church in East Dorset." "They'll say that's because he's family." "They won't say that about the rest of the people on the Hill; they're going over the mountain with him. Mr. Lawrence said if Dr. Steele could come out there in the winter to stop his wife from bleeding to death and then take some jars of pickles for his trouble, he wasn't having much to do with a church that wouldn't bury his dead.

"It's not a family thing; after all those sermons about charity, dedicating our lives to imitating the life of Christ, turning the other cheek, not judging, and that's how they act. Well, some of the old ones will go out of habit, but I'm not going to be seen there, not with a minister wearing his top hat instead of a head, and without anything to tie his head onto his heart; that's what they said up in East Hadley, and I don't think they said half enough." She stared up at Ella as if she were one of the guilty parties.

"It's good of you," Ella said. "Of us? With our jars of pickles and Mr. Weston weaving around the common sending for your father at four in the morning? Good of his patients? Don't joke," she scolded; "we're not being good." "It looks like Reverend Pierce will be pierced," Ella quipped. "It does, doesn't it?" "Anna wouldn't have liked it." "Anna won't be here to see it; that's one blessing," Sarah sighed. William came in and put his hand on Ella's shoulder. "We better go," he told his wife; "we better see about your parents." "You always come; someone from that house always comes," Sarah said wonderingly. "Like the Japanese beetle," said Bill. "Oh, get on with you." Sarah walked them out.

John lost his bet and spent a day on rounds with Martin. The Sunday after the burial, a number of sleighs, estimates varied from ten to thirty, reined up a short distance in front of the church; they stayed there until the last bells rang summoning the congregation to worship. Then, when the doors closed, they started up their horses, drove by the church jangling their harness bells, and drove over to the Methodist church in East Dorset. There was no mistaking the nature of the event; it was a quiet, irreversible mutiny. The Steeles noted it with grim satisfaction, but it was the satisfaction of a moment. It was the Moffats and their children who gloried in the outcome; they were the religious ones. Edna did not understand it. She would have asked John about it, but it was so hard to talk to him. He had moved into the cottage and came in later and later at night. Now, when she awoke, she could never be sure if he would be there. He had dragged an old lounge from the attic and set it up in the cottage. More and more frequently, he slept there, under carriage blankets.

He liked the solitude; no, he needed it, he finally told Edna, after she flared up one night. She never knew where he was; when she woke up she didn't know where he'd gone. She would become frantic worrying if he were alive or dead. The first few months she had gone out and looked in the window but she had given that up. She had tried to persuade herself she didn't care whether he was dead or alive, and she was getting better at it, she screamed at him.

There were mornings she didn't care whether he was

alive or dead, and now *he* complained when she wasn't to be found when he came in. Well, she was in Ten's room, that's where she was; Ten was still more company than he was. He didn't care how she felt any longer. He tried to keep away from her as much as he could. He wasn't even living in the same house anymore; all he cared about was his picture making, those horrible, dead pictures, and breathing in that poison, forgetting to open the ventilators she invented for him. He wanted to get away from her so much he was trying to kill himself; wouldn't he be happy until he watched her bury everyone in the family? All her life she had cared about him more than anyone else, and this was what it was like, silence and more silence. If she came into the cottage when he was working he just pretended she wasn't there. Well, she couldn't endure it another day; she was going to Boston tomorrow, or she would go to Boston tomorrow, if the roads were clear.

"Aren't you a bit old to be running home to Mother?" John asked. "That is just what I mean," Edna shrilled; "that is just it exactly. It's like talking to a piece of ice. We buried them; they didn't bury us. I can't live like this anymore." She stared straight at him, dry-eyed. "You don't have to." "Is that your last word on the subject, your last will and testament?" she asked, feeling herself growing older. How long could he take to answer her? she wondered, her pride holding her straight in her chair. She looked at the table her elbow rested on. There was a pewter candlestick, the one she carried back and forth between her room and Ten's at night. "Answer me," she screamed, picking it up and throwing it at him. He ducked; the candlestick buried itself in the heavy velvet draperies. She stared at it; she had no idea she was so strong. "You could have killed me with that." "I don't care," she sobbed; "I don't care. You're doing that anyway. I would have just hurried things up for you."

He was staring at her, the tears rolling out of her big green eyes, as if she were a stranger, as if he were watching an enemy, a rain cloud, cry; as if she weren't human. She sat there, upright, looking at him, then covered her face with her hands. She couldn't stand it, seeing him look at her that way. She ought to have died when the others did. She had died when the others died; perhaps they had both died then. They just hadn't realized it yet.

She started in her chair; it was the feeling of hands resting on her shoulders. "I'm sorry," John said gruffly; "I'm sorry. There's something wrong. I can't stand to have anyone look at me." "Not even me?" she asked, staring straight ahead. "Not yet, not yet. Look at me if you want to; look at me." She slowly turned to see him. His cheeks were wet. "I wake up at night, and I start crying. I can't stop. It's like convulsions. I'm going off my head." "No, you're not," Edna whispered; "I do the same thing." "It's different; it's all I think about, the way she looked on that piece of wood, how fast it went back toward the house; how she came out of the house again, how it was all my fault. And that face, that dead face, it didn't look any different than it did the day before. You'd think," he talked through his thick sobs, "after all the dead faces I'd seen . . ." He stopped, unable to continue.

"I know," Edna said; "I know. We're the only ones who know. The others, they're younger. They're in the middle of their families; this didn't cut out any holes in their skies. They're missing a star; that's what's happened to them. The lights in the sky can't even break through to us. We're the only ones who know, and we're sealing each other up in separate rooms. We should have planned a family crypt," she went on bitterly; "we could have moved into our separate compartments there. That would have been more honest." "Don't!" John cried; "I know what I've been doing." "But you're not going to stop," Edna answered, cold. That coldness; it kept coming back into her voice. "I don't know if I can, not yet." "And you're not going to try." "I didn't say that." "Then what did you say?" "I didn't say anything. I want it to stop. I'm getting to like it less and less out there. Alone."

"If you want to sleep in the snow," Edna answered, "there's nothing I can do about it." She couldn't soften her voice. "I don't want to sleep in the snow," he answered pathetically. "Then come into bed." "Do you mean that? After you threw that thing at me?" "I don't like you very much, not now, but I want you back in bed." John shook his head, discouraged. "We can't," she began, "just erase it all, not as if it took place on a blackboard; it's changed us." "Forever?" "I can't see that far ahead; I don't think so. People don't change that much. Come into bed," she pleaded. She got up stiffly and began undressing; she forgot to brush her hair. She got back out of bed. She forgot to open the window a crack. She got back out of bed. She forgot to latch the door. She got back out of bed again. "All right," she sighed, settling in.

"Did we ever," John finally asked, "have hopes for the children?" "No, I don't think so," Edna answered, surprised; "we just expected them to grow up." "We wouldn't have been surprised if they'd taken up cracker peddling." "No," Edna agreed; "it's a good thing we didn't have high hopes." "We had high hopes. We hoped they'd grow up, grow old. We never hoped they'd freeze to death in the snow." She started crying. "We're not being fair to the others," she finally whispered. "That's because she was our favorite." "Which one?" "Which one?" John repeated; "that's a good question." She turned on her side stiffly and stiffly touched his cheek; she had forgotten he was alive, warm. "You're cold," John told her, feeling the touch of her hand. "I know; I'm never warm enough." "Are you warmer now?" he asked, holding her so tightly she wanted to cry out. She was, she realized, warm. For the first time since the funeral, she was warm. "Yes," she said happily, "and my left ribs are cracking." "Oh, Lord," John sighed with relief. "Let's go to Boston for the weekend and let the mummies take care of us." "We'll go tomorrow," she agreed. "I hope the surprise doesn't kill them." "Don't say it," Edna sighed, squeezing closer.

They spent their week in Boston. Mrs. Siddons took one look at them and treated *them* as invalids; meals on trays arrived at their room. The Siddonses canceled all their engagements; they sat up in front of their high, tiled fireplace reading the papers in the flickering light. "You would think," Mr. Siddons said, looking up, "an important paper could find something better to write about than this: 'A Kansas Sunday-School Boy under Arrest—Says His Father, a Deacon, Compelled Him to Steal.' The headline is almost as long as the article," he complained. " 'George Styman, a ten-year-old boy, is under arrest on the charge of robbing the contribution box at the Baptist Sunday school at Buggham, near Wichita, Kansas. For more than six months money has been missed and action was taken to expel the treasurer of the school, Miss Effie Twintingham, from the church, and have her arrested for embezzlement, as she could not account for the missing money, amounting to only one hundred dollars. When arrested, the boy was almost paralyzed with fear and said that his father had threatened him and forced him to steal.' Idiots!" Mr. Siddons exclaimed, "expelling Miss Effie Twitwit, who's probably over two hundred, with a whole congregation of ruffians sitting right there." "Baptists." Edith shook her head. Since learning of the incident at the cemetery, she and Mr. Siddons had begun attending the Episcopal church; the choir was better, she explained guiltily to Edna. Edna and John smiled. "I think I'll go up to bed," Edna said at last; she knew her mother wanted to talk to John. "I'm going up, too," Mr. Siddons said. "I hope you still remember which room is which," Edna teased him. "I think I've forgotten," he called back. They had won through to the end, she thought, contented, going into her room.

"John," Edith said, "do you mind terribly if I talk to you about your sister? I know how close you were to her." "No, no, I don't." He wanted to talk about her; it was a relief, he understood at last, talking to someone who didn't live in the house. "I felt," Edith said, rubbing her arms, "as if part of me went in there with her. I was so mad at her for dying first; she would have said I'm still childish as ever." "Something like that." "I want her back," Edith said, starting to cry; "when I was a very little girl, and broke a Chinese doll, I kept saying, 'I want her back'; a lot of good it did me," she sniffed, ladylike, into her handkerchief. "A lot of good it does anyone. "It wasn't right of her; she never seemed any older." "You don't, either. Women like you and Ten and your daughter ought to prepare all the others. You might walk around in old-age masks part of the time. Then it wouldn't seem so sudden."

"It would have seemed sudden twenty years from now, wouldn't it?" Edith asked. "It always does; I don't know why, but it always does." "Ella sent on the letter she wrote me; she said you and Edna would be at each other like two tomcats." "She never did get her sexes straight, at least not in her figures of speech." He smiled, puffing at his pipe. He had taken it up since Ten and Anna died.

909

"She said you would have a portrait of Ten for me; you know, one taken after she left us." "Edna has it. We took quite a few of them. Everyone wanted one; it was a good thing she died in cold weather." "*Have* you and Edna been at each other?" "Like two tomcats." "Oh, dear," Edith sighed; "she didn't tell me what to do about it. She just said to tell you she'd be back for you if you didn't behave and she'd come disguised as the Reverend Pierce." "I'm cured"; John grinned; "you don't have to worry. We've gotten more peaceable. Look," he said, stretching out his hand: "velvet paws. Edna has a new cat. She brings it into the cottage. I don't chase her out. We're starting to talk again. Or cry. Sometimes, I think there's never going to be one without the other." "You're wrong there," Edith said; "it will end as something nice and warm, as soon as the corners wear off." "The tears should have worn them off long ago." "Well, perhaps they have, and you just haven't noticed it." John looked at her surprised.

After he and Edna returned from the trial, Edna commented how her mother had changed. Ella was incensed. "She hasn't changed," their daughter protested angrily; "you've just let her out of that cage you've kept her in. You're the one who's changed." They chatted on about Ten; the longer they talked, the closer toward them she came. "I've done my share of crying," Edith admitted at last. "If Ten is hovering around the room," John teased, pretending to look into the corners, "she's probably trying to drop handkerchiefs into our laps." "Or stones on our heads," Edith said, trying to smile; "she was always unpredictable." "Predictably there." Edith nodded. "Well," John said, "up to bed with you. We want to keep you as long as we can." "Sentences like that add years to a life"; she smiled. He escorted her up, as if to a ball.

"Edna," he said later, "we have to do something about Lettie. We can't just cut her out." "I'm not about to discuss Lettie this weekend." "Ella was right about the wreath she sent." "A lot of trouble she went to," Edna grumbled; "going to that fancy store and sending a wreath of silk roses." They lay in bed, remembering. Edna had refused to keep "the thing" in the house, but Ella grabbed it from her hand. "Mother," she said, "this is the best she can do. I'll keep it in our room." "Throw it *out*," Edna ordered her. "I will not," Ella answered, furious; "just because she's not like Anna, just because she's not like the rest of us, doesn't mean she isn't human. I'm going to write a thank-you note and I think you should sign it." Edna glared. "I don't see why you, of all people, should defend her," her mother said. "Because the more she's missing, the more she needs to be pitied. We don't have to like her to pity her. She didn't ask to be a member of this family." "I didn't ask to have a daughter like her!" "Isn't that too bad?" Ella said; every day she sounded more and more like Ten. "At least," she told Edna, "when your mother is gone, you'll have Lettie as a living reminder. That should make her worth something." "Not much."

"Mother," Ella objected, "isn't it about time you got something straight? You aren't going to change people. You couldn't change Anna and you can't change Lettie, and none of us changed you. You wouldn't have liked it, either, if we'd tried." "What would you have tried to change?" "Just think about it," Ella answered, turning on her heel. An hour later, the wreath of silk roses hung over the mantel; Edna had not disturbed it. The next night, she and John began talking, or screaming, or whatever one would call it. "Well, we had better do something," Edna conceded to the waiting silence; "but could we wait a week?" "I doubt if Lettie will notice," John allowed; "you've given up mourning, I see." "What do you mean?" "You're coming to bed in your skin, not those black silk gowns." "That's because it's warmer," Edna said, guilty. "It isn't," John said, sliding his hand down her back. "It is," she contradicted, turning to face him. The moon shone in on their smiling faces.

"The country is gone; the snow has covered it. All things float now. At night, especially. The farmhouses with their one light look like ships marooned. The sea is white; the sky is white; day, the rivers run pearl gray between the drifts of white snow; there is the arbitrary design of black trees, black twigs. The roads narrow like old veins; the frozen snowdrifts gray and blacken. The dirt freezes; pebbles eat into it. During the day, after the snow has been standing as if it would stay forever, it rains. Then the houses, trees, hills, cows, are black outlines; they are dissolving like a grainy photograph. They are in a middle state; they are either decomposing or recomposing or both. Chimneys turn black from their own smoke. The blue jays stay all winter. In the summer no one will prefer them. They add color, the color of dawns, sunset after the sun goes down. The barns are red and gray, keeping things alive until the next season. That is important to believe when the gray sky becomes the gray frozen water, the clouds loosened chunks of ice when the river above breaks up. The weather vanes define themselves, effigies of animals. Perhaps they are not alive; perhaps even the animals wish to escape the pull of the earth. The horse and its carriage turn under the sky high above the earth. It rises.

"The pine trees are stubborn in their greenness. There are dead leaves on the ivy vines; they hang now like dead rope. There is a stone wall where drifts melt irregularly; the ice melts on the roofs, scalloping them. There is ice on the twigs; the trees have turned to glass. The earth becomes breakable. People become fragile; it is possible to see through them. At certain angles, the snow glitters. It looks hard, harder than stone. The sun is a gray button; it is remote. Some thick twigged trees on the bank have fuzzy gray hair. They are old women, sharing their secrets. The birches have grown like lightning, malignantly out of the snow. Ice beards on rocks and the earth ages. Some water still trickles through the ice beards; the cliffs are old beyond counting. The dull red gold of lost autumns lingers in their leaves. Blood, spilled and dried. The streams are green. Their water runs green over the ice just under the water, a pale, lichenous green. The whole stream runs black, black with dark green tints; it is a snake. The blue jays and cardinals stay behind; they have the answer. The old trees told them. They were once human and older than the trees. I must remember all these things. The worst sin is forgetfulness. Whenever the voice speaks it says remember, remember. It uses the wind for its voice. The wind has many other things to say, but I have not learned enough of its words."

It was Ella who found this paper in Anna's room; her parents were in Boston. She read it once, once again, took it to her room, and burned it. "Ashes to ashes, dust to dust," she whispered, tears streaming down her cheeks.

That was the end of her sister. They were each burying the dead in their own way.

Gradually, the dead kept more and more to themselves; life in the house began returning to normal. John worked on his pictures. When Edna went out to the cottage, which she did more and more frequently, John flipped the two little wooden handles opening the little ventilators Edna had designed for him. She knew he had regarded the cottage as his own private coffin which linked him to the dead, but now it had shed its chrysalis; it was again an object in the ordinary world. He had gone down to Boston to see Lettie; she seemed happy, but uneasy, he told Edna, as if there was something she had forgotten. Her husband was another matter altogether. John felt sorry for him. As often as he could, he stole—that was the only word for it—his own children and took them on swan boats, to the common, riding, to the country on picnics; he lived for their affection. He was more and more successful, but when he and John went out for the papers, he looked at the front page, handed it to John saying there was nothing new he wanted to know about, for he might decide he wanted it. He had meant it as a joke, but he wasn't joking; he was serious. If it weren't for the children, John believed Lettie would have been widowed long ago, and in the same way her grandmother had been. She seemed, at times, a travesty of Edith, a moral cartoon of her. "We should have them down here more often," he concluded. The others agreed, suspiciously looking at Edna, who nodded her head in assent. "There are enough of us," she said; "we can each stand a fifteen-minute dose; we can call in Alice and her brood." Everyone smiled at her. At that instant, she understood she had gotten over nothing; she had only fallen back into the old, strong habits. The old emotions, they were as powerful as anything else, but they had been jerking her about like puppet strings. She was still frozen somewhere inside.

It was late afternoon in April when John found her sitting alone in the kitchen. There was no one else in the house. She held a picture of little Minnie in one hand and a book in the other. He had never seen a face so covered with tears, so soaked with them; the front of her dress was so wet it clung to her breasts. John stood behind her, his hand on her shoulder. He looked at the picture of little Minnie. She was propped up on what looked like a raccoon skin, her dark almond eyes wide open, her little mouth open, too, as if she had just seen something incredible. She wore a little white lace dress, the bodice in the Napoleonic style, its belt across where her breast would someday be, but now really crossing her enormous little stomach. Her chubby hands lay on her starched white skirt and her huge shoes peeped out from beneath its lace rim. Anna had parted her hair in the middle, and, in a vain attempt to keep it in place, had pushed it behind her ears, but one strand had escaped and hung down. It made her look as if she were really there: that one strand of hair.

"What have you been reading?" he asked. Edna turned the book face up on the table. "Bacon?" he asked; "I've never seen anyone cry over Bacon." She pointed to the title. *Bacon and Other Essayists*. "Edna," he said, "I'm too worn out for guessing games. Can you tell me what you're crying about?" "I can't believe," she answered, as if she were still not crying, "it's been six months since they died. Everything's turning green." "Is that what you're crying about?" "No, the book." She opened it. " 'We have made too untimely a departure and too remote a recess from particulars,' " she read to him; " 'whosoever shall entertain high and vaporous imaginations instead of a laborious and sober inquiry of truth, shall beget hopes and beliefs of strange and impossible shapes.' " She turned several pages; he saw the book was carefully marked. " 'Our persons live in the view of heaven, yet our spirits are included in the caves of our own complexions and customs which minister unto us infinite errors and vain opinions if they be not recalled to examination.' " She stared up at him. "This was the Bible we needed," she said, flipping to another page; "I taught her all the wrong things."

"There was no teaching her." " 'Mere power,' " Edna read out loud, " 'and mere knowledge exalt human nature, but do not bless it. We must gather from the whole store of things such as make most for the uses of life.' " "He sounds," John put in, trying to lighten her mood, "as if he were speaking of going to market." "We did and we came home with all the wrong things," she cried on. It was useless talking to her; listening, that was the only thing that would do any good. Even, he thought, sighing inwardly, if he had to listen to the whole of *Novum Organum.*

She turned to another page. " 'The empire of man over things depends wholly on the arts and sciences. For we cannot command nature except by obeying her.' This would have done Anna some good," she said, her voice muffled. John sighed. "If we had given it to her in her cradle, perhaps then. But I doubt it." She went on to the next passage. " 'Custom is the principal magistrate of man's life.' He says it is 'everywhere visible,' and that men go about 'as if they were dead images and engines moved by the wheels of custom.' He says it is a good idea to observe from the mountain of truth and to see 'the errors and wanderings, and mists, and tempests in the vale below.' " His wife paused. " 'So always that this prospect be with pity.' " "He really believes custom determines life," John said, breaking his resolution of silence. "Or childhood the nature of the woman. Nothing can be done about it. That's what he says, Edna. The only adequate response is pity. Isn't that what he's saying? Only a few change, or grow into lives which fit them? And no one at all can do anything about it? Isn't that what he's saying? Edna?" She stared, helpless. "Read some more," he asked; would this sadness never end?

" 'Make the time to come the disciple of the time past and not the servant.' " "That, should be the new motto for this family; at least," he went on, searching his wife's face, "for a while." "John, listen to this," she said excitedly, the weeping continuing as naturally as breathing. " 'All things are full of panic terrors; human beings most of all; so infinitely tossed and troubled as they are with superstition especially in seasons of hardship, anxiety, and adversity.' " "So we're not so unique, after all," he murmured, tugging a strand of her hair loose. "Emerson," Edna said, trying to push his hand away, "says that nature is the immense shadow of man. He thinks we can change it by changing ourselves. I wonder"—she looked at him—"if Anna read Emerson."

"I doubt it; I doubt it very much." "This is the worst part," Edna told him, turning to the page with the corner bent down; "it's by an anonymous writer. They think it may be Christopher Smart. 'We are living on this planet, blown here by an ill wind.' 'Life would be unacceptable otherwise; now it is glorious and mysterious. We know ourselves changelings, seeking our true parents. We are lost in a deep wood where no moss grows.' That seems to encompass everything," she said; she wept as she breathed in and out. "We know ourselves changelings," John repeated slowly; "the deep woods. I don't really understand it. It seems true. If we don't belong here, that would make things easier to accept. Our lives, I mean." She nodded. John put his hand over hers. She closed the book, but they sat there in the darkening kitchen, the tears streaming down her face. When the clock struck seven, and the light was finally dying in the cement sky of the window, she wiped her eyes and smiled at him. As if she had never been upset.

That night, Edna heard someone knocking at the door. She got up and went down in her robe. Bridget had taken to leaving a kerosene lamp on the hall table; John to latching the children's doors. Edna opened the front door. Outside, a young woman was standing in the snow. She looked something like Anna, Edna thought, but not really. Her face was a more definite heart shape; she was taller. She had her black cloak with its hood clutched about her; Edna could not tell the color of her hair. It was entirely hidden by the dark fur rim of her hood. She must need some help; perhaps she had come for one of the boys. "Just a minute," Edna said cheerfully, going back for the light. When she came back, the snow-covered lawn was blank. She had gone. I should have asked her in, Edna thought; I should follow her and bring her back. That was when she noticed there were no tracks in the snow, and the snow had stopped falling. Then how had she gotten there? Her healthy red cheeks, her beautiful face, were vivid in her sight. She had seemed so kind, waiting so patiently. She must have been a ghost. There was no other explanation, even though she had never believed in such things.

She woke in the morning in a state of bliss approaching ecstasy. Then she remembered the night's event. It must have been a dream, she told herself; she had not felt so happy, so at peace, for a long time. She finished dressing and went out into the hall. John was still sound asleep. Poor man; she had worn him out. It was about time *they* went for a picnic, back to the old meadow. She went down to the kitchen. "What about a picnic basket?" she asked Bridget. "A picnic basket?" Bridget quavered in disbelief; "in this weather?" "What's wrong with this weather?" Edna asked; "it's spring." "Spring, is it?" Bridget asked; "just look out the window." Edna walked over. The grounds, as far as the eye could see, were covered with snow. The mountains rising beyond the fields were covered with snow. "A fine thing for Miss Ten's geraniums," Bridget muttered; "a good thing for them I won't let them out until May. Can't tell a thing about the weather up here until the middle of May." "You sound like you think we're living in the Arctic circle. It's been no picnic for you, I guess." "I guess not."

Then it had not been a dream. The snow was real. But this happiness was genuine; the sadness over not having brought the girl inside with her; that was real, too. It must have been a ghost, she decided, puzzled. A good ghost. She told John about it later; he didn't laugh at her. "After the doings of our clock, nothing surprises me. Maybe someone was saying goodbye." "But her feet left no tracks, and I didn't know who she was." "Anna's feet left no tracks, either." "Now they are completely covered up," she said. He looked at her again. It was peace, he thought; peace had knocked on the door last night. He was happy Edna had gone to the door. Perhaps no one else could have believed it, have taken it in. He smiled at her. "Let's go sliding," he teased. "Let's go!" she agreed, surprising him. He warned her they would both come home with broken legs, but she only laughed, saying they would be worth it, sliding in April. They left in the sleigh before the others were up.

1891

Time passed. Alice looked at her diaries. They reminded her of something; they had always reminded her of something. She began keeping a diary in 1845. They were lined up on the shelf in her bedroom on top of her vanity now.

All of them, except for the last one, were black. They varied in height and thickness. Yes, that was it; they reminded her of tombstones. She had no idea why she kept them. 1867 was long and thin. The months were decorated with signs of the zodiac. The Civil War had been in the air still. After the year's calendar came "Memorable Events in the Secession Rebellion Together with the Fluctuations in Gold." Eight pages. Together with the fluctuations in gold. Whoever had written that could have written her diaries. She picked up the diary for 1849.

"January 1: Weather moderating. Signs of rain. Washing day in the afternoon. Went to the village. Called on Mrs. Grimsby and brother Lucretius. Found her more comfortable than I expected. Came back and stopped at Julia's a while" (she had been gone over twenty years now); "Great Oyster Supper at Joneses' in Rupert; got Florence a book and Florence a corn popper." Monday, that was a Monday. She didn't have to look at the top of the entry to know that; Monday was a washing day.

"Tuesday, January 2. Moderate winter weather. Amos drawed a load of wood to the blacksmith. Moved J. M. Perkins from the tavern to J. Fisher's. Drawed a load of sawdust for P. M. Kellogg from Sherwood's Mill to the village. Elvira Davis called and took dinner. Received the first number of *The Rural American Teacher*.

"January 3. Weather about like yesterday. Howard and William been piling balsa wood boards at the mill. This afternoon Elvira and Laura Hopgood gone back to Bennington to school. Florence and I have done housework and sewed some. I mended Florence's nightdress, etc.

"January 4. Some appearance of a thaw in the forenoon but it proved otherwise before nine o'clock in the evening. It was cold as Greenland. Howard got a load of sawdust this afternoon. I cut out a pair of overalls and sewed most of the day except getting the meals. S. Frank called, also Mrs. Lakey in the P.M.

"January 5. The coldest day we have had yet. William chopped wood all day. Howard drawed another load of sawdust for himself and I have nearly finished a pair of overalls. Freddie and Lois ran over to Mrs. Post's for a flying visit. Visited to Mrs. Post's yesterday. It is so cold we had no callers today.

"January 6. Still very cold. Howard chopped wood until

3 o'clock, then went home. Howard did his chores and went to the village in the evening. Carried Aunt Eliza some cheese and buttermilk. Newcomb and Hat and several of the young people met here to sing. Florence went home with them.

"January 7. Today colder than yesterday. No one went to church but the teacher. Florence staying over the Sabbath with Aunt Hat. Ed Jameson came over here to get some medicine Howard got for him to the store. Came very near freezing his face. Mrs. Platt handed Howard the first number of *The Advocate* and *Guardian* for 1847.

"January 8. The cold more severe today than yesterday. So cold Charles did not come to work. Emily's plants froze last night. The teacher and six or seven of his scholars went to a union spelling school this evening at the village. We think the weather moderating a little this evening, etc.

"January 9. Weather a little more moderate today. So much so that I went to East Dorset after Mrs. Brock and Lucretius. Florence came from school this afternoon to supper. Charles chopped wood a part of the day. I carried a cheese to John Chalmers. Left it first to Elder's grocery to be weighed; it weighed 52 pounds.

"January 10. Weather several degrees warmer today than yesterday. Mrs. Block and I went to the village this morning to get some trimming for our dresses. Came home and went to baking. Howard drawed a load of wood to Mrs. Caulder. Got his horses shod. I cooked a part of a sparerib.

"January 11. Quite comfortable weather. This morning signs of a storm of some kind. Howard and Charles worked in the woods all day. The singers all met to Oldman's for a sing this evening. Florence stayed all night. Florence swept the chamber in the A.M. I've done general housework.

"January 12. Very moderate weather. Snowing a little. Howard and Charles getting wood from the woods all day. I've sewed considerable today. Almost finished a dress skirt. Mrs. Poole made us a call this afternoon. She said Mrs. Eggerton was sick.

"January 13. Our thaw a short one. A little rain and a little snow and a sudden turnabout and freeze-up. The boys did not accomplish much in the way of work in the forenoon. Charles chopped in the afternoon. Howard drawed a load of wood to Mrs. Caulder. Oldman and his wife here a while in the evening. I got some cloth for a frock.

"January 14. Sunday. Very cold again. Been growing cold all day. Mrs. Griffin went to church Sabbath-School Concert in the vestry. Mrs. Poole and I went to see Mrs. Eggerton. Found her quite cheerful. She was operated upon again Friday, the fifth of the month. I don't see much chance for her recovery."

So much for January, Alice thought. It was always colder in February. She flipped the pages.

"February 12. Our freeze-up was a regular rainstorm. Icicles froze on the fence and on the trees and no work done out of doors. Charles tore down one of the grain bins upstairs. I washed 3 woolen sheets and at four o'clock Howard went to the schoolhouse after Florence. Went up to Farwood's in the evening.

"February 13. Not very cold but everything covered up with ice. Howard drawed Amanda another load of wood; found her quite feeble. Was operated on again yesterday, poor woman. I fear she will not want much wood or anything else. Jack Lawson called, also Uncle Haddock.

"February 14. A cold east wind. About one o'clock it began to snow. It was tedious being out in the evening. It began to rain at ten. Was raining hard. Freddie went to Derrick's court; Derrick got it adjourned. Again witnesses turned out for nothing, as they have several times before. Howard out in the rain. Nearly 11 o'clock P.M.

"March 10. This week has been about as cold as any we have had this winter. Neither of them able to work much. Howard got a hard cold and Charles a lame side. Florence got up to Uncle Oldman's again to stay all night. I mended Florence's hoops and delaine dress. Glad Saturday has come again.

"March 11. Sunday. The wind has blowed from the east all day. Began to snow towards night. Will probably rain towards morning. Howard went over to Oldham's. To come home with Florence this evening. I've been quite off the hooks all day. Florence gone most of the week." So much for the year altogether, Alice thought.

1880. The months were illustrated by signs of the zodiac, but drawn into scenes. The Interest Laws. Domestic

Postage. Foreign Postage. Interest Table. Population of States and Territories. Principal Territories. Principal Cities. Presidents of the United States. R. B. Hayes the last name.

"January 1. 30 degrees above. Pleasant all day. The old year calmed down some before it left us. Howard went to the mill. Got a check of $91.36. After doing housework for a while, I cut out an underwaist for Lois Ann.

"January 2. 40 degrees above zero. A very strong south wind. Looked like a thaw but the wind has got in the west. Colder again. John Haddock talks of moving to Dorset in the spring, if not before. I cut out an underwaist for myself.

"January 3. Cold but pleasant till just at night. It clouded up and is storming this evening. Charles went to Dorset. Howard went down and carried Lois Ann to the street. Got the money of his milk check. So far we are having an open winter. More wagons than sleighs running.

"January 4. 40 degrees above zero at noon thawing. Has rained nearly all the afternoon. Howard and I have been alone all day and I enjoy it so much, so quiet, such a good time to read. Wrote a letter to Aunt Hat Foote this evening.

"January 7. 30 degrees above zero. Very pleasant all day. Dried our lard. Howard salted his pork. A post office order from Mrs. Poole for $11.27. Young Jack died this morning. Too pleasant to last long." Alice shivered. At least she could control the seasons when she read. She flipped to July.

"July 23. 60 degrees above zero. A passable hay day. Howard mowed the orchard north of the barn. He began to seed sowed corn three days ago. I tried to cut a few carpet rags and it has made my hands very lame."

By 1880, Alice thought, I began summarizing the months and their weather, as if making another entry. By 1880, noting the events was not enough; I began charting them. She turned to the diary's last pages and the familiar lists: Deaths in 1880. The lists are getting longer now, she thought.

"Mrs. John Haddock, Augusta, Wisconsin. February 7.

Mrs. Daniel Foote, Manchester. February 7.

Mrs. Henry Ring, Barumsville. January 4.

Morton Parker, Williamsville. February 15.

Mrs. Eunice Hopgood, Williamsville. March 1.

Miss Narcissus Underhill, Williamsville. April 22.

Joseph Sherwood, Williamsville. April 30.

Josephine Hopgood, Williamsville. March 1.

Mrs. Fanny Pierce, Williamsville. May 5.

Miss Calist Pierce, Williamsville. May 5.

Leonard Pierce, Williamsville. May 5.

Miss Florence Pierce, Williamsville. May 13.

Fred Camp, Williamsville. May 14.

Bertha Camp, Williamsville. May 15.

Ellen Camp, Williamsville. May 15.

Miss Celia Camp, Williamsville. May 16.

Eugenia Camp, Williamsville. May 16.

Frank Aiken, Fredonia, Kansas. November 15.

Harriet Smith, Centerville, California. November 3.

Ann Cranford, Durango, Colorado. December 25.

Mrs. Ralph Eggerton, Arlington. December 8.

Twenty-one deaths in 1880. Everyone must have been remarkably healthy. What had Anna called these events, these deaths, the births? The mere alphabet and accidence of life. Whole families gone. They went everywhere; they died everywhere. What would they think of her? Alice wondered, looking at her diaries patiently waiting in lines on their shelves. Would they think of her as an old woman, growing cranky and morbid and religious? She was all of those things, some of the time. Would anyone guess why she wrote these diaries: that the entries were epitaphs for each day, the volumes epitaphs for each year? Would anyone understand they were a measure of the value she placed upon them? And how could they?

"Today I regulated our house. I shall not keep a fire through the night as I did last night. The old adage of the shepherd that he'd rather see his wife on a bier than see Candlemas cold and clear was verified today. Five tramps were here just at night. The city boarders went on a tilt somewhere. A calf and a horse were killed by lightning. The city boarders are to hie away to their city homes again. The clothes froze on the line. Howard left his harness to be oiled. Lucy Bliss died far away from her family on a visit. Her home was in Indiana. The townsmen have gone to clean up the cemetery." No, there was no sign of her, of Alice Moffat, in 1880. Perhaps she would come across herself in 1879.

"Howard is washing the buckets, so sugaring is ended for this year. Afflicted parents, I know how to sympathize with you. The city teams begin to play merrily. We set out rat traps. We caught the gentleman in both, one foot in each trap. I don't see anyone that seems to take much comfort. I am manuring my roses. We went to the quarry. We were well paid for going, for we had a good time. Jane Camp died from falling down cellar steps. The peddler took a dinner here. If I stay up much longer it will be already morning. Not much news flying about. Father's burial today. The ground was frozen like a rock. A man passes twice a day on a velocipede. The north wind howls dismally. I shall keep a fire all night to keep things from freezing in the house for the first time this winter. It is discouraging for a farmer to see crops cut down by frosts when it is too late to replant. City teams stopped to admire my double sunflowers.

"The Coes' boarders have taken French leave. Howard is sawing wood at the door. The clothes are back in the tub. This is a rather cold night to be turned out of house and home by fire. It is probably the last Sabbath I shall spend in the house. I can't realize the sad truth, but change will come to us all. We went back to the old house. It doesn't look much like home now, everything is so changed there. I swept the front yard, blacked the kitchen stove. An old woman stopped to rest and a man wanted to stay in the barn but we didn't keep him. Three children of John Rice dead. All died since the 14th of October; yesterday. It is eat, drink, and wash dishes all the time, or nearly so.

"The horse got frightened, capsized the wagon, threw two ladies into some bushes. The oats were thrashed by a machine for the first time. There was a sad accident in Barnumsville. There were rowdies all about the rum shop. Mr. Oldham shot his only son. The wind blew considerable plate off the roof of the Old Stone Church and made the timbers fly generally. The spire will probably go next. The funeral of Lois Ann was held here. Nothing else to do, of course, but attend it. Edna had to come on top of the wall partway. The hens were well astonished to find themselves prisoners. I had a good time to read and improved it, too. I improved the time. There has been frost on the windows for some days. I have been as ever. I am working and thinking. I took some subscriptions for ornamental shrubbery. A good day for gardening and I improved it, too. I improved the time. I improved the time."

Alice dropped the diary in her lap, crying softly. So many years. She was nowhere to be found in them. Where was the body? It sat here holding the years in her lap like so many small stones. No one could really find it. 1891. She was seventy-four. Howard was seventy-four. Edna was sixty. John was seventy-two. Minnie was forty-two. Martin was forty-two. Ten would have been ninety-four. She still noted her birthdays in her diaries. Ten's ninety-fourth birthday; she had just written that. Ella was forty-one. Lettie was forty. Matthew would have been forty-one. Jack was thirty-four.

Jack. He had come as the biggest surprise of all. He had gone off to the medical college, just as the others had done, and then on to Fredonia, where Ten had lived; he wrote back he'd always been fascinated with the place because of his aunt's stories. That, naturally, was the first any of them knew she ever talked about it. She must have kept something of herself for everyone, dividing herself up as if she were already property to be distributed by a will after her own death, but keeping the process going during her whole life. Then he had gone on to California and joined up with Edmund Munyan. Edmund was the sheriff, and farmed. Jack stayed with him until he had his practice established.

This led to a friendship with the Munyans which joined the Moffats and Steeles to yet another family. Jack had, of course, married a Munyan in California. On the other side of the world. Why was it Edna's children were sure to do something like that, cross an entire continent to marry someone they had gone to school with in Williamsville? He married Katherine Munyan after her husband died. From all accounts, the marriage had been very stormy. There had been no children. When cholera hit Centerville and left two six-month-old twins orphaned, Jack brought them home. Now everyone in Williamsville called them Jack's orphans, but, Alice sighed, he was too far away to hear of it. Two years after Anna's death, John and Edna had crossed the country, sending back letters describing every inch of the trip, but they were really heading straight for Centerville.

"The children," Edna wrote them, "are marvelous. But I think Edmund Munyan is too generous. He has taken in a couple from Williamsville; I don't know if you will remember them. Remember how the town used to talk about the Turners? Whatever people did, nothing improved them? The townspeople cleaned their house and grounds once a year and the next day everything was back to normal? Well, Edmund has taken in their son, Oscar, and his wife, Julia. We think they take advantage of him, but we are not certain, and Edmund doesn't care enough about such things to keep an eye on them, so John guesses they could carry the house off on their backs, if only they were slightly bigger turtles, without Edmund noticing. He says it is a good thing he has the children, since they are the practical ones, and watch out for their father and mother. He has also set them to watching Edmund. The Turners will cause trouble later, we are sure of that."

And the trip had meant so little to her. And to John. Edna told her it was like seeing a brighter series of paintings than normal; well, yes, of course it was interesting, she had answered Alice, annoyed, but after two weeks, it just faded. It wasn't as if they'd beeen scalped by Indians, nothing so memorable. No, she remembered the people, although she was perfectly willing to describe every detail of every landscape they'd seen. Arizona, that was what had impressed her most, with its landscapes like paintings of oblivion itself. And the dangers of life so evident in the bright snakes and the huge insects. She couldn't live there. It was the extreme of the world, the heat, she went on; it fell like stones. She had never seen so much light; she hoped never to see so much at once again. Although she did wish they had been able to spend a night in the desert; she was sure there were whispers in the canyons, voices, she didn't know quite what. But, of course, it wasn't safe. Not that it was her decision, she said, shrugging her shoulders; John wouldn't hear of it. He said he intended to come home sitting up and talking, just as he had left.

"Well," Alice said, "you would probably like Montana, too, or any of those Arctic places." "Oh yes," Edna bubbled happily on, "but of course, we went in the summer and there was no chance at all of seeing one of their famous blizzards; *theirs* couldn't even compare, or so I've been told." "Why?" Alice asked; "did you want to see all those cattle freezing to death in the snow?" "Oh, Alice," Edna complained; she finally realized her friend was laughing at her. "It's just that I wanted another point on my compass." "The perfection of frozen things," Alice said, thinking back. "*Broken* things," Edna corrected; "no, this was different." And she was sorry to have missed the blizzards; she had hoped winter would start up early, on their return trip, but she hadn't had any luck there at all. "At least the other passengers had luck," Alice laughed, shaking her head. "Still, I would like to see it," Edna said, her lips narrowing. "Well, you can't have everything." "No." In her sixties, and still not resigned to that small fact of life.

Life at the Steeles' and the Moffats' continued as it always had; instead of going on rounds, John and Edna accompanied the boys on theirs; infrequently, and with quite a new purpose: John was along to take pictures, although, whenever asked, he gave advice. Edna was happy to go as ever; John was there with her. Added was a series of more and more frequent meetings in which the families read letters from the West aloud to one another. Fred Munyan had become a raving hypochondriac. Every deed was the "last deed I shall ever do." This had been so funny and so horrible that when Edmund came down with diphtheria, poor Fred began to fear he would never live through coping with his brother's estate should he have to settle it; he had not made out a will, or if he had, he was sure the Turners had hidden it. "I don't know," he wrote, "as I shall live to see the estate settled up but while I do live I shall take charge of it. I am entirely ignorant," he wrote Oscar, his brother who had stayed behind in Dummerston, "how you ever learned of Edmund's affairs.

"You say he may be taken away before he makes his wishes known. I do not see why you want to hurry him off the face of the earth. Jack Steele fully believes he will recover, and he is usually correct. He has been in his full senses for nearly six weeks since he was taken with the diphtheria and the doctor told him at the start he would never get well, but only because he did not think there was any other way to shake him into action, and he did have two children to provide for. He told him if he had any business he wished to fix that he should attend to it at once, but he told Jack he had fixed all, and he desired no change.

"The Turners are still there, but I know he intends to do nothing more for them than he has already done. The Turners have been there for ten years and Turner has not yet done a day's work, which was Edmund's purpose in taking him in, although now he will probably be shipped off to Jack, who is susceptible to the worst people skipping along the face of this earth. As far as I am concerned, I shall discharge my responsibilities to the fullest, and if this illness should prove Edmund's last, which I very much doubt, I shall discharge my duties and see to the erection of his monument, undoubtedly the last deed I shall perform on this earth. You must tell me how much I am to spend. I believe we can erect quite a respectable monument for $250.00, but I believe we should not write Edmund anything about this as he now believes he is in the best of health, and I think so too. I should like to know where you get all your queer information, and what makes you trust others more than your own brother. The Turners were never more than rotten potatoes in the cellar in Williamsville and the warm air in Centerville has just given the mold on them a head start. I myself am in very feeble health and wholly unable to do anything for myself. And my house is in such a condition that I cannot use it until it is set up on the foundation and repaired. At least you have no earthquakes in Williamsville.

"A contractor looked at it and said he would charge $102.00 to put it up and repair the woodwork. Then it would cost nearly as much more to plaster it and build the chimney and repair the windows. I don't know when I will be able to have it done as I cannot sell it for anything in its present condition nor can I mortgage it, either. I have sent my wife and children off to Jack's as I am living in an outhouse ten feet by ten feet square, north only, and an oil stove to cook on as the doors of the house are in such shape I could not get out the cookstove.

"The earthquake was a dreadful calamity and you have no idea what suffering and loss it has caused here. The quake was a hard blow to this portion of the state, and it hit me very hard, but people seem to think I should be thankful to escape with my family and my life, and no doubt you will, too, as you waste no sympathy on me but spend all your time suspecting me of everything imaginable. But with my feeble health and in my present condition, life is not much of a prize while the poorhouse is staring me in the face all the time, but my time is nearly up and I will probably not have too long to suffer. You may wonder why the poorhouse is staring me in the face, but I can tell you no one is worrying about spraying their crops with my invention while they have no houses to live in, so I can take no chances. You accuse me of becoming miserly; I should like to know what you would like to do in my place."

Letters from Jack were more interesting, if less amusing. He was drawn to fame; his picture was constantly in the paper: "Pioneer of Medicine Discovers New Medicine in California." "It reminds me," Edna said, looking at it, "of Dr. Talbott and his Nervine Tonic," but John said this was real medicine. He was, however, puzzled by Jack. He wrote them all about his gooseberry garden, claiming it was the most famous in the state, of the condition of his grape vines—he insisted Ella's daughter Wilma had lost herself in them during her last visit. He wrote endlessly about the children and almost nothing about the driving force of his life: his desire to make a permanent name for himself in medicine. They only knew, he reminded Edna, from Edmund's letters their son's great ambition was to see his name set down in every textbook of communicable diseases. They wondered a great deal about his desire for fame; he was the first in the family to find himself possessed by worldly ambition.

The Munyans always trotted over with all the letters from their children; all three families pronounced Edmund's letters scandalous, but they were, they admitted a little guiltily, hilarious. "We had two cases of Lynch Law here on the second. One of them had been arrested for horse stealing and was out on bail, and the next night a mob under my direction went to the the house and took him and his brother out, and the next day they were found 'looking up the limb of a tree,' with ropes around their necks preventing them from falling to the ground and getting hurt. I, of course, was not there to see it since I had a knitted stocking over my head. The civil authorities, including myself, have not yet offered any reward for the men who did it and no one seems very anxious to find out who they were. Jack examined them and solemnly said they were fit for burying and not much else. He looked at me most suspiciously, but he kept quiet. I suppose it is my sister's excellent moral influence working silently upon him.

"Several persons left this vicinity about this time who, had they stopped a few days longer, would undoubtedly have received a lift up in the world in the same way, but they seemed to take the hint from the other horse thieves and very modestly declined such marked favors, and emigrated to some portion of the country where such *high* honors could not be thrust upon them without more familiar acquaintance enabling them to ride good horses for a while without fearing a public reception and a through ticket to the 'Holy Land of Canaan.' "

There were endless letters from Jack's children to Ella's and Minnie's; Wilma, Ella's first child, had developed trouble with her lungs which improved dramatically in California; she was now staying permanently with Jack. The young man escorting her to picnics, to her teaching, to Sunday-school concerts, appeared destined to become her future husband, which could make Alice and Edna both great-grandmothers. Alice was not, she thought, thoroughly prepared for that. A grandmother, well, a grandmother was still young, but a great-grandmother, that went back before Christ. Could she really, she wondered, be seventy-four? And could Edna's mother really be ninety-four? They worried about her, the Steeles, she knew that.

Edith had recently written her daughter to say she hoped she would not outlive her; that would seem terribly unnatural. It still felt unnatural, after all this time, she said, to have outlived Ten, except she could not believe Ten was gone. Wasn't Edna happy now she had so many children? Edith asked. That, Alice imagined, was the closest Edith would come to mentioning Anna's death. Anna, Edith wrote, had been so young; she had been the very image of her own daughter. Edith was still confused, so Edna said, because it had been like hearing and seeing her own daughter buried. But Edna was alive; she was fine. Edith, Mr. Siddons had written of his wife, had been quite unhinged after she had seen Anna's death portraits. She could barely endure the delay thrust upon travelers between Boston and Williamsville, so anxious was she to see for herself that her own daughter was still alive! What a fancy way the man had of putting things! Alice thought, admiring; she was always after Edna for one of his letters. She took them home and studied them, although, at her age, she wasn't likely to acquire such a remarkable talent for written correspondence.

And she remembered it all so clearly! The funeral must have had the same effect on Edna, although no one, not even Edna herself, had guessed it: as if she had indeed seen herself dead. Her mother's delight in her physical existence, that *had* kept Edna up. And John. There was still nothing he feared but the death of his wife. Alice wondered why he did not think more of his own health; not one letter arrived from the California troop failing to inquire after John's cough. Did he still have it? Had it gotten worse? Was it caused by smoking or by chemicals? Did plants make him sneeze? Everyone three thousand miles away worried about him, but no worrying of Edna's could stop him from working in his cottage until all hours, with the vents, as usual, closed.

Anna's death had changed him in some way. There were times, Alice thought, staring down at her diary, when she thought he was trying to hurry his death toward him; he didn't want to outlive his wife. She didn't want to outlive him. If was as if they were in some kind of contest. You would think, if they only knew what they were doing, they would drive that carriage off a cliff. Well, she had thought that often enough before. She had never said anything to them about it; she could not find the words. She told William, though.

Bill said something to John; he told her that a week afterwards. He said John had dropped the pen he was using to label a plate, stared at him sadly, and then gone right on about his business. Finally, he said something like Bill was probably right, but he couldn't change, not anymore. Besides, he had grinned, about that driving a carriage off a cliff: he couldn't do that to his wife. Oh, he

had looked gray when he said that, Bill told her, and he
also said he couldn't take a chance on cheating himself
out of the days which might be left, even if, he had
paused, they might only gain two more. Two more would
still be worth everything.

Well, Alice sighed, she felt the same way, too. At least
she and Howard were the same age. It had taken Ten's
death to bring them together in the same way Edna and
John had always been. After so many years to fall in love
with one's husband, or to realize it: that was what Edna
said happened. They *had* finally realized it. Of course,
they weren't the Steeles; they didn't have the same passionate natures. They didn't think as much; they were two
comfortable old horses who pulled the same wagon all
their lives, but if one died in harness, the other would fall
down, too. She knew that now. She wished she knew how
to say things better; they were more than two horses who
had grown old together.

They had grown into each other, as ivy grew into nooks
and crannies of stone walls. She supposed she had Edna
to thank for her growing dissatisfaction with her inability
to put things into words. Especially now, when it seemed
so useless, but she was getting used to it, better at it, and
the better at it she got, and Howard got, the sharper their
emotions. She supposed there was something to be said for
talk, and also, she thought, puzzled, a great deal to be
said for its absence. She used to say she and Howard were
comfortable together, but she knew a word for it now:
that made it easier to keep in sight. To keep. It was a
kind of bliss. Grace. Well, she had known that word all
along. She just never thought of using it to describe their
lives. Edna thought of things like that.

How could she ever communicate the exquisite bliss
she felt when she read letters from the grandchildren?
They were so silly, so trivial. She was beginning to think
the trivia of life, that was what Edna called it—she
couldn't take credit for words like that—were code things;
inside were true messages. The trivial things, those were
the real Books of Revelation. At least for mortals. She
did not intend to venture into the waters of heresy. Of
course, she had abandoned the Old Stone Church and
gone with her brother's family to the new Methodist
church; well, it wasn't so new any longer. Nothing was.

But William and Minnie: they stuck at the old church. They said their presence there embarrassed everyone and it ought, too. The Reverend Pierce had taken several Sunday looks at them; they behaved as if nothing had ever happened—and he decided to take advantage of an invitation to teach at a Connecticut seminary. Alice insisted that was all their doing. They looked pleased enough, but modestly denied it. They now had the Reverend Case; he was a good man. Perhaps now she and Howard could return to the church in Williamsville. She would, but her brother would never go back. There was no human in the world as stubborn and loyal as Lucretius. He must have been a bulldog in a previous life, she thought, smiling into the empty room.

The letters from the children, though. Edna sensed how she felt about them and turned them all over to her. The Steeles wanted no part of clippings announcing Jack's latest discoveries; still, they let her have them. She didn't understand them. She treasured those clippings. He had been at her house so much when he was a child, in her trees, her roses, her pumpkins, her swamps, she half thought of him as her own. She couldn't understand why John and Edna didn't want the clippings she cared for so deeply, pasting them carefully into an old book on agriculture; that was her scrapbook. She had never lost her old habits of economy. Not even if the children rained money down on her like the north wind. She even had a beautiful scrapbook all the children had given her, but she thought it too beautiful to use, its red plush cover and mother-of-pearl decorations, its faint designs of flower and statuary in pale green on each cream-colored page. When they discovered she was doing nothing more with her treasured family portraits than stacking them neatly in an old hatbox she had gotten from Ella, John took some new pictures of the children and made them up for the extravagantly beautiful album the women brought back from Boston. Mrs. Siddons made it up specially, and they were all amused, she knew, at the way she handled it, treating it as spun glass, insisting one of them insert the new pictures lest she tear a page, and she would sit so still with it on her lap, opening and closing the beautiful, magnificently wrought silver clasp. With her initials on it. There was no denying whose it was. Whenever she picked it up, she thought or said the same thing: "I don't deserve something this good. It doesn't belong in a farmhouse. I'm just a farmer's wife." They loved hearing her say it, she knew that. They were beyond understanding.

Now, she laughed at herself, she had gotten so daring she slipped the childrens' letters between the fancy pages of the magnificent scrapbook—but she wasn't daring enough to paste them in. Jack's twins were so sweet: Cora and Blanche. And Wilma's letters so sad. "Mrs. Pete came to see Mrs. Polk and stayed until Sunday. It made her feel so bad to see her flowers nearly all pulled up and everything all torn up. I don't think I ever told you they pulled up nearly all the flowers and cut the rose bushes even with the floor of the porch, but they are beginning to grow, and all that framework that was around the pump is torn down; everything is so changed that I don't think anyone would know the place." Her granddaughter. How often she sounded like Edna. And then, some of their letters; they reminded her of old letters of Anna's, written to her grandmother in Boston. The twins went on so about a little dog named Foxy, it became a great fear Foxy would finally do something to get himself shot. The grandchildren were always in a fever for the mail; Foxy, what had happened to Foxy? His fame was spreading all over the county.

Alice put the diaries and the letters down, one ear listening for Howard returning. What *would* they say of her, know about her, when she was gone? It was the grandchildren who made her ask such questions, with their anguished letters about willow trees chopped down, rose bushes cut down, old places changed so, and Cora and Blanche only nine and already bemoaning lost bushes, puppies, trees; they sensed the end already. Yet they would forget all about it when they discovered that marvelous invention, romance. It was only at her age that one began remembering again. What would they say about her? she thought, staring at her row of diaries. That she must have been a trivial person to have kept a record of such trivial things? They would never know what she was like, not once she was gone. And to tell the truth, she couldn't see why anyone would want to. She was not important. The most important thing she had done was value every day.

She had loved every day. She had loved the touch of things, keeping things alive, keeping things growing, living under the high-domed ceiling of the weather. No one would understand from those diaries how she felt about the weather; it was a force, not human, but somehow permitting them to exist. How she loved the weather. No one would understand that. How she had loved everything. How she had loved the world with all its doings. How she looked out the window and whispered to herself, "It is the Lord's work and it is marvelous in our eyes." No matter what happened. She could not write things like that in her diary. She stared at each of the familiar objects in her bedroom. Everything. Everything. She loved everything. Everything was marvelous in her eyes. But it would make no difference. Not when John's and Edna's eyes closed. Not when Howard's closed. Not when her eyes closed. Not when any of their eyes closed. Still, the world was marvelous in her eyes. That was something, she asked herself defiantly, wasn't it?

Edna, at sixty-two, had given up trying to deprive her husband of his cough. She pointed out that Howard was seventy-four, and never coughed, or hardly ever coughed, and Alice, who was seventy-four, never coughed. But he was dedicated to his daguerreotypes as ever and for some reason incapable of flipping the ventilator sticks for himself. There were times she wondered if he was trying to absorb enough fumes to embalm himself, the first picture in three dimensions. There were other times she was sure he had simply never gotten over the deaths of Anna and Ten. At the time, it seemed as if the youngest and the oldest were taken, even though that had not been the case. Still, she knew she had seen it that way, as if death had pruned not only the branches but the roots of the tree.

John left her alone in her meditations on time and gave up trying to deprive her of a small series of photographs and portraits he found her staring at so often. One afternoon, particularly, it took all his self-restraint to prevent his snatching the photographs from her hand. She had left her journal open carelessly, one page up, and without realizing he was doing so, he read it. "Anna was right about our being possessed. Our minds: what are they for? They are only here to use our bodies; they thank us by giving us occasional glimpses of a landscape. I cannot stop thinking about the railway in Manhattan, its spidery vaultings. The mind is like it, its endless tracks; if we are lucky, we follow one. I did. From my window, I caught glimpses of others going by in carriages, white faces pressed to sun-struck glass. Sometimes they wore linen dusters; sometimes they were under carriage blankets. Frequently, they had handkerchiefs pressed to their mouths to avoid the dust. Anna's train stays somewhere in my mind, on some ghostly tracks. It ought to be buried in the dust, but the winds of memory keep blowing it out. Perhaps there is a special place for memory, after all. Now Anna's train is changing its track. Now she goes into the earth. Now she comes back. Ella's Tenney looks just like me, and therefore also like Anna. So the dead do return, after all. So there is one kind of reincarnation."

It was not her journal keeping, the odd turns it took, which upset John most, but her persistent fascination with the floating death portrait of little Mat. Edna often stared at it upside down, so that the child appeared drowned, and its robes, lighter, catching more air, floating up to the surface first. The head, if she looked at it long enough, seemed to be swaying back and forth like a loose weed in some kind of dark water. At other times, because of the peculiar nature of the picture, which seemed to have missed the rim of the dead child's head, the infant's skull caught in the mud.

Oddly, the child looked more alive upside down; the shadows under his eyes more natural. What appeared the clamped, tight lips of the dead looked, upside down, like an open mouth with a tiny tongue protruding. There was even a fullness in the cheeks. And the head seemed made of inferior porcelain, the same stuff the children's toys were made of. Its sad infuriated look did not soften. Regardless of how many years passed, he refused to be comforted or pacified. Once John asked her why it was that picture, always that picture she studied so, always holding it the same way, her hand half curled around it, gently holding it, her hand resting on the edge of the table so that she could hold and hold it without tiring and dropping it. Especially when she had the other picture of little Minnie to torture herself. Well, if one was to study death portraits, he asked, what was wrong with the one of little Minnie which came into their hands a year after the child's death?

That had been taken by an amateur photographer, who finally directed it to the proper place, and it was, John insisted, a comforting picture. There was little Minnie, lying back against her soft, stuffed pillow which was so big for her it looked like two pillows where her little body, from the waist up, was pressed against it. Some neighbor had combed the child's hair; the cheeks were still fat. It looked much as she had in life, even if her lips, too, seemed clenched, one corner of her mouth drawn down, again as if in protest, her little hands folded across her stomach in the position of prayer.

There was something wrong with the sheets; that was all Edna said the first time he mentioned it. The second time, she practically screamed there was something wrong with the sheets, and she knew what it was. Some idiot had placed the huge family Bible over the child's pelvis and knees and it pulled the blankets down. Look, she had cried, look, you can see its wings here and here, and here is the joining for the binding, and here is the outline of its covers, and couldn't he see Minnie never had such a large pillow and she must be in a large bed. She must have been in her mother's bed; otherwise that Bible would have slid off. What a weight to put on a child, she had cried, and of course, by the end of it all, she was weeping steadily. It was that idea: that the dead child had been put in its mother's bed, as if Minnie were prophesying later events. It was more than Edna could stand. Minnie, too, looked asleep and dead in the snow, that was what it was.

The more John looked at it, the less he liked it. The more he inspected it, the more he saw how much of a hand the neighbors had in properly illustrating the dead for the book of heaven. Above the child's folded hands (he never mentioned any of his feelings to his wife) he finally spotted the faint silhouette of a black paper angel blowing a bugle. Once he recognized it, he couldn't imagine how he'd been foolish enough to imagine that dark spot was a shadow cast by the child's thumbs; they were tucked under. The longer he peered at it, the deeper, the more rigid the pillows seemed, their deep, dark creases darkening into the face of the child. As if nothing had happened. That, Edna said, was the worst part of it; the other picture made no pretense about it. Something had happened.

But in this one, the child seemed to have fallen back in a vision of ecstasy induced by reading the Great Book. Edna had no doubt, she told him, bitter, that someone had opened it to the Book of Revelation. How could anyone, looking at the child, believe in an afterlife? He had not answered either of her questions, but she knew the answers to them already. "Then," she had told him in a flat voice, "the picture to study is the one I do study. It's easier on everyone's nerves than taking up the study of a real skull. It is something," she went on, rebellious, "we have to learn, that end point."

John objected, saying it was human nature to learn by experience, and one's own experience. Contemplating the dead bodies of others: well, that did no good. It was only one's own body, one's own dead body, that could convince, and it was the tragedy of every human that when it appeared, it was too late to teach anyone anything about it. Not even the death of a child, not even the death of a wife, he insisted, could take the place of one's own experience of death, and that just came; there was no preparing for it. Really, there was no preparing for it. It might be better, he suggested, to contemplate an emptied place: for instance, their old house. He thought he had a picture of that. *It* might have more of an effect on her; it was an old picture, one of the few he had taken with a wet-plate camera; before, he smiled at her, *he* had learned better than to point a camera into the sun. Well, you could see the house well enough, he supposed, but the deeper you looked into the picture, the lighter, more transparent, the objects seemed to become; they became almost porous. The top of the house seemed lifting into dust or light.

Funny, he said; the two back wings of the house were really invisible unless you knew where to look for them. The gates, of course, those were clear enough, and the hitching posts, but what did she think about the two twisters of light, one rising out of the bush on the right side of the picture, the other having risen from the bushes on the left side, and ascending, already having obliterated

937

most of the great elm. No one lived there now, he mused on, not since Lois Ann's death, but there had been people living in the house at one time. It had been full; still, it appeared empty.

A space where something was once, and now was not; yes, he thought you needed something that large. If only, when someone died, a torn space appeared in the blue sky with nothing but emptiness visible behind it, perhaps that would make it more real. If it stayed there, if gradually more and more of the sky one saw disappeared, until there was only a silhouette of oneself left. Then it might be possible to believe in what was coming, as if one had become a bird of some kind, alone in the sky, with nothing to distract the fastened attention of the guns. Then one would feel the threat, as one did in epidemics, or in houses filled with those already dead; but it was impossible, as it was, to feel that threat long enough to remember the sensation. He couldn't do that, he finished; not even after all the death portraits he had taken.

There was one study he had done when Mr. Siddons was there; he always came back to it. It was of a series of meadows, trimmed with a stone wall, and a man sitting in the distance on the highest point, overlooking the landscape, thinking his own thoughts. Soon he would be gone, for whatever reason. That, he told her, had become his picture of the end of things. Although he did not imagine he would ever be able to see the end of things, his things, in his lifetime. He did not tell her he *might* have seen the end of things when they had filed past Anna's casket for the last time, when it seemed to him he was looking down at his wife. That had seemed the world's end, the emptied sky. But then she had been standing next to him. So the sensation had faded; but it was still there. He had never really lost it.

Edna took a deep breath, and turned, one arm around his shoulders, one around his head. It was time he was asleep, not up with her talking about death portraits. He hadn't, she remembered, been able to endure waiting for her mother's last visit; *she* would be able to tell her, Edna had thought, if John really was thinner, or if it was just her imagination at work. But Edith's eyesight was worse and worse. He looked just as ever to her, she told Edna, bewildered. Now, she supposed, she would have to wait for the next, purposeless visit of her daughter Lettie; she would be only too happy to point out signs of encroaching decrepitude and decomposition in any of them.

Well, the last time she came, it was all they could do to endure her; she spoke only in questions. How *could* they survive in such cold? How could they endure the lack of society? How could they live properly without satisfying their appetite for music, for drama, for conversation? Edna knew at once *their* conversation was as useless and unintelligible to Lettie as the twitter of wild birds. How could they put up with the suspense as to the next season's fashions? She would have to send additional fashion papers. To which Minnie had gently answered they had all the new ones, and she was welcome to them if she would like to amuse herself. She had flushed, glaring at Minnie. Minnie confused her. She hated to be confused. Of course, Edna thought, eyelids becoming heavier, it was harder and harder for Lettie to be confused by bonnets, musicales, "conversation," or her husband, who, fortunately, had become a specialist in the art of "badinage." Well, that had been a terrible visit. Her husband, Richard, had obviously been taken with Ella. He sought out every opportunity to be with her.

One day he caught up with her in the grape arbor; Ella turned; he was smiling at her. "You're the only Richard in the family, I believe"; Ella smiled again, trying to break the silence. He still stood immobile, looking at her. "Are you terribly bored here?" she asked at last; "we used to spend so much time in Boston, I know how much of a change it is." His eyes seemed fastened to hers. "Come, come," Ella coaxed, flushing, "you must think me worth at least *one* word." He turned tomato red. "It's not that, believe me," he said hurriedly; "it's just that I don't know what to say to you. To all of you," he corrected himself quickly; "all of you seem so sophisticated." "Sophisticated!" Ella flushed, angry; "it isn't kind to amuse yourself by ridiculing us!"

Why wouldn't he think of what to say? "Please; no ridicule was intended. It's just that all of you do so much. You have four children, don't you? I'm afraid I can't keep the children clear. Everyone seems to belong to everyone else except when they fall down and scrape a knee." She finally began to smile. "Then you might mistake my mother for their mother," she teased. "Well," he sighed— he was deciding whether or not he should try again— "you manage all those children, and then you go out on rounds with your husbands. Mrs. Siddons gave me an inkling of what they must be like, and there always seems to be something important you're up to, and then all of you read. There must be three rooms lined with books."

"Minnie doesn't read much," she said into the sunset; "her eyes are weak." "Now you are ridiculing me." "No. You overestimate all of us. We do nothing important. We're concerned with our families and other people's families." "What could be more important than that?" "Oh, come," Ella protested, "and with all the talk in the air of your becoming our next President." That would just suit Lettie, Edna thought, to be officially labeled First Lady. "The country," he said, "is made up of families. If I became President," he went on, "what would be my sacrifice? I doubt that I would spend less time with my children. I would certainly spend no less time with my wife. But that wouldn't be your position, or your husband's; you would have far more to sacrifice." Ella nodded. The presidency. What a horrid idea. She supposed she ought not to view it that way; someone had to be President. Probably people looked at William and thought that—someone had to be a doctor. Someone had to be everything, she thought in exasperation, trying to clear her head. She was not sure what she felt for him, whether it was pity or something more dangerous.

"If you become President," she went on, trying to change the course of the stream, "your wife would be a perfect ornament. The sophisticated women here would be perfect encumbrances." "I was unaware that a man wanted an ornament for a wife." He was bitter. Ella shook her head slightly. This was impossible; this could not go on. But she might be flattering herself. "Your sister," he said, "used to go on so about your marrying a farmer's son." "I always thought she must have done," Ella said. The roses were melting into the grays of the sky. The sky was dusty with their scent. "She didn't see how you could manage to love him." "It was hardly a question of managing; I couldn't help it, really. It was an illness." "Did it prove incurable?" "It did." "It is still incurable?" "Terminal, I am afraid," Ella answered, staring into the far sky; "isn't yours?" "I'm afraid not." "I'm sorry."

The compassion in her voice shook him; he was used to everything else. "I had some foolish hopes," he murmured; "I thought perhaps Lettie was right. Perhaps our respective mates would predecease us, as they say in wills. Perhaps we could meet somewhere in this world." "We have met, and that's all we can say. In any case," she added after a long pause, "I would not marry again." "How can you be sure?" he asked, curiously defeated. "I suppose in the same manner my aunt was sure." "One riddle for another." "No, no; it's a sense of my own nature." "I'm sorry to hear that." "You ought not to be; we've chosen our lives. And," she went on more cheerfully, "only think of what such doings would mean to your career." "The more I think about that, the less a career seems to mean." "You'll change your mind once you return to the city." Her tone stopped all further conversation on the subject.

She would have liked to touch him, to hold him, but it would be wrong, even if she did want to hold him as she would have wanted to hold one of her own children. But he was no child; that made it worse, she thought; he was alone in a room emptied of all the adult toys. "Richard!" Lettie's voice cut into the twilight like cold metal; "where have *you* been? You've missed rounds and rounds of croquet. Surely you will come in for euchre." "Do you play?" he asked Ella courteously. "Not tonight; I have to go to East Caulder with William. Something fascinating"—she grinned at her sister—"skin eruptions and two carbuncles in need of lancing and dressing." "Ugh!" Lettie exclaimed. "Then you don't want to come?" Ella asked her. "*We* certainly do not," Lettie answered huffily, taking her husband's arm and marching off with him as if he were a parcel she had forgotten and returned to retrieve.

Ella told no one about the incident, not then, but she knew her mother suspected something. Otherwise, she thought, why would her mother try, at this late date, to talk some sense into Lettie? "Why, we're perfectly happy!" Lettie cried, indignant; "you've lived here so long, Mother, I am sorry to say it, but you cannot imagine happiness unless there is a cow and a horse somewhere on the premises, and they do not belong in brownstones on the Hill, I can tell you."

Even Edna gave up after that. As for Ella, she kept her own secrets for some time. The table in Ten's room, covered with portraits of all members of the family, had not looked quite right the day after Lettie and Richard returned to Boston. She inspected it. Her portrait was missing. She went into her mother's room and took the duplicate, replacing it on Ten's table. No one would notice its absence in her mother's room, or, if they did, they would make nothing of it. Her father was forever going with portraits. But if it were to be missed here—so she had replaced it and said nothing. She only hoped Lettie would never find it in her husband's possession. She would be sure she had placed it there to embarrass her. This when she was forty-two and Lettie forty-one. Finally, she told her mother every word he had said.

Edna felt sorry for Richard; no, more than sorry. Whatever he felt for Ella was genuine, and he was capable of great feeling; she knew that. What she didn't understand was how Lettie ever persuaded him he wanted to marry her. Perhaps he hadn't known himself well enough then. Now, whenever she read of the new formulas sure to produce gold, she thought of Richard in Boston, and his head of fool's gold perpetually resting on the pillow beside him. What must he think, waking in the middle of the night, seeing that beautiful head asleep? The little deaths, that was what John called sleeps. She supposed he wished the little death was a real one, but he would never say or do anything; he was, after all, a good man.

Still, that head on the pillow. Perhaps he would be the only one prepared for death. From the gray look he always had when he appeared with Lettie, he must have done what she wished to do: contemplated his own skull, his own skeleton. Perhaps to be too ready for death was a sickening away from life. Yet she believed the fullest life could only be lived by those not ready for death, those who could feel it, live with it, as a tangible thing.

That was a paradox, and she could not see how to undo it. Unless the sickening, the repulsion against life, was temporary, and brought immunity, as with an inoculation against smallpox. But even there was a problem. Was it Anna or Lettie who had been inoculated ten times and still not gotten a "take"? Eventually, the inoculation had taken, although she had to have serum taken from a cow; the little boy whose arm they had used couldn't affect her. She had better go to sleep and cut off that line of thought; Lettie and the cow. She had promised herself to stop thinking such thoughts about her daughter.

Life at their house had taken on a peculiar quality. Watching the boys go off on rounds with their wives, day in and day out, it seemed as if she were watching a version of her life with John multiplied, but it was the form without the content. Of course, they went frqeuently enough to satisfy any longings they still had for such activity: John had to take his pictures. And she had become far more interested in the garden than she ever would have expected. Her black thumb had turned green when Ten died. She would go out into the garden, prune the rose bushes, weed the flower beds, automatically pushing her sun-wet hair back from her forehead and her eyes, and when she came in, three or four or five hours had passed; it seemed more like five minutes. She had no idea what happened to the time. Perhaps it dissolved into the shrubbery and the flowers; everything was so healthy. And the grandchildren: they kept her occupied. And it was odd, how much easier they were to understand than her own children had been, how little she resented their small, constant invasions.

And now she and John spent a great deal of their time together in his cottage; she loved watching pictures emerge from the empty plates. That, she thought, was a kind of resurrection. On days when she was too tired to sit in the dark for hours, she would have John ring a bell; it sounded in her room. Then she would go out and watch the forms and the faces swim up from under the water into the light. She never lost her hope, or fancy—perhaps that was a better word for it—one of them would quicken, jump up, walk out the door, wave, disappear down the path.

They would sit there, in the dark, or with the skylight open, talking about newspapers, about the children; neither of them, they agreed, could get the right name for the right child when they wanted it. Both of them had taken to using Ten's tricks, pointing and addressing the improperly behaved child as "miss" or "sir." Of course, if one of them showed up for some important reason, because a doll had lost its shoe, or one of the boys decided to have a mock burial using one of the younger girls' stuffed toys, then they would have solemn conversations; then they had no trouble remembering names. They loved them passionately, Edna said, but sometimes it seemed to her they loved the pictures of the children more; they were more vivid. Perhaps because, John thought, the pictures were theirs alone.

Edna took to studying a series of photographs she carefully took out and filed separately; she called them "The Seen a Ghost" portraits. There was one of a young woman: all high forehead, thin lips, and the largest ears anyone had ever seen, but the arresting thing was her eyes, which seemed to see something ghastly, invisible. Edna was surprised at how often that look appeared, regardless of the time of day, of the person's age, of the nature of the face.

She had found one tiny tintype which she labeled and slipped in at the head of John's portraits. She looked at it for hours. It was the size of a small cameo; the woman had a protruding, high forehead, hair parted as neatly and smoothly as a baby's, pulled back tight. Her cheeks had been tinted to give the face some color, but her eyes were open so wide they looked as if they had somehow jammed. If only it were possible, Edna thought, each time she looked at it, to get close enough to the picture and see what image was reflected on her retina. That might be the important vision. She was convinced there was nothing whatever to the notion that a vision of the next life appeared at the moment of death. She and John had long ago concluded all deaths were peaceful; not the moments before, perhaps, but at the moment of death, there was no pain; there was nothing. Which was, she supposed, appropriate. The haunted and haunting picture of Anna at Minnie's bedside: how could she have kept her eyes open long enough for that picture to be taken? She never ceased to wonder at it. She looked as if she had gone into a trance. Perhaps she had. Perhaps they should have been forewarned by that portrait.

There were three others she tried to avoid; two were of Anna's children, one of them the little boy on the Gothic pillar, his unhappy look already prefiguring the one in his final portrait, little Minnie next to him with a strange look, as if she were asking the most dangerous question there was: what happens next? And the two of them in the perambulator, with the opposite vision: there was no end to life and its delights. And the picture of Anna herself newly married, in her velvet jacket. There were times now when she came across it and wondered why, at this stage of her life, *she* was wearing such strange clothes. She was, she noticed recently, wearing the chain and medallion she gave her daughter the night before she married. But that was in the beginning. She always turned the picture of Anna to its other side. There was something comical, reassuring about the message on the back: "Donner Studios, 25 Elm Street, New Bedford, Massachusetts." And on the bottom: "Streetcars Run by Studio." As if there would be permanent transportation for anyone immortalized in their portraits. "Copies always available." How lovely, Edna sighed; "copies always available."

Their lives, she thought now, seemed more and more ordinary; why had she ever thought them otherwise? When Wilma had visited, one of her schoolmates promptly showed up on the doorstep, hat in hand. John Ware. They thought he might not have lost his lady love if only he had not stayed so late. Everyone in the house teased her. Ella scolded her for jeopardizing her health, and wondered why John Ware would be so careless of her health. Then, too, Wilma began to tire of talking while becoming sleepier and sleepier, even if her eyelids were drooping under the lids of her admirer. "It takes," John sighed, "a very intense love affair to keep a girl who awoke at seven o'clock awake until midnight; yes, and it had better be a very entertaining man, too." "Our salvation," he told Edna, "was going to bed whenever we pleased, before we married. Never before," he told her, "did I realize how lucky we were to spend our courtship in the same house until the ceremony." After that, of course, he sighed, bedtime varied with the general state of affairs and had very little to do with sleepiness.

Poor Mr. Ware. He had the bad luck to come courting when they were absolutely swollen with visitors; for the first time, they had to use a parlor for a bedroom, and who had been staying in it but old Mr. Hewitt, who had arrived for some comforting, along with his wife. Mr. Ware's late visits kept him in such a fury they began to worry the hasty-tempered old man would fire the house. It was a good thing, Martin said, he couldn't disinherit them, and John Ware often chose the wrong parlor, and Wilma, too shy to say anything, often would stay up with him, sitting by the hour on old Mr. Hewitt's temporary sofa bed, which the old man was dying to get into. "You would think," cranked old Mr. Hewitt, "when a girl starts yawning a man would head for the hills. He's so dumb and selfish," the old man growled at breakfast, "the family ought to hire a milkman to come rattle his cans before the door and to whoop a lot around the house."

They went through the papers, clipping things of interest for the other. Edna particularly liked advertisements which seemed to comment on life, either in themselves, or by juxtaposition. She often wondered if the editor put them together to tell a story, or if they appeared next to each other accidentally, or if perhaps there was some purpose to it. She had clipped two advertisements, the topmost advertising New London Business College, and showing three men climbing a ladder toward a huge sack of money labeled with a dollar sign. "At the Top," read the big black letters. "Success comes from climbing," the text began. And right under it, an advertisement for H. H. Bond, Undertaker and Embalmer, an engraved picture of his team pulling a decorative hearse in black silhouette, and the message at the bottom: "Telephone: Day, call 22-3; Night, call 75-2." Or the advertisement for the Temperance Society placed atop that for a cold cure, whose most prominent line was "Your Life May Depend on Having a Little Bottle Handy."

They collected instances of humor as assiduously as John collected faces; they were as interested as ever in incidents of violence, in aberrations, but more and more they managed to convert one into the other. Howard's last fit over the loss of his corn crop had alarmed all of them; he had taken on so over it. "It's the last time I'm going to try; I'm just giving up. When your luck goes against you, it's no use at all." Alice came over a week later, saying one or two doses of her new medicine had taken care of Howard, whereupon all wanted to know what she had done. *Someone* or other in the Steele house was always ready to give up, although it was usually one of the children when they reached twelve, thirteen, or fourteen. She asked him, she said, how he was going to find a way out.

He had gone on and on about how she didn't understand what it was like to be responsible for a family and a home and know if he did away with himself she would have no one to provide for her, at least not a husband. Finally, she told him she had a favor she wanted to ask of him: "Don't die in the house." And, she said, before he had a chance to answer, she went on with it: "Because it would be so unpleasant for the children and me." It would be terrible to have so many awful associations in every room, and she wouldn't like it, either, if they had to bury him at the four corners with a stake driven through him, even if there was some slender hope that people finally would forget he ever had anything to do with them. She wouldn't like to have to tell people she was the widow of a coward, or her children were the children of a coward. They would say that, though, when they found out how he died. Only a coward would do himself in, leaving his wife to fight on alone. She never wanted to hear him mention such a thing again. It was bad enough, she said, to live with a bitter man, but she wasn't going to talk about it again; a discouraged man was one thing, but someone who threatened to wiggle out of things was another and she objected to it. He had snapped out of it fast, she could tell them that.

They sat in each other's parlor and discussed clippings about life at home. Mrs. Pinkham's cures always interested them. She had lately taken to advertising cures for "The Blues": "A Graphic Description of the Dreadful Feeling. What is Meant by This Form of Acute Misery—Where Doctors Make Mistakes." Howard relished those passages. "When a cheerful, brave, lighthearted woman is suddenly plunged into that perfection of misery, the BLUES, it is a sad picture. It is usually this way: She has been feeling out of sorts for some time; head has ached; and back also; has slept poorly." Alice interrupted to say she described a new mother perfectly. Edna nodded.

"It gets worse," Howard promised cheerfully. They settled back. "She's been quite nervous, and nearly fainted once or twice; head dizzy, and heartbeat very fast; then that bearing-down feeling. Her doctor says, 'Cheer up, you have dyspepsia; you'll be better soon.' " "Did you ever say that?" Edna asked John. "No; I should have." How guilty he looked! "I wouldn't have let you in the house if you'd told me to cheer up. Howard could have done that much." Howard glared at her, and went on.

"But she doesn't get 'all right.' She grows worse by the day, till all at once she realizes that a distressing female complaint is established. Her doctor has made a mistake." All made faces at John. "She has lost faith in him; hope vanishes; then comes the brooding, morbid, melancholy, everlasting BLUES. Her doctor, if he knew, should have told her and cured her, but he did not, and she was allowed to suffer. By chance she came across one of Mrs. Pinkham's books, and in it she found her very symptoms described, and an explanation of what they meant. Then she wrote to Mrs. Pinkham, at Lynn, for advice, feeling that she was telling her troubles to a woman. Speedy relief followed and vigorous health returned. Lydia E. Pinkham's Vegetable Compound instantly asserts its curative powers in all those peculiar ailments of women. It has been the standby of intelligent women for twenty years, and the story recited above is the true story of hundreds of women, whose letters of gratitude are to be found on file in Mrs. Pinkham's library."

"Do you think those things work?" Alice asked. "I don't know," Edna said; "but I love reading them. They always remind me of Ten's ludicrous novels. Such perils, and then rescued by a vegetable compound." "It's probably getting an answer; that's what cures them," Alice decided. "Probably," John said; "that's what they need."

They examined advertisements for sound sleep, usually ushered in by a picture of a distraught woman cowering under a blanket, as if faced by the visible ghost of a slaughtered victim who had just then decided to open her door. "The highly organized, finely strung nervous system of a woman subjects them to terrors of nervous apprehension which no man can ever appreciate." The advertisement went on to say this medicine was the "only medicine which makes the coming of a baby safe and comparatively easy." The personal letter appended read, "I was a sufferer and was cured by Dr. Pierce's wonderful medicine. When I commenced the medicine, I could neither eat nor sleep. My hands and feet were constantly cold; I had a wasting, troublesome drain for three months, and my monthly periods were never regular. I took Dr. Pierce's Favorite Prescription and it cured me. I feel well. I thank the World's Dispensary Medical Association." "I don't know," Alice remarked; "I never have trouble sleeping at night and I don't see why that medicine should do so many tricks." "I never have trouble sleeping, either," Edna said. "It must be for the rich ones," Howard said, and then flushed. "Well, you don't act rich enough for me to remember," he grumbled; that was his way of apologizing to the Steeles.

Edna and John spent more and more time at the Moffat house; there were so many fewer there, and this had the happy result of keeping Howard home nights. Whatever they were doing, they agreed, it was good for them. At their ridiculous ages, they were positively blooming. Then they would have to remember to make an exception for Edna; she was, they always said, still a baby. She was only sixty-two. They talked about poverty in Dummerston. William was called into a "suspicious-looking" house; the good people of the town "suspected" the children should be taken from their unfit mother. Bill found her dying of consumption, unable to do anything; the house was so cold that water froze on the floor; there was no wood for a fire. They had no food and mattresses. One old thing made of straw ticking had been given over to the mother. She died three days after William arrived, and two of her five children followed within the week. This threw Bill into such a rage he went to the Reverend Case, who went along with him to inspect the ruin, and preached a thundering sermon on charity at home and forgetting about the heathens and the lepers, taking care of the needy and the starving on one's own streets. The poor poor, Edna joked, were now really afflicted with attention, although most seemed to enjoy it, but almost all of them expressed a wish that it not end before they did. Which was, John agreed, the real problem.

They talked about visits of condolence; they wished people would make fewer of them. There was nothing, Edna said sadly, which was the right thing to say. A presence, that was all the bereaved could be expected to endure. They remembered Jane Camp, who had gone to every funeral; she had once gone without her usual preparation and research; after viewing the remains, she asked someone sitting next to her, "Did the corpse leave a widow?" That was probably the first and last time a near relation burst out laughing in the middle of a funeral. It did them good to talk about such things without the children for witnesses. No matter how old they got, they would be sure to misunderstand, to mistake their irony, their laughter, for callousness. They could never talk so in front of them. Of course, in other ways, they agreed, it was always the children who kept them up and going.

Alice would chat on about a new way to keep plants without a fire at night.

They looked with puzzlement at the telephone on the wall of Alice's parlor. She and Edna hardly ever used theirs, unless one or the other was sick in bed, or the weather truly impossible. Edna held it at arm's length, shouting into its speaker. They seemed, in spite of the telephone, to visit back and forth more frequently now, although they dutifully called each other, much to the amusement of their husbands, to announce their impending calls. It didn't occur to them to make use of the instrument for ordinary conversation. The boys, of course, adored the thing; they considered it, as they often said, the best invention since the sun. It simplified their practice. They knew where they were going before they left; it saved endless miles, and wear and tear on the horses, and the longer they went on, singing its praises, the blanker the looks from the parents. "Spooky." That was all Howard had to say about it. John and Edna talked about it alone; they didn't like it. No; they decided they hated it. It was the signal of their lives coming to an end. It was that strange. They wondered at others who grew used to it so quickly.

They complained about the local newspapers and the city papers. They still reported important doings, John commented, sarcastic: "The sidewalk in front of one of the churches needs better attention." "The papers," John said, "are as bad as the advertisements"; "Frank Prideman has a broad smile on his face. It is a boy this time." Immediately followed, John told them, by "John Gold's baby died Wednesday morning in a spasm. The baby had not been well lately and was subject to spasms."

They deplored the increasing incendiarism, the seemingly greater and greater number of adults raping children and stepchildren: "thirteen years of continuous wrong with a sixteen-year-old." That one gave them pause. They thought about the tarring-and-feathering case that was evidently to go on forever; some townsmen had tarred and feathered a stranger for rowdyism. They could make nothing of a letter to the editor written by one of the townsmen's wives. "Those in the mob, they were mostly a set of lazy loafers that infest the grocery store, and tavern, and there are no more than two or three that pay more than a poll tax, and one pays no tax at all. One thousand dollar list would be as much as they all pay. The strata of that particular district at this time is like a crater emitting lots of fire and smoke. Your correspondent was evidently no resident of this part of Williamsville, but has been a resident of New York City, and picked up in the slums, where drunkenness and night raids run riot. I think your correspondent must have been very close to the mob or he would not have known how near the women resembled the Tiger Cats. It was not Bourne's girls who ruined the minister's hat." They promptly examined the previous issues of that paper and could find no reference whatever to the minister, much less to his hat; there was no mention of the Bourne girls. The writer, they concluded, would be the next taken off to the Retreat.

So the nights passed and passed, and the days. As they lost their distinctive character, Edna noticed, surprised, they became more and more dear. It had taken so long to accept life; she hadn't realized until recently just how long it had taken her to do that, or to do it at least as well, or as badly, as she had. She supposed something similar was happening to John, Howard, and Alice. But still, she was puzzled. If that was so, why didn't John open his ventilator when he worked? Well, things still changed, she thought, lying in bed, waiting for John to wake.

Her etiquette books had been supplanted by her collection of humorous jokes, assiduously snipped out of newspapers, magazines, letters. Had she been looking in the wrong places all this time? she wondered, thinking over her latest clippings. One day, while Howard was retailing a joke, it occurred to her that people laughed at what they feared. Well, that had been no great discovery. But, she reasoned, what they were afraid of had to be common enough, real enough, to deserve becoming the butt of a joke. Yes, the subject of jokes. Jokes were the bombs that needed defusing, the mines buried in the field. The Bible, she now thought, the books of etiquette, told you what you ought to believe in; the jokes, she reasoned, told you what you did in fact believe in, why you needed a Bible, etiquette books. They were antidotes. So she clipped them out, although John found her dogged pursuit of humor somewhat comical in itself. And she was beginning to find they sorted themselves into categories: professional jokes, that was one category: jokes about doctors, dentists, undertakers, usually those in the feared professions.

Her interest in etiquette, she thought, that had been her idea; it was Howard—Edna wouldn't have known he could read if it hadn't been for his endless reading aloud of jokes, curious facts, humorous matters, and "little bits"—who had begun her on this. It was odd where roads began; yes, it was. She crept silently out of bed; she didn't know why, but she objected to John's observing her in the act of studying her clippings, especially when it had never bothered her if he came upon her in her previous studies. Well, she thought, picking up her scrapbooks and going through the door into the adjoining room, he would sleep for a while. *He* didn't seem to obey the rule he had once set down: that the older one got, the less sleep one needed.

On the other hand, his habits confused her; he now stayed up later and later, making more and more of his pictures. If Bridget didn't regularly betray him, she sighed, she would never know how late he came to bed, how much to scold him. Bridget, she thought sadly, opening her book. Ninety-four years old. As old as Ten would have been. She hoped Bridget would last forever. Lately, she hoped everyone older than she was would last forever. She shook her head disapprovingly at herself. As long, she thought, opening the first book, as she didn't take to thinking her desires had anything to do with anything.

She came across one of her favorites: "The criminal lawyer's view: 'So you murdered nobody but your cousin himself?' 'Only him.' 'That's unfortunate. If you had killed yourself, we might have pleaded insanity.'" She giggled like a child whenever she read it; but the others, including

John, all made the same mistake. They all thought the lawyer meant it was too bad he hadn't killed the whole family. She should note that: when the humor became too bizarre or savage, there was a tendency to ignore it. Or change it.

She had found only one widow joke; she kept it in a special place. "They had mourned him as dead, but, like Enoch Arden, or the cat, he had come back. His little wife sat on his knee, the joy shining in her eyes. 'Are you really glad I came back?' he asked. 'Glad! I had just made up my mind to don a widow's outfit, but there was the loveliest picture hat, with bright ribbon all over it in spots, that I have been longing for and now I can get it. Glad!' " She went on to the next one. Society, these had to do with society: " 'I don't know what you women find to talk about at your literary circle,' he sneered. She gave him a pitying look. 'You must remember, Harry, that all the members are never present at every meeting.' " She thought again about Lettie's husband; she wished they could do something for Richard. She wondered if he had seen this joke; she didn't know whether she ought to hope he had or hadn't. Howard loved that joke; he had copied it out into a little book of his own; she imagined his standard diary had received it.

There was a category of jokes she didn't know what to make of; she thought, perhaps, they represented an incipient rebellion against the whole order of things; perhaps they were defenses against insanity. They were insane, irrational in their own way, but they did, she thought, keep one amused or interested enough to permit safe passage "through the ordeal of daily life": "Now is the time to transplant croquet hoops." "Trees have their time to leave and never leave without a bough." "There has been a run on the snowbanks." "We are credibly informed that the morning which broke has since been mended." "A competent authority says you must lie with your feet to the equator. Liars will please take notice of this." "One of our agents was bitten by a dog the other day. After lingering some time, death put an end to the sufferings of the dog." "A lad with a good appetite swallowed a small leaden bullet. His friends were very much alarmed about it. The doctor was found, heard the dismal tale, and with as much unconcern as he would manifest in a case of common headache, wrote the following laconic note to the lad's father: 'Don't alarm yourself. If, after three weeks, the bullet is not removed, give the boy a charge of powder. Yours, etc. P.S. Don't shoot the boy at anybody.' "

"The world is to come to an end in the year 1921, at three minutes past seven o'clock A.M., July 13. Any little matters which ought to be settled before that time should be at once adjusted." "A Connecticut man recently went to see a friend in an insane retreat. He stood a few minutes before a fine-looking man he had seen before at the institution, and inquired his name. 'Julius Caesar, sir,' said the lunatic. 'Why, you were Alexander when I was here before, were you not?' 'Oh, why yes, but that was by a former wife,' said the crazy man, not at all disconcerted."

Her perpetual favorites, the ones she never tired of, the ones she suspected of hiding the door to some important, secret place, came from an old issue of a magazine she had found in a pile in her mother's attic on their last visit to Boston: "January, the first month of the year, took its name from Janus. We don't know what Janus did without his name afterwards." "The bulbs appear this month. Book your secrets early. Protect your tulip beds. Sit up with them all night and keep your blunderbuss loaded. Examine the roots of your dahlias. Never mind if you offend them; it will do them good. If you keep a boardinghouse, attend to your boarders. February used to come before January. This, however, has since been set straight, to avoid confusion. Begin to get your annuals ready for next year. Give out your snowstorm stories to be written at midsummer. Pot off well-rooted cuttings of calceolaria. This is good rifle practice. Sow cabbage, but take care that your thread is strong enough. March used to be called the spring month. In leap year, however, the name is more properly applied to February. Keep your beds as tidy as you can. Rake and water them carefully. If this won't do, consult an experienced bedmaker. You may nail wall fruit this month, if no one is looking.

"There is a full moon this month. Let us say on the twelfth day, 9h. 51m. P.M., but you may fix any other time if you think it better. Weed your walks and throw weeds over the neighbor's wall. Sow climbers and sit down and watch them; this requires patience. Plant a biennial, and give him the slip; this is an awful lark and well repays the trouble. Lads and lasses in the olden time used to repair to the woodlands at the dawn of May morning to gather May on other people's property. Many of them having gotten into trouble, this fine old practice has subsided. You should remove bulbs this month. Remove those belonging to the people next door if you can. This is a good month to throw bottle ends and brickbats over the wall into the next-door people's garden. Finish potting the layers of picotees; also pot your old roosters. Replant your shrubberies—two or three times a day. Take up your dahlias sharply, especially if they are pert. Play your cornet to the cabbages; it encourages them. Dig a hole and fill it up again. Get over the wall and break the next-door people's spade. Dig up everything. Dig up all small shrubs and transplant them. Do this four or five times a day. Get up a row among the cabbages. Get over the wall and pull up the next-door people's roses. If the weather is open, shut it up. Have the garden paved."

These, Edna thought tearfully, should have been in *The Floral Cabinet;* the garden had not been the same since Ten had gone, not even after all her efforts. On the other hand, Alice had gotten over the wall and helped tend to things; they were improving. People took gardens so seriously: as if they finally had some control of life and death. And the hatred of the neighbors when your roses lived and theirs did not. The room was brightening. Her absolute favorite, she thought, without bothering to turn to it, was "Truth crushed to earth will rise again, but it isn't so with eggs." She was so busy collecting these things she rarely had time to think about them; but *that* was her favorite.

Her mind wandered off to the last days of Lettie's visit. "Don't you think," Lettie asked Ella, "my daughter has a remarkable voice?" "I certainly do," said Ella, "but you are not to worry about it. She may outgrow it yet." Poor Lettie; she did not like jokes. She did not, Edna decided, like anything.

She stirred restlessly in her chair. She hadn't thought John would sleep long enough so that she would reach her second scrapbook and its small collection of what people considered curious facts. Was he never going to wake?

She listened. No sound. She turned her attention to the clippings in the second book:

"Music has a tendency to make its professors mad or apoplectic. Forty-eight eminent musicians who died of apoplexy are enumerated in *The Musical Directory*."

"Among the assigned causes of insanity in patients received at the Taunton Lunatic Asylum, during eighteen years, spiritualism is given in 53 cases, religious excitement in 151, use of tobacco in 6, and intemperance in 703."

Edna gazed at her hands. She still had an uncontrollable tendency to save clippings which might interest Anna: she had two about women buried alive. One man buried his wife without adequately checking to see if she was really dead; that became apparent when she appeared at his door in her winding sheet. The Pope declared the marriage invalid, and she married her first love.

She wondered if Anna had come across many stories like that. She had clipped an article about men who lived for centuries. She had one about the oldest man now living; he resided in Brazil and was said to be one hundred and seventy-nine years old. None of her behavior, she decided, was precisely rational. She picked up her first scrapbook and thumbed to another familiar page: "Lady to a little girl of four years: 'What are you going to call your new doll?' Little girl answers, heaving a deep sigh, like some anxious mother: 'I shall call it Rosa—if it lives.'" If it lives, she repeated; if it lives. She was getting old.

There was a knock at the door. "Mother?" Martin said, poking his head in; "is Father up yet?" "No, dear," she answered without looking up. "What are you doing?" he asked, sitting down opposite her. "Oh, only studying my jokes." "Studying your jokes?"—Martin grinned at her— "you're not supposed to do that. You're supposed to laugh at them. That's what they're for. To cheer you up, not send you into meditations." "You laugh at your jokes and I'll study mine. What do you want with your father?"

"We thought he might be willing to help us out today." Edna glared at him. "Well, you know he still has the fastest fingers of all of us, and Elder Coe just shot his son and someone's got to take out the bullet and no one can do a better job than Father." "You know how to take out bullets." "I know," Martin said. He was irritated; he didn't like to ask for help. "But they got into some kind of argument about Frank's marriage. Elder didn't approve of it, and he didn't want the intended brought to his house, and for some reason Frank hit his sister in the face; no one knows why, but Elder got furious and took out a pistol or revolver. He had it in his pocket and fired a shot into his son's back, so that's where he lies. Coma, critical. Taking out a bullet isn't hard work, Mother."

"And where else are you going?" "Well, typhoid in East Hadley." "Typhoid!" Edna exclaimed; "why? Are you trying to kill him off?" "He's already had it," Martin said. "I suppose that's all there is on the agenda?" "Two cases of consumption." "Just what your father needs, with his cough." "He's been exposed to that all his life." "He's not going," Edna said flatly. "Edna, old girl," John said behind her, "how about reviving old habits and coming on rounds with me?" She sat, frozen with rage. "The weather is terrible," she snapped; "you don't go out taking pictures in weather like this. We'll come back on an oxcart; I never saw such mud." "Have you looked out the window yet?" "I don't have to look out the window; I know the sound of that rain." "I'm going in ten minutes," John told her. "All right," she said, getting up; "Don't expect me to be happy about it." "You ought to be happy about it," Martin told her; "at least he won't be in his cottage with his fumes." "That's just about enough from you." Edna glared at him. Martin knew when to beat a retreat. "Don't treat me as if I had one foot in the grave," John asked gently, his hand on her shoulder. "Have everything your own way," Edna said, angry; "you never change." "Now *that* makes me feel better." "Idiot," she said, but more softly.

"Well," she said as they set off in the carriage. "Well, what?" "Well, when are you going to stop this?" "When are *you* going to stop?" John asked. "Don't be so childish." He sighed and fell silent. She was right; it was muddy. And the odd thing, he thought, was that she didn't worry about anything, not unless it was something concerning him. "What do you think about that compact with the devil business?" he asked a while later. "I don't

have the faintest idea of what you're talking about."
"Edna," he observed, "at least it's not dusty today." She
continued glaring at the gray, dripping landscape. Mists
were rising up from the ground: the mountains were ob-
scured.

"That man Frederickson," John continued, undaunted;
"the one who says his criminal nature comes from a pact
he made with the devil when he was only eleven. He said
he had to serve him until he was twenty-five." "Very interesting," his wife answered; "are we stopping in to see
him, too?" "He killed a Mr. Whitney. He said something
about wishing he could feel sorry about killing him, but
he was just as happy as could be, and it was all the devil's
fault. He said things about trying to run away from the
devil, but he always caught up with him and pulled chairs
out from under him and he stood around laughing while
he killed Mr. Whitney; it's incredible. He goes on and on
about how if he dies before February 1902 he'll never
get away from the devil for all eternity, so he wants them
to hang him then. He sounds insane." "Really?" "Howard
said the latest papers reported he fell on a board when
he was a child and a nail went straight into his head."
"And," she finished for him, "he had fits and was given
to queer behavior; it's always the same thing." "Are you
going to keep this up all day?" John asked. His wife refused to answer him. "Why, pray tell, did you come? It
isn't a pleasant prospect, and you're not helping." She
sighed audibly.

"What do you think about the new invention the type-
writer?" he asked, exasperated. "I think," she answered,
"there will be a great deal more nonsense in the world,
now that it's easier to write it down." "They say it doesn't
need a treadle like the sewing machine." "Well, it isn't a
sewing machine, is it?" "The assistants at the newspapers
seem delighted with it," he persevered. "How lovely for
them." "I give up," he said. "Good."

They rode on and on. "Retired!" Edna finally muttered
bitterly. "That is the last straw," John roared; "I'll stop at
one of the houses and have them carry you back home."
"Never mind that," she answered icily; "I'll cheer up eventually." "In this life, I hope." "Did you see Hattie's essay
about the habits of cats?" she asked at last. "No." "Are
you starting now?" "Well, you can't blame me for being

off the hooks, can you?" "I suppose not." "I brought it with me." "Good."

"Would you like me to read it?" "Please yourself." "You can stop now; that's enough of my own medicine." The corners of her husband's mouth relaxed. "Read some of it." " 'Cats are full of curiosity, and if a new chair or other piece of furniture is brought in when they are out, as soon as they see it, they walk around it, smell of it, touch it, and sometimes climb up on it, sit a while, and go off satisfied.' " "There we have the explanation of Jimmie's attachment to you"—John grinned—"a new object." Edna raised her eyebrows at him. *"That* was true love. My first." The air was softening between them.

"What else do cats do?" he asked. "When hungry they stick out the tongue, elevate the tail, and follow someone around, or pull at the clothing of the arm or lap to attract attention to their needs. When satisfied with eating and drinking, they lower their tail. Scratching at the doors is a sign for wanting to go out, also. Shaking the head or jerking the foot is not only an effort to free feet and ears from water, but it means unhappiness or dislike. Rubbing the head is an effort to attract attention, as well as a sign of friendship. Purring means happiness or worry. A large yellow cat of my sister's thought to follow the hired hand to the cow and sit on a log until the milking was over, and always came back happy and stuffed up with milk.' "

"What a precise little mind. It sounds just like the things Anna used to write at that age." "Yes, doesn't it?" Edna said, thinking; now everything they said or did reminded them of something already over. Life as a repetition of pleasures. There was nothing wrong with that, she thought, but it meant something; the milestone markers were getting closer together on the road. It wasn't amusing, as it had been in the joke about the ignorant foreign woman who wanted to shorten her trip by putting the markers on the way closer together.

She put her hand on John's knee. He smiled over at her. "John," she asked, "do you think after this we could take a vacation? Go to some cottage near the house and just swim around, lie in the meadow, things like that?" "It sounds like our honeymoon." "Yes." "I don't see why we can't," he considered; "the photography can wait.

959

Really, I don't intend to make a habit of this. But you know they're not as good at taking bullets out as I am; the bullet's near the spine, too." "I wish they'd get a surgeon." "I'm a surgeon." "But you're not supposed to be; it's an accident you're so good at it." "Edna," he warned. "All right, all right," she said, falling silent.

"Besides, no surgeon in his right mind would come out here and get paid pickle relish for his trouble." "I suppose not. Well, do you think you can do it?" "Who knows? You ought to know better than to ask before we take a look." And, she thought, he wouldn't be unhappy whatever the result, not as long as he tried. Well, he would probably succeed and the concerned father would inspect the wound and cause an infection.

John did, in fact, remove the bullet successfully; Edna arranged to have one of the East Hadley Camps come down as a nurse. The Camps were enough to drive anyone to the insane asylum, they were so diligent. It was less than Elder Coe deserved, she told John, but not much less. *She* never changed, either, he thought.

It was a long, long day, and they arrived home exhausted. Neither John nor Edna had the energy to talk; she sat in silence, thinking about her collection of jokes. There were a number, she thought, about funerals. No, not funerals, never funerals, but events which took place after the death: inscriptions on tombstones, doings of the undertaker, the comments he made after death occurred. They usually made the dead person seem silly, useless, insignificant. Then there were the doctor jokes. They were nasty. Well, that made sense enough; the doctor did so little good most of the time, and even when he did, the family directed their anger at him, as if he were responsible for the patient coming down with the illness in the first place. And lawyer jokes, more and more of them about the plea of insanity as the defense used it. They made sense, too; that particular plea made everyone doubt their own minds. It also loosened everyone's sense of boundaries. No wonder lawyers enraged people.

But she kept coming back to the others, her favorites. "Now is the time to transplant croquet hoops." Things like that, they seemed to go along with the puns; men liked the puns better than the women, or at least so it seemed. The two types seemed to go together, she thought, too tired to move her hand, as if something were struggling to expression, something too dangerous to talk about, that thing she kept sensing: that lunacy flowing under all life. And the hatred of the neighbors; how it showed up in all of them. As if they all hated each other. Once she had thought the hatred grew from jealousy, envy of those who had not yet lost things, but now, driving home, watching the mist cover more and more of the familiar markings of her world, she thought, no, that was not it; it had to do with one's sense of everyone else's fragility. That was what they hated; what she hated.

The fragile nature of other humans. And the neighbors. If they weren't walled out, then they were too close. Hatred between loved ones, yes, she decided; that was the most intense. In dreams, she attacked Anna physically, clawing at her face, slapping her, pushing her against a wall. As if she wanted to kill her in dreams. And she did want to kill her because she had died. That was the worst thing Anna could have done, and she had done it deliberately. Religion, how people mocked that, as if ministers were as ineffective as doctors. They were only sympathetic when they became the butts of their congregation. Well, they were like doctors; even the believers laughed at them. That convinced her others were not as secure in their faith as they thought they were. Of course, some people did not think such jokes were funny, but she didn't know of any such people herself.

"Almost home," John said at last; it was obviously an effort to speak. He began coughing. Edna shook her head but kept quiet. She ought to help him down this time, but he would never forgive her. They wove into the house like two drunkards. John was asleep on the bed before she had time to turn around. Edna took a deep breath, began undressing. She frightened so easily lately; yes, she thought, lying down, she had to get hold of herself. She was doing no one any good this way. She wrapped herself around John, even if he was already asleep. He was thinner, she thought groggily, and older. Much older than she was. Twelve years; they were making a difference now. She knew she looked much, much younger; she wished she did not. She wished she looked twelve, twenty years older. A tear slid down her cheek. She scolded herself asleep; she did not want to wake him up.

The rain continued for two days; then the pendulum swung to the bright blue end of the spectrum. This was the day they were waiting for, John said happily; everyone helped them pack their traps into the carriage. They set off under the new green fluttering leaves. The whole world seemed in motion, talking to itself in its various tongues. John suddenly stopped the carriage. "Come out," he told Edna; "let's go to the old meadow." They wandered down the lane. Before they came to its end, where it broadened out suddenly into its thick plushes, they heard the sound of voices; they peered through the fringed trees. Several couples were having a picnic. "We'll have to find another," he said sadly. "I know another one," Edna said; "Ella found it last month chasing after Hattie and that little boy." John seemed happy to go, but she felt very depressed; the blues. At her side, John felt the same sensation; neither of them wanted to mention it.

"Where are we going?" she asked after they ate dinner. "Peru." "Peru? How far away is it?" "Twenty miles." "We have to go farther and farther away to get back where we began," she murmured. "I was just thinking the same thing, but at least we can get there." "At least we have a place to go." "At least we want to go," John concluded. Forty-five years of marriage, Edna thought, and it was still as it had been. Except that their lives, like their faces, had wrinkled a bit; the sheets were not so smooth, but they had made the right bed, and they were happy to lie in it.

The two weeks passed so quickly; John wondered at it. They were always near the river, or on it. They floated up and down between banks, taking turns holding Edna's white lace parasol. John wore his straw hat; Edna, as usual, kept her head uncovered. Her hair, she said, as she always did, was hat enough for her. When there was a chill in the air, they drove by and looked carefully at the oldest houses. They both seemed to find peculiar delight in the cave-like appearances of many of them, the heavy vines having climbed the pillars and porches, shutting the house off from sight under its thick green arches, as if the very leaves themselves were protective of the structure, the inhabitants, which had supported them so long.

They passed three men and two women walking on a dusty road between two stone walls; one woman held her hat against the wind, one man held a little girl's arm. The men had thrown their jackets over their shoulders. The women had not worn any. Their starched white blouses shone like snow in the heat.

They had both come to love driving by porches; there was one big house in particular they always passed on an isolated lane; it reminded them of theirs. A young woman was doing some needlework, her mother bent over it, worried. Someone, probably her sister, leaned her head on her hand, her elbow on the windowsill, staring out at them in boredom. At the other window, another woman stared out; she was watching the mother and daughter. Her look was disapproving. On the other side of the door, farther down the porch, an old man and old woman sat on the wicker chairs, talking and rocking. Probably they were no older than she and John were, Edna realized, surprised. At the next house, a crowd of young people had gathered, jauntily dressed. One particularly raffish young man lounged on the porch roof. He must have climbed out a bedroom window. The other young men loafed on the lawn in white suits and soft caps, the young girls floating lazily among them in muslin, some of them having commandeered the caps of the men for their own. A little girl sat primly on the porch, as if disapproving of such doings, but her propriety was rather spoiled by her position; her knees were wide apart, her heels together, toes pointing apart, forming another "V."

They passed a woman in flowered muslin lying on a hammock; she opened her eyes lazily, like a salamander, looked at them as they passed, then flicked her eyes to her son, who sat, perched for flight, mischief in his eyes, on a green wicker rocker. Another porch and a woman in a checked shirt held a small baby; she was badly overdressed for the weather. The light fell on the ivy framing her porch so that it appeared cast iron; the far fields blazed in the brilliant sunlight. The mother kept the child's back to the light.

They passed one of the great houses; four stories high

and the vines had almost covered it. A young woman, perhaps sixteen, was perched on the banister, staring idly out. She seemed held prisoner by the leaves, the only person left in a world of plants. Another, newer house was under attack. New trellises were hammering themselves against the walls; a young man waited impatiently next to his velocipede. The handlebars were almost as high as his nose. The man driving the tea and coffee wagon had stopped to let his son play with the dog on the grass. Two horses were in back of the veterinary wagon, which was pulled by two more. A double-decker trolley was leaving for an outing somewhere.

It got darker. They passed a group of men, heads bent, standing in front of some sort of monument covered with an American flag, an eight-year-old child about to pull the rope and unveil it. They must be, Edna decided, veterans of the Civil War, or Masons, or Odd Fellows. As they were driving home, they passed a collection of eight children spread across the road like a roadblock. The biggest girl was in the center, pulling a smaller child in a homemade carriage. Someone had stuck a flower behind the tallest boy's ear. One of the smaller boys was about to run ahead. Another, dragged along, looked down at the road, carrying his jacket. The boy on the far right strode menacingly down the road, holding his bat like a club. They kept walking until the last instant, then scattered to both sides like chipmunks.

At night, they climbed into bed early, read, talked; they discussed the humorous material Edna collected; they reminisced. They wore no clothes and forgot there were such things as knocks at the door. It was never to end. John's cough, however, was far worse. Edna worried intermittently; finally John told her *his* father's cough had always worsened in the summer, but when winter came, it disappeared entirely. He hoped his father's bones were still peacefully at rest when he finished *that* story. He would see about some medication when he got home; he dismissed the subject. But it did hurt now when he coughed. Edna was not immediately pacified. "Well," he said, "listen to my chest." "Thump-bump, thump-bump." "Pulse, please," he said, extending his arm. "It's just the same," she said, puzzled. "Then will you stop worrying?"

"Yes," she sighed, leaning back ecstatically. And then they had to return home.

Ella met them at the door. "Everything," she reassured them wearily, "is just the same, except that seven of the children have measles." "Let's go back," Edna begged John, but he dragged her in the door; he was, he said, too old to carry her, and she wouldn't dream of asking him, would she? Three days later, after she had been checking on the various rooms filled with spotted children, Edna noticed John was not down yet. Either that, she thought, exasperated, or he was already out in the cottage. She went back to their room; he was still in bed. It was after eleven o'clock; dinner was almost ready. "I'm just tired," he said, opening his eyes as soon as he heard her come in.

She marched over to the bed and put her hand on his forehead. "You're hot," she said accusingly. "The soles of my feet aren't." "That only works with little babies; besides," she said, feeling them, "they are, too, hot. Wrap up." "Wrap up? In this heat?" he asked, coughing; "Send in one of the Stethoscopes; I refuse to be examined by an amateur." She forced herself to smile. He had never been examined by anyone else before. "It seems," he told her later, "I have congestion of the lungs. Now popularly called pneumonia." He coughed violently. He saw her lips tighten. "That hurts, I see," she said. "Well, that's why I called in the boys. I'm a dreadful coward."

That was the first day. The second was more coughing and more fever. The third day brought more coughing, the same fever, and less appetite. By the end of the week, John seemed to be losing his interest in food altogether, although Edna sat at the side of the bed coaxing him as if he were three weeks old. "It's too much trouble"; he coughed; his voice was hoarse. "You'll be better soon," she constantly promised. He nodded; she suspected him of humoring her. "Promise me something," John said, waking up midafternoon. "What?" she asked, suspicious. "That you'll live as long as I will," he coughed. "You idiot." "Promise," he insisted. "I promise, I promise," she answered; "you promise me something." "What?" "To eat." "I'll try." Did she imagine it, or was his breathing becoming labored? His pulse, she found, when he fell back asleep, was faster.

By the end of the week, John slept most of the day, coughing even in his sleep; he could rest only propped up on pillows, semi-reclining. "You tell me the truth!" Edna screamed at Martin late that night; "I know almost as much as you do!" "Calm down, calm down," Ella ordered; she was beginning to worry about *her*. "Martin," Ella ordered, "tell her the truth." "He has pneumonia," he told his sister defensively; "I told Mother that right away." "Tell her," Ella said patiently, "how dangerous a condition it is." Howard and Alice, who were there all the time now, sat silent as statues on chairs against the wall.

"Mother, it's very dangerous. Pneumonia is always dangerous in someone his age. You know that," her son said sadly. "Is he *failing?*" Edna demanded shrilly. "He is not gaining," Bill said, taking over. She stood, looking up at him. Her lips had turned to stone; they would not move. "But," Bill said hopefully, "he can suddenly improve; you know you've seen it happen time and time again." "He can also," she whispered, hopeless, "take a turn for the worse." "It's either one or the other," William said firmly. "Yes, yes, I know." "His spirits will vary with yours," Bill reminded her. "I'm in a very cheerful mood." "He can always sense your mood, Mother," Ella warned. "What do you all expect of me?" Edna demanded, shrill. "Mother," Bill said to Alice, "would you put her to bed in our room?" "No," Edna protested, refusing to be pulled; "who will watch with him?" "I will," Alice promised. "I'll only go as far as the next room." "That's better than nothing," Alice sighed, taking her off.

The first week turned into the second, the second into the third. With growing misery, the two families watched the familiar spectacle on a new stage; time working with its myriad hands, changing the lines of John's face, deepening the vertical scores from his nose to the corners of his mouth, deepening the cleft in his chin, hollowing out the space between the cheekbones, digging deeper and deeper into the marble of the skull, the eyes burrowing back like small exhausted animals returning to their deep, deep homes.

How like a sculptor's dream, Edna thought, sitting

silently on a small, straight chair: leaving the clay out in the wind and the sand, waking up in the morning, or some indefinite time later, finding the statue complete, finished to the last touch of the chisel, the sands blowing and blowing over the body, taking the full face down to its essentials, bringing out the important features, the cheekbones, the hollows for the eyes, the sharpness of the nose, thinning the skin over the bones, bringing out the chin, whitening with each change. No, this was no trouble; this was something which had been done again and again, and would be again. Yes, there it was, the developing skull, still veiled in its skin.

Edna sat interminably on her chair, learning to sleep sitting up, waking at the slightest sound from the bed, sleeping on if the noise came from another room, or behind her. Every four or six hours, the two boys would consult; he couldn't last much longer, another hour, another two hours, but then he would wake, open his eyes, his head perpetually turned toward Edna's chair, and the struggle to breathe was renewed; it went on.

Finally, they spoke to Alice. "He's keeping alive," Martin said slowly, "because of her." "I know that; but he might make it. You know what his ambition was in Sabbath school? To say at the end, 'I have fought a good fight, I have finished my course, I have kept the faith.' " "That's just it, Mother," Bill said; "he *has* finished his course; it's cruel to keep him going." "What are you saying?" Alice cried; "none of us can do anything about how long he lives. I wish we could." "But he doesn't want to die because of *her*," Bill whispered intensely. "That's the story of his life," Alice answered; "isn't it?" She fell silent. "I don't see what you're getting at," she said finally.

"Someone," Bill began, avoiding his mother's eyes, "has to convince her to let go of him." "I don't understand," Alice said again. "Someone has got to convince her it's useless; someone has got to convince him she'll be fine without him. That she'll be able to go on without him." "Are you saying," Alice asked, "that you want me to convince him he ought to die?" Her son looked at Martin. "No. Someone has got to convince my mother she has to let go of him. She has to make it easier for him. Someone has got to talk to *her*." "I can't do it, Martin," she pleaded, "we're all the same age, John, Howard, and me. It would be like asking me to tell the rest of us to go. I can't," she said, anguished. "I will," Ella said from behind her. Alice turned suddenly. "Don't do it, Ella," she begged; "she'll never forgive you." "She'll forgive me. She won't be angry at any one of us. You don't understand, Alice," she said; "she'll never forgive the world."

"Do you mean," Alice gasped, "she'll end the way Anna did?" "No, no," Ella said; "everything will stop for her. Time will stop for her; she'll keep going, but the world won't be forgiven. Not by her. You don't understand me, do you?" She hesitated. Explaining her mother; now that was a task. "When I first came home, after the two Stethoscopes brought us back from the medical college, she had a nightmare. It had something to do with Father dying in a river or in an overturned carriage or something like that, and she kept saying it was the last winter, or the last summer. Before the next one came, she would be through with this earth. Then she woke up and said—she was still dreaming somehow—'I won't miss it. There's nothing left of it; it's ashes, all of it.'

"Then she woke up altogether and said something about the day of small things; then she said, 'All these are the beginnings of sorrows. Have I been babbling?' " I told her yes and she told me something about the dream. I said it was about the weather and she said it was a premonition, and I teased her about it for years. And she finally said I didn't understand; it was a premonition she would die last, or that he would die before she did, and I didn't have much patience that day. Wilma had stuck her hand on the iron and was screaming her head off about how there was blood coming out of her body, and I told her, Mother, I mean, she should have expected that when she married someone so much older."

"Did she ever talk to you about it again?" Alice asked. "Oh yes, but she would always look at me in a new way, as if I had caught her pretending a sock was a monkey or her doll was a princess. I never much liked talking about it, either, not after that. But she did talk to me about it. Yes; we've talked about it often." "Lately?" "Not since Father got sick, if that's what you mean." "That's what we meant. I don't know, Ella," Bill said, "it's a lot to ask of you. They're your parents; you know what they've been to each other." "That's why I should do it," Ella said softly, fiddling with a paper knife. "I would do the same for you," she said, looking up at her husband. "Would you?" "Yes, I would."

"Why?" Alice asked. "Because anything else would be too selfish. That's enough!" Ella exploded abruptly. "All right, you talk to her whenever you want to," William said. "Thank you"; she sounded bitter. She looked down. She had sawed right through the damask cloth. "I didn't ask you to do it!" Bill was angry. Ella got up and flew out of the room. "Leave her alone," Alice said; "she's mad at the world, too." "I guess she has every right." "I'd say so," Howard mumbled. Minnie sat through it all, silent.

Meanwhile, the anger in the house began pointing its accusing finger toward Ella; more than a day had elapsed and still she had not spoken to her mother. "Don't anyone say a word," Howard growled from his corner. "I won't," Minnie promised. "No one's worried about you," snapped Alice. It sounded, Martin thought, as if they hated each other. Ella, through it all, was nowhere to be found. She had gone out on her favorite horse, tethered it on the common, and started walking. The day was beautiful; it was always beautiful when someone was dying. She wandered aimlessly under the canopying leaves; they flickered their laces. They could not get her attention. Well, then, death was like that, she thought, opening her parasol; nothing got one's attention. She nodded at people; she didn't recognize them. Was time passing? Was that why her feet were so tired? Poor Mother, she sighed, finally finding a place to sit down. The grass was so green. The world finally swam back into focus.

She was in the church burying ground; she was sitting behind Anna's headstone, at the other side, where it was blank, without inscription. She leaned back against it; it was cool and strong against her. "Well, Anna," she murmured, "what should I do now? It's happening again, only this time it's Mother and Father. He doesn't want to die and she doesn't want to let him go. It's easier to take the little deaths. And the ones that come suddenly. Think what you missed, Anna," she continued bitterly, "by dying so young. Now, was that right, when you know all the passages from the Bible? I don't suppose you have anything helpful to say now? I thought not. I suppose the best I can do, Anna, is go back and tell them not to take any pages from your book. My dear sister. Dear sister Anna, what kind of love was it you had for *your* husband? 'Do not despise the day of small things.' He used to love that text so. You betrayed him, my dear sister. You didn't keep the faith. Do you have any idea, any idea, of how much harm you've done? I don't know if Father would be dying now if it hadn't been for you. You, you're the one who sent him into that cottage day and night. Now we'll never know what killed him. Perhaps *you* did it, Anna. Perhaps we should have put that stake through your heart, just the way Mrs. Moffat threatened her husband. Murderer! Murderess!" she hissed; "I hope they catch you, sister Anna, with that angelic look of yours. So this is how you became perfect, is it?"

A chill was in the air, hovering. Ella shivered, wiped her eyes, and stood up. "You'll have company soon enough," she said, looking down at the mound with its endless supply of fresh flowers. "Why don't you come home and help me out?" she whispered bitterly; "why don't *you* talk to Mother? Why don't *you* do something besides hang on to us like a stone? Perfect, perfect, perfect!" she taunted the headstone. "Well, Anna, rest in peace. No one else does; they want me to pry Mother's hand away from Father's. That way he rests and she lives in misery. You understand why that's fair, perfect sister Anna? Someone ought to. I don't believe you're in heaven," she whispered, kicking a pebble at the stone; "why don't you tell me how fast scars heal, especially ones in the earth? That was the only kind you bothered with. My dear, dear sister." She kicked over the vase of flowers with the tip of her boot. "Smell," she told the stone nastily.

"Where," William asked, "have *you* been?" "Out. Singing in the choir. Visiting a house of ill repute. Getting in the harvest. Swarming bees. Getting a new dress cut." "All right!" William snapped, seizing her wrist, squeezing it until she winced. "Let go of me!" He dropped her arm. She went into her parents' room. "Mother," she whispered, "I have to talk to you." "Not now." "Now," she said, adamant. "First get Alice." "Well?" Edna asked, once in Ella's bedroom; "what can possibly be so important?"

"You're being selfish," she began without preliminary; "he's staying alive for your sake. It's torture for him. You have to let him go; you have to tell him you'll be all right. You'll have to lie and say you'll be happy. You have to do it." "I can't; I can't." She was so tiny, Ella thought. She looked so small, a prematurely aged child. "Do you want it to end this way?" her daughter asked; "do you want this to be the last time you'll spend together? So that he'll take his last breath feeling he's failed you? After all this time, he has to die knowing he can't make you happy? Do you want that? Do you want him to die knowing he's disappointed you, that you're disappointed in him?" Edna stared at her; Ella shivered.

Her mother looked as if she had caught a glimpse of something unmentionable: a lost ghost, an emptiness. Ella waited. "No," her mother said finally, still staring: what was she seeing? "We have never seen a daguerreotype of heaven," her mother murmured; "that was what Reverend Pierce once said at one of his services. We have never seen a daguerreotype of heaven." "That doesn't mean there isn't one." "No, no, it doesn't." "It doesn't mean there is one, either," Ella said, without thinking. "No." "Perhaps you have seen heaven," Ella said suddenly. "Yes. I saw it and couldn't keep it. Isn't there a nursery rhyme that sounds something like that?" "I think so." "I'll go back in now, dear." Ella got up, steadying her. "I don't envy you," she whispered. "Fair is fair; in this unfair world—enjoying something is believing in its permanence. Nothing permanent was meant for time; nothing. That's the word to time's one song: nothing. That's what I sit there thinking all day and all night: Nothing. Nothing. Nothing. It sticks in your head like a sad mass. It fits all the hymns. It fits everything. Well," she said, stopping.

Alice saw them in the doorway, and left. "Should I stay with you?" "Please don't," Edna whispered, sitting down next to the bed. "He's sound asleep," she said, waiting for the latch to fall into place. Click, click. Like two beats of a clock. She waited. Time passed; she was defeated. She knew that. John's head turned on the pillow. "Edna," he gasped. "I'm sitting right here." "Have you been there for a long time?" "Probably. I don't have too many places to go. The patients don't send for me." He smiled faintly. His face, she thought; it wasn't the same face she remembered. The voice was the same; he was the same man. She had to remember that.

"I love you," he said. "I know." "You were life," he said, hoarse. "And you were mine." "No"; he shook his head impatiently; "you were life." "Life; I never knew what it was until I met you. The sky was too far away before I met you. There was no one real. It was all a game. As if the world were made of paper." "Yes," he said. "John. Dear, you need some sleep. You need to sleep. I can wait until you wake up." "You're crying." "It's just that I'm tired." "Just?" "What else could it be?" "I love you so," he said, staring at her. "It's just that I'm tired," Edna said. "I love you so, even when you cry." He took a deep breath. Each one racked his body; "I am persuaded that neither death, nor life, nor angels shall be able to separate us." "Blasphemer," she said. "I am persuaded," he whispered again. How blue his skin looked! "Don't talk so." "It makes no difference." "No, dear." "I love you, Edna." "More than you ever loved Serepta?" She smiled through her tears. "Not quite that much." "Villain!" She smiled, and meanwhile, every nerve in her body was crying.

"Well, I never loved you; I married you for your fortune, you know that." "And my cat." "And your cat. Poor Jimmie," she sighed. "Poor everyone," John gasped. "John," she said, taking his hand, "I have had the best life. I will never believe anyone had a life like mine. And it isn't even over. There are all the children; too much happiness, well, it brings stupidity, it brings peace. Peace. I am peaceful, dear. Really, I am." He was searching her face.

"Move over," she said finally. "What?" he gasped, smiling. "I'll help you"; his body was so light, she thought, pulling him over to his side of the bed by the sheet on which he rested. "You never change," he said. "No, I suppose I don't," she said, climbing up on her side of the bed without removing her shoes; she had no time to unbutton them. "I don't suppose you're comfortable on your side?" He shook his head no. "You always were inconsiderate in bed," she scolded; "pulling the covers off in the middle of the winter, turning over on me, hitting me in the eye with your elbow, taking my pillow because it had more feathers." He smiled. "I never made you sleep on the floor." "That's something, isn't it? But you never got enough sleep; I spent too much time in this bed alone." "Then you're used to it," he said. "I certainly am, but you need more sleep. I can wait until you wake up," she said again. "Can you?" He was staring at her as if trying to see into her bones. "Of course I can; I always did." She turned on her side, putting one arm over his chest, another across the top of his head. "Will you go to sleep?" "Will you wait for me?" "I promise; close your eyes." "You're so warm," he murmured, closing his eyes slowly, opening them, looking at her, looking around the room, looking again at Edna, closing his eyes.

"That's a change," Edna purred. His eyes flickered open, looking at her. "You're taking a picture?" she teased; he nodded. "Close your eyes," she sang softly; "go to sleep." "You'll wait?" he asked again. "Happily, happily. Nothing has changed. Nothing will ever change." "Nothing," John repeated, serene. "Nothing," she said again. He closed his eyes. "Mmmmm," he sighed, rubbing his cheek against her arm; "I am tired," he said. "I know; so am I. I'll be here when you wake up." He nodded, eyes closed; his breathing deepened. Edna was suddenly exhausted. She watched the rise and fall of his chest. Under the quilt, its emaciation was hidden. Tired, she was tired. She fell asleep.

It was dark when she awoke; there was something missing in the room. She knew that immediately. The ticking of the clock, that was too loud. Her breathing was too loud. It was because it was so quiet; her eyes flicked around the room like a lizard's. It was her room. The candle flickered its tongues against the walls. The only sound of breathing was her own. She raised herself up on one arm. The only sound of breathing in the bed was hers. She felt John's head. It was cold. She felt his pulse. It was gone. "Nothing," she whispered to herself, crying silently. "You won't wake up?" she pleaded, looking at him. He didn't answer. "Not even if I shake you?" She shook him slightly. "You won't wake up," she said, toneless. "I lied; I will never wait happily. There is nothing to wait for. It's over. I'll stay in the play as an extra. As I promised. I always keep my promises," she said through her tears. "I'm a fool." She cried silently so that no one outside could hear her, not until early morning. Then she went out.

"He's dead," she told Martin. "When?" "Just now." William, emerging from a cloud, grabbed for her arm; Ella took the other. "Get in our bed," Ella pleaded. Her mother offered no resistance. "He's been dead all night," Martin told Alice, bewildered. Alice sat down next to the body on the bed, crying. Howard came in and put his hands on her shoulders. "One gone," he said sadly. "The best one," Alice cried. Howard nodded, afraid to speak.

"We have to do something about the funeral," Howard said. "Give her some time," Alice pleaded. "That's what I meant; if we do it, she'll have more time." "But we'll have to ask her." "Not about having the body laid out, not about a coffin." "No, I guess not," Alice agreed, "but she'll never have him painted up." "That's true." "We have to get ice," Alice said. "Yes." "It's awfully hot." "Two days," Howard said; "we can give her two days, then . . ." Alice got up, taking his arm. "She's asleep," Ella told them, "or at least she's pretending to sleep. She won't open her eyes." "She's not dead?" Alice asked, worried. "She's as alive as we are," William assured her. "I don't know about that," Minnie muttered. "Well, physically, anyhow," Bill said. "Don't start fighting," Alice warned. "We can keep the children at George's for a while," Ella said. "Then we better go in and talk," Martin decided.

They sat glumly in the parlor. "Someone better start," Ella said, almost whining. "I've had enough for some time." "I sent for Mrs. Greenwood," Martin volunteered. "Remarkable"; Ella glared. "The problem is the funeral," he went on, ignoring his sister; "everyone will want the funeral service in the church." "Why?" Ella asked. *"Why!"* Alice exclaimed; "because most of the people alive around here owe their lives to him." "She won't like it," Ella predicted. "We'll tell her Father wanted it that way"; Martin glowered. "Well, he would have," he exploded at his sister. She just peered steadily at him. "Will you stop that?" Howard asked; "squabble, squabble, squabble; they never get tired of it."

The younger ones finally smiled; it was a relief, being scolded again, like children. "But a church service," Alice thought aloud; "that would be awfully hard on her." "I doubt if she'd notice," Ella said; "she won't notice much of anything for a while. I don't think she's coming out of her room until the funeral." "Our room," William corrected. "Stop it!" Howard roared; "you can sleep in at our house if you can't find a room in our barn." Bill and Ella looked down at their shoes. "Where will we bury him?" Minnie asked. "In the ground, where else?" Howard growled. "She may not want to bury him in the churchyard," Minnie persisted. "I don't see there's any choice; not right now," Alice said. "I suppose not," Martin said. "Then there's nothing to do but wait out the two days; and then we have to talk to her. Well, we do," Bill said, seeing their accusing stares turn to him.

One by one, during the following hours, they went in to say goodbye, to convince themselves. It was Martin who came in with the camera from the cottage. The day was unnaturally bright; he pushed back all the curtains. The others helped him move the bed to the window. "I think that's enough light," he decided at last. He took a series of pictures. "The last of a series; not to be continued," he said sadly, putting the plates back in their cases. "Do you think she'll want them?" Minnie asked, her gray eyes wide. "Eventually," someone said. "Should we sit up with the body?" Minnie asked. "I doubt if Mother would want that," Ella said. "No," Martin agreed; "it's still their room."

Alice went in to tell Edna the funeral would be in three days, on Thursday. She could tell Edna was listening, but she didn't open her eyes, or move. "Well," Alice said, as if nothing unusual had happened, "we'll talk about it on Wednesday. In the morning." Wednesday morning, Edna came down, neatly dressed, immaculate, her hair combed, dressed in black. "We have some things to discuss." Her voice had a mechanical, metallic sound. They told her the townspeople wanted the funeral held at the church. "What do they have to do with him?" she asked in the same flat voice; "they've already taken more than their share." "Mother," Martin interrupted. "I don't see why it's necessary," she answered, looking straight at him. He looked beseechingly at his sister. "Mother," Ella began, "Father never believed in futile gestures. 'If it does them good, and it doesn't do any harm, give it to them.' That's what he always said." They waited.

"What kind of service do they want?" "A normal one; except they want the choir to sing. In his honor." "I don't see why it's necessary," she said again. "Does it make any difference?" Amos' gruff voice asked from the doorway. He stood there awkwardly, like the uninvited guest at the christening. His voice, when it touched Edna, seemed to wound her physically. "No, I guess it doesn't. Sit down, Amos," she said gently. "Yes, miss." He was one of the people who had begun with them. "What do you say?" she asked. "He'd want you to do it, miss; he didn't spend all that time going after them if he didn't like them some. Anyway, you know he'd agree with anything at all to make a person feel better." "All right," she said; "but I don't want him buried in the churchyard." There was an impatient stir at the table. "He can be buried there temporarily, but after that, I'm building a monument for us on the grounds.

"I'll put up a high gate around it; no one has to worry about the children. I intend to be buried right there with him. Anyone who wants to join us is welcome to," she finished harshly.

"There's no harm in that," Alice said; "if it's what you want." "It's what I want; the last house. I want it to look like a house. I want to design one more house." "You'll be separating members of the family," William said. "It won't hurt people to be reminded there are such things as fatal separations; after we're safe inside, it's up to the rest of you. You can leave everyone where they are, or move them. As for where you make your beds, that's your choice; it always has been." "She has a right to say it"; Howard glowered around the table. "The funeral," he told her, "is at eleven." "I'll be ready," she said, getting up.

"What do you think?" Ella asked after she left the room. "She'll be fine until after," Amos said; "then she'll have a real fit. Then she'll walk around." They all peered at him. "When she walks around," Martin asked him slowly, "what will she be like?" "Like a cow that's lost its calf." "Will she be all right?" Ella asked. "She won't start up sleeping in the snow." "But will she be all right?" Ella insisted. "She'll live"—Amos shrugged—"that's all."

Thursday was gray and misty. Edna refused to have her mother notified. She would go to Boston eventually and tell her herself. At her age, Edith didn't need surprises. She didn't need to worry about her daughter, either, especially a daughter in her sixties. So it was the immediate family, accompanied by Amos, Bridget, and the rest of the servants, who set off for the church. "It's crowded," Edna said, seeing the long line of carriages. "He had an awful many patients," Minnie said. As if she didn't know.

She supposed they were right; that this is what John would have wanted. But she didn't like it; she didn't see why they had to have the same last look at him she did. But then, they wouldn't; they couldn't. They could never see the same thing. "Did you make it clear to the Reverend Case," she asked, "that the service was to be simple? Brief, brief?" she asked, suspiciously. They all nodded. "But it will take some time," Bill warned, "for everyone to go by the casket and back out again." She shuddered. "We can go into the vestry," he told her, "and wait until everyone's settled." She nodded.

They went in through the back entrance. "All right," William said, "everyone's waiting." He took Edna's arm; she didn't seem to want her children touching her. They went around in front of the pulpit. The casket was resting on two chairs. It was completely covered with flowers: roses, tulips, daisies, she had never seen so many flowers. There were so many wreaths they were laid around the casket and along the edge of the pulpit. Edna was taken aback by the gratitude she felt. The organ was playing "Nearer My God to Thee." Edna stood still, listening. The way the voices rose and fell; the words of the song: it did make you want to believe. John, she thought, would have liked "Amazing Grace" better; but she doubted the choir would have wanted to sing it, not after John and Howard had mauled it so at Anna's funeral. Her mind went blank; she observed it happening without surprise, a photographic plate overexposed to the light. It was hot, but inside the church it was cool. Her thoughts stopped there.

The rest of them moved her here and there like a

somnambulist. She knew she was standing at the side of a grave. Again. She knew she was hearing the funeral service again. "Our Heavenly Father, we commend our brother to thy heavenly care in the certainty that we will meet again on the golden shore and live forever in thy abounding grace." "Amen," said someone who had come from the church. "I am the resurrection and the life: he that believeth in me, though he were dead, yet he shall live. And whosoever liveth, and believeth in me, shall never die. Except a crown of wheat fall into the ground and die, it abideth alone: but if it die, it bringeth forth much fruit. He that loveth his life shall lose it; and he that hateth his life in this world, shall keep it unto life eternal. In my Father's house are many mansions. I go to prepare a place for you, I will come again and receive you unto myself; that where I am, there ye may be also. Behold, the hour cometh, yea, is now come, that ye shall be scattered every man to his own, and shall leave me alone, and yet I am not alone, because the Father is with me. Little children, it is the last time. I am Alpha and Omega, the beginning and the end, the last and the first. Amen," the Reverend Case said. A chorus of voices echoed him.

The family proceeded slowly back to their carriages. Edna stumbled. "It's the heat," she said; it was the same mechanical voice they had been hearing since the previous morning. They were surprised at how calm she had been. Even though, as John had constantly teased, only Catholics had hysterics, still, they expected hysterics of her. "The fit"; Amos had predicted it. The ride home seemed endless, as if the air itself resisted their progress. "Reverend Case explained that there were to be no visitors," Minnie said to the clouds. If it were not for a slight motion of Edna's head, they would not have known she had heard. Alice raised her eyebrows sympathetically at her daughter; Minnie stared out at the landscape. None of them looked at each other. William helped Edna out of the carriage, and they started toward the house, Amos hobbling valiantly after her.

They were almost at the door when Edna saw the funeral wreath someone had put up in their absence. "No!" she screamed without warning, pulling back. William had all he could do to hold on to her. "No!" she kept screaming rhythmically; she sank down onto the ground. Her clothes surrounded her like a pool of black water. "Edna, get up," Howard growled. "No, no, no, no," she kept moaning, rocking back and forth. Amos pushed him aside. "Miss Edna," he said gruffly, "you get up off that grass. John told me to look after you and I can't stand here like a fence all day; come on into the barn, come on. Up." To their astonishment, she got up, docilely following him. "Where are you sleeping?" they heard him ask her. "In my own room," she answered, crying; "it's our room, isn't it?" "I don't know who else it belongs to," he answered, and then they were too far off to be heard.

"Will it be good for her?" Minnie asked; "I mean, sleeping in that room, after the body was there so long?" The rest of them looked at her, pitying. After this, what was or was not good for her would be her own decision. There was no one in the world who could influence her now. "What," Bill asked his father, "was all that commotion at the other end of the burying ground?" "They struck into another grave." "Whose?" "Old Probst's; the one who shot Martin's dog. The shovel went clear through his skull; it was all crumbling up. I had to look. They practically had Bertie Coe's shoes planted in his head." "They're getting careless," Alice said. "It's about time Probst got a kick in the head," Howard mumbled; "even if it did take this long." "Well, maybe moving Ten isn't such a bad idea. Before someone kicks her," Alice thought. "Let's leave all that for later," Ella said sharply.

They all watched Edna move through the following weeks as if her life was something someone had set going, a broken clock which had been repaired, which ran, marking the hours against her will. Gradually, she seemed less stiff; when the weather turned chilly, she busied herself taking in Ten's geraniums. Now Alice had a good excuse to be there all the time. Edna was still helpless when it came to flowers; she was busily potting weeds when Alice came up the first morning. Slowly, the old ways seemed to be asserting themselves. Yet she reminded Alice of those eggs emptied for Easter, then painted; they had nothing inside.

They took to visiting George's in a vain attempt to break old, painful associations. Alice and Howard ransacked the papers. "A woman got poisoned for rejecting a suit—with arsenic," Howard read. Edna nodded, as if making a note to be opened later. "Poor Mrs. Coe," Alice sighed; "she had to go to the poorhouse. Why, she must be almost one hundred! Those rotten Coes! And it's all because that bank failed in Dudley. It says here she was supported by an in-law, but when the crash came, he was sent to jail, and he couldn't do it anymore. She's gone and been sent to the county farm." "That's terrible," Edna commented in her expressionless voice. Earthquakes, people buried alive, bigamy, a minister's son who shot his father because he couldn't go out riding: everything brought the same response, or lack of it.

Alice consulted Amos. "Wait," he advised. "For what? Do you think she'll change?" "Maybe. Can't tell." She waited for him to say something more, but he had said all he had to say. Then one night when she drove over, the Steele house was in an uproar. Martin was shouting at his mother—she could have been killed. What on earth was she thinking about? Edna stood in the middle of the room, listening to them babble at her, confused. "What," Alice asked severely, "is this all about? Don't you think it's too many of you at one bird?"

"They're mad at me about the tramp," Edna said. "What tramp?" The others were all glaring at Edna. "Oh, well," she began, sitting down, "one came by this morning when everyone was out, and the upstairs chambers, the ones we use for spare rooms, needed cleaning. So I didn't see why he shouldn't do it. Well, it says in the Bible, 'If any would not work neither should they eat,' so I told him we had a carpet upstairs which needed shaking and cleaning, and two carpets to beat, and some weeds to pull up, and I said he could have breakfast if he'd do those things right after he finished eating." "Oh, Mother, for pity sake!" Ella exclaimed. "Will you keep quiet?" Alice asked.

"He certainly ate enough," Edna said, shaking her head; "he ate five roasted potatoes, four slices of bread and butter, some biscuits, half of one of your cheeses, three chopped onions in vinegar, three cups of coffee and a whole pie. He ate up everything except the cloth. Then it turned out he had no intention of working. I lost my temper; and that's what they're losing their tempers about.

He was putting on his hat, picking up his satchel, and getting all ready to leave without even saying thank you. I was angry, that's all. So I reminded him of what he was supposed to be doing; I said he'd eaten his breakfast and I'd pay him what I promised when he finished working. He couldn't get around me," she explained to Alice; "I was standing in the doorway.

"But then he started complaining he didn't know a thing about dirty work like that, so I asked him if he would manage to help me carry out the carpet, and he said he would, and he started up the steps. So that's when I took his satchel and hid it." "You could have been killed!" Minnie cried. Alice stopped her daughter with a look. "When, then, after we got out the miserable carpet, he wouldn't hang it on the line, but he came back after his satchel, and I said he couldn't have it until he put up the carpet, brushed it, beat it, shook it, folded it, and brought it in clean enough for the floor. I don't know why they're so excited," she said, confused.

For the first time since John's death, Alice noted some shading in her voice. "He did what I told him to. He did it very well, too, as if he'd never done anything else in his life, and I gave him a dollar and told him I would have given him two if he'd kept his promise in the first place and didn't force me to act like an idiot, running around hiding his satchel as if he was a child. That's all there was to it," she sighed; "such a fuss."

"Well, Edna," Alice said, "I don't think I'd have been so daring. There aren't any policemen walking around here, and no neighbors within screaming distance." "You don't have to be afraid of tramps," Edna said; "they're all cowards. Most of them just have bad habits anyway, because they can't get steady work, and once they're tramps, hardly anyone gives them work, so they get used to doing nothing. That's why they don't want to do anything. They're not used to it. And," she finished, looking severely at the others, "I really didn't see how I could send off a hungry person just because I had high principles and knew he wasn't too likely to do his work. I should think someone like that would be more dangerous the hungrier and more desperate he was, just like a starved cat. Well, that's all I did, and that's what all this caterwauling is about."

"The last time I took in two tramps for a meal," Alice said, "they ate all right, about as well as your caller, and they were supposed to dig out a patch and rake it out for the potatoes, and I put some things up to boil and kept looking out the window at them. I didn't trust them much, I can tell you. Every time they picked up a shovel with dirt on it, they looked all around and looked at the patch to see how much smaller it had just got, and they kept showing each other their palms, which were pink as tongues, and such faces! Such sympathy for each other; I tell you, it was something. Then the next time I looked out, what should I see? They hadn't even dug one row and they dropped the spades and jumped the fence and disappeared like two weasels. You're a lot braver than I am, I can tell you that." Edna shrugged.

"Brave!" Ella exclaimed; "that's not the word for it." "Stupid, that's what it was!" Martin put in. "I've heard enough about it," Edna said, raising her voice; "Alice, come and tell me more about the child who shot his father." They stared after her, furious and helpless. It was true. There was no one who could tell her anything now. "His father whipped him for taking the horse, and he blew his head off in the corncrib, where he hid himself," they heard Alice saying. "I guess that's about the best we can expect," Ella fumed; "she still doesn't understand the country." "Yup," Minnie chimed in; "and it could be worse." "That's the truth," Bill said. "Don't let's start looking for trouble again," Minnie implored them. "And I wouldn't mention it again, if I were any of us," said Martin. "It's going to be like having another child," Ella pronounced.

Martin came down early one morning in October, looked out the window, and saw the first snow squalls heralding a real snowstorm. Then he saw a large sheet of paper folded in the middle of the table, standing there in the center like a tent. It was a note from his mother. "I've gone to Boston for a while," Edna wrote; "I thought a change of scene would be good for all of us. Please don't notify *my* mother until I get around to it. I have some shopping to do and won't be staying with them for the first few days. You are not to worry about me. I'm quite accustomed to traveling to Boston alone, and will get back safely the same way. Your Mother." That sounded innocent enough; he showed Bill the note as he came in. "Good idea," he said, putting it back. The others agreed. Alice muttered something about it not being like Edna to leave so suddenly, but the others said that was Edna all over. She never did anything she was expected to, and she always did the things she wasn't. So the family went on with its ways, its skinned knees, its plans for sliding, sleighing, last picnics, whippings over taking out the wrong horses, rounds and more rounds, alarms of scarlet fever, the beginning of a new epidemic of measles. Occasionally, during the first week of her absence, they thought about her, but no more and no less than when she went into Boston to meet John while that interminable trial dragged on. She was staying at the Parker House. That was where she always stayed.

Amos had driven Edna to the Brattleboro station. "You coming back?" he asked, awkwardly waiting beside her. "Where else do I have to go? Besides," she said, trying to smile, "I have to build that little house." "Well, don't forget it." "Go on back," she told him after a while; "the horses have more trouble getting their dinner than I do. Go on, scat," she teased; "you always used to leave me here before and I always got there." "That was different." "Everything was different; but I still know how to get on a train. Go, go on; I'll be back. If Ten and John were here," she said finally, playing her best card, "they'd tell you to listen to me." "Would they, Miss Edna?" "Yes," she said, "they would."

The train, Edna decided, settling back, was a good place to think. She began sketching her little monument on a little pad of paper. The more she worked on it, the more it resembled the house she had originally built, as it had originally been. Well, that was what it was going to look like, she concluded, resigning herself, filling in the details of the sketch. She would have to ask Mr. Siddons to recommend someone. He was too old for marble, he wrote remorsefully in his last letter; it would be all porcelain figurines for him now. The terrible tragedy had at last occurred: his hand shook. He was reduced to employing a tribe of starving artists to paint the creations and to finish off the finer curves and angles, although he could do a great deal more in that way than he would have thought ever since one of the young men had built a platform bracket for his arm. It was adjustable, and he had a little handle which tightened it and tightened his hand, steadying it, even if he couldn't do it himself. It was certainly nice of both of them to have stayed alive long enough for her; if she had anything against her mother, she would have to forgive her now.

The miles went by smoothly. The snow stopped half an hour out of Williamsville, and the train ran smoothly on, the one time when she did not care if she got into Boston; certainly not *when*. She would get off the train at the Back Bay station; there was no one she wanted to meet. Bits of the funeral kept floating back; she took out the little packet of photographs she had wrapped into her coat pocket for proof against these moments. She studied the pictures of John; she studied the death portraits. He was too thin in them, too old. She put them in the back, and looked at the earlier ones she had had taken before the trial. That was how he had always looked, tall, unshakable. This last wind had been too great for him, she thought, eyes filling. She had never liked too much light. She pulled down the shade next to her seat.

It was odd to be traveling back to Boston alone, again in mourning, as she had come that first time to Williamsville, as if she had reversed the process set in motion when she had first been sent to her Aunt Ten's. She had been sixteen then; she was almost sixty-three now. Was that why she was going back? In some vague hope that when she returned things would be just the same as they had been when she first arrived? Still, it was about time. She found herself humming snatches of "Nearer My God to Thee." That had always happened when she came back from Anna's. She would walk around the house singing "Amazing Grace," "A Mighty Fortress Is Our God," singing and dressing, singing and reading. "You're singing," John used to say, grinning. "Am I?" she always asked, surprised. "She comes back converted every time," Ten said; "her conversions don't last long, fly little thing." She turned her head against the headrest, smiling at them.

She would be spending more and more time with their voices now. She was exhausted, she realized, closing her eyes. It was so nice to be out of everyone's sight. What a sense of freedom! She could go completely mad if she so decided without her bodyguards rushing in with blunderbusses of rationality. "Jabber, jabber, jabber," she said softly, trying it. No one was close enough to hear her. "Jabber, jabber, jabber," she said again, a little louder. No one was interested; she wasn't much amused by the exercise. And the trouble, she was sure, would be that if she did manage to go off her head, she wouldn't even have the satisfaction of knowing she was doing it. She pouted at the air, then closed her eyes; would she ever get over missing the feel of John's body next to hers? And it was no use pretending anyone else could take his place. Her daughter had tried climbing into bed with her, probably because she remembered how they used to climb into bed with her when they were children.

No, the only thing that helped was sleeping on his side of the bed, and even then, she had to put herself into a trance, telling herself again and again, it didn't happen, it didn't happen. Well, she thought, closing her eyes, she was keeping her word. She was staying, waiting for him to wake up. As long as she could. She hadn't added *that*, not that last time she had climbed into bed next to him. As long as she could. The train pulled into the Back Bay station. Edna took down her own trap. She had packed two dresses and several nightgowns. "Where to, miss?" the hansom driver asked. "The Massachusetts Infirmary," she answered, leaning back.

"Well, well, Mrs. Steele, is it?" "Yes, it is," she said, sitting down; "is there a room reserved for me?" "Don't you think we should find out if there's anything wrong with you first? This isn't a hotel." "There's something wrong with me," she said pleasantly, "and it's in my left breast." "You seem familiar," the doctor mused, staring down at his sheet: "Mrs. John Steele." He repeated the name several times. "You do seem familiar." "Not the part of me we were just discussing." The poor thing was flushing. Well, she shouldn't do that. He was only a little older than Martin, probably William's age. "Mrs. John Ashbel Steele," she prompted. He looked at her, pencil poised.

"The doctor who testified at the Griffin trial?" "He's my husband." "He's a doctor; he should have come with you if it's what you think. He seemed to be a good person. We had to study that case in school; it's in the textbooks now. Did you know that?" "No, I didn't." Well, she thought, taking a deep breath. "You must have been a child then," she said. "Not quite a child; but my parents read about it in the papers; it seemed so vivid. It's a hard case to forget. My parents talked about it for years, how my brothers and sisters would end up like the two girls if we didn't stop tormenting each other. Then I came across it again in school." "I thought people would have forgotten about it by now." "Well, how long have you noticed it?" he asked; he *must* be a doctor, she thought, to change subjects so abruptly. She looked at his badge; Dr. Undset. "For five years." "Five years! You were married to a doctor for five years and he didn't notice anything?" "Well, it's in a difficult place to find, especially if the lady takes up lying on her left side." "You mean you hid it from him?" "Yes, yes, I did."

"What made you stop?" This was no concern of his, but he found himself fascinated by her; she looked so young and small, but the chart said her age was sixty-two and five months. "He died." "He died?" "After the burial I didn't think he'd notice"; Edna smiled. He studied her carefully. "Didn't the papers say two of your sons were doctors?" "Yes, they are; but if I had told either of them, they would have told my husband. Only one of them lives in the state; the other doctor in the house is a son-in-law." "Where's your other son?" "In California." "California: Dr. John Ashbel Steele, Jr.; he's in our textbooks, too. Is he any relation?" "He's my other son." He sat, thinking. "You didn't tell him, either?" "*He* would have been the last one to keep quiet; he was the baby of the house. There always comes a point when the baby decides he should take care of his father and mother. I didn't want him bothering anyone." "And that's all there was to it? That's why you hid it for five years?" "Not exactly; I thought I'd have time enough for it when my husband died." "Time enough for it," he repeated, staring at her. "Come," she said energetically; "do your duty. Examine me."

He began struggling with her buttons. "I'll do that," she said, unbuttoning them deftly. "You have a surgeon's fingers." "I've had to help out." "Jack Steele," he mused, waiting for her to finish; "isn't he the one who wins all the prizes?" "Yes," she answered, unlacing her bodices; "but he's really very pleasant." "I didn't mean to imply anything else." The poor doctor was blushing again. "I just don't understand how you could have acted like this coming from such a family." "They had worries enough." What should she tell him? That after her husband died any time would be time enough? Any time would be too much time?

The poor thing was having trouble moving her breast out of her tournure corset, the perfect garment, she thought, smiling to herself; he was afraid to take hold of her. "Why don't you just drag it right out?" she suggested helpfully. He turned the color of the red exit sign. "Let me do it," she suggested, pulling the corset down over her skirt; "there, that's all of me there is above the waist." Her breasts were still strong and firm as they had always been, but wrinkled, like fine parchment. "Good firm breasts," he said admiringly. "For a woman my age." "For a woman any age," he said, beginning to examine her left breast. "I don't feel anything yet," he said after a minute. "It's in back of the nipple, to the left of it, on the inside." He shook his head, but examined the area she had described.

"Well, you're right," he said finally; "there's a lump there, all right." "How large is it?" "That's hard to tell; reasonably large." "Then you'll have to remove it," she said as he moved his chair over to her right side; "did you reserve a room for me?" "For some reason I did; it must have been all the medical talk in the letter. I thought you'd already been to someone else." "Well?" she asked as he finished examining the other breast. "Nothing here." "Well, that's good; at least I'll be able to sleep on my right side. I always slept on my right side. Just one thing, though. I want ether. No chloroform. They always said ether was better."

"And if I told you we didn't use ether?" "Then I'd get drunk and bite the bullet." "You sound like a doctor's wife; the old breed." "Why, thank you." She smiled happily. This was more like life. "Why don't you like chloroform?" he asked curiously; "half the people I know think it's better than a glass of warm milk to put them to sleep. I've got to watch my own wife to make sure she doesn't get any into the house." "Well, tell her I said not to; we watched someone die from liver poisoning after chloroform. He'd be alive now if we'd had ether."

"Are you going to be one of those difficult patients who tell the doctor where to cut with the scalpel? I don't mind holding hands, but not when I have a scalpel in mine." "I don't know a thing about surgery," she answered peaceably. "What about your relatives? Are they coming?" "They are not coming." "Mrs. Steele," he said patiently, "an operation of this kind is distressing. You ought to notify your relatives." "Not a single one of them." "You'll be sorry later." "Then I'll be sorry later." "Didn't you have a mother living in Boston?" he asked after a while; this woman fascinated him. He'd never come across such stubbornness; *everyone's* stubbornness broke down when it came to surgery. "You'll never find her." "That's right; you don't have the same family names." "Aha!"—she grinned at him—"the fly in the ointment!" He wondered vaguely about her sanity. "Don't worry," she told him; "I've already made my will." "How encouraging"; the doctor sighed; "and to whom shall I send it?"

"My address and telephone number, and my mother's, are in my clothes somewhere; if you'll promise me not to look for them before the operation, I'll tell you where they are." She meant business. "I promise, I promise," he said hurriedly. "Under the lining of my right boot; I presumed I wouldn't need them in here." He was observing her as if she came from another planet. "I'll call them myself as soon as I come out of the anesthetic." "You can give yourself an hour or two. If you've waited this long." "When is the surgery to be?" "I have some free time this evening." "It's a date," Edna sighed, relieved; if there was one thing she dreaded, it was a long delay.

She woke in the morning, a dull pain in her left breast. She moved. "Ouch!" she gasped. Well, he had done it, then. She looked at her watch; it was John's watch, really. It chimed the hours. She had turned the chimes off out of consideration for others on the ward. Six o'clock. Well, what was she to do now? She couldn't simply pick up that phone and call her mother, not without asking Dr. Undset to prepare another room first. She wondered, vaguely, if it was possible to call Alice from this distance; she thought it was. But that wouldn't do any good. It was her mother she wanted to see, someone from the family: no, her mother. She would call Richard, she thought, contented. Lettie's husband; she could call him at his office if she waited until after ten o'clock.

She closed her eyes and went back to sleep. She had a vague sense of hands fussing over her, a hand on her head; then she was awake again. Dr. Undset was sitting next to her bed. "Was the lump interesting?" she asked. "Interesting and large," he said severely. "Very, very large?" "Large enough." "Large enough for what?" "To kill time fast," he said; he already had a sense of her. She would have her sons sending for the medical charts.

"Then am I going to die soon?" She sounded so cheerful as she asked it; he was thunderstruck. "I doubt it. I think all of it came out; it was encapsulated." Her face fell. She *was* a strange one. "If you wanted to be a suicide, there would have been easier ways." "Oh no; I made a promise." "Do you always keep them?" "Always." "Then when are you going to call one of your relatives?" "At ten o'clock, when he gets to his office." Dr. Undset looked at his watch: "You have half an hour." "I can still tell time." "I was just reminding you." "Unnecessary." "Are you going to come down with an infection?" "No," she drawled; "I have no luck." "I'll be back later." "I should hope so. Well, go on. I have to use that instrument there." She glared at the telephone. He couldn't help smiling at her. She was a curiosity, he thought, going down the hall.

Edna contemplated that menacing object, the telephone. "Yes, *yes*," she said, exasperated; "Richard Knowles. K. As in 'kitchen.' " She shook her head. "Well, then, as in 'cat.' " The operator promptly announced she would make the connection. "Richard?" Edna began; "this is your mother-in-law. . . . Where am I? I'm in the Massachusetts Infirmary. . . . Oh no, it's nothing to worry about; I must have swallowed a stone and it settled in the wrong place." She listened. "An unmentionable place above the waist. Is that a good hint? . . . No, no, you don't have to come right over. No, I'm enjoying it; there's no one here watching me every minute to see if my mind's going. . . . Yes, I'd prefer that. I think they'll let you in at seven. . . .

Really?" she asked, laughing. Oh, dear, laughing was painful. "Then don't send the Infirmary any more money. . . . No, they've been very good to me. . . . Dr. Undset. Write his name down. . . . Oh, that's a relief. Please don't tell Lettie." She hesitated. "It's just that I don't want to see any blood relations just yet." He said he understood. "I'll wait for you, then," she said; "they won't let me out for ten days. . . . Yes, that's the problem: telling Mother. All right, then," she said awkwardly. How in the world did one end a phone conversation properly? That wasn't in any of her etiquette books; she hadn't even come across any telephone jokes yet. She lay back blissfully; her mind was empty, emptier and emptier. She hadn't really been sick, she thought, since Jack was born.

"Well," Richard said, coming in. "You *are* full of surprises. Everyone's going to be mad as hell at you, you know. For not telling them." "I've had enough of them." "You don't mean that." "If you say so." "Well, perhaps you are tired of them; at least you've got a lot to be tired of." "You should have had more children," she said. "I don't think that would have helped. Would it have helped if you had more children at home?" "Of course not; I'm sorry," she said, taking his hand. "Did my letter come as a shock? About John?" "Yes." "Did you have trouble keeping Lettie quiet?" "No. I told her she'd have to take care of your mother day and night, she'd be so upset when she heard the news. That did it." "Ella is fine," she told him; "this life is full of strange turns, isn't it?" "It is. Did you know about this before?" he asked, suspicious. She told him the same things she had told the doctor. "I'm not going to scold you; it makes all too much sense to me."

"What are we going to do about my mother?" They were conspirators, hiding from their parents in the dark. "I'll go over," Richard promised. "But what will you tell her?" "I'll tell her you were coming down to surprise her, got sick on the train, called me, and I reserved this room, and while you were here, they found something minor and you had some surgery. Doesn't that sound convincing?" "No, it doesn't, but Mother will believe it." "Then we'll all be back in the morning; I'm glad you're here," he said, squeezing her hand. He sounded so desolate, more than she was.

"How could you do it?" Edith demanded shrilly the next morning; "just come here without telling anyone about it?" She understood everything at once. Richard's deceptions hadn't worked. That, Edna thought, was a real surprise. "You could have *died*, Edna," her mother went on, "and none of us would have been here with you." "Mother," she defended herself weakly, "death scenes aren't terribly interesting and they're a terrible drain." "And not to have told me about John and Ten. When you knew how attached to them I was! Twice! I thought after Ten died you'd have more sense than to do that again. I don't want to be protected; it's worse this way," she said urgently; "I never know what's happening. I used to be able to assume," she flared out, "that no news is good news. Well, now, Edna, what *am* I to think? You could go into Brattleboro and pick up a telephone if you didn't want the others listening. And the mails are still coming all the way through to Boston.

"Oh, I am angry with you! I suppose," she said after a pause, "you feel awfully miserable. And I don't mean about the surgery." "I do." Edith took her hand. Mr. Siddons sat disconsolate on his chair. "He was so young," he volunteered. Edna began crying, crying and smiling. "It's so good to see you," she said, looking up at her mother. "Oh, dear," Edith wailed, hugging her awkwardly about the shoulders; "you always were such a willful child. I don't know what to say to you," she told her, helpless. Edna shook her head, still crying, her lips quavering into a smile. "Edna, it's a pity," she finally said with more energy; "it was such a wonderful marriage." "I don't believe it's over; I don't think of it as over," Edna finally answered. "Then it isn't," Mr. Siddons said; "believe what makes you happiest." "Yes," Edith agreed; "that does seem sensible."

"What will you do now?" Edith asked. "Oh, I'll go home. I'll help scold your great-grandchildren; it looks as if we'll have one more from Wilma soon. I'll drift around with the boys when they go on calls. I'll study my jokes. I've taken to studying jokes," she explained. Her mother nodded; it wouldn't surprise her if her daughter took to studying fruit tarts. "And I'm designing a monument for the family, on the family grounds," she told her, fishing for the plans in the drawer next to her bed. "Here"—she gave it to Mr. Siddons—"I want to move John into it, and then I'll go in eventually, too. There's a great deal of land. I don't think it will depress anyone, and I want it to have stained-glass windows, and I was hoping," she continued enthusiastically, "Mr. Siddons could design them." "Tiffany does a better job," he admitted. "I'd still rather have you do it; especially," she coaxed, "if you could make use of some of the sketches of Minnie you made when the boys were at the medical college." "Oh, he'll like *that*," Mrs. Siddons said. "I would," her husband agreed. "I thought you could do the drawing and perhaps supervise the execution." "Yes, that would be lovely; I would be honored to do it." "And there's a cat to be carved on my stone. I'll explain later," she said hastily, seeing her mother's eyebrows twitch upwards. "Well, good," she sighed, settling back. "And I collect buttons. Della Robbia buttons particularly," she added as an afterthought.

"Edna," her mother interrupted, "when are you going to tell the others?" "Tomorrow." "What's wrong with calling them today?" "Oh, they'll start in inspecting me again; they'll send someone down to bring me back. I don't want to be bothered by any one of them, not just now. When I leave, I'll go back with a nurse if that will cheer you up." "It certainly would!" "But I thought, I hoped I might stay with you for a week or two after I came out of here." "You don't have to ask, Edna," Mr. Siddons told her.

Two weeks later they put her back on a train to Brattleboro. Yes, Ella had said, Amos would be there to meet her; no, if she didn't want any of them, Amos would come alone. Edith and Mr. Siddons stood on the platform waving goodbye; Edna dangled out the window. It all *reminded* her of so much. The silent John would be silent now. And it would be so cold. At least Edna didn't mind that.

Ella

Mother died four years after her surgery. It seemed one day she was coming back from Boston, and the next day she was gone. I imagine the years seemed much longer to her. She was buried in her stone gingerbread house with her husband, my father. She would not have liked her funeral. We had to go through another church service when she died. There were at least as many people in attendance as at Father's; perhaps more. They played "Amazing Grace" for her, and "Nearer My God to Thee." Lucretius Sargent, Alice's brother, came in the middle of mourning his second wife. There were people none of us knew, people neither Martin nor Bill remembered. A great many husbands and wives came alone. I suppose those were the ones she sat with while Father did his work. At the last minute, she surprised us: she wanted to be buried with a small packet of Father's pictures. Martin asked if she wasn't suddenly superstitious. She said no, but if she woke up after she was buried, she wanted to have something to look at. He reminded her it would be dark inside. She said she would bite down on them, then. She would run her fingers over them. She would pretend she could see them. Furthermore, she had no intention of arguing about it. It was written into her will and that was that. She *would* resort to such measures to get her own way.

Minnie asked her if she was afraid to die, and she said she wasn't. We suspected her of looking forward to it; she told William she was. She had kept her promise to wait for John until he woke up, and, since it was taking him so long, she had decided to go to sleep with him. Yes, she was happy about it. Life tired her out, all the new things in it: cars, telephones, the new Grand Central Station. She didn't like traveling. The "elevated" in New York City upset her; the trains ran, she said, in midair. She had seen it when it was first constructed. People were afraid to go near it. They expected it to fall down into the street.

993

Then one by one they began climbing up, deciding it might be nice above the streetcars, away from the tired horses and their smells, the coal carts, the express wagons, the ragmen's carts covered with cowbells. Well, the next year, it took up to four cars to carry people back and forth; they never got out of the cars. She supposed it was a good thing; you could look down and see the iron railings and the gardens. It was nice to look into third-story windows, and look down at the crowd beneath.

It was a puzzle where they were all going. There were white-capped nurses, the babies all fancily dressed, little velocipedes, not at all like the constructions they were used to in Williamsville, businessmen and businesswomen; more women with laundry baskets of neatly ironed clothes, women out shopping; the mail carrier in his gray suit, the market lady with the basket on her head and a bag of vegetables in her arms. It passed the brownstones; some of them had "To Let" signs in the windows. Some people were having trouble with their lives. You could see into the narrow streets where everything was crumbling, just as she was, and under some of the windows, green plants in cups and tins and boxes. Well, they must paint themselves, she thought; poor flowers, like fancy women, they looked so out of place, so vivid, in the city.

She had met a man who went on and on about sleigh rides; how he used to go sleigh riding every Saturday with his father, and how they took the oxen through the deep drifts, even the baby, and then they would get more children and babies from another house and fill up the sled and everyone was so interested in everyone else and those were such social times, and it wasn't that way anymore, and she realized she was as old as he was, and she had lived long enough, really. Sixty-six, that was a good age. She never expected to live so long, in any case. She teased us, right before she died. She wanted to know what we were going to do when we got tired of steam travel and decided it was too slow for us? She supposed we would want wings, but as for her, she wasn't really interested, not anymore. She died in her sleep.

Well, we missed her. It was the end of the older ones. And it gave us a stronger sense of ourselves, as if more of ourselves had somehow flowed back to us. We were stronger in ourselves, in each other, in our trust in each other. Our children grew up and got married, and they had children. I don't know how it happened, how my parents became so mythical in my family. One of us must have said something. Or perhaps Alice did. Something simple. For example: there weren't marriages like that anymore. But we never believed that; we knew they had their ups and downs, and we couldn't believe our lives had been any less, although, I suppose, it is time to be honest, and say our lives were less intense.

Well, none of us had anything to worry about as far as material existence went. Father had left all his money to Mother. Ten had left hers to both of them; Mr. and Mrs. Siddons left their money to Mother, although Mrs. Siddons, our grandmother, outlived Mother by six years. They both died when they were ninety-seven years old. Mother would have envied them. They were driving happily along in the brougham when a runaway milk wagon crashed into the side of their carriage, slamming them against the cobblestones and under the milk tins; it took a great many men to lift them off and remove the bodies; but they had died together. That would have been the best end for our parents.

We talked about the monument she built. She liked it, she said, because it was just as the house was when she was first married. It would be so much more permanent. She went on and on about that: how the heat and the light and the dust and the snow and the rain would take so much longer to eradicate it. The house: she didn't think that would last long, and if, later on, no one knew who was buried in the little house, well, then, whoever had the house could just take them out and do whatever they did with buried bodies by then, and turn it into a doll's house. She would have loved such a doll's house when she was a child, and very young children wouldn't know what it was for, and perhaps, by the time they found out, they would be used to that kind of house. She certainly did die happy.

Howard Moffat died a year after Mother; Alice died two years after that. For a while it seemed as if it was one funeral after another. Then they stopped for a long time. Well, and what happened to us? Jack got more and more famous in California; he finally won the highest honors they gave for medical research. His wife, Kate

Munyan, never had children of her own, but they collected people, children, dogs, flowers; they were very happy. Martin and Bill, Minnie and I, followed in Mother's and Father's footsteps; we spent our lives at home or on rounds. Gradually, everyone began to die; you see, I am over one hundred, perhaps one hundred and twenty. No one really knows how old I am. All of our records burned up one night. A dog tipped over a kerosene lamp and burned them up.

It was odd, though, the way Mother never wanted anything to do with Father's photographs. She preferred the ones from the local photographer, and the ones he took of Father particularly. She took them with her wherever she went. Mother. Even now it is hard to believe she is dead, or that Father is. They were such presences. "Edna, Edna, Edna"; I can still hear him saying her name. They seemed to love each other's names. Even when they fought; well, I suppose I refuse to bury them. Or they refuse to be buried.

And Mother was wrong about the old house. The whole tribe is still living in it; it costs the fortune of the Pharaohs to keep it up, and fortunately, we have the fortune. The great-great-great-grandchildren, or whatever relation they are to me, treasure me up. They tend to keep me secret. It isn't often they bring anyone in to see me, anyone who doesn't belong to the family, I mean. And the family has become so famous.

Yesterday, I heard one of the children saying, "There's no such thing as marriage anymore"; then Kate drifted in to talk and said the same thing. I said that was ridiculous, but she told me I came from another world. And how did I get here? I asked her; by spaceship? She muttered something about things being simpler then, and I had her sit down and told her all about the Griffin trial, and the incest, and then *I* started thinking about the families around the common. There were the three Camps who promised never to marry, and never did. There was the man who attacked his wife with a pitchfork. Jane Camp was taken off to the Retreat for a while; she was mad. I think it was Fred Camp, their father, who tried to kill his wife with a pitchfork. There was the woman found wandering on the common in the middle of the winter. The Coes, they were unhinged. Elder Coe shot his son when he didn't approve of his new bride-to-be. Around the common: one of the Camps taken to the Retreat. In four houses, there were simpleminded triplets, two madwomen, a family of three, in their seventies, still keeping a vow never to marry.

There were two poisonings in the houses. Dishes flew from the Reverend Pierce's window, and everyone blamed his wife. She ran away after he left for the Seminary. My own sister went to sleep in the snow; she was mad as a hatter when she died. And she thought—Kate did—life was simpler then. Well, I guess she knows better now. If she believes me. They usually believe me, at least when I tell them what they want to hear, and usually, when I tell them the truth.

Life became so strange; all of a sudden we had voices in the parlor. Usually the parlor was empty unless it was used for courting or someone was laid out there. People didn't come to call as often, not after they got accustomed to the telephone. And the children used to be so terrified of the radio programs! So many imaginary disasters! I remember one about a monkey's paw, and someone sneaked out while they were all sitting in the barn listening to that onmipresent box and just opened the door and stood there in a dark coat and held up a chicken's foot and it took us hours to collect them all again.

Well, I forgot to account for Mother's death; it was distinctive. We all said that at the time, even if she did finally die in her sleep. She grew more and more interested in Della Robbia buttons. Matthew had given her her first one, and courting chains, and she ended giving lectures to groups of ladies. The courting chains were already becoming very rare; Mother had several, and she was horrified when she discovered Hattie Coe, another member of the button club (or whatever they called themselves), had faked one; she must have taken some old buttons and gotten busy. I remember Mother telling me, more indignant than I'd ever seen her, that the woman actually dipped the thread in oil so it would look antique and then put it in her dust in the carpet sweeper so it would seem old. She was infuriated for days. Well, Mother's button collection was notable; that was what people said. I think Lettie has it, although how anyone had the nerve to name anyone after my sister is a puzzle to me.

Mother was lecturing on Della Robbia buttons to the Slab Hollow Valley Club; she was just lecturing away when she stopped and stood there. After about four or five minutes, people began to think something was wrong, and a woman led her away and they brought her home. William said she had had a stroke; we never knew whether it had to do with the lump in her breast. At the time, we didn't think so. Bill didn't expect her to speak again, but she regained consciousness and talked and talked for three days, and then she died in her sleep. Somehow it was like her, managing to die right in the middle of something, or starting to die anyway, right in the middle of things.

Right now, I am scheming again. I want them to take me to the hospital. My friend Jennie Pritchett is dying; she's almost as old as I am. I met her after I went blind. She was a friend of the Munyans and acted in serials on the radio. It was so nice knowing her, especially after I lost my sight and I could listen to her voice on the radio. But now I can see again, and I intend to go see her in the hospital, no matter what the others say about it. She taught me how to change voices and for a while I went down to the studio and was all kinds of people. It *was* fun. She was very, very good, much better than I was, and when television appeared—well, that was a shock, but not so much as the telephone—I used to love watching her. She could cry on cue. She told me they had instructions: tears, five seconds. I asked her to demonstrate that for me, and she did it, too. Well, I am going to see her before she dies, and they will just have to take me. I will think of something.

The blindness was not such a dreadful thing, although everyone felt so sorry for me. Cataracts: I could hardly see a thing when Bill died, which was, I imagine, just as well. Then, when I was ninety-nine, the family doctor said there was a new kind of operation, and they could take off the cataracts; I could see again. Well, I was so excited they had to give me something to calm me down. A Dr. Cooper did the operating; I was awake the whole time, and then they bandaged up my head and I just lay there for what seemed forever.

Everyone thought I would be delighted when I started peeping around again, but I can tell you, I wasn't. I assumed everything was just as it was when I lost my sight.

We were still living in the same house, after all, but what should I see when I went up on the hill? A superhighway: that's what it's called, cutting across our land one thousand feet from the house. Of course, they can't see us, hidden behind the trees the way we are, but it annoys me they are where they are. And I thought we were so insulated.

And then the house was in such a state! The children just dropped things wherever they finished with them, and the older girls, their mothers, can't be bothered. So I beat a retreat to my room and not one piece of furniture has come into it or gone out. At least everything is the same in here. I started to make rag rugs, although no one can see the point when it's so easy to get things from the store, and I never used to make them when I was younger, either. I suppose the rugs remind me of Bridget.

It took me some time to get used to their clothes, too. I didn't think they had any on for a long time; and the children, the little ones, *didn't* have any on. I suppose I am getting to feel as Mother said she did: as if there has been enough change in my life for any one person to take in. But I will see Jennie first. She is not going to die among strange creatures in short dresses.

As for the Munyans; they ended well, I suppose. Or ended, since no one seems to know anything about them. Everyone in the town always said they were going downhill as fast as possible, but no one knew how deep down they were going.

Well, to tell the truth, I miss the old clothes and the old ways; things were more formal then, the way everyone dressed and posed next to their fancy chairs or against elaborate scenes. At least for us. We were the rich ones. And things were more ceremonial. Now there are snapshots. The old pictures seemed to fix points in time, but this new way is truer to the nature of things, the way one flows into the other, and the group stays a group, but one wanders off, and another one takes that one's place, and finally the group is entirely new. And death was so much closer to us then. Well, it was supposed to be; but did any of us ever believe we would die? Or that anyone close to us would? We all had our filters. Well, sometimes I believe that is what life is, under its surface (and the surface is wonderful enough)—avoiding death. Perhaps Mother and Father didn't; perhaps that was what made them so special, so unique, so valued. And then so missed. Life is peculiar; so Alice Moffat always said.

After Jack died, we learned he had been almost as well known for his silly humor as for his doctoring. I can't imagine what it must have been like: his idea of humor. He and Father used to joke in just the same way. "Have you retired yet?" he asked Father on one of his visits. Father pretended he hadn't, saying, "I'm waiting to get mature, ripe on the vine." Jack said, "It was very easy for me, like slipping on a banana peel." They could go on and on that way until even Mother refused to listen to them.

It is very difficult to finish telling the story of our family. Undoubtedly, that is why I've taken the long way around. I was not given to note taking, diaries, personals, journals of any sort. I knew what was happening from day to day, and that was enough for me, although I hear Mother's voice often enough: "When your husband dies, that's when you feel the cosmic chill." She never actually said that aloud; we found it written in her papers.

And how did we die? Pneumonia seemed to have a particular fondness for our family. William went swimming with some of the children and took our big white dog, Major; he could swim two miles and retrieve any human being wearing a shirt. One of the children threw a stick for Major, who went right for it, but he landed on Bill's wrist, breaking it. It seemed an innocent enough event, especially in our family, but William had swallowed a great deal of water, and that morning had just attended a patient whose pneumonia was contagious. So he died of it, too. "The great illness for which there is no cure." Martin said that, looking down at him. Minnie used to wonder who was taking it harder: colleague or wife. I suppose Martin looked at William as if he were looking into a mirror.

I didn't do any looking into anything. First Bill was there; then he was gone, and then he was back. He believed we would meet on the golden shore; I never did and still don't. This shore was my golden shore. There is no describing what his death was like. I was in a fury. Other women I had read of climbed into their husbands' coffins. My own sister did that. I sat up one night with

the body; out of respect, no one came in. I lectured him
and called him names and told him I would never forgive
him. That lasted until two o'clock in the morning, when
I began remembering all the things I still remember. I remember his letters, their shape and texture, especially the
little white ones that looked like little iced cakes. I remember when we had our first son and nothing could
keep him safe in his crib and finally I decided to build a
higher frame around it and made it out of chicken wire,
but he climbed right up to the top of that fence; it was
too high for him, though. He wouldn't jump over it. We
used to rescue him when we heard him screaming. Later
Edward (we named him for my mother, I suppose) would
rock back and forth in his crib until he had driven it over
to the window, where he would stand and count the carriages going by; one carriage, one lady, another carriage,
some more ladies, another carriage, big sticks, one velocipede, one man on it, one horse running away, one lady
lying in our road.

Minnie heard him say that and went tearing out of the
house, and we found a fine case of a sprained back; we
had her on our hands for two weeks. Bill, another son,
said he would go into finance, but he didn't. He became
a doctor. For some time we thought they became doctors
because they couldn't think of what else to do. One of the
grandchildren ran away "to sea," and when he got finished washing decks and leaning over the rail, came back
and became a doctor. It had gotten into the blood, and
whether we liked it or not, there wasn't much any of us
could do about it. Then, when the new discoveries began,
stopping them was hopeless, at least for the two generations following ours.

I remember Wilma throwing an orange from her tin
plate right into the middle of her father's soup; I remember Bill making Edward a round chair on wheels so he
wouldn't bump into everything in the house. That child
was the first observable flying saucer. I remember fishing,
catching hornpout, cooking them, eating them; I remember
William taking one off a hook in a hurry—that was long
before we were married—and getting the sticker caught
in his hand. I remember the touch of his hand as I took
it out. I remember myself, and Reverend Pierce teaching
us that God was in three persons and how I sniffed

around for months trying to decide which three they were; I finally concluded they were Ten, Mother, and Father. He also said something about no intercessors being necessary between a man and his God, and I got it through my head he meant there were no cesspools or chamber pots necessary for the religious, and I was quite a case. You see, our privy was always called "the necessary." Aunt Ten never forgot it. She reminded me of it each time my own children acted up.

Well, William's death. We discussed the square tent set up for the church fair on the town common, the new birdbath (it's as green as a boat sunken for centuries now) in three layers, each ascending circle smaller than the one before; the birds didn't like it. We talked about things like that. He said he was happy he'd been smart enough not to marry the kind of wife who would sit next to his bed stitching away at a beaded scene for the inside of his coffin lid. I swore the inside of his coffin lid would have an early picture of me, my tongue sticking out at him. When he died, I couldn't think of anything to do but cry, so that is what I did. If I think about it now, I will begin crying again, but I am not going to think about it because I will start in coughing and the children will never take me to the hospital to visit Jennie. What was it like? As if the world had become flat. As if someone had made it into a piece of paper jaggedly ripped from a blank notebook. That is enough of that; I do want to go to the hospital.

Martin and Minnie had the worst luck of us all. Martin's boy Howard turned out very wild. Martin and Bill were forever at the jail getting him out of one scrape after another: first stealing a chicken, then drunkenness, then frequenting houses of ill repute. Two years after Bill died (that was how it was for me: after William died, or before he died), Howard decided he wanted to go into the ministry. He had always been curious about Anna, and Minnie told him about her, and also about Matthew. He entered the Seminary; he came home for his first vacation. The girls were already getting married. Martin got an emergency call. There had been a bad accident at Three Corners. That was all he knew. When he got there, there was the usual crowd milling about. They were waiting for the doctor to officially pronounce the victims dead, and their heads were covered. When Martin pulled a blanket back, he saw one of the village boys. Then he pulled back the other blanket. It was Howard. He nearly retired, or expired, on the spot.

And Minnie. She was more concerned with her husband than her son. She was like that; William was, too. What was over, was over; what was not, had to be attended to, and she did. Then their other son took some time to settle down and at the time there was considerable suspicion that one of Lenore Sweeney's illegitimate children had been fathered by him. That was too much for poor Minnie. She said she couldn't bear to look at that baby's face just in case he might look like her son. Then later he married a Catholic, and came down with tuberculosis. As he got poorer, he had to move from his house to an apartment in Maine; he couldn't seem to get far enough away from the rest of us, and, of course, he would accept no financial help.

When he moved, his address stayed the same. He went from 34 Marshall Street, Brattleboro, to 34 Marshall Street in Rutland. Poor Minnie! She had a great deal to put up with. Her daughter took up the bass violin and the child's friend was perpetually at the house; she played the trombone. When she played, Minnie's daughter accompanied her on the piano. After all these years, I have to pronounce it a repulsive scene: the spit hole on the trombone, the girl playing and spitting. Minnie always had to have a pile of newspapers on the floor. I suppose she had some luck: Martin died quickly. He was operating on a patient whose wound had become infected. The man's wife was hysterical and accidentally stuck Martin's finger with a sharp edge of the iron piece he had already extracted. He finished the operation and died of blood poisoning less than forty-eight hours later. She married again, but not for five years. And she kept Martin's picture with her as long as she lived.

She married Lettie's husband, Richard. Lettie, I think, died very nicely. The newspaper reported the sad event. My dear departed sister had become so absorbed in a performance of *La Traviata* that she leaned farther and farther over the railing of her box. *We* all knew she was observing someone's hairdress. She tumbled over in her crimson evening dress. She had recently discovered that color set off her hair and did not make her look foolish, but exceptionally striking, and she was diligently hunting up other bits and pieces of useful information which would allow her to enhance the effect. Wild flowers *or* roses. She did not want to look like a woman she once saw who evinced the following comment: that woman's hair needs mowing. At any rate, she turned twice in the air, seemed to land unhurt on her feet, like a cat, and then collapsed; the impact had crushed her spine.

When Richard came up here with her body (she requested she be buried at home; she must have decided our family was more distinguished than his), he followed after me, but I had enough of finding and losing things. Then the same charm that caught Mr. Siddons began to catch him. It wasn't quite the proper time, but he was kind to her, talked to her, began to visit her more frequently. She had a serious conversation with the Reverend Case, who assured her nothing like incest would result from such a marriage; she married him. They died in a flu epidemic in Boston. She took excellent care of his children when they needed it; they were too old to have more of their own.

George and Ellen lived and died more happily than anyone could imagine. Ellen had been raised on a farm; she was a farm girl, after all. Oh, she kept after George. He used to say she got up early and went out to brush and comb the hens. Yes, she turned out to be the industrious one, the respectable one. They had five children; she became a churchgoing woman—that was how George described her. We thought that would kill him. George died first, in the classic manner. He stepped on something in the manure pile; it went through his shoe. He died of lockjaw. He was, I think, seventy-six. Ellen was prostrate for three days, but she was used to managing. She managed her married son who remained on the farm a bit too much. Every month, she moved a little further up in the house, a little farther away from the main rooms. We expected to find her living in the cupola.

But she died six months after George. She insisted on teaching one of the grandchildren to swim; it wasn't safe for a country child to live if he couldn't swim. She kept saying that. She drowned giving a demonstration of the necessary skills. The current was very strong that day and it was some time before anyone on the shore could reach her. It would never have occurred to any of us to swim in the lake; we were always in the river. The only people who saw her going under were fishing on the shore. They did their best, but there wasn't much they could do. And then the rest of us had our hands full with the child. Someone made up a fairy tale about his grandmother floating off to China to see the Emperor. He finally took to the water like a duck. Although he *did* finally move to Arizona, and all he wrote about was how there was no water at all in that part of the country.

Alice and Howard died so appropriately we were tempted to put something to that effect on their tombstone. They were buried in the vault with the rest of us; they were no longer strangers. They were like vice-presidents who ascended to the highest office when the first in command died. Alice was off hunting for a new kind of lily which made its appearance in the woods; she found what she wanted, and also a severe case of poison ivy. Nothing could be done to prevent her scratching at it. We had to burn her clothes afterwards and we couldn't touch her without special gloves, which we had to burn later as well. She died of an infection which set in from the scratching.

Fortunately for those of us left, she died after Howard, but when she died the silence in the house was so thick it seemed the air had hardened into some death-like rigor of its own. She was the last of them. She took Howard's death far harder than any of us expected, although his death, like Lettie's, was not the most pathetic. He was milking his favorite cow when the needlepoint milking stool Minnie had made for him suddenly collapsed. He was so angry at the stool he kicked it and sent pieces of it flying, and one piece struck the flank of the cow, who was old and nervous, and she began moving back and forth in her stall. Howard was still flying around in a rage, and where his foot was was where the cow's foot was, and the next thing, *his* foot had to be amputated. First the nail came off, then there was the reddening of the small veins and capillaries, and then the leg.

He died of the shock of the operation. Alice's sorrow was like mine; it took the form of fury. She lectured the coffin; she went into the monument and harangued the grave. "You silly old ass," we heard her; "after so many years to get stepped on by your own cow! To leave me unprovided for! I want you to understand, Howard, when I meet you on the golden shore, I intend to cut you dead." It sounds comical now, but it was just dreadful then. None of us could go down to the graves without listening to that unending diatribe. She kept it up for almost six months; not even the snow hampered her progress toward the stone.

Amos died in his sleep in the barn; Bridget in the kitchen. I don't remember what took Bertha or Ella, probably because they returned to their families before they died. We buried Bridget and Amos with the rest of us, thus unintentionally creating a scandal in the town, but it was one of the last we were to cause.

It is always the little things I remember. Reverend Case punishing the congregation. He had a young minister to train up, and the poor thing was so dreadfully boring that everyone flocked to the new church when they saw him pacing up and down, studying a sermon for the Sabbath. Reverend Case knew what was up, so he asked the minister at the other church if he wouldn't like a rest, and volunteered the fledgling's services. He asked the young man to preach the very same excellent sermon he had that morning, and naturally, the young man was pleased beyond containment, so that when Reverend Case's congregation fled to the other church's afternoon services and sat through the same tedious buzzing of flies and mumbled words, they knew they had been taken, and stopped church shopping. That was what Mr. Case called it.

I remember holding the baby up to the mirror and how astonished she was. I remember poor Richard in the arbor. "Despise not the day of little things." Everyone in the family had their motto, and that was mine. (It was supposed to be Anna's also.) I never did. I hope they will write that as my epitaph: "She did not despise the day of little things." Although that may be hard on the old stone-cutter, who will probably prefer "devoted wife, mother and grandmother and great-grandmother and great-great-great-grandmother." Now *that* begins to sound difficult and tiring, so perhaps I shall have my way, after all.

We never stopped living in the house; I believe I said that. But I am getting weary of finding myself treated as an antique doll. And the new crop of children; they never weary of intellectual discussions. They go off to college and come home and talk about atoms and electrons and theories of relativity and the earth falling into the sun, and their parents won't listen to them, so I do, or at least pretend to do so. But they do not seem happy. One of them died of an overdose of Darvon on New Year's Eve. I said it was just as well, for, had she recovered, she would have been nothing more than a vegetable. She was strangely paralyzed; the paralysis set in at the toes and crept up higher and higher until finally it covered her altogether. Two more have decided to leave the evils of civilization and are living somewhere in a cabin in the Maine woods. One of the younger boys ran off with his cousin's wife, and his father had to bring him back. Everyone says they will settle down. I have my favorite, of course, but she is very intense. At my age, that is wearing, if interesting. She has to sit in a low chair because I can't look up at her. It's too hard. And I do tire more easily. She is always at me for advice. I find out what she really wants to do and tell her to do it. Naturally, she thinks me wiser than the Sphinx. I am certainly almost as old.

When I close my eyes, the picture that fills me is one of Bill's house, that simple house of white wood siding, black shutters, its spindled porch railing, an ornamental railing along the top of the porch, a striped shade half lowered to cool at least part of it. Morning glories growing up the strings playing their invisible music. I still hear it. The ancient hydrangea tree spilling its cones over the lawn, from inside, almost screening the window with its leaves. The lawn is neat as ever. Alice never liked clutter, and if Howard would not mow the grass on time, she would. It is not William I see standing there at the edge of the porch step, at the top, looking out at me, coming up the road, but Alice: in her neat starched print dress, her thick white hair parted in the middle and drawn back.

Old age had rounded her stomach; it protruded like a baby's. The wild grass begins right at the edge of the lawn, which stops at the border of the house. The flowers riot. The trees are gray and fading, as if a storm was coming from the north, threatening to blow us all away. I don't know how many times I see that picture, or vision, and each time I am closer and closer to Alice. It is difficult to climb up the hill to her house, which stands isolated in the middle of the field, which is also a hill, and stands on its crest; people were so afraid of miasmas then. Still, even if nothing had surrounded the house, it would have been impossible to see from the road. You would have had to know where to break through the dense growth at the edge of the road to see it. I suppose we seemed isolated and lonely to others; I suppose some of us were. And sometimes, when I close my eyes, face after face swims past in a dark water, one fish after another. They are faces I've never seen before. I wonder if they have already died or if they have not yet come into being. And in the dream about Alice—it is not only harder and harder to walk up the hill; sometimes I slip and fall and cannot get up at all, but she stands there, waiting patiently. I always wake before reaching her. It is a dreadful dream.

With her great-granddaughter's collusion, the scheme Ella had been concocting was put into execution Wednesday morning. Kate found out when Jennie could be visited. Jennie's relatives objected to nothing that might cheer her up, and as soon as she heard of Ella's impending arrival, Jennie wanted her needles taken out, her hair brushed, her cheeks rouged, and suddenly developed a talent for talking. They obliged her in everything except the knitting needles.

Now it was Ella's turn. "Edna," she announced to her granddaughter, or great-granddaughter, loudly, "if you will not take me there, I shall call a taxicab." "I will pull the phone right out of the wall," Edna answered calmly. "Then I will go downstairs and break my neck and you will have yourself to blame." Others began rushing in. Ella picked up her silver hairbrush and tried to throw it. "Will you stop?" Edna demanded; "you know you're not supposed to exert yourself!" Ella picked up her silver shoehorn. Kate promptly burst into hysterical tears. "You'll kill her; you'll kill her," she sobbed. "At least eat your lunch," Edna coaxed; she hoped Ella would forget about the hospital once she had worn herself out chewing. "I'm not eating until I go to the hospital." Ella clamped her jaws shut. What a face, Edna thought; Ella would not let them replace her teeth. She had one left. A face all eyes and shadows. Edna put the tray down before her; she knocked it to the carpet. "Mother!" Kate cried.

Edna went out and telephoned her husband. "All right," Edna told her, coming back; "have your way. The limousine is coming up, but there's one condition. We have to go with you." "I don't care who comes with me." "Go get your brothers," Edna told Kate; "we'll have to carry her down. Tell them to throw her"—she glared at Ella—"into the front seat and put her wheelchair in the trunk." The two boys carried her down and set her in the car. The limousine began its slow wind and descent through the curving avenues, then speeded up as it reached the highway. "Is there no end to your ridiculous ideas?" Edna asked. "No," Ella answered shortly; "I don't like these things; I never did. I liked them better when they had vases for flowers in them, but this looks like a hearse," she grumbled. "It's because the windows are bulletproof, you know that," Edna snapped. "No one ever told you to be motes in the public eye."

"I believe it began with *your* father," Edna told her, nasty. "The photographs are in the archives?" Ella suddenly asked. "We've told you and told you." Jack had been the only one who wanted them; they had eventually come to Ella. Edna's husband, Richard, had them placed in the Harvard Archives. More and more people were taking an interest in them, trying to reproduce them. They found it difficult. Ella found their difficulties comical.

"Traffic," Ella grumbled as they went through the edge of Boston on their way to Massachusetts General. "If you want to turn back," Edna began, but a look from Ella smothered her sentence. "I suppose it's nice to come and go whenever you please," she said, almost to herself. Edna smiled. The old bat would never admit to liking things in this new world; she suspected her of harboring a desire to try on a bikini and wiggle. Perhaps she ought to have Kate leave one of hers in Ella's room. She grinned to herself. "Here we are," she told Ella. "I can see, I can see." They placed her in her wheelchair and took the elevator up to the fifth floor. Ella regarded it with suspicion.

Jennie was dying of cancer. None of them could imagine what good this meeting would do either of the old women, but they could do nothing to stop them. "Leave us alone," Jennie commanded as soon as Ella was wheeled up. Another one, Edna sighed silently, leaving. "Well," Ella said. "Well," Jennie said. They sat staring at each other for over five minutes, eyes brimming. Ella put her hand over her friend's. "I don't believe you had the nerve to come here," Jennie said, admiring. "So cancer's got you?" Ella asked. "At least it's growth. It got my mother, a long time ago." "I know."

They began jabbering as fast as they could, one toothless, one weak. "Do you remember," Jennie asked, "when we did the voices for Snow White?" Ella nodded. "Mirror, mirror, on the wall, who's the fairest of them all?" Jennie intoned, just as she once had. "You are," Ella answered in a quavering child's voice. "No, you are," Jennie answered in the Queen's voice. "There goes the script," Ella teased, imitating the director. "We never stuck to one, did we?" Jennie asked. "Of course we did," Ella contradicted; "we're following it now, even if it is the strangest version of *Romeo and Juliet* I've ever heard of." "Are you going to be buried next to your William?" "Naturally." "Me, too." "What, next to Bill?" "No, next to Lazarus. I'm sorry, dear. That *was* his name." They laughed; they both began coughing.

"Oh, Jennie, you just reminded me of something. There was a family named Camp in our town; they took an oath to stay together and never marry. There were two sisters and one brother. Well, when the first sister died—it was Jane Camp, I think—her sister Bertha was sitting up next to her, watching with her. Jane woke all at once, very excited. 'There's something very important I have to tell you.' 'What is it?' her devoted sister asked, leaning over. 'You have to promise not to forget,' Jane kept saying; she was terrified her sister would forget. 'Don't worry, Jane; I won't forget,' Bertha promised her.

"Oh, I don't know when I've had such a good time telling stories," Ella sighed in a transport; "are you interested?" Jennie nodded. "Well, Jane told her she'd seen heaven; that's what she said. 'I saw heaven last night and there's something I have to tell you, but you have to promise not to forget.' 'I promise,' poor Bertha said again.

'Well, then,' Jane said, lifting her head, 'when you get to heaven you walk two blocks straight ahead, and then you come to a church on the left. You go in there and sit down in the first pews on the right. Don't forget. On the right. That's where our family sits. I don't want you to get lost. Can you remember?' 'Oh, I can,' Bertha assured her. 'Then I can die in peace,' her sister said, and that's just what she did.

"Well, Bertha was happy the rest of her life, because she knew just where to go, and Jane, she died happy. You don't think there's anything to the dream she had?" "Well," Jennie said, "if we're going anywhere, we'll find out soon enough. We haven't disgraced ourselves enough to be thrown out of the family plots, so I guess we'll be with our family anyhow." "You don't think that's what she meant?" Ella asked, horrified; "not after all the faith I've put in that story all these years?" "You don't want me to start lying now, do you?" "I suppose not; but, Jennie! It made them so happy, that dream. I *want* to believe there was something to it." "Then go ahead." "Oh, well," Ella sighed; "it's hard to give up those things." "It is," Jennie agreed. "At least"—Ella grinned—"you get to lie down next to Lazarus." "Nothing's fair in life and war." "They're the same," Ella said, tired.

"I'm getting worn out by life," Ella finally admitted. "Just like an old dress," Jennie commiserated. "I can't swallow any more of it," Ella said; "you know what they did to me last year? Our town was having its centennial parade and they wanted me to sit in front as the oldest citizen in town. So what do you think they did? They put me in a carriage, right in front of everything, showed me off to everyone, took me all the way down Main Street, and then, out of concern for my health, took me straight back home. Well, I was furious as a wet cat, I can tell you. I didn't see *anything*, not one thing. And after all that trouble getting my sight back. And on top of it, they were so proud of themselves because I was safe and sound. Well, I hope they don't have any more parades; they can take a mummy for all I care. It's ridiculous being as old as I am. They wouldn't be so inconsiderate to any other human, would they? Oh, well," she murmured, "at least I got to see some trees and was jostled a little more than usual. Even if I couldn't unbend my elbow for three days."

Jennie shook her head at her, amused. "Parades. You're still caught up in all that." "I'm a little old for the films." "True; *my* skin doesn't even like the air. The light hurts my eyes. Dust has me sneezing. Still, I won't be happy to go." "We don't have any choice." "That's true enough; I'm awfully glad you came. You know, I get terribly off the hooks in this place. It's not hard to believe the carriages are going by outside, is it? While we're together, I mean?" "Oh, they are," Ella assured her. "Yes, so they are," Jennie agreed.

"Visiting hours are over," the nurse announced. "Who ever heard of such a barbaric invention?" Jennie asked her friend; "visiting hours? Hours at home, afternoon calls: that made sense. But visiting hours for the sick, whether they're better or not? She tells me"—Jennie looked icily at the nurse—"they're more flexible when you're gasping your last." "How nice of them," Ella said; "just when you want to talk away." She glared at the nurse. "I didn't arrange it that way," the poor girl said. "Of course not, dear," Ella said, sympathetic; "everyone knows you don't run the hospital. *My* idiotic family does. Goodbye, dear," she told Jennie, turning to her; "I'm afraid I'll have to blow you a kiss. If I bend over, we'll both be in that bed." "You don't need to tell me; I understand."

"Well, Ella, I guess we better get on with it, hadn't we?" "Yes, I suppose. But I won't say goodbye." "Stubborn as ever"; Jennie smiled. "Visiting hours really are over," the nurse interjected nervously. The two women looked at each other. "Call my bodyguards," Ella told the nurse; "the two hulks with long hair hanging down in the hall." The limousine slowly made its way back. Ella glared at the superhighway. It ruined half her enjoyment of the trip, having to see it. "Satisfied?" Edna asked. She ignored her. Of course she was satisfied.

Well, Ella thought, settled again in bed, I had better get on with it. Tiresome, this binding up of things. She was extremely sleepy. Voices began coming back to her. "Children should not marry." "We are always coming to the end of something. We shall come to the close of our last day, take our last walk, write our last letter, say our last good-night. We shall not miss dying." That was Matthew. "Every hour comes with some little faggot of God's will fastened on its back." How the meaning of words changed. "Which of you being anxious can add one cubit to his stature." "The heart is deceitful above all things and desperately wicked." She did not believe that. "O grave, I will be thy destruction." "I am persuaded that neither death, nor life, nor angels . . ." "We must not despise the day of small things." "Edna! *Edna!* How long can it take to put on a pair of boots?" "Will someone get Minnie out of those eggs?" "She is slower than time in the primer." "Yet a little while and time shall be no longer." "It is the Lord's work and it is marvelous in our eyes."

We did not any of us feel very well.
I did not go out and no one came.
Nothing of interest to record.
Father buried today.
Howard went down after the doctor for Mrs. Jackson and got stuck in the snow out to Charles Harris' and left the horses.
Mrs. Obadiah Olney died and was brought back to be buried.
I felt stupid enough today.
Thanksgiving seemed strange in every respect.
The terrific announcement that Edna was dead.
It is such a pity to have the old trouble return.
I am the only one at present that is able to go and come regularly.
We are holding our parlor on the upper hall landing while the kitchen is being renovated.
We went down to hear the chime of bells ring for the first time.
It has been windy and pleasant.
It has been warm and pleasant.
I went raspberrying just at night.
Some snow fell just at night.
It has been cloudy and rained.
It has been pleasant, but cool and windy.
Oats, washing sheep, sugaring off, logs for the barn raising, washing, ironing, the woodpile, killing the

hogs, beef, shearing the sheep. The fourth anniversary of Florence's death. The first anniversary of Father's death. The first anniversary of Mother's death. The only anniversary of William's death.
It is getting late and I had better get back.
She is poor as a crow.
It has been warm and pleasant.
It has been warm and pleasant.
As men with eyes half open, like him that saw men as trees walking.
How I pity you, Matilda.
A dead soul in a living body; a dead child in the womb.

More got in my blood than I intended. Should I tell them I want them to write that I went down the last flight of steps without anything in my hand: a scalpel, a photograph, the Father, the Son, and the Holy Ghost, fame, a husband who became God? That I went down into the ground with the clear sky in my eyes? That is my victory, Mother, Father. We must have our victories. Ten always said that.

Everything tastes like ashes and I do not mind.
It is clear and cool.
It is clear and breezy.
As it was in the beginning, is now, and ever shall be.
World without end.

Nothing changes. Nothing ever changes. This is not the right world for us, but I have loved it. This world is a changeling, or we are. Someone left us on the threshold and there was nothing to do but go through.
I was happy. Yes, I was happy. World without end. Nothing ever changes. As it was in the beginning, is now, and ever shall be. The weather continues, and the light, and the dust blows in. In my last dream, I saw Mother sweeping and sweeping; she could not keep ahead of the dust. Mother? Oh, good. I have seen the same thing. I meant to tell you what a good idea the stone house was. Don't go on rounds today. I'm expecting something. I should record the weather, but there is none today. World without end, Mother. As it was in the beginning, is now,

and ever shall be. Why won't anyone believe it? Stop asking questions and go to sleep, John said. Do as your father says, Edna said firmly. Mother, I am still angry at Anna. Go to sleep, dear. Someone turned on the television; there's the sound of guns firing. Tears, five seconds. That was time, and time enough. Ella closed her eyes.